EXILES

BY DAVID BRIN

The Practice Effect
The Postman
Heart of the Comet (with Gregory Benford)
Earth
Glory Season
Otherness
Foundation's Triumph
Kil'n People
Existence

The Uplift Books
Sundiver
Startide Rising
The Uplift War
Brightness Reef
Infinity's Shore
Heaven's Reach

Uplift: The Complete Original Trilogy (omnibus edition)
Exiles: The Second Uplift Trilogy (omnibus edition)

EXILES

The Second Uplift Trilogy

This omnibus edition includes
Brightness Reef
Infinity's Shore
Heaven's Reach

DAVID BRIN

orbit

www.orbitbooks.net

ORBIT

First published in Great Britain in 2012 by Orbit
Reprinted 2013

Copyright © 2012 by David Brin

Brightness Reef
First published in Great Britain in 1996 by Orbit
Copyright © 1995 by David Brin
Map of Jijo by Kevin Lenagh

Infinity's Shore
First published in Great Britain in 1997 by Orbit
Copyright © 1996 by David Brin

Heaven's Reach
First published in Great Britain in 1998 by Orbit
Copyright © 1998 by David Brin

The moral right of the author has been asserted.

A CIP catalogue record for this book
is available from the British Library.

ISBN 978-1-84149-490-6

Typeset in New Aster by M Rules
Printed and bound in Great Britain by
Clays Ltd, St Ives plc

Papers used by Orbit are from well-managed forests
and other responsible sources.

 MIX
Paper from
responsible sources
FSC
www.fsc.org FSC® C104740

Orbit
An imprint of
Little, Brown Book Group
100 Victoria Embankment
London EC4Y 0DY

An Hachette UK Company
www.hachette.co.uk

www.orbitbooks.net

BRIGHTNESS REEF

To Herbert H. Brin
Poet, journalist, and lifelong champion of justice

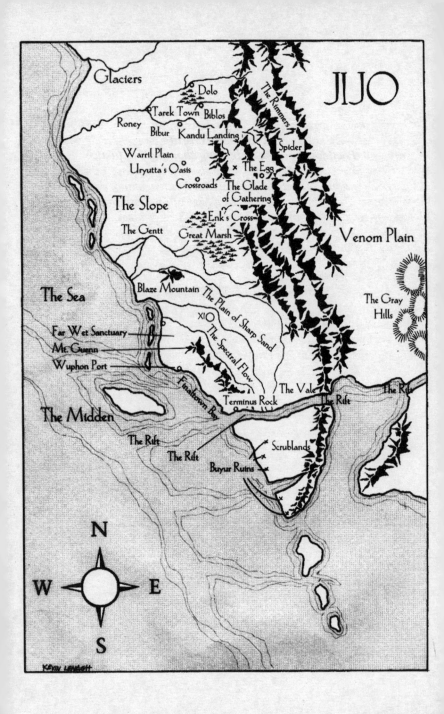

I must ask your permission. You, my rings, my diverse selves.

Vote now! Shall i speak for all of us to the outer world? Shall we join, once more, to become Asx?

That is the name used by humans, qheuens, and other beings, when they address this stack of circles. By that name, this coalition of plump, traeki rings was elected a sage of the Commons, respected and revered, sitting in judgment on members of all six exile races.

By that name – Asx – we are called upon to tell tales.
Is it agreed?

Then Asx now bears witness ... to events we endured, and those relayed by others. 'I' will tell it, as if this stack were mad enough to face the world with but a single mind.

Asx brews this tale. Stroke its waxy trails. Feel the story-scent swirl. There is no better one i have to tell.

Pain is the stitching holding him together ... or else, like a chewed-up doll or a broken toy, he would have unraveled by now, lain his splintered joins amid the mucky reeds, and vanished into time.

Mud covers him from head to toe, turning pale where sunlight dries a jigsaw of crumbly plates, lighter than his dusky skin. These dress his nakedness more loyally than the charred garments that fell away like soot after his panicky escape from fire. The coating slakes his scalding agony, so the muted torment grows almost companionable, like a garrulous rider that his body hauls through an endless, sucking marsh.

A kind of music seems to surround him, a troubling ballad of scrapes and burns. An opus of trauma and shock.

Striking a woeful cadenza is the *hole* in the side of his head.

Just once, he put a hand to the gaping wound. Fingertips, expecting to be stopped by skin and bone, kept going horribly inward, until some faraway instinct made him shudder and withdraw. It was too much to fathom, a loss he could not comprehend.

Loss of *ability* to comprehend ...

The mud slurps greedily, dragging at every footstep. He has to bend and clamber to get through another blockade of crisscrossing branches, webbed with red or yellow veins. Caught amid them are bits of glassy brick or pitted metal, stained by age and acid juices. He avoids these spots, recalling dimly that once he had known good reasons to keep away.

Once, he had known lots of things.

Under the oily water, a hidden vine snags his foot, tripping him into the mire. Floundering, he barely manages to keep his head up, coughing and gagging. His body quivers as he struggles back to his feet, then starts slogging forward again, completely drained.

Another fall could mean the end.

While his legs move on by obstinate habit, the accompanying pain recites a many-part fugue, raw and grating, cruel without words. The sole sense that seems intact, after the abuse of plummet, crash, and fire, is *smell*. He has no direction or goal, but the combined stench of boiling fuel and his own singed flesh help drive him on, shambling, stooping, clambering and stumbling forward until the thorn-brake finally thins.

Suddenly, the vines are gone. Instead a swamp sprawls ahead – dotted by strange trees with arching, spiral roots. Dismay clouds his mind as he notes – the water is growing deeper. Soon the endless morass will reach to his armpits, then higher.

Soon he will die.

Even the pain seems to agree. It eases, as if sensing the futility of haranguing a dead man. He straightens from a buckled crouch for the first time since tumbling from the wreckage, writhing and on fire. Shuffling on the slippery muck, he turns a slow circle . . .

. . . and suddenly confronts a pair of *eyes*, watching him from the branches of the nearest tree. Eyes set above a stubby jaw with needle teeth. Like a tiny dolphin, he thinks – a *furry* dolphin, with short, wiry legs . . . and forward-looking eyes . . . and ears . . .

Well, perhaps a dolphin *was* a bad comparison. He isn't thinking at his best, right now. Still, surprise jars loose an association. Down some remnant pathway spills a relic that becomes almost a word.

'Ty . . . Ty . . .' He tries swallowing. 'Ty – Ty – t-t-t—'

The creature tips its head to regard him with interest, edging closer on the branch as he stumbles toward it, arms outstretched—

Abruptly, its concentration breaks. The beast looks up toward a sound.

A liquid splash . . . followed by another, then more, repeating in a purposeful tempo, drawing rhythmically nearer. Swish and splash, swish and splash. The sleek-furred creature squints past him, then grunts a small disappointed sigh. In a blur, it whirls and vanishes into the queer-shaped leaves.

He lifts a hand, urging it to stay. But he cannot find the words. No utterance to proclaim his grief as frail hope crashes into a chasm of abandonment. Once more, he sobs a forlorn groan.

'Ty . . . ! Ty . . . !'

The splashing draws closer. And now another noise intervenes – a low rumble of aspirated air.

The rumble is answered by a flurry of alternating clicks and whistled murmurs.

He recognizes the din of speech, the clamor of sapient beings, without grasping the words. Numb with pain and resignation, he turns – and blinks uncomprehendingly at a *boat*, emerging from the grove of swamp trees.

Boat. The word – one of the first he ever knew – comes to mind slickly, easily, the way countless other words used to do.

A boat. Constructed of many long narrow tubes, cleverly curved and joined. Propelling it are figures working in unison with poles and oars. Figures he knows. He has seen their like before. But never so close together.

Never cooperating.

One shape is a cone of stacked rings or toruses, diminishing with height, girdled by a fringe of lithe tentacles that grasp a long pole, using it to push tree roots away from the hull. Nearby, a pair of broad-shouldered, green-cloaked bipeds paddle the water with great scooplike oars, their long scaly arms gleaming pale in the slanting sunlight. The fourth shape consists of an armored blue hump of a torso, leather-plated, culminating in a squat dome, rimmed by a glistening ribbon eye. Five powerful legs aim outward from the center, as if the creature might at any moment try to run in all directions at once.

He knows these profiles. Knows and fears them. But true despair floods his heart only when he spies a final figure, standing at the stern, holding the boat's tiller, scanning the thicket of vines and corroded stone.

It is a smaller bipedal form, slender, clothed in crude, woven fabric. A familiar outline, all too similar to his own. A stranger, but one sharing his own peculiar heritage, beginning near a certain salty sea, many eons and galaxies distant from this shoal in space.

It is the last shape he ever wanted to see in such a forlorn place, so far from home.

Resignation fills him as the armored pentapod raises a clawed leg to point his way with a shout. Others rush forward to gape, and he stares back, for it is a sight to behold – all these faces and forms, jabbering to one another in shared astonishment at the spectacle of him – then rushing about, striving together as a team, paddling toward him with *rescue* their clear intent.

He lifts his arms, as if in welcome. Then, on command, both knees fold and turbid water rushes to embrace him.

Even without words, irony flows during those seconds, as he gives up the struggle for life. He has come a long way and been through much. Only a short time ago, *flame* had seemed his final destiny, his doom.

Somehow, this seems a more fitting way to go – by drowning.

I

THE BOOK OF THE SEA

You who chose this way of life –
to live and breed and die in secret on this
wounded world,
cowering from star-lanes you once roamed,
hiding with other exiles in a place forbidden
by law –
what justice have you any right to claim?

The universe is hard.
Its laws are unforgiving.
Even the successful and glorious are punished
by the grinding executioner called Time.
All the worse for you who are accursed,
frightened of the sky.

And yet there are paths that climb,
even out of despair's sorrow.

Hide, children of exile!
Cower from the stars!
But watch, heed and listen –
for the coming of a path.

—The Scroll of Exile

ALVIN'S TALE

On the day I grew up enough for my hair to start turning white, my parents summoned all the members of our thronging cluster to the family khuta, for a ceremony giving me my proper name – *Hphwayuo*.

I guess it's all right, for a hoonish tag. It rolls out from my throat sac easy enough, even if I get embarrassed hearing it sometimes. The handle's supposed to have been in the lineage ever since our sneakship brought the first hoon to Jijo.

The sneakship was utterly gloss! Our ancestors may have been sinners, in coming to breed on this taboo planet, but they flew a mighty star-cruiser, dodging Institute patrols and dangerous Zang and Izmunuti's carbon storms to get here. Sinners or not, they must have been awfully brave and skilled to do all that.

I've read everything I can find about those days, even though it happened hundreds of years before there was paper on Jijo, so all we really have to go on are a few legends about those hoon pioneers, who dropped from the sky to find g'Keks, glavers, and traeki already hiding here on the Slope. Stories that tell how those first hoon sank their sneakship in the deep Midden, so it couldn't be traced, then settled down to build crude wooden rafts, the first to sail Jijo's rivers and seas since the Great Buyur went away.

Since it has to do with the sneakship, I guess my given name can't be too bad.

Still, I really like to be called *Alvin*.

Our teacher, Mister Heinz, wants us upper graders to start journals, though some parents complain paper costs too much here at the southern end of the Slope. I don't care. I'm going to write about the adventures me and my friends have, both helping and heckling the good-natured sailors in the harbor, or exploring twisty lava tubes up near Guenn Volcano, or scouting in our little boat all the way to the long, hatchet-shadow of Terminus Rock.

Maybe someday I'll turn these notes into a book!

And why not? My Anglic is real good. Even grumpy old Heinz says I'm a whiz at languages, memorizing the town copy of *Roget's* by the time I was ten. Anyway, now that Joe Dolenz, the printer, has come set up shop in Wuphon, why should we have to count on the traveling librarian's caravan for new things to read? Maybe Dolenz would even let me set the type myself! That is, if I get around to it before my fingers grow too big to fit around those little backward letters.

Mu-phauwq, my mother, calls it a great idea, though I can tell she's partly humoring a childish obsession, and I wish she wouldn't patronize me that way.

My *dad*, Yowg-wayuo, acts all grumpy, puffing his throat sac and telling me not to be such a human-mimicker. But I'm sure he likes the idea, deep down. Doesn't *he* keep taking borrowed books on his long voyages to the Midden, even though you're not supposed to, because what if the ship sank and maybe the last ancient copy of *Moby Dick* went down with the crew? Wouldn't that be a *real* disaster?

Anyway, didn't he used to read to me almost from the day I was born? Booming all the great Earthling adventure tales like *Treasure Island*, *Sinbad*, and *Ultraviolet Mars*? So who's *he* to call *me* a humicker!

Nowadays, Dad says I should read the new hoon writers, those trying to go past imitating old-time Earthers, coming up with literature by and for our own kind.

I guess maybe there *should* be more books in languages other than Anglic. But Galactic Two and Galactic Six seem so darn stiff for story-telling. Anyhow, I've tried some of those writers. Honestly. And I've got to say that not one of them can hold a peg to Mark Twain.

Naturally, *Huck* agrees with me about that!

Huck is my best friend. She picked that name even though I kept telling her it's not a right one for a girl. She just twists one eyestalk around another and says she doesn't care, and if I call her 'Becky' one more time, she'll catch my leg-fur in her spokes and spin till I scream.

I guess it doesn't matter, since g'Keks get to change sex after their training wheels fall off, and if she wants to stay female, that's her business. As an orphan, Huck's lived with the family next door ever since the Big Northside Avalanche wiped out the weaver clan that used to squat in Buyur ruins up that way. You'd expect her to be a bit strange after living through that and then being raised by hoons. Anyway, she's a great friend and a pretty good sailor, even if she is a g'Kek, and a girl, and doesn't have legs to speak of.

Most times, *Pincer-Tip* also comes on our adventures, specially when we're down by the shore. He didn't need a nickname from some story, since all red qheuens get one the minute they set five claws outside the brooding pen. Pincer's no big reader like Huck and me, mostly because few books can stand the salt and dampness where his clan lives. They're poor, living off wrigglers they find in the mudflats south of town. Dad says the qheuens with red shells used to be servants to the grays and blues, before their sneakship brought all three to hide on Jijo. Even after that, the grays kept bossing the others for a while, so Dad says the reds aren't used to thinking for themselves.

Maybe so, but whenever Pincer-Tip comes along, *he's* usually the one chattering – with all leg-mouths at once –about sea serpents, or lost Buyur treasure, or other things he swears he's seen ... or else he heard of somebody who knows someone else who might've seen something, just over the horizon. When we get into trouble, it's often on account of something he thought up inside that hard dome where he keeps his brain. Sometimes I wish I had an imagination a dozenth as vivid as his.

I should include *Ur-ronn* in the list, since she comes along sometimes. Ur-ronn's almost as much of a book maniac as Huck and me. Still, she's *urrish*, and there's a limit to how much of a humicker any urs can be, before planting four feet and saying whoa.

They don't take to nicknames, for instance.

Once, when we were reading a mess of old Greek myths, Huck tried calling Ur-ronn 'Centaur.' I guess you *could* say an urs sort of looks like one of those fabled creatures – if you'd just been conked on the head by a brick and can't see or think too well from the pain. But Ur-ronn disliked the comparison and showed it by swinging her long neck like a whip, nearly taking off one of Huck's eyestalks with a snap of her three-way mouth.

Huck only said 'Centaur' just that once.

Ur-ronn is a niece of Uriel, who runs a forge next to fiery lava pools, high up on Mount Guenn. She won a scholarship to 'prentice as a smith instead of staying with the herds and caravans on the grassy plain. Too bad her aunt keeps Ur-ronn busy most of the time and won't *ever* let her go off in the boat with us, on account of urs can't swim.

Ur-ronn used to read a lot, back in that prairie school. Books we never heard of in this hick corner of the Slope. She tells us the stories she can recollect, like all about Crazy Horse and Genghis Khan, and urrish hero-warriors from those big battles they had with the humans, after Earthers came to Jijo but before the Commons got patched together and they started the Great Peace.

It'd be uttergloss if our gang could be a complete Six, like when Drake and Ur-jushen and their comrades went on the Big Quest and were the very first to set eyes on the Holy Egg. But the only traeki in town is the pharmacist, and that *er* is too old to make a new stack of rings we could play with. As for humans, *their* nearest village is several days from here. So I guess we're stuck being just a foursome.

Too bad. Humans are gloss. They brought books to Jijo and speak Anglic better than anybody, except me and maybe Huck.

Also, a human kid's shaped kind of like a small hoon, so he could go nearly all the same places I can with my two long legs. Ur-ronn may be able to run fast, but she can't go into water, and Pincer can't wander too far from it, and poor Huck has to stay where the ground is level enough for her wheels.

None of them can climb a tree.

Still, they're my pals. Anyway, there are things they can do that I can't, so I guess it evens out.

It was Huck who said we ought to plan a really burnish adventure for the summer, since it would likely be our last.

School was out. Mister Heinz was on his yearly trip to the great archive at Biblos, then to Gathering Festival. As usual, he took along some older hoon students, including Huck's foster sister, Aph-awn. We envied their long voyage – first by sea, then riverboat to Ur-Tanj town, and finally by donkey-caravan all the way up to that mountain valley where they'd attend games and dramas, visit the Egg, and watch the sages meet in judgment over all six of Jijo's exile races.

Next year we may get our turn to go, but I don't mind saying the prospect of waiting another seventeen months wasn't welcome. What if we didn't have a single thing to do all summer except get caught loafing by our parents, then sent to help pack dross ships, unload fishing boats, and perform a hundred other mindless chores? Even more depressing, there wouldn't be any new books till Mister Heinz got back – that is *if* he didn't lose the list we gave him!

(One time he returned all excited with a big stack of old Earth *poetry* but not a single novel by Conrad, Coopé, or Coontz. Worse, some grown-ups even claimed to *like* the stuff!)

Anyway, it was Huck who first suggested heading over the Line, and I'm still not sure whether that's giving a friend due credit or passing on blame.

'I know where there's something to read,' she said one day, when summer was just getting its early start here in the south.

Yowg-wayuo had already caught us, vegetating under the pier, skipping rocks at dome-bobbers and bored as noors in a cage. Sure enough, he right-prompt sent us up the long access ramp to repair the village camouflage trellis, a job I always hate and I'll be glad when I'm too big to be drafted into doing it anymore. We hoon aren't as fond of heights as those tree-hugging humans and their chimp pets, so let me tell you it can be dizzifying having to crawl atop the wooden lattice arching over all the houses and shops of Wuphon, tending a carpet of greenery that's supposed to hide our town against being seen from space.

I have doubts it'd really work, if *The Day* ever comes that everyone frets about. When sky-gods come to judge us, what good will a canopy of leaves do? Will it spare us punishment?

But I don't want to be called a heretic. Anyway, this ain't the place to talk about that.

So there we were, high over Wuphon, all exposed with the bare sun glaring down, and Huck blurts her remark like a sudden burst of hollow hail.

'I know where there's something to read,' she says.

I put down the lath strips I was carrying, laying them across a clump of black iris vines. Below, I made out the pharmacist's house, with its chimney spilling distinct traeki smells. (Do you know that different kinds of plants grow above a traeki's home? It can be hard working there if the pharmacist happens to be making medicine while you're overhead!)

'What're you talking about?' I asked, fighting a wave of wooziness. Huck wheeled over to pick up one of the laths, nimbly bending and slipping it in where the trellis sagged.

'I'm talking about reading something no one on the Slope has ever seen,' she answered in her crooning way, when she thinks an idea's gloss. Two eyestalks hovered over her busy hands, while a third twisted to watch me with a glint I know too well. 'I'm talking about something *so* ancient, it makes the oldest Scroll on Jijo look like Joe Dolenz just printed it, with the ink still wet!'

Huck spun along the beams and joists, making me gulp when she popped a wheelie or swerved past a gaping hole, weaving flexible lath canes like reeds in a basket. We tend to see g'Keks as frail beings, because they prefer smooth paths and hate rocky ground. But those axles and rims are nimble, and what a g'Kek calls a road can be narrow as a plank.

'Don't give me that,' I shot back. 'Your folk burned and sank their sneakship, same as every race who skulked down to Jijo. All they *had* were Scrolls – till humans came.'

Huck rocked her torso, imitating a traeki gesture that means, *Maybe you're right, but i/we don't think so.*

'Oh, Alvin, you know even the first exiles found things on Jijo to read.'

All right, so I wasn't too swift on the grok. I'm plenty smart in my own way – steady and thorough is the hoonish style – but no one ever accused me of being quick.

I frowned, mimicking a human 'thoughtful' expression I once saw in a book, even though it makes my forehead hurt. My throat sac throbbed as I concentrated.

'Hrrrrrm ... Now wait just a minute. You don't mean those wall markings sometimes found—'

'On the walls of old Buyur buildings, yes! The few not smashed or eaten by mulc-spiders when the Buyur left, a million years ago. Those same markings.'

'But weren't they mostly just street signs and such?'

'True,' she agreed with one dipping eyestalk. 'But there were really strange ones in the ruins where I first lived. Uncle Lorben was translating some into GalTwo, before the avalanche hit.'

I'll never get used to how matter-of-factly she can speak about the disaster that wiped out her family. If anything like it happened to me, I wouldn't talk again for years. Maybe ever.

'Uncle swapped letters with a Biblos scholar about the engravings he found. I was too little to understand much. But clearly there are savants who want to know about Buyur wall writings.'

And others who wouldn't like it, I recall thinking. Despite the Great Peace, there are still folk in all six races ready to cry *heresy* and warn of an awful penance, about to fall from the sky.

'Well, it's too bad all the carvings were destroyed when ... you know.'

'When the mountain killed my folks? Yeah. Too bad. Say, Alvin, will you pass a couple more strips over to me? I can't quite reach—'

Huck teetered on one wheel, the other spinning madly. I gulped and passed over the lengths of slivered boo. 'Thanks,' Huck said, landing back on the beam with a shuddering bounce, damped by her shocks. 'Now where was I? Oh yeah. Buyur wall writings. I was going to suggest how we can find some engravings no one's ever seen. At least none of us exile Sixers.'

'How could that be?' My throat sac must have fluttered in confusion, making burbly sounds. 'Your people came to Jijo two thousand years ago. Mine almost as long. Even *humans* have been here a few hundred. Every inch of the Slope is explored, and each Buyur site poked into, scores of times!'

Huck stretched all four eyes toward me.

'*Exactly!*'

Floating from her cranial tympanum, the Anglic word seemed stressed with soft accents of excitement. I stared for a long time and finally croaked in surprise.

'You mean to *leave* the Slope? To sneak beyond the Rift?'

I should have known better than to ask.

All it would have taken was a shift in the roll of Ifni's dice, and this would be a very different tale. Things came *that* close to going the way Huck wanted.

She kept badgering me, for one thing. Even after we finished repairing the lattice and went back to loitering near the ships moored under huge, overhanging gingourv trees, she just kept at it with her special combination of g'Kek wit and hoonlike persistence.

'Come on, Alvin. Haven't we sailed to Terminus Rock dozens of times and dared each other to keep on going? We even *did* it, once, and no harm ever came!'

'Just to the middle of the Rift. Then we scurried home again.'

'So? Do you want that shame sticking forever? This may be our last chance!'

I rubbed my half-inflated sac, making a hollow, rumbling sound. 'Aren't you forgetting, we already *have* a project? We're building a bathy, in order to go diving—'

She cut loose a blat of disgust. 'We talked it over last week and you agreed. The bathy reeks.'

'I agreed to *think* about it. *Hrm*. After all, Pincer has already built the hull. Chewed it himself from that big garu log. And what about the work the rest of us put in, looking up old Earthling designs, making that compressor pump and cable? Then there are those wheels you salvaged, and Ur-ronn's porthole—'

'Yeah, yeah.' She renounced all our labors with a dismissive twirl of two stalks. 'Sure, it was fun working on that stuff during winter, when we had to sit indoors anyway. *Especially* when it looked like it'd never actually happen. We had a great game of pretend.

'But things are getting serious! Pincer talks about actually making a deep dive in a month or two. Didn't we agree that's crazy? Didn't we, Alvin?' Huck rolled closer and did something I've never heard another g'Kek do. She rumbled an *umble* at me, mimicking the undertone a young hoon female might use if her big, handsome male was having trouble seeing things her way.

'Now wouldn't you rather come with me to see some uttergloss writings, so burnish and ancient they were written with *computers* and *lasers* and such? Hr-rm? Doesn't that beat drowning in a stinky dross coffin, halfway to the bottom of the sea?'

Time to switch languages. While I normally find Anglic more buff than smug old star-god tongues, even Mister Heinz agrees that its 'human tempos and loose logical structure tend to favor impetuous enthusiasms.'

Right then, I needed the opposite, so I shifted to the whistles and pops of Galactic Two.

'*Consideration of (punishable) criminality – this has not occurred to thee?*'

Unfazed, she countered in GalSeven, the formal tongue most favored by humans.

'*We are minors, friend. Besides, the border law is meant to thwart illicit breeding beyond the permitted zone. Our gang has no such intent!*'

Then, in a quick flip to Galactic Two—

'—*Or hast thee (perverted) designs to attempt (strange, hybrid) pro-creation experiments with this (virginal female) self?*'

What a thought! Plainly she was trying to keep me off balance. I could feel control slip away. Soon I'd find myself vowing to set sail for those dark ruins you can dimly see from Terminus Rock, if you aim an urrish telescope across the Rift's deep waters.

Just then, my eye caught a familiar disturbance under the placid bay. A ruddy shape swarmed up the sandy bank until a dappled crimson carapace burst forth, spraying saltwater. From that compact pentagonal shell, a fleshy dome raised, girdled by a glossy black ring.

'Pincer!' I cried, glad of a distraction from Huck's hot enthusiasm. 'Come over and help me talk to this silly—'

But the young qheuen burst ahead, cutting me off even before water stopped burbling from his speech vents.

'M-m-mo-mo-mon—'

Pincer's not as good at Anglic as Huck and me, especially when excited. But he uses it to prove he's as humicking modern as anyone. I held up my hands. 'Easy, pal! Take a breath. Take five!'

He exhaled a deep sigh, which emerged as a pair of bubble streams where two spiky legs were still submerged. 'I s-s-seen 'em! This time I *really* s-seen 'em!'

'Seen what?' Huck asked, rolling across squishy sand.

The vision band rimming Pincer's dome looked in all directions at once. Still, we could feel our friend's intense regard as he took another deep breath, then sighed a single word.

'*Monsters!*'

II

THE BOOK OF THE SLOPE

Legends

The better part of a million years has passed since the Buyur departed Jijo, obeying Galactic rules of planetary management when their lease on this world expired. Whatever they could not carry off, or store in lunar caches, the Buyur diligently destroyed, leaving little more than vine-crusted rubble where their mighty cities once towered, gleaming under the sun.

Yet even now, their shadow hangs over us – we cursed and exiled savages – reminding us that gods once ruled on Jijo.

Living here as illegal squatters – as 'sooners' who must never dwell beyond this strip between the mountains and the sea – we of the Six Races can only look with superstitious awe at eroded Buyur ruins. Even after books and literacy returned to our Commons, we lacked the tools and skills to analyze the remains or to learn much about Jijo's last lawful tenants. Some recent enthusiasts, styling themselves 'archaeologists,' have begun borrowing techniques from dusty Earthling texts, but these devotees cannot even tell us what the Buyur looked like, let alone their habits, attitudes, or way of life.

Our best evidence comes from folklore.

Though glavers no longer speak – and so are not counted among the Six – we still have some of the tales they used to tell, passed on by the g'Keks, who knew glavers best, before they devolved.

Once, before their sneakship came to Jijo, when glavers roamed the stars as full citizens of the Five Galaxies, it is said that they were on intimate terms with a race called the Tunnuctyur, a great and noble clan. In their youth, these Tunnuctyur had been clients of another species – the patron that uplifted them, giving the Tunnuctyur mastery of speech, tools, and sapiency. Those patrons were called Buyur, and they came from Galaxy Four – from a world with a huge carbon star in its sky.

According to legend, these Buyur were known as clever designers of small living things.

They were also known to possess a rare and dangerous trait — a sense of humor.

—*Mystery of the Buyur*
by Hau-uphtunda. Guild of Freelance
Scholars, Year-of-Exile 1908.

Hear, my rings, the song i sing. Let its vapors rise amid your cores, and sink like dripping wax. It comes in many voices, scents, and strengths of time. It weaves like a g'Kek tapestry, flows like a hoon aria, gallops and swerves in the manner of urrish legend, and yet turns inexorably, as with the pages of a human book.

The story begins in peace.

It was springtime, early in the second lunar cycle of the nineteen hundred and thirtieth year of our exile-and-crime, when the Rothen arrived, manifesting unwelcome in our sky. Shining sunlike in their mastery of air and ether, they rent the veil of our concealment at the worst of all possible times – during the vernal gathering-of-tribes, near the blessed foot of Jijo's Egg.

There we had come, as so often since the Emergence, to hear the great ovoid's music. To seek guidance patterns. To trade the produce of our varied talents. To settle disputes, compete in games, and renew the Commons. Above all, seeking ways to minimize the harm done by our ill-starred presence on this world.

Gathering – a time of excitement for the young, work for the skilled, and farewells for those nearing the end of years. Already there had spread rumors – portents – that this assembly would be momentous. More than a usual quota from each clan had come. Along with sages and roamers, grafters and techies, many simple folk of two legs, four and five – and of wheel and ring – followed drumbeats along still-frosted mountain tracks to reach the sacred glades. Among each race, manifold had felt the tremors – stronger than any since that provident year when the Egg burst from Jijo's mother soil, shedding hot birth-dust, then settling to rule our fractious passions and unite us.

Ah, Gathering.

This latest pilgrimage may not yet have solidified as waxy memory. But try to recall slowly wending our now-aged pile of rings aboard ship at Far Wet Sanctuary, to sail past the glistening Spectral Flow and the Plain of Sharp Sand.

Did not those familiar wonders seem to pale when we reached the Great Marsh and found it in bloom? Something seen once in a traeki lifetime? A sea of color – flowering, fruiting, and already dying gaudily before our senses. Transferring from boat to barge, we travelers rowed amid great pungency, under avenues of million-petalled sylph canopies.

Our companions took this as an omen, did they not, my rings? The humans in our midst spoke of mysterious Ifni, the capricious one, whose verdicts are not always just but are ever-surprising.

Do you recall other sights/experiences? The weaver villages? The mulc-spiders and hunting camps? And finally that arduous climb, twist by twist of our straining footpads, through the Pass of Long Umbras to reach this green vale where, four traeki generations ago, geysers steamed and rainbows danced, celebrating the dark ovoid's emergence?

Recollect, now, the crunch of volcanic gravel, and how the normally obedient rewq-beast trembled on our head-ring, mutinously refusing to lay itself over our eyelets, so that we arrived in camp barefaced, unmasked, while children of all Six Races scurried, shouting, *'Asx/Asx! Asx, the traeki, has come!'*

Picture the other High Sages – colleagues and friends – emerging from their tents to walk, slither, roll, and greet us with this epithet. This label they regard as permanently attached to 'me' – a fiction that i humor.

Do you recall all that, my rings?

Well, patience then. Memories congeal like dripping wax, simmering to coat our inner core. Once there, they can never be forgotten.

On Jijo there is a deep shine in the section of sky farthest from the sun. We are told this is rare on worlds catalogued by the Great Galactics, an effect of carbon grains – the same ones that seed the hollow hail – grains sent by Izmunuti, the glaring star-eye in a constellation humans call Job's Torment. It is said our ancestors studied such traits of their new home before burning and burying their ships.

It is also said that they simply 'looked it all up' in a portable branch of the Galactic Library – before consigning even that treasure to flames on the day called Never-Go-Back.

There was no hollow hail that spring morning, when the other sages emerged to salute our rings, calling us/me Asx. As we gathered under a pavilion, i learned that our rewq was not the only one grown skittish. Not even the patient hoon could control his translation-helper. So we sages conferred without the little symbionts, fathoming each other by word and gesture alone.

Of all whose ancestors chose hopeless exile on this world, the g'Kek are senior. So to Vubben fell the role – Speaker of Ignition.

'Are we guilty for the failure of rantanoids?' Vubben asked, turning each eye toward a different point of the compass. 'The Egg senses pain in the life-field whenever potential is lost.'

'Hrrrm. We argue the point endlessly,' the hoon sophist, Phwhoon-dau, replied. 'Lark and Uthen tell of a *decline*. Rantanoids aren't yet extinct. A small number remain on an Yuqun Isle.'

The human sage, Lester Cambel, agreed. 'Even if they are past hope, rantanoids are just one of countless species of root-grubbers. No reason to figure they were specially blessed.'

Ur-Jah retorted that her own ancestors, long ago and far away, had been *little root-grubbers*.

Lester conceded with a bow. 'Still, we aren't responsible for the rise and fall of every species.'

'How can you know?' Vubben persisted. 'We who lack most tools of science, left to flounder in darkness by our selfish forebears, cannot know what subtle harm we do by stepping on a leaf or voiding our wastes in a pit. None can predict what we'll be held accountable for, when The Day comes. Even *glavers*, in their present state of innocence, will be judged.'

That was when our aged qheuenish sage, whom we call Knife-Bright Insight, tilted her blue carapace. Her voice was a soft whisper from one chitin thigh.

'The Egg, our gift in the wilderness, knows answers. Truth is its reward to an open mind.'

Chastened by her wisdom, we fell into meditation.

No longer needed, the errant rewq slipped off our brows and gathered in the center, exchanging host-enzymes. We took up a gentle rhythm, each sage adding a line of harmony – of breath and beating hearts.

My rings, do you recall what chose then to occur?

The fabric of our union was ripped by booming *echoes*, cast arrogantly by the Rothen ship, proclaiming its malign power, before it even arrived.

We emerged to stare, dismayed, at the riven sky.

Soon sage and clanfolk alike knew The Day had finally come.

Vengeance is not spared upon the children of the fallen.

THE FAMILY OF NELO

The paper-crafter had three offspring – a number worthy of his noble calling, like his father, and his father's father. Nelo always supposed the line would go on through his own two sons and daughter. So he took it hard when his strong-jawed children deserted the water mill, its sluiceways, and wooden gears. None heeded the beckoning rhythm of the pulping hammer, beating cloth scavenged from all six races, or the sweet mist spread by the sifting screens, or the respectful bows of traders, come from afar to buy Nelo's sleek white pages.

Oh, Sara, Lark, and Dwer were happy to *use* paper! Dwer, the youngest, wrapped it around arrowheads and lures for the hunt. Sometimes he paid his father in piu nodules, or grwon teeth, before fading into the forest again, as he had done since turning nine. Apprenticed to Fallon the Tracker, Dwer soon became a legend across the Slope. Nothing he sought escaped his bow, unless it was shielded by law. And rumors said the fierce-eyed lad with jet-black hair killed and ate whatever he liked, when the law wasn't looking.

As focused as Dwer was wild, *Lark* used paper to plot vast charts on his study wall, some parts almost black with notes and diagrams. Elsewhere, large spaces gaped blank, a waste of Nelo's art.

'It can't be helped, Father,' Lark explained near wooden shelves filled with fossils. 'We haven't found which species fill those gaps. This world is so complex, I doubt even the Buyur ever fully grasped Jijo's ecosystem.'

Nelo recalled thinking that an absurd thing to say. When the Buyur leased Jijo, they had been full citizens of the Community of the Five Galaxies, with access to the fabled Great Library, dwarfing all the paper books in Biblos! With a word, the Buyur could beckon any answer under the sun. Under a *billion* suns, if tales of the past could be trusted.

At least the sages approved of Lark's work. But what of *Sara*? Always Nelo's favorite, she used to love the smells, rhythms and textures of papermaking – till age fourteen, when she stumbled on a *talent*.

Nelo blamed his late wife, who had entered his life so strangely, long ago, and used to fill the kids' heads with odd tales and ambitions.

Yes, he decided. *It was all Melina's fault—*

A low cough jarred Nelo's drifting resentment. He blinked as a pair of deep brown eyes peered over his pitted desk. Dark fur framed a face so nearly human that unwary traeki sometimes gave *chimpanzees* the courtesy due full members of the Commons.

'Are you still here?' Nelo snapped.

The face winced, then nodded to the left, toward the paper storeroom, where one of Nelo's aides slowly gathered torn sheets from a discard bin.

He cursed. 'Not that garbage, Jocko!'

'But Master, you said to fetch waste scraps we can't sell—'

Nelo ducked under the Great Shaft, a rotating horizontal shank of hardwood, carrying power from the village dam to nearby workshops. He shooed Jocko away. 'Never mind what I said. Go back to the vats – and tell Caleb to put less water through the millrace! It's four months till rainy season. He'll have us out of business in two!'

Nelo scanned the shelves for himself, finally choosing two reams of slightly flawed sheets, bound in liana vines. They weren't quite rejects. Someone might have paid cash for them. On the other hand, what was there to save for? Didn't the sages warn against investing much pride or care in tomorrow?

For all strivings will be judged, and few will win grace . . .

Nelo snorted. He wasn't a religious man. He made *paper*. The profession implied some faith in the essential goodness of time.

'These'll do for your mistress, Prity,' he told the little chimp, who rounded the desk, holding out both hands. Mute as a rewq, she served Nelo's daughter in ways no other being on Jijo could manage. Ways that few could comprehend. He handed over one of the heavy packages.

'I'll carry the other. It's time I dropped by anyway, to see if Sara's getting enough to eat.'

Mute or not, the ape was expressive with rolled eyes. She knew this was just an excuse for Nelo to have a look at Sara's mysterious house-guest.

Nelo growled. 'Come along and no dawdling. Some of us work for a living, you know.'

A covered walkway linked the dam/factory to the forest, where most villagers dwelled. Fierce sunlight filtered through a canopy of living camouflage. At noon it took an optimist to think the screen would hide the buildings against a resolute scan from space – and among the Six, optimism was viewed as a mild type of heresy.

Alas, it was *not* the type of heresy followed by Nelo's eldest son.

Concealment seemed doubly problematic for the great dam itself. Unlike the ones qheuenish colonists made, bottling small ponds behind barriers that mimicked landslides or piles of logs, this dam spanned half an arrowflight from end to end. False boulders and cascades of melon creepers blurred its outline. Still many called it the most blatant artifact on the Slope – outside of some ancient Buyur site. Each year, on Denouncement Day, radicals harangued for its destruction.

And now Lark is one of them. Nelo cast a stock complaint toward his dead wife's spirit. *Do you hear, Melina? You brought the boy with you, when you came from the far south. We're taught genes don't matter as much as upbringing, but did I raise a son to be a rabble-rousing apostate? Never!*

Instead of camouflage, Nelo put his faith in the promise of the founding ancestors who planted their truant seed on Jijo, claiming there would be *no* determined scan from space. Not for half a million years or so.

He once stressed that point in an argument with Lark. To his surprise, the lad agreed, then said it did not matter.

'I urge drastic measures not because I'm afraid of being caught, but because it's the right thing to do.'

Right? Wrong? A cloud of dizzying abstractions. Lark and Sara kept bringing up such fluff – arguing with each other for miduras about fate and destiny. Sometimes Nelo found *Dwer*, the wild boy of the forest, the easiest of his children to understand.

The village carpenter's shop spewed sawdust, making pipe for Jobee, the rotund village plumber, to splice into homes, bringing fresh water and taking away waste to the septic pits. The comforts of a civilized life.

'Deep shade, Nelo,' Jobee drawled in a manner that invited a soul to stop and chat a spell.

'Cloudy sky, Jobee,' Nelo replied with a polite nod, and kept walking. Not that a few duras' idle banter would hurt. *But if he learns I'm visiting Sara, he'll drop by later with half the town to find out what I learned about her new pet . . . the stranger with the hole in his head.*

Once upon a time, it had been a fallen chipwing with a broken tail rudder, or a wounded toyo pup. Anything sick or hurt used to wind up in his storeroom, where Sara tended it in a box lined with his finest felt. Nelo had figured his adult daughter finally past that phase – till she returned from a routine gleaning trip a few days ago, with a wounded man thrashing on a stretcher.

Once Nelo might have opposed an outsider, even a sick one, lodging in his daughter's treehouse. Now he was glad to see anything draw her from a year's hard work and isolation. One of Sara's guildmasters had written to him recently, complaining that she was shirking a principal duty of a woman of her caste, prompting Nelo to write back, rebuking the fellow's impudence. Still, any interest Sara showed in a man was cause for guarded hope.

From the covered walkway, Nelo spied the town exploser and his young son, inspecting an anchor-pier of the great dam. Forbidding and earnest, with deep-chiseled features, Henrik reached into a recessed hole and withdrew a bulb-ended clay tube. Scrutinizing the charge, the exploser held it for his son to sniff.

Nelo was suddenly acutely aware of the mighty lake, lurking behind the dam, ready to sweep away the locks and factories if ever a signal came from Henrik to do his duty. He also felt a pang of *jealousy* over that knowing tête-à-tête between father and child – the sort that he once had with his own sire. One he hoped to share again, with someone who loved paper as he did.

If only one of the three kids would give me an heir.

I'll have one yet, he vowed. *If I must bribe the sages to command it!*

Henrik slipped the tube back inside, resealing the hole with clay.

A low sigh hissed to Nelo's left, where he saw another person also watching the explosers. *Log Biter*, matriarch of the local qheuenish hive, squatted by a tree stump with all five legs drawn in. Nervous exhalations stirred dust beneath her blue carapace, and she wore a rewq over her vision strip – as if that would tell her much about Henrik and son!

Anyway, what was Log Biter worried about? Surely this was just routine maintenance. Dolo's human villagers would never sacrifice the dam, source of their wealth and prestige. Only a few orthodox fools wanted that.

And Nelo's eldest son.

Everyone's edgy, he thought, turning away. *First an abnormal winter, then Ulkoun's proposition, and Lark's heresy. And now Sara comes home with a mysterious outsider.*

Is it any wonder I have trouble sleeping?

Most villagers' homes lay safe from the glowering sky, nestled high in the trunks of mighty garu trees, where strains of edible moss flourished on wide branch-top gardens. It seemed a niche made for Earthlings, just as blue qheuens loved lakes, and dry plains suited urrish tribes.

Nelo and Prity had to stop briefly while children herded braying bush-turkeys across the forest loam. A pair of opal-skinned glavers, perturbed while rooting for grubs, lifted their round heads and sniffed haughtily. The children laughed, and the glavers' bulging eyes soon dimmed, the light of anger costing too much effort to maintain.

It was the familiar rhythm of village life, and Nelo would happily go on taking it for granted, but for his eldest son's words before leaving for Gathering, when Lark explained the reason for his heresy.

'*Nature is taking hold of this world again, Father, moving beyond the patterns imposed by its former tenants.*'

Nelo had been doubtful. How could unsapient life change a world in less than a million years? Without a guiding race to tend it, as a farmer manages a garden?

'It's what declaring a world fallow is all about,' Lark went on. 'Letting it rest and recover without interference.'

'Without the likes of us, you mean.'

'That's right. We aren't supposed to be on Jijo. We do harm simply living here.'

It was the moral dilemma of the Six. The ancestors of each race had felt they had strong reasons to come so far in sneakships, planting outlaw seed on a forbidden world. The Scrolls spoke of crime blended with desperate *hope*. But Nelo's son stressed only the felony. Moreover, Lark and his comrades planned finally doing something about it. A grand gesture at this year's Gathering, atoning for generations of guilt with an act of devotion, both holy and terrible.

'What foolishness!' Nelo had protested. 'When civilization finally resettles this galaxy, there'll be no sign our kind ever lived here. Not if we live righteously, by Egg and Oath. What you plan will make no difference!'

In any quarrel with *Dwer*, there would have been defiant shouting. But Lark was even more frustrating to talk to, masking his purist heresy behind an obstinate civility he must have inherited from his mother.

'It doesn't matter if our crime is never discovered, Father. What matters is we don't belong here. We simply should not exist.'

Villagers saluted their paper-crafter as Nelo and Prity passed by. But today he only glowered, wishing acridly that his offspring wouldn't vex him so – first by neglecting his wishes, then by inflicting the ferment of their disturbing ideas.

Several boats lay berthed at the town dock. Nimble, sleek-furred noor beasts scampered across the masts, tending lines and camouflage shrouds, as their kind had been trained to do for centuries by the tall, long-snouted hoon. The crew of one vessel helped some local men load a cargo of glass and metal, scavenged from a Buyur site upriver, destined for reprocessing by the smiths of Ur-Tanj town, or else bound for the dross pits, far out to sea.

Normally, Nelo might have paused to watch, but Prity tugged his sleeve, urging him upward, into the blue-gray branches of the grove.

As they turned, sudden shouts blared. Men dropped their burdens and hoon sailors crouched, splaying shaggy legs. Creaking tree trunks swaying like the ship masts as lines snapped and ripples stitched the water. A cloud of leaves poured from the forest, filling the air with spinning spiral forms. Nelo recognized the basso rumble of a quake! Spine-tingling fear mixed with a strange *thrill* as he pondered whether to try for open ground.

The tumult passed before he could decide. Branches kept sway-ing, but the walkway planks ceased vibrating and the watery ripples vanished like dreams. Relieved sailors snorted. Villagers made rev-erent hand gestures, for Jijo's flexings were sacred omens of the planet's healing force, even when they brought riotous ruin. Once, a century ago, a more violent quake had brought forth the Holy Egg, a blessing worth all the pain that accompanied its birth.

Oh, Mother Jijo, Nelo prayed as the last temblors faded. *Let things go well at Gathering. Let the sages talk Lark and his friends out of their foolish plan.*

And perhaps, he dared add, *let Dwer also meet a girl of good family and settle down?*

He knew better than to ask a third wish. Sara wouldn't want him invoking a deity in her favor. Not unless it were Ifni, the impartially capricious goddess of numbers and fate.

When his pulse steadied, Nelo signaled for Prity to lead. Their route now spiraled up a massive garu, then along branch-tops spanned by rope guideways. Nelo's feet moved by habit and he barely noticed the height, but the bundle of paper grew heavy in his hands.

Sara's treehouse perched so high that daylight spread for hours across one wattle wall. Nelo gripped a guide-rope while crossing the last stretch. The naked sun was so unsettling, he nearly missed noticing a square-sided cage, made of braced rods, that hung from a pulley next to Sara's sky porch.

A lift! Why is a lift attached to my daughter's home?

Then he recalled. *It's because of the Stranger.*

Pungent aromas wafted from the house – tart, musty, and sweetly slimy. Peering inside, Nelo made out slanting rays of light, stabbing through louvered blinds. Sara's voice could be heard, mut-tering unhappily from another room. His hand raised to knock on the jamb, but paused when a pair of shadows loomed from within – one a cone-shaped outline of circular tubes, taller than Nelo's head. Nubby feet propelled the bottommost ring, making squishy sounds as it neared.

Two roller-hoops framed the smaller creature, whose slim torso ended with a pair of graceful arms and four eye-tipped feelers that peered all ways at once. One wheel squeaked as this entity rolled forward, revealing the spotted brain case and droopy eyestalks of an elderly g'Kek.

If any two citizens of Dolo Village could make Nelo feel spry at his age, it was this pair. In all the life-history of their two species, no g'Kek or traeki had ever climbed a tree.

'Cloudy skies, papermaker,' the wheeled one said.

'Deep shade, Doctor Lorrek. And to *you*, Pharmacist.' Nelo bowed twice. 'How goes your patient?'

Lorrek's Anglic was superb after years serving Dolo's mostly human populace.

'Astonishingly, the injured man gains strength, soothed by Pzora's special unguents' – the doctor bent a stalk toward the traeki whose ninth torus looked flushed from hard medicinal labor – 'and helped by the care he receives in this clean air.'

This *was* a surprise. The Stranger had seemed a goner.

'But his wounds! The hole in his head—?'

Shrugging had originally been a human gesture, but no one did it with more poise than a g'Kek.

'A fatal mutilation, I feared. Clearly the outlander owes his life to Pzora's secretions, and your daughter's swift action, hauling him from that foul swamp.'

The traeki pharmacist then spoke, turning its jewel-like sense organs, its voice wavering like an untuned metal harp.

'i/we help gladly, though our synthesis rings near-swoon from the effort. Unguents of rare potency were needed. Yet it seems difficult to please.'

'How do you mean?'

'Only here, up height where germs are scarce, might the work be done. Miss Sara's abode is ideal, and she will let no other take the patient. Yet she complains so! Aggrieved, she speaks longingly of an end to her work-disruption. Toward getting us all *out of her hair.*'

'It's just a metaphor,' Lorrek explained.

'As i/we assumed. Its paradoxical dissonance we/i esteem highly. May her selves understand that.'

'I'll see that she does,' Nelo told Pzora, smiling.

'Thank you all, excellent Nelos,' the young traeki responded, slipping into plural form, 'i/we hope for serene work, when we return this evening.'

Lorrek wrapped his eyestalks, and Nelo needed no rewq to read the old g'Kek's silent laughter. 'Serenity *is* good,' he agreed dryly, coughing behind a hand.

He braced the elevator cage, first for the heavy traeki to shuffle aboard. Then Lorrek rolled in, his left wheel wobbling from unbeatable degenerative axle disease. Nelo pulled the signal rope, calling an operator far below to start the weight-driven winch.

'Has anything been learned about the Stranger's identity?' Lorrek asked while waiting.

'Not that I heard. Though I'm sure it's just a matter of time.'

So far, even merchant traders had failed to recognize the unconscious man, implying he came quite a distance, perhaps from the coast settlements or even The Vale. *No one in Dolo knew Melina, either, when she arrived long ago, with a letter of introduction and a baby on her hip. The Slope is a bigger place than we're used to thinking.*

The g'Kek sighed. 'We must resolve soon whether it will better serve the patient to send him on, now that he's stabilized, to be examined in—'

The case shuddered, then dropped swiftly, cutting Lorrek off mid-sentence.

Ah well, Nelo thought, watching the car vanish steadily below moss-heavy branches. *That'd explain the shouting. Sara wouldn't want her pet sent to specialists in Tarek Town – even if she does complain about disrupted work.*

Would she ever learn? The last time Sara's nurturing instincts took over – succoring a convalescing bookbinder, in Biblos – it led to a love affair that ended in tragedy, scandal, and alienation from her guild. Nelo hoped the cycle wasn't repeating.

Even now she could win it all back – both her position and marriage to a respected sage. True, I never liked that sour-pussed Taine, but he offers a more secure life than she'd have had with that frail lover of hers.

Anyway, she can still do math while making me some grandkids.

The little chimp plunged into the house first. Sara's voice called from shadows, 'Is that you, Prity? It's been nothing but interruptions, but I think I finally whipped that integral. Why don't you look it ov—'

There was a flat sound. A large bundle, landing on a table.

'Ah, the paper. Wonderful. Let's see what the old man sent us this time.'

'Whatever *the old man* sends is good enough for one who don't *pay* for it,' Nelo groused, shuffling while his eyes adapted. Through the gloom, he saw his daughter rise from a desk covered with notebooks and obscure symbols. Sara's round face spread with a smile *he* always thought beautiful, though it might have helped if she'd taken more after her mother.

My looks and Melina's wild brains. Not a blend I'd wish on a sweet lass.

'Father!' She hurried over to embrace him. 'You gave me a start.'

Her black hair, cut like a boy's, smelled of pencil dust and Pzora's unguents.

'No doubt.' He frowned at the shambles of her quarters, worse now with a mattress by her desk. A jumble of texts, some bearing emblems of the great Biblos trove, lay amid notes on the 'new direction' her research had taken, combining mathematics and *linguistics*, of all things.

Prity took one of Sara's papers and perched on a stool. The chimp worked her lower kip, scanning one line of symbols at a time, silent collaborator in an arcane art Nelo would never understand.

He glanced toward the sleeping porch, where sunlight spread across a blanket, outlining two large feet.

'With both of the lads gone, I thought I'd come see how you're doing.'

'Well, I'm all right, as you can see.' She gestured, as if the firetrap of a treehouse were a model of home-tending. 'And I have Prity to take care of me. Why, I even recall to eat, most days!'

'Well ...' he muttered. But Sara had taken his arm and was gently maneuvering him toward the door. 'I'll come visit tomorrow,' she vowed, 'when Lorrek and old Stinky want me out of the way. We'll go to Belonna's for a nice meal, hm? I'll even wear a clean gown.'

'Well – that'd be fine.' He paused. 'Just remember, the elders will assign you help, if all this gets to be too much fuss and work.'

She nodded. 'I know how this looks to you, Father. "Sara's gone obsessive again," right? Well don't worry. It's not like that, this time. I just think this place is ideal for preventing infection of those horrid wounds—'

A low moan floated from the back of the house. Sara hesitated, then held up a hand. 'I'll be a moment.'

Nelo watched her hasten toward the shuttered porch, then he followed, drawn by curiosity.

Prity was wiping the injured stranger's brow, while his dark hands trembled outward, as if warding off something deadly. Livid scars laced the man's arms, and yellow fluid leaked through a gauze dressing near his left ear. The last time Nelo had seen the man, his skin was ashen with a pallor of approaching death. Now the eyes, with near-black irises, seemed to flame with awful passion.

Sara took the wounded man's hands, speaking insistently, trying to soothe the abrupt fit. But the outsider clutched her wrists, clamping down so hard that Sara cried out. Nelo rushed to her side, plucking vainly at the strong fingers gripping his daughter.

'Ge – ge – ge – *dow*!' the stranger stammered, yanking Sara toward the floor.

At that moment, the sky cracked open.

A savage roar blew in the shutters, knocking pottery off kitchen shelves. The entire garu tree *leaned*, as if a great hand shoved it, knocking Nelo off his feet. With ringing ears, father and daughter clutched floor planks as the tree swung over so far, Nelo glimpsed the *ground* through a gaping window. More crockery spilled.

Furniture slid toward the open door. Amid a storm of swirling paper, Prity shrieked, and the wide-eyed stranger howled in harmony.

Nelo managed one dumbfounded thought. *Could it be another quake?*

The garu whipped them back and forth like beads in a rattle, for a terrifying interval that felt like eternity – and must have lasted all of a minute.

Amazingly, the house clung to its cleft between two branches. Vibrations thrummed along the tree's abused spine as the wail in Nelo's skull abated at last, trailing to numbed silence. Reluctantly, he let Sara help him rise. Together, they joined the stranger, who now clutched the windowsill with bone-white knuckles.

The forest was a maelstrom of dust and fluttering leaves. No trees had toppled, much to Nelo's surprise. He sought the great dam and found that it held, thank God. The paper-mill appeared intact.

'Look!' Sara gasped, pointing *above* the forest toward the southeast sky.

A thin white trail showed where, high overhead, the air had been riven by something titanic and fast – something that still sparkled in the distance as they glimpsed it streak past the valley's edge, toward the white-tipped peaks of the Rimmer Range. So high and so fleet it seemed – so arrogantly untimid – Nelo did not have to speak his dread aloud. The same fear lay in his daughter's eyes.

The stranger, still tracking the distant, dwindling glitter, let out a foreboding sigh. He seemed to share their anxiety, but in his weary face there was no hint of surprise.

ASX

Do you recall, my rings, how the rothen ship circled thrice over the glade of Gathering, blazing from its hot descent, chased by the roaring protest of a cloven sky? Stroke the wax-of-memory, and recollect how mighty the vessel seemed, halting dramatically, almost overhead.

Even the human tribe – our finest tech-crafters – stared in the round-eyed manner of their kind, as the great cylinder, vast as a glacier, settled down just ninety arrowflights away from the secret sacred hollow of the Holy Egg.

The people of the Six Races came before us, moaning dread.

'Oh, sages, shall we flee? Shall we hide, as the law demands?'

Indeed, the Scrolls so command us.

Conceal your tents, your fields, your works and very selves. For from the sky shall come your judgment and your scourge.

Message-casters asked – 'Shall we put out the Call? Shall villages and burghs and herds and hives be told to raze?'

Even before the law was shaped – when our Commons had not yet congealed out of sharp enmities – even then our scattered outcast bands knew where danger lay. We exiles-on-Jijo have cowered when survey probes from the Galactic Institutes made cursory audits from afar, causing our sensor-stones to light with warning fire. At other times, shimmering globe-swarms of *Zang* fell from the starry vault, dipping to the sea, then parting amid clouds of stolen vapor. Even those six times when new bands of misfits settled on this desert shore, they went ungreeted by those already here, until they burned the ships that brought them.

'Shall we try to hide?'

Recall, my rings, the confused braying as folk scattered like chaff before a whirlwind, tearing down the festival pavilions, hauling dross from our encampment toward nearby caves. Yet amid all this, some were calm, resigned. From each race, a few understood. This time there would be no hiding from the stars.

Among the High Sages, Vubben spoke first, turning an eyestalk toward each of us.

'Never before has a ship landed right in our midst. Clearly, we are already seen.'

'*Perhaps not,*' Ur-Jah suggested in hopeful Galactic Seven, stamping one hoof. Agitated white fur outlined her flared urrish nostril. '*They may be tracking emanations of the Egg! Perhaps if we hide swiftly ...*'

Ur-Jah's voice trailed off as Lester, the human, rocked his head – a simple gesture of negation lately fashionable throughout the Commons, among those with heads.

At this range, our infrared signatures would be unmistakable. Their onboard library will have categorized us down to each subspecies. If they didn't know about us before entering the atmosphere, they surely do by now.'

Out of habit, we took his word for such things, about which humans oft know best.

'Perhaps they are refugees like us!' burst forth our qheuenish sage, venting hope from all five leg-vents. But Vubben was not sanguine.

'You saw the manner of their arrival. Was that the style of refugees, treading in fear, hiding from Izmunuti's stare? Did any of *our* ancestors come thus? Screaming brutishly across the sky?'

Lifting his forward eye to regard the crowd, Vubben called for order. 'Let no one leave the festival valley, lest their flight be tracked to our scattered clans and holds. But seek all glavers that have come to browse among us, and push those simple ones away, so our guilt won't stain their reclaimed innocence.

'As for those of the Six who are here now, where the ship's dark shadow fell ... we all must live or die as fate wills.'

i/we sensed solidification among the rings of my/our body. Fear merged into noble resignation as the Commons saw truth in Vubben's words.

'Nor shall we scurry uselessly,' he went on. 'For the Scrolls also say – *When every veil is torn, cower no more. For that day comes your judgment. Stand as you are.*'

So clear was his wisdom, there rose no dissent. We gathered then, tribe by tribe, did we not, my rings? From many, we coalesced as one.

Together our Commons turned toward the ship, to meet our destiny.

DWER

The weird noor still dogged his heels, leering down at him from tree branches, being an utter pest. Sometimes the sleek, black-pelted creature vanished for a while, raising Dwer's hopes. Perhaps it finally had tired of dusty alpine air, so far from the swamps where most noor dwelled.

Then it reappeared, a grin splitting its stubby snout, perched on some ledge to watch Dwer hack through thorn-hedges and scramble over upended slabs of ancient pavement, kneeling often to check footprint traces of a runaway glaver.

The scent was already cool when Dwer had first noticed the spoor, just outside the Glade of Gathering. His brother and the other pilgrims had continued toward sounds of gala music, floating from the festival pavilions. But alas for Dwer, it was *his* job to stop glavers who took a strange notion to leave the cozy lowlands and make a break for perilous freedom. Festival would have to wait.

The noor barked high-pitched yelps, pretending to be helpful, its sinuous body streaking along at root level while Dwer had to chop and scramble. Finally, Dwer could tell they were gaining. The glaver's tired footprints lay close together, pressing the heel. When the wind changed, Dwer caught a scent. *About time*, he thought, gauging how little mountain remained before a cleft led to the next watershed – in effect another world.

Why do glavers keep doing this? Their lives aren't so rough on this side, where everyone dotes on them. Beyond the pass, by contrast, lay a poison plain, unfit for all but the hardiest hunters.

Or tourists, he thought, recalling Lena Strong's offer to pay him to lead a trip east. A journey whose sole aim was *sightseeing* – a word Dwer had only heard in tales from Old Earth.

These are crazy times, he thought. Yet the 'tour organizers' claimed to have approval from the sages – under certain conditions. Dwer shook his head. He didn't need idiotic ideas clouding his mind right now, with a quarry just ahead.

The noor, too, showed signs of fatigue, though it kept snuffing along the glaver's track, then rising on its hind legs to scan with black, forward-facing eyes. Suddenly, it gave a guttural purr and took off through the montane thicket – and soon Dwer heard a glaver's unmistakable squawl, followed by the thud of running feet.

Great, now he's spooked it!

At last Dwer spilled from the undergrowth onto a stretch of ancient Buyur highway. Sprinting along the broken pavement, he sheathed the machete and drew his compound bow, cranking the string taut.

Sounds of hissing confrontation spilled from a narrow side canyon, forcing Dwer to leave the old road again, dodging amid vine-crusted trees. Finally he saw them, just beyond a screen of shrubs – two creatures, poised in a showdown of sable and iridescent pale.

Cornered in a slit ravine, the glaver was obviously female, possibly pregnant. She had climbed a long way and was pulling deep breaths. Globelike eyes rotated independently, one tracking the dark noor while the other scanned for dangers yet unseen.

Dwer cursed both of them – the glaver for drawing him on a profitless chase when he had been looking forward to festival, and the meddlesome noor for daring to interfere!

Doubly cursed, because now he was in its debt. If the glaver had reached the plains beyond the Rimmer Range, it would have been no end of trouble.

Neither creature seemed to notice Dwer – though he wouldn't bet against the noor's keen senses. *What is the little devil doing up here? What's it trying to prove?*

Dwer had named it Mudfoot, for the brown forepaws marring an ebony pelt, from a flattish tail to whiskers that twitched all around a stubby snout. The black-furred creature kept still, its gaze riveted on the flighty glaver, but Dwer wasn't fooled. *You know I'm watching, show-off.* Of all species left on Jijo when the ancient Buyur departed, Dwer found noor the least fathomable, and fathoming other creatures was a hunter's art.

Quietly, he lowered the bow and unfastened a buckskin thong, taking up his coiled lariat. Using patient, stealthy care, he edged forward.

Grinning with jagged, angular teeth, Mudfoot reared almost to the glaver's height – roughly as tall as Dwer's thigh. The glaver retreated with a snarl, till her bony back plates brushed rock, causing a rain of pebbles. In her forked tail she brandished a stick – some branchlet or sapling with the twigs removed. A sophisticated tool, given the present state of glaverdom.

Dwer took another step and this time could not avoid crushing some leaves. Behind the noor's pointy ears, gray spines jutted from the fur, waving independently. Mudfoot kept facing the glaver, but something in its stance said – '*Be quiet, fool!*'

Dwer didn't like being told what to do. Especially by a noor. Still, a hunt is judged only by success, and Dwer wanted a clean capture. Shooting the glaver now would be to admit failure.

Her loose skin had lost some opal luster since leaving familiar haunts, scavenging near some village of the Six, as glavers had done for centuries, ever since their innocence was new.

Why do they do this? Why do a few try for the passes, every year?

One might as well guess the motives of a *noor*. Among the Six, only the patient hoon had a knack for working with the puckish, disruptive beasts.

Maybe the Buyur resented having to quit Jijo and left noor as a joke on whoever came next.

A buzzing lion-fly cruised by, under filmy, rotating wings. The panting glaver tracked it with one eye, while the other watched the swaying noor. Hunger gradually prevailed over fear as she realized Mudfoot was too small to murder her. As if to enhance that impression, the noor sat back on its haunches, nonchalantly licking a shoulder.

Very clever, Dwer thought, shifting his weight as the glaver swung both eyes toward the hovering meal.

A jet of sputum shot from her mouth, striking the fly's tail.

In a flash, Mudfoot bounded left. The glaver squealed, struck out with the stick, then whirled to flee the other way. Cursing, Dwer sprang from the undergrowth. Moccasins skidded on spoiled granite, and he tumbled, passing just under the flailing club. Desperately, Dwer cast the lariat – which tautened with a savage yank that slammed his chin to the ground. Though starving and weak, the glaver had enough panicky strength to drag Dwer for a dozen meters, till her will finally gave out.

Shivering, with waves of color coursing under her pale skin, she dropped the makeshift club and sank to all four knees. Dwer got up warily, coiling the rope.

'Easy does it. No one's gonna hurt you.'

The glaver scanned him with one dull eye. '*Pain exists. Marginally,*' she crooned, in thickly slurred Galactic Eight.

Dwer rocked back. Only once before had a captured glaver spoken to him. Usually they kept up their unsentient pose to the last. He wet his lips and tried answering in the same obscure dialect.

'*Regrettable. Endurance suggested. Better than death.*'

'*Better?*' The weary eye squinted as if vaguely puzzled and unsure it mattered.

Dwer shrugged. '*Sorry about the pain.*'

The faint light drifted out of focus.

'*Not blamed. Dour melody. Now ready to eat.*'

The flicker of intellect vanished once more under a bolus of animal density.

Both amazed and drained, Dwer tethered the creature to a nearby tree. Only then did he take account of his own wincing cuts and bruises while Mudfoot lay on a rock, basking in the last rays of the setting sun.

The noor couldn't talk. Unlike the glaver, its ancestors had never been given the knack. Still, its open-mouth grin seemed to say – 'That was fun. Let's do it again!'

Dwer recovered his bow, started a fire, and spent the day's last half-midura feeding the captive from his meager rations. Tomorrow he'd find it a rotten log to root under for grubs – a favorite, if undignified pastime for members of what had once been a mighty starfaring race.

Mudfoot sidled close when Dwer unwrapped some hard bread and jerky. Dwer sighed and tossed some to the noor, who snatched chunks out of midair and ate with dainty care. Then Mudfoot sniffed at Dwer's gourd canteen.

He had seen the beasts use gourds aboard hoon-crewed river-boats. So after a dubious pause, he pulled the cork stopper and handed it over. The creature used both six-fingered forepaws – nearly as deft as true hands – to adroitly slosh quick dollops over its tongue, smacking loudly.

Then it poured the remainder over its head.

Dwer shot to his feet, cursing. But Mudfoot blithely tossed the empty vessel aside. Rivulets ran down its glossy back, dribbling dark splatters in the dust. The noor chirped happily and began to groom.

Dwer shook the canteen, winning a few drops. 'Of all the selfish, ungrateful—'

It was already too late to hike to the nearest stream, down a narrow, treacherous trail. A waterfall growled, close enough to hear but over a midura away by foot. This was no crisis; he'd done without before. Still, the sound would give him dry-mouth, all night long.

Never stop learning, said the sage Ur-Ruhols. Tonight, Dwer had learned one more thing about noor. All told, the price of the lesson was pretty cheap.

He decided to arrange for a wakeup call. For that, he would need a clock teet.

There were good reasons to get an early start. He might still make it back to the yearly Gathering of the Six, before all the unpledged human boys and girls chose partners for jubilee dancing. Then there was his annual report to Danel Ozawa, and Lena Strong's ridiculous 'tourism' idea to oppose. Also, if he led the glaver away before dawn, he just might manage to leave Mudfoot snoring by the coals. Noor loved sleep almost as much as upsetting the routines of villagers, and this one had had a long day.

So after supper Dwer brought forth a sheaf of paper folders, his cache of practical things. Many of the wrappers had come from his brother's wastebasket, or Sara's.

Lark's handwriting, graceful and controlled, usually traced some living species on Jijo's complex order of life. Dwer used Lark's castoff notes to store seeds, herbs, and feathers – things useful in the hunt.

Sara's hand was expansive yet tense, as if imagination and order held each other in check. Her discards swarmed with baffling mathematics. (Some failed equations weren't just scratched out but *stabbed* to death in fits of frustration.) Dwer used his sister's worksheets to hold medicines, condiments, and the powders that made many Jijoan foods edible to humans.

From one folded page he drew six *tobar* seeds – plump, hard, and fragrant – which he spread across a rock some way downwind. Holding his breath, he used his knife to split one open, then fled a rising, pungent cloud. The glaver mewed unhappily, and the noor glared at him until the breeze swept most of the intense aroma away.

Back in his sleeping roll, Dwer waited as the stars came out.

Kalunuti was a hot reddish pinpoint, set high on the leering face of Sargon, pitiless enforcer of laws. More starry patterns followed, *eagle, horse, dragon* – and *dolphin*, beloved cousin, grinning with her jaw thrust in a direction some said might lead to Earth.

If we exiles are ever caught, Dwer pondered. *Will the Great Galactic Library make a file about our culture? Our myths? Will aliens read our constellation myths and laugh?*

If all went as planned, no one would ever hear of this lonely colony or recall its tales. *Our descendants, if any, will be like glavers – simple, and innocent as the beasts of the field.*

Fluttering wings grazed the firelight. A squat form landed near the tobar seeds, with wings of grayish plates that slid like overlapping petals. The birdling's yellow beak quickly devoured the nut Dwer had cracked.

Mudfoot sat up, eyes glinting.

Dwer warned the noor, half-dozing – 'You bother it, an' I'll have yer hide fer a hat.'

Mudfoot sniffed and lay down again. Soon there came a rhythmic tapping as the teet started pecking at the next nut. It would take its time, consuming one kernel each midura – roughly seventy minutes – until the last was gone. Then, with a chattering screech, it would fly off. One didn't need a printout from the Great Library to know what function the Buyur had designed this creature to fill. The living alarm clock still worked as programmed.

Lark is wrong about our place on this world, Dwer thought, lulled by the unvaried tapping. *We do a service. Jijo would be a sad place without people to use its gifts.*

There were dreams. Dwer always had dreams.

Shapeless foes lurked beyond sight as he wandered a land covered with *colors*, like a rainbow that had melted, flowed across the ground, then frozen in place. The harsh hues hurt his eyes. Moreover, his throat felt parched, and he was unarmed.

The dream shifted. All of a sudden, he found himself alone in a forest of trees that seemed to stretch up past the moons. For some reason, the trees were even more threatening than the colored landscape. He fled, but could find no exit from the forest as their trunks glowed, burst into flame, then started to *explode*.

The furious intensity of the nightmare yanked him awake, sitting up with a racing heart. Dwer stared wide-eyed, glad to find the *real* woods intact, though dark and threaded by a chill breeze. There was no raging firestorm. He had dreamed the whole thing.

Still, uneasiness gnawed. Something felt *wrong*.

He rubbed his eyes. Different constellations swarmed the sky, fading in the east under a wash of predawn gray. The biggest moon, Loocen, hovered over silhouetted peaks, its sunlit face spangled with bright pinpoints – the domes of long-abandoned cities.

So what's wrong?

It wasn't just intuition. The clock teet had stopped. Something must have disturbed it before the time to chatter its alarm. He checked the area and found the noor snoring on quietly. The glaver tracked Dwer dully with one thoughtless eye, the other still closed.

All at once, he knew the problem.

My bow!

It wasn't where he'd left it, within arm's reach. It was gone.

Stolen!

Anger flooded the predawn dimness with blinding adrenaline outrage. Dozens had spoken enviously of his bow – a masterpiece of laminated wood and bone, fashioned by the qheuenish craftsmen of Ovoom Town. But who . . . ?

Calm down. Think.

Could it be Jeni Shen? She often joked about luring him into a poker game, with the bow at stake. Or might it be—

Stop!

He took a deep breath, but it was hard disciplining his young body, so full of need to act.

Stop and hear what the world has to say . . .

First, he must calm the furious spilling of his own unspoken words. Dwer pushed aside all noisy thoughts. Next he made himself ignore the rasping sound of breath and pulse.

The distant, muttering waterfall was by now familiar, easy to cancel out. The wind's rustle, less regular, soon went away too.

One hovering sound might be the clock teet, cruising in hope of more tobar seeds. Another flutter told of a honey bat – no, a mated pair – which he also disregarded. The noor's snoring he edited, and the soft grind of glaver-molars as the prisoner rechewed her cud.

There! Dwer turned his head. Was that a scrape on gravel? Pebbles rattling down a scree, perhaps. Something, or someone – bipedal? Almost man-size, he guessed, and hurrying away.

Dwer took off after the sound. Gliding ghostlike in his moccasins, he ran some distance before noting that the thief was heading in the *wrong direction*. Away from the coast. Away from the Slope. Higher into the Rimmer Range.

Toward the Pass.

Padding up the rocky trail, Dwer's angry flush gave way to the scrupulous cadence of pursuit – a tense, almost ecstatic concentration on each thrust of heel and toe; the efficiency of motion needed for silence; an eager probing beyond his own soft noise to seize any trace of the pursued. His head felt clear, no longer poisoned by fury. Whatever the reason for this chase, he could not help feeling a kind of joy. This was his art, the thing he loved best.

Dwer was near the notch of gray light separating two shadowy peaks, when a problem occurred to him.

Wait a minute!

He slowed to a trot, then down to a walk.

This is stupid. Here I am, chasing off after a sound I'm not even sure I heard – maybe a hangover of a dream – when the answer was there all along!

The noor.

He stopped, beating his fist against his thigh and feeling like an idiot.

It's just what a noor would do – stealing things. Swapping a villager's chipped cup for a treasure, or vice versa.

When he returned, would a pile of ligger turds sit where the bow had lain? Or a diamond wrested from the crown of some long dead Buyur king? Or would they all – noor, bow, and glaver – simply be gone? Mudfoot had been quite an actor, snoozing by the coals. Did the beast cackle when he hightailed off, chasing his own outraged imagination?

Alongside anger, there arose a grudging appreciation.

A good one. He really got me.

Then again, this noor might have a surprise coming. Of all the humans on Jijo, perhaps only Dwer was qualified to *find* the beast and get even.

It would be a difficult chase. Maybe impossible.

Or else the hunt of a lifetime.

Sudden insight filled Dwer with wonder. Was *that* the noor's gift? To offer Dwer—

Ahead of him, in the vague dimness, the corner of a shadow moved.

His unfocused eyes had been open to peripheral vision, habituated to a static scene. A reflex hunter's trick that made one especially sensitive to motion – as when a 'boulder' shifted to the left, then moved onward toward the Pass.

Ears snatched distant tickling scrapes, softer than the wind. Dwer's eyebrows knotted as he started forward again, slowly at first, then stealthily faster.

When the blurry shadow stopped, *he* stopped, splaying his arms for balance.

Profiled against predawn gray, the silhouette waited a few duras more, then turned and continued on its way.

Trust your instincts, Fallon the Tracker used to teach. The old man was nobody's fool.

Mudfoot *had* been the obvious suspect. Perhaps that was *why* it didn't occur to Dwer, back at the campsite. He would have wasted valuable time blaming the logical culprit. His first impulse had been right, after all. The initial clue, a true one.

The shadow turned again. Dwer traced a human shape, alarmed now, fleeing with his purloined bow. This time he sprinted, forsaking stealth for speed. Pebbles flew, rattling the pass with echoes. The other swiveled too, leaping away like a striped gusul in flight.

Only three humans on Jijo could outrun Dwer, and none at all in rough terrain.

Endgame, he thought, bearing down for a final dash.

When his quarry turned, he was ready. When it drew a knife, he knew this was no joke. Dwer launched into a tackling dive, primed to hear shouts of anger and dismay.

Unexpected was the thief's face, looming as he hurtled forward.

Human.

Female.

Terribly young.

Above all – a complete and total stranger.

ASX

Fate had fallen from the sky.

To Jijo.

To the Slope.

To the Glade of Gathering.

To the nexus of our fears, much sooner than expected.

Across megaparsecs, a ship from the Five Galaxies had come! Such a vast distance ... the least we poor exiles could do was march a short way to where it landed, and courteously greet it.

Vubben declined the honor of leading. Jijo's gravity so hobbles our dear g'Kek, they must rely solely on wheels, using their stilt-legs for balance only, moving over rough ground almost as slowly as a traeki. So, Vubben and i hobbled along, urging our hoon, qheuen-ish, human, and urrish counterparts to forge ahead.

Do i/we sense a foul odor of *envy* fuming in our central core? Do some of you, my several selves, resent our awkward slowness compared to those long hoonish legs or nimble urrish feet? Things might have been different had our traeki exile-ship come equipped with the full menagerie of rings our kin were said to own. Legends tell of adroit running limbs – gifts of the mighty Oailie – limbs to make even a heavy stack like ours as speedy as a song jackal. Speedy as a *Jophur*.

But then, would we also have carried Oailie arrogance? Their madness? Would we have fought *wars*, the way qheuens and urs and hoons and men did for centuries here on Jijo, bickering until the Commons grew strong enough for peace? Those traeki who fled to Jijo had reasons to leave some rings behind. Or so we believe.

But again, *digression* thwarts our tale. Discipline, my rings! Give the fumes another spin. Stroke the waxy imprints, and remember—

Recall how we marched, each at ers own pace, toward the side valley where the intruder ship had set down. Along the way, Vubben recited from the Book of Exile, greatest of Scrolls, the one least altered by quarrel, heresy, or waves of new arrivals.

'*The right to live is tentative*,' Vubben chanted in a voice that seemed to caress the soul.

'*Material things are limited, though the mind is free.*

'*Of protein, phosphorus, nor even energy is there ever enough to slake all hungers. Therefore, show not affront when diverse beings vie over what physically exists. Only in thought can there be true generosity. So let thought be the focus of your world.*'

Vubben's voice had a calming way with our people. The slim-boled welpal trees seemed to resonate his words, tuned as they are to the music of the Egg.

And yet, while Vubben spoke of equanimity, my/our basal segment kept trying to stop, turn its feet around, and carry us away! Dimly, that bottommost ring realized that danger lay ahead, and sensibly voted to flee. Our upper tiers had to apply scent-throbs to urge it onward.

i/we find strange how *fear* functions in non-traeki. They say it infuses all parts of a body, and hence must be fought everywhere at once! Once, i/we asked Lester Cambel how humans keep calm in times of crisis. His answer was that generally they don't!

How strange. Humans always seem so much in control. Is it just a grand act, to fool both others *and* themselves?

Do not digress, Oh Asx. Stroke the wax. Go on. Go on toward the ship.

Henrik seemed reluctant to set off his charges.

At first this surprised Sara. Wasn't this crisis what an exploser always dreamed of? A chance to make things go boom? To destroy works that others spent their lives building?

In fact, Henrik seemed less avid than many of the citizens crowding the Meeting Tree in panic that night, after witnessing a fireball rattle the forest to its ancient roots. Two gardeners and a worker chimp had fallen from high branches to their deaths, and scores of others had had narrow escapes. The farmers were in a state.

Carved from the specious heart knot of a grandfather garu, the great hall was crammed with nearly every sapient adult within a rapid day's hike. Like a steaming minnow pie, the room seemed stuffed with perspiring humanity.

A cluster of other folk were also present – hoon sailors mostly, their pale scaly skins and shaggy white leg fur offset by dark green cloaks, cinched with wooden brooches below their puffing throat sacs. Some also wore trembling rewq over their eyes, to help interpret this stew of human emotions.

Near the north entrance, where it was less humid, a few urrish tinkers chafed and stamped, uneasily switching their braided tails. Sara even spied one forlorn g'Kek pilgrim, anxious green sweat dripping from a single eyestalk, while the other three lay curled like socks in a drawer, hiding from the raucous ferment.

Doctor Lorrek had been wise, it seemed, volunteering to spend the evening watching the wounded Stranger.

Pzora, the town pharmacist, had a defense against having ers lower rings trampled. If pressed too closely, the traeki just vented a little pungent steam, and even the most agitated citizen gave er room.

No doubt it was like this wherever folk had seen the dread specter in the sky. Right now *human* visitors were attending qheuen or hoon assemblies and even urrish tribal conclaves, beside roaring fires on the open plains.

The Great Peace is our finest accomplishment, Sara thought. *Maybe it will weigh in our favor, when we're judged. We've come far since the days of war and slaughter.*

Alas, from the rancor of tonight's meeting, the Commons still had a long way to go.

'Minor repairs?'

Chaz Langmur, the master carpenter, protested from the stage, normally used for concerts and theatricals. 'We're talking about losing everything below the flood line, and that don't count the dam itself! You ask how many *years* to rebuild, if this turns out to be a false alarm? Let's talk *lifetimes*!'

Merchants and craft workers supported Langmur with shouts but were opposed by cries of 'Shame!' from many wearing the gray garb of farmers. Overhead, excited apelike shrieks joined in. Though not voting citizens, tradition let local chimps clamber up the wall tapestries to observe from slit vents high above. How much they understood was debatable. Some screamed lustily for whichever speaker seemed most impassioned, while others were as partisan as Sara's father, who clapped the carpenter's back with encouragement.

It had gone this way for hours. Angry men and women taking turns citing scripture or bemoaning costs, each side waxing ever louder as their fear and irritation grew. Nor were humans the sole partisans. Log Biter, matriarch of the local qheuenish hive, had spoken urgently for preserving Dolo Dam, while her cousin from Logjam Pond proclaimed it a 'gaudy monstrosity.' Sara feared a melee would ensue between two huge armored matrons, until the chief elder, Fru Nestor, interposed her small human form, the rewq on her brow flashing soothing colors until both qheuens finally backed down.

The audience was no better. A woman stepped on Sara's foot. Someone else must not have bathed this week, comparing badly to Pzora's worst secretions. Sara envied Prity, a tiny figure perched high on a windowsill next to several human kids too young to vote. Unlike other chimps, she seemed to find her notebook more engaging than the shouting speakers, tugging at her lower lip while she studied lines of complex mathematics.

Sara envied Prity's escape into abstraction.

One of the tree farmers rose to speak – a dark man named Jop, whose pale yellow hair curled around his ears. He clenched two large hands, knotty with lifelong calluses.

'Penny pinching and farsightedness!' Jop dismissed the carpenter's plea. 'What would you preserve? A few workshops and docks? Passing toys like plumbing and paper? Dross! All dross! Some paltry comforts that our sinner ancestors let us poor exiles keep for a while, softening our first steps on the road toward grace. But the Scrolls say *none* of it will last! It's all destined for the sea!'

Jop turned to his partisans, clutching both hands together. 'It was planned long ago – what we're sworn to do when starships come. Or else, why've we supported a guild of explorers all this time?'

Sara glanced again at Henrik and son, seated at the back of the dais. The boy, Jomah, betrayed unease with a slow twisting of his cap between nervous young hands. But his pa might have been a statue. Henrik had remained silent throughout, except to report tersely that his charges were ready.

Sara always pictured their craft as a frustrating profession, probably unique to Jijo. After so many years of preparation – performing endless tests in a small canyon in the hills – wouldn't they hanker to see it all finally put to use? *I know I would*.

Long ago, she and Lark and little Dwer used to sit in their attic room, watching moonlight spill over the rumbling water wheel and thrilling each other with lurid tales of what they might see if ever *the* moment came when Henrik lit his fuses. With delicious mock-terror pounding in their chests, they counted down heartbeats until – kablam!

Dwer loved making sound effects, especially the pretend detonation that finished off the dam, accompanied by waving arms and lots of saliva. Sara's younger brother then gleefully described the wall of water tossing proud boats like trifles, smashing Nelo's drying racks, and driving toward their bedroom window like a fist.

Lark took over then, thrilling and terrifying the younger kids as he portrayed their attic being sheared off by a watery blast, sent careening through the garu forest while farmers stared down in pity. Each pretend near-miss made Sara and Dwer cry out till they leaped on their laughing older brother, pummeling to make him stop.

And yet – after Dwer and Lark had done their best to scare her, *they* would toss and turn, while Sara never had nightmares. When she did dream about the dam bursting, she used to picture a great wave simply taking them in the palm of its gentle hand. As froth concealed all of Jijo, it magically transformed into the fluffy, charged substance of a cloud. Always, the fantasy ended with her body lighter than mist, fearless, soaring through a night radiant with stars.

A roar of approval yanked her back to the present. At first she could not tell if it came from the party wanting quick action, or from those resolved not to wreck nine generations' work on the mere evidence of their own eyes.

'We have no idea what it was we saw!' her father declared, combing his beard with gnarled fingers. 'Can we be sure it was a spaceship? Perhaps a *meteor* grazed by. That'd explain all the noise and ruckus.'

Sneers and foot-stamps greeted this suggestion. Nelo hurried on. 'Even if it was a ship, that doesn't mean we've been discovered!

Other vessels have come and gone – Zang globes, for instance, come to siphon water from the sea. Did we wreck everything then? Did the older tribes burn their towns when we *humans* came? How do we know it wasn't another sneakship, bringing a seventh exile race to join our Commons?'

Jop snorted derisively.

'Let me remind the learned papermaker – sneakships *sneak*! They come under the shadow of night an' cloud an' mountain peak. This new vessel made no such effort. It aimed straight at the Glade of the Egg, at a time when the pavilions of Gathering are there, along with the chief sages of the Six.'

'Exactly!' Nelo cried. 'By now the sages should be well aware of the situation and would have farcast if they felt it necessary to hair—'

'*Farcasting?*' Jop interrupted. 'Are you serious? The sages remind us over an' over again that it can't be trusted. In a crisis, farcasts may be just the thing to *attract* attention! Or else' – Jop paused meaningfully – 'or else there may have been no calls for a more terrible reason.'

He let the implication sink in, amid a scatter of gasps. Almost everyone present had a relative or close friend who had taken pilgrimage this year.

Lark and Dwer – are you safe? Sara pondered anxiously. *Will I ever see you again?*

'Tradition leaves it up to each community. Shall we shirk, when our loved ones may've already paid a dearer price than some buildings and a stinkin' dam?'

Cries of outrage from the craft workers were drowned out by support from Jop's followers. 'Order!' Fru Nestor squeaked, but her plaint was lost in the chaos. Jop and his allies shouted for a vote.

'Choose the Law! Choose the Law!'

Nestor appealed for order with upraised hands, clearly dreading the dismemberment of her town – its reduction to a mere farming hamlet, rich in reverence but little else. 'Does anyone else have something to say?'

Nelo stepped up to try again but wilted under a stream of catcalls. Who had ever seen a *papermaker* treated thus? Sara felt his shame and dishonor, but it would be far worse when his beloved factory was blown to oblivion before an all-destroying flood.

Sara had a strange thought – should she sneak up to her old attic room and wait for the wave? Who had prophesied right? Dwer and Lark? Or those images *she* had foreseen in dreams? It would be a once-in-a-lifetime chance to find out.

Resumed chanting tapered off as someone new moved forward

from behind the crowd of pale hoon sailors. It was a centauroid figure with a long sinuous body of mottled suede that branched into a pair of stubby shoulderless arms and a powerful snakelike neck. The narrow-pointed head contained three black eyes, one of them lidless and faceted, all set around a triangular mouth. It was an urrish tinker Sara recognized from past visits to Dolo, buying scraps of glass and metal, selling simple Buyur tools reclaimed from some ruin. The urs stepped daintily, as if worried her hooves might catch in the rough floorboards. She had one arm raised, exposing a glimpse of the bluish brooding pouch underneath, an act that might have different connotations in a meeting of her own kind, but Fru Nestor took it as a request to speak, which she granted with a bow.

Sara heard a human mutter – '*hinney!*' – a rude callback to days when newcomer Earthlings fought urrish tribes over land and honor. If the tinker heard the insult, she ignored it, carrying herself well for a youngish urs with just one husband pouch tenanted by a squirming bulge. Among so many humans, the urs could not use a plains dialect of Galactic Two but made do with Anglic, despite the handicap of a cloven upper lip.

'I can ve called Ulgor. I thank you for your courtesy, which is vlessed among the Six. I wish only to ask questions concerning the issues discussed tonight. Ny first question follows—

'Is this not a natter vest decided vy our sages? Why not let those wise ones rule whether the great tine of judgment has arrived?'

With an exaggerated show of mannerly patience, Jop replied, 'Learned neighbor, the Scrolls call on all villages to act independently, to erase all signs that might be seen from the sky! The order's simple. No complicated judgment is needed.

'Besides,' he concluded. 'There's no time to hear from the sages. They're all far away, at Gathering.'

'Forgive.' Ulgor bowed her forelegs. '*Not* all. A few linger in residence at the Hall o'Vooks, in Vivlos, do they not?'

There was confusion as people looked at one another, then Fru Nestor cried out. 'The Hall of *Books*, in *Biblos*! Yes, that's true. But Biblos is still many days away, by boat.'

Again Ulgor bent her neck before dissenting. 'Yet I have heard that, fron the highest tree in Dolo, one can see across the quicksand marsh to the glass cliffs overlooking Vivlos.'

'With a good telescope,' Jop acknowledged, wary that this was sapping the crowd's passionate momentum. 'I still don't see how it helps—'

'*Fire!*'

Faces turned toward Sara, who had shouted while the thought was still half formed.

'We'd see flames as the library burned!'

Muttering, the crowd stared at her, till she explained. 'You all know I used to work at Biblos. They have a contingency plan like everyone else. If the sages command it, the librarians are to carry off what volumes they can, then ignite the rest.'

This brought on a somber hush. Wrecking Dolo's dam was one thing, but loss of Biblos would truly signal an ending. No place was more central to human life on Jijo.

'Finally, they are to blow the pillars holding up the roof-of-stone and bring it down on the ashes. Ulgor's right. We could see any change that big, especially with Loocen rising at this hour.'

Fru Nestor spoke a terse command. 'Send someone aloft to see!'

Several boys leaped up and vanished through the windows, accompanied by a string of hooting chimpanzees. A nervous murmur ensued while the crowd waited. Sara felt uncomfortable under the regard of so many, and lowered her eyes.

That was the sort of thing Lark *would do. Boldly taking over a meeting at the last minute, compelling others to act. Joshu had that impulsiveness, too – till the sickness took him in those final weeks ...*

Gnarled fingers grasped hers, halting the bleak gyre of her thoughts. She looked up and saw that Nelo had aged in the last hour. Now the fate of his beloved mill rested on news from above.

As the slow duras passed, the full import of her prediction sank in.

Biblos.

The Hall of Books.

Once already, fire had taken a terrible toll there. Even so, the remaining archive was humanity's greatest contribution to the Commons and a cause of both envy and wonder among the other races.

What will we become, if it's gone? True pastoralists? Gleaners, living off remnants swiped from ancient Buyur sites? Farmers all?

That was how the other five had seemed, when humans first came. Bickering primitives with their barely functioning commons. Humanity introduced new ways, changed the rules, almost as much as the arrival of the Egg several generations later.

Now shall we slide downslope faster? Losing the few relics that remind us we once roamed galaxies? Shucking our books, tools, clothes, till we're like glavers? Pure, shriven innocents?

According to the Scrolls, that was one path to salvation. Many, like Jop, believed in it.

Sara tried to see hope, even if word came back of flames and dust in the night. At any time, hundreds of books were outside Biblos, on loan to far-flung communities.

But few texts in Sara's specialty ever left their dusty shelves. *Hilbert. Somerfeld. Witten and Tang. Eliahu* – names of great minds she knew intimately across centuries and parsecs. The intimacy of pure, near-perfect thoughts. *They'll burn. The sole copies.* Lately her research had swung to other areas – the chaotic ebb and flow of language – but still she called mathematics home. The voices in those books had always seemed soul-alive. Now she feared learning they were gone.

Then abruptly, another notion occurred to her, completely unexpected, glancing off her grief at a startling angle.

If Galactics really have come, what do a few thousand paper volumes really matter? Sure, they'll judge us for our ancestors' crime. Nothing can prevent that. But meanwhile, aboard their ships ...

It occurred to Sara that she might get a chance to visit a completely different *kind* of library. One towering over the Biblos cache, the way the noon sun outblazed a candle. *What an opportunity! Even if we're all soon prisoners of the galactic Lords of Migration, destined for some prison world, they can hardly deny us a chance to read!*

In accounts of olden days she had read about 'accessing' computer databases, swimming in knowledge like a warm sea, letting it fill your mind, your pores. Swooping through clouds of wisdom.

I could find out if my work is original! Or if it's been done ten million times, during a billion years of Galactic culture.

The thought seemed at once both arrogant and humbling. Her fear of the great starships was undiminished. Her prayer remained that it was all a mistake, or a meteor, or some illusion.

But a rebel corner of her roiling mind felt something new – a wakened hunger.

If only ...

Her thought broke against an interruption. Suddenly, high overhead, a boy stuck his head through a slit window. Hanging upside down, he cried – *'No fires!'*

He was joined by others, at different openings, all shouting the same thing. Chimps joined in, shrieking excitement across the crowded meeting hall.

'No fires – and the roof-of-stone still stands!'

Old Henrik stood, then spoke two words to the elders before departing with his son. Amid the flustered babble of the throng, Sara read the exploser's expression of resolve and the decisive message of his lips.

'We wait.'

Our caravan of races marched toward where the alien ship was last seen – a blazing cylinder descending beyond a low hill. Along the way, Vubben continued chanting from the Scroll of Danger.

Voices cried out ahead. Crowds jostled along a ridge-top, hissing and murmuring. We must nudge past men and hoon to win our way through.

Whereupon, did we not gaze across a *nest*? A new clearing lined with shattered trees, still smoking from whatever ray had cut them down.

And poised amid this devastation – shimmering from its heat of entry – lay the cause.

Nearby, human and urrish crafters argued in the strange dialect of the engineering caste, disputing whether this nub or that blister might be weaponry or sensors. But which of us on Jijo has the expertise to guess? Our ships long ago went down to join this planet's melting crust. Even the most recent arrivals, humans, are many generations removed from starfarers. No living member of the Commons ever saw anything like this.

It *was* a ship of the Civilization of the Five Galaxies. That much the techies could tell.

Yet where was the rayed spiral? The symbol required to be carried on the forward flank of every sanctioned ship of space?

Our worried lore-masters explain – the spiral is no mere symbol. Silently, it rides. Impartially, it records. Objectively, it bears witness to everything seen and done, wherever the vessel may fly.

We peered and sought, but in the ordained place there lay only a *burnished shine*. It had been rubbed away, smoother than a qheuenish larva.

That was when confusion gave way to understanding. Realization of what this ship represented.

Not the great Institutes, as we first thought.

Nor the righteous, mighty, legalistic star-clans – or the mysterious Zang.

Not even exiles like ourselves.

None of those, but *outlaws*. Felons of an order worse than our own ancestors.

Villains.

Villains had come to Jijo.

III

THE BOOK OF THE SEA

It is a Paradox of Life that all species breed
past mere replacement.
Any paradise of plenty soon fills, to become
paradise no more.
By what right, then, do we exiles claim a
world that was honorably set aside,
to nurture frail young-life in peace,
and be kept safe from hungry nations?

Exiles, you should fear the law's just wrath,
to find you here, unsanctioned, not yet
redeemed.
But when judgment comes, law will also be
your shield, tempering
righteous wrath with justice.

There is a deeper terror, prowling the angry
sky.
It is a different peril. One that stalks in
utter absence of the law.

—*The Scroll of Danger*

All right, so I'm not as quick as some. I'll never think as fast as Huck, who can run verbal circles around me. It's just as well, I guess. I could've grown up in this little hoon port thinking I was such a clever fellow – as witty and gloss as my literary nickname-sake – just 'cause I can read any Anglic book and fancy myself a writer. Good thing I had this little g'Kek genius living in the khuta next door, to remind me that an above-average hoon is still a hoon. Dull as a brick.

Anyway, there I was, squatting between two of my best friends while they fussed over what we should do with the coming summer, and it never occurred to me that both Huck and Pincer were ring-coring me at more than one level.

Pincer only spent a few duras trying to tell us about his latest 'monsters' – grayish shapes he *thought* he glimpsed through the murk, while bored, tending his hive's lobster pens. He's pulled that one on us so many times, we wouldn't listen if he brought us a molar from Moby-Dick, with a peg leg jammed like a toothpick on one end. Sighing from all five vents at once, he gave up babbling about his latest sighting, and switched over to defending his *Project Nautilus*.

Pincer was upset to learn that Huck wanted to abandon the scheme. Legs lifted on opposite sides of his hard shell, hissing like tubes on a calliope.

'Look, we already *agreed-deed*. We just *gotta* finish the bathy, or else what've we been working-king on for a year now-ow!'

'You did most of the carpentry and testing,' I pointed out. 'Huck and I mostly drew up plans for—'

'Exactly!' Huck interrupted, two eyes bobbing for emphasis. 'Sure, we helped with designs and small parts. That was fun. But I never signed on to actually *ride* the dam' thing to the bottom of the sea.'

Pincer's blue cupola lifted all the way up, and his slit-of-eyes seemed to spin. 'But you *said* it was interesting-ing! You called the idea utter-gloss-loss!'

'True,' Huck agreed. 'In theory, it's totally puff. But there's one problem, friend. It's also jeekee *dangerous*.'

Pincer rocked back, as if the thought had never occurred to him. 'You . . . never said anything about that before.'

I turned to look at Huck. I don't think I ever heard her speak that word till then. *Dangerous*. In all our adventures growing up, *she* always seemed the one ready to take a chance, sometimes daring the rest of us with cutting taunts, the way only a g'Kek can on those rare occasions when they put away politeness and *try* to be nasty. With Huck an orphan, and Ur-ronn and Pincer coming from low-kay races, no one was going to miss them much if they died. So it normally fell on *me* to be the voice of caution – a role I hated.

'Yeah,' Huck said. 'Well, maybe it's time someone pointed out the difference between taking a calculated risk and committing flat-out *suicide*. Which is what it'd be if we ever took a ride aboard that contraption of yours, Pincer!'

Our poor qheuenish friend looked like someone had stuck him in a leg-vent with a stick. His cupola went all wobbly. 'You all know-ow I'd never ask my friends-ends—'

'To go anywhere *you* wouldn't go?' Huck retorted. 'Big of you, since you're talking about dragging us around underwater, where *you're* built to be perfectly comfortable.'

'Only at first-irst!' Pincer retorted. 'After some test dives, we'll go deeper. And I'll be in there with you, taking all the same chances-ances!'

'Come on, Huck,' I put in. 'Give the poor guy's shell a buff.'

'Anyway-ay,' Pincer retaliated, 'what about *your* plan? At least the bathy would be lawful and upright. *You* want to break the rules and do *sooner* stuff-uff!'

Now it was Huck's turn to go defensive. 'What sooner stuff? None of us can breed with each other, so there's no chance of committing *that* crime while we're over the border. Anyhow, hunters and inspectors go beyond the markers.'

'Sure. *With* permission from the sages-ages!'

Huck shrugged two stalks, as if to say she couldn't be bothered with petty legalistic details. 'I still prefer a misdemeanor over flat-out suicide.'

'You mean you prefer a silly little trip to some broken-down Buyur ruin, just to read boring ol' wall markings-ings, over a chance to see the *Midden-idden*? And real live *monsters*?'

Huck groaned and spun a disgusted circle. Earlier, Pincer had told us about a thing he glimpsed that morning, in the shallows south of town. Something with silvery-bright scales swooped by, he swore, flapping what looked in the murky distance like underwater *wings*. After hearing similar stories almost since Pincer's molting day, we didn't give this one a lot of credit.

That was when both of them turned to *me* to decide!

'Remember, Alvin,' Huck crooned. 'You just promised—'

'You promised *me*, months ago!' Pincer cried, so avid that he didn't stutter.

Right then I felt like a traeki standing between two piles of really ripe mulch. I liked the notion of getting to see the deep Midden, where everything slick and Galactic had gone since the Buyur went away. An undersea adventure like in books by Haller or Verne.

On the other hand, Huck was right about Pincer's plan being Ifni-spit. The risk might seem worth it to a low-kay qheuen, who didn't even know for sure who his mother was, but I know *my* folks would sicken awful if I went off and died without leaving even my heart-spine behind for soul-grinding and vuphyning.

Anyway, Huck offered a prospect almost as gloss – to find writings even more ancient than the books humans brought to Jijo. Real *Buyur* stories, maybe. The idea set off tingles in my sucker pads.

As it turns out, I was spared having to decide. That's because my noor, Huphu, arrived right then, darting under Pincer's legs and Huck's wheels, yapping something about an urgent message from Ur-ronn.

Ur-ronn wanted to see us.

More than that – she had a big surprise to share.

Oh, yes. Huphu needs introducing.

First off, she's not really *my* noor. She hangs around me a lot, and my rumble-umbles seem to work, getting her to do what I want a good part of the time. Still, it's kind of hard to describe the relationship between hoon and noor. The very word – relationship – implies a lot of stuff that's just not there. Maybe this is one of those cases where Anglic's flexibility, usually the most utterbuff thing about it, simply falls apart into vagueness.

Anyway, Huphu's no talker-decider. Not a *sapient* being, like us members of the Six. but since she comes along on most of our adventures, I guess she's as much a part of the gang as anyone. Lots of folks say noors are crazy. For sure, they don't seem to care if they live or die, so long as they're seeing something *new*. More have probably perished of curiosity than from liggers on land or sea-starks offshore. So I knew how Huphu would vote in our argument, if she could talk.

Fortunately, even Pincer knows better than to suggest ever letting *her* decide anything.

So there we were, arguing away, when this little noor bounds up the jetty, yipping like mad. Right off we can tell it's a semaphore message she's relaying, on account of it makes sense. Noors can't speak Galactic Two or any other language anyone's ever grokked, but they *can* memorize and repeat any short mirror-flash signal they happen to pick up with their sharp eyes. They can even tell from the opener-tag who a message is for. It's a gloss talent that'd be awfully useful – if only they did it reliably, instead of just when they felt like it.

Huphu sure must've felt like it, 'cause next thing you know she's yelping the upper denotation train of a GalTwo memorandum. (I figure an old Morse code telegraph operator like Mark Twain could've managed GalTwo, if he tried.)

As I said before, the message was from our urrish pal, Ur-ronn, and it said – *WINDOW FINISHED. COME QUICK. OTHER VERY WEIRD STUFF HAPPENING!*

I put an exclamation point at the end 'cause that's how Huphu finished reciting the bulletin she'd seen flash down from Mount Guenn, terminating her report with a bark of ecstatic excitement. I'm sure the phrase 'weird stuff' was what had her bounding in circles, biting at her shadow.

'I'll get my water bag,' Pincer-Tip said after a short pause.

'I'll fetch my goggles,' Huck added.

'I'll grab my cloak and meet you at the tram,' I finished. There was no need for discussion. Not after an invitation like *that*.

IV

THE BOOK OF THE SLOPE

Legends

There is a fable told by the g'Kek, one of the oldest handed down since their sneakship came to Jijo, passed on orally for almost two thousand years, until it was finally recorded on paper.

The saga tells of a youth whose 'thread skating' prowess was renowned in one of the orbital cities where g'Keks dwelled, after losing their homeworld on a wager.

In this particular city, unhampered by the drag of solid ground, young wheel-lords of a space-born generation fashioned a new game — skimming with flashing rims along the thinnest of colored strands — cables that they strung at angles throughout the vast inner cavity of their artificial world. One skater, the tale says, used to take on dare after dare, relishing risk, hopping among gossamer strands and sometimes even flying free, wheels spinning madly before catching the next cord, swooping in ecstatic abandon.

Then, one day, a defeated opponent taunted the young champion. *'I'll bet you can't skim close enough to wrap a thread round the sun!'*

Today's Jijoan scholars find this part of the tale confusing. How could a *sun* be within reach, *inside* a hollow, spinning rock? With much of our Space Technologies section destroyed, the Biblos Scholarium is ill-equipped to interpret such clues. Our best guess is that the story became garbled over time, along with most other memories of a godlike past.

The technical details do not matter as much as the moral of the tale — the imprudence of messing with forces beyond your comprehension. A fool doing so can get burned, like the skater in the tale, whose dramatic end ignited a storm of slender, blazing trails, crisscrossing the doomed city's suddenly fiery inner sky.

—Collected Fables of Jijo's Seven,
Third Edition. Department of Folklore and
Language, Biblos, Year 1867 of Exile.

DWER

Since finishing his apprenticeship, Dwer had visited nearly every village and farm in Jijo's settled zone, including the islands and one or two secret places he was sworn never to speak of. He had met a great many settlers from every race, including most of the Slope's human population.

He grew more certain with each passing dura that the new prisoner wasn't one of them.

Surprise flustered Dwer. Irrational guilt made him doubly angry.

'Of all the stupid things to do,' he told the girl rubbing her head by the cold campfire, 'stealing my bow ranks pretty high. But pulling a *knife* tops all! How was I to know you were just a kid, up there in the dark? I might've broke your neck in self-defense!'

It was the first time either of them had spoken since her skull smacked the ground, leaving her body limp to be slung over a shoulder and lugged back to camp. Never quite losing consciousness, the strange youth had recovered most of her wits by the time he sat her down near the coals. Now she kneaded her bruised head, watched by the glaver and the noor.

'I ... thought you was ... a ligger,' she stammered at last.

'You stole my bow, ran away, then thought you were being chased by a *ligger*?'

This much could be said in her favor – she was a lousy liar. By dawn's light, her small frame sat bundled in garments of poorly tanned leather, stitched with sinew. Her hair, tied in a chopped-off ponytail, was a wavy reddish brown. Of her face – what could be made out under smudges – the stand-out features were a nose that had once been broken and a nasty burn scar along her left cheek, marring a face that might otherwise have been pretty, after a good scrubbing.

'What's your name?'

She lowered her chin and muttered something.

'What was that? I couldn't hear.'

'I said, it's *Rety*!' She met his eyes for the first time, her voice now edged with defiance. 'What're you gonna do with me?'

A reasonable question, under the circumstances. Rubbing his chin, Dwer couldn't see where he had much choice. 'Guess I'll take you to Gathering. Most of the sages are there. If you're old enough, you've got a grievance to answer, or else your parents will be fetched. By the way, who are they? Where do you live?'

The glowering silence returned. Finally, she muttered – 'I'm thirsty.'

Both the glaver and the noor had taken turns nuzzling the empty canteen, then scolding him with their eyes. *What am I?* Dwer thought. *Everybody's daddy?*

He sighed. 'All right, let's head for water. Rety, you go stand over by the glaver.'

Her eyes widened. 'Does – does it bite?'

Dwer gaped back at her. 'It's a *glaver*, for Ifni's sake!' He took her by the hand. 'You'd have reason to fear it if you were a grubworm, or a pile of garbage. Though now that I mention it—'

She yanked back her hand, glaring.

'Okay, sorry. Anyway, you're going to lead, so's I can keep an eye on you. And this will make sure you don't scoot off.' He tied the free end of the glaver's tether to her belt, in back where she could only reach it with difficulty.

Dwer then hoisted his pack and the bow. 'Hear the waterfall? We'll take a break for jerky when we get there.'

It was a strange trek – the sullen leading the apathetic, followed by the confused, all tailed by the inveterately amused. Whenever Dwer glanced back, Mudfoot's leering grin seemed only a little strained as the noor panted in the bone-dry morning air.

Some folk barred their doors when they heard a noor was nearby. Others put out treats, hoping to entice a change in luck. Dwer sometimes saw wild ones in the marshes, where flame trees flourished on the forested backs of drifting acre-lilies. But his strongest memories were from his father's mill, where young noor came each spring to perform reckless, sometimes fatal dives from the ponderously turning power wheel. As a child, Dwer often scampered alongside, taking the same exhilarating risks, much to his parents' distress. He even tried to bond closer to those childhood playmates, bribing them with food, teaching them tricks, seeking a link like Man once had with his helpmate – *dog*.

Alas, noor were *not* dogs. In time, as his life-path took him farther from the gentle river, Dwer came to realize noor were clever, brave – and also quite dangerous. Silently, he warned Mudfoot, *Just because you weren't the thief, don't think that makes me trust you one bit*.

A steep trail looks and feels different going down than heading up. At times, this one seemed so wild and untamed, Dwer could squint and imagine he was on a *real* frontier, untouched by sapient hands since the world was new. Then they'd pass some decayed Buyur remnant – a cement-aggregate wall, or a stretch of rubbery pavement missed by the roving deconstructors when Jijo was laid fallow – and the illusion vanished. Demolition was never perfect. Countless Buyur traces were visible west of the Rimmers.

Time was the true recycler. Poor Jijo had been assigned enough to restore her eco-web, or so said his brother, Lark. But Dwer rarely thought on such a grand scale. It robbed magic from the Jijo of today – a wounded place, but one filled with wonders.

Rety needed help over some steeper patches, and the glaver often had to be lowered by rope. Once, after wrestling the lugubrious creature down to a stretch of old road, Dwer swiveled to find the girl *gone*.

'Now where did the little—' He exhaled frustration. 'Oh, hell.'

Rety's affront deserved some penalty, and her mystery shouted to be solved, but fetching stray glavers came first. After delivering this one, perhaps he'd return to pick up the girl's trail, even though it would make him miss most of Gathering—

He rounded a sheer stone corner and almost stumbled over the girl, squatting face to face with Mudfoot. Rety looked up at Dwer.

'It's a *noor*, right?' she asked.

Dwer covered his surprise. 'Uh, it's the first you've seen?'

She nodded, bemused by Mudfoot's flirtatious grin.

'Nor ever met a glaver, it seems.' Dwer asked – 'How far east do you people live?'

The scar on her cheek grew livid as her face flushed. 'I don't know what you—'

She stopped as the extent of her slip-up sank in. Her lips pressed in a pale line.

'Don't fret it. I already know all about you,' he said, gesturing at her clothes. 'No woven cloth. Hides sewn with gut. Good imla and sorrl pelts. Sorrl don't grow that big, west of the Rimmers.'

Reading her dismay, he shrugged. 'I've been over the mountains myself, several times. Did your folks say it's forbidden? That's true, mostly. But *I* can range anywheres I want, on survey.'

She looked down. 'So I wouldn't've been safe even if I—'

'Ran faster and made it over the pass? Cross some imaginary line and I'd have to let you go?' Dwer laughed, trying not to sound too unfriendly. 'Rety, go easy on yourself. You stole the wrong fella's bow, is all. I'd've chased you beyond the Sunrise Desert if I had to.'

That was bluster, of course. Nothing on Jijo was worth a two thousand-league trek across volcanoes and burning sands. Still, Rety's eyes widened. He went on.

'I never spotted your tribe in any of my expeditions east, so I'd guess you're from quite a ways *south* of east, beyond the Venom Plain. Is it the Gray Hills? I hear that country's so twisty, it could hide a small tribe, if they're careful.'

Her brown eyes filled with a weary pang. 'You're wrong. I don't come from ... that place.'

She trailed off lamely, and Dwer felt sympathy. He knew all about feeling awkward around one's own kind. The loner's life made it hard getting enough experience to overcome his own shyness.

Which is why I have to make it to Gathering! Sara had given him a letter to deliver to Plovov the Analyst. Coincidentally, Plovov's daughter was a beauty, and unbetrothed. With luck, Dwer might get a chance to ask Glory Plovov out for a walk, and maybe tell a story good enough to impress her. Like how he stopped last year's migration of herd-moribul from stampeding over a cliff during a lightning storm. Perhaps he wouldn't stammer this time, making her giggle in a way he didn't like.

Suddenly he was impatient to be off. 'Well, no sense worrying about it now.' He motioned for Rety to lead the glaver again. 'You'll be assigned a junior sage to speak for you, so you won't face the council alone. Anyway, we don't hang sooners anymore. Not unless we have to.'

His attempt to catch her eye with a wink failed, so the joke went flat. She studied the ground as he retied the tether, and they resumed moving single file.

A rising humidity turned into mist as they neared the noise of plunging water. Where the trail rounded a switchback, a streamlet fell from above, dropping staccato spatters across an aquamarine pool. From there, water spilled over a sheer edge, resuming its steep journey toward the river far below, and finally the sea.

The way down to the pool looked too treacherous to risk with Rety and the glaver, so he signaled to keep going. They would intersect the brook again, farther along.

But the noor leaped from rock to rock. Soon they heard him splashing joyfully as they plodded on.

Dwer found himself thinking of another waterfall, way up where the Great Northern Glacier reached a towering cliff at the continent's edge. Every other year, he hunted brankur pelts there, during spring thaw. But he really made the journey in order to be on hand when the ice dam finally broke, at the outlet of Lake Desolation.

Huge, translucent sheets would tumble nearly a kilometer, shattering to fill the sky with crystal icebows, bringing the mighty falls back to life with a soul-filling roar.

In his fumbling way, he once tried describing the scene to Lark and Sara – the shouting colors and radiant noise – hoping practice would school his clumsy tongue. Reliably, his sister's eyes lit up over his tales of Jijo's marvels beyond the narrow Slope. But good old cheerful Lark just shook his head and said – *'These fine marvels would do just as well without us.'*

But would they? Dwer wondered.

Is there beauty in a forest, if no creature stops and calls it lovely, now and then? Isn't that what 'sapience' is for?

Someday, he hoped to take his wife-and-mate to Desolation Falls. If he found someone whose soul could share it the way his did.

The noor caught up a while later, sauntering by with a smug grin, then waiting to shake its sleek back, spraying their knees as they passed. Rety laughed. A short sound, curt and hurried, as if she did not expect any pleasure to last long.

Farther down the trail, Dwer halted where an outcrop overlooked the cascade, a featherlike trickle, dancing along the cliff face. The sight reminded Dwer of how desperately dry he felt. It also tugged a sigh, akin to loneliness.

'Come on, sprig. There's another pool down a ways, easy to get to.'

But Rety stood for a time, rooted in place, with a line of moisture on her cheek, though Dwer guessed it might have come from floating mist.

ASX

They do not show their faces. Plans might go astray. Some of us might survive to testify. So naturally, they hide their forms.

Our Scrolls warn of this possibility. Our destiny seems foredoomed.

Yet when the starship's voice filled the valley, the plain intent was to reassure.

'(Simple) scientists, we are.
Surveys of (local, interesting) lifeforms, we prepare.
Harmful to anyone, we are not.'

That decree, in the clicks and squeaks of highly formal Galactic Two, was repeated in three other standard languages, and finally – because they saw men and pans among our throng – in the wolfling tongue, Anglic.

'Surveying (local, unique) lifeforms, in this we seek your (gracious) help.
'Knowledge of the (local) biosphere, this you (assuredly) have.

'Tools and (useful) arts, these we offer in trade.
'Confidentially, shall we (mutually) exchange?'

Recall, my rings, how our perplexed peoples looked to one another. Could such vows be trusted? We who dwell on Jijo are already felons in the eyes of vast empires. So are those aboard this ship. Might two such groups have reason for common cause?

Our human sage summed it up with laconic wit. In Anglic, Lester Cambel muttered wisely—

'Confidentially, my hairy ancestors' armpits!'

And he scratched himself in a gesture that was both oracular and pointedly apropos.

LARK

The night before the foreigners came, a chain of white-robed pilgrims trekked through a predawn mist. There were sixty, ten from each race.

Other groups would come this way during festival, seeking harmony patterns. But this company was different – its mission more grave.

Shapes loomed at them. Gnarled, misgrown trees spread twisted arms, like clutching specters. Oily vapors merged and sublimed. The trail turned sharply to avoid dark cavities, apparently bottomless, echoing mysteriously. Knobs of wind-scoured rock teased form-hungry agents of the mind, stoking the wanderers' nervous anticipation. Would the next twisty switchback, or the next, bring *it* into sight – Jijo's revered Mother Egg?

Whatever organic quirks they inherited, from six worlds in four different galaxies, each traveler felt the same throbbing call toward oneness. Lark paced his footsteps to a rhythm conveyed by the rewq on his brow.

I've been up this path a dozen times. It should be familiar by now. So why can't I respond?

He tried letting the rewq lay its motif of color and sound over the real world. Feet shuffled. Hooves clattered. Ring nubs swiveled and wheels creaked along a dusty trail pounded so smooth by past pilgrims that one might guess this ritual stretched back to the earliest days of exile, not a mere hundred or so years.

Where did earlier folk turn, when they needed hope?

Lark's brother, the renowned hunter, once took him by a secret way up a nearby mountain, where the Egg could be seen *from above*, squatting in its caldera like the brood of a storybook dragon, lain in a sheersided nest. From that distant perspective, it might have been some ancient Buyur monument, or a remnant of some *older* denizens of Jijo, eons earlier – a cryptic sentinel, darkly impervious to time.

With the blink of an eye, it became a grounded *starship* – an oblate lens meant to glide through air and ether. Or a *fortress*, built of some adamantine essence, light-drinking, refractory, denser than a neutron star. Lark even briefly pictured the shell of some titanic being, too patient or proud to rouse itself over the attentions of mayflies.

It had been disturbing, forced to rethink his image of the sacred. That epiphany still clung to Lark. Or else it was a case of jitters over the speech he was supposed to give soon to a band of fierce believers. A sermon calling for extreme sacrifice.

The trail turned – and abruptly spilled into a sheer-walled canyon surrounding a giant oval form, a curved shape that reared fantastically before the pilgrims, two arrowflights from end to end. The pebbled surface curved up and over those gathered in awe at its base. Staring upward, Lark knew.

It couldn't be any of those other things I imagined from afar.

Up close, underneath its massive sheltering bulk, anyone could tell the Egg was made of *native stone*.

Marks of Jijo's fiery womb scored its flanks, tracing the story of its birth, starting with a violent conception, far underground. Layered patterns were like muscular cords. Crystal veins wove subtle dendrite paths, branching like nerves.

Travelers filed slowly under the convex overhang, to let the Egg sense their presence, and perhaps grant a blessing. Where the immense monolith pressed into black basalt, the sixty began a circuit. But while Lark's sandals scraped gritty powder, chafing his toes, the peacefulness and awe of the moment were partly spoiled by memory.

Once, as an arrogant boy of ten, an idea took root in his head – to sneak behind the Egg and take a *sample*.

It all began one jubilee year, when Nelo the Paper-maker set out for Gathering to attend a meeting of his guild, and his wife, Melina the Southerner, insisted on taking Lark and little Sara along.

'*Before they spend their lives working away at your paper mill, they should see some of the world.*'

How Nelo must have later cursed his consent, for the trip changed Lark and his sister.

All during the journey, Melina kept opening a book recently

published by the master printers of Tarek Town, forcing her husband to pause, tapping his cane while she read aloud in her lilting southern accent, describing varieties of plant, animal, or mineral they encountered along the path. At the time, Lark didn't know how many generations had toiled to create the guidebook, collating oral lore from every exile race. *Nelo* thought it a fine job of printing and binding, a good use of paper, or else he would have forbidden exposing the children to ill-made goods.

Melina made it a game, associating real things with their depictions among the ink lithographs. What might have been a tedious trip for two youngsters became an adventure outshadowing Gathering itself, so that by the time they arrived, footsore and tired, Lark was already in love with the world.

The same book, now yellow, worn, and obsolete thanks to Lark's own labors, rested like a talisman in one cloak-sleeve. *The optimistic part of my nature. The part that thinks it can learn*.

As the file of pilgrims neared the Egg's far side, he slipped a hand into his robe to touch his other amulet. The one he never showed even Sara. A stone no larger than his thumb, wrapped by a leather thong. It always felt warm, after resting for twenty years next to a beating heart.

My darker side. The part that already knows.

The stone felt *hot* as pilgrims filed by a place Lark recalled too well.

It was at his third Gathering that he finally had screwed up the nerve – a patrician artisan's son who fancied himself a scientist – slinking away from the flapping pavilions, ducking in caves to elude passing pilgrims, then dashing under the curved shelf, where only a child's nimble form might go, drawing back his sampling hammer ...

In all the years since, no one ever mentioned the scar, evidence of his sacrilege. It *shouldn't* be noticeable among countless other scratches marring the surface up close. Yet even a drifting mist didn't hide the spot when Lark filed by.

Should he still be embarrassed by a child's offense, after all these years?

Knowing he was forgiven did not erase the shame.

The stone grew cooler, less restive, as the procession moved past.

Could it all be illusion? Some natural phenomenon, familiar to sophisticates of the Five Galaxies? (Though toweringly impressive to primitives hiding on a forbidden world.) Rewq symbionts also came into widespread use a century ago, offering precious insight into the moods of other beings. Had the Egg brought them forth, as some said, to help heal the Six of war and discord? Or were they just another quirky marvel left by Buyur gene-wizards, from back when this galaxy thronged with countless alien races?

After poring through the Biblos archives, Lark knew his confusion was typical when humans puzzled over the sacred. Even the great Galactics, whose knowledge spanned time and space, were riven by clashing dogmas. If mighty star-gods could be perplexed, what chance had *he* of certainty?

There's one thing both sides of me can agree on.

In both his scientific work and the pangs of his heart, Lark knew one simple truth—

We don't belong here.

That was what he told the pilgrims later, in a rustic amphitheater, where the rising sun surrounded the Egg's oblate bulk with a numinous glow. They gathered in rows, sitting, squatting, or folding their varied torsos in attentive postures. The qheuen apostate, Harullen, spoke first in a poetic dialect, hissing from several leg vents, invoking wisdom to serve this world that was their home, source of all their atoms. Then Harullen tilted his gray carapace to introduce Lark. Most had come a long way to hear his heresy.

'We're told our ancestors were criminals,' he began with a strong voice, belying his inner tension. 'Their sneakships came to Jijo, one at a time, running the patrols of the great Institutes, evading wary deputy globes of the Zang, hiding their tracks in the flux of mighty Izmunuti, whose carbon wind began masking this world a few thousand years ago. They came seeking a quiet place to perform a selfish felony.

'Each founding crew had excuses. Tales of persecution or neglect. All burned and sank their ships, threw their godlike tools into the Great Midden, and warned their offspring to beware the sky.

'From the sky would come judgment, someday – for the crime of survival.'

The sun crept past the Egg's bulk, stabbing a corner of his eye. He escaped by leaning toward his audience.

'Our ancestors invaded a world that was set aside after ages of hard use. A world needing time for its many species, both native and artificial, to find restored balance, from which new wonders might emerge. The civilization of the Five Galaxies has used these rules to protect life since before half of the stars we see came alight.

'So why did our ancestors flout them?'

Each g'Kek pilgrim watched him with two eyestalks raised far apart and the other two tucked away, a sign of intense interest. The typical urrish listener pointed her narrow head not toward Lark's face but his midriff, to keep his center of mass in view of all three black slits surrounding her narrow snout. Lark's rewq highlighted these signs, and others from hoon, traeki, and qheuen.

They're with me so far, he saw.

'Oh, our ancestors tried to minimize the harm. Our settlements lie in this narrow, geologically violent zone, in hopes that volcanoes will someday cover our works, leaving no evidence behind. The sages choose what we may kill and eat, and where to build, in order to intrude lightly on Jijo's rest.

'Still, who can deny harm *is* done, each hour we live here. Now rantanoids go extinct. Is it our fault? Who knows? I doubt even the Holy Egg can tell.'

A murmur from the crowd. Colors flowed in the rewq veil over his eyes. Some literalistic hoon thought he went too far. Others, like the g'Kek, were more comfortable with metaphor.

Let their rewq handle the nuances, Lark thought. *Concentrate on the message itself.*

'Our ancestors passed on excuses, warnings, rules. They spoke of tradeoffs, and the Path of Redemption. But I'm here to say that none of it is any good. It's time to end the farce, to face the truth.

'*Our* generation must choose.

'We must choose to be the last of our kind on Jijo.'

The journey back skirted dark caves, exhaling glistening vapors. Now and then, some deep natural detonation sent echoes rolling from one opening, then another, like a rumor that dwindled with each retelling.

Rolling downhill was easier for the g'Keks. But several traeki, built for life in swampy fens, chuffed with exertion as they twisted and turned, striving to keep up. In order to ease the journey, hoonish pilgrims rumbled low atonal music, as they often did at sea. Most pilgrims no longer wore their exhausted rewq. Each mind dwelled alone, in its own thoughts.

Legend says it's different among machine intelligences, or the Zang. Group minds don't bother with persuasion. They just put their heads together, unify, and decide.

It wouldn't be that easy convincing the common citizenry of the Six to go along with the new heresy. Deep instincts drove each race to reproduce as best it could. Ambition for the future was a natural trait for people like his father.

But not here, not on this world.

Lark felt encouraged by this morning's meeting. *We'll convince a few this year. Then more. First we'll be tolerated, later opposed. In the long run, it must be done without violence, by consensus.*

Around noon, a mutter of voices carried up the trail – the day's first regular pilgrims, making an outward show of reverence while still chattering about the pleasures of Gathering. Lark sighted white-robed figures beyond some vapor fumaroles. The leaders called greetings to Lark's group, already returning from devotions, and began shuffling aside to give up right of way.

A crack of thunder struck as the two parties passed alongside, slamming their bodies together and flapping their robes. Hoons crouched, covering their ears, and g'Kek eyestalks recoiled. One poor qheuen skittered over the edge, clutching a gnarled tree with a single, desperate claw.

Lark's first thought was of another gas discharge.

When the ground shook, he pondered an *eruption*.

He would later learn that the noise came not from Jijo, but the sky. It was the sound of fate arriving, and the world he knew coming abruptly to an end, before he ever expected it.

ASX

Those within the starship induced a small opening in its gleaming side. Through this portal they sent an emissary, unlike anything the Commons had seen in living memory.

A robot!

my/our ring-of-associations had to access one of its myriad moist storage glands in order to place its contours, recalling an illustration we/i once perused in a human book.

Which book? Ah, thank you my self. *Jane's Survey of Basic Galactic Tools*. One of the rarest surviving fruits of the Great Printing.

Exactly as depicted in that ancient diagram, this floating mechanism was a black, octagonal slab, about the size of a young qheuen, hovering above the ground at about the level of my ring-of-vision, with various gleaming implements projecting above or hanging below. From the moment the hatch closed behind it, the robot ignored every earthly contour, leaving a trail where grass, pebbles, and loam were pressed flat by unseen heaviness.

Wherever it approached, folk quailed back. Just one group of beings kept still, awaiting the creature of not-flesh. We sages. *Responsibility* was our cruel mooring, so adamant that even my basal segment stayed rigid, though it pulsed with craven need to flee. The robot – or its masters in the ship – thus knew who had the right/duty to parlay. It hesitated in front of Vubben, appearing to contemplate our eldest sage for five or six duras, perhaps sensing

70

the reverence we all hold for the wisest of the g'Kek. Then it backed away to confront us all.

i/we watched in mystified awe. After all, this was a *thing*, like a hoonish riverboat or some dead tool left by the vanished Buyur. Only the tools *we* make do not fly, and Buyur remnants show no further interest in doing so.

This thing not only moved, it *spoke*, commencing first with a repeat of the earlier message.

'Surveying (local, unique) lifeforms, in this we seek your (gracious) help.
'Knowledge of the (local) biosphere, this you (assuredly) have.
'Tools and (useful) arts, these we offer in trade.
'Confidentially, shall we (mutually) exchange?'

Our rewq were useless – shriveling away from the intense flux of our distress. We sages nonetheless held conference. By agreement, Vubben rolled forward, his roller-wheels squeaking with age. In a show of discipline, all eyestalks turned toward the alien device, though surely over-surfeited with its frightening stimulus.

'Poor castaways, are we,' he commenced reciting, in the syncopated pops and clicks of formal Galactic Two. Although our urrish cousins find that language easiest and use it among themselves, all conceded that Vubben, the g'Kek, was peerless in his mastery of the grammar.

Especially when it came to telling necessary lies.

'Poor castaways, ignorant and stranded.
'Delighted are we. Ecstatic at this wondrous thing.
'Advent of rescue!'

SARA

Some distance below Dolo village, the river felt its way through a great marsh where even hoon sailors were known to lose the main channel, snagging on tree roots or coming aground on shifting sandbars. Normally, the brawny, patient crew of the dross-hauler *Hauph-woa* would count on wind and the river's rhythmic rise-and-fall to help them slip free. But these weren't normal times. So they folded their green cloaks – revealing anxious mottles across their lumpy backbone ridges – and pushed the *Hauph-woa* along with poles made of lesser-boo. Even passengers had to assist, now and then, to keep the muddy bottom from seizing the keel and holding them fast. The uneasy mood affected the ship's contingent of flighty noor, who barked nervously, scampering across the masts, missing commands and dropping lines.

Finally, just before nightfall, the captain-pilot guided the *Hauphwoa*'s ornate prow past one last fen of droopy tallgrass to Unity Point, where the river's branches reconverged into an even mightier whole. The garu forest resumed, spreading a welcome sheltering canopy over both banks. After such an arduous day, the air seemed all at once to release passengers and crew from its moist clench. A cool breeze stroked skin, scale, and hide, while sleek noor sprang overboard to splash alongside the gently gliding hull, then clambered the masts and spars to stretch and preen.

Sara thanked Prity when her assistant brought supper in a wooden bowl, then the chimp took her own meal to the side, in order to flick overboard the spicy greens that hoon chefs loved slicing into nearly everything they cooked. A trail of bubbles showed that river creatures, feeding on the scraps, weren't so finicky. Sara didn't mind the tangy taste, though most Earthlings wound up defecating bright colors after too many days of shipboard fare.

When Prity later brought a pair of blankets, Sara chose the plushest to tuck over the Stranger, sleeping near the main hold with its neatly stacked crates of dross. His brow bore a sheen of perspiration, which she wiped with a dry cloth. Since early yesterday, he had shown none of the lucidity so briefly displayed when the ill-omened bolide split the sky.

Sara had misgivings about hauling the wounded man on a hurried, stressful trek. Still, there *was* a good clinic in Tarek Town. And this way she might keep an eye on him while performing her other duty – one rudely dropped in her lap last night, after that frenzied conclave in the Meeting Tree.

Pzora stood nearby, a dark tower, dormant but ever-vigilant over the patient's condition. The pharmacist vented steamy puffs from the specialized ring that routinely performed ad hoc chemistry beyond the understanding of Jijo's best scholars or even the traeki themselves.

Wrapping her shoulders in another soft g'Kek-spun blanket, Sara turned and watched her fellow passengers.

Jomah, the young son of Henrik, the Exploser, lay curled nearby, snoring softly after the excitement of leaving home for the first time. Closer to the mast sat Jop, the bristle-cheeked delegate of Dolo's farmers and crofters, peering in the half-light at a leather-bound copy of some Scroll. Over by the starboard rail, Ulgor, the urrish tinker who had spoken at the village meeting, knelt facing a qheuenish woodcarver named Blade, one of many sons of the matriarch, Log Biter. Blade had lived for years among the sophisticated Gray Qheuens of Tarek Town, so his choice as representative of Dolo Hive seemed natural.

From a moss-lined pouch, Ulgor drew a quivering rewq symbiont, of the type suited for lean urrish heads. The trembling membrane crawled over each of her triple eyes, creating the Mask-That-Reveals. Meanwhile, Blade's rewq wrapped itself around the seeing-strip bisecting his melonlike cupola. The qheuen's legs retracted, leaving only the armored claws exposed.

The pair conversed in a bastard dialect of Galactic Two, at best a difficult tongue for humans. Moreover, the breeze carried off the treble whistle-tones, leaving just the lower track of syncopated clicks. Perhaps for those reasons the two travelers seemed unconcerned anyone might listen.

Maybe, as often happened, they underrated the reach of human hearing.

Or else they're counting on something called common courtesy, she thought ironically. Lately Sara had become quite an eavesdropper, an unlikely habit for a normally shy, private young woman. Her recent fascination with language was the cause. This time though, fatigue overcame curiosity.

Leave them alone. You'll have plenty of chances to study dialects in Tarek Town.

Sara took her blanket over to a spot between two crates marked with Nelo's seal, exuding the homey scents of Dolo's paper mill. There had been little time for rest since that frenetic town meeting. Only a few miduras after adjournment, the village elders had sent a herald to wake Sara with this assignment – to lead a delegation downriver in search of answers and guidance. She was chosen both as one with intimate knowledge of Biblos and also to represent the Dolo craft workers – as Jop would speak for the farmers, and Blade for the upriver qheuens. Other envoys included Ulgor, Pzora, and Fakoon, a g'Kek scriven-dancer. Since each was already billeted aboard the *Hauph-woa*, with business in Tarek Town, they could hardly refuse. Together with the ship's captain, that made at least one representative from all Six exile races. A good omen, the elders hoped.

Sara still wondered about Jomah. Why would Henrik dispatch the boy on a trip that promised danger, even in quiet times?

'*He will know what to do,*' the taciturn explorer had said, putting his son in Sara's nominal care. '*Once you reach Tarek Town.*'

If only I could say as much for myself, Sara worried. It had been impossible to turn down this assignment, much as she wanted to.

It's been a year since Joshu died – since shame and grief made a hermit of you. Besides, who is going to care that you made a fool of yourself over a man who could never be yours? That all seems a small matter, now that the world we know is coming to an end.

Alone in the dark, Sara worried.

Are Dwer and Lark safe? Or has something dreadful already happened at Gathering?

She felt Prity curl up alongside in her own blanket, sharing warmth. The hoonish helmsman rumbled a crooning melody, with no words in any language Sara knew, yet conveying a sense of muzzy serenity, endlessly forbearing.

Things work out, the hoonish umble seemed to say.

Sleep finally climbed out of her body's fatigue to claim Sara as she thought—

I ... sure ... hope ... so.

Later, in the middle of the night, a dream yanked her bolt upright, clutching the blanket close. Her eyes stared over the peaceful river, lit by two moons, but Sara's heart pounded as she quailed from an awful nightmare image.

Flames.

Moonlight flickered on the water, and to her eyes it became fire, licking the Biblos roof-of-stone, blackening it with the heat and soot of half a million burning books.

THE STRANGER

Unconscious, he is helpless to control dark images roiling across the closed universe of his mind.

It is a tight universe – narrow and confined – yet teeming with stars and confusion. With galaxies and remorse. With nebulae and pain.

And water. Always water – from dense black ice fields all the way to space-clouds so diffuse, you might never know they thronged with beings the size of planets. Living things as slow and thin as vapor, swimming through a near-vacuum sea.

Sometimes he thinks water will never leave him alone. Nor will it let him simply die.

He hears it right now, water's insistent music, piercing his delirium. This time it comes to him as a soft lapping sound – the sluicing of wooden boards through gentle liquid, like some vessel bearing him along from a place he can't remember, toward another whose name he'll never learn. It sounds reassuring, this melody, not like the sucking clutch of that awful swamp, where he had thought he was about to drown at last—

—as he so nearly drowned once, long ago, when the Old Ones forced him, screaming, into a crystal globe they then filled with a fluid that dissolved everything it touched.

—or as he once fought for breath on that green-green-green world whose thick air refused to nourish while he stumbled on and on half-blind toward a fearsome glimmering Jophur tower.

—or the time his body and soul felt pummeled, squeezed, unable even to gasp as he threaded a narrow passage that seemed about to strip him to his spine ... before abruptly spilling him into a realm where shining light stretched on and on until—

His mind rebels, quailing from brief, incoherent images. Fevered, he has no idea which of them are remembered, which are exaggerated, and which his damaged brain simply invented out of the pitchy stuff of nightmare—

—like a starship's vapor contrail (water!) cleaving a blue sky that reminded him of home.

—or the sight of beings like himself (more water!) living on a world where they clearly don't belong.

Amid the chaos of fevered hallucinations, another impression penetrates. Somehow he knows that it comes from beyond his delusion – from someplace real. It feels like a touch, a stroke of softness on his brow. A brush, accompanied by murmurs in a voice that soothes. He can make no sense of the words, but still he welcomes the sensation, even knowing that it should not be. Not here. Not now.

It is a comfort, that touch, making him feel just a little less alone.

Eventually, it even pushes back the fearsome images – the memories and dreams – and in time he slips from delirium into a quietude of sleep.

V

THE BOOK OF THE SEA

When judgment comes, you will be asked
about the dead.

What living species, beautiful and unique,
exist no more because you squatters chose
a forbidden place to live?

And what of your own dead?
Your corpses, cadavers, and remains?
Your tools and cold-made things?
How have you disposed of them?

Be righteous, sooners of Jijo.
Show how hard you tried.
Make small the consequences of your crime.
(The offense of living.)

Felonies – and their punishment –
can be made smaller, by the simple fact
of doing less harm.

—The Scroll of Advice

ALVIN'S TALE

The Mount Guenn tram climbs a steep route from Wuphon Port all the way up to the workshops of Uriel the Smith. The railway is small and hard to see, even when you're looking for it. Still, it's allowed by the sages only because it's important for getting Uriel's forgings down to market. Also, it uses no artificial power. Water from a hot spring, high up on the mountain, pours into a tank aboard whichever car is waiting at the top station. Meanwhile, the bottom car's tank is emptied, so it's much lighter, even with passengers aboard. When the brake is cut, the heavier car starts down, pulling the cable, which in turn hauls the bottom car *up*.

It sounds gimmicky, but in fact it goes pretty fast and can even get scary for a few seconds in the middle, when the other car seems to be rushing right at you along the same set of slim wooden rails. Then you reach a split section where that car streaks past in a blur. What a thrill!

It's a trip of over forty arrowflights, but the water's still near boiling hot in the first car's tank when it reaches bottom – one reason folks like it when Uriel ships her wares down to port on laundry day.

Ur-ronn says one piece of salvaged Buyur cable is what makes it all possible. A real treasure that can't ever be replaced.

Mount Guenn was behaving itself that day, so there wasn't much ash in the air and I didn't really need my cloak. Huck wore her goggles anyway, one strapped over each eyebulb, and Pincer still had to spray his red cupola as the air got thinner, and Wuphon turned into a toy village under its blanket of camouflage greenery. Thick stands of lowland boo soon gave way to hedgerows of multitrunked gorreby trees, followed by tufts of feathery shrubs that got sparser as we climbed. This was *not* red-qheuen country. Still, Pincer was excited over the news from Ur-ronn.

'You see? The window's done! The last big piece we needed for the bathy. A little more work an' it'll be ready-eady!'

Huck sniffed disdainfully. She did a good job of it, too, since that's one of those human gestures you read about that we actually get to see pretty often, whenever Mister Heinz, our local schoolmaster, hears an answer he doesn't like.

'Great,' Huck remarked. 'Whoever rides the thing can *see* whatever's about to eat him.'

I had to laugh. 'Hrrrm. So now you admit there might be sea monsters after all?'

Huck swiveled three stalks toward me in a look of surprise. It's not often I can catch her like that.

'I'll admit I'd want more than just a slab of urrish glass between me and whatever's down there, twenty thousand leagues under the sea!'

I confess being puzzled by her attitude. This bitterness wasn't like Huck at all. I tried lightening the mood.

'Say, I've always wondered. Has anybody ever figured out exactly how long a league *is*?'

Two of her eyes gazed at each other, then back at me with a glint of whimsy.

'I looked in the dictionary once, but I couldn't *fathom* the answer.'

Pincer complained, 'Look, are you two about to start—'

I interrupted, 'If anyone *does* know the answer, I'd sure like to meter.'

'Heh!' Huck made a thrumming sound with her spokes. 'That's assuming you could parsec what she says.'

'Hrrrm. I don't know if I can take this furlong.'

'Oh-oh-oh-oh-oh!' Pincer complained, feigning agony with all five mouths at once.

That's how we passed the time while climbing into chilly badlands bare of life, and I guess it shows my dad's right about us being humickers. But GalTwo and GalSix aren't any fun for word games. You can't pun in them at all! You *can* in GalSeven, but for some reason it just doesn't hurt as much.

The mountainside got even more stark as we neared the top, where steam vents mark Mount Guenn's broad shoulders and mask the hot breath of Uriel's forges. Here some of the old volcanic spills crystallized in special ways that reflect shimmering colors, shifting as your eye moves. Only a short journey from here, the same kind of stuff stretches as far as you can see across a poison plain that's called the Spectral Flow.

That day, my imagination was unhoonly active. I couldn't help pondering all the power bubbling away, deep under the mountain. Nowhere do Jijo's innards churn more intensely than under the region we exiles call the Slope. We're told that's why all the different ancestor-ships planted their seed in the same part of the planet. And nowhere else *on* the Slope do folks live in closer daily contact with that pent-up power than my hometown. No wonder we were never assigned a family of explosers to prepare our village for destruction. I guess everyone figures Wuphon will be blessed by the volcano anyway, inside the next hundred years. A thousand at most. Maybe any day now. So why bother?

We're told it's proper that no trace of our homes will be left after that happens. Still, Jijo can take her own sweet time, as far as I'm concerned.

Despite dozens of tram trips, I still find it kind of surprising whenever the car nears the end of the climb and suddenly a great big cave seems to open out of nowhere, with the rail heading straight for it. Maybe it was all that earlier talk of monsters, but this time I felt a twirl in my heart-spine when that black hollow gaped wide and we plunged toward what looked an awful lot like a hungry *mouth*, set in the face of an angry, impulsive mountain.

The dark stillness inside was suddenly hot and dry as dust. Urronn waited for us when the car came to a jarring halt. She seemed skittish, dancing clip-clop with all four hooves while her stubby work-arms held the door and I helped Huck roll out of the car. Little Huphu rode on Pincer-Tip's back, eyes all aglitter, as if ready for anything.

Maybe the *noor* was ready, but Huck, Pincer, and I were thrown completely off balance by what our urrish friend said at that point. Ur-ronn spoke in GalSix, since it's easier for an urs to speak without lisping.

'I am glad in my pouches that you, my friends, could come so soon. Now swiftly to Uriel's observatory, where she has, for several days, been tracking strange objects in the sky!'

I confess, I was struck dumb. Like the others, I just stared at her for several duras. Finally, we all unfroze at once.

'Hrrrrm, you can't—'

'What do you—'

'Surely you don't mean—'

Ur-ronn stamped her front-left foot. *'I do mean it! Uriel and Gybz claim to have perceived one or more starships, several days ago! Moreover, when last sighted, one or all of them seemed poised to land!'*

VI

THE BOOK OF THE SLOPE

Legends

It seems ironic that most of Jijo's nighttime constellations were named by humans, the youngest exile sept. None of the prior six had thought of giving fanciful labels to groups of unrelated stars, associating them with real and mythical beasts.

The quaint habit clearly derives from humanity's unique heritage as an orphaned race – or as self-evolved wolflings – who burst into space without guidance by a patron. Every other sapient species had such a mentor – as the hoon had the Guthatsa and g'Keks had the Drooli – an older, wiser species, ready to teach a younger one the ropes.

But not humans.

This lack scarred *Homo sapiens* in unique ways.

Countless bizarre notions bloomed among native Terran cultures during humanity's dark lonely climb. Outlandish ideas that would never occur to an uplifted race – one taught nature's laws from the very start. Bizarre concepts like connecting dots in the sky to form fictitious creatures.

When Earthlings first did this on Jijo, the earlier groups reacted with surprise, even suspicion. But soon the practice seemed to rob the stars of some of their terror. The g'Kek, hoon, and urs started coming up with sky-myths of their own, while qheuens and traeki were glad to have tales made up about them.

Since the advent of peace, scholars have disagreed in their assessment of this practice. Some say its very primitiveness helps the Six follow in the footsteps of the glavers. This meets with approval from those who urge that we hurry as quickly as possible down the Path of Redemption.

Others claim it is like the trove of books in Biblos, a distraction from achieving the simple clarity of thought that will help us exiles achieve our goal.

Then there are those who like the practice simply because it feels good, and makes for excellent art.

—Cultural Patterns of the Slope, by Ku-Phuhaph Tuo, Ovoom Town Guild of Publishers, Year-of-Exile 1922.

Who would have imagined that a robot might display *surprise*? Yet did we not discern an unmistakable yank, a twitch, in response to Vubben's manifest lie? An impromptu falsehood, contrived out of sudden necessity by Ur-Jah and Lester, whose quick wits do their hot-blooded tribes proud?

The first Scrolls – a mere ten kilowords, engraved on polymer bars by the original g'Kek pioneers – warned of several ways that doom might fall from heaven. New Scrolls were added by glaver, hoon, and qheuen settlers, first jealously hoarded, then shared as the Commons slowly formed. Finally came human-sept and its flooding gift of paper books. But even the Great Printing could not cover all potentialities.

Among likely prospects, it was thought the Galactic Institutes charged with enforcing quarantine might someday find us. Or titanic cruisers of the great patron clans would descry our violation, if/when the glaring eye, Izmunuti, ceased spewing its wind of masking needles.

Among other possibilities, we pondered what to do if a great globeship of the hydrogen-breathing Zang came to one of our towns, dripping freezing vapors in wrath over our trespass. These and many other contingencies we discussed, did we not, my rings?

But seldom *this* thing which had come to pass – the arrival of *desperados*.

If malefactors ever did come to Jijo, we reasoned, why should they make themselves known to us? With a world to sieve for riches, would they even deign to notice the hovels of a few coarse savages, far devolved from ancient glory, clumped in one small corner of Jijo's expanse?

Yet here they have come into our midst with a boldness that terrifies.

The robot emissary contemplated Vubben's proclamation for ten duras, then responded with a single terse interrogation.

'Your presence on this world, it is a (query) accident?'

Do you recall, my rings, the brief thrill that coursed our linking membranes? The robot's masters were set aback! Against all reason or proportionality of force, the initiative was ours, for a moment.

Vubben crossed two eyestalks in a gesture of polite aloofness.

*

'Your question, it insinuates doubt.

'More than doubt, it suggests grave assumptions about our nature.

'Those assumptions – might they lay upon our ancestors' necks a shackling suspicion?

'(Query) suspicion of heinous crimes?'

How resilient was Vubben's misdirection. How like the web of a mulc-spider. He denies nothing, tells no explicit lie. Yet how he implies!

'Forgiveness for (unintended) insults, we implore,' the machine ratcheted hastily. *'Descendants of castaways, we take you for. An illfated vessel, your ancestors' combined ship must have been. Lost on some noble errand, this we scarcely doubt.'*

Now *they* were the liars, of that *we* had no doubt at all.

DWER

Leaving the craggy rimmer range, Dwer led Rety and the others into that region of undulating hills, gently slanting toward the sea, that was called the Slope. The domain of the Six. Dwer tried getting his mysterious young prisoner to talk about herself. But his first efforts were answered in morose monosyllables. Clearly, Rety resented the fact that he could tell so much from her appearance, her animal skin clothes, her speech and manner.

Well, what did you expect? To sneak over the mountains and walk into one of our villages, no questions asked?

Her burn scar alone would mark her for attention. Not that disfigurement was rare on the Slope. Accidents were common, and even the latest traeki unguents were crude medicine by Galactic standards. Still, people would notice Rety anywhere she went.

At meals, she gaped covetously at the goods he drew from his backpack. His cup and plate, the hammered aluminium skillet, his bedroll of fleecy hurchin down – things to make life a bit easier for those whose ancestors long ago forsook the life of star-gods. To Dwer there was a simple beauty in the woven cloth he wore, in boots with shape-treated tree sap soles, even the elegant three-piece urrish fire-starter – all examples of primitive cunning, the sort his wolfling ancestors relied on through their lonely isolation on old Earth. Most people took such things for granted on the Slope.

But to a clan of sooners – illegal squatters living jealous and filthy beyond the pale – they might seem marvels, worth any risk to steal.

Dwer wondered, was this the only time? Perhaps Rety was just the first to get *caught*. Some thefts blamed on noors might be the fault of other robbers, sneaking over the mountains from a far-off hermit tribe.

Was that your idea? To swipe the first worthwhile thing you came across and scoot home to your tribe, a hero?

Somehow, he figured more than that must be involved. She kept peering around, as if looking for something in particular. Something that mattered to her.

Dwer watched Rety lead the captive glaver by a rope tied to her waist. The girl's saucy gait seemed meant to defy him, or anyone else who might judge her. Between clumps of grimy hair, he was nauseated to see puckered tracks made by borer bees, a parasite easily warded off with traeki salve. But no traekis lived where she came from.

It forced uncomfortable thoughts. What if his own grandparents had made the same choice as Rety's? To flee the Commons for whatever reason, seeking far reaches to hide in? Nowadays, with war – and war's refugees – a thing of the past, sooners were rather rare. Old Fallon had found only one squatter band in many years roaming across half a continent, and this was Dwer's first encounter.

What would you do if you were raised that way, scraping for a living like animals, knowing a land of wealth and power lay beyond those mountains to the west?

Dwer had never thought of the Slope that way before. Most Scrolls and legends emphasized how far the six exile races had already fallen, not how much farther there was yet to go.

That night, Dwer used tobar seeds to call another clock teet, not because he wanted an early wakeup, but to have the steady, tapping rhythm in the background while he slept. When Mudfoot yowled at the burst of aroma, covering his snout, Rety let out a soft giggle and her first smile.

He insisted on examining her feet before bed, and she quietly let him treat two blisters showing early signs of infection. 'We'll have healers look you over when we reach Gathering,' he told her. Neither of them commented when he kept her moccasins, tucking them under his sleeping roll for the night.

As they lay under a starry canopy, separated by the dim campfire coals, he urged Rety to name a few constellations, and her curt answers helped Dwer eliminate one momentous possibility – that some *new* group of human exiles had landed, destroying their ship and settling to brute existence far from the Slope. Rety couldn't realize the importance of naming a few patterns in the sky, but Dwer erased one more pinprick of worry. The legends were the same.

At dawn Dwer awoke sniffing something in the air – a familiar odor, almost pleasant, but also *nervous* – a sensation Lark once explained mysteriously as 'negative ions and water vapor.' Dwer shook Rety awake and hurriedly led the glaver under a rocky overhang. Mudfoot followed, moving like an arthritic g'Kek, grumbling hatred of mornings with every step. They all made it to shelter just as a sheet-storm hit – an undulating curtain of continuous rain that crept along the mountainside from left to right, pouring water like a translucent drapery that pummeled everything beneath, soaking the forest, one wavy ribbon at a time. Rety stared wide-eyed as the rainbow-colored tapestry swept by, drenching their campsite and ripping half the leaves off trees. Obviously she had never witnessed one before.

The trek resumed. Perhaps it was a night's restful sleep, or the eye-opening start to the day. But Rety now seemed less sullen, more willing to enjoy sights like a meadow full of bumble flowers – yellow tubes, fringed with black fuzz, which rode the steady west wind, swooping and buzzing at the end of tether-stems. Rety's eyes darted, enthralled by the antic dance of deception and pollination. The species did not exist in the stagnant weather shadow beyond the Rimmers, where a vast plain of poison grass stretched most of the way to the Gray Hills.

Just getting here across all that was an accomplishment, Dwer noted, wondering how she had managed it.

As alpine sheerness gave way to gentler foothills, Rety gave up hiding her fierce curiosity. She began by pointing and asking – 'Are those wooden poles holding up your backpack? Don't they make it heavy? I'll bet they're hollow.'

Then – 'If you're a hunter, where's the rest of your stalking gang? Or do you always hunt alone?'

In rapid succession more questions followed. 'Who made your bow? How far can you hit somethin' the size of my hand?

'Did you live in one place the whole time you were little? In a . . . *house*? Did you get to hold on to stuff you wanted to keep, 'stead of leavin' it behind when you moved?

'If you grew up by a river, did you ever see any *hoon*? What're they like? I hear they're tall as a tree, with noses long as your arm.

'Are the *trikki* really trick? Are they made of tree sap? Do they eat garbage?

'Do noors ever slow down? I wonder why Buyur made 'em that way.'

Other than her habit of turning *Buyur* into a singular proper name, Dwer couldn't have phrased the last question any better himself. Mudfoot was a perpetual nuisance, getting underfoot, chasing shrub critters, then laying in ambush somewhere along the path, squeaking in delight when Dwer failed to pick him out of the overhanging foliage.

I could shake you easily, if I didn't have a glaver and a kid in tow, Dwer thought at the grinning noor. Yet he was starting to feel pretty good. They would make quite an entrance at Gathering, sure to be the talk of the festival.

Over lunch, Rety used his cooking knife to prepare a scrub hen he had shot. Dwer could barely follow her whirling hand as the good parts landed in the skillet with a crackling sizzle, while the poison glands flew to the waste pit. She finished, wiping the knife with a flourish, and offered it back to him.

'Keep it,' Dwer said, and she responded with a hesitant smile.

With that he ceased being her jailor and became her guide, escorting a prodigal daughter back to the embrace of clan and Commons. Or so he thought, until some time later, during the meal, when she said – 'I really ha' seen some of those before.'

'Seen some of what?'

Rety pointed at the glaver, placidly chewing under the shade of a stand of swaying lesser-boo.

'You thought I never saw any, 'cause I feared she'd bite. But I seen 'em, from afar. A whole herd. Sneaky devils, hard to catch. Took the guys all day to spear 'un. They taste awful gamey, but the boys liked it fine.'

Dwer swallowed hard. 'Are you saying your tribe *hunts and eats* glavers?'

Rety looked back with brown eyes full of innocent curiosity. 'You don't on this side? I'm not surprised. There's easier prey, an' better eatin'.'

He shook his head, nauseated by the news.

Part of him chided – *You were willing to shoot this particular glaver down, stone dead, if it crossed over the pass.*

Yes, but only as a last resort. And I wouldn't eat her!

Dwer knew what people called him – the Wild Man of the Forest, living beyond the law. He even helped nurse the mystique, since it meant his awkward speech was taken for something more manly than shyness. In truth, killing was the part of any hunt he did as capably and swiftly as possible, never with enjoyment. Now, to learn people beyond the mountains were devouring *glavers*? The sages would be appalled!

Ever since surmising that Rety came from a sooner band, Dwer had known his duty would be to guide a militia expedition to round up the errant clan. Ideally, it would be a simple matter of firm but gentle ingathering, resettling lost cousins back into the fold of the Commons. But now, Rety had unknowingly indicted her tribe with another crime. The Scrolls were clear. *That which is rare, you shall not eat. That which is precious, you must protect.* But, above all – *You may not devour what once flew between the stars.*

Irony was ashen in Dwer's mouth. For after the sooners were brought back for trial, his job then would be to collect every glaver living east of the Rimmers – and slaughter those he could not catch.

Ah, but that won't make me a bad person ... because I won't eat them.

Rety must have sensed his reaction. She turned to stare at the nearby stand of great-boo, its young shoots barely as thick as her waist. The tubelike green shafts swayed in rippling waves, like fur on the belly of the lazy noor, dozing by her foot.

'Are they gonna hang me?' the girl asked quietly. The scar on her face, which was muted when she smiled, now seemed stretched and livid. 'Old Clin says you slopies hang sooners when you catch 'em.'

'Nonsense. Actually, each race handles its own—'

'The old folks say it's slopie law. Kill anyone who tries to make a free life east o' the Rimmers.'

Dwer stammered, suddenly awash in irritation, 'If – if you think that, why'd you come all this way? To – to stick your head in a noose?'

Rety's lips pressed. She looked away and murmured low. 'You wouldn't believe me.'

Dwer repented his own flash of temper. In a gentler tone, he asked – 'Why don't you try me? Maybe ... I might understand better than you think.'

But she withdrew once more into a cocoon of brooding silence, unresponsive as a stone.

While Dwer hastily rinsed the cooking gear, Rety tied herself in place ahead of the glaver, even though he had said she could walk free. He found his cooking knife by the smothered coals, where she must have laid it after those sharp words.

The gesture of rejection irked him, and he muttered gruffly, 'Let's get out of here.'

We had chosen to feign a small distinction between two crimes. At best a slightly lesser felony – that of *accidental* rather than planned colonization.

No one could deny the obvious – that our ancestors had loosed unsanctioned offspring on a fallow world. But Vubben's artful evasion implied an act of culpable carelessness, rather than villainy by design.

The lie would not hold for long. When archaeological traces were sifted, forensic detectives from the Institutes would swiftly perceive our descent from many separate landings, not one mixed crew stranded by mishap on this remote shore. Moreover, there was the presence of our juniormost sept – the human clan. By their own bizarre tale, they are a *wolfling race*, unknown to Galactic culture until just three hundred Jijoan years ago.

Then why even try such a bluff?

Desperation. Plus a frail hope that our 'guests' have not the skill or tools for archaeology. Their goal must be to swoop in for a quick sampling of hidden treasures. Then, covering their tracks, they would wish a swift, stealthy departure with a ship's hold full of contraband. To this mercenary quest, our strange, forlorn colony of miscreants offers both opportunity and a threat.

They must know we possess firsthand knowledge of Jijo, valuable to their needs.

Alas, my rings. Are we not also potential witnesses to their villainy?

SARA

Nobody expected an ambush.

It was the perfect place for one. Still, no one aboard the *Hauph-woa* had any idea of danger until it actually happened. A century of peace had blurred the once-jealously guarded domains of old. Urrish and g'Kek settlers were few, since the former could not raise young near water, and the latter preferred smooth terrain. Still, all types were seen crowding tiny docks when the *Hauph-woa* glided by, eager to share scant news.

Alas, there had been none from downstream since that terrible spectacle crossed the sky.

Mostly, the river folk were reacting constructively, rushing to reinforce their facade screens, cleaning the baffles of their smoke-stacks or hauling boats under cover – but one forlorn tribe of traeki marsh-dwellers had gone much further, burning their entire stilt village in a spasm of fear and fealty to the Scrolls. Pzora's topknot shivered at the aroma of woebegone ring-stacks, floundering in the ashes. The *Hauph-woa*'s captain promised to spread word of their plight. Perhaps other traeki would send new basal segments for the locals to wear, making them better suited for evacuation inland. At worst, the swamp traeki could get rotting matter, settle on top, and shut down higher functions till the world became a less scary place.

The same could not be said for an urrish trade caravan they passed later, stranded with their pack beasts on the desolate west bank, when the panicky citizens of Bing Village blew up their beloved bridge.

The hoonish boat crew back-pedaled with frantic haste, rowing against the current to avoid getting caught in a tangle of broken timbers and mulc-fiber cables, shattered remnants of a beautiful span that had been the chief traverse for an entire region. A marvel of clever camouflage, the bridge used to resemble a jagged snag of jumbled logs. But even that apparently wasn't enough for local orthodox Scroll thumpers. *Maybe they were burning it while I had my nightmare last night*, Sara thought, observing charred timbers and recalling images of flame that had torn her sleep.

A crowd of villagers stood on the east bank, beckoning the *Hauph-woa* to draw near.

Blade spoke up. 'I would not approach,' the blue qheuen hissed from several leg-vents. He wore a rewq over his vision-ring while peering at the folk on shore.

'And why not?' Jop demanded. 'See? They're pointing to a way past the debris. Perhaps they have news, as well.'

Sure enough, there did appear to be a channel, near the shore, unobstructed by remnants of the broken bridge.

'I don't know,' Blade went on. 'I sense that ... something is wrong.'

'You're right about that,' Ulgor added. 'I'd like to know why they have done nothing for the stranded caravan. The villagers have boats. The urs could have been ferried across by now.'

Sara wondered. It certainly would not be fun for any of Ulgor's race to ride a little coracle, with icy water lapping just an arm's breadth away. 'The urs may have refused,' she suggested. 'Perhaps they're not that desperate yet.'

The captain made his decision, and the *Hauph-woa* turned toward the village. As they drew near, Sara saw that the only construct still intact was the hamlet's camouflage lattice. Everything else lay in ruins. *They've probably sent their families into the forest*, she thought. There were plenty of garu trees for humans to live in, and qheuenish citizens could join cousins upstream. Still, the toppled village was a depressing sight.

Sara pondered how much worse things might be if Jop ever got his wish. If Dolo Dam blew up, every dock, weir, and cabin they had seen below the flood line would be swept away. Native creatures would also suffer, though perhaps no more than in a natural flood. *Lark says it is species that matter, not individuals. No eco-niches would be threatened by demolishing our small wooden structures. Jijo won't be harmed.*

Still, it seems dubious, all of this burning and wrecking just to persuade some Galactic big shots we're farther along the Path of Redemption than we really are.

Blade sidled alongside, his blue carapace steaming as dew evaporated from the seams of his shell – a sure sign of anxiety. He rocked a complex rhythm among his five chitinous legs.

'Sara, do you have a rewq? Can you put it on and see if I'm mistaken?'

'Sorry. I gave mine up. All those colors and raw emotions get in the way of paying close attention to language.' She did not add that it had grown painful to wear the things, ever since she made the mistake of using one at Joshu's funeral. 'Why?' she asked. 'What's got you worried?'

Blade's cupola trembled, and the rewq that was wrapped around it quivered. 'The people onshore – they seem ... strange somehow.'

Sara peered through the morning haze. The Bing Villagers were mostly human, but there were also hoon, traeki, and qheuens in the mix. *Likes attract*, she thought. Orthodox fanaticism crossed racial lines.

As does heresy, Sara noted, recalling that her own brother was part of a movement no less radical than the folk who had brought down this bridge.

Several coracles set forth from tree-shrouded shelters, aiming to intercept the riverboat. 'Are they coming to pilot us through?' young Jomah asked.

He got his answer when the first grappling hook whistled, then fell to the deck of the *Hauph-woa*.

Others swiftly followed.

'*We mean you no harm!*' shouted a thick-armed man in the nearest skiff. '*Come ashore, and we'll take care of you. All we want is your boat.*'

That was the wrong thing to say to the proud crew of a river-runner. Every hoon but the helmsman ran to seize and toss overboard the offending hooks. But more grapplers sailed aboard for every one they removed.

Then Jomah pointed downstream. 'Look!'

If anyone still wondered what the Bing-ites planned for the *Hauph-woa*, all doubts vanished at the sight of a charred ruin, blackened ribs spearing upward like a huge, half-burned skeleton. It triggered an umble of dismay from the crew, resonating down Sara's spine and sending the noor beasts into frenzied fits of barking.

The hoon redoubled their efforts, tearing frantically at the hooks.

Sara's first instinct was to shield the Stranger. But the wounded man seemed safe, still unconscious under Pzora's protecting bulk.

'Come on,' she told Blade. 'We better help.'

Pirates often used to attack ships this way until the Great Peace. Perhaps the attackers' own ancestors used the technique in deadly earnest, during the bad old days. The grapples, made of pointy Buyur metal, dug deep when the cables tautened. Sara realized in dismay that the cords were mulc fiber, treated by a traeki process that made them damnably hard to cut. Worse, the lines stretched not just to the coracles but all the way to shore, where locals hauled them taut with blocks and tackle. Hoon strength, helped by Blade's great claws, barely sufficed to wrestle the hooks free. Still, Sara tried to help, and even the g'Kek passenger kept lookout with four keen eyes, shouting to warn when another boat drew near. Only Jop leaned against the mast, watching with clear amusement. Sara had no doubt who the orthodox tree farmer was rooting for.

The beach loomed ever closer. If the *Hauph-woa* made it past midpoint, she'd have the river's pull on her side. But even that force might be too little to break the strong cords. When the keel scraped sand, it would spell the end.

In desperation, the crew hit on a new tactic. Taking up axes, they chopped away at planks and rails, wherever a grapple had dug in, tearing out whole wooden chunks to throw overboard, attacking their own vessel with a fury that was dazzling to behold, given normal hoon placidity.

Then, all at once, the deck jerked under Sara's feet as the whole boat suddenly shuddered, slewing, as if the center mast were a pivot.

'They've hooked the rudder!' someone cried.

Sara looked over the stern and saw a massive metal barb speared through the great hinged paddle the helmsman used to steer the ship. The rudder could not be pulled aboard or chopped loose without crippling the *Hauph-woa*, leaving it adrift and helpless.

Prity bared her teeth and screamed. Though shivering with fear, the little ape started climbing over the rail, till Sara stopped her with a firm hand.

'It's my job,' she said tersely, and without pause shrugged out of her tunic and kilt. A sailor handed her a hatchet with a strap-thong through the haft.

Don't everybody speak up all at once to argue me out of doing this, she thought sardonically, knowing no one would.

Some things were simply obvious.

The hatchet hung over one shoulder. It wasn't comforting to feel its metal coolness stroke her left breast as she climbed, even though the cutting edge still bore a leather cover.

Clothes would have been an impediment. Sara needed her toes, especially, to seek footholds on the *Hauph-woa*'s stern. The clinker construction style left overlaps in the boards that helped a bit. Still, she could not prevent shivering, half from the morning chill and partly from stark terror. Sweaty palms made it doubly hard, even though her mouth felt dry as urrish breath.

I haven't done any climbing in years!

To nonhumans, this must look like another day's work for a tree-hugging Earthling. Kind of like expecting *every* urs to be a courier runner, or all traekis to make a good martini. In fact, *Jop* was the logical one for this task, but the captain didn't trust the man, with good reason.

The crew shouted tense encouragement as she clambered down the stern, holding the rudder with one arm. Meanwhile, derisive scorn came from the coracles and those ashore. *Great. More attention than I ever had in my life, and I'm stark naked at the time.*

The mulc cable groaned with tension as villagers strained on pulleys to haul *Hauph-woa* toward the beach, where several gray qheuens gathered, holding torches that loomed so frighteningly close that Sara imagined she could hear the flames. At last, she reached a place where she could plant her feet and hands – bracing her legs in a way that forever surrendered all illusions of personal modesty. She had to tear the leather cover off the ax with her teeth and got a bitter electrical taste from the reddish metal. It made her shudder – then tense up as she almost lost her grip. The boat's churning wake looked oily and bitter cold.

Jeers swelled as she hacked at the rubber blade, sending chips flying, trying to cut a crescent around the embedded hook. She soon finished gouging away *above* the grapple and was starting on the tougher part below, when something smacked the back of her left hand, sending waves of pain throbbing up her arm. She saw *blood* ooze around a wooden sliver, protruding near the wrist.

A *slingshot* pellet lay buried halfway in the plank nearby.

Another glanced off the rudder, ricocheting from the boat's stern, then skipping across the water.

Someone was *shooting* at her!

Why you jeekee, slucking, devoluted . . .

Sara found an unknown aptitude for cursing, as she went through a wide vocabulary of oaths from five different languages, hacking away with the hatchet more vehemently than ever. A steady drumbeat of pebbles now clattered against the hull, but she ignored them in a blur of heat and fury.

'Otszharsiya, perkiye! Syookai dreesoona!'

She ran out of obscenities in Rossic and was starting to plumb urrish GalTwo when the plank abruptly let out a loud *crack*! The attached cable moaned, yanking hard at the grappling hook—

—and the tortured wood gave way.

The hook snatched the ax out of her hand as it tore free, glittering in the sunlight. Thrown off balance, Sara struggled to hold on, though her hands were slippery from sweat and blood. With a gasp she felt her grip fail and she dropped, sucking in deeply, but the Roney slammed her like an icy hammer, driving air from her startled lungs.

Sara floundered, battling first to reach the surface, then to tread water and sputter a few deep breaths, and finally to keep from getting tangled in all the ropes that lay strewn across the water. A shiny hook passed a frightening hand's width from her face. Moments later, she had to dive down to avoid a snarl of cords that might have trapped her.

The boat's turbulent wake added to her troubles, as the *Hauph-woa* took advantage of its chance to flee.

Her chest ached by the time she hit surface again – to come face to face with a lanky young man, leaning on the rim of a coracle, clutching a slingshot in one hand. Surprise rocked him back when their eyes met. Then his gaze dropped to notice her bareness.

He *blushed*. Hurriedly, the young man put aside his weapon and started shrugging out of his jacket. To give to her, no doubt.

'Thanks . . .' Sara gasped. 'But I gotta . . . go now.'

Her last glimpse of the young villager, as she swam away, showed a crestfallen look of disappointment. *It's too soon yet for him to be a hardened pirate*, Sara thought. *This new, hard world hasn't yet rubbed away the last traces of gallantry.*

But give it time.

Now she had the river's current behind her as she swam, and soon Sara glimpsed the *Hauph-woa* downstream. The crew had the boat turned and were stroking to stay in place, now that they had reached a safe distance from Bing Village. Still, it was a hard pull to reach the hull at last and start up the rope ladder. She only made it halfway before her muscles started to cramp, and the helpful sailors had to haul it in the rest of the way by hand.

I've got to get stronger, if I'm going to make a habit of having adventures, she thought as someone wrapped a blanket around her.

Yet, Sara felt strangely fine while Pzora tended her wound and the cook made her some of his special tea. Sara's hand ached, and her body throbbed, yet she felt also something akin to a *glow*.

I made decisions, and they were right ones. A year ago, it seemed every choice I made was wrong. Now, maybe things have changed.

Clutching her blanket, Sara watched as the *Hauph-woa* labored back upstream along the *west* bank, to a point where they could take aboard the stranded caravan, ferrying the urs and their beasts far enough to have no worries about local fanatics. The calm teamwork of passengers and crew was such an encouraging sight, it boosted her morale about 'big' issues, almost as much as the brief fight had lifted something else inside her.

My faith in my own self, she thought. *I didn't think I was up to any of this. But maybe Father's right, after all.*

I stayed in that damn treehouse long enough.

ASX

Shortly after Vubben spoke, the portal reopened and there emerged from the ship several more floating machines, growling disconcertingly. Each hesitated on reaching the onlookers lining the valley rim. For several duras, the folk of the Commons held their ground, though trembling in foot, wheel, and ring. Then the robots turned and swept away, toward every point of the compass, leaving cyclones of broken grass in their wake.

'*Survey probes – these shall commence their duties*,' the first messenger explained, buzzing and clicking primly in a formal version of Galactic Two.

'*(Preliminary) analyses – these surrogates shall provide.*

'*Meanwhile, toward a goal of both profit and rescue – let us, face-to-face discussions, commence.*'

This caused a stir. Did we understand correctly? Our dialects have drifted since our devolution. Did the phrase 'face-to-face' mean what it seemed?

Below, the ship's doorway began reopening once more.

'Bad news,' Lester Cambel commented gruffly. 'If they're willing to let us see them in person, it means—'

'—that they are not worried anyone will be left after they depart, to *tell* whose face was seen,' finished Knife-Bright Insight.

Our hoon brother, Phwhoon-dau, shared the gloomy diagnosis. His aged throat sac darkened from somber thought. 'Their confidence is blatant, unnerving. *Hrrhrm*. As is their haste.'

Vubben turned an eyestalk toward my/our sensor ring and winked the lid – an efficient, human-derived gesture conveying irony. Among the Six, we traeki and g'Keks hobble like cripples on this heavy world, while hoon stride with graceful power. Yet those dour, pale giants claim to find the rest of us equally frantic and wild.

Something, or rather *two* somethings, stirred within the shadowy air-lock. A pair of bipedal forms stepped forward – walkers – slim, stick-jointed, and somewhat tall. Clothed in loosely draped garments that concealed all but their bare hands and heads, they emerged into the afternoon light to peer upward at us.

From the Commons there erupted a low collective sigh of shock and recognition.

Was this a hopeful sign? Out of all the myriad space-faring races in the Civilization of the Five Galaxies, what impossibly remote chance decreed that our discoverers might turn out to be *cousins*? That the crew of this ship should be cogenetic with one of our Six? Was this the work of our capricious goddess, whose luck favors the anomalous and strange?

'Hyoo-mans-s-s . . . ' Ur-Jah, our eldest sage, aspirated in Anglic, the native tongue of our youngest sept.

From Lester Cambel, there escaped a sound i had never heard before, which these rings could not decipher at the time. Only later did we comprehend, and learn its name.

It was despair.

DWER

Rety led single file along a track that now ran atop a broad shelf of bedrock, too hard for great-boo to take root. The slanting, upthrust granite ledge separated two broad fingers of cane forest, which Dwer knew stretched for hundreds of arrowflights in all directions. Although the rocky trail followed a ridgetop, the boo on either side grew so tall that only the highest peaks could be seen above the swaying ocean of giant stems.

The girl kept peering, left and right, as if in search of something. As if she *wanted* something, rather urgently, and did not want to walk past it by mistake. But when Dwer tried to inquire, all she gave back was silence.

You'll have to watch it with this one, he thought. *She's been hurt all her life, till she's prickly as a dartback hare.*

People weren't his specialty, but a forester uses empathy to grasp the simple needs and savage thoughts of wild things.

Wild things can know pain.

Well, in another day or so she won't be my problem. The sages have experts, healers. If I meddle, I may just make things worse.

The stone shelf gradually narrowed until the footpath traced a slender aisle between crowded ranks of towering adult boo, each stem now over twenty meters tall and as thick as several men. The giant green stalks grew so close that even Mudfoot would have trouble getting far into the thicket without squeezing between mighty boles. The strip of sky above pinched gradually tighter, becoming a mere ribbon of blue as the trail constricted. At some points, Dwer could spread his arms and touch mighty cylinders on both sides at the same time.

The compressed site played tricks with perspective as he pictured two vast walls, primed to press together at any instant, grinding their tiny group like scraps of cloth under Nelo's pulping hammer.

Funny thing. This stretch of trail hadn't felt nearly so spooky on his way *uphill*, two days ago. Then, the slender avenue had felt like a funnel, channeling him briskly toward his quarry. Now it was a cramped furrow, a pit. Dwer felt a growing tightness in his chest. *What if something's happened up ahead. A landslide blocking the way. Or a fire? What a trap this could be!*

He sniffed suspiciously, picking up only a gummy reek *of greenness* given off by the boo. Of course, anything at all could be going on downwind, and he wouldn't know of it until—

Stop this! Snap out of it. What's gotten into you?

It's her, he realized. *You're feeling bad because she thinks you're a bastard.*

Dwer shook his head.

Well, ain't it so? You let Rety go on thinking she might be hanged, when it would have been easy enough to say—

To say what? A lie? I can't promise it won't happen. The law is fierce because it has to be. The sages can show mercy. It's allowed. But who am I to promise in their name?

He recalled his former master describing the last time a large band of sooners was discovered, back when old Fallon had been an apprentice. The transgressors were found living on a distant archipelago, far to the north. One of the hoon boat-wanderers – whose job it was to patrol at sea the same way human hunters roamed the forests and urrish plainsmen ranged the steppes – came upon a thronging cluster of her kind, dwelling amid ice floes, surviving by seeking the caves of hibernating rouol shamblers and spearing the rotund beasts as they slept. Each summer, the renegade tribe would come ashore and set fires across the tundra plains, panicking herds of shaggy, long-toed gallaiters, sending the frightened ungulates tumbling over cliffs by the hundreds, so that a few might be butchered.

Ghahen, the boat-wanderer, had been drawn by the smoke of one mass killing and soon began dealing with the crime in the manner of her folk. Patient beyond human fathoming, gentle in a way that gave Dwer nightmares to hear of it, she had taken an entire year to winnow the band, one by one, painlessly confiscating from each member its precious life bone, until all that remained was a solitary male elder, whom she seized and brought home to testify, ferrying the dejected captive in a boat piled high with the fifth vertebra of all his kin. After reciting his tale – a crooning lament lasting fourteen days – that final seagoing sooner was executed by the hoon themselves, expiating their shame. All the impounded vertebrae were ground to dust and scattered in a desert, far from any standing water.

The forbidding memory of that story filled Dwer's heart with leaden worry.

Spare me, please, from being asked to do as Ghahen did. I couldn't. Not if all the sages ordered it. Not if Lark said the fate of all Jijo hung in the balance. There's got to be a better way.

Just where the rocky shelf seemed about to narrow down to nothing, letting the divided tracts of boo converge and obliterate the trail, a clearing abruptly opened ahead. A bowl-shaped depression, nearly a thousand meters across, with an algae-crusted lake in its center and a narrow outlet at the far end. A fringe of great-boo lined the crater's outer rim, and spindly tufts of the tenacious plant sprouted from crevices between jagged boulders that lay tumbled across the silent mountain vale. The lake's watery shore was outlined by a dense hedge, appearing at a distance like rank moss, from which radiated countless twisted tendrils, many of them broken stumps. Even where Dwer stood, ropy fibers could be seen half-buried in the dust, some as thick as his leg.

The peaceful quiet was belied by an eerie sense of *lifelessness*. The dust lay undisturbed by footprints, only the scrape of wind and rain. From prior visits, Dwer knew why prudent creatures avoided this place. Still, after the strangling confinement of that tunnel-trail, it felt good to see sky again. Dwer had never much shared the prevailing dread of crossing open ground, even if it meant walking for a short time under the glaring sun.

As they picked their way past the first boulders, the glaver began to mew nervously, creeping alongside Rety to keep in her shadow. The girl's eyes roved avidly. She seemed not to notice drifting off the trail, at an angle that would skirt the fringe of the lake.

Dwer took several long strides to catch up. 'Not that way,' he said, shaking his head.

'Why not? We're headin' over there, right?' She pointed to the only other gap in the outer wall of boo, where a narrow, scummy stream leaked through the valley's outlet. 'Quickest way is past the lake. Looks easier, too, except right by the shore.'

Dwer gestured toward a relic webbery of dun strands, draping the nearby jagged boulders. 'Those are—' he began.

'I *know* what they are.' She made a face. 'Buyur didn't only live on the Slope, y'know, even if you westies do think it's simply the best place to be. We got mulc-spiders over the hill too, eatin' up old Buyur ruins.

'Anyway, what're you so scared of? You don't think this one's still alive, do you?' She kicked one of the desiccated vines, which crumbled to dust.

Dwer controlled himself. *It's that chip on her shoulder talking. Her people must have been awful to her*. Taking a breath, he replied evenly.

'I don't *think* it's alive. I know it is. What's more – this spider's crazy.'

Rety's first reaction was to raise both eyebrows in surprised fascination. She leaned toward him and asked in a hushed voice – '*Really?*'

Then she tittered, and Dwer saw she was being sarcastic. 'What's it do? Put out sticky lures full o' berry-sugar an' sweet gar, to snatch little girls who're bad?'

Taken aback, Dwer finally grunted. 'I guess you could say something like that.'

Now Rety's eyes widened for real, brimming with curiosity. 'Now this I gotta see!'

She gave the rope at her waist a sudden yank. The formidable-looking knot fell apart, and she took off, dashing past several craggy stones. The gaily squeaking noor pursued with excited bounds.

'Wait!' Dwer yelled futilely, knowing it useless to chase her through the boulder maze. Scrambling up a nearby talus slope of rocky debris, he managed to glimpse her ragged ponytail, bobbing as she ran toward where the rocky slabs converged in a tumbled labyrinth rimming the lake shore.

'Rety!' he screamed into the wind. 'Don't touch the—'

He stopped wasting breath. The same breeze that pushed the lake's musty pungency against his face stole his words before they could reach her ears. Dwer slid back down to the trail, only to realize – damn! Even the *glaver* was gone!

He finally found it half an arrowflight uphill, shambling back the way they had come, following whatever instinct sometimes drove its kind to wander doggedly east, away from comfort and protection and toward near-certain death. Growling under his breath, Dwer seized the mare's tether and sought something, anything, to tie her to, but the nearest stand of gangly boo lay too far away. Dropping his pack, he whipped out a length of cord. 'Sorry about this,' he apologized, using his hip to lever the glaver over. Ignoring her rumbling complaint, he proceeded to hobble her rear legs, where he hoped she couldn't reach the rope with her teeth.

'Pain, frustration – both quite tedious are.'

'Sorry. I'll be back soon,' he answered optimistically, and took off after the sooner child.

Stay uphill and downwind, Dwer thought, angling to the right of her last heading. *This might just be a trick to let her circle around and head for home.*

A little later, he noticed he had reflexively unlimbered his bow, cranking the string tension for short range, and had loosed the clamp securing the stubby arrows in his thigh quiver.

What good will arrows do, if she makes the spider angry?

Or worse, if she catches its interest?

Toward the valley's rim, many stones retained a semblance to their ancient role, segments of whatever Buyur structure once stood proudly on this site, but as Dwer hurried inward, all likeness to masonry vanished. Ropy strands festooned the boulders. Most appeared quite dead – gray, desiccated, and flaking. However, soon his eye caught a greenish streak here ... and over there a tendril oozing slime across a stony surface, helping nature slowly erase all vestiges of former scalpel-straight smoothness.

Finally, raising a creepy feeling down his back, Dwer glimpsed tremors of *movement*. A wakening of curling strands, roused from sleep by some recent disturbance.

Rety.

He dodged through the increasingly dense maze, leaping over some ropy barriers, sliding under others, and twice doubling back with an oath when he reached impassable dead ends. This Buyur site was nowhere near as vast as the one north and east of Dolo Village, where each local citizen dutifully took part in crews gleaning for items missed by the deconstructor spider. Dwer used to go there often, along with Lark or Sara. That spider was more vigorous and alive than this crotchety old thing – *yet far* less dangerous.

The thicket of pale cables soon grew too crowded for an adult to pass, though the girl and noor might have gone on. In frustration, Dwer whirled and slapped a rounded knob of rock.

'Ifni sluck!' He waved his stinging hand. 'Of all the bloody damn jeekee . . .

He slung the bow over one shoulder, freeing both hands, and started scrambling up the jagged face of a boulder three times his height. It was no climb he would have chosen, given time to work out a better route, but Dwer's racing heart urged him to hurry.

Mini-avalanches of eroded rock spilled over his hair and down his collar, stinging with a dusty redolence of decayed time. Flakey vines and dried tendrils offered tempting handholds, which he strove to ignore. Rock was stronger, though not always as reliable as it looked.

While his fingers traced one fine crack, he felt the outcrop under his left foot start to crumble and was forced to trust his weight to one of the nearby crisscrossing mulc-cables.

With a crackling rachet, the vine gave but a moment's warning before slipping. He gasped, suspending his entire weight with just his fingertips. Dwer's torso struck the stone wall, slamming air out of his lungs.

His flailing legs met another strand, thinner than the first, just seconds before his grip would have failed. With no other choice, Dwer used it as a springboard to pivot and launch himself leftward, landing on a slim ledge with his right foot. His hands swarmed along the almost sheer face – and at last found solid holds. Blinking away dust, he inhaled deeply till it felt safe to resume.

The last few meters were less steep but worn slick by countless storms since the boulder had been dragged here, then left in place by the weakening vines. Finally, he was able to get up on his knees and peer ahead, toward the nearby shore.

What had seemed a uniform hedge, lining the lake's perimeter, was now a thick snarl of vines, varying from man-height to several times as tall. This near the water, the cables' gray pallor gave way to streaks of green, yellow, even bloodred. Within the tangle he glimpsed specks of yet other colors, sparkling in shafts of sunlight.

Beyond the thorny barrier, the scummy pond seemed to possess a geometric essence, both liquid and uncannily *corrugated*. Some areas seemed to pulse, as if to a cryptic rhythm – or enduring anger.

One-of-a-Kind, he thought, not really wanting to evoke the name but unable to resist. He pulled his gaze away, scanning for Rety. *Don't hurt her, One-of-a-Kind. She's only a child.*

He didn't want to converse with the mulc-spider. He hoped it might be dormant, as when the lake was a harmless cranny in the winter snowscape. Or perhaps it was dead, at last. The spider was surely long past due to die. A grisly *hobby* seemed to be all that kept this one alive.

He shivered as a creeping sensation climbed the nape of his neck.

[Hunter. Fellow-seeker. Lonely one. How good for you to greet me. I sensed you pass nearby some days ago, hurrying in chase. Why did you not pause to say hello?

[Have you found what you sought?

[Is it this 'child' you speak of?

[Is she different from other humans?

[Is she special in some way?]

Scanning for traces of Rety, Dwer tried to ignore the voice. He had no idea why he sometimes held conversations with a particular corrosive alpine puddle. Though psi talent wasn't unknown among the Six, the Scrolls warned darkly against it. Anyway, most psi involved links among close kin – one reason he never told anyone about this fey channel. Imagine the nicknames, if people learned of it!

I probably imagine it all, anyway. Must be some weird symptom of my solitary life.

The tickling presence returned.

[Is that still your chief image of me? As a figment of your mind? If so, why not test it? Come to me, my unowned treasure. My unique wonder! Come to the one place in the cosmos where you will always be prized!]

Dwer grimaced, resisting the hypnotic draw of the algae patterns, still scanning amid the rocks and tangles for Rety. At least the spider hadn't taken her yet. Or was it cruel enough to lie?

There! Was that a flicker to the left? Dwer peered westward, shading his eyes against the late afternoon sun. Something rustled near the coiled vines, just a dozen or so meters closer to the lake, hidden by the bulk of several stone slabs, but causing a section of hedge to quiver. Squinting, Dwer wished he hadn't been so hasty in dropping his pack, which contained his priceless handmade ocular.

It might be a trap, he thought.

[Who would trap you, Special One? You suspect me? Say you don't mean it!]

The wind had died down a bit. Dwer cupped his hands and called, 'Rety!'

Queer echoes scattered among the rocks, to be sucked dry by pervasive moss and dust. Dwer looked around the alternatives. He could slip down to ground level and hack this way inward, using the machete sheathed at his back. But that would take forever, and how would One-of-a-Kind react to having its fingers sliced off?

His only real option was to go *over*.

Dwer backed up till his heels hung over empty space, then took a deep breath and sprang forward ... one, two, three paces, and *leaped* – sailing over a jungle of interlacing tendrils – to land with a jarring thud atop the next slab. This one slanted steeply, so there was no time to recover. He had to scramble fast to reach a long knife-edged ridge. Standing up, he spread his arms and gingerly walked heel-and-toe, teetering for ten paces before reaching a boulder with a flatter top.

Dwer's nostrils filled with sour, caustic odors from the lake. More nearby tendrils throbbed with veins now, flowing acrid tinctures. He skirted puddles of bitter fluid, collecting in cavities of etched stone. When his boot scraped one pool, it left fine trails of ash and a scent of burning leather.

The next time he took a running leap, he landed hard on hands and knees.

'Rety?' he called, crawling to the forward edge.

The shoreline barrier was a dense-woven knot of green, red, and yellow strands, twisted in roiling confusion. Within this contorted mass, Dwer spied *objects* – each nestled in its own cavity. Each sealed, embedded, within a separate crystal cocoon.

Golden things, silvery things. Things gleaming like burnished copper or steel. Tubes, spheroids, and complex blocky forms. Things shining unnatural hues of pigment or nanodye. Some resembled items Dwer had seen dragged from Buyur sites by reclaimer teams; only those had been decomposed, worn by passing centuries. *These* samples of past glory looked almost new. Like bugs trapped in amber, their cocoons preserved them against the elements, against time. And each item, Dwer knew, was one of a kind.

Not every sample was a Buyur relic. Some had once been alive. Small animals. Insectoids. Anything that strayed too close and caught the mad spider's collecting fancy. It seemed a wonder that a being devoted to destruction – one *designed* to emit razing fluids – could also secrete a substance that conserved. All the more astonishing that it would want to.

The rustling resumed, coming from his left. Dwer slithered that way, dreading to find the girl trapped and suffering. Or else some small creature he would have to put out of misery with his bow.

He edged forward ... and gasped.

What he saw netted in the profuse tangle, just a few meters ahead, came as a complete surprise.

At first sight it resembled a bird – a Jijoan avian – with the typical clawed stilt for a landing leg, four broad-feathered wings, and a tentacle-tail. But Dwer swiftly saw that it was no species he knew – or any genus listed on his brother's charts. Its wings, flapping desperately against a surrounding net of sticky threads, articulated in ways Dwer thought unnatural. And they beat with a power he found suspicious in any living thing that size.

Feathers had been ripped or burned away in several places. Within those gaps, Dwer glimpsed flashes of glistening metal.

A machine!

Shock made him release the screen on his thoughts, allowing the tickling voice to return.

[Indeed, a machine. Of a type I never before owned. And see, it still operates. It lives!]

'I see that, all right,' Dwer muttered.

[And you don't yet know the half of it. Is this my day, or what?]

Dwer hated the way the mulc-spider not only slipped into his mind but somehow used what it found there to produce perfect Anglic sentences, better than *Dwer* could manage, since the spider never stammered or seemed at a loss for words. He found that obnoxious, coming from a being lacking a face to talk back to.

The false bird thrashed in its snare. Along its feathered back gleamed clear, golden droplets that it fought to shake off, flicking most aside before they could harden into a shell of adamant, preserving crystal.

What on Jijo could it be? Dwer wondered.

[I was hoping, now that I have you, to learn the answer.]

Dwer wasn't sure he liked the way One-of-a-Kind put that. Anyway, there wasn't time to bandy words. Dwer pushed aside pity for the trapped creature. Right now he must keep *Rety* from becoming yet another unique specimen in the mulc-spider's collection.

[So, as I suspected. The small human is *special!]*

Dwer quashed the voice with the best weapon he had – anger.

Get out of my mind!

It worked. The presence vanished, for now. Once more, Dwer lifted his head and shouted. 'Rety! Where are you!'

An answer came at once, from surprisingly close by.

'I'm here, fool. Now be quiet, or you'll scare it!'

He swiveled, trying to stare in all directions at once. 'Where? I don't see—'

'Right below you, so shut up! I've been followin' this thing for weeks! Now I gotta figure how to get it outta there.'

Dwer slid further left to peer into the crisscrossing network just below – and found himself staring straight into the beady black eyes of a grinning noor! Stretched out across a dormant vine as if it were a comfy roost, Mudfoot tilted his head slightly, squinting back at Dwer. Then, without warning, the noor let loose a sudden sneeze.

Dwer rocked back, cursing and wiping his face, while Mudfoot grinned innocently, happily.

'Quiet, you two! I think I see how to get a little closer—'

'No, Rety. You mustn't!' Ignoring the noor, Dwer crept back to the edge and found her at last, close to the ground, perched with a leg on either side of a giant vine, squinting through the gloomy tangle at the mysterious avian.

'Took you long enough to catch up,' Rety commented.

'I ... had some distractions,' he replied. 'Now just wait a second, will you? There's – some things you ought to know about this – about this here mulc-spider.' He motioned at the snarled mesh surrounding them. 'It's more, well, *dangerous* than you realize.'

'Hey, I been exploring webs since I was little,' she replied. 'Most are dead, but we got a few big ones in the Hills, still full o' sap and nasty stuff. I know my way around.' She swung her leg over the branch and slipped forward.

In a panic, Dwer blurted out – 'Did any of those spiders *try* to catch you?'

She stopped, turned to face him again, and smirked.

'Is that what you meant by crazy? Oh, hunter. You got some imagination.'

Maybe you're right, he pondered. That *could* be why he never heard of anyone else holding conversations with shrubs and lakes.

[What, again? How many times must we speak before you are convinced—]

Shut up and let me think!

The spider's presence backed off again. Dwer bit his lip, trying to come up with something, anything, to keep the girl from venturing deeper into the thicket.

'Look, you've been following that bird-machine for some time, right? Is that what led you west in the first place?'

She nodded. 'One day some o' the boys saw a critter swoop out of a marsh, down by the Rift. Mean ol' Jass winged it, but it got away, leaving a feather behind.'

She plucked something out of her leather blouse. Dwer glimpsed a brief metal sparkle before she put it away.

'I swiped it from Jass before I snuck out to go after the bird. Poor thing must've been hurt, 'cause by the time I picked up the trail, it wasn't flyin' so good. Kind of gliding for a stretch, then hoppin' along. I only got one good look. Upslope to the Rimmers it started pullin' ahead. Then I reached the Slope, and it came to me that I risked getting hanged every dura that I stayed.'

She shivered, a memory of fear.

'I was about to give up and head back home for a beatin', when I heard a tapping sound in the night. I followed it, and for a minute I thought the clock teet was *my* bird!' She sighed. 'That's when I saw you, snorin' away, with that fancy bow of yours lyin' nearby. Figured it'd make Jass an' Bom happy enough to forget knockin' my teeth out for runnin' off.'

Dwer had never heard their names before but decided a rope was too good for some sooners.

'That's why you came all this way? To follow that bird-thing?'

Rety answered with a shrug. 'I don't spect you'd understand.'

On the contrary, he thought. It was what he himself would have done, if something so strange ever crossed his path.

[As would I, were I not rooted to this spot, ensnared by my own limitations. Are we not alike?]

Dwer chased the spider out – and the next instant an idea glimmered, offering a possible way out of this mess, as Rety slid off the branch and began to sidle forward, holding a slim blade that Dwer had never found when he searched her, the day before. It gleamed with razor sharpness.

'Wait. I – think about it, Rety. Shouldn't we work together? Wouldn't we do a better job getting it out?'

She stopped and seemed to consider the idea, looking up through the branches. 'I'm listenin'.'

Dwer frowned, concentrating on getting the words right. 'Look ... nobody on the Slope has seen an active Buyur machine since – well, long before humans came to Jijo. This is important. I want to get that thing out of there as much as you do.'

All of which was true, or would have been if his first concern weren't saving the girl's life and his own. *Stall for time*, Dwer thought. *There's only a midura of daylight left. Get her to retreat till tomorrow. Then you can drag her away by force if you have to.*

'Go on,' Rety said. 'You want to come down an' chop with your big knife? I bet you'd splatter, hacking at live vines. Lotta pain that way, if the sap goes spraying around.' Still, she seemed interested.

'Actually, I know a way that won't bruise a single branch but might spread a hole big enough to get your bird-thing out. We'd use some of the – um, natural resources handy hereabouts.'

'Yeah?' She frowned. 'The only stuff around here is rock, and dirt, and—'

Her eyes lit. 'Boo!'

He nodded. 'We'll cut some young shoots, trim them tonight, and return in the morning with bridges and ladders to cross on top of the boulders – and enough pry bars to spread a path through all this' – he waved at the surrounding thicket – 'without spilling any acid or gunk ourselves. We'll get your birdie-thing out long before it's sealed in a crystal egg, and march right up to the sages with a surprise that'll make a hoon's spine pop. How does that sound?'

Dwer saw distrust in her eyes. She was naturally suspicious, and he had never been a very good liar. When she glanced back at the trapped mystery machine, he knew she must be gauging whether it could hold out overnight. 'It still looks strong,' he told her. 'If it lasted in there several days, one more night shouldn't make that much difference.'

Rety lowered her head, pondering. 'Might even be good if its wings got stickier. Won't be able to fly off when we free it.' She nodded. 'All right. Let's go cut us some boo.'

With one hesitant, longing scan behind her, Rety swung her legs over the thick branch and reached up to begin climbing. She carefully examined each hand or foothold before committing herself, eyeing it for caustic leaks, then testing whether the next vine would bear her weight. Clearly, she was an experienced explorer.

But Rety had never ventured through a spider like this one. When she was about a third of the way through the twisty tangle, she suddenly winced, withdrawing her hand and staring at a single pale-golden droplet, glistening on the back of her wrist. It did not burn, or she would have screamed. For a moment, she seemed more entranced by the color than afraid.

'Quick, shake it off!' Dwer cried.

She complied. The glob flew into the foliage. But instantly there followed two more soft splatting sounds. A drop appeared on her shoulder, and one in her hair. Rety looked up to see where they came from – and took one more in the middle of her forehead. Cursing, she tried wiping it off – but managed only to smear it down her cheek. Rety backed away rapidly.

'Not that way!' Dwer urged. He saw some active vines snake toward her, golden dew oozing from crevices. Rety hissed in dismay, taking more drops in her hair as she scrambled in a new direction.

[Tell her not to fight. There need be no pain.]

Dwer's angry snarl was voiceless, inarticulate, hurling the spider's mind-touch away. He shrugged the bow off his shoulder, leaving it atop the boulder, and began clambering down to the girl. Vaguely, he was aware that the noor had departed, sensibly fleeing danger. *Unlike some fools I know*, Dwer thought, slipping the machete out of its sheath.

'I'm coming, Rety,' he said, testing his weight on a branch. Dwer saw Rety try to ascend by another route, easily evading the sluggishly pursuing vines.

'Don't bother!' she called. 'I'm all right. I don't need your hel – ack!'

The branch she was holding, which had seemed inert moments before, suddenly beaded a line of golden moisture. Rety recoiled, cursing. Several drops adhered to her hand. 'Don't rub them!' Dwer urged.

'I'm not an idiot!' she retorted, backing away. Unfortunately, that took her deeper into the morass.

Dwer's machete, an artfully reshaped length of Buyur metal, gleamed as he took a swipe at one of the vines between them. It looked lifeless, but he was ready to leap back in case—

It severed neatly, a crumbling, decaying tube, spilling nothing but cloying dust. A good thing he had decided against using it as a foothold, then. This place wasn't forgiving of mistakes.

He let the machete hang by the pommel loop while he lowered himself one level, to what seemed a stable vine, setting his weight down gingerly; then he sidled along the horizontal span seeking a way downward. The next foothold seemed thinner, less anchored, but he didn't have much choice. At least it didn't gush acid or try to wrap his ankle like a snake. *How did she get this far in the first place?* he wondered, glad that most of the tendrils were dead. The hedge would have been impassable when the mulc-spider was in its prime.

'Dwer!'

He swiveled, wobbling as the ropy strand rocked to and fro. Peering past shadows, he watched Rety climb a chimneylike funnel, offering what seemed a way out. Only now, halfway up the slim gap, she saw something begin twisting into place above. Another clump of living vines ... moving in to block the promise of escape. Meanwhile, the chimney's base was closing the same way. Her face betrayed rising panic. Flushed, she held out her slim blade, eyes darting for some vital spot to stab her foe. But all she could do was saw at some nearby strand, hoping it would not gush vitriol or golden death.

A short way beyond, Dwer saw the bird-thing, still struggling within its own trap.

Let her go, One-of-a-Kind, Dwer thought as he crouched, then leaped with both hands outstretched for another cable – which fortunately held as he swung across a dark opening to land straddling another almost horizontal branch, as thick as a sapling's trunk. *Let her go, or I'll—*

His mind seemed to strangle on the demand, not knowing how one intimidated a mulc-spider. Could he do more than irritate it with a machete? He might threaten to depart and return with tools to destroy the ancient thing, with flame and explosives, but somehow Dwer knew that would seem too abstract. The spider appeared to have little sense of perspective or cause and effect, only immediacy and *avarice*, combined with enough patience to make a hoon seem like a cranky noor.

Anyway, by the time Dwer could carry out his retribution, Rety would be sealed in a golden cocoon, preserved for all time . . . and dead as a stone.

Let's talk a trade, One-of-a-Kind, he projected as he took up the machete once more. *What will you take in exchange for her?*

There was no answer. Either One-of-a-Kind was too busy pushing vines and fluids around, acting with unaccustomed haste, or else—

The spider's silence felt eerie, predatory. Smug. As if it felt no need for conversation when it had two treasures and seemed about to get a third. Grimacing, Dwer sidled deeper into the quagmire. What else could he do?

He hacked at three more vines. The last sent streams of caustic sap arcing between crisscrossing branches. Smoke curled up from the rubbish-strewn floor below, adding to the acrid stench.

'Dwer, help me!'

Rety was fully hemmed in now, and touchy pride no longer suppressed the normal panic of a frightened child. Seen through a matrix of ensnaring mulc-twine, her hair glistened like an urrish tinker's mane on a dewy morning, coated with a fine dusting of golden droplets. A vine parted under her sawing knife – and two more slithered in to take its place.

'I'm coming!' he promised, splitting two more cables, then dropping to the next stable-looking branch. It sagged, then Dwer's footing went slippery as it seeped a clearish, greasy liquor. He shouted, and his feet slid out from under him.

The same dense tangle he'd been cursing saved him from a broken neck. His windmilling arms caught a vine, wrapping round it desperately as his legs swung in midair. But his sigh of relief turned into a gagging gasp. Under his chin, livid veins pulsed with some vile, crimson solution. Blisters formed as corrosive liquid welled beneath the thinnest of membranes. Dwer's eyes stung from escaping vapor.

[No, no. Don't think I would ever harm you so! You are much too precious for that.]

Before Dwer's tear-blurred gaze, the blisters stopped rising – then reddish fluid seemed to drain out of the throbbing arteries.

[That nectar is for plain stone. For you, my unique one, only the gold.]

Dwer grimaced. *Thanks a lot!*

Peering to one side, he found another tangle within reach of his feet. Risking that perch, he pushed away from the loathsome branch that had broken his fall.

[Think nothing of it]

Dwer was almost at Rety's level now, close enough to see grim determination replace panic in her eyes as she sawed another vine in half. A fine spray rewarded her, gilding the forearm she raised to protect her face. All of a sudden, Dwer realized – *She's cutting in the wrong direction!*

Instead of taking the most direct route toward daylight, she was heading deeper into the morass – toward the mechanical bird-thing!

Of all the times to chase an Ifni-slucking obsession!

Sudden liquid coolness brushed Dwer's wrist. A shimmering meniscus bead lay amid the dark hairs. He moved aside quickly, before another drop could fall from the seep-pore overhead. Dwer shook the droplet off, but even after it was gone, the spot still felt chilled, touched with a not-unpleasant numbness, like when the village dentist spread powdered Nural leaves along a patient's gums, before spinning his hand-cranked drill.

The machete now wore its own streaked coating, already starting to crystallize in places. Certainly it was an artifact worth collecting, a slab of star-god stuff, adapted by a tribe of primitives to new use in a twilight place, between the gritty earth and urbane sky. Grimly, he raised his weapon and set to with a will.

Concentration was vital, so he ignored the stench and grinding dust with a hunter's narrow-minded focus. Sweat beaded his brow, face, and neck, but he dared not wipe. No doubt he already looked like Rety, who now glittered like some fairy confection, dusted with beads of honey. Dwer did not bother shouting for her to turn and head toward him. Given her obstinacy, he might as well save his breath.

Glancing back, he saw his escape route still looked clear – a tunnel lined by chopped branches and dangling severed vines. One-of-a-Kind could marshal more, but the mulc-spider was old, slow. As Dwer neared Rety's cage, he felt sure he could thwart the spider's move, when it came.

Now he called, hoarsely.

'Okay, Rety. No foolin'. Let's get outta here.'

The girl was over at the far end of her funnel opening, staring at the bird-thing past the branches that blocked her way. 'Hey, it noticed me! It's turning around!'

Dwer wouldn't care if it stood on its head and gave Drake's Farewell Address in Buyur-accented Galactic Three. He sliced another cable and coughed as fumes flowed from both writhing ends. 'Rety, we haven't got time!'

When the smoke cleared, he sidled closer and saw that the bird-thing had risen up within its cell, peering skyward and ignoring droplets that settled, mistlike, on its feathered back. Rety, too, seemed to notice its attention shift. She turned to look upward, as Dwer heard a shrill, chittering sound from the same general direction.

It's just the bloody noor.

Beyond the diffracting crisscross of vines, he saw Mudfoot, returned from wherever it had fled. Only now the creature stood on its hind legs, sinuous body upraised, whiskered snout pulled back, snarling at something out of sight, to the south.

Another flicker caught Dwer's eye. Like an epileptic snake, a kinked vine twisted into view, crossing part of the opening Dwer had cut through the hedge. Its jerky fits and starts seemed pathetic, all alone – but that tendril was followed by another, and another still.

'Rety!' He shouted, preparing to slash at the remaining barrier between them. The trap's closing. It's now or never!'

On her face lay the frustration of coming within arm's reach of her grail, only to have it snatched away by cruel fate. Not waiting for her answer, he lifted the heavy machete with both weary arms and cried out, splitting with three hard strokes the heavy cable blocking his way forward. *Don't throw it away, Rety*, he pleaded inside, knowing it would do no good to say anything more aloud.

With a cry of frustration, Rety whirled around, forsaking her treasure, hurling herself at smaller vines with her tiny blade, then squeezing between others with lithe, squirmy agility. The tight passage smeared gold drops until she resembled a streaked pastry of swirled nut cream. Dwer sliced relentlessly and at last was close enough to stretch one arm into the morass.

Rety's hand clasped his wrist.

Dwer planted his feet and hauled backward, drawing her through a dark, fetid funnel. A low moan accompanied the passage. He could not tell if it came from her, or himself, or both of them at once.

She slid free at last and clung to him with sudden fury, wrapping his torso, in quivering arms and legs. Underneath all her macho bravado, Dwer knew she must have been terrified in there.

'We've got to hurry,' he said tugging at one arm.

Rety resisted but a moment, then slithered off. She inhaled. 'Okay, let's go.'

He gave her a boost with his hands, sending her clambering into the tunnel-chimney he had carved through the hedge.

[Oh, going so soon? Have I been so poor a host?]

'Dry up and burn, One-of-a-Kind,' Dwer muttered under ragged breaths as he climbed after Rety, trusting her strong instincts to lead the way.

[Someday I surely will. But by then I'll have preserved a legacy.

[Think on it! When Jijo's fallow age ends, and new tenants possess this world for an eon of shining glory, they will gaze in wonder at this collection I've gathered. Amid their glittering city towers, they'll cherish my samplings of the interregnum, setting my prize pieces on pedestals for all to see. And paramount among those specimens will be you, *my trophy, my treasure. Perhaps the best-conserved exemplar for your by then long-extinct wolfling race.]*

Dwer puzzled – how did the spider sink hooks into his brain to draw forth words he didn't recall ever learning, like *exemplar* and *interregnum*? Lark might have used them in his presence sometime, when perhaps they lodged somewhere deep in memory.

You're the one who's going to be extinct, spider! You and your whole damn race.

This time his blistering reply did not shove away the entity's mind-touch.

[By then, certainly. But our type-design is always to be found in the Great Galactic Library, and we are far too useful ever to be forgotten. Whenever a world must be evacuated, tidied up, and allowed to lay fallow once more – whenever the mighty works of some former tenant race must be rubbed down to recycled dust – then we shall always rise again.

[Can your tribe of ignorant monkeys claim such usefulness, my precious? Can you claim any 'purpose' at all? Save a tenacious will to keep on existing?]

This time Dwer did not answer. He needed to conserve his strength. If the earlier descent had been awful, ascending became pure hell. It was twice as hard craning backward to hack away at vines overhead as it had been striking down. In addition to danger from whipping cables and spurting acid, he and Rety had to climb through a mist of shimmering drops. It was no longer a matter of shaking them off one by one, but of dodging the thicker drifts and somehow preventing them from adhering to their eyes, noses, and ears. Through that luminous miasma, Dwer saw more creepers twist and flop into a gathering mesh above, more quickly than he would have believed possible. Clearly, One-of-a-Kind had been holding back till now.

[What did you expect? That I would show you all the things that I am capable o—

[... that I would show you all the ...

[... that I would show ...]

When the voice in Dwer's head trailed off, his first reaction was relief. He had other worries, like an agonizing crick in his neck and a right arm that looked as if it had been dipped in a jeweler's vat, and that seemed about to cramp from the repetitive hacking, hacking, hacking. Now if only the chattering *noor* would shut up too, with its shrill keening. Mudfoot's piercing chitters crescendoed, rising in pitch beyond the limit of Dwer's direct hearing but not past ability to scrape a vexing runnel under his skull.

Through it all, a nagging worry bothered Dwer.

I left the glaver all tied up. Will she die of thirst if I never make it back?

'Left!' Rety shouted. He quickly obeyed, swinging as far as possible, trusting her swift reflexes to warn of jets of yellow sap.

'Okay, clear!' she called.

The machete slipped. Dwer fumbled at the wrist strap three times before getting a grip to resume chopping the slender vines filling the chimney overhead, cutting off the swiftly failing twilight. If they didn't make it out by full nightfall, every advantage would belong to the crazy mulc-spider.

Now a sound he had dismissed as background noise grew too loud to ignore. A low rumbling counterbass overrode the noor's yapping. All around Rety and Dwer, the hedge began vibrating. A number of brittle vines shuddered to dust while others sprouted cracks and dripped fluids – red, orange, and milky – noxious additions to a fog that already stung human eyes. Through that blur, Dwer blinked upward to see Mudfoot, perched nimbly atop the hedge of vines, withdrawing in snarling defiance as something new entered view from the south – something that *hovered* in the air, without any visible means of support!

A machine! A symmetrical, slab-sided form with gleaming flanks that reflected the sunset, drifting to a point just above the shuddering hedge.

Suddenly, its belly blazed forth a bitter light that diffracted past the vines. The slender beam lanced right past Rety and Dwer, as if probing for something deeper ...

'It's hunting the bird!' Rety crouched beside Dwer, seizing his arm and pointing.

'Never mind the damn bird!' he cursed. The hedge was shaking worse than ever. Dwer dragged her behind him just as a sundered tube whipped past, spurting caustic fluid, splattering a trail of fizzing agony along his back as he shielded the girl. Purple spots swarmed across his field of vision, and the machete slipped its thong to fall, clattering off branches on its way down.

Now it seemed as if the hedge were alive with stark, fleeing shadows, as the floating machine's searchlight narrowed to a searing needle that scorched anything it touched.

By the same light Dwer glimpsed the bird-thing, trapped inside its cage of ropy mesh and coated with a golden patina, erupting now in a dance of evasion, leaping back and forth as it tried to *dodge* the burning ray of light, its feathers already smoldering in spots. Rety let out a throaty cry of anger, but it was all the two humans could do simply to hold on.

Finally, the bird-thing seemed to give up. It stopped ducking and instead spread its four wings in a pitiful effort to create a shielding canopy, which began to smoke as the blazing shaft struck home and stayed. Only the little bird-machine's head poked out, snaking upward to gape toward the aggressor with one open, staring eye.

Dwer was watching in horrified amazement, mixed with stunned pity, when that dark, jadelike eye abruptly *exploded*.

The blinding flash was the last thing he clearly remembered for a long time to come.

VII

THE BOOK OF THE SEA

Do not make poisons
that you cannot use.

Use all of the poisons
that you make.

If others must clean up
after you,

Do not act offended
when they exact a price.

—*The Scroll of Advice*

ALVIN'S TALE

So there we were, just arrived at the top-end tram platform after a long ride from Wuphon Port, and no sooner do Huck, Pincer, and me step off the tram car (with little Huphu riding Pincer's shell for luck) than our urrish pal, Ur-ronn, gallops up all flushed and bothered. Without offering so much as a greeting-preamble, she commences to prancing, snaking her narrow head back and forth, and hissing at us in that awful version of GalTwo she must've picked up back when she was grub-sized, foraging in the grass out on the Warril Plain. You know the dialect I mean – the one that drops every other double-click phrase stop, so at first all I could make out was a bunch of basso tone pulses conveying frenzied excitement.

Worse, a moment later she starts *nipping* at us, like we were a bunch of pack donkeys to be herded down the hall!

'Hrrm! Now hold it right there,' I insisted. 'Nothing ever gets done right by letting yourself get so *igsee* frantic. Whatever you've got to say can surely wait for a proper hello to friends you haven't seen in weeks. After all – *yi-houongwa!*'

Yes, that was a hoonish throat-blat of pain. Huck had rolled one of her main-wheels over my left foot.

'Varnish it, Alvin. You sound just like your father!'

My father? I thought. *How utterly ungloss*.

'Haven't you been *listening* to Ur-ronn?' Huck went on.

My sac panted a few times as I ran back over the last few duras, piecing together some of what Ur-ronn was nattering about.

It was a wild tale all right, and we've told each other some whoppers.

'Hr-r-r – a *starship*?' I stared at our urrish pal. 'You *mean* it this time? It's not just a comet, like you tried fooling us with a year ago?'

Ur-ronn stamped a forefoot, knowing I had her nailed. Switching to Anglic, she swore. 'This time for real! Velieve ne! I heard Uriel and Gyfz talking. They caught it on flates!'

On plates, I translated from the way her cleft upper lip mangles some Anglic consonants. *Photographic plates*. Maybe Ur-ronn wasn't having us on, after all. 'Can we see?' I asked.

An urrish moan of frustration. 'You jeekee file of scales and fur! That's where I veen trying to take you guys since the tran stoffed!'

'Oh.' I bowed with a sweep of one arm. 'Well then, what are we waiting around here for? Let's go!'

*

Years ago, Uriel the Smith inherited the Mount Guenn works from Ur-tanna, who was liege-heir to Ulennku, who got the sprawling underground mill from her own dying master, the great Urnunu, who rebuilt those mighty halls after quakes shook the Slope like a wet noor during the Year of the Egg. Before that, the gale goes back to a misty time before humans brought paper memory to Jijo, when wisdom had to fit in someone's living head or else be lost. Back to days when urrish settlers had to fight and prove themselves more than mere galloping savages, roaming the grassy plains, beholden to high-caste qheuens for everything they owned.

Ur-ronn used to recite the legend during our adventure trips. Even allowing for exaggeration, those must've been brave urs who climbed fuming volcano heights to build the first crude forges near fiery lava springs, toiling through cinders and constant danger to learn the secret of reworking Buyur metal and break the Gray Queens' tool-monopoly forever.

It kind of makes you glad humans didn't come any sooner, 'cause the answers would've been right there in some book – how to make knives and lenses and windows and such. Sure, it would've made it easier for the other exile races to free themselves from dominion by qheuenish woodcarvers. On the other hand, all you have to do is hear Ur-ronn's lisping tale to know what pride her folk won from all that work and sacrifice.

They did it themselves, you see, earning liberty and self-respect. Ask any hoon how *we'd* feel without our swaying ships. Earthling lore has made improvements, but no one *gave* us the sea! Not our far-off Guthatsa patrons, or the Great Galactic Library, or our selfish ancestors who dumped us on Jijo, naive and unready. It's a proud thing to have done it for ourselves.

Pride can be important, when you don't have much else.

Before entering the forge-inferno, Pincer-Tip draped a water-soaked mantle over his soft red carapace. I gathered my cloak around me while Huck checked her goggles and axle-guards. Then Ur-ronn led us past overlapping leather curtains into the Works.

We hurried along a walkway of treated boo, hung between bubbling pools that glowed white with Jijo's blood heat. Cleverly diverted updrafts guided smoldering vapors into stone baffles, venting them outside to look no different than any other smoker on Mount Guenn's flank.

Huge buckets dangled overhead – one filled with reclaimed Buyur scrap and the other with a sandy mix – each waiting to be dipped in that blazing heat, then to pour into clay molds. Urrish workers hauled pulleys and ladles. Another twirled a big glob of liquid glass at the end of a tube, spinning it round and round to form a flat whirling disk that turned solid as it thinned and cooled, a *window* destined for homes far away from here.

They were assisted by several gray qheuens who, in one of Jijo's ironies, turned out to be the other sept well suited to these conditions. The grays may even be happier than when their queens used to dominate the Commons. But I never could read much expression on their stony cupolas. I often wonder how our wild, emotional Pincer could be related to them.

Farther from the heat, half a dozen g'Keks skittered across the smooth floor, handling account ledgers, while a traeki specialist with throbbing synthi rings tasted each mix to certify the mill's products would rust or decay in less than two hundred years, as required by the sages.

Some orthodox Scroll-pounders say we shouldn't have smithies at all – that they're vanities, distracting us from salvation through forgetfulness. But I think the place is gloss, even if the smoke frets my throat sac and sets my spine-scales itching.

Ur-ronn led us through more curtains into the Laboratory Grotto, where Uriel studies the secrets of her art – both those hard-won by her ancestors and others delved from human texts. Clever breezes freshened the air, allowing us to loosen our protections. Pincer gratefully doffed his heavy mantle and doused his red carapace at a shower-alcove. Huphu splashed eagerly while I sponged my sac. Ur-ronn kept her distance from the water, preferring a brief roll in some clean dry sand.

Huck skittered down a hallway lined with many doors, peering into various laboratory chambers. 'Hsst! Alvin!' she whispered urgently, waving me over with one arm and two eyestalks. 'Come look. Care to guess who's here again?'

'Who is it?' Pincer whistled, leaving five wet trails of prints behind him. Ur-ronn daintily avoided the moist tracks with her rattling hooves.

I already had a pretty good idea who Huck was talking about, since no ship passenger enters Wuphon without being known to the harbor master – my mother. She hadn't announced anything, but I knew from overheard snatches that the latest dross ship had brought an important human visitor, one who debarked at night, heading straight to the Mount Guenn tram.

'Hrrrm. I'll bet you a sweetboo cane it's that sage again,' I ventured before arriving at the door. 'The one from Biblos.'

Huck's rear-facing eye looked disappointed, and she groused – 'Lucky guess' – while making space for the rest of us.

I knew this room. Many's the previous visit I used to stand at the doorway and stare at the goings-on within. The huge chamber held

Uriel's mystery machine – a gimcrackery of gears, cables, and revolving glass that seemed to fill the vaulted cavern with grinding motion like one of those Victorian factories you read about in books by Dickens. Only *this* device didn't make a single blessed thing, as far as any of us could ever tell. Only countless glitters of light as whirling crystal disks spun like hundreds of ghostly little g'Keks, rolling against each other madly, futilely, going noplace the faster they spun.

I glimpsed the human visitor, bent over a trestle table with a precious-looking folio spread open before him, pointing at a diagram, while *Uriel* rocked in a circle, lifting one leg at a time, shaking her pelted head in disagreement. The smith's gray-fringed nostril blew exasperation.

'With all due resfect, Sage Furofsky, you night have gone to Gathering instead of coming all this way. I cannot see how this vook is relevant to our frovlen – to our quandary.'

The human wore the black cloak of a lesser sage, the kind who dwell in the sacred halls of Biblos with half a million printed tomes for company, tending wisdom handed down for three hundred years. He was hoonish-handsome, which happens when one of their males gets gray head fleece and lets his facial fur grow long, an effect enhanced by a noble long nose. This worthy jabbed again at the ancient page, so hard I feared he'd hurt the priceless text.

'But I tell you this algorithm is exactly what you need! It can be executed in a tenth the space, with far fewer parts, if you'd just consider—'

I can't write what followed, because it was in that dialect of Anglic called Engineering, and even my hoonish memory won't help me write words I can't understand or spell. The sage must have come to help Uriel in her project. Anyone who knew her could predict Uriel's resistance.

Beyond those two we saw *Urdonnol*, a younger urrish techie, who the Master trusted with general upkeep of this whatever-it-is machine, stretching beyond the farthest reach of the single overhead skylight. Urdonnol peered through the shuddering, squeaking assembly, reaching in to tighten an elastic belt or lubricate a bearing. As senior apprentice, she was two hooves toward being Uriel's heir.

The sole other candidate was *Ur-ronn*, partly because of our pal's school scores, and also because she's the nearest of Uriel's scent-cousins to survive from steppe-grub to adult. No doubt Urdonnol worked here – tending the Master's personal project – to improve her chances, though she clearly hated the big machine.

Miniature centaur figures moved amid the whirling disks, making delicate adjustments. Urrish *males*, normally rare to see outside their wives' pouches, tightened belts and gears under Urdonnol's terse direction. Striking a blow for equality, I guess.

I bent and whispered to Huck, 'So much for all that talk about – hr-hrrm – *starships*! If they really saw one, they wouldn't be fooling with toy gadgets right now!'

Ur-ronn must've overheard me. She swung her long muzzle, wearing a wounded look. Two out of three eyes narrowed. 'I *heard* Uriel and Gyfz,' she hissed. 'Anyhow, what does a snarty-fants like you know?'

'Enough to know all these whirling glass yo-yos don't have hair on a qheuen's backside to do with visiting spaceships!'

Even if we *hadn't* been snapping at each other, it wasn't easy for a gang like ours to *peer discreetly* into a room, the way you read about humans doing in detective stories. Still, those inside mightn't have noticed us, if Huphu the noor hadn't chosen that moment to go bounding in, yipping at those spinning pulleys and disks. Before we knew it, she leaped onto a leather belt and was running in place like mad, snapping toward a pair of cringing urs husbands.

Urdonnol noticed, waving her arms, displaying the bright glands under both brood pouches.

'*This event signifies? It signifies?*' the apprentice demanded with slurred interrogative trills. Her agitation grew as the Master snaked a grizzled snout around to peer at the commotion.

Despite stereotypes, a hoon can act quickly if he sees a clear need. I rushed over to snatch Huphu, rumbling my very best umble, and rejoined the others, girding for a group tongue-lashing.

'*Behavior that is (astonishingly, horrifyingly) unacceptable,*' declared Urdonnol in GalTwo. '*Interruption of an important congress by (knavish, microcephalic, unhousebroken)—*'

Uriel cut in, breaking Urdonnol's insult-stream before the fuming, stamping Ur-ronn could be provoked to responding in kind.

'That will do, Urdonnol,' the Master commanded in GalSeven. 'Kindly take the youngsters to Gybz, who has business of ers own with them, then hurry back. We have several more models to run before we are through for the day.'

'It shall be done,' Urdonnol replied in the same tongue. Turning to us with an aggressive neck-stretch, the older prentice said – 'Come along, you gaggle of jeekee *adventurers.*'

She said it with dripping scorn, which is possible in GalSeven, though not as harsh as Anglic.

'Come swiftly. It's been decided to take you up on your offer.

'Your grand plan.

'Your one-way expedition to Hell.'

VIII

THE BOOK OF THE SLOPE

Legends

It is said that glavers are an example to us all. Of the seven races to plant exile colonies on the Slope, they alone have escaped this prison where their ancestors consigned them. They did this by finding, and traveling, the Path of Redemption.

Now they are innocent, no longer criminals, having become one with Jijo. In time, they may even be renewed, winning that blessed rarity – a second chance at the stars.

It is a source of some frustration to Earthlings – the youngest sept to come here – that humans never got to meet glavers as thinking, speaking beings. Even the hoon and urs arrived too late to know them at their prime, when glavers were said to have been mighty intellects, with a talent for deep race memory. Watching their descendants root through our garbage middens, it is hard to picture the race as great starfarers and the patrons of three noble client-lines.

What desperation brought them here, to seek safety in oblivion?

The g'Keks tell us, by oral tradition, that it was the result of financial setbacks.

Once (according to g'Kek lore), glavers were said to be among those rare breeds with a knack for conversing with *Zang* – the hydrogen-breathing civilization existing aloofly in parallel to the society of races that use oxygen. This aptitude enabled glavers to act as intermediaries, bringing them great wealth and prestige, until a single contractual mistake reversed their fortunes, landing them in terrible debt.

It is said that the great Zang are patient. The debt falls due in several hundred thousand years. Yet so deep is the usury that the glaver race, and all its beloved clients, were hopelessly forfeit.

Glavers had but one thing left to trade, a precious thing they might yet sell, providing they could find the right path.

That thing was themselves.

—Collected Fables of Jijo's Seven,
Third Edition. Department of Folklore and Language, Biblos. Year 1867 of Exile.

The plunder ship soon departed as it came, amid a storm of whirling fragments of our poor, shattered forest. A tornado leaned in its wake, as if Jijo's own ghostly hand were reaching, clasping, trying to restrain it.

Alas, this departure was no cause for joy, for the crew vowed an early return. Surety of this promise squatted near the steaming scar where the ship had lain – a black *cube*, half an arrowflight wide, featureless save where a ramp led to a gaping hatch.

Nearby, two frail cloth pavilions had been transplanted from Gathering, at the request of star-gods who had stayed behind when their ship departed. One to serve as a place of liaison, and a large tent for 'examining specimens.' Already a small foray party of star-humans worked under that canopy, feeding dark mysterious machines with samples of Jijoan life.

Shock still throbbed throughout the Commons. Despite unity-entreaties by their sages, the many septs and clans cleaved, each seeking shelter among its own kind. Emissaries darted among these cloistered groups, parleying in hushed secrecy. All save the youngest of the Six, whose envoys were rebuffed.

For the moment no one, not even the traeki, wants to speak to humans.

SARA

Around midafternoon, the river spilled into canyon country. As if remembering some urgent errand, the water hastened through a terrain of thorny scrub, clinging to eroded slopes. Sara recalled these badlands from childhood fossil-hunting trips with Dwer and Lark. Those had been good times, despite the heat, stale food, and gritty dust. Especially when Melina used to come along, before the final lingering illness that took her away, leaving Nelo an old man.

Their mother's soft accent used to grow stronger, Sara recalled, the farther south they traveled. The open sky never seemed to cause her any dread.

In contrast, the crew of the *Hauph-woa* grew restless with each southward league, especially after the morning's episode of inept piracy, by the shattered bridge. Clearly the hoon sailors would prefer tying up for the rest of the day under some rocky shelter. The captain reminded them, with a farty blat from his violet sac, that this was no leisurely dross run but an urgent mission for the Commons.

A prevailing west wind normally filled the sails of craft climbing upstream. In places where the river's current pushed strongest, trusty hoon operators offered winch tows from cleverly camouflaged windmills – shaped like upright eggbeaters – that tapped the funneled breeze under cliff overhangs. But the first set of lonely vanes swept in and out of sight before anyone could emerge from the attached hut to answer their hails, and half a midura later, the overseer of the next windmill barely finished a rumbling courtesy-preamble before the river hauled the *Hauph-woa* beyond range.

Like the tug of time, Sara thought. *Pulling you into the future before you're ready, leaving behind a wake of regrets.*

If only life let you catch a friendly tow rope now and then, to climb back into the past, offering a chance to change the flow of your own life-stream.

What would she do, with the last year or two to live over again? Could any amount of foresight have averted the sweet pain of giving her heart where it did not belong? Even with foreknowledge of Joshu's nature, would or could she have rejected in advance all those months of heady joy, when she had pretended in her own mind that he could be hers alone?

Might any amount of prophecy have helped save his *life*?

An image came to her, unbeckoned and unwelcomed out of memory. Recollection of the very day she fled Biblos Citadel, clutching her books and charts, rushing home to that treehouse overlooking Dolo Dam, to drown herself in study.

—black banners flapping in a zephyr that blew past the castle's heavy roof-of-stone ...

—murmur-kites, tugging at their tether strings, moaning their warbling lament during the mulching ceremony for Joshu and the other plague victims ...

—a tall, fair-skinned woman, newly come by boat from far-off Ovoom Town, standing by Joshu's bier, performing a wife's duty, laying on his brow the wriggling torus that would turn mortal flesh into gleaming, crystal dust ...

—the poised, cool face of Sage Taine, rimmed by a mane of hair like Buyur steel, approaching to graciously forgive Sara's year-long indiscretion ... her 'fling' with a mere bookbinder ... renewing his offer of a more seemly union ...

—her last sight of Biblos, the high walls, the gleaming libraries, with forest-topped stone overhead. A part of her life, coming to an end as surely as if *she* had died.

The past is a bitter place, said the Scrolls. *Only the path of forgetfulness leads ultimately to redemption.*

A sharp, horrified gasp was followed by a clatter and crash of fallen porcelain.

'Miss Sara!' an aspirated voice called. 'Come quickly, please. All of you!'

She hurried from the starboard rail to find Pzora puffing in agitation, ers delicate arms-of-manipulation reaching out imploringly. Sara's heart leaped when she saw the Stranger's pallet *empty*, blankets thrown in disarray.

She spied him, backed between three barrel-caskets of human dross, clutching a jagged pottery shard. The wounded man's eyes gaped, wide and wild, staring at the traeki pharmacist.

He's terrified of Pzora, she realized. *But why?*

'Do not fear,' she said soothingly in GalSeven, stepping forward slowly. 'Fear is inappropriate at this time.'

Eyes showing white above the irises, his gaze swung from her to Pzora, as if unable to picture the two of them in the same frame, the same thought.

Sara switched to Anglic, since some coastal human settlements used it almost exclusively.

'It's all right. It is. Really. You're safe. You've been hurt. Terribly hurt. But you're getting better now. Really. You're safe.'

Some words prompted more reaction than others. He seemed to like 'safe,' so she repeated it while holding out her hand. The Stranger glanced anxiously at Pzora. Sara moved to block his view of the traeki, and some tension diminished. His eyes narrowed, focusing on her face.

Finally, with a resigned sigh, he let the jagged sliver fall from trembling fingers.

'That's good,' she told him. 'No one's going to harm you.'

Though the initial flood of panic was over, the Stranger kept glancing toward the Dolo Village pharmacist, shaking his head with surprise and evident loathing.

'Bedamd ... bedamd ... bedamd ...'

'Now be polite,' she chided, while sliding a folded blanket behind his head. 'You wouldn't be taking a nice boat trip to Tarek Town without Pzora's unguents. Anyway, why should you be afraid of a traeki? Who ever heard of such a thing?'

He paused, blinked at her twice, then commenced another pathetic attempt to speak.

'A-jo ... A-joph ... j-j-jo – joph ...'

Frustrated, the Stranger abruptly stopped stammering and shut his mouth, squeezing his lips in a tight, flat line. His left hand raised halfway to the side of his head – toward the bandage covering his horrible wound – then stopped just short, as if touching would make his worst fears real. The arm dropped and he sighed, a low, tremulous sound.

Well, he's awake at least, Sara thought, contemplating a miracle. *Alert and no longer feverish*.

The commotion attracted gawkers. Sara called for them to move back. If a *traeki* could set off hysteria in the wounded man, what about the sight of a qheuenish male, with sharp clambering spikes up and down each leg? Even these days, there were humans who disliked having other members of the Six close by.

So the next sound was the last thing Sara expected to hear—

Laughter.

The Stranger sat up, eyeing the gathered passengers and crew. He gaped at Jomah, the exploser's son, who had climbed Blade's broad back, clasping the head-cupola jutting from the qheuen's blue carapace. Blade had always been gentle and popular with the kids of Dolo, so Sara thought little of it. But the Stranger sucked breath, pointed, and guffawed.

He turned and saw a sailor feeding tidbits to a favorite noor, while another hoon patiently let Prity, the chimpanzee, perch on his broad shoulder for a better view. The Stranger let out a dry, disbelieving cackle.

He blinked in puzzled surprise at the sight of the g'Kek scrivendancer, Fakoon, who had spun over to rest wheels between Pzora and the urrish tinker, Ulgor. Fakoon ogled the injured human with a pair of waving eyestalks, turning the other two toward his neighbors as if to ask – *'What's going on?'*

The Stranger clapped hands like a delighted child, laughing uproariously as tears flowed tributaries down his dark, haggard cheeks.

ASX

It was as if a century's enlightenment by our Holy Egg – and all the earlier hard work to establish the Commons – were forgotten in the aftermath. Few rewq could be seen anywhere, as suspicion-poisons drove them off our brows to sulk in moss-lined pouches, leaving us to rely on mere words, as we had done in ages past, when mere words often led to war.

my/our own folk brought samples of recent noxious rumors, and i laid our base segment over/upon the vileness, letting its vapors rise up our central core, bringing distasteful understanding of *these* odious thoughts—

—*our human neighbors are not trustworthy anymore, if they ever were.*
—*they will sell us out to their gene-and-clan cousins in the foray party.*
—*they lied with their colorful tale of being poor, patronless wolflings, scorned among the Five Galaxies.*
—*they only feigned exile, while spying on us and this world.*

Even more bitter was this gossipy slander—

—*they will depart soon with their cousins, climbing to resume the godlike life our ancestors forsook. Leaving us to molder in this low place, cursed, forgotten, while they roam galaxies.*

That was the foulest chattering stench, so repugnant that i/we vented a noisome, melancholy steam.

The humans ... might they really do that? Might they abandon us?

If/when that happened, night would grow as loathsome as day. For we would ever after have to look up through our darkness and see what they had reclaimed.

The stars.

LARK

The forayer biologist made him nervous. Ling had a way of looking at Lark – one that kept him befuddled, feeling like a savage or a child.

Which he *was*, in comparison, despite being older in duration-years. For one thing, all his lifetime of study wouldn't fill even one of the crystal memory slivers she dropped blithely into the portable console slung over her one-piece green coverall.

The dark woman's exotic, high cheekbones framed large eyes, a startling shade of creamy brown. 'Are you ready, Lark?' she asked.

His own pack held four days' rations, so there'd be no need to hunt or forage, but this time he would leave behind his precious microscope. That treasure of urrish artifice now seemed a blurry toy next to the gadgets Ling and her comrades used to inspect organisms down to the level of their constituent molecules. *What could we tell them that they don't already know?* he pondered. *What could they possibly want from us?*

It was a popular question, debated by those friends who would still speak to him, and by those who turned their backs on any human, for being related to invaders.

Yet the sages charged a human – and a heretic at that – to guide one of these thieves through a forest filled with treasure. To begin the dance of negotiating for our lives.

The Six had one thing to offer. Something missing from the official Galactic Library entry on Jijo, collated by the Buyur before they departed. That thing was *recent* data, about how the planet had changed after a million fallow years. On that, Lark was as 'expert' as a local savage could be.

'Yes, I'm ready,' he told the woman from the starship.

'Good, then let's be off!' She motioned for him to lead.

Lark hoisted his pack and turned to show the way out of the valley of crushed trees, by a route passing far from the cleft of the Egg. Not that anyone expected its existence to stay secret. Robot scouts had been out for days, nosing through the glens, streams, and fumaroles. Still, there was a chance they might mistake the Egg for just another rock formation – that is, until it started to *sing*.

Lark's chosen path also led away from the canyon where the innocents had been sent – the children, chimpanzees, lorniks, zookirs, and glavers. Perhaps the plunderers' eyes weren't omniscient, after all. Maybe precious things could be hidden.

Lark agreed with the sages' plan. Thus far.

Clots of spectators normally gathered at the valley rim to watch the black cube drink sunlight without reflections or highlights. When the two humans reached those heights, one group of urrish onlookers backed away nervously, hooves clattering like pebbles on hard stone. They were all young unbrooded females with empty mate pouches. Just the sort to have an itch for trouble.

Conical heads bobbed and hissed, lowering toward the humans, displaying triangles of serrated teeth. Lark's shoulders tensed. The rewq in his belt pocket squirmed as it sensed rancor in the air.

'Stop that!' he warned, when Ling started pointing an instrument toward the milling urs. 'Just keep walking.'

'Why? I only want to take—'

'Of that I'm sure. But now's not a good time.'

Lark held her elbow, urging her along. From first contact he could tell she was quite strong.

A rock shot past them from behind and struck the ground ahead. An aspirated shout followed.

'Skirlsss!'

Ling started to turn in curiosity, but Lark kept her moving. Added voices joined in.

'Skirls!'

'Jeekee skirlsss!'

More stones pelted around them. Ling's eyes showed dawning concern. So Lark reassured her, dryly, 'Urs don't throw very well. Lousy aim, even after they learned about bows and arrows.'

'They are your enemies,' she observed, quickening the pace on her own accord.

'That's putting it too strong. Let's just say that humans had to fight a bit for our place here on Jijo, early on.'

The urrish rabble followed, easily keeping up, shouting and stoking their nerve – until one of their own kind galloped in from the east, swerving suddenly in front of the throng. Wearing the brassard of a Proctor of Gathering, she spread her arms wide, displaying two full mating pouches and active scent glands. The mob stumbled to a halt as her head bobbed bold, aggressive circles, snapping and shooing them away from the two humans.

Law and order still function, Lark thought, with relief. *Though for how much longer?*

'What were they shouting at us?' Ling asked after marching farther under a canopy of fine-needled vor trees. 'It wasn't in GalSix or GalTwo.'

'Local dialect.' Lark chuckled. '*Jeekee* was originally a hoonish curseword, now in common use. It means smelly – as if those randy little unwed urs should talk!'

'And the other word?'

Lark glanced at her. 'Insults are important to urs. Back in pioneer days, they wanted something to call us. Something humans would find both offensive and apropos. So, during an early truce, they very nicely asked our founders to tell 'em the name of an animal familiar to us. One that lived in trees and was known for being silly.'

Her eyes, taken straight on, were large and exquisite. Hardly the sort you'd expect on a pirate.

'I don't get it,' Ling said.

'To them we're tree-climbers. Just as they must have reminded our ancestors of horses, hinneys, grass-browsers.'

'So? I still don't—'

'So we make an effort to act really insulted, when an angry urs calls one of us a *squirrel*. It makes them so happy, you see.'

She looked puzzled, as if many parts of his explanation confused her. 'You *want* to please your enemies?' she asked.

Lark sighed. 'No one on the Slope has enemies anymore. Not on that kind of scale.'

That is, not until lately, he added silently.

'Why?' he continued, trying to turn the interrogation around. 'Are enemies common where you're from?'

It was her turn to sigh. 'The galaxies are dangerous. Humans aren't well-liked by many.'

'So said our ancestors. It's because humans are wolflings, right? Because we uplifted ourselves, without the help of a patron?'

Ling laughed. 'Oh, *that* old myth!'

Lark stared. 'Do you ... You can't mean ... ?'

'That we know the truth? Our origin and destiny?' She smiled, an expression of serene knowing. 'Goodness, lost child of the past, you people *have* been away a long time. Do you mean that you have never heard of our gracious lords, the Rothen? The beloved patrons of all humankind?'

His foot caught a stone, and Ling grabbed his arm to steady him. 'But we can discuss that later. First I want to talk about these – what did you call them – *skirrils*?'

She held out a finger adorned with a bulbous ring Lark guessed must be a recording device. It took an effort of will to switch mental tracks, suppressing his flare of curiosity about galactic issues.

'What? Oh, that's *squirrels*.'

'You imply they are arboreal and humanlike. Will we get to see any along the way?'

He blinked at her, then shook his head. 'Um, I don't think so. Not this trip.'

'Well, what can you tell me about them? For instance, do they show any aptitude for tool use?'

Lark needed neither psi nor rewq to read the mind of his lovely guest. He carried her question toward its unmistakable aim.

Do they show a talent for machinery? For war and commerce? For philosophy and art?

Do they have Potential? The magic essence that it takes to profit from the right kind of help?

Do they have the rare tincture, the promise, that makes a patron's push worthwhile? The stuff to become starfarers someday?

Are they prospects for uplift?

Lark concealed his surprise over her ignorance. 'Not to the best of my knowledge,' he answered honestly, since the only squirrels he'd seen were in ancient, faded pictures from old Earth. 'If we pass near any, you can see for yourself.'

Clearly, the star-forayers were here seeking bio-treasure. What else might poor Jijo offer that was worth sneaking past the sentries of the Migration Institute, slipping through star-lanes long ceded to the strange, menacing civilization of the Zang, than braving Izmunuti's deadly carbon wind?

What else? Lark pondered. *Except refuge? Ask your own ancestors, boy.*

The newcomers made no pretense, as Lark might have expected, of representing a galactic agency or feigning a legal right to survey Jijo's biosphere. Did they think the exiles had no memory of such things? Or did they simply not care? Their goal – data about changes since the Buyur left – made Lark's lifework more precious than he ever imagined. So much that Lester Cambel had ordered him to leave his notebooks behind, lest they fall into alien hands.

The sages want me to play it close. Try to find out at least as much from her as she learns from me.

A foredoomed plan, of course. The Six were like infants, ignorant of the rules of a deadly game. Still, Lark would do his best, so long as his agenda and the sages' remained the same. Which might not always be the case.

They know that. Surely they've not forgotten I'm a heretic?

Fortunately the forayers had assigned their least intimidating member to accompany him. It might just as easily have been *Rann*, a huge male with close-cropped gray hair, a booming voice, and a wedgelike torso that seemed about to burst from his snug uniform. Of the two others who emerged from the black station, *Kunn* was nearly as masculinely imposing as Rann, with shoulders like a young hoon's, while pale-haired *Besh* was so dramatically female that Lark wondered how she moved so gracefully with a body that prodigiously curved. Compared to her colleagues, Ling seemed almost normal, though she would have caused a stir growing up in any Jijoan town – no doubt provoking many duels among hot-tempered suitors.

Don't forget your vow, Lark reminded himself, puffing in exertion while climbing a steep part of the trail. Perspiration stained the front of Ling's blouse, which clung to her in provocative ways. He forced himself to look away. *You made a choice, to live for a goal greater than yourself. If you wouldn't forsake that aim for an honest woman of Jijo, don't even think about giving it up for a raider, an alien, an enemy of this world.*

Lark found a new way to direct the heat in his veins. Lust can be blocked by other strong emotions. So he turned to anger.

You plan to use us, he mused silently. *But things may turn out different than you think.*

That attitude, in turn, roused an obstinate layer, overcoming his natural curiosity. Earlier, Ling had said something about humans no longer being considered *wolflings,* out among the stars. No longer orphans, without patrons to guide them. From the look in her eye, she had clearly expected this news to cause a stir. No doubt she wanted him to beg for further information.

I'll beg if I must – but I'd rather buy, borrow, or steal it. We'll see. The game's just in its opening rounds.

Soon they passed stands of lesser-boo. Ling took samples of some segmented stems – each no more than ten centimeters across – deftly slicing near-transparent sections into her analyzer.

'I may be a dumb native guide,' he commented. 'But I'll wager boo doesn't show much sign of pre-sapience.'

Her head jerked when he said the word. Thus Lark ended one pretense.

We know why you're here.

Ling's dusky skin did not hide a flush. 'Did I suggest any such thing? I just want to track genetic drift since this species was planted by the Buyur. We'll need a benchmark to compare trends in animals. That's all.'

So we begin the outright lies, he thought. From fossil evidence, Lark knew that boo already thrived on Jijo long before the Buyur won their lease, twenty million years ago. Perhaps it was imported by a previous tenant. Whole ecosystems had coevolved around the successful vegetal type, and countless animals now relied on it. But things must have been rough for the first eon or so, as boo pushed native flora out of many watersheds.

Lark knew little about the biochemical level, but from fossils he was sure the genus hadn't changed much in a hundred million years.

Why would she lie about something so unimportant? The Scrolls taught that deceit was not only wrong, but also a fickle, dangerous ally. And habit forming. Once you start lying, it's hard to stop. Eventually it is small, needless lies that get you caught.

'Speaking of pre-sapience,' Ling said, folding her sample case, 'I can't help wondering where you folks stashed your chimpanzees. I'm sure *they* must have drifted in interesting ways.'

It was Lark's turn to give away too much with an involuntary twitch. Denial was useless. *Humans don't need rewq to play this game with each other – reading clues in each other's faces. Lester must know I'll betray as much as I learn.*

'Chimps are like children. Naturally we sent them away from possible danger.'

Ling looked left and right. 'Do you see any danger?'

Lark almost burst out with sardonic laughter. In Ling's eyes danced a complexity of things he could only guess. But some thoughts were clear without being spoken aloud.

You know that I know. I know that you know that I know. And you know that I know that you know that I know …

There is another emotion that can overcome hormonal lust, or the fury of anger.

Respect.

He nodded to his adversary, meeting her gaze full on. 'I'll let you know if we pass near any chimps, so you can see for yourself.'

Ling had extremely sharp vision and proved it frequently by spotting movements Lark would have missed – forest creatures foraging, browsing, hunting or tending their young. In this, she reminded him of Dwer. But Ling also owned many *tools*, which she brought swiftly to bear on whatever crawling, flitting, or ambling thing caught her attention.

She must really have studied those old Buyur records, for their progress was slowed by frequent sighs of recognition, when she would classify a species of shrub, tree, or four-winged bird, then ask Lark to add whatever quaint name the locals used. Lark gave cautious answers – just enough to support his value as a local expert.

Sometimes Ling would pause and mutter into her ring, as if contemplating what she had learned. Lark realized with a shiver that she must be in contact with her base. This was *speech at a distance*, not like semaphore, farcasting, or even rare psi-telepathy, but the high-tech kind mentioned in books, perfect and reliable. The voice of the person at the other end could barely be made out as a whisper. He guessed it must be projected somehow, compactly, to the region near her ear.

At one point, Ling murmured in a dialect form of Anglic, rather hard to follow.

'Yea, yea … Oright. A'll try to speed ip. But yigotta chuz – distince er ditail.'

The other party must have been persuasive, for Ling picked up the pace when the march resumed – until the next excited discovery caused her to forget her promise and go right back to dawdling over some intriguing detail. Lark found this character flaw – how easily she was distracted by the sight of living things – the first thing he honestly liked about her.

Then Ling spoiled it by patronizing him, defining – in slow, simple words – what 'nocturnal' meant. Lark quashed resentment. He had read enough adventure novels as a kid to know how a native guide was supposed to act. So he thanked her respectfully. There might be future advantages to be had in letting her maintain her stereotypes.

For all of Ling's enthusiasm and keen eyesight, she was no hunter like Dwer. Even to Lark, the surroundings frothed with signs – footprints and broken stems, feces and territory marks, wisps of fur, scale, feather, and torg. Any child of the Six could read such stories, found along the path. But Ling seemed aware only of what was currently alive.

Thinking about Dwer made Lark smile. *By the time he gets back from his mundane glaver hunt, I'll be the one with wild stories to tell, for a change.*

At intervals, Ling unfolded an instrument with twin 'holio screens,' one showing a forest scene that rippled and moved as Lark stared over her shoulder, showing someplace nearby, he could tell from the foliage. The other screen displayed charts and figures he found indecipherable – which was humbling. He had read nearly every biology text in Biblos and figured he should at least understand the vocabulary.

Maybe the 'Yes, bwana' routine isn't such an act. Turns out I may be illiterate, after all.

Ling explained this was data from one of the robot probes, climbing the same path some distance ahead. 'Could we move faster now?' she asked eagerly. 'The robot has subdued some interesting specimens. I want to reach them before they deteriorate.'

She had been the one dawdling. Still, Lark only nodded.

'Whatever you say.'

The first specimen was a hapless wuankworm whose burrow had been sliced open with scalpel-smoothness. A web of fibrous stuff defied repeated battering by the worm's bony head, as it fought futilely to escape.

Ling spoke into her ring. 'This feral form seems related to ore-gleaners the Buyur imported from Dezni, three eons ago. Dezni-evolved organisms *should* estivate after injection with clathrate of methane. We'll try a larger dose now.'

She aimed a device that sent a slender tube flashing like a resolute predator, piercing a crease between two armor plates. The worm flinched, then slumped, quivering.

'Good. Now let's see if encephalization has changed during the last megayear.' She turned to Lark and explained. 'That's to see if they have more brain matter.'

Now that I knew, he thought, but restrained himself and remarked instead, 'How perfectly amazing.'

Lark learned to pass instruments, draw blood, and assist his employer as required. At one point the raspy tongue of an angry longsnout whipped between the strands of its cage and would have torn off strips off Ling's arm, if he had not yanked it away in time. After that, Ling seemed to realize her 'native guide' had uses beyond toting, carrying, and being impressed whenever she spoke.

Though the robot's specimens were 'brainy' types, living by their wits as hunters or omnivorous gatherers, Lark thought none of them likely prospects for uplift. *Maybe in ten million years, when this galaxy is reopened for legal settlement. By then, longsnouts or leap raptors may be ready, tested by evolution and Ifni's luck, primed for adoption by some kindly elder race.*

Yet, watching her use sorcerous rays and probes to appraise a mangy-looking carrion snorter, Lark could not help but imagine the beast responding by rearing up on its hind legs and reciting an ode to the comradeship of living things. Ling's group clearly thought they might find something precious, emerging on Jijo ahead of schedule. *Once potential is there, all it takes is help from a patron to set a new race on the Upward Path.*

A few texts in Biblos disagreed. A birth does *not* always need a midwife, they claimed.

Lark chose to follow up that idea during the next part of the trek.

'A while back you implied Earthlings aren't as wolflings anymore.'

Ling smiled enigmatically. 'Some still believe that old myth. But others have known the truth for quite a while.'

'The truth?'

'About where we came from. Who gave humanity the boon of thought and reason. Our true patrons. The Rothen mentors and guides we owe everything we are, and ever will be.'

Lark's heart beat faster. A few tomes on the subject had survived the fire that ravaged the Biblos xenology shelves, so he knew the debate was still raging when the sneakship *Tabernacle* left for Jijo, three centuries ago. In those days, some speculated that humanity *had* been helped, in secret by clandestine benefactors, long before the historical era. Others held out for the model of Darwin – that intelligence could evolve all by itself, without outside help, despite the skepticism of Galactic science. Now Ling insisted the debate was settled.

'Who are they?' Lark asked in a hushed voice. 'Did some Rothen come to Jijo with you?'

That smile returned, a knowing look, tugging her high

cheekbones. 'Truth for truth. First *you* tell me the real story. What's a pack of humans doing here on this dreary little world?'

'Uh . . . which pack are you talking about? Yours or mine?'

Her silent smile was his only answer, as if to say – '*Go ahead and be coy, I can wait.*'

Ling followed tracers left by the relentless robot, leading from one sedated creature to the next. As the day waned, she picked up the pace until they reached the crest of a long ridge. From there, Lark saw several more plateaus to the north, slanting up toward Rimmer peaks. Instead of the usual covering of native trees, the nearest mesa bore a blanket of darker green, a dense sward of giant boo – stems so huge that individuals could be made out even from where he stood. A few streaks of stone, and one of water, broke the expanse of gently swaying tubes.

Their final specimen was an unfortunate rock-staller, no more than a curled-up ball of spines when they cut away the webbing the robot used to restrain its victims. Ling prodded the creature with a tool that emitted a short, sharp spark, but got no reaction. She repeated, at a higher setting. Lark's stomach turned as he caught a stench from curling smoke.

'It's dead,' he diagnosed. 'I guess your robot ain't perfect, after all.'

Lark dug a latrine ditch and prepared a fire. His meal was leaf-wrapped bread and cheese. Hers bubbled when she broke the foil seals, stinging Lark's nose with unfamiliar, enticing tangs. It wasn't quite dark by the time he gathered her empty packets to be carried back and sealed as dross.

Ling seemed inclined to resume their conversation.

'Your sage, Cambel, says that no one recalls exactly why your ancestors came. Some sooners sneak into fallow worlds as rogue breeding groups. Others are fleeing war or persecution. I'd like to know what your own founders told the races already here, when they arrived.'

Among the Six, the term *sooner* applied to small bands who slinked away from the Slope to invade territory forbidden under the sacred Scrolls. *But I guess we're all 'sooners' in that sense. Even those living on the Slope.* In his heart, Lark had always known it.

Still, he had been commanded to lie.

'You are mistaken,' he said. Deceit tasted foul. 'We're castaways. Our combined ship—'

The forayer woman laughed. 'Please. That clever trick set us back a day or so. But before our ship left, we knew. The story is impossible.'

Lark's lips pressed. No one had expected the bluff to last long. 'How do you figure?'

'It's simple. Humans have only been in Galactic space four centuries or so – three hundred and fifty Jijoan cycles. It's quite impossible for Earthlings to have been aboard the same ship that brought g'Keks to this world.'

'Why is that?'

'Because, my good rustic cousin, by the time humans entered the galactic scene, there *weren't* any g'Kek to be found.'

Lark blinked while she continued.

'When we saw you all there, lining the valley rim, we recognized most of the types. But we had to look up the g'Kek. Imagine our surprise when one word flashed, right at the top.

'The word was – *extinct.*'

Lark could only stare.

'Your wheeled friends are rare,' Ling concluded. 'Those here on Jijo are surely the last of their kind.'

And just when I was starting to like you . . .

Lark could swear there was a kind of satisfaction in her eyes, over the shock her news caused.

'So you see,' Ling added, 'each of us has truths to share. I've just told you one. I hope you'll be as open with me.'

He kept his voice even. 'You haven't found me helpful so far?'

'Don't get me wrong! Your sages have been so obscure about certain matters. They may not have understood our questions. As you and I converse at greater length, some issues may clarify.'

Lark saw what was going on. *Divide and interrogate.* He had not been present when the sky-humans met with the sages. She was sure to catch him in a net of discrepancies if he weren't extremely careful.

'For instance, when Kunn asked about sightings of other spacecraft, since the first sooners came to Jijo, we were told about visits by Zang globes, dipping down to lick the sea, and some distant lights long ago that might have been Institute survey ships. But we're *really* interested in occurrences that might have taken place much more—'

A sharp trill interrupted her. Ling lifted the blue finger-ring. 'Yes?'

Her head tilted, listening to a whisper projected near one ear.

'For *sure?*' she demanded, surprise infecting her voice. Ling's hands flapped at her belt pouch, pulling forth the pocketbook receiver, whose twin screens came alight with forest images, moving ahead through the lowering evening gloom. *Machines don't sleep*, Lark observed.

'Switch view from probe four to probe five,' Ling requested. The scene changed abruptly to a blur of static. On the right, all the charts and graphs showed the flat slashes that denoted 'zero' in Galactic Six.

'When did it happen?' the forayer woman demanded of her unseen colleague. Lark watched her face, wishing he could hear more of the other end of the conversation than a vague murmur.

'Replay the last ten minutes before the probe failed.'

The left-hand screen soon lit with images, showing a narrow green corridor with a ribbon of sky above and a stream of scummy water below. The close walls consisted of closely packed stems of towering great-boo.

'Go to double speed,' Ling asked, impatiently. The great columns swept by in a blur. Lark leaned closer, finding the scene familiar.

Abruptly, the slim aisle spilled into a shallow crater, a rubble-strewn bowl with a small lake at its center, rimmed by a thorny barricade of looping vines.

Wait a minute. I know this place . . .

A set of livid cross-hairs crawled across the holio display, converging near the frothy lake shore, while the right-hand screen flashed red symbols in technical GalSix. Lark had to labor, but managed to make out certain words—

. . . anomaly . . . unknown source . . . strong digital activity . . .

His stomach churned as the camera-eye sped toward the disturbance, swooping by slabs of ancient Buyur masonry, as crimson symbols clustered toward the central field of view. Everything inside that tunnel of attention grew more vivid, while the periphery dimmed. Seething emblems flashed preparations that Lark read with dismay – the readying of *weapons*, powering up for use.

Dwer always said this mulc-spider was nastier than most and warned people to stay away. But what on Jijo could the robot have to worry about?

Another thought struck him.

My God, isn't this the direction Dwer was headed, chasing after that runaway glaver?

The machine decelerated. Lark recognized the thick tangle of an aged mulc-spider, its vines splayed across the remains of some ancient Buyur structure.

The robot's view skimmed past a pale figure, hunched on the ground, and Lark blinked.

Was that a glaver, lying in the open? Ifni, we went to such trouble hiding them, and this machine shoots past one without noticing.

Another surprise slipped by the camera's periphery as it slowed. A lean animal, four-footed and wiry, black fur nearly blending with the dark tangle. The white teeth of a *noor* flashed briefly, chattering surprised defiance at the onrushing machine, then vanishing to one side as the robot cruised on, single-mindedly.

A *noor*? Up in the mountains? Without knowing why, Lark tasted bile.

The machine slowed to a crawling hover. Red cross-hairs converged downward toward a point throbbing with rhythms of crimson menace ... *digital cognizance* ... *level nine or greater* ... the GalSix symbols throbbed. Little could be made out in the gloomy snarl below, except some vague flutterings near the center of the cross-hairs. The robot must be targeting with senses other than vision.

... *autonomous decision* ... *terminate threat immediately* ...

Suddenly, the dim scene flashed with brilliance. The central field blazed white as shafts of angry lightning tore into the morass, slicing the mulc-spider's medusa limbs. Boiling juices sprayed from whipping, severed vines while red targeting circles danced back and forth, seeking something that kept dodging randomly within a confined space.

Ling was reading the data-filled right-hand screen, cursing the robot's inability to make a clean kill. So Lark felt sure he alone glimpsed a brief outline at one edge of the holio panel. It flashed just an instant but seemed to sear his optic nerve.

One – no, *two* clusters of arms and legs, intermeshed among the shuddering vines, cowering from the burning fury above.

Static again filled the displays.

'No, I can't head over there right now. It's half a mictaar from here. My guide and I would flounder in the dark. It'll have to wait until—'

Listening again, Ling sighed. 'All right, I'll ask him.' She lowered her ring and turned.

'Lark, you know this country. Is there a trail—'

She stopped, and stood up quickly, peering left, then right.

'Lark?'

She called into the night, now a velvet blackness dusted with the winking luster of this galaxy's third brightest spiral arm.

'Lark! Where are you?'

Wind stirred branches overhead, brushing the forest silence. There was no way of knowing how long it was since he had left, or in which direction.

With a sigh, Ling lifted her hand and reported the abandonment.

'How should I know?' she replied to a curt query. 'Can't blame the nervous monkey for spooking. Never saw a robot's cut-beam at work before. He may be halfway home by now, if he stops before the coast—

'Yes, yes. I know we hadn't decided about that, but it's too late now. Hardly matters, anyway. All he got away with are a few hints and clues. We've got plenty more to bribe the natives with. And there's more where he came from.'

ASX

Dissension grows.

The Commons writhes against itself like a traeki whose rings were cruelly stacked, without nurturing rapport between the married toruses.

Word arrives by galloping urrish courier from settlements downslope, where anxiety and chaos reign like despotic qheuenish empresses of old. Some villages topple their water tanks, their grain silos, solar heaters, and windmills, claiming authority in the sacred Scrolls, overruling the rescript that our sage Council sent in haste the day the ship came – a policy urging that all folk wait-and-see.

Meanwhile, others protect their barns and docks and weirs, laboring to pile concealing vegetation – and violently repelling angry neighbors who approach their precious property bearing torches and crowbars.

Should we not do better here at Gathering? Did not the finest of the Six come together here for yearly rites of union? Yet poison also roils in this place.

First discord – foul suspicion of our youngest sept. Might our human neighbors be allied with invaders? With plunderers? If not now, could they grow tempted, in time?

Oh, dire notion! Theirs is the highest grasp of science among the Six. What hope have we, without their aid, ever to pierce the deceits of godlike felons?

So far, some faith has been restored by the noble example of Lester and his deputies, who swear devotion to Jijo and our Holy Egg. Yet do not rumors and odious doubts still fly, like whirling soot, amid these gentle glades?

Dissension multiplies. A harvest team returns from one of the deep caves where wild rewq breed, to find the cavern walls deserted, no rewq to be seen. And the ones within our pouches languish. They will not sup our vital fluids, nor help us share the secrets of each other's souls.

*

Further discord – in each race many are tempted by a siren song. Sweet utterances by our unwelcome guests. Unctuous promises, words of comradeship.

And not merely words.

Do you recall, my rings, when the star-humans spread word they would *heal*?

Under a canopy brought over from the festival grounds – shaded by their dark, cubic outpost – they call forth the lame, sick, and hurt. We sages can but watch, helpless and confused, as queues of our wounded brethren limp inside, then amble out elated, transformed, in some part cured.

In truth, many seemed palliated only in their pain. But for some others – miraculous change! Death's door is transmuted, now a portal to restored youth, vigor, potency.

What can we do, forbid? Impossible. Yet what profuse samplings do the healers gain! Vials brimming with specimens of our diverse biologies. Whatever gaps once filled their dossiers, they now know all about our strengths and weaknesses, our genes and latent natures.

Those returning from the healing, are they well-greeted? Some call their own sept-mates traitor. Some perceive defilement, turning away in hatred.

So we divide. In fresh enmity, we *sub*divide.

Are we a gathering any longer? Are we a Commons?

Did not you, my/our own third basal ring – ailing for a year with the ague known as torus plaque – did you not attempt to twist this aging pile toward that green pavilion where wonder cures are offered, though not unselfishly? If dissension infests this entity which others call *Asx*, can a society of individuals cohere any better?

The heavens above have always been our dread. But disharmony now swarms these very meadows, filling our frustrated days and nights until Jijo's *soil* now seems as fearsome as her sky.

Can we hope, my rings?

Tonight we do pilgrimage. The most sage of the Six shall travail under darkness, arduously, past fuming pits and misty cliffs, to reach the place of the Holy Egg.

This time, will it answer us? Or shall the fell silence of recent weeks go on?

Can we still hope?

There is a sensation we traeki have learned to describe only since meeting humans on Jijo. Yet never till now have i felt this pang so terribly. It is a desolation not well rendered in Galactic languages, which emphasize tradition and close relations, subsuming thoughts of self to those of race and clan. But in Anglic the feeling is central and well known.

Its name is – *alone*.

DWER

They took turns rescuing each other.

It wasn't easy. Consciousness kept threatening to drown under surges of pain from his many cuts and burns. To make matters worse, Dwer suspected he was deaf.

Rety kept stumbling, yet she would not use her arms for anything except to clutch her treasure tightly to her breast.

That prize very nearly finished them both off, a while ago, when she plunged screaming back into the maelstrom of fire and acid steam, desperately seeking remnants of her precious 'bird' amid smoldering stumps and glowing wreckage of the horrible machine that fell from the burning sky.

Dwer had just about had it by the time he got her out of there a second time.

You go back in again, and you can stay for all I care.

For a distance of two arrowflights, he had carried her with aching lungs and scalded skin, fleeing the burning mulc-spider till the worst stench, heat, and suffocating vapors lay well behind. Finally, he had put her down by the muddy creek at the lake's outlet and plunged his face and arms into the cooling stream. The slaking liquid cut his agony in half, and *that* was almost more shock than his system could bear. Gasping some water into his lungs, he pushed back, gagging and coughing. When his hands slipped, he fell into the muck, floundering weakly. If Rety had not caught his hair and dragged him out, he might have drowned right there.

A hiccup of ironic laughter joined his hacking cough. *After all that . . . what a way to go . . .*

For some time they lay there, exhausted and shivering side-by-side, stirring only to scoop mud and slather it over each other's seared nakedness. It coated raw nerves and offered some small guard against the deepening night chill. Dwer thought of the warm clothes in his pack, nestled amid the boulders somewhere back there amid the fires.

And my bow, left on a boulder. He suppressed that worry with a silent curse. *Forget the damn bow! Come back for it later. Now just get out of here.*

He tried to gather strength to rise. Rety was pursuing the same goal, with identical results, sagging back with a moan after each effort. Finally, Dwer managed to sit up. The stars swayed as he teetered, pushed by a wintry wind.

Get moving, or you'll freeze.

Insufficient reason. Not enough to overcome shock and fatigue.

The girl then. Get her moving, or—

Or what? Dwer somehow doubted even twice this much suffering could kill Rety. Trouble would not spare her yet. Trouble must find her too useful as an ally and friend.

But he was on the right track, Dwer felt sure. There was something else. Another duty. Someone awaited his return . . .

The glaver. Dwer's mud-crusted eyelids opened. *I left her hobbled. She'll starve. Or a ligger will get her.*

With quaking limbs, he fought his way up to his knees – and found he could rise no further.

Rety struggled up too and sagged against him. They rested, leaning against each other for support. *When folks find our frozen bodies lying together this way, someone's sure to think we must've liked each other.*

That, alone, was good reason to move. But messages to his arms and legs weren't obeyed.

A soft moistness stroked his cheek . . .

Stop that, Rety.

It repeated. Wet and scratchy.

What's the kid doing now – licking me? Of all the weird . . .

Again a wet tongue – rather long and raspy for a little sooner girl. Dwer managed to turn his head . . . and blinked at the sight of two huge bulging eyes, rotating independently on each side of a broad rounded head. The glaver's mouth opened again. This time the tongue abraded a path right up Dwer's lip and over both nostrils. He flinched, then managed to wheeze—

'H-how . . . how-w . . . ?'

Vaguely, distantly, he heard his own words. So he wasn't completely deaf, after all.

Knowing a better perch when she saw it, Rety transferred her one-armed grip from his neck to the glaver's. The other hand still clenched her prize – a fragment of knobs, lumps, and scorched metal feathers.

Dwer didn't pause to question fortune. He flung himself over the glaver's other side, sucking warmth from her downy hide.

Patiently – or apathetically – the creature let both humans hang on, till Dwer finally found the strength to gather his feet and stand.

One of the glaver's hind legs still bore remnants of a rope hobble, chewed off at the knot. Behind her, the cause of this miracle grinned with the other end in its mouth. Mudfoot leered at Dwer, eyes glittering.

Always gotta make sure to get full credit, don't you? Dwer thought, knowing it was ungrateful but thinking it anyway.

Another brilliant explosion sent rays of brightness cutting through black shadows, all centered on the fiery site by the lake. Two more reports followed within a few duras, erasing any thought of going back after his supplies. Flames continued to spread.

He helped Rety up, leaning on the glaver for support. *Come on,* Dwer said, with a slight incline of the head. *Better to die in motion than just lying here.*

Even stumbling in the dark, numbed by cold, pain, and weariness, Dwer couldn't help pondering what he'd seen.

One little bird-machine might have been rare but explainable – a surviving relic of Buyur days, somehow preserved into this era, wandering confused across a continent long abandoned by its masters. But the *second* machine – that daunting, floating menace – was no dazed leftover of vanished Jijoan tenants. It had been powerful, resolute.

A new thing in the world.

Together they weaved unsteadily down another avenue between two forests of boo. The channel spared them from the frigid wind, and also from having to make any decisions. Each step took them farther from the lakeside conflagration, which suited Dwer fine.

Where there's one death machine, might there be more?

Could another levitating minifortress come to avenge its brother? With that thought, the narrow, star-canopied aisle ceased seeming a refuge, rather an awful trap.

The boo-lined corridor ended at last, spilling the four of them onto a meadow of knee-high grass swaying before a stiff, icy wind that drained their bodies as they shuffled along. Frost flurries whirled all around. Dwer knew it was just a matter of time before they collapsed.

A grove of scrubby saplings clustered by a small watercourse, some distance from the path. Shivering, he nudged the glaver across the crunching, crackling grass. *We're leaving tracks,* the hunter in him carped. Lessons drilled by old Fallon floating to mind. *Try keeping to bare rock or water . . . When you're being stalked, head downwind . . .*

None of which was helpful now. Instinct led him to a rocky ledge, an outcrop shrouded by low bushes. Without his fire-lighter or even a knife or piece of flint, their best hope lay in finding shelter. Dwer yanked Rety off the glaver's neck, pushing till she understood to bend and crawl under the shelf. The glaver shuffled inward on all four knees, Mudfoot hitching a ride on her corrugated back. Dwer yanked some fallen branches where the wind would pile leaves on top. Then he also dropped, slithering to join an interspecies tangle of limbs, fur, skin – and someone's fetid breath not far from his face.

Snowflakes sublimed off flesh as body heat spread through the confined space. *Just our luck to have a late flurry, so far into spring*, he thought. Old Fallon used to say there were just two seasons in the mountains. One was called Winter. The other was *also* winter, with some green stuff growing to trick the unwary.

He told himself the weather wasn't really so bad – or wouldn't be if their clothes hadn't been burned off their bodies, or if they weren't already in shock, or if they had supplies.

After a while, Dwer realized the deafness must be fading. He could hear someone's teeth chattering, then a *murmur* of some sort, coming from behind him. That was followed by a sharp jab on his shoulder.

'I *said* could you *move* jes a bit?' Rety shouted, not far from his ear. 'You're lying on my—'

He shifted. Something bony slid from under his ribcage. When he lay back down, his flank scraped icy grit. Dwer sighed.

'Are you all right?'

She squirmed some more. 'What'd you say?'

He writhed around to see her blurry outline. 'Are you okay?' he shouted.

'Oh, sure. Never better, dimmie. Good question.'

Dwer shrugged. If she had energy to be nasty, she was probably far from death's door.

'You got anything to eat?' Rety added.

He shook his head. 'We'll find something in the morn. Till then, don't speak 'less you must.'

'Why?'

Because robots probably have ears, he almost said. But why worry the kid?

'Save your strength. Now be good and get some sleep.'

A slight vibration might have been the girl, mimicking his words sarcastically under her breath. But he couldn't be sure – a blessed side effect to the beating his ears had taken.

With a series of sharp jabs, Mudfoot clambered up his leg to settle in the wedge between his body and Rety's. Dwer squirmed to a position where his head was less sheltered by the glaver's warm flank.

A bitter chill greeted his face as he peered back at the trail they had just left – the narrow avenue between two vast stands of boo. As a makeshift hunter's blind, this wasn't bad – if only more snow would fill in the trampled trail they had left in the broken grass.

We got away from you, One-of-a-Kind, he thought, savoring a victory he had not won. Many patches of skin still seemed too numb, too cool for even the glaver's warmth to heat up, tracing where the spider's golden preserving fluid had stuck. No way to clean them right now – if the droplets ever *would* come off.

Still, we got away, didn't we?

A faint touch seemed to stroke his mind. Nothing he could pinpoint, but it triggered a tickle of worry. Surely the crazy old mulc-deconstructor couldn't have survived the inferno by the lake?

It's just my imagination. Forget it.

Unfortunately, his imagination also supplied what One-of-a-Kind would surely reply.

Ah, my precious. Is that not what you always say?

Shivering from more than mere cold, Dwer settled for a long watch, eyeing the funnel-avenue for other strange things sneaking over the pass through the Rimmer Range.

A sound roused Dwer from a dream filled with sensations of failure and paralysis. His eyes flinched when he opened them to a chill wind. Listlessly, he tried focusing on what had yanked him awake. But all that came to mind was a preposterous notion that someone had called his *name*.

The Dolphin was up near zenith, its flank shimmering with blue-white stars, seeming to dive between milky waves.

Clouds. And more snow was falling.

He blinked, trying to stare. Something was moving out there.

Dwer lifted a hand to rub his eye, but the fingers would not uncurl. When they touched his face, they seemed petrified – a sign of shock compounded by frostbite.

Over there. Is that it?

Something *was* moving. Not another robot, wafting on smug pillars of force, but a shambling bipedal figure, hurrying upslope at a pace Dwer found professionally lacking. At that rate, whoever-it-was would tire much faster than necessary. No errand was worth taking such risks in this kind of weather.

Of the Six, only a hoon or human could make it this high in a snowfall, and no hoon would let himself get into that much of a hurry.

Hey, you! Don't go up through the boo! There's danger thataway!

Dwer's voice produced only a croak, barely loud enough to rouse the noor, causing Mudfoot to lift its head.

145

Hey, fool. Can't you see our trail in the grass and snow? It's like a Buyur highway out there! Are you blind?

The figure plowed right on by, disappearing into the dark cathedral-like aisle between twin walls of vaulting boo. Dwer slumped, hating himself for his weakness. *All I had to do was shout. That's all. Just a little shout.*

Glassy-eyed, he watched more flakes fill the runnel in the grass, slowly erasing all signs leading to this rocky cleft. *Well, you wanted to hide, wasn't that the idea?*

Perhaps the four of them would never be found.

Dwer lacked the strength to feel irony.

Some hunter. Some mighty hunter . . .

THE STRANGER

It will take some getting used to, this curious unlikely voyage, rushing along in a wooden boat that glides down rocky canyons, swooping past high stone walls, giving a sense of incredible speed. Which is odd, since he knows he used to travel much, much faster than this . . . though right now it's hard to recall exactly how.

Then there are his fellow passengers, a mixture of types he finds amazing to behold.

At first, several of them had filled him with raw terror – especially the squishy thing, looking like a stack of phlegmy doughnuts piled up high, venting complex stinks that scrape-tickled his nose and tongue. The mere sight of its corrugated cone wrenched feelings of blank horror –until he realized that something was quite different about this *particular Joph—*

His mind refuses to bring forth the epithet, the name, even though he trolls and sifts for it.

Words refuse to come easily. Most of the time, they do not come at all.

Worse, he cannot speak or form ideas, or comprehend when others send shaped-sounds toward him. Even names, *the simplest of labels, refuse to rest within his grasp but wriggle off like slippery things, too angry or fickle to bear his touch.*

No matter.

He resolves to wait, since there is no other choice. He even manages to hold back revulsion when the doughy cone-creature touches him, since healing seems its obvious intent, and since the pain always lessens a bit, each time it wraps oily tendrils round his throbbing head.

In time, the contact becomes oddly pleasant.

Anyway, she is usually there, speaking to him gently, filling the tunnel-view of his attention with her smile, providing an excuse for frail optimism.

He doesn't recall much about his former life, but he can dimly remember something about the way he used to live ... not so much a philosophy as an attitude—

If the universe seems to be trying to destroy you, the best way to fight back is with hope.

IX

THE BOOK OF THE SEA

Scrolls

In order to be blessed,
And to bring redemption,
Forgetfulness cannot come at random.

Aspects of oblivion
Must come in the right order.

First must come detachment from the driving
need
To coerce the material world,
Or to shape other beings to your needs.

To be shaped is your goal.
First by nature,
And later by hands and minds
Wiser than your own.

—*The Scroll of Promise*

So there we were, way up in the thin, dry air atop Mount Guenn, surrounded by heat and dust and sulfury smells from Uriel's forge, and what does Gybz the Alchemist want to talk to us about?

The traeki tells us we're being sent to a different *kind* of hell.

But hold on, Alvin. Spin the yarn the way an old-time human storyteller would. Describe the scene, *then* the action.

Gybz concocts recipes for metal and glass in a grimy workshop, quite unlike Uriel's prim, spotless hall of spinning disks. Mineral powders spill across stained wooden shelves and earthenware jars stink with noxious liquids. One slit window overlooks a northern vista stretching all the way down to a splash of painful color that could only be the Spectral Flow, which means the chamber is about as high as you can get without tumbling into Mount Guenn's simmering caldera.

Below the window, flies swarmed over a pile of nicely aged kitchen mulch. I hoped we weren't interrupting Gybz at dinner.

The four of us – Huck, Pincer, Ur-ronn, and me – had come up to the alchemy lab at the command of Uriel, the great blacksmith, ruler of this fortress of industry perched on Jijo's trembling knee. At first I figured she sent us away just to get rid of some irritating youngsters, while she conferred with a human sage over how to improve her beloved mobile of gears, pulleys, and whirling glass. The chief assistant, Urdonnol, muttered disapproval while shepherding us up a long ramp to the traeki's mixing room. Only our pal Ur-ronn seemed cheerful, almost ebullient. Huck and I exchanged a glance, wondering why.

We found out when Gybz shuffled its mottled, conical bulk around from behind a workbench. Words bubbled from a speaking tube that puckered the third-from-the-top ring.

'*Bright youths of four races, be made welcome! Sublime news for you, it is an honor to relate. A decision to approve your expedition, this has occurred. Your endeavor to reach, visit, explore the nearest reaches of the Upper Midden, this you may attempt.*'

Gybz paused, venting puffs from a purple synthi ring. When the traeki resumed, it was in warbling, uneven Anglic, with a voice that sounded strained.

'The attempt will have ... the full backing of Mount Guenn Forge. As evidence of this support, behold – your completed window!'

The Master of Mixes gestured with a wraparound tentacle toward a wooden crate near the wall, with its cover removed. Amid drifts of fine sawdust, there gleamed a curved pane of thick glass, flawless to the eye.

Pincer-Tip danced excitedly, his red-clawed feet noisy on the stone floor. 'Beautiful-iful!'

Gybz agreed. 'It has been treated with proper coatings – for clear vision in the planned environment.'

Ur-ronn snaked her long neck around to inspect the bubble-pane.

'This last phase was delicate. Thank you, Gyfz, for the exquisite coatings!'

Ur-ronn turned to explain to Huck and me, 'After months of delay, Uriel suddenly agreed just three days ago to allow the casting. And since the results were good on the first try, she will let this count toward a *kun-uru*!'

That was urrish plains dialect for a master work. One qualifying the maker for craftsman status. It would take Ur-ronn a long way toward fulfilling her ambitions.

None of the rest of us have started professions, or even decided what we want to do, I thought, a little jealously. *On the other hand, urs have to hurry. They don't get that much time.*

I glanced at Urdonnol, who was Ur-ronn's top rival as Uriel's heir. I didn't need a rewq to read her annoyance with all this fuss over what she called a 'childish hobby' – the making of an experimental deep diving craft.

You should know better, I thought, feeling a bit sorry for Urdonnol. *Uriel also has a useless pastime, that room full of spinning disks. Ur-ronn's project shares that just-for-the-hell-of-it quality. It's a similarity between them that goes beyond mere kin-scent.*

To Ur-ronn, then, this had also been a smart career move. I felt happy for our friend.

'The glass was tested to withstand hydrostatic pressures exceeding those at fifty cords depth,' she commented with evident satisfaction. 'And when you add the lanterns and other gear Uriel is kindly lending us—'

'Us?' Huck cut in, breaking the mood. She spun to face Ur-ronn with three outthrust eyes. 'What you mean *us*, honky? You're volunteering to come along, then?'

Ur-ronn's narrow head snapped back, staring at Huck. Then her neck slumped in an S-curve.

'I will . . . if I can.'

'Huck!' I chided. It was mean to rub Ur-ronn's nostril in her limitations. I could hear Huck's spokes vibrate with tension.

Gybz interrupted with another venting, this time pungent like rusty metal.

'If possible, an urrish presence will be called for.' The traeki seemed short of breath. 'But even if that proves impossible, fear not. A member from Mount Guenn shall ... accompany this bold undertaking ... to its deepest depths.'

I had trouble following Gybz's halting, accented Anglic. Huck and I shared a confused look.

'It is *i/we* ... who shall part-wise accompany ... this august group,' Gybz explained, wheezing through the topmost ring. With that, the traeki showed us something none of us expected, shuffling around to expose an oozing blister on its far side, halfway up the fleshy stack. It was no normal swelling, where the traeki might be making another tentacle or readying chemicals for the mill. A *crack* split the swollen zone, exposing something slick and wriggly within.

Staring, I realized – the traeki was *vlen-budding* before our eyes!

While the crevice widened, the Masters of Mixes seemed to flutter. A complex gurgle of vaguely sickening noises accompanied something that began to *emerge*, slithering through the opening, then sliding down the traeki's sloping flank, trailing loose fibers behind it.

'Gosh-osh-osh-osh-osh ...' Pincer repeated in turn from each legvent, his sensor strip spinning frantically. Urdonnol edged away nervously while Huck rolled back and forth, torn between curiosity and revulsion. I felt sharp, biting sensations as little Huphu, our noor beast mascot, scrambled up my back and onto my shoulder, growling anxiously. Half-consciously I stroked her sleek pelt, rumbling an umble that must have sounded more confident than I felt.

Glistening with slime, the thing landed on the floor with a plopping sound and lay almost still, ripples coursing around its quadruple torus of miniature rings. Meanwhile, realignments quivered under the flaccid skin of the traeki parent.

'Not to ... be concerned,' a somewhat altered voice burbled from the oration peak of the old stack of rings. 'i/we adjust ... reconfigure.'

Reassuring words, but everyone knows vlenning is a dangerous time for a traeki, when the unity of the former stack is challenged and sometimes fails. For that reason, most of them reproduce externally, growing new rings singly, in pens, or buying them from expert breeders, exchanging and swapping for the full set of traits they want in an offspring. Still, vlenning has advantages, I hear. Mister Heinz claims to have witnessed several, but I bet he never saw a four-tier bud emerge like this, already stacked and moving on its own!

This newly detached self may be addressed – for the time being – as *Ziz*. To that word-phrase it might answer, if engraved training patterns take hold. After performing its function with merit, it may then return for augmentation as a candidate for full life. Meanwhile, it is schooled ... to serve your quest, coming with traits you may require.'

'I don't know.' Ur-ronn's head swayed an oval of confusion. 'Do you mean—'

Huck muttered, 'Gybz, what are we supposed to—'

The traeki cut in.

'i/we no longer answer to that name. Our rings vote among ourselves now. Please do not speak or interfere.'

We fell silent, watching in awe as the creature literally wrestled with itself, *within* itself. A rippling seemed to rise from the base segment all the way up, terminating in a belch of yellow vapor. Waves flowed back and forth, crosswise as well as vertical. This went on for many duras, while we feared Gybz was about to tear erself apart.

Finally, the tremors lessened, then faded away. The traeki sensory organs refocused. Words bubbled from the puckered speech mouth, in a voice transformed.

'It is decided.

'Provisionally, you may call us/me *Tyug* and have good odds that this stack will answer.'

Another pulse of throbbing.

'That *i* will answer. Please inform Uriel that this thing is done. Furthermore, tell her that my/our major skill cores seem to be intact.'

Only then did I realize what had been at risk during the vlenning. The Master of Mixes is a vital member of Uriel's team. If Gybz – if *Tyug* – failed to remember all of its tricks of the trade, Mount Guenn alloys might not shine or cut as well, or decay so completely with the passage of time.

Foolish me. I'd been worried the whole time about the poor traeki's *life*.

Huphu slithered down my back and approached the new-formed traeki half-entity, which was already gathering an array of flipper-like feet under its bottommost segment, waving clumsy tentacles from its stubby top ring. The noor sniffed suspiciously, then settled back with a satisfied trill.

Thus Huphu was first to welcome Ziz – newest member of our band.

Now if only we had a human kid, we'd be a true six.

Omens can be good things, as any sailor knows. Luck is utter-gloss. *Fickle*, but a damn sight better than the alternative.

I had a feeling we were going to need all of Ifni's help we could get.

X

THE BOOK OF THE SLOPE

Legends

Among qheuens, it is said that fleeing to Jijo was not as much a matter of survival as of culture.

There is dispute among the legends that have been passed down by the armored ones, since their landing on Jijo over a thousand years ago. Grays, blues, and reds each tell their own versions of events before and after their sneakship came.

Where they agree is that it all began in Galaxy One, where the sept found itself in trouble with its own alliance.

According to our surviving copy of Basic Galactic Socio-Politics, by Smelt, most starfaring races are members of clans – a relationship based on the great chain of uplift. For example, Earthclan is among the smallest and simplest, consisting of humans and their two clients – neo-chimps and neo-dolphins. If the patrons who supposedly raised up *Homo sapiens* are ever found, it could link Earthlings to a vast 'family' stretching back ages, possibly even as far back as the Progenitors, who began the uplift cycle a billion years ago. With membership in such a clan, Earthlings might become much stronger. They might also become liable for countless ancient debts and obligations.

Another, quite separate network of allegiance seems to be based on philosophy. Many of the bitter feuds and ornate wars-of-honor dividing Galactic culture arose out of disputes no member of the Six can now recall or comprehend. Great alliances fought over arcane differences in theology, such as the nature of the long-vanished Progenitors.

It is said that when qheuens dwelled among the stars, they were members of the Awaiters Alliance – a fealty they inherited from their Zhosh patrons, who found and adopted primitive qheuens from sea-cliff hives, dominated by fierce gray queens.

Things might have been simpler had the Zhosh only uplifted the grays, but they gave the same expansion of wit and mind to the servant castes as well. Nor was this the end, for according to lore, the Awaiter philosophy is egalitarian and pragmatic. The alliance saw useful talents in the reds and blues. Rulings were made, insisting that the bonds of obeisance to the grays be loosened.

Certain qheuens *fled* this meddling, seeking a place to preserve their 'natural way' in peace.

That, in brief, is why they came here.

On Jijo, the three types disagree to this day over who first betrayed whom. Grays claim their colony began in harmony, discipline, and love. All went well until urs, and then humans, stirred up blue discontent. Other historians, such as River-Knife and Cuts-Coral, forcefully dissent from this view.

Whatever the cause, all agree that Jijo's qheuenish culture is now even more untraditional than the one their ancestors fled.

Such are the ironies when children ignore their parents' wishes and start thinking for themselves.

—*Collected Fables of Jijo's Seven,*
Third Edition. Department of Folklore and Language, Biblos.
Year 1867 of Exile.

Suddenly, their questions take a new turn. An edge of tension – not quite fear, but a cousin to that universal passion – abruptly colors the invaders' speech.

Then, in a single night, their apprehension takes hasty physical form.

They have buried their black station!

Do you recall the surprise, my rings? At dusk there it was, serene, arrogantly uncaring of the open sky. A cubic shape, blatant in its artificiality.

When we returned at dawn, a great heap of dirt lay there instead. From the size of the mound, Lester surmised the station must have scooped a hole, dropped itself inside, and piled the detritus on top, like a borer-beetle fleeing a digbat.

Lester's guess is proven right when Rann, Kunn, and Besh emerge from below, ascending a smooth, dark tunnel to resume discussions under the canopy-of-negotiation. This time they choose to focus on *machines*. Specifically – what devices remain from Buyur days? They want to know if ancient relics still throb with vital force.

This happens on some fallow worlds, they say. Sloppy races leave countless servant drones behind when they depart, laying their worlds down for an eon of rest. Near-perfect and self-repairing, the abandoned mechanisms can last a long time, wandering masterless across a terrain void of living voices.

They ask – have we seen any mechanical orphans?

We try to explain that the Buyur were meticulous. That their cities were dutifully scraped away, or crushed and seeded with deconstructors. Their machine servants were infected with meme-compulsions, driving those still mobile to seek nests in the deep trench we call the Midden. All this we believe, yet the sky-humans seem to doubt our word.

They ask (again!) about *visitations*. What clues have we seen of other ships coming stealthfully, for purposes vaguely hinted at but never said aloud?

As planned, we dissemble. In old human tales and books, it is a technique oft used by the weak when confronted by the strong.

Act stupid, the lore suggests. *Meanwhile, watch and listen closely*.

Ah, but how much longer can we get away with it? Already Besh questions those who come for healing. In their gratitude, some will surely forget our injunctions.

The next stage will start soon, while our preparations are barely begun.

The fourth human forayer, Ling, returns from her research trip. Did she not leave with the young heretic, Lark? Yet she comes back alone.

No, we tell her. *We have not seen him. He did not come this way. Can you tell us why he abandoned you? Why he left you in the forest, his assigned task undone?*

We promise her another guide. The qheuen naturalist, Uthen. Meanwhile, we placate.

If only our rewq had not abandoned us! When i/we ask Lester about the woman's mood – what he can read from her demeanor – he only shudders and says he cannot say.

SARA

A concert was arranged by an impromptu group of passengers and crew, on the fantail of the *Hauph-woa*, to welcome the Stranger back among the living.

Ulgor would play the violus, a stringed instrument based on the Earthling violin, modified to suit deft, urrish fingers. While Ulgor tuned, Blade squatted his blue-green carapace over a mirliton-drum, stroking its taut membrane with his massive, complex tongue, causing it to rumble and growl. Meanwhile, all five legs held jugs filled to varied levels with water. Tentative puffs from his speech vents blew notes across each opening.

Pzora, the traeki pharmacist, modestly renounced any claim to musical talent but agreed to take up some metal and ceramic chimes. The hoonish helmsman would sing, while the professional scriven-dancer honored the makeshift group by agreeing to accompany them in the g'Kek manner, with graceful motions of his eyestalks and those famous dancing arms, calling to mind the swaying of trees, or wind-driven rain, or birds in flight.

They had asked Sara to round out a six, but she declined. The only instrument she played was her father's piano, back in Nelo's house by the great dam, and even at that her proficiency was unremarkable. *So much for the supposed correlation between music and mathematics*, she thought ironically. Anyway, she wanted to keep an eye on the Stranger, in case events threw him into another hysterical fit. He seemed calm so far, watching through dark eyes that seemed pleasantly surprised by nearly everything.

Was this a symptom? Head injuries sometimes caused loss of memory – or even ability to *make* memories – so everything was forever new.

At least he can feel some joy, she thought. Take the way he beamed, every time she approached. It felt strange and sweet for someone to be so reliably happy to see her. Perhaps if she were prettier, it wouldn't be so befuddling. But the handsome dark outlander was a sick man, she recalled. Out of his proper mind.

And yet, she pondered further, *what is the past but a fiction, invented by a mind in order to go on functioning?* She had spent a year fleeing memory, for reasons that had seemed important then.

Now it just doesn't amount to much.

She worried about what was going on up in the Rimmers. Her brothers stayed close to her thoughts.

If you'd accepted Taine's original proposal of marriage, you might have had little ones by now, and their *future to fret about, as well.*

Refusing the august gray-headed sage had caused a stir. How many other offers would there be for the hand of a shy papermaker's daughter without much figure, a young woman with more passion for symbols on a page than dancing or the other arts of dalliance? Soon after turning Taine down, Joshu's attentions had seemed to ratify her decision, till she realized the young bookbinder might only be using her as a diversion during his journeyman year in Biblos, nothing more.

Ironic, isn't it? Lark could have his pick of young women on the Slope, yet his philosophy makes him choose celibacy. My conclusions about Jijo and the Six are the opposite to his. Yet I'm alone too.

Different highways, arriving at the same solitary dead end.

And now come gods from space, diverting us all onto a road whose markings we can't see.

They still lacked a sixth for the concert. Despite having introduced string instruments to Jijo, humans traditionally played flute in a mixed sextet. *Jop* was an adept, but the farmer declined, preferring to pore over his book of Scrolls. Finally, young Jomah agreed to sit in for luck, equipped with a pair of spoons.

So much for the vaunted contributions of Earthlings to musical life on Jijo.

Hidden under Blade's heavy shell, the mirliton groaned a low, rumbling note, soon joined by a mournful sigh from one of the jugs under Blade's left-front leg. The qheuen's seeing-band winked at

Ulgor, and the urs took her cue to lift the violus, laying the double bow across the strings, drawing twin wavering notes, embellishing the mirliton's basso moan. A multilevel chord was struck. It held ...

The moment of duet harmony seemed to stretch on and on. Sara stopped breathing, lest any other sound break the extraordinary consonance. Even Fakoon rolled forward, visibly moved.

If the rest is anything like this ...

Pzora chose the next instant to pile in, disrupting the aching sweetness with an eager clangor of bells and cymbals. The Dolo pharmacist seemed zealously unaware of what er had shattered, rushing ahead of the beat, halting, then pushing on again. After a stunned instant, members of the hoonish crew roared with laughter. Noor on the masts chittered as Ulgor and Blade shared looks that needed no rewq to interpret – equivalents to a shrug and a wink. They played on, incorporating Pzora's enthusiasm in a catchy four-part rhythm.

Sara recalled being taught piano by her mother, from music that was actually *written down*, now a nearly forgotten art. Jijoan sextets weaved their impromptu harmonies out of separate threads, merging and diverging through one congenial coincidence after another. *Human* music used to work that way in most pre-Contact cultures, before the Euro-West hit on symphonies and other more rigorous forms. Or so Sara had read.

Overcoming shyness, Jomah started rattling his spoons as Blade puffed a calliope of breathy notes. The hoonish helmsman inflated his air sac to answer the mirliton's rumble, singing an improvisation, without words in any known language.

Then Fakoon wheeled forward, arms swaying delicately, reminding Sara of gently rising smoke.

What had been exquisite, then humorous, soon took on a quality even more highly prized.

Unity.

She glanced at the Stranger, his face overcome with emotion, eyes delighting in Fakoon's opening moves. The left hand thumped his blanket happily, beating time.

You can tell what kind of man he used to be, she mused. *Even horribly mutilated, in awful pain, he spends his waking time enthralled by good things.*

The thought seemed to catch in her throat. Taken by surprise, Sara turned away, hiding a choking wave of sadness that abruptly blurred her vision.

Tarek Town appeared soon after, perched between the merging rivers Roney and Bibur.

From afar it seemed no more than a greenish knoll, like any other hill. Grayish shapes studded the mound, as if boulders lay strewn over the slopes. Then the *Hauph-woa* rounded one last oxbow turn, and what had seemed solid from a distance now spread open – a huge, nearly hollow erection of *webbing*, festooned with greenery. The 'boulders' were the protruding *tips* of massive towers, enmeshed in a maze of cables, conduits, rope bridges, netting, ramps, and sloping ladders, all draped under lush, flowing foliage.

The air filled with a humid redolence, the scent of countless flowers.

Sara liked to squint and imagine Tarek in other days, back when it was but a hamlet to the mighty Buyur, yet a place of true civilization, humming with faithful machines, vibrant to the footsteps of visitors from far star systems, thronging with sky-craft that settled gracefully on rooftop landing pads. A city lively with aspirations that she, a forest primitive, might never imagine.

But then, as the hoon crew poled the *Hauph-woa* toward a concealed dock, no amount of squinting could mask how far Tarek had fallen. Out of a multitude of windows, only a few still shone with million-year-old glazing. Others featured crude chimneys, staining once-smooth walls with the soot of cook fires. Wide ledges where floating aircraft once landed now supported miniature orchards or coops for noisy herd chicks. Instead of self-propelled machines, the streets swarmed with commerce carried on the backs of tinkers and traders, or animal-drawn carts.

High up a nearby tower, some young g'Kek sped around a railless ramp, heedless of the drop, their spokes blurry with speed. Urban life suited the wheeled sept. Rare elsewhere, g'Kek made up the town's largest group.

Northward, crossing Tarek's link to the mainland, lay a 'recent' ruin of stone blocks – the thousand-year-old city wall, erected by the Gray Queens who long ruled here, until a great siege ended their reign, back when the Dolo paper mill was new. Scorch marks still smeared the fallen bulwark, testimony to the violent birth of the Commons-of-Six.

However many times she passed through Tarek Town, it remained a marvel. Jijo's closest thing to a cosmopolitan place, where all races mixed as equals.

Along with hoon-crewed vessels, countless smaller boats skimmed under lacy, arching bridges, rowed by human trapper-traders, bringing hides and wares to market. River-traeki, with amphibious basal segments, churned along the narrow canals, much faster than their landbound cousins managed ashore.

Near the river confluence, a special port sheltered two hissing steam-ferries, linking forest freeholds on the north bank to southern grasslands where urrish hordes galloped. But on a sloping beach nearby, Sara saw some blue qheuens climb ashore, avoiding ferry tolls by *walking* across the river bottom, a talent useful long ago, when blue rebels toppled the Queens' tyranny – helped by an army of men, traeki, and hoon.

In all the tales about that battle, none credits the insurgents with a weapon I think crucial – that of language.

It took some time for the *Hauph-woa* to weave through a crowd of boats and tie up at a cramped wharf. The jammed harbor helped explain the lack of upstream traffic.

Soon as the moorings were tied, *Hauph-woa*'s contingent of noor squalled and blocked the gangways, demanding their pay. Rumbling a well-pleased umble song of gratitude, the ship's cook went down the row of black-furred creatures, handing out chunks of hard candy. Each noor tucked one sourball in its mouth and the rest into a waterproof pouch, then leaped over the rail to cavort away between bumping, swaying hulls, risking death by narrow margins.

As usual, the Stranger watched with a complex mixture of surprise, delight, and sadness in his eyes. He spurned a stretcher, and went down the ramp leaning on a cane, while Pzora puffed with pride, having delivered a patient from death's door to the expert healers of Tarek Town. While Prity went to hail a rickshaw, they observed the hoonish crew strain with block and tackle, lifting crates from the hold, many of them bound from Nelo's paper works for various printers, scribes, and scholars. In their place, stevedores gently lowered ribboned packages, all bound from Tarek for the same destination.

– Pottery shards and slag from urrish forges.

– Used-up ceramic saws from qheuenish woodcarving shops.

– Worn-out printers' type and broken violin strings.

– Whatever parts of the deceased that could not be counted on to rot away, such as the bones of cremated humans and urs, hoonish vertebrae, g'Kek axles, and traeki wax crystals. The glittering dust of ground-up qheuen carapaces.

– And always lots of ancient Buyur junk – it all wound up on dross boats, sent to the great Midden, to be cleansed by water, fire, and time.

An urrish rickshaw driver helped them usher the injured man onto her low four-wheeled cart, while Pzora stood behind, holding the Stranger's shoulders with two tendril-hands. 'You're sure you don't need me to come along?' Sara asked, having second thoughts.

Pzora waved her gently away. 'It is a short distance to the clinic, is it not? Have you not urgent matters to attend? Have i not our own tasks to perform? All-of-you shall meet all-of-us again, tonight. And our lucky patient will your fine selves perceive on the morrow.'

The Stranger's dark eyes caught hers, and he smiled, patting her hand. There was no sign of his former terror of the traeki.

I guess I was wrong about his injury. He does acquire memories. Maybe in Tarek we can find out who he is. If family or friends can be brought, they'll help him more than I ever could. That evoked a pang, but Sara reminded herself that she was no longer a child, tending a wounded chipwing. *What matters is that he's well cared for. Now Pzora's right. I've got other matters to attend.*

The anarchic style of Tarek Town meant there was no one 'official' at the dock to greet them. But merchants hurried to the quay, eager for their cargoes. Others came in search of news. There were rumors of horrible events up north and east. Of landings by frost-covered Zang ships, or whole towns leveled by titanic rays. Gossip told of a populace herded toward mass trials, conducted by insectoid judges from the Galactic Institute of Migration. One credulous human even argued with Jop, insisting the farmer was mistaken, since everyone knew Dolo Village was destroyed.

That explains why no boats came upstream, Sara thought. From Tarek, the intruder ship must have seemed to lay a streak of fire right over Sara's hometown.

Rumors were a chief stock in trade of all harbors, but surely cooler heads prevailed elsewhere?

Prity signaled that all of Nelo's crates were signed for, save the one she pulled on a wheeled dolly to be hand carried to Engril the Copier. Sara bade farewell to the other Dolo emissaries, agreeing to meet them again tonight and compare notes.

'Come, Jomah,' she told Henrik's son, who was staring at the bustle and tumult of city life. 'We'll take you to your uncle first.'

Voices seemed subdued in the harborside market; the haggling was sullen, perfunctory. Most buyers and sellers did not even wear rewq while dickering with members of other races – a sure sign they were only going through the motions.

One shopkeeper, an elegant gray qheuen with intricate, gold-fleck shell decorations, held up two claw-hands and counted nine jagged toepads, indicating by a slant of her cupola that it was her final offer. The trader, a rustic-looking red, hissed in dismay, gesturing at the fine salt crystals she had brought all the way from the distant sea. While passing, Sara overheard the city qheuen's reply.

'Quality or amount, what difference does it make? The price, why should you or I care?'

The answer shocked Sara. An urbane gray, indifferent over a commercial transaction? The locals must be in a state, all right.

As if we in Dolo were any better?

Townsfolk mostly gathered in small groups, gossiping in dialects of their own kind. Many of the hoons carried iron-shod canes – usually a perquisite of captains – while urrish tinkers, herders, and traders kept close to their precious pack beasts. Each urs carried an ax or machete sheathed at her withers, useful tools in the dry woods and plains where they dwelled.

So why did the sight make Sara feel edgy?

Come to think of it, many *humans* were behaving much the same, walking in close company, armed with tools suitable for chopping, digging, hunting – or uses Sara did not want to think about. The g'Kek populace kept to their apartments and studios.

I'd better find out what's going on, and soon, Sara thought.

It was a relief when the tense market zone ended at the glaring brightness of the Jumble.

Till now, they had walked in shade, but here an opening gaped under the shelter-canopy. Once towering structures lay in heaps, their neat geometries snapped, splintered and shoved together, giving the place its name. Scummy fluid shimmered between the shattered stones, where oily bubbles formed and popped, relics of a time when this place was caustic, poisonous, and ultimately restoring.

Jomah shaded his eyes. 'I don't see it,' he complained.

Sara resisted an impulse to pull him back out of the light. 'See what?'

'The *spider*. Isn't it s'pozed to be here, in the middle?'

'This spider's dead, Jomah. It died before it could do much more than get started. That's why Tarek Town isn't just another swamp full of chewed-up boulders, like we have east of Dolo.'

'I know *that*. But my father says it's still here.'

'It is,' she agreed. 'We've been passing beneath it ever since the boat docked. See all those cables overhead? Even the ramps and ladders are woven from old mulc-spider cords, many of them still living, after a fashion.'

'But where's the *spider*?'

'It was in the cables, Jomah.' She motioned toward the criss-crossing web, twining among the towers. 'United, they made a life form whose job was to demolish this old Buyur place. But then one day, before even the g'Kek came to Jijo, this particular spider got sick. The vines forgot to work together. When they went wild, the spider was no more.'

'Oh.' The boy pondered this awhile, then he turned around. 'Okay, well there's another thing I *know* is around here—'

'Jomah,' Sara began, not wanting to squelch the child, who seemed so much like Dwer at that age. 'We have to get—'

'I heard it's here near the Jumble. I want to see the horse.'

'The ho—' Sara blinked, then exhaled a sigh. 'Oh! Well, why not. If you promise we'll go straight to your uncle's, right after. Yes?'

The boy nodded vigorously, slinging his duffel again. Sara picked up her own bag, heavy with notes from her research. Prity wheeled the dolly behind.

Sara pointed. 'It's this way, near the entrance to Earthtown.'

Ever since the Gray Queens' menacing catapults were burned, Tarek Town had been open to all races. Still, each of the Six had a favored section of town, with humans holding the fashionable south quarter, due to wealth and prestige generated by the book trade. The three of them walked toward that district under a shaded loggia that surrounded the Jumble. The arching trellises bloomed with fragrant bowlflowers, but even that strong scent was overwhelmed as they passed the sector where urs traders kept their herds. Some unmated urrish youths loitered by the entrance. One lowered her head, offering a desultory snarl at Sara.

Suddenly, all the urs lifted their long necks in the same direction, their short, furry ears quivering toward a distant rumble that came rolling from the south. Sara's reflex thought was *thunder*. Then a shiver of concern coursed her spine as she turned to scan the sky.

Can it be happening again?

Jomah took her arm and shook his head. The boy listened to the growling echo with a look of professional interest. 'It's a test. I can tell. No muffling from confinement or mass loading. Some exploser is checking his charges.'

She muttered – 'How reassuring.' But only compared to the brief, fearsome thought of more god-ships tearing across the heavens.

The young urs were eyeing them again. Sara didn't like the look in their eyes.

'All right then, Jomah. Let's go see the horse.'

The Statuary Garden lay at the Jumble's southern end. Most of the 'art works' were lightly scored graffiti, or crude caricatures scratched on stone slabs during the long centuries when literacy was rare on the Slope. But some rock carvings were stunning in their abstract intricacy – such as a grouping of spherical balls, like clustered grapes, or a jagged sheaf of knifelike spears, jutting at pugnacious angles – all carved by the grinding teeth of old-time gray matriarchs who had lost dynastic struggles during the long qheuenish reign and were chained in place by victorious rivals, whiling away their last days under a blazing sun.

A sharply realistic bas-relief, from one of the earliest eras, lay etched on a nearby pillar. Slow subsidence into corrosive mud had eaten away most of the frieze. Still, in several spots one could make out *faces*. Huge bulging eyes stared acutely from globelike heads set on bodies that reared upward with supple forelegs raised, as if straining against the verdict of destiny. Even after such a long time, the eyes seemed somehow lit with keen intelligence. No one on Jijo had seen expressions of such subtlety or poignancy on a glaver's face for a very long time.

In recent years, Tarek's verdant canopy had been diverted over this part of the Jumble, putting most of the carvings under shade. Even so, orthodox zealots sometimes called for all the sculptures to be razed. But most citizens reasoned that Jijo already had the job in hand. The mulc-spider's ancient lake still dissolved rock, albeit slowly. These works would not outlive the Six themselves.

Or so we thought. It always seemed we had plenty of time.

'There it is!' Jomah pointed excitedly. The boy dashed toward a massive monument whose smooth flanks appeared dappled by filtered sunshine. *Humanity's Sacrifice* was its title, commemorating the one thing men and women had brought with them to Jijo that they esteemed above all else, even their precious books.

Something they renounced forever, as a price of peace.

The sculpted creature seemed poised in the act of bounding forward, its noble head raised, wind brushing its mane. One had but to squint and picture it in motion, as graceful in full gallop as it was powerful. Mentioned lovingly in countless ancient human tales, it was one of the great legendary wonders of old Earth. The memorial always moved Sara.

'It isn't like a donkey at all!' Jomah gushed. 'Were horses really that big?'

Sara hadn't believed it herself, till she looked it up. 'Yes, they got that big, sometimes. And don't exaggerate, Jomah. Of *course* it looks quite a bit like a donkey. They were cousins, after all.'

Yeah, and a garu tree is related to a grickle bush.

In a hushed voice Jomah asked, 'Can I climb up on top?'

'Don't speak of that!' Sara quickly looked around. No urrish faces were in sight, so she relented a little and shook her head. 'Ask your uncle. Maybe he'll take you down here at night.'

Jomah looked disappointed. 'I bet *you've* been up there, haven't you?'

Sara almost smiled. She and Dwer had indeed performed the

ritual when they were teens, late on a chill winter's eve, when most urs were snug among their wallow mates. No triple-eyes, then, to grow inflamed at a sight that so enraged them for the first century after Earthlings landed – that of humans being magnified by symbiosis with a great beast that could outrun any urs. Two creatures, amplified into something greater than either one alone.

They thought, after the second war, that it would put us down forever to demand all the horses, then wipe the species out.

I guess they learned different.

Sara shook off the bitter, unworthy thought. It all happened so long ago, before the Great Peace or the coming of the Egg. She glanced up past the stone figure and the flower-draped skeleton of the ancient Buyur town, toward a cloud-flecked sky. *They say when poison falls from heaven, its most deadly form will be suspicion.*

The Explosers Guild occupied a building whose formal name was Tower of Chemistry, but that most Tarekians called the Palace of Stinks. Tubes of treated boo climbed the spire's flank like parasitic vines, puffing and steaming so the place vaguely resembled Pzora after a hard day in the pharmacy. Indeed, after humans, traeki were most numerous among those passing through the front portal, or riding a counter-weighted lift to upper floors, where they helped make items coveted throughout the Slope – matches for lighting cook stoves, oils to treat qheuen shells against Itchyflake, soaps for cleaning human and hoon garments, lubricants to keep elderly g'Kek rolling after Dry-Axle set in – as well as paraffin for reading lamps, ink for writing, and many other products, all certified to leave no lasting trace in Jijo's soil. Nothing to worsen punishment when the inevitable Day of Days came.

Despite smells that made Prity chuff in disgust, Sara felt a lightening of her spirit inside the tower. All races mixed in the lobby, without any of the cliquishness she'd seen elsewhere in town. The hustle of commerce, with crisp murmurs in the language of science, showed some folk weren't letting the crisis drive them to gloom or hostility. There was just too much to do.

Three floors up, Explosers Hall seemed to boil with confusion. Men and boys shouted or hurried by, while guildswomen with clipboards told hoon helpers where to push barrels of ingredients. Off in a corner, gray-headed human elders bent over long tables, consulting with traeki colleagues whose hardworking secretion rings were adorned with beakers, collecting volatile drippings. What had seemed chaotic gradually resolved as Sara saw patterned order in the ferment.

This crisis may be confusing to others, but it's what explosers have spent all their lives thinking about. In this place, the mood would be fierce dedication. It was the first justification for optimism Sara had seen.

Jomah gave Sara a swift, efficient hug, then marched over to a man with a salt-and-pepper beard, poring over schematics. Sara recognized the paper, which Nelo made in special batches once a year, for painters and explosers.

A family resemblance went beyond features of face or posture, to the man's expression when he set eyes on Jomah. A lifted eyebrow was all Kurt the Exploser betrayed as Jomah placed a long leather tube in his calloused palm.

Is that all? I could have delivered it for Henrik myself. No need to send the boy on what might be a perilous mission.

If anyone knew about events up the Rimmer, it would be those in this room. But Sara held back. The explosers seemed busy. Besides, she had her own source of information, nearby. And it was time to go there.

Engril the Copier refilled cups of tea while Sara read a slim sheaf of pages – a chronology of events and conjectures that had arrived from the Glade of Gathering, by urrish galloper, this very morning. Sara's first emotion was a flood of relief. Till now, there had been no way of knowing which rampant rumor to believe. Now she knew the landing in the mountains had occurred without casualties. Those at Gathering were safe, including her brothers. For the time being.

In the next room, Engril's aides could be seen duplicating photostats of the report's pen-and-ink illustrations, while an offset press turned out printed versions of the text. Soon copies would reach notice boards in Tarek Town, then surrounding hives, hamlets, and herds.

'Criminals!' Sara sighed, putting down the first page. She couldn't believe it. 'Criminals from space. Of all the possibilities—'

'It always seemed the most far-fetched,' Engril agreed. She was a portly, red-headed woman, normally jovial and motherly but today more somber than Sara recalled. 'Perhaps it wasn't much discussed because we dared not think of the consequences.'

'But if they came illegally, isn't that better than Institute police putting us all under arrest? Crooks can't report us without admitting their own crime.'

Engril nodded. 'Unfortunately, that logic twists around the other way. Criminals cannot afford to let *us* report *them*.'

'How reasonable a fear is that? It's been several thousand years since the g'Kek came, and in all that time there's been just this one direct contact with Galactic culture. The ancients calculated a half-million-year gap before the next orbital survey, and *two* million before a major inspection.'

'That's not so very long.'

Sara blinked. 'I don't get it.'

The older woman lifted a steaming pot. 'More tea? Well, it's like this. Vubben suspects these are gene raiders. If true, the crime has no – what did the ancients call it? – no *sculpture of limitations*? No time limit for punishing perpetrators. Individuals from the foray party might be long dead, but not the species or Galactic clan they represent, which can still be sanctioned, from the eldest patron race down to the youngest client. Even a million years is short by the reckoning of the Great Library, whose memory spans a thousand times that long.'

'But the sages don't think we'll even be around in a million years! The ancestors' plan – the Scrolls—'

'Gene raiders can't count on that, Sara. It's too serious a felony.'

Sara shook her head. 'All right, let's say some distant descendants of the Six are still around by then, telling blurry legends about something that happened long ago. Who would believe their story?'

Engril lifted her shoulders. 'I can't say. Records show there are many jealous, even feuding, factions among the oxygen-breathing clans of the Five Galaxies. Perhaps all it would take is a hint, just a clue, to put rivals on the scent. Given such a hint they might sift the biosphere of Jijo for stronger proof. The entire crime could come unraveled.'

Silence fell as Sara pondered. In Galactic society, the greatest treasures were biological – especially those rare natural species rising now and then out of fallow worlds. Species with a spark called Potential. Potential to be *uplifted*. To be adopted by a patron race and given a boost – through teaching and genetic manipulation – crucial to cross the gap from mere clever beasts to starfaring citizens. Crucial, unless one believed Earthlings' legend of lonely transcendence. But who in all the Five Galaxies credited *that* nonsense?

Both wilderness and civilization had roles to play in the process by which intelligent life renewed itself. Neither could do it alone. The complex, draconian rules of migration – including forced abandonment of planets, systems, even whole galaxies – were meant to give biospheres time to recover and cultivate feral potential. New races were then apportioned for adoption, according to codes time-tested over eons.

The raiders hoped to bypass those codes. To find something precious here on Jijo, off limits and ahead of schedule. But then, even if they made a lucky strike, what could they do with their treasure?

Take some mated pairs far away from here, to some world the thieves already control, and seed the stock quietly, nudging them along with gene infusions so they fit into a natural-seeming niche. Then wait patiently for millennia, or much longer, till the time seems right to 'find' the treasure, right under their noses. Eureka!

'So you're saying,' she resumed, 'the raiders may not want to leave witnesses. But then why land here on the Slope? Why not beyond the Sunrise Desert, or even the small continent on the far side of Jijo, instead of barging in on us!'

Engril shook her head. 'Who can say? The forayers claim to want our expertise, and they say they're willing to pay for it. But we are the ones likely to pay in the end.'

Sara felt her heart thud. 'They – have to kill us all.'

'There may be less drastic answers. But that's the one that strikes the sages as most practical.'

'Practical!'

'From the raiders' point of view, of course.'

Sara absorbed this quietly. *To think, part of me looked forward to meeting Galactics, and maybe asking to peek at their portable libraries*.

Through the door to Engril's workshop, she glimpsed the copier's assistants hard at work. One girl piloted a *coelosat*, a big mirror on a long arm that followed the sun, casting a bright beam through the window onto whatever document was being duplicated. A moving slit scanned that reflected light across a turning drum of precious metal, cranked by two strong men, causing it to pick up carbon powder from a tray, pressing it on fresh pages, making photostatic duplicates of drawings, art works, designs – anything but typescript text, which was cheaper to reproduce on a printing press.

Since this technology came to Jijo, nothing so dire had ever been copied.

'This is awful news,' Sara murmured.

Engril agreed. 'Alas, child, it's not the worst. Not by far.' The old woman motioned toward the report. 'Read on.'

Hands trembling, Sara turned more sheets over. Her own memory of the starship was of a blurry tablet, hurtling overhead, shattering the peaceful life of Dolo Village. Now sketches showed the alien cylinder plain as day, even more fearsome standing still than it had seemed in motion. Measurements of its scale, prepared by engineering adepts using arcane means of triangulation, were hard to believe.

Then she turned another page and saw two of the plunderers themselves.

She stared, dismayed, at the portrayal.

'My God.'

Engril nodded. 'Indeed. Now you see why we delayed printing a new edition of the *Dispatch*. Already some hotheads among the qheuens and urs, and even a few traeki and hoon, have begun muttering about *human collusion*. There's even talk of breaking the Great Peace.

'Of course, it may never come to that. If the interlopers find what they seek soon enough, there may not be time for war to break out among the Six. We human exiles may get to prove our loyalty in the most decisive way – by dying alongside everyone else.'

Engril's bleak prospect made awful sense. But Sara looked at the older woman, shaking her head.

'You're wrong. That's *not* the worst thing.'

Engril looked back at her, puzzled. 'What could be worse than annihilation of every sapient being on the Slope?'

Sara lifted the sketch, showing a man and a woman, unmistakably human, caught unawares by a hidden artist as they looked down haughtily on Jijo's savages.

'Our lives mean nothing,' she said, tasting bitter words. 'We were doomed from the moment our ancestors planted their outlaw seed on this world. But these' – she shook the paper angrily – 'these fools are dabbling in an ancient game no human being could possibly know how to play well.

'They'll perform their theft, then slay us to erase all witnesses, only to get caught anyway.

'And when that happens, the real victim will be *Earth*.'

ASX

They have found the valley of the innocents.

We tried hard to conceal it, did we not, my rings? Sending them to a far-off vale – the glavers, lorniks, chimpanzees, and zookirs. And those children of our Six who came to Gathering with their parents, before the ship pierced our lives.

Alas, all efforts at concealment were unavailing. A robot from the black station followed their warm trail through the forest to a sanctuary that was not as secret as we hoped.

Among our sage company, Lester was the least surprised.

'They surely expected us to try hiding what we value most. They must have sought the deep-red heat spoor of our refugees, before it could dissipate.' His rueful smile conveyed regret but also respect. 'It's what I would have done, if I were them.'

Anglic is a strange language, in which the subjunctive form allows one to make suppositions about impossible might-have-beens. Thinking in that tongue, i (within my/our second ring-of-cognition) understood Lester's expression of grudging admiration, but then i found it hard to translate for my/our other selves.

No, our human sage is not contemplating betrayal.

Only through insightful empathy can he/we learn to understand the invaders.

Ah, but our foes learn about *us* much faster. Their robots flutter over the once-secret glen, recording, analyzing – then swooping to nip cell or fluid samples from frightened lorniks or chimps. Next, they want us to send individuals of each species for study, and seek to learn our spoken lore. Those g'Kek who know zookirs best, the humans who work with chimps, and those qheuens whose lorniks win medallions at festivals – these 'native experts' must come share their rustic expertise. Though the interlopers speak softly of paying well (with trinkets and beads?), there is also implied compulsion and threat.

Our rings quiver, surprised, when Lester expresses satisfaction.

'They must think they've uncovered our most valued secrets.'

'Have they not?' complains Knife-Bright Insight, snapping a claw. 'Are not our greatest treasures those who depend on us?'

Lester nods. 'True. But we could never have hidden them for long. Not when higher life-forms are the very thing the invaders desire. It's what they *expect* us to conceal.

'But now, if they are smug, even satiated for a while, we may distract them from learning about *other* things, possible advantages that offer us – and our dependants – a slim ray of hope.'

'How can that ve?' demanded Ur-Jah, grizzled and careworn, shaking her black-streaked mane. 'As you said – what can we conceal? They need only pose their foul questions, and those profane rovots gallop forth, piercing any secret to its hoof and heart.'

'Exactly,' Lester said. 'So the important thing is to keep them from asking the right questions.'

DWER

His first waking thought was that he must be buried alive. That he lay – alternately shivering and sweltering – in some forgotten sunless crypt. A place for the dying or the dead.

But then, he wondered muzzily, what stony place ever felt like this? So *sweaty*. Threaded by a regular, thudding rhythm that made the padded floor seem to tremble beneath him.

Still semi-incoherent – with eyelids stubbornly stuck closed – he recalled how some river hoons sang of an afterlife spent languishing within a narrow fetid space, listening endlessly to a tidal growl, the pulse-beat of the universe. That fate seemed all too plausible in Dwer's fading delirium, while he struggled to shake off the wrappers of sleep. It felt as if fiendish imps were poking away with sharp utensils, taking special pains with his fingers and toes.

As more roiling thoughts swam into focus, he realized the clammy warmth was *not* the rank breath of devils. It carried an aroma much more familiar.

So was the incessant vibration, though it seemed higher-pitched, more uneven than the throaty version he'd grown up with, resounding through each night's slumber, when he was a boy.

It's a water wheel. I'm inside a dam!

The chalky smell stung his sinuses with memory. *A qheuen dam.*

His rousing mind pictured a hive of twisty chambers, packed with spike-clawed, razor-tooth creatures, scrambling over each other's armored backs, separated by just one thin wall from a murky lake. In other words, he was in one of the safest, most heartening places he could ask.

But . . . how? The last thing I recall was lying naked in a snowstorm, halfway gone, with no help in sight.

Not that Dwer was astonished to be alive. *I've always been lucky,* he thought, though it dared fate to muse on it. Anyway, Ifni clearly wasn't finished with him quite yet, not when there were still more ways to lure him down trails of surprise and fate.

It took several tries to open his heavy, reluctant eyelids, and at first the chamber seemed a dim blur. Tardy tears washed and diffused the sole light – a flame-flicker coming from his left.

'Uh!' Dwer jerked back as a dark shape loomed. The shadow resolved into a stubby *face*, black eyes glittering, tongue lolling between keen white teeth. The rest of the creature reared into view, a lithe small form, black pelted, with agile brown paws.

'Oh . . . it's you,' Dwer sighed in a voice that tasted scratchy and stale. Sudden movements wakened flooding sensations, mostly unpleasant, swarming now from countless scratches, burns, and bruises, each yammering a tale of abuse and woe. He stared back at the grinning noor beast, amending an earlier thought.

I was always lucky, till I met you.

Gingerly, Dwer pushed back to sit up a bit and saw that he lay amid a pile of furs, spread across a sandy floor strewn with bits of bone and shell. That untidy clutter contrasted with the rest of the small chamber – beams, posts, and paneling, all gleaming in the wan light from a candle that flickered on a richly carved table. Each wooden surface bore the fine marks of qheuen tooth-work, all the way down to angle brackets sculpted in lacy, deceptively strong filigrees.

Dwer held up his hands. White bandages covered the fingers, too well wrapped to be qheuen work. He felt hesitant relief on counting to ten and gauging their length to be roughly unchanged – though he knew sometimes frostbite stole the tips even when doctors saved the rest. He quashed an urge to tear the dressings with his teeth and find out right away.

Patience. Noting you do now will change what's happened. Stabbing pins-and-needles told him that he was alive and his body was struggling to heal. It made the pain easier to handle.

Dwer kicked aside more furs to see his feet – which were still there, thank the Egg, though his toes also lay under white wrappings. *If* there were still any toes down there. Old Fallon had gone on hunting for many years, wearing special shoes, after one close call on the ice turned his feet into featureless stumps. Still, Dwer bit his lip and concentrated, sending signals, meeting resistance, nevertheless *commanding* movement. Tingling pangs answered his efforts, making him wince and hiss, but he kept at it till both legs threatened cramps. At last, he sagged back, satisfied. He could wriggle the critical toes, the smallest and largest on each foot. They might be damaged, but he would walk or run normally.

Relief was like a jolt of strong liquor that went to his head. He even laughed aloud – four short, sharp barks that made Mudfoot stare. 'So, do I owe you my life? Did you dash back to the Glade, yapping for help?' he crooned.

For once, Mudfoot seemed set aback, as if the noor knew it was being mocked.

Aw, cut it out, Dwer told himself. *For all you know, it might even be true*.

Most of his other hurts were the sort he had survived many times before. Several were sewn shut with needle and thread, crossstitched by a fine, meticulous hand. Dwer stared at the seam-work, abruptly recognizing it from past experience. He laughed again, knowing his rescuer from tracks laid across his own body.

Lark. How in the world did he know?

Clearly, his brother had managed to find the shivering group amid the snowdrifts, dragging him all the way to one of the qheuen freeholds of the upper hills. *And if I made it, Rety surely did. She's young and would chew off Death's arm, if He ever came for her*.

Dwer puzzled for a while over blotchy, pale stains on his arms and hands. Then he recalled. *The mulc-spider's golden fluid – some-one must have peeled it off, where it stuck*.

Those places still felt strange. Not exactly *numb* so much as *pre-served* – somehow offset in time. Dwer had a bizarre inkling that bits of his flesh were *younger* now than they had been before. Perhaps those patches would even outlive his body for a while, after the rest of him died.

But not yet, One-of-a-Kind, he mused.

It's the mulc-spider who's gone. Never got to finish her collection.

He recalled flames, explosions. *I better make sure Rety and the glaver are all right.*

'I don't guess you'd run and fetch my brother for me, would you?' he asked the noor, who just stared back at him.

With a sigh, Dwer draped a fur over his shoulders, then gin-gerly pushed up to his knees, overruling waves of agony. Lark would resent him popping any of those fine stitches, so he took it easy, standing with one hand pressed against the nearest wall. When the dizziness passed, he shuffled on his heels to the ornate table, retrieving the candle in its clay holder. The doorway came next, a low, broad opening covered by a curtain of hanging wooden slats. He had to stoop, pushing through the qheuen-shaped portal.

A pitch-black tunnel slanted left and right. He chose the leftward shaft, since it angled upward a bit. Of course, blue qheuens built their submerged homes to a logic all their own. Dwer used to get lost even in familiar Dolo Dam, playing hide-and-seek with Blade's creche-mates.

It was painful and awkward keeping most of his weight gingerly on the heels. Soon he regretted the stubborn impulse that sent him wandering like this, away from his convalescent bed. But a few duras later, his stubbornness was rewarded by sounds of anxious conversation, echoing from somewhere ahead. Two speakers were clearly human – male and female – while a third was qheuen. None were Lark or Rety, though mumbled snatches rang familiar. And *tense*. Dwer's hunter-sensitivity to strong feelings tingled like his frostbitten fingers and toes.

'. . . our peoples are natural allies. Always have been. Recall how our ancestors helped yours throw off the tyranny of the grays?'

'As my folk succored *yours* when urrish packs stalked humans everywhere outside Biblos Fortress? Back when our burrows shel-tered your harried farmers and their families, till your numbers grew large enough to let you fight back?'

The second voice, aspirated from two or more leg-vents, came from a qheuen matron, Dwer could tell. Probably lord of this snug mountain dam. He didn't like the snatches of conversation he had heard so far. He blew out the candle, shuffling toward the soft glow of a doorway up ahead.

'Is that what you are asking of me now?' the matriarch went on, speaking with a different set of vents. The timbre of her Anglic accent changed. 'If refuge is your need against this frightful storm, then I and my sisters offer it. Five fives of human settlers, our neighbors and friends, may bring their babes and chimps and smaller beasts. I am sure other lake-mothers in these hills will do the same. We'll protect them here until your criminal cousins depart, or till they blast this house to splinters with their almighty power, setting the lake waters boiling to steam.'

The words were so unexpected, so free of any context in Dwer's foggy brain, that he could not compass them.

The male human grunted. 'And if we ask for more?'

'For our *sons*, you mean? For their rash courage and spiky claws? For their armored shells, so tough and yet so like soft cheese when sliced by Buyur steel?' The qheuen mother's hiss was like that of a bubbling kettle. Dwer counted five overlapping notes, all vents working at once.

'That *is* more,' she commented after a pause. 'That is very much more indeed. And knives of Buyur steel are like whips of soft boo, compared to the new things we all fear.'

Dwer stepped around the corner, where several lanterns bathed the faces of those he had been listening to. He shielded his eyes as two humans stood – a dark stern-looking man in his mid-forties and a stocky woman ten years younger, with light-colored hair severely tied back from a broad forehead. The qheuen matron rocked briefly, lifting two legs to expose flashes of claw.

'What new things do you fear, revered mother?' Dwer asked hoarsely. Turning to the humans, he went on. 'Where are Lark and Rety?' He blinked. 'And there . . . was a glaver, too.'

'All are well. All have departed for the Glade, bearing vital information,' the qheuen whistle-spoke. 'Meanwhile, until you recover, you honor this lake as our guest. I am known as Tooth-Slice Shavings.' She lowered her carapace to scrape the floor.

'Dwer Koolhan,' he answered, trying awkwardly to bow with arms crossed over his chest.

'Are you all right, Dwer?' the man asked, reaching toward him. 'You shouldn't be up and about.'

'I'd say that's up to Captain Koolhan himself,' the woman commented. 'There's much to discuss, if he's ready.'

Dwer peered at them.

Danel Ozawa and . . . Lena Strong.

He knew her. They had been scheduled to meet at Gathering, in fact. Something having to do with that stupid *tourism* idea.

Dwer shook his head. She had used a word, strange and dire-sounding.

Captain.

'The militia's been called up,' he reasoned, angry with his mind for moving so slowly.

Danel Ozawa nodded. As chief forester for the Central Range, he was nominally Dwer's boss, though Dwer hardly saw him except at Gatherings. Ozawa was a man of imposing intellect, a deputy sage, sanctioned to make rulings on matters of law and tradition. As for Lena Strong, the blond woman was aptly named. She had been a crofter's wife until a tree fell – accidentally, she claimed – on her shiftless husband, whereupon she left her home village to become one of the top lumberjack-sawyers on the river.

'Highest-level alert,' Ozawa confirmed. 'All companies activated.'

'What … *all*? Just to collect a little band of *sooners*?'

Lena shook her head. 'The girl's family beyond the Rimmers? This goes far beyond that.'

'Then—'

Memory assailed Dwer. The blurry image of a hovering monster, firing bolts of flame. He croaked, 'The flying machine.'

'That's right.' Danel nodded. 'The one you encountered—'

'Lemme guess. Some hotheads dug up a *cache*.'

Dreamers and ne'er-do-wells were always chasing rumors of a fabled hoard. Not rubble but a sealed trove buried on *purpose* by departing Buyur. Dwer often had to round up searchers who strayed too far. What if some angry young urs actually found an ancient god-weapon? Might they test it first on two isolated humans, trapped in a mulc-spider maze, before going on to settle larger grudges?

Lena Strong laughed out loud.

'Oh, he's a wonder, Danel. What a theory. If only it were true!'

Dwer lifted a hand to his head. The vibration of the water wheel seemed labored, uneven. 'Well? What *is* true?' he demanded testily, then stared at the expression on Ozawa's face. The older man answered with a brief eye-flick heavenward.

'No,' Dwer whispered.

He felt strangely remote, detached.

'Well then iz all over, an' I'm out of a job – no?'

The two humans grabbed his arms as he let go of the thing that had kept him going until now, the force that had dragged him upward out of unconsciousness in the first place: duty.

Galactics. Here on the Slope, he thought as they bore his weight back down the hall. *So it's come at last. Judgment Day.*

There was nothing more to do. No way he could make any difference at all.

Apparently, the sages didn't agree. They thought fate might yet be diverted, or at least modified somehow.

Lester Cambel and his aides are making plans, Dwer realized the next morning as he met the two humans again, this time by the shore of the forest-shrouded mountain lake. Even the dam wore trees, softening its graceful outline, helping root the structure firmly to the landscape. Stretched out on an elegant wooden bench, Dwer sipped a cool drink from a goblet of urrish glass as he faced the two envoys who had been sent all the way to see him.

Clearly the leaders of Earthling-Sept were playing a complex, multilayer game – balancing species self-interest against the good of the Commons as a whole. Bluff, open-faced Lena Strong seemed untroubled by this ambivalence, but not Danel Ozawa, who explained to Dwer the varied reactions of other races to the invaders being human.

I wish Lark had stayed. He could have made sense of all this. Dwer's mind still felt woozy, even after a night's restoring sleep.

'I still don't get it. What are *human* adventurers doing out here in Galaxy Two? I thought Earthlings were crude, ignorant trash, even in their own little part of Galaxy Four!'

'Why are *we* here, Dwer?' Ozawa replied. 'Our ancestors came to Jijo just decades after acquiring star drive.'

Dwer shrugged. 'They were selfish bastards. Willing to endanger the whole race just to find a place to breed.'

Lena sniffed, but Dwer kept his chin raised. 'Nothing else makes sense.'

Our ancestors were self-centered scoundrels – Lark had put it one day.

'You don't believe the stories of persecution and flight?' Lena asked. 'The need to hide or die?'

Dwer shrugged.

'What of the g'Keks?' Ozawa asked. 'Their ancestors claimed persecution. Now we learn their race *was* murdered by the Inheritors' Alliance. Does it take genocide to make the excuse valid?'

Dwer looked away. None of the g'Keks *he* knew had died. Should he mourn millions who were slaughtered long ago and far away?

'Why ask me?' he murmured irritably. 'Can anything I do make a difference?'

'That depends.' Danel leaned forward. 'Your brother is brilliant but a heretic. Do you share his beliefs? Do *you* think this world would be better off without us? *Should* we die out, Dwer?'

He saw they were testing him. As a top hunter, he'd be valuable to the militia – if he could be trusted. Dwer sensed their eyes, watching, weighing.

Without doubt, Lark was a deeper, wiser man than anyone Dwer knew. His arguments made sense when he spoke passionately of higher values than mere animal reproduction – certainly more sense than *Sara's* weird brand of math-based, what-if optimism. Dwer knew firsthand about species going extinct – the loss of something beautiful that would never be recovered.

Maybe Jijo *would* be better off resting undisturbed, according to plan.

Still, Dwer knew his own heart. He would marry someday, if he found the right partner, and he would sire as many kids as his wife and the sages allowed, drinking like a heady wine the love they gave, in return for his devotion.

'I'll fight, if that's what you're askin',' he said in a low voice, perhaps ashamed to admit it. 'If that's what it takes to survive.'

Lena grunted with a curt, satisfied nod. Danel let out a soft sigh.

'Fighting may not be necessary. Your militia duties will be taken up by others.'

Dwer sat up. 'Because of this?' He motioned toward the bandages on his feet and left hand. Those on the right were already off, revealing that the middle finger was no longer the longest, a disconcerting but non-crippling amputation, healing under a crust of traeki paste.

'I'll be up and around soon, good as ever.'

'Indeed, I am counting on it.' Ozawa nodded. 'We need you for something rather arduous. And before I explain, you must swear never to inform another soul, *especially* your brother.'

Dwer stared at the man. If it were anyone else, he might have laughed scornfully. But he trusted Ozawa. And much as Dwer loved and admired his brother, Lark was without any doubt a heretic.

'It's for the good?' he asked.

'I believe so,' the older man said, in apparent sincerity.

Dwer sighed unhappily. 'All right then. Let's hear what you have in mind.'

ASX

The aliens demanded to see chimpanzees, then marveled over those we brought before them, as if they had never seen the like before.

'Your chimps do not speak! Why is that?'

Lester proclaims mystification. Chimpanzees are capable of sign language, of course. But have other traits been added since the *Tabernacle* fled to Jijo?

The invaders seem unimpressed with Lester's demurral, and so are some of our fellow Sixers. For the first time, i/we sense something hidden, deceitful, in the manner of my/our human colleague. He knows more than he tells. But our skittish rewq balk at revealing more.

Nor is this our sole such worry. Qheuens refuse to speak further regarding lorniks. Our g'Kek cousins reel from the news that they are the last of their kind. And all of us are appalled to witness alien robots returning to base laden with gassed, sleeping *glavers*, kidnapped from faraway herds for analysis under those once-gay pavilions we lent our guests.

'Is *this* the return of innocence, promised in the Scrolls?' Ur-Jah asks, doubt dripping like fumes from her lowered snout. 'How could a blessing arise out of base crime?'

If only we could *ask* the glavers. Is this what they wanted, when they chose the Path of Redemption?

LARK

'Well, look who it is. I'm surprised you have the nerve to show your face around here.'

The forayer woman's grin seemed at once both sly and teasing. She peeled off elastic gloves, turning from a glaver on a lab bench with wires in its scalp. There were several of the big trestle tables, where human, g'Kek, and urrish workers bent under cool, bright lamps, performing rote tasks they had been taught, helping their employers test animals sampled from sundry Jijoan ecosystems.

Lark had dropped his backpack by the entrance. Now he picked it up again. 'I'll go if you want.'

'No, no. Please stay.' Ling waved him into the laboratory shelter, which had been moved to a shielded forest site the very night Lark last saw the beautiful intruder, the same evening the black station buried itself under a fountain of piled dirt and broken vegetation. The basis for both actions was still obscure, but Lark's superiors now thought it must have to do with the violent destruction of one of the interlopers' robots. An event his brother must have witnessed at close hand.

Then there was the testimony of Rety, the girl from over the mountains, supported by her treasure, a strange metal machine, once shaped like a Jijoan bird. Was it a Buyur remnant, as some supposed? If so, why should such a small item perturb the mighty forayers? Unless it was like the tip of a red qheuen's shell, innocuous at first sight, poking over a sand dune, part of much more than it seemed? The 'bird' now lay in a cave, headless and mute, but Rety swore it used to move.

Lark had been ordered back down to the Glade before his brother could confirm the story. He knew he shouldn't worry. Danel Ozawa was qualified to tend Dwer's wounds. Still, he deeply resented the recall order.

'Will you be needing me for another expedition?' he asked Ling.

'After you abandoned me the last time? We found human tracks when we finally got to where our robot went down. Is that where you rushed off to? Funny how you knew which way to go.'

He shouldered his pack. 'Well, if you don't need me, then—'

She swept a hand before her face. 'Oh, never mind. Let's move on. There's plenty of work, if you want it.'

Lark glanced dubiously at the lab tables. Of Jijo's Six, all three of the races with good hand-eye coordination were employed. Outside, hoons and qheuens also labored at the behest of aliens whose merest trinkets meant unimaginable wealth to primitive savages. Only traeki were unseen among the speckled tents, since the ringed ones seemed to make the raiders nervous.

Sepoy labor. That was the contemptuous expression Lena Strong had used when she brought Lark new orders at Tooth-Slice Shavings' Dam. An old Earth term, referring to aborigines toiling for mighty visitors, paid in beads.

'Oh, don't look so sour.' Ling laughed. 'It *would* serve you right if I put you to work staining nerve tissue, or shoveling the longsnout pens ... No, stop.' She grabbed Lark's arm. All signs of mockery vanished. 'I'm sorry. There really *are* things I want to discuss with you.'

'Uthen is here.' He pointed to the far end of the tent, where his fellow biologist, a large male qheuen with a slate gray carapace, held conference with Rann, one of the two male forayers, a tall massive man in a tight-fitting uniform.

'Uthen knows incredible detail about how different species relate to each other,' Ling agreed with a nod. 'That's not easy on a planet that has had infusions of outsider species every twenty million years or so, for eons. Your lore is impressive, given your limitations.'

Had she any idea how far Jijoan 'lore' really went? So far, the sages had not released his detailed charts, and Uthen must be dragging all five feet, cooperating just enough to stay indispensable. Yet the aliens seemed easily impressed by sketchy glimmers of local acumen, which only showed how insultingly low their expectations were.

'Thanks,' Lark muttered. 'Thanks a lot.'

Ling sighed, briefly averting her dark eyes. 'Crampers, can't I say *anything* right, today? I don't mean to offend. It's just ... look, how about we try starting from scratch, all right?' She held out a hand.

Lark looked at it. What was he expected to do now?

She reached out with her left hand to take his right wrist. Then *her* right hand clasped *his*.

'It's called a handshake. We use it to signify respect, amicable greeting, or agreement.'

Lark blinked. Her grip was warm, firm, slightly moist.

'Oh, yes ... I've rea – heard of it.'

He tried to respond when she squeezed, but it felt so strange, and vaguely *erotic*, that Lark let go sooner than she seemed to expect. His face felt warm.

'Is it a common gesture?'

'Very common, I hear. On Earth.'

You hear? Lark leaped on the passing phrase and knew it had begun again – their game of hints and revelations, mutual scrutiny of clues and things left unsaid.

'I can see why we gave it up, on Jijo,' he commented. 'The urs would hate it; their hands are more personal than their genitals. Hoons and qheuens would crush our hands and we'd squash the tendrils of any g'Kek who tried it.' His fingers still felt tingly. He resisted an urge to look them over. Definitely time to change the subject.

'So,' Lark said, trying for a businesslike tone of equality, 'you've never been to Earth?'

One eyebrow raised. Then she laughed. 'Oh, I knew we couldn't hire *you* for just a handful of biodegradable toys. Don't worry, Lark; you'll be paid in answers – *some* answers – at the end of each day. After you've earned them.'

Lark sighed, although in fact the arrangement did not sound unsatisfactory.

'Very well, then. Why don't you tell me what it is you want to know.'

ASX

Each day we strive to mediate stress among our factions, from those urging cooperation with our uninvited guests, to others seeking means to destroy them. Even my/our subselves war over these options. Making peace with felons, or fighting the unfightable. Damnation or extinction.

And still our guests question us about *other visitors*! Have we seen other outsiders lately, dropping from the sky? Are there Buyur sites we have not told them about? Sites where ancient mechanisms lurk, alert, still prone to vigorous action?

Why this persistence? Surely they can tell we are not lying – that we know nothing more than we have told.

Or is that true, my rings? Have all Six shared equally with the Commons, or are some withholding vital information, needed by all?

That i should think such a thing is but another measure of how far we are fallen, we unworthy, despicable sooners. We, who surely have farther yet to fall.

RETY

Under a smaller, shabbier tent, in a dense grove some secret distance from the research station, Rety threw herself onto a reed mat, pounding it with both fists.

'Stinkers. Rotten guts an' rancy meat. Rotten, rotten, *rotten*!'

She had good reason to thrash in outrage and self-pity. That liar, Dwer, had told her the sages were good and wise. But they turned out to be horrid!

Oh, not at the beginning. At *first*, her hopes had shot up like the geysers back home in the steaming Gray Hills. Lester Cambel and the others seemed *so* kind, easing her dread over being punished for her grandparents' crime of sneaking east, over the forbidden mountains. Even before questioning her, they had doctors tend her scrapes and burns. It never occurred to Rety to fear the unfamiliar g'Kek and traeki medics who dissolved away drops of clinging mulc-fluid, then used foam to drive off the parasites that had infected her scalp for as long as she could remember. She even found it in her to forgive them when they dashed her hopes of a cure for the scars on her face. Apparently, there was a limit even to what Slopies could accomplish.

From the moment she and Lark strode into the Glade of Gathering, everyone seemed awfully excited and distracted. At first Rety thought it was because of her, but it soon grew clear that the real cause was visitors from the sky!

No matter. It still felt like coming home. Like being welcomed into the embrace of a family far bigger and sweeter than the dirty little band she had known for fourteen awful years.

At least it felt that way for a while.

Till the betrayal.

Till the sages called her once again to their pavilion and told her their decision.

'It's all Dwer's fault,' she muttered later, nursing hot resentment. 'Him an' his rotten brother. If only I could've snuck in over the mountains without being seen. No one would've noticed me in all this ruckus.' Rety had no clear notion what she would have done after that. The oldsters back home had been murky in their handed-down tales about the Slope. Perhaps she could make herself useful to some remote village as a trapper. Not for food – Slopies had plenty of that – but for soft furs that'd keep townfolk from asking too closely where she came from.

Back in the Gray Hills, such dreams used to help her pass each grinding day. Still, she might never have found the guts to flee her muddy clan but for the beautiful bright bird.

And now the sages had taken it away from her!

'We are grateful for your part in bringing this enigmatic wonder to us,' Lester Cambel said less than an hour ago, with the winged thing spread on a table before him. 'Meanwhile though, something terribly urgent has come up. I hope you'll understand, Rety, why it's become so necessary for you to go back.'

Back? At first, she could not bring herself to understand. She puzzled while he gabbed on and on.

Back?

Back to Jass and Bom and their strutting ways? To the endless bullying of those *big, strong hunters*? Always boasting around the campfire about petty, vicious triumphs that grew more exaggerated with each telling? To those wicked oafs who used fire-tipped sticks to punish anyone who dared to talk back to them?

Back to where mothers watched half their babies waste away and die? To where that hardly mattered, because new babies kept on coming, coming and coming, till you dried up and died of old age before you were forty? Back to all that hunger and dirt?

The human sage had muttered words and phrases that were supposed to sound soothing and noble and logical. But Rety had stopped listening.

They meant to send her back to the tribe!

Oh, it might be fine to see Jass's face when she strode into camp, clothed and equipped with all the wonders the Six could offer. But then where would she be? Condemned once more to that awful life.

I won't go back. I won't!

With that resolution, Rety rolled over, wiped her eyes, and considered what to do.

She could try running away, taking shelter elsewhere. Rumors told that all was not in perfect harmony among the Six. So far, she had obeyed Cambel's request not to blab the story of her origins. But Rety wondered – might some urrish or qheuen faction pay for the information? Or invite her to live among them?

It's said the urs sometimes let a chosen human ride upon their backs, when the human's light enough, and worthy.

Rety tried to picture life among the galloping clans, roaming bold and free across the open plains with wind blowing through her hair.

Or what about going to sea with hoons? There were islands nobody had ever set foot on, and flying fish, and floating mountains made of ice. What an adventure *that* would be! Then there were the traeki of the swamps . . .

A new thought abruptly occurred to her. *Another* option that suddenly appeared to lie open. One so amazing to contemplate that she just lay there silently for several duras, hands unclenching at last from their tightly clutched fists. Finally, she sat up, pondering with growing excitement a possibility beyond any other ambition she had ever conceived.

The more she thought about it, the better it began to seem.

XI

THE BOOK OF THE SEA

Animals think nothing of race, clan, or philosophy.
Nor of beauty, ethics, or investment
in things that will long outlast their lives.
All that matters to beasts is the moment.
All that counts is self.

Mates/offspring/siblings, and hive-consorts,
All these offer continuity of self.
To even a loving beast, altruism has deep roots,
founded in self-interest.

Sapient beings are not beasts.
Loyalty binds even the innately egotistic
to things nobler, more abstract,
than mere continuity, or self.
To race, clan, or philosophy.
To beauty, ethics, or investment
in fruits you and I will never harvest.

If you seek the downward trail, the long
road to redemption —
If you want a second chance, shriven of your
grief and worry —
Seek that path by returning to the soil,
In forgetfulness of race, clan, or philosophy.

Yet beware! Lest the road take you too far.

Keep faith in something greater than you are.

Beware resumed obsession with the self.

To those who have tasted vacuum and Stardust,
that way lies damnation.

—*The Scroll of Redemption*

The others are asleep now. It's late, but I want to get all this down, 'cause things are about to get busy and I don't know when I'll have another chance.

Tomorrow we head back down the mountain, loaded with all kinds of gear lent to us by Uriel the Smith – so much good stuff that we're feeling pretty dumb right now about our former plans.

To think, we were willing to trust our lives to some of the junk *we* designed!

Uriel already sent messages to our parents, calligraphed on heavy cloth paper and sealed with her signet as a sage of the Commons. So there's not much Huck's folks or mine can do to stop us.

Not that I looked forward to facing them, anyway. What would I say? *'Hey, Pop. It'll be just like Twenty Thousand Leagues Under the Sea! Remember how often you read it to me, when I was little?'*

I recall now how that tale ended for Captain Nemo's submarine crew, and I can see why Yowg-wayuo regrets what a humicker I've become. If my father confronts me over this, I'll discuss it in a language other than Anglic, to show that I really have thought it out several ways. This trip is more than a passing kid-obsession but something meaningful for our village and our race. Me and the others are going to make history. It's important for a hoon to be involved, from notion to motion to recollection.

Once she decided, Uriel really got things rolling. Pincer-Tip headed out the very same evening after Ziz was vlenned, taking the newly budded traeki to his home hive for water-adapting in the tidepools south of Wuphon. Pincer will also use the smith's authority to hire some red-shelled cousins to haul the bathy's wooden hull to a meeting point down near the Rift. The rest of us will come overland with supply wagons.

Test dives start in just five days!

The choice of a site was vital. There's just one place where the Midden's deep watery trench plunges like a scythe blade toward the coast. Where it sends a deep rupture of jagged canyons passing right next to Terminus Rock. By deploying a boom from an overhanging ledge, we won't even need to hire a ship.

It's a relief to have a decision made at last. Even Huck admits the die is cast, accepting destiny with a shrugged rubbing of two eyestalks.

'At least we'll be right there at the border, where I want to be anyway. When we finish, Uriel will owe us. She'll *have* to write us a warrant to go over the line and visit some Buyur ruins.'

There's an Anglic word – *tenacity* – that comes out as *stubbornness* when I translate into GalSix. Which is one more reason why human speech best describes my pal Huck.

All of us, even Ur-ronn, are more than a little surprised by how Uriel is throwing resources at our 'little adventure' all of a sudden. We talked about the smith's outbreak of helpfulness during our last evening on Mount Guenn, after a long day spent packing crates and going over inventory lists, waiting for the factory complex to settle down for the night.

'It nust have to do with the *starshifs*,' Ur-ronn said, lifting her muzzle from the straw of her sleeping pallet.

Huck turned two stalks toward Ur-ronn – leaving just one buried in her well-thumbed copy of *Lord Valentine's Castle*. She groaned. 'Not that again! What in the world could *our* dumbass little diving trip have to do with Galactic cruisers coming to Jijo? Don't you think Uriel would have more important things on her mind?'

'Vut Gyfz said, a week ago—'

'Why not just admit you overheard Gybz wrong? We asked er again today, and that traeki doesn't recall seeing any spaceships.'

'Not *that* traeki,' I corrected. 'We never had a chance to ask *Gybz* anything, before the vlenning. It's *Tyug* who said er doesn't remember.'

'Tyug, Gybz. The difference can't be that great. Not even a vlenned traeki would forget something like that!'

I wasn't so sure about that. Traeki memory wax can be tricky stuff, I hear.

Then again, I'm hardly ever as sure of *anything* as Huck is of *everything*.

Of course, there was one other person we could ask, but in the course of stowing gear and going over plans, I guess the fiery old smith dazzled us out of bringing the subject up. *Intimidated* may be a better word, though I'm not sure, since I'm writing this by candlelight without my handy dictionary. All during the last few days, Uriel galloped from her normal duties, to talks with her human guest, to tending her precious hall of disks, to flooding us with more details we never thought of during all our long months planning an undersea adventure – a voyage none of us ever *really* expected to come true. In all the rushing about, there never seemed time to raise other questions. Or else Uriel made it plain that some things weren't any of our business.

At one point I did try to ask about all the changes she had made in our plan.

'We always figured on starting by exploring the shallows near home. Then redesign and refit before trying deeper water from a boat. Maybe going down ten or twenty cords. Now you're talking about doing *thirty*, right from the start!'

'Thirty cords is not so very nuch,' Uriel dismissed with a snort. 'Oh, I agree that your old air circulators wouldn't have veen uf to it. That's why I reflaced the systen with a suferior one we had on hand. Also, your gaskets would have leaked. As for the hull itself, your design will do.'

I couldn't help wondering – where did all the equipment come from? We hadn't figured on needing a gas pressure regulator, for instance. Good thing Uriel pointed out the mistake and happened to have a beautiful handmade one in stock. But *why* did she already have one? Why would even the Smith of Guenn Volcano need such a thing?

Huck admitted, it wasn't hurting our chances to have Uriel's competence behind us. Yet I worried. An air of mystery shrouded the enterprise.

'All will ve nade clear when you get to the Rock, and everything is ready to go. I'll check the gear out nyself, then I'll exflain what *you* can do for *ne*.'

Barring day trips to Wuphon, Uriel hardly ever left her forge. Now she wanted to take two *weeks* off, adventuring with us? Never in my life has a single piece of news struck me the way that one did – at once both reassuring and terrifying. Perhaps my nick-namesake felt the same way when, exploring the deep catacombs under Diaspar, he found something unimaginable, a mystery tunnel leading all the way to faraway Lys.

So there we were, Huck, Ur-ronn, and me, all packed up and ready to set off in the morn, on an exploit that would either make us famous or kill us. Before that, though, there was one bit of business we *had* to take care of. We waited till night settled fully over Mount Guenn, when sunshine no longer filled the hundred clever skylights, leaving nothing to compete with the lava pools and glowing forges. The ore buckets and casting furnaces went silent and laborers downed tools. Soon after evening meal, seven gongs clanged, summoning urrish workers to perform their ritual grooming before settling down to sleep.

Ur-ronn didn't like moving about at that hour – what urs does? – but she knew there was no other choice. So we set forth single file from the warehouse chamber where Urdonnol had us barracked, picking our way without lanterns. Huck led, with two eyestalks stretched ahead as she spun quickly along a swooping stone ramp. The eyes facing backward seemed to glare at us each time she passed under a sky-duct, catching glimmers of moonlight.

'Come on, you guys! You're so jeekee slow!'

Ur-ronn muttered. 'Who had to carry *her* across rock-fields for three days, when we went exploring the Yootir Caves? I still have sfoke scars in ny flanks.'

An exaggeration. I know how tough urrish hide is. Still. Huck does have a way of recalling only whatever seems convenient at the time.

She had to stop and wait, huffing impatiently, at intersections to let Ur-ronn show the way. Soon that meant exiting the warren of underground passages and following a trail of pounded pumice across a rocky plain that looked even more eerily alien, more starkly un-Jijoan, by night than it did by day. In fact, we were crossing terrain much like pictures I've seen of Earth's moon.

Speaking of moons, great Loocen sat low in the west, the largest of Jijo's satellites, a familiar reddish crescent, though right now the main part facing us was dark, so no sunlight sparkled off the cold, dead cities the Buyur left there intact, as if to taunt us.

Stars glittered overhead like ... well, before writing this down, I racked my brain for a comparison out of some book I've read, but Earthling authors never had anything in their sky like the Dandelion Cluster, a giant puff-ball of sparkling pinpoints taking up almost a quarter of the sky, skimming the southern horizon. I know 'cause if they did, they'd have competed to describe it over and over, in a million different ways. Visitors from the crowded north part of the Slope always act amazed to see it in its glory, so I guess the Dandelion's one good thing about living here at the southmost boonies.

It's also one chief reason why Uriel's predecessor built a telescope on that spot, and a dome to protect it against rain and ash from old Guenn's frequent mini-eruptions.

Ur-ronn says there's just one part of the mountain where the observatory can take advantage of the sea breeze and not have heat currents ruin the seeing. There are probably much better places for astronomy on the Slope. But this spot has one advantage – it's where Uriel lives. Who else has the time, wealth, and knowledge to maintain such a hobby? No one, except perhaps the savants of Great Biblos.

The heavy cinderblock structure seemed to rise against the dazzling starry cluster, reminding me of a glaver's muzzle, taking a bite out of a big gutchel pear. The sight made my back scales frickle. Of course at this altitude, with no clouds in the sky, the air had a chilly bite.

Whistling dismay, Ur-ronn halted in a sudden plume of dust, causing Huck to ram into me, eyestalks pronging outward, squinting in all directions at once. Little Huphu reacted by digging her claws into my shoulder, ready to leap and abandon us at the first sign of peril.

'What is it?' I whispered urgently.

'*The roof is open,*' Ur-ronn explained, slipping into GalTwo as her pointed snout sniffed greedily. '*The mercury float bearing, I do scent; therefore the telescope (probably) is in use. We must now undertake (swiftly) to return to our beds, not raising suspicion.*'

'The hell you say,' Huck cursed. 'I'm for sneakin' in.'

They looked to me for the deciding vote. I shrugged, human-style. 'We're here. Ought to at least take a look.'

Ur-ronn corkscrewed her neck. She snorted a sigh. '*Stay behind me, in that case. And in vain hope of Ifni's luck, do remain quiet!*'

So we neared the dome and made out that the roof line was split open, exposing blocky shapes to the shimmering sky. The path ended at a ground-level door – ajar – revealing dim shadows within. Huphu trembled on my shoulder, either from eagerness or from anxiety. I already regretted taking her along.

Ur-ronn was an outline, pressed against the outer wall, snaking her head through the door.

'Of all utterjeekee things, what could top *her* scouting ahead at night?' Huck groused. Urs can't see in the dark any better'n a glaver can at noon. Oughta let me do it.'

Yeah, I thought. *As if g'Keks are built for stealth.* But I kept silent, except for a low umble to prevent Huphu jumping off.

Switching her braided tail nervously, Ur-ronn twisted her neck inside – and her long body followed, twisting nimbly through the doorway. Huck followed close behind, all eyestalks erect and quivering. Taking up the rear, I kept swiveling to check for anyone creeping *behind*, though of course there was no reason to imagine someone would want to.

The main floor of the observatory looked deserted. The big scope glittered faintly under starlight. On a nearby table, one hooded lantern spilled a red-filtered glow onto a clipboarded sky chart and a pad covered with what might be mathematical markings – lots of numbers plus some symbols that weren't part of any alphabet ... though now that I think about it, maybe Mister Heinz *did* show some of them to our class, hoping to hook an interest.

'*Listen and note,*' Ur-ronn said. '*The motor for tracking objects in compensation against Jijo's rotation; that device is still turned on.*'

Sure enough, a low, hoonlike rumble transmitted from the telescope's case, and I smelled faint exhaust from a tiny fuel cell motor.

Another extravagance almost unknown elsewhere on the Slope but allowed here because Mount Guenn is a sacred place, certain to cleanse itself of all toys, conceits, and unreverent vanities, if not tomorrow then sometime in the next hundred years.

'That means it may still be pointed wherever they were looking before they left!' Huck responded eagerly.

Who says 'they' have left? – I was about to add. Turning around again, I noticed a closed door outlined by a pale rim of light. But Huck rushed on.

'Alvin, give me a boost so I can look!'

'Hr-r-rm? But—'

'Alvin!' A wheel stroked one of my footpads, as a warning to do what I was told.

'What? A boost?' I saw no ramp or other way for Huck to reach the scope's eyepiece, only a chair resting next to the table. Still, the best course would be to let her have her way, as quickly and silently as possible, rather than forcing an argument.

'Hrrrm . . . well, all right. But keep it quiet, will you?'

I stepped behind Huck, squatted down, and slung both arms under her axle frame. I grunted, lifting her to bring one stalk level with the eyepiece.

'Hold still!' she hissed.

'I am . . . hrm-rm . . . *trying* . . .'

I let my arm bones slip slightly, so the elbow joints clicked into a locked position – a trick I'm told humans and urs are jealous of, since even the strongest human who tried this would have to do it using muscle power alone. Even so, Huck had put on weight, and holding her in place meant standing in a bent-over half-squat. Whenever I grunted, she'd twist a free stalk round to glare, just a handsbreadth from my face, as if I was annoying her on purpose.

'Hold it, you unbuff hoon! . . . Okay, I can see now . . . a whole lot of stars . . . more stars . . . Hey, there's *nothing* but stars in here!'

'Huck,' I murmured, 'did I ask you to keep it quiet?'

Ur-ronn whistled a sigh. 'Of *course* there's only stars, you hoof-stinky g'Kek! Did you think you could count the fortholes on an orviting starshif with this little telescofe? At that height, it'll twinkle like any other foint source.'

I was impressed. We all know Ur-ronn is the best mechanic in our bunch, but who figured she knew astronomy, as well?

'Here, give ne a chance to look. It's fossible I can tell which star *isn't* a star, if its fosition changes in relation to others.'

Huck's wheels spun angrily in the air, but she could no more deny the fairness of Ur-ronn's request than keep me from lowering her to the ground. I straightened with relief, and some crackling of cartilage, as she rolled away, grumbling. Ur-ronn had to put both forehooves on the chair in order to rise up and peer through the eyepiece.

For a few moments, our urrish pal was silent; then she trilled frustration. 'They really *are* all just stars, far as I can tell. Anyway, I forgot – a starshif in orvit would drift out of view in just a few duras, even with the tracking engine turned on.'

'Well, I guess that's it,' I said, only half disappointed. 'We'd better head on back now—'

That's when I saw Huck was gone. Whirling, I finally spied her, heading straight for the doorway I had seen earlier!

'Remember what we discussed?' she called rearward at us, speeding toward the back-lit rectangle. 'The *real* evidence will be on those photographic *plates* you say Gybz spoke of. That's what we came up here to look at in the first place. Come on!'

I admit staring like a stranded fish, my throat sac blatting uselessly while Huphu gouged my scalp, gathering purchase for a spring. Ur-ronn took off in a mad scramble after Huck, trying desperately to tackle her by the spokes before she reached the door—

—which *swung open*, I swear, at that very instant, casting a painful brightness that outlined a *human* silhouette. A short, narrow-shouldered male whose fringe of head hair seemed aflame in the glare of several lanterns behind him. Blinking, raising a hand to shade my eyes, I could dimly make out several easels in the room beyond, bearing charts, measuring rules, and slick glass plates. *More* square plates lay racked on shelf after shelf, crowding the walls of the little room.

Huck squealed to a stop so suddenly her axles glowed. Ur-ronn nearly rammed her, halting in frantic haste. We all froze, caught in the act.

The human's identity wasn't hard to guess, since only one of his race lived on the mountain at the time. He was *only* known far and wide as the most brilliant of his kind, a sage whose mind reached far, even for an Earthling, to grasp many of the arcane secrets that our ancestors once knew. One whose intellect even the mighty self-assured *Uriel* bowed before.

The Smith of Mount Guenn was *not* going to be pleased with us for intruding on her guest.

Sage Purofsky stared for a long moment, blinking into the darkness beyond the doorway, then he raised a hand straight toward us, pointing.

'You!' he snapped in a strangely distracted tone of voice. 'You surprised me.'

Huck was the first of us to recover.

'Um, sorry ... uh, master. We were just, er. ... '

Cutting her off, but without any trace of rancor, the human went on.

'It's just as well, then. I was about to ring for somebody. Would you kindly take these notes to Uriel for me?'

He held out a folded sheaf of papers, which Huck accepted in the grasp of one quivering tentacle-arm. Her half-retracted eyestalks blinked in surprise.

'That's a good lad,' the savant went on absentmindedly, and turned to go back into the little room. Then Sage Purofsky stopped and swiveled to face us once more.

'Oh, please also tell Uriel that I'm now sure of it. Both ships are gone. I don't know what happened to the bigger one, the first one, since it appeared only by lucky accident on one early set of plates, before anyone knew to look for it. That orbit can't be solved except to say I think it may have landed. But even a rough calculation based on the last series shows the *second* ship de-orbiting, heading into an entry spiral down to Jijo. Assuming no later deviations or corrections, its course would have made landfall some days ago, north of here, smack dab in the Rimmers.'

His smile was rueful, ironic.

'In other words, the warning we sent up to the Glade may be somewhat superfluous.' Purofsky rubbed his eyes tiredly and sighed. 'By now our colleagues at Gathering probably know a lot more about what's going on than we do.'

I swear, he sounded more disappointed than worried over the arrival of something the exiles of Jijo had feared for two thousand years.

We all, even Huphu, stared for a long time – even after the man thanked us again, turned around, and closed the door behind him, leaving us alone with our only company millions of stars, like pollen grains scattered on a shimmering ocean, stretching over our heads. A sea of darkness that suddenly felt frighteningly near.

XII

THE BOOK OF THE SLOPE

Legends

There is a word we are asked not to say too often. And to whisper, when we do.

The *traeki* ask this of us, out of courtesy, respect, and superstition.

The word is a name – with just two syllables – one they fear ever to hear again.

A name they once called themselves.

A name presumably still used by their cousins, out on the star-lanes of the Five Galaxies.

Cousins, who are mighty, terrifying, resolute, pitiless, and single-minded.

How different that description seems to make our own sept of ringed ones, from those who still roam the cosmos, like gods. Those *Jophur*.

Of all the races who came to Jijo in sneakships, some, like qheuens and humans, were obscure and almost unknown in the Five Galaxies. Others, like g'Keks and glavers, had reputations of modest extent, among those needing their specialized skills. Hoon and urs had made a moderate impression, so much that Earthlings knew of them before landing, and worried.

But it is said that every oxygen-breathing, starfaring clan is familiar with the shape of stacked rings, piled high, ominous and powerful.

When the traeki sneakship came, the g'Kek took one look at the newcomers and went into hiding for several generations, cowering in fright until, at last, they realized – these were *different* rings.

When qheuen settlers saw them already here, they very nearly left again, without unloading or even landing their sneakship.

How came our beloved friends to have such a reputation to live down? How came they to be so different from those who still fly in space, using that awful name?

—*Reflections on the Six,*
Ovoom Press, Year-of-Exile 1915

ASX

Either the invaders are trying to confuse us, or else there is something strange about them.

At first, their powers and knowledge appeared as one might expect – so far above us that we seem as brutish beasts. Dared we contrast our own meager wisdom, our simple ways, against their magnificent, unstoppable machines, their healing arts, and specially the erudition of their piercing questions about Jijoan life? Erudition showing the vast sweep and depth of records at their command, surely copied from the final survey of the world, a million years ago. Yet ...

They seem to know nothing about lorniks or zookirs.

They cannot hide their excitement, upon measuring specimen glavers, as if they have made a great discovery.

They make puzzling, nonsensical remarks concerning chimpanzees.

And now they want to know everything about mulc-spiders, asking naïve questions that even this inexpert stack of manicolored rings could answer. Even if all of our/my toruses of sapiency were vlenned away, leaving nothing but instinct, memory, and momentum.

The sigil of the Great Library was missing from the bow of the great vessel that left their station here. We thought its absence a mere emblem of criminality. A negative symbol, denoting a kind of skulking shame.

Can it mean more than that? Much more?

SARA

From Engril's shop on Pimmin Canal, it was but a short walk to the clinic where Pzora had taken the Stranger yesterday. Engril agreed to meet Sara there with Bloor the Portraitist. Time was short. Perhaps Sara's idea was foolish or impractical, but there would be no better moment to broach it, and no better person to present it to than Ariana Foo.

A decision had to be made. So far, the omens weren't good.

The emissaries from Dolo Village had gathered last night, in a tavern near the Urrish Quarter, to discuss what each of them had learned since the *Huaph-woa* docked. Sara showed a copy of the sages' report, fresh from Engril's copy shop, expecting it to shock the others. But by that evening even Pzora knew most of the story.

'I see three possibilities,' the stern-browed farmer Jop had said, nursing a mug of sour buttermilk. 'First – the story's an Egg-cursed lie. The ship really *is* from the great Institute, we're about to be judged as the Scrolls say, but the sages are spreading a pebble-in-my-hoof fable about bandits to justify musterin' the militia, preparin' for a fight.'

'That's absurd!' Sara had complained.

'Oh yeah? Then why've all the units been called up? Humans drilling in every village. Urrish cavalry wheelin' in all directions, and the hoons oilin' their old catapults, as if they could shoot down a starship by hurlin' rocks.' He shook his head. 'What if the sages've got some fantasy about resisting? It wouldn't be the first time leaders were driven mad by an approaching end to their days of petty power.'

'But what of these sketches?' asked the scriven-dancer, Fakoon. The g'Kek touched one of Engril's reproductions, portraying a pair of humans dressed in one-piece suits, staring brazenly at sights both new to them and yet somehow pathetic in their eyes.

Jop shrugged. 'Ridiculous on the face of it. What would *humans* be doin' out here? When our ancestors left Earth on an aged third-hand tub, not a single human scientist understood its workings. The folks back home couldn't have caught up with galactic standard tech for another ten thousand years.'

Sara watched Blade and the hoon captain react with surprise. It was no secret, what Jop had said about human technology at the time of exile, but they must find it hard to picture. On Jijo, *Earthlings* were the engineers, the ones most often with answers.

'And who would want to ferfetrate such a hoax?' Ulgor asked, lowering her conical head. Sara read tension in the ur's body stance. *Uh-oh*, she thought.

Jop smiled. 'Why, maybe some bunch that sees opportunity, amid the chaos, to besmirch our honor and have one last chance at revenge before Judgment Day.'

Human and urs faced each other, each grinning a bright display of teeth – which could be taken equivocally as either friendly or threatening. For once, Sara blessed the sickness that had caused nearly everyone's rewq to curl up and hibernate. There would have been no ambiguity with symbionts to translate the meaning in Jop's and Ulgor's hearts.

At that moment, a squirt of pinkish steam jetted between the two – a swirling fume of cloying sweetness. Jop and Ulgor retreated from the cloud in opposite directions, covering their noses.

'Oops, i express repentance on our/my behalf. This pile's digestive torus still retains, processes, deletes the richness of esteemed hoonish shipboard fare.'

Unperturbed, the captain of the *Hauph-woa* said – 'How fortunate for you, Pzora. As to the subject at hand, we must still decide what advice to send back to Dolo Village and the settlements of the Upper Roney. So let me ask Jop ... *Hrrm* – what if we consider a simpler theory – there is *no* hoax by the honored sages, *hrr*?'

Jop still waved the air in front of his face, coughing. 'That brings us to possibility number two – that we are being tested. The Day has come at last, but the noble Galactics are undecided what to do with us. Maybe the great Institutes hired human actors to play this role, offering us a chance to nip the scales one way through right action, or the other by choosing incorrectly. As for what advice we send upriver, I say we counsel that demolition should proceed according to the ancient plan!'

Blade, the young qheuen delegate, reared back on three legs, lifting his blue carapace, stammering and hissing so that his initial attempts at Anglic came out garbled. He switched to Galactic Two.

'Madness you betray! This (lunatic) thing, how can you say? Our mighty dam (glorious to see and smell) must fall? For what reason, if our (illicit) existence on Jijo be already known?'

Jop explained, 'True, we can't hide our crime of colonization. But we *can* start the process of removing our works from this scarred world. By showing our good intentions, we'll prove we merit leniency.

'What we must *not* do – and I fear our sages may be fooled – is offer any cooperation to these humans who pretend to be gene raiders. No bribes or service, since that, too, must be part of the test.'

Ulgor snorted doubt. 'And fossivility three? What if they turn out to ve felons, after all?'

Jop had shrugged. 'Then the same answer holds. Passive resistance. Fade into the countryside. Tear down our cities—'

'Burn the libraries,' Sara cut in, and Jop glanced her way, then nodded, curtly.

'Above all else. They are the roots of conceit. Our outrageous pretense at remaining civilized.' He waved around him at the old Buyur chamber that had been converted to a tavern, the soot-stained walls adorned with spears, shields, and other souvenirs of the bloody siege of Tarek Town. 'Civilized!' Jop laughed again. 'We're like parrot-ticks, reciting verses we do not understand, pathetically miming the ways of the mighty. If pirates have indeed come, such vanities can only lessen our skill at burrowing down.

Our only chance of survival will be to blend in with Jijo's animals. To *become* the innocents that glavers are, in their blessed salvation. A salvation we might have achieved by now, had humans not foiled nature with our so-called Great Printing.

'So you see it does not matter,' he concluded with a shrug of finality. 'Whether the visitors from space are noble chancellors from the Institute of Migration or the foulest criminals to prowl space. Either way, they are our judgment, come at last. Our sole option remains the same.'

Shaking her head in bemusement, Sara had commented, 'You're starting to sound like Lark.'

But Jop saw nothing ironic in that. His radicalization had intensified each day since the deafening, terrifying specter shook the tree farms, leaving trails of noise and heat that seared the sky.

'This is a bad thing,' Blade had said to Sara, later that evening, after Jop left to meet friends and fellow believers. 'He seems sure of his reasoning and virtue – like a gray queen, unshakably convinced of her righteousness.'

'Self-righteousness is a plague that afflicts all races, except the traeki,' answered Fakoon, bowing two stalks toward Pzora. 'Your folk are lucky to be spared the curse of egotism.'

The Dolo Village pharmacist had vented a soft sigh, 'i/we urge you to make no simple assumptions, dear comrades. It is said that we, too, once possessed that talent, whose partner is the gift/curse of ambition. To excise it from our natures meant leaving behind some of our greatest treasures, our finest rings. It must not have been an easy thing to do.

'One of the things we/i fear most about restored contact with Galactics is something you other species and beings may not understand – we fear temptation by an enticing offer.

'We fear an offer to be made whole.'

The clinic was a place of wheels – of g'Kek surgeons and patients on push-chairs. Many of the traeki pharmacists used skooter-wagons, pushing along faster than most could walk alone. No wonder the smooth planarity of city life appealed to two of the Six.

The Stranger's room was on the fifth floor, looking out across the confluence of the rivers Roney and Bibur. Both steam ferries could be seen moored under screening arbors, now operating only at night, since vigilante groups had threatened to burn them if they budged by day. And this morning confirming word came down from the Glade. The High Sages, too, wanted no unnecessary signs of technology revealed by the Six. *Destroy nothing. Conceal everything.*

It only added to a growing sense of confusion among common folk. Was this Judgment Day or not? Sounds of raucous argument were heard in all parts of town. *We need some goal to unite us,* Sara thought, *or we'll start coming apart, skin and pelt, shell and spokes.*

A traeki attendant motioned Sara through to the private chamber that had been given the Stranger. The dark man looked up when she entered, and smiled with clear delight to see her. He laid aside a pencil and pad of pale paper, on which Sara glimpsed the scene outside the window – one of the steam ferries, outlined with subtle countershading. Pinned to the wall was another sketch depicting the shipboard concert on the fantail of the *Hauph-woa*, capturing a gentle interlude amid the storm of crisis.

'Thank you for coming,' said an elderly, sallow-faced woman seated by the Stranger's bedside, looking surprisingly like a g'Kek, in coloration, her startling blue eyes, and also the way a wheelchair framed her blanket-shrouded form. 'We have been making progress, but there are some things I wanted to try only after you arrived.'

Sara still wondered why Ariana Foo, of all people, had taken an interest in the wounded man. With Lester Cambel and most other sages away, she was the highest ranking human savant left this side of Biblos. One might expect her to have more urgent things on her mind right now, than focusing her keen intellect on the problem of the Stranger's origins.

The g'Kek doctor rolled forward, his voice mellow, with a cultured accent.

'First, Sara, please tell us – have you recalled anything further about our patient's aspect, the day you pulled him from the swamp all burned and torn?'

She shook her head silently.

'His clothing, none was recovered?'

'There were a few scraps, mostly charred. We threw them out while treating the burns.'

'Did those scraps go to dross barrels?' he asked eagerly. 'Those very barrels aboard the *Hauph-woa* right now?'

'There were no ornaments or buttons, if that's what you're looking for. The scraps went to recycling, which in the case of old cloth means going straight to my father's pulping machine. Would they have helped?'

'Perhaps,' answered the old woman, clearly disappointed. 'We try to consider all possibilities.'

The Stranger's hands lay folded on his lap, and his eyes darted back and forth, focusing on faces as if he were fascinated not by words but the sounds themselves.

'Can' – she swallowed – 'can you do anything for him?'

'That depends,' the doctor replied. 'All burns and contusions are healing well. But our finest unguents are useless against structural damage. Our enigmatic guest has lost part of his left temporal lobe, as though it had been torn out by some horrid predator. I am sure you know this area is where you humans process speech.'

'Is there any chance—'

'Of recovering what he has lost?' A g'Kek shrug, twining two eye-stalks, had never become fashionable among the other races. 'If he were very young or female, there might be some transfer of speech facility to the *right* lobe. A few stroke victims do this. But the feat is rare for adult males, whose brain structures are more rigid, alas.'

The light in the dark Stranger's eyes was deceptive. He smiled amiably, as if they were discussing the weather. His reliable cheerfulness tore at Sara's heart.

'Nothing can be done?'

'Out in the Galaxy, perhaps.'

It was an old expression, almost habitual, whenever one hit the limits of the crude arts available on the Slope.

'But we can do no more. Not in *this* place.'

There was something in the doctor's tone. All four eyes stared inward – as if a human being were studying his fingernails, waiting for someone else to say the unspoken.

Sara looked to Ariana Foo, whose face was composed.

Too composed. Sara leaped on the doctor's hanging implication.

'You can't be serious.'

The sage briefly closed her eyes. When they reopened there was a daring glitter.

'Word comes down that our invaders are plying mass opinion, winning converts with drugs, potions, and miracle cures. Already, unsanctioned caravans of the sick and lame have set out from Tarek and other sites, hobbling up the hard trails in desperate search of remedies. I admit, the thought even crossed *my* mind.' She lifted her stick-thin arms from her fragile body. 'Many may die on the trek, but what matters such risk against the lure of hope?'

Sara paused. 'Do you think the outsiders can help him?'

Ariana shrugged in the hoonish manner, with a puff of air in her cheeks. 'Who can say? Frankly, I doubt even Galactics could repair such damage. But they may have palliatives to improve his lot. Anyway, all bets are off if my suspicion is true.'

'What suspicion?'

'That our Stranger is no poor savage at all.'

Sara stared, then blinked. '*Ifni*,' she breathed.

'Indeed.' Ariana Foo nodded. 'Shall we see if our guest truly was delivered to us by our goddess of luck and change?'

Sara could barely manage a nod. While the old woman rummaged in her valise, Sara pondered. *This must be why everyone was in awe of her, when she was chief human sage before Cambel. They say genius is a knack for seeing the obvious. Now I know it's true.*

How could I have been so blind!

Ariana took up several of the sheets recently copied on Engril's machine. 'I thought of asking a Sensitive to sit in, but if I am right, we'll want this kept quiet. So we'll make do by watching how he reacts. Note that he is probably the only person in Tarek Town who has not seen these yet. Everybody pay close attention, please.'

She rolled closer to the patient, who watched attentively as Ariana laid a single sheet on the coverlet.

His smile gradually thinned as he picked up the drawing, touching the fine expert lines. Mountains framed a bowlike vale littered with shattered trees – nest lining for a thick javelin, adorned with jutting spines whose contours Sara had first seen hurtling above her shaken home. Fingertips traced the sloping curves, trembling. The smile was gone, replaced by a look of agonised perplexity. Sara sensed that he was trying to *remember* something. Clearly there was familiarity here, and more, much more.

The Stranger looked up at Ariana Foo, eyes filled with pain and questions he could not pose.

'What can this prove?' Sara asked, writhing inside.

'He finds the image of the ship troubling,' Ariana answered.

'As it would any thoughtful member of the Six,' Sara pointed out.

The older woman nodded. 'I had expected a happier response.'

'You think he's one of *them*, don't you?' Sara asked. 'You think he *crashed* into the swamp east of Dolo, aboard some kind of flying machine. He's a galactic. A criminal.'

'It seemed the simplest hypothesis, given the coincidence in timing – a total stranger, burned amid a humid swamp, appearing with injuries unlike anything our doctors have seen. Let's try another one.'

The next sketch showed the same little valley, but with the starship replaced by what the sages called a 'research station', assigned the task of analyzing Jijoan life. The Stranger peered at the black cube, intrigued and perhaps a little frightened.

Finally, Ariana presented a drawing showing two figures with strong, confident faces. A pair who had come a hundred thousand light-years to plunder.

This time a sharp gasp escaped him. The Stranger stared at the human forms, touching the symbol-patches on their one-piece exploration suits. It did not require fey sensitivity to read despair in his eyes. With an incoherent cry, he crumpled the sketch and flung it across the room, then covered his eyes with an arm.

'Interesting. *Very* interesting,' Ariana murmured.

'I fail to understand,' the doctor sighed. 'Does this mean he is from off-Jijo or not?'

'It is too soon to tell, I fear.' She shook her head. 'But let's say it turns out he *is* from the Five Galaxies? If the forayers are seeking a mislaid confederate, and we have him in hand to offer in trade, it might work to our advantage.'

'Now just a darn—' Sara began, but the older human only continued, thinking aloud.

'Alas, his reaction isn't one I'd call *eager* to be reunited with lost comrades. Do you think he might be an escaped foe? That somehow he survived imprisonment, even attempted murder, just a day or so before the foray ship came down to land? If so, how ironic his particular injury, which prevents him from telling so much! I wonder if *they* did it to him ... the way barbaric kings of old Earth used to rip out an enemy's tongue. How horrible, if true!'

The range of possibilities rattled off by the sage left Sara momentarily stunned. There was a long stretch of silence, until the doctor spoke once more.

'Your speculations intrigue and terrify me, old friend. Yet now I must ask that you not agitate my patient further.'

But Ariana Foo only shook her head in somber pondering. 'I had thought to send him up to the Glade right away. Let Vubben and the others decide for themselves what to do next.'

'*Indeed?* I could never allow you to move one so seriously—'

'Of course an opportunity to offer him Galactic-level treatment of his injuries would make a fine synergy, combining pragmatism with kindness.'

The g'Kek medic's oral flap opened and shut soundlessly, as he worked to find a way past Ariana's logic. Finally, his stalks contracted unhappily.

The retired sage sighed. 'Alas, the point seems moot. From what we've seen, I doubt very much that our guest here will be willing to go.'

Sara was about to tell the old woman where *she* could go, with her intent to meddle in a man's life. But just then the subject of their deliberations lowered his arm. He looked at Ariana and Sara. Then he picked up one of the sketches.

'G-guh ... ?' He swallowed, and his brow furrowed with intense concentration.

All eyes stared back at him. The man lifted one of the drawings, showing the starship nestled in a bower of shattered trees. He stabbed the scene with his index finger.

'G-g-g-oh!'

Then he looked into Sara's eyes, pleadingly. His voice dropped to a whisper.

'*Go.*'

After that, discussion of Sara's plan seemed almost anticlimactic. *I won't be going back to Dolo on the next boat, after all. I'm on my way to see the aliens.*

Poor Father. All he ever wanted was to raise a gaggle of safe little papermakers. Now every heir goes rushing into danger's pincers, just as fast as our legs can carry us!

Engril and Bloor, the portraitist, arrived, bearing portable tools of their trades.

Bloor was a short, fair-skinned man with ringlets of yellow hair showering over his shoulders. His hands were stained blotchy from years creating the delicate emulsions required by his art. He held up a plate of metal, as wide as his palm, which shimmered with finely etched lines and depressions. From certain angles, those acid-cut shapes coalesced to form sharp profiles of shadow and light.

'It's called the *Daguerre* process,' he explained. 'Actually, it is quite a simple technique for creating permanent images. One of the first methods of photography ever invented by wolfling humans, back on Old Earth. Or so say our reference books. We don't employ the procedure for portraits nowadays, as paper is faster and safer.'

'And paper decays,' Ariana Foo added, turning the plate over in her hands. Depicted on the etched metal was an urrish warrior of high rank, with both husbands perched on her back in a formal pose. The female's sinuous neck was painted with garish, zigzag stripes, and she held a large crossbow, as if cradling a beloved scent-daughter.

'Indeed,' the portraitist conceded. 'The fine papers produced by Sara's father are guaranteed to corrupt in less than a century, leaving no traces to betray our descendants. This sample daguerreotype is one of only a few not sent to the dross middens since our strengthened Commons started promoting wider respect for the Law. I have special permission to hold on to this excellent example. See the fine detail? It dates from before the third urrish-human war. The subject is a chieftain of the Sool tribes, I believe. Note the tattoo scars. Marvelous. As crisp and clear as the day it was taken.'

Sara leaned forward as Ariana passed the slim plate over. 'Has anyone used this process on Jijo since then?'

Bloor nodded. 'All members of my guild create one daguerreotype, as part of our master work. Nearly all are then sent to the Midden, or given to smiths for remelting, but the capability remains.' He lifted a satchel, causing a faint clinking of bottles. 'There's enough acid and fixative here to treat and develop several dozen plates – but I have only about twenty of the plates themselves. If we want more, they must be ordered from Ovoom Town, or one of the volcano smithies.'

Sara felt a tap on her shoulder and turned to see the Stranger holding out his hand. She gave him the small photograph, and he traced the finely etched grooves with his fingertips.

Now that her mind had shifted to encompass Ariana's theory, everything the wounded man did seemed to refract differently. Was he smiling now over the crudeness of this photographic technology, or expressing enchantment at its cleverness? Or was the sparkling delight in his eyes a reaction to the depicted image of a savage warrior, whose bow and lance had been such a scourge during that age of heroic struggle, ten generations ago?

Ariana Foo rubbed her chin. 'Twenty plates. Let's say you get good pictures with just half—'

'A generous estimate, my sage, since the technique requires long exposure times.'

Ariana grunted. A half-dozen successes, then. And several must be handed over to the forayers, in order for a threat to be believable.'

'Copies can be made,' Engril put in.

'We won't need copies,' Sara said. 'They'll *have* to assume we have plenty of others. The crucial point is, can these pictures last a million years?'

The portraitist blew at a strand of yellow hair. From his throat, there emerged a soft strangling sound, like a qheuen sigh. 'Given the right storage conditions, this metal oxidizes a nice protective layer . . .' He laughed nervously, looking from Sara to Ariana. 'You aren't *serious*, are you? A bluff is one thing. We're desperate enough to clutch at straws, but do you *really* imagine you can store evidence somewhere until the next Galactic survey?'

The g'Kek doctor twisted two eyestalks to stare in opposite directions. 'It appears we have entered into entirely new realms of heresy.'

ASX

It may have been a mistake to have striven so hard to suppress psi powers among the Six.

For most of the long millennia of our exile, it seemed the wisest move. Was not our greatest goal to remain hidden? We had only to build modestly, in harmony with nature, and let the inverse square law do the rest.

But psi channels are fey, nonlinear. Or so say books printed by the humans who admit that their kind knew little about the subject when their ancestors fled this way.

When the Holy Egg first gave us rewq, some among the Six feared the symbionts worked by psi, which might make our fugitive enclave more detectable. Despite satisfying proof it is not so, that old slander has now returned, once more stirring friction among us.

Some even contend that the Holy Egg *itself* may have attracted our ruin! After all, why do pirates come *now*, a mere century after the blessed day the Egg emerged? Others point out that we might by now know much more about our invaders, if only we had bred adepts of our own, instead of the few sensitives and truth-scryers we have today.

Regret is a silly, useless thing, i might as well pine for the rings our ancestors were said to have abandoned, simply because those toroids were tainted with sin.

Oh, how many things the legends say those rings once let us do! To run before the wind, as fleet as any urs. To swim like qheuens and walk beneath the sea. To touch and handle the world at all levels of its grainy texture. Above all, to face this dire, dread-filled universe, with a self-centered confidence that was utterly, biologically serene. No uncertainty to plague our complex community of selves. Only the towering egotism of a central, confident 'I'.

DWER

The blue qheuens of the mountains had different traditions than their cousins who lived behind mighty Dolo Dam. Molting rituals back home always seemed informal. Human youngsters from the nearby village ran free with their chitinous friends, while grownups shared nectar-beer and celebrated the coming-of-age of a new generation.

In this alpine sanctuary, the chants and hissing rituals felt more solemn. Guests included the local g'Kek doctor, some traeki gleaners, and a dozen human neighbors, who took turns at a warped window pane, to view events in the larva creche next door. The hoons who fished the lake behind the dam had sent the usual regrets. Most hoon felt incurably squeamish toward the qheuen way of reproduction.

Dwer was here out of gratitude. If not for this kindly hive, he might be flexing stumps instead of a nearly full set of fingers and toes, still tender but recovering. The occasion also came as a break from tense preparations with Danel Ozawa. When beckoned to the window by Carving Tongue, the local matriarch, Dwer and Danel bowed to the matriarch, and to the human tutor, Mister Shed.

'Congratulations to you both,' Ozawa said. 'May you have a fine clutch of graduates.'

'Thank you, honored sage.' Carving Tongue's breathy sigh seemed edgy. As head female, she laid more than half the eggs. Many of the throbbing shapes next door would be her offspring, preparing to emerge at last. After waiting twenty years or more, some strain was expected.

Mister Shed had no genetic investment in the young qheuens transforming next door, but anxiety wrote across the instructor's gaunt face.

'Yes, a fine clutch. Several will make excellent senior students, when their shells harden and they take names.'

Carving Tongue added – 'Two are already precocious chewers of wood – though I believe our tutor refers to other talents.'

Mister Shed nodded. 'There is a school downslope, where local tribes send their brightest kids. Elmira should qualify, if she makes it through—'

The matriarch erupted a warning hiss. *'Tutor! Keep your private nicknames to yourself. Do not jinx the larvae on this sacred day!'*

Mister Shed swallowed nervously. '*Sorry, matron.*' He rocked side to side, in the manner of a qheuen boy, caught stealing a crayfish from the hatchery ponds.

Fortunately, a traeki caterer arrived then with a cauldron of vel nectar. Humans and qheuens crowded the table. But Dwer saw that Ozawa felt as he did. Neither of them had time for a euphoric high. Not while preparing for a deadly serious mission.

Too bad, though, Dwer thought, noting how the traeki spiked each goblet with a race-specific spray from its chem-synth ring. Soon the mood in the chamber lightened as intoxicants flowed. Carving Tongue joined the throng at the cauldron, leaving the three humans alone by the window.

'That's it, my beauties. Do it gently,' murmured the scholar

209

contracted to teach qheuen children reading and math – a long patient task, given the decades larvae spent in one muddy suite, devouring wrigglers and slowly absorbing the mental habits of sapient beings. To Dwer's surprise, Mister Shed slipped a functioning rewq over his face. Lately, most of the symbionts had gone dormant, or even died.

Dwer peered through the window, a rippled convex lens with a broken stem in the middle. A greasy pool filled the center of the next room, which dim shapes traversed, casting left and right as if in nervous search. Those may have been Mister Shed's beloved pupils a few days ago, and some would be again, after molting into adolescent qheuens. But this play hearkened back millions of years, to a time log before the patrons of the qheuen race meddled and reshaped them into starfarers. It had a bloody logic all its own.

'That's right, children, do it softly—'

Shed's hopeful sigh cut off with a yelp as the pond erupted in froth. Wormlike forms flipped out of the water in a thrashing tangle. Dwer glimpsed one shape that was already nearly five-sided, with three legs flailing under a glistening carapace of aquamarine. The new shell bore livid marks of recent raking. Trailing were tatters of white tissue, the larval body mass that must be sloughed.

Legend said that qheuens who still roamed the stars had ways to ease this transition – machines and artificial environments – but on Jijo, molting was much the same as when qheuens were clever animals, hunting the shallows of the world that gave them birth.

Dwer recalled running home in tears, the first time he saw a molting, seeking comfort and understanding from his older brother. Even then, Lark had been serious, learned, and a bit pedantic.

'Sapient races have many reproductive styles. Some focus all their effort on a few offspring, which are cherished from the start. Any good parent will die to save her child. Hoons and g'Keks are like humans in this so-called High-K approach.

'Urs breed much like fish in the sea – that's Low-K – casting hordes of offspring to live wild in the bush, until the survivors sniff their way back to blood relatives. Early human settlers thought the urrish way heartless, while many urs saw our custom as paranoid and maudlin.

'Qheuens fall in between. They care about their young but also know that many in each clutch must die, so that others can live. It's a sadness that lends poignancy to qheuen poetry. Truly, I think the wisest of them have a better grasp of life and death than any human ever could.'

Sometimes Lark got carried away. Still, Dwer saw truth in what his brother said. Soon a new generation would shamble out of the humid nursery, to a world that would dry their shells and make them citizens. Or else no survivors would emerge at all. Either way, the bitter-sweetness was so intense, anyone wearing rewq, like Mister Shed, must be crazy or a masochist.

He felt a touch on his arm. Danel motioned – time to make a polite exit, before the rituals resumed. They had work, provisions and weapons to prepare, as well as the *Legacy* they were to take over the mountains.

This morning, Lena Strong had returned from the Glade with another young woman Dwer recognized with a wince – Jenin, one of the big, strapping Worley sisters – along with five donkey-loads of books, seeds, and ominous sealed tubes. He had been expecting Rety as well, but Lena reported that the sages wanted to talk to the sooner girl for a while longer.

No matter. With or without her as a guide, Dwer was ultimately responsible for getting the small expedition to its goal.

And once there? Would there be violence? Death? Or a brave beginning?

Sighing, Dwer turned to follow Ozawa.

Now we'll never know if Sara would've turned out to be right, or Lark. Whether the Six were bound on the Low Road, or the High.

From here on, it's all about survival.

Behind him, Mister Shed pressed both hands against the warped pane, his voice hoarse with anguish over small lives that were not his to adore or rightfully to mourn.

THE STRANGER

He wonders how he knows the thing he knows.

It used to be so easy, back when wisdom came in compact packages called words. Each one carried a range of meanings, subtly shaded and complex. Strung together, they conveyed a multitude of concepts, plans, emotions . . .

And lies.

He blinks as that one word comes slickly into mind, the way so many used to do. He rolls it around his tongue, recognizing both sound and meaning at the same time, and this brings on a wash of joy mixed with awe. Awe to imagine that he once did the same thing countless times during the span of any breath, knowing and using innumerable words.

He relishes this one, repeating it over and over.

Lies . . . lies . . . lies . . .

And the miracle redoubles as another, related word slips in—
Liars ... liars ...

*On his lap he sees the crumpled sketch, now smoothed almost flat
again, a detailed rendition of human figures with expressive faces,
staring disdainfully past a multirace crowd of primitive beings. The
newcomers wear uniforms with bright emblems he finds somehow
familiar.*

*He used to know a name for people like this. A name – and reasons
to avoid them.*

*So why had he been so eager to go see them, just a little while ago?
Why so insistent? At the time it seemed as if something welled up
from deep inside him. An urgency. A need to travel, whatever the cost,
to the far-off mountain glen shown in the drawing. To go confront
those depicted on a rumpled sheet of off-white paper. The journey had
seemed terribly important, though right now he cannot quite remember why.*

*A cloudy haze covers most of his memory. Things that had waxed
vivid during his delirium now can barely be glimpsed as fleeting
images—*

—like a star *that appears dwarfed by a surrounding* structure, *a
made-thing consisting of countless angles and divided ledges, enclosing a reddish sun's brittle heat within a maze of plane surfaces.*

*—or a world of water, where metal isles jut like mushrooms and
the sea is a slow poison to touch.*

*—or one particular shallow place in space, far from the deep oases
where life normally gathers. Nothing lives in that shoal, far beyond the
shining spiral arm. Yet amid the strange flatness there clusters a vast
formation of globelike forms, strangely bright, floating timelessly,
resembling a fleet of moons ...*

*His mind flees from that last impression, reburying it with all the
other half-real memories. Losing it along with his past, and almost
certainly his future.*

XIII

THE BOOK OF THE SEA

Sapient beings are frequently tempted
to believe in purpose.
That they exist in the universe for a reason.

To serve something greater –
– a race or clan,
– patrons or gods,
– or on esthetic aim.

Or else to seek individual goals –
– wealth and power,
– reproduction,
– or enhancement of a personal soul.

Deep Philosophers call this search for purpose
nothing more than vanity,
a frantic need to justify
an inherited drive to exist.

But why would our ancestors
have brought us here, so for from race, clan,
patrons, gods, or wealth or power,
if not to serve a purpose higher than all
those things?

—*The Scroll of Contemplation*

ALVIN'S TALE

I always thought myself a city boy. After all, Wuphon is the biggest port in the south, with almost a thousand souls, if you include nearby farmers and gleaners. I grew up around docks, warehouses, and cargo hoists.

Still, the Deploying Derrick is really something. A long, graceful shape made of hundreds of tubes and reamed and cured boo, it was pieced together in a matter of days, crisscrossed and joined by a team of qheuen carpenters, who listened politely each time Urdonnol berated them for straying from the design illustrated on page five hundred and twelve of her precious text, *Pre-Contact Terran Machinery, Part VIII: Heavy Lifting Without Gravities*. Then, with a respectful spin of their cupolas, the qheuens went back to lacing and gluing the crane in their own way, applying lessons learned in real life.

Urdonnol should be more flexible, I thought, watching Uriel's humorless assistant grow ever more frustrated. *True, the books hold great wisdom. But these guys aren't exactly working with titanium here. We're castaways who must adapt to the times*.

I was glad to see that our pal, *Ur-ronn*, seemed satisfied with the work so far, after peering and sniffing at every brace, strut, and pulley. Still I'd rather *Uriel* were here, supervising as she had for the first two days, when our group set up camp under the stark shadow of Terminus Rock. The master smith was a pernickety, demanding taskmistress, often insisting a job be done over, and over again, till it was damn well perfect.

I guess we four *might* resent the bossy way she took over what used to be our own private project. But we didn't. Or not much. Her attention to detail was nerve-racking, but each time Uriel finally admitted something was done right, my confidence rose a notch that we might actually come back alive. It came as a blow when she went away.

An urrish courier had raced into camp – breathless, exhausted, even *thirsty*, for Ifni's sake – holding an envelope for Uriel to snatch and tear open. On reading the message, she drew aside Tyug, the traeki, and whispered urgently. Then she galloped off, hurrying back toward her precious forge.

Since then, things didn't exactly fall apart. The plan moves ahead step by step. But I can't say our mood's quite the same. Especially after our first test dive near-to drowned the passenger.

By then the crane was a beautiful thing, a vaulting arm so

graceful, you'd never guess sixteen steel bolts thick as my wrist anchored it to the ledge, hanging far over the deep blue waters of the Rift. A big drum carried more than thirty cables of Uriel's best hawser, all of it ending at our gray-brown vessel, which we named *Wuphon's Dream*, in hope of placating our parents – and those in the local community who think we're doing blasphemy.

Another derrick stands alongside the first, linked to an even bigger drum. This one doesn't have to carry the bathy's weight, but its job is just as vital – keeping a tangle-free length of double *hose* attached to our little craft, so that clean air goes in and bad air goes out. I never got a chance to ask what the hoses are made of, but it's much stronger than the stitched skink bladders we four had planned using, back when we started thinking about this adventure.

Uriel had made other changes – a big pressure regulator, high strain gaskets, and a pair of *eiklites* to cast bright beams down where sunshine never reaches.

Again, I wondered – where did all this stuff come from?

It surprised us that Uriel never messed much with the bathy itself – carved from a single hollowed-out garu trunk, with Ur-ronn's beautiful window sealed at one end. In front, we installed two hinged grabber arms that Ur-ronn copied out of a book. Our little craft also bore *wheels*, four in all, mounted so *Wuphon's Dream* might roll along the muddy sea bottom.

Even after being fitted with superwide treads, the wheels looked familiar. Especially to Huck. She had kept them as private mementos out of the wreckage of her home, back when her real g'Kek parents were killed in that awful avalanche. With typical grim humor, Huck named them Auntie Rooben, Uncle Jovoon Left, and Uncle Jovoon Right. The fourth one was simply Dad – till I made her stop the grisly joke and call them One through Four instead.

Using wheels would normally be impossible without Galactic technology. A turning axle would tear any gasket apart. But Huck's macabre stash of spare parts offered a solution. Those wondrous g'Kek magnetic hubs and motivator spindles can be placed on either side of the hull, without actually piercing the wood. Huck will steer the forward pair of wheels, while I'll use a rotary crank to power the driver pair in back.

Which covers all our jobs during a dive, except 'Captain' Pincer-Tip, whose world of bright blue water we'll pass through on our way to depths no qheuen has seen since their sneakship sank, a thousand years ago. His place is right in the bubble nose, controlling the eiklamps and shouting instructions how the rest of us are to steer and push or grab samples.

Why does *he* get to be in charge? Pincer surely never impressed anyone as the brightest member of our gang.

First, all this was his idea from the start. He hand – or rather mouth – carved most of the *Dream* all by himself, during scarce free time between school and day-work in the crustacean pens.

More important, if that beautiful window ever starts to fail – or any of the other gaskets – he's the one least likely to panic when salt water starts spraying about the cabin. If that ever happens, it'll be up to Pincer to get the rest of us out somehow. We've all read enough sea and space tales to know *that's* a pretty good definition of a captain – the one you all better listen to when seconds count the difference 'tween life and death.

He'd have to wait a while, though, before taking command. Our first test would have just one passenger, a volunteer who was literally 'born' for the job.

That morning, Tyug, the traeki, laid a trail of scento-mones to draw the little partial stack, Ziz, from its pen to where *Wuphon's Dream* waited, gleaming in the sunshine. Our good ship's hull of polished garuwood was so bright and lovely – too bad the open blue sky is normally taken as a bad omen.

So it seemed to the onlookers watching our crew from a nearby bluff. There were hoon from Wuphon Port, plus some local reds, and urs with caravan dust on their flanks, as well as three humans who must have come a hard three-day trek from The Vale – all of them with nothing better to do than trade hearsay about the starship, or ships, said to have landed up north. One rumor said everyone at the Glade was already dead, executed on the spot by vengeful Galactic judges. Another claimed the Holy Egg had wakened fully at last, and the lights some saw in the sky were the *souls* of those lucky enough to be at Gathering when the righteous of the Six were transformed and sent back as spirits to their ancient homes among the stars.

Shave my legs if some of the stories weren't beautiful enough to make me wish I'd made 'em up.

Not all the onlookers were protestors. Some came out of curiosity. Huck and I had some fun with Howerr-phuo, who is second nephew by adoption to the Mayor's junior half-mother, but who dropped out of school anyway, on account of he claimed not to like the way Mister Heinz smells. But everyone knows Howerr-phuo is lazy, and anyway, *he* shouldn't talk about the hygienic habits of *others*.

At one point Howerr slinked up to ask about the *Dream* and its mission. Nice polite questions, mind you. But he seemed to barely hear our answers.

Then he sort of eased over to asking questions about *traekis*, gesturing over at Tyug, who was feeding Ziz in ers pen.

True, we have a pharmacist in Wuphon Town, but still there's some mystery about the ringed ones. Sure enough, Huck and I soon got the gist of what Howerr-phuo was going on about. He and some of his backwash friends had a wager going, about *traeki sex life*, and he'd been elected to run the matter past *us*, as local experts!

Sharing a wink, Huck and I quickly emptied his head of all the nonsense it had been stuffed with – then proceeded to fill it back up with our own imaginative version. Howerr soon looked like a sailor who just had a loose tackle-pulley carom off his skull. Glancing furtively at his feet, he hurried off – no doubt to check for 'ring spores,' lest he start growing little traekis in places where he'd been neglectful about washing.

I don't feel much guilt over it. Anyone standing downwind from Howerr-phuo, from now on, oughta thank us.

I was going to ask Huck if we were ever that dumb – then I recalled. Didn't *she* once convince me that a g'Kek can manage to be her own mother *and* father? I swear, she had made it sound plausible at the time, though for the life of me, I still can't figure out how.

For the first couple of days, the spectators mostly lurked beyond a line in the sand, drawn by Uriel and her sage's baton. No one said much while the master smith was around. But after she left, some took to yelling slogans, mostly objecting that the Midden is sacred, not a place for conceited gloss-addicts to go sight-seeing. Once the Vale humans arrived, the protests got better organized, with banners and slogans chanted in unison.

I found it pretty exciting, like a scene from *Summer of Love* or *Things to Come*, all full of righteous dissent for a cause. To a humicker like me, nothing could be more buff than forging ahead with an adventure *against* popular opinion. Seems nearly all the romantic tales I've read were about intrepid heroes persisting despite the doubts of stick-in-the-mud parents, neighbors, or authority figures. It reminded me of the book my nickname comes from – where the people of Diaspar try to keep Alvin from making contact with their long-lost cousins in faraway Lys. Or when the Lysians don't want him going back home with news of their rediscovered world.

Yeah, I know that's fiction, but the connection stoked my resolve. Huck and Ur-ronn and Pincer-Tip said they all felt the same.

As for the mob, well, I know that folks who're scared can get unreasonable. I even tried once or twice to see it from their point of view. Really, I did.

Boy, what a bloat-torus of jeekee, Ifni-slucking skirls. Hope they all sit on bad mulch and get spin vapors.

XIV

THE BOOK OF THE SLOPE

Legends

It is said that humans on Earth spent untold generations living in brute fear, believing a myriad things that no sensible person would ever imagine. Certainly not anyone who had been handed truth on a silver platter – the way it was given to nearly every sapient race in the Five Galaxies.

Earthlings had to figure it all out for themselves. Slowly, agonizingly, humans learned how the universe worked; abandoning most of the fanciful beliefs they carried through their long, dark loneliness. This included belief in—

—the divine right of egotistical kings,

—the mental incapacity of women,

—the idea that a wise state knows all,

—the idea that the *individual* is always right,

—the sick-sweet addiction that transforms a doctrine from a mere model of the world into something sacred, worth killing for.

These and many other wild concepts eventually joined pixies and ufos in the trunk where humans finally put away such childish things.

A very large trunk.

Even so, the newly contacted Galactics saw Earthlings as superstitious primitives, as *wolflings*, prone to weird enthusiasms and peculiar, unprovable convictions.

How ironic, then, is the role reversal that we see on *Jijo*, where Earthlings found the other five far regressed down a road humans had traveled before, wallowing in a myriad fables, fantasies, grudges, and vividly absurd notions. To this maelstrom of superstition, settlers fresh off the *Tabernacle* contributed more than paper books. They also brought tools of logic and verification – the very things Earthlings had to fight hardest to learn, back home.

Moreover, with their own history in mind, Earthlings became voracious collectors of folklore, fanning out among the other five to copy down every tale, every belief, even those they demonstrated to be false.

Out of their wolfling past came this strange mixture – reasoning skepticism, plus a deep appreciation of the peculiar, the bizarre, the extravagantly vivid.

Amid the darkness, humans know that it is all too easy to lose your way, if you forget how to tell what is true.

But it is just as urgent never to let go of the capacity to dream. To weave the illusions that help us all make it through this dark, dark night.

—from *The Art of Exile*,
by Auph-hu-Phwuhbhu

The tiny robot was a wonder to behold. No larger than a g'Kek's eyeball, it lay pinned down to the ground by a horde of attacking privacy wasps, covered by their crowded fluttering wings.

Lester was the first sage to comment, after the initial surprise.

'Well, now we know why they're called *privacy wasps*. Did you see the way they swarmed over that thing? Otherwise, we'd never have known it was there.'

'A device for spying,' surmised Knife-Bright Insight, tipping her carapace to get a closer look at the machine. 'Minuscule and mobile, sent to listen in on our council. We would have been helpless, all our plans revealed, if not for the wasps.'

Phwhoon-dau concurred with a deep umble.

'Hr-um ... We were used to seeing the insects as minor irritants, their presence required by tradition for certain ceremonies. But the Buyur must have designed the wasps for just such a purpose. To patrol their cities and homes thwarting would-be eavesdroppers.'

'*Using a (specifically) designed life-form to deal with the (annoying) threat – indeed, that would have been the Buyur way,*' added Ur-Jah.

Lester leaned close to peer at the wasps, whose wings rippled in front of the robot's tiny eyes, beating a maze of colors that reminded me/us of rewq.

'I wonder what the wasps are showing it,' murmured our human sage.

Then Vubben spoke for the first time since the wasps attacked the intruder.

'Probably exactly what it *wants* to see,' he suggested confidently.

Do you recall, my rings, how we all nodded, sighed, or umbled respectful agreement? Vubben spoke the words so well, in such tones of wise credibility. Only later did it occur to we/us to ask ourselves—

What?

What in the world could he possibly mean by that?

During two thousand years of illicit settlement, Lark was hardly the first member of the Six to fly. He wasn't even the first human.

Soon after the sneakship *Tabernacle* sank forever into the Midden's sucking embrace, men and women used to soar like kites, riding steady offshore winds from the blue ocean all the way to the white peaks of the Rimmer Range. Back in those days, lacy airfoils used to catch sky-currents, lofting brave pilots to survey their new world from above.

The last silky glider now lay under glass in a Biblos museum, a wonder to behold, made of the mystical materials *monomolecular carbon* and *woven stress polymer*, which the brightest wizards of the Chemists' Guild could not reproduce today, even if the sages allowed it. Time and mishaps eventually smashed all the others, leaving later human generations to walk the heavy ground like everybody else, and erasing one more cause of jealousy among the Six – though lately, since the Great Peace, groups of ambitious youths had resumed a crude version of the pastime, occasionally risking their lives on spindly frames of hollow boo, covered with hand-woven sheets of wic-cotton. Or else urrish middlings rode bulging *balloons*, wafting upward on puffs of torrid air. Sometimes success caused a local sensation, but none of the efforts had much lasting effect. Available materials were too heavy, weak, or porous. The wind was much too strong.

Some, with ardent piety, claimed this was a good thing. The sky was not where redemption would be found. Nor in clinging to vanities of the past. Lark normally agreed with the orthodox view, but in this case, he mused—

Such a modest dream. To waft a few leagues through the lower air. Is that so much to ask, when once we had the stars?

He was never one to waste time on idle fancies, though. Certainly Lark never expected *personally* to spy down on Jijo's mountains from a great height.

But look at me now!

Ling had clearly enjoyed watching his expression, when she told him of today's plan.

'We'll be gone most of the day, to pick up some specimens our robots have snared. Later, as the drones roam farther afield, we'll go for trips of several days at a time.'

Lark had stared at the alien flying machine, a slender arrow with stubby wings that unfolded after it exited a narrow tunnel from the buried research station. The hatch gaped like a pair of hungry jaws.

How like Ling to spring this on him without warning!

While Besh loaded supplies, the big blond man, Kunn, shouted, 'Come on, Ling! We're running late. Coax your pet aboard to get another.'

Lark set his jaw, determined to show no emotion as he followed her up a ramp. He expected a cave-like interior, but it turned out to be more brightly lit than any enclosed space he'd ever seen. There was no need to let his eyes adapt.

Not wanting to gawk like a yokel, he aimed for a padded seat next to a window and dropped his pack nearby. Lark sat down gingerly, finding the voluptuous softness neither comfortable *nor* comforting. It felt as if he had settled onto the lap of something fleshy and perhaps queerly amorous. Moments later, Ling added to his unease by strapping a belt across his waist. The hissing closure of the metal hatch made his ears feel funny, increasing his disorientation. The moment the engines came on, Lark felt a strange tickling at the base of his neck, as if a small animal were breathing on the hairs back there. He could not help lifting a hand to brush away at the imaginary creature.

Takeoff was surprisingly gentle, a wafting motion, rising and turning, then the sky-boat swept away so quickly that he had no chance to survey the Glade and its surroundings, or to seek the hidden valley of the Egg. By the time he turned around to press close against the window, the continent was already sweeping underneath as they hurtled southward, many times faster than a catapulted stone. Only minutes later, they dropped away from the alpine hills, streaking over a wide open plain of steppe grass, which bowed and rippled like the ever-changing surface of a phosphorescent sea. At one point, Lark spotted a drove of galloping stem-chompers, a genus of native Jijoan ungulates, which trumpeted distress and reared away from the airboat's passing shadow. A band of urrish herders stretched their sinuous necks in expressions of curiosity mixed with dread. Near the adults, a group of early middlings gamboled and snapped in mock battle, ignoring their elders' sudden, dark focus on the heavens.

'Your enemies certainly are graceful creatures,' Ling commented.

Lark turned and stared at her. *What's she going on about now?*

Ling must have misinterpreted his look, hurrying as if to placate. 'Of course I mean that in a strictly limited sense, the way a horse or other animal can be graceful.'

Lark pondered before answering. 'Hrm. It's too bad your visit disrupted Gathering. We'd normally be having the Games about now. That's when you'd see real grace in action.'

'Games? Oh, yes. Your version of the fabled Olympics. Lots of running and jumping around, I suppose?'

He nodded guardedly. 'There are speed and agility events. Others let our best and bravest test their endurance, courage, adaptability.'

'All traits highly prized by those who brought humanity into being,' Ling said. Her smile was indulgent, faintly condescending. 'I don't imagine any of the six species go up against each other *directly* in any events, do they? I mean, it's hard to picture a g'Kek outrunning an urs, or a qheuen doing a pole vault!' She laughed.

Lark shrugged. Despite Ling's hint regarding a subject of great moment – the question of human origins – he found himself losing interest in the conversation.

'Yes, I suppose it could be. Hard. To picture.'

He turned to look back out the window, watching the great plain sweep by – wave after wave of bending grass, punctuated by stands of dark boo or oases of gently swaying trees. A distance requiring several days to cross by caravan was dismissed in a few brief duras of blithe flight. Then the smoldering mountains of the southern range swarmed into view.

Besh, the forayer pilot, banked the craft to get a closer look at Blaze Mountain, circling at an angle so that Lark's window stared vertiginously on a vast lava apron where past eruption layers spilled across a country that was both ravaged and starkly renewed. For an instant, he glimpsed the smelters that lay clustered halfway up the mighty eminence. Fashioned to resemble native magma tubes and floes, the forge vented steam and smoke no different from that exhaled by nearby wild apertures. Of course, the camouflage was never meant to endure scrutiny as close as this.

Lark saw Besh share a knowing glance with Kunn, who tapped one of his magical viewing screens. Out of several score glowing red lights, outlining the mountain's shape, *one* was marked by sharp symbols and glowing arrows. Dotted lines traced underground passages and workrooms where famed urrish smiths labored to make tools out of those special alloys sanctioned by the sages, second in quality only to those produced farther south, near the peak of towering Mount Guenn.

Incredible, Lark thought, trying to memorize the level of detail shown on Kunn's screen, for his report to Lester Cambel. Clearly that monitor had little to do with the ostensible purpose of this mission – scouting for advanced 'candidate' life-forms. From a few brief exchanges, Lark reckoned Kunn was no biologist. Something in the man's stance, his way of moving, reminded one of Dwer stalking through a forest, only *more* deadly. Even after generations of relative tranquility, a few men and women on the Slope still carried themselves like that, experts whose chief job was to circulate each summer from village to village, training local human militias.

Just in case.

Each of the other five races had similar specialists. A prudent policy, since even now there were regular minor crises – a criminal act here, a wayward tribe of sooners there, and spates of hot-tempered friction between settlements. Enough to make 'peacetime warrior' no contradiction in terms.

The same *might* also be true of Kunn. Looking lethally competent didn't mean he was coiled, preparing to wreak murder.

What's your purpose, Kunn? Lark wondered, watching symbols flash across the screen, crisscrossing reflections of the outlander's face. *What, exactly, are you looking for?*

Blaze Mountain fell behind them as the little vessel now seemed to leap ahead at a new angle, spearing across a brilliant whiteness known as the Plain of Sharp Sand. For a long time, low dunes swept past, undulating in windswept perfection. Lark saw no caravans laboring across the sparkling desert, carrying mail or trade goods to isolated settlements of The Vale. But then, no one sane ranged those searing wastes by day. There were hidden shelters down there, where travelers awaited nightfall, which even Kunn's rays shouldn't be able to pick out, amid the glaring immensity.

The pale dazzle was nothing compared to the *next* sudden transition, crossing over from the sand ocean to the Spectral Flow, a blurry expanse of shifting colors that made Lark's eyes sting. Ling and Besh tried to peer at it past their sheltering hands, before finally giving up, while Kunn muttered sourly at the static on his display. Lark struggled against a natural reflex to squint, endeavoring instead to *loosen* his habitual way of focusing. Dwer had once explained that it was the only way to let oneself see in this realm where exotic crystals cast an ever-changing wildness of luminance.

That had been shortly after Dwer won master hunter status, when he hurried home to join Lark and Sara at their mother's bedside, during the illness that finally took her away, turning Nelo almost overnight into an old man. Melina accepted no food during that final week, and very little drink. Of her two eldest, whose minds she had doted on, day in, day out, ever since arriving in Dolo to be a papermaker's wife, she now seemed to need nothing. But from her youngest child, she devoured tales of his wanderings, the sights, sounds, and sensations of far corners of the Slope where few ever trod. Lark recalled feeling a jealous pang when he saw the contentment Dwer's stories gave in her last hours, then chiding himself for having such unworthy thoughts.

That memory swept over him starkly, apparently triggered by the stabbing colors.

Some credulous folk among the Six said these layers of poison stone had magical properties, poured into them by eons of overlapping volcanic effusions. 'Mother Jijo's blood,' they called it. At that moment, Lark could almost credit the superstition, so struck was he by uncanny waves of *familiarity*. As if he had been here before, sometime long ago.

With that thought, his eyes seemed to adjust – to *open up*, letting the muddle of swirling hues blossom into mirage canyons, figment valleys, ghost cities, and even whole phantom civilizations, vaster than the greatest Buyur sites ...

Then, just as he was starting to enter fully into the experience, the blur of illusion suddenly ended, cut off as the Spectral Flow plunged into the sea. Besh banked the craft again, and soon the sweeping domain of color vanished like a dream, replaced on the left by a more normal desert of windswept igneous rock.

The line of crashing surf became like a fabled highway, pointing toward lands unknown. Lark fumbled to unfasten his seat belt, moving across the aisle to stare over the great ocean. *So vast*, he thought. Yet this was nothing compared to the immensities Ling and her comrades spanned with hardly a thought. His eyes peered in hopes of spotting a camouflaged dross-hauler, its gray-green sails slicing the wind, bearing sacred caskets to their final rest. From this height, he might even glimpse the Midden itself, dark blue waters-of-forgetfulness covering a plunge so deep that its trench could take all the arrogant excesses of a dozen mighty civilizations and still bless them with a kind of absolution – oblivion.

They had already dashed beyond the farthest of Lark's lifetime travels, seeking data for his ever-hungry charts. Even looking with a practiced eye, he found few scattered traces of sapient habitation – a hoonish fishing hamlet, a red qheuen rookery – tucked under rocky clefts or bayou-root canopies. Of course, at this speed something important might sweep by in the time it took to switch windows, which he did frequently as Besh rolled the craft, playing instruments across both shore and sea.

Even those few signs of settlement ceased when they reached the Rift, crossing a few hundred arrowflights west of the distant, hatchet-shape of Terminus Rock.

A series of towering cliffs and deep subsea canyons split the land here. Jagged promontories alternated with seemingly bottomless fingers of dark sea, as if some great claw had gouged parallel grooves almost due east, to form a daunting natural barrier. Dwelling beyond this border labeled you an outlaw, cursed by the sages and by the Holy Egg. But the alien flier made quick work of the realm of serrated clefts and chasms, dismissing them like minor ruts across a well-traveled road.

League after league of sandy scrublands soon passed by, punctuated at long intervals by stark fragments of ancient cities, eroded by wind, salt, and rain. Explosions and pulverizing rays must have shattered the mighty towers, just after the last Buyur tenant turned off the lights. In time, the ceaseless churning of the Midden and its daughter volcanoes would grind even these sky-stabbing stumps to nothing.

Soon the sky-boat left the continent altogether, streaking over chains of mist-shrouded isles.

Even Dwer never dreamed of going this far.

Lark decided not to mention this trip to the lad without discussing it first with Sara, who understood tact and hurt feelings better than either brother.

Then reality hit home. *Sara's back in Dolo. Dwer may be sent off east, hunting glavers and sooners. And when the aliens finish their survey, we all may meet our end, far from those we love.*

Lark sank into his seat with a sigh. For a while there, he had actually been enjoying himself. *Damn* memory, for reminding him the way things were!

For the rest of the trip he kept low key and businesslike, even when they finally landed near forests eerily different from those he knew, or while helping Ling haul aboard cages filled with strange, marvelous creatures. Professionalism was one pleasure Lark still allowed himself – a relish for studying nature's ways. But there remained little zest or wonder in the thought of flying.

It was after nightfall when Lark finally shuffled back to his own shabby tent near the Glade – only to find Harullen waiting there with news.

The low massive figure took up fully half the shelter. At first, standing in the entry with only dim moonlight behind him, Lark thought it was *Uthen*, his friend and fellow naturalist. But this qheuen's ash-colored carapace wasn't scarred from a lifetime digging into Jijo's past. *Harullen* was a bookworm, a mystic who spoke with aristocratic tones reminiscent of Gray Queens of old.

'The zealots sent a message,' the heretic leader announced portentously, without even asking Lark about his day.

'Oh? Finally? And what do they say?' Lark dropped his daypack by the entrance and sagged onto his cot.

'As you predicted, they desire a meeting. It is arranged for tonight at midnight.'

Echo-whispers of the final word escaped speaking vents in back, as the qheuen shifted his weight. Lark suppressed a groan. He still had a report to prepare for the sages, summarizing everything he'd learned today. Moreover, Ling wanted him bright and early the next morning, to help evaluate the new specimens.

And now this?

Well, what can you expect when you play games of multiple loyalty? Old-time novels warn how hard things can get when you serve more than one master.

Events were accelerating. Now the rumored, secretive rebel organization had finally offered to talk. What choice had he but to go?

'All right,' he told Harullen. 'Come get me when it's time. Meanwhile, I have work to do.'

The gray qheuen departed silently, except for a faint clicking of claws on the rocky trail. Lark struck a match that sputtered rank fumes before settling enough to light his tiny oil lamp. He unfolded the portable writing table Sara had given him when he graduated from the Roney School, what seemed a geologic age ago. Pulling out a sheet of his father's best writing paper, he then shaved black powder from a half-used ink stick into a clay mortar, mixed the dust with fluid from a small bottle, and ground the mixture with a pestle till all the lumps were gone. Lark used his pocket knife to sharpen his tree-staller quill pen. At last he dipped the tip into the ink, paused for a moment, and began to write his report.

It was true, Lark realized later, during a tense conclave by the wan opal glow of Torgen, the second moon. Tentatively, suspiciously, the zealots were indeed offering alliance with Harullen's loose-knit society of heretics.

Why? The two groups have different aims. We seek to reduce, then end, our illegal presence on this fragile world. The zealots only want the old status quo back, our hidden secrecy restored, as it was before the raider ship came – and perhaps a few old scores settled along the way.

Still, envoys of the two groups gathered in the dead of night, near a steaming fumarole, by the winding path leading to the silent nest of the Egg. Most of those in the conspiracy wore heavy cloaks to hide their identities. Harullen, who was among the few still to possess a functioning rewq, was asked to remove the squirming symbiont from his sensory cupola, lest the delicate creature burn itself out in the atmosphere of strained intrigue. Creatures of the Great Peace, rewq were not suited for times of war.

Or is it because the zealots don't want us to see too much, Lark pondered. Not for nothing were rewq called the 'mask that reveals.'

Their near-universal hibernation was as troubling as the heavy silence of the Egg itself.

Before starting, the zealots first cracked open several jars, releasing swarms of privacy wasps around the periphery – an ancient ritual whose origins had been lost but that now made earnest sense, after discoveries of the last few days. Then the urrish spokesman for the cabal stepped forward, speaking in Galactic Two.

'Your association sees opportunity in the (greatly lamented) coming of these felons,' she accused. The whistles and clicks were muffled by a cowl, obscuring all but the tip of her muzzle. Still, Lark could tell she wasn't many seasons past a middling, with at most one husband pouched under an arm. Her diction implied education, possibly at one of the plains academies where young urs, fresh from the herd, gathered within sight of some steaming volcano, to apprentice in their finest arts. *An intellectual, then. All full of book learning and the importance of her own ideas.*

Yeah, a part of him answered honestly. *In other words, not too different from yourself.*

Harullen answered the rebel's challenge, making a political point by speaking Anglic.

'What do you mean by that strange proposition?'

'We mean that you perceive, in these (disliked/unwelcome) aliens, a chance to see your ultimate goals fulfilled!'

The urs stamped a foreleg. Her insinuation sent angry murmurs through the heretic delegation. Yet Lark had seen it coming.

Harullen's gray carapace rocked an undulating circle. A traeki gesture, which the ringed ones called Objection to Unjust Impeachment.

'You imply that we condone our own murder. And that of every sapient on Jijo.'

The urrish conspirator imitated the same motion, but in reverse – Reiteration of Indictment.

'I do so (emphatically) imply. I do so (in brutal frankness) mean. All know this is what you heretics (misguidedly) desire.'

Lark stepped forward. If the zealots' murmur included any anti-human slurs, he ignored them.

'That is not (negation reiterated) what we desire!' Lark complained, garbling the qualifier trill-phrase in his haste to speak up.

'There are two reasons for this,' he continued, still struggling in GalTwo.

'First among our grounds (for rebuttal) is this – the aliens (greedy to extreme fault) must not only eliminate all sapient witnesses (to crime/to theft) who might testify in a Galactic court. They must also wipe out the native stock of any (unlucky) species they steal from Jijo!

Otherwise, how embarrassing would it be someday, when the (foolish) thieves announce their adoption of a new client race, only to be confronted with proof that it was stolen from this world? For this reason they must exterminate the original population, when they depart.

'This we (in righteousness) cannot allow! Genocide of innocent life is the very crime our group was (in selfless righteousness) formed to fight!'

Harullen and the other heretics shouted approval. Lark found his throat too dry to continue in Galactic Two. He had made the gesture. Now he switched to Anglic.

'But there is another reason to resist being slaughtered by the aliens.

'There is no honor in simply being killed. Our group's goal is to seek agreement, consensus, so that the Six shall do the right thing slowly, painlessly, *voluntarily*, by means of birth control, as an act of nobility and devotion to this world we love.'

'The effect, in the end, would be identical,' the urrish speaker pointed out, slipping into the same language Lark used.

'Not when the truth is finally revealed! And it *will* be, someday, when this world has new legal tenants, who take up the common hobby of archaeology.'

That statement triggered confused silence. Even Harullen rotated his cupola to stare at Lark.

'Exflain, flease.' The urrish rebel bent her forelegs, urging him to continue. 'What difference will archaeology signify, once we and all our descendants are long gone, our hoof bones littering the wallows of the sea?'

Lark drew himself up, fighting fatigue.

'Eventually, despite all efforts to live by the Scrolls and leave no permanent marks, this story *will* someday be told. A million years from now, or ten, it will become known that a society of sooners once dwelled here, descendants of selfish fools who invaded Jijo for reasons long forgotten. Beings who nonetheless *transcended* their ancestors' foolishness, teaching themselves where true greatness lies.

'*That* is the difference between seeking dignified self-extinction and being foully murdered. For honor's sake, and by all the blessings of the Egg, the choice must be *ours*, every individual's, not imposed on us by a pack of criminals!'

Harullen and his other friends were clearly moved. They shouted, hissed, and umbled fervent support. Lark even heard some approving murmurs among the cowled zealots. Without benefit of rewq, he could tell he was managing to sound convincing – although deep inside, he scarcely believed his own words.

Ling's bunch don't seem to fear archaeological hobbyists of some future eon.

In fact, Lark didn't give a damn either, whether some obscure historical footnote said nice things about the Six, far in the distant future.

Good laws don't need rewards or recognition to make them right. They're true and just on their own account and should be honored even if you know that no one else is watching. Even if no one ever knows.

Despite all the well-recited flaws of Galactic civilization, Lark knew the rules protecting fallow worlds were *right*. Though he'd been born flouting them, it was still his duty to help see to it they were obeyed.

Contrary to his own words, he had no objection, in principle, to Ling's bunch eliminating local witnesses, if the means were gentle. *Take a gene-tailored plague, one leaving everyone healthy but sterile. That might handle their witness predicament and solve Jijo's problem as well.*

Ah, but Lark also had a duty to oppose the raiders' gene-stealing scheme. That, too, was a violation of Jijo, not unlike rape. With the sages apparently waffling, only the zealot conspiracy seemed willing to fight the alien threat.

Hence Lark's impassioned lie, meant to build trust between two very different radical bands. He wanted a coalition with the zealots, for one simple reason. If there were plans afoot, Lark wanted a say in them.

Cooperate for now, he told himself as he spoke on, using his best oratorical skills to soothe their suspicions, arguing persuasively for alliance.

Cooperate, but keep your eyes open.

Who knows? There may come a way to accomplish both goals with a single stroke.

ASX

The universe demands of us a sense of irony.

For example, all the effort and good will that forged the Great Peace was worthwhile. We folk of the Commons became better, wiser because of it. We also supposed it would work in our favor, if/when Galactic inspectors came to judge us. Warring nations do more harm to a world than those who calmly discuss how best to tend a shared garden. It would surely weigh well that we were courteous and gentle criminals, not rapacious ones.

Or so we reasoned. Did we not, my rings? Alas, no judges dropped from the sky, but thieves and liars. Suddenly, we must play deadly games of intrigue, and those skills are not what they were in days before Commons and Egg.

How much more capable we might have been, if not for peace!

We rediscovered this truth with sharp pangs today, when a panting galloper showed up with dispatches from the forge-study of Uriel the Smith. Words of warning. Dire admonitions, telling of sky-portents, urging that we brace ourselves for visitation by a starship!

Oh, tardy premonition! A caution that arrived too late by far.

Once, stone citadels nestled on bitter-cold peaks, from north of Biblos all the way down to the tropic settlements of the Vale, flashing messages via cleverly fashioned mirrors, outracing the swiftest urrish couriers or even racing birds. With their semaphore, humans and their allies mobilized speedily for battle, making up skillfully for their lack of numbers. In time, urs and hoon developed systems of their own, each clever in its way. Even we traeki formed a network of scent-spore trackers, to warn of possible danger.

None of these feats survived peace. The semaphore was abandoned, the system of signal rockets allowed to lapse. Until lately, commerce alone simply did not justify such costly media – though ironically just last year investors had begun speaking of reoccupying those frigid stone aeries, resuming the network of flashed messages.

Had they moved faster, would we have received Uriel's warning in time?

Would receiving it have made any difference in our fate?

Ah, my rings. How vain it is to dwell on might-have-beens. Other than solipsism, it may be the most mad thing that unitary beings waste their time doing.

RETY

'Do you have something for me?'

Rann, the tall, stern-looking leader of the sky-humans, held out his hand toward her. In the late twilight, with wind rustling a nearby thicket of pale boo, it seemed to Rety that each of his calloused fingers was like her entire wrist. Moonlight brought out shadows on Rann's craggy features and wedgelike torso. She tried not to show it, but Rety felt all too insignificant in his presence.

Are all men like this, out there among the stars?

The thought made her feel funny, like earlier, when Besh told her it was possible to smooth away her scars.

First had come bad news.

'We cannot do anything about it here in our little clinic,' the for-ayer woman had told her, during Rety's brief turn at the aliens' sick call, near their buried station.

She had been standing in line for half the morning, a horrid wait, spent shuffling between a g'Kek with a wheezy, lopsided wheel and an aged urs whose nostril dripped a ghastly gray fluid. Rety tried hard not to step in it each time the queue moved forward. When her chance finally came to be examined under bright lights and probing rays, her hopes soared, then crashed.

'This kind of dermal damage would be easy to repair back home,' Besh had said, while ushering Rety toward the tent flap. 'Bio-sculpting is a high art. Experts can mold a pleasant form out of even .primitive material.'

Rety wasn't offended. *Primitive material. It's what I am, all right.* Anyway, at the time she was dazed from imagining – what if Galactic wizardry could give her a face and body like Besh, or Ling?

She set her feet, refusing to budge till Besh let her speak.

'They – they say you may take some humans with you, when you go.'

Besh had looked down at her with eyes the color of golden-brown gemstones.

'Who says such things?'

'I . . . hear stuff. Rumors, I guess.'

'You should not believe all rumors.'

Had there been extra emphasis on the word *all*? Rety leaped on any excuse for hope.

'I also hear you pay good when folks bring things you want – or news you need.'

'That much is true.' Now the eyes seemed to glitter a little. From amusement? Or greed?

'And if the news is really, *really* valuable? What'd be the reward then?'

The star-woman smiled, a grin full of friendship and promise. 'Depending on how helpful or precious the information – the sky's the limit.'

Rety had felt a thrill. She started to reach into her belt pouch. But Besh stopped her. 'Not now,' the woman said in a low voice. 'It is not discreet.'

Looking left and right, Rety realized there were other patients around, and employees of the forayers – members of the Six serving as assistants in the aliens' many enterprises. Any one could be a spy for the sages.

'Tonight,' Besh had told her in a low voice. 'Rann goes walking each evening, down by the stream. Wait next to the stand of *yellow* boo. The one just coming into bloom. Come alone, and speak to no one you see along the way.'

Great! Rety had thought jubilantly on leaving the tent. *They're interested! It's exactly what I was hoping for. And just in the nick o' time.*

All might have been lost if it had taken much longer to make contact. The chief human sage had decreed she must leave tomorrow, accompanying a small donkey caravan aimed up into the mountains, along with two silent men and three big women she had never met before. Nothing was said, but she knew the goal was to catch up with Dwer, and from there head back to the wilderness she came from.

No chance of that! she had thought, relishing tonight's rendezvous. *Dwer's welcome to go play hunter in the forest. While he's scratchin' for eats in the Gray Hills, I'll be living high an' mighty, up on the Dolphin's Tail.*

That was the constellation where, rumor had it, the forayers came from, although the crablike sage, Knife-Bright Insight, once tried explaining to Rety about galaxies and 'transfer points' and how the route back to civilization was twisty as a mulc-spider's vine. None of it made sense, and she figured the old qheuen was probably lying. Rety far preferred the idea of going to a star she could clearly see – which meant she would someday look *back* at Jijo from the beautiful Galactic city where she'd gone to live, and stick her tongue out every night at Jass and Bom and their whole stinking tribe. And Dwer and the sages, for that matter, along with everyone else on this rancy planet who was ever mean to her.

All day after meeting Besh she had avoided the sages and their servants, seeking the clearings several arrowflights to the west, where some pilgrims were trying to restore a few of the festivities of Gathering. Pavilions that had been taken down in panic were now restored, and many folk had come out of hiding. There was still plenty of tension. But some people seemed determined to get on with life, even if just for a little while.

She visited one tent where craft-workers showed wares brought from all over the Slope. Their goods would have impressed Rety even yesterday. But now she smiled scornfully, having seen the bright machines the sky-humans used. At one panel discussion, she watched hoon, g'Kek, and human experts discuss improved techniques for weaving rope. The atmosphere was hushed, and few in the audience asked questions.

Nearby, a traeki ring-breeder displayed some flabby donut shapes with slender arms, eye buds, or stubby feet. A trio of mature traeki stood near the pen, perhaps pondering additions to a newborn stack they were building back home. Or maybe they were just browsing.

Farther along, in a sun-dappled glade, chimp acrobats performed for a crowd of children, and an all-race sextet played by a simmering hot spring. It all might have seemed quite gay if Rety didn't sense a pall, spoiling the mood. And if she had not already hardened her heart to all things Jijoan.

These Slopies think they're so much better than a pack of dirty sooners. Well, maybe it's so. But then, everybody *on Jijo is a sooner, ain't they?*

I'm going far away, so it won't matter to me anymore.

In a rougher clearing, she passed much of the afternoon watching human kids and urrish middlings vie in a game of Drake's Dare.

The playing field was a strip of sand with a stream along one side. The other border was a long pit filled with coals, smoldering under a coating of gray ash. Wisps of hot smoke wafted into Rety's face, tugging painful memories of Jass and Bom. Her scars tightened till she moved a ways uphill, sitting under the shade of a dwarf garu.

Two contestants arrived – a human boy starting at the north end of the field and a burly urrish middling at the south – sauntering and hurling insults as they neared the center, where two umpires waited.

'Hey, hinney! Get ready to take a bath!' the boy taunted, trying to swagger but hindered by his left arm, which was trussed back with cloth bindings. He wore a leather covering from crotch to chin, but his legs and feet were bare.

The young urs had her own protections and handicaps. Tough, transparent junnoor membranes stretched tight over her delicate pouches and scent glands. As the middling drew close, she tried to rear up threateningly – and almost fell over, to the amusement of onlookers. Rety saw the reason – her hind pair of legs were hobbled together.

'Silly skirl!' the urs shouted at her adversary, retaining her balance to hop forward once more. 'Vavy skirl gonna get vurned!'

Along both boundaries – beyond the coal bed and across the stream – crowds of other youths gathered to watch. Many wore leather or membrane protectors, hanging jauntily open, while waiting for their own turn in the arena. Some boys and girls smeared salve over livid reddish streaks along their calves and thighs and even their faces, making Rety wince. True, none of the burns looked anywhere near as deep or wounding as her own. No blisters or horrid, charred patches. Still, how could they risk getting scorched *on purpose*?

The thought both nauseated and queerly fascinated Rety.

Was this so very different from her own story, after all? She had known that standing up to Jass would have consequences, yet she did it anyway.

Sometimes you just gotta fight, that's all. Her hand lifted briefly to touch her face. She regretted nothing. Nothing.

Some urrish spectators also bore marks of recent combat, especially on their legs, where swaths of fur had gone mangy or sloughed off. Strangely, there wasn't any clear separation along race lines – no human cheering section versus an urrish one. Instead, there was a lot of mixing, preliminary sparring, and friendly comparing of techniques and throws. Rety saw one human boy joke with a middling urs, laughing with his arm on her sleek mane.

A sizable group of zookirs and chimps screeched at each other in excitement, making wagers of piu nodules and pounding the ground with their hands.

Some distance beyond the coals, Rety saw another makeshift arena being used by juvenile traekis with newly wedded rings, engaged in a different kind of sport with g'Kek youngsters so light and agile, they spun wheelies and even lifted to stride briefly on their rear pusher legs. That tournament seemed to involve a sort of rolling, whirling dance. Rety couldn't make out the point, but clearly the pastime was less violent than Drake's Dare.

A pair of qheuen umpires – one gray and one blue – awaited the two contestants in the middle of the sandy strip. They carefully inspected the human's sleeve for weapons, then checked the middling's teeth for caps on her scythelike incisors. The blue qheuen then backed away into the stream while the gray extended armored legs and, to Rety's blinking surprise, stepped daintily onto the bed of steaming coals! From then on it kept shifting its weight, lifting two clawed feet at a time high above the fuming surface, then switching to another pair, and so on.

After ritually – and warily – bowing to each other, the boy and middling began circling, looking for weakness.

Abruptly, they sprang at each other, grappling, each trying to push, twist, or throw the other in the direction he or she least wanted to go. Now Rety saw the reason for the handicaps. With both hind legs tied, the urs could not stomp her opponent or simply power her way to victory. Likewise, the boy's strong, agile arms might throttle the middling, unless one was bound to his side.

'*drak's dare! drak's dare! yippee yooee!*'

The tiny, squeaky voice startled Rety, coming from much closer than the crowd of shouting onlookers. She swiveled, seeking the source, but saw no one nearby till a tug on her tunic made her look down.

'pouch-safe? yee talk! you me pouch-safe and yee talk you!'

Rety stared. It was a tiny urs! No bigger than her foot, it danced delicately on four miniature hooves while still plucking at her garment. The little creature tossed its mane, rotating a sinuous neck to peer around behind it, nervously, *'yee need pouch! need pouch!'*

Rety turned to follow its anxious stare and glimpsed what had it terrified. A sleek black shape crouched in the undergrowth, panting slightly, a lolling tongue hanging between rows of sharp white teeth. At first, Rety felt a shock of recognition, thinking it was Mudfoot, grouchy old Dwer's funny companion in the mountains. Then she saw this one had no brown paw patches. A different noor, then.

The predator raised its head and leered at the tiny urs, taking a step, then another.

On impulse, Rety scooped up the quivering prey and slipped it in her leather hip-pouch.

The noor gave her a look of puzzled disappointment, then turned to vanish in the shrubs.

Cheers, boos, and excited snorts made her look up in time to see the human contestant tumble through a cloud of billowing ash. To Rety's amazement, the boy was not instantly set ablaze but rolled erect, dancing from bare foot to bare foot on the coals, swiftly but calmly brushing embers from crevices in his leather garment. He waved off the gray qheuen, who had hurried protectively to his side. The youth ran a hand along his collar one more time, then sauntered across more glowing cinders back to the sandy arena.

Rety was impressed. Slopies seemed tougher than she'd thought.

'hot-hot, but not much heat!' the little voice squeaked from her pouch, as if pleased by her surprise. All memory of flight from the hungry noor seemed forgotten, *'boy make boo-boo. slip and fall, but not again, not this boy! he tops! watch silly hinney get wet!'*

Rety wrestled with her own amazement, unable to decide which thing dumbfounded her more, the contest below or the entity in her pocket, providing running commentary.

Combat won her attention as the young human launched at his opponent once more. Whatever his mistake the first time, the boy seemed bent on making up for it as he bobbed and weaved, then leaped to catch a handful of the middling's mane. She snorted and snapped, pushing vainly with both slim handling-arms to break his grip. She tried lifting a foreleg to tug with its stubby grasping paw, but that just left her teetering dangerously.

'*drak's dare!*' the tiny urs shouted gleefully, '*drak say to Ur-choon. you-me tussle, tussle 'stead of kill!*'

Rety caught her breath.

Oh, I remember now.

She had heard the legend when she was little, told round the campfire by one of the old grandpas. A tale that died with the old man, since Jass and the young hunters preferred exaggerated retellings of their own exploits over stories of life beyond the mountains.

To Rety's best recollection, there once had been a man named Drak – or Drake – a hero mightier and bolder than any human before or since. Once, when Earthlings were still new on Jijo, a giant urrish chieftain fought Drak in a wrestling match. For three days and nights they grappled, pounding and tearing at each other, making the ground shake, drying up rivers, ripping all the countryside between a fiery mountain and the sea, till both volcano and ocean vanished in curling steam. When the clouds finally cleared, a bright region glowed from horizon to horizon with all the colors one could paint by mixing urrish and human blood.

Then, out of the smoke and mist, two heroes strode forth – he missing an arm and she a leg – leaning on each other, inseparable from that day forth.

While there would be more wars between the tribes, from that day forth all were fought with honor, in memory of Drak and Ur-choon.

'*watch!*' the little urs called.

The boy faked a leftward lean, then planted his right foot and heaved. Snorting dismay, the urs could not keep her greater weight from pivoting over his hip, sailing head-over-withers to crash into the nearby stream. There came a shrill sigh as she floundered, slipping in the mud. Finally, the blue qheuen surfaced behind her, using one clenched foot to give a helpful shove. With a grateful cry, the middling dove into the sand, raising plumes of dust.

'*hee! go roll in hot ash, silly hinney! sand too slow! hair gonna rot!*'

Rety gazed down at the tiny urs. It was no baby, as first she thought. Somewhere she recalled hearing that urrish newborns stayed in their mothers' pouches for a few months, then were spilled by the dozen into tall grass to fend for themselves. Anyway, infant urs couldn't talk.

It must be a male! Rety saw that its throat and muzzle looked unlike a female's, lacking the flashy neck colors or pendulous cloven lip, which explained why it could speak Anglic sounds a female could not.

Back in the arena, the boy crouched for a third round, but the urrish youth lowered her head, conceding. The human raised a red-streaked arm in victory, then helped guide the limping loser off the playing field. Meanwhile, two new contestants flexed and stretched, while helpers trussed their handicapped limbs.

Wistfully, Rety watched the human kids, joking with friends from the other septs. She wondered how the boy had managed to get just slightly singed by the coals – but could not bring herself to approach with questions. They might only laugh at her unkempt hair, her uncouth speech, and her scars.

So forget 'em, anyway, she thought bitterly. All the dry heat and smoke was making her face itch. In any case, she had important business. An item to retrieve from her tent before dark. Something to use as down payment on a ticket *away* from here, to a place none of these big handsome kids would ever see, despite all their pride and skill and strutting around. A place where no one from her past would bother her. That was lots more important than watching savages play violent games with fire and water.

'Look, I gotta go,' she told the little urrish male, rising to her feet and looking around. 'I think the nasty ol' noor's gone away, so you can be off now too.'

The tiny creature peered at her, his tail and muzzle drooping. Rety cleared her throat.

'Um, can I drop you off somewhere? Isn't your – uh – *wife* prob'ly worried about you?'

The dark eyes glittered sadly. *'Uf-roho need yee no more, pouch home now full of slimy newbrats. push yee out. right-pouch still husband-full, yee must find new pouch, or grass burrow to live/die in. but no sweet grass in mountain! just rocks!'*

That last was sung mournfully. It sounded like an awful thing to do to a helpless little guy, and Rety felt mad just thinking about it.

'this nice *pouch, this one.'* He crooned a strange reverberating melody, surprisingly low for a creature so small. Rety's skin tingled where he lay closest.

'yee serve new wife good, do good things she want.'

Rety stared at him, dazed to think of what he offered. Then she burst out laughing, leaning on a tree, guffawing till her sides hurt. Through clouded eyes, she saw that *yee* seemed to laugh too, in his own fashion. At last she wiped her face and grinned. 'Well, you done one thing for me, already. Ain't chortled so good in I dunno how long.

'An' you know what else? Come to think of it, there *is* somethin' you might be able to do. Somethin' that'd make me even happier.'

'yee do anything! new wife feed yee. yee make wife happy!'

Rety shook her head, amazed once more at the twists and turns life seemed to push on the unwary. If her new idea worked out, this could turn out to be an awfully lucky break.

'Do you have something for me?'

Rann held out his enormous hand. In the dim twilight, with the yellow boo rustling nearby, Rety stared at the man's calloused fingers, each like her wrist. His craggy features and massive torso – so much greater than the biggest boy-wrestler playing Drake's Dare that day – made her feel callow, insignificant.

Rety wondered – *Are all men like this, out there among the stars? Could I ever trust anyone with hands like those, to have a husband's power over me?*

She had always thought she'd rather die than marry.

Yet now she *had* a husband, purring next to her belly.

Rety felt yee's warm tongue on her hand as she stroked his silky neck.

Rann seemed to note her ironic smile. Did it make her seem more confident?

She reached past yee to pluck a slender object, fluffy at one end, pointy-hard at the other, and laid the feather on Rann's open palm. Puzzled, he drew forth an instrument to shine at it from several sides, while her mind still cycled round-and-round the events leading to this moment, when her hopes hung in the balance.

On her way here, Rety had passed other members of the Six, each waiting alone by some landmark along Rann's regular evening stroll. As instructed, no one spoke or made eye contact, though Rety spied observers – a g'Kek, two hoons, and a human – taking notes from a distance.

Rety didn't give a damn what they told Lester Cambel about her 'treason.' After tonight, the sages wouldn't make plans for her anymore.

On arriving at the yellow boo, she had waited nervously, petting yee and biting her fingernails. A few duras before Rann appeared, a soft whine announced one of the mighty robots – eight-sided, intimidating – and a wave of horrid memory recalled another floating monster, firing savagely into the mulc-spider's lair ... and Dwer's strong arms yanking her out of the path of a searing beam, holding her fiercely against falling, sheltering her with his body.

Rety bit her lip, quashing any thought, any memory, that might shake her resolve. Now was no time to go sappy and soft. That was what the sages wanted.

As she had done countless times back home – making herself stand up to Jass despite horrid punishments – she had stopped cowering from the dark robot, standing straight, forcing her chin out.

You can't harm me, she projected defiantly. *You wouldn't dare!*

But an unwelcome thought fizzed up from below.

One of these killed the bird.

The bird fought it and died.

A surge of guilt nearly made her spin around and flee. But then the robot had swerved aside, vanishing into the night, and Rann took its place, holding out his massive hand.

'Do you have something for me?' he had asked, smiling till Rety handed over the feather.

Now she watched him grow excited as he played instruments over the souvenir, once her prize possession. Pressing lips together, she bore down to reinforce her resolve.

Hell yes, I have somethin' for you, Mister Star-Man. Somethin' I bet you want pretty bad.

The point is – you better have somethin' for me, too!

XV

THE BOOK OF THE SEA

The Path takes time, so time
you must clearly buy.

When the lawful seek you – hide.
When they find you – be discreet.
When you are judged – do not quail.

What you have tried to do is rightly banned.
But there is a beauty in it, if done well.

On this, most agree.

—*The Scroll of Redemption*

I've got my Anglic dictionary and usage guide with me right now, so I'm going to try an experiment. To capture some of the drama of what happened next, I'm going to try my narrative skill in *present tense*. I know it's not used in many of the Old Earth stories I've read, but when it's done right, I think it lends a buff sense of *immediacy* to a story. Here goes.

I left off with little Ziz – the traeki partial we all witnessed being vlenned a week ago, on the day Gybz turned erself into Tyug and forgot all about starships – slithering its way from pen to derrick, where we were about to test the bathy for the first time. Ziz had spent the last week voring a rich feed-mix and had grown a lot. Still, it made a pretty short stack. Nobody expects miracles of strength or brilliance from a half-pint traeki that barely reaches my bottom set of knees.

Ziz follows Tyug's scentomone trail almost to the edge of the cliff, where you can stare straight down into the Great Midden as it takes a sharp hook, stabbing the continent with a wound so deep and wide, our ancestors chose it as a natural boundary for settler life on Jijo.

The towering bulk of Terminus Rock casts a long morning shadow, but *Wuphon's Dream*, our pride and joy, dangles just beyond, shimmering in a blaze of sunlight. Instead of slithering up the ramp to the sealed cabin hatch, Ziz glides into a little cage mounted under the bulb window, in front of eighteen heavy ballast stones. As it passes Tyug, Ziz and the full-size traeki exchange puffs of vapor in a language no other member of the Six is equipped to even try to understand.

The cage closes. Urdonnol whistles a call, and gangs of hoon and qheuens set to work, first swinging the bathy gently away, then lowering it toward the sea, unreeling both the taut hawser and the double hose. The drums turn to a slow steady beat, singing over and over—

rumble-dum-dumble-um-rumble-dum-dumble-um ...

It draws us. Hoon all over the mesa – even protestors – get caught up in the pulselike cadence of joyful labor. A rhythm of teamwork, sweat, and a job under way.

Being the only noor present, Huphu seems to think it her duty to scamper like a wild thing, taking perches high on the derricks like they're ship masts, arching her back and stretching as if the umble is being sung just for her, a physical hand petting her back, stroking the bristles on her head. Her eyes sparkle, watching our bathy dip lower and lower with Ziz visible as a single tentacle dangling from the wire cage.

It occurs to me that maybe Huphu thinks the little traeki is being used as *bait* at the end of a really big fishing line! Maybe Huphu's curious what we're trying to catch.

That, in turn, brings to mind Pincer's wild tales of 'monsters' in the deep. Neither he nor Huck has mentioned a word about it since we arrived, each for his or her own reasons, I guess. Or am I the only one who hasn't forgotten, amid all the recent excitement?

Wuphon's Dream descends below the cliff face, and we rush near the edge to keep her in sight. Qheuens don't like heights and react by hunkering down, scraping their abdomens, clutching the ground. That's where I go too, lying prone and screwing up my courage to slide forward. Huck, on the other hand, just rolls up to the stony rim, teeters with her pusher legs jutting back for balance, then sticks two of her eyestalks over as far as they'll go.

What a girl. So much for g'Keks being cautious, hi-kay beings. Watching her, I realize I can't do any less, so I creep my head over the rim and force my eyelids apart.

Looking west, the ocean is a vast carpet stretching to a far horizon. Pale colors dominate where the sea covers only a few cables' depth of continental shelf. But a band of dark blue-gray tells of a *canyon*, stabbing our way from the giant planetary scar called the Midden. That deep-deep gorge passes almost directly under our aerie, then drives on farther east, splitting the land like a crack in the clinker boards of a doomed ship. The far shore is just a hundred or so arrowflights away, but rows of razor-sharp crags and near-bottomless ravines parallel the Rift, making it a daunting barrier for anyone wishing to defy the law.

I'm no scientist; regrettably, I don't have the mind for it. But even I can tell the jagged spires must be new, or else wind and surf and rain would've worn them down by now. Like Mount Guenn, this is a place where Jijo is actively renewing itself. (We felt two small quakes since setting up camp here.) No wonder some think Terminus Rock a sacred spot.

The surf is a crashing, spuming show elsewhere, but here the sea settles down mysteriously – glassy smooth. A slight out-tow draws gently *away* from the cliff. Ideal conditions for our experiment – *if* they're reliable. No one ever thought to make soundings in the Rift before, since no dross ships ever come this way.

Wuphon's Dream drops lower, like a spiderfly trailing twin filaments behind her. It gets hard to tell exactly how far she is from the surface. Huck's eyestalks are spread as far apart as possible, trying to maximize depth perception. She murmurs.

'Okay, here we go, into the drink ... *now!*'

I hold my breath, but nothing happens. The big drums keep feeding out cable and hose. The bathy gets smaller.

'Now!' Huck repeats.

Another dura passes, and *Wuphon's Dream* is still dry.

'Sure is a long way down-own-own,' Pincer stutters.

'You can say that again,' adds Ur-ronn, stamping nervously.

'But please don't,' Huck snaps, showing pique. Then in GalSix – '*Reality merges with expectation when—*'

It serves her right – a splash cuts off whatever deep insight she was about to share. The big drums' song slows and deepens as I stare across the vast, wet stillness where the *Dream* vanished.

roomble—doom—doomble—oom—roomble—doom— doomble ...

It sounds like the world's biggest hoon. One who never has to take a break or a breath. Based on that umble, the big derrick would've won the title of Honorary Captain of the South if it came to a vote then and there.

Huphu is all the way out at the end of the deployer crane, back arched with pleasure. Meanwhile, someone counts off.

'One *cable, forty* ...

'One cable, *sixty* ...

'One cable, *eighty* ...

'*Two cables!*

'Two cables, *twenty* ...

The chant reminds me of Mark Twain's tales of river pilots on the romantic Mississippi, especially one scene with a big black man-human up at the bow of the *Delta Princess*, swinging a weight on a line, calling out shoals in a treacherous fog, saving the lives of everyone aboard.

I'm an ocean hoon. My people sail *ships*, not sissy boats. Still, those were among my father's favorite tales. And Huck's too, back when she was a little orphan, toddling around on her pusher legs, four eyes staring in lost wonder as Dad recited tales set on a wolfling world that never knew the stifling wisdom of Galactic ways. A world where ignorance wasn't exactly noble, but had one virtue – it gave you a chance to see and learn and do things no one else had ever seen or learned or done before.

Humans got to do that back on Earth.

And now we're doing it here!

Before I even know I'm doing it, I sit up on my double-fold haunches, rock my head back, and belt out an umble of joy. A mighty, rolling hoot. It resounds across the mesa, strokes the grumbling equipment, and floats over the serrated stones of the Great Rift.

For all I know, it's floating out there still.

Sunshine spills across calm waters at least twenty cables deep. We imagine *Wuphon's Dream*, drifting ever downward, first through a cloud of bubbles, then a swollen wake of silence as the light from above grows dimmer and finally fails completely.

'Six cables, *sixty* …

'Six cables, *eighty* …

'*Seven cables!*'

When we go down, this is where we'll turn on the eik lights and use the acid battery to send sparks up the hawser, telling those above that all is well. But *Ziz* has no lights, or any way to signal. The little stack is all alone down there – though I guess no traeki ever feels entirely lonely. Not when its rings can argue endlessly among themselves.

'*Eight cables!*'

Someone brings a jar of wine for me and some warm simla blood for Ur-ronn. Huck sips pungent galook-ade from a long curvy straw, while Pincer sprays his back with salt water.

'*Nine cables!*'

This experiment's only supposed to go to ten, so they begin gently increasing pressure on the brake. Soon they'll reverse the drums to bring *Wuphon's Dream* back to the world of air and light.

Then it happens – a sudden twang, like a plucked violus string, loud as thunder.

The deployer chief cries – '*Release the brake!*'

An operator leaps for a lever … too late as bucking convulsions hit the derrick, like a backlash on a fishing pole when a big one gets away. Only this recoil is massive, unstoppable.

We all gasp or vurt at the sight of *Huphu*, a small black figure clinging to the farthest spar as the crane whips back and forth.

One paw, then another, loses its grip. She screams.

The tiny noor goes spinning across space, barely missing the hawser's cyclone whirl amid a frothing patch of sea. Staring in helpless dismay, we see our mascot plunge into the abyss that already swallowed Ziz, *Wuphon's Dream*, and all the hopes and hard work of two long years.

XVI

THE BOOK OF THE SLOPE

Legends

The urs tell of a crisis of breeding.

Out among the stars, they were said to live longer than they do on Jijo, with spans much enhanced by artificial means. Moreover, an urs never stops wanting a full pouch, tenanted either with a husband or with brooding young. There were technical ways to duplicate the feeling, but to many, those methods just weren't the same.

Galactic society is harsh on overbreeders, who threaten the billion-year-old balance. There is a constant dread of another 'wildfire' – a conflagration of overpopulation, like one that burned almost half the worlds in Galaxy Three, a hundred or so million years ago.

Especially, those species who reproduce slowly, like hoon, seem to have a deep-set fear of 'low-K' spawners, like urs.

Legend tells of a conflict over this matter, heading between the lines of ornate urrish oral history, it seems the bards must be telling of a *lawsuit* – one judged at the higher levels of Galactic society.

The urs lost the suit, and a bitter war-of-enforcement that followed.

Some of the losers did not wish to settle, even then. They turned one ship toward forbidden spaces, there to search for a wild prairie they could call home.

A place to hear the clitter-clatter of a myriad little urrish feet.

A strange message has come all the way from Tarek Town, sent by Ariana Foo, emeritus High Sage of human sept.

The exhausted urrish runner collapsed to her knees after dashing uphill from the Warril Plain, so spent that she actually craved water, raw and undiluted.

Center now, my rings. Spin your ever-wavering attention round the tale of Ariana Foo, as it was read aloud by Lester Cambel, her successor. Did not the news send vaporous wonder roiling through my/our core – that a mysterious injured outlander showed up one day near the Upper Roney? A stranger who might possibly be some *lost comrade* of the star-god visitors who now vex our shared exile! Or else, she speculates, might he be one who *escaped* these far-raiding adventurers? Could his wounds show evidence of shared enmity?

Ariana recommends we of the Council cautiously investigate the matter at our end, perhaps using truth-scryers, while she performs further experiments at Biblos.

The forayers *do* seem to have other interests beyond seeking presentient species to ravish from Jijo's fallow peace. They feign nonchalance, yet relentlessly query our folk, offering rewards and blandishments for reports of 'anything strange.'

How ironic those words, coming from *them*.

Then there is the bird.

Surely you recall the metal bird, my rings? Normally, we would have taken it for yet another Buyur relic, salvaged from the entrails of a dead-dying mulc-spider. Yet the sooner girl swears she saw it move! Saw it travel great distances, then fight and kill a Rothen machine!

Was that not the very evening the forayers buried their station, as though *they* were now fearful of the dread sky?

Our finest techies examine the bird-machine, but with scant tools available they learn little, save that energies still throb within its metal breast. Perhaps the contingent Lester has sent east – to ingather the human sooner band according to our law – will find out more.

So many questions. But even with answers, would our dire situation change in the least?

Were there time, i would set my/our varied rings the task of taking up different sides and arguing these mysteries, each question pouring distinct scents to coat our moist core, dripping syllogisms like wax, until only truth shines through a lacquered veneer. But there is no time for the traeki approach to problem solving. So we sages debate in the dry air, without even rewq to mediate the inadequacies of language. Each day is spent buying futile delays in our destiny.

As for Ariana's other suggestion, we *have* employed truth-scryers during discussions with the sky-humans. According to books of lore, this passive form of psi should be less noticeable than other techniques.

'*Are you seeking anybody in particular?*' This we asked, just yesterday. '*Is there a person, being, or group we should look for in your name?*'

Their leader – the one answering to the name-label Rann – seemed to grow tense, then recovered swiftly, confidently, smiling in the manner of his kind.

'*It is always our desire to seek strangeness. Have you observed strange things?*'

In that moment of revealed strain, one of our scryers claimed to catch something – a brief flash of *color*. A dark shade of gray, like the hue of a Great Qheuen's carapace. Only this surface seemed more supple, with a lissome litheness that undulated nimbly, free of adornment by hair, scale, feather, or torg.

The glimpse ended quickly. Still the scryer felt an association – with *water*.

What else did she describe, my rings, during that scant fey moment?

Ah, yes. A swirl of bubbles.

Scattered in formations, numerous as stars.

Bubbles growing into globes the size of Jijo's moons. Glistening. Ancient. Ageless.

Bubbles filled with distilled wonder ... sealed in by time.

Then nothing more.

Well and alas, what more could be asked? What are we but amateurs at this kind of game? Phwhoon-dau and Knife-Bright Insight point out that even this slim 'clue' might have been laid, adroitly, in the scryer's thoughts, in order to distract us with a paradox.

Yet at times like these, when our rewq and the Holy Egg seem to have abandoned us, it is such slender stems that offer wan hope to the drowning.

In her message, Ariana promised to send another kind of help. An expert whose skill may win us leverage with our foes, perhaps enough to make the invaders willing to bargain.

Oh, Ariana, how we/i have missed your wily optimism! If fire fell from heaven, you would see a chance to bake pots. If the entire Slope shuddered, then sank into the Midden's awful depths, you would find in that event cause to cry out – *opportunity*!

Despite urgent orders to hide by day, the steamship *Gopher* broke her old record, bolting upstream from Tarek Town, against the Bibur's springtime flood, boilers groaning as pistons beat their casings, an exuberance of power unsurpassed by anything else on Jijo, save her sister ship, the *Mole*. Mighty emblems of human technology, they were unapproachable even by clever urrish smiths, laboring on high volcanoes.

Sara recalled her own first ride, at age fifteen, newly recruited to attend advanced studies in Biblos and fiercely proud of her new skills – especially the knack of seeing each clank and chug of the growling steam engine in terms of temperatures, pressures, and pounds of force. Equations seemed to tame the hissing brute, turning its dismaying roar into a kind of music.

Now all that was spoiled. The riveted tanks and pulsing rocker-arms were exposed as primitive gadgets, little more advanced than a stone ax.

Even if the star-gods leave without doing any of the awful things Ariana Foo predicts, they have already harmed us by robbing us of our illusions.

One person didn't seem to mind. The Stranger lingered near the puffing, straining machinery, peering under the rockers, insisting with gestures that the engine chief open the gear box and let him look inside. At first, the human crew members had been wary of his antics; but soon, despite his mute incapacity with words, they sensed a kindred spirit.

You can explain a lot with hand motions, Sara noted. Another case of language adapting to needs of the moment – much as each wave of Jijoan colonists helped reshape the formal Galactic tongues they had known, culminating when humans introduced half a million texts printed mostly in Anglic, a language seemingly built *out of* chaos, filled with slang, jargon, puns, and ambiguity.

It was a warped mirror image of what had happened back on Earth, where billion-year-old grammars were pushing human culture *toward* order. In both cases the driving force was a near monopoly on knowledge.

That was the *obvious* irony. But Sara knew another – her unusual theory about language and the Six – so heretical, it made *Lark's* views seem downright orthodox.

Maybe it is *past time I came back to Biblos, to report on my work . . . and to confront everything I'm afraid of.*

The Stranger seemed happy, engrossed with his fellow engineers and closely observed by Ariana Foo from her wheelchair. So Sara left the noisy engine area, moving toward the ship's bow, where a thick mist was cleaved by the *Gopher's* headlong rush. Tattered breaks in the fog showed dawn brightening the Rimmer peaks, south and east, where the fate of the Six would be decided.

Won't Lark and Dwer be surprised to see me!

Oh, they'll probably yell that I should have stayed safe at home. I'll answer that I have a job to do, just as important as theirs, and they shouldn't be such gender-menders. And we'll all try hard not to show how happy we are to see each other.

But first, Sage Foo wanted this side trip to check her notion about the Stranger, despite Sara's instinct to protect the wounded man from further meddling.

Those instincts have caused me enough trouble. Is it not time to temper them with reason?

One ancient text called it 'nurturing mania,' and it might have seemed cute when she was a child, nursing hurt creatures of the forest. Perhaps it would have posed no problem, if she followed the normal life path of Jijoan women, with children and a fatigued farmer-husband tugging at her, demanding attention. What need, then, to *sublimate* maternal instincts? What time for other interests, without all the labor-saving tools tantalizingly described in Terran lore? Plain as she was, Sara felt certain she would have been successful at such a modest life and made some simple, honest man happy.

If a simple life was what I wanted.

Sara tried to shrug the wave of introspection. The cause of her funk was obvious.

Biblos. Center of human hopes and fears, focus of power, pride, and shame, the place where she once found love – or its illusion – and lost it. Where the prospect of a 'second chance' drove her off in panicked flight. Nowhere else had she felt such swings of elation and claustrophobia, hope and fear.

Will it still be standing when we round the final bend?

If the roof-of-stone had already fallen—

Her mind shied away from the unendurable. Instead, she drew from her shoulder bag the draft manuscript of her second paper on Jijoan language. It was past time to consider what to say to Sage Bonner and the others, if they confronted her.

What have I been doing? Demonstrating on paper that chaos *can be a form of progress. That noise can be informing.*

I might as well tell them I can prove that black is white, and up is down!

*

Evidence suggests that long ago, when Terran tribes were nomadic or pre-agricultural, most language groups were more rigidly structured than later on. For example, Earth scholars tried rebuilding proto-Indo-European, working backward from Latin, Sanskrit, Greek, and German, deriving a mother tongue strictly organized with many cases and declensions. A rule-based structure that would do any Galactic grammar proud.

In the margin, Sara noted a recent find from her readings, that one native North American tongue, Cherokee, contained up to seventy pronouns – ways to say 'I' and 'you' and 'we' – depending on context and personal relationship – a trait shared with GalSix.

To some, this implies humans must have once had patrons, who uplifted Earthling man-apes. Teachers who altered our bodies and brains and also taught a stern logic, through languages tailored to our needs.

Then we lost our guides. Through our own fault? Abandonment? No one knows.

After that, the theory goes, all Earthly languages devolved, spiraling back toward the apelike grunts protohumans used before uplift. At the time our ancestors left Earth for Jijo, Galactic advisers were counseling that Anglic and other 'wolfling' tongues be dropped in favor of codes designed for thinking beings.

Their argument can be illustrated by playing the game of Telephone.

Take a dozen players, seated in a circle. Whisper a complex sentence to one, who then whispers the same message to the next, and so on. Question: how soon is the original meaning lost amid confusion and slips of the tongue? Answer: in Anglic, noise can set in from the very start. After just a few relays, a sentence can become hilariously twisted.

The experiment yields different results in Rossic and Nihanic, human grammars that still require verb, noun, and adjective endings specific to gender, ownership, and other factors. If a mistake creeps into a Rossic Telephone message, the altered word often stands out, glaringly. Acute listeners can often correct it automatically.

In pure Galactic languages, one might play Telephone all day without a single error. No wonder the game was unknown in the five Galaxies, until humans arrived.

*

Sara had quickly recognized a version of *Shannon coding*, named after an Earthling pioneer of information theory who showed how specially coded messages can be restored, even from a jumble of static. It proved crucial to digital speech and data transmission, in pre-Contact human society.

Indo-European was logical, error-resistant, like Galactic tongues that suit computers far better than chaotic Anglic.

To many, this implied Earthlings *must* have had patrons in the misty past. But watching the Stranger commune happily with other engineers, in a makeshift language of grunts and hand gestures, reminded Sara—

It wasn't Indo-European speakers who invented computers. Nor users of any prim Galactic language. The star-gods received their mighty powers by inheritance.

In all the recent history of the Five Galaxies, just one folk independently invented computers – and nearly everything else needed for starfaring life – from scratch.

Those people spoke Rossic, Nihanic, French, and especially the fore-runner of Anglic, wild, undisciplined English.

Did they do it despite their chaotic language?

Or because of it?

The masters of her guild thought she chased phantoms – that she was using this diversion to evade other obligations.

But Sara had a hunch. Past and present held clues to the destiny awaiting the Six.

That is, if destiny had not already been decided.

Dawn spilled quickly downslope from the Rimmers. It was in clear violation of emergency orders for the *Gopher* to continue, but nobody dared say it to the captain, who had a crazed look in his eye.

Probably comes from spending so much time around humans, Sara thought. The steamers had as many men and women on the crew – to tend the machines – as hoon sailors. Grawph-phu, the pilot and master, knew the river with sure instincts that arose out of his heritage. He also had picked up more than a few Earthling mannerisms, like wearing a knit cap over his furry pate and puffing a pipe that fumed like the steamer's chimney. Peering through the dawn haze, the captain's craggy features might have come from the flyleaf of some seafaring adventure tale, chosen off the shelves in the Biblos Library – like some piratical old-timer, exuding an air of confidence and close acquaintance with danger.

Grawph-phu turned his head, noticed Sara looking at him, and closed one eye in a sly wink.

Oh, spare me, she sighed, half expecting the hoon to spit over the side and say – '*Arr, matie. 'Tis a fine day for sailin'. Full speed ahead!*'

Instead, the *Gopher*'s master pulled the pipe from his mouth and pointed.

'Biblos,' he commented, a low, hoonish growl accented by a salty twang. 'Just beyond the curve after next. Hr-rm ... A day sooner 'n you expected to arrive.'

Sara looked ahead once more. *I should be glad,* she thought. *Time is short.*

At first she could make out little but Eternal Swamp on the left bank, stretching impassably all the way to the Roney, an immensity of quicksand that forced the long detour past Tarek Town. On the right began the vast Warril Plain, where several passengers had debarked earlier to arrange overland passage. Taking a fast caravan were Bloor, the Portraitist, and a petite exploser carrying dispatches for her guild. Both were slight enough to ride donkeys all the way and with luck might reach the glade in three days. Prity and Pzora also went ashore at Kandu Landing to hire carts in case the Stranger must be taken before the High Sages – to be decided during this trip to Biblos.

As the fog cleared, there now reared to the right a wall of stone, rising from the water line, getting taller with each passing dura. The cliff shimmered, almost glassy smooth, as though impervious to erosion or time. Arguments raged as to whether it was natural or a Buyur relic.

Against these mirror-like cliffs, Ulgor had said the citizens of Dolo Village might see flames from burning books. Two centuries ago, settlers *had* witnessed such a sight, horrible even from afar. A disaster never equaled since, not by the massacre at Tolon, or when Uk-rann ambushed Drake the Elder at Bloody Ford.

But we saw no flames.

Still, tension reigned until the steamer turned a final bend ...

Sara let out a tense sigh. *The Archive ... it stands.*

She stared for some time, awash in emotion, then hurried aft to fetch the Stranger and Ariana Foo. Both of them would want to see this.

It was a *castle*, adamant, impervious, carved with tools that no longer existed. Godlike tools, sent to the deep soon after they cut this stronghold. A citadel of knowledge.

The original granite outcrop still jutted like a finger into the curving river, with its back braced against the shiny-smooth cliff. From above, it probably looked much as it always had, with woody thickets disguising atrium openings that let filtered daylight into courtyards and reading groves below. But from the dock where the *Gopher* tied up, one saw imposing defensive battlements, then row after row of massive, sculpted pillars that held up the natural plateau, suspending its undermined weight as a roof against the sky.

Inside this abnormal cave, wooden buildings protected their precious contents against rain, wind, and snow – all except the inferno that once rocked the southern end, leaving rubble and ruin. In a single night, fully a third of the wisdom left by the Great Printing had gone up in smoke and despair.

The sections that would have been most useful today. Those devoted to Galactic society, its many races and clans. What remained gave only sketchy outlines of the complex bio-social-political relationships that fluxed through the Five Galaxies.

Despite the crisis, dawn summoned a stream of pilgrims from hostelries in the nearby tree-shrouded village, scholars who joined the *Gopher* passengers climbing a zigzag ramp toward the main gate. Traeki and g'Kek students caught their breath at resting spots. Red qheuens from the distant sea paused now and then to spray salt water over their cupolas. Ulgor and Blade gave them wide berth.

A donkey-caravan edged by the line of visitors, heading downhill. Wax-sealed crates told of precious contents. *They're still evacuating,* Sara realized. *Taking advantage of the sages' delaying tactics.*

Would she find empty shelves inside, as far as the eye could see?

Impossible! Even if they could somehow move so many volumes, where would they store them all?

The Stranger insisted on pushing Ariana's wheelchair, perhaps out of respect, or to show how far his physical recovery had come. In fact, his dusky skin now had a healthy luster, and his deep laughter was hearty. He stared in wonder at the mighty stone walls, then the drawbridge, portcullis, and militia guards. Instead of the token detail Sara recalled, now a full platoon patrolled the parapets, equipped with spears, bows, and arbalests.

Ariana looked pleased by the Stranger's reaction. The old woman glanced at Sara with an expression of satisfaction.

He's never been here before. Even the damage he's suffered could not have erased a memory as vivid as Biblos. Either he is a rube from the farthest, most rustic human settlements, or else . . .

They passed the final battlements, and the Stranger gazed in amazement at the buildings of the Archive itself. Wooden structures, modeled after stone monuments of Earth's revered past – the Parthenon, Edo Castle, and even a miniature Taj Mahal, whose minarets merged into four heavy pillars holding up part of the roof-of-stone. Clearly, the founders had a taste for the dramatically ironic, for all the ancient originals had been built to *last*, dedicated in their day to vain resistance against time, while *these* buildings had a different goal – to serve a function and then vanish, as if they had never been.

Even that was too much for some people.

'Arrogance!' muttered Jop, the tree farmer, who had chosen to come along when he learned of this expedition. 'It all has to go, if we're ever to be blessed.'

'In time, it must,' Ariana Foo nodded, leaving vague whether she meant next week, or in a thousand years.

Sara saw fresh clay smeared over holds at the base of several great pillars. *Just like back home*, she realized. *The explosers are making sure all is ready*.

She could not help turning to glance behind Jop. Taking up the rear were the last two *Gopher* passengers, young Jomah, Henrik's son, and his uncle, Kurt. The elder exploser bent to point out structural features to the boy, using hand motions that made Sara think of tumbling chunks of ancient granite. She wondered if the Stranger, staring about in apparent delight, had any idea how little it would take to turn all this into rubble, indistinguishable from a hundred other places demolished by the Buyur when they departed, leaving the planet to revert to nature.

Sara felt a return of the old tightness in her shoulder blades. It hadn't been easy, at first, being a student in this place. Even when she had taken her books to the forest up top, to read under the shade of a homey garu tree, she could never shake off a sense that the whole plateau might shudder and collapse beneath her. For a while, the nervous fantasies had threatened her studies – until Joshu came along.

Sara winced. She had known it would all come back if she returned to this place. Memories.

'Nothing lasts forever,' Jop added as they neared the Athenian portico of Central Hall, unaware how stingingly the words struck Sara's private thoughts.

Ariana agreed. 'Ifni insists on it. Nothing can resist the goddess of change.'

If the elder sage meant the remark to be sardonic, Sara missed her point. She was too deep in reminiscence to care, even as they neared the giant double doors – carved from the finest wood as a gift from the qheuen race, then bound with urrish bronze, lacquered by traeki secretions and painted by g'Kek artists. The work towered ten meters high, depicting in ornate symbolism the thing most treasured by all, the latest, best, and most hard-won accomplishment of Jijo's Commons in Exile.

The Great Peace.

This time, Sara hardly noticed when the Stranger gasped in appreciation. She couldn't share his pleasure. Not when all she felt within this place was sadness.

ASX

The portraitist did not even ask to rest after the long, hard trek from Kandu Landing. He set to work at once, preparing his materials – caustic chemicals and hard metals whose imperviousness to time make them suspect under Commons law – yet ideal for blackmail.

Others of his guild were already here, having come to Gathering in order to sell paper photographs of visitors, guildmasters, winners at the games – anyone vain enough to want a graven image keepsake to last out a lifetime, maybe two. A few of these skilled likeness-peddlers had offered to secretly record the invaders, but to what purpose? Paper portraits are designed to fade and rot, not last eons. Better not to risk the aliens catching them in the act, and so discovering some of our hidden arts.

But Ariana, Bloor, and young Sara Koolhan appear to have come up with something different, have they not, my rings? Despite exhaustion from the road, Bloor appeared at once before us to show off the *daguerreotype*. An implausibly precise image stored on etched metal, centuries in age. Ur-Jah trembled as she fondled the accurate depiction of a great tattooed chieftain of old.

'If we attempt this, secrecy is essential. Our foes must not know how few pictures were taken,' Phwhoon-dau pointed out, while privacy wasps swarmed our hidden tent-of-conclave, fluttering drops of bitter color from their glowing wings.

'The sky-gods must imagine that we have scribed *hundreds* of plates already safely hidden far from here, in so many deep places they could never find them all.'

'True,' Vubben added, his eyestalks weaving a dance of caution. 'But there is more. For this to work, the portraits cannot simply show the human invaders' faces. Of what use will that be as evidence, a million years hence? They must include the aliens' machines, and clear Jijoan landmarks, and also the local animals they inspect as candidates for ravishment.'

'And their costumes, their garish garb,' Lester Cambel inserted urgently. 'Any identifiers to show they are *renegade* humans. Not representatives of our sept on Jijo, or on Earth.'

We all assented to this last request, though it seems futile to satisfy. How could a few etched plates express such fine distinctions to prosecutors so long after we are gone?

We asked Bloor to consult with our agents, bearing all these criteria in mind. If anything comes of this, it will indeed be a miracle.

We *believe* in miracles, do we not, my rings? Today, the rewq in our/my pouch came out of dormant state. So did that of Vubben, our Speaker of Ignition. Others report stirrings.

Is it possible to call this cause for hope? Or have they only begun awakening, as rewq sometimes do in the last stages of illness, shortly before they roll up and die?

DWER

The trail over the Rimmers was steep and broken.

That never mattered during Dwer's prior trips into the eastern wilderness – survey sweeps sanctioned by the sages – carrying just his bow, a map, and a few necessities. The first time, right after old Fallon's retirement, he got so elated that he *ran* down to the misty plains letting gravity yank him headlong, yelling as he leaped from one teetering foothold to the next.

There was none of that now. No exhilaration. No contest of youth and skill against Jijo's ardent hug. This was a sober affair, coaxing a dozen heavily laden donkeys over patches of unsteady footing, using patient firmness to overcome the animals' frequent bouts of stubbornness. He wondered how Urrish traders made it look so easy, guiding their pack trains with shrill, clipped whistles.

And they say these things come from Earth? he wondered, dragging yet another donkey out of trouble. Dwer wasn't warm to the idea of being a close genetic cousin to such creatures.

Then there were the *human* charges he must also shepherd into the wilderness.

In fairness, it could have been worse. Danel Ozawa was an experienced forester, and the two women were strong, with their own unique skills. Still, nothing back on the tame slope compared to this kind of trekking. Dwer found himself frequently moving up and down the train, helping his companions out of jams.

He wasn't sure which unnerved him more, the stolid indifference of Lena Strong or the gawky friendliness of Jenin Worley, frequently catching his eye with a shy smile. They had been obvious choices, since Jenin and Lena were already at Gathering to lobby for their 'tourism' idea – hoping to enlist Dwer's help, and approval from the sages, to start taking groups of 'sightseers' over the Rimmers.

In other words, bright people with too much time on their hands, overly influenced by notions they found in old Earth books.

I was going to fight it. Even same-sex groups risked violating the anti-sooner covenant.

But now – I'm part of a scheme to break the law I'm sworn to uphold.

He couldn't help glancing repeatedly at the two women, the same way they were surely appraising him.

They sure looked ... healthy.

You're a true wild man now. Learn to prize the honest virtues of wild females.

There would be women in the Gray Hills, too, but Rety said most of them began childbirth at fourteen. Few kept more than half their teeth past age thirty.

There was supposed to be a second group of volunteer exiles from the Slope, following behind this one. For their sake, Dwer smeared dabs of porl paste on prominent landmarks every half a midura or so, blazing a trail any moderately competent Jijoan could follow, but that should be untraceable by Galactic raiders or their all-seeing machinery.

Dwer would rather be home at the bitter end, preparing to fight hopelessly against the aliens, alongside other militia soldiers of the Six. But no one was better qualified to lead this expedition to the Gray Hills, and he had given Danel his word.

So now I'm a tour-guide, after all, he thought.

If only he sure it was right.

What are we doing? Fleeing to another place we don't belong, just like our sinner ancestors? It made Dwer's head ache to think about such things. *Just please don't let Lark find out what I'm doing. It'd break his heart.*

The trek grew a little easier when they spilled off the mountain onto a high steppe. But unlike his other expeditions, this time Dwer turned *south*, toward a rolling domain of bitter yellow grass. Soon they were stomping through a prairie of calf-high shoots, whose florets had sharp tips, forcing the humans – and even the donkeys – to wear leather leggings for protection.

No one complained, or even murmured discomfort. Danel and the others took his guidance without question, wiping sweat from their hat brims and collars as they slogged alongside the stolid donkeys. Fortunately, scattered oases of real forest helped Dwer pilot the company from one water source to the next, leaving markers for the next group.

Rety must've been dogged to cross all this, chasing after her damn bird.

Dwer had suggested waiting for the girl. 'She's your real guide,' he had told Danel.

'Not true,' Ozawa demurred. 'Would you trust her advice? She might steer us wrong in some misguided gesture to protect her loved ones.'

Or to avoid ever seeing them again. Still, Dwer wished Rety had made it back in time to depart with this group. He kind of missed her, sullen sarcasm and all.

He called a halt at a large oasis, more than an hour before sunset. 'The mountains will cut off daylight early,' he told the others. Westward, the peaks were already surrounded by the nimbus of yellow-orange. 'You three should clear the water hole, tend the animals, and set up camp.'

'And where are *you* going?' Lena Strong asked sharply, mopping her brow.

Dwer strapped on his hip quiver. 'To see about shooting some supper.'

She gestured at the sterile-looking steppe. 'What, here?'

'It's worth a try, Lena,' Danel said, slashing at some yellow grass with a stick. 'With the donkeys unable to eat this stuff, our grain must last till we hit hill country, where they can forage. A little meat for the four of us could help a lot.'

Dwer didn't bother adding anything to that. He set out down one of the narrow critter byways threading the spiky grass. It was some distance before he managed to put the donkey stench behind him, as well as the penetrating murmur of his companions' voices.

It's a bad idea to be noisy when the universe is full of things tougher than you are. But that never stopped humans, did it?

He sniffed the air and watched the sway of thigh-high grass. In this kind of prairie, it was even more imperative to hunt upwind not only because of scent, but so the breeze might help hinder the racket of your own trampling feet from reaching the quarry – in this case a covey of bush quaile he sensed pecking and scratching, a dozen or so meters ahead.

Dwer nocked an arrow and stepped as stealthfully as he could, breathing shallowly, until he picked out soft chittering sounds amid the brushing stems ... a tiny ruckus of claws scratching sandy loam ... sharp beaks pecking for seeds ... a gentle, motherly cluck ... answering peeps as hatchlings sought a feathery breast ...

the faint puffs of junior adults, relaying news from the periphery that all is well. All is well.

One of the sentries abruptly changed its muted report. A breath of tentative alarm. Dwer stooped to make his profile lower and kept stock still. Fortunately, the twilight shadows were deepest to his back. If only he could manage to keep from spooking them for a few more . . .

A sudden crashing commotion sent four-winged shapes erupting into the air. *Another predator*, Dwer realized, raising his bow. While most of the quaile scattered swiftly across the grasstops and vanished, a few spiraled back to swoop over the intruder, distracting it from the brood-mother and her chicks. Dwer loosed arrows in rapid succession, downing one – then another of the guardians.

The ruckus ended as swiftly as it began. Except for a trampled area, the patch of steppe looked as if nothing had happened.

Dwer shouldered his bow and pulled out his machete. In principle, nothing that could hide under grass should be much of a threat to him, except perhaps a root scorpion. But there were legends of strange, nasty beasts in this realm southeast of the gentle Slope. Even a famished ligger could make a damned nuisance of itself.

He found the first bird where it fell.

This should make Lena happy for a while, he thought, realizing that might be a lifelong task, from now on.

The grass swayed again, near where he'd shot the second bird. He rushed forward, machete upraised. 'Oh, no you don't, thief!'

Dwer braked as a slinky, black-pelted creature emerged with the other quaile clutched between its jaws. The bloody arrow trailed in the dust.

'You.' Dwer sighed, lowering the knife. 'I should've known.'

Mudfoot's dark eyes glittered so eloquently, Dwer imagined words.

That's right, boss, glad to see me? Don't bother thanking me for flushing the birds. I'll just keep this juicy one as payment.

He shrugged in resignation. 'Oh, all right. But I want the arrow back, you hear?'

The noor grinned, as usual betraying no sign how much or how little it understood.

Night fell as they ambled toward the oasis. Flames flickered under a sheltering tree. The shifting breeze brought scents of donkey, human, and simmering porridge.

Better keep the fire small enough to seem a natural smolder, he reminded himself.

Then another thought occurred to Dwer.

Rety said noor never came over the mountains. So what's this one doing here?

Rety hadn't lied about there being herds of *glaver*, southeast of the Rimmers. After two days of swift trekking, loping at a half-jog beside the trotting donkeys, Dwer and the others found clear signs – the sculpted mounds where glavers habitually buried their feces.

'Damn ... you're right ...' Danel agreed, panting with hands on knees. The two women, on the other hand, seemed barely winded. 'It looks ... as if things ... just got more complicated.'

You could say that, Dwer thought. Years of careful enforcement by hunters like himself had all been in vain. *We always figured the yellow grass could be crossed only by well-equipped travelers, never glavers. That's why we aimed most of our surveys farther north.*

The next day, Dwer called a halt amid another jog, when he spied a throng of glavers in the distance, scrounging at one end of a scrub wadi. All four humans took turns observing through Danel Ozawa's urrish-made binoculars. The pale, bulge-eyed creatures appeared to be browsing on a steppe-gallaiter, a burly, long-legged beast native to this region, whose corpse lay sprawled across a patch of trampled grass. The sight stunned them all, except Jenin Worley.

'Didn't you say that's how to survive on the plains? By eating animals who *can* eat this stuff?' She flicked a stem of the sharp yellow grass. 'So the glavers have adapted to a new way of life. Isn't that what we're gonna have to do?'

Unlike Danel Ozawa, who seemed sadly resigned to their mission, Jenin appeared almost *avid* for this adventure, especially knowing it might be their destiny to preserve the human race on Jijo. When he saw that zealous eagerness in her eyes, Dwer felt he had more in common with the sturdy, square-jawed Lena Strong. At least Lena looked on all this much the way he did – as one more duty to perform in a world that didn't care about anyone's wishes.

'It's ... rather surprising,' Danel replied, lowering the glasses and looking upset. 'I thought it wasn't possible for glavers to eat red meat.'

'Adaptability,' Lena commented gruffly. 'One of the hallmarks of presentience. Maybe this means they're on their way back up, after the long slide down.'

Danel seemed to consider this seriously. 'So soon? If so, I wonder. Could it mean—'

Dwer interrupted before the sage had a chance to go philosophical on them. 'Let me have those,' he said, taking the glass-and-boo magnifiers. 'I'll be right back.'

He started forward at a crouch. Naturally, Mudfoot chose to tag along, scampering ahead, then circling repeatedly to stage mock-ambushes. Dwer's jaw clenched, but he refused to give the beast the satisfaction of reacting. *Ignore it. Maybe it'll go away.*

That hadn't worked so far. Jenin seemed thrilled to have Mudfoot as a mascot, while Danel found its tenacity intriguing. Lena had voted with the others, overruling Dwer's wish to send it packing. *'It weighs next to nothing,'* she said. *'Let it ride a donkey, so long as it fetches its own food and stays out of the way.'*

That it did, scrupulously avoiding Lena, posing for Danel's pensive scrutiny, and purring contentedly when Jenin petted it by the campfire each evening.

In my case, it acts as if being irritated were my heart's desire.

While creeping toward the wadi, Dwer kept mental notes on the lay of the land, the crackling consistency of the grass stems, the fickleness of the breeze. He did this out of professional habit, and also in case it ever became necessary to do this someday for real, pursuing the glaver herd with arrows nocked and ready. Ironically that would happen only in the event of *good* news. If word came from the Slope that all was well – that the gene-raiders had departed without wreaking the expected genocide – then this expedition would revert to a traditional Mission of Ingathering – a militia enterprise to rid this region of all glavers *and* humans, preferably by capture, but in the end by any means necessary.

On the other hand, assuming the worst did happen out west and all the Six Races were wiped out, their small group would *join* Rety's family of renegades as exiles in the wilderness. Under Danel's guidance, they would tame Rety's cousins and create simple, wise traditions for living in harmony with their new home.

One of those traditions would be to forbid the sooners from ever again hunting glavers for food.

That was the bloody incongruity Dwer found so hard to take, leaving little option or choice. *Good* news would make him a mass-killer. Contrariwise, horrible news would make him a gentle neighbor to glavers and men.

Duty and death on one side. Death and duty on the other. Dwer wondered, *Is survival really worth all this?*

From a small rise, he lifted the binoculars. Two families of glavers seemed to be feeding on the gallaiter, while others kept watch. Normally, such a juicy corpse would be cleaned down to a white skeleton, first by liggers or other large carnivores, then hickuls with heavy jaws for grinding bones, and finally by flyers known simply as vultures, though they looked like nothing in pictures from Old Earth.

Even now, a pack of hickuls swarmed the far periphery of the clearing.

A glaver rose up on her haunches and hurled a stone. The scavengers scattered, whining miserably.

Ah. I see how they do it.

The glavers had found a unique way to live on the steppe. Unable to digest grass or boo, or to eat red meat, they apparently used cadavers to attract hordes of *insects* from the surrounding area, which they consumed at leisure while others in the herd warded off all competition.

They seemed to be enjoying themselves, holding squirmy things before their globelike eyes, mewling in approval, then catching them between smacking jaws. Dwer had never seen glavers act with such – *enthusiasm*. Not back where they were treated as sacred fools, encouraged to root at will through the garbage middens of the Six.

Mudfoot met Dwer's eyes with a revolted expression.

Ifni, what pigs! All right if we charge in there now? Bust 'em up good, boss. Then herd 'em all back to civilization, like it or not?

Dwer vowed to curb his imagination. Probably the noor simply didn't like the smell.

Still he chided Mudfoot in a low voice.

'Who are *you* to find *others* disgusting, Mister lick-myself-all-over? Come on. Let's tell the others, glavers haven't gone carnivorous, after all. We have more running ahead, if we're to make it out of this sting-grass by nightfall.'

ASX

More word arrives from the far south, sent by the smith of Mount Guenn Forge.

The message was sparse and distorted, having come partly by courier, and partly conveyed between mountain peaks by inexperienced mirror-flashers, in the partly-restored semaphore system.

Apparently, the alien forayers have begun visiting all the fishing hamlets and red qheuen rookeries, making pointed inquiries. They even landed in the water, far out at sea, to badger the crew of a dross-hauler, on its way home from holy labors at the Midden. Clearly the interlopers feel free to swoop down and interrogate our citizens wherever they dwell, with questions about 'strange sights, strange creatures, or lights in the sea.'

Should we make up a story, my rings? Should we fabulate some tale of ocean monsters to intrigue our unwanted guests and possibly stave off fate for a while?

Assuming we dare, what would they do to us when they learn the truth?

LARK

All that morning, Lark worked next to Ling in a state of nervous tension, made worse by the fact that he did not dare let it show. Soon, with luck, he would have his best chance to line things up just right. It would be a delicate task though, doing spywork at the behest of the sages while also probing for information *he* needed, for reasons of his own.

Timing would be everything.

The Evaluation Tent bustled with activity. The whole rear half of the pavilion was stacked with cages made by qheuenish crafters out of local boo, filled with specimens brought from all over this side of Jijo. A staff of humans, urs, and hoon labored full time to keep the animals fed, watered, and healthy, while several local g'Kek had shown remarkable talent at running various creatures through mazes or performing other tests, supervised by robots whose instructions were always in prim, flawless Galactic Two. It had been made clear to Lark that it was a mark of high distinction to be asked to work *directly* with one of the star-humans.

His second airborne expedition had been even more exhausting than the first, a three-day voyage beginning with a zigzag spiral far out to sea, cruising just above the waves over the dark blue expanse of the Midden, then hopping from one island to the next along an extended offshore archipelago, sampling a multitude of wildly varied life-forms Lark had never seen before. To his surprise, it turned out to be a much more enjoyable trip than the first.

For one thing, Ling grew somewhat less condescending as they worked together, appreciating each other's skills. Moreover, Lark found it stirring to see what evolution had wrought during just a million fallow years, turning each islet into a miniature biological reactor, breeding delightful variations. There were flightless avians who had given up the air, and gliding reptiloids that seemed on the verge of earning wings. Mammiforms whose hair grew in horny protective spikes, and zills whose coatings of fluffy torg shimmered with colors never seen on their bland mainland cousins. Only later did he conclude that some of the diversity might have been enhanced from the start, by Jijo's last legal tenants. Perhaps the Buyur seeded each isle with different genetic stock as part of a *very* long scale experiment.

Ling and Besh often had to drag him away when it came time to leave a sampling site, while Kunn muttered irascibly by his console, apparently happy only when they were aloft. On landing, Lark was always first to rush out the hatch. For a while, all the dour brooding of his dreams lay submerged under a passion for discovery.

Still, as they cruised home on the last leg – another unexplained back-and-forth gyration over open sea – he had found himself wondering. *This trip was marvelous, but* why *did we go? What did they hope to accomplish?* Even before humans left Earth, biologists knew – higher life-forms need *room* to evolve, preferably large continents. Despite the wild variety encountered on the archipelago, there wasn't a single creature the star-folk could hope to call a candidate for uplift.

Sure enough, when he rejoined Ling the next day, the outlander woman announced they would return to analyzing rock-stallers, right after lunch. Besh had already resumed her intensive investigation of glavers, clearly glad to be back to work on her best prospect.

Glavers. The irony struck Lark. Yet he held back his questions, biding his time.

Finally, Ling put down the chart they had been working on – duplicating much that already covered the walls of his Dolo Village study – and led him to the table where machines offered refreshments in the sky-human fashion. The light was very good there, so Lark gave a furtive nod to a small man, cleaning some animal pens. The fair-haired fellow moved toward a stack of wooden crates, used for hauling food-stuffs for the raucous zoo of captive creatures.

Lark positioned himself at the south end of the table so he would not block the man's view of Ling, as well as Besh and everything beyond. Especially Ling. For this to work, he must try to keep her still for as long as possible.

'Besh seems to think you've found yourselves a first-class candidate species.'

'Mm?' The dark-eyed woman looked up from a complex machine lavishly dedicated to producing a single beverage – a bitter drink Lark had tried just once, appropriately named *coughee*.

'Found what?' Ling stirred a steaming mug and leaned back against the edge of the table.

Lark gestured at the subject Besh studied, complacently chewing a ball of sap while a contraption perched on its head, sifting neurons. There had been a spurt of excitement when Besh swore she heard the glaver 'mimic' two spoken words. Now Besh seemed intent, peering through her microscope, guiding a brain probe with tiny motions of her hands, sitting rock still.

'I take it glavers have what you seek?' Lark continued.

Ling smiled. 'We'll know better when our ship returns and more advanced tests are made.'

Out the corner of his eye, Lark saw the small man remove the cover from a hole in one side of a box. There was a soft sparkle of glass.

'And when *will* the ship be back?' he asked, keeping Ling's attention.

Her smile widened. 'I wish you folks would stop asking that. It's enough to make one think you had a reason for caring. Why should it matter to you when the ship comes?'

Lark blew his cheeks, hoon fashion, then recalled that the gesture would mean nothing to her. 'A little warning would be nice, that's all. It takes *time* to bake a really big cake.'

She chuckled, more heartily than his joke deserved. Lark was learning not to take umbrage each time he suspected he was being patronized. Anyway, Ling wouldn't be laughing when shipboard archives revealed that glavers – their prime candidate for uplift – were *already* Galactic citizens, presumably still flitting around their own backwater of space, in secondhand ships.

Or would even the star-cruiser's onboard records reveal it? According to the oldest Scrolls, glavers came from an obscure race among the myriad sapient clans of the Five Galaxies. Maybe, like the g'Kek, they had already gone extinct and no one remembered them, save in the chilly recesses of the largest-sector branch Libraries.

This might even be the moment foretold long ago by the final glaver sage, before humans came to Jijo. A time when restored innocence would shrive their race, peel away their sins, and offer them a precious second chance. A new beginning.

If so, they deserve better than to be adopted by a pack of thieves.

'Suppose they prove perfect in every way. Will you take them with you when you go?'

'Probably. A breeding group of a hundred or so.'

Peripherally, he glimpsed the small man replacing the cover of the camera lens. With a satisfied smile, Bloor the Portraitist casually lifted the box, carrying it outside through the back tent flap. Lark felt a knot of tension release. Ling's face might be a bit blurry in the photo, but her clothes and body stood a good chance of coming through, despite the long exposure time. By good fortune, Besh, the glaver, a robot, and a sleeping rock-staller had remained still the entire time. The mountain range, seen through the open entrance, would pin down location and season of the year.

'And what of the rest?' he asked, relieved to have just one matter on his mind now.

'What do you mean?'

'I mean what will happen to all the glavers you leave behind?'

Her dark eyes narrowed. 'Why should anything happen to them?'

'Why indeed?' Lark shifted uncomfortably. The sages wanted to maintain the atmosphere of tense ambiguity for a while longer rather than confront the aliens directly over their plans. But he had already done the sages' bidding by helping Bloor. Meanwhile, Harullen and the other heretics were pressuring Lark for answers. They must decide soon whether to throw their lot in with the Zealots' mysterious scheme.

'Then ... there is the matter of the rest of us.'

'The rest of you?' Ling arched an eyebrow.

'We Six. When you find what you seek, and depart – what happens to us?'

She groaned. 'I can't count the number of times I've been asked about this!'

Lark stared. 'Who—?'

'Who *hasn't*?' She blew an exasperated sigh. 'At least a third of the patients we treat on clinic day sidle up afterward to pump us about how we'll *do it*. What means do we plan to use when we finally get around to killing every sentient being on the planet? Will we be gentle? Or will it come as firebolts from heaven, on the day we depart? It gets so repetitious, sometimes I want to— agh!' She clenched her fist, frustration apparent on her normally composed features.

Lark blinked. He had planned edging up to the very same questions.

'Folks are frightened,' he began. 'The logic of the situation—'

'Yes, yes. I know,' Ling interrupted impatiently. 'If we came to steal presapient life-forms from Jijo, we can't afford to leave any witnesses. And especially, we can't leave any native stock of the species we stole! Honestly, where do you people get such ideas?'

From books, Lark almost answered. *From the warnings of our ancestors.*

But, indeed, how well could those accounts be trusted? The most detailed had been lost to fire soon after humans arrived. Anyway, weren't humans naive newcomers on the Galactic scene back in those days, worried to the point of paranoia? And wasn't it the *most* paranoic who had boarded the *Tabernacle*, smuggling themselves to a far, forbidden world to hide?

Might the danger be exaggerated?

'Seriously, Lark, why should we fear anything a bunch of sooners might say about us? The odds of another Institute inspection team arriving at Jijo in under a hundred thousand years are very small. By the time one does, if any of you are still around, our visit will surely have dissolved into vague legends. We have no need to commit genocide – as if we could *ever* bring ourselves to do such a horrid thing, however strong the reason!'

For the first time, Lark saw beyond Ling's normal mask of wry sardonicism. Either she deeply believed what she was saying, or she was a very skilled actress.

'Well then, how *do* you plan to adopt any presentient species you find here? Surely you can't admit you picked them up on a restricted world.'

'At last, an intelligent question.' She seemed relieved. 'I confess, it won't be easy. They must be planted in another ecosystem for starters, along with any symbionts they need, and other evidence to imply they've been there for some time. Then we must wait quite a while—'

'A million years?'

Ling's smile returned, thinly. 'Not quite so long. We have a couple of advantages going for us, you see. One is the fact that on most worlds the bio-record is a jumble of phylogenic anomalies. Despite rules to minimize harmful cross-flow, each time a new starfaring clan wins tenant rights to a world, they inevitably bring in their favorite plants and animals, along with a host of parasites and other hangers-on. Take glavers, for instance.' She nodded over at the subject. 'I'm sure we'll find records of places where similar genes flowed in the past.'

Now it was Lark's turn to smile, briefly. *You don't know the half of it.*

'So you see,' Ling went on. 'It won't matter much if a residual population stays on Jijo, as long as we have time to modify the borrowed stock, artificially enhancing the apparent rate of genetic divergence. And that will happen anyway when we begin the process of uplift.'

So, Lark realized, *even if the forayers eventually find glavers unsuitable, they might still make off with some other promising species and turn a nice profit from their crime.*

Moreover, they appeared completely comfortable seeing it as no crime at all.

'And your other advantage?' he asked.

'Ah, now that's the real secret.' A shine seemed to enter the woman's dark eyes. 'You see, what it really comes down to is a matter of *skill*.'

'Skill?'

'On the part of our blessed patrons.' Now her words struck a reverent tone. 'The Rothen are past masters at this art, you see. Witness their greatest success so far – the human race.'

There it was again, mention of the mysterious clan that had the utter devotion of Ling, Rann, and the others. The star-humans had started out reticent. Ling had even made it clear that Rothen was not their real name. But with time she and the others grew more talkative, as if their pride could not be contained.

Or else, because they had no fear the tale would spread.

'Imagine. They managed to uplift humanity in complete secrecy, subtly altering the records of the Migration Institute so that our homeworld, Earth, remained untouched, on fallow status, for an incredible half a *billion* years! They even kept their gentle guidance unknown to our own ancestors, leaving them with the fantastic but useful illusion that they were uplifting themselves!'

'Amazing,' Lark commented. He had never seen Ling so animated. He wanted to ask, *'How could such feats be feasible?'* But that might imply he doubted her, and Lark wanted this openness to continue. 'Of course, self-uplift is impossible,' he prompted.

'Completely. It's been known since the fabled days of the Progenitors. Evolution can bring a species all the way up to pre-sapience, but the final leap needs help from another race that's already made it. This principle underlies the life-cycle of all oxygen-breathing races in the Five Galaxies.'

'So why did our ancestors believe they raised themselves up?'

'Oh, the most insightful always suspected we had help from beyond. It explains the depth of feeling underlying most religions. But the true source of our gift of sapiency remained mysterious for most of the time that hidden hands guided our path. Only the Danikites – early precursors of our group – knew the secret all along.'

'Even the Tergens Council—'

'The *Terragens* Council.' Her voice soured. 'The idiots guiding Earth and her colonies during these dangerous times? Their obstinacy hardly matters. Even this *Streaker* business, sending half the fanatics in the universe into a frenzy, howling for Earthling blood, even this will come out all right, despite the Terragens fools. The Rothen will see to things. Don't worry.'

Lark *hadn't* been worried. Not on the scale she referred to. Not till that moment. Now he found her words anything but reassuring.

From other conversations with the Danik sky-humans, the sages had already pieced together hints that some great crisis was setting the Five Galaxies in an uproar. It might even explain why the gene raiders were here right now, taking advantage of the turmoil to do a little burglary.

What could a feeble clan of Earthlings have done to cause such commotion? Lark wondered.

With some effort, he pushed the thought aside as much too vast to be grappled with right now.

'When did the Rothen revel the truth to you ... Dakkins?'

'Longer back than you might think, Lark. Even before your ancestors headed off in their creaky junkyard starship, taking their foolish wild gamble in coming to this world. Soon after humanity entered interstellar space, a few men and women were chosen by the Rothen to receive the word. Those who had already been keeping faith, holding steadfast vigil. Some stayed on Earth to help guide the race in secret, while others went off to dwell in joy among the Rothen, aiding them in their work.'

'And what work is that?'

She had a look Lark sometimes saw on the faces of those returning from pilgrimages to the Egg, on those blessed occasions when the sacred stone sang its serene harmonies. An expression of having experienced splendor.

'Why, rescuing the lost, of course. And nurturing what might-yet-be.'

Lark worried she might drift into complete mysticism. 'Will we get to meet some Rothen?'

Her eyes had defocused while pondering vistas of time and space. Now they turned and glittered sharply.

'Some of you may, if you are lucky.

'In fact, a few of you may get luckier than you ever dreamed.'

Her implication set his head awhirl. Could she mean what he thought she meant?

That evening, by candlelight, he went over his calculations one more time.

From our best measurements, the starship had a volume of about half a million cubic meters. If you stacked every human on Jijo like frozen cordwood, we just might fit – providing you left no room for anything else.

The first time he had worked out the numbers, his intent was simply to dispel rumors among some younger urs and qheuens that the human settlers would soon abandon Jijo. It was physically impossible, he showed, for the youngest sept to forsake the Commons for a ticket back to the stars. At least with this ship alone.

But she said 'some of you.'

Even after loading aboard hundreds of wuankworms, longsnouts, or glavers, there'd still he room for a few lost cousins. Those who had proved useful.

Lark knew a bribe when he heard one.

Much as he condemned the ancestors' choice to come here, Lark loved this world. He would feel a pang if he ever left, and for all his days thereafter.

Yet if things were different, I'd go in a shot. Who wouldn't?

The zealots are right. No human can be completely trusted these days. Not when any of us might be suborned. Bought with an offer to be made into a god.

In fact, he had no idea what the zealots planned. Only that they felt free to act without advice or approval from the dithering sages. There were humans in the cabal, of course. What could be accomplished without Earthling skill and lore? But men and women were excluded from the inner circle.

So what have I learned?

He looked down at a blank sheet. Surely the sages and zealots had other feelers out. Even Harullen must be hedging his bets. Still, Lark knew his words carried weight.

If Ling is telling the truth, and the zealots believe it, they might call off whatever action they planned. What do they care if a few glavers or rock-stallers are taken off planet, so long as the intruders leave us in peace, as we were before?

But what if Ling was lying? Might the zealots lose their best chance to strike, for nothing?

On the other hand, suppose no one believed Ling, but she really *was* telling the truth? The zealots might attack, and fail, only to goad the very response they feared!

At the opposite extreme of radicalism from the fiery zealots, some of the most radical *heretics* actually *favored* their own destruction, along with the rest of the Six. Some hoon and urs members of Harullen's society yearned for a time of transcendent ending – the urrish apostates because of their hot blood, and the hoon precisely *because* their passions stirred slowly, but once whipped, they stopped for nothing.

If our extremists think Ling's folk haven't the guts to do the job, they may plot to provoke genocide! This despite his speech, urging that the Six cede their place on Jijo by consensus and birth control.

Then there was this scheme to try *blackmailing* the forayers. Lark had helped Bloor set up candid shots, but were the sages aware of how the scheme might backfire?

Did they think they had nothing to lose?

Lark rubbed his stubbled chin, feeling wearier than his years.

What a tangled web we weave, he pondered. Then he licked the tip of his pen, dipped it in the ink, and began to write.

THE STRANGER

This place makes him want to laugh. It makes him want to cry.

So many books *– he even remembers that word for them – lay stacked high all around him, in row after mighty row, vanishing around corners or up twisty, spiral ramps. Books bound in the leather of unknown animals, filling the air with strange scents, especially when he cracks some volume taken off a shelf at random and inhales the fumes of paper and ink.*

It jolts something within him, dredging up memories more effectively than anything since he regained consciousness.

Suddenly, he recalls a cabinet of books like these, in his room when he was very young ... and that brings back the pinch and crinkling flex of paper pages, covered with bright pictures. Grown-ups did not use books very much, he remembers. Adults needed the constant flash and jangle of their machines. Machines that talked at you faster than a child was trained to hear, or cast flickering beams directly at the eyeball, filling it with facts that faded the moment you blinked. That was one reason he used to like the solid promise of paper – where a favorite story would not go away like smoke, or vanish when the infoscreens went dark.

Another image leaps out from childhood – holding his mother's hand while strolling in a public place filled with busy, important people. Several walls were rimmed with bound volumes, much like the books surrounding him right now. Big books without pictures, filled with black, unmoving dots. Filled with words and nothing else. Hardly anyone used them anymore, his mother had explained. But they were important nonetheless, as decorations lining many of the places most sacred or important to human beings.

They were reminders of something ... of something he cannot quite recall right now. But it must have been important. That much he knows.

Patiently, he waits for the two women – Sara and Ariana Foo – to finish their meetings and return for him. Passing the time, he sketches on a pad of rich, almost luminous paper, first refining some of his drawings of the machinery aboard the steamship, then trying to capture the eerie perspectives of the stone cavern where all these odd wooden buildings lay sheltered from the sky – under a cave whose roof is propped up by incredible, massive stone pillars.

A few names are coming easier now, so he knows that it is Prity who brings him a cup of water, then checks his dressing to make sure it's still tight. Her hands seem to flutter and dance before her, then his do likewise. He watches, fascinated, as his own fingers make movements independent of his will or command. It might be frightening to behold ... except that Prity suddenly grins broadly and slaps her knee, chuffing hoarse, appreciative chimpanzee laughter.

He feels a wash of pleasure to know his joke had pleased her. Though it puzzles and slightly miffs him that his hands never saw fit to share the humor with him.

Well, well. The hands seem to know what they are doing, and he draws some satisfaction from their work. Now they pick up the pencil once again, and he lets time slip away, concentrating on the moving pencil, and on the sketch and tilt of line and shadow. When Sara returns for him, he will be ready for whatever comes next.

Perhaps it might even be possible to find a way to save her and her people.

Maybe that was what his hands had said to Prity, just a little while ago.

If so, no wonder the little chimp broke out in wry, doubtful laughter.

XVII

THE BOOK OF THE SEA

Should you succeed in following the Path of Redemption –
to be re-adopted, uplifted anew, given a second chance –
that will not mean an end to all your strivings.

First you must prove yourselves
as noble clients, obedient and true
to the new patrons who redeemed you.

Later you will rise in status, and uplift clients of your own,
generously passing on the blessings that you earned.

But then, in time, there oft begins to glimmer a light
on the horizon of the species' life, hinting at other realms,
beckoning the tired, the worthy.

This is said to be a sign post.
Some will call it The Lure,
or else The Enticement.

Eon after eon, old ones depart,
seeking paths that younger
races can't perceive.

They vanish from our midst,
those who find these paths.

Some call it transcendence.
Others call it death.

—The Scroll of Destiny

ALVIN'S TALE

One thing always struck me about the way tales are told in Anglic – or any of the other Earthling tongues I've learned – and that's the problem of keeping up *suspense*.

Oh, some human authors of Twencen and Twenty-One had it down cold. There've been times that I stayed up three nights straight, taken with some yarn by Conrad or Cunin. What's puzzled me, ever since I got the notion of becoming a writer myself, is *how* those old-timers managed it.

Take this account I've been scribbling lately, whenever I get a chance to lie down on this hard deck with my notebook, already gone all ragged at the corners from the places I've taken it, scrawling clumsy hoon-sized letters with a chewed-up pencil clutched in my fist. From the very start I've been telling my story in 'first person' – like a diary, only with all sorts of fancy-gloss tricks thrown in that I've picked up from my reading over the years.

Why first person? Well, according to *Good Fiction* by Anderson, that 'voice' makes it a whole lot easier to present the reader with a single, solid-feeling point-of-view, even though it means my book will have to be translated if a traeki's ever to understand it.

But the trouble with a first person chronicle is this – whether it's real-life history or a piece of make-believe, *you know the hero survived!*

So during all the events I'm about to relate, you who are reading this memoir (hopefully after I've had a chance to rewrite it, have a human expert fix my grammar, and pay to have it set in type) you already know that I, Alvin Hph-wayuo, son of Mu-phauwq and Yowg-wayuo of Wuphon Port, and intrepid explorer extraordinaire, simply *have* to escape alive the jam I'm about to describe, with at least one brain, one eye, and a hand to write it all down.

I've lain awake some nights, trying to see a way around this problem using some other language. There's the GalSeven tentative case, for instance, but that doesn't work in past-explicit tense. And the quantum-uncertain declension, in Buyur-dialect GalThree, is just too *weird*. Anyway, who would I be writing for? Huck's the only other GalThree reader I know, and getting praise from *her* is kind of like kissing your sister.

Anyway, the waters of the Rift were all a-froth at the point where I last left our tale. The hatchet shadow of Terminus Rock cut across a patch of ocean where both hawser and hose still whirled, chopping the normally placid surface, spinning with tension energy released just moments before, by a disaster.

It was all too easy to picture what would happen to *Wuphon's Dream*, our little vessel for exploring the great unknown below. In reluctant imagining I saw the hollow wooden tube – its wheels spinning uselessly, the bulbous glass nose broken – tumbling into black emptiness trailing its broken leash, carrying Ziz, the little traeki partial stack, to perdition along with it.

As if that weren't enough, we all had fresh in memory the sight of little *Huphu*, our noor-beast mascot, thrown by the recoiling crane, screeching and gyrating till her tiny black figure vanished into the blue waters of the Rift. As Huck's Earthling nicknamesake might've said – 'It warn't a happy sight. Nor a lucky wun.'

For a long time, everybody just stared. I mean, what could we do? Even the protestors from Wuphon Port and The Vale were silent. If any felt smug over our comeuppance as heretics, they felt wiser to withhold jubilation.

We all back away from the ledge. What point in peering at a velvety-smooth grave?

'Retrace the hawser and hose,' Urdonnol commanded. Soon the drums began rotating the other way, rewinding what had unreeled so hopefully just duras before. The same hoonish voice called out depths, only this time the numbers grew steadily smaller, and there was no great, booming enthusiasm in the throaty baritone. Finally, at two and a half cables, the hawser's frayed end popped out of the sea, dripping water like white lymph fluid from a traeki's wounded, dangling tentacle. Those cranking the drum sped up, eager to see what had happened.

'Acid vurn!' Ur-ronn declared in shock, when the severed end was swung onto the bluff. She lisped in anger. 'Savotage!'

Urdonnol seemed reluctant to leap to conclusions, but the older urs technician kept swinging her narrow head back and forth, low and snakelike, from the burned cable to the crowd of protestors standing on the bluff, gaping at our tragedy. The urrish apprentice's dark suspicion was clear.

'Get away from here!' Huck shouted angrily, rolling toward the dissenters, spinning up gravel with her rims. She swerved, just missing the toes of several humans and hoon, who backed off nervously. Even a couple of reds withdrew their clawed, armored legs, scuttling away a pace or two, before recalling that a flail-eyed g'Kek isn't much physical threat to a qheuen. Then they moved forward again, hissing and clicking.

Pincer and I rushed to Huck's side. It might've gotten ugly, but then a bunch of big grays and burly urrish smiths from Mount Guenn Forge hurried up behind us, some carrying cudgels, ready to back up Huck's demand with angry force. The rabble took note and quit our worksite, moving toward their makeshift camp.

'Bastards!' Huck cursed after them. 'Horrid, jeekee murderers!'

Not by law, I thought, still numb from shock. Neither Huphu nor little Ziz had strictly been citizens of the Commons. Nor even honorary ones, like glavers, or members of any threatened species. So it wasn't murder, exactly.

But close enough, by my reckoning. My hands clenched, and I sensed something *give* as my back flexed with fight-hormones. Anger is slow to ignite in a hoon and hard to snuff once lit. It's kind of disturbing to look back on how I felt then, even though the sages say what you feel isn't evil, only what you do about it.

No one said a word. We must've moped for a while. Urdonnol and Ur-ronn argued over what kind of a message to send to Uriel.

Then a stuttering whistle pierced our pit of mourning, coming from behind us, toward the sea. We turned to see Pincer-Tip, teetering bravely at the edge, blowing dust as he piped shrilly from three leg-vents while motioning with two claws for us to come back.

'Look-ook-ook!' came his aspirated stammer. 'Huck, Alvin – hurry!'

Huck claimed later she realized right off what Pincer must've seen. I guess in retrospect it *is* kind of obvious, but at the time I had no idea what could have him so excited. On reaching the edge, I could only peer down in amazement at what had popped out of the belly of the Rift.

It was our bathy! Our beautiful *Wuphon's Dream* floated upright, almost peaceful in the bright sunshine. And on its curved top sat a small black figure, wet and bedraggled from nose to tail. It didn't take a g'Kek's vision to tell that our little noor was as amazed to be alive as we were to see her. Faint whispers of her yelping complaint floated up to us.

'But how—' Urdonnol began.

'Of course!' Ur-ronn interrupted. 'The vallast cane loose!'

I blinked a couple of times.

'Oh, the *ballast*! Hr-rm. Yes, the *Dream*'d be buoyant without it. But there was no crew to pull the release, unless—'

'Unless *Ziz* did it!' Huck finished for me.

'*Insufficient explanation*,' Urdonnol interjected in GalTwo. '*With eight cables of (heavy, down-seeking) metal hawser weighing the diving device, the (minuscule) air pocket within our vessel ought to have been (decisively) overwhelmed.*'

'Hrm-rm, I think I see what made the difference,' I suggested, shading my eyes with both hands. 'Huck, what is that ... *thing* surrounding the bathy?'

Again, our wheeled friend teetered at the edge, spreading two eye-stalks far apart and sticking out a third for good measure. 'It looks like a *balloon* of some sort, Alvin. A tube, wrapped around the *Dream* like a life preserver. A circular – *Ziz*!'

That matched my own guess. A traeki torus, inflated beyond anything we might have thought possible.

Everybody turned to stare at Tyug, the Mount Guenn Master of Mixes. The full-sized traeki shuddered, letting out a colored cloud that smelled like released tension.

'A precaution. One that i/we contemplated in consultation with our lord, Uriel. A safeguard of unknown, untried efficacy.

'Glad we/i are to have vlenned a success. These rings, and those below, anticipate relishing recent events. Soon. In retrospect.'

'In other words-ords,' Pincer interpreted, 'stop staring like a bunch of day-blind glavers. Let's go fetch 'em *back-ack-ack*!'

XVIII

THE BOOK OF THE SLOPE

Legends

It is said that earlier generations interpreted the Scrolls in ways quite different than we do now, in our modern Commons.

Without doubt, each wave of immigrants brought to the Slope a new crisis of faith, from which beliefs emerged restructured, changed.

At the start, every fresh arrival briefly held advantages, bearing godlike tools from the Five Galaxies. Newcomers kept these powers for intervals ranging from a few months to more than eight years. This helped each sept establish a secure base for their descendants, as humans did at Biblos, the hoon on Hawph Island, and the g'Kek at Dooden Mesa.

Yet each also knew its handicaps – a small founding population and ignorance about how to live a primitive existence on an unknown world. Even the haughty gray queens conceded they must accept certain principles, or risk vendetta from all the others combined. The Covenant of Exile set rules of population control, concealment, and Jijo-preservation, as well as proper ways to handle dross. These fundamentals continue to this day.

It is all too easy to forget that other matters were settled only after mordant struggle.

For instance, bitter resistance to the reintroduction of metallurgy, by urrish smiths, was only partly based on qheuens protecting their tool-monopoly. There was also a sincere belief, on the part of many hoon and traeki, that the innovation was sacrilege. To this day, some on the Slope will not touch reforged Buyur steel or let it in their villages or homes, no matter how many times the sages rule it safe for 'temporary' use.

Another remnant belief can be seen among those puritans who despise books. While paper itself can hardly be faulted – it decays well and can be used to reprint copies of the Scrolls – there is still a dissident minority who call the Biblos trove a vanity at best, and an impediment to those whose goal should lie in blessed ignorance. In the early days of human life on Jijo, such sentiments were exploited by urrish and qheuen foes – until the great smiths discovered profit in the forging of type, and book-addiction spread unstoppably throughout the Commons.

Strangely, it is the most recent crisis-of-faith that shows the least leftover effects today. If not for written accounts, it would be difficult to believe that, only a century ago, there were many on the Slope who loathed and feared the newly arrived Holy Egg. Yet at the time there were serious calls for the Explosers Guild to destroy it! To demolish the stone-that-sings, lest it give away our hiding place or, worse, distract the Six away from following the same path already blazed by glavers.

'If it is not in the Scrolls, it cannot be sacred.'

That has always been the declaration of orthodoxy, since times immemorial. And to this day it must be confessed – there is no mention in the Scrolls of anything even remotely like the Egg.

Dark, clammy, stifling.

Rety didn't like the cave.

It must be the stale, dusty air that made her heart pound so. Or else the painful scrapes on her legs, after sliding down a twisty chute to this underground grotto, from a narrow entrance in a boo-shrouded cleft.

Or maybe what made her jumpy was the way *shapes* kept crowding in from all sides. Each time Rety whirled with her borrowed lantern, the creepy shadows turned out to be knobs of cold, dead rock. But a little voice seemed to say – *Always ... so far! But a real monster may wait around the next bend.*

She set her jaw and refused to listen. Anyone who called *her* scared would be a liar!

Does a scared person slink into dark places at night? Or do things they was told not to do, by all the big fat chiefs of the Six?

A weight wriggled in her belt pouch. Rety reached past the fur-lined flap to stroke the squirming creature. 'Don't spook, yee. It's just a big hold in the groun'.'

A narrow head and a sinuous neck snaked toward her, three eyes glittering in the soft flamelight. A squeaky voice protested.

'yee *not* spooked! dark good! on plains, li'l man-urs love hidey-holes, till find warm wife!'

'Okay, okay. I didn't mean—'

'yee *help* nervous wife!'

'Who're *you* calling nervous, you little—'

Rety cut short. Maybe she should let yee feel needed, if it helped him keep his own fear under control.

'ow! not so tight!' The male yelped, echoes fleeing down black corridors.

Rety quickly let go and stroked yee's ruffled mane. 'Sorry. Look, I bet we're gettin' close, so let's not talk so much, okay?'

'okay, yee shut up. wife do too!'

Rety's lips pressed. Then anger flipped into a sudden urge to laugh. Whoever said male urs weren't smart must've never met her 'husband', yee had even changed his *accent*, in recent days, mimicking Rety's habits of speech.

She raised the lantern and resumed picking her way through the twisty cavern, surrounded by a sparkle of strange mineral formations, reflecting lamplight off countless glittering facets. It might have been pretty to look at, if she weren't obsessed with one thing alone. An item to reclaim. Something she once, briefly, had owned.

My ticket off this mudball.

Rety's footprints appeared to be the first ever laid in the dust – which wasn't surprising, since just qheuens, and a few humans and urs, had a knack for travel underground, and she was smaller than most. With luck, this tunnel led toward the much larger cave she had seen Lester Cambel enter several times. Following the chief human sage had been her preoccupation while avoiding the group of frustrated men and women who wanted her to help guide them over the mountains. Once she knew for sure where Cambel spent his evenings, she had sent yee scouring the underbrush till he found this offshoot opening, bypassing the guarded main entrance.

The little guy was already proving pretty darn useful. To Rety's surprise, married life wasn't so bad, once you got used to it.

There was more tight wriggling and writhing. At times, she had to squirm sideways or slide down narrow chutes, making yee complain when he got squeezed. Beyond the lantern's dim yellow puddle, she heard soft tinkling sounds as water dripped into black pools, slowly sculpting weird underground shapes out of Jijo's raw mineral juices. With each step Rety fought a tightness in her chest, trying to ignore her tense imagination, which pictured her in the twisty guts of some huge slumbering beast. The rocky womb kept threatening to close in from all sides, shutting the exits, then grinding her to dust.

Soon the way narrowed to a corkscrew horizontal tube that was tight even for her. She had to send yee ahead before attempting the contorted passage, pushing the lantern along in front of her.

yee's tiny hooves clattered on gritty limestone. Soon she heard a welcome hoarse whisper.

'is good! hole opens up, little ways more, come wife, faster!'

His chiding almost made her snort angrily – not a wise idea with her cheek, nose, and mouth scraping rank dust. Contorting her body to turn the next corner, she suddenly felt *certain* the walls were moving!

She recalled what Dwer's brother had said about this region, when he led her down that last stretch to the Glade, past steaming sulfur vents. Lark had called this a land of earthquakes, and seemed to think it a *good* thing!

Twisting uneasily, her hip jammed in a stone cleft.

I'm caught!

Thought of entrapment sent a whimpering moan surging past flecked lips as she thrashed, banging her knee agonizingly. The world really was closing in!

Her forehead struck stone, and pain-dazzles swarmed her dimming vision. The candle lantern rattled from her clutching fingertips, almost toppling over.

'easy, wife! stop! stay!'

The words bounced off the warped mirror of her panic. Stubbornly, Rety kept striving against cold stone, groaning and pushing futilely ... until ...

Something *clicked* inside her. All at once, she went limp, suddenly resigned to let the mountain do whatever it wanted with her.

Moments after she stopped fighting, the walls miraculously seemed to stop moving. Or had it been her, all along?

'better now? good-good, now move left leg ... left! good, stop now. okay roll other way. go-o-o-ood wife!'

His tiny voice was a lifeline she clutched for the few duras – for the *eternity* – that it took to win free. At last, the clutch of the stony passage eased, and she slithered down a sandy bank in a flowing, almost liquid liberation that felt just like being born.

When next she looked up, yee had the lantern cradled in both arms, bowing with forelegs bent.

'good brave wife! no wife *ever* like yee's amazing wife!'

This time Rety could not hold it in. She covered her mouth with both hands, yet her escaping laughter bounced off the fluted walls. Combed by stalactites, it came back as a hundred soft echoes of her joy to be alive.

The sage was pondering *her* bird.

He peered at it, wrote on a notepad, then poked it with some shiny tool.

Rety seethed. The gold-green machine was hers. Hers! She had pursued it from the southern marshes to the Rimmers, rescued it from a greedy mulc-spider, *won* it with her sweat, suffering, and dreams. *She* would choose who, if anybody, got to study it.

Anyway, what was a savage shaman going to achieve with his crude glass lenses and such? The tools lying near the bird might have impressed the old Rety, who thought Dwer's hunting bow was so great. But all that changed after meeting Besh, Rann, and the other starhumans. Now she knew – despite all his airs, Lester Cambel was just like Jass or Bom, or any of the other idiots back in the Gray Hills. Stupid braggards. Bullies. Always taking things that didn't belong to them.

Under the bright flare of a mirrored oil lamp, Cambel flipped through a book. Its pages crackled, as if they had not been turned in a very long time. Rety couldn't make out much from her vantage point, perched on a cleft high up one craggy cavern wall. Not that she could read, anyway. Most of each page seemed to be taken up with drawings with lots of little crisscrossing lines. Nothing much resembled a bird.

Come on, yee, she thought, restlessly. *I'm countin' on you!*

She was taking a big risk. The little male had assured her he could handle it, but what if he got lost while sneaking around to the other side? Or forgot his lines? Rety would be furious if the little guy wound up getting hurt!

Cambel's assistant stood up and left the chamber, perhaps on some brief errand, or else to retire for the night. Either way, this was a perfect time! *Come on, yee!*

After so long writhing through dark passages, always fearful the little candle would go out, Rety found the cool brilliance of the sage's lamp harsh to the eyes. With reluctance she had blown out her own light while creeping the last few meters, lest its glow draw attention. Now she regretted it. *What if I have to retreat the way I came?* She couldn't willingly face that path again. But as a last resort, if someone were chasing her ... ?

Too bad she had no way to restart the candle. *Maybe I should've learned to use one of those 'match' things the Slopies boast about.* She had been too awed by the sudden burst of flame to pay close attention when Dwer, and later Ur-Jah, tried showing how they worked. It was all the fault of Jass and Bom, of course, who didn't like womenfolk controlling fire on their own.

But fire's just fine for scaring or burning women, ain't it? she pondered angrily, touching her face. *Maybe I'll come back someday, Jass. Maybe I'll bring another kind of fire.*

Rety reentered her favorite fantasy, flying off to live with the sky-humans on their home star. Oh, at first she'd start out as a sort of pet or mascot. But just give her time! She'd learn whatever it took in order to rise up, until she became so important ...

So important that some great Rothen prince would put a ship – a *fleet* of ships! – at her command, to go with her back to Jijo.

It was fun picturing the look on Jass's smug handsome face, when the sky over the Gray Hills went dark at noon, and then *her* words booming from above—

'you wise mister human sir?'

The tiny voice shook her back to the present. She sought down below – and spied yee trotting nervously near the leg of Lester Cambel's chair.

'Hm? What was that?' Cambel asked, yee jumped as the chair scraped back, pushed by the sage, who peered about in confusion.

'message for wise human! message from wise grandma urs, Ur-Jah!'

Now Cambel looked down, first amazed, then quizzically intrigued.

'Yes, small one? And how did you get down here past the guard?'

'guard he look out for danger, look right past yee. is yee danger?'

The tiny urs laughed, mimicking Rety's own nervous giggle. She hoped Cambel didn't recognize the similarity.

The sage nodded, gravely. 'No, I suppose not. Unless someone gets you angry, my friend, which I'll strive not to do. So now, what's this about a message at this time of night?'

yee did a little dance with his hooves and lifted both arms dramatically, 'urgent time for talk-talk, look at dead birdie later! go Ur-Jah now. now!'

Rety feared his vehemence would rouse suspicion. But the balding human put down his tools at once and stood up. 'Well then, let's go.'

Rety's hopes soared, then sank as Cambel lifted the *bird* with both hands.

No! Put it down!

As if prodded by her tense mental urging, the sage paused, shook his head, and put the machine back, picking up his notebook instead.

'Lay on, MacDuff,' he said to yee, motioning with a sweep of one arm.

'great sage says what?' the small urs tilted his head.

'I said ... oh, never mind. An obscure allusion. Guess I'm just tired. Shall I carry you, sir?'

'no! yee lead wise human, walk this way! *this* way!' and he scampered off eagerly, pausing impatiently and backtracking several times as the sage followed ploddingly behind.

When they both had vanished up the tunnel leading toward the main entrance, Rety wasted no time slithering down the crumbly, slanting limestone wall till she tumbled bottom-first onto the floor of the laboratory cave. She scrambled up and hurried to the table where her bird lay, headless as it had been ever since the fight with the alien robot.

Its breast lay spread open like a carcass at a feast, exposing innards like none Rety had ever seen, glittering like jewels. *What did the stinker do, gut it like a herd chick?* She fought to check her rage. *Rann might not pay if the fools have ruined it by mucking inside!*

She looked closer. The opening was too clean to have been hacked with a knife. In fact, when she hesitantly touched the bird's ribcage, it seemed to roll smoothly around the line where it was still connected – like the *hinged* door she had seen on a big cabinet, and marveled at, while visiting the forayers' medical tent.

I see. You just close it like ... this.

She lifted the smaller section through an arc, till it swung shut with a decisive click.

Now Rety regretted her haste. There was no more chance to look closer at the little flashings inside. *Oh, well. None of my biznis, anyway*, she thought, and plucked up her prize. *At least I don't pretend I'm anythin' but a sooner an' a savage.*

Though not forever. Once I get off Jijo, I'll learn. I'll learn all right!

The bird was heavier than she recalled. Briefly, her heart felt full. She had her treasure back! She crammed the heavy bird-thing into her pouch, bypassing the books strewn across the table as she hurried off, following the same path yee and Lester Cambel had taken, an easy stand-up trail leading toward the outside world.

The way was lit by little lamps, hanging from a thin boo pipe stapled to the wall. Tiny flames flickered an eerie blue color, leaving wide pools of shadow in between. Dim light also spilled from several side chambers, now mostly empty of workers as it was night-time outside. One cell, however, seemed to blaze with bulky lanterns. Before tiptoeing past, Rety warily eyed two human occupants – who were luckily turned away, murmuring with low voices. Drawings of the star-gods, their aircraft, and other tools lay tacked on a dozen or so easels. The cube-shaped station – which Rety had never seen unburied – lay revealed in fine detail, more grand than some shattered Buyur site. Yet it seemed minute next to the monstrous tube depicted on the *next* sketch, floating above the forest.

My starship, she mused, though cowed by the thought of boarding the huge vessel when it returned for the forayers. She must remember to hold her chin up that day and show no fear.

The artists had caught Rann's distant amused gaze, and Kunn's sharp hunter's glare as he adjusted the claw arm of a hovering robot. The pale intensity of Besh balanced Ling's dusky half-cynical expression. Rety knew they were only drawings, like the ones some old grandpas used to scratch on a cliff overlooking the wintering cave, back in the Gray Hills. Still, the lifelike accuracy seemed spooky and magical. *The Slopies are studying the star-men. What could it mean?*

Rety almost tripped in her haste to get away. *Whatever they're planning it won't come to much*. She set her mind back to getting out of this place and making the rendezvous in time.

The mustiness began to lift and the harsh echoes softened. Soon she heard voices ahead ... Lester Cambel trading words with a second human. Rety tiptoed to the next bend and peered around. The human sage could be seen talking to the cave guard, who looked down at yee with a chagrined expression.

'Privacy wasps may stop the tiniest robots,' Cambel said. 'But what about something the size of this little fellow?'

'Honestly, sir. I can't imagine how he got past—'

Cambel waved off the apology. 'There was no harm done this time, son. It's mostly their contempt that protects us – their confidence we have nothing worth spying on. Just be more careful from now on, eh?'

He patted the young man's arm and turned to follow as yee hurried outside. The path seemed brightly lit by moonshine, piercing through gently waving forest branches. Still clearly perplexed, the guard set his jaw and gripped his weapon – a kind of pole with a sharp-looking knife-thing at one end – standing with legs slightly apart, in the center of the entrance. When the scrape of Cambel's footsteps faded, Rety counted twenty duras, then made her own move. Faking calm, she sauntered toward the young guard, who swiveled when she was close.

Rety gave a smile and an easygoing wave. 'Well, guess I'm all done for the night.' She yawned, sidling past his bulk, sensing his startled indecision. 'Boy I'll tell ya, that science sure is hard work! Well g'night.'

Now she was outside, gratefully inhaling fresh mountain air and trying not to break into a run. *Especially* when he shouted – 'Hey, stop right there!'

Swiveling around but continuing to walk backward down the path, Rety delayed him a few more seconds by grinning broadly. 'Yeah? You need somethin'?'

'What . . . who *are* you—?'

'Got something here I figure the sage'd want to be seein',' she replied with deceptive truthfulness, patting her belt pouch and still backing away.

The guard started toward her.

With a joyful shout, Rety spun about and took off into the forest, knowing pursuit was hopeless at this point. He had lost his chance, the stinker!

Still, she was kind of glad that he tried.

yee met her where they had agreed, by the log bridge, halfway to the place where she was to join Rann. On spying her, the little urs yelped and seemed to fly into her arms.

He was less pleased on trying to burrow into his accustomed place, only to find a cold hard object taking up the pouch. Rety tucked him into the folds of her jacket, and after a moment he seemed to find that acceptable.

'yee tell wife, yee see—'

'We did it!' Rety chortled gleefully, unable to contain the rush of an adventure so well closed. The chase had been a perfect way to finish, leaping and laughing as she ran through the forest, leaving the big oaf to flounder in the dark while she circled around, then slinked right past the noisy guard on her way back to the Glade.

'You were great, too,' she told yee, sharing credit. 'Would've been harder to do it without you.' She hugged his little body till he complained with a series of short grunts. 'Did you have any trouble getting away from Cambel?' she asked.

'wiseman human no problem, yee get 'way good, but then—'

'Great, then it's over. We better go now, though. If Rann has to wait, he may not be in as good a mood as—'

'—but then yee *see* something on way to meet wife! whole *herd* of urs ... qheuens ... hoons ... men ... all going sneak-sneak in dark, carry big boxes!'

Rety hurried down a side trail leading toward the rendezvous point. 'Hm-hm? Do tell? Prob'ly one of those silly pilgrim things, headin' up to pray to that big rock they think is a god.' She had only contempt for the superstitions of planet-grubbing sooners. To her, all the talk she'd heard about the Slopies' fabulous 'Egg' was just more scare-you-in-the-dark stuff, like those tales of ghosts and huge beasts and spirit glavers that were common campfire fare back in the Gray Hills, especially since Jass and Bom took over. Whenever times were hard, the hunters would argue into the night, seeking some reason why the prey animals might be angry, and ways to appease them.

'herd of sneakers *not* go holy rock!' yee protested, 'head wrong way! no white robes, no sing-songs! just sneak-sneak, I say! sneak with boxes to 'nother cave!'

Rety's interest was almost piqued. yee sure seemed to think it important ...

But just then the trail turned to overlook the little valley where the sky-humans dwelled. Moonlight spilled across pavilions that seemed strangely less well camouflaged now, in the vivid dimness.

A soft hum warbled from the west, and a *glint* drew her eye as a glistening teardrop shape floated into view, folding away two delicate wings as it descended. Rety felt a tingle, recognizing the small flying boat of the forayers, returning from another mysterious expedition. She watched, transfixed, as the lovely thing settled gracefully to the valley floor. A hole opened, swallowing it into the ground.

Excitement filled Rety's lungs, and her heart felt light.

'Hush, husband,' she told yee when he complained of being ignored. 'We got some tradin' and dickerin' to do.'

'Now's when we'll see if they pay what they promised.'

My rings, you need not my weakly focused musings to inform you. Surely all of you must feel it, deep within each oily torus core?

The Egg. Slowly, as if rising from a deep torpor, it wakens!

Perhaps now the Commons will be filled once more with comity, with union of spirit, with the meshed resolve that once bound jointly our collective wills. Oh, let it be so!

We are so fractured, so far from ready. So far from worthy.

Oh, let it be so.

SARA

The stacks were infested with polisher bees, and the music rooms thronged with hungry, biting parrot fleas, but the chimps on the maintenance staff were too busy to fumigate for minor pests.

While taking some air in the west atrium, Sara watched several of the hairy workers help a human librarian pack precious volumes into fleece-lined crates, then seal them with drippings from a big red candle. Gobbets of wax clung to the chimps' matted fur, and they complained to each other with furtive hand signs.

This is not correct, Sara interpreted one worker's flurry of gestures and husky grunts. *In this intemperate haste, we are making regrettable errors.*

The other replied, *How true, my associate! This volume of Auden should not go in among Greek classics! We shall never get these books properly restacked when this crisis finally blows over, as surely it must.*

Well, perhaps she was generous in her mental translation. Still, the chimps who labored in these hallowed halls were a special breed. Almost as special as Prity.

Overhead towered the atrium of the Hall of Literature, spanned by bridges and ramps that linked reading rooms and galleries, all lined with shelves groaning under the weight of books, absorbing sound while emitting a redolence of ink, paper, wisdom, and dusty time. Weeks of frantic evacuation, hauling donkey-loads to faraway caves, had not made a dent in the hoard – still crammed with texts of every color and size.

Sage Plovov called this hall – dedicated to *legend*, *magic*, and *make-believe* – the House of Lies. Yet Sara always felt this place less burdened by the supremacy of the past than in those nearby structures dedicated to science. After all, what could Jijo's savages ever add to the mountain of facts brought here by their godlike ancestors? A mountain said to be like a sand grain next to the Great Galactic Library. But the tales in *this* hall feared no refutal by ancient authority. Good or bad, great or forgettable, no work of literature was ever provably 'false.'

Plovov said – *'It's easy to be original when you don't have to care whether you're telling the truth. Magic and art arise from an egomaniac's insistence that the artist is right, and the universe wrong.'*

Of course, Sara agreed. On the other hand, she *also* thought Plovov was jealous.

When humans came to Jijo, the effect on the other five races must have been like when Earth met Galactic culture. After centuries with just a handful of engraved scrolls, the urs, g'Kek, and others reacted to the flood of paper books with both suspicion and voracious appetite. Between brief, violent struggles, nonhumans devoured Terran fables, dramas, and novels. When they wrote stories of their own, they imitated Earthly forms – like ersatz Elizabethan romances featuring gray-shelled queens, or Native North American legends recast for urrish tribes.

But lately, a flowering of new styles had also started emerging, from heroic adventures to epic poems set in strange meters and rhymes, unraveling the last shreds of order from dialects of GalSeven, and even GalTwo. Printers and binders had as many orders for new titles as reprints. Scholars debated what it all might mean – an outbreak of heresy? Or a freeing of the spirit?

Few dared use the term *renaissance*.

All of which may end in a matter of days or weeks, Sara pondered glumly. News from the glade – brought by a kayak pilot braving the Bibur rapids – showed no change in the sages' grim appraisal of the alien gene-raiders, or their intent.

Well, Bloor should be there by now. Sara's plan might not dissuade the sky-humans from genocide, but a folk as helpless as the Six must be willing to try anything.

Including Ariana's crazy notion. Even if it's cruel.

The voice of the elderly sage carried from the chamber behind Sara.

'There now, dear. You've struggled long enough with that one. Let's see what you can make of this nice book. Have you ever seen symbols and words like these before?'

Sighing, Sara turned around to reenter the Children's Wing.

The Stranger sat near Ariana Foo's wheelchair, surrounded by volumes bearing bright colors and simple text, printed in large friendly type. Though his face was haggard, the tall dark man resignedly accepted yet another book and ran his hand over the dots, slashes, and bars of a GalTwo teaching rhyme – a primer meant for young urrish middlings. Sara was unsurprised when his lips pursed and his tongue clicked as he worked across the page, laboriously. His eyes recognized the symbols, but clearly, no sense was being made of the sentence-phrase itself.

It had been the same with books in GalSix, Anglic, and GalSeven, tearing Sara's heart to see his frustration turn into torment. Perhaps only now was the injured man coming to know fully what had been ripped away from him. What he had forever lost.

Ariana Foo, on the other hand, seemed eminently satisfied. She beamed at Sara. 'This is no rube from the outer hamlets,' the old woman ruled. 'He was an educated person, familiar with every language currently in use among the Six. If we have time, we *must* take him to the Linguistics Wing and try some of the forgotten dialects! Galactic Twelve would clinch it. Only three scholars on Jijo know any of it today.'

'What's the point?' Sara asked. 'You've made your case. Why not let him be?'

'In a minute, dear. One or two more, then we'll be off. I've saved the best for last.'

Two library staff members watched nervously as Ariana reached over to a stack of books by her side. Some were priceless, with rings set in their spines where chains normally kept them locked to their shelves. The archivists clearly did not like seeing them pawed by a speechless barbarian.

Unwilling to watch, Sara turned away.

The rest of the Children's Wing was placid – and contained few children. Scholars, and traveling librarians from all six races came here to study, copy, or select books to borrow, carrying their precious cargo by cart, boat, or pack donkey to settlements throughout the Slope. Sara observed a red qheuen carefully gather some of the heavy, brass-bound albums required by her kind, assisted by two lorniks trained as assistants and page-turners. One lornik swatted at a polisher bee that was working its way across the cover of a book, rubbing its abdomen amorously across the jacket, buffing it to a fine sheen and erasing part of the title. No one knew what function the insectoids once served for the departed Buyur, but they were a damned nuisance nowadays.

Sara saw others from every race, educators who refused to let a mere crisis interfere with the serious task of instructing the next generation. Beyond the qheuen, an elderly traeki selected volumes treated to resist the fluids emitted by new stacks of rings, too clumsy to control their secretions.

A low moan brought Sara back around to see the Stranger holding before him a long, slim book so old, the colors had gone all dingy and gray. The man's dark features clouded with clashing emotions. Sara had no time to read the title, only to glimpse a skinny black feline figure on the cover, wearing a red-and-white-striped stovepipe hat. Then, to the librarians' gasping dismay, he clutched the volume tightly to his chest, rocking back and forth with eyes closed.

'Something from his childhood, I'll warrant,' Ariana Foo diagnosed, scribbling on her pad. 'According to the indexes, this fable was widely popular among children in northwestern Earth civilization almost continuously for over three centuries, so we can tentatively localize his cultural origins ...'

'How nice. Then you're finished?' Sara demanded, caustically.

'Hm? Oh, yes, I suppose so. For now. Get him settled down will you, pet? Then bring him along. I'll be waiting in the main Listening Parlor.' With that, Ariana nodded briskly to the chimp assigned to push her chair, leaving Sara behind to deal with the upset Stranger.

He was muttering to himself, as he did from time to time, repeating the same short phrase, over and over. Something that wormed its way out, despite the damage to his brain. In this case, it was clearly nonsense, sparked by intense emotion.

'... *wocket in my pocket* ...' he said again and again, chortling poignantly, '... *a wocket in my pocket* ...'

Gently, firmly, Sara managed to pry the ancient tome out of his trembling hands, returning the treasure to the disapproving librarians. With patience she encouraged the wounded man to stand, though his dark eyes were fogged with a kind of misery Sara found she could fathom. She too had lost someone precious to her.

Only the one *he* was mourning was himself.

Two g'Kek servants met them by the entrance to the Listening Parlor, physician researchers who had examined the Stranger soon after he arrived in Biblos. One now took him by the hand.

'Sage Foo wishes you to attend her in the observing room, next door,' the other one said. One eyestalk gestured toward an opening farther down the hall. When the Stranger looked at Sara questioningly, she gave him an encouraging nod. His trusting smile only made her feel worse.

The observing room was dimly illuminated by light streaming in through two circular windows – exquisite slabs of spun glass, flawless except for the characteristic central stem – which looked into another chamber where the two g'Kek doctors could be seen seating the Stranger before a large box with a crank on one side and a trumpetlike horn rising from the other.

'Come in, pet. And please close the door.'

It took several duras for Sara's eyes to adapt and see who sat with Ariana. By then it was too late to flee.

The whole party from Tarek Town was present, along with two humans dressed in scholars' robes. Ulgor and Blade had reason to be here, of course. Blade had helped rescue the Stranger from the swamp, and Ulgor was an honorary delegate from Dolo Village. Even Jop had an official interest. But why were Jomah and Kurt the Exploser in the room? Whatever cryptic guild business brought them from Tarek, the old man and boy now watched the proceedings with the silent intensity that was a trademark of their family and craft.

The human scholars turned toward her.

Bonner and Taine – the very persons she had hoped to avoid during this visit.

Both men rose to their feet.

Sara hesitated, then bowed at the waist. 'Masters.'

'Dear Sara.' Bonner sighed, leaning on his cane more than she recalled when she had last seen the balding topologist. 'How we've missed you in these dusty halls.'

'As I've missed you, master,' she replied, surprised how true it was. Perhaps in the numbness after Joshu's passing, she had closed off too many good memories as well as bad. The warmth of the old savant's hand on her arm recalled their many walks, discussing the arcane, endlessly fascinating habits of *shapes*, the sort that could be described with symbols but never seen by human eyes.

'Please don't call me master anymore,' he asked. 'You are an adept now, or should be soon enough. Come, have a seat between us, like old times.'

A bit *too* much like old times, Sara realized, meeting the eyes of the other mathematician-sage. The tall, silver-haired algebraist seemed unchanged, still distant, enigmatic. Taine nodded and spoke her name, then sat again facing the windows. Typically, he had chosen the position farthest from the nonhumans in the room.

Sage Taine's discomfort around the other septs was not rare. A minority felt that way in every race, a reaction deep-rooted in ancient drives. What mattered was how you dealt with it, and Taine was unfailingly polite to the urs or g'Kek teachers who came to consult him about the binomial theorem. Given the handicap, it was just as well the tall savant could live a scholar's cloistered life ... like the one Sara herself had expected—

—until a visiting bookbinder became an unlikely suitor, filling Sara's heart with unexpected possibilities.

—until she boldly announced to her confused colleagues a new focus for her studies, *language,* of all things.

—until Joshu sickened when pepper pox swept through the Valley of the Bibur, a plague that took its victims with agonizing suddenness, and she had to watch another woman perform the rites of mourning, knowing that everyone was watching, to see how she'd react.

—until, after the funeral, Sage Taine approached her with stiff formality and renewed his earlier proposal of marriage.

—until, in a rush, she fled this place of dust and memories, running home to her treehouse overlooking the great dam where she was born.

Now it all circled around again. Taine had seemed so austerely beautiful when she first came to Biblos in her teens, a towering figure, impressive beyond compare. But things had changed inside her since. *Everything* had changed.

Abruptly, Taine's aristocratic bearing broke as he cursed and slapped his neck, then peered at his hand, frowning in disappointment. Sara glanced at Bonner, who whispered, 'Parrot ticks. Such annoyances. If one gets in your ear, Ifni help you. I heard everything double for a week, till Vorjin fished the damn thing out.'

Ariana Foo made an emphatic throat-clearing sound, drawing their attention forward. 'I've already explained to the others, Sara, my belief that your Stranger is a man from the stars. Further research illuminates the nature of his injuries.'

Her chimp assistant passed out sheets of paper, streaked from hasty, hand-cranked photocopying, showing the stylized profile of a man's head, with arrows and captions pointing to parts. Most of the words were gibberish to Sara, though Lark might have found them familiar.

'I recalled reading about this once and was lucky enough to find the reference quickly. It seems that when our ancestors departed Earth, experiments had been taking place with the objective of creating direct connections between computers and living human brains.'

Sara heard an awed hiss from somewhere in back. To many of the Six, the word *computer* carried superstitious power. The crews of every sneakship to reach Jijo had melted all their digital calculating engines, down to the very smallest, before sinking their star cruisers in the depths of the Midden. No other possession had such potential for betraying illegal sapience on a forbidden world.

Sara had read a few gaudy stories from Earth days, in which the author used mind-to-computer links in the narrative. She had always dismissed them as a metaphor, like legends of humans flying with feathers glued to their arms. But Ariana said the notion was once taken seriously.

'This illustration shows some of the brain areas being proposed for neural-electronic junctions at the time our ancestors departed,' Ariana continued. 'Research surely proceeded during the three hundred years since. In fact, it's my belief that our Stranger possessed the product – an aperture which let him commune with computers and other devices, inset just above the left ear.'

Now it was Sara's turn to gasp. 'Then his—'

Ariana held up a hand. 'It is a safe guess that his burns and lesser injuries resulted when his ship or flying craft crash-landed in the Eternal Swamp, not far from where Sara and her friends found him. Alas, his miraculous escape from fiery death was spoiled by one bit of bad luck, when the artificial connector attached to his head was violently ripped away, taking with it portions of his left temporal lobe.

'I needn't add, this is the portion of the human brain most closely identified with speech.'

Sara could only blink. Through the glass, she saw the man Ariana referred to, eyes bright and interested, watching the g'Kek doctors prepare their apparatus.

'I'd have thought such damage would kill him,' Bonner said, summarizing her own surprise.

'Indeed, he seems to have made a remarkable recovery. Were he not adult and male, with a rigid synaptic structure, perhaps he might have roused speech from the semi-dormant *right* temporal lobe, as some children and women do, after suffering damage to the left side. As things stand, there remains one possib—' She paused, noticing a waving of eyestalks in the next room.

'Well, I see our good doctors are ready, so let's proceed.'

Ariana opened a listening vent under the nearest pane of glass. At almost the same moment, Sara felt a sudden sharp pain on her thigh, and Taine slapped his neck again. 'Damn pests!' he muttered, and glanced sideways at Sara. 'Things have been going to hell in more ways than one around here.'

Good old, cheerful Taine, she thought, quashing an urge to brush at her own neck. Parrot ticks were generally harmless – another mysterious vestige of Buyur times. Who would ever want the 'symbiosis' of a creature who attached itself to one of your veins and repaid you by reiterating every sound you heard? The Buyur must have been strange beings indeed.

In the next room, one of the g'Kek doctors opened a large album whose thick sleeves held several dozen slim black disks. The physician delicately removed one and laid it on a round platform which began to spin.

'An elenentary sfring action device,' Ulgor explained. 'Easily constructed from scraf netal and slices of voo.'

'A primitive but effective analog storage and retrieval system,' Taine elucidated.

'Safely nondigital,' Bonner added.

'Yesss,' the blue qheuen, Blade, hissed in agreement. 'And I hear it plays *music*. Sort of.'

The g'Kek doctor gently lowered a wooden armature until a slender stylus touched the rim of the spinning disk. Almost at once, low strains of melody began crooning from the machine's hornlike speaker. A strange *tinny* melody – accompanied by faint crackling pops – which seemed to tickle the roots of Sara's hair.

'These disks are originals,' Ariana Foo said, 'pressed by the *Tabernacle* colonists at the same time as the Great Printing. Nowadays, only a few experts play them. Earthly musical forms aren't popular in the modern Commons, but I'm betting our Stranger won't agree.'

Sara had heard of the disk-playing device. It seemed bizarre to listen to music with no living performer involved. Almost as bizarre as the music itself, which sounded unlike anything she had heard. Sara quickly recognized some instruments – violins, drums, and horns – which was natural, since string and wind instruments had been introduced to Jijo by Earthlings. But the arrangement of notes was strange, and Sara soon realized – what seemed most eerie was its *orderliness*.

A modern Jijoan sextet involved the blending of six solo performers, each spontaneously merging with the others. Half the excitement came from waiting for unpredictable, felicitous blendings of harmony, emerging and then vanishing once more, much like life itself. No two performances were ever the same.

But this is purely human music. Complex chords coiled and gyred in sequences that reiterated with utter disciplined precision. *As in science, the point is to make something repeatable, verifiable.*

She glanced at the others. Ulgor seemed fascinated, twitching her left hand-cluster – the one used for fingering notes on a violus. Blade rocked his heavy carapace in bewilderment, while young Jomah, sitting next to his stolid uncle, seemed twitchy with confused ennui.

Although she'd never heard its like, something felt ineffably familiar about the orderly sweep and flow of harmony. The notes were like ... *integers*, the phrases like geometric figures.

What better evidence that music can be like mathematics?

The Stranger was reacting, as well. He sat forward, flushed, with clear recognition in his squinting eyes. Sara felt a wave of concern. Too much more emotional turbulence might push the poor exhausted man past his limit.

'Ariana, is all of this going somewhere?' she asked.

'In a minute, Sara.' The sage held up her hand once more. 'That was just the overture. Here comes the part we're interested in.'

How does she know? Sara wondered. Apparently, the breadth of Ariana's eclectic knowledge stretched even to obscure ancient arts.

Sure enough, in moments the instrumental arrangement crescendoed and paused. Then a new element joined in – the unmistakable twang of human voices. After missing the first few stanzas, Sara bent forward, concentrating to make out queerly accented words.

For today our pirate 'prentice
  rises from indenture freed,
Strong his arm and keen his scent is,
  he's a pirate now indeed.

The effect on the Stranger was profound. He stood up, trembling. The emotion spilling across his face was not simply recognition, but joyful *surprise*.

Then – to his own clear amazement as much as Sara's – he opened his mouth and sang along!

Pour, oh pour, the pirate sherry,
  fill, oh fill, the pirate glass.
And to make us more than merry,
  let the pirate bumper pass!

Sara stood up too, staring in astonishment. From Ariana Foo came a shout of satisfaction.

'Aha! A hit with the very first try! Even with the cultural cue, I expected to work through many before finding one he knew.'

'But his injury!' objected Taine. 'I thought you said—'

'Quite right,' Bonner cut in. 'If he can't speak, how can he sing?'

'Oh, that.' Ariana dismissed the miracle with a wave. 'Different functions. Different parts of the brain. There are precedents in the medical references. I'm told it's even been observed here on Jijo, once or twice.

'No, what startles *me* is the cultural persistence this experiment demonstrates. It's been three hundred years. I'd have thought by now Galactic influences would overwhelm all native Earthly—' The old woman paused, as if realizing she was running off on a tangent. 'Well, never mind that. Right now what matters is that our off-planet visitor seems to have found a way to communicate, after all.'

Even in the dimness, Ariana's smile was broad and anything but humble.

Sara laid her hand on the glass, feeling its cool slickness vibrate to the music in the next room, which had passed on to a new song. The cadence slowed and melody changed, though apparently not the topic.

She closed her eyes and listened as the Stranger plunged ahead with throaty joy, outracing the recording in his eagerness to be heard at last.

> *Away to the cheating world go you,*
> *where pirates all are well-to-do.*
> *But I'll be true to the song I sing . . .*
> *and live and die a Pi-i-rate King!*

XIX

THE BOOK OF THE SEA

Scrolls

Of galaxies, it is said,
there were once seventeen,
linked and bound together,
by tubes of focused time.

One by one, those frail tubes snapped,
sundered as the universe
stretched its ageing seams.
Of galaxies, the Progenitors
knew eleven.

Six more have parted ways,
in the ages since, stranding
distant cousins to unknown fates.
Of galaxies, our immediate ancestors knew
five.

What if it should happen
once again, while we seek redemption
in this fallow spiral?
Will anyone come down to claim us,
once our innocence is restored?

In our own sky, of Galaxies we see but one.

—*The Scroll of Possibilities*

I don't wish to dwell too much on my own role in what came next. Let's just say that as a young male hoon, I seemed best suited to dangle at the end of the redeployed hawser, sitting in a makeshift sling while the crew lowered me toward the dark blue waters of the Rift.

After dropping below the edge, all I could see of the others were a few hoon and urrish faces, plus a pair of g'Kek eyestalks, peering down at me. Then even those blended into the rocks and I was alone, dangling like bait on a hooked line. I tried not to look at the long drop below, but soon a gusting wind set the hawser swaying, reminding me of the slender support overhead.

During the lonely descent I had time to ask myself – *'What the heck am I doing here?'*

It became a kind of *mantra*. (If I recall that word right, since it's not in the dictionary I have with me in this cold, hard place.) Repeated often enough, the phrase soon lost some of its horrid fascination, instead taking on a queerly pleasant cadence. By the halfway point, I was umbling—

'What the heck. I am *doing*. Here!'

In other words, a deed is being done, and I'm the one doing it, so why not do it right? An Anglic way of phrasing a very hoonish thought.

Anyway, I guess I did a good job of convincing myself, 'cause I didn't panic when they overshot at the end. My furry legs got well dunked before the brakes firmed and the tether stopped jouncing. It took a moment to gather breath and start umbling at Huphu, calling her to swim over from *Wuphon's Dream*, almost an arrowflight away. Haste was vital, since the bathy was slowly drifting out from the placid water under Terminus Rock. Soon she'd hit the Rift Current, and we might never see her again.

This time Huphu didn't make me wait. She dove in and swam toward me like a little black dartfish, clearly not badly harmed by her plummet off the bluff.

What's that sick joke they tell about noors? If you ever *have* to kill one, it will take a quart of traeki poison, a qheuen's claw, a human's arrow, and a rack of urrish insults. That assumes a hoon first distracts the beast with a first-class umble, and even so, it's best to have a g'Kek roll back and forth over the corpse a few times, just to be sure.

All right, it's juvenile humor, but also *respectful* in a way. I couldn't help spine-laughing over it while waiting for our indestructible Huphu. Finally, she clambered up my leg and into my arms, wallowing in my happy umble. I sensed she was still frightened, since for once she made no effort to pretend nonchalance or to hide her happiness to see me.

Still, time was short. Soon as I could, I slipped a harness of tough cord over Huphu's shoulders and urged her back down to the sea.

Urdonnol's plan seemed a good one ... that is, *if* Huphu understood my instructions ... *if the Dream* hadn't already drifted beyond reach ... *if* Huphu managed to hook the cable's end onto the bathy's grommet fixture ... *if the* subtraeki, Ziz, could hold on awhile longer in its hugely distended form, bearing up the weight of all that dangling metal ... *if the* re-spliced hawser would bear the burden when the crew above hauled away ...

There were so many ifs. Is this why Earthlings chose to call their goddess of luck and chance Ifni? Her capricious whims sure do swing back and forth. As on that day, when she first cursed our enterprise with calamity, then tossed her dice again the other way. Throughout the following tense midura, we all worried and wondered what her next clattering roll would bring – till at last Huphu and I stood atop the cliff together, dripping beside the beautiful flank of *Wuphon's Dream*, staring in amazement as Tyug carefully deflated and tended Ziz. Meanwhile, Pincer and Huck rolled round and round the bathy, inspecting nervously for damage, and Ur-ronn supervised the crew hauling in the rest of the dangling cable.

Finally, the two severed ends lay side by side on the stony mesa, burned, frayed, and torn.

'This will *not* haffen again!' I overheard our urrish friend mutter. It was in that tone of voice an urs uses when she makes a prediction, a vow, and means she'll rip the neck off anyone who tries to make a liar out of her.

The next day Uriel returned, galloping into camp accompanied by armed assistants, and a retinue of pack donkeys. With her came messages that had arrived by semaphore-and-runner relay from the far north, which she read aloud that evening, with the Dandelion Cluster as a shimmering backdrop above the glistening Rift. Wearing the robes of a lesser sage, the smith summarized what had occurred at Gathering – the coming not just of starships but star-*criminals*. Beings capable of bringing an end to the Great Peace, the Commons, and perhaps every member of the Six.

I couldn't see Huck's reaction when Uriel told in passing that the g'Kek race was now extinct among the stars, their last survivors reduced to savages, wheeling primitive tracks in the dust of Jijo. My tunnel of attention was still centered on other startling news.

The forayers were humans!

Everyone knows Earthlings weren't much more than animals in the eyes of the Galactic god-clans, only three hundred years ago. So what were mere *humans* doing, trying to pull a complicated theft across such distances?

Then I realized, since Uriel was addressing us in formal GalTwo, I'd been thinking in that tongue, seeing events the way a Galactic would. Things looked quite different when I rephrased the question in Anglic.

Three hundred years? That's an eternity! In that time humans moved from sailboats to their first starships. By now, who knows? Maybe they own half the universe!

All right, I've probably read way too much stuff by Doc Smith and 'Star-Smasher' Feng. But while most folks on the bluff that night expressed shock that wise, cultured human beings could ever do such things, I knew an inner truth about them. One that weaves through Earthling literature like a never-absent umble tone.

As long as their race survives, some among them will be wolves.

It amazed us all when Uriel said the project would continue.

Amid talk of militia call-ups, emergency camouflage repairs, and possibly having to fight for our lives against overwhelming power, I expected the smith to order us all back to Wuphon and Mount Guenn at once, putting our backs to labor for the common good. So we stared when instead she acted as if *this* were important, this silly diving expedition of ours.

I even said so to her face.

'Why are you doing this?' I asked the next day as Uriel oversaw resplicing the hawser and air hose. 'Don't you have urgent things to worry about?'

Her neck stretched upward, lifting the center, pupilless eye almost even with my own.

'And what would you have us do instead? Turn out *weapons*? Convert our forge into a factory of death?' Her single nostril flared, revealing the twisty membranes that lock in moisture, making urrish breath as dry as wind off the Plain of Sharp Sand.

'We urs know death well, young Hph-wayuo. It scales our legs and dries our husvand fouches all too soon. Or else we hurry it along with fights and feuds, as if glory could ever requite our haste to die. A great nany urs look fondly on those days when Earthlings were our finest foes, when heroes roared across the frairie, wheeling and charging recklessly.

'I, too, feel that call. And like others, I resist. This is an age for another kind of hero, young fellow. A warrior who *thinks*.'

Then she turned back to her labors, directing workers with severe attention to detail. Her response left me confused, unsatisfied ... but also, in some way I could not quite fathom, just a bit more proud than I had been before.

It took two days to complete the overhaul and triple-check all systems. By that time, the mass of onlookers had changed. Many of the originals had hurried home on hearing Uriel's news. Some had militia duties, or were eager to perform destructive sacraments prescribed by the oldest Scrolls. Others rushed back to save their property *against* premature drossing by the devout, or simply to be with loved ones during the expected last of days.

Those departing were replaced by others even angrier than the first, or frightened by things they had seen. Only yesterday, observers from Wuphon Port all the way to Finaltown Bay beheld a narrow, winged specter – a pale *aircraft* – that paused over the useless camouflage lattices, as if to say *I see you*, before resuming a twisty course along the coast, then out to sea.

No one had to say it. Whatever Uriel wanted to accomplish here, we didn't have a lot of time.

XX

THE BOOK OF THE SLOPE

Legends

The first sooner races arrived at Jijo knowledgeable, but they lacked a safe way to store that knowledge. The names of many archival tools come down to us, from *data plaques* to *memo-slivers* and *info-dust*, but all of these had to be consigned to the deep.

Earthlings possessed a secure, undetectable way to store information. The secret of paper – pulping and screening vegetable fibers with clays and animal products – was a uniquely wolfling invention. But the *Tabernacle* crew left Earth so soon after Contact, the data published in the Great Printing was sparse in galactology, especially concerning other 'sooner infections' elsewhere in the Five Galaxies.

This makes it hard to put our Jijoan Commons in perspective. How different are we from other cases of illegal settlement on fallow worlds? Have we done a better job at minimizing the harm we do? What are our chances of avoiding detection? What kinds of justice were meted out to other squatters who were caught? How far down the Path of Redemption must a race travel before they cease being criminals and become blessed?

The Scrolls offer some guidance on these matters. But since most date from the first two or three landings, they shed little light on one of the greatest mysteries.

Why *did* so many come to this small patch of ground, in such a short span of time?

Against the half a million years since the Buyur left, two thousand years is not very much. Moreover, there are many fallow worlds – so why Jijo? There are many sites on Jijo – so why the Slope?

Each question has answers. The great carbon-spewing star, Izmunuti, began shielding local space only a few millennia ago. We are told this phenomenon somehow disabled robot sentinels patrolling routes to this system, easing the way for sneakships. There are also vague references to omens that a 'time of troubles' would soon spread upheavals across the Five Galaxies. As for the Slope, its combination of robust biosphere and high volcanic activity assures that our works will be destroyed, leaving few traces we were ever here.

To some, these answers suffice. Others wonder, still.

Are we unique?

In some Galactic languages, the question does not even parse as sane. One can find a precedent for anything in the archives of a billion years. Originality is an illusion. Everything that is also was.

Perhaps it is symptomatic of our low state – our uncivilized level of consciousness, compared with the godlike heights of our ancestors – but one still is tempted to wonder.

Might something unusual be going on here?

—Spensir Jones, A Landing Day Homily

We sages preach that it is foolish to assume. Yet, during this, our greatest crisis, the invaders often turn out to know much that we thought safely hidden.

Should this surprise us, my rings? Are they not star-gods from the Five Galaxies?

Worse, have *we* been united? Have not many of the Six rashly exercised their right of dissent, currying favors from the sky-humans against our advice? Some of these have simply vanished – including the sooner girl who so vexed Lester with her ingratitude, daring to steal back the treasure she had brought, which intrigued our human sage for days on end. Does she even now dwell within the buried station, pampered as a g'Kek might groom a favorite zookir? Or else, did the sky-felons simply delete her, as a traeki voids its core of spent mulch, or as Earthling tyrants used to eliminate quislings who had finished serving their purpose?

For every secret the raiders uncover, there are as many ways they seem shockingly ignorant, for sky-gods.

It is a puzzlement – and small solace as we contemplate the proud, intimidating visitor who this morn came before the Council of Sages.

My rings, has memory of this event yet coated your waxy cores? Do you recollect the star-human, Rann, making his request? Asking that several from his group be invited along, when next we commune with the Holy Egg?

The request was courteous, yet it had aspects of a command.

We should not be surprised. How could the aliens *not* notice what is happening?

At first discernible only to the most sensitive, the tremors strengthen till now they pervade this corner of our world.

—curling the mists that rise from geysers and steam pools,
—guiding patterned flocks of passing birdlings,
—waking dormant rewq, both in caves and in our pouches,
—even permeating the myriad blue colors of the sky.

'We have heard much about your sacred stone,' Rann said. 'Its activity triggers fascination in our sensoria. We would see this wonder for ourselves.'

'Very well,' Vubben answered for the Six, wrapping three eye-stalks in a gesture of assent. Indeed how could we refuse?

'Pray tell – how many will be in your party?'

Rann bowed again, imposing for a human, as tall as any traeki, broad in the shoulders as a young hoon. 'There will be three. Myself and Ling, you have met. As for the third, his revered name is *Rokenn*, and it is incumbent to realize how you are about to be honored. Our master must be shown all expressions of courtesy and respect.'

With varied eyes, visors, and sight patches, we sages winked and winced amazement. All save Lester Cambel, who muttered softly next to our traeki stack,

'So the blood Dakkins had one underground with them, all along.'

Humans are surprising creatures, but Lester's breach in tact so stunned our rings that 'i' was unanimously amazed. Did he not fear being overheard?

Apparently not. Through our rewq, i read Lester's ill-regard for the man across from us, and for this news.

As for the rest of the Council, it did not take rewq to note their *curiosity*.

At long last, we were about to meet the Rothen.

LARK

Dear Sara,

The caravan bearing your letter took some time to get here, because of troubles on the plains. But how wonderful to see your familiar scrawl, and to hear you're well! And Father, when you saw him last. These days, there are few enough reasons to smile.

I'm dashing this off in hopes of catching the next brave kayak-courier to head down the Bibur. If it reaches Biblos before you leave, I hope I can persuade you not to come up here! Things are awful tense. Recall those stories we told each other about the dam, back home? Well, I wouldn't sleep in that attic room right now, if you smell my smoke. Please stay somewhere safe till we know what's happening.

As you asked, I've inquired carefully about your mysterious stranger. Clearly the aliens are seeking someone or something, beyond their goal of illicitly adopting a candidate species for uplift. I can't prove your

wounded enigma-man isn't the object of their search, but
I'd bet he's at most a small part of the picture.

I could be wrong. Sometimes I feel we're like kitchen-
ants peering upward, trying to comprehend a human
quarrel from the stir of shadows overhead.

Oh, I can picture your look right now! Don't worry, I'm
not giving up! In fact, I have a different answer to the
question you're always asking me ... Yes, I have met a
girl. And no, I don't think you'd approve of her. I'm not
sure this boy does, either.

Smiling ironically, Lark finished the first page of the letter and
put down his pen. He blew on the paper, then picked up his
portable blotter, rolling the felt across the still damp lines of ink. He
took a fresh sheet out of the leather portfolio, dipped the pen in the
ink cup and resumed.

Along with this note you'll get a hand-cranked copy of
the latest report the sages are sending throughout the
Commons, plus a confidential addendum for Ariana
Foo. We've learned some new things, though so far
nothing likely to assure our survival when the Rothen
ship returns. Bloor is here, and I've been helping him
put your idea into effect, though I see potential
drawbacks to threatening the aliens, the way you
recommend.

Lark hesitated. Even such veiled hints might be too much to
risk. In normal times it would be unthinkable for anyone to
tamper with someone's else's mail. But such things used to be
done by frantic factions during ancient Earthly crises, according
to historical accounts. Anyway, what good would it do Sara to
worry? Feeling like a wastrel, he crumpled the second sheet and
started fresh.

Please tell Sage Foo that young Shirl, Kurt's daughter,
arrived safely along with B—r, whose work proceeds as
well as might be expected.

Meanwhile, I've followed up on your other queries. It's
delicate questioning these space people, who always make
me pay with information useful to their criminal goals. I
must also try not to arouse suspicion over why I want to
know certain things. Still, I managed to bargain for a few
answers.

*One was easy. The star humans do not routinely use
Anglic, or Rossic, or any other 'barbaric wolfling tongue.'
That's how Ling put it the other day, as if those languages
were much too vulgar and unrigorous for a properly
scientific person to use. Oh, she and the others speak Anglic
well enough to converse. But among themselves, they
prefer GalSeven.*

He paused to dip his pen in the cup of fresh ink.

*It fits our notion that these humans do not come from the
main branch of the race! They aren't representatives of
Earth, in other words, but come instead from an offshoot
that's bound in loyalty to the Rothen, a race claiming to be
the long-lost patrons of humankind.*

*Recall how Mother used to have us debate the Origins
Question? One of us arguing the Danikenite side and the
other supporting the Darwinists? At the time it seemed
interesting but pretty pointless, since all our facts were
out of texts three hundred years old. Who would think
we'd live to see an answer proclaimed on Jijo, before our
eyes?*

*As to the validity of the Rothen claim, I can't add
anything to the report except that Ling and the others
seem passionately to believe.*

Lark took a sip from an earthenware cup of springwater. He
dipped the pen again.

*Now for the big news everyone's excited about. It seems
we're about to get our first glimpse of one of these
mysterious beings! Within hours, one or more Rothen are
scheduled to emerge from their buried station and join a
pilgrimage to the reawakening Egg! All this time, we never
guessed their starship had left any of them behind with
Rann and the others.*

*The Commons is tense as a violus that's been strung too
tight. You could cut the anxiety here with an overused
metaphor.*

*I'd better wrap this up if I'm to slip it in the mail
packet.*

*Let's see. You also asked about 'neural taps.' Do the
aliens use such things to communicate directly with
computers and other devices?*

I was going to answer yes. Ling and the rest do carry tiny devices that bring them voice and data information, arriving as if by magic from afar.

Then I reread your account of the Stranger's injury and reconsidered. The forayers command their machines by voice and gesture. I never saw anything like a brain-direct computer link, or the sort of 'instant man-machine rapport' Ariana spoke of.

Now that I think about it

Lark dipped the pen again, poised to continue, then stopped.

Footsteps clattered on the gravel path beyond his tent. He recognized the heavy, scrape-ratchet of a gray qheuen. Nor was it the casual, unpretentious rhythm of Uthen. This was a stately twist-and-swivel cadence, using a complex ripple of alternating feet – a difficult aristocratic step, taught by chitinous matriarchs who sometimes styled themselves royal queens.

Lark laid down his pen and closed the portfolio. A low, wide silhouette loomed against the tent flap. Harullen's voice was accompanied by fluting sighs from three speech vents, each singing a different note in a high qheuenish dialect of Galactic Six.

'Friend Lark, are you within? Please greet me. I come bearing precious gifts.'

Lark lifted the flap, shading his eyes as he emerged from dimness to face the lowering sun, poking sharp rays between rows of forest giants. 'I greet you, Harullen, faith-comrade,' he replied in the same language.

Harullen wore pilgrim's robes draped across his pentagonal carapace, leaving the central cupola uncovered. The g'Kek-woven finery shimmered under glancing sunshine. It took a moment for Lark's adapting eyes to spot what else was different – something wound around the qheuen's ash-colored cupola.

'Aha,' he commented, slipping into a more relaxed sevenish dialect. 'So it's true. The mask renews its offer.'

'To take nourishment of our bodies in exchange for revelation of the soul. Indeed. The mask returns among us. Caves which had seemed barren now swarm with labile young rewq, even as the Egg resumes its patterning song. Are these not good omens? Shall we rejoice?'

With a snap of one claw, Harullen signaled to a lornik, which had been crouching out of view behind its master. The small servant creature hurried around the qheuen's great flank, scuttling and twisting in a four-legged imitation of Harullen's own stately walk. With small, three-fingered hands it bore a box of polished wood, showing fluted traces of personal tooth-carving.

'From among this crop of cave fledglings, there were many shaped for noble human brows,' Harullen continued. 'Please accept these to choose from, as offerings of deep esteem.'

Lark took the box from the lornik, knowing better than to thank or make eye contact with the shy creature. Unlike chimps and zookirs, lorniks seemed able to bond only with the race that brought their ancestors to Jijo, nearly a thousand years ago.

He lifted the delicately grooved lid of the gift box, which by qheuenish tradition had been gnawed by the giver and could never be used again for any other purpose. Inside, resting on a bed of garu sawdust, several clusters of brown-speckled tendrils quivered, coupled by colored bands of translucent film.

There's been so little time. I've had so many duties. This really is a fine favor ...

Still, all told, Lark would rather have gone to the caves and picked his next rewq for himself, as he had done on three other occasions since passing puberty. It seemed strange to choose one out of a box. What was he to do with the others?

Several tentacles raised tentatively, reaching toward the light, then twisting, searching. Only one pair showed no indecision, wafting gently in Lark's direction, spreading a gossamer web between them.

Well, it's a humaniform rewq, all right, he thought. *It looks new, robust.*

To feel diffident was only natural. A person usually held on to a personal rewq for many years. It had been painful to watch helpless as the last one wasted in its moss-lined pouch, during the many weeks the Egg was silent. Nor could he share someone else's symbiont. Among humans, one was more likely to pass around a toothbrush than a rewq.

'My gratitude is manifest in acceptance of this unexcelled gift,' he said. Though reluctant, Lark lifted the squirming mass to his brow.

His former rewq had been like a pair of old shoes – or a favorite pair of urrish-made sunglasses – comfortable and easy to use. This one twitched and wriggled in agitated eagerness, palpating his temples in avid search of rich surface veins where it might feed. The gauzy membrane spread taut over Lark's eyes, rippling with the rewq's own excitement, conveying nothing more useful than a wave of vertigo. It would take time to reach an understanding with the new creature. Ideally you let your old one teach the new, during an overlapping time before the elderly rewq died.

Ifni's miracles often have ironic timing. We had to face the aliens for so long without the help rewq might have offered. Now, at a critical moment, they return so suddenly that they may only prove a distracting hindrance.

Still, for courtesy's sake, he pretended pleasure, bowing and thanking Harullen for the fine gift. With luck, Harullen's own rewq would be noisy too, and not convey any of Lark's own mixed feelings.

The heretic leader's satisfaction was evident in a mincing, clattering dance of feet and dangling claws. The film over Lark's eyes added a blur of sparks that *might* be translated qheuenish emotions – or else just static from the excited, untrained rewq.

Then Harullen abruptly changed the subject, slipping into Anglic.

'You know that the time of pilgrimage is almost at hand?'

'I was just writing a letter. I'll don my robe and join our group at the Wheel Stone in a midura.'

Partly because Ling requested Lark's presence, the Sages had granted the heretical faction two sixes among the twelve twelves selected to make the first climb, setting forth to greet the rousing Egg. Since hearing the news, Lark had felt a familiar heat coming from the knob of stone that hung by a thong around his neck. His reminder and penance. No pilgrimage was ever easy wearing that amulet.

'Very well, then,' Harullen replied. 'At the Wheel Stone we shall consider the zealots' latest entreaty before proceeding to join . . .'

The heretic's voice trailed off, muffling as he crouched down, drawing all five legs into his carapace, bringing his sensitive tongue into contact with the ground. This time, Lark's rewq conveyed a vivid image of emotions – a halo depicting distaste mixed liberally with disapproval.

Harullen resumed. 'There is another on the trail. One whose stone-hard lineage is belied by disorderly foot-haste.'

One whose *what* is *what*? Lark puzzled. Sometimes the way other races used Anglic left him confused. Maybe it wasn't such a good thing the chaotic human language had become so popular on Jijo.

Soon he also felt ground-tremors, tickling the soles of his feet. A five-beat vibration even more familiar than Harullen's earlier footsteps. *Similar* to that rhythmic beat, yet simpler, less aristocratic, a pace too hurried and eager to waste time on etiquette or show.

Another armored form burst into view, trailing twigs and leaves. Like Harullen, Uthen the Taxonomist was dressed for pilgrimage – in a carelessly draped, once-white rag that flapped behind him like somebody's old bedsheet. His carapace was a slightly deeper shade of slate than his disdainful cousin's. Like Harullen, Uthen wore a new rewq, which might explain his stumbling progress, twice veering off the path as if distracted by swarms of buzzing insects. Lark peeled his own reluctant symbiont back from his eyes. He needed no help reading his colleague's excitement.

'Lark-ark, Harullen-en,' Uthen stammered out of several vents, in unmatched timbres. Harullen scornfully turned his cupola while the newcomer caught his breath.

'Come quickly, both of you. They've come out!'

'*Who's* come—?' Lark began, before realizing that Uthen could mean but one thing.

He nodded. 'Just give me a dura.'

Lark ducked back under the tent flap, fumbled for his own pilgrimage robe, then paused by the writing desk. He snatched the unfinished letter from under the folio and slid it into a sleeve, along with a sharpened pencil. Ink was more elegant and wouldn't smudge. Still, Sara wouldn't give a damn, so long as the letter got there and contained the latest news.

'Come on!' Uthen urged, impatiently, when Lark re-emerged. 'Hop aboard and let's hoof it!' The gray qheuen scientist dipped one end of his shell to the ground. This time, Harullen groaned annoyance. Sure, kids did it all the time, but it wasn't dignified for an adult gray – especially one with ancestry like Uthen's – to go around carrying a human on his back. Still, they would move faster now, toward the Meadow of Concealed Aliens, hurrying to see the wonder that had emerged.

If anything, Ling understated when she called them beautiful.

Lark had never envisioned anything quite like them. Not when leafing through ancient picture books, or reading pre-Contact works of space fiction. Not even in his dreams.

In the vernacular of Jijo's exiled tribes, it was common to call all Galactics 'star-gods.' Yet here, strolling a forest clearing, were beings that seemed all but literally worthy of the name, so exquisite were they to behold. Lark could stand it only for moments at a stretch, then had to look away lest his eyes fill with tears and his chest begin to ache.

Ling and the other forayer humans formed a guard of honor around their noble patrons, while vigilant robots hovered. Occasionally, one of the tall stoop-shouldered Rothen crooked a finger, beckoning Rann or Besh to lean upward and explain something, like children called on to recite, gesturing at a nearby tree, one of the tent-pavilions, a herd of spline beasts, or a shy infant g'Kek.

Crowds gathered. Proctors of Gathering, armed with red-dyed sticks, kept people from pressing too close, but there seemed small likelihood of a shameful outburst. Hardly anyone even whispered, so thick was the atmosphere of awe.

The effect seemed greatest on the humans present, most of whom stared with hushed wonderment and bewildered *familiarity*. Rothen were humanoid to an uncanny degree, with high noble foreheads, wide sympathetic eyes, eloquent noses, and droopy, soft-fringed eye-brows that seemed to purse with sincere, attentive interest in anyone or everything they encountered. Nor were these parallels coincidental, Lark supposed. Physical and emotional affinities would have been cultivated during the long process of uplift, tens of thousands of years ago, when Rothen experts tinkered and modified a tribe of graceless but promising apes back on Pliocene Earth, altering them gradually into beings almost ready for the stars.

That assumed these creatures really *were* humanity's long-hidden patrons, as Ling claimed. Lark tried to retain an attitude of cautious neutrality but found it hard in the face of such evidence. How could this race be any other than humankind's lost patrons?

When the two august visitors were introduced to the assembled High Sages, Lark drew comfort from the serene expressions of Vubben, Phwhoon-dau, and the others, none of whom wore rewq for the occasion. Even Lester Cambel remained composed – at least on the outside – when presented to *Ro-kenn* and *Ro-pol*, whose names Rann proclaimed for all to hear.

By human standards, Ro-kenn appeared to be male. And though Lark tried not to be overly influenced by analogies, the more delicate-featured Ro-pol struck him as possibly female. The crowd murmured when the two *smiled* – revealing small white teeth – conveying apparent pleasure at the meeting. Ro-pol's grin creased in ways that might even be called dimples. The word *merry* tempted Lark, as a way to describe the slighter Rothen's cheerful mien. It wouldn't be hard to like a face like that, so warm, open, and filled with understanding.

It makes sense, Lark thought. *If the Rothen really are our patrons, wouldn't they have ingrained us with similar esteem patterns?*

Nor were Earthlings alone affected. After all, the Six Races had a lot of experience with each other. You didn't have to be a qheuen to sense the charisma of a stately queen, so why shouldn't an urs, or hoon, or g'Kek sense this potent humanoid magnetism? Even without rewq, most of the nonhumans present seemed caught up in the prevailing mood – *hope.*

Lark recalled Ling's assurance that the forayer mission would succeed without incident, and Jijo's Commons needn't be changed in any but positive ways. '*It will all work out,*' she had said.

Ling had also told him the Rothen were special beings, even among high Galactic clans. Operating in deliberate obscurity, they had quietly arranged for Old Earth to lie fallow, off the colonization lists, for half a billion years, an accomplishment with implications Lark found hard to imagine. Needing no fleets or weapons, the Rothen were influential, mystical, mysterious – in many ways godlike even compared with those beings whose vast armadas thundered across the Five Galaxies. No wonder Ling and her peers thought themselves above so-called 'laws' of migration and uplift, as they sifted Jijo's biosphere for some worthy species to adopt. No wonder she seemed fearless over the possibility of being caught.

The newly cave-fledged rewq also appeared dazzled, ever since the tall pair emerged from the buried research station. The one on Lark's brow trembled, casting splashy aurae around the two Rothen till he finally had to peel it back.

Lark tried to wrest control over his thoughts, reclaiming a thread of skepticism.

It may be that all advanced races learn to do what the Rothen are doing now – impressing those beneath them on the ladder of status. Perhaps we're all extra-susceptible on account of being primitives, having no other experience with Galactics.

But skepticism was slippery as the Rothen emissaries conversed with the sages in voices that seemed warm, compassionate. A robot amplified the discourse for all to hear.

'*We two now express grateful and respectful honors for your hospitality,*' Ro-kenn said in a very prim, grammatically perfect GalSixish.

'*Furthermore, we now express regret for any anxiety our presence may have generated among your noble Commons,*' Ro-pol added. '*Only of late have we come to realize the depth of your unease. Overcoming our natural reticence – our shyness, if you will – we now emerge to soothe your quite unwarranted fears.*'

Again, whispers of tentative hope from the crowd – not an easy emotion for Jijoan exiles.

Ro-kenn spoke again.

'*Now we express joy and appreciation to have been invited to attend your sacred rites. One of us shall accompany you on this eve, to witness the wonderment inherent in, and remarkably expressed by, your renowned and Holy Egg.*'

'*Meanwhile,*' Ro-pol continued, '*the other of us shall withdraw to contemplate how best to reward your Commons for your pains, your worries, and your hard sequestered lives.*'

Ro-pol appeared to muse on the problem for a moment, choosing her words.

'*Some gift, we foresee. Some benefaction to help you through the ages ahead, as each of your cojoined races seeks salvation down the long, courageous path known as Return-to-Innocence.*'

A murmur coursed the ranks of onlookers – pleasure at this surprising news.

Now each of the sages took turns making a welcoming speech, starting with Vubben, whose aged wheels squeaked as he rolled forward to recite from one of the oldest Scrolls. Something apropos about the ineffable nature of mercy, which drifts upward from the ground when least expected, a grace that cannot be earned or even merited, only lovingly accepted when it comes.

Lark let the neophyte rewq slip back over his eyes. The Rothen pair remained immersed in a nimbus of confused colors, so while Vubben droned on, he turned and scanned the assembled onlookers.

Of course rewq offered no magic window to the soul. Mostly, they helped make up for the fact that each race came equipped with brain tissue specifically adapted for reading emotional cues from its own kind. Rewq were most effective when facing *another* rewq-equipped being, especially if the two symbionts first exchanged empathy hormones.

Is that why the sages aren't wearing theirs now? In order to protect secret thoughts?

From the throng he picked up ripples of fragile optimism and mystical wonder, cresting here and there with spumelike waves of near-religious fervor. There were other colors, however. From several dozen qheuens, hoon, urs, and men – proctors and militia guards – there flowed cooler shades of duty. Refusal to be distracted by anything short of a major earthquake.

Another glittering twinkle Lark quickly recognized as a *different* kind of duty, more complex, focused, and vain. It accompanied a brief reflection off a glass lens. *Bloor and his comrades at work*, Lark guessed. *Busy recording the moment*.

Lark's symbiont was working better now. In fact, despite its lack of training, it might never again be quite this sensitive. At this moment almost every rewq in the valley was the same age, fresh from caves where they had lately mingled in great piles, sharing unity enzymes. Each would be acutely aware of the others, at longer than normal range.

I should warn Bloor. His people shouldn't wear rewq. If it lets me spot them, it might help robots, too.

Another swirl caught his eye, flashing bitterly from the far end of the Glade, standing out from the prevailing mood like a fire burning on an ice-field. There was no mistaking a flare of acrid *hate*.

Finally he made out a shaggy snakelike neck, rising from the profile of a small centaur. Rewq-mediated colors, like a globe of distilled loathing, obscured the head itself.

The wearer of that distant, powerful symbiont suddenly seemed to notice Lark's focused regard. Shifting her attention from aliens and sages, she turned to face Lark directly. Across a crowd of shifting, sighing citizens, they watched each other's colors. Then, in unison each pulled back their rewq.

In clear light, Lark met her unblinking stare – the urrish leader of the zealot cause. A rebel whose malice toward invaders was stronger than Lark had realized. With those three fierce eyes turned his way, Lark needed no symbiont to translate the zealot's feelings toward *him*.

Under the late afternoon sun, her neck twisted and she snarled an urrish smile of pure, disdainful contempt.

The pilgrimage commenced at dusk, with long forest shadows pointing toward a hidden mountain pass. Twelve twelves of chosen citizens represented all the Commons, along with two star-humans, four robots, and one tall ancient being whose shambling gait hinted great strength under glossy white robes.

Judging by his so-humanlike smile, Ro-kenn seemed to find delight in countless things, especially the rhythmic chanting – a blending of vocal contributions from all races – as the assembly set out past steaming vents and sheer clefts, weaving its slow way toward the hidden oval Valley of the Egg. The Rothen's long-fingered hands stroked slim-boled welpal trees, whose swaying resonated with emanations from that secret vale. Most humans would hear nothing till they got much closer.

In Lark's heart, dark feelings churned. Nor was he alone. Many, especially those farthest from Ro-kenn's cheerful charisma, still felt uneasy about guiding strangers to this sacred place.

The procession marched, rolled, and slithered, wending higher into the hills. Soon the heavens glittered with formations of sparkling lights – brittle bright clusters and nebulae – divided by the dark stripe of the Galactic disk. If anything, the sight re-inforced the starkly uneven order of life, for tonight's guests would shortly cross those starscapes, whether they departed in peace or betrayal. To them, Jijo would become another quaint, savage, per-haps mildly interesting spot they had visited once in long, deified lives.

The last time Lark came up this way – so earnest about his self-appointed mission to save Jijo from invaders like himself – no one had any thought of starships cruising Jijo's sky.

Yet they were already up there, preparing to land.

What is more frightening? The danger you already dread, or the trick the universe hasn't pulled on you yet? The one to make all prior concerns seem moot.

Lark hoped none of this gloom carried into his letter to Sara, which he had finished in a hurried pencil scrawl by the headwaters of the Bibur after the Rothen emerged. The kayak pilot added Lark's note to a heavy bundle from Bloor, then set off in a flash of oars, speeding down the first set of spuming rapids in a pell-mell rush toward Biblos, two days' hard rowing away.

On his way back to rendezvous with the other heretics, he had stopped to watch the alien aircraft glide out of its dark tunnel like a wraith, rising on whispering engines. Lark glimpsed a small human silhouette, hands and face pressed against an oval window, drinking in the view. The figure looked familiar ... but before he could raise his pocket ocular, the machine sped away, eastward, toward a cleft where the largest moon was rising above the Rimmer Range.

Now, as the evening procession entered a final twisty canyon leading to the Egg, Lark tried putting temporal concerns aside, preparing for communion. *It may be my last chance*, he thought, hoping this time he might fully take part in the wholeness others reported, when the Egg shared its full bounty of love.

Drawing his right arm inside his sleeve, he grasped the rocky flake, despite its growing heat. A passage from the Scroll of Exile came to mind – an Anglic version, modified for Earthlings by one of the first human sages.

We drift, rudderless, down the stream of time,
*   betrayed by the ancestors who left us here,*
blind to much that was, hard-learnt by other ages,
fearful of light and the law,
but above all, anxious in our hearts
that there might be no God,
no Father,
*   no heavenly succor,*
or else that we are already lost to Him,
*   to fate,*
*   to destiny.*

Where shall we turn, in banished agony,
*   with our tabernacle lost,*
*   and faith weighed down by perfidy?*
What solace comes to creatures lost in time?

One source of renewal,
*   never fails.*
With rhythms long,
*   its means are fire and rain,*
*   ice and time.*
*   Its names are myriad.*
To poor exiles it is home.
*   Jijo.*

The passage ended on a strange note of combined reverence and defiance.

> *If God still wants us, let him find us here.*
> *Till then, we grow part of this,*
>   *our adopted world.*
> *Not to hinder, but to serve Her cyclic life.*

> *To sprout humble goodness out of the foul seed of crime.*

Not long after that Scroll gained acceptance in the human sept, one winter's day, good tremors shook the Slope. Trees toppled, dams burst, and a terrible wind blew. Panic swept from mountains to sea amid reports that Judgment Day had come.

Instead, bursting through a cloud of sparkling dust, the *Egg* appeared. A gift out of Jijo's heart.

A gift which must be shared tonight – with aliens.

What if they achieved what he had always failed? Or worse, what if they reacted with *derisive laughter*, declaring that the Egg was a simple thing that only yokels would take seriously – like fabled Earth-natives worshipping a music box they found on the shore?

Lark struggled to push out petty thoughts, to tune himself with the basso rumble of the hoon, the qheuens' calliope piping, the twanging spokes of the g'Keks, and all of the other contributions to a rising song of union. He let it take over the measured pace of his breathing, while warmth from the stone fragment seemed to swell up his hand and arm, then across his chest, spreading relaxed detachment.

Close, he thought. A tracery of soft patterns began taking shape in his mind. A weblike meshing of vague spirals, made up partly of images, partly of sound.

It's almost as if something is trying to—

'Is this not *exciting*?' a voice broke in from Lark's right, splitting his concentration into broken shards. 'I believe I can feel something now! It's quite unlike any psi phenomenon I have experienced. The motif is highly unusual.'

Ignore her, Lark thought, clinging to the patterns. *Maybe she'll go away*.

But Ling kept talking, sending words clattering up avenues that could not help hearing them. The harder he tried holding on, the quicker detachment slipped away. Lark's hand now clenched a clammy ball of rock and twine, warm with his body heat alone. He let go in disgust.

'We picked up some tremors on instruments several days ago.

The cycles have been rising in strength and complexity for some time.'

Ling seemed blithely unaware of having done anything wrong. That, in turn, made Lark's simmering resentment seem both petty *and* futile. Anyway, her beauty by moonlight was even more unnerving than usual, cutting through his anger to a vulnerable loneliness within.

Lark sighed. 'Aren't you supposed to be guarding your boss?'

'Robots do the real guarding – as if we have anything to fear. Rokenn gave Rann and me permission to look around while he talks to your sages, preparing them for what's about to happen.'

Lark stopped so suddenly, the next pilgrim in line had to stumble to avoid him. He took Ling's elbow. 'What are you talking about? *What's* about to happen?'

Ling's smile carried a touch of the old sardonicism.

'You mean you haven't guessed by now? Oh, Lark. Think about the *coincidences*.

'For two thousand years sooners of various races lived on this world, squabbling and slowly devolving. Then humans came and everything changed. Though you started few and helpless, soon your culture became the most influential on the planet.

'Then, just a few generations after your arrival, a miracle suddenly erupts out of the ground, this spirit guide you all revere.'

'You mean the Egg,' he said, brow furrowing.

'Exactly. Did you really think the timing *accidental*? Or that your patrons had forgotten you?'

'Our patrons.' Lark frowned. 'You mean . . . you're implying the Rothen knew all along—'

'About the voyage of the *Tabernacle*? Yes! Ro-kenn explained it to us this morning, and now everything makes sense! Even our own arrival on Jijo is no accident, dear Lark. Oh, our mission *is* partly to seek deserving pre-sapients, to join our clan. But more than that, we came for *you*. Because the experiment is finished!'

'Experiment?' He felt an involuntary disorientation.

'An arduous trial for your small branch of humanity, cast away and forgotten – or so you thought – on a savage world. It sounds harsh, but the road of uplift is hard when a race is destined for the heights our patrons plan for us.'

Lark's mind whirled. 'You mean our ancestors were *meant* to sneak down to Jijo? As part of an ordeal that's supposed to . . . transform us somehow? The Egg was – is – part of some Rothen scheme—'

'Design,' Ling corrected, a kind of elation invading her voice. 'A *grand* design, Lark. A *test*, which your folk passed brilliantly, I'm told, growing stronger, smarter, and more noble even as this awful place tried to grind you down.

'And now the time has come to graft this successful offshoot back onto the main trunk, helping all of humanity to grow, thrive, and better face the challenges of a dangerous universe.'

Her grin was joyful, exuberant.

'Oh, Lark, when I spoke to you last, I thought we might be taking a few human castaways with us, when we go.

'But *now* the news is pure and grand, Lark.

'*Ships* are coming. So many ships!

'It is time to bring you *all* back home.'

ASX

Astonishment!

This news bellows through our waxy cavities, driving out the Egg's pattern/resonance with acrid vapors of surprise.

we/i/we/i/we ... cannot coalesce as Asx. Nor contemplate these tidings with any sense of unity.

The worst rumors of recent months – spread by irredentist urrish chiefs and bitter gray queens – claimed that humans might abandon Jijo, departing with their sky-cousins, leaving the other five to fester and be damned.

Yet even *that* dark fantasy left one solace to the rest of us.

One comfort.

The Egg.

Now, we are told—
(disbelieve it!)
(but how?)
—that the holy ovoid was *never* ours! Only *humans'*, all along! Its dual purpose – to guide Earthlings toward greatness while at the same time soothing, *domesticating* we other Five!

Taming the other septs, in order to keep humans safe during their brief stay on Jijo.

Now this is topped by insulting 'kindness,' as Ro-kenn says the Egg will be left as a parting gift.

Left as a token,
a trifle,
a gratuity for our pains.
Left to shame us all!

Pause, my rings. Pause. Ensure fairness. Stroke vapors across the wax drippings. Remember.

Did not Lester Cambel seem as dismayed as the rest of us?

Did not all the sages resolve to conceal this news? Lest rumors do great harm?

It is useless. Even now, eavesdropping citizens rush off, dispersing exaggerated versions of what they overheard, casting a poison up and down the chain of pilgrims, shattering the rhythms that had been uniting us.

Yet from the majestic Rothen, we sense cheerful unawareness that anything is wrong!

Is this what it means to be a god? To know not what harm you do?

Ripples of infection spread along the twisty trail. The worship-chant breaks apart, dissolving into many twelves of muttering individuals.

Now, from my/our highest peak, we perceive *another* disturbance, propagating from the *front* of the procession! The two disruptions meet like waves on a storm-tossed lake, rolling through each other in a great spume of noise.

'*The way is blocked,*' a galloping messenger cries, hastening back with word. '*A rope harrier bars the path, with a banner upon it!*'

NO INFIDEL DESECRATION
KEEP SKY FILTH AWAY
JIJO WILL NOT BE MOCKED!

This can only be the work of zealots.

Frustration spins round our core. The fanatics chose a fine time to make their gesture!

We sages must go see. Even Vubben makes haste, and my basal segments labor to keep up. Ro-kenn strides with graceful ease, seeming unperturbed.

And yet, my rings, is this *variance* we observe, in Ro-kenn's aura? Through our rewq, we sense discrepancy between parts of his face, as if the Rothen's outward calm masks a canker of seething *wrath*.

Can rewq read so much from an alien form we just met, this very day? Is it because i have one of the few *older* rewq, surviving from earlier days? Or do we notice this because traeki are tuned to perceive disunity of self?

Ahead – the defiant banner.

Above – perched on cliffs, shouting youths brandish foolish (but brave!) weapons.

Below – Phwhoon-dau, with his booming voice, calls to them, asking them to state their demands.

Their reply? Echoing down canyons and steam-fumaroles – a command that the aliens depart! Never to return. Or else suffer vengeance by the greatest force on Jijo.

!?!?

The zealots threaten the Rothen with the *Egg*?

But did not Ro-kenn just claim the great ovoid as *his* to command?

Across the Rothen's visage flows what i interpret as *cool amusement*. He calls the zealots' bluff.

'*Shall we see who has the power to back up their claims?*' the star-god asks. '*This night the Egg, and all Jijo, will sing our truth.*'

Lester and Vubben plead for restraint, but Ro-kenn ignores them. Still smiling, he commands robots to each side of the gorge, to seize the anchor bolts holding the barrier in place. Overhead, the rebel leader stretches her long neck, keening a curse in plains dialect, invoking the sacred power of Jijo to renew. To cleanse impudent dross with fire.

The young zealot is a fine showman, stamping her hooves, foretelling awful punishments. Our more credulous rings find it possible, for a moment, to believe—

—to believe—

—to believe—

> What is happening?
> What – is – happening?
> What impressions pour
>> in
>> now,
>> faster than
>> wax can melt?
>> Then penetrate
>> awareness,
>> ring after
>> ring
> in a manner that
>> makes
>> all events
>> equal in both
>> timing and
>> import?
> What is happening?

*

—twin lightning bolts outline many twelves of pilgrims, their shadows fleeing from white flame ...

—crackling metal complains ... shattered ... unable to fly ... a pair of tumbling cinders ...

—after-image of demolition ... two junk piles smolder ... more dross to collect and send to sea ...

With other eye-patches, we/i glimpse horrified surprise on the face of Rann, the sky-human.

—surrounding Ro-kenn, a schism of variance ... like a traeki sundered between one ring that is jolly and a neighbor filled with wrath ...

And now, though surfeited with impressions, suddenly there is more!

—with eye-patches on the opposite side, we are first to glimpse a fiery spike ...

—a searing brightness climbs the western sky ... rising from the Glade of Gathering ...

—the ground beneath us trembles ...

—actual sound takes a while longer to arrive, battling upward through thin air to bring us a low groan, like thunder!

At last, the pace of events slows enough for our spinning vapors to keep up. Happenings occur in order. Not disjointed, parallel.

Review, my rings!

Did we perceive two robots *destroyed*, even as they tore down the zealots' barrier?

Then were we dazzled by some vast explosion *behind* us? Toward the Glade of Gathering?

What had been a pilgrimage of union dissolves into a mob. Small groups hurry downhill toward a dusty, moonlit pall, left by that brief flame. Humans hang close together, for protection, clinging to their remaining hoonish and qheuenish friends, while other qheuens and many urs clatter by, aloof, scornful, even threatening in their manner.

Ro-kenn no longer walks but rides a cushioned plate between his two remaining robots, speaking urgently into a hand-held device, growing more agitated by the moment. His human servants seem in shock.

The female, Ling, holds the arm of Lark, our young human biologist. Uthen offers a ride, and they climb aboard his broad gray back. All three vanish down the trail after Ro-kenn.

Bravely, Knife-Bright Insight proposes similarly to carry *this* pile of rings, this Asx!

Can i/we refuse? Already, Phwhoon-dau totes Vubben in his strong, scaly arms. The hoon sage lugs the g'Kek so both might hurry downhill and see what has happened.

By majority ballot, our rings choose to accept the offer. But after several duras of jouncing qheuenish haste, there are calls for a recount! Somehow, we clamp down, managing to hang on to her horny shell, wishing we had walked.

Time passes through a gelatin of suspense, teasing us with idle speculation. Darkness swallows wisdom. Glittering stars seem to taunt.

Finally, at an overlooking bluff, we jostle with others for a view.

Can you sense it, my rings?

Unified now, in shock, i see a steaming *crater*, filled with twisted metal. The sanctuary where Ro-kenn and the sky-humans dwelled among us for weeks. Their buried outpost – now a fiery ruin.

Acting with hot-blooded decisiveness, Ur-Jah and Lester call for volunteers to leap into that smoky pit, reckless of their own lives, heroically attempting rescue. But how could anyone survive within the wrecked station? Can anyone be found alive?

We all share the same thought. All members of the Six. All of my rings.

Who can doubt the power of the Egg? Or the fury of a planet scorned?

THE STRANGER

Doors seem to open with every song he rediscovers, as if old melodies are keys to unlock whole swaths of time. The earlier the memory, the more firmly it seems attached to a musical phrase or snippet of lyrics. Nursery rhymes, especially, take him swiftly down lanes of reclaimed childhood.

He can picture his mother now, singing to him in the safety of a warm room, lying sweetly with ballads about a world filled with justice and love – sweet lies that helped fix his temperament, even when he later learned the truth about a bitter, deadly universe.

A string of whimsical ditties brings back to mind the bearded twins, two brothers who for many years shared the Father Role in his family-web, a pair of incurable jokers who routinely set all six of the young web-sibs giggling uncontrollably at their quips and good-natured antics. Reciting some of the simplest verses over and over, he finds he can almost comprehend the crude punchlines – a real breakthrough. He knows the humor is puerile, infantile, yet he laughs and laughs at the old gag-songs until tears stream down his cheeks.

Arianafoo plays more records for him, and several release floods of excitement as he relives the operettas and musical plays he used to love as in late adolescence. A human art form, to help ease the strain as he struggled, along with millions of other earnest young men and women, to grasp some of the lofty science of a civilization older than most of the brightest stars.

He felt poignant pain in recovering much of what he once had been. Most words and facts remain alien, unobtainable – even his mother's name, or his own, for that matter – but at least he begins to feel like a living being, a person with a past. A man whose actions once had meaning to others. Someone who had been loved.

Nor is music the only key! Paper offers several more. When the mood strikes, he snatches up a pencil and sketches with mad abandon, using up page after page, compelled to draw even though he knows each sheet must cost these impoverished folk dearly.

When he spies Prity doodling away, graphing a simple linear equation, he delightedly finds that he understands! Math was never his favored language, but now he discovers a new love for it. Apparently, numbers hadn't quite deserted him the way speech had.

There is one more communion that he realizes while being treated by Pzora, the squishypile of donut-rings that used to frighten him so. It is a strange rapport, as foreign to words as day is to night. Robbed of speech, he seems better attuned to notice Pzora's nuances of smell and touch. Tickling shimmers course his body, triggered by the healer's ever-changing vapors. Again, his hands seem to flutter of their own accord, answering Pzora's scent-queries on a level he can only dimly perceive.

One does not need words to notice irony. Beings shaped much like this one had been his deadly foes – this he knew without recalling how. They were enemies to all his kind. How strange then that he should owe so much to a gentle pile of farting rings.

All these tricks and surprises offer slim rays of hope through his desolation, but it is music that seems the best route back to whoever he once was. When Arianafoo offers him a choice of instruments, laid out in a glass case, he selects one that seems simple enough to experiment with, to use fishing for more melodies, more keys to unlock doors.

His first awkward efforts to play the chosen instrument send clashing noises down the twisty aisles of this strange temple of books, hidden beneath a cave of stone. He strives diligently and manages to unloose more recollections of childhood, but soon discovers that more recent memories are harder to shake free. Perhaps in later life he had less time to learn new songs, so there were fewer to associate with recent events.

Events leading to a fiery crash into that horrid swamp.

The memories are there, he knows. They still swarm through his dreams, as they once thronged his delirium. Impressions of vast, vacuum vistas. Of vital missions left undone. Of comrades he feels shamed to have forgotten.

Bent over the instrument with its forty-six strings, he hammers away, one and two notes at a time, seeking some cue, some tune or phrase that might break the jam-up in his mind. The more it eludes him, the more certain he grows that it is there.

He begins to suspect it is no human song he seeks, but something quite different. Something both familiar and forever strange.

That night, he dreams several times about water. It seems natural enough, since Sara had made it clear they would be departing on the steamboat tomorrow, leaving behind the great hall of paper books, heading for the mountain where the starship landed.

Another ship voyage might explain the vague, watery images.

Later, he knew better.

XXI

THE BOOK OF THE SEA

In traveling the downward path,
that of redemption,
be not unaware of what you seek

To divorce your racial destiny,
from your former clan,
from your associations,
from the patrons who first gave
your species speech,
and reason,
and starflight.

You are saying that they failed
the first time.
That someone else should have
a new chance to adopt your kind
and try again.

There is nobility in this gamble.
Nobility and courage.

But do not expect gratitude from
those you have spurned.

—*The Scroll of Exile*

ALVIN'S TALE

The day came. After all our fantasies, preparations, and endless details, there we were at last, the four of us, standing by the open hatch of *Wuphon's Dream*.

'Shoulda built a raft instead,' Huck muttered nervously, while static from her nearest wheel hub made my leg hair stand out. 'There's lots of rivers we could've explored all summer, all by ourselves. Done some nice quiet fishing, too.'

I was hyperventilating my throat sacs, as if packing their livid tissues with pure oxygen would help much where we were going! Fortunately, Tyug had provided each of us with mild relaxant drugs, which might explain Ur-ronn's easy composure.

'*I* couldn't've gone on a raft,' Ur-ronn replied, in flat deadpan tones. 'Id've gotten wet.'

We all turned to stare at her, then each of us, in our own way, burst out laughing. Pincer whistled, Huck guffawed, and I umbled till it hurt. Oh, Ur-ronn – what a character!

'You're right,' added Pincer-Tip. 'The hot-air balloon would have been a *much* better plan. Let's talk Uriel into doing a retrofit-fit.'

'Hush up, you two!' Huck chided, a little unfairly, since she had started it. We all turned as Uriel approached, Tyug following two paces behind. The traeki's little partial, Ziz, now recovered from its distending ordeal, lay back in its assigned cage, under the *Dream*'s bubble window.

'You have your charts?' Uriel inspected Pincer's pouch to make sure. Made of laminated plastic by a human-invented process, the sheets were tough, durable, and therefore somewhat less than legal. But we were heading for the Midden anyway, so wasn't it all right? We had studied the course chosen by Uriel, to follow as soon as the *Dream*'s wheels touched the muddy bottom.

'Compass?'

Both Pincer and Ur-ronn were equipped. Huck's magnetically driven axles shouldn't interfere much, if she didn't get too excited.

'We've gone over contingency tactics and rehearsed as nuch as fossifle, given our haste. I hope.' Uriel shook her head in the manner of a human expressing regret. 'There's just one thing left to cover, an ovject you are to seek out, while down there. A thing I need you to find.'

Huck craned an eyestalk around to semaphore me.

See? I told you so! she flashed in visual GalTwo. Huck had maintained for days that there must be some item Uriel desperately wanted. An ulterior motive for all this support. Something we alone, with our amateur bathy, were qualified to find. I ignored her smug boast. The problem with Huck is that she's right just often enough to let her think it's a law of nature.

'This is what you are looking for,' Uriel said, lifting up a sketch pad so that no one but we four could see, showing a *spiky* shape with six points, like a piece in a child's game of jacks. Tendrils, or long cables, stretched outward from two of the arms, trailing in opposite directions off the page. I wondered if it might be some kind of living thing.

'It is an artifact we need rather urgently,' Uriel went on. 'Even nore infortant than the artifact, however, is the strand of wire running away fron it. It is this strand that you seek, that you shall seize and fasten with the retrieval cord, so that we can haul it vack.'

Sheesh, I thought. The four of us were modernist gloss-junkies who would gladly raid the Midden for treasure, even in defiance of the Scrolls. But now to have a *sage* order us to do that very thing? No wonder she preferred not letting nearby citizens in on this heresy!

'Will do!' Pincer exclaimed, briefly teetering on two legs in order to salute with three. As for the rest of us, we already stood on the ramp. What were we going to do? Use this as an excuse to back out?

All right, I considered it. So strap me to the Egg and sing till I confess.

I was the last one aboard – unless you count Huphu, who scampered through my legs as I was about to dog the hatch. I tightened the wheel and the skink-bladder seals spread thin, oozing like immunity caulk between a traeki's member rings. The closing shut us off from nearly all sound – except the hissing, gurgling, rumbling, and sighing of four frightened kids just coming to realize what a fix all their humicking daydreams had gotten them into.

It took half a midura to make certain the air system and dehumidifiers worked. Pincer and Ur-ronn went over a checklist up front and Huck tested her steering bars, while I squatted in the very back with nothing to do but stroke the crank that I would use, whenever the *Dream* needed the services of an 'engine.' To pass the time, I umbled Huphu, whose claws were a welcome distraction, scratching a nervous itch that tickled the outer surface of my heart spine.

If we die, please let Uriel at least drag our bodies home, I thought, and maybe it was a prayer, like humans often do in tight spots, according to books I've read. *Let my folks have a life-bone for vuphyning, to help them in their grief and disappointment over how I misspent the investment of their love.*

XXII

THE BOOK OF THE SLOPE

Legends

Anyone who travels by riverboat, and listens to the compelling basso of a hoonish helmsman, knows something of the process that once made them starfaring beings.

For one thing, the sound is clearly where their race-name comes from. According to legend, the Guthatsa patrons who originally adopted and uplifted presapient hoon were entranced by the musical trait. While splicing in speech, reason, and other niceties, the Guthatsa also worked to enhance the penetrating, vibrant output of the hoonish throat sac, so that it might enrich their clients' adulthood, when they took up mature responsibilities in Galactic society.

It would, the Guthatsa predicted, help make the hoon better patrons when their turn came to pass on the gift of wisdom, continuing the billion-year-old cycle of intellect in the Five Galaxies.

Today we know our hoonish neighbors as patient, decent folk, slow to anger, though doughty in a fix. It is hard to reconcile this image with the reaction of urrish and later human settlers, on first learning that the Tall Ones dwelled on Jijo – a response of animosity and fear.

Whatever the initial reasons for that loathing, it soon ebbed, then vanished within a single generation. Whatever quarrels divided our star-god ancestors, we on Jijo do not share them. These days, it is hard to find anyone among the Six who can claim not to like the hoon.

Yet there remains a mystery – why do they dwell on Jijo at all? Unlike other races of the Six, they tell no tale of persecution, or even of a quest for breeding space. When asked why their sneakship defied great odds to seek this hidden refuge, they shrug and cannot answer.

A sole clue lies in the Scroll of Redemption, where we read of an inquiry by the last glaver sage, who asked a first-generation hoonish settler why his folk came, and got this deeply-umbled answer—

'To this (cached) haven, we came, (in hope) seeking.
'On a (heartfelt) quest to recover the (lamented) spines of (lost) youth.
'Here we were sent, on the advice of (wise, secret) oracles.
'Nor was the (danger-ridden) trip in vain.
'For behold what, in (delighted) surprise, we already have won!'

At that point, the hoon colonist was said to point at a crude raft, fashioned from boo logs and sealed with tree sap — earliest precursor of all the vessels to follow, plying Jijo's rivers and seas.

From our perspective, a thousand years later, it is hard to interpret the meaning of it all. Can any of us today imagine our shaggy friends without boats? If we try to picture them cruising space in starships, do we not envision those, too, running before storm and tide, sluicing their way between planets by keel, rudder, and soil?

By the logic, does it not follow that urs once 'galloped' across Galactic prairies, with stellar winds blowing their waving tails? Or that any starcraft fashioned by humans ought to resemble a tree?

—from *A Re-Appraisal of Jijoan Folklore*, by Ur-Kintoon and
Herman Chang-Jones
Tarek City Printers, Year-of-Exile 1901.

DWER

It was a midura past nightfall when the ember crossed the sky, a flicker that grew briefly as it streaked by, crossing the heavens to descend southeast. Dwer knew it was no meteor, because the spark traveled below the clouds.

Only after it was gone, dropping beyond the next rank of forested knolls, did he hear a low, muttering purr, barely above the rustling of the tree branches.

Dwer might never have noticed if his dinner had agreed with him. But his bowels had been shaky ever since the four humans began supplementing their meager supplies with foraged foods. So he sat at the makeshift latrine, in a cleft between two hills, waiting for his innards to decide whether to accept or reject his hard-won evening meal.

The others were no better off. Danel and Jenin never complained, but Lena blamed Dwer while her intestines growled.

'Some mighty hunter. You've been over the pass dozens of times and can't tell what's poison from what's not?'

'Please, Lena,' Jenin had asked. 'You know Dwer never crossed the Venom Plain. All he can do is look for stuff that's like what he knows.'

Danel tried his hand at peacemaking. 'Normally, we'd eat the donkeys as their packs lightened. But they're weak after recent stream-crossings, and we can't spare any from carrying our extra gear.'

He referred to the weight of books, tools, and special packages that were meant to make human life beyond the Rimmers somewhat more than purely savage. *If* it was finally decided to stay here forever. Dwer still hoped it wouldn't come to that.

'One thing we do know,' Danel went on. 'Humans *can* survive here in the Gray Hills, and without all the vat processes we're used to back home. Right now we're adjusting to some local microbes, I'm sure. If the sooner band got used to them, so can we.'

Yes, Dwer had thought, *but survival doesn't mean comfort. If Rety's any indication, these sooners are a grumpy lot. Maybe we're getting a taste of how they got that way.*

Things might improve once Danel set up vats of his own, growing some of the yeasty cultures that made many Jijoan foods palatable to humans, but there would be no substitutes for the traeki-refined enzymes that turned bitter ping fruit and bly-yoghurt into succulent treats. Above all, Dwer and the other newcomers would count on the sooners to explain which local foods to avoid.

Assuming they cooperate. Rety's relatives might not appreciate having the new order-of-life explained to them. *I wouldn't either, in their position*. While Danel was skilled at negotiation and persuasion, Dwer's role would be to back up the sage's words, giving them force of law.

From Rety's testimony, her tribe likely totaled no more than forty adults. The social structure sounded like a typical macho-stratified hunting band – a standard human devolution pattern that old Fallon long ago taught Dwer to recognize – with a fluid male ranking order enforced by bluster, personal intimidation, and violence.

The preferred approach to ingathering such a group, worked out by Dwer's predecessors, was to make contact swiftly and dazzle the sooners with gifts before shock could turn into hostility, buying time to map the web of alliances and enmities within the band. After that, the procedure was to choose some promising middle-ranked males and help those candidates perform a *coup*, ousting the formerly dominant group of bully boys, whose interest lay in keeping things as they were. The new leaders were then easy to persuade to 'come home.'

It was a time-tested technique, used successfully by others faced with the task of retrieving wayward human clans. Ideally, it shouldn't prove necessary to kill anybody.

Ideally.

In truth, Dwer hated this part of his job.

You knew it might come to this. Now you pay for all the freedom you've had.

If gentle suasion didn't work, the next step was to call in militia and hunt down every stray. The same hard price had been agreed to by every sept in the Commons, as an alternative to war and damnation.

But this time things are different.

This time we don't have any law on our side – except the law of survival.

Instead of bringing illegal settlers back to the Slope, Ozawa planned to *take over* Rety's band. Guiding them toward a different way of life, but one still hidden from sight.

Only if the worst happens. If we're the last humans alive on Jijo.

Dwer's mind reeled away from that awful notion, as his innards wrestled with the remnants of his meal. *If this keeps on, I'll be too weak to win a wrestling match, or however else Jass and Bom settle their tribal ranking. It may come down to Lena and her tools, after all*.

Throughout the journey, the stocky blond woman carefully

tended one donkey carrying the gadgets of her personal 'hobby' – a human technology passed down since the first ancestors landed on Jijo, one so brutal that it had been seldom used, even during the urrish wars. 'My equalizers,' Lena called the wax-sealed wooden crates, meaning their contents made her able to enforce Danel's verdicts, as thoroughly as Dwer's muscle and physical skill.

It won't come to that! he vowed, commanding his body to shape up. Dwer touched several fingertips whose frostbite damage might have been much worse. *I've always been luckier than I deserved.*

According to Sara, who had read extensively about Earth's past, the same thing could be said about the whole bloody human race.

That was when the glowing ember crossed the sky, streaking overhead while Dwer sat at the makeshift latrine. He would never have noticed the sight had he been facing another way or engaged in an activity more demanding of his attention. As it was, he stared glumly after the falling spark while the rumbling thunder of its passage chased up and down nearby canyons, muttering echoes in the night.

They faced more stream crossings the next day.

It was hard country, which must have influenced the sooners' ancestors to come this way in the first place. Guarded first by the Venom Plain, then ravines and whitewater torrents, the Gray Hills were so forbidding that surveyors checked the region just once per generation. It was easy to imagine how Fallon and the others might overlook one small tribe in the tortured badlands Dwer led the party through – a realm of sulfurous geysers and trees that grew more twisted the deeper they went. Low clouds seemed to glower and sulk, giving way to brief glimpses of sunshine. Green moss beards drooped from rocky crevices, trickling oily water into scummy pools. Animal life kept its skittish distance, leaving only faint spoor traces for Dwer to sniff and puzzle over.

They lost several donkeys crossing the next rushing stream. Even with a rope stretched from bank to bank, and both Lena and Dwer standing waist-deep in the frigid water to help them along, three tired animals lost their footing on slippery stones. One got tangled in the rope, screaming and thrashing, then perished before they could free it. Two others were carried off. It took hours, sloshing through shallows, to retrieve their packs. Dwer's fingers and toes seemed to burn the whole time with a queer icy-hot numbness.

Finally, drying off by a fire on the other side, they measured the damage.

'Four books, a hammer, and thirteen packets of powder missing,' Danel said, shaking his head over the loss. 'And some others damaged when their waterproofs tore.'

'Not to mention the last fodder for the beasts,' Jenin added. 'From now on they forage, like it or not.'

'Well, we're almost there, ain't we?' Lena Strong cut in, cheerful for once as she knelt butchering the donkey that had strangled. 'On the bright side, we eat better for a while.'

They rested that night, feeling better – if a bit guilty – with the change in diet. The next morning they marched just one arrowflight east to face a mighty ravine, with sheer walls and a raging torrent in its heart.

Dwer headed upstream while Lena struck off to the south, leaving Jenin and Danel to wait with the exhausted donkeys. Two days out and two back, that was the agreed limit. If neither scout found a way by then, they might have to make a raft and try the rapids. Not a prospect Dwer relished.

Didn't I tell Danel we should wait for Rety? I may be a tracker, but she came out through this desolation all by herself.

More than ever he was impressed by the girl's unswayable tenacity.

If there is a second party, and she's with them, Rety's probably chortling over me falling into this trap. If she knows some secret shortcut, they may reach the tribe before us. Now won't that screw up Danel's plans!

Even moving parallel with the river was awkward and dangerous, a struggle up steep bluffs, then back down the slippery bank of one icy tributary after another. To Dwer's surprise, Mudfoot came along, forsaking Danel's campfire and Jenin's pampering attention. The trek was too hard for any of the noor's standard antics, ambushing Dwer or trying to trip him. After a while, they even began helping each other. He carried the noor across treacherous, foamy creeks. At other times, Mudfoot sped ahead to report with squeals and quivers which of two paths seemed better.

Still, the river and its canyon tormented them, appearing almost to open up, then abruptly closing again, narrower and steeper than before. By noon of the second day, Dwer was muttering sourly over the obstinate nastiness of the terrain. *Fallon warned me about the Gray Hills. But I always figured I'd get to go through the old man's notes and maps. Pick a path based on the trips of earlier hunters.*

Yet none of them had ever found any trace of Rety's band, so maybe they relied *too* much on each other's advice, repeatedly taking the same route in and out of these badlands. A route the sooners knew to avoid. Maybe all this horrid inaccessibility meant Danel's group was getting near the tribe's home base.

That's it, boy. Keep thinkin' that way, if it makes you feel better.

Wouldn't it be great to struggle all this way, and back, only to learn that *Lena* had already found a good crossing, just a little ways downstream? That thought tortured Dwer as he shared food with Mudfoot. Going on seemed futile, and he'd have to call the trip a loss in a few hours anyway. Dwer's fingers and toes ached, along with overstrained tendons across his back and legs. But it was the pounding roar of rushing water that really wore away at him, as if a clock teet had been hammering inside his head for days.

'Do *you* think we oughta head back?' he asked the noor.

Mudfoot cocked its sleek head, giving Dwer that deceptively intelligent expression, reminding him of legends that said the beasts could grant wishes – if you wanted something so bad, you didn't care about the cost. Workmen used the expression 'Let's consult a noor' to mean a problem couldn't be solved, and it was time to soften frustration with a set of stiff drinks.

'Well,' Dwer sighed, hoisting his pack and bow, 'I don't guess it'd hurt to go on a ways. I'd feel silly if it turned out we missed a good ford just over the next rise.'

Thirty duras later, Dwer crawled up a thorny bank, cursing the brambles and the slippery wetness that soaked his skin, wishing he was on his way back to a hot meal and a dry blanket. Finally, he reached a place to stand, sucking an oozing scratch across the back of his hand.

He turned – and stared through a mist at what lay ahead.

A crashing waterfall, whose roar had been masked by the turbulent river, stretched low and wide from far to the left all the way to the distant right. A wide curtain of spray and foam.

Yet that was not what made Dwer gape.

Just *before* the roaring plummet, traversing the river from bank to bank, lay a broad expanse of rocky shallows that appeared nowhere more than ankle deep.

'I guess this settles the question of whether or not to *proceed*.' He sighed.

Shortly, he and Mudfoot stood at last on the other shore, having sloshed easily across to prove the ford was safe. From there an obvious game trail zigzagged through the forest, departing the canyon eastward.

On my way back downstream I'll scout an easier path for Danel and the others to get up here. Success took much of the sting out of his aches and pains. *There's a chance Lena beat me to a way across. Still, I found this place, and maybe I'm the first! If all this stupid alien stuff blows over and we get to go home, I'll check Fallon's maps to see if anyone's named this spot since the Buyur went away.*

The broad falls reminded him of the spillway back at Dolo

Village, a thought that was sweet, but also a bitter reminder of why he was here, so far from Sara and everyone else he loved.

I'm here to survive. It's my job to cower and have babies with women I barely know, while those on the Slope suffer and die.

The pleasure of discovery evaporated. *Shame* he displaced with a wooden determination to do the job he had been commanded to do. Dwer started to head back across the shallows ... then paused in his tracks, acutely aware of a tickling sensation in the middle of his back.

Something was wrong.

Frowning, he slipped off the bow and drew the string-tightening lever. With an arrow nocked, he flared his nostrils to suck humid air. It was hard to make out anything in the musty dankness. But judging from Mudfoot's arched spines, the noor felt it too.

Someone's here, he thought, moving swiftly inland to get under the first rank of trees. *Or was here, recently*.

Away from the shore, the place stank with a terrible muddle of scents, which was natural next to the only river crossing for many leagues. Animals would come to drink, then leave territorial markings. But Dwer sensed something else, inserting a wary hint of threat.

Painfully aware that open water lay at his back, he moved deeper into the forest.

I smell ... burnt wood – someone had a fire, not too long ago.

He scanned. Sniffing and peering.

It was over ... there.

Amid the shadows, half a stone's throw away, he made out the remnants, set in a modest clearing. A large pit of black ashes.

Some of Rety's band? He worried. Might Jass and Bom be watching right now, picking their best shot at an intruder from the dreaded west?

Clues lay in the brushing rustle of wind in the branches, the furtive movements of insects and birds. But this terrain and wildlife were strange to him, and the racket from the waterfall would drown out a militia company on maneuvers.

Mudfoot made a low chuffing growl and sniffed close to the ground while Dwer scanned the complex dimness beyond the next rank of trees. 'What is it?' he asked, kneeling where Mudfoot scratched a layer of freshly fallen leaves.

A familiar odor struck him fully.

'Donkey shit?'

He risked a quick glance – and didn't need a second look.

Donkeys? But Rety said the sooners didn't have any!

With dark-adapting eyes he now picked out traces of pack beasts all over the clearing. Hoofprints and droppings from at least a dozen animals. A stake where a remuda line was tethered. Flattened spots where cargo carriers must have lain.

He lowered the bow. So a second expedition *had* set out, passing the first by a better route, no doubt led by Rety herself.

Well, at least we won't be quite so outnumbered by the sooners, even if contact doesn't happen in the order Danel planned.

An element of relief was more personal, if ungallant. *My choice in a future mate might go beyond Jenin, Lena, or some surly cousin of Rety's.*

Something still nagged at Dwer however, making him reluctant to put down the bow. He was counting wallows – the depressions made by donkeys as they lay – and realized there were just too many. Or rather, there were two different *kinds* of wallow. Nearer the fire they were smaller, closer . . .

No. It can't be.

Anywhere else, scent would have hit him long before this. Now a sharp, familiar pungency smacked Dwer in his sinuses. He bent to pluck a clump of stringy fur, still coated from when the owner rolled in ash after an unpleasantly wet river crossing.

Glossy strands from an urrish mane.

It had been generations since the last war. Regardless, instinctive fear surged in Dwer's chest – a heart-pounding wave of angst.

An urrish caravan in these parts could not be up to anything good.

Here in the wilderness, far from the restraint of sages and the Commons, with the Six possibly already extinct back home, all the old rules were clearly moot. As in days before the Great Peace, Dwer knew how dangerous these beings would be to have as enemies.

Silent as a ghost, he crept away, then crossed the river in a zigzag dash, leaping behind a boulder, then swiveling to cover the opposite bank while Mudfoot came splashing behind, clearly as eager to get out of there as he was.

Dwer kept wary watch for a whole midura, till long after his pounding pulse finally settled.

At last, when it seemed safe, he slung his bow and set off downstream, running when and where he could, hurrying southward with news.

Can you see the smoke, oh my rings? Spiraling from a fresh cavity in Jijo's ruptured soil? Two moons cast wan beams through that sooty pall, piercing a crater wherein twisty metal shapes flicker and burn.

Distracting thoughts rise from our second torus-of-cognition. What is it that you say, my ring? That this is a *very* large amount of dross? Dross that will not degrade back to nature on its own?

Indeed it is. Shall we hope that the aliens themselves will clean up the mess? It would take a hundred donkey-caravans to haul so much hard waste down to sea.

Another ring suggests a stream be diverted, to form a lake. A transplanted mulc-spider might dissolve the sinful wreckage over the course of centuries.

By mass vote, we send these thoughts to waxy storage for later reflection. For now, let us watch events flow in real time.

A roiling mob of onlookers teems the slopes overlooking this savaged vale, held in check by stunned, overworked proctors. Higher on tree-shrouded hills, we glimpse murky ranks of disciplined silhouettes, wheeling and maneuvering – militia units taking up positions. From here we cannot tell the companies' intent. Are they preparing, counter to all hope, to defend the Commons against overpowering vengeance? Or else have inter-sept grudges finally torn the Great Peace, so that we hasten doomsday tearing each other apart with our own bloody hands?

Perhaps even the commanders of those dark battalions don't yet know for sure.

Meanwhile, closer to the heat, Ur-Jah and Lester Cambel supervise teams of brave urs, men, hoon, and gray qheuens, who descend into the pit armed with ropes and tools of Buyur steel.

Ro-kenn protests at first, does he not, my rings? In hasty GalSeven, the Rothen emissary decries those he calls 'wanton looters.' One of the remnant robots rises, unfolding spiky organs of punishment.

Vubben urges that Ro-kenn look again. Can he not recognize sincere efforts at *rescue*? For two tense duras we poise on a precipice. Then, with a grudging mutter, the Rothen recalls his death machine – for now.

From Ro-kenn's charismatic, human-handsome face, our steady old rewq translates undertones of grief and rage. True, this race is new to us, and rewq can be fooled. Yet what else should we expect from one whose home/campsite lies in ruins? Whose comrades languish, dead or dying, in the twisted tangle of their buried station?

The male sky-human, Rann, wears torment openly as he rides the other robot, shouting at those working through the rubble, directing their efforts. A tense but encouraging sign of cooperation.

Ling, the other sky-human, appears in shock, leaning against young Lark as he pokes his foot through debris at the crater's rim. He bends to lift a smoldering plank, sniffing suspiciously. We perceive his head rock back, exclaiming surprise.

Ling draws away, demanding an explanation. Through our rewq, we perceive Lark's reluctance as he shows her the smoky plank, a strip of burned wood from a Jijoan box or crate.

Ling drops her hand from his arm. She spins about, hurrying toward Rann's hovering robot steed.

Much closer to this stack of rings, Ro-kenn has become embroiled in argument. A delegation accosts the Rothen emissary, demanding answers.

Why did he earlier claim the right and power to *command* the Holy Egg, since it is now clear that the sacred stone violently rejects him and his kind?

Furthermore, why did he seek to sow dissension among the Six with his baseless calumny about the human sept? His groundless lie, claiming that our Earthling brethren are *not* descendants of sinners, just like the other Five.

'You Rothen may or may not be the high patrons of humanity,' the spokesman contends. 'But that takes nothing from our ancestors who came here on the *Tabernacle*. Not from their crime, or their hope, when they set us on the Path of Redemption.'

There is anger in the voice of the human intercessor. But we/i also descry thick brushstrokes of *theater*. An effort to smother the fire of disharmony that Ro-kenn ignited with his tale. Indeed, urrish voices rise in approval of his anger.

Now our second cognition-torus vents yet another thought-hypothesis.

What is it, my ring? You suggest disharmony was Ro-kenn's *intent*, all along? A deliberate scheme to create strife among the Six?

Our fourth ring rebuts – what purpose might such a bizarre plot serve? To have Five gang up on One? To cause vendetta against the very sept these Rothen claim as beloved clients?

Store and wick this weird postulate, oh my rings. Argue it later. For now the Rothen prepares to respond. Drawing himself up, he surveys the crowd with an expression that seems awesome both to humans and to those who know them – to rewq-wearers and those without.

There is kindness in his expressive gaze. Overstrained patience and love.

'Dear, misguided children. This explosive manifestation was not rejection by Jijo, or the Egg. Rather, some malfunction of the mighty forces contained in our station must have released—'

Abruptly, he stops as Rann and Ling approach, each riding a robot. Each wearing looks of dark anger. They murmur into devices, and the Rothen stares back, listening. Again, my rewq reveals dissonance across his features, coalescing at last in raging fury.

Ro-kenn speaks.

'So, now the (dire) truth is known. Learned. Verified!

'No accident, this (slaying) explosion.

'No (unlikely) malfunction – nor any rejection by your (overly-vaunted) Egg.

'Now it is known. Verified. That this was (foul, unprovoked) murder!

'Murder by deceit, by subterfuge.

'By use of subterranean explosives. By sneak attack.

'By you!'

He points, stabbing with a long, graceful finger. The crowd reels back from Ro-kenn's fierce wrath, and this news.

At once it is clear what the zealots have done. Secretly, taking advantage of natural caverns lacing these hills, they must have laboriously burrowed deep beneath the station to lay chests of eruptive powder – crude but plentiful – which then awaited a signal, the right symbolic moment, to burst forth flame and destruction.

'With scanners tuned for chemical sleuthing, we now perceive the depth of your shared perfidy. How undeserved were the rewards we planned conferring on murderous half-beasts!'

He might say more to the cowering throng, adding terrible threats. But at that moment, a *new* disturbance draws our focus toward the smoldering pit. The crowd parts for a phalanx of soot-stained rescuers, coughing and gasping as they bear pitiable burdens.

Rann cries out, bounding from his mount to inspect a crumpled form, borne upon a litter. It is Besh, the other female sky-human. From her mangled figure, our rewq reads no life flicker.

Again, the crowd divides. This time it is *Ro-kenn* who exclaims a distinctly unhuman wail. The litter brought before him bears the other of his race, Ro-pol, whom we guessed to be female. (His mate?)

This time, a slim thread of *breath* swirls in the near infrared, from the victim's soot-stained but still splendid face. Ro-kenn bends close, as if seeking some private communion.

The poignant scene lasts but a few moments. Then the reed of living tension is no more. A second corpse lies in the hollow, under bitter-bright stars.

The living Rothen stands to his full height, a terrible sight, emoting vast anger.

'Now comes the reward (foul) treachery deserves!' Ro-kenn cries, reaching skyward, his voice reverberating with such wrath that every rewq in the valley trembles. Some humans drop to their knees. Do not even gray queens whistle awe and dismay?

'For so long you have feared (righteous) judgment from above. Now behold its incarnate form!'

Along with the others, we/i look up, our gaze following Ro-kenn's extended arm.

There, crossing the sky, we perceive a single glaring spark. A pitiless glimmer that ponderously *moves*, passing from the Spider's Web into the constellation humans call The Sword.

The great ship is still a distant point, but it does not wink, nor does it twinkle. Rather, it seems to *throb* with an intensity that hurts those who watch for long.

One can hardly fault the zealots' timing, suggests our ever-thoughtful second-torus-of-cognition. *If their objective was to bring an end to pretense, they could have chosen no better way.*

SARA

Sage Taine wanted to speak with her before she left for Kandu Landing. So did Ariana Foo. Both wished she would delay her departure, but Sara was eager to be off.

Yet with just a midura to go before the *Gopher* set sail, she decided on impulse to visit her old office, high in the cathedral-tower housing the Library of Material Science.

West from the Grand Staircase, her ascent first took her by the vast, rambling stacks of physics and chemistry, where the recent evacuation had taken a visible toll. The maze of shelves showed frequent gaps. Scraps of paper lay in place of absent volumes, to help staff put things back if the present crisis passed. In places, the wood surface looked almost new, implying this was the first time a book had budged since the Great Printing.

Glancing down one crooked aisle, Sara glimpsed young Jomah, teetering under a load of heavy volumes, lumbering gamely behind his uncle to begin the ornate rituals-of-borrowing. None too soon if they hoped to make the *Gopher* in time. The explosers and quite a few others were bound the same way as Sara, first by boat, then donkey-caravan to the Glade of Gathering.

The winding labyrinth triggered complex emotions. She used to get lost back in the early days, but never cared, so happy had she been to dwell in this splendid place. This temple of wisdom.

Her long year away had hardly changed her little office, with its narrow window overlooking the green-flanked Bibur. Everything seemed much as she had left it, except for the dust. *Well, I always figured I'd be back before this.* Many competed to be chosen by human sept for this life, subsidized by a race of farmers and gleaners whose one great sinful pride lay in their books.

Tacked to the far wall lay a chart showing the 'devolution' of various dialects spoken on the Slope. Like branches splitting off from parent roots, there were multiple downward shoots for each Galactic language in current use. This older depiction showed the bias of scholars over in Linguistics, and was colored by one unassailable fact – the billion-year-old Galactic languages had once been perfect, efficient codes for communication. Deviation was seen as part of a foretold spiral toward the innocence of animal-like grunts – the *Path of Redemption* already blazed by glavers – a fate variously dreaded or prayed for by folk of the Slope, depending on one's religious fervor.

Human tongues were also traced backward, not over a billion years but ten thousand. Earthling authorities like Childe, Schrader, and Renfrew had carefully rebuilt ancestral languages and many of those grammars were more primly structured, better at error-correction, than the 'bastard' jargons that followed. What better evidence that human devolution began long before the landing on Jijo? Did not all Earth cultures have legends of a lost Golden Age?

One conclusion – the missing Patrons of Earth must have been interrupted in their work, forced to leave humanity half finished. True, the ensuing fall was masked by some flashy tricks of precocious technology. Still, many scholars believed Earthlings had much to gain from any road leading toward re-adoption and a second chance, especially since they appeared to be heading that way anyway.

That's the orthodox view. My model takes the same data, but projects a different outcome.

Her most recent chart resembled this one – *turned upside down*, with lightless roots transformed into trees, showing the Six heading in a new direction.

In many *directions.*

If no one interferes.

Yesterday, she had shown her latest work to Sage Bonner, whose enthusiasm reignited the pleasure of a colleague's praise.

'Well, my dear,' said Jijo's oldest mathematician, stroking his bald pate, 'you do seem to have a case. So let's schedule a seminar! Interdisciplinary, of course.'

He punctuated his enthusiasm with a sloppy GalTwo emotion trill of anticipation.

'We'll invite those stuffy pedants from Linguistics. See if they can bear to hear a bold new idea for a change. Heh. Heh-cubed!'

Bonner probably hadn't much followed her discussion of 'redundancy coding' and chaos in information theory. The elderly topologist just relished the prospect of a brisk debate, one that might knock down some ensconced point of view.

If only you knew how good an example you are of my thesis, she had thought affectionately. Sara hated to disappoint him.

'We can have it when I get back from Gathering, with luck.'

Alas, there might be no return from her coming journey. Or else, it might be to find that the explorers had done their duty at last, bringing down the stony roof, and with it a prophesied age of darkness and purity. She was turning to go, when a low *thunk* announced a message ball, landing on her desk. Above the in-box, a fleshy tube bounced in recoil, having spit the ball from a maze of pipes lacing the Biblos complex.

Oh no. Sara backed away, hoping to leave before the furry sphere unrolled. If the messenger found no one home, it would simply reenter the tube and report the fact to whoever sent it.

But the ball uncoiled swiftly and a tiny mouselike form scrambled up the box to see her, squeaking delight over achieving the purpose bred into it by the ancient Buyur – to deliver brief messages via a network of cross-linked tunnels and vines. With a sigh, Sara put out her hand, and the courier spat a warm *pellet* into her palm. The pill squirmed.

Suppressing distaste, she raised the little symbiont – a larger cousin of a parrot tick – and let it writhe inside her ear.

Soon, as she feared, it began speaking with the voice of Sage Taine.

'*Sara, if this reaches you, I'd like to talk before you go … it is essential to clear up our misunderstanding.*'

There came a long pause, then the voice hurried on.

'*I've thought about it and have lately come to believe that this situation is largely my fau—*'

The message stopped there. The record bug had reached its limit. It began repeating the message over again, from the beginning.

Fault? Was 'fault' the word you were about to say?

351

Sara tipped her head until the bug realized it wasn't wanted anymore and crawled out of her ear. Taine's voice grew distant, plaintive, as she tossed the bug back to the furry little messenger, who snatched it, tweaking it between sharp jaws, making the bug receptive for Sara's reply.

I'm sorry, she almost said aloud.

I should have made allowances. You were tactless, but meant well, in your haughty way.

I should have been honored by your proposal, even if you first made it out of a sense of duty.

I reacted badly when you renewed the offer at Joshu's funeral.

A month ago, I was thinking about finally saying yes. There are worse lives on the Slope than the one you offered.

But now everything had changed. The aliens had seen to that. *Dwer* had what it would take in the new era to come. He'd thrive and sire generations of fine hunter-gatherers, if an age of innocence really was at hand.

And if it's death the aliens have in mind for us? Well, Dwer will fool them too and survive.

That thought made Sara poignantly glad.

Either way, what use will Jijo have for intellectuals like us, Taine?

The two of them would soon be more equal than ever, alike in useless obsolescence, before the end.

Sara said nothing aloud. The messenger ball gave a stymied squeak. It popped the bug into one cheek, then reentered the tube, vanishing into the maze-work of conduits that laced Biblos like a system of arteries and veins.

You're not the only one. Sara cast a thought after the frustrated creature. *There's more than enough disappointment to go around.*

The *Gopher* was already putting on steam when Sara hurried to the dock. Ariana Foo waited nearby, the twilight shrouding her wheelchair so that she resembled some human-g'Kek hybrid.

'I wish I could have a few more days with him,' she said, taking Sara's hand.

'You've done wonders, but there's no time to spare.'

'The next kayak pilot may bring vital news—'

'I know. And I'd give anything to hear from Lark. But that reasoning will only take us in circles. If something urgent happens, you can send a galloper after us. Meanwhile I have ... a feeling that we'd better hurry.'

'More dreams?'

Sara nodded. For several nights her sleep had been disturbed by ill-defined impressions of alpine fire, then watery suffocation. It might just be a return of the claustrophobia she felt years ago, as a youthful newcomer under the overhanging roof-of-stone. Or else maybe her nightmares echoed something real. An approaching culmination.

Mother believed in dreams, she recalled. *Even as she drilled into Lark and me a love of books and science, it was* Dwer *whom she heeded, whenever he woke with those powerful visions, back when he was little – and then the week before she died*.

The steam packet hissed, its boilers straining. Two dozen donkeys thumped and whinnied, tethered at the stern alongside sealed crates of books.

Contrasting strangely, a different sound came from the ship's bow. Delicate, melodic *music* consisting of parallel chains of halting notes, somewhat twangy. Sara tilted her head.

'He's getting better fast.'

'He has motivation,' the sage replied. 'I expected him to choose a simpler instrument, like a flute or violus. But he pulled the dulcimer off the museum shelf and seemed to draw some deep satisfaction out of counting its strings. It's simple to learn, and he can sing along, when a tune spills out of memory. Anyway, he's fit for a journey, so' – she took a deep breath, looking weary and old – 'give Lester and the other High Mucketies my regards, will you? Tell them to behave.'

Sara bent to kiss Ariana's cheek. 'I'll do that.'

The retired sage gripped her arm with unexpected strength. 'Safe journey, child. Ifni roll you sixes.'

'Safe house,' Sara returned the blessing. 'May she roll you long life.'

Ariana's chimp aide pushed her upslope, toward the comfort of an evening fire. It was becoming a habit for Sara to doubt she would ever see someone again.

The captain gave the order to cast off, guiding his precious boat gingerly away from the camouflage shelter. Jop and Ulgor joined Sara at the rail, along with several morose-faced librarians, appointed to carry precious volumes to uncertain safety in the wilderness. Soon the churning shove of the paddle wheels settled to a reassuring rhythm, working with the Bibur's current to turn them downstream.

The spaceman played along with focused monomania. Hunched over a small, wedgelike instrument, he hammered its strings with two small curved mallets, faltering often but radiating passion. The music laced through bittersweet memory as Sara watched the mighty fortress slip by, with its many-windowed halls. The stone canopy seemed to hover like a patient fist of God.

I wonder if I'll ever be back.

Soon they passed the westernmost edge of laser-cut stone – the mulching grounds. There were no banners today, or mourners, or busy little subtraekis consuming flesh, preparing white bones for the sea. But then, amid the dusky gloom, she did spy a solitary figure overlooking the river. Tall and straight-backed, with a sleek mane of silver-gray, the human leaned slightly on a cane, though he seemed far from frail. Sara's breath caught as the *Gopher* swept by.

Sage Taine nodded – a friendly, even ardent display for such a diffident person. Then, to Sara's surprise, he lifted an arm, in a gesture of unadorned goodwill.

At the last moment she gave in, raising her own hand. *Peace*, she thought.

Biblos fell behind the chugging steamboat, swallowed by gathering night. Nearby, the Stranger's voice broke in, singing words to a song about a voyage of no return. And while she knew the lyrics expressed his own sense of loss and poignant transition, they also rubbed, both sweetly and painfully, against conflicts in her own heart.

> *For I am bound beyond the dark horizon,*
> *And ne'er again will I know your name ...*

XXIII

THE BOOK OF THE SEA

g'Kek roller, can you stand and gallop
across the heavy ground?
Traeki stack, can you weave a tapestry,
or master the art of fire?
Royal qheuen, will you farm the forest heights?
Can you heal with your touch?
Hoonish sailor, will you endure the plains,
or spin along a cable, stretched up high?
Urrish plainsman, would you sail to sea,
or sift fine pages out of slurried cloth?
Human newcomer, do you know this world?
Can you weave, or spin, or track Jijo's song?
Will all or any of you follow
in the trail blazed by glavers?
The Trail of Forgiveness
through oblivion?
If you do, save room to remember
this one thing –
You were one part of a union
greater than its parts.

—*The Scroll of the Egg*
—*(unofficial)*

I didn't begrudge my position crammed way back, far from the window. At least not during the long descent down the cliff face with the sea looming ever-closer, closer. After all, I'd seen this part before and the others hadn't. But once we hit water, and my friends started cooing and oohing over what they saw through the bubble up front, I started getting a little resentful. It also put me in a bind as a *writer*, faced with having to describe the descent later, to my readers. At best I could see a bare patch of blue over the backs of my compeers.

Looking back on it, I suppose I could solve the problem, in several ways.

First, I could *lie*. I mean I haven't decided whether to turn this story into a novel, and according to Mister Heinz, fiction is a kind of lying. In a later draft I might just write in a window aft. That way my character could describe all sorts of things I only heard about from the others. Or else I could pretend I was up front all along. In fiction, you can be captain if you want to be.

Or maybe I should rewrite it from *Pincer*'s point of view. After all, it was his boat, more than any of ours. And he had the best view of what happened next. That would mean having to write believably from a *qheuen*'s perspective. Not as alien as a traeki's, I suppose. Still, maybe I'm not ready to take on that kind of a challenge, just yet.

All of this assumes I live to do a rewrite, or that anyone else survives who I'd care to have read my tale.

Anyway, for now, this semitruthful journal style will have to do, and that means telling what I really saw, felt, and heard.

The deploying drums transmitted a steady vibration down the hawser. The fresh air inlet hissed and gurgled by my left ear, so it was hardly what I had pictured as a serene descent into the silent deep. Now and then, Ur-ronn would gasp – 'What was that?' – and Pincer identified some fish, piscoid, or skimmer – creatures a hoon usually saw dead in a net-catch, and an urs likely never glimpsed at all. Still, there were no monsters of fantasy. No faery minarets of undersea cities, either. Not so far.

It got dark pretty fast as we dropped. Soon all I made out were little streaks of phosphor that Tyug had smeared in vital spots around the cabin, such as the tips of my motor cranks, the depth gauge, and the ballast release levers. With nothing to do, I catalogued the odors assailing me from my friends. Familiar aromas, but never quite so pungent as now. And this was just the beginning.

A reason to be glad no human came along, I thought. One of many problems contributing to friction between urs and earthlings had been how each race *smelled* to the other. Even today, and despite the Great Peace, I don't figure either sept would much enjoy being cooped up in an oversized coffin with the other for very long.

Ur-ronn started calling out depths from the pressure-bladder gauge. At seven cables she turned a switch, and the eik light came on, casting twin beams into cool, dark waters. I expected those in front to resume their excited exclamations, but apparently there was less to see at this depth. Pincer identified something only every few duras, in a voice that seemed disappointed.

We all tensed at nine cables, since trouble had struck there the first time. But the milestone passed uneventfully. It should, since Uriel had inspected every hoof of the hawser personally.

At eleven and a half cables, a sudden chill swept the cabin, causing fog briefly to form. Every hard surface abruptly went damp and Huck cranked up the dehumidifier. I reached out to touch the garu-wood hull, which seemed markedly cooler. *Wuphon's Dream* turned and tilted slightly, facing a new tug, no longer the same languid downward drift. From soundings, we had known to expect a transition to a deep frigid current. Still, it was unnerving.

'Adjusting ballast for trim,' Huck announced. Closest to dead center, she used Uriel's clever pumps to shift water among three tanks till the spirit levels showed an even keel. That would be vital on reaching bottom, lest we topple over at the very moment of making history.

I thought about what we were doing. In Galactic terms, it was consummately primitive, of course. Earth history makes for much more flattering comparisons – which may be one reason we four find it so attractive. For instance, when Jules Verne was writing *Twenty Thousand Leagues Under the Sea*, no human had ever gone as far down into the oceans of Terra as we were heading today. We savages of Jijo.

Huck shouted – 'Look! Is that something down below?'

Those eyes of hers. Even peering past Pincer and Ur-ronn, she had glimpsed bottom first. Ur-ronn turned the eik beams and soon the three of them were back at it again, driving me crazy with oohs, ahs, and k-k-k-k wonderment clicks. In frustration I turned the crank, making the rear wheels thrash till they yelled at me to quit, and agreed to describe what they saw.

'There's a wavy kind of plant,' Pincer said, his voice no longer stuttering. 'And another kind that's all thin and skinny. Don't know how they live, with no light getting down here. There's lots of that kind, sort of waving about. And there are snaky trails in the mud, and some kind of weird fishes dodging in and out of the skinny plants ...'

After a bit more of that, I would've gladly gone back to wonderment clicks. But I kept quiet.

'... And there are some kurtle crabs – bright red and bigger than any I ever seen before! And what's that, Ur-ronn, a mudworm? You think so? What a mudworm! ... Hey, what's that thing? Is that a dro—'

Ur-ronn interrupted, 'Half a cavle to bottom. Signaling the surface crew to slow descent.'

Sharp electric sparks broke the cabin's darkness as she touched a contact key, sending coded impulses from our battery up an insulated strand, woven through the hawser. It took a few duras for the rumbling grumble of the deploying drums to change pitch as the brakes dug in. *Wuphon's Dream* jerked, giving us all a start. Huphu's claws raked my shoulder.

The descent slowed. It was specially agonizing for me, not knowing how much farther bottom lay, when we'd make contact, or with how much force. Naturally, nobody was confiding in good old Alvin!

'Hey, fellas,' Pincer resumed, 'I think I just saw—'

'Adjusting trim!' Huck announced, peering with one eye at each of the spirit levels.

'Refocusing the lights,' Ur-ronn added. 'Ziz shows one yellow tentacle to starvoard. Current flowing that direction, five knots.'

Pincer murmured – 'Fellas? I *thought* I just saw ... oh, never mind. Bottom appears to slope left, maybe twenty degrees.'

'Turning forward wheels to compensate,' Huck responded. 'Alvin, we may want a slow rearward crank on the driver wheels.'

That jerked me out of any resentful mood. 'Aye-aye,' I said, turning the zigzag bar in front of me, causing the rear set of wheels to rotate. At least I *hoped* they were responding. We wouldn't know for sure till we hit the ground.

'Here it comes,' Huck announced. And then, apparently recollecting her missed estimates during the trial run, she added – 'This time for sure. Brace yourselves!'

When I write about all this someday from these notes, perhaps I'll describe sudden billows of mud as we plowed into the ocean floor, gouging a long furrow, sending vegetation tumbling and blind subsea creatures fleeing in panic. Maybe I'll throw in fierce saltwater spray from a blown seal or two, tightened frantically by the heroic crew, in the nick of time.

What I probably *won't* admit in print is that I couldn't even tell the exact moment when our wheels touched down. The event was, well, more than a bit *murky*. Like sinking a probe fork into the rind of a shuro fruit and not being quite sure whether you've speared the core nut yet.

'Murky' also described the scene around us as slime-swirls spiraled, slowly settling to reveal a dead-black world, except down twin corridors of dazzling blue cast by the eiks. What I could see of those narrow tunnels showed a slanting plain of mud, broken here and there by pale slim-stemmed 'plants' that needed no sunlight to thrive, though I couldn't begin to guess what else they lived on. Their leaves or fronds seemed to wave back and forth, as if in a breeze. No animal life moved in our beams, which wasn't that surprising. Wouldn't we top-dwellers hide if some weird vessel plunged into our midst from above, casting forth both noise and a searing gaze?

Forcing the comparison, I wondered if any suboceanic locals thought *their* judgment day had just come.

With her telegraph key, Ur-ronn pulsed the message everyone above waited to hear. *We are down*, she sent. *All is well.*

Yes, it lacks the poetic imagery of flags planted, eagles landed, or infinitives boldly split. I shouldn't complain. Not all urs are born to recite epic sagas on demand. Still, I think I'll change it in rewrite – if I ever get the chance, which right now seems pretty unlikely.

Again, sparks jumped the tiny gap, this time without Ur-ronn touching it. A reply from above.

Welcome news. Proceed.

'Ready, Alvin?' Pincer called back. 'All ahead, one quarter.'

I responded – 'Ahead one quarter, aye, Captain.'

My back and arm muscles flexed. The crank seemed reluctant at first. Then I felt the magnetic clutch take hold – a strange sense of attachment to once-living g'Kek parts that I tried not thinking about. The special mud treads worked as I felt resistance. *Wuphon's Dream* shuddered forward.

I concentrated on maintaining a steady pace. Pincer shouted steering instructions at Huck while holding Uriel's map for reference. Ur-ronn correlated our bearing with her compass. The hawser and air hose resumed transmitting the distant rumble of deployer drums, unreeling more tether so we might wander ever farther from safety. The confined space resonated with my deep work umble, but no one complained. The sound wrapped itself around me till I felt encircled by hoonish shipmates, making the cramped confinement more bearable. Like a ship far at sea, we were all alone, dependent on Ifni's luck and our resourcefulness to make it home again.

Time passed. We fell into a rhythmic routine. I pushed, Huck steered, Ur-ronn aimed the headlights, and Pincer was pilot. Pretty soon, it began to feel like we were old hands at this.

Huck asked – 'What were you saying, Pincer, just before we landed? Something you saw?'

'Sonething with lots of *teeth*, I vet!' Ur-ronn teased. 'Isn't this just avout when we're suffosed to see nonsters?'

Monsters, I thought. My umble annexed a laugh-quaver.

Pincer took the teasing well. 'Give it time, chums. You never can tell when ... there! Over to the left; that's what I saw before!'

The *Dream* listed a bit as Huck and Ur-ronn leaned forward to look, causing the rear wheels to lose half their traction. 'Hey!' I complained.

'Well, I be despoked—' Huck murmured.

'And I vee drenched,' Ur-ronn added.

All right, so I whined a bit – 'Come *on*, you grass-fed bunch of sour-mulching—'

Just then the ground slanted a bit more, and my narrow tunnel view finally swept across the scene they'd all been staring at.

'Hr-rm-rm!' I exclaimed. 'So *that's* what got you all stirred up? A bunch of *dross coffins*?'

They lay scattered across the ocean floor, canted at all angles, many half buried in the mud. Scores of them. Mostly oblong and rectangular, though a few were barrel-shaped. Naturally, all traces had vanished of the ribbons that once bedecked them, honoring the bones or spindles or worn-out tools cast off by some earlier generation of sooners.

'But dross ships never come into the Rift,' Huck complained, pushing two stalks toward my face. 'Ain't that right, Alvin?'

I twisted to peer past her damn floating eyes.

'They don't. Still, the Rift is officially part of the Midden. Another section of the same down-sucking whatsit.'

'A tectonic suvduction zone,' Ur-ronn put in.

'Yeah, thanks. So it's a perfectly legal place to dump dross.'

'But if no ships come, how did it get here?'

I was trying to make out which kinds of coffins were present and which were missing. That could help pin down when the spill had been made. There were no human-style chests or urrish reed baskets, which wasn't surprising. So far I'd only seen g'Kek and qheuenish work, which could make the site pretty darn old.

'The cartons arrived the same way we did, Huck,' I explained. 'Somebody dumped them off the cliff at Terminus Rock.'

Huck gasped. She started to speak, then paused, and I could almost hear wheels turning in her head. Dumping from land just isn't done. But she must have already reasoned that this place was an acceptable exception. If a portion of the Midden really did pass right underneath Terminus Rock, and assuming there must have once been settlements nearby, this would have been a cheaper way of burying Grandpa than sending his coffin out to sea by boat.

'But then how did the boxes get so far from land? We've come cables and cables by now.'

'Tides, mudslides,' Pincer answered. But I rumbled negation.

'You forget how the Midden's supposed to work. It *sucks* stuff *in*, isn't that right, Ur-ronn?'

Ur-ronn whistled despair over my insistent oversimplifying. She motioned with two hands. 'One tectonic flate slides under the other, you see, creating a trench and drawing old sea floor along with it.'

'To be dragged underground, melted, and renewed, pushing underneath the Slope and making volcanoes. Yeah, I get it.' Huck turned all four stalks forward, pensively. 'Hundreds of years since these were dumped, and the dross has only come this far from where it fell?'

Only few seconds ago, she had been amazed by how *great* a distance the crates had come from the cliff! I guess it goes to show how different time can seem, when you shift from the perspective of a person's lifetime to the life cycles of a world. In comparison, I don't suppose humans have much to brag about, living twice as long as urs. We're all bound for Jijo's slow digestion soon enough, whether or not alien invaders leave us alone.

Pincer and Ur-ronn consulted their maps, and shortly we were under way again, leaving that boneyard where another generation of sinners made their slow way toward pardon in melted stone.

About half a midura later, with a sense of great relief, we found Uriel's 'jack.'

By that time my arms and legs ached from row-boating the crank handle at least a couple of thousand times, responding to Pincer's insistent commands of '*speed up!*' or '*slow down!*' or '*can't you go any faster?*' Of the four of us, he alone seemed to be enjoying himself, without any qualms or physical ague.

We hoon elect our captains, then obey without question while any sort of emergency is going on – and this whole voyage qualified in my mind as a screaming emergency – so I tucked away any resentment for later, when I pictured getting even with Pincer in many colorful ways. Maybe the gang's next project *should* be a hot-air balloon. Make him the first qheuen to fly since they gave up starships. It'd serve him right.

By the time Huck finally yelled 'Eureka!' my poor muscles and pivots felt as if we'd covered the entire width of the Rift, and then some. My first relieved thought was – *No wonder Uriel provided so much hawser and hose!*

Only after that did I wonder – *How did she know where to tell us to look for this jeekee thing?*

It stood half buried in the mud, about twelve cables south of where we first touched down. Judging from the portion that was visible from my 'vantage point' way in back, it consisted of long spikes, each pointed outward in a different direction, as if aimed toward the six faces of a cube. Each spike had a big knob at the end, hollow I guessed, to prevent sinking in the muck. It was obviously meant to be found, being colored a garish swirl of reds and blues. Red to really stand out at short range, since the color's almost totally absent underwater, and blue to be visible from farther away, if your beam happened to sweep across it in the deep darkness. Even so, you had to be within less than a cable to see the thing, so we'd never have come across it without Uriel's instructions. Still, it took two search spirals before we stumbled on the jack.

It was the strangest thing any of us had ever encountered. And don't forget, I've heard a g'Kek umble and witnessed a traeki vlen.

'Is it Buyur-uyur?' Pincer asked, superstitious awe invading his voice vents, along with a returned stammer.

'I bet a pile of donkey mulch *that's* not Buyur-made,' Huck said. 'What do you think, Ur-ronn?'

Our urs pal stretched her neck past Pincer, her muzzle drying a patch of the bubble window. 'No way the Vuyur would've vuilt anything so frightful-ghastly,' she agreed. 'It's not their style.'

'Of *course* it's not their style,' Huck continued. 'But I know whose it is.'

We all stared at her. Naturally, she milked the moment, pausing till we were on the verge of pummeling her.

'It's *urrish*,' she concluded with a tone of smug conviction.

'Urrish!' Pincer hissed. 'How can you be so—'

'Exflain,' Ur-ronn demanded, snaking her head to peer at Huck. 'This ovject is sophisticated. Uriel could forge nothing like it. Not even Earthlings have such craft.'

'Exactly! It's not Buyur, and no one currently living on the Slope could make it. That leaves just one possibility. It must have been left here by an original sooner starship, when one of the Six Races – seven if you include glavers – first arrived on Jijo, before the settlers scuttled their craft and joined the rest of us as primitives. But *which* one left it? I'd eliminate us g'Keks on account of we've been here so long that I'll bet the jack would've moved a lot farther into the Rift by now. The same probably holds for glavers, qheuens, and traeki.

'Anyway, the clincher is that Uriel knew exactly where to find it!'

Fur riffled around the rim of Ur-ronn's nostril. Her voice turned colder than the surrounding ocean. 'You suggest a conspiracy.'

g'Kek stalks twined, a shrug.

'Not a horribly vile one,' Huck assured. 'Maybe just a sensible precaution.

'Think about it, mates. Say you've come to plant a sooner colony on a forbidden world. You must get rid of anything that'd show on a casual scan by some Institute surveyor, so your ship and complex gear have to go. Nearby space is no good. That's the first place cops'd check. So you sink it amid all the stuff the Buyur dumped when they left Jijo. Sounds good so far.

'But then you ask yourself – what if an unforeseen emergency crops up? What if someday your descendants need something high-tech to help 'em survive?'

Ur-ronn lowered her conical head. In the dimness I could not tell if it denoted worry or rising anger. I hurried to cut in.

'Hr-rm. You imply a long view of things. A secret kept for generations.'

'For centuries,' Huck agreed. 'Uriel no doubt was told by her master, and so on back to the first urrish ancestors. And before Ur-ronn snaps one of my heads off, let me rush to add that the urs sages showed great restraint over the years, never seeking to use this cache during their wars with qheuens, then humans, even when they were getting their tails whipped.'

That was meant to calm Ur-ronn? I rushed to save Huck from mutilation. 'Perhaps – hrm – humans and qheuens had their own caches, so there was a standoff.' Then my own words sank in. 'Maybe those caches are being sought now, while we serve as Uriel's dipping claw, in search of this one.'

There was a long silence.

Then Pincer spoke.

'Sheesh-eesh-eesh. Those aliens up at the Glade must really have the grown-ups spooked.'

Another pause, then Huck resumed. 'That's what I'm *hoping* all of this is about. The aliens. A mutual effort of the Six, pooling resources, and not something else.'

Ur-ronn's neck twisted nervously. 'What do you mean?'

'I mean, I'd have liked Uriel's word of honor that we're down here seeking powers for the defense of *all* the Commons.'

Not simply to arm urrish militia, in some of the grudge fights we've heard rumors about, I thought, finishing Huck's implication. There was a tense moment when I could not predict what would happen next. Had tension, worry, and Tyug's drugs strung our urrish friend to the point where Huck's baiting would make her snap?

Ur-ronn's neck slowly untwisted. An effort of will, I saw by the dim light of the phosphors. 'You have ...' she began, breathing heavily. 'You have the oath of *this* urs, that it will ve so.'

And she repeated the vow in Galactic Two, following it with a laborious effort to *spit* on the floor, not an easy act for one of her kind. A sign of sincerity.

'Hr-rm, well, that's great,' I said, umbling for peace. 'Not that any of us ever thought any different. Right, Huck? Pincer?'

Both of them hurried to agree, and some of the tension passed. Underneath, however, seeds of worry had been laid. *Huck*, I thought, *you'd bring a jar full of scorpions in a lifeboat, then drop it just to see who swims the best*.

We got under way again and soon were near enough to see how big the jack really was. Each of the bulbous balloonlike things at its spiky tips was larger than *Wuphon's Dream*. 'There's one of the cables Uriel talked about,' Pincer announced, waving a claw toward one spike, from which a glossy black strand made a relatively straight line, though buried in places, aimed north, in the direction we had come.

'I bet anything that line's broken somewhere tween here and the cliffs,' Huck ventured. 'Prob'ly used to go all the way to some secret cleft or cave near Terminus Rock. From there the cache might've been hauled in without an urs ever having to get her hooves wet. That end point may've gotten cut in an avalanche or quake, like the one that killed my folks. This jack thing is a backup, so the cord can be picked up again, even if the first end point is lost.'

'Good thinking. It does explain one thing that had me puzzled – why Uriel had so much equipment on hand. Stuff that proved so useful for diving. In fact, it makes me wonder why she needed us at all. Why didn't she have a hidden bathy of her own in the first place?'

Ur-ronn was getting over her funk. 'A g'Kek accountant inventories the forge warehouse regularly. He'd notice anything as un-urrish as a *suvnarine*, just lying around, ready to ve used.'

Her voice was sarcastic. Yet Huck agreed.

'The difficult parts were there, the pumps and valves and gaskets. I'm sure Uriel and her predecessors figured they could whip up a hull and the rest in a matter of months. Who ever expected an emergency to strike so quick? Besides, we bunch of crazy kids offered a perfect cover story. No one will associate us with god-caches from the Galactic past.'

'I prefer to think,' Pincer interjected, with a dramatically miffed tone of voice, 'that the real reason Uriel begged pretty-please to be allowed to join our team was the superior design and craftsmanship of our ship-hip.'

We quit bickering to stare at him for a moment – then laughter filled the tiny cabin, making the hull vibrate and waking Huphu from her nap.

The four of us felt better then, ready to get on with the mission. The hard part was over, it appeared. All we had to do now was order Ziz to attach a clamp to the cord on the jack's other side and signal Uriel to haul away. There would then be a long wait while we slowly rose up toward the surface, since g'Keks and urs are even more likely than humans to get the bends if air pressure changes too rapidly. From books we knew it's an awful way to die, so a tedious ascent was an accepted necessity. We had all packed snacks, as well as personal articles to help pass the time.

Still, I was anxious to get on with it. Claustrophobia was nothing compared with the ordeal that would commence when everyone onboard – each in his or her unique way – started feeling the need to go, as some Earthling books politely put it, 'to the bathroom.'

There would be, it seemed, one slight difficulty in clamping onto the second cord.

We saw the problem at once, upon rolling around to look at the jack's other side.

The second cord was missing.

Or rather, it had been *cut*. Fresh-looking metal fibers waved gently in the subsea currents, hanging like an unbraided urrish trail from one of the jack's spiky ends.

Nor was that all. When Ur-ronn cast our beams across the ocean floor, we saw a wavy trail in the mud, meandering south, in which direction the cord apparently had been dragged. None of us knew how to tell if this was done days, or jaduras, or years ago. But the word *recent* came to mind. No one had to say it aloud.

Electric sparks flashed as Ur-ronn reported the situation to those waiting in the world of air and light. Surprise was evident in a long delay. Then an answer came back down, crackling pulses across the tiny spark gap.

If in good health, follow trail for two cables, then report.

Huck muttered. 'As if we've got any choice, with Uriel controlling the winch. Like a little case of narcosis or the cramp-jitters would make a difference to her?'

This time, Ur-ronn didn't turn around, but both tails switched Huck's torso sharply, just below the neckline.

'Ahead one half, Alvin,' Pincer commanded. With a sigh, I bent over to begin again.

So we set forth, keeping one beam focused on the snake-trail through the mud, while Ur-ronn cast the other searchlight left and right, up and down. Not that seeing a threat in advance would give us any kind of useful warning. There was never a vessel as unarmed, slow, and helpless as *Wuphon's Dream*. That severed cord we had seen – it had been made by beings using Galactic technology, intended to survive millennia underwater and still retain immense strength. Whatever had sliced it apart wasn't anything I wanted to make angry.

A deeper, more solemn mood filled the cabin as we crept onward. After cranking for more than a midura against the ever-changing traction of slippery muck, my arms and back were starting to feel the stinging tingle of second-stage fatigue. I was too tired to umble. Behind me, Huphu expressed her boredom by rummaging through my backpack, tearing open a package of pish fish sandwiches, nibbling part of it and scattering the rest through the bilge. Splashing noises and a wet tickling on my toe-pads told of water accumulating down there – whether from excess humidity, or some slow leak, or our own disgusting wastes, I didn't care to guess. The aroma inside was starting to get both complex and pretty damn ripe. I was fighting another onset of confinement dread when Pincer let out a shrill yell.

'Alvin, stop! Back up! I mean engines back full!'

I wish I could report that I saw what caused this outburst, but my view was blocked by frenzied silhouettes. Besides, I had my hands full fighting the momentum of the crank, which seemed determined to keep turning in the same direction despite me, driving the wheels ever forward. I held the wooden rods in a strangle grip and heaved with all my might, feeling something pop in my spine. Finally, I managed to slow the axles, then at last bring them to a stop. But for all my grunting effort, I could not make them turn the other way.

'I'm getting a list!' Huck announced. 'Tilting forward and to port.'

'I didn't see it coming!' Pincer cried out. 'We were climbing a little hill, then it just came out of nowhere, I swear!'

Now I could feel the tilt. The *Dream* was definitely tipping forward even as Huck frantically pumped ballast aft. The eik beams seemed to flail around the darkness up ahead, offering an unsettling view of yawning emptiness where before there had been a gently sloping plain.

I finally managed to get the crank turning backward, but any sense of victory was short-lived. One of the magnetic clutches – attached to a wheel salvaged from Huck's aunt, I believe – gave way. The remaining roller bit hard into the mud, with the effect of abruptly slewing us sideways.

The beams now swung *along* the lip of the precipice we were poised upon. Apparently, what we had thought was the main floor of the Rift had been but a shelf along the outskirts of the *actual* trench. The true gash now gaped, ready to receive us, as it had received so many other things that would never again partake in affairs up where stars glittered bright.

So many dead things, and we were about to join them.

'Shall I cut ballast?' Huck asked, frantically. 'I can cut ballast. Pull the signal cord to have Ziz inflate. I can do it! Shall I do it?'

I reached out and took two eyestalks, gently stroking them in the calming way I had learned over the years. She wasn't making any sense. The weight of all the steel hawser we trailed was greater than a few bricks slung under the belly of *Wuphon's Dream*. If we cut the hawser too, we might rise all right. But then what would keep the air hose from tangling and snapping as we spun and tumbled? Even if it miraculously survived, unsnarled, we would shoot up like the bullet-ship in Verne's *First Men in the Moon*. Even Pincer would probably die of the bends.

More practical with death looming before us, Ur-ronn fired off rapid spark-pulses, telling Uriel to yank us home without delay. Good idea. But how long would it take, I wondered, for the crew above to haul in all the slack? How fast could they do it without risking a crimp in the air hose? How far might we fall before two opposite pulls met in a sudden jerk? That moment of truth would be when we discovered just how well we'd built the *Dream*.

Helplessly, I felt the wheels lose contact with the muddy shelf as our brave little bathy slid over the edge, starting a long languid fall into darkness.

That, I guess, would be a nice, dramatic place to end a chapter, with our heroes tumbling into the black depths. A true-to-life cliff hanger.

Will the crew ever make it home again?

Will they survive?

Yeah, that'd make a good stopping point. What's more, I'm tired and hurting. I need to call for help, so I can make it to the bucket in the corner of this dank place and get some relief.

But I won't stop there. I know a better place, just a bit farther down the stream of time, as *Wuphon's Dream* slowly fell, rotating round and round, and we watched the eik beams sweep a cliff face that rose beside us like the wall of an endless tomb. Our tomb.

We dropped half of our ballast, which helped slow the plunge – till a current yanked ahold of the *Dream*, dragging us faster. We dropped the remainder but knew our sole chance lay in Uriel reacting perfectly, and then a hundred other things working better than there was any hope of them working.

Each of us was coming to terms with death in our own way, alone, facing the approaching end of our personal drama.

I missed my parents. I mourned along with them, for my loss was in many ways as bitter to me as it would be to them, though I wouldn't have to endure for years the sorrow they'd carry, on account of my foolish need for adventure. I stroked and umbled Huphu, while Ur-ronn whistled a plains lament and Huck drew all four eyes together, looking inward, I supposed, at her life.

Then, out of nowhere, Pincer shouted a single word that overrode the keening of our fears. A word we had heard from his vents before, too many times, but never quite like this. Never with such tones of awe and wonder.

'*Monsters-ers-ers!*' he yelled.

Then, with rising terror and joy, he cried it out again.

'*Monsters!*'

No one has come to answer my call. I'm stuck lying here with a back that won't bend and a terrible need for that bucket. My pencil is worn down and I'm almost out of paper ... so while I'm waiting I might as well push on to the *real* dramatic moment of our fall.

All was confusion inside *Wuphon's Dream* as we plunged toward our doom. We tumbled left and right, banging against the inner hull, against cranks, handles, levers, and each other. The view outside, when I could see past my wildly gesturing comrades, was a jumbled confusion of phosphorescent dots caught in the eik beams, plus occasional glimpses of a rising cliff face, and then quick flashes of something else.

Something – or *some things* – lustrous and gray. Agile, flitting movements. Then curious strokings, rubbing our vessel's hull, followed by sharp raps and bangs all along the flanks of our doomed boat.

Pincer kept babbling about monsters. I honestly thought he'd gone crazy, but Ur-ronn and Huck had changed their wailing cries and were leaning toward the glass, as if transfixed by what they saw. It was all so noisy, and Huphu was clawing my aching backside between frenzied attacks on the walls.

I felt sure I made out Huck saying something like—

'*What – or who – could they possibly be?*'

That's when the whirling shapes divided, vanishing to both sides as a *new* entity arrived, causing us all to gasp.

It was huge, many times the size of our bathy, and it swam with easy grace, emitting a growl as it came. From my agonizing prison at the back, I could not make out much except two great eyes that seemed to shine far brighter than our failing eik beams.

And its mouth. I recall seeing *that* all too well, as it spread wide, rushing to meet us.

The hull groaned, and there were more sharp bangs. Ur-ronn yelped as a needle spray of water jetted inward, ricocheting back at me.

Numb with fear, I could not stop my whirling brain long enough to have a single clear thought, only a storm of notions.

These were *Buyur ghosts*, I guessed, come to punish living fools who dared invade their realm.

They were *machines*, cobbled together from relics and remnants that had tumbled into the Rift since long before the Buyur, in epochs so old, even the Galactics no longer recalled.

They were home-grown sea monsters. Jijo's own. Products of the world's most private place.

These and other fancies flashed through my muddled brain as I watched, unable to look away from those terrible onrushing jaws. The *Dream* buffeted and bucked – in sea currents, I now suppose, but at the time it felt she was struggling to get away.

The jaws swept around us. A sudden surge brought us hurtling to one side. We hit the interior of the great beast's mouth, crashing with such force that the beautiful glass bubble *cracked*. Frosted patterns spread from the point of impact. Ur-ronn wailed, and Huck rolled her eyestalks tight, like socks, going in a drawer.

I grabbed Huphu, ignoring her tearing claws, and took a deep breath of stale air. It was awful stuff, but I figured it would be my last chance.

The window gave up at the same moment the air hose snapped.

The dark waters of the Rift found their rapid way into our shattered ship.

XXIV

THE BOOK OF THE SLOPE

Legends

It took twenty years to recover the first human band of sooners — a sizeable group who fled to the scrublands south of the Vale, rejecting the Covenant of Exile that their leaders had signed, just before the *Tabernacle* went tumbling to the depths. They risked both desolation and the law in order to get away, and had to be dragged back, shuddering in dread, all because they could not bring themselves to trust hoon or *traeki.*

In retrospect this seems so ironic, since it was qheuens and urs who caused human settlers grief during two subsequent centuries of war. Why then did so many earthlings fear the peaceful ringed ones, or our cheerful friends with the broad shoulders and booming voices? The star-cousins of both traeki and hoon must have seemed quite different when our ancestors' first starships emerged onto the lanes of Galaxy Four.

Unfortunately, most galactology records burned in the Great Fire. But other accounts tell of relentless hostility by mighty, enigmatic star-lords calling themselves Jophur, who took a leading role in the *Sequestration of Mudaun.* That fearsome atrocity led directly to the *Tabernacle* exodus — an outrage executed with single-minded precision and utter resoluteness. Traits not often observed in traeki here on the Slope.

It is also said that *hoon* were at Mudaun, portrayed in the accounts as dour, officious, unhappy beings. A race of stern accountants, dedicated to population control and tabulating the breeding rates of other races, un-swayed by appeals to mercy or forbearance.

Could anyone recognize, in these descriptions, the two most easygoing members of the Six?

No wonder hoon and traeki seem the least prone to nostalgia about 'good old days,' back when they flew about as gods of space.

—Annals of the Jijoan Commons

SARA

With dawn bleaching the eastern sky, weary travelers trudged into Uryutta's Oasis after a long night march across the parched Warril Plain – a teeming, thirsty crowd of donkeys and simlas, humans and hoon. Even urrish pilgrims stepped daintily to the muddy shore and dipped their narrow heads, wincing at the bitter, unmasked taste of plain water.

Full summer had broken over the high steppe, when hot winds ignited rings of circle grass, sending herds stampeding amid clouds of dust. Even before the present crisis, wayfarers avoided the summer sun, preferring the cool moonlight for travel. Urrish guides bragged they would know the plain blindfolded.

That's fine for them, Sarah thought, swishing her aching feet in the oasis spring. *An urs doesn't fall on her face when a chance stone turns underfoot. Me, I like to see where I'm going.*

Predawn light revealed mighty outlines to the east. *The Rimmers*, Sara thought. The mixed-race expedition was making good time, hurrying to reach the Glade before events there reached a climax. On the plus side, she was anxious to see her brothers, and to learn how well Bloor was implementing her idea. There might also be medical help for her ward, the Stranger, if it seemed safe to reveal him to the aliens. A big if. Nor had she quite given up on getting to see one of the fabled library consoles of the Great Galactics.

Yet there was also much to fear. If the star-gods did plan on wiping out all witnesses, it would surely start at the Glade. Above all, Sara worried that she might be taking the Stranger into the hands of his enemies. The dark, ever-cheerful man seemed eager to go, but did he really understand what was involved?

A whistling sigh fluted from Pzora's corrugated cone, as the traeki siphoned water from the pond, fatigued despite having ridden all the way in a donkey-drawn chariot. A new rewq draped across Pzora's sensor ring, one of two Sara had bought from the fresh supply at Kandu Landing, to help the traeki pharmacist treat the wounded alien, even though she wasn't keen on the symbionts herself.

A chain of bubbles broke the surface near Sara's foot. By Loocen's silver light, she made out *Blade*, from Dolo Village, resting underwater. The hasty trek had been hard on red qheuens, and blues like Blade, as well as those humans too big to burden a donkey. Sara had been allowed to mount every even-numbered midura. Even so, her body ached. *Serves me right for leading a book-ish, cloistered life*, she thought.

A raucous cheer rose up where urrish donkey-drivers piled grass and dung to make a campfire. Simla blood was drained into a tureen, followed by chopped meat, and soon they were slurping tepid sanguinary stew, lifting their long necks to swallow, then bending for more – sinuous silhouettes whose rise and fall was eerily accompanied by the Stranger's plinking dulcimer. Meanwhile a hoon cook, proud of her multirace cuisine, banged pots and sprinkled powders until spicy aromas finally overcame the stench of roast simla, restoring even Sara's queasy appetite.

A little while later, full dawn revealed stunning tan-and-green mountains towering across the eastern horizon. The Stranger laughed as he worked shirtless, helping Sara and the other humans do a typical camp-chore assigned to earthlings – erecting shelters of g'Kek blur cloth, to shade travelers and beasts through the blazing day. The star-man's muteness seemed no handicap at working with others. His pleasure at being alive affected all those around him, as he taught the others a wordless song to help pass the time.

Two more days, Sara thought, glancing up toward the pass. *We're almost there*.

The oasis was named for a nomad warrior who had lived soon after urrish settlement on Jijo, when their numbers were still small, and their planet-bound crafts pitifully crude. In those olden times, Uryutta fled east from the rich grazing lands of Znunir, where her tribal chiefs had vowed fealty to mighty Gray Queens. Uryutta led her fellow rebels to this wadi in the vast dry plain, to nurse their wounds and plot a struggle for freedom from qheuen dominance.

Or so went the legend Sara heard that afternoon, after sleeping through the hottest part of the day – a slumber during which she had dreamed vaguely of water, cool and clear, raising a terrible thirst. She slaked it at the spring, then rejoined the other travelers under the big tent for another meal.

With a few hours still to go before dusk, and a leaden heat still pressing outside, tinkers and pack-handlers gathered around a story-teller, accompanying her recital with foot-stamps and switched braided tails. Even after gaining books and printing, urs still loved the oral tradition, its extravagance and impromptu variations. When the bard's chant reached the Battle of Znunir Trading Post, elongated heads swayed together. Triplet eyes stared past the poet toward times gone by.

*

So the traitor cavalry scattered
Willing slaves, the cowards were driven
Into the trap Uryutta had fashioned
Tumbling screaming through Deep Stink Crevasse
There to mix sulfurous death smells
With their own dry-pouch, death-fearing rankness.

Listeners hissed contempt for gutless renegades. Sara pulled out her notebook and took notes on the antiquated story-telling dialect, already devolved from GalTwo, long before humans came.

Then wheeled Uryutta, ready to confront
The dread footmen of gray qheuen matrons
Males in armor, males with weapons
Of sharp-edged hardwood, flashing so brightly
And clattering claws, keen to tear hide,
Poised now to flay us in shreds for their mothers.

This time the urs listeners vented repeated low grunts, marking respect for a tough foe, a sound humans first heard the third generation after arriving, when Earthlings won their own place in the pre-Commons chaos.

Now is the time! Our chief gives the signal.
Bring forth the weapons, tools newly fashioned.
Bring forth the longsticks, come forth you strongbacks.
Stab now to miss, but stab hard below!
Bear now the burden. Bear it, you strongbacks!
Heave! Claws a-flashing, over they go!

At first Sara had trouble following the action. Then she understood Uryutta's combat innovation – using 'long-sticks,' or rods of boo, to tip over the invincible qheuen infantry. Urrish volunteers served as living fulcrums, braving snapping claws and crushing weight while their fellows heaved, toppling one qheuen after another.

Despite the ecstatic song of vengeful slaughter, Sara knew the historical Uryutta's victories had been shortlived, as qheuens adjusted their tactics. It took a later breed of heroes – the warrior smiths of Blaze Mountain – to finally drive gray tyrants off the high plains. And still the queens thwarted the rising Commons, until humans brought new-old skills to the art of war.

Not all the urs were celebrating past glories. The caravan chief and her aides knelt on a peko-skin rug, planning the next trek.

From their gestures over a map, they clearly meant to skip the next oasis and make a hard dash for the foothills by sunrise.

Oh, my aching feet, Sara thought.

The chief raised her conical head, hissing as one human pilgrim neared a tent flap.

'Got to go,' explained Top, the Dolo tree farmer.

'What, leaking again? Are you ill?'

Jop had spent most of the journey immersed in a copy of the Scroll of Exile, but now he seemed affable. He laughed. 'Oh, no. I jest drank too much lovely spring water. Time to give it back to Jijo. That's all.'

While the flap was briefly up, Sara glimpsed bubbles in the pond again. Blade was back under, soaking for the next hard march. Was he also blocking out the storyteller's victory paean over defeated qheuens?

The flap fell, and Sara looked around the pavilion-shelter.

Kurt the Exploser used a compass to draw loopy arcs on sheets of graph paper, growling over his labors, making a papermaker's daughter wince as he crumpled one sheet after another in frustration. Nearer to Sara, *Prity* also drew abstract figures, more economically, in a patch of sand. Pulling at her furry chin, she consulted a topology text Sara had brought from Biblos.

My, what an intellectual caravan, Sara observed sardonically. *A would-be priest, a designer of things that go bang, a geometrical chimpanzee, and a fallen mathematician, all hurrying toward possible destruction. And that just begins our list of oddities.*

Over to the left, the Stranger had set aside his dulcimer to watch Kurt's nephew, young Jomah, play a game of *Tower of Haiphong* with a red-qheuen salt peddler, a pair of Biblos librarians, and three hoonish pilgrims. The contest involved moving colored rings over a hexagonal array of posts, stuck in the sand. The goal was to pile a stack of rings on your Home Post in the right order, largest at the bottom, smallest on top. In the advanced game, where ring colors and patterns signified *traeki* attributes, one must wed various traits to form an ideal traeki.

Pzora seemed more entranced by the storyteller than the game. Sara had never heard of a traeki taking offense at *Tower of Haiphong*, even though it mimicked their unique mode of reproduction.

'See here?' the boy explained the game to the Stranger. 'So far I got swamp flippers, a mulching core, two memory rings, a Sniffer, a Thinker, and a Looker.'

The star-human showed no sign of frustration by Jomah's rapid speech. He watched the apprentice exploser with an expression of intelligent interest – perhaps he heard Jomah's warbling voice as something like musical notes.

'I'm hoping for a better base, to let my traeki move around on land. But Horm-tuwoa snatched a walker torus I had my eye on, so it looks like I'm stuck with flippers.'

The hoon to the boy's left crooned a low umble of gratification. You had to think fast, playing *Tower of Haiphong*.

'Build me a dream house, oh my dear,
  fourteen stories high.
Basement, kitchen, bedroom, bath,
  I'll love you till I die.'

Jomah and the others all stopped what they were doing to stare at the Stranger, who rocked back and laughed.

He's getting better at this, Sara thought. Still, it seemed eerie whenever the star-man came up with the verse to some song, perfectly apropos to what was going on at the time.

With a glitter in his eye, the Stranger waited till the other players were engrossed once more in their own stacks. Then he nudged Jomah, covertly pointing out a game piece ready to draw from the reserve box. The boy stared at the rare torus called *Runner*, trying so hard to stifle a yelp of joy that he coughed, while the dark alien patted him on the back.

Now how did he know that? Do they play Tower of Haiphong, *among the stars?* She had pictured space-gods doing – well, *godlike* things. It was encouraging to think they might use games with simple pieces – hard, durable symbols of life.

Of course, most games are based on there being winners ... and losers.

The audience hissed appreciatively as the bard finished her epic and left the low platform to accept her reward, a steaming cup of blood. *Too bad I missed the end*, Sara thought. But she would likely hear it again, if the world lasted beyond this year.

When no one else seemed about to take the stage, several urs stretched and started drifting toward the nearest tent flap, to go outside and check their animals, preparing for tonight's trek. But they stopped when a fresh volunteer abruptly leaped up, clattering hooves on the dais. The new storyteller was *Ulgor*, the tinker who had accompanied Sara ever since the night the aliens passed above Dolo Village. Listeners regathered around as Ulgor commenced reciting her tale in a dialect even older than the one before.

Ships fill your thoughts   right now,
Fierce, roaming   silently,
Ships fill your dreams   right now,
Far from all   watery seas.

Ships cloud your   mind-scape now,
Numberless   hordes of them,
Ships dwarf *your*   mind-scape now,
Than mountains,   vasterfar.

A mutter of consternation. The caravan chief corkscrewed her long neck. This was a rare topic, widely thought in poor taste, among mixed-races. Several hoonish pilgrims turned to watch.

Ships of the   Urrish-ka
Clan of strong   reverence.
Ships of the   Urrish host,
Clan bound for   vengeance!

Bad taste or no, a tale under way was sacrosanct till complete. The commander flared her nostril to show she had no part in this breach, while Ulgor went on evoking an era long before urs colonists ever set hoof on Jijo. To a time of space armadas, when god-fleets fought over incomprehensible doctrines, using weapons of unthinkable power.

Stars fill your thoughts   right now.
Ships large as   mountain peaks,
Setting stars   quivering,
With planet-sized   lightings.

Sara wondered – *why is she doing this?* Ulgor had always been tactful, for a young urs. Now she seemed out to *provoke* a reaction.

Hoon sauntered closer, air sacs puffing, still more curious than angry. It wasn't yet clear that Ulgor meant to dredge up archaic vendettas – grudges so old they made later, Jijo-based quarrels with qheuens and men seem like tiffs over this morning's breakfast.

On Jijo, urs and hoon share no habitats and few desires. No basis for conflict. It's hard to picture their ancestors slaughtering each other in space.

Even the *Tower of Haiphong* game was abandoned. The Stranger watched Ulgor's undulating neck movements, keeping tempo with his right hand.

Oh ye, native	*listeners*
So-smugly	*ignorant,*
Planet-bound minds,	*dare you*
Try to	*conceive?*
Of planet-like	*holes in space,*
In which dwell	*entities,*
That planet-bound	*minds like yours*
Cannot	*perceive?*

Several hoon umbled relief. Perhaps this *wasn't* about archaic struggles between their forebears and the urs. Some space-epics told of awesome vistas, or sights baffling to modern listeners, reminders of what the Six had lost, but might regain someday – ironically, by forgetting.

Cast back your	*dread-filled thoughts,*
To those ships,	*frigidly,*
Cruising toward	*glory's gate,*
Knowing not	*destiny.*

If the first bard had been ardent, chanting bloody glory, Ulgor was coolly charismatic, entrancing listeners with her bobbing head and singsong whistle, evoking pure essences of color, frost, and fear. Sara put her notebook down, spellbound by vistas of glare and shadow, by vast reaches of spacetime, and shining vessels more numerous than stars. No doubt the yarn had grown in retelling, countless times. Even so, it filled Sara's heart with sudden jealousy.

We humans never climbed so high before our fall. Even at our greatest, we never possessed fleets of mighty star-ships. We were wolflings. Crude by comparison.

But that thought slipped away as Ulgor spun her rhythmic chant, drawing out glimpses of infinity. A portrait took shape, of a great armada bound for glorious war, which fate lured near a dark region of space. A niche, mysterious and deadly, like the bitter hollows of a mulc-spider's lair. A place wise travelers skirted, but not the admiral of this fleet. Steeped in her own invincibility, she plotted a course to fall on her foes, dismissing all thought of detour.

Now from one	*black kernel,*
Spirals out	*fortune's bane,*
Casting its	*trap across,*
Throngs of	*uneasy stars . . .*

*

With a sudden jerk, Sara's attention was yanked back to the present by a hard tug on her right arm. She blinked. *Prity* gripped her elbow, tight enough to grow painful – until Sara asked – 'What is it?'

Letting go, her chimp consort signed.

Listen. Now!

Sara was about to complain – *That's what I was doing, listening* – then realized Prity did not mean the story. So she tried to sift past Ulgor's mesmerizing drone ... and finally picked up a low mutter coming from *outside* the pavilion.

The animals. Something's upsetting them.

The simlas and donkeys had their own camouflaged shelter, a short distance away. Judging from a slowly rising murmur, the beasts weren't exactly frightened, but they weren't happy, either.

The Stranger also noticed, along with a couple of librarians and a red qheuen, all of them backing away, looking around nervously.

By now the caravan chief had joined the crowd of rising-falling urrish heads, lost in a distant place and time. Sara moved forward to nudge the expedition leader – carefully, since startled urs were known to snap – but all at once the chief's neck went rigid of its own accord, anxious tremors rippling her tawny mane. With a hiss, the urs matron roused two assistants, yanking a third back to reality with a sharp nip to the flank. All four stood and began trotting toward the tent flap—

—then skittered to a halt as phantom *shapes* began rising along the shelter's western edge – shadowy centauroid outlines, creeping stealthily, bearing spiky tools. A dismayed screech escaped one of the caravan-lieutenants, just before chaos exploded on all sides.

The audience burst into confusion. Grunts and whistling cries spilled from stunned pilgrims as the tent was ripped in a dozen places by flashing blades. War-painted fighters stepped through the gaps, leveling swords, pikes, and arbalests, all tipped with bronze-colored Buyur metal, driving the churned mass of frightened travelers back toward the ash pit at the center.

Prity's arms clasped Sara's waist while young Jomah clung to her other side. She wrapped an arm around the boy, for whatever comfort it might offer.

Urrish militia? she wondered. These warriors looked nothing like the dun-colored cavalry that performed showy maneuvers for Landing Day festivals. Slashes of sooty color streaked their flanks and withers. Their weaving, nodding heads conveyed crazed resolve.

A caravan-lieutenant bolted toward the stand where weapons were kept, mostly to ward off liggers, khoobras, or the occasional small band of thieves. The trail boss shouted in vain as the young urs dove for a loaded arbalest – and kept going, toppling through the stand and skidding along a trail of sizzling blood. She tumbled to a stop, riddled with darts, at the feet of a painted raider.

The expedition leader cursed the intruders, deriding their courage, their ancestry, and especially her own complacency. Despite rumors about trouble in far corners of the plains, peacetime habits were hard to break, especially along the main trail. Now her brave young colleague had paid the price.

'*What do you want?*' she demanded in GalTwo. '*Do you have a leader? Show her (criminal) muzzle, if she dares to speak!*'

The tent flap nearest the oasis lifted, and a burly urrish warrior entered, painted in jagged patterns that made it hard to grasp her outline. The raider chieftain high-stepped delicately over the lieutenant's bloody trail, cantering to a halt just before the caravan commander. Surprisingly, both of her brood-pouches were full, one with a husband whose slim head peered under the fighter's arm. The other pouch was blue and milk-veined, bulging with unfledged offspring.

A full matron was not usually prone to violence, unless driven by duty or need.

'*You are not one to judge our (praiseworthy) daring,*' the raider captain hissed in an old-fashioned, stilted dialect. '*You, who serve (unworthy) client/masters with too-many or too-few legs, you are not fit to valuate this band of sisters. Your sole choice is to submit (obsequiously), according to the (much revered) Code of the Plains.*'

The caravan chief stared with all three eyes. '*Code? Surely you do not mean the (archaic, irrelevant) rituals that old-time (barbaric) tribes used, back when—*'

'*The code of war and faith among (noble, true-to-their-nature) tribes. Confirmed! The way of our (much revered) aunts, going back generations before (recent, despicable) corruption set in. Confirmed! Once again, I ask/demand – do you submit?*'

Confused and alarmed, the caravan chief shook her head, human style, blowing air uncertainly like a hoon. With a low aspiration, she muttered in Anglic,

'Hr-r-r. Such jeekee nonsense for a grownuf adult to kill over—'

The raider sprang upon the merchant trader, wrapping their necks, shoving and twining forelegs till the caravan chief toppled with a groan of agony, wheezing in shock. Any Earthly vertebrate might have had her spine snapped.

The raider turned to the pilgrims with her head stretched far forward, as if to snap anyone in reach. Frightened prisoners pressed close together. Sara tightened her grip on Jomah, pushing the boy behind her.

'Again I ask/demand – who will (unreservedly) submit, in the name of this (miserable excuse for a) tribe?'

A dura passed. Then out of the circle staggered a surviving lieutenant – perhaps pushed from behind. Her neck coiled tightly, and her single nostril flared with dread as she stumbled toward the painted harlequin. Trembling, the young urs crouched and slowly pushed her head along the ground till it rested between the raider's forehooves.

'Well done,' the corsair commented. 'We shall make a (barely acceptable) plainsman of you.'

'As for the rest, Iam called UrKachu. In recent (foolish) days I was known as Lord High Aunt of Salty Hoof Clan, a useless honorary title, bereft of (real) power or glory. Now banished from that (ungrateful) band, I co-lead this new company of cousin-comrades. United, we resurrect one of the (great, lamented) warrior societies – the Urunthai!'

The other raiders raised their weapons, bellowing a piercing cry.

Sara blinked surprise. Few humans grew up ignorant of that name, fearsome from bygone days.

'This we have done because (so-called) aunts and sages have betrayed our glory race, falling into a (reviled) human trap. A scheme of extermination, planned by alien criminals.'

From an abstract corner of her mind, Sara noted that the raider was losing control over her tailored, old-fashioned GalTwo phrasing, giving way to more modern tones, even allowing bits of hated Anglic to slip in.

The other raiders hissed supportive counterpoint to their leader's singsong phrasings. UrKachu leveled her head toward the pilgrims, twisting and searching, then stopped before a tall, dark human male – the Stranger.

'Is this he? The star-demon?'

The spaceman smiled back, as if not even bloody murder could break his good humor. This, in turn, seemed to set the painted urs back momentarily.

'Is this the (selected, sought-after) one?' UrKachu went on. 'Sky-cousin to those two-legged devils we have lived among for (long-suffering) generations?'

As if trying to perceive a new form of life, the crippled star-alien flipped the veil of his new rewq over his eyes, then off again, comparing perspectives on the urrish marauder. Perhaps, with meaning robbed from words, he found some in the riot of emotion-laden colors.

A new voice spoke up, as smooth and coolly magnetic as the warrior chief was fiery-fierce, answering from *behind* the mass of huddled pilgrims.

'*This is the one,*' Ulgor assured, emerging from the tight-packed, sweaty crowd, stepping toward UrKachu. Like the Stranger, she showed no trace of fear.

'*It is the (promised) prize, recovered from far-off Dolo Town. Recently confirmed by a human sage to be one of the star-demons, not Jijo born.*'

While the pilgrims muttered dismay at Ulgor's betrayal, UrKachu's hooves clattered joy. '*Those from space will pay (dearly) for his return. For this they may offer one thing valuable above all else – survival for some (though not all) urs on Jijo.*'

Many things suddenly made sense. The motive for this raid, as well as Ulgor's spellbinding performance on the storytelling platform, designed to keep the caravan crew inside while the *Urunthai* moved stealthily into position.

A slim shadow fell between the two urrish leaders. A new voice cut in, speaking Anglic.

'Don't forget friends, we'll be demandin' a bit more'n just that.'

A human form stood in the torn entry. Moving away from the late-afternoon glare, it resolved as *Jop*, the Dolo Village tree farmer. 'There's a whole list o' things we'll be needin' if they're to get their boy back, hale and whole' – Jop glanced at the Stranger's scarred scalp – 'or as whole as the poor veg will ever be.'

Sara realized. *He went outside to signal the raiders while Ulgor kept us distracted.*

A strange alliance. A human purist helping urrish fanatics who named their group after the ancient Earthling-hating Urunthai Society.

A *frail* alliance, if Sara overheard rightly when UrKachu muttered sideways to Ulgor—

'*Would things not prove simpler without this one?*'

Tellingly, the painted warrior winced and shut up when Ulgor gave her leg a sharp kick, out of view of the other urs.

Sara detached Jomah and Prity, sheltering them in the crowd before taking a step forward.

'You can't do this,' she said.

Jop's smile was grim. 'And why not, little bookworm?'

It was a victory to keep a tremor out of her voice.

'Because he may not be one of the gene-thieves at all! I have reason to believe he may actually be an enemy of theirs.'

Ulgor looked the Stranger up and down, nodding. 'A fossivility that natters not at all. What counts is – we have goods to sell and can set a frice.'

That price Sara could envision. For UrKachu, a return to glory days of wild warriors roaming free – not incompatible with *Jop's* goal to have all the dams, machines, and books cast down, speeding humanity along the Path of Redemption.

Neither seemed to fear the chance of renewed war, so clear was the contempt each held for the other. At the moment, it hardly mattered.

We are in the hands of maniacs, Sara thought. *Fools who will ruin us all.*

ASX

And now returns the Rothen ship. Back from its cryptic mission probing nearby space for some unknown god-purpose.

Back to collect the station it left behind, and its crew of biological prospectors.

Back to gather up a treasure-hold of purloined genes.

Back to cover up their crime.

Only now, that erstwhile-buried station gapes before us, a twisted ruin. One Rothen and a sky-human lie on makeshift biers, robbed of life, while the surviving visitor-invaders rage choleric, vowing retribution. If any doubted their intent before, my rings, can it be ambiguous anymore? We are bound to be punished. Only means and extent remain in doubt.

This is what the rebel zealots desired. No more confusion. An end to hints and sweet, lying promises. Only the cleanliness of righteous opposition, however uneven our powers against those we must resist. Let us be judged, the zealots demand, by our courage and faith, not our hesitation.

The hot, unwinking star moves across our pre-dawn sky, orbiting slowly closer, an angel – or demon – of vengeance. Do those aboard already know what has happened? Are they even now plotting the storm to come?

The zealots argue we must seize the survivors – Ro-kenn, Ling, and Rann – as hostages for the protection of every member of the Commons. And the remaining star-man, Kunn, when his aircraft returns to its shattered base.

Horrified, our qheuenish High Sage, Knife-Bright Insight, skewers the zealot logic.

'You would pile one crime on another? Did they harm us, these aliens? Did they strike the first blow, with their *clinics* and high-paying *jobs*? You have slain two of them based on mere speculation of ill intent! Now you would kidnap the rest? Let us imagine that those on the ship *agree* to your demands, promising not to attack the Six. What is to stop them changing their minds, once the hostages go free?'

The zealot chief replies—

'*Who says they will go free? Let them dwell among us for the rest of their natural spans, living as deterrents to alien vileness.*'

'And after that? How foolish to think in terms of mere lifespans! Star-gods pondering long thoughts. They plan long plans. To slay us now or in fifty years, what difference will that make, in the grand scheme of things?'

Some onlookers murmur agreement. To others, however, it is as if the sage has made a fine joke. They laugh in various ways and shout, 'It makes a big difference to those now alive!'

'*Anyway*,' the urrish leader of the zealots adds – '*You are wrong to say they had not yet attacked us, or attempted (villainous) harm. To the contrary, our (justified) explosive feat stopped their (vile) scheme just in time!*'

Soot-stained and fatigued, Lester Cambel sits on a nearby boulder. Now he lifts his head from his hands, and asks—

'What do you mean by that?'

'*I mean their (foul) intent was to begin a program of annihilation by igniting (fratricidal) war among the Six!*'

The gathered onlookers absorb this silently.

Knife-Bright Insight demands – 'Can you prove this?'

'*Solid (irrefutable) evidence is on the way. But first, should you not hear (supportive) testimony from your own (highly revered) fellow sage?*'

Confusion reigns, until Phwhoon-dau steps forward to speak. Our hoonish colleague has been strangely silent, taking little part in events, save to carry Vubben downhill from the ill-starred pilgrimage. Now his long, scaly spine unbends, as if glad to pass a heavy burden.

'It is too short a time that I have had to ruminate upon these matters,' he demurs.

'You would ruminate a geologic age, dear friend,' Lester Cambel jests in a gentle way. 'Even your most tentative wisdom is greater than any other, except the Egg's. Please share it with us.'

A deep, rolling sound emanates from Phwhoon-dau's pendulous, vibrating sac.

'Hr-r-rm ... For almost two jaduras, I have kept careful records of statements made by our guests from space, especially those spoken formally, as if written by someone else for the sky-humans to say aloud. I had several linguistic reference works from Biblos, which I sometimes consult when judging disputes between individuals of different races, speaking different tongues. Despite our local dialect devolution, these works contain useful charts regarding syntax and variable meaning. I do not claim great expertise – just a backwoods practicality – in scrutinizing the aliens' statements.'

'But you reached conclusions?'

'Hr-r. Not conclusions. Correlations perhaps. Indicating a possible pattern of intent.'

'Intent?'

'Intent ... r-r-rm ... to incite divisiveness.'

Ur-Jah comments from the wallow where she curls in exhaustion from the futile rescue effort, scratching for survivors amid the smoky ruin of the aliens' station.

'This is not the first time such a susficion has veen raised. We all have anecdotes to tell, of innocent-sounding remarks which sting gently at first, like a shaedo-fly, laying eggs that fester a wound that never heals. Now you say there is a consistent fattern? That this was vart of a deliverate flan? Why did you not sfeak of this vefore?'

Phwhoon-dau sighs. 'A good scholar does not publish provisional data. Also, the aliens seemed unaware that we have retained this skill, charting the meaning in phrases. Or rather, that we recovered it with the Great Printing. I saw no reason to leak the fact too soon.'

He shrugs like a traeki, with a left-right twist. 'I finally became convinced when Ro-kenn spoke to us all, during the pilgrimage. Surely it occurred to some of you that his aim was to strike sparks of dissension with his words?'

'It sure did!' Lester Cambel growls. Assent echoes loudly from many humans present, as if to convince others of their sincerity. Hoofed urs stamp uncertainly, their hot tempers clearly frayed from the long enervating night. Only hard-won habits of the recent Peace have kept things calm till now.

Phwhoon-dau continues. 'The formal dialect of Galactic Six used by the Rothen star-god allows little room for ambiguity. Ro-kenn's disconcerting words can have but two possible interpretations. Either he is tactless to a degree beyond all stupidity, or else the objective was to incite a campaign of genocide against human-sept.'

'Against their own veloved clients?' Ur-Jah asks, incredulous.

'That is irrelevant. Even if the Rothen claim of patronhood is true, why should they care about one small, isolated band of feral humans, long cut off from the race as a whole, genetically inbred and several hundred years out of date, perchance even defective, psychologically backward, polluted by—'

'You've made your point,' Lester interrupts testily. 'But in that case, why *pick* on us?'

Phwhoon-dau turns to our human peer, umbling apologetically. 'Because among the Six, man-sept is greatest in its technic lore, in its imperfect-but-useful recollection of Galactic ways, and in its well-remembered skill at the art of war.'

There rises a muttering from some qheuenish and urrish listeners, yet no actual disagreement. Not from anyone who knows the tale of Battle Canyon, or Townsend's Ambush, or the siege of Tarek Town.

'All of these factors make your kind the obvious first target. Moreover, there is another reason. The effect your race has had upon the rest of us. As newcomers, when your rank was lowest, still you opened your sole treasure, your library, to all. After your great victories, when your status towered highest, you refused many privileges of dominance, instead bowing to the sages, accepting limits called for by the Great Peace.

'It is this record of *restraint* that makes you dangerous to Rothen plans. For what good is it to incite war, if your intended victims choose *not* to fight?'

Yes, my rings, we observe/note the crowd's reaction. A hush as Phwhoon-dau evokes images of reconciliation, gently dousing still-simmering sparks of resentment. It is a masterwork of mediation.

'Once men-sept is gone,' Phwhoon-dau goes on, 'it would prove simple to goad disaffection among the rest, pretending secret friendships, offering assistance. Handing over tailored plagues, for instance, letting each race come up with clever ways to deliver death bugs to their foes. Within less than a generation the job would be complete. The sparse record left in Jijo's soil would show only that six sooner races once sank low here, never reaching redemption.'

Uneasy silence greets this scenario painted by our hoonish sage.

'Of course, none of this is proven,' Phwhoon-dau concludes, rounding to stab a finger toward the zealot chieftain. 'Nor does it justify the horrors we have seen this night, perpetrated rashly, without consulting the sages or the Commons.'

The urrish rebel lifts her head high, in order to peer over the crowd toward the east. With a glad snort, she turns back to Phwhoon-dau.

'*Now arrives your proof!*' She whistles jubilantly, helping shove an opening through the ranks of spectators, as dawn reveals dusty figures galloping down the trail from the Holy Glade.

'*Here, also, is your justification.*'

Harullen called down from the crater's edge. 'You two had better come up now!' the heretic shouted. 'Someone's going to catch you and it'll mean trouble. Besides – I think something's happening!'

Physical and emotional exhaustion had taken their toll of the gray aristocrat's polished accent. He sounded frantic, as if serving as reluctant lookout were as risky as poking through perilous wreckage.

'*What's* happening?' Uthen shouted back. Though a cousin to the qheuen above, Lark's fellow biologist looked like a different species, with his scarred carapace streaked by gummy ash. 'Are they sending a robot this way?'

Harullen's leg-vents fluted overtones of worry. 'No, the machines still hover protectively over Ro-kenn, and the two servant-humans, and the cadavers, all surrounded by a crowd of local sycophants. I refer to a commotion over where the sages have been holding court. More zealots have arrived, it seems. There is ferment. I'm certain we are missing important news!'

Harullen may be right, Lark thought. Yet he was reluctant to leave. Despite the stench, heat and jagged stubs of metal – all made more dangerous by his own fatigue – dawn was making it easier to prowl the ruins of the buried station in search of anything to help make sense of it all.

How many times had he seen Ling vanish down a ramp into these secret precincts, wondering what lay inside? Now it was a blackened hell.

I aided the zealots, he recalled. *I gave them copies of my reports. I knew they were going to do something.*

But I never figured anything as brutal as this.

Neither had the star-gods, who clearly never guessed that angry primitives might still know how to make things go boom.

They never asked the right questions.

'I tell you something's happening!' Harullen shouted again, making no effort at originality. 'The sages are in motion – toward the aliens!'

Lark glanced over at Uthen and sighed. 'I guess he means it, this time.'

His friend had been silent for some time, standing over the same spot. When Uthen replied, it was in a low voice that barely disturbed the ash beneath his feet.

'Lark, would you please come look at this?'

Lark knew that tone from past field trips, exploring for evidence of Jijo's complex living past. He picked his way toward the qheuen, slipping gingerly between torn metal braces and seared, buckled plating, lifting his feet to kick up as little of the nasty dust-ash as possible.

'What is it? Did you find something?'

'I – am not sure.' Uthen lapsed into GalSix. *'It seems I have seen this before. This symbol. This representation. Perhaps you can confirm?'*

Lark bent alongside his friend, peering into a recess where the rising sun had yet to shine. There he saw a jumble of rectangular lozenges, each thick as his hand and twice as long. Uthen had scraped aside some half-melted machinery in order to reveal the pile. One slab lay near enough to make out a symbol, etched across its dark brown surface.

A double spiral with a bar through it. Now where have I seen—

Lark's hand reached where Uthen could not, stroked the rectangle, then picked it up. It felt incredibly light, though now it dawned on him that it could be the weightiest thing he had ever touched.

'Are you thinking what I'm thinking?' he asked, turning it in the light.

Uthen plucked the slab from his hand, holding it in a trembling claw.

'How can I not be?' the qheuenish scholar replied. 'Even half-animal, reverted primitives should recognize the glyph of the Great Galactic Library.'

The 'evidence' lay strewn across the trampled grass. Ro-kenn's piercing eyes surveyed a tangle of wires and glossy spheroids that the zealots had recently brought down from the Valley of the Egg. Clogs of dirt still clung to a necklace of strange objects, from where it had till lately been buried, next to the holiest site on Jijo.

Two clusters of onlookers formed semicircles, one backing the assembled sages, the other reverently standing behind the star-god. Many in the second group had been patients at the forayers' clinic or believed their claims of righteousness above all law. Among the humans on that side, faith in their rediscovered patrons seemed to glow, depicted by Lark's new rewq as intense red fire, surrounding their faces.

Gone was the Rothen's prior mien of furious wrath. Ro-kenn's humanoid features once more conveyed charismatic poise, even serene indulgence. He spent another dura looking over the jumble of parts, then spoke in prim Galactic Seven.

'I see nothing here of interest. Why do you show me these things?'

Lark expected the young urrish radical – leader of the rebel zealots – to answer, as both plaintiff and defendant, justifying her group's violence by diverting blame to the aliens. But the young dissenter kept well back, huddling with a crowd of humans and urs, consulting texts.

The hoonish sage, Phwhoon-dau, stepped forward to confront the Rothen emissary.

'We seek to ascertain whether these tools of high acumen are yours. Tools which some of our children found, within the last turning of Jijo's axis. Tools which *someone* buried surreptitiously, in close contact with our beloved Egg.'

Lark watched Ling's reaction. Since he already knew her pretty well, no rewq was needed to translate her shock of recognition. Nor the embarrassment that followed as she worked things out in her own head. *That's all I needed to know*, Lark thought.

Ro-kenn seemed nonchalant. 'I can only guess that some among you natives placed it there – as your foolish rebels placed explosives under our station.'

Now Ling's reaction was to blink in surprise. *She didn't expect to hear him lie. At least not so badly, with no time to prepare a smooth performance.*

Glancing to one side, the star-woman noticed Lark's scrutiny and quickly looked away. Lark wasn't proud of the satisfaction he felt, over the reversal of their moral positions. Now it was *her* turn to feel ashamed.

'Use your instrumentalities,' Phwhoon-dau urged the tall Rothen. 'Analyze these implements. You will find the technology far beyond anything we Six can now produce.'

Ro-kenn shrugged with an elegant roll of his shoulders. '*Perhaps they were left by the Buyur.*'

'In that place?' Phwhoon-dau boomed amusement, as if Ro-kenn had made a good-natured jest. 'Only a century ago, that entire valley glowed white-hot from the Egg's passage to the upper world. These tendrils would not have survived.'

The crowd murmured.

Lark felt a tug on his sleeve. He glanced around to see that a short blond figure – Bloor the Portraitist – had slinked up behind, bearing a box camera and tripod.

'Let me shoot under your arm!' the photographer whispered urgently.

Lark felt a frisson of panic. Was Bloor mad? Trying this in the open, with the robots at their wariest? Even if Lark's body shielded *that* angle, people on both sides would see. Despite Phwhoon-dau's masterful performance, could they count on loyalty from *everyone* in the milling throng?

With a helpless sigh, he lifted his left arm enough for Bloor to aim at the confrontation on the Glade.

'*Then I have no other explanation for these items,*' Ro-kenn answered referring to the snarled mess of gear. '*You are welcome to speculate to the extent that you are able, until our ship arrives.*'

Ignoring the implied threat, the hoonish sage went on with an air of calm reason that made the Rothen seem edgy by comparison.

'Is speculation required? It's been asserted that several sets of eyes *observed* your robots, on a recent foggy night, deliberately implanting these devices underneath our sacred stone—'

'*Impossible!*' Ro-kenn burst forth, temper once more flaring. '*No life-forms were in any position to witness on that night. Careful scans beforehand showed no sentient beings within range when—*'

The Rothen emissary trailed off midsentence, while onlookers stared, awed and amazed that an urbane star-god could be suckered by so obvious a ploy.

He must be awfully accustomed to getting his way, Lark thought, *to fall for such a simple trap*.

Then a strange notion occurred to him. *Many Earthly cultures, from ancient Greece and India to High-California, depicted their gods as spoiled, temperamental adolescents.*

Could that be racial memory? Maybe these guys really are our long-lost patrons, after all.

'Thank you for the correction,' Phwhoon-dau answered, with a graceful bow. 'I only said it was so *asserted*. I shall rebuke those who suggested it. We will take your word that there were no witnesses on the night that you *now admit* your robots planted these strange, alien devices next to our Egg. Shall we leave that aspect now and proceed to *why* they were planted in the first place?'

Ro-kenn appeared to be chewing on his mistake, working his jaw like a human grinding his teeth. Lark's rewq showed a discolored swath that seemed to ripple across the upper part of the Rothen's face. Meanwhile Bloor whispered contentment as he took another picture, pushing a cover slide over the exposed plate. *Go away*, Lark silently urged the little man, to no avail.

'I see no further purpose to be served by this session,' the alien finally announced. He turned and began to move away, only to stop when confronted by the gaping crater where his station once lay, recalling that he had no place to go.

Of course Ro-kenn *could* climb aboard a robot and simply fly off. But till either Kunn's aircraft or the starship arrived, there was only wilderness to flee to. No shelter beyond this glade filled with inconvenient questions.

A shout rose up from the cluster of urs and men over to the left.

The huddle broke, revealing a beaming Lester Cambel, burdened by several large-format volumes as he hurried forward. 'I think we found it!' he announced, kneeling with several assistants beside one of the spheroidal knobs that ran along the tangled mass of cable. While an aid pried at the box, Lester explained.

'Naturally, none of us has the slightest idea *how* this device works, but Galactic tech is so refined and simplified, after a billion years, that most machines are supposed to be pretty easy to use. After all, if *humans* could pilot a creaky, fifth-hand starship all the way to Jijo, the things must be darn near idiot-proof!'

The self-deprecating jest drew laughter from both sides of the crowd. Pressing close to watch, the throng left no easy or dignified avenue for Ro-kenn or his servants to escape.

'In this case,' Cambel continued, 'we assume the gadget was meant to go off when all the pilgrims were in place near the Egg, at our most impressionable, perhaps as we finished the invocation. A good guess would be either a timer or some remote control trigger, possibly a radio signal.'

An aide succeeded in getting the cover off, with an audible pop. 'Now let's see if we can find something like the standard manual override switch they show on page fifteen-twelve,' Lester said, crouching closer, consulting one of the open volumes.

Ro-kenn stared at the book, filled with crisp diagrams, as if he had just seen something deadly creep out of his own bedsheets. Lark noticed that Ling was looking at him once again. This time, her expression seemed to say, *What have you been hiding from me?*

Although she lacked a rewq, Lark figured a wry smile would convey his reply.

You assume too much, my dear. It blinded you, preventing you from asking sound questions. It also made you patronizing, when we might have been friends.

All right, maybe that was too complex to transmit by facial expression alone. Perhaps what his smirk actually said was – Such nerve! *You* accuse *me* of hiding things?

'I protest!' interjected the male sky-human, Rann, towering over all but the hoon and a few traeki as he stepped forward. 'You have no right to meddle with the property of others!'

Phwhoon-dau crooned softly, 'Hr-r – then you avow *ownership* of this invasive thing, placed without permission in our most sacred site?'

Rann blinked. Clearly he hated the present weakness of the aliens' position, having to fence words with savages. Confused, the tall sky-human turned to Ro-kenn for guidance. While they conferred, heads close together, Lester Cambel continued.

'The *purpose* of this contraption was what had us stymied for a while. Fortunately, I'd already been doing some research on Galactic technologies, so the texts were somewhat familiar. Finally, I found it listed under *psi emitters*!'

'Here's the switch, sir,' an aide declared. 'Ready when you are.'

Lester Cambel stood up, raising both hands.

'People! This is a first and final warning. We've no idea what we're about to set off. I assume nothing fatal, since our guests aren't flying out of here at top speed. However, since we've no time for careful experiments, I advise you to at least step back. The cautious among you may retreat some greater distance, perhaps twice the diameter of the Egg. I'll count down from ten.'

Uthen wanted to stay and watch, Lark thought. *But I made him go hide those library disk-things we found.*

Did I actually do him a favor?

Cambel drew a deep breath.

'Ten!'

'Nine!'

'Eight!'

Lark had never seen a g'Kek outrace an urs before. But as the crowd dissolved, some of the Six showed surprising haste to depart. Others remained, tethered by curiosity.

Courage is one trait that binds any true union, he thought with some pride.

'Seven!'

'Six!'

Now Ro-kenn himself glided forward. '*I avow ownership of this device, which—*'

'Five!'

'Four!'

Ro-kenn hurried louder to be heard past the tumult. '*—which consists merely of instrumentation, innocently emplaced—*'

'Three!'

'Two!'

Faster, in frantic tones. '*—to study patterns cast by your revered and sacred—*'

'One!'

'Now!'

Some humans instinctively brought their hands up to their ears, crouching and squinting as if to protect their eyes against an expected flash. Urs pressed arms over pouches. g'Keks drew in their eyes, while qheuens and traeki squat-hugged the ground. Rewq cringed, fleeing the intense emotions pouring from their hosts. Whatever a 'psi emitter' might be, everyone was about to find out.

Lark tried to ignore instinct, taking his cue instead from Ling. Her response to the countdown seemed a queer mix of anger and curiosity. She clasped both hands together, turning to meet his eyes at the very moment Cambel's aide stroked a hidden switch.

ASX

Confusion brims our central core, oozing through the joint-seals that bind us/we/i/me, seeping bewilderment down our outer curves, like sap from a wounded tree.

This voice, this rhythmic recitation, can it be what we know it not to be?

The Egg's patternings have stroked us so many ways. *This* ruction has familiar elements, like the Sacred One's way of singing ...

Yet – there is also a metallic *tang*, simplistic, lacking the Egg's sonorous pitch and timbre.

One sub-cadence draws us toward it, clattering like a hasty quintet of claws, pulling our attention, as if down a dark underground funnel.

Suddenly, i/we coalesce, submerging into strange existence as a *unified* being. One encased in a *hard shell*.

Pentagonal resentment surges. This 'me' is filled with rage.

How dare they tell me I am free!

What unnatural law is this Code of the Commons? This rule that 'liberates' my kind from the sweet discipline we once knew, imposed by our gracious queens?

We who are blue – we who are red – surely we yearn to serve, deep in our throbbing bile nodes! To work and fight selflessly, assisting gray dynastic ambitions! Was that not our way among the stars, and before?

The native way of all qheuens?

Who dared bring an end to those fine days, forcing alien notions of liberty into carapaces too stiff for a deadly drug called freedom?

Humans dared impose these thoughts, breaking up the union of our well-ordered hives! Theirs is the fault, the shell-bound debt to pay.

And pay they shall!

After that, there will be other scores to settle ...

i/we writhe, experiencing what it feels like to crouch and run on five strong legs. Legs meant for *service*. Not to a mere nest, crouched behind some puny dam, or to some vast abstraction like the Commons, but to grand gray matrons, noble, gorgeous, and strong.

Why does this vivid perception flood through our dazzled core?

It must be the Rothen artifice – their psi-device – part of their scheme to influence each race of the Six. Tricking us into doing their will.

Quivers of surprise shake our/my rings. Even after so many years of friendship, i/we had never realized – the qheuen point of view is *so weird*!

Yet no weirder than the *next* sensation that comes barging into our shared consciousness.

The feel of galloping hooves.

A hot breath of the dry steppes.

The burning flare of a psyche at least as egocentric as any human being.

Now I am urrish-ka! Solitary, proud as the day I emerged from the grass, little more than a beast. Nervous, but self-reliant.

I may join the tribe or clan that adopts me off the plain.

I may obey a leader – for life has hierarchies that one must endure. Yet inside I serve one mistress. Me!

Can humans ever know how their gross smell scrapes my nostril membranes? They make good warriors and smiths, it's true. They brought fine music to Jijo. These are valid things.

Yet one conceives how much better the world would be without them.

We had fought our way up high before they came. From the plains to fiery mountaintops, we stretched our necks over all others on Jijo – till these bipeds dragged us down, to be just another race among Six.

Worse, their lore reminds us – (me!) – how much we have lost. How much is forgotten.

Each day they make me recall how low and brief my life is doomed to be, here on this spinning ball of mud, with bitter oceans all around ...

The indignant narration gallops past our ability to follow. Its resentful thread is lost, but another takes its place, imposed from the outside by a force that throbs through the little mountain vale.

This beat is much easier to follow. A cadence that is heavy, slow to anger – and yet, once roused, its ire seems hopeless to arrest short of death.

It is not a rhythm to be rushed. Still, it beckons us ...

Beckons us to ponder how often the quicker races tease we poor, patient hoon,

how they swirl around us,
how often they seem to talk fast on purpose,
how they set us to the most dangerous tasks,

to face the sea alone, although each lost ship wrenches a hundred loved ones, tearing our small families apart with wrenching pain.

Humans and their stinking steamboats, they have kept the skills, pretending to share, but not really. Someday they will leave us rotting here, while they go off on ships made of pure white light.

Should this be allowed? Are there ways they can be made to pay?

Confusion reigns.

If these pernicious messages were meant for each separate race – to sway it toward aggression – then why are we/i receiving *all* of them? Should the Rothen not have targeted each sept to hear *one* theme, alone?

Perhaps their machine is damaged, or weak.

Perhaps *we* are stronger than they thought.

Breaking free of the hoonish rhythm, we sense that two layers of bitter song remain. One is clearly meant for *Earthlings*. Reverence is its theme. Reverence and pride.

We are superior. Others specialize but we can do anything! Chosen and raised by mighty Rothen, it is proper that we be greatest, even as castaways on this Slope of savages.

If taught their place, others might learn roles of worthy service ...

we/i recall a phrase. *Direct empathic transmission* – a technique used by Galactic science for the better part of half a billion years.

Knowing makes the manipart stream of voice seem more artificial, tinny, even self-satirical. Of course, this message was to have been amplified somehow through our Holy Egg, at a time when we would be most receptive. Even so, it is hard to imagine such prattle winning many believers.

Did they actually think we would fall for this?

Another fact penetrates our attention: *There is no layer for the wheeled ones!* Why is that? Why are the g'Kek left out? Is it because of their apparent uselessness in a program of genocidal war?

Or because they were already extinct, out there among the stars?

One resonance remains. A drumbeat, like hammers pounding on stacks of stiff round tubes. A reverberation that howls in a manner this composite self finds eerily familiar.

Yet, in some ways it is the most alien of all.

<MACRO-ENTITY PRIESTLY DECLARATION, DIRECT FROM ORATION PEAK OF KNOWING-*iD* IRATE HOSTILITY.

<RESPONSE=VOWED END TO PERSONAL INSULT! LET PERPETRATORS (EARTHLING) FACE ANNIHILATION . . . >

We shrivel back, dismayed. *This* egomania is far greater than any of the other broadcasts, even those aimed at urs and men! And yet – it is aimed at *traeki*!

Do you see what is happening, my rings? Is *this* a taste of the proud willfulness that used to flow from coercive despot-toruses? Those tyrant psyches that once dominated our cognition rings? Overlord-collars that were abandoned on purpose by the traeki founders, when they fled to Jijo?

Is this is how resentment tasted to those haughty *Jophur*? (Yes, shudder at the name!)

Mighty beings who still prowl the stars, in our image. Ring cousins whose waxy cores are ruled by monomaniacal ravings.

If so, why do these rantings mean so little to our manicolored segments? Knowing them for what they are, why do they seem so banal? So uncompelling?

The demonstration ends. All the scraping emissions fade as power runs out of the alien device. No matter. We now know the purpose of this tangle of cables and balls. To cast poison, amplified and lent credibility by passage through the Egg.

All around the meadow, anger seethes at this blasphemy, at this puerile appeal to our basest animosities. Passions that were obsolete even before the Egg appeared.

Is this how poorly you think of us, star-lords? That we might be fooled into doing your dirty work?

We perceive the crowd regathering, a muttering fuming throng, contemptuous of the bobbing hissing robots. Humans, urs, and others mix more freely now, sharing a heady kind of elation, as if we Six have passed an awful test. Passed it stronger and more unified than ever.

Is this the worst they can do to us?

That is a question i overhear several times.

Yes, my rings, it occurs to us that the Glade is but a small part of the Slope, and we present here make up only a fragment of the Commons.

Is this the worst they can do to us?

Alas, if only it were so.

The Urunthai liked to travel fast and light, not burdening their donkeys any more than necessary. The Urunthai also believed in the Path of Redemption – they did not much approve of books.

The librarians never had a chance.

Still, the trio of gray-robed archivists protested desperately when they saw the late afternoon bonfire. Two humans and their chimp assistant tore frantically at their bonds, pleading, entreating, trying to throw themselves across the wax-sealed crates they had been escorting to safety.

The ropes saved their lives. Watching with arbalests cocked, the painted Urunthai guards would not have flinched at shooting a clutch of pasty-skinned text-tenders.

'You like fire?' one warrior taunted in thickly accented Anglic. 'Fire *cleanses*. It vurns away dross. It can do the same thing with *flesh*. Hoonan flesh, vurns so nice.'

The librarians were reduced to silent weeping as flames licked the wax, then split the wooden chests, tumbling cascades of volumes that fluttered like dying birds. Paper pages flared as brief meteors, yielding whatever ink-scribed wisdom they had preserved for centuries.

Sara was glad Lark and Nelo couldn't see this.

Many texts were copied, during the Great Printing or after. The loss may not be as bad as it looks.

Yet how much longer would those duplicates endure this kind of age, filled with self-righteous sects and crusades, each convinced of their own lock on truth?

Even if the star-gods never wreck Biblos, or force the explosers to do it for them, fanatics like Jop and UrKachu will only grow more numerous and bold as the social fabric unravels.

As if to illustrate the point, a squadron of Jop's comrades entered camp before sundown – a dozen hard-looking men equipped with bows and swords, who slaked their parched throats at the oasis without turning their backs on UrKachu's clansmen, but glanced with satisfaction at the pyre of dying books.

The two groups have a common goal. An end to literary 'vanities.' Replacing the current sages. Hewing closer to the dictates of the Scrolls.

Later, when we're all firmly on the Path, we can return to slaughtering and ambushing each other, deciding who's top predator on a sinking pyramid of redeemed animals.

The blaze collapsed, spewing sparks and curled paper scraps that seemed to swoop in whirling air currents. Standing next to Sara, the Stranger caught one in his hand and peered, as if trying to read what it once said. Perhaps he recognized something that was much like him, in a poignant way. Once eloquent, it had now lost the magic of speech.

The librarians weren't alone watching with horrified, soot-streaked faces. A young mated pair of hoonish pilgrims clutched each other, umbling a funeral dirge, as if a loved one's heart spine lay in the filthy coals. Several qheuens stared in apparent dismay, along with – *lest we forget* – a handful of sorrowful urrish traders.

The smoke-stench made her think of darkness. The kind that does not end with dawn.

'All right, everybody! Your attention, please. Here is the plan.'

It was Jop, breaking the somber silence, approaching as part of a foursome, with UrKachu, Ulgor, and a grim, sunburned man whose rugged face and flinty hardness made him seem almost a different species from the soft, bookish librarians. Even the Urunthai treated this human with grudging deference. Painted warriors stepped quickly out of his way. Sara found him *familiar* somehow.

'We'll be leaving in two groups,' Jop went on. 'The larger will proceed to Salty Hoof Marsh. If any militia platoons hear o' this raid and care to give chase that's the first place they'll look, so some of you may be "rescued" in a week or so. That's fine by us.

'The smaller group's gonna go faster. Humans will ride, switchin' to fresh donkeys every half midura. Don't cause trouble or even *think* of sneakin' off in the dark. The Urunthai are expert trackers, and you won't get far. Any questions?'

When no one spoke, Jop shoved a finger at the Stranger. 'You. Over there.' He gestured where the biggest, strongest-looking beasts were tethered single file, beside the oasis pond. The Stranger hesitated, glancing at Sara.

'It's all right. She can go along. Can't have our hostage goin' sick on us, eh?' Jop turned to Sara. 'I expect you'll be willin' to take care of him awhile longer.'

'If I can take my bags. And Prity, of course.'

The four leaders muttered among themselves. UrKachu hissed objections, but Ulgor sided with the humans, even if it meant sacrificing some of the booty robbed from the caravan merchants. Two donkeys had their trade goods dumped on the ground, to make room.

Another argument erupted when the Stranger straddled the animal he had been assigned, with his feet almost dragging on both sides. He refused to surrender the dulcimer, keeping the instrument clutched under one arm. With ill temper, UrKachu snorted disgust but gave in.

From her own perch on a sturdy donkey, Sara watched the hard-faced man gesture toward Kurt the Exploser, sitting with his nephew, silently watching events unfold.

'And you, Lord Exploser,' Jop told Kurt with a respectful bow, 'I'm afraid there are questions my friends want to ask, and this is no place to persuade you to answer 'em.'

Ignoring the implied threat, the gray-bearded man from Tarek Town carried his satchel over to the donkey train, with Jomah close behind. When a pair of Urunthai reached for the valise, Kurt spoke in a soft, gravelly voice.

'The contents are ... delicate.'

They backed away. No one interfered as he chose a pack beast, dumped its load of plunder on the ground, and tied the valise in place.

Equal numbers of human radicals and Urunthai warriors made up the rest of the 'fast group.' The men looked almost as ungainly on their donkeys as the tall Stranger, and more uncomfortable. For many, it must be their first experience riding.

'You aren't coming?' Sara asked Jop.

'I've been away from my farm too long,' he answered. 'Also, there's unfinished business in Dolo. A certain *dam* needs tendin' to, the sooner the better.'

Sara's head jerked, but it wasn't Jop's statement of destructive intent that made her blink suddenly. Rather, she had glimpsed something over his shoulder: a stream of bubbles, rising to the surface of the pond.

Blade. He's still underwater, listening to everything!

'Don't worry, lass,' Jop assured, misconstruing her briefly dazed look. 'I'll make sure your dad gets out, before the cursed thing blows.'

Before Sara could reply, UrKachu cut in.

'*Now it is (well past) time to end delays and perform actions! Let us be off?*'

One of her tails switched the lead donkey's rump, and the queue jostled forward.

Abruptly, Sara slid off her saddle and planted her feet, causing her mount to stutter in confusion, sending a ripple of jerks down the chain in both directions. One of the rough men tumbled to the ground, raising amused snorts from some Urunthai.

'No!' Sara said, with grim determination. 'First I want to know where we are going.'

Jop urged in a low voice, 'Miss Sara, please. I don't even know myself—'

He cut off, glancing past her nervously as the flinty-eyed hunter approached.

'What seems to be the problem?' His deep voice seemed strangely cultured for his rough appearance. Sara met his steady gray eyes.

'I won't mount till you tell me where we're going.'

The hunter lifted an eyebrow. 'We could tie you aboard.'

Sara laughed. 'These little donkeys have enough trouble carrying a willing rider, let alone one who's throwing her weight around, trying to trip the poor beast. And if you truss me like a bag o' spuds, the bouncing will break my ribs.'

'Perhaps we're willing to take that chance,' he began – then frowned as the Stranger, Kurt, and Prity slid off their beasts as well, crossing their arms.

The warrior sighed. 'What difference can it possibly make to you, knowing in advance?'

The more he spoke, the more familiar he sounded. Sara felt *sure* she had met him before!

'My ward needs medical attention. So far, we've held off infection with special unguents provided by our traeki pharmacist. Since you don't plan to bring er's chariot along with your "fast group," we had better ask Pzora for a supply to take with us.'

The man nodded. 'That can be arranged.' He motioned for the Stranger to go join Pzora.

Unwrapping the rewq that had lately replaced his gauze bandages, the spaceman exposed the gaping wound in the side of his head. On seeing it, several desert-men hissed and made superstitious gestures against bad luck. While his symbiont joined Pzora's rewq in a tangled ball, exchanging enzymes, the Stranger made a flutter of rapid hand motions to the traeki – Sara thought she caught a brief snatch of *song* – before he bowed to present his injury for cleaning and treatment.

She spoke again.

'Furthermore, any stock Pzora provides will stay good for just a few days, so you better figure on taking us someplace with *another* expert pharmacist, or you may have a useless hostage on your hands. The star-gods won't pay much for a dead man, whether he's their friend or foe.'

The renegade looked at her for a long, appraising moment, then turned to confer with UrKachu and Ulgor. When he returned, he wore a thin smile.

'It means a slight detour, but there is a town so equipped, not far from our destination. You were right to point this out. Next time, however, please consider simply voicing the problem, without starting out quite so confrontationally.'

Sara stared at him, then burst out with a guffaw. It seemed to cut some of the tension when he joined with a booming chuckle – one that took Sara back to her earliest days as a student, underneath the overhanging fist-of-stone.

'Dedinger,' she said, breathing the name without voice.

The smile was still thin, disdainfully bitter.

'I wondered if you'd recognize me. We labored in different departments, though I've followed your work since I was expelled from paradise.'

'A paradise you sought to destroy, as I recall.'

He shrugged. 'I should have acted, without trying for consensus first. But collegial habits were hard to break. By the time I was ready, too many people knew my beliefs. I was watched night and day until the banishment.'

'Aw, too bad. Is *this* your way of getting another chance?' She motioned toward the bonfire.

'Indeed. After years in the wilderness, ministering to a flock of the fallen – humans who have progressed furthest along the Path – I've learned enough—'

UrKachu's shrill whistle of impatience was not in any known language, yet its short-tempered insistence was plain. Again, Dedinger lifted an eyebrow.

'Shall we go, now?'

Sara weighed trying again to get him to name a destination, out loud. But Dedinger was insane, not stupid. Her insistence might rouse suspicions and maybe even give Blade away.

With an acquiescent shrug, she clambered back aboard the patient donkey. Watching with narrowed eyes, the Stranger remounted too, followed by Kurt and Prity.

The remaining survivors of the ill-starred caravan seemed both pitying and relieved to be less important to the Urunthai. As the fast group rode out of the oasis, heading south, the facing bonfire wafted bitter odors, along with dust and pungent animal smells.

Sara glanced back toward the moonlit pool.

Did you hear any of that, Blade? Were you asleep? Was it a garbled blur of uncertain noise?

Anyway, what good could a lone blue qheuen do, in the middle of a parched plain? His best bet was to stay by the pond till help came.

A mutter of beasts lifted behind Sara as the second party got under way, more slowly, following the same path.

Makes sense. The larger bunch will trample the trail of the smaller. At some point, UrKachu will veer us off, letting any pursuers keep following the main party.

Soon they were alone on the high steppe. Urunthai trotted alongside, agile and contemptuous of the awkward humans, who winced, dragging their toes as they rode. In reaction, the men began taking turns sliding off their mounts to run at a steady lope for several arrowflights before swinging back aboard. This shut up the derisive urs and also seemed a good way to avoid saddle sores.

Alas, Sara knew she was in no physical condition to try it. *If I live through this, I'm definitely getting into shape*, she thought, not for the first time.

The man with slate eyes ran next to Sara for a few duras, sparing her a wry, eloquent smile. He was so wiry and strong, it amazed Sara that she recognized him. The last time she had seen Savant Dedinger, he was a pale intellectual with a middle-aged paunch, an expert on the most ancient Scrolls, and author of a text Sara carried in her own slim luggage. A man once honored with status and trust, till his orthodox fanaticism grew too extreme for even the broadminded High Council.

These days, the sages preached a complex faith of divided loyalty, split evenly between *Jijo*, on the one hand, and the ancestors' outlaw plan, on the other. It was a tense trade-off. Some solved it by choosing one allegiance over the other.

Sara's brother gave his full devotion to the *planet*. Lark saw wisdom and justice in the billion-year-old Galactic ecological codes. To him, no fancied 'path of redemption' could ever make up for flouting those rules.

Dedinger took the opposite extreme. He cared little about ecology or species preservation, only the racial deliverance promised by the Scrolls. Seeking pure innocence as a way to better days. Perhaps he also saw in this crisis a way to regain lost honors.

By moonlight, Sara watched the banished sage move with wiry grace – alert, focused, powerful – living testimony for the simpler style that he preached.

Deceptively simple, she thought. *The world has countless ways of not being quite as it seems.*

The Urunthai slowed after a while, then stopped to rest and eat. Those with pouched husbands or larvae needed warm simla blood every midura or so, although the human raiders chafed and complained, preferring a steady pace over the urrish fashion of hurry-and-relax.

Soon after the second of these breaks, UrKachu veered the party onto a stony ledge that extended roughly southeast like the backbone of some fossilized behemoth. Rougher terrain slowed the pace, and Sara took advantage to dismount, giving respite to the donkey and her own bottom. Exercise might also take some chill stiffness out of her joints. She kept her right arm on the saddle though, in case some unseen stone made her stumble in the dark.

The going went a little easier with second moonrise. Back-lit by silvery Torgen, the mountains seemed to loom larger than ever. Northside glaciers drank the satellite's angled light, giving back a peculiar blue luminance.

The Stranger sang for a while, a sweet, soft melody that made Sara think of loneliness.

I am a bar'n island,
apart in the desult sea,
and the nearest skein of land
is my stark thought o' thee.

O' say I were a chondrite,
tumblin' sool an' free,
would you be my garner-boat?
An' come to amass me?

It was Anglic, though of a dialect Sara had never heard, with many strange words. It was problematical how much the star-man still grasped. Still, the unrolling verses doubtless roused strong feelings in his mind.

Am I the ice that slakes your thirst
that twinkles your bright rings?
You are the fantoom angel-kin,
whose kiss gives planets wings ...

The recital ended when UrKachu trotted back, nostril flaring, to complain about *unbearable Earthling caterwauling*. A purely personal opinion, Sara felt, since none of the other urs seemed to mind. Music was on the short list of things the two races tended to agree about. Some urs even said that, for bringing the violus to Jijo, they could almost overlook human stench.

For an auntie, UrKachu seemed a particularly irritable sort.

The man from space fell silent, and the group traveled in a moody hush, punctuated by the clip-clop of the animals' hooves on bare stone.

The next blood-stop took place on the wind-sheltered lee side of some towering slabs that might be natural rock forms but in the dimness seemed like ruins of an ancient fortress, toppled in a long-ago calamity. One of the weathered desert-men gave Sara a chunk of gritty bread, plus a slab of bushcow cheese that was stale, but tasty enough to one who found herself ravenously hungry. The water ration was disappointing, though. The urs saw little point in carrying much.

Around midnight, the party had to ford a wide, shallow stream that flowed through a desert wadi. Always prepared, Ulgor slipped on sealed booties, crossing with dry feet. The other urrish rebels slogged alongside the humans and animals, then dried each other's legs with rags. After that, the Urunthai seemed eager to run for a while, till the moisture wicked out of their fibrous ankle fur.

When the pace slackened again, Sara slid off her mount to walk. Soon a low voice spoke from her right.

'I meant to tell you – I've read your paper on linguistic devolution from Indo-European.'

It was the scholar-turned-hunter, Dedinger, striding beyond her donkey's other flank. She watched him for a long moment before answering.

'I'm surprised. At fifty pages, I could afford to get only five photocopies cranked, and I kept one.'

Dedinger smiled. 'I still have friends in Biblos who send me engaging items, now and then. As for your thesis, while I enjoyed your ideas about grammatical reinforcement in pre-literate trading clans, I'm afraid I can't bring myself to accept your general theory.'

Sara didn't find it surprising. Her conclusions ran counter to everything the man believed in.

'That's the way of science – a cycle of give-and-take. No dogmatic truth. No rigid, received word.'

As opposed to my own slavish devotion to a few ancient Scrolls that no human had a hand in writing?' The flinty man laughed. 'I guess what it comes down to is which direction you think people are heading. Even among conservative Galactics, *science* is about slowly improving your models of the world. It's future-oriented. Your children will know more than you do, so the truth you already have can never be called "perfect."'

'That's fine when your destiny lies *upward*, Sara. But tradition and a firm creed are preferable if you're embarked on the narrow, sacred road downhill, to salvation. In that case, argument and uncertainty will only confuse your flock.'

'Your flock doesn't seem confused,' she acknowledged.

He smiled. 'I've had some success winning these hard men over to true orthodoxy. They dwell much of each year on the Plain of Sharp Sand, trapping the wild spike-sloths that lurk in caves, under the dunes. Most don't read or write, and their few tools are handmade, so they were already far down the Path. It may prove harder convincing some other groups.'

'Like the Explosers Guild?'

The former scholar nodded.

'An enigmatic clan. Their hesitation to do their duty, during this crisis, is disturbing.'

Sara raised her eyes toward Kurt and Jomah. While the senior exploser snored atop an ambling donkey, his nephew held another one-sided conversation with the Stranger, who smiled and nodded as Jomah chattered. The star-man made an ideal, uncritical audience for a shy boy, just beginning to express himself.

'Maybe they figure they can blow it all up just once,' Sara commented. 'Then they'll have to scratch for a living, like everyone else.'

Dedinger grunted. 'If so, it's time someone reminded them, respectfully, of their obligations.'

She recalled Jop's talk of taking Kurt somewhere to be 'persuaded.' In more violent times, the expression carried chilling implications.

We may be headed back to such times.

The flinty insurgent shook his head.

'But never mind all that. I *really* want to discuss your fascinating paper. Do you mind?'

When Sara shrugged, Dedinger continued in an amiable tone, as if they sat in a Biblos faculty lounge.

'You admit that proto-Indo-European, and many other human mother tongues, were more rigorous and rational than the dialects that evolved out of them. Right so far?'

'According to books carried here by the *Tabernacle*. All we have is inherited data.'

'And yet you *don't* see this trend as an obvious sign of decay from perfection? From original grammars designed for our use by a patron race?'

She sighed. There might be weirder things in the universe than holding an abstract chat with her kidnapper under a desert sky, but none came to mind.

'The structure of those early tongues could have risen out of selective pressure, operating over generations. Primitive people *need* rigid grammars, because they lack writing or other means to correct error and linguistic drift.'

'Ah yes. Your analogy to the game of *Telephone*, in which the language with the highest level of shaman coding—'

'That's *Shannon* coding. Claude Shannon showed that any message can carry within itself the means to correct errors that creep in during transit. In a *spoken* language, this redundancy often comes embedded in grammatical rules – the cases, declensions, modifiers, and such. It's all quite basic information theory.'

'Hm. Maybe for you. I confess that I failed to follow your mathematics.' Dedinger chuckled dryly. 'But let's assume you're right about that. Does not such clever, self-correcting structure *prove* those early human languages were shrewdly designed?'

'Not at all. The same argument was raised against biological evolution – and later against the notion of self-bootstrapped intelligence. Some folks have a hard time accepting that complexity can emerge out of Darwinian selection, but it does.'

'So you believe—'

'That the same thing happened to preliterate languages on Earth. Cultures with stronger grammars could hang together over greater distances and times. According to some of the old-timer linguists, Indo-European may have ranged all the way from Europe to Central Asia. Its rigid perfection maintained culture and trade links over distances far beyond what any person might traverse in a lifetime. News, gossip, or a good story could travel slowly, by word of mouth, all the way across a continent, arriving centuries later, barely changed.'

'Like in the game of *Telephone*.'

'That's the general idea.'

Sara found herself leaning on the donkey as fatigue prickled her calves and thighs. Still, it seemed a toss-up – aching muscles if she stayed afoot versus shivering on a bruised coccyx if she remounted. For the little donkey's sake, she chose to keep walking.

Dedinger had his teeth in the argument.

'If all you say is true, how can you deny those early grammars were superior to the shabby, disorganized dialects that followed?'

'What do you mean, "superior"? Whether you're talking about proto-Indo-European, proto-Bantu, or proto-Semitic, each language served the needs of a conservative, largely changeless culture of nomads and herders, for hundreds or thousands of years. But those needs *shifted* when our ancestors acquired agriculture, metals, and writing. Progress changed the very notion of what language was for.'

An expression of earnest confusion briefly softened the man's etched features.

'Pray, what could language *be* for, if not to maintain a culture's cohesion and foster communication?'

That was the question posed by members of Dedinger's former department, who spurned Sara's theory at its first hearing, embarrassing her in front of Sages Bonner, Taine, and Purofsky. Had not the majestic civilization of the Five Galaxies been refining its twenty or so standard codes since the days of the fabled Progenitors, with a single goal – to promote clear exchange of meaning among a myriad citizen races?

'There is another desirable thing,' Sara replied. 'Another product of language, just as important, in the long run, as cohesion.'

'And that is?'

'*Creativity*. If I'm right, it calls for a different kind of grammar. A completely different way of looking at error.'

'One that *welcomes* error. Embraces it.' Dedinger nodded. 'This part of your paper I had trouble following. You say Anglic is better because it *lacks* redundancy coding. Because errors and ambiguity creep into every phrase or paragraph. But how can *chaos* engender inventiveness?'

'By shattering preconceptions. By allowing illogical, preposterous, even obviously *wrong* statements to parse in reasonable-sounding expressions. Like the paradox – "This sentence is a lie" – which can't be spoken grammatically in any formal Galactic tongue. By putting manifest contradictions on an equal footing with the most time-honored and widely held assumptions, we are tantalized, confused. Our thoughts stumble out of step.'

'This is good?'

'It's how creativity works, especially in humans. For every good idea, ten thousand idiotic ones must first be posed, sifted, tried out, and discarded. A mind that's afraid to toy with the ridiculous will never come up with the brilliantly original – some absurd concept that future generations will assume to have been "obvious" all along.

'One result has been a profusion of new words – a vocabulary vastly greater than ancient languages. Words for new things, new ideas, new ways of comparing and reasoning.'

Dedinger muttered, 'And new disasters. New misunderstandings.'

Sara nodded, conceding the point.

'It's a dangerous process. Earth's bloody past shows how imagination and belief turn into curses unless they're accompanied by critical judgment. Writing, logic, and experimentation help replace some of the error-correction that used to come embedded in grammar. Above all, mature people must consider that most unpleasant of all possibilities – that their own favorite doctrines *might* prove wrong.'

She watched Dedinger. Would the man catch on that she had aimed that barb at *him*?

The exiled pedagogue gave Sara a wry smile.

'Has it occurred to you, Miss Sara, that your last statement could apply to *you* and your own beloved hypothesis?'

Now it was Sara's turn to wince, then laugh aloud.

'Human nature. Each of us thinks *we* know what we're talking about and those disagreeing are fools. Creative people see Prometheus in a mirror, never Pandora.'

Dedinger spoke with an ironic edge. 'Sometimes the torch I carry scorches my fingers.'

Sara could not tell how much he meant the remark in jest. Often she found it easier to read the feelings of a hoon, or g'Kek, than some members of her own enigmatic race. Still, she found herself enjoying the conversation, the first of its kind in quite some time.

'As for trends here on Jijo, just look at the new rhythmic novels being published by some of the northern urrish tribes. Or the recent burst of hoonish romantic poetry. Or the GalTwo haiku imagery coming out of the Vale—'

A sharp whistle cut her short – a guttural, stop-command piped by UrKachu's upstretched throat. The queue of tired animals jostled to a halt, as the Urunthai leader pointed north of a stone spire, decreeing that a camouflaged shelter be raised in its long, tapered shadow.

In its shadow ...

Blinking, Sara looked around to see that the night was over. Dawnlight filtered over the peaks, sifting through an early-morning haze. They had climbed *among* the mountains, or at least the rocky foothills, leaving behind the parched Warril Plain. Alas, they were by now far south of the well-worn trail leading to the Glade of Gathering.

Dedinger's courtliness clashed with his rough appearance, as he excused himself to organize his men. 'I've enjoyed matching wits,' he told her with a bow. 'Perhaps we can resume later.'

'Perhaps.'

Although the discussion had been a pleasant diversion, she had no doubt the man would sacrifice her, along with all of her ideas, on the altar of his faith. Sara vowed to be ready for any occasion to sneak her friends away from these fanatics.

Right. An old man, a boy, a chimpanzee, a wounded alien, and an out-of-shape intellectual – even if we got a huge head start, these urs and desert-men would catch us faster than you can transform a sine wave.

Still, she gazed north toward high peaks where momentous events were taking place in hidden valleys, and thought – *We'd better move fast, or else Ifni, God, and the universe will surely move on without us.*

Now comes *our* turn to threaten.

Proctors fight to hold back a furious throng, hemming our erstwhile guests inside a circle of rage. The remaining alien-lovers, mostly humans, form a protective ring around the star-beings, while the twin robots swoop and dive, enforcing a buffer zone with bolts of stinging lightning.

Lester Cambel steps forward, raising both hands for calm. The raucous noise ebbs, as members of the mob ease their pressure on the harried proctors. Soon silence reigns. No one wants to miss the next move in this game, wherein all of us on Jijo are tokens being gambled, to be won or lost, counting on our skill and luck.

Lester bows to the Rothen emissary. In one hand he bears a stack of metal plates.

'Now let's drop all pretense,' he tells the star-god. 'We know you for what you are. Nor can you trick us into genocidal suicide, doing your dirty work.

'Furthermore, should you try to do the job yourselves, annihilating all witnesses to your illegal visit, you will fail. All you'll accomplish is to increase your list of crimes.

'We recommend that you be satisfied. Take what you will from this world, and go.'

The male star-human bursts forth, outraged. 'How dare you speak so to a patron of your race!' Rann chastises, red-faced. 'Apologize for your insolence!'

But Lester ignores Rann, whose status has diminished in the eyes of the Six. A toady/servant does not dictate to a sage, no matter what godlike powers he wields.

Instead, our human envoy offers one of the metal plates to Rokenn.

'We are not proud of this art form. It uses materials that won't age or degrade back into Mother Jijo's soil. Rather, it is adamant. Resistant to time. Properly stored, its images will last until this world again teems with legal sapient life.

'Normally, we would send such dross to where Jijo can recycle it in fire. But in this case, we'll make an exception.'

The Rothen emissary turns the plate in the morning light. Unlike a paper photograph, this kind of image is best viewed from certain angles. we/i know what it depicts, do we not, my rings? The plate shows Ro-kenn and his comrades just before that ill-starred pilgrimage – a journey whose horrors still drop vexingly down our waxy core. Bloor the Portraitist developed the picture to serve as an instrument of blackmail.

'Other images depict your party in various poses, performing surveys, testing candidate species, often with backgrounds that clearly portray this place, this world. The shape of glaciers and eroding cliffs will set the date within a hundred years. Perhaps less.'

The rewq covering our/my torus-of-vision reveals ripples criss-crossing Ro-kenn's face, again a dissonance of clashing emotions – but which ones? Are we getting better at reading this alien life-form? The second of our cognition rings seems deeply curious about the clashing colors.

The Rothen holds out an elegant hand.

'May I see the others?'

Lester hands them over. 'This is but a sampling. Naturally, a detailed record of our encounter with your ship and crew has also been etched on durable metal, to accompany these pictures into hiding.'

'Naturally,' Ro-kenn answers smoothly, perusing one plate after another, turning them in the sunshine. 'You have retained unusual arts, for self-accursed sooners. Indeed, I have never seen the like, even in civilized space.'

This flattery draws some murmurs from the crowd. Ro-kenn is once more being charming.

Lester continues, 'Any acts of vengeance or genocide against the Six will also be chronicled this way. It is doubtful you can wipe us out before hidden scribes complete such a record.'

'Doubtful indeed.' Ro-kenn pauses, as if considering his options. Given his earlier arrogance, we had expected outrage over being blackmailed in this way, plus indignation over the implied disrespect. It would not surprise us to see open contempt for an effort by half-beasts to threaten a deity.

Instead, do we now perceive something like *cautious calculation* cross his features? Does he realize we have him cornered? Ro-kenn shrugs in a manner not unlike a human. 'What shall be done, then? If we agree to your demands, how can we be certain these will not reappear anyway, to plague our descendants someday? Will you sell these records to us now, in return for our promise to go in peace?'

Now it is Lester who laughs. Turning half toward the crowd, he gestures with one hand. 'Had you come after the Commons experienced another century or two of peace, we might have trustingly accepted. But who among us has not heard stories told by old-timers who were *there* when Broken-Tooth deceived Ur-xouna near False Bridge, at the end of the old wars? What human has not read moving accounts of some great-grandfather who escaped the slaughter at Truce Gorge, during the Year of Lies?'

He turned back to Ro-kenn. 'Our knowledge of deceit comes self-taught. Peace was hard-won – its lessons not forgotten.

'No, mighty Rothen. With apologies, we decline simply to take you at your word.'

This time a mere flick of one slender hand holds back the outraged Rann, checking another outburst. Ro-kenn himself seems amused, although the strange dissonance once more cuts his visage.

'Then what guarantee have *we* that you will destroy these items, and not leave them in a place where they may be found by future tenants of this world? Or worse, by Galactic Institutes, as little as a thousand years from now?'

Lester is prepared with an answer.

'There is irony here, Oh mighty Rothen. If we, as a people, remember you, then we are still witnesses who can testify against your crime. Thus, if we retain memory, you have reason to act against us.

'If, on the other hand, we successfully follow the path of redemption and forgetfulness, in a thousand years we may already be like glavers, innocuous to you. No longer credible to testify. If so, you will have no cause to harm us. To do so would be senseless, even risky.'

'True, but if you have by that time forgotten our visit, would you not also forget the hiding places where you cached these images?' Ro-kenn holds up a plate. 'They will lie in ambush, like lurker missiles, patiently awaiting some future time to home in on our race.'

Lester nodded. 'That is the irony. Perhaps it can be solved by making a vow of our own – to teach our descendants a song – a riddle, as it were – something simple, that will resonate even when our descendants have much simpler minds.'

'And what function will this puzzle serve?'

'We will tell our children that if ever beings come from the sky who know the riddle's answer, they must retrieve these items from sacred sites, handing them over to the star-lords – your own successors, Oh mighty Rothen. Naturally, if we Six retain *detailed* memory of your crime, we sages will *prevent* the hand-over, for it will be too soon. But *that* memory will not be taught to children, nor passed on with the same care as we teach the riddle. For to remember your crime is to hold on to a poison, one that can kill.

'We would rather forget how and why you ever came. Only then will we be safe from your wrath.'

It is an ornately elaborate bargain that Lester offers. In Council he had been forced to explain its logic three times. Now the crowd mutters, parsing the idea element by element, sharing bits of understanding until a murmur of admiration flows like molten clarity around the circle of close-pressed beings, Indeed, the bargain contains inherent elegance.

'How shall we know that all the items will be accounted for in this way?' Ro-kenn asks.

'To some extent, you must trust to luck. You were gamblers coming on this mission in the first place, were you not, mighty Rothen? I can tell you this. We have no grand desire to have these images arrive across the ages for Institute lawyers to pore over, looking for reasons to punish our own species-cousins, still roaming the stars. In their hardness and durability, these plates are an insult to our own goal on this world, to be shriven down to innocence. To earn a second chance.'

Ro-kenn ponders this.

'It seems we may have come to Jijo a few thousand years too soon. If you succeed in following your Path, this world will be a treasure trove.'

His meaning is not clear at first, then a mutter passes through the crowd, from urrish snorts to qheuenish hisses and finally booming hoonish laughter. Some are impressed by Ro-kenn's wit, others by the implied compliment – that the Rothen would wish to adopt any presentient races that we Six might become. But that reaction is not universal. Some of those assembled seethe angrily, rejecting any notion of adoption by Ro-kenn's folk.

Don't we/i find this anger silly, my rings? Have client races any control over who becomes their patron? Not according to lore we've read.

But those books will be dust long before any of this comes to pass.

'Shall we swear oaths?' Ro-kenn asks. 'This time based on the most pragmatic assurance of all – mutual deterrence?

'By this new arrangement, we shall depart in our ship, waiting only till our scout craft returns from its final mission, choking back whatever bitterness we feel over the foul murder of our comrades. In return, you all vow to forget our intrusion and our foolish effort to speak through the voice of your Holy Egg.'

'It is agreed,' replies Knife-Bright Insight, clicking two claws. 'Tonight we'll confer and choose a riddle whose secret key will be told to you. When next your kind comes to Jijo, may it be to find a world of innocents. That key will guide you to the hiding place. You may then remove the dross images. Our deal will be done.'

Hope washes over the crowd, striking our rewq as a wave of soft green tremors.

Can we credit the possibility, my rings? That the Six might live to see a happy ending? To the zealots this seems all that they desired. Their young leader dances jubilation. Now there will be no punishment for their violent acts. Rather, they will be known as heroes of the Commons.

What do you say, my ring?

Our second cognition-torus reminds us that some *heretics* might *prefer* that angry fire and plagues rid Jijo of this infestation called the Six. And yes, there is yet another, even smaller heretical fringe. Eccentrics who foresee our destiny lying in a different direction – scarcely hinted by sacred Scrolls. Why do you bring this up, my ring? What possible relevance can such nonsense have, at this time and place?

Scribes write down details of the pact. Soon High Sages will be called to witness and assent. (Prepare, my lower rings!) Meanwhile, we ponder again the anomaly brought to our waxy notice by the rewq, which still conveys vexing colors from Ro-kenn. Could they be shades of *deceit*? Deceit and *amusement*? Eager gladness to accept our offer, but only in appearance, buying time until—

Stop it, we command our second ring, which gets carried away all too easily. It has read too many novels. We do not know the Rothen well enough to read subtle, complex meanings in his alien visage.

Besides, don't we have Ro-kenn trapped? Has he not reason to fear the images on those plates of hard metal? Logically, he dare not risk them being passed on to incriminate his race, his line.

Or does he know something we do not?

Ah – what a silly question to ask, when pondering a star-god!

While hope courses the crowd, i/we grow more nervous by the dura. *What if they care nothing about the photographs?* Then Ro-kenn might agree to anything, for it would not matter what vows were signed, once his almighty ship arrives. From that point on, with his personal safety assured . . .

. . .

we never get a chance to complete that dripping contemplation. For suddenly, something new happens! Far too quickly for wax to ooze.

. . .

It begins with a shrill human cry—

One of the sycophants, a devoted Rothen-follower, points *behind* the star-beings, toward the raised bier where their two dead comrades lay—

Silky cloths had been draped across the two who were slain in the explosion. But now we see those coverings are *pulled back*, exposing the late Rothen and the late sky-human—

Do we now perceive *Bloor* the Portraitist, poised with his recording device, *attempting to photograph the faces of the dead*?

Bloor ignores growls of anger rising from those-who-follow-the-Rothen-as-patrons. Calmly, he slides out one exposed plate and inserts another. He appears entranced, focused on his art, even as attention turns his way from Rann, then an outraged Ro-kenn, who screams in terse Galactic Six—

Bloor glimpses the swooping robot and has time to perform one last act of professionalism. With his fragile body, the portraitist shields his precious camera and dies.

Have patience, you lesser rings that lie farthest from the senses. You must wait to caress these memories with our inner breath. For those who squat higher up our tapered cone, events come as a flurry of muddled images.

Behold – the livid anger of the star-gods, apoplectic with affronted rage!

Observe – the futile cries of Lester, Vubben, and Phwhoon-dau, beseeching restraint!

Witness – Bloor's crumpled ruin, a smoldering heap!

Note – how the crowd backs away from the violence, even as other dark-clad figures rush inward from the forest rim!

Quail – from the roaring robots, charging up to strike, ready to slay at command!

Above all, *stare* – at the scene right before us, the one Bloor was photographing when he died . . .

An image to preserve as long as this tower of rings stands.

Two beings lay side by side.

One, a human female, seems composed in death, her newly washed face serene, apparently at peace.

The other figure *had* seemed equally tranquil when we saw it last, before dawn. Ro-pol's visage was like an idealized human, impressive in height and breadth of brow, in strong cheekbones and the set of her womanlike chin, which in life had sustained a winning smile.

That is not what we see now!

Rather, a quivering *thing*, suffering its own death tremors, creeps *off* Ro-pol's face . . . taking much of that face with it! The very same brow and cheek and chin we had been pondering – these make up the *body* of the creature, which must have ridden the Rothen as a rewq rides one of the Six, nestled so smoothly in place that no join or seam was visible before.

Does this explain the dissonance? The clashing colors conveyed by our veteran rewq? When some parts of Ro-kenn's face relayed tart emotions, others always seemed cool, unperturbed, and friendly.

It crawls aside, and onlookers gasp at what remains – a sharply narrower face, chinless and spiny, with cranial edges totally unlike a human being's.

Gone is the mirage of heavenly comeliness in Earthling terms. Oh, the basic shape remains humanoid, but in a tapered, *predatory* caricature of our youngest sept.

'Hr-rm ... I have seen this face before,' croons Phwhoon-dau, stroking his white beard. 'In my readings at Biblos. An obscure race, with a reputation for—'

Rann whips the coverings back over the corpse, while Ro-kenn shrilly interrupts, '*This is the final outrage!*'

Our rewq now clearly show Ro-kenn as *two* beings, one a living mask. Gone is the patient amusement, the pretense at giving in to blackmail. Until now, we had nothing to blackmail *with*.

Until now.

The Rothen points to Rann, commanding – '*Break radio silence and recall Kunn, now!*'

'The prey will be warned,' Rann objects, clearly shaken. 'And the hunters. Dare we risk—'

'*We'll take that chance. Obey now! Recall Kunn, then clear all of these away.*'

Ro-kenn motions at the crowd, the sycophants, and all six sages. '*No one leaves to speak of this.*'

The robots start to rise, crackling with dire strength. A moan of dread escapes the crowd.

Then – as is sometimes said in Earthling tales – All Hell Breaks Loose.

THE STRANGER

He strums the dulcimer slowly, plucking one low note at a time, feeling nervous over what he plans to attempt, yet also pleased by how much he is remembering.

About urs, *for instance. Ever since first regaining consciousness aboard the little riverboat, he had tried to pin down why he felt so friendly toward the four-footed beings, despite their prickly, short-tempered natures. Back at the desert oasis, before the bloody ambush, he had listened to the ballad recited by the traitor Ulgor, without understanding more than a few click-phrases, here and there. Yet the rhythmic chant had seemed strangely familiar, tugging at associations within his battered brain.*

Then, all at once, he recalled where he heard the tale before. In a bar, on faraway—

—on faraway—

Names are still hard to come by. But now at least he has an image, rescued from imprisoned memory. A scene in a tavern catering to low-class sapient races like his own, frequented by star travelers sharing certain tastes in food, music, and entertainment. Often, songs were accepted as currency in such places. You could buy rounds of drinks with a good one, and he seldom had to pay cash, so desired were the tunes warbled by his talented crewmates.

... crewmates ...

Now he confronts another barrier. The tallest, harshest wall across his mind. He tries once more but fails to come up with a melody to break it down.

Back to the bar, then. With that recollection had come things he once knew about urs. Especially a trick he used to pull on urrish companions when they dozed off, after a hard evening's revelry. Sometimes he would take a peanut, aim carefully, and—

The Stranger's train of thought breaks as he realizes he is being watched. UrKachu glares at him, clearly irritated by the increasing loudness of the thrumming dulcimer. He quickly mollifies the leader of the urrish ambushers by plucking at the string more softly. Still, he does not quite stop. At a lower, quieter level, the rhythm is mildly hypnotic, just as he intended it to be.

The other raiders – both urs and men – lie down or snooze through the broiling middle of the day. So does Sara, along with Prity and the other captives. The Stranger knows he should rest too, but he feels too keyed up.

He misses Pzora, though it does seem strange to long for the healing touch of a Jophur—

No, that is the wrong word. Pzora is not one of those fearsome, cruel beings, but a traeki – something quite different. As he grows a little better at names, he is going to have to remember that.

Anyway, he has work to do. In the time remaining, he must learn to use the rewq that Sara bought for him – a strange creature whose filmy body covers his eyes, causing soft colors to waft around every urs and human, turning the shabby tent into a pavilion of revealing hues. He finds unnerving the way the rewq quivers over his flesh, using a sucker to feed from veins near the gaping wound in his head. Yet he cannot turn down a chance to explore yet another kind of communication. Sometimes the confusing colors coalesce to remind him of the last time he communed with Pzora, back at the oasis. There had been a moment of strange clarity when their cojoined rewqs seemed to help convey exactly what he wanted.

Pzora's answering gift lies inside the hole in his head – the one place the raiders would never think to search.

He resists an urge to slip his hand inside, to check if it's still there.

All in good time.

While he sits and strums, the oppressive heat slowly mounts. Urrish and human heads sink lower to the ground, where night's lingering coolness can still be dimly felt. He waits and tries to remember a little more.

His biggest blank zone – other than the loss of language – covers the recent past. If ten fingers represent the span of his life up to now, most of the final two digits are missing. All he has are the shreds that cling whenever he wakes from a dream. Enough to know he once roamed the linked galaxies and witnessed things none of his kind ever saw before. The seals holding back those memories have resisted everything he's tried so far – drawing sketches, playing math games with Prity, wallowing in Pzora's library of smells. He remains fairly certain the key will be found in music. But what music?

Sara snores softly nearby, and he feels a swelling of grateful fondness in his heart ... combined with a nagging sense that there is someone else he should be thinking about. Another who had his devotion before searing fate swatted him out of the sky. A woman's face flickers at a sharp angle to his thoughts, passing too swiftly to recognize – except for the wave of strong feelings it evokes.

He misses her ... though he can't imagine that she feels the same, wherever she may be.

Whoever she may be.

More than anything else, he wishes he could put his feelings into words, as he never did during all the dangerous times they spent together ... times when she was pining for another ... for a better man than he.

This thought thread is leading somewhere, he realizes, feeling some excitement. Avidly, he follows it. The woman in his dreams ... she longs for a man ... a hero who was lost long ago ... a year or two ago ... lost along with crewmates ... and also along with ...

... along with the Captain ...

Yes, of course! The commander they all missed so terribly, gone ever since a daring escape from that wretched water world. A world of disaster and triumph.

He tries conjuring an image of the Captain. A face. But all that comes to mind is a gray flash, a whirl of bubbles, and finally a glint of white, needle-like teeth. A smile unlike any other. Wise and serene.

Not human.

And then, out of nowhere, a soft warbling emerges. A sound never before heard on the Slope.

*My good silent friend ...
   Lost in winter's dread stormcloud ...
      Lonely ... just like me ... *

The whistles, creaks, and pops roll out of his mouth before he even knows he's speaking them. His head rocks back as a dam seems to shatter in his mind, releasing a flood of memories.

The music he'd been looking for was of no human making, but the modern tongue of Earth's third sapient race. A language painfully hard for humans to learn, but that rewarded those who tried. Trinary was nothing like Galactic Two or any other speech, except perhaps the groaning ballads sung by great whales who still plumbed the home-world's timeless depths.

Trinary.

He blinks in surprise and even loses his rhythm on the plucked dulcimer. A few urs lift their heads, staring at him blankly till he resumes the steady cadence, continuing reflexively while he ponders his amazing rediscovery. The familiar/uncanny fact that had eluded him till now.

His crewmates – perhaps they still await him in that dark, dreary place where he left them.

His crewmates were dolphins.

XXV

THE BOOK OF THE SEA

Beware, ye damned who seek redemption.
Time is your friend, but also your great foe.

Like the fires of Izmunuti,
It can fade before you are ready.
Letting in, once more,
The things from which you fled.

—*The Scroll of Danger*

ALVIN'S TALE

I tried reading *Finnegan's Wake* once upon a time.

Last year.

A lifetime ago.

It's said that no non-Earthling has ever grokked that book. In fact, the few *humans* who managed the feat spent whole chunks of their lifespans going over Joyce's masterpiece, word by obscure word, with help from texts written by *other* obsessed scholars. Mister Heinz says no one on the Slope has any hope at all of fathoming it.

Naturally, I took that as a challenge, and so the next time our schoolteacher headed off to Gathering, I nagged him to bring a copy back with him.

No, I'm not about to say I succeeded. Just one page into it, I knew this was a whole different venture from *Ulysses*. Though it looks like it's written in prespace English, the *Wake* uses Joyce's own language, created for a single work of art. Hoonish patience would not solve this. To ever begin to understand, you have to share much of the author's *context*.

What hope had I? Not a native speaker of Irish-English. Not a citizen of early twentieth-century Dublin. Not human. I've never been inside a 'pub' or seen a 'quark' close up, so I can only guess what goes on in each.

I recall thinking – maybe a little arrogantly – *If I can't read this thing, I doubt anyone else on Jijo ever will.*

The crisp volume didn't look as if anyone had tried, since the Great Printing. So why did the human founders waste space in Biblos with this bizarre intellectual experiment from a bygone age?

That was when I felt I had a clue to the *Tabernacle* crew's purpose, in coming to this world. It couldn't be for the reasons we're told on holy days, when sages and priests read from the sacred Scrolls. Not to find a dark corner of the universe to engage in criminally selfish breeding, or to resign from the cosmos, seeking the roads of innocence. In either of those cases, I could see printing how-to manuals, or simple tales to help light the way. In time, the books would turn brittle and go to dust, when humans and the rest of us are ready to give them up. Kind of like the Eloi folk in H. G. Wells's *The Time Machine*.

In neither case did it make any sense to print copies of *Finnegan's Wake*.

Realizing this, I picked up the book once more. And while I did not understand the story or allusions any better than before, I *was* able to enjoy the flow of words, their rhythms and sounds, for their own extravagant sake. It wasn't important anymore that I be the only person to grok it.

In fact, there came a warm feeling as I turned the pages and thought – *someday, someone else is going to get more out of this than I did*.

On Jijo, things get stored away that seem dead, but that only sleep.

I've been pondering that very thought while lying here in constant pain, trying to bear it stoically whenever strange, silent beings barge into my cell to poke me with heat, cold, and prickly sharpness. I mean, should I feel *hope* as metal fingers probe my wounds? Or sour gloom that my blank-faced tenders refuse to answer any questions, or even to speak? Shall I dwell on my awful homesickness? Or on the contrary *thrill* over having discovered something wonderfully strange that no one on the Slope ever suspected, not since the g'Keks first sent their sneakship tumbling into the deep?

Above all, I wondered – am I prisoner, patient, or *specimen*?

Finally I realized – I just don't have any framework to decide. Like the phrases in Joyce's book, these beings seem at once both strangely familiar and completely unfathomable.

Are they machines?

Are they denizens of some ancient submarine civilization?

Are they invaders? Do they see *us* as invaders?

Are they *Buyur*?

I've been avoiding thinking about what's really eating away at me, inside.

Come on, Alvin. Face up to it.

I recall those final duras, when our beautiful *Wuphon's Dream* shattered to bits. When her hull slammed against my spine. When my friends spilled into the metal monster's mouth, immersed in cold, cold, cold, cruel water.

They were alive then. Injured, dazed, but alive.

Still alive when a hurricane of air forced out the horrid dark sea, leaving us to flop, wounded and half dead, down to a hard deck. And when sun-bright lights half-blinded us, and creepy spider-things stepped into the chamber to look over their catch.

But memory blurs at that point, fading into a hazy muddle of images – until I awoke here, alone.

Alone, and worried about my friends.

XXVI

THE BOOK OF THE SLOPE

Legends

We know that in the Five Galaxies, every star-faring race got its start through the process of uplift, receiving a boost to sapience from the patrons that adopted them. And those patrons were bestowed the same boon by earlier patrons, and so on, a chain of beneficence stretching all the way back to misty times when there were more than five linked galaxies – back to the fabled Progenitors, who began the chain, so very long ago.

Where did the Progenitors *themselves* come from?

To some of the religious alliances that wrangle testily across the space lanes, that very question is anathema, or even likely to provoke a fight.

Others deal with the issue by claiming that the ancient ones must have come from 'somewhere else,' or that the Progenitors were transcendent beings who descended graciously from a higher plane in order to help sapient life get its start.

Of course one might suggest that such facile answers simply beg the question, but it's unwise to suggest it too loudly. Some august Galactics do not take it kindly when you point out their inconsistencies.

Finally, there is one *cult – the Affirmers* who hold the view that the Progenitors must have self-evolved on some planet, boot-strapping to full sapiency all by themselves – a prodigious, nigh-impossible feat. One might imagine that the Affirmers would be more friendly to Earthlings than most of the more fanatical alliances. After all, many Terrans still believe our race did the very same thing, uplifting ourselves in isolation, without help from anyone.

Alas, don't expect much sympathy from the Affirmers, who see it as arrogant hubris *for mere wolflings* to make such a claim. Self-uplift, they maintain, is a phenomenon of the highest and most sacred order – not for the likes of creatures like us.

A Pragmatist's Introduction to Galactology, by Jacob Demwa, reprinted from the original by Tarek Printers Guild, Year-of-Exile 1892.

It did no good to shout or throw stones at the glavers. The pair just retreated to watch from a distance with blank, globelike eyes, then resumed following when the human party moved on. Dwer soon realized there would be no getting rid of them. He'd have to shoot the beasts or ignore them.

'You have other things to keep you busy, son,' Danel Ozawa ruled.

It was an understatement.

The clearing near the waterfall still reeked of urs, donkey, and simla when Dwer warily guided Danel's group across the shallow ford. From then on, he borrowed a tactic from the old wars, reconnoitering each day's march the night before, counting on urrish diurnal habits to keep him safe from ambush – though urs were adaptable beings. They *could* be deadly even at night, as human fighters used to find out the hard way.

Dwer hoped this group had lazy habits, after generations of peace.

Rising at midnight, he would scout by the light of two smaller moons, sniffing warily each time the trail of hoofprints neared some plausible ambuscade. Then, at dawn, he would hurry back to help Danel's donkey train plod ahead by day.

Ozawa thought it urgent to catch up with the urrish band and negotiate an arrangement. But Dwer worried. *How does he expect they'll react? Embracing us like brothers? These are criminals. Like Rety's band. Like us.*

The spoor grew fresher. Now the urs were just a week ahead of them, maybe just a few days.

He began noting *other* traces. Soft outlines in the sand. Broken stone flakes. Fragments of a moccasin lace. Smudged campfires more than a month old.

Rety's band. The urs are heading straight for the heart of their territory.

Danel took the news calmly. 'They must figure as we did. The human sooners know a lot about life in these hills. That's valuable experience, whether it can be bought, borrowed—'

'Or tortured out of 'em,' Lena Strong finished, whetting one of her knives by the evening's low red coals. 'Some urrish clans used to keep human prisoners as drudges, before we broke —'em of the habit.'

'A habit *they* learned from the queens. There's no call to assume slavery is a natural urs behavior. For that matter, back on Old Earth *humans* used to—'

'Yeah, well, we still have a problem,' Dwer interrupted. 'What to do when we catch up.'

'Right!' Lena inspected the knife-edge. 'Do we pounce fast, taking the urs all bunched together? Or do it hoon-style – picking them off one at a time.'

Jenin sighed unhappily. 'Oh, Lena. Please stop.' She had been cheerful throughout the journey, until hearing all this talk of fighting. Jenin had joined this trek in order to be a founding mother of a new race, not to hunt down beings who had once been her neighbors.

Dwer's heart felt the same pain as Jenin, though his pragmatic side agreed with Lena.

'If we have to, I'd rather do it fast,' he muttered, glancing at the donkey carrying their most secret, unspeakable 'tools.'

'It shouldn't come to that,' Danel insisted. 'First let's ascertain who they are and what they want. Perhaps we can make common cause.'

Lena snorted. 'Send an emissary? Give away our presence? You heard Dwer. There's over a dozen of 'em!'

'Don't you think we should wait for the second group, then?' Jenin asked. 'They were supposed to be right behind us.'

Lena shrugged. 'Who knows how long they'll take? Or if they got lost? The urs could find us first. And there's the human tribe to consider.'

'Rety's old band.'

'Right. Want to let them get killed or enslaved? Just on account of we're too scared to—'

'Lena!' Danel cut her off. 'That will do for now. We'll see what's to be done when the time comes. Meanwhile, poor Dwer should get some sleep. We owe him whatever rest he can get.'

'That ain't half what he's owed,' Lena muttered, causing Dwer to glance her way, but in the pre-moonrise dimness, he could make out only shadows.

'G'night all,' he said, and slipped away to seek his bedroll.

Mudfoot looked up from the blanket, chuttering testily over having to move. The creature *did* help warm things up at night, which partly made up for its vexing way of licking Dwer's face while he slept, harvesting perspiration from his forehead and lip.

Dwer lay down, turned over – and blinked in surprise at two pairs of giant round eyes, staring back at him from just three meters away.

Jeekee glavers.

Normally, one simply ignored the placid creatures. But he still couldn't shake the memory of that pack of them, clustered greedily around a dead gallaiter.

He tossed a dirt clod vaguely their way. 'Go on! Get!'

Just as vaguely, the pair turned and sauntered off. Dwer glanced at Mudfoot.

'Why not make yourself a *bit* useful and keep those pests away?'

The noor just grinned back at him.

Dwer pulled the blanket over his chin, trying to settle down. He was tired and ached from sore muscles and bruises. But slumber came slowly, freighted with troubling dreams.

He woke to a soft touch, stroking his face. Irritably, he tried to push the noor away.

'Quit it, furball! Lick a donkey turd, if you want salt so bad.'

After a surprised pause, a hushed voice answered.

'Reckon I never been welcomed to a man's bed half so sweetly.'

Dwer rolled onto an elbow, rubbing one eye to make out a blurred silhouette. A woman.

'Jenin?'

'Would you prefer her? I won the toss, but I'll fetch her if you like.'

'Lena! What – can I do for you?'

Dwer made out a white glint – her rare smile.

'Well, you *could* invite me in from the cold.' Her voice sounded soft, almost shy.

Lena was buxom and sanguinely female, yet *soft* and *shy* were two words Dwer had never linked with her before. 'Uh – sure ...'

Am I still dreaming? he wondered as she slid alongside, strong hands working to loosen his clothes. Her smooth skin seemed to blaze with ardent heat.

I must be. The Lena I know never smelled this good.

'You're all knotted up,' she commented, kneading his neck and back with uncanny, forceful accuracy. At first, Dwer's gasps came from released muscle strain. But Lena somehow also made each jab or digging twist of her calloused fingers seem feminine, erotic.

She got halfway through the massage before Dwer passed his limit of self-control and turned over to gently but resolutely reverse their positions, taking her beneath him, repaying her vitality with a vigor that welled from weeks of pent-up tension. Hoarded worry and fatigue seemed to explode into the air, into the forest, into her as she clutched and sighed, pulling him closer.

*

426

After she slipped away, he pondered muzzily – *Lena thinks I may die, since my job is to be upfront in any fight. This might be the last ... the only chance ...*

Dwer drifted into a tranquil, dreamless repose – a slumber so blank and relaxing that he actually felt rested by the time *another* warm body slid into the bedroll next to him. By then, his unconscious had worked it out, crediting the women with ultimate pragmatism.

Danel will probably be around later, so it makes sense to use whatever I have to give, before it's gone.

It wasn't his place to judge the women. Theirs was the harder job, here in the wilderness. His tasks were simple – to hunt, fight, and if need be, to die. Theirs was to go on, whatever it took.

Dwer did not even have to rouse all the way. Nor did Jenin seem offended that his body performed but half awake. There were all sorts of duties to fulfill these days. If he was going to keep up, he would simply have to catch what rest he could.

Dwer woke to find it already a midura past midnight. Though he felt much better now, he had to fight a languid lethargy to get dressed and check his gear – the bow and quiver, a compass, sketch pad, and hip canteen – then stop by the dim coals to pluck the leaf-wrapped package Jenin left for him each night, the one decent meal he would eat while away.

For most of his adult life he had traveled alone, relishing peace and solitude. Yet, he had to admit the attractions of being part of a team, a community. Perhaps, under Ozawa's guidance, they might come to feel like *family*.

Would that take some of the bitter sting out of recalling the life and loved ones they had left behind, in the graceful forests of the Slope?

Dwer was about to head off, following the urrish track farther in the direction of the rising moons, when a soft sound made him pause. Someone was awake and talking. Yet he had passed both women, snoring quietly and (he liked to imagine) happily. Dwer slipped the bow off his shoulder, moving toward the low speech sounds, more curious than edgy. Soon he recognized the murmured whisper.

Of course it was Danel. But who was the sage talking to?

Beyond the bole of a large tree, Dwer peered into a small clearing where satiny moonlight spilled over an unlikely pair. Danel was kneeling low to face the little black creature called Mudfoot. Dwer couldn't make out words, but judging from tone and inflection, Ozawa was trying to ask it *questions*, in one language after another.

The noor responded by licking itself, then glancing briefly toward Dwer, standing in the shadows. When Ozawa switched to GalTwo, Mudfoot grinned – then twisted to bite an itch on one shoulder. When the beast turned back, it was to answer the sage with a gaping yawn.

Danel let out a soft sigh, as if he had expected to fail but felt it worth an effort.

What effort? Dwer wondered. Was the sage seeking magical aid, as ignorant lowlanders sometimes tried to do, treating noor like sprites in some fairy tale? Did Ozawa hope to *tame* Mudfoot, the way hoon sailors did, as agile helpers on the river? Few nonhoon had ever managed that feat. But even if it worked, what use was *one* noor assistant? Or would Dwer's next assignment – after dealing with urrish sooners and then Rety's band – be to run back and collect more of Mudfoot's kind?

That made no sense. If by some miracle the Commons survived, word would be sent calling them all home. If the worst happened, they were to stay as far from the Slope as possible.

Well, Danel will tell me what he wants me to know. I just hope this doesn't mean he's gone crazy.

Dwer crept away and found the urrish trail. He set off at a lope that soon strained forward, pulling him with unwilled eagerness to see what lay beyond the next shadowy rise. For the first time in days, Dwer felt whole and strong. It wasn't that all worries had vanished. Existence was still a frail, perilous thing, all too easily lost. Still, for this narrow stretch of time he pounded onward, feeling vibrantly alive.

RETY

The dream always ended the same way, just before she woke shivering, clutching a soft blanket to her breast.

She dreamed about the bird.

Not as it appeared the last time she had seen it –headless, spread across Rann's laboratory bench in the buried station – but as she recalled first glimpsing the strange thing. Vivid in motion, with plumage like glossy forest leaves, alert and lustrous in a way that seemed to stroke her soul.

As a child she had loved to watch native birds, staring for hours at their swooping dives, envying their freedom of the air, their liberty to take wing, leaving their troubles far behind. Then one day Jass returned from a long journey to the south, bragging about all the beasts he had shot. One had been a fantastic flying thing that they took by surprise as it emerged from a tidal marsh. It barely got away after an arrow tore one wing, flapping off toward the northwest, leaving behind a feather harder than stone.

That very night, risking awful punishment, she stole the stiff metal fragment from the tent where the hunters snored, and with a pack of stolen food she ran off, seeking this fabled wonder for herself. As luck had it, she guessed right and crossed its path, spotting the fluttering creature as it labored onward with short, gliding bounds. In a throat-catching instant of recognition, Rety knew the bird was like her – wounded by the same man's taste for senseless violence.

Watching it hop-glide ever westward, never resting, she knew they shared one more trait. Persistence.

She wanted to catch up with it, to heal it, talk to it. To learn its source of power. To help it reach its goal. To help find its home. But even disabled, the bird soon outdistanced her. For a heart-aching time, she thought she had lost it forever . . .

At that point of harsh emotion, without transition, the dream shifted to another scene. Suddenly, the bird was right in front of her, closer than ever, fluttering inside a jeweled cage, dodging a mist of golden, cloying drops . . . then cowering away from searing knives of flame!

Frustration choked Rety, unable to give aid. Unable to save it.

Finally, when all seemed lost, the bird did as Rety herself would have done. It lashed out with desperate strength, dying to bring down its oppressor, the agent of its torment.

For several nights in a row the dream ended the same way, with someone's insistent arms holding her back in shameful safety while the bird fired its own head upward toward a hovering, shadowy form. A dark rival with dangling, lethal limbs.

It seemed revenge was going to be another of those things that didn't turn out quite the same in real life as she'd imagined.

For one thing, in her heart, Rety never reckoned on Jass taking pain so well.

The hunter lay strapped to a couch inside the scout aircraft, his ruggedly handsome features twisting as Kunn kept the promise he had made. A promise Rety regretted a bit more each time Jass clamped back another moan, choking it behind gritted teeth.

Who would've thought he'd turn out to be brave, she pondered, recalling all the times Jass used to brag, bluster, and harass other members of the tribe. Bullies were supposed to be cowards, or so one of the tribe's aged grandfathers used to mutter when he was sure the young hunters wouldn't hear. Too bad the old geep would never know how wrong he'd been. That battered patriarch had died during the months since Rety left these hills.

She tried steeling her heart during the contest of wills between Kunn and Jass, one Jass was bound to lose. *You want to find out where the bird came from, don't you?* she asked herself. *Anyway, don't Jass deserve everything he's getting? Ain't his own stubbornheadedness bringing this on himself?*

Well, in truth, Rety had played a role in stiffening the hunter's resistance, thus extending his torment. Kunn's patient, insistent questions alternated with grunts of pure glaverlike obstinacy from Jass, sweating and contorting under jolts applied by Kunn's robot partner.

When she could take no more without getting sick, Rety silently slipped out the hatch. If anything changed, the pilot could call her on the tiny comm button the sky-humans had installed under the skin near her right ear.

She set off toward the campsite, trying to appear casual in case any sooners watched from the shrubby undergrowth.

That was how she thought of them. *Sooners*. Savages. No different in kind from those puffed-up barbarians on the Slope, who thought themselves *so* civilized with their fancy books but who were still little more than half-animals, trapped on a dirty world they could never leave. To a sky-being like herself, they were all the same, whichever side of the Rimmers they led their dirt-scratching lives.

She smelled the camp before reaching it. A familiar musty blend of wood smoke, excrement, and poorly tanned hides, all mixed with a sulfury pungence rising from the steam pools that always drew the tribe here this time of year – a fact that had made it easy to guide Kunn to this pocket canyon, high in the Gray Hills. Rety paused halfway to the campsite, smoothing down the sleek jumpsuit Ling had given her, soon after she became the first Jijoan to enter the underground station, that wonderland of luxuries and bright marvels. Ling had also bathed Rety, treated her scalp, and applied potions and rays to leave her feeling cleaner, stronger, even *taller* than before. Only the livid scar on one side of her face still marred the mirror's transformed image and that would be tended, she was assured, when they all went 'home.'

My home too, Rety mused, resuming a brisk pace until all moaning traces of the hunter's torment faded behind her. She drove out memory of Jass's squirming agony by calling to mind those images the sky-foursome had shown her – of a splendid, jewellike city, tucked inside a steep-walled valley. A city of fairy towers and floating castles, where one lucky branch of humanity lived with their beloved patrons, the wise, benevolent Rothen.

That part didn't quite appeal to her – this business of having *masters* who told you what to do. Nor did the Rothen themselves, when she met the two living aboard the station, who seemed too pretty and prim, too smugly happy, by far. But then, if Ling and Besh loved them, she supposed she could get used to that idea too. Anyway, Rety was willing to do or put up with anything to reach that city of lights.

I always knew I belonged someplace else, she thought, rounding a bend in the forest. *Not here. Not in a place like this*.

Before her stretched a debris-strewn clearing dotted by half a dozen ragged shelters – animal hides thrown over rows of bent saplings – all clustered round a cook fire where soot-smudged figures hunched over a carcass. Tonight's meal. A donkey with a neat hole burned through its heart. A gift, courtesy of Kunn's handy hunter-killer robot.

People dressed in poorly tanned skins moved about at chores or simply slouched through the middle of the day. Their complexions were filthy. Most had matted hair, and they stank. After meeting the Slopies – and then Ling and Besh – it was hard to picture these savages as the same *race* as herself, let alone her own tribe.

Several male figures loafed near a makeshift pen where the new prisoners huddled, having barely moved since they were herded into camp a couple of nights back. Some of the men chopped at tree stumps with machetes swiped from the newcomers' supplies, marveling at the keen blades of Buyur metal. But the men kept well away from the pile of crates Kunn had forbidden them to touch, awaiting his decision which to destroy.

A handful of boys straddled a new fence of laser-split logs, passing the time by spitting, then laughing as angry complaints rose from the captives.

Shouldn't let 'em do that, Rety thought. *Even if the outlanders are nosy fools who oughtn't have come*.

Kunn had assigned her the task of finding what brought the prisoners to these parts, violating their own sacred law. But Rety felt reluctant, even disgusted.

Dawdling, she turned to survey a way of life she once thought she'd never escape.

Despite the tumult of the last few days, tribal life went on. Kallish, the old clubfoot, still labored by the stream bed, hammering stone cores into flake arrowheads and other tools, convinced the recent influx of iron implements would be a passing fad. He was probably right.

Upstream, women waded through shallows, seeking the trishelled juice oysters that ripened in volcanic heat this time of year, while farther upslope, beyond the steamy pools, a cluster of girls used poles to beat Illoes trees, gathering the tart fallen berries in woven baskets. As usual females were doing most of the hard work. Nowhere was this more evident than near the cook fire, where grouchy old Binni, her arms bloody past the elbows, took charge of preparing the donkey for roasting. The headwoman's hair was even grayer than before. Her latest baby had died, leaving Binni irritable with swollen, tender breasts, hissing at her two young helpers through wide gaps between yellow-brown teeth.

Despite such signs of normality, most tribe-folk moved in a state of sluggish distraction. Whenever anyone glanced Rety's way, they *flinched*, as if she were the last thing on Jijo they ever expected to see. More shocking than a glaver standing upright.

Rety, the god.

She held her head high. *Tell your stinky brats about it by the campfire, till the end of time. Tell 'em about the girl who talked back to big mean hunters, no matter what they did to her. A girl who wouldn't take it anymore. Who dared to do what you never imagined. Who found a way to leave this stinking hell and go live on a star.*

Rety felt a thrill each time someone briefly met her gaze and quickly looked away.

I'm not one of you. Never was. And now you know it too.

Only Binni showed no trace of being overwhelmed by the deity Rety had become. The same old disdain and disappointment lay in those metal-gray eyes. At age twenty-eight, Binni was younger than any of the forayers, even Ling. Still, it seemed nothing on Jijo, or in heaven, would ever surprise her.

It had been years since Rety last called the old woman 'Mama.' She wasn't tempted to resume now.

With her back straight, she walked past the chefs and their grisly work. Inside, though, she wavered.

Maybe it wasn't such a good idea to come back here. Why mix with these ghosts when she could be in the aircraft, relishing victory over her lifelong enemy? The punishment being executed on Jass seemed rightful and good, now that she didn't have to face his agony up close. That contradiction made Rety nervous, as if something were missing. Like trying to use moccasins without laces.

'wife! there you are, wife! bad wife, to leave yee alone so long!'

Several clansmen scurried out of the way, making room for a four-legged creature, galloping past their ankles like some untouchable, all-powerful being. Which the little urrish male *was*, in a sense, since Rety had loudly promised horrors to anyone laying a hand on her 'husband.'

yee leaped into her arms, squirming with pleasure even as he scolded.

'wife leave yee alone too long with female foes! they offer yee soft, warm pouch, temptresses!'

Rety flared jealousy. 'Who offered you a pouch! If any of those hussies—'

Then she saw he was teasing. Some of the tension in her shoulders let go as she laughed. The little critter was definitely good for her.

'relax, wife,' he assured her. 'just one pouch for yee. go in now?'

'In now,' she replied, unzipping the plush hip bag Ling had provided. yee dove inside, wriggled around, then stuck out his head and long neck to peer at her.

'come now, wife, visit Ul-Tahni. that sage ready talk now.'

'Ah, is she? Well now, isn't that awfully nice of her.'

Rety didn't relish going to see the leader of the outlanders. But Kunn had given her a job, and now was as good a time as any.

'All right,' she said. 'Let's hear what the hinney has to say.'

DWER

The urs, it appeared, had done the small human expedition a favor. In receiving death and devastation, they had left a warning.

A tale of callous murder was clear to read through the dawn light – in seared and shattered trees, blackened craters, and scattered debris, pushed by a gusty, dry wind. The violence that took place here – just a few days ago by Dwer's estimate – must have been brief but horrible.

The plateau's terraced outlines were still visible after ages of softening by erosion and vegetation. It was a former Buyur site, going back to the last race licensed to use this world – legal residents dwelling in heaven-like towers, who went through their daily lives unafraid of the open sky.

Dwer traced the terror that recently fell upon this place. All too vividly he pictured the panicked urrish settlers, rearing and coughing with dread, coiling their long necks, with slim arms crossed to shield their precious pouches as the ground around them exploded. He could almost hear their screams as they fled the burning encampment, down a steep trail leading into a narrow defile – where *human* footprints swarmed in abruptly from both sides, tracked by crude moccasins, mingling with urrish hooves chaotically.

He picked up shreds of home-twisted twine and leather cord.

From countless signs, Dwer pictured ropes and nets falling to trap the urs, taking them prisoner.

Couldn't they tell they were being herded? The aircraft aimed off to the sides and all around, to drive them. So why didn't the urs scatter instead of clumping in a mass to be caught?

Several patches of sticky sand gave him an answer. The overall intent might have been capture, but the flying gunner had few qualms about enforcing the round-up with a corpse or two.

Don't judge the urs too harshly. Do you know how you'll react when lightning bolts start falling all around? War is messy, and we're all out of practice. Even Drake never had to cope with anything like this.

'So, we're facing an alliance between the human sooners and the aliens,' Lena concluded. 'Kind of changes things, don't it?'

Danel Ozawa wore a bleak expression. 'This entire region is compromised. Whatever fate befalls the Slope will now surely happen here, as well. Whether by plague, or by fire, or hunting their victims one at a time with machines – they'll scourge the area as thoroughly as back home.'

Danel's task had been to carry a legacy into the wilderness – both knowledge and fresh genes to invigorate the human tribe already living here – to preserve something of Earthling life in case the worst came to pass. It was never a joyous enterprise, more like the mission of a lifeboat captain in some ancient tale about a shipwreck. But at least that endeavor had been based on a slim hope. Now his eyes lacked all trace of that emotion.

Jenin protested, 'Well, didn't you just say the sooners and aliens were allies against the urs? The star-gods wouldn't turn on the tribe now, would they?'

She stopped as the others looked at her, their expressions answering better than words.

Jenin paled. 'Oh.'

Moments later, she lifted her chin once more.

'Well, they still don't know we exist, right? So why don't we just *leave*, right now? The four of us. What about *north*, Dwer? You've been up that way before. Let's go!'

Danel kicked some debris left by the urs' riotous flight and the looting that followed. He pointed to a narrow cleft in the rocks. 'We can build a pyre over there.'

'What are you doing?' Jenin asked, as Dwer led the donkeys where the sage indicated and began unloading their packs.

'I'll set the grenades,' Lena said, prying open a container. 'We'd best add some wood. I'll gather these broken crates.'

'Hey! I asked you guys – what's going *on*?'

Danel took Jenin's arm while Dwer hauled a portion of their supplies to one side – food and clothing plus a few basic implements, none containing any metal. Left behind in a stack were all the books and sophisticated tools they had taken from the Slope.

The sage explained.

'We brought this legacy in order to maintain some minimal semblance of human culture in exile. But four people can't establish a civilization, no matter how many books they have. We must prepare for the likelihood that all of this must be destroyed.'

Clearly the prospect gnawed at Ozawa. His face, already haggard, now seemed sliced by pain. Dwer averted his gaze, concentrating on the work at hand, separating only supplies helpful to a small party of fugitives on the run.

Jenin chewed on the news and nodded. 'Well, if we must live and raise families without books, I guess that just puts us ahead of schedule, no? A bit farther along the Path of—'

She stopped. Danel was shaking his head.

'No, Jenin. That is not the way things will be.

'Oh, we four might as well try to survive. But even if we *did* make it to some far-off valley, beyond reach of whatever demise the aliens have planned, it's unlikely we'd adapt to a strange ecosystem in time. Rety told us that her band lost half its first generation to accidents and allergic reactions. That's typical for sooner groups, till they learn what's safe to eat or touch. It's a deadly, trial-and-error process. Four just isn't enough.'

'I thought—'

And that leaves out the problem of inbreeding—'

'You can't mean—'

'But even if we could solve all of those dilemmas, it still wouldn't work, because we *aren't* going to start a band of fallen savages, spiralling into ignorance, even if the Scrolls give that fate all sorts of fancy names. Human beings never came to Jijo for the Path of Redemption.'

Dwer looked up from his work. Lena halted as well, holding a thick tube with a clockwork fuse at one end. Up to that point, Ozawa had been explaining what Dwer already knew. But now silence reigned. No one was going to move or speak until the sage explained.

For a second time, Danel Ozawa sighed deeply.

'The secret is passed on to a few, each generation. But I see no point in concealing it from you three, whom I now think of as kin, as family.

'Some of the other five races were appalled when we built Biblos. The Great Printing seemed to imply we had no intention of ever forgetting. Our founders did some smooth talking to explain the flood of books. A *temporary measure*, they called it. A way to help all races live in enough comfort to concentrate on developing their souls, till we're spiritually ready to move on down the Path.

'Officially, it's the long-term goal of each of the Six. But the *Tabernacle* founders never meant their descendants to devolve down to speechless proto-humans, ready for some race of star-gods to adopt and uplift.'

The sage paused until Dwer finally broke in. 'Then why *are* we here?'

Danel shrugged. 'Everyone knows that each race had ulterior motives. Those forbidden to breed at home sought a place where they can have offspring as they please. Or take the g'Keks, who tell of persecutors, hounding them throughout the star lanes.'

'So humans came to Jijo because folks on Earth weren't sure they'd survive?'

Ozawa nodded. 'Oh, we'd made a few friends, who helped Earth get a Library branch. And having uplifted two client races, we won low-level patron status. Still, Galactic history doesn't offer much hope for a wolfling race like ours. We already had enemies. The Terragens Council knew Earth would be vulnerable for a long time to come.'

'So the *Tabernacle* crew *weren't* outcasts?'

Danel ticked a thin smile. 'A cover story, in case the colonists were caught, so the Council could disavow them as renegades. In fact, our ancestors were sent to find a hidden refuge for humankind.' The sage raised his hands. 'But where? Despite rumors, no route is known *beyond* the Five Galaxies. *Within* them, every star is catalogued, many with lease-holders to watch over 'em. So the Terragens searched the Great Library to see what other races did in our position.

'Despite flaws, the "sooner" phenomenon showed promise.'

Lena shook her head. 'There's a lot you're leavin' out. Like what we're supposed to be *doing* here, while hiding, if our mission isn't to go down the Path.'

'If Lester or the others know, they haven't told me,' Danel answered. 'Maybe we're to sit tight and wait for the universe to change. Anyway, that hardly matters now. If our culture's finished, I won't have any part in going on as wretched fragments, whelping kids who will be no more than savage brutes.'

Jenin started to speak, but then pressed her lips.

'At least we know Earth *has* survived a few hundred years,' Dwer said.

'Though the forayers say there's a crisis,' Lena noted. 'With Earth in the middle of it.'

Danel looked away, his jaw set.

'Hey,' Dwer said, 'aren't the *sky-humans* exactly what that Terra Council wanted? To have a branch of humans off somewhere safe from whatever happens to Earth? Those guys you met back at the Glade have these Rothen characters to protect them.'

Danel exhaled. 'Perhaps, though who knows if they'll *remain* human under that influence? The irony of being murdered by cousins seems too much to bear.'

The sage shook himself, as if shedding cobwebs.

'Let's prepare that pyre. If these items cannot serve a civilized tribe of exile Earthlings, then we can at least do our duty by this world and leave no dross. Lena, set the timer to go off one day from now, if we don't return.'

'Return?' Lena looked up from her preparations. 'I thought we were giving up—'

She rocked back as the sage whirled, with some of the old fire in his eyes.

'Who said anything about giving up! What's the matter with you three? Look at your faces. Are you going to let one little setback get you down?'

A little setback? Dwer wondered, glancing at the blast scars and shattered trees surrounding the urrish encampment. 'I don't get it. You said we can't finish our mission.'

'So?' Danel Ozawa demanded. 'We're adaptable We'll *switch missions*! We're not colonists anymore – so what?

'We can still be warriors.'

RETY

The prisoners lay dejected in muddy wallows, necks drooping, already stinking after two days' confinement in the dank pen. Thirteen urs who would have preferred the arid plateau where they had settled, till a warcraft screeched over their camp without warning, casting lightning, driving the survivors toward Jass and the other hunters, waiting with rough ropes.

Thus Kunn had fulfilled his side of a bargain, ridding the hills of a recent, hated urrish infestation. In return, Jass was to guide Kunn to the site where he and Bom first saw the flying bird-thing. No one knew why the deal later broke down – why Jass abruptly changed his mind, preferring the robot's caresses over giving the pilot what he wanted.

No one except Rety.

Binni used to say – why defy men, who can beat you if you make them mad? Use words to nudge and guide the brutes. Make 'em think it was their idea all along.

But I kept talking back, didn't I?

Well, I finally tried it your way, Binni, and know what? You were right. Nothing I could do to Jass could ever hurt him like he's hurting himself right now.

Bom was guarding the gate to the prisoners' pen. The burly hunter hurriedly obeyed her command to open up, not once meeting Rety's eyes. He knew where his pal was now. Just two things kept Bom from sharing the same fate. First was his notoriously poor sense of direction. Alone, he could never find the place where he and Jass had spotted the metal bird.

The other thing was Rety's whim. Bom's abject cringing pleased her more than screams. *This* bully was scared half out of his breech-clout.

When she glared at the boys spitting at the prisoners, they jumped off the wall and ran. She cast curt laughter after them. The tribe-kids never used to speak to her in the old days, either.

She entered the pen.

Ul-Tahni, leader of the unlucky urs, greeted Rety with a fluid bow of her long neck. From a gray-fringed snout, she launched into a series of whistles and clicks, till Rety broke in.

'None o' that now!' she admonished. 'I don't follow that jabber.'

Wincing, Ul-Tahni switched to Anglic.

'I afologize. Your attire deceives the eye into seeing a Galactic-level entity.'

Rety lifted her head. 'You weren't dee-seeved. That's exactly what I am.'

I hope, she added inside. Rann and the others could change their minds before the ship returned, especially once she gave them all she had in trade. Even if the forayers kept their word, she *would*, in time, have to learn all those crazy languages they used among the stars.

'Again, regret for having offended. Is it true, then? You have veen adofted off Jijo's forlorn desert into the running-clan of star creatures? What a fortunate youngling you are.'

'Yeah,' Rety agreed, wondering if the urs was being sarcastic. 'So, yee says you're ready to tell us what your bunch was doing out here, beyond the Rimmers.'

A long sigh blew the gray fringe.

'We arrived, disgracefully, to set uf a colony, freserving our kind in a secret sanctuary.'

Rety grunted. 'That much is obvious. But why here? Why now?'

'It is a site already ascertained to ve havitavle ... suitavle for sustaining earthlings, and therefore the donkeys we rely on. You yourself testified to that fact.'

'Ah.' Ul-Tahni must have been one of the junior sages in the pavilion when Rety told her story to the High Council. 'Go on.'

'As to our haste – we sought to elude the fate soon to fall on the Slofe, annihilation at the hands of star-felons.'

Rety reacted angrily. 'I've heard that damned lie before. They'd *never do* a thing like that!'

Ul-Tahni rocked her head. 'I stand corrected. Clearly such fine entities would not slay folk who had done them no hurt, nor cast death without warning from a cloudy sky.'

This time the sarcasm was thick. Rety glanced at a young middling urs with a nasty burn along one flank, from the flying robot's heat beam.

'Well, I guess it's just your tough luck we had reason to come visit, asking directions, and found you already at war with my old family.'

'Not war. A transient discord. One we did not initiate. Naturally, your cousins were shocked to see us. Our idea was to vanquish their reflex hostility with resolute friendliness. To induce cordiality with gifts and offers of assistance.'

'Yeah, right.' Rety knew how early human settlers had been treated by urrish clans of yore. 'I bet you also counted on having better weapons than any they had here.'

Again, a snorted sigh. 'As *your* associates crushed *us*, using fower far greater than our own? It kindles wonder – could this chain of uneven strength ve extrafolated?'

Rety didn't like the bemused look in those beady urrish eyes. 'What do you mean?'

'A conjecture. Could there exist forces as far suferior to your new lords as they are over us? In all the wide galaxies, can one *ever be* sure one has chosen the right side?'

The words sent twinges up Rety's spine, reminding her of recent disturbing dreams.

'You don't know *nothin'* about galaxies an' such, so don't you pretend—'

At that moment a sudden yelp cut her short, as yee popped his head out of the pouch, mewling with unease. A ripple of reaction spread among the prisoners' husbands, who emerged howling, swinging their heads to face south. Soon the larger females followed suit, clambering to their feet.

Rety worried – was it a revolt? But no, clearly something was unnerving them.

'What d'you hear?' she demanded of yee.

'*engine!*' the little urs answered, corkscrewing his agile neck.

A moment later Rety sensed it too. A distant whine. She brought a hand to the bump near her ear and pressed.

'Hey, Kunn! What's going on?'

There followed a long pause, during which the open line relayed cabin sounds – switches being thrown, motors revving. Finally, the pilot's voice buzzed near her skull.

'*Jass chose to cooperate, so we're off now in search of the source of your metal bird.*'

'But I want to go too!'

Kunn's reply was cool.

'*Jass told me everything, including the* reason *he resisted so hard. It seems you convinced him I'd finish him off the moment he told what he knew. That he would live only until then. Now why did you tell the poor bastard such a thing. Rety? It caused inconvenience and unnecessary pain.*'

Rety thought – *Unnecessary for you, but darn important to me!* Revenge was only half of her rationale for manipulating Jass. But it would have been enough all by itself.

'Kunn, don't leave me. I'm one of you now. Rann an' Besh, an' even Ro-pol said so!'

Suddenly she felt small and very vulnerable, with urs in front of her and Bom behind at the gate, surrounded by others who would surely love to bring her down. She covered her mouth and lowered her voice, whispering urgently for the little transmitter, 'The sooners'll turn on me, Kunn. I know it!'

'*Perhaps you should have thought of that before.*' Another long pause followed. Then – '*If Rann hadn't insisted on long-range radio silence, I could talk it over with the others before deciding.*'

'Deciding what?'

'*Whether to bring you back, or to leave you where you began.*'

Rety fought down a trembling that coursed her body, in response to Kunn's harsh words. Her hopes were a bright tower that seemed about to crash.

'*I'll tell you what, I'll leave the robot to protect you, Rety. It will do what you say till I get back. Do not abuse the privilege.*'

Her heart leaped at the phrase – *till I get back*.

'I promise!' she whispered urgently.

'*Treat this as a second chance. Question the urs. Destroy their weapons. Don't let anyone leave the valley. Do a good job and we may wipe the slate clean when I return – providing my hunt flushes out the prey at last.*

'*Kunn out.*'

The line clicked, cutting off the cabin sounds. Rety quelled an urge to press the button and choke out another plea to be taken along. Instead she set her teeth grimly and climbed the fence rails to stare as a silvery dart lifted out of the narrow canyon, turned in the morning light, then streaked southward, leaving her with a heart as cold and barren as a glacier.

DWER

The sooner village was a simmering place that squatted at the base of a canyon filled with dense, sulfurous, listless air.

A hellish place, from an urrish point of view.

Dwer's high vantage point looked down at the captives, in their cramped pen. Long necks drooped, and they lay like the atmosphere, barely moving.

'I count about a dozen, not including dead ones, just as you said,' Lena noted, peering through her compact telescope. 'I guess you'll do as a tracker, fella-me-boy.'

'Thanks, Oh Mistress of Forbidden Devices,' Dwer answered. He was getting used to Lena's ways. She always had to get a little *bite* in, even when making a compliment. It was like a noor, purring on your lap, who repays your petting by dipping its claws briefly into your thigh. The funny thing was – he'd actually been getting used to the idea of making a life with this woman, along with Jenin, Danel, and the lost tribe of human exiles. Even discovering the urrish invasion hadn't made the notion absurd. Danel had been right. There *might* have been room for common cause.

But now all such ideas were obsolete. Over to the left lay the reason why – a silver-gray machine, shaped like a hoonish cigar with stubby wings. It was the first alien thing. Dwer had seen, since almost being killed with Rety by a floating robot that evening in a mulc-spider's lair.

The sky-car should not be here in the badlands.

It meant the demolishment of all their plans.

It also had no business being so beautiful.

Dwer was proud of this overlook, high on the canyon wall, which surveyed from the village, past the steam pools, all the way to the flying machine, sitting in a nest of crushed vegetation.

'I wish the yokels would stop movin' around. It's hard gettin' a good count,' Lena complained. 'At least the kid said the local bully-boys won't let women use weapons, so they aren't combatants to worry about.'

She sniffed disdain over such a stupid waste of resources.

Dwer would prefer not to fight Jijoan humans, as well as the alien kind. Anyway, their only real chance lay in achieving complete surprise.

Sharing the cramped ledge, Dwer felt Lena's breast pressing against his arm, yet it provoked no arousal. Their bodies seemed to grasp that a change had occurred. There would be no more passionate episodes. No life-affirming gestures. Sex and gender were important to colonists planning to raise families, not to a raiding party bent on destruction. All that mattered now were skills. And an ability to count on one another.

'It looks like a standard atmospheric scout,' Danel Ozawa said. 'Definitely a fighter. I wish we brought along just *one* text on Galactic technology. Give me the glass, will you?'

Like Dwer's and Lena's, Danel's face now bore jagged, charcoal slashes that were supposed to muddle the pattern-recognizing optics of alien killer machines. Dwer preferred thinking of it as war paint.

'Well, I'll be—' Danel muttered. 'Here, take a look. I guess now we know how the star-gods found this place.'

When Dwer got the telescope, the first thing he noticed was that the flyer's hatch now lay ajar, revealing part of the interior, including banks of control panels. *If only we were close right now,* he thought. *With the door open and no guard robot in sight …*

'Look to the right, up the trail a ways,' Danel urged.

Dwer shifted the spyglass, sweeping till he glimpsed a small figure dressed in one of the aliens' one-piece garments, moving toward the sooner encampment.

'Great Ifni's Egg!' he yelped.

'What is it?' Lena demanded, grabbing the scope as Dwer rolled on his back, staring past tangled branches at a murky sky.

'Well, well,' Lena muttered. 'Looks like she caught up with us, after all.'

'I should've strangled her when she stole my bow. I should've left her to the damn spider.'

'You don't mean that, son,' Danel chided.

Dwer knew the sage was right. Still, he grumbled. 'Oh, don't I? She was a pain from the start. Now she's ruined everything.'

'Perhaps Rety was coerced.' But the sage sounded unconvinced as they took turns with the telescope. Each of them had seen the girl's clothes, her freshly coifed hair, and her confident stride, swaggering into camp like she owned the place.

'She's gone to see the prisoners,' Lena reported, a little later. 'Talking to one of 'em now ... Those urs sure look ragged, poor things.' Lena tsked, and her sympathy was clearly more than sarcastic. 'I wish I could make out—'

She stopped as Dwer suddenly gripped her arm, reacting to a faint, a high keening that seemed to scrape the inside of his skull. The noor beast chuttered irritably, shaking its head and sneezing. Soon the noise deepened and grew loud enough for the rest of them to hear. Even Jenin, who was on lookout duty upslope, hissed a worried query.

The clamor came from the *aircraft*. It made Dwer's teeth feel as if they were loosening in their moorings.

'Something's coming out!' Lena exclaimed, turning the telescope. 'It's the robot!'

Dwer saw a hovering black dot with dangling tendrils separate from the ship, whose hatch then closed. The air shimmered from expelled dust as humming motors lifted the scout off the ground. The gray arrowhead was larger than the house Dwer grew up in, yet it *wafted* upward and turned lightly, stopping when its nose pointed almost due south. Then the heavens echoed its fierce growl as it plunged away, receding faster than anything he had ever seen.

'Damn,' Danel cursed. 'We missed our best opportunity.'

Lena wasn't watching the departing scout. Instead, her eyes followed the black robot, now cruising toward the tribal village.

'Don't worry,' she assured. 'I expect we'll get another chance.'

The glavers were back. Of all irksome times for the stupid things to tag along!

They must have followed, at their own lazy pace, all the way from last night's campsite. Now they mewled unhappily at the sights and smells of the fetid ravine, but that did not keep them from following Dwer as he left the shelter of the forest, heading toward the cluster of rude huts.

Dwer glanced back at Lena Strong, crouched at the edge of the last line of trees. With raised eyebrows, she asked if he wanted her to shoot the idiotic beasts. He said no with a terse headshake. They were dangerous only to a man who was trying to hide. And he did not mind being conspicuous at this point. In fact, that was the general idea.

Still, when he passed a rotting log, he gave it several swift kicks, exposing a rich trove of grubs swarming the interior. The distracted glavers crooned delight and dove in for the kill.

Which left just one irritation, the scampering noor beast, who darted through the meadow grass and between his legs.

Trying to ignore Mudfoot and carrying his bow slung over one shoulder, Dwer walked with feigned nonchalance past a devastation of jagged tree stumps toward the bustling sooner tribe. The prisoners' pen lay a quarter of an arrowflight to the left, the huts to the right. Straight ahead, a cook fire fumed smoke that hovered lazily, as if reluctant to depart.

Come on, people, Dwer mused when he was over halfway across the pocket meadow and still unnoticed. *Don't you have any sort of sentry system?*

He pursed his lips and whistled a tune – 'Yankee Doodle,' the first thing to come to mind.

Finally, one of the kids peering at the urrish captives glanced his way, did a gaping double take, and began screaming, pointing at Dwer.

Well, whatever works.

Their reaction might have been different as recently as a week ago. For generations these people had seen no outsiders at all. Now, after making contact with an urrish band, then flying aliens and a lost cousin transformed into a goddess, they took his arrival pretty well. Only three out of four ran away, howling in terror. Hesitantly, with goggle-eyes that showed white around the rims, the remainder gathered to stare at him, edging forward in a clump when he showed no sign of aggression.

Dwer motioned for one boy to come forward.

'Yeah, that's right, you! Don't worry, I won't bite.'

He squatted down in order to seem less imposing. The boy, a filthy urchin, looked like one for whom *bravado* was as important as life. Dwer knew the type. With others watching, the lad would rather die than let himself show fear. Puffing his chest out, the kid took several steps toward Dwer, glancing back to make sure his courage was being noted.

'What a fine young man,' Dwer commented. 'And what would your name be?'

The boy looked nonplussed, as if no one had ever asked him that before. Didn't everybody in the world grow up knowing each other's names?

'Well, never mind,' Dwer said, aware the throng was growing larger as curiosity overcame dread. 'I want you to run an errand for me. If you do, I'll give you something special, understand? Good. Please go to *Rety*. Tell her someone she knows is waiting for her—' Dwer turned and pointed the way he came '—over there. By the trees. Can you remember that?'

The boy nodded. Already, calculating avarice had replaced fear. 'What'll I get?'

Dwer pulled a single arrow from his quiver. It was made by the best fletchers of Ovoom Town, perfectly straight, with a tip of razor-sharp Buyur metal that gleamed in the sunshine. The boy reached out, but Dwer snatched it back.

'*After* you bring Rety.'

Their eyes met in brief understanding. With a blasé shrug, the boy swiveled and was gone, squeezing past the crowd, shouting for all he was worth. Dwer stood up, winked at the staring tribesmen, and began sauntering back toward the forest, whistling casually. Glancing back, he saw a good part of the clan following at a distance. So far, so good.

Oh, hell, he cursed when he saw the glavers. *Get out of the way, will you?*

They had finished browsing at the rotten log and now sauntered toward him. Dwer worried – when they saw the villagers, might they panic and bolt toward the prisoners' pen? The female glaver turned one globelike eye toward the approaching crowd. The other eye then followed, a sure sign of concern. She snorted, and her mate reared backward in surprised dismay. They whirled – and fled in exactly the direction Dwer feared!

With a tracker's sense of light and shadow, he noted Jenin Worley crouching by a tree, where the forest came nearest the prison-corral. One of Dwer's objectives had been to attract notice *away* from there.

He had the bow off his shoulder and an arrow drawn when *Mudfoot* suddenly reared out of the tall grass, waving its forepaws in front of the glavers, hissing. The glavers skidded to a halt and reversed course with astonishing spryness, cantering away with the noor yipping close behind.

For some reason the locals found all of this terrifically funny. It didn't seem to matter that they had never seen a noor before. They guffawed, pointing and laughing uproariously at the glavers' distress, clapping as if Dwer had put on a show for their benefit. He turned around, grinning as he reslung the bow. Anything to keep their regard riveted this way.

Abruptly, the crowd fell silent as a shadow fell across Dwer. A low, eerily familiar whine raised shivers up his spine. Shading his eyes against the sun, he looked up toward a hovering black shape, all jutting angles and hanging tendrils, like a certain demon that still haunted his dreams – the fire-spitting monster that had finished off the old mulc-spider of the mountains. Despite a penumbral glare surrounding it like a fierce halo, he made out the same octagonal symmetry. Only this one wore a rounded silhouette, perched on one jutting shoulder.

'So. You made it all the way here, after all,' the silhouette commented. 'Not bad for a Slopie. You're no fluff-baby, I guess – though the trip seems to've wore you down to a rag man. I seen you look better, Dwer.'

'Thanks, Rety,' he said, edging aside so the sun would not blind him. He also wanted to get closer to the forest. 'You, on the other hand, never looked so good. Been taking it easy?'

She answered with a curt chuckle that sounded husky, as if she hadn't laughed a lot lately. 'I turned down the offer your sages made – to have me hike all the way back here afoot, guiding a bunch o'geeps. Why walk, I figured, when I can ride?'

Now he could make her out clearly. Except for the old scar, she seemed quite *made over*, as they said in certain parts of Tarek Town. Yet the same sullen wariness lay in her eyes.

It was also his first chance to have a good look at an alien machine. Eight even rectangles made up its sides, black without highlights, as if sunshine had trouble glancing off it. Below, a pair of tendril-arms dangled menacingly on either side of a globe that was studded with glass facets and metal tubes. Danel had warned him to watch out for that globe. On top, where Rety sat in a lashed-on saddle, the robot's surface looked flat, except for a spire rising from the center. An 'antenna,' Danel had identified it.

Dwer nodded toward the hovering machine.

'Seems you've been making new friends, Rety.'

The girl laughed again – a sharp bark. 'Friends who'll take me places *you* never saw.'

He shrugged. 'I'm not talking about star-gods, Rety. I mean the friend giving you a ride, right now. Last time I saw one of these things, it was trying to kill us both—'

She cut in. 'A lot's changed since, Dwer.'

'—and oh, yeah, it was burning the hell out of that *bird* thing you cared so much about. Ah, well. I guess sometimes it just pays better to join those who—'

'Shut up!'

The robot reacted to its rider's anger by bobbing toward him. Retreating, he noted movement by the spherical cluster of lenses and tubes under the machine's blocky torso, turning fluidly to track him. On a hunch, Ozawa had called it a weapons pod, and Dwer's every clawing instinct confirmed the guess.

A crowd gathered beyond Rety, most of the human tribe, watching this confrontation between a ragged stranger and one of their own who had harnessed a flying devil. It must seem a pretty uneven matchup.

Some things are exactly as they seem.

Dwer caught a flash of movement toward the prison-pen. Jenin, making her move.

'Well?' Rety demanded, glaring down at him.

'Well what?'

'*You* sent for me, idiot! Did you hike halfway round the world just to try and make me feel guilty? Why didn't you stay away, once you saw what's going on here?'

'I could ask you the same question, Rety. What are you doing? Showing off for the folks? Getting some payback? Did the star-gods have some special reason to need a guide to this armpit of Jijo?'

Complex emotions crossed her face. What finally won was curt laughter.

'—*armpit?* Heh. That just about tells it all.' She chuckled again, then leaned closer. As for what Kunn is lookin' for, I can't tell ya. It's a secret.'

Rety was a lousy bluffer. *You don't have the slightest idea*, Dwer pondered, *and it galls you*.

'So, where's that pack of Slopies you were gonna lead out here?' she demanded.

'In hiding. I came ahead to make sure it's safe.'

'Why shouldn't it be? Nothin' dangerous here, except maybe my nasty ol' cousins . . . an' a bunch of smelly hinneys—'

When she said that, a piping whistle, like faint, piccolo laughter, vented from a padded pouch at her waist.

'And killers from outer space?' Dwer added. 'Planning to wipe out every thinking being on the planet?'

Rety frowned. 'That's a damn lie! They ain't gonna do it. They promised.'

'And what if I showed you *proof*?'

Her eyes darted nervously. 'More lies. They just wouldn't do nothing like that!'

'Like they wouldn't shoot a poor, unsuspecting bird-thing, I suppose. Or attack those urs without warning.'

Rety turned red as Dwer hurried on.

'Come along. I'll show you what I'm talking about.'

Before she could refuse, he turned to walk back toward the forest. 'I left it over there, behind that stump.'

The girl grumbled but followed on her robot steed. Dwer worried that the machine might be more sophisticated than Ozawa guessed. The reference works the sage had studied were three hundred years out of date and sparse on details. What if the robot both understood speech and could tell he was lying? What if it could read his *thoughts*!

The tree stump was thicker than most. The sooners must have worked hard with their primitive tools to hack it down, when they made this clearing. Dwer bent to pick up two things he had stashed on the far side. One, a slender tube, he slid up his tunic sleeve. The other was a leather-bound book.

'What is it?' Rety demanded, nudging the robot to drop closer. Atop the machine's flat upper surface there protruded short tentacle-things with glossy ends. Three swiveled toward Dwer, while the fourth watched for danger from the rear. So far, Danel Ozawa had been right about the robot's mechanical organs. If these were 'eyes,' then that narrow spindle jutting up from the robot's center—

'Show me!' Rety demanded, dropping closer still, peering at the small volume, containing about a hundred paper pages, a treasure from Danel's Legacy.

'Oh, it's a book,' she muttered with contempt. 'You think you can prove anything with *this*? The Rothen-kin have pictures that move, an' talk, an' tell you anythin' you want to know!'

Exactly, Dwer thought. *They can create images to show exactly what you want to see.*

But he answered with a friendly nod. 'Oh, sorry, Rety. I forgot, you can't read. Well, open it up, and you'll find this book has pictures, too. I'll explain them, if you like.'

This part had been Danel's idea. Back at Gathering, the lesser sage had seen Rety flip through dozens of picture books in apparent fascination – when she felt no one was watching. Dwer was trying to mix insult with encouragement, shame with curiosity, so the girl would have no choice but to look at this one.

Wearing an unhappy grimace, Rety reached down further and accepted the book. She sat up and riffled the paper leaves, clearly puzzled. 'I don't get it. What page should I look at?'

The robot's hover-fields brushed Dwer's leg, making all the hairs stand on end. His mouth felt dry, and his heart pounded. He fought a wave of anticipation-weakness by pure force of will.

'Oh, didn't I open it to the right picture? Here, let me show it to you.'

As Rety turned toward him, the robot dropped lower. Dwer raised his arms, reaching toward the book, but staggered when he bumped the robot's side.

It was fiery death if the thing thought it was being attacked. Would the machine recognize normal human clumsiness and make allowances?

Nothing happened. The robot didn't fear his touch.

'Hey, watch it,' he complained. 'Tell your pal here to take it easy, will you?'

'What? It's not any o' *my* doin'.' She kicked the machine. 'Leave him be, you stupid thing!'

Dwer nodded. 'All right, let's try again.'

Both hands went up. His legs were like coiled springs – and Dwer's life seemed to float above him like a sound, ready to flee on the wind.

He leaped.

The robot's brief hesitation ended in a sudden yowl, joined instantly by a series of sharp detonations, coming from the nearby forest. *Heat* flared between Dwer's legs as he yanked two of the sensor-heads, using them as handholds to swarm desperately up the machine's flank, away from the deadly ball. Pain erupted along one thigh, the split instant before he hauled his torso atop the gyrating machine. He clutched the bucking thing with his left hand while his right brought forth the slender tube.

The world was a blur of trees and clouds and whirling sky. More explosions pealed, accompanied by horrible *sizzling* sounds. Desperately, Dwer shoved the tube at the robot's central spindle and squeezed.

Traeki enzymes combined and emerged in an acrid, fizzing stream, vanishing down openings at the spindle's base. Dwer kept squirting despite the robot's wild pirouettes, until his aim was spoiled by *Rety*, shoving his arm away. Only then did Dwer note her screams amid the general tumult. When her *teeth* clamped on his wrist, Dwer's own howl joined in. The half-empty tube escaped his convulsing hand, tumbling away.

Purple steam rose from the robot's center. The spindle began to slump. Dwer shook Rety off and with a reckless cry threw himself on the drooping antenna, taking it in both hands, heaving with all his might. He shouted an ululation of triumph when the whole thing tore free at the base, though it left him rolling across the flat surface, clutching futilely for a hold.

Flailing, he tumbled off the edge, falling toward the meadow floor.

Dwer never worried, during that brief interval, about striking some rock or jagged tree stump. The machine would likely dice him to bits before he ever hit the ground.

But he was *not* sliced. Nor did he strike the rough meadow. Blinking in surprise, he found that a pair of *arms* had caught him!

Relief was tempered when he saw the arms belonged to the robot.

Oh, great. Out of the frying pan and into the—

There came another series of detonations, and the hovering machine rocked as if slammed along one side. Hanging below the octagonal body, Dwer saw part of the globe underneath explode in a spray of steel and glass. The weapons-ball was already a smoking ruin. Not a single lens or tube appeared intact.

Great work, Lena, Dwer thought, proud of how well she used the terrible devices that only she and a few others on the Slope were trained to use. Firearms that did not use a bit of metal. He turned his head in time to see more brief flares as Lena or Danel fired again from the forest edge. The machine rocked as another exploding shell impacted. This time one of the dangling tentacles holding Dwer shuddered and went limp.

That was definitely Lena's work. *What a clever girl*, he thought, half-dazed from pain. *The sages chose well. I would've been a lucky boy, if things had gone according to—*

He got no chance to finish the thought, as the robot whirled around to flee, zigzagging across the meadow, using his body as a shield between it and danger. Dwer saw Lena rise and take aim with her launcher, then lower it, shaking her head.

'No! Shoot, dammit!' he screamed. 'Don't worry about me!'

But the rushing wind of flight carried off his words. Lena dropped her weapon and hurried to a figure lying on the ground nearby, slumped beside a second missile tube. She turned Danel Ozawa over, revealing a red river pouring from his chest.

The robot's next zigging turn spun that poignant scene away. Now Dwer spied terrified villagers cowering beyond a low hill of garbage near the prisoners' pen. So dismayed were they by the battle that they seemed unaware of the group now circling around *behind* them – Jenin Worley and a dozen newly released urs. The former captives held ropes and arbalests. Dwer prayed this part of Danel's plan would turn out all right.

'All or nothing,' Ozawa had said. *'Either we live together as civilized beings, or let's end it. End it now – bringing as much harm to our enemy as we can.'*

Dwer had time for one benedictory thought, as Rety's cousins grew aware of the reversal taking place behind their backs.

Learn to be wise ...

Then the village vanished as the fleeing machine streaked around a bend, whipped through a forest aisle, and plunged almost straight downhill, accelerating.

Rety was still shrieking from her perch, wailing for it to stop. From Dwer's point of view, dangling underneath, the ground seemed to sweep by in a blur. Fighting the buffeting wind, he brought up both arms to grab the base of the tendril wrapped around his torso, holding him horizontal to the rushing terrain. If he tore it loose, the fall might kill him, but anything would be better than this torment.

He tugged with all his might, but the tentacle would not budge. It *flexed* occasionally, yanking him up in time to miss being smashed against some boulder or shrub. Soon they were swooping beside the canyon's central stream, an obstacle course of sudden turns and bitter, stinging spray. Disorientation forced Dwer to close his eyes, moaning.

Faintness took hold, threatening to haul him the rest of the way to unconsciousness.

Come on, he chided. *Now's not the time to give up. If you can't escape, at least check and see if you're bleeding to death!*

Pain helped him concentrate, ignoring the looming vertigo. It came in a nagging medley, from a searing ache in his left thigh, to Rety's teethmarks that still oozed blood from his right hand, to the chafing rub of the robot's arm, all the way to a series of awful, biting scratches that clawed into his hip, then his abdomen, and finally his chest – as if someone were stabbing him with clusters of sharp needles, working their way up along his battered body.

He opened his eyes – and shrieked at the sight of a gaping mouth, filled with horrible, glistening fangs!

'Oh, Ifni . . .' he moaned. 'Oh, God oh God oh God . . .'

Even when he knew the truth about the specter that loomed inches from his face, it didn't help much. At this point, and for a while longer, all Dwer could manage was a frail, thready whimper.

Mudfoot, the noor, yawned a second time, then settled into the narrow space between Dwer's chest and the robot's hard shell. The beast watched the boy – gibbering from one shock over his limit. With a sigh of affectionate scorn, it started chuttering, less to comfort Dwer than for its own simple pleasure, making a sound somewhat like that of a hoon sailor, umbling a song about the joys of travel.

ASX

If the Commons survives – if we six endure into times to come – no doubt it will be called the Battle of the Glade.

It was brief, bloody, and tactically decisive, was it not, my rings?

And strategically futile. An interval of flame and terror that made my/our manicolored bands so very glad/sorrowful that we are traeki.

Sorrowful because these stacks of rings seemed so useless, so helpless to match the frantic pace of other beings whose antic warlike fury drives them so quickly in a crisis. With such speed that waxy imprints cannot form within our core, except duras behind actual events.

Sorrowful that we could not help, except to serve as chroniclers-after-the-fact, bearing testimony to what already took place.

And yet we are also *glad*, are we not, my rings? Glad because the full impact of violence never quite fills our central cavity with a searing steam of dread. Not until the action is already over, leaving the dead like smoky embers, scattered on the ground. That is a blessing, is it not, my rings? To us, horror is seldom an experience, only a memory.

It was not always so. Not for the beings we once were, when our kind roamed the stars and were a terror on the Five Galaxies. In those days, creatures like us wore bright shining rings. Not only the ones given to us by our patrons, the Poa, but *special* collars, donated by the meddlesome Oailie.

Rings of power. Rings of rapid decisiveness and monumental ego. Had we possessed such rings but moments ago, they might have spurred us to move swiftly, in time to help our friends during the struggle.

But then, if the old tales are true, those same rings might have kept us from having friends in the first place.

Stroke the wax. Trace the images, frozen in fatty drippings.

Images of atrocity and dread.

There lies Bloor, the Portraitist, a smoldering ruin, draped over his precious camera.

Nearby, can we trace the slithering path of a dying creature? A symbiont crawling off the face and brow of the dead Rothen named Ro-pol? Revealing in its wake a sharp, angular visage, humanoid, but much *less* so than we had thought. Less charismatic. Less winsomely womanlike than we were led to believe.

If Bloor died for seeing this, are all eyes now accursed?

There, screams Ro-kenn, ordering Rann, the star-human servant, to call back the fierce sky-car from its distant errand, even if it means 'breaking' something called 'radio silence.'

There, screams Ro-kenn once more, ordering his slave-demons, his robots, aloft to – 'clear all of these away.'

Meaning us. All witnesses to this abrupt revelation. All who know the secret of Bloor's Bane.

Up, *up* rise the awful instrumentalities, meting out slashing doom. From their bellies lash spears of cold flame, slicing through the stunned host, turning it into a roiling, screaming mob. Four-legged urs bound high into the air, screeching panic. Qheuens cower low, trying to burrow away from rays that carve chitin as easily as flesh. Humans and hoon throw themselves flat on the ground, while poor g'Keks spin their wheels trying to back away.

We traeki – those left at Gathering after weeks of silent departures – mostly stand where we were, venting multi-fragranced fumes of woe, erupting wet fear-stench as cutting beams slice through popping toruses, spilling rich liquor, setting our stacks afire.

But *look*! Stroke the image layers one more time, my rings. See the darkly clad ones? Those who rush forward *toward* the terror, not away? Our vision spots scry little, even by daylight, for their clothing blurs them in uncanny ways. Nonetheless, we/i trace squat qheuen shapes, running with humans crouched on their backs, and urrish troops sweeping alongside. There comes, as well, a booming noise, a rarely heard sound, that of lethal *hoonish* ire. From their midst, these dim shapes raise strange tubes, even as the soaring demons turn their killing rage upon the newcomers, slashing at them mercilessly.

There is a place ...

It is here, in our core, where the wax depicts only a *roar* – a flash – an overload of searing afterimages – and then ...

What followed now lies before us.

Cinders – where the robots fell to sully Jijo's holy soil, shattered and reduced to dross.

Three sky-lords – stunned to find themselves held captive, taken prisoner, stripped of their godlike tools.

A poignant field – strewn with lamented dead. So many dead.

A makeshift infirmary – where even more wounded writhe and grimace, crying diverse plaints of pain.

Here, at last, is something we can do in real time. Perhaps they can use the assistance of an old retired pharmacist.

Is it agreed, my rings?

Wonderful unanimity. It makes easier the unaccustomed haste as i hurry forth to help.

SARA

The hard march had taken nothing from the tension between the two rebel groups. UrKachu's painted warriors and Dedinger's dun-clothed hunters eyed each other warily while eating separate meals under an aged canopy of patched and weathered blur-cloth, never wandering far from their weapons. Members of each group took turns sleeping after supper, no more than six at a time, while the rest kept watch. Sara found it hard to imágine this alliance lasting a dura longer than it was in both sides' perceived self-interest.

What if fighting broke out? In these close quarters it would be no artful exercise in maneuver and strategy but a roiling tumble of slashing, grappling forms.

She recalled the frontispiece illustration in volume one of *The Urrish-Earthling Wars*, by Hauph-hutau, one of the most popular titles published since the Great Printing. In small type, the great historian acknowledged copying the scene from a *Tabernacle*-era art book, showing the sculpture frieze that once surrounded the Parthenon, in ancient Greece. That famous relief depicted a long row of mighty figures, clenched in mortal combat – naked men brawling with furious monsters, half human and half horse, who reared, kicked, and slashed at their foes in a bitter fight to the death. According to myth, the feud broke out during a festival of peace and concluded with extinction for the centaur race.

Of course, an urs had almost nothing in common with a centaur, beyond having four legs and two arms. Yet the symbolism of the frieze was so eerie, so unnerving, that it became notorious during the age of struggle, helping steel the resolve of both sides. Sara had no wish to see such a bloody scene enacted in front of her.

Of the others taken captive at Uryutta's Oasis, young Jomah was already out like a snuffed candle, curled in his bedroll, fast asleep. The Stranger picked away at his meal of corn mush, frequently putting down his spoon to pluck a series of soft notes from his dulcimer, or else performing the ritual of counting its strings. Numbers, it seemed, were like music to him – a window to what he once had been, more faithful than the knack at sentences, that he had lost.

Kurt, the Exploser, doodled on his notepad, occasionally picking up one of the little books he kept so secretively, either in his valise or the inner pocket of his gown. He covered his work whenever any human or urs passed close but seemed not to mind that *Prity* lingered nearby, after bringing his meal. Putting on her best I'm-just-a-dumb-critter act, Prity spent some time pretending to inspect her leg for lice. But soon the little chimp was peering over the exploser's shoulder, rubbing her chin, drawing her lips past her gums, exposing a grin of silent, delighted interest.

Sara had to squelch an urge to laugh out loud. At the same time, she worried.

The Urunthai and desert-men are politely leaving Kurt alone, for now. The habit of deference to explosers runs deep and is hard to break. But they also promised 'persuasion' when we reach our destination. Does Kurt really imagine he can keep his work secret then?

He'd be better off throwing his notebooks into the fire.

Sara restrained her own curiosity. Explosers were a mysterious, formidable sect. Frankly, she doubted the wisdom of the Urunthai in messing with them.

'We won't wait till nightfall, vefore setting forth,' Ulgor told Sara, passing near her bedroll. 'I'd catch uf on sleef, if I were you.'

The urrish tinker's unpainted pelt, well-kept mane, and piercing black true-eyes set her apart from her wild cousins. There was no air of antagonism, no anti-human hostility. After all, Ulgor had visited Dolo Village dozens of times, always on friendly terms.

Sara shook her head. 'I can see what drives the others. Religion can be a strong motive when you think your descendants' salvation is at stake. But what do *you* get out of all this, Ulgor? I know it can't be profit.'

The narrow, conical head split in a triangular grin. Sara did not need a rewq to know the expression was sardonic.

'Why exclude the overt reason? Earnings. Fersonal gain.'

Sara quoted scripture: '"What use will be all your wealth and goods, two leagues down Redemption's Road?"'

Ulgor breathed a soft whistle of laughter. 'Little good at all. On the other hoof, hero status can ve useful in a clan of savages. Ferhafs I will ve one of the great chiefs of the plains, higher in renown than Ur-Chown!'

Ulgor's self-mocking tone dismissed that idea, while encouraging Sara to keep guessing.

Sara suddenly felt tired. 'You're right, Ulgor.'

'You think so?'

'Indeed I do. It *would* be a good idea to catch up on sleep, while I can.'

The tinker stared, twisting her neck a half spiral. 'I thought you wanted to know—'

Sara covered a yawn. 'Please be assured, Ulgor, that I am very sorry I asked.'

With that she turned away to lie down on her bedroll. Prity hurried over to tuck the blanket around Sara, then chuffed at Ulgor, shooing her away. Sara listened to the urbane traitor's hooves pound a nervous retreat, as if burdened by Sara's contempt.

She really was exhausted. Her muscles throbbed from several days' unaccustomed exertion, and her tailbone from jarring contact with the hard leather saddle. And there was an emotional element.

I was given a job to do. Several of them. Now it looks like I won't complete even one.

A low, repetitive thrum pervaded the pavilion, like the synchronous, pulselike snoring of the urs. It was the Stranger, plucking his dulcimer's lowest string, so softly and regularly that no one, not even UrKachu, might find any cause for complaint, creating a lulling rhythm, resembling less a heartbeat than the rise-and-fall cadence of ribcages – both urrish and human – as members of both parties slept.

Ariana figured he'd develop new skills, to compensate for those be lost, she thought. *I guess this musical sensitivity is part of that.*

Just after dawn, while the two radical groups worked to set up camp, the spaceman had played for the urrish males, briefly released from the close confines of their wives' pouches, taking advantage of the break to stretch their legs in the fresh air. A few males kept close watch on maturing larvae, with six short legs and no arms, almost ready to be spilled onto the plains and fend for themselves.

Using two curved mallets to strike the dulcimer strings, the Stranger had accompanied himself as he sang a chain of children's melodies, familiar enough to flow smoothly from undamaged memory. Sara even recognized a few. Among the rest, one seemed especially apropos.

'I had a little husband, no bigger than my thumb,
I put him in a pint pot, and there I bid him drum;
I bought a little handkerchief, to wipe his little nose,
And a pair of little garters, to tie his little hose.'

He repeated the verse several times, and soon, under his encouragement, the males were beating time to the song, crooning along. Sara recalled thinking, if he wound up stranded on Jijo and had no future in any other profession, the fellow could certainly find employment in one of those modern Tarek Town day-care centers.

If we still have such luxuries when all this is done.

Prity plopped herself in front of Sara. Sniggering softly, the little chimp flattened a patch of sand and began drawing figures with a stick – mostly convex, parabolalike shapes that climbed, turned over, and fell once more to zero. Prity chuffed and pointed, as if eager to share a joke. But Sara could not concentrate. Fatigue overcame the throbbing of her abused body, drawing her down to helpless slumber.

She dreamed of Urchachka – world of grass – its plains whipped endlessly by hot winds, seared by frequent fires, or else swept by scorching rains of glittering volcanic dust. After each scalding episode, the plains seemed strewn with ashy death – yet bright stems always burst forth in prolific flashes, pushing skyward fast enough to be tracked by a patient eye.

On busy Urchachka, water seldom stayed long on the ground. *Life* sucked it up, caching it in buried tuber reservoirs that meshed across whole continents, or else in bulbous, multihued spore-pods, or in the lush grass stems themselves. These, in turn, were browsed by herds of grazing beasts – nervous brutes whose three-pronged horns used to wave threateningly toward danger, till they found themselves tended in great herds, protected by creatures more formidable than any past predator.

In the manner of dreams, Sara dwelled concurrently both within and outside the images. At one level, her mind's eye peered through a forest of waving fronds, feeling wary and fearful, alert to dodge being trampled by the great beasts, or worse, being gobbled by accident in their ever-crunching maws.

Holes in the fecund loam led down to underground warrens – a lightless, crowded realm of sweet roots and frequent violent encounters – a domain that had lately begun to seem all too cramped, confining. The world of light above now appeared paradise by comparison – for those large enough to snake their necks above the tips of wafting grass.

With a slim, detached portion of her mind – the fragment that *knew* she was dreaming – Sara marveled at the power of imagination. A gift allowing her to inflate what little anyone on Jijo knew about Urchachka – from terse entries in a prelanding encyclopedia, plus a few fables passed by urrish storytellers. Tales about days before their fallow breed was discovered on its torrid home world, by a patron race who dropped from the sky to claim that strain of clever herders, guiding them upon the Rising Path. The road of uplift, toward the stars.

The detached part could observe but had no other power over a fantasy like this one. A *color* dream, potent, forceful, and emotional. A fey fantasm, with momentum all its own. A vision of clouded, insentient paranoia.

Darting between bulbous stems, evading the big dumb herbivores, she followed a smell of drifting smoke and came upon the trampled circle surrounding a smoldering pit of ashes, with a crowd of lanky four-legged figures lounging around its rim. She peered cautiously at the Big Ones. Only lately had she recognized them as larger versions of herself, older cousins and aunts, instead of dangerous horrors with flashing hooves and alarming tempers. Now she spied on them, creeping closer, fighting an ever-growing temptation.

An urge to step forward, out of the grass, and announce herself.

She had seen others do so, from time to time. Other small ones like herself, shaking off the dust of their burrows and stretching out their necks. Boldly moving to assert their claim, their birthright to a place by the fire. About a third of those who did so were ignored, then tolerated, accepted, and finally welcomed into the tight web of intermeshing loyalties. The rest did not meet happy ends. There seemed to be a trick of timing involved. A ritual of twisting necks and groveling abasement that varied from group to group.

Then there was *smell*. It was best to approach a band that had a good aroma. One like your own.

Stealing closer, she watched the party of adults, some with pouches that squirmed with lucky males who had found safe refuge from the dangerous world. Dimly, she recalled having once lived in such a place. But now she was much too big.

The adults lay sheltered by tall stems from the beating sun, resting with their long necks curled round upon their backs. Now and then, one of them snorted when her breathing fell briefly out of phase with the others. The third eye – the simple one without lids – kept watch.

Overhead, a swarm of tiny flying things hovered in parasitic avarice, wary for any chance to dive and briefly suck at an exposed lip, or pouch flap, or even a blood-rich eyelid, and get away again before quick hands or jaws snapped. Sara watched as one unlucky bug was snatched before landing. In a fluid motion, the adult popped the buzzing bloodsucker into her mouth, crunching away without bothering to rouse from her slumber.

I don't recall diving insects when I read about the urs' homeworld, pondered the detached part of Sara's drowsy mind, *or in any tale of Urchachka*.

Gradually, it dawned on her that she wasn't making it all up. Rather, her unconscious was borrowing from events in the real world. Her eyes were open just a crack, and through the dreamlike diffraction of her interlaced lashes, she was watching *actual* urs do what she had thought she imagined.

As before, half of the *Urunthai* lay curled on sandy wallows, breathing with uncanny unison under the blur-cloth canopy. Nothing seemed much changed from when she had last gazed at her captors. But then something happened that correlated eerily with her dream – a low, buzzing sound, accompanied by whizzing motion through the air. A small, insectlike object darted from left to right, toward one of the dozing urs. In a flash, the sleeper snatched the hurtling speck out of the air with her gaping, three-jawed mouth, chewing contentedly with both main eyes still closed.

The central one, unlidded and faceted, retained the glassy dullness of full sleep as the warrior settled back down, snoring heavily.

I've never seen that happen before, Sara pondered. *Are there bugs here in the foothills that attack urs like those on their homeworld?*

Taut, bowstring tension ran up Prity's spine as the little chimp edged backward, pressing against Sara with an elbow. Sara slowly lifted her head to scan the Urunthai. Those awake fondled their arbalests and switched their tails nervously, as if beginning to suspect that something was wrong. Their long necks stretched, waving left all at the same time, then at Dedinger's desert men, and onward to the right. When they turned away again, there came another low twanging buzz, so familiar it almost seemed unnoticeable. Once more, a small shape sped toward a dozing urs. Again, it was snatched from the air and consumed without rousing the sleeper.

Sara followed the arc of that brief flight, backward across the tent to where the *Stranger* sat at his dulcimer, still plucking at the lowest note, creating a steady hypnotic rhythm. The rewq draped over his eyes only partly masked an enigmatic smile.

Sara realized two others were watching the star-man – Dedinger and Kurt the Exploser.

Sniffing at the humid air, UrKachu motioned for Ulgor to join her outside. The four painted warriors on duty went back to tending their weapons.

The Stranger bided his time, softly plucking the string. He kept up a slow, soothing cadence until the wary Urunthai guards settled back down. Then, with his left hand, the Stranger touched the side of his head and slipped two fingers under the filmy covering provided by the rewq – reaching *into* the hole in his head, Sara realized, with a touch of nausea. When the fingers emerged, they held a tiny object, a pellet, about the size of one of the message balls used in the Biblos Library. While his right hand plucked the string another time, his left brought the pellet forth, poising it for the next stroke.

He's using the dulcimer as a launcher! Sara realized, watching in fascination.

She noted a slight difference in the sound, a buzzing dissonance as the tiny pill spun through the air toward another sleeping urrish rebel. It missed this time, dropping half a body length short of the target.

Dedinger was in motion, surreptitiously nudging his comrades, using furtive hand signs, telling them quietly to prepare. *He doesn't know what's going on, but he wants to be ready when the pulp hits the screen.*

The tent flap opened, and UrKachu reentered, without Ulgor.

The chieftain sauntered over to one of the sleeping Urunthai and prodded her – an action that normally would have a wiry urs on her feet in an instant. But there was no response. The raider kept on snoring.

Alarmed, UrKachu began jabbing, then kicking the sleeping warriors. Others hurried over to help. In moments it grew clear – of eight who had gone down to sleep, all but two were lost in a soporific stupor.

The dulcimer twanged again, and several things happened at once.

UrKachu swiveled angrily and shouted in Anglic – 'Stof that infernal racket now!'

Meanwhile, a tiny object sailed over the dying coals, toward the confused warriors. One of them snapped reflexively, taking it with her jaws. Almost instantly, her nostril flared and her neck stretched to full extension, trembling along its length. The urs began to wobble at the knees.

Sara would not have thought she could react so fast, scrambling backward with Prity, gathering up the blanket-swathed Jomah, hauling the sleeping boy to the rear of the tent. Swift as ghosts, Dedinger's men were already deploying in a crescent, surrounding the Urunthai, with arrows nocked and drawn.

'What's going on?' Jomah asked, rubbing his eyes.

The wobbly urs drifted to one side, fell against another, and collapsed, ribcage heaving slowly, heavily.

'Remain calm,' Dedinger announced. 'I urge you to lay down your weapons. You are in no condition to fight.'

UrKachu stared blankly, dismayed by the sudden reversal of power. Her group *had* outnumbered the humans. But now her remaining followers stood in a cluster, unready, at the Earthlings' mercy. The Urunthai leader growled.

'*So, in this (perfidious) treason, the nature of human (so-called) friendship is revealed.*'

'Yeah.' Dedinger laughed, a little smugly. 'As if *you* planned things any different, when the chance came. Anyway, there is no cause for panic over this. We'll still keep our side of the bargain, only as *senior* partners, with a few slight changes, such as the destination for tonight's march. Once there, we'll let you send a message—'

He might have meant to sound soothing, but the words only infuriated UrKachu, who cut in with a shrill battle cry, hurling herself toward Dedinger, unsheathed knives flashing.

'No!' screamed the Stranger in an outburst of reflex horror as feathered shafts sprouted from the thorax of the Urunthai leader. 'No dammit! dammit! dammit!'

UrKachu's remaining followers followed her example, charging into a hail of arrows. Half were riddled during the first half dura. The survivors leaped among their bipedal foes, slashing and drawing some blood before being dragged down by weight of human numbers.

Finally, with no living Urunthai left on their feet, the panting, wild-eyed desert men began turning their knives on the unconscious ones, those whose drugged stupor never let them take part or defend themselves.

To the Stranger, this was the final straw. Screaming curses, he threw himself on the nearest human, throttling his neck ganglia. The hunter struggled briefly, then sagged with a moan. The starman leaped at another, hurling streams of epithets.

Sara pushed Jomah toward the tent flap and cried – 'Prity, take him to the rocks!'

In the blurry muddle of split instants, she saw three of Dedinger's hunters turn and assail the Stranger. One tumbled away, tossed by some tricky twist of the alien's body, while another found herself suddenly burdened with a new problem – *Sara* hammering at his ribcage from behind.

If only I listened, when Dwer tried to teach me how to fight.

For a moment things went well. Sara's short-but-burly adversary groaned and turned around, only to catch her knee in the gut. That didn't stop the hard-muscled hunter, but it slowed him, letting Sara get in two more blows. Meanwhile, the Stranger threw his remaining foe aside in a dazed heap and started to turn, coming to her aid—

The avalanche hit then. A tide of male-human wrath that dragged both of them down. Sara struck ground with enough force to knock the breath from her lungs. Someone yanked her arms back and sharp agony made her gasp, wondering if the limbs were about to tear off.

'Don't harm them, boys,' Dedinger commanded. 'I said ease off!'

Distantly, through a muzzy fog of pain, she heard blows landing as the former sage slapped and hauled his men back from the brink of murderous revenge. Desperately, Sara managed to swing her head around to see the Stranger, pinned down, red-faced, and bleeding from the nose, but well enough to keep up a faint, hoarse stream of inventive profanity. The outpouring was as eloquently expressive, though not quite as fluent as song. Sara worried that shouting and straining so hard might reopen his injuries.

The leader of the human rebels knelt by the Stranger, taking his face in both hands.

'It's too bad you can't understand me, fella. I don't know what you did to the urs, but I truly am grateful. Made a complicated situation simple, is what it did. For that reason, and because your living carcass is still valuable to us, I'll hold back my guys. But if you don't settle down, I may be forced to get unpleasant with your friend here.'

With that he nodded pointedly at Sara.

The Stranger glanced at her, too, and somehow seemed to grasp the threat. His stream of scatological curses tapered, and he ceased heaving against the men holding him down. Sara felt relieved that he stopped straining so hard – and strangely moved to be the reason.

'That's better,' Dedinger said in the same smooth, reasonable voice he had used before UrKachu's fatal charge. 'Now, let's take a look at what you've got hidden in that handy little hole in your head.'

The ex-sage began to peel back the Stranger's rewq, revealing the wound from which he had taken the mysterious pellets.

'No!' Sara shouted, despite sharp pain when two men yanked her arms. 'You'll give him an infection!'

'Which his star-friends will cure, if they so choose, once we make our exchange,' Dedinger answered. 'Meanwhile, this stuff he was feeding the urs seems worth looking into. It could prove powerfully handy during the years ahead.'

Dedinger had finished pulling back the rewq and was about to insert his hand, when a new voice broke in, whistling a trill-stream of rapid Galactic Two.

'Sara, I (earnestly) urge you to (swiftly) close your eyes!'

She turned her head and glimpsed *Kurt*, the Tarek Town exploser, holding a small brown tube. A burning string dangled from one end, giving off sparks at a furious pace. The exploser cranked his arm and threw the tube in a high arc, at which point Kurt dove for cover.

Sara squeezed her eyes shut tight as Dedinger began to shout a warning to his men—

A flash like a thousand lightning bolts filled all reality, stabbing through her eyelids. At the same instant, roaring noise shook her like a bird in a ligger's jaws, rolling the mass of sweaty men off, releasing her twisted arms, so that waves of *relief clashed* with agonizing sensory overload.

It was over almost the moment that it happened – except for howling reverberations, rebounding off the stony pillars that now could be seen towering over the shredded tent ... or perhaps they were shock waves hammering inside her own head. Hurriedly she fled the tangle of screaming men, who clutched their useless eyes.

Blinking past purple spots, she made out one other human who could stand and see: Dedinger, who would also have understood Kurt's brief warning. The desert prophet peered ahead while holding forth a gleaming blade of Buyur metal.

He yelled past the bedlam in her ears and charged at Kurt, knocking the old man down before the exploser could bring a new weapon to bear. Sara recognized a *pistol* from pictures in ancient texts.

'So much for exploser neutrality!' Dedinger shouted, twisting Kurt's arm until the old man groaned and the weapon fell. 'We should have searched you, and tradition be damned.'

Overriding pain, Sara tried to spring at the ex-sage, but he lashed out with a savage backhand, knocking her down amid a swirl of spinning stars. Consciousness wavered. Only gritty resolution let her rise again, turning on her knees to try one more time.

There came another flash-and-roar, as Dedinger fired the pistol just past her and then tried awkwardly to cock for a second shot – before being bowled over by two hairy forms, hitting him from both sides. Sara somehow managed to fling herself into the fray, joining Ulgor and Prity in subduing the former scholar, whose wiry strength was astonishing for his age.

Fanaticism has rewards, she thought, as they finally managed to tie Dedinger's hands and feet.

Recovering his weapon, Kurt backed away, taking a rocky perch where he could watch the moaning remnants of the desert gang, as well as the surviving urs. Especially Ulgor. The tinker's sudden return might have been fortuitous, but that would not make him trust her.

A sticky sensation made Sara stare at her hands, trying to separate red stains from vision-blotches left by Kurt's stun bomb. The stains had the color and scent of *blood*.

It isn't me – and Ulgor wouldn't bleed this shade of—

It was *Prity* stanching a crimson flow from a deep gash in her side. Sara took the trembling little chimp into her arms and fought a sudden fit of weary sobs.

The wrecked tent was a horror scene of dead or delirious Urunthai and flash-blinded men. The Stranger seemed in better shape than most, when he finally staggered to his feet. At least he could see well enough to help Ulgor bind the arms of Dedinger's crew, while young Jomah returned to hobble the legs of sedated urs. Still, it soon grew clear that the battered man from the stars could not hear a blessed sound.

Against every instinct that urged her to be thorough, Sara forced herself to make do with a pressure compress over Prity's wound. It did not seem immediately life-threatening, and someone else might yet be saved by quick action. So with the chimp's grunt of approval, she hurried over to one wheezing quadruped, a young urs thrashing feebly with an arrow through her neck, whose labored breathing made noisy, purple bubbles—

—and who died with a shuddering gasp of despair, before Sara could do a thing to help her.

ASX

Battle-echoes gouged the land, only a few short duras ago.

Firebolts lashed from heaven, scourging the Six, laying open flesh, chitin, and bone.

Traekis gushed molten wax across the tortured valley, or else burst aflame, ignited by searing beams.

Oh my rings, what images lay seared throughout our trembling core!

The dead.

The dying.

The prudent ones, who fled.

The rash heroes, who came.

Their blur-cloth tunics are now grimy with mud and grue, no longer quite as slippery to the eye. Young tree farmers and donkey-drivers. Simple keepers of lobster pens. Junior hands on the humblest fishing coracles. Volunteers who never imagined their weekend training might come to this.

Our brave militia, who charged into that maelstrom, that cauldron of slicing rays. Amateurs, soft and unready after generations of peace, who now wince silently, clenching their limbs while horrid wounds are dressed or while life slips away. Bearing agony with the gritty resolve of veterans, the suffering eased by the only balm that soothes.

Victory.

Was it only yesterday, my rings, that we feared for the Commons? Feared that it might fly apart in jealous hatreds fostered by crafty star-devils?

That dread fate may yet come to pass, along with a thousand other terrors. But not today. Right now the arrogant aliens stand captive, staring about in surprise, stripped of their godlike tools, their hellish robots destroyed by the crude fire-tubes of our brave militia.

A day of reckoning may not be far off. It could swoop at any moment from an unforgiving sky.

Yet there is exhilaration. A sense of relief. The time of ambiguity is over. No more subtle games of misdirection and innuendo. No more pretense or intrigue. Ifni's dice have been shaken and cast. Even now they tumble across Jijo's holy ground. When they stop rolling, we will know.

Yes, my second ring. You are right to point this out. Not *everyone* shares a sense of grim elation. Some see in recent events cause for nihilism. A chance to settle old grudges, or to spread lawlessness across the land.

One vocal minority – 'Friends of the Rothen' – demands the release of Ro-kenn. They advise throwing ourselves prostrate before his godlike mercy.

Others call for the hostages to be done away with at once.

'The starship may have means to track its lost members,' they claim, *'perhaps by brain emanations, or body implants. The sole way to be sure is to grind their bones and sift the dust into a lava pool!'*

These and other testy groups might think differently, if the full truth were told. If only we sages could divulge the plans already set in motion. But secrets are innately unfair. So we hold our peace.

To the folk of the Six, we say only this—

'Go to your homes. See to your lattice screens and blur-webs. Prepare to fight if you can. To hide if you must.

'Be ready to die.

'Above all, keep faith with your neighbors – with the Scrolls – with Jijo.

'And wait.'

Now our survivors hurry to pull down pavilions, to pack up valuables, to bear the wounded off on litters. Children of all races spend one sacred midura scouring the Glade for every scrap of dross they can find. Alas, that midura is all we can spare for tradition. There will be no festive mulching ceremony. No gaudy caravan, bearing ribboned crates down to the sea and ships – the most joyous part of any Gathering.

Such a pity.

Anyway, the aliens' ruined station will take generations to haul away, one donkey-back at a time. That task must wait for after the crisis. If any of us remain alive.

*

The hostages are spirited off. Caravans depart toward plains, forest and sea, like streams of sentient wax, creeping in liquid haste to flee a fire.

The sun retreats, as well. Bitter-bright stars now span that vast domain called The Universe. A realm denied the Six, but where our foes roam at will.

A few of us remain, rooted to this sacred vale, awaiting the starship.

Are we/i in agreement, my rings? To linger near the Holy Egg, resting our base on hard stone, sensing complex patterns vibrate up our fatty core?

Yes, it is far better to rest here than to go twisting up some steep, rocky trail, hauling this old stack toward an illusion of safety.

We shall stay and speak for the Commons, when the great ship lands.

It comes now, roaring out of the west, where the sun lately fled.

A fitting replacement, the ship hovers angrily, erupting a brilliance that puts daylight to shame, scanning the valley floor with rays that sear and scrutinize. Scanning first the ruined station, then the surrounding countryside.

Searching for those it left behind.

XXVII

THE BOOK OF THE SEA

Animals exist in a world of struggle,
in which all that matters is one result –
continuity of self and the genetic line.

Sapient beings dwell in nests of obligations,
to their colleagues, patrons, clients, and
ideals.
They may choose fealty to a cause,
to a godhead or philosophy,
or to the civilization that enabled them
to avoid living animal lives.

Knots of allegiance cling to us all,
even after treading down
the Path of Redemption.

Still, children of exile, remember this –

– in the long run, the Universe
as a whole
owes you nothing.

—*The Scroll of Hope*

Perhaps the spider-things find me as eerie as I find them. Maybe they are trying their best to help. Given the little that I know, it seems best to take an attitude of wait-and-see.

We hoon are good at that. But I can only imagine what poor Huck is going through, if they put her in a cell like this one. A steel room with barely enough room to spin her wheels before hitting a wall, with the ceaseless drone of some weird kind of engine humming in the background. She's got no patience and may have gone quite loco by now.

If Huck's still alive.

She seemed to be, when last I saw her, after our plummet into the Midden's icy depths was stopped by crashing into a sea monster's gaping mouth. I recall seeing Huck sprawled on a metal surface, wheels spinning, kicking feebly with her pusher legs, while the floor and walls shook under a roaring wind that scraped my ears with incredible screeching pressure.

That pressure saved us, driving out the crushing mass of water before we drowned. But at the time, all I could do was scream, wrapping my arms around my head while my back convulsed from the blow I'd taken, escaping from our broken *Wuphon's Dream*.

Vaguely, I was aware of someone else howling. Ur-ronn huddled in a far corner, sliced and torn by slivers of her precious shattered window and further panicked by the drenching wetness.

Looking back, it seemed a miracle she was breathing at all, after the *Dream* broke up and harsh sea pounded in from all sides. The force of that blow slammed me against the garuwood hull, while my friends spun away, heads over hooves and rims.

I had never before seen an urs try to swim. It's not a pretty sight.

I remember thinking it would be my *last* sight, until that explosive cloud of bubbles poured in from a hundred wall slits, splitting the water with a foaming roar. The bubbles frothed together, merging into that screeching wind, and we survivors flopped onto the splintered wreckage of our beautiful bathy, gasping and gagging into dark, oily puddles.

Of the four of us, only Pincer seemed to come through with any power of movement. I seem to recall him clumsily trying to tend Ur-ronn's wounds, pinning her against a wall with his scarred carapace while fumbling with two claws, pulling shards of glass out of her hide. Ur-ronn wasn't cooperating much. She didn't seem coherent. I couldn't blame her.

Then a door opened, opposite the clamshell mouth that bit through the *Dream*. It was a smaller portal, barely offering clearance for two *demons* to emerge, one at a time.

They were horrible-looking, six-legged beasts, with horizontal bodies longer than a hoon is tall, flaring wide in back and bulging up front with huge, glassy bubble-eyes, black and mysterious. They stamped into the chamber, awkwardly crushing both Uriel's depth gauge and Ur-ronn's compass underfoot, looking like waterbugs, whose spindly appendages met along a tubelike body that glistened and flexed with fleshy suppleness. Smaller limbs, dangling in front, looked like mechanical tools.

All right, I'm describing a lot of stuff I couldn't have seen all that well at the time. It was dark until the spider-things entered, except in the sharp glare of two beams cast from opposite walls. Also, I was half conscious and in shock, so nothing I write can be taken as reliable testimony.

Especially my impressions of what came next.

Waving their own dazzling lanterns, the two shadowy forms began inspecting their catch, first pausing to illuminate and stare at Pincer and Ur-ronn, then poor Huck, wheeling vainly on her side, and finally me. I tried to move and nearly fainted. When I fought to speak or umble, I found my bruised throat sac would not take air.

Funny thing, I could swear the monsters talked to one another while they looked us over, something they never do now, when they enter my cell in teams to tend me. It was an eerie, trilling, and ratcheting kind of speech, totally unlike GalTwo or any other Galactic language that I know. And yet something about it felt familiar. Each time their lights fell on another of us for the first time, I swear the beasts sounded *surprised*.

When they reached me, part of my terror was eased by the sudden appearance of *Huphu*. Somewhere in my addled mind, I'd been worried about our mascot. Abruptly, there she was, rearing in front of me, chattering defiance at the towering spider-things.

The creatures rocked back, amazement now so evident that I might have been watching them with perfectly tuned rewq. One of the things crouched down and murmured hurriedly, excitedly, either talking excitedly *about* the little noor or right *at* her. I couldn't tell which.

Can I trust that dreamlike impression? At this point, as they say in some Earthling books, I was fading to vacuum, fast. In retrospect, it seems an illusion.

One thing I *know* I fantasized. Something that comes back now more as notion than memory. Yet the image clings, flickering the same way consciousness flickered, just before dimming out.

Without warning, a final figure crept into view, crawling from under a slab of our poor shattered bathy. Half-flattened and deformed, *Ziz* regathered its conical shape while the two monsters staggered backwards, as if they had seen something deadlier than a poison-skenk. One of them swung a gleaming tube at the battered traeki partial and fired a searing bolt that blew a hole in the poor stack's middle ring, flinging it against the wall near Huck.

My overtaxed brain shut down about then. (Or had it done so already?) Yet there *is* just one more vague, dreamlike impression that clings to me right now, like a shadow of a phantom of a ghost of stunned astonishment.

Somebody spoke, while the midget traeki oozed sap across the sodden floor. Not in the trilling whistles the creatures used before. Not in GalSeven or any other civilized tongue – but in Anglic.

'*My God*—' it said, in tones of disbelief, and it struck me as a human female's voice, with a strange accent I never heard before.

'*My God – all these – and a Jophur too!*'

XXVIII

THE BOOK OF THE SLOPE

Legends

It is said that we are all descended from unlucky races.

According to many of the tales told by the Six, there is endless war, persecution, suffering, and fanaticism amid the Five Galaxies. But if this really were typical, that civilization could not have lasted even a million years, let alone a billion or more.

If it were typical, places like Jijo would be teeming with countless sooner infestations, not just half a dozen.

If it were typical, worlds like Jijo would have been used up long ago.

Other accounts tell that the vast majority of star-faring races are relatively calm. That they manage their interests, raise their clients, and tend their leased worlds with serene attentiveness to good manners and the ancient codes, while treading the Upward Path toward whatever transcendence awaits them. They see the abrasive antics of zealous, fanatical alliances as tasteless, immature – but why intervene when it is simpler and safer just to keep your head (or heads) down and mind your own business?

Clients lucky enough to be adopted into such moderate clans grow up peaceful and secure, except during those intervals – legendary Times of Change – when upheaval overwhelms even the cautious and discreet.

Then it is the hardy that tend to thrive. Those toughened by scrappy interactions in the back alleys of space.

These alleys claim victims, though. It is said that we Six count among the bleeding refugees who slunk away from lost causes and broken dreams, seeking a place to hide. To heal. To seek another path.

To search in quest of one last chance.

SARA

It was a muddle, any way you looked at it.

The stun-bomb had driven the pack animals into hysterical flight, yanking free of their tethers to run wild through the maze of stony spires. Someone would have to go search for them, but only after the wounded were tended with what skill Sara possessed.

Those humans who were blinded – perhaps temporarily – needed to be calmed, then fed by hand. Later, the dead must be dragged to a flat spot where a pyre could be raised, to sear their corpses down to ineluctable dross – a neat transportable pile to be gathered and sent to sea.

There was an added complication. Several dead Urunthai had been carrying husbands or larvae. Sara herded together the strongest that crawled out of pouches – those with any chance of surviving – into a makeshift pen where the diminutive males took charge of their offspring, chewing and regurgitating small bits of meat for the pasty, caterpillarlike, pre-infant urs.

In tales praising the glory of war, they never talk about the hard stuff that comes after a battle. Maybe people wouldn't fight as much if they knew they'd have to clean up the awful mess.

Kurt and Jomah finally got her to sit down around sunset, to eat and rest for a while. By then the day had dimmed, and the campfire's glow flickered across two ranks of sullen captives – human and urrish – who stared at each other, sulky, half-blind, and petulant. None seemed more melancholy than the former sage, the scholar-turned-prophet who had argued with Sara so confidently half a day before. Dedinger glared calculatingly at Kurt, who cradled the pistol carefully, never letting any of the prisoners out of his sight.

Before sitting down, Sara first checked Prity's stitches, which still oozed enough to worry her. It had been difficult sewing the wound, with the chimp understandably twitching and with Sara's eyes blurry from the stun-bomb. After she had done all she could for her little assistant and friend, Sara looked around for the Stranger. He had been a great help all afternoon, but she had not seen him in over an hour, and it was past time for his medicine.

Kurt said, 'He went off thataway' – indicating southward, into the rocks – 'to try catching some donkeys. Don't worry. That fellow seems to know how to take care of himself.'

Sara quashed her initial reaction – to berate the explorer for

472

letting the star-man head into an unfamiliar wilderness all alone. The alien was a cripple, after all, and might get hurt or lost.

But then, she recalled, he was a strangely *competent* cripple. Clever and skilled in ways that had little to do with words. And for a man with such a peaceful demeanor, he fought very well.

With a shrug, Sara accepted what could not be changed and sat down to partake of the desert warriors' wafer bread and a jug of leathery-tasting water.

'In the morning we must gather wood for a pyre, since we haven't any scavenger toruses for proper mulching,' she said between mouthfuls, speaking more loudly than normal, because everyone was still rather hard of hearing. At best, it took a shout to carry over the steady ringing in her own ears. 'And we should send someone for help.'

'I'll go,' Jomah volunteered. 'I'm the only one who wasn't banged up in the battle. I'm strong an' I've got a compass. Uncle Kurt knows I won't get lost. And I can move real fast.'

The senior exploser looked uncomfortable. His nephew was very young. Still, after a moment's reflection, Kurt nodded. 'It makes sense. He can head—'

'Of course *I* an the one to send,' Ulgor interrupted, turning from tending the campfire. 'I can run faster and farther than the child, and I know these hills well.'

Sara choked. 'Not a chance! I can't believe we haven't tied you up yet with the others! Let you *go*? So you can hurry off and collect more of your fanatic friends?'

Ulgor turned her narrow head to peer at Sara sideways. 'As if those friends are not *already* on their way, dear daughter of Nelo? UrKachu sent envoys ahead, don't forget. Let us suffose that Kurt's nephew could reach the Glade without encountering a ligger, or a fack of khoov-rahs. If he heads north, I guarantee the first folks he encounters will ve UrKachu's allies, hurrying to join us.'

Now it was Kurt's turn to interrupt, with a short, hard laugh.

'And who says we're headin' north?'

Both Ulgor and Sara looked at him. 'What do you mean? Obviously we have to . . .'

Her voice trailed off as she saw the exploser smile. *Come to think of it, Kurt never explicitly said the Glade was his destination.* She had assumed, quite naturally, that his urgent business lay there. *But he might have planned to leave our group at Crossroads, where the rest of us would turn uphill toward the Egg.*

'Others of my guild have already gone to help the High Sages. But the boy and I have interests in another direction. And while we're on the subject, I suggest you should consider coming along, Sara. For one thing, it's the last direction the Urunthai are likely to look.'

It was the longest speech she had ever heard Kurt make, and her mind churned with implications. For instance, why was he saying this *in front* of Ulgor?

Because any determined urs could track a bunch of humans and donkeys over a fresh trail. Obviously, Ulgor has to come along, or else be eliminated.

But then, didn't the same logic require that they murder all the other survivors, too? Kurt surely knew that Sara would never permit that. Anyway, the problem would not go away simply because they got a couple of days' head start. A good tracker, like Dwer, could hunt them even over a trail that had gone cold.

She started to raise these matters, then stopped, realizing that Kurt could not give a satisfactory answer with the seething outlaws listening nearby.

'You know I can't go,' she said at last, shaking her head. 'These men and urs will die if left here like this, all trussed up, and we clearly can't release them.'

If she had any doubts about that, one look into Dedinger's wrath-filled eyes settled the matter. That cold fury was a problem only a great deal of time and distance would solve. The more the better. 'I'll stay and take care of them till their friends arrive,' she added. 'The Urunthai will probably protect me, since I fought to help save some of them – though they may still keep me prisoner. I may even be able to stop 'em from slaughtering Dedinger's gang.

'But you and Jomah ought to go ahead. Assuming we get some of the donkeys back, you can take Prity and the Stranger along. With tons of luck you might get them somewhere with a pharmacist and a strong militia outfit. I'll follow for several arrowflights and brush away your trail, then I'll use more donkeys to trample a mess of false paths leading out of here.'

A soft whistle of grudging respect escaped Ulgor. 'You are, indeed, your vrother's sister.'

Sara turned and pointed at the elegant tinker. 'Of course this means *you* have used up the free time you earned by helping us at the battle's end.' She bent to pick up a length of tent rope. 'It's time for you to join the others by the fire, neighbor.'

Ulgor backed away. '*You and who else plan on enforcing that ruling?*' she asked in defiant GalSix.

Kurt cocked the pistol. 'Me and my magic wand, Ulgor. You just stop right there.'

Ulgor's long neck slumped in defeat. 'Oh, all right,' she

murmured, disconsolately. 'If you're going to ve so insistent. I suffose I can stand it for a little while.'

Amid Ulgor's stream of placating words, it took a dura or two for Sara to realize – *she's still backing up!*

Confused by mixed signals, Kurt wavered until Dedinger cried out. *'She's faking*, you fools!'

In a blur, Ulgor whipped around and plunged into the twilight dimness. Kurt fired once – and missed – as the urrish rump vanished amid the rocks. Their last sight of Ulgor was a flourish of twin braided tails. The captive urs lifted their heads from drug-hangover misery to chortle with amused glee. Several *human* captives laughed at the exploser's discomfiture.

'You need more practice with that thing, grandpa,' Dedinger observed. 'Or else hand it to a guy who *hit* something the one time he tried.'

Prity bared her teeth and snarled at the ex-sage, who sarcastically feigned terror, then laughed again.

He spent time around chimps in Biblos, Sara thought, laying a hand on Prity's knee to restrain her. *He should know better.*

Then again, there's no fool like a bright fool.

'Well, that tears it,' Kurt muttered to Sara. 'It's my fault. I should've listened to you. Tied her up, even though she helped save my life. Now she can lurk out there watching us. Or run and bring her gang before we get far enough away.'

Sara shook her head. *Far enough away for what?* Surely Ulgor's escape only hastened the inevitable.

The exploser motioned for her to come closer. When she sat down, Kurt's lips pressed together hard before he finally decided to speak, so softly that her battered ears could barely hear.

'I've been thinkin' lately, Sara ... it seemed a gift from the Egg to find you traveling with us. A fluke-blessing of Ifni. Your skills could prove quite useful to something ... a project I'm involved with. I was going to ask you at Crossroads.'

'Ask me what?'

'To come south with us' – his voice lowered further still – 'to Mount Guenn.'

'*To Mount—*' Sara blurted, standing up.

At Kurt's panicked expression, she sat back down and dropped her voice. 'You're kidding, right? You know I have business at the Glade. *Important* business. If the radicals think the Stranger is important enough to kill over, don't you think the *sages* ought to have a chance to look him over and decide what to do? Besides, if the aliens *are* his friends, it's our duty to help him get modern medical—'

Kurt waved a hand. 'All quite true. Still, with the path from here to the Glade blocked, and with another task waiting that could be more important—'

Sara stared at the man. Was he crazy as Dedinger? What could possibly be more important?

'—a task one of your colleagues has been working on, down at the place I mentioned, for several weeks now—'

One of my colleagues? Sara blinked. She had seen Bonner and Taine, a few days ago, at Biblos. Plovov was at Gathering. Then who ... ?

One name came to mind.

Purofsky the astronomer? Down at Mount Guenn? Doing what, in the Egg's name?

'—a task which seems to cry out for your expertise, if I might be so bold.'

She shook her head. 'That – place – is all the way beyond the Great Swamp, past the desert and the Spectral Flow! Or else you must take the long way around by river and then by sea—'

'We know a shortcut,' Kurt put in, absurdly.

'—and just a while ago we were plotting a mad dash just to reach the nearest *village*, as if it were as hopeless as a journey to a moon!'

'I never said it would be easy.' Kurt sighed. 'Look, all I want to know right now is this. If I *could* convince you it was possible, would you come?'

Sara bit back her initial reply. Kurt had already pulled miracle powers and god-machines out of that satchel of his. Did he also have a magic carpet in there? Or a fabled antigravity sled? Or a gossamer-winged glider to catch the offshore wind and loft them to a distant mountain of fire?

'I can't waste time talking nonsense.' She stood up, worried about the Stranger. It was getting dark fast, and though Ulgor had fled to the northwest, there was no guarantee she would not circle around to seek and surprise the man from space. 'I'm going to go look—'

A scream interrupted, making her jump. A shrill ululation of surprise and outrage that warbled melodically, almost like a snatch of frantic song, rebounding off the rocks so many times that her bruised ears could not pin down where it came from. Sara's back shivered with empathic terror at the awful sound.

Prity snatched up one of the long urrish knives and stepped closer to the nervous prisoners. Jomah fondled the smallest of the desert hunters' bows, nocking an arrow against the string. Sara flexed her hands, knowing that a weapon should be in them, but the thought of holding one felt obscene. She could not bring herself to do it.

A character flaw, she admitted, a bit dazedly. *One I shouldn't pass on to kids. Not if we're headed into an age of violence and 'heroes.'*

Tension built as the wail intensified. An eerie howl that seemed one part pain, one part despair, and eight parts humiliation, as if death would be preferable to whatever the screamer was going through. It grew louder and more frenzied with each passing dura, causing the prisoners to crowd together, peering anxiously into the gloom.

Then another sound joined, in basso counterpoint. A rapid, unrhythmic thumping that made the ground tremble like an approaching machine.

Kurt cocked the pistol, holding it in front of him.

Suddenly, a shadow took form at the western fringe of firelight. A monstrous shape, slanted and heavy, protruding forward at a rising angle, leading with an appendage that flailed and thrashed like a cluster of waving arms and legs. Sara gasped and stepped back.

A moment later it resolved itself, and she let out a shuddering sigh, recognizing *Ulgor* as the protrusion, moaning in distress and shame, held up in the air by the adamant embrace of two armored, pincer-equipped, chitinous arms.

Qheuenish arms. The remaining three out of five stumbled forward clumsily, fighting for balance as the writhing urs fought to break free.

'*Resistance is useless*,' a scratchy but familiar voice whistled from two leg-vents, a voice dry with the same caked dust that fooled Sara at first, into thinking the armor was slate gray. Only near the fire did a hint of the true shade of blue glimmer through.

'Hello f-f-folks,' croaked Blade, son of Log Biter of Dolo Dam. 'Could anybody s-s-spare a drink of water?'

The night was clear, windy, and extremely cold for this time of year. They nursed their fuel supply for the fire and draped fragments of the shredded tent over huddled groups of captives to help them retain body heat. Darkness hauled the urs – including a tightly bound Ulgor – down toward sleep, but the human insurgents muttered together under their makeshift shelter, making Sara ponder glumly what they must be scheming. Clearly they had less desire than the surviving members of UrKachu's band to see more Urunthai arrive over the hilltops, tomorrow or the next day. If they sawed or chewed through their bindings in the darkness, what deterrence value would Kurt's pistol hold in the event of a sudden charge?

Granted, many of the men were flash-blinded. And *Blade* was a comfort to have around. Even wheezing dust, and with the softer chitin of a blue, he was an intimidating figure. With him present, Sara and the others might even risk taking turns trying to get some sleep.

If only we knew what's happened to the star-man, she worried.

He'd been gone for several miduras. Even with Loocen now up

to shed a wan glow across the countryside, it was all too easy to imagine the poor fellow getting lost out there.

'The gunshot helped lead me to your camp,' Blade explained once Sara and Jomah had sponged out his vents and eye circle, using up much of their precious water. 'I was becoming rather desperate, unable to follow your trail in the fading light, when I heard the bang. A bit later there was the reflection of your fire off yonder spire.'

Sara looked up. A flicker did seem to dance across the tall stone tower. Perhaps it would guide the Stranger home.

'Imagine my surprise, though, when someone came running forth to greet me!' Blade chuckled out three vents. 'Of course, my shock was nothing like *Ulgor's* when she saw me!'

The qheuen's tale was simple, if valiant. He had waited underwater, back at Uryutta's Oasis, until UrKachu's fast group departed, followed by the slower expedition of captives and booty. Blade spent the time contemplating his options. Should he strike out for Crossroads or some other settlement? Or else try to follow and give help when help might do the most good? Either decision would mean dehydration and pain – not to mention danger. Sara noticed that Blade never mentioned a third option: to wait at the oasis until someone came along. Perhaps it never occurred to him.

'One thing I didn't expect – to find you four *in charge*, having overcome both groups all by yourselves! It appears you never needed rescue, after all.'

Jomah laughed from atop Blade's carapace, where he was sponging off the qheuen's scent-slits. The boy hugged his blue cupola. 'You saved the day!'

Sara nodded. 'You're the biggest hero of all, dear, dear friend.'

There seemed no more to say after that. Or else, everyone was too tired for more words. They watched the flames in silence for a while. At one point Sara stared at Loocen, observing the bright, reflected-sunlight twinkle of abandoned Buyur cities, those enduring reminders of the might and glory that once filled this solar system and that would again, someday.

We sooners are like Jijo's dreams, she thought. *Ghostlike wraiths who leave no trace when we are gone. Passing fantasies, while this patch of creation rests and makes ready for the next phase of achievement by some godlike race.*

It was not a comforting contemplation. Sara did not *wish* to be a dream. She wanted what she did and thought in life to matter, if only as contributions to something that grew better with time, through her works, her children, her civilization. Perhaps this desire was rooted in the irreverent upbringing provided by her mother, whose offspring included a famous heretic, a legendary hunter, and a believer in crazy theories about a different kind of redemption for all of the races of the Six.

She thought back to her conversation with Dedinger.

We'll probably never know which of us would have been right, if the Commons had been left alone to go its own way. Too bad. Each of us believes in something that's beautiful, in its own way. At least, a whole lot more beautiful than extinction.

Silence allowed some of the world's natural sounds to grow familiar once again, as residual tintinnations in her ears slowly ebbed.

I should be glad not to be completely deaf or blind at this point – let alone dead. If there's any permanent damage, I'll manage to live with it.

The Stranger set a good example, ever cheerful despite horrific loss of much that had made him who he was. She decided, at times like these, any attitude but gritty stoicism simply made no sense at all.

Of the sounds brought forth by the night, some were recognizable. A floating cadence of sighs that was wind, stroking the nearby prairie and then funneling through the columns of twisted stone. A distant, lowing moan told of a herd of gallaiters. Then came the grumbling rattle of a ligger, warning all others to stay out of its territory, and the keening of some strange bird.

While she listened, the keening changed in pitch, waxing steadily in volume. Soon she realized. *That's no bird.*

It wasn't long before the sound acquired a throaty power, steadily increasing until it took over possession of the night, pushing all competitors aside. Sara stood up and the bulging tent fragments rippled as others reacted to the rising clamor – a din that soon climaxed as a bawling roar, forcing her hands over her tender ears. Blade's cupola shrank inward, and the captive urs bayed unhappy counterpoint, rocking their long necks back and forth. Pebbles fell from the nearby rocky spires, worrying Sara that the towers might topple under the howling shove of disturbed air.

That sound – I heard it once before.

The sky grew radiant as something *bright* passed into view – decelerating with a series of titanic booms – a glowing, many-studded tube whose heat was palpable, even at a distance of—

Of what? Sara had glimpsed a starship only once before, a far-off glitter from her treehouse window. Beyond that, she had pictures, sketches, and dry, abstract measurements to go on – all useless for comparison, as her mind went numb.

It *must* still be high up in the atmosphere, she realized. Yet it seemed so *big* . . .

The god-ship passed from roughly southwest to northeast, clearly descending, slowing down for a landing. It took no great ingenuity to guess its destination.

For all its awesome beauty, Sara did not feel anything this time but a sour churn of dread.

LARK

It was hard to make out much from a distance. The blaze of light coming from the Glade was so intense, it cast long shadows, even down the forested lanes of a mountainside, many leagues away.

'Now you see what you're up against,' Ling told him, standing nearby, watched by a half-dozen wary militiamen. 'This won't be anything like taking down a couple of little bodyguard robots.'

'Of that I have no doubt,' Lark answered, shading his eyes to peer against the glare, as searchlights roved across the crater where the alien station lay in ruins. After two days without sleep, the far-off engines reminded him of a growl of a she-ligger, just returned from a hunt to find her pup mauled and now nursing a killing rage.

'It's still not too late, you know,' Ling went on. 'If you hand over your zealot rebels – and your High Sages – the Rothen *may* accept individual rather than collective guilt. Punishment doesn't have to be universal.'

Lark knew he should get angry. He ought to whirl and decry the hypocrisy of her offer – reminding her of the evidence everyone had seen and felt earlier, proving that her masters planned genocide all along.

Two things stopped him.

First, while everyone now knew the Rothen planned inciting bloody civil war, aimed foremost at the *human* population of Jijo, the details were still unclear.

And the devil lies in the details.

Anyway, Lark was too tired to endure another mental tussle with the young Dakkin biologist. He turned his head in a neck-twist that mimicked an urrish shrug, and hiss-clicked in GalTwo—

'Have we not (much) better things to do, than to discuss (intensely) absurd notions?'

This brought approving snickers from the guards, accompanying the two of them into hiding. Other groups were escorting Rann and Ro-kenn to separate concealed places, dispersing the hostages as far apart as possible.

Yes, but why did they put me in charge of Ling?

Maybe they figure she'll be too busy constantly fighting with me to plan any escape.

For all he knew, the two of them might be stuck together for a long time to come.

Silence reigned as they watched the mighty starship cruise back and forth, shining its fierce beam onto every corner of the Glade, every place where a pavilion had stood, only miduras before. From a remote mountainside, it was transfixing, hypnotic.

'Sage, we must be going now, it's still not safe.'

That was the militia sergeant, a small wiry woman named Shen, with glossy black hair, delicate features, and a deadly compound bow slung over one shoulder. Lark blinked, at first wondering who she was talking to.

Sage – ah, yes.

It would take some getting used to. Lark had always figured his heresy would disqualify him, despite his training and accomplishments.

But only a sage can rule in matters of life or death.

As the group resumed their trek, he could not help glancing at Ling. Though half the time he 'wanted to strangle her,' that was only a figure of speech. Lark doubted he could ever carry out his duty, if it came to that. Even now, smudged and gaunt from exhaustion, her face was too lovely by far.

A midura or so later, a blaring cry of dismay filled the mountain range, echoing round frosted peaks to assail them from all sides, setting trees quivering. A militia soldier pointed back along the trail to where the starship's artificial glow had just grown impossibly brighter. They all ran to the nearest switchback offering a view southwest and raised their hands to shield their eyes.

'Ifni!' Lark gasped, while guards clutched their crude weapons, or each other's arms, or made futile hand gestures to ward off evil. Every face was white with reflected radiance.

'It ... can't ... be ...' Ling exhaled heavily, sighing each word.

The great Rothen ship still hovered over the Glade – as before, bathed in light.

Only *now* the light blazed down upon it from *above* – cast by a new entity.

Another ship.

A much, much bigger ship, like a grown urs towering over one of her larvae.

Uh ... went Lark's mind as he stared, struggling to adjust to the change in scale. But all he could come up with was a blaspheming thought.

The new monster was huge enough to have *laid* the Holy Egg and still have room inside for more.

Trapped underneath the behemoth, the Rothen craft gave a grinding noise and trembled, as if straining to escape, or even to move. But the light pouring down on it now seemed to take on qualities of physical substance, like a solid shaft, pressing it ever lower toward the ground. A *golden* color flowed around the smaller star-craft as it scraped hard against Jijo's soil. The dense lambency coated and surrounded it, congealing like a glowing cone, hardening as it cooled.

Like wax, Lark thought, numbly. Then he turned with the others and ran through the forest night for as long and as hard as his body could bear it.

ASX

What is this, my rings? This shivering sensation, coursing through our stack?

It feels like dread familiarity.

Or a familiar dread.

Amid this horrible glare, we stand rooted in the festival glade with the Rothen ship grounded nearby, encased in a bubble of frozen time, with leaves and twigs caught motionless, mid-whirl, next to its gold-sealed hull.

And above, this new power. This new titan.

The searing lights dim. Humming an overpowering song, the monstrous vessel descends, crushing every remaining tree on the south side of the valley, shoving a new bed for the river, filling the sky like a mountain.

Can you feel it, my rings?

Can you feel the premonition that throbs our core with acid vapors?

Along the vast flank of the starship, a hatch opens, large enough to swallow a small village.

Against the lighted interior, silhouettes enter view.

Tapered cones. Stacks of rings.

Frightful kinfolk we had hoped never to see again.

The stranger hurried into camp a while after the second ship passed overhead. By then, Sara had recovered enough to bring her mind back down to matters close at hand.

Matters she could do something about.

The star-man came from the south, herding a half-dozen weary donkeys. He seemed excited, feverish with need to tell of something. His mouth opened and closed, gabbling incoherently, as if trying to force words by sheer will.

Sara felt his forehead and checked his eyes.

'I know,' she said, trying to calm his overwrought nerves. 'We saw it too. A huge damn thing, bigger than Dolo Lake. I wish you could tell us whether it was *your* ship, or someone you don't like much.'

In fact, she wasn't even sure the man could hear her voice, let alone follow her meaning. He had been closer to the stun-grenade and less prepared.

Nevertheless, something seemed strange about his excitement. He did not point at the sky, as she would have expected, nor to the north, where the two ships were last seen descending, one after the other. Instead, he gestured *southward*, in the direction he had just come.

The Stranger's gaze met hers, and he shuddered. His brow furrowed in concentration as he took several deep breaths. Then, with a light suddenly in his eyes, he sang,

> *'Blacks and bays, dapples and grays,*
> *Coach and six white horses,*
> *Hush-a-bye, don't you cry,*
> *Go to sleep, little baby.'*

His voice was raspy and Sara saw tears. Still, he went on, triggering verses that he knew by heart – that lay ready, even after many decades, creased in undamaged folds of his brain.

> *'When you wake,*
> *you shall have cake,*
> *and all the pretty*
> *little horses'*

Sara nodded, trying to sift meaning out of the lullaby.

'All the pretty litt— oh, Ifni!'

She whirled to face the explosers.

'He's seen more urs! They're here already, swinging south to take us from behind!'

Kurt blinked a couple of times, then began to open his mouth – but was cut off by a fluting whistle of jubilation from the prisoners.

Ulgor stretched her neck toward them. 'I *told* you our allies would not take long arriving. Now cut these cords so I can intercede, and fersuade our Urunthai friends not to treat you too badly.'

'Sara,' Kurt said, taking her elbow. But she shrugged him off. There was no time to spare.

'Kurt, you take Jomah, Prity, and the Stranger into the rocks. The Urunthai can't follow well in rough terrain. You might reach high ground if Blade and I stall them. Try to find a cave or something. Go!'

She swiveled to face the blue qheuen. 'Are you ready, Blade?'

'I am, Sara!' The blue clacked two fierce pincers and stepped forward, as if prepared to fight the Battle of Znunir Trading Post all over again.

More laughter made her turn around. This time it was *Dedinger*. The former sage chortled amusement.

'Oh, don't mind me, sister. Your plan sounds delightful. It'll save my life and those of my men. So by all means, Kurt, do as she says! Head for the rocks. Go!'

Sara quickly saw what Dedinger meant. If Urunthai reinforcements found they could not follow the fugitives through a boulder field, or down some narrow grotto, or up a garu tree, that could force them to renew their broken alliance with the band of human radicals, forgoing vengeance – at least for as long as it took the desert trappers to hunt Kurt and the others down.

She sagged, seeing the futility of it all.

We've been through so much, only to come right back where we started.

'Sara—' Kurt said again. Then the old man stopped what he had been about to say and cocked his head. 'Listen.'

The clearing went silent. Moments later, she heard it too – the approaching clatter of rushing hooves. A great many of them. She could feel their rumbling haste through the soles of her feet.

Too late to come up with another plan. Too late for anything but dignity.

She took the Stranger's arm. 'Sorry I didn't catch on when you first tried to warn us,' she said, brushing the worst streaks of dust off his clothes and straightening his collar. If he was to be their prize, he should at least look the part of a valuable hostage, not some ragamuffin drifter. He repaid her with a tentative smile. Together, they turned south, to face the onrushing cavalry.

The newcomers swelled out of the darkness, from between giant pillars of stone. *They're urs, all right*, she thought. Burly, powerful and well-armed, they spilled into the clearing in a disciplined skirmish pattern, taking positions on all sides, brandishing their arbalests, scanning for danger signs. Sara was startled, and a bit insulted, when the vanguard simply ignored the standing humans and Blade, finding them no threat at all.

More surprisingly, they paid little more heed to the trussed-up prisoners, leaving them right where they were.

Sara noticed that the war paint of the new arrivals was unlike that of UrKachu's band – more restrained, dabbed in smoother, more flowing lines. Could that mean they weren't Urunthai, after all?

From the dismayed look on Ulgor's face, Sara realized this was not the band of 'friends' the tinker was expecting. She nursed a slim reed of hope. Could they be militia? They wore no formal brassards or tunics, nor did they *act* like the typical urrish militia unit – local herdsmen who drilled for fun every eighth day, when the weather was good.

Who are these guys?

Skirmishers whistled that the area was clear. Then a senior matron with a gray-fringed muzzle sauntered into the firelight. She approached the Dolo Villagers and lowered her neck, respectfully.

'We regret our tardiness, friends. It is sad you were inconvenienced, vut we are glad to see you overcane your trouvles, without help.'

Sara stared as Kurt touched noses with the aged urs. 'You're not late if you arrive in the nick of time, Ulashtu. I knew you'd scent our affliction and come for us ...'

At that point, Sara lost track of the conversation. For the Stranger pulled her about, squeezing her arm tight while a nervous, excited quaver throbbed along his skin.

More figures were approaching out of the darkness.

Perplexing shapes.

At first she thought it was another party of urs, outfitted for war. Very *large* urs, with strange, stiff necks and an odd way of moving. For an instant she recalled the ancient illustration that once rimmed the Parthenon – the one depicting savage, mythical *centaurs*.

A moment later, she sighed.

Silly thing. It's only men riding donkeys. Ifni! This darkness would make anything ordinary seem mysterious, especially after all we've been thr—

She blinked and stared again.

They were *big* donkeys. The human riders' feet did not drag but perched high off the ground, astride great torsos that seemed to pulsate with raw animal power.

'It's them!' Jomah cried. 'They're real! They weren't all killed off, after all!'

To Sara it felt like witnessing dragons, or dinosaurs, or stag-griffins come alive off the pages of a storybook. A dream made real – or a nightmare to some. The Urunthai prisoners let out a howl of anger and despair when they realized what was stepping into the firelight. This meant their one great achievement – their league's sole claim to fame – was in fact a failure. A farce.

The riders dismounted, and Sara realized they were all women. She also saw that several more of the great beasts followed behind, bearing saddles but otherwise unburdened.

No, she thought, realizing what was about to be asked of her. *They can't seriously expect me to climb onto one of those things!*

The nearest beast snorted as the Stranger reached up to stroke its mammoth head. The creature easily outmassed four or five urs, with jaws big enough to swallow a person's arm, whole. Yet, the man from space pressed his cheek against its great neck.

With tears in his eyes, he sang again.

When you wake,
you shall have cake,
and all the pretty
little horses.

EPILOGUE

It is a strange universe.

He ponders this without putting it in words. It's easier that way.

Lately, he has found quite a few means to express ideas without the swarm of busy, smacking, humming, clattering noises that used to run through all his thoughts.

Music and song. Numbers. Pencil sketches. Feelings. And the strange colors cast by those funny living-visors people sometimes wear on this world.

Rewq.

He can think the name of the beasts and is proud of the accomplishment.

As he slowly gets better, he finds he can contemplate important names more clearly.

Sara, Jomah, Prity . . .

And some other words, occasionally two or three at a time.

Memory, too, is becoming more clarified. He can recall the scoutship, for instance, blasted as he tried a futile diversion, attempting to draw a hunter ship away from its prey.

He failed, taking a jolting series of blows, and there had followed a period that was still a blur to him, a vague impression of rapid movement and change . . . after which he found himself plummeting, on fire, crashing—

No, no. Think of something else.

Riding. That was a much nicer thing to muse upon. Riding a saddled animal. A spirited *horse*. The heady, surprising joy of it, with cool wind in his face, bringing a thousand amazing smells.

How strange to find so many things to like about this new world! About a life robbed of the one thing that makes most humans *human*. A command of words.

And now he remembers. Something very much like this injury of his happened *before*. To a friend.

To his captain.

An image swirls through his mind. A handsome, sleek-gray figure. Flukes thrashing through water filled with tiny bubbles. A narrow, bottle-shaped jaw, filled with pointy, grinning teeth. A brain, wounded, but still profoundly wise.

Silently, he mouths three syllables.

Crei ... dei ... ki ...

And all at once this triggers *more* memories. More friends. A ship. A mission. A need.

An image of watery depths. So deep and black that no light could ever penetrate – a hiding place, but no sanctuary. In all the vast cosmos, there is no sanctuary.

But now, as if released from the prison of his illness, one more thing swarms through his mind, surprising him with sudden recognition.

A name.

My ... name.

Slippery from pent-up frustration, it shoots out from wherever it had lain, dammed up for so long. Caroming back and forth, it finally settles down within reach.

It ought never to have gone away. It should be the most familiar word in a person's life, yet only now does it return, as if to say 'welcome back.'

Riding through a night washed with exotic moonlight, surrounded by curious beings and a culture unlike any he had ever known, he now laughs aloud, ecstatic to be able to do this simple thing. This one, cherished act.

My ... name ... is ... Emerson.

ACKNOWLEDGMENTS

For those familiar with my other work, this volume may seem a departure from my normal custom of trying to write novels that stand on their own. That was my intention this time, but the story kept growing, evolving beyond even the length of huge tomes like *Earth* and *Glory Season*, leaving me no alternative but to 'go the trilogy route.' There is no shame in the practice – trilogies have their own lavish, wide-screen, Technicolor attraction. But in future I trust that I'll plan better.

I hope to bring out volumes two and three promptly.

I'd like to thank the following people for helping with their comments and criticism to make this complicated story work, among them – Gregory Benford, Anita Everson, Joy Crisp, Mark James, Dr Bruce Miller, Jim Richards, Prof. Jim Moore, and Dr Steinn Sigurdsson. Also my gratitude to members of SPECTRE, the Caltech science fiction club: Aaron Petty, Teresa Moore, Dustin Laurence, Damien Sullivan, Micah Altman, John Langford, Eric Schell, Robin Hanson, Grant Swenson, Ruben Krasnopolsky, and Anita Gould. Special thanks are due Stefan Jones and Kevin Lenagh for helping enhance and embellish my poor efforts. My deep appreciation also goes to Jennifer Hershey, Ralph Vicinanza, and Cheryl Brigham, for their dedication and wisdom.

David Brin, March 1995

In Memory of Dr James Neale,
Kiwi third-baseman,
healer and friend.

INFINITY'S SHORE

To
Ariana Mae, our splendid envoy,
who will speak for us at the threshold of
the fantastic twenty-second century.

Those who hunger after wisdom often seek it
in the highest heights, or profound depths.

Yet, marvels are found in shallow sites
where life starts, burgeons, and dies.

What pinnacle, or lofty mount,
offers lessons as poignant
as the flowing river –
a crashing reef –
or the grave?

—from a Buyur wall inscription
found half-buried in a marsh
near Far Wet Sanctuary

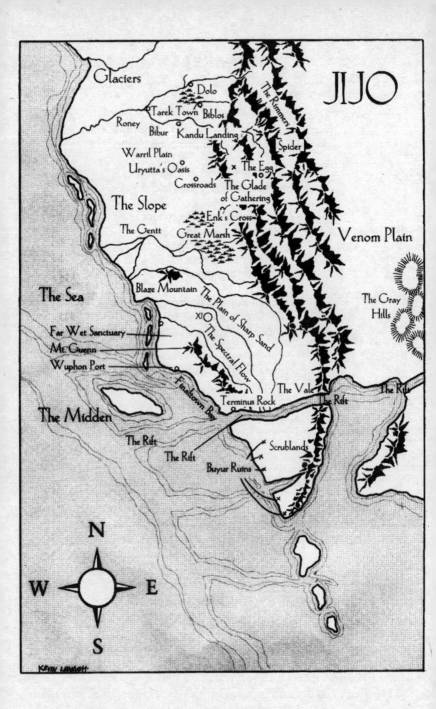

STREAKERS

[Five Jaduras Earlier]

KAA

> * What strange fate brought me,
>   * Fleeing maelstroms of winter,
>   * Past five galaxies? *
>
> * Only to find refuge,
>   * On a forlorn planet (nude!)
>   * In laminar luxury! *

So he thought while performing swooping rolls, propelling his sleek gray body with exhilarated tail strokes, reveling in the caress of water against naked flesh.

Dappled sunlight threw luminous shafts through crystal shallows, slanting past mats of floating sea florets. Silvery native creatures, resembling flat-jawed fish, moved in and out of the bright zones, enticing his eye. Kaa squelched the instinctive urge to give chase.

Maybe later.

For now, he indulged in the liquid texture of water sliding around him, without the greasiness that used to cling so, back in the oily seas of Oakka, the green-green world, where soap-like bubbles would erupt from his blowhole each time he surfaced to breathe. *Not that it was worth the effort to inhale on Oakka. There wasn't enough good air on that horrid ball to nourish a comatose otter.*

This sea also tasted good, not harsh like Kithrup, where each excursion outside the ship would give you a poison dose of hard metals.

In contrast, the water on Jijo world felt clean, with a salty tang reminding Kaa of the gulf stream flowing past the Florida Academy, during happier days on far-off Earth.

He tried to squint and pretend he was back home, chasing mullet near Key Biscayne, safe from a harsh universe. But the attempt at make-believe failed. One paramount difference reminded him this was an alien world.

Sound.

—a beating of tides rising up the continental shelf – a complex rhythm tugged by three moons, not one.

—an echo of waves, breaking on a shore whose abrasive sand had a strange, sharp texture.

—an occasional distant groaning that seemed to rise out of the ocean floor itself.

—the return vibrations of his own sonar clicks, tracing schools of fishlike creatures, moving their fins in unfamiliar ways.

—above all, the engine hum just behind him ... a cadence of machinery that had filled Kaa's days and nights for five long years.

And now, another clicking, groaning sound. The clipped poetry of duty.

> * *Relent, Kaa, tell us,*
> > * *In exploratory prose,*
> > > * *Is it safe to come?* *

The voice chased Kaa like a fluttering, sonic conscience. Reluctantly, he swerved around to face the submarine *Hikahi*, improvised from ancient parts found strewn across this planet's deep seafloor – a makeshift contraption that suited a crew of misfit fugitives. Clamshell doors closed ponderously, like the jaws of a huge carnivore, cycling to let others emerge in his wake ... if he gave the all clear.

Kaa sent his Trinary reply, amplified by a saser unit plugged into his skull, behind his left eye.

> * *If water were all*
> > * *We might be in heaven now.*
> > > * *But wait! I'll check above!* *

His lungs were already making demands, so he obeyed instinct, flicking an upward spiral toward the glistening surface. *Ready or not, Jijo, here I come!*

He loved piercing the tense boundary of sky and sea, flying weightless for an instant, then broaching with a splash and spume of exhalation. Still, he hesitated before inhaling. Instruments predicted an Earthlike atmosphere, yet he felt a nervous tremor drawing breath.

If anything, the air tasted better than the water! Kaa whirled, thrashing his tail in exuberance, glad Lieutenant Tsh't had let him volunteer for this – to be the first dolphin, the first Earthling, ever to swim this sweet, foreign sea.

Then his eye stroked a jagged, gray-brown line, spanning one horizon, very close.

The shore.

Mountains.

He stopped his gyre to stare at the nearby continent – inhabited, they now knew. But by whom?

There was not supposed to be any sapient life on Jijo.

Maybe they're just hiding here, the way we are, from a hostile cosmos.

That was one theory.

At least they chose a pleasant world, he added, relishing the air, the water, and gorgeous ranks of cumulus hovering over a giant mountain. *I wonder if the fish are good to eat.*

* As we await you,
    * Chafing in this cramped airlock,
        * Should we play pinochle? *

Kaa winced at the lieutenant's sarcasm. Hurriedly, he sent back pulsed waves.

* Fortune smiles again,
    * On our weary band of knaves.
        * Welcome, friends, to Ifni's Shore. *

It might seem presumptuous to invoke the goddess of chance and destiny, capricious Ifni, who always seemed ready to plague *Streaker*'s company with one more surprise. Another unexpected calamity, or miraculous escape. But Kaa had always felt an affinity with the informal patron deity of spacers. There might be better pilots than himself in the Terragens Survey Service, but none with a deeper respect for fortuity. Hadn't his own nickname been 'Lucky'?

Until recently, that is.

From below, he heard the grumble of clamshell doors reopening. Soon Tsh't and others would join him in this first examination of Jijo's surface – a world they heretofore saw only briefly from orbit, then from the deepest, coldest pit in all its seas. Soon, his companions would arrive, but for a few moments more he had it to himself – silken water, tidal rhythms, fragrant air, the sky and clouds . . .

His tail swished, lifting him higher as he peered. *Those aren't normal clouds*, he realized, staring at a great mountain dominating the eastern horizon, whose peak wore shrouds of billowing white. The lens implanted in his right eye dialed through a spectral scan, sending readings to his optic nerve – revealing steam, carbon oxides, and a flicker of molten heat.

A volcano, Kaa realized, and the reminder sent his ebullience down a notch. This was a busy part of the planet, geologically speaking. The same forces that made it a useful hiding place also kept it dangerous.

That must be where the groaning comes from, he pondered. Seismic activity. An interaction of miniquakes and crustal gas discharges with the thin overlaying film of sea.

Another flicker caught his notice, in roughly the same direction, but much closer – a pale swelling that might also have been a cloud, except for the way it moved, flapping like a bird's wing, then bulging with eagerness to race the wind.

A sail, he discerned. Kaa watched it jibe across the stiffening breeze – a two-masted schooner, graceful in motion, achingly familiar from the Caribbean seas of home.

Its bow split the water, spreading a wake that any dolphin might love to ride.

The zoom lens clarified, magnified, until he made out fuzzy bipedal forms, hauling ropes and bustling around on deck, like any gang of human sailors.

. . . Only these weren't human beings. Kaa glimpsed scaly backs, culminating in a backbone of sharp spines. Swathes of white fur covered the legs, and froglike membranes pulsated below broad chins as the ship's company sang a low, rumbling work chant that Kaa could dimly make out, even from here.

He felt a chill of unhappy recognition.

Hoons! What in all Five Galaxies are they doing here?

Kaa heard a rustle of fluke strokes – Tsh't and others rising to join him. Now he must report that enemies of Earth dwelled here.

Kaa realized grimly – this news wasn't going to help him win back his nickname anytime soon.

She came to mind again, the capricious goddess of uncertain destiny. And Kaa's own Trinary phrase came back to him, as if reflected and reconverged by the surrounding alien waters.

> * Welcome . . .
>> * Welcome . . .
>>> * Welcome to Ifni's Shore . . . *

SOONERS

THE STRANGER

Existence seems like wandering through a vast chaotic house. One that has been torn by quakes and fire, and is now filled with bitter, inexplicable fog. Whenever he manages to pry open a door, exposing some small corner of the past, each revelation comes at the price of sharp waves of agony.

In time, he learns not to be swayed by the pain. Rather, each ache and sting serves as a *marker*, a signpost, confirming that he must be on the right path.

His arrival on this world – plummeting through a scorched sky – should have ended with merciful blankness. What luck instead hurled his blazing body from the pyre to quench in a fetid swamp?

Peculiar luck.

Since then, he has grown intimate with all kinds of suffering, from crass pangs to subtle stings. In cataloging them, he grows learned in the many ways there are to hurt.

Those earliest agonies, right after the crash, had screeched coarsely from wounds and scalding burns – a gale of such fierce torment that he barely noticed when a motley crew of local savages rowed out to him in a makeshift boat, like sinners dragging a fallen angel out of the boggy fen. Saving him from drowning, only to face more damnations.

Beings who insisted that he fight for his broken life, when it would have been so much easier just to let go.

Later, as his more blatant injuries healed or scarred, other types of anguish took up the symphony of pain.

Afflictions of the mind.

Holes gape across his life, vast blank zones, lightless and empty, where missing memories must once have spanned megaparsecs and life years. Each gap feels chilled beyond numbness – a raw vacancy more frustrating than an itch that can't be scratched.

Ever since he began wandering this singular world, he has probed the darkness within. Optimistically, he clutches a few small trophies from the struggle.

Jijo is one of them.

He rolls the word in his mind – the name of this planet where six castaway races band together in feral truce, a mixed culture unlike any other beneath the myriad stars.

A second word comes more easily with repeated use – *Sara*. She who nursed him from near death in her tree house overlooking a rustic water mill ... who calmed the fluxing panic when he first woke to see pincers, claws, and mucusy ring stacks – the physiques of *hoons*, *traekis*, *qheuens*, and others sharing this rude outcast existence.

He knows more words, such as *Kurt* and *Prity* ... friends he now trusts almost as much as *Sara*. It feels good to think their names, the slick way all words used to come, in the days before his mangling.

One recent prize he is especially proud of.

Emerson ...

It is his own name, for so long beyond reach. Violent shocks had jarred it free, less than a day ago – shortly after he provoked a band of human rebels to betray their urrish allies in a slashing knife fight that made a space battle seem antiseptic by comparison. That bloody frenzy ended with an explosive blast, shattering the grubby caravan tent, spearing light past Emerson's closed lids, overwhelming the guardians of reason.

And then, amid the dazzling rays, he had briefly glimpsed ... his captain!

Creideiki ...

The blinding glow became a luminous foam, whipped by thrashing flukes. Out of that froth emerged a long gray form whose bottle snout bared glittering teeth. The sleek head *grinned*, despite bearing an awful wound behind its left eye ... much like the hurt that robbed Emerson of speech.

Utterance shapes formed out of scalloped bubbles, in a language like none spoken by Jijo's natives, or by any great Galactic clan.

> * In the turning
>   of the cycloid,
> * Comes a time
>   to break for surface.
>
> * Time to resume
>   breathing, doing.
> * To rejoin the
>   great sea's
>   dreaming.
>
> * Time has come
>   for you *my old friend.*
> * Time to wake
>   and see what's churning ...*

Stunned recognition accompanied waves of stinging misery, worse than any fleshy woe or galling numbness.

Shame had nearly overwhelmed him then. For no injury short of death could ever excuse his forgetting—

Creideiki ...

Terra ...

The dolphins ...

Hannes ...

Gillian ...

How could they have slipped his mind during the months he wandered this barbarian world, by boat, barge, and caravan?

Guilt might have engulfed him during that instant of recollection ... except that his new friends urgently needed him to act, to serve the brief advantage offered by the explosion, to overcome their captors and take them prisoner. As dusk fell across the shredded tent and torn bodies, he had helped Sara and Kurt tie up their surviving foes – both urrish and human – although Sara seemed to think their reprieve temporary.

More fanatic reinforcements were expected soon.

Emerson knew what the rebels wanted. They wanted *him*. It was no secret that he came from the stars. The rebels would trade him to sky hunters, hoping to exchange his battered carcass for guaranteed survival.

As if anything could save Jijo's castaway races, now that the Five Galaxies had found them.

Huddled round a wan fire, lacking any shelter but tent rags, Sara and the others watched as terrifying portents crossed bitter-cold constellations.

First came a mighty titan of space, growling as it plunged toward nearby mountains, bent on awful vengeance.

Later, following the very same path, there came a *second* behemoth, this one so enormous that Jijo's pull seemed to lighten as it passed overhead, filling everyone with deep foreboding.

Not long after that, golden lightning flickered amid the mountain peaks – a bickering of giants. But Emerson did not care who won. He could tell that neither vessel was *his* ship, the home in space he yearned for ... and prayed he would never see again.

With luck, *Streaker* was far away from this doomed world, bearing in its hold a trove of ancient mysteries – perhaps the key to a new galactic era.

Had not all his sacrifices been aimed at helping her escape?

After the leviathans passed, there remained only stars and a chill wind, blowing through the dry steppe grass, while Emerson went off searching for the caravan's scattered pack animals. With donkeys, his friends just might yet escape before more fanatics arrived ...

Then came a rumbling noise, jarring the ground beneath his feet. A rhythmic cadence that seemed to go—

taranta, taranta,
taranta, taranta

The galloping racket could only be urrish hoofbeats, the expected rebel reinforcements, come to make them prisoners once again.

Only, miraculously, the darkness instead poured forth *allies* – unexpected rescuers, both urrish and human – who brought with them astonishing beasts.

Horses.

Saddled horses, clearly as much a surprise to Sara as they were to him. Emerson had thought the creatures were extinct on this world, yet here they were, emerging from the night as if from a dream.

So began the next phase of his odyssey. Riding southward, fleeing the shadow of these vengeful ships, hurrying toward the outline of an uneasy volcano.

Now he wonders within his battered brain – is there a plan? A destination?

Old Kurt apparently has faith in these surprising saviors, but there must be more to it than that.

Emerson is tired of just running away.

He would much rather be running toward.

While his steed bounds ahead, new aches join the background music of his life – raw, chafed thighs and a bruised spine that jars with each pounding hoofbeat.

taranta, taranta, taranta-tara
taranta, taranta, taranta-tara

Guilt nags him with a sense of duties unfulfilled, and he grieves over the likely fate of his new friends on Jijo, now that their hidden colony has been discovered.

And yet ...

In time Emerson recalls how to ease along with the sway of the saddle. And as sunrise lifts dew off fan-fringed trees near a river-bank, swarms of bright bugs whir through the slanted light, dancing as they pollinate a field of purple blooms. When Sara glances back from her own steed, sharing a rare smile, his pangs seem to matter less. Even fear of those terrible starships, splitting the sky with their angry engine arrogance, cannot erase a growing elation as the fugitive band gallops on to dangers yet unknown.

Emerson cannot help himself. It is his nature to seize any possible excuse for hope. As the horses pound Jijo's ancient turf, their cadence draws him down a thread of familiarity, recalling rhythmic music quite apart from the persistent dirge of woe.

> *tarantara, tarantara,*
> *tarantara, tarantara*

Under insistent stroking by that throbbing sound, something abruptly clicks inside. His body reacts involuntarily as unexpected *words* surge from some dammed-up corner of his brain, attended by a melody that stirs the heart. Lyrics pour reflexively, an undivided stream, through lungs and throat before he even knows that he is singing.

> *'Though in body and in mind,* *{tarantara, tarantara}*
> *We are timidly inclined,* *{tarantara!}*
> *And anything but blind,* *{tarantara, tarantara}*
> *To the danger that's behind—* *{tarantara!}'*

His friends grin – this has happened before.

> *'Yet, when the danger's near,* *{tarantara, tarantara}*
> *We manage to appear,* *{tarantara!}*
> *As insensible to fear,*
> *As anybody here,*
> *As an-y-bo-dy here!'*

Sara laughs, joining the refrain, and even the dour urrish escorts stretch their long necks to lisp along.

> *'Yet, when the danger's near,* *{tarantara, tarantara}*
> *We manage to appear,* *{tarantara!}*
> *As insensible to fear,*
> *As anybody here,*
> *As anybody here!'*

1

Each of the sooner races making up the Commons of Jijo tells its own unique story, passed down from generation to generation explaining why their ancestors surrendered godlike powers and risked terrible penalties to reach this far place – skulking in sneakships past Institute patrols, robot guardians, and Zang globules. Seven waves of sinners, each coming to plant their outlaw seed on a world that had been declared off-limits to settlement. A world set aside to rest and recover in peace, but for the likes of us.

THE g'Kek arrived first on this land we call the Slope, between misty mountains and the sacred sea – half a million years after the last legal tenants – the Buyur – departed Jijo.

Why did those g'Kek founders willingly give up their former lives as star-traveling gods and citizens of the Five Galaxies? Why choose instead to dwell as fallen primitives, lacking the comforts of technology, or any moral solace but for a few engraved platinum scrolls?

Legend has it that our g'Kek cousins fled threatened extinction, a dire punishment for devastating gambling losses. But we cannot be sure. Writing was a lost art until humans came, so those accounts may be warped by passing time.

What we do know is that it could not have been a petty threat that drove them to abandon the spacefaring life they loved, seeking refuge on heavy Jijo, where their wheels have such a hard time on the rocky ground. With four keen eyes, peering in all directions at the end of graceful stalks, did the g'Kek ancestors see a dark destiny painted on galactic winds? Did that first generation see no other choice? Perhaps they only cursed their descendants to this savage life as a last resort.

NOT long after the g'Kek, roughly two thousand years ago, a party of traeki dropped hurriedly from the sky, as if fearing pursuit by some dreaded foe. Wasting no time, they sank their sneakship in the deepest hollow of the sea, then settled down to be our gentlest tribe.

What nemesis drove them from the spiral lanes?

Any native Jijoan glancing at those familiar stacks of fatty toruses, venting fragrant steam and placid wisdom in each village of the Slope, must find it hard to imagine the traeki having enemies.

In time, they confided their story. The foe they fled was not some other race, nor was there a deadly vendetta among the star gods of the Five Galaxies. Rather, it was an aspect of their own selves. Certain rings — components of their physical bodies — had lately been modified in ways that turned their kind into formidable beings. Into *Jophur*, mighty and feared among the noble Galactic clans.

It was a fate those traeki founders deemed unbearable. So they chose to become lawless refugees — *sooners* on a taboo world — in order to shun a horrid destiny.

The obligation to be great.

IT is said that glavers came to Jijo not out of fear, but seeking the Path of Redemption — the kind of innocent oblivion that wipes all slates clean. In this goal they have succeeded far better than anyone else, showing the rest of us the way, if we dare follow their example.

Whether or not that sacred track will also be ours, we must respect their accomplishment — transforming themselves from cursed fugitives into a race of blessed simpletons. As starfaring immortals, they could be held accountable for their crimes, including the felony of invading Jijo. But now they have reached a refuge, the purity of ignorance, free to start again.

Indulgently, we let glavers root through our kitchen middens, poking under logs for insects. Once mighty intellects, they are not counted among the sooner races of Jijo anymore. They are no longer stained with the sins of their forebears.

QHEUENS were the first to arrive filled with wary ambition.

Led by fanatical, crablike gray matrons, their first-generation colonists snapped all five pincers derisively at any thought of union with Jijo's other exile races. Instead, they sought dominion.

That plan collapsed in time, when blue and red qheuens abandoned historic roles of servitude, drifting off to seek their own ways, leaving their frustrated gray empresses helpless to enforce old feudal loyalties.

OUR tall *hoonish* brethren inhale deeply, whenever the question arises — 'Why are you here?' They fill their prodigious throat sacs with low meditation umbles. In rolling tones, hoon elders relate that their ancestors fled no great danger, no oppression or unwanted obligations.

Then why did they come, risking frightful punishment if their descendants are ever caught living illegally on Jijo?

The oldest hoons on Jijo merely shrug with frustrating cheerfulness, as if they do not know the reason, and could not be bothered to care.

Some do refer to a legend, though. According to that slim tale, a Galactic oracle once offered a starfaring hoonish clan a unique opportunity, if they dared take it. An opportunity to claim something that had been robbed from them, although they never knew it was lost. A precious birthright that might be discovered on a forbidden world.

But for the most part, whenever one of the tall ones puffs his throat sac to sing about past times, he rumbles a deep, joyful ballad about the crude rafts, boats, and seagoing ships that hoons invented from scratch, soon after landing on Jijo. Things their humorless star cousins would never have bothered looking up in the all-knowing Galactic Library, let alone have deigned to build.

LEGENDS told by the fleet-footed *urrish* clan imply that their foremothers were rogues, coming to Jijo in order to breed — escaping limits imposed in civilized parts of the Five Galaxies. With their short lives, hot tempers, and prolific sexual style, the urs founders might have gone on to fill Jijo with their kind ... or else met extinction by now, like the mythical centaurs they vaguely resemble.

But they escaped both of those traps. Instead, after many hard struggles, at the forge and on the battlefield, they assumed an honored place in the Commons of Six Races. With their thundering herds, and mastery of steel, they live hot and hard, making up for their brief seasons in our midst.

FINALLY, two centuries ago, Earthlings came, bringing chimpanzees and other treasures. But humans' greatest gift was paper. In creating the printed trove Biblos, they became lore masters to our piteous commonwealth of exiles. Printing and education changed life on the Slope, spurring a new tradition of scholarship, so that later generations of castaways dared to study their adopted world, their hybrid civilization, and even their own selves.

As for *why* humans came all this way — breaking Galactic laws and risking everything, just to huddle with other outlaws under a fearsome sky — their tale is among the strangest told by Jijo's exile clans.

—*An Ethnography of the Slope,*
by Dorti Chang-Jones and Huph-alch-Huo

SOONERS

ALVIN

I had no way to mark the passage of time, lying dazed and half-paralyzed in a metal cell, listening to the engine hum of a mechanical sea dragon that was hauling me and my friends to parts unknown.

I guess a couple of days must have passed since the shattering of our makeshift submarine, our beautiful *Wuphon's Dream*, before I roused enough to wonder, What next?

Dimly, I recall the sea monster's face as we first saw it through our crude glass viewing port, lit by the *Dream*'s homemade searchlight. That glimpse lasted but a moment as the huge metal thing loomed toward us out of black, icy depths. The four of us – Huck, Pincer, Urronn, and me – had already resigned ourselves to death ... doomed to crushed oblivion at the bottom of the sea. Our expedition a failure, we didn't feel like daring subsea adventurers anymore, but like scared kids, voiding our bowels in terror as we waited for the cruel abyss to squeeze our hollowed-out tree trunk into a zillion soggy splinters.

Suddenly this enormous shape erupted toward us, spreading jaws wide enough to snatch *Wuphon's Dream* whole.

Well, *almost* whole. Passing through that maw, we stuck a glancing blow.

The collision shattered our tiny capsule.

What followed still remains a painful blur.

I guess anything beats death, but there have been moments since that impact when my back hurt so much that I just wanted to rumble one last umble through my battered throat sac and say *farewell* to young Alvin Hph-wayuo – junior linguist, humicking writer, utter-gloss daredevil, and neglectful son of Mu-phauwq and Yowg-wayuo of Wuphon Port, the Slope, Jijo, Galaxy Four, the Universe.

But I stayed alive.

I guess it just didn't seem *hoonish* to give up, after everything my pals and I went through to get here. What if I was sole survivor? I owed it to Huck and the others to carry on.

My cell – a prison? hospital room? – measures just two meters, by two, by three. Pretty skimpy for a hoon, even one not quite fully grown. It gets even more cramped whenever some six-legged, metal-sheathed demon tries to squeeze inside to tend my injured spine, poking with what I assume (hope!) to be clumsy kindness. Despite their efforts, misery comes in awful waves, making me wish desperately for the pain remedies cooked up by Old Stinky – our traeki pharmacist back home.

It occurred to me that I might never walk again ... or see my family, or watch seabirds swoop over the dross ships, anchored beneath Wuphon's domelike shelter trees.

I tried talking to the insecty giants trooping in and out of my cell. Though each had a torso longer than my dad is tall – with a flared back end, and a tubelike shell as hard as Buyur steel – I couldn't help picturing them as enormous *phuvnthus*, those six-legged vermin that gnaw the walls of wooden houses, giving off a sweet-tangy stench.

These things smell like overworked machinery. Despite my efforts in a dozen Earthling and Galactic languages, they seemed even less talkative than the *phuvnthus* Huck and I used to catch when we were little, and train to perform in a miniature circus.

I missed Huck during that dark time. I missed her quick g'Kek mind and sarcastic wit. I even missed the way she'd snag my leg fur in her wheels to get my attention, if I stared too long at the horizon in a hoonish sailor's trance. I last glimpsed those wheels spinning uselessly in the sea dragon's mouth, just after those giant jaws smashed our precious *Dream* and we spilled across the slivers of our amateur diving craft.

Why didn't I rush to my friend, during those bleak moments after we crashed? Much as I yearned to, it was hard to see or hear much while a screaming wind shoved its way into the chamber, pushing out the bitter sea. At first, I had to fight just to breathe again. Then, when I tried to move, my back would not respond.

In those blurry instants, I also recall catching sight of *Ur-ronn*, whipping her long neck about and screaming as she thrashed all four legs and both slim arms, horrified at being drenched in vile water. Ur-ronn bled where her suede-colored hide was pierced by jagged shards – remnants of the glass porthole she had proudly forged in the volcano workshops of Uriel the Smith.

Pincer-Tip was there, too, best equipped among our gang to survive underwater. As a red qheuen, Pincer was used to scampering on five chitin-armored claws across salty shallows – though our chance tumble into the bottomless void was more than even he had bargained for. In dim recollection, I *think* Pincer seemed alive ... or does wishful thinking deceive me?

My last hazy memories of our 'rescue' swarm with violent images until I blacked out ... to wake in this cell, delirious and alone.

*

Sometimes the phuvnthus do something 'helpful' to my spine, and it hurts so much that I'd willingly spill every secret I know. That is, if the phuvnthus ever asked questions, which they never do.

So I never allude to the mission we four were given by Uriel the Smith – to seek a taboo treasure that her ancestors left on the seafloor, centuries ago. An offshore cache, hidden when urrish settlers first jettisoned their ships and high-tech gadgets to become just one more fallen race. Only some dire emergency would prompt Uriel to violate the Covenant by retrieving such contraband.

I guess 'emergency' might cover the arrival of alien robbers, plundering the Gathering Festival of the Six Races and threatening the entire Commons with genocide.

Eventually, the pangs in my spine eased enough for me to rummage through my rucksack and resume writing in this tattered journal, bringing my ill-starred adventure up to date. That raised my spirits a bit. Even if none of us survives, my diary might yet make it home someday.

Growing up in a little hoonish village, devouring human adventure stories by Clarke and Rostand, Conrad and Xu Xiang, I dreamed that people on the Slope would someday say, 'Wow, that Alvin Hph-wayuo was some storyteller, as good as any old-time Earther.'

This could be my one and only chance.

So I spent long miduras with a stubby charcoal crayon clutched in my big hoon fist, scribbling the passages that lead up to this one – an account of how I came to find myself in this low, low state.

—How four friends built a makeshift submarine out of skink skins and a carved-out garu log, fancying a treasure hunt to the Great Midden.

—How Uriel the Smith, in her mountain forge, threw her support behind our project, turning it from a half-baked dream into a real expedition.

—How we four snuck up to Uriel's observatory, and heard a human sage speak of *starships* in the sky, perhaps bringing foretold judgment on the Six Races.

—And how *Wuphon's Dream* soon dangled from a pole near Terminus Rock, where the Midden's sacred trench passes near land. And Uriel told us, hissing through her cloven upper lip, that a ship had indeed landed up north. But this cruiser did not carry Galactic magistrates. Instead another kind of criminal had come, worse even than our sinner ancestors.

So we sealed the hatch, and the great winch turned. But on reaching the mapped site, we found that Uriel's cache was already missing! Worse – when we went looking for the damned thing, *Wuphon's Dream* got lost and tumbled off the edge of an undersea cliff.

Flipping back some pages, I can tell my account of the journey was written by someone perched on a knife-edge of harrowing pain. Yet, there is a sense of *drama* I can't hope to match now. Especially that scene where the bottom vanished beneath our wheels and we felt ourselves fall toward the *real* Midden.

Toward certain death.

Until the phuvnthus snatched us up.

So, here I am, swallowed by a metal whale, ruled by cryptic silent beings, ignorant whether my friends still live or if I am alone. Merely crippled, or dying.

Do my captors have anything to do with starship landings in the mountains?

Are they a different enigma, rising out of Jijo's ancient past? Relics of the vanished Buyur perhaps? Or ghosts even older still?

Answers seem scarce, and since I've finished recounting the plummet and demise of *Wuphon's Dream*, I daren't waste more precious paper on speculation. I must put my pencil down, even if it robs my last shield against loneliness.

All my life I've been inspired by human-style books, picturing myself as hero in some uttergloss tale. Now my sanity depends on learning to savor *patience*.

To let time pass without concern.

To live and think, at last, just like a hoon.

ASX

you may call me Asx.

you manicolored rings, piled in a high tapered heap, venting fragrant stinks, sharing the victual sap that climbs our common core, or partaking in memory wax, trickling back down from our sensory peak.

you, the rings who take up diverse roles in this shared body, a pudgy cone nearly as tall as a hoon, as heavy as a blue qheuen, and slow across the ground like an aged g'Kek with a cracked axle.

you, the rings who vote each day whether to renew our coalition.

From you rings i/we now request a ruling. Shall we carry on this fiction? This 'Asx'?

Unitary beings – the humans, urs, and other dear partners in exile – stubbornly use that term, Asx, to signify this loosely affiliated pile of fatty toruses, as if we/i truly had a fixed *name*, not a mere label of convenience.

Of course unitary beings are all quite mad. We traeki long ago resigned ourselves to living in a universe filled with egotism.

What we could not resign ourselves to – and the reason for our exile here on Jijo – was the prospect of becoming the most egotistical of all.

Once, our/my stack of bloated tubes played the role of a modest village pharmacist, serving others with our humble secretions, near the sea bogs of Far Wet Sanctuary. Then others began paying us/me homage, calling us 'Asx,' chief sage of the Traeki Sept and member of the Guiding Council of the Six.

Now we stand in a blasted wasteland that was formerly a pleasant festival glade. Our sensor rings and neural tendrils recoil from sights and sounds they cannot bear to perceive. And so we are left virtually blind, our component toruses buffeted by the harsh fields of two nearby starships, as vast as mountains.

Even now, awareness of those starships fades away . . .

We are left in blackness.

What has just happened!

Be calm, my rings. This sort of thing has transpired before. Too great a shock can jar a traeki stack out of alignment, causing gaps in short-term memory. But there is another, surer way to find out what has happened. Neural memory is a flimsy thing. How much better off we are, counting on the slow/reliable wax.

Ponder the fresh wax that slithers down our common core, still hot-slick, imprinted with events that took place recently on this ill-fated glade, where once gay pavilions stood, and banners flapped in Jijo's happy winds. A typical festival, the annual gathering of Six Races to celebrate their hundred-year peace. Until—

Is this the memory we seek?

Behold . . . a starship comes to Jijo! Not sneaking by night, like our ancestors. Not aloofly, like a mysterious Zang globule. No, this was an arrogant cruiser from the Five Galaxies, commanded by aloof alien beings called *Rothen*.

Trace *this* memory of our first sight of Rothen lords, emerging at

last from their metal lair, so handsome and noble in their conde-
scension, projecting a majestic charisma that shadowed even their
sky-human servants. How glorious to be a star god! Even gods who
are 'criminals' by Galactic law.

Did they not far outshine us miserable barbarians? As the sun
out-glows a tallow candle?

But we sages realized a horrifying truth. After hiring us for local
expertise, to help them raid this world, the Rothen could not afford
to leave witnesses behind.

They would not leave us alive.

No, that is too far back. Try again.

What about these other livid tracks, my rings? A red flaming
pillar erupting in the night? An explosion, breaking apart our
sacred pilgrimage? Do you recall the sight of the Rothen-Danik station, its girders, twisted and smoking? Its cache of biosamples
burned? And most dire – one Rothen and a sky human killed?

By dawn's light, foul accusations hurled back and forth between
Ro-kenn and our own High Sages. Appalling threats were
exchanged.

*No, that still took place over a day ago. Stroke wax that is more
recent than that.*

Here we find a broad sheet of terror, shining horribly down our oily
core. Its colors/textures blend hot blood with cold fire, exuding a
smoky scent of flaming trees and charred bodies.

Do you recall how Ro-kenn, the surviving Rothen master, swore
vengeance on the Six Races, ordering his killer robots forward?

'Slay everyone in sight! Death to all who saw our secret revealed!'

But then behold a marvel! Platoons of our own brave militia.
They spill from surrounding forest. Jijoan savages, armed only with
arrows, pellet rifles, and courage. Do you now recall how they
charged the hovering death demons ... and prevailed!

The wax does not lie. It happened in mere instants, while these
old traeki rings could only stare blankly at the battle's awful ruin,
astonished that we/i were not ignited into a stack of flaming tubes.

Though dead and wounded lay piled around us, victory was
clear. Victory for the Six Races! Ro-kenn and his godlike servants
were disarmed, wide-eyed in their offended surprise at this turn of
Ifni's ever-tumbling dice.

Yes, my rings. i know this is not the final memory. It took place
many miduras in the past. Obviously something must have happened since then. Something dreadful.

Perhaps the Danik scout boat came back from its survey trip, carrying one of the fierce sky-human warriors who worship Rothen patron masters. Or else the main Rothen starship may have returned, expecting a trove of bioplunder, only to find their samples destroyed, their station ruined, and comrades taken hostage.

That might explain the scent of sooty devastation that now fills our core.

But no later memories are yet available. The wax has not congealed.

To a traeki, that means none of it has really happened.

Not yet.

Perhaps things are not as bad as they seem.

It is a gift we traeki reacquired when we came to Jijo. A talent that helps make up for the many things we left behind, when we abandoned the stars.

A gift for wishful thinking.

RETY

The fierce wind of flight tore dampness from her streaming eyes, sparing her the shame of tears running down scarred cheeks. Still, Rety could weep with rage, thinking of the hopes she'd lost. Lying prone on a hard metal plate, clutching its edge with hands and feet, she bore the harsh breeze as whipping tree branches smacked her face and caught her hair, sometimes drawing blood.

Mostly, she just held on for dear life.

The alien machine beneath her was supposed to be her loyal servant! But the cursed thing would not slow its panicky retreat, even long after all danger lay far behind. If Rety fell off now, at best it would take her days to limp back to the village of her birth, where less than a midura ago there had been a brief, violent ambush.

Her brain still roiled. In just a few heartbeats her plans had been spoiled, and it was all *Dwer's* fault!

She heard the young hunter moan, held captive by metal arms below her perch. But as the wounded battle drone fled recklessly onward, Rety turned away from Dwer's suffering, which he had only brought on himself, trekking all the way to these filthy Gray Hills from his safe home near the sea – *the Slope* – where six intelligent races lived at a much *higher* level of ignorant poverty than her own birth clan of wretched savages. Why would slopies hike past two thousand leagues of hell to reach this dreary wasteland?

What did Dwer and his pals hope to accomplish? To conquer Rety's brutish relatives?

He could *have* her smelly kinfolk, for all she cared! *And* the band of urrish sooners Kunn subdued with fire from his screeching scout boat. Dwer was welcome to them all. Only, couldn't he have waited quietly in the woods till after Rety and Kunn finished their business here and flew off again? Why did he have to rush things and attack the robot with her aboard?

I bet he did it out of spite. Prob'ly can't stand knowing that I'm the one Jijo native with a chance to get away from this pit hole of a planet.

Inside, Rety knew better. Dwer's heart didn't work that way.

But mine does.

When he groaned again, Rety muttered angrily, 'I'll make you even sorrier, Dwer, if I don't make it off this mudball 'cause of you!'

So much for her *glorious homecoming*.

At first it had seemed fun to pay a return visit, swooping from a cloud-decked sky in Kunn's silver dart, emerging proudly to amazed gasps from the shabby cousins, who had bullied her for fourteen awful years. What a fitting climax to her desperate gamble, a few months ago, when she finally found the nerve to flee all the muck and misery, setting forth alone to seek the fabled Slope her great-grandparents had left behind, when they chose the 'free' life as wild sooners.

Free of the sages' prying rules about what beasts you may kill. Free from irky laws about how many babies you can have. Free from having to abide neighbors with four legs, or five, or that rolled on humming wheels.

Rety snorted contempt for the founders of her tribe.

Free from books and medicine. Free to live like animals!

Fed up, Rety had set out to find something better or die trying.

The journey had nearly killed her – crossing icy torrents and parched wastes. Her closest call came traversing a high pass into the Slope, following a mysterious metal bird into a mulc-spider's web. A web that became a terrifying trap when the spider's tendrils closed around her, oozing golden drops that horribly *preserved* . . .

Memory came unbidden – of *Dwer* charging through that awful thicket with a gleaming machete, then sheltering her with his body when the web caught fire.

She recalled the bright bird, glittering in flames, treacherously cut down by an attacking robot just like her 'servant.' The one now hauling her off to Ifni-knew-where.

Rety's mind veered as a gut-wrenching swerve nearly spilled her overboard. She screamed at the robot.

'*Idiot!* No one's shooting at you anymore! There were just a few slopies, and they were all afoot. Nothing on Jijo could catch you now!'

But the frantic contraption plunged ahead, riding a cushion of incredible god force.

Rety wondered, Could it sense her contempt? Dwer and two or three friends, equipped with crude fire sticks, had taken just a few duras to disable and drive off the so-called war bot, though at some cost to themselves.

Ifni, what a snarl. She pondered the sooty hole where Dwer's surprise attack had ripped out its antenna. *How'm I gonna explain this to Kunn?*

Rety's adopted rank as an honorary star god was already fragile. The angry pilot might simply abandon her in these hills where she had grown up, among savages she loathed.

I won't go back to the tribe, she vowed. *I'd rather join wild glavers, sucking bugs off dead critters on the Poison Plain.*

It was all Dwer's fault, of course. Rety hated listening to the young fool moan.

We're heading south, where Kunn flew off to. The robot must be rushin' to report in person, now that it can't far-speak anymore.

Having witnessed Kunn's skill at torture, Rety found herself hoping Dwer's leg wound would reopen. Bleeding to death would be better by far.

The fleeing machine left the Gray Hills, slanting toward a tree-dotted prairie. Streams converged, turning the brook into a river, winding slowly toward the tropics.

The journey grew smoother and Rety risked sitting up again. But the robot did not take the obvious shortcut over water. Instead, it followed each oxbow curve, seldom venturing past the reedy shallows.

The land seemed pleasant. Good for herds or farming, if you knew how, and weren't afraid of being caught.

It brought to mind all the wonders she had seen on the Slope, after barely escaping the mulc-spider. Folk there had all sorts of clever arts Rety's tribe lacked. Yet, despite their fancy windmills and gardens, their metal tools and paper books, the slopies had seemed dazed and frightened when Rety reached the famous Festival Glade.

What had the Six Races so upset was the recent coming of a *starship*, ending two thousand years of isolation.

To Rety, the spacers seemed wondrous. A ship owned by unseen Rothen masters, but crewed by *humans* so handsome and knowing that Rety would give anything to be like them. Not a doomed savage with a scarred face, eking out a life on a taboo world.

A daring ambition roused ... and by pluck and guts she had made it happen! Rety got to know those haughty men and women – *Ling*, *Besh*, *Kunn*, and *Rann* – worming her way into their favor. When asked, she gladly guided fierce Kunn to her tribe's old camp, retracing her earlier epic journey in a mere quarter day, munching Galactic treats while staring through the scout boat's window at wastelands below.

Years of abuse were repaid by her filthy cousins' shocked stares, beholding her transformed from grubby urchin to *Rety, the star god*.

If only that triumph could have lasted.

She jerked back when Dwer called her name.

Peering over the edge, Rety saw his windburned face, the wild black hair plastered with dried sweat. One buckskin breech leg was stained ocher brown under a makeshift compress, though Rety saw no sign of new wetness. Trapped by the robot's unyielding tendrils, Dwer clutched his precious hand-carved bow, as if it were the last thing he would part with before death. Rety could scarcely believe she once thought the crude weapon worth stealing.

'What do you want now?' she demanded.

The young hunter's eyes met hers. His voice came out as a croak. 'Can I ... have some water?'

'Assumin' I have any,' she muttered, 'name one reason I'd share it with you!'

Rustling at her waist. A narrow head and neck snaked out of her belt pouch. Three dark eyes glared – two with lids and one pupilless, faceted like a jewel.

'wife be not liar to this one! wife has water bottle! yee smells its bitterness.'

Rety sighed over this unwelcome interruption by her miniature 'husband.'

'There's just half left. No one tol' me I was goin' on a trip!'

The little urrish male hissed disapproval. 'wife share with this one, or bad luck come! no hole safe for grubs or larvae!'

Rety almost retorted that her marriage to yee was not real. They would never have 'grubs' together. Anyway, yee seemed bent on being her portable conscience, even when it was clearly every creature for herself.

I never should've told him how Dwer saved me from the mulc-spider. They say male urs are dumb. Ain't it my luck to marry a genius one?

'Oh . . . all right!'

The bottle, an alien-made wonder, weighed little more than the liquid it contained. 'Don't drop it,' she warned Dwer, lowering the red cord. He grabbed it eagerly.

'No, fool! The top don't *pull* off like a stopper. *Turn* it till it comes off. That's right. Jeekee know-nothin' slopie.'

She didn't add how the concept of a screw cap had mystified her, too, when Kunn and the others first adopted her as a provisional Danik. Of course that was before she became sophisticated.

Rety watched nervously as he drank.

'Don't spill it. An' don't you *dare* drink it all! You hear me? That's enough, Dwer. Stop now. *Dwer!*'

But he ignored her protests, guzzling while she cursed. When the canteen was drained, Dwer smiled at her through cracked lips.

Too stunned to react, Rety knew – she would have done exactly the same.

Yeah, an inner voice answered. *But I didn't expect it of him.*

Her anger spun off when Dwer squirmed, tilting his body toward the robot's headlong rush. Squinting against the wind, he held the loop cord in one hand and the bottle in the other, as if waiting for something to happen. The flying machine crested a low hill, hopping over some thorny thickets, then plunged down the other side, barely avoiding several tree branches. Rety held tight, keeping yee secure in his pouch. When the worst jouncing ended she peered down again . . . and rocked back from a pair of black beady eyes!

It was the damned *noor* again. The one Dwer called *Mudfoot.* Several times the dark, lithe creature had tried to clamber up from his niche, between Dwer's torso and a cleft in the robot's frame. But Rety didn't like the way he salivated at yee, past needle-sharp teeth. Now Mudfoot stood on Dwer's rib cage, using his forepaws to probe for another effort.

'Get lost!' She swatted at the narrow, grinning face. 'I want to see what Dwer's doin'.'

Sighing, the noor returned to his nest under the robot's flank.

A flash of blue came into view just as Dwer threw the bottle. It struck watery shallows with a splash, pressing a furrowed wake. The young man had to make several attempts to get the cord twisted so the canteen dragged with its opening forward. The container sloshed when Dwer reeled it back in.

I'd've thought of that, too. If I was close enough to try it.

Dwer had lost blood, so it was only fair to let him drink and refill a few more times before passing it back up.

Yeah. Only fair. And he'll do it, too. He'll give it back full.

Rety faced an uncomfortable thought.

You trust him.

He's the enemy. He caused you and the Daniks heaps of trouble. But you'd trust Dwer with your life.

She had no similar confidence in Kunn, when it came time to face the Rothen-loving stellar warrior.

Dwer refilled the bottle one last time and held it up toward her. 'Thanks, Rety ... I owe you.'

Her cheeks flushed, a sensation she disliked. 'Forget it. Just toss the cord.'

He tried. Rety felt it brush her fingertips, but after half a dozen efforts she could never quite hook the loop. *What happens if I don't get it back!*

The noor beast emerged from his narrow niche and took the cord in his teeth. Clambering over Dwer's chest, then using the robot's shattered laser tube as a support, Mudfoot slithered closer to Rety's hand. *Well*, she thought. *If it's gonna be helpful ...*

As she reached for the loop, the noor sprang, using his claws as if her arm were a handy climbing vine. Rety howled, but before she could react, Mudfoot was already up on top, grinning smugly.

Little yee let out a yelp. The urrish male pulled his head inside her pouch and drew the zipper shut.

Rety saw blood spots well along her sleeve and lashed in anger, trying to kick the crazy noor off. But Mudfoot dodged easily, inching close, grinning appealingly and rumbling a low sound, presenting the water bottle with two agile forepaws.

Sighing heavily, Rety accepted it and let the noor settle down nearby – on the opposite side from yee.

'I can't seem to shake myself loose of *any* of you guys, can I?' she asked aloud.

Mudfoot chittered. And from below, Dwer uttered a short laugh – ironic and tired.

ALVIN

It was a lonely time, confined in gnawing pain to a cramped metal cell. The distant, humming engine reminded me of umble lullabies my father used to sing, when I came down with toe pox or itchysac. Sometimes the noise changed pitch and made my scales frickle, sounding like the moan of a doomed wooden ship when it runs aground.

Finally I slept . . .

. . . then wakened in terror to find that a pair of metal-clad, six-legged monsters were tying me into a contraption of steel tubes and straps! At first, it looked like a pre-contact torture device I once saw in the Doré-illustrated edition of *Don Quixote*. Thrashing and resisting accomplished nothing, but hurt like bloody blue blazes.

Finally, with sonic embarrassment, I realized. It was no instrument of torment but a makeshift *back brace*, shaped to fit my form and take weight off my injured spine. I fought to suppress panic at the tight metal touch, as they set me on my feet. Swaying with surprise and relief, I found I could walk a little, though wincing with each step.

'Well thanks, you big ugly bugs,' I told the nearest of the giant phuvnthus. 'But you might've warned me first.'

I expected no answer, but one of them turned its armored torso – with a humped back and wide flare at the rear – and tilted toward me. I took the gesture as a polite bow, though perhaps it meant something different to them.

They left the door open when they exited this time. Slowly, cringing at the effort, I stepped out for the first time from my steel coffin, following as the massive creatures stomped down a narrow corridor.

I already figured I was aboard a submarine of some sort, big enough to carry in its hold the greatest hoonish craft sailing Jijo's seas.

Despite that, it was a hodgepodge. I thought of Frankenstein's monster, pieced together from the parts of many corpses. So seemed the monstrous vessel hauling me to who-knows-where. Each time we crossed a hatch, it seemed as if we'd pass into a distinct ship, made by different artisans . . . by a whole different *civilization*. In one section, the decks and bulkheads were made of riveted steel sheets. Another zone was fashioned from some fibrous substance – flexible but strong. The corridors changed proportions – from wide to painfully narrow. Half the time I had to stoop under low ceilings . . . not a lot of fun in the state my back was in.

Finally, a sliding door hissed open. A phuvnthu motioned me ahead with a crooked mandible and I entered a dim chamber much larger than my former cell.

My hearts surged with joy. Before me stood my friends! All of them – alive!

They were gathered round a circular viewing port, staring at inky ocean depths. I might've tried sneaking in to surprise them, but qheuens and g'Keks literally have 'eyes in the back of their heads,' making it a challenge to startle Huck and Pincer.

(I *have* managed it, a couple of times.)

When they shouted my name, Ur-ronn whirled her long neck and outraced them on four chattering hooves. We plunged into a multispecies embrace.

Huck was first to bring things back to normal, snapping at pincer.

'Watch the claws, Crab Face! You'll snap a spoke! Back off, all of you. Can't you see Alvin's hurt? Give him room!'

'Look who talks,' Ur-ronn replied. 'Your left wheel just squished his toes, Octofus Head!'

I hadn't noticed till she pointed it out, so happy was I to hear their testy, adolescent whining once more.

'Hr-rm. Let me look at you all. Ur-ronn, you seem so much ... *drier* than I saw you last.'

Our urrish buddy blew a rueful laugh through her nostril fringe. Her pelt showed large bare patches where fur had sloughed after her dousing. 'It took our hosts a while to adjust the hunidity of ny guest suite, vut they finally got it right,' she said. Her torso showed tracks of hasty needlework – the phuvnthus' rough stitching to close Ur-ronn's gashes after she smashed through the glass port of *Wuphon's Dream*. Fortunately, her folk don't play the same mating games as some races. To urs, what matters is not appearance, but *status*. A visible dent or two will help Ur-ronn show the other smiths she's been around.

'Yeah. And now we know what an urs smells like after actually taking a *bath*,' Huck added. 'They oughta try it more often.'

'*You* should talk? With that green eyeball sweat—'

'All right, all right!' I laughed. 'Just stopper it long enough for me to look at you, eh?'

Ur-ronn was right. Huck's eyestalks needed grooming and she had good reason to worry about her spokes. Many were broken, with new-spun fibers just starting to lace the rims. She would have to move cautiously for some time.

As for Pincer, he looked happier than ever.

'I guess you were right about there being monsters in the deep,' I told our red-shelled friend. 'Even if they hardly look like the ones you descr—'

I yelped when sharp needles seemed to lance into my back, clambering up my neck ridge. I quickly recognized the rolling growl of *Huphu*, our little noor-beast mascot, expressing gladness by demanding a rumble umble from me right away.

Before I could find out if my sore throat sac was up to it, Ur-ronn whistled from the pane of dark glass. 'They turned on the search-light again,' she fluted, with hushed awe in her voice. 'Alvin, hurry. You've got to look!'

Awkwardly on crutches, I moved to the place they made for me. Huck stroked my arm. 'You always wanted to see this, pal,' she said. 'So gaze out there in wonder.

'Welcome to the Great Midden.'

ASX

Here is another memory, my rings. An event that followed the brief Battle of the Glade, so swiftly that war echoes still abused our battered forest canyons.

Has the wax congealed enough yet? Can you stroke-and-sense the awesome disquiet, the frightening beauty of that evening, as we watched a harsh, untwinkling glow pass overhead?

Trace the fatty memory of that spark crossing the sky, brightening as it spiraled closer.

No one could doubt its identity.

The Rothen cruiser, returning for its harvest of bioplunder, looted from a fragile world.

Returning for those comrades it had left behind.

Instead of genetic booty, the crew will find their station smashed, their colleagues killed or taken.

Worse, their true faces are known! We castaways might testify against them in Galactic courts. Assuming we survive.

It takes no cognition genius to grasp the trouble we faced. We six fallen races of forlorn Jijo.

As an Earthling writer might put it – we found ourselves in fetid mulch. Very ripe and very deep.

SARA

The journey passed from an anxious blur into something exalting ... almost transcendent.

But not at the beginning.

When they perched her suddenly atop a galloping creature straight out of mythology, Sara's first reaction was terrified surprise.

With snorting nostrils and huge tossing head, the *horse* was more daunting than Tarek Town's stone tribute to a lost species. Its muscular torso flexed with each forward bound, shaking Sara's teeth as it crossed the foothills of the central Slope by the light of a pale moon.

After two sleepless days and nights, it still seemed dreamlike the way a squadron of the legendary beasts came trotting into the ruined Urunthai campsite, accompanied by armed urrish escorts. Sara and her friends had just escaped captivity – their former kidnappers lay either dead or bound with strips of shredded tent cloth – but she expected reenslavement at any moment. Only then, instead of fresh foes, the darkness brought forth these bewildering saviors.

Bewildering to everyone except Kurt the Exploser, who welcomed the newcomers as expected friends. While Jomah and the Stranger exclaimed wonder at seeing real-life horses, Sara barely had time to blink before she was thrust onto a saddle.

Blade volunteered to stay by the bleak fire and tend the wounded, though envy filled each forlorn spin of his blue cupola. Sara would trade places with her qheuen friend, but his chitin armor was too massive for a horse to carry. There was barely time to give Blade a wave of encouragement before the troop wheeled back the way they came, bearing her into the night.

Pounding hoofbeats soon made Sara's skull ache.

I guess it beats captivity by Dedinger's human chauvinists, and those fanatic Urunthai. The coalition of zealots, volatile as an exploser's cocktail, had joined forces to snatch the Stranger and sell him to Rothen invaders. But they underestimated the enigmatic voyager. Despite his crippling loss of speech, the starman found a way to incite urs-human suspicion into bloody riot.

Leaving us masters of our own fate, though it couldn't last.

Now here was a *different* coalition of humans and centauroid urs! A more cordial group, but just as adamant about hauling her Ifni-knew-where.

When limnous Torgen rose above the foothills, Sara got to look over the urrish warriors, whose dun flanks were daubed with more subtle war paint than the garish Urunthai. Yet their eyes held the same dark flame that drenched urs' souls when conflict scents fumed. Cantering in skirmish formation, their slim hands cradled arbalests while long necks coiled, tensely wary. Though much smaller than horses, the urrish fighters conveyed formidable craftiness.

The human rescuers were even more striking. Six *women* who came north with nine saddled horses, as if they expected to retrieve just two or three others for a return trip.

But there's six of us. Kurt and Jomah. Prity and me. The Stranger and Dedinger.

No matter. The stern riders seemed indifferent about doubling up, two to a saddle.

Is that why they're all female? To keep the weight down?

While deft astride their great mounts, the women seemed uneasy with the hilly terrain of gullies and rocky spires. Sara gathered they disliked rushing about strange trails at night. She could hardly blame them.

Not one had a familiar face. That might have surprised Sara a month ago, given Jijo's small human population. The Slope must be bigger than she thought.

Dwer would tell stories about his travels, scouting for the sages. He claimed he'd been everywhere within a thousand leagues.

Her brother never mentioned horse-riding amazons.

Sara briefly wondered if they came from off-Jijo, since this seemed the year for spaceships. But no. Despite some odd slang, their terse speech was related to Jijoan dialects she knew from her research. And while the riders seemed unfamiliar with this region, they knew to lean away from a migurv tree when the trail passed near its sticky fronds. The Stranger, though warned with gestures not to touch its seed pods, reached for one curiously and learned the hard way.

She glanced at Kurt. The exploser's gaunt face showed satisfaction with each league they sped southward. The existence of horses was no surprise to him.

We're told our society is open. But clearly there are secrets known to a few.

Not *all* explosers shared it. Kurt's nephew chattered happy amazement while exchanging broad grins with the Stranger . . .

Sara corrected herself.

With *Emerson* . . .

She peered at the dark man who came plummeting from the sky months ago, dousing his burns in a dismal swamp near Dolo Village. No longer the near corpse she had nursed in her tree house, the star voyager was proving a resourceful adventurer. Though still largely mute, he had passed a milestone a few miduras ago when he began thumping his chest, repeating that word – *Emerson* – over and over, beaming pride over a feat that undamaged folk took for granted. Uttering one's own name.

Emerson seemed at home on his mount. Did that mean horses were still used among the god worlds of the Five Galaxies? If so, what purpose might they serve, where miraculous machines did your bidding at a nod and wink?

Sara checked on her chimp assistant, in case the jouncing ride reopened Prity's bullet wound. Riding with both arms clenched round the waist of a horsewoman, Prity kept her eyes closed the whole time, no doubt immersed in her beloved universe of abstract shapes and forms – a better world than this one of sorrow and messy nonlinearity.

That left *Dedinger*, the rebel leader, riding along with both hands tied. Sara wasted no pity on the scholar-turned-prophet. After years preaching militant orthodoxy, urging his desert followers toward the Path of Redemption, the ex-sage clearly knew patience. Dedinger's hawklike face bore an expression Sara found unnerving.

Serene calculation.

The tooth-jarring pace swelled when the hilly track met open ground. Soon Ulashtu's detachment of urrish warriors fell behind, unable to keep up.

No wonder some urs clans resented horses, when humans first settled Jijo. The beasts gave us mobility, the trait most loved by urrish captains.

Two centuries ago, after trouncing the human newcomers in battle, the original Urunthai faction claimed Earthlings' beloved mounts as war booty, and slaughtered every one.

They figured we'd be no more trouble, left to walk and fight on foot. A mistake that proved fatal when Drake the Elder forged a coalition to hunt the Urunthai, and drowned the cult's leadership at Soggy Hoof Falls.

Only, it seems horses weren't extinct, after all. How could a clan of horse-riding folk remain hidden all this time?

And as puzzling – *Why emerge now, risking exposure by rushing to meet Kurt?*

It must be the crisis of the starships, ending Jijo's blessed/cursed isolation. What point in keeping secrets, if Judgment Day is at hand?

Sara was exhausted and numb by the time morning pushed through an overcast sky. An expanse of undulating hills stretched ahead to a dark green marsh.

The party dismounted at last by a shaded creek. Hands aimed her toward a blanket, where she collapsed with a shuddering sigh.

Sleep came laced with images of people she had left behind.

Nelo, her aged father, working in his beloved paper mill, unaware that some conspired its ruin.

Melina, her mother, dead several years now, who always seemed an outsider since arriving in Dolo long ago, with a baby son in her arms.

Frail Joshu, Sara's lover in Biblos, whose touch made her forget even the overhanging Fist of Stone. A comely rogue whose death sent her spinning.

Dwer and Lark, her brothers, setting out to attend festival in the high Rimmer glades ... where starships were later seen descending.

Sara's mind roiled as she tossed and turned.

Last of all, she pictured Blade, whose qheuen hive farmed crayfish behind Dolo Dam. Good old Blade, who saved Sara and Emerson from disaster at the Urunthai camp.

'*Seems I'm always late catching up,*' her qheuen friend whistled from three leg vents. '*But don't worry, I'll be along. Too much is happening to miss.*'

Blade's armor-clad dependability had been like a rock to Sara. In her dream, she answered.

'*I'll stall the universe ... keep it from doing anything interesting until you show up.*'

Imagined or not, the blue qheuen's calliope laughter warmed Sara, and her troubled slumber fell into gentler rhythms.

The sun was half-high when someone shook Sara back to the world – one of the taciturn female riders, using the archaic word *brekkers* to announce the morning meal. Sara got up gingerly as waves of achy soreness coursed her body.

She gulped down a bowl of grain porridge, spiced with unfamiliar traeki seasonings, while horsewomen saddled mounts or watched Emerson play his beloved dulcimer, filling the pocket valley with a sprightly melody suited for travel. Despite her morning irritability, Sara knew the starman was just making the best of the situation. Bursts of song were a way to overcome his handicap of muteness.

Sara found Kurt tying up his bedroll.

'Look,' she told the elderly explorer, 'I'm not ungrateful to your friends. I appreciate the rescue and all. But you can't seriously hope to ride horses all the way to ... *Mount Guenn.*' Her tone made it sound like one of Jijo's moons.

Kurt's stony face flickered a rare smile. 'Any better suggestions? Sure, you planned taking the Stranger to the High Sages, but that way is blocked by angry Urunthai. And recall, we saw *two* starships last night, one after the other, headed straight for Festival Glade. The Sages must have their hands and tendrils full by now.'

'How could I forget?' she murmured. Those titans, growling as they crossed the sky, had seared their image in her mind.

'You *could* hole up in one of the villages we'll pass soon, but won't Emerson need a first-rate pharmacist when he runs out of Pzora's medicine?'

'If we keep heading south we'll reach the Gentt. From there a riverboat can take us to Ovoom Town.'

'Assuming boats are running ... and Ovoom still exists. Even so *should* you hide your alien friend, with great events taking place? What if he has a role to play? Some way to help sages and Commons? Might you spoil his one chance of goin' home?'

Sara saw Kurt's implication – that she was holding Emerson back, like a child refusing to release some healed forest creature into the wild.

A swarm of sweetbec flies drifted close to the starman, hovering and throbbing to the tempo of his music, a strange melody. Where did he learn it? On Earth? Near some alien star?

'Anyway,' Kurt went on, 'if you can stand riding these huge beasts awhile longer, we may reach Mount Guenn sooner than Ovoom.'

'That's crazy! You must pass *through* Ovoom if you go by sea. And the other way around is worse – through the funnel canyons and the Vale.'

Kurt's eyes flickered. 'I'm told there's a ... more direct route.'

'Direct? You mean due *south*? Past the Gentt lies the Plain of Sharp Sand, a desperate crossing under good conditions – which these aren't. Have you forgotten that's where Dedinger has followers?'

'No, I haven't forgotten.'

'Then, assuming we get past the sandmen and flame dunes, there comes the *Spectral Flow*, making any normal desert seem like a meadow!'

Kurt only shrugged, but clearly he wanted her to accompany him toward a distant simmering mountain, far from where Sara had sworn to take Emerson. Away from Lark and Dwer, and the terrible attraction of those fierce starships. Toward a starkly sacred part of Jijo, renowned for one thing above all – the way the planet renewed itself with flaming lava heat.

ALVIN

Maybe it was the compressed atmosphere we breathed, or the ceaseless drone of reverberating engines. Or it could have been the perfect darkness outside that fostered an impression of incredible depth, even greater than when our poor little *Wuphon's Dream* fell into the maw of this giant metal sea beast. A single beam – immeasurably brighter than the handmade eik light of our old minisub – speared out to split the black, scanning territory beyond my wildest nightmares. Even the vivid imagery of Verne or Pukino or Melville offered no preparation for what was revealed by that roving circle as we cruised along a subsea canyon strewn with all manner of ancient dross. In rapid glimpses we saw so many titanic things, all jumbled together, that—

Here I admit I'm stumped. According to the texts that teach Anglic literature, there are two basic ways for a writer to describe unfamiliar objects. First is to catalog sights and sounds, measurements, proportions, colors – saying *this* object is made up of clusters of colossal *cubes* connected by translucent rods, or *that* one resembles a tremendous sphere caved in along one side, trailing from its crushed innards a glistening streamer, a liquidlike banner that somehow defies the tug of time and tide.

Oh, I can put words together and come up with pretty pictures, but that method ultimately fails because at the time I *couldn't tell how far away anything was!* The eye sought clues in vain. Some objects – piled across the muddy panorama – seemed so vast that the huge vessel around us was dwarfed, like a minnow in a herd of *behmo* serpents. As for colors, even in the spotlight beam, the water drank all shades but deathly blue gray. A good hue for a shroud in this place of icy-cold death.

Another way to describe the unknown is to *compare* it to things you already recognize ... only that method proved worse! Even Huck, who sees likenesses in things I can't begin to fathom, was reduced to staring toward great heaps of ancient debris with all four eyestalks, at an utter loss.

Oh, *some* objects leaped at us with sudden familiarity – like when the searchlight swept over rows of blank-eyed windows, breached floors, and sundered walls. Pushed in a tumbled mound, many of the sunken towers lay upside down or even speared through each other. Together they composed a city greater than any I ever heard of, even from readings of olden times. Yet someone once scraped the entire metropolis from its foundations, picked it up and dumped it here, sending all the buildings tumbling down to be reclaimed the only way such things can be reclaimed – in Mother Jijo's fiery bowels.

I recalled some books I'd read, dating from Earth's Era of Resolution, when pre-contact humans were deciding on their own how to grow up and save their homeworld after centuries spent using it as a cesspit. In Alice Hammett's mystery *The Case of a Half-Eaten Clone*, the killer escapes a murder charge, only to get ten years for disposing of the evidence at sea! In those days, humans made no distinction between midden trenches and ocean floor in general. Dumping was dumping.

It felt strange to see the enormous dross-scape from two viewpoints. By Galactic law, this was a consecrated part of Jijo's cycle of preservation – a scene of devout caretaking. But having grown up immersed in human books, I could shift perspectives and see *defilement*, a place of terrible sin.

The 'city' fell behind us and we went back to staring at bizarre shapes, unknown majestic objects, the devices of star-god civilization, beyond understanding by mere cursed mortals. On occasion, my eyes glimpsed flickerings in the blackness *outside* the roving beam – lightninglike glimmers amid the ruins, as if old forces lingered here and there, setting off sparks like fading memories.

We murmured among ourselves, each of us falling back to what we knew best. Ur-ronn speculated on the nature of materials, what things were made of, or what functions they once served. Huck swore she saw *writing* each time the light panned over a string of suspicious shadows. Pincer insisted every other object must be a starship.

The Midden took our conjectures the same way it accepts all else, with a patient, deathless silence.

Some enormous objects had already sunk quite far, showing just their tips above the mire. I thought – *This is where Jijo's ocean plate takes a steep dive under the Slope, dragging crust, mud, and anything else lying about, down to magma pools that feed simmering volcanoes. In time, all these mighty things will become lava, or precious ores to be used by some future race of tenants on this world.*

It made me ponder my father's sailing ship, and the risky trips he took, hauling crates of sacred refuse, sent by each tribe of the Six as partial payment for the sin of our ancestors. In yearly rituals, each village sifts part of the land, clearing it of our own pollution and bits the Buyur left behind.

The Five Galaxies may punish us for living here. Yet we lived by a code, faithful to the Scrolls.

Hoonish folk moots chant the tale of Phu-uphyawuo, a dross captain who one day saw a storm coming, and dumped his load before reaching the deep blue of the Midden. Casks and drums rolled overboard far short of the trench of reclamation, strewing instead across shallow sea bottom, marring a site that was changeless, unrenewing. In punishment, Phu-uphyawuo was bound up and taken to the Plain of Sharp Sand, to spend the rest of his days beneath a hollow dune, drinking enough green dew to live, but not sustain his soul. In time, his heart spine was ground to dust and cast across a desert where no water might wash the grains, or make them clean again.

But this is the Midden, I thought, trying to grasp the wonder. *We're the first to see it.*

Except for the phuvnthus. And whatever else lives down here.

I found myself tiring. Despite the back brace and crutches, a weight of agony built steadily. Yet I found it hard to tear away from the icy-cold pane.

Following a searchlight through suboceanic blackness, we plunged as if down a mine shaft, aimed toward a heap of jewels – glittering objects shaped like needles, or squat globes, or glossy pancakes, or knobby cylinders. Soon there loomed a vast shimmering pile, wider than Wuphon Bay, bulkier than Guenn Volcano.

'Now, *those* are definitely ships!' Pincer announced, gesturing with a claw. Pressed against the glass, we stared at mountainlike piles of tubes, spheres, and cylinders, many of them studded with hornlike protrusions, like the quills of an alarmed rock staller.

'Those must be the *probability whatchamacallums* starships use for going between galaxies,' Huck diagnosed from her avid reading of *Tabernacle*-era tales.

'*Probability flanges*,' Ur-ronn corrected, speaking Galactic Six. In matters of technology, she was far ahead of Huck or me. '*I think you may be right*.'

Our qheuenish friend chuckled happily as the searchlight zeroed in on one tremendous pile of tapered objects. Soon we all recognized the general outlines from ancient texts – freighters and courier ships, packets and cruisers – all abandoned long ago.

The engine noise dropped a notch, plunging us toward that mass of discarded spacecraft. The smallest of those derelicts outmassed the makeshift *phuvnthu* craft the way a full-grown traeki might tower over a herd-chick turd.

'I wonder if any of the ancestor vessels are in this pile,' Huck contemplated aloud. 'You know, the ones that brought our founders here? The *Laddu'kek* or the *Tabernacle*.'

'Unlikely,' Ur-ronn answered, this time in lisping Anglic.

'Don't forget, we're in the *Rift*. This is nothing vut an *offshoot* canyon of the Nidden. Our ancestors likely discarded their shifs in the nain trench, where the greatest share of Vuyur trash went.'

I blinked at that thought. *This, an offshoot? A minor side area of the Midden?*

Of course she was right! But it presented a boggling image. What staggering amounts of stuff must have been dumped in the main trench, over the ages! Enough to tax even the recycling power of Jijo's grinding plates. No wonder the Noble Galactics set worlds aside for ten million years or more. It must take that long for a planet to digest each meal of sapient-made things, melting them back into the raw stuff of nature.

I thought of my father's dross ship, driven by creaking masts, its hold filled with crates of whatever we exiles can't recycle. After two thousand years, all the offal we sooners sent to the Midden would not even show against this single mound of discarded starships.

How rich the Buyur and their fellow gods must have been to cast off so much wealth! Some of the abandoned vessels looked immense enough to swallow every house, khuta, or hovel built by the Six Races. We glimpsed dark portals, turrets, and a hundred other details, growing painfully aware of one fact – those shadowy behemoths had been sent down here to rest in peace. Their sleep was never meant to be invaded by the likes of us.

Our plummet toward the reef of dead ships grew alarming. Did any of the others feel we were heading in awful *fast*?

'Maybe this is their home,' Pincer speculated as we plunged toward one twisted, oval ruin, half the size of Wuphon Port.

'Maybe the phuvnthus are made of, like, *parts* of old machines that got dumped here,' Huck mused. 'And they kind of put themselves together from whatever's lying around? Like this *boat* we're on is made of all sorts of junk—'

'Ferhafs they were servants of the Vuyur—' Ur-ronn interrupted. 'Or a race that lived here even vefore. Or a strain of nutants, like in that story vy—'

I cut in. 'Have any of you considered the simplest idea? That maybe they're just like us?'

When my friends turned to look at me, I shrugged, human style.

'Maybe the phuvnthus are sooners, too. Ever stop to think of that?'

Their blank faces answered me. I might as well have suggested that our hosts were noor beasts, for all the sense my idea made.

Well. I never claimed to be quick-witted, especially when racked with agony.

We lacked any sense of perspective, no way to tell how close we were, or how fast we were going. Huck and Pincer murmured nervously as our vessel plunged toward the mountain-of-ships at a rapid clip, engines running hard in reverse.

I think we all jumped a bit when a huge slab of corroded metal moved aside, just duras before we might have collided. Our vessel slid into a gaping hole in the mountain of dross, cruising along a corridor composed of spaceship hulls, piercing a fantastic pile of interstellar junk.

Read the newly congealed wax, my rings.

See how folk of the Six Races dispersed, tearing down festival pavilions and bearing away the injured, fleeing before the Rothen starship's expected arrival.

Our senior sage, Vubben of the g'Kek, recited from the Scroll of Portents a passage warning against disunity. Truly, the Six Races must strive harder than ever to look past our differences of shape and shell. Of flesh, hide, and torg.

'Go home,' we sages told the tribes. 'See to your lattice screens. Your blur-cloth webs. Live near the ground in Jijo's sheltered places. Be ready to fight if you can. To die if you must.'

The *zealots*, who originally provoked this crisis, suggested the Rothen starship might have means to track Ro-kenn and his lackeys, perhaps by sniffing our prisoners' brain waves or body implants. 'For safety, let's sift their bones into lava pools!'

An opposing faction called *Friends of the Rothen* demanded Ro-kenn's release and obeisance to his godlike will. These were not only humans, but some qheuens, g'Keks, hoons, and even a few urs, grateful for cures or treatments received in the aliens' clinic. Some think redemption can be won in this lifetime, without first treading the long road blazed by glavers.

Finally, others see this chaos as a chance to settle old grudges. Rumors tell of anarchy elsewhere on the Slope. Of many fine things toppled or burned.

Such diversity! The same freedom that fosters a vivid people also makes it hard to maintain a united front. Would things be better if we had disciplined order, like the feudal state sought by Gray Queens of old?

It is too late for regrets. Time remains only for *improvisation* – an art not well approved in the Five Galaxies, we are told.

Among poor savages, it may be our only hope.

Yes, my rings. We can now remember all of that.

Stroke this wax, and watch the caravans depart toward plains, forests, and sea. Our hostages are spirited off to sites where even a starship's piercing scrutiny might not find them. The sun flees and stars bridge the vast territory called the Universe. A realm denied us, that our foes roam at will.

Some remain behind, awaiting the ship.

We voted, did we not? We rings who make up Asx? We volunteered to linger. Our cojoined voice would speak to angry aliens for the Commons. Resting our basal torus on hard stone, we passed the time listening to complex patterns from the Holy Egg, vibrating our fatty core with strange shimmering motifs.

Alas, my rings, none of these reclaimed memories explains our current state, that something terrible must have happened?

Here, what of *this* newly congealed waxy trail?

Can you perceive in it the glimmering outlines of a great vessel of space? Roaring from the same part of the sky lately abandoned by the sun?

Or *is* it the sun, come back again to hover angrily above the valley floor?

The great ship scans our valley with scrutinizing rays, seeking signs of those they left behind.

Yes, my rings. Follow this waxy memory.

Are we about to rediscover the true cause of terror?

LARK

Summer pressed heavily across the Rimmer range, consuming the unshaded edges of glaciers far older than six exile races. At intervals, a crackling static charge would blur the alpine slopes as countless grass stems wafted skyward, reaching like desperate tendrils. Intense sunshine was punctuated by bursts of curtain rain – water draperies that undulated uphill, drenching the slopes with continuous liquid sheets, climbing until the mountaintops wore rainbow crowns, studded with flashes of compressed lightning.

Compact reverberations rolled down from the heights, all the way to the shore of a poison lake, where fungus swarmed over a forty-hectare thicket of crumbling vines. Once a mighty outpost of Galactic culture, the place was now a jumble of stone slabs, rubbed featureless by abrading ages. The pocket valley sweltered with acrid aromas, as caustic nectars steamed from the lake, or dripped from countless eroding pores.

The newest sage of the Commons of Jijo plucked yellow moss from a decaying cable, one of a myriad of strands that once made up the body of a half-million-year-old creature, the mulc-spider responsible for demolishing this ancient Buyur site, gradually returning it to nature. Lark had last seen this place in late winter – searching alone through snow flurries for the footprints of Dwer and Rety, refugees from this same spider's death fury. Things had changed here since that frantic deliverance. Large swathes of mulc cable were simply gone, harvested in some recent effort that no one had bothered explaining when Lark was assigned here. Much of what remained was coated with this clinging moss.

'*Spirolegita cariola.*' He muttered the species name, rubbing a sample between two fingers. It was a twisted, deviant cariola variety. Mutation seemed a specialty of this weird, astringent site.

I wonder what the place will do to me – to all of us – if we stay here long.

He had not asked for this chore. To be a *jailor*. Just wearing the title made him feel less clean.

A chain of nonsense syllables made him turn back toward a blur-cloth canopy, spanning the space between slablike boulders.

'It's a *clensionating sievelator* for *refindulating* excess torg . . .'

The voice came from deep shade within – a strong feminine alto, though somewhat listless now, tinged with resignation. Soft clinking sounds followed as one object was tossed onto a pile and another picked up for examination.

'At a guess, I'd say *this* was once a *glannis truncator*, probably used in rituals of a chihanic sect . . . that is, unless it's just another Buyur joke-novelty device.'

Lark shaded his eyes to regard Ling, the young sky-born scientist and servant of star-god Rothen, in whose employ he had worked as a 'native guide' for many weeks . . . until the Battle of the Glade reversed their standing in a matter of heartbeats. Since that unexpected victory, the High Sages had assigned her care and custody to him, a duty he never asked for, even if it meant exalted promotion.

Now I'm quite a high-ranking witch doctor among savages, he thought with some tartness. *Lord High Keeper of Alien Prisoners.*

And maybe executioner. His mind shied from that possibility. Much more likely, Ling would be traded to her Danik-Rothen comrades in some deal worked out by the sages. Or else she might be rescued at any moment by hordes of unstoppable robots, overpowering Lark's small detachment of sword-bearing escorts like a pack of *santi* bears brushing aside the helpless buzzing defenders of a zil-honey tree.

Either way, she'll go free. Ling may live another three hundred years on her homeworld, back in the Five Galaxies, telling embroidered tales about her adventure among the feral barbarians of a shabby, illicit colony. Meanwhile, the best we fallen ones can hope for is bare survival. To keep scratching a living from poor tired Jijo, calling it lucky if some of the Six eventually join glavers down the Path of Redemption. The trail to blissful oblivion.

Lark would rather end it all in some noble and heroic way. Let

Jijo's Six go down defending this fragile world, so she might go back to her interrupted rest.

That was his particular heresy, of course. Orthodox belief held that the Six Races were sinners, but they might mitigate their offense by living at peace on Jijo. But Lark saw that as hypocrisy. The settlers should *end* their crime, gently and voluntarily, as soon as possible.

He had made no secret of his radicalism ... which made it all the more confusing that the High Sages now trusted him with substantial authority.

The alien woman no longer wore the shimmering garb of her Danik star clan – the secretive band of humans who worshiped Rothen lords. Instead she was outfitted in an ill-fitting blouse and kilt of Jijoan homespun. Still, Lark found it hard to look away from her angular beauty. It was said that sky humans could buy a new face with hardly a thought. Ling claimed not to care about such things, but no woman on the Slope could match her.

Under the wary gaze of two militia corporals, Ling sat cross-legged, examining relics left behind by the dead mulc-spider – strange metallic shapes embedded in semitransparent gold cocoons, like archaic insects trapped in amber. Remnants of the Buyur, this world's last legal tenants, who departed half a million years ago when Jijo went fallow. A throng of egglike preservation beads lay scattered round the ashen lakeshore. Instead of dissolving all signs of past habitation, the local mulc-spider had apparently chosen relics to seal away. *Collecting* them, if Lark believed the incredible story told by his half brother, Dwer.

The luminous coatings made him nervous. The same substance, secreted from the spider's porous conduits, had nearly smothered Dwer and Rety, the wild sooner girl, the same night two alien robots quarreled, igniting a living morass of corrosive vines, ending the spider's long, mad life. The gold stuff felt queer to touch, as if a strange, slow liquid sloshed under sheaths of solid crystal.

'*Toporgic*,' Ling had called the slick material during one of her civil moments. '*It's very rare, but I hear stories. It's said to be a pseudo-matter substrate made of organically folded time.*'

Whatever that meant. It sounded like the sort of thing Sara might say, trying to explain her beloved world of mathematics. As a biologist, he found it bizarre for a living thing to send 'folded time' oozing from its far-flung tendrils, as the mulc-spider apparently had done.

Whenever Ling finished examining a relic, she bent over a sheaf of Lark's best paper to make careful notes, concentrating as if each child-like block letter were a work of art. As if she never held a pencil before, but had vowed to master the new skill. As a galactic voyager, she used to handle floods of information, manipulating multidimensional displays, sieving data on this world's complex ecosystem, searching on behalf of her Rothen masters for some biotreasure worth stealing. Toiling over handwritten notes must seem like shifting from starship speeds to a traeki's wooden scooter.

It's a steep fall – one moment a demigoddess, the next a hostage of uncouth sooners.

All this diligent note taking must help take her mind off recent events – that traumatic day, just two leagues below the nest of the Holy Egg, when her home base exploded and Jijo's masses violently rebelled. But Lark sensed something more than deliberate distraction. In scribing words on paper, Ling drew the same focused satisfaction he had seen her take from performing any simple act well. Despite his persistent seething anger, Lark found this worthy of respect.

There were folk legends about mulc-spiders. Some were said to acquire odd obsessions during their stagnant eons spent chewing metal and stone monuments of the past. Lark once dismissed such fables as superstition, but Dwer had proved right about this one. Evidence for the mulc beast's collecting fetish lay in countless capsules studding the charred thicket, the biggest hoard of Galactic junk anywhere on the Slope. It made the noxious lakeshore an ideal site to conceal a captured alien, in case the returning starship had instruments sifting Jijo for missing crew mates. Though Ling had been thoroughly searched, and all possessions seized, she might carry in her body some detectable trace element – acquired growing up on a far Galactic world. If so, all the Buyur stuff lying around here might mask her presence.

There were other ideas.

Ship sensors may not penetrate far underground, one human techie proposed.

Or else, suggested an urrish smith, *a nearby lava flow may foil alien eyes.*

The other hostages – Ro-kenn and Rann – had been taken to such places, in hopes of holding on to at least one prisoner. With the lives of every child and grub of the Six at stake, anything seemed worth trying. The job Lark had been given was important. Yet he chafed, wishing for more to do than waiting for the world to end. Rumors told that others were preparing to fight the star criminals. Lark knew little about weapons – his expertise was the natural flux of living species. Still, he envied them.

A burbling, wheezing sound called him rushing to the far end of the tent, where his friend Uthen squatted like an ashcolored chitin mound. Lark took up a makeshift aspirator he had fashioned out of boo stems, a cleft pig's bladder, and congealed mulc sap. He pushed the nozzle into one of the big qheuen's leg apertures and pumped away, siphoning phlegmy fluid that threatened Uthen's ventilation tubes. He repeated the process with all five legs, till his partner and fellow biologist breathed easier. The qheuen's central cupola lifted and Uthen's seeing stripe brightened.

'Th-thank you, L-Lark-ark ... I am – I am sorry to be so – be So – to be a burden-en-en ...'

Emerging uncoordinated, the separate leg voices sounded like five miniature qheuens, getting in each other's way. Or like a traeki whose carelessly stacked oration rings all had minds of their own. Uthen's fevered weakness filled Lark's chest with a burning ache. A choking throat made it hard to respond with cheerful-sounding lies.

'You just rest up, claw brother. Soon we'll be back in the field ... digging fossils and inventing more theories to turn your mothers blue with embarrassment.'

That brought a faint, gurgling laugh. 'S-speaking-king of here-sies ... it looks as if you and Haru ... Haru ... Harullen-ullen, will be getting your wish.'

Mention of Lark's other gray qheuen friend made him wince with doubled grief. Uthen didn't know about his cousin's fate, and Lark wasn't about to tell him.

'How do you mean?'

'It seems-eems the raiders-raiders found a way to rid Jijo of at least *one* of the S-S-Six P-p-pests ...'

'Don't say that,' Lark urged. But Uthen voiced a common thought. His sickness baffled the g'Kek medic resting in the next shelter, all four eyes curled in exhaustion. The malady frightened the militia guards. All knew that Uthen had been with Lark in the ruined Danik station, poking among forbidden things.

'I felt sorrow when-henn zealots-lots blew up the alien base.' Uthen's carapace shuddered as he fought for breath.

'Even when the Rothen tried to misuse our Holy Egg ... sending false dreams as wedges-edges ... to drive the Six Races apart-part ... Even *that* did not justify the ... inhospitable-able murder of strangers.'

Lark wiped an eye. 'You're more charitable than most.'

'Let me finish-ish. I was-as going to say that *now* we know what the outsiders were up to all along-long ... something worse than dreams. Designing-ing *bugs* to bring us downown-own.'

So, Uthen must have overheard the rumors – or else worked it out for himself.

Biological warfare. Genocide.

'Like in *War of the Worlds*.' It was one of Uthen's favorite old novels. 'Only with the roles reversed.'

Lark's comparison made the gray qheuen laugh – a raspy, uneven whistle.

'I ... always-ways did identify ... with those ... with those poor Martians-ans-ans ...'

The ribbon eye went foggy, losing the light of consciousness as the cupola sank. Lark checked his friend's breathing, and found it no worse. Uthen was simply tired.

So strong, he thought, stroking the rigid shell.

We picture grays as toughest of the tough. But chitin won't slow a laser ray.

Harullen found that out. Death came to Uthen's cousin during the brief Battle of the Glade, when the massed militia of Six Races barely overcame Ro-kenn's robot assassins. Only the advantage of surprise had carried that day. The aliens never realized that savages might have books showing how to make rifled firearms – crude, but potent at short range.

But victory came late for Harullen. Too dedicated or obstinate to flee, the heretic leader spent his last frenzied moments whistling ornate pleas for calm and reason, crying in five directions at once, beseeching everyone to lay down their arms and talk things over – until Harullen's massive, crablike body was cleaved in uneven parts by a killer drone, just before the machine was itself blown from the sky.

There will be mourning among the gray matrons of Tarek Town, Lark thought, resting both arms across Uthen's broad shell, laying his head on the mottled surface, listening to the strained labor of his friend's phlegmy breathing, wishing with all his heart that there was more he could do.

Irony was but one of many bitter tastes in his mouth.

I always figured, if the end did come, that qheuens would be the last to go.

EMERSON

Jijo's countryside flows rapidly past them now, as if the mysterious horsewomen fear any delay might turn faint hope to dust.

Lacking speech, Emerson has no idea where they are riding in such a hurry, or why.

Sara turns in her saddle now and then, to give an encouraging smile. But rewq-painted colors of misgiving surround her face – a nimbus of emotion that he can read the way he used to find meaning in letters on a data display. Perhaps he should find her qualms unnerving, since he depends on her guidance in this strange, perilous world. Yet Emerson cannot bring himself to worry. There are just too many other things to think about.

Humidity closes in as their caravan veers toward a winding river valley. Dank aromas stir memories of the swamp where he first floundered after the crash, a shattered cripple, drenched in agony. But he does not quail. Emerson welcomes any sensation that might trigger random recall – a sound, a chance smell, or else a sight around the next bend.

Some rediscoveries already float across a gulf of time and loss, as if he has missed them for quite a while. Recovered names connect to faces, and even brief snatches of isolated events.

Tom Orley ... so strong and clever. Always a sure eye for trouble. He brought some back to the ship, one day. Trouble enough for Five Galaxies.

Hikahi ... sweetest dolphin. Kindest friend. Dashing off to rescue her lover and captain ... never to be seen again.

Toshio ... a boy's ready laughter. A young man's steady heart. Where is he now?

Creideiki ... captain. Wise dolphin leader. A cripple like himself.

Briefly, Emerson wonders at the similarity between Creideiki's injury and his own ... But the thought provokes a searing bolt of pain so fierce that the fleeting thought whirls away and is lost.

Tom ... Hikahi ... Toshio ... He repeats the names, each of them once attached to friends he has not seen for ... well, a very long time.

Other memories, more recent, seem harder to reach, more agonizing to access.

Suessi ... Tsh't ... Gillian ...

He mouths each sound repeatedly, despite the tooth-jarring ride and difficulty of coordinating tongue and lips. He does it to keep in practice – or else how will he ever recover the old handiness with language, the skill to roll out words as he used to, back when he was known as such a clever fellow ... before horrid holes appeared in both his head and memory.

Some names come easy, since he learned them *after* waking on Jijo, delirious in a treetop hut.

—*Prity*, the little chimp who teaches him by example. Though mute, she shows flair for both math and sardonic hand speech.

—*Jomah* and *Kurt* ... sounds linked to younger and older

versions of the same narrow face. Apprentice and master at a unique art, meant to erase all the dams, towns, and houses that unlawful settlers had built on a proscribed world. Emerson recalls *Biblos*, an archive of paper books, where Kurt showed his nephew well-placed explosive charges that might bring the cave down, smashing the library to dust. If the order ever came.

—The captive fanatic, *Dedinger*, rides behind the explosers, deeply tanned with craggy features. Leader of human rebels with beliefs Emerson can't grasp, except they preach no love of visitors from the sky. While the party hurries on, Dedinger's gray eyes rove, calculating his next move.

Some names and a few places – these utterances have meaning now. It is progress, but Emerson is no fool. He figures he must have known *hundreds* of words before he fell, broken, to this world. Now and again he makes out snatches of half meaning from the 'wah-wah' gabble as his companions address each other. Snippets that tantalize, without satisfying.

Sometimes the torrent grows tiresome, and he wonders – might people be less inclined to fight if they talked less? If they spent more time watching and listening?

Fortunately, words aren't his sole project. There is the haunting familiarity of music, and during rest stops he plays math games with Prity and Sara, drawing shapes in the sand. They are his friends and he takes joy from their laughter.

He has one more window to the world.

As often as he can stand it, Emerson slips the *rewq* over his eyes ... a masklike film that transforms the world into splashes of slanted color. In all his prior travels he never encountered such a creature – a species used by all six races to grasp each other's moods. If left on too long, it gives him headaches. Still he finds fascinating the auras surrounding Sara, Dedinger, and others. Sometimes it seems the colors carry more than just emotion ... though he cannot pin it down. Not yet.

One truth Emerson recalls. Advice drawn from the murky well of his past, putting him on guard.

Life can be full of illusions.

Legends tell of many precious texts that were lost one bitter evening, during an unmatched disaster some call the Night of the Ghosts, when a quarter of the Biblos Archive burned. Among the priceless volumes that vanished by that cruel winter's twilight, one tome reportedly showed pictures of Buyur – the mighty race whose lease on Jijo expired five thousand centuries ago.

Scant diary accounts survive from witnesses to the calamity, but according to some who browsed the Xenoscience Collection before it burned, the Buyur were squat beings vaguely resembling the *bullfrogs* shown on page ninety-six of *Cleary's Guide to Terrestrial LifeForms*, though with elephantine legs and sharp, forward-looking eyes. They were said to be master shapers of useful organisms, and had a reputation for prodigious wit.

But other sooner races already knew that much about the Buyur, both from oral traditions and the many clever servant organisms that flit about Jijo's forests, perhaps still looking for departed masters. Beyond these few scraps, we have very little about the race whose mighty civilization thronged this world for more than a million years.

HOW could so much knowledge be lost in a single night? Today it seems odd. Why weren't copies of such valuable texts printed by those first-wave human colonists, before they sent their sneakship tumbling to ocean depths? Why not place duplicates all over the Slope, safeguarding the learning against all peril?

In our ancestors' defense, recall what tense times those were, before the Great Peace or the coming of the Egg. The five sapient races already present on Jijo (excluding glavers) had reached an edgy balance by the time starship Tabernacle slinked past Izmunuti's dusty glare to plant Earthlings illicitly, the latest wave of criminal colonists to plague a troubled world. In those days, combat was frequent between urrish clans and haughty qheuen empresses, while hoonish tribes skirmished among themselves in their ongoing ethical struggle over traeki civil rights. The High Sages had little influence beyond reading and interpreting the Speaking Scrolls, the only documents existing at the time.

Into this tense climate dropped the latest invasion of sooner refugees, who found an unused eco-niche awaiting them. But human colonists were not content simply to take up tree farming as another clan of illiterates. Instead, they used the *Tabernacle*'s engines one last time before sinking her. With those godlike forces they carved Biblos Fortress then toppled a thousand trees, converting their pulp into freshly printed books.

The act so astonished the Other Five, it nearly cost human settlers their lives. Outraged, the queens of Tarek Town laid siege to the vastly outnumbered Earthlings. Others, equally offended by what seemed heresy against the Scrolls, held back only because the priest sages refused sanctioning holy war. That narrow vote gave human leaders time to bargain, to cajole the different tribes and septs with practical advice from books, bribing them with useful things. Spoke cleats for g'Kek wheels. Better sails for hoonish captains. And, for urrish smiths, the long-sought knack of brewing clear glass.

How things had changed just a few generations later, when the new breed of scholar sages gathered to affirm the Great Peace, scribing their names on fresh paper and sending copies to each hamlet on the Slope. Reading became a common habit, and even writing is no longer viewed as sin.

An orthodox minority still objects to the clatter of printing presses. They piously insist that literacy fosters memory, and thus attachment to the same conceits that got our spacefaring ancestors in trouble. Surely, they claim, we must cultivate detachment and forgetfulness in order to tread the Path of Redemption.

Perhaps they are right. But few these days seem in a hurry to follow glavers down that blessed trail. Not yet. First, we must prepare our souls.

And wisdom, the New Sages declare, can be nurtured from the pages of a book.

from *Forging the Peace,*
a Historical Meditation-Umble,
by Homer Auph-puthtwaoy

STREAKERS

KAA

Stranded, by unyielding fate, on Ifni's shore.

Stranded, like a beached whale, barred from ever going home.

Five ways stranded—

First, cut off from Earth by hostile aliens bearing a death grudge toward Terrans in general, and the *Streaker* crew in particular, though Kaa never quite understood why.

Second, banished from Earth's home *galaxy*, blown off course, and off-limits, by a caprice of hyperspace – though many on the crew still blamed Kaa, calling it 'pilot's error.'

Third, starship *Streaker* taking refuge on a taboo world, one scheduled to have a respite from sapient minds. An ideal haven, according to some. A trap, said others.

Fourth, when the vessel's weary engines finally ceased their labors, depositing the *Streaker* in a realm of ghosts, deep in this planet's darkest corner, far from air or light.

And now this, Kaa thought. *Abandoned, even by a crew of castaways!*

Of course Lieutenant Tsh't didn't put it that way, when she asked him to stay behind in a tiny outpost with three other volunteers for company.

'This will be your first important command, Kaa. A chance to show what you're made of.'

Yeah, he thought. *Especially if I'm speared by a hoonish harpoon, dragged onto one of their boats, and slit open.*

That almost happened yesterday. He had been tracking one of the native sailing craft, trying to learn its purpose and destination, when one of his young assistants, Mopol, darted ahead and began surfing the wooden vessel's rolling bow wake ... a favorite pastime on Earth, where dolphins frequently hitched free rides from passing ships. Only here it was so dumb, Kaa hadn't thought to forbid it in advance.

Mopol offered that lawyerly excuse later, when they returned to the shelter. 'B-besides, I didn't do any harm.'

'No harm? You let them see you!' Kaa berated. 'Don't you know they started throwing *spears* into the water, just as I got you out of there?'

Mopol's sleek torso and bottle beak held a rebellious stance.

'They never saw a dolphin before. Prob'ly thought we were some local kind of fish.'

'And it's gonna stay that way, do you hear?'

Mopol grunted ambiguous assent, but the episode unnerved Kaa.

A while later, dwelling on his own shortcomings, he worked amid clouds of swirling bottom mud, splicing optical fiber to a cable the submarine *Hikahi* had laid, on its return trip to *Streaker's* hiding place. Kaa's newly emplaced camera should let him spy more easily on the hoon colony whose sheltered docks and camouflaged houses lay perched along the nearby bay. Already he could report that hoonish efforts at concealment were aimed *upward*, at shrouding their settlement against the sky, not the sea. That might prove important information, Kaa hoped.

Still, he had never trained to be a spy. He was a pilot, dammit!

Not that he ever used to get much practice during the early days of *Streaker's* mission, languishing in the shadow of Chief Pilot Keepiru, who always got the tough, glamorous jobs. When Keepiru vanished on Kithrup, along with the captain and several others, Kaa finally got a chance to practice his skill – for better and worse.

But now Streaker's *going nowhere. A beached ship needs no pilot, so I guess I'm expendable.*

Kaa finished splicing and was retracting the work arms of his harness when a flash of silver-gray shot by at high speed, undulating madly. Sonar strafed him as waves of liquid recoil shoved his body. Clickety dolphin laughter filled the shallows.

> * *Admit it, star seeker!*
> * *You did not hear or see me.*
> * *Sprinting from the gloom!* *

In fact, Kaa had known the youth was approaching for some time, but he did not want to discourage Zhaki from practicing the arts of stealth.

'Use Anglic,' he commanded tersely.

Small conical teeth gleamed in a beam of slanted sunshine as the young Tursiops swung around to face Kaa. 'But it's much easier to speak Trinary! Sometimes Anglic makes my head hurt.'

Few humans, listening to this exchange between two neodolphins, would have understood the sounds. Like Trinary, this underwater dialect consisted mostly of clipped groans and ratchetings. But the *grammar* was close to standard Anglic. And grammar guides the way a person thinks – or so Creideiki used to teach, when that master of Keeneenk arts lived among the *Streaker* crew, guiding them with his wisdom.

Creideiki has been gone for two years, abandoned with Mr. Orley and others when we fled the battle fleets at Kithrup. Yet every day we miss him – the best our kind produced.

When Creideiki spoke, you could forget for a while that neodolphins were crude, unfinished beings, the newest and shakiest sapient race in the Five Galaxies.

Kaa tried answering Zhaki as he imagined the captain would.

'The pain you feel is called *concentration*. It's not easy, but it enabled our human patrons to reach the stars, all by themselves.'

'Yeah. And look what good it did them,' Zhaki retorted. Before Kaa could answer, the youth emitted the *need-air s*ignal and shot toward the surface, without even performing a wariness spiral to look out for danger. It violated security, but tight discipline seemed less essential as each Jijoan day passed. This sea was too mellow and friendly to encourage diligence.

Kaa let it pass, following Zhaki to the surface. They exhaled and drew in sweet air, faintly charged with distant hints of rain. Speaking Anglic with their gene-modified blowholes out of the water called for a different dialect, one that hissed and sputtered, but sounded more like human speech.

'All right-t,' Kaa said. 'Now report.'

The other dolphin tossed his head. 'The red crabs suspect nothing. They f-fixate on their crayfish pensss. Only rarely does one look up when we c-come near.'

'They aren't crabs. They're *qheuens*. And I gave strict orders. You weren't to go near enough to be seen!'

Hoons were considered more dangerous, so Kaa had kept that part of the spy mission for himself. Still, he counted on Zhaki and Mopol to be discreet while exploring the qheuen settlement at the reef fringe. *I guess I was wrong.*

'Mopol wanted to try some of the reds' delicaciesss, so we p-pulled a diversion. I rounded up a school of those green-finned fishies – the ones that taste like Sargasso eel – and chased 'em right through the q-qheuen colony! And guess what? It turns out the crabs have *pop-up nets* they use for jussst that kind of luck! As soon as the school was inside their boundary, they whipped those things up-p and snatched the whole swarm!'

'You're lucky they didn't snag you too. What was Mopol doing, all this time?'

'While the reds were busy, Mopol raided the crayfish pens.' Zhaki chortled with delight. 'I saved you one, by the way. They're delisssh.'

547

Zhaki wore a miniharness fastened to his flank, bearing a single manipulator arm that folded back during swimming. At a neural signal, the mechanical band went to his seamed pouch and drew out a wriggling creature, proffering it to Kaa.

What should I do? Kaa stared at the squirmy thing. Would accepting it only encourage Zhaki's lapse of discipline? Or would rejection make Kaa look stodgy and unreasonable?

'I'll wait and see if it makes you sick,' he told the youth. They weren't supposed to experiment on native fauna with their own bodies. Unlike Earth, most planetary ecosystems were mixtures of species from all across the Five Galaxies, introduced by tenant races whose occupancy might last ten million years. So far, many of the local fishoids turned out to be wholesome and tasty, but the very next prey beast might have its revenge by poisoning you.

'Where is Mopol now?'

'Back doing what we were told,' Zhaki said. 'Watching how the red crabs interact with hoonsss. So far we've seen 'em pulling two sledge loads toward the port, filled with harvested ssseaweed. They came back wth cargoes of wood. You know ... ch-chopped tree trunks.'

Kaa nodded. 'So they do trade, as we suspected. Hoons and qheuens, living together on a forbidden world. I wonder what it means?'

'Who knows? If they weren't mysterious, they wouldn't be eateesss. C-can I go back to Mopol now?'

Kaa had few illusions about what was going on between the two young spacers. It probably interfered in their work, but if he raised the issue, Zhaki would accuse him of being a prude, or worse, 'jealous.'

If only I were a real leader, Kaa thought. *The lieutenant should never have left me in charge.*

'Yes, go back now,' he said. 'But only to fetch Mopol and return to the shelter. It's getting late.'

Zhaki lifted his body high, perched on a thrashing tail.

 * *Yes, oh exalted!*
  * *Your command shall be obeyed,*
   * *As all tides heed moons.* *

With that, the young dolphin did a flip and dived back into the sea. Soon his dorsal fin was all Kaa saw, glinting as it sliced through choppy swell.

Kaa pondered the ambiguous insolence of Zhaki's last Trinary burst.

In human terms – by the cause-and-effect logic the patron race taught its dolphin clients – the ocean bulged and shifted in response to the gravitational pull of sun and moon. But there were more ancient ways of thinking, used by cetacean ancestors long before humans meddled in their genes. In those days, there had never been any question that tides were the most powerful of forces. In the old, primal religion, *tides* controlled the *moon*, not vice versa.

In other words, Zhaki's Trinary statement was sassy, verging on insubordination.

Tsh't made a mistake, Kaa mused bitterly, as he swam toward the shelter. *We should never have been left here by ourselves*.

Along the way, he experienced the chief threat to his mission. Not hoonish spears or qheuen claws, or even alien battlecruisers, but Jijo itself.

One could fall in love with this place.

The ocean's flavor called to him, as did the velvety texture of the water. It beckoned in the way fishlike creatures paid him respect by fleeing, but not too quick to catch if he cared to.

Most seductive of all, at night throbbing *echoes* penetrated their outpost walls – distant rhythms, almost too low to hear. Eerie, yet reminiscent of the whale songs of home.

Unlike Oakka, the green-green world – or terrible Kithrup – this planet appeared to have a *reverent* sea. One where a dolphin might swim at peace.

And possibly forget.

Brookida was waiting when Kaa cycled through the tiny airlock, barely large enough for one dolphin at a time to pass into the shelter – an inflated bubble, half-filled with water and anchored to the ocean floor. Against one wall, a lab had been set up for the metallurgist geologist, an elderly dolphin whose frailty had grown as *Streaker* fled ever farther from home.

Brookida's samples had been taken when the *Hikahi* followed a hoonish sailboat beyond the continental shelf, to a plunging abyssal trench, where the ship had proceeded to dump its cargo overboard! As casks, barrels, and chests fell into the murk, a few were snagged by the submarine's gaping maw, then left here for analysis as the *Hikahi* returned to base.

Brookida had already found what he called 'anomalies,' but something else now had the aged scientist excited.

'We got a message while you were out. Tsh't picked up something amazing on her way to *Streaker*!'

Kaa nodded. 'I was here when she reported, remember? They found an ancient cache, left by illegal settlers when—'

'That's nothing.' The old dolphin was more animated than Kaa had seen Brookida in a long time.

'Tsh't called again later to say they rescued a bunch of *kids* who were about to drown.' Kaa blinked.

'Kids? You don't mean—'

'Not human or fin. But wait till you hear who they are … and how they came to be d-down there, under the sea.'

SOONERS

ALVIN

A few scant duras before impact, part of the wall of debris ahead of us began to move. A craggy slab, consisting of pitted starship hulls, magically slipped aside, offering the phuvnthu craft a long, narrow cavity.

Into it we plummeted, jagged walls looming near the glass, passing in a blur, cutting off the searchlight beam and leaving us in shadows. The motors picked up their frantic backward roar ... then fell away to silence.

A series of metallic clangs jarred the hull. Moments later the door to our chamber opened. A clawed arm motioned us outside.

Several phuvnthus waited – insectoid-looking creatures with long, metal-cased torsos and huge, glassy-black eyes. Our mysterious saviors, benefactors, captors.

My friends tried to help me, but I begged them off.

'Come on, guys. It's hard enough managing these crutches without you all crowding around. Go on. I'll be right behind.'

At the intersection leading back to my old cell, I moved to turn left but our six-legged guides motioned right instead. 'I need my stuff,' I told the nearest phuvnthu-thing. But it gestured *no* with a wave of machinelike claws, barring my path.

Damn, I thought, recalling the notebook and backpack I had left behind. I figured I'd be coming back.

A twisty, confused journey took us through all sorts of hatches and down long corridors of metal plating. Ur-ronn commented that some of the weld joins looked 'hasty.' I admired the way she held on to her professionalism when faced with awesome technology.

I can't say exactly when we left the sea dragon and entered the larger base/camp/city/hive, but there came a time when the big phuvnthus seemed more relaxed in their clanking movements. I even caught a snatch or two of that queer, ratcheting sound that I once took for speech. But there wasn't time for listening closely. Just moving forward meant battling waves of pain, taking one step at a time.

At last we spilled into a corridor that had a feel of permanence, with pale, off-white walls and soft lighting that seemed to pour from the whole ceiling. The peculiar passage curved gently *upward* in both directions, till it climbed out of sight a quarter of an arrowflight to either side. It seemed we were in a huge *circle*, though what use such a strange hallway might serve, I could not then imagine.

Even more surprising was the reception committee! At once we faced a pair of creatures who could not look more different from the phuvnthus – except for the quality of having six limbs. They stood upright on their hind pair, dressed in tunics of silvery cloth, spreading four scaly webbed hands in a gesture I hopefully took to mean welcome. They were small, rising just above my upper knees, or the level of Pincer's red chitin shell. A frothy crown of moist, curly fibers topped their bulb-eyed heads. Squeaking rapidly, they motioned for us to follow, while the big phuvnthus retreated with evident eagerness.

We four Wuphonites consulted with a shared glance ... then a rocking, qheuen-style shrug. We turned to troop silently behind our new guides. I could sense Huphu purring on my shoulder, staring at the little beings, and I vowed to drop my crutches and grab the noor, if she tried to jump one of our hosts. I doubted they were as helpless as they looked.

All the doorways lining the hall were closed. Next to each portal, something like a *paper strip* was pasted to the wall, always at the same height. One of Huck's eyestalks gestured toward the makeshift coverings, then winked at me in Morse semaphore.

SECRETS UNDERNEATH!

I grokked her meaning. So our hosts did not want us to read their door signs. That implied they used one of the alphabets known to the Six. I felt the same curiosity that emanated from Huck. At the same time, though, I readied myself to stop her, if she made a move to tear off one of the coverings. There *are* times for impulsiveness. This was not one of them.

A door hatch slid open with a soft hiss and our little guides motioned for us to enter.

Curtains divided a large chamber into parallel cubicles. I also glimpsed a dizzying array of shiny machines, but did not note much about them, because of what then appeared, right in front of us.

We all stopped in our tracks, facing a quartet of familiar-looking entities – an urs, a hoon, a red qheuen, and a young g'Kek!

Images of ourselves, I realized, though clearly not reflections in a mirror. For one thing, we could see right *through* the likenesses. And as we stared, each figure made beckoning motions toward a different curtained nook.

After the initial shock, I noticed the images weren't perfect portraits. The urrish version had a well groomed pelt, and my hoonish counterpart stood erect, without a back brace. Was the difference meaningful? The hoonish caricature smiled at me in the old-fashioned way, with a fluttering throat sac, but no added grimace of mouth and lips that Jijoan hoons had added since humans came.

'Yeah right,' Huck muttered, staring at the ersatz g'Kek in front of her, whose wheels and spokes gleamed, tight and polished. 'I am *so* sure these are *sooners*, Alvin.'

I winced. So my earlier guess was wrong. There was no point rubbing it in.

'Hr-rm ... shut up, Huck.'

'These are holographic frojections,' Ur-ronn lisped in Anglic, the sole Jijoan language suitable for such a diagnosis. The words came from human books, inherited since the Great Printing.

'Whatever you s-say,' Pincer added, as each ghost backed away toward a different curtained cell. 'What d-d-do we do now?'

Huck muttered. 'What choice do we have? Each of us follows our own guy, and see ya on the other side.'

With an uneven bumping of her rims, she rolled after the gleaming g'Kek image. A curtain slid shut after her.

Ur-ronn blew a sigh. 'Good water, you two.'

'Fire and ash,' Pincer and I replied politely, watching her saunter behind the urrish cartoon figure.

The fake hoon waved happily for me to enter the cubby on the far right.

'Name, rank, and serial number only,' I told Pincer.

His worried – 'Huh?' – aspirated from three leg vents in syncopation. When I glanced back, his cupola eye still whirled indecisively, staring in all directions *except* at the translucent qheuen in front of him.

A hanging divider closed between us.

My silent guide in hoonish form led me to a white obelisk, an upright slab, occupying the center of the small room. He pantomimed stepping right up to it, standing on a small metal plate at its base. When I did so, I found the white surface *soft* against my face and chest. No sooner were my feet on the plate than the whole slab began to *tilt* ... rotating down and forward to become a table, with my own poor self lying prone on top. Huphu scrambled off my shoulders, muttering guttural complaints, then yowled as a *tube* lifted up from below and snaked toward my face!

I guess I could have struggled, or tried to flee. But to what point? When colored gas spilled from the tube, the odor reminded me of childhood visits to our Wuphon infirmary. The House of Stinks, we kids called it, though our traeki pharmacist was kindly, and always secreted a lump of candy from an upper ring, if we were good . . .

As awareness wavered, I recall hoping there would be a tasty sourball waiting for me this time, as well.

'G'night,' I muttered, while Huphu chittered and wailed. Then things kind of went black for a while.

ASX

Stroke the fresh-flowing wax, my rings, streaming hot with news from real time.

Here, trace this ululation, a blaring *cry of dismay* echoing round frosted peaks, setting stands of mighty greatboo a-quivering.

Just moments earlier, the Rothen ship hovered majestically above its ruined station, scanning the Glade for signs of its lost spore buds, the missing members of its crew.

Angry the throbbing vessel seemed, broody and threatening, ready to avenge.

Yet we/i remained in place, did we not, my rings? Duty rooted this traeki stack in place, delegated by the Council of Sages to parley with these Rothen lords.

Others also lingered, milling across the trampled festival grounds. Curious onlookers, or those who for personal reasons wished to offer invaders *loyalty*.

So we/i were not alone to witness what came next. There were several hundred present, staring in awe as the Rothen starship probed and palped the valley with rays, sifting the melted, sooty girders of its ravaged outpost.

Then came that abrupt, awful sound. A cry that still fizzes, uncongealed, down our fatty core. An alarm of anguished dread, coming from the ship itself!

Shall we recall more? Dare we trace this waxy trail yet further? Even though it gives off painful molten heat?

Yes?

You are brave, my rings . . .

Behold the Rothen ship – suddenly bathed in light!

Actinic radiance pours onto it *from above* . . . cast by a new entity, shining like the blazing sun.

It is no sun, but *another* vessel of space! A ship unbelievably larger than the slim gene raider, looming above it the way a full-stacked traeki might tower over a single, newly vlenned ring.

Can the wax be believed? Could anything be as huge and mighty as that luminous mountain-thing, gliding over the valley as ponderous as a thunderhead?

Trapped, the Rothen craft emits awful, grating noises, straining to escape the titanic newcomer. But the cascade of light now presses on it, pushing with force that spills across the vale, taking on qualities of physical substance. Like a solid shaft, the beam thrusts the Rothen ship downward against its will, until its belly scours Jijo's wounded soil.

A deluge of saffron color flows around the smaller cruiser, covering the Rothen craft in layers – thickening, like gobs of cooling sap. Soon the Rothen ship lies helplessly encased. Leaves and twigs seem caught in midwhirl, motionless beside the gold-sealed hull.

And above, a new power hovered. Leviathan.

The searing lights dimmed.

Humming a song of overpowering might, the titan descended, like a guest mountain dropping in to take its place among the Rimmers. A stone from heaven, cracking bedrock and reshaping the valley with its awful weight.

Now the wax stream changes course. The molten essence of distilled chagrin veers in a new direction.

Its heading, my rings?

Over a precipice.

Into hell.

RETY

Rety thought about her bird. The bright bird, so lively, so unfairly maimed, so like herself in its stubborn struggle to overcome.

All her adventures began one day when Jass and Bom returned from a hunting trip boasting about wounding a mysterious flying creature. Their trophy – a gorgeous metal feather – was the trigger she had been waiting for. Rety took it as an omen, steadying her resolve to break away. A sign that it was time, at last, to leave her ragged tribe and seek a better life.

I guess everybody's looking for something, she pondered, as the robot followed another bend in the dreary river, meandering toward the last known destination of Kunn's flying scout craft. Rety had the same goal, but also dreaded it. The Danik pilot would deal harshly with Dwer. He might also judge Rety, for her many failings.

She vowed to suppress her temper and grovel if need be. *Just so the starfolk keep their promise and take me with them when they leave Jijo.*

They must! I gave 'em the bird. Rann said it was a clue to help the Daniks and their Rothen lords search . . .

Her thoughts stumbled.

Search for what?

They must need somethin' awful bad to break Galactic law by sneakin' to far-off Jijo.

Rety never swallowed all the talk about 'gene raiding' – that the Rothen expedition came looking for animals almost ready to think. When you grow up close to nature, scratching for each meal alongside other creatures, you soon realize *everybody* thinks. Beasts, fish . . . why, some of her cousins even prayed to trees and stones!

Rety's answer was – *so what?* Would a gallaiter be less smelly if it could read? Or a wallow kleb any less disgusting if it recited poetry while rolling in dung? By her lights, nature was vile and dangerous. She had a bellyful and would gladly give it up to live in some bright Galactic city.

Rety never believed Kunn's people came across vast space just to teach some critters how to blab.

Then what was the real reason? And what were they afraid of?

The robot avoided deep water, as if its force fields needed rock or soil to push against. When the river widened, and converging tributaries became rivers themselves, further progress proved impossible. Ever a long detour west offered no way around. The drone buzzed in frustration, hemmed by water on all sides.

'Rety!' Dwer's hoarse voice called from below. 'Talk to it again!'

'I already did, remember? You must've wrecked its ears in the ambush, when you ripped out its antenna thing!'

'Well . . . try again. Tell it I might . . . have a way to get across a stream.'

Rety stared down at him, gripped by snakelike arms. 'You tried to kill it a while back, an' now you're offerin' to help?'

He grimaced. 'It beats dying, wandering in its clutches till the sun burns out. I figure there's food and medicine on the flying boat. Anyway, I've heard so much about these alien humans. Why should you get all the fun?'

She couldn't tell where he stopped being serious, and turned sarcastic. Not that it mattered. If Dwer's idea proved useful, it might soften the way Kunn treated him.

And me, she added.

'Oh, all right.'

Rety spoke directly to the machine, as she had been taught.

'Drone Four! Hear and obey commands! I order you to let us down so's we can haggle together about how to pass over this here brook. The prisoner says he's got a way mebbe to do it.'

The robot did not respond at first, but kept cruising between two high points, surveying for any sign of a crossing. But finally, the humming repulsors changed tone as metal arms lowered Dwer, letting him roll down a mossy bank. For a time the young man lay groaning. His limbs twitched feebly, like a stranded fish.

More than a little stiff herself, Rety hoisted her body off the upper platform, wincing at the singular touch of steady ground. Both legs tingled painfully, though likely not as bad as Dwer felt. She got down on her knees and poked his elbow.

'Hey, you all right? Need help gettin' up?'

Dwer's eyes glittered pain, but he shook his head. She put an arm around his shoulder anyway as he struggled to sit. No fresh blood oozed when they checked the crusty dressing on his thigh wound.

The alien drone waited silently as the young man stood, unsteadily.

'Maybe I can help you get across water,' he told the machine. 'If I do, will you change the way you carry us? Stop for breaks and help us find food? What d'you say?'

Another long pause – then a chirping note burst forth. Rety had learned a little Galactic Two during her time as an apprentice star child. She recognized the upward sliding scale meaning yes.

Dwer nodded. 'I can't guarantee my plan'll work. But here's what I suggest.'

It was actually simple, almost obvious, yet she looked at Dwer differently after he emerged from the stream, dripping from the armpits down. Before he was halfway out, the robot edged aside from its perch above Dwer's head. It seemed to glide down the side of the young hunter's body until reaching a point where its fields could grip solid ground.

All the way across the river, Dwer looked as if he wore a huge, eight-sided hat, wafting over his head like a balloon. His eyes were glazed and his hair stood on end as Rety sat him down.

'Hey!' She nudged him. 'You all right?'

Dwer's gaze seemed fixed far away. After a few duras though, he answered.

'Um . . . I . . . guess so.'

She shook her head. Even Mudfoot and yee had ceased their campaign of mutual deadly glares in order to stare at the man from the Slope.

'That was *so* weird!' Rety commented. She could not bring herself to say 'brave,' or 'thrilling' or 'insane.'

He winced, as if messages from his bruised body were just now reaching a dazed brain. 'Yeah . . . it was all that. And more.'

The robot chirruped again. Rety guessed that a triple upsweep with a shrill note at the end meant – *That's enough resting. Let's go!*

She helped Dwer onto a makeshift seat the robot made by folding its arms. This time, when it resumed its southward flight, the two humans rode in front with Mudfoot and little yee, sharing body heat against the stiff wind.

Rety had heard of this region from those bragging hunters, Jass and Bom. It was a low country, dotted with soggy marshes and crisscrossed by many more streams ahead.

ALVIN

I woke feeling woozy, and high as a chimp that's been chewing ghigree leaves. But at least the agony was gone.

The soft slab was still under me, though I could tell the awkward brace of straps and metal tubes was gone. Turning my head, I spied a low table nearby. A shallow white bowl held about a dozen familiar-looking shapes, vital to hoon rituals of life and death.

Ifni! I thought. *The monsters cut out my spine bones!*

Then I reconsidered.

Wait. You're a kid. You've got two sets. In fact, isn't it next year you're supposed to start losing your first . . .

I really was *that* slow to catch on. Pain and drugs can do it to you. Looking in the bowl again, I saw all my baby vertebrae. Normally, they'd loosen over several months, as the barbed adult spines took over. The accident must have jammed both sets together, pressing the nerves and hurrying nature along. The phuvnthus must have decided to take out my old verts, whether the new ones were ready or not.

Did they guess? Or were they already familiar with hoons?

Take things one at a time, I thought. *Can you feel your toe hooks? Can you move them?*

I sent signals to retract the claw sheaths, and sensed the table's fabric resist as my talons dug in. So far so good.

I reached around with my left hand, and found a slick bulge covering my spine, tough and elastic.

Words cut in. An uncannily smooth voice, in accented Galactic Seven.

'The new orthopedic brace will actively help bear the stress of your movements until your next-stage vertebroids solidify. Nevertheless, you would be well advised not to move in too sudden or jerky a manner.'

The fixture wrapped all the way around my torso, feeling snug and comfortable, unlike the makeshift contraption the phuvnthus provided earlier.

'Please accept my thanks,' I responded in formal GalSeven, gingerly shifting onto one elbow, turning my head the other way. 'And my apologies for any inconvenience this may have cause—'

I stopped short. Where I had expected to see a phuvnthu, or one of the small amphibians, there stood a whirling shape, ghostly, like the *holographic projections* we had seen before, but ornately abstract. A spinning mesh of complex lines floated near the bed.

'There was no inconvenience.' The voice seemed to emerge from the gyrating image. 'We were curious about matters taking place in the world of air and light. Your swift arrival – plummeting into a sea canyon near our scout vessel – seemed as fortuitous to us as *our* presence was for you.'

Even in a drugged state, I could savor multilevel irony in the whirling thing's remarks. While being gracious, it was also reminding me that the survivors of *Wuphon's Dream* owed a debt – our very lives.

'True,' I assented. 'Though my friends and I might never have fallen into the abyss if *someone* had not removed the article we were sent to find in more shallow waters. Our search beyond that place led us to stumble over the cliff.'

The pattern of shifting lines took a new slant of bluish, twinkling light.

'You assert ownership over this thing you sought? As your property?'

Now it was my turn to ponder, wary of a trap. By the codes laid down in the Scrolls, the cache Uriel had sent us after should not exist. It bent the spirit and letter of the law, which said that sooner colonists on a forbidden world must ease their crime by abandoning their godlike tools. It made me glad to be speaking a formal dialect, forcing more careful thought than I might have used in our local patois.

'I assert ... a right to *inspect* the item ... and reserve an option to make further claims later.'

Purple swirls invaded the spinning pattern, and I could almost swear it seemed amused. Perhaps this strange entity already had pursued the same line of questioning with my pals. I may be articulate – Huck says no one can match me in GalSeven – but I never claimed to be the brightest one in our gang.

'The matter can be discussed another time,' the voice said. 'After you tell us of your life, and recent events in the upper world.'

This triggered something in me ... call it the latent trading instinct that lurks in any hoon. A keenness for the fine art of dickering. Carefully, tenderly, I sat up, allowing the supple back brace to take most of the strain.

'Hr-r-m. You're asking us to give away the only thing we have to barter – our story, and that of our ancestors. What do you offer in exchange?'

The voice made a pretty good approximation of a rueful hoonish rumble.

'Apologies. It did not occur to us that you would look at it that way. Alas, you have already told us a great deal. We will now return your information store. Please accept our contrition over having accessed it without expressed permission.' A door slid open and one of the little amphibian creatures entered the cubicle, bearing in its four slim arms my backpack!

Better yet, on top lay my precious journal, all battered and bent, but still the item I most valued in the world. I snatched up the book, flipping its dog-eared pages.

'Rest assured,' the spinning pattern enounced. 'Our study of this document, while enlightening, has only whetted our appetite for information. Your economic interests are undiminished.'

I thought about that. 'You read my journal?'

'Again, apologies. It seemed prudent, when seeking to understand your injuries, and the manner of your arrival in this realm of heavy wet darkness.'

Once again, the words seemed to come at me with layers of meaning and implications I could only begin to sift. At the time, I only wanted to end the conversation as soon as possible, and confer with Huck and the others before going any further.

'I'd like to see my frends now,' I told the whirling image, switching to Anglic.

It seemed to quiver, as if with a nod.

'Very well. They have been informed to expect you. Please follow the entity standing at the door.'

The little amphibian attended while I set foot on the floor, gingerly testing my weight. There were a few twinges, just enough to help me settle best within the support of the flexible body cast. I gripped the journal, but glanced back at my knapsack and the bowl of baby vertebrae.

'These items will be safe here,' promised the voice.

I hope so, I thought. *Mom and Dad will want them ... assuming that I ever see Mu-phauwq, and Yowg-wayuo again ... and especially if I don't.*

'Thank you.'

The speckled pattern whirled.

'It is my pleasure to serve.'

Holding my journal tight, I followed the small being out the door. When I glanced back at the bed, the spinning projection was gone.

ASX

Here it is, at last. The image we have sought, now cool enough to stroke.

Yes, my rings. It is time for another vote. Shall we remain catatonic, rather than face what will almost certainly be a vision of pure horror?

Our first ring of cognition insists that duty must take precedence, even over the natural traeki tendency to flee unpleasant subjectivities.

Is it agreed? Shall we be *Asx*, and meet reality as it comes? How do you rule, my rings?

stroke the wax ...
follow the tracks ...
see the mighty starship come ...

Humming a song of overwhelming power, the monstrous vessel descends, crushing every remaining tree on the south side of the valley, shoving a dam across the river, filling the horizon like a mountain.

Can you feel it, my rings? Premonition. Throbbing our core with acrid vapors?

Along the starship's vast flank a hatch opens, large enough to swallow a small village.

Against the lighted interior, *silhouettes* enter view. Tapered cones. Stacks of rings.

Frightful kin we had hoped never again to see.

SARA

Sara looked back fondly at last night's wild ride, for now the horses sped up to a pace that made her bottom feel like butter.

And to think, as a child I wished I could gallop about like characters in storybooks.

Whenever the pace slackened, she eyed the enigmatic female riders who seemed so at home atop huge, mythological beasts. They called themselves Illias, and their lives had been secret for a long time. But now haste compelled them to travel openly.

Can it really be just to get Kurt the Exploser where he wants to go?

Assuming his mission is vital, why does he want my help? I'm a theoretical mathematician with a sideline in linguistics. Even in math, I'm centuries out of date by Earth standards. To Galactics I'd be just a clever shaman.

Losing altitude, the party began passing settlements – at first urrish camps with buried workshops and sunken corrals hidden from the glowering sky. But as the country grew more lush, they skirted dams where blue qheuen hives tended lakebottom farms. Passing a riverside grove, they found the 'trees' were ingeniously folded masts of hoonish fishing skiffs and khuta boats. Sara even glimpsed a g'Kek weaver village where sturdy trunks supported ramps, bridges, and swaying boardwalks for the clever wheeled clan.

At first the settlements seemed deserted as the horses sped by. But the chick coops were full, and the blur canopies freshly patched. *Midday isn't a favorite time to be about, especially with sinister specters in the sky.* Anyone rousing from siesta glimpsed only vague galloping figures, obscured by dust.

But attention was unavoidable later, when members of all six races scurried from shelters, shouting as the corps of beasts and riders rushed by. The grave Illias horsewomen never answered, but Emerson and young Jomah waved at astonished villagers, provoking some hesitant cheers. It made Sara laugh, and she joined their antics, helping turn the galloping procession into a kind of antic parade.

*

When the mounts seemed nearly spent, the guides veered into a patch of forest where two more women waited, dressed in suede, speaking that accent Sara found tantalizingly familiar. Hot food awaited the party – along with a dozen fresh mounts.

Someone is a good organizer, Sara thought. She ate standing up – a pungent vegetarian gruel. Walking helped stretch kinked muscles.

The next stage went better. One of the Illias showed Sara a trick of flexing in her stirrups to damp the jouncing rhythm. Though grateful, Sara wondered.

Where have these people lived all this time?

Dedinger, the desert prophet, caught Sara's eye, eager to discuss the mystery, but she turned away. The attraction of his intellect wasn't worth suffering his character. She preferred spending her free moments with Emerson. Though speechless, the wounded starman had a good soul.

Villages grew sparse south of the Great Marsh. But *traeki* flourished there, from tall cultured stacks, famed for herbal industry, all the way down to wild quintets, quartets, and little trio ring piles, consuming decaying matter the way their ancestors must have on a forgotten homeworld, before some patron race set them on the Path of Uplift.

Sara daydreamed geometric arcs, distracting her mind from the heat and tedium, entering a world of parabolas and rippling wave-like forms, free of time and distance. By the time she next looked up, dusk was falling and a broad river flowed to their left, with faint lights glimmering on the other bank.

'Traybold's Crossing.' Dedinger peered at the settlement, nestled under camouflage vines. 'I do think the residents have finally done the right thing ... even if it inconveniences wayfarers like us.'

The wiry rebel appeared pleased. Sara wondered.

Can he mean the bridge? Have local fanatics torn it down, without orders from the sages?

Dwer, her well-traveled brother, had described the span across the Gentt as a marvel of disguise, appearing like an aimless jam of broken trees. But even that would not satisfy fervent scroll thumpers these days.

Through twilight dimness she spied a forlorn skeleton of charred logs, trailing from sandbar to sandbar.

Just like at Bing Hamlet, back home. What is it about a bridge that attracts destroyers?

Anything sapient-made might be a target of zealotry, these days.

The workshops, dams, and libraries may go. We'll follow glavers into blessed obscurity. Dedinger's heresy may prove right, and Lark's prove wrong.

She sighed. *Mine was always the unlikeliest of all.*

Despite captivity, Dedinger seemed confident in ultimate success for his cause.

'Now our young guides must spend days trying to hire boats. No more rushing about, postponing Judgment Day. As if the explosers and their friends could ever have changed destiny.'

'Shut up,' Kurt said.

'You know, I always thought your guild would be on *our* side, when the time came to abandon vanities and take redemption's path. Isn't it frustrating, preparing all your life to blow up things, only to hold back at the crucial moment?'

Kurt looked away.

Sara expected the horsewomen to head to a nearby fishing village. Hoonish coracles might be big enough to ferry one horse at a time, though that slow process would expose the Illias to every gawking citizen within a dozen leagues. Worse, Urunthai reinforcements, or Dedinger's own die-hard supporters, might have time to catch up.

But to her surprise, the party left the river road, heading west down a narrow track through dense undergrowth. Two Illias dropped back, brushing away signs of their passage.

Could their settlement lie in this thicket?

But hunters and gleaners from several races surely went browsing through this area. No secret horse clan could remain hidden for more than a hundred years!

Disoriented in a labyrinth of trees and jutting knolls, Sara kept a wary eye on the rider in front of her. She did not relish wandering lost and alone in the dark.

Gaining altitude, the track finally crested to overlook a cluster of evenly spaced hills – steep mounds surrounding a depression filled with dense brush. From their symmetry, Sara thought of Buyur ruins.

Then she forgot about archaeology when something else caught her eye. A flicker to the west, beckoning from many leagues away.

The mountain's wide shoulders cut a broad wedge of stars. Near its summit, curved streaks glowed red and orange.

Flowing lava.

Jijo's blood.

A volcano.

Sara blinked. *Might they already have traveled to—*

'No,' she answered herself. 'That's not Guenn. It's *Blaze Mountain*.'

'If only that *were* our destination, Sara. Things'd be simpler.' Kurt spoke from nearby. 'Alas, the smiths of Blaze Peak are conservative.

564

They want no part of the hobbies and pastimes that are practiced where we're headin'.'

Hobbies? Pastimes? Was Kurt trying to baffle her with riddles?

'You can't still reckon we're going all the way to—'

'To the other great forge? Aye, Sara. We'll make it, don't fret.'

'But the bridge is out! Then there's desert, and after that, the Spec . . .'

She trailed off as the troop turned downward, into the thorn brake between the hills. Three times, riders dismounted to shift clever barriers that looked like boulders or tree trunks. At last, they reached a small clearing where the guides met and embraced another group of leather-clad women. There was a campfire . . . and the welcome aroma of food.

Despite a hard day, Sara managed to unsaddle her own mount and brush the tired beast. She ate standing, doubtful she would ever sit again.

I should check Emerson. Make sure he takes his medicine. He may need a story or a song to settle down after all this.

A small figure slipped alongside. chuffing nervously.

No – Go – Hole – Prity motioned with agile hands. *Scary – Hole.*

Sara frowned.

'What hole are you talking about?'

The chimp took Sara's hand, pulling her toward several Illias, who were shifting baggage to a squat, boxy object.

A *wagon*, Sara realized. A big one, with four wheels, instead of the usual two. Fresh horses were harnessed, but to haul it where? Surely not through the surrounding thicket!

Then Sara saw what 'hole' Prity meant – gaping at the base of a cone hill. An aperture with smooth walls and a flat floor. A thin glowing stripe ran along the tunnel's center, continuing downhill before turning out of sight.

Jomah and Kurt were already aboard the big wagon, with Dedinger strapped in behind, a stunned expression on his aristocratic face.

For once Sara agreed with the heretic sage.

Emerson stood at the shaft entrance and whooped, like a small boy exploring a cave first with his own echoes. The starman grinned, happier than ever, and reached for her hand. Sara took his while inhaling deeply.

Well, I bet Dwer and Lark never went anywhere like this. I may yet be the one with the best story to tell.

I found my friends in a dim chamber where frigid fog blurred every outline. Even hobbling with crutches, my awkward footsteps made hardly a sound as I approached the silhouettes of Huck and Ur-ronn, with little Huphu curled on Pincer's carapace. All faced the other way, looking downward into a soft glow.

'Hey, what's going on?' I asked. 'Is this any way to greet—' One of Huck's eyestalks swerved on me.

'*We're-glad-to-see-you're-all-right-but-now-shut-up-and-get-over-here*.'

Few other citizens of the Slope could squeeze all that into a single GalThree word-blat. Not that skill excused her rudeness.

'*Hr-rm. The-same-to-you-I'm-sure, oh-obsessed-being-too-transfixed-to-offer-decent-courtesy*,' I replied in kind.

Shuffling forward, I noted how my companions were transformed. Ur-ronn's pelt gleamed, Huck's wheels were realigned, and Pincer's carapace had been patched and buffed smooth. Even Huphu seemed sleek and content.

'What is it?' I began. 'What're you all staring . . .'

My voice trailed off when I saw where they stood – on a *balcony* without a rail, overlooking the source of both the pale glow and the chill haze. A cube – two hoon lengths on a side, colored a pale shade of brownish yellow – lay swathed in a fog of its own making, unadorned except by a symbol embossed on one face. A *spiral* emblem with five swirling arms and a bulbous center, all crossed by a gleaming vertical bar.

Despite how far the people of the Slope have fallen, or how long it's been since our ancestors roamed as star gods, that emblem is known to every grub and child. Inscribed on each copy of the Sacred Scrolls, it evokes awe when prophets and sages speak of lost wonders. On this frosted obelisk it could only mean one thing – that we stood near more knowledge than anyone on Jijo could tally, or begin to imagine. If the human crew of sneakship *Tabernacle* had kept printing paper books till this very day, they could have spilled only a small fragment of the trove before us, a hoard that began before many stars in the sky.

The Great Library of the Civilization of the Five Galaxies.

I'm told moments like these can inspire eloquence from great minds.

'J-j-jeez,' commented Pincer.

Ur-ronn was less concise.

'The questions ...,' she lisped. 'The questions we could ask ...'

I nudged Huck.

'Well, you said you wanted to go find something to *read*.'

For the first time in all the years I've known her, our little wheeled friend seemed at a loss for words. Her stalks trembled. The only sound she let out was a gentle keening sigh.

ASX

If only we/i had nimble running feet,
   i/we would use them now, to flee.
If we/i had burrowers' claws,
   i/we would dig a hole and hide.
If we/i had the wings,
   i/we would fly away.

Lacking those useful skills, the member toruses of our composite stack nearly vote to draw permanently, sealing out the world, negating the objective universe, waiting for the intolerable to go away.

It will not go away.

So reminds our second torus of cognition.

Among the greasy trails of wisdom that coat our aged core, many were laid down after reading learned books, or holding lengthy discussions with other sages, These tracks of philosophical wax agree with our second ring. As difficult as it may be for a traeki to accept, the cosmos does not vanish when we turn within. Logic and science appear to prove otherwise.

The universe goes on. Things that matter keep happening, one after another.

Still, it is *hard* to swivel our trembling sensor rings to face toward the mountain dreadnought that recently lowered itself down from heaven, whose bulk seems to fill both valley and sky.

Harder to gaze through a hatchway in the great ship's flank – an aperture broad as the largest building in Tarek Town.

Hardest to regard the worst of all possible sights – those cousins that we traeki fled long ago.

Terrible and strong – the mighty Jophur.

How gorgeous they seem, those glistening sap rings, swaying in their backlit portal, staring without pity at the wounded glade their vessel alters with its crushing weight. A glade thronging with half-animal felons, a miscegenous rabble, the crude descendants of fugitives.

Exiles who futilely thought they might elude the ineludible.

Our fellow Commons citizens mutter fearfully, still awed by the rout of the smaller Rothen ship – that power we had held in dread for months – now pressed down and encased in deadly light.

Yes, my rings. i/we can sense how some nearby Sixers – the quick and prudent – take to their heels, retreating even before the landing tremors fade. Others foolishly mill *toward* the giant vessel, driven by curiosity, or awe. Perhaps they have trouble reconciling the shapes they see with any sense of danger.

As harmless as a traeki, so the expression goes. After all, what menace can there be in tapered stacks of fatty rings?

Oh, my/our poor innocent neighbors. You are about to find out.

LARK

That night he dreamed about the last time he saw Ling smile – before her world and his forever changed.

It seemed long ago, during a moonlit pilgrimage that crept proudly past volcanic vents and sheer cliffs, bearing shared hope and reverence toward the Holy Egg. Twelve twelves of white-clad celebrants made up that procession – qheuens and g'Keks, traekis and urs, humans and hoons – climbing a hidden trail to their sacred site. And accompanying them for the first time, guests from outer space – a Rothen master, two Danik humans, and their robot guards – attending to witness the unity rites of a quaint savage tribe.

He dreamed about that pilgrimage in its last peaceful moment, before the fellowship was splintered by alien words and fanatical deeds. Especially the smile on her face, when she told him joyous news.

'Ships are coming, Lark. So many ships!
'It's time to bring you all back home.'

Two words still throbbed like sparks in the night. Rhythmically hotter as he reached for them in his sleep.

... ships ...
... home ...
... ships ...
... home ...

One word vanished at his dream touch – he could not tell which. The other he clenched hard, its flamelike glow increasing. Strange light, pushing free of containment. It streamed past flesh, past bones. A glow that clarified, offering to show him *everything*.

Everything except . . .

Except now *she* was gone. Taken away by the word that vanished.

Pain wrenched Lark from the lonely night phantasm, tangled in a sweaty blanket. His trembling right hand clenched hard against his chest, erupting with waves of agony.

Lark exhaled a long sigh as he used his left hand to pry open the fingers of his right, forcing them apart one by one. Something rolled off his open palm—

It was the stone fragment of the Holy Egg, the one he had hammered from it as a rebellious child, and worn ever since as penance. Even as sleep unraveled, he imagined the rocky talisman throbbing with heat, pulsing in time to the beating of his heart.

Lark stared at the blur-cloth canopy, with moonlight glimmering beyond.

I remain in darkness, on Jijo, he thought, yearning to see once more by the radiance that had filled his dream. A light that seemed about to reveal distant vistas.

Ling spoke to him later that day, when their lunch trays were slipped into the tent by a nervous militiaman.

'Look, this is stupid,' she said. 'Each of us acting like the other is some kind of devil spawn. We don't have time for grudges, with your people and mine on a tragic collision course.'

Lark had been thinking much the same thing, though her sullen funk had seemed too wide to broach. Now Ling met his eyes frankly, as if anxious to make up for lost time.

'I'd say a collision's already happened,' he commented. Her lips pressed a thin line. She nodded.

'True. But it's wrong to blame your entire Commons for the deeds of a minority, acting without authority or—'

He barked a bitter laugh. 'Even when you're trying to be sincere, you still condescend, Ling.'

She stared for a moment, then nodded 'All right. Your sages effectively sanctioned the zealots' attack, *post facto*, by keeping us prisoner and threatening blackmail. It's fair to say that we're already—'

'At war. True, dear ex-employer. But you leave out our own *casus belli*.' Lark knew the grammar must be wrong, but he liked showing that even a savage could also drop a Latin phrase. 'We're fighting for our lives. And now we know genocide was the Rothen aim from the start.'

Ling glanced past him to where a g'Kek doctor drew increasing amounts of nauseating fluid from the air vents of a qheuen, squatting unconscious at the back of the shelter. She had worked alongside Uthen for months, evaluating local species for possible uplift. The gray's illness was no abstraction.

'Believe me, Lark. I know nothing of this disease. Nor the trick Ro-kenn allegedly pulled, trying to broadcast psi-influentials via your Egg.'

'Allegedly? You suggest *we* might have the technology to pull off something like that, as a frame-up?'

Ling sighed. 'I don't dismiss the idea entirely. From the start you Jijoans played on our preconceptions. Our willingness to see you as ignorant barbarians. It took weeks to learn that you were still literate! Only lately did we realize you must have hundreds of books, maybe thousands!'

An ironic smile crossed his face, before Lark realized how much the expression revealed.

'More than that? *A lot more?*' Ling stared. 'But where? By Von Daniken's beard – how?'

Lark put aside his meal, mostly uneaten. He reached over to his backpack and drew forth a thick volume bound in leather.

'I can't count how many times I wanted to show you this. Now I guess it doesn't matter anymore.'

In a gesture Lark appreciated, Ling wiped her hands before accepting the book, turning the pages with deliberate care. What seemed reverence at first, Lark soon realized was inexperience. Ling had little practice holding paper books.

Probably never saw one before, outside a museum.

Rows of small type were punctuated by lithographed illustrations. Ling exclaimed over the flat, unmoving images. Many of the species shown had passed through the Danik research pavilion during the months she and Lark worked side by side, seeking animals with the special traits her Rothen masters desired.

'How old is this text? Did you find it here, among all these remnants?' Ling motioned toward a stack of artifacts preserved by the mulc-spider, relics of the long-departed Buyur, sealed in amber cocoons.

Lark groaned. 'You're still doing it, Ling. For Ifni's sake! The book is written in *Anglic*.'

She nodded vigorously. 'Of course. You're right. But then who—'

Lark reached over and flipped the volume to its title page.

A PHYLOGENETIC INTERDEPENDENCE PROFILE
OF ECOLOGICAL SYSTEMS ON THE JIJOAN SLOPE

'This is part one. Part two is still mostly notes. I doubt we'd have lived long enough to finish volume three, so we left the deserts, seas, and tundras for someone else to take on.'

Ling gaped at the sheet of linen paper, stroking two lines of smaller print, below the title. She looked at him, then over toward the dying qheuen.

'That's right,' he said. 'You're living in the same tent with both authors. And since I'm presenting you with this copy, you have a rare opportunity. Care to have both of us autograph it? I expect you're the last person who'll get the chance.' His bitter sarcasm was wasted. Clearly she didn't understand the word *autograph*. Anyway, Ling the biologist had replaced the patronizing alien invader. Turning pages, she murmured over each chapter she skimmed.

'This would have been incredibly useful during our survey!'

'That's why I never showed it to you.'

Ling answered with a curt nod. Given their disagreement over the rightness of gene raiding, his attitude was understandable.

Finally, she closed the volume, stroking the cover. 'I am honored by this gift. This *accomplishment*. I find I cannot grasp what it must have taken to create it, under these conditions, just the two of you ...'

'With the help of others, and standing on the shoulders of those who came before. It's how science works. Each generation's supposed to get better, adding to what earlier ones knew ...'

His voice trailed off as he realized what he was saying.

Progress? But that's Sara's apostasy, not mine!

Anyway, why am I so bitter? So what if alien diseases wipe out every sapient being on Jijo? Weren't you willing to see that as a blessing, a while ago? Didn't it seem an ideal way to swiftly end our illegal colony? A harmful invasion that should never have existed in the first place?

Over the course of Uther's illness, Lark came to realize something – that death can sometimes seem desirable in abstract, but look quite different when it's in your path, up close and personal.

If Harullen the Heretic had lived, that purist might have helped Lark cling to his belief in Galactic law, which for good reason forbade settlements on fallow worlds. *It was our goal to atone for our ancestors' egotistical sin. To help rid Jijo of the infestation.*

But Harullen was gone, sliced to bits by a Rothen robot, and now Lark grappled with doubts.

I'd rather Sara were right. If only I could see nobility here. Something worth enduring. Worth fighting for.

I don't really want to die.

Ling pored through the guidebook again. Better than most, she could appreciate the work he and Uther spent their adult lives creating. Her professional esteem helped bridge the chasm of their personalities.

'I wish I had something of equal value to give you,' she said, meeting his eyes again.

Lark pondered.

'You really mean that?'

'Of course I do.'

'All right then, wait here. I'll be right back.'

At the rear of the shelter, the g'Kek physician indicated with twined eyestalks that Uthen's condition was unvaried. Good news, since each change till now had been for the worse. Lark stroked his friend's chitin carapace, wishing he could impart comfort through the gray's stupor.

'Is it my fault you caught this bug, old friend? I made you go with me into the station wreckage, rummaging for alien secrets.' He sighed. 'I can't make up for that. But what's in your bag may help others.'

He lifted Uthen's private satchel and took it back to Ling. Reaching inside, he felt several slablike objects, cool to the touch.

'Earlier, we found something that you might help me learn to read. If you meant your promise.'

He put one of the flat lozenges in her hand – pale brown and smooth as glass, with a spiral shape etched on each face.

Ling stared at it for several duras. When she looked up, there was something new in her countenance. Was it respect for the way he had cornered her? Trapping her with the one other trait they shared – a compelling sense of honor?

For the first time since they met, Ling's eyes seemed to concede that she was dealing with an equal.

ASX

Calm down, my rings. No one can force you to *stroke wax against your will*.

As traeki we are each of us sovereign, free not to recall intolerable memories before we are ready.

Let the wax cool a little longer – a majority of rings demands – *before we dare look again.*

Let the most recent terror wait.

But our second cognition ring demurs. It insists – we/i should delay no longer confronting the dread news about Jophur, our terrible cousins, arriving on Jijo.

Our second ring of cognition reminds us of the Quandary of Solipsism – the riddle that provoked our traeki founders to flee the Five Galaxies.

Solipsism. The myth of the all-important self.

Most mortal sapient beings hold this conceit, at one level or another. An individual can perceive others by sight, touch, and empathy, yet still reckon them as mere figments or automatons. Caricatures, of little importance.

Under solipsism, the world exists for each solitary individualist.

Examined dispassionately, it seems an insane concept. Especially to a traeki, since none of us can thrive or think alone. Yet egotism can also be useful to ambitious creatures, driving their single-minded pursuit of success.

Madness seems essential in order to be 'great.'

Terran sages knew this paradox from their long isolation. Ignorant and lonely, humans wallowed in one bizarre superstition after another, frantically trying concepts that no uplifted species would consider for even a dura. According to wolfling tales, humans wrestled endlessly with their own overpowering egos.

Some tried *suppressing* selfness, seeking detachment. Others subsumed personal ambition in favor of a greater whole – family, religion, or a leader.

Later they passed through a phase in which individualism was extolled as the highest virtue, teaching their young to inflate the ego beyond all natural limits or restraint. Works from this mad *era of the self* are found in the Biblos Archive, with righteous, preening rage flowing across every page.

Finally, just before contact, there emerged another approach.

Some of their texts use the word *maturity*.

We traeki – newly uplifted from the pensive swamps of our homeworld – seemed safe from achieving greatness, no matter how many skills our patrons, the blessed Poa, inserted in our rings. Oh, we found it pleasant to merge in tall, wise stacks. To gather learned wax and travel the stars. But to our patrons' frustration, we never found appealing the fractious rivalries that churn the

Five Galaxies. Frantic aspiration and zeal always seemed pointless to our kind.

Then the Poa brought in experts. The *Oailie*.

The Oailie pitied our handicap. With great skill, they gave us tools for achievement. For greatness.

The Oailie gave us new rings—

Rings of power.

Rings of self-centered glory.

Rings that turned mere traeki into *Jophur*.

Too late, we and the Poa learned a lesson – that ambition comes at a cost.

We fled, did we not, my rings?

By a fluke, some traeki managed to shuck these Oailie 'gifts,' and escape.

Only a few wax-crystal remembrance cells survive from those days. Memories laced with dread of what we were becoming.

At the time, our ancestors saw no choice but flight.

And yet ... a pang of conscience trickles through our inner core. *Might there have been another way?*

Might we have stayed and fought somehow to tame those awesome new rings? Futile as our forebears' exodus now seems ... was it also wrong?

Since joining the High Sages, this traeki Asx has pored over Terran books, studying their lonely, epochal struggle – a poignant campaign to control their own deeply solipsistic natures. A labor still under way when they emerged from Earth's cradle to make contact with Galactic civilization.

The results of that Asx investigation remain inconclusive, yet i/we found tantalizing clues.

The fundamental ingredient, it seems, is courage.

Yes, my rings?

Very well then. A majority has been persuaded by the second ring of cognition.

We/i shall once again turn to the hot-new-dreadful waxy trail of recent memory.

Glistening cones stared down at the confused onlookers who remained, milling on the despoiled glade. From a balcony high a-flank the mountain ship, polished stacks of fatty rings dripped luxuriously as they regarded teeming savages below – we enthralled members of six exile races.

Shifting colors play across their plump toruses – shades of rapid disputation. Even at a great distance, i/we sense controversy raging among the mighty Jophur, as they quarrel among themselves. Debating our fate.

Events interrupt, even as our dribbling thought-streams converge.

Near.

At last we have come very near the recent. The present.

Can you sense it, my rings? The moment when our dreadful cousins finished arguing what to do about us? Amid the flashing rancor of their debate, there suddenly appeared forceful decisiveness. Those in command – powerful ring stacks whose authority is paramount – made their decree with stunning confidence.

Such assuredness! Such certainty! It washed over us, even from six arrowflights away.

Then something else poured from the mighty dreadnought.

Hatchet blades of infernal light.

EMERSON

He has never been especially fond of holes. This one both frightens and intrigues Emerson.

It is a strange journey, riding a wooden wagon behind a four-horse team, creaking along a conduit with dimpled walls, like some endless stretched intestine. The only illumination – a faintly glowing stripe – points straight ahead and behind, toward opposite vanishing points.

The duality feels like a sermon. After departing the hidden forest entrance, time became vague – the past blurry and the future obscure. Much like his life has been ever since regaining consciousness on this savage world, with a cavity in his head and a million dark spaces where memory should be.

Emerson can feel this place tugging associations deep within his battered skull. Correlations that scratch and howl beyond the barriers of his amnesia. Dire recollections lurk just out of reach. Alarming memories of abject, gibbering terror, that snap and sting whenever he seeks to retrieve them.

Almost as if, somehow, they were being guarded.

Strangely, this does not deter him from prodding at the barricades. He has spent much too long in the company of pain to hold it in awe any longer. Familiar with its quirks and ways, Emerson figures he now knows pain as well as he knows himself.

Better, in fact.

Like a quarry who turns at bay after growing bored with running – and then begins hunting its pursuer – Emerson eagerly *stalks* the fear scent, following it to its source.

The feeling is not shared. Though the draft beasts pant and their hooves clatter, all echoes feel muffled, almost deathlike. His fellow travelers react by hunching nervously on the narrow bench seats, their breath misting the chill air.

Kurt the Exploser seems a little less surprised by all this than Sara or Dedinger, as if the old man long suspected the existence of a subterranean path. Yet, his white-mirrored eyes keep darting, as if to catch dreaded movement in the surrounding shadows. Even their guides, the taciturn women riders, appear uneasy. They must have come this way before, yet Emerson can tell they dislike the tunnel.

Tunnel.

He mouths the word, adding it proudly to his list of recovered nouns.

Tunnel.

Once upon a time, the term meant more than a mere hole in the ground, when his job was fine-tuning mighty engines that roamed the speckled black of space. Back then it stood for . . .

No more words come to mind. Even images fail him, though oddly enough, *equations* stream from some portion of his brain less damaged than the speech center. Equations that explain *tunnels*, in a chaste, sterile way – the sort of multidimensional tubes that thread past treacherous shoals of hyperspace. Alas, to his disappointment, the formulas lack any power to yank memories to life.

They do not carry the telltale spoor of fear.

Also undamaged is his unfailing sense of direction. Emerson knows when the smooth-walled passage must be passing under the broad river, but no seepage is seen. The tunnel is a solid piece of Galactic workmanship, built to last for centuries or eons – until the assigned time for dismantling.

That time came to this world long ago. This place should have vanished along with all the great cities back when Jijo was lain fallow. By some oversight, it was missed by the great destroyer machines and living acid lakes.

Now desperate fugitives use the ancient causeway to evade a hostile sky, suddenly filled with ships.

While still vague on details, Emerson knows he has been fleeing starships for a very long time, along with *Gillian, Hannes, Tsh't,* and the crew of *Streaker.*

Faces flicker, accompanying each name as recall agony makes him grunt and squeeze his eyelids. Faces Emerson pines for ... and desperately hopes never to see again. He knows he must have been sacrificed somehow, to help the others get away.

Did the plan succeed? Did *Streaker* escape ahead of those awful dreadnoughts? Or has he suffered all of this for nothing?

His companions breathe heavily and perspire. They seem taxed by the stale air, but to Emerson it is just another kind of atmosphere. He has inhaled many types over the years. At least this stuff nourishes the lungs ...

... unlike the wind back on the green-green world, where a balmy day could kill you if your helmet failed ...

And his helmet *did* fail, he now recalls, at the worst possible time, while trying to cross a mat of sucking demi-veg, running frantically toward—

Sara and Prity gasp aloud, snapping his mental thread, making him look up to see what changed.

At a brisk pace the wagon enters a sudden widening of the tunnel, like the bulge where a snake digests its meal. Dimpled walls recede amid deep shadows, where dozens of large objects dimly lurk – tube-like vehicles, corroded by time. Some have been crushed by rock falls. Piles of stony debris block other exits from the underground vault.

Emerson lifts a hand to stroke a filmy creature riding his forehead, as lightly as a scarf or veil. The *rewq* trembles at his touch, swarming down to lay its filmy, translucent membrane over his eyes. Some colors dim, while others intensify. The ancient transit cars seem to shimmer like specters, as if he is looking at them not through space, but time. It is almost possible to imagine them in motion, filled with vital energies, hurtling through a network that once girdled a living, global civilization.

The horsewomen sitting on the foremost bench clutch their reins and peer straight ahead, enclosed by a nimbus of tension made visible by the rewq. The film shows Emerson their edgy, superstitious awe. To them, this is no harmless crypt for dusty relics, but a macabre place where phantoms prowl. Ghosts from an age of gods.

The creature on his brow intrigues Emerson. How does the little parasite translate emotions – even between beings as different as human and traeki – and all without words? Anyone who brought such a treasure to Earth would be richly rewarded.

To his right, he observes Sara comforting her chimpanzee aide, holding Prity in her arms. The little ape cringes from the dark, echoless cavern, but the rewq's overlaid colors betray a fringe of *deceit* in Prity's distress. It is partly an act! A way to distract her mistress, diverting Sara from her own claustrophobic fears.

Emerson smiles knowingly. The hues surrounding Sara reveal what the unaided eye already knows – that the young woman thrives on being needed.

'It's all right, Prity,' she soothes. 'Shh. It'll be all right.'

The phrases are so simple, so familiar that Emerson understands them. He used to hear the same words while thrashing in his delirium, during those murky days after the crash, when Sara's tender care helped pull him back from that pit of dark fire.

The vast chamber stretches on, with just the glowing stripe to keep them from drifting off course. Emerson glances back to see young Jomah, seated on the last bench with his cap a twisted mass between his hands, while his uncle Kurt tries to explain something in hushed tones, motioning at the distant ceiling and walls – perhaps speculating what held them up . . . or what explosive force it would take to bring them crashing down. Nearby, with fastened hands and feet, the rebel, Dedinger, projects pure hatred of this place.

Emerson snorts annoyance with his companions. What a gloomy bunch! He has been in spots infinitely more disturbing than this harmless tomb . . . some of them he can even remember! If there is one sure truth he can recall from his former life, it is that a cheerful journey goes much faster, whether you are in deep space or the threshold of hell.

From a bag at his feet, he pulls out the midget dulcimer Ariana Foo had given him back at the Biblos Archive, that ornate hall of endless corridors stacked high with paper books. Not bothering with the hammers, he lays the instrument on his lap and plucks a few strings. Twanging notes jar the others from their anxious mutterings to look his way.

Though Emerson's ravaged brain lacks speech, he has learned ways to nudge and cajole. Music comes from a different place than speech, as does song.

Free association sifts the shadowy files of memory. Early drawers and closets, undammed by the traumas of later life. From some cache he finds a tune about travel down another narrow road. One with a prospect of hope at the end of the line.

It spills forth without volition, as a whole, flowing to a voice that's unpracticed, but strong.

> *'I've got a mule, her name is Sal,*
> *Fifteen miles down the Erie Canal.*
> *She's a good old worker and a good old pal,*
> *Fifteen miles down the Erie Canal.*

We've hauled some cargo in our day,
Filled with lumber, coal, and hay,
And we know every inch of the way,
From Albany to Buffalo-o-o ...'

Amid the shadows, they are not easily coaxed from their worries. He too can feel the weight of rock above, and so many years. But Emerson refuses to be oppressed. He sings louder, and soon Jomah's voice joins the refrain, followed tentatively by Sara's. The horses' ears flick. They nicker, speeding to a canter.

The subterranean switching yard narrows again, walls converging with a rush. Ahead, the glowing line plunges into a resuming tunnel.

Emerson's voice briefly falters as a flicker of memory intrudes. Suddenly he can recall another abrupt plunge ... diving through a portal that opened into jet vacuum blankness ... then falling as the universe converged on him from all sides to *squeeze* ...

And something else.

A row of pale blue eyes.

Old Ones ...

But the song has a life of its own. Its momentum pours unstoppably from some cheerful corner of his mind, overcoming those brief, awful images, making him call out the next verse with a vigor of hoarse, throaty defiance.

'Low bridge, everybody down!
Low bridge! 'Cause we're comin' to a town.

And you'll always know your neighbor,
Always know your pal,
If you ever navigate along the Erie Canal.'

His companions lean away from the rushing walls. Their shoulders press together as the hole sweeps up to swallow them again.

III

Once a lengthy eopisode of colonization finally comes to an end, subdution recycling is among the more commonly used methods for clearing waste products on a life world. Where natural cycles of plate tectonics provide a powerful indrawing force, the planet's own hot convection processes can melt and remix elements that had been fashioned into tools and civilized implements. Materials that might otherwise prove poisonous or intrusive to newrising species are thus removed from the fallow environment as a world eases into the necessary dormant phase.

What happens to these refined materials, after they have been drawn in, depends on mantle processes peculiar to each planet. Certain convection systems turn the molten substance into high-purity ores. Some become lubricated by water seeps, stimulating the release of great liquid magma spills. Yet another result can be sudden expulsions of volcanic dust, which briefly coat the planet and can later be traced in the refractory-metal enrichment of thin sedimentary layers.

Each of these outcomes can result in perturbations of the local biosphere, and occasional episodes of extinction. However, the resulting enrichment fecundity usually proves beneficial enough to compensate, encouraging development of new presapient species ...

from *A Galactographic Tutorial for Ignorant Wolfing Terrans*, a special publication of the Library Institute of the Five Galaxies, year 42 EC, in partial satisfaction of the debt obligation of 35 EC

STREAKERS

HANNES

Suessi felt nostalgic about being human. Now and then, he even wished he were still a man.

Not that he was ungrateful for the boon the Old Ones had granted him, in that strange place called the Fractal System, where aloof beings transformed his aged, failing body into something more durable. Without their gift, he would be stone dead – as cold as the giant corpses surrounding him in this dark ossuary of ships.

The ancient vessels seemed peaceful, in dignified repose. It was tempting to contemplate resting, letting eons pass without further care or strife.

But Suessi was much too busy to spare time for being dead.

'*Hannes,*' a voice crackled directly to his auditory nerve.

'*Two minutes, Hannes. Then I think-k we'll be ready to resume cut-t-ting.*'

Shafts of brilliant illumination speared through the watery blackness, casting bright ovals toward one curved hull segment of the Terran starship *Streaker*. Distorted silhouettes crisscrossed the spotlight beams – the long undulating shadows of workers clad in pressurized armor, their movements slow, cautious.

This was a more dangerous realm than hard vacuum.

Suessi did not have a larynx anymore, or lungs to blow air past one if he had. Yet he retained a voice.

'Standing by, Karkaett,' he transmitted, then listened as his words were rendered into groaning saser pulses. 'Please keep the alignment steady. Don't overshoot.'

One shadow among many turned toward him. Though cased in hard sheathing the dolphin's tail performed a twist turn with clear body-language meaning.

Trust me ... do you have any choice?

Suessi laughed – a shuddering of his titanium rib cage that replaced the old, ape-style method of syncopated gasps. It wasn't as satisfying, but then, the Old Ones did not seem to have much use for laughter.

Karkaett guided his team through final preparations while Suessi monitored. Unlike some others in *Streaker*'s crew, the engineering staff had grown more seasoned and confident with each passing year. In time, they might no longer need the encouragement – the supervising crutch – of a member of the patron race. When that day came, Hannes would be content to die.

I've seen too much. Lost too many friends. Someday, we'll be captured by one of the eatee factions pursuing us. Or else, we'll finally get a chance to turn ourselves in to some great Institute, only to learn Earth was lost while we fled helter-skelter across the universe. Either way, I don't want to be around to see it.

The Old Ones can keep their Ifni-cursed immortality.

Suessi admired the way his well-trained team worked, setting up a specially designed cutting machine with cautious deliberation. His audio pickups tracked low mutterings – *keeneenk* chants, designed to help cetacean minds concentrate on explicit thoughts and tasks that their ancestral brains were never meant to take on. Engineering thoughts – the kind that some dolphin philosophers called the most painful price of uplift.

These surroundings did not help – a mountainous graveyard of long-dead starcraft, a ghostly clutter, buried in the kind of ocean chasm that dolphins traditionally associated with their most cryptic cults and mysteries. The dense water seemed to amplify each rattle of a tool. Every whir of a harness arm resonated queerly in the dense liquid environment.

Anglic might be the language of engineers, but dolphins preferred Trinary for punctuation – for moments of resolution and action. Karkaett's voice conveyed confidence in a burst phrase of cetacean haiku.

> * *Through total darkness*
> > * *Where the cycloid's gyre comes never . . .*
> > > * *Behold – decisiveness!* *

The cutting tool lashed out, playing harsh fire toward the vessel that was their home and refuge . . . that had carried them through terrors unimaginable. *Streaker*'s hull – purchased by the Terragens Council from a third-hand ship dealer and converted for survey work – had been the pride of impoverished Earthclan, the first craft to set forth with a dolphin captain and mostly cetacean crew, on a mission to check the veracity of the billion-year-old Great Library of the Civilization of the Five Galaxies.

Now the captain was gone, along with a quarter of the crew. Their mission had turned into a calamity for both Earthclan and the Five Galaxies. As for *Streaker*'s hull – once so shiny, despite her age – it now lay coated by a mantle of material so black the abyssal waters seemed clear by comparison. A substance that drank photons and weighed the ship down.

Oh, the things we've put you through, dear thing.

This was but the latest trial for their poor ship.

Once, bizarre fields stroked her in a galactic tide pool called the Shallow Cluster, where they 'struck it rich' by happening upon a vast derelict fleet containing mysteries untouched for a thousand eons. In other words, where everything first started going wrong.

Savage beams rocked her at the Morgran nexus point, where a deadly surprise ambush barely failed to snare *Streaker* and her unsuspecting crew.

Making repairs on poisonous Kithrup, they ducked out almost too late, escaping mobs of bickering warships only by disguising *Streaker* inside a hollowed-out Thennanin cruiser, making it to a transfer point, though at the cost of abandoning many friends.

Oakka, the green world, seemed an ideal goal after that – a sector headquarters for the Institute of Navigation. Who was better qualified to take over custody of their data? As Gillian Baskin explained at the time, it was their duty as Galactic citizens to turn the problem over to the great institutes – those august agencies whose impartial lords might take the awful burden away from *Streaker*'s tired crew. It seemed logical enough – and nearly spelled their doom. Betrayal by agents of that 'neutral' agency showed how far civilization had fallen in turmoil. Gillian's hunch saved the Earthling company – that and a daring cross-country raid by Emerson D'Anite, taking the conspirators' base from behind.

Again, *Streaker* emerged chastened and worse for wear.

There *was* refuge for a while in the Fractal System, that vast maze where ancient beings gave them shelter. But eventually that only led to more betrayal, more lost friends, and a flight taking them ever farther from home.

Finally, when further escape seemed impossible, Gillian found a clue in the Library unit they had captured on Kithrup. A syndrome called the 'Sooner's Path.' Following that hint, she plotted a dangerous road that might lead to safety, though it meant passing through the licking flames of a giant star, bigger than Earth's orbit, whose soot coated *Streaker in* layers almost too heavy to lift.

But she made it to Jijo.

This world looked lovely from orbit. Too bad we had only that one glimpse, before plunging to an abyssal graveyard of ships.

Under sonar guidance by dolphin technicians, their improvised cutter attacked *Streaker's* hull. Water boiled into steam so violently that booming echoes filled this cave within a metal mountain. There were dangers to releasing so much energy in a confined space. Separated gases might recombine explosively. Or it could make their sanctuary detectable from space. Some suggested the risk was too great ... that it would be better to abandon *Streaker* and instead try reactivating one of the ancient hulks surrounding them as a replacement.

There were teams investigating that possibility right now. But Gillian and Tsh't decided to try this instead, asking Suessi's crew to pull off one more resurrection.

The choice gladdened Hannes. He had poured too much into *Streaker* to give up now. *There may be more of me in her battered shell than remains in this cyborg body.*

Averting his sensors from the cutter's actinic glow, he mused on the mound of cast-off ships surrounding this makeshift cavern. They seemed to speak to him, if only in his imagination.

We, too, have stories, they said. *Each of us was launched with pride, flown with hope, rebuilt many times with skill, venerated by those we protected from the sleeting desolation of space, long before your own race began dreaming of the stars.*

Suessi smiled. All that might have impressed him once – the idea of vessels millions of years old. But now he knew a truth about these ancient hulks.

You want old? he thought. *I've seen old.*

I've seen ships that make most stars seem young.

The cutter produced immense quantities of bubbles. It screeched, firing ionized bolts against the black layer, just centimeters away. But when they turned it off at last, the results of all that eager destructive force were disappointing.

'That-t's all we removed?' Karkaett asked, incredulously, staring at a small patch of eroded carbon. 'It'll take years to cut it all away, at-t this rate!'

The engineer's mate, Chuchki, so bulky she nearly burst from her exo-suit, commented in awed Trinary.

* Mysteries cluster
    * Frantic, in Ifni's shadow—
        * Where did the energy go! *

Suessi wished he still had a head to shake, or shoulders to shrug. He made do instead by emitting a warbling sigh into the black water, like a beached pilot whale.

> * Not by Ifni's name,
>   * But her creative employer—
>   * I wish to God I knew. *

GILLIAN

It isn't easy for a human being to pretend she's an *alien*.

Especially if the alien is a Thennanin.

Shrouds of deceitful color surrounded Gillian, putting ersatz flesh around the lie, providing her with an appearance of leathery skin and a squat bipedal stance. On her head, a simulated crest rippled and flexed each time she nodded. Anyone standing more than two meters away would see a sturdy male warrior with armored derma and medallions from a hundred stellar campaigns – not a slim blond woman with fatigue-lined eyes, a physician forced by circumstances to command a little ship at war.

The disguise was pretty good by now. It ought to be. She had been perfecting it for well over a year.

'Gr-phmph pltith,' Gillian murmured.

When she first started pulling these charades, the Niss Machine used to translate her Anglic questions into Thennanin. But now Gillian figured she was probably as fluent in that Galactic dialect as any human alive. Probably even Tom.

It still sounds weird though. Kind of like a toddler making disgusting fart imitations for the fun of it.

At times, the hardest part was struggling not to break out laughing. That would not do, of course. Thennanin weren't noted for their sense of humor.

She continued the ritual greeting.

'Fhishmishingul parfful, mph!'

Chill haze pervaded the dim chamber, emanating from a sunken area where a beige-colored cube squatted, creating its own wan illumination. Gillian could not help thinking of it as a magical box – a receptacle folded in many dimensions, containing far more than any vessel its size should rightfully hold.

She stood at a lipless balcony, masked to resemble the former owners of the box, awaiting a reply. The barred-spiral symbol on its face seemed slippery to the eye, as if the emblem were slyly looking back at her with a soul far older than her own.

> 'Toftorph-ph parfful. Fhishfingtumpti parffful.'

The voice was deeply resonant. If she had been a real Thennanin, those undertones would have stroked her ridge crest, provoking respectful attentiveness. Back home, the Branch Library of Earth spoke like a kindly human grandmother, infinitely experienced, patient, and wise.

'I am prepared to witness,' murmured a button in her ear, rendering the machine's words in Anglic. 'Then I will be available for consultation.'

That was the perpetual trade-off. Gillian could not simply demand information from the archive. She had to give as well.

Normally, that would pose no problem. Any Library unit assigned to a major ship of space was provided camera views of the control room and the vessel's exterior, in order to keep a WOM record for posterity. In return, the archive offered rapid access to wisdom spanning almost two billion years of civilization, condensed from planet-scale archives of the Library Institute of the Civilization of Five Galaxies.

Only there's a rush, Gillian thought.

Streaker was not a 'major ship of space.' Her own WOM units were solid, cheap, unresponsive – the only kind that impoverished Earth could afford. This lavish cube was a far greater treasure, salvaged on Kithrup from a mighty war cruiser of a rich starfaring clan.

She wanted the cube to *continue* thinking it was on that cruiser, serving a Thennanin admiral. Hence this disguise.

'Your direct watcher pickups are still disabled,' she explained, using the same dialect. 'However, I have brought more recent images, taken by portable recording devices. Please accept-and-receive this data now.'

She signaled the Niss Machine, her clever robotic assistant in the next room. At once there appeared next to the cube a series of vivid scenes. Pictures of the suboceanic trench that local Jijoans called the 'Midden' – carefully edited to leave out certain things.

We're playing a dangerous game, she thought, as flickering holosims showed huge mounds of ancient debris, discarded cities, and abandoned spacecraft. The idea was to pretend that the Thennanin dreadnought *Krondor's Fire* was hiding for tactical reasons in this realm of dead machines ... and to do this without showing *Streaker's* own slender hull, or any sign of dolphins, or even revealing the specific name and locale of this planet.

If we make it home, or to a neutral Institute base, we'll be legally bound to hand over this unit. Even under anonymous seal, it would be safest for it to know as little as we can get away with telling.

Anyway, the Library might not prove as cooperative to mere Earthlings. Better to keep it thinking it was dealing with its official leaseholders.

Ever since the disaster at Oakka, Gillian had made this her chief personal project, pulling off a hoax in order to pry data out of their prize. In many ways, the Library cube was more valuable than the relics *Streaker* had snatched from the Shallow Cluster.

In fact, the subterfuge had worked better than expected. Some of the information won so far might prove critically useful to the Terragens Council.

Assuming we ever make it home again . . .

Ever since Kithrup, when *Streaker* lost the best and brightest of her crew, that had always seemed a long shot, at best.

In one particular area of technology, twenty-second-century humans had already nearly equaled Galactic skill levels, even before contact.

Holographic imagery.

Special-effects wizards from Hollywood, Luanda, and Aristarchus were among the first to dive confidently into alien arts, undismayed by anything as trivial as a billion-year head start. Within mere decades Earthlings could say they had mastered a single narrow field as well as the best starfaring clans—

Virtuosity at lying with pictures.

For thousands of years, when we weren't scratching for food we were telling each other fables. Prevaricating. Propagandizing. Casting illusions. Making movies.

Lacking science, our ancestors fell back on magic. The persuasive telling of untruths.

Still it seemed a wonder to Gillian that her Thennanin disguise worked so well. Clearly the 'intelligence' of this unit, while awesome, was of a completely different kind than hers, with its own limitations.

Or else maybe it simply doesn't care.

From experience, Gillian knew the Library cube would accept almost anything as input, as long as the show consisted of credible scenes it had never witnessed before. So Jijo's abyss flashed before it – this time the panoramas came over fiber cable from the western sea, sent by Kaa's team of explorers, near the settled region called the Slope. Ancient buildings gaped – drowned, eyeless, and windowless – under the scrutiny of probing searchlight beams. If anything, this waste field was even greater than the one where *Streaker* took refuge. The accumulated mass of made-things collected by a planetary culture for a million years.

Finally, the cascade of images ceased.

There followed a brief pause while Gillian waited edgily. Then the beige box commented.

'The event stream remains disjointed from previous ones. Occurrences do not take place in causal-temporal order related to inertial movements of this vessel. Is this effect a result of the afore-mentioned battle damage?'

Gillian had heard the same complaint – the very same words, in fact – ever since she began this ruse, shortly after Tom brought the captured prize aboard *Streaker* ... only days before he flew away to vanish from her life.

In response, she gave the same bluff as always.

'That is correct. Until repairs are completed, penalties for any discrepancies may be assessed to the *Krondor's Fire* mission account. Now please prepare for consultation.'

This time there was no delay.

'Proceed with your request.'

Using a transmitter in her left hand, Gillian signaled to the Niss Machine, waiting in another room. The Tymbrimi spy entity at once began sending data requisitions, a rush of flickering light that no organic being could hope to follow. Soon the info flow went bi-directional – a torrential response that forced Gillian to avert her eyes. Perhaps, amid that flood, there might be some data helpful to *Streaker*'s crew, increasing their chances of survival.

Gillian's heart beat faster. This moment had its own dangers. If a starship happened to be scanning nearby – perhaps one of *Streaker*'s pursuers – onboard cognizance detectors might pick up a high level of digital activity in this area.

But Jijo's ocean provided a lot of cover, as did the surrounding mountain of discarded starships. Anyway, the risk seemed worth-while.

If only so much of the information offered by the cube weren't confusing! A lot of it was clearly meant for starfarers with far more experience and sophistication than the *Streaker* crew.

Worse, we're running out of interesting things to show the Library. Without fresh input, it might withdraw. Refuse to cooperate at all.

That was one reason she decided yesterday to let the four native kids come into this misty chamber and visit the archive. Since Alvin and his friends didn't yet know they were aboard an Earthling vessel, there wasn't much they could give away, and the effect on the Library unit might prove worthwhile.

Sure enough, the cube seemed bemused by the unique sight of an urs and hoon, standing amicably together. And the existence of a living g'Kek was enough, all by itself, to satisfy the archive's passive curiosity. Soon afterward, it willingly unleashed a flood of requested information about the varied types of discarded spaceships surrounding *Streaker* in this underwater trash heap, including parameters used by ancient Buyur control panels.

That was helpful. But we need more. A lot more.

I guess it won't be long until I'm forced to pay with real secrets.

Gillian had some good ones she could use ... if she dared.

In her office, just a few doors down, lay a mummified cadaver well over a billion years old.

Herbie.

To get hold of that relic – and the coordinates where it came from – most of the fanatic, pseudo-religious alliances in the Five Galaxies had been hunting *Streaker* since before Kithrup.

Pondering the chill beige cube, she thought—

I'll bet if I showed you one glimpse of ol' Herb, you'd have a seizure and spill every datum you've got stored inside.

Funny thing is ... nothing would make me happier in all the universe than if we'd never seen the damned thing.

As a girl, Gillian had dreamed of star travel, and someday doing bold, memorable things. Together, she and Tom had planned their careers – and marriage – with a single goal in mind. To put themselves at the very edge, standing between Earth and the enigmas of a dangerous cosmos.

Recalling that naive ambition, and how extravagantly it was fulfilled, Gillian very nearly laughed aloud. But with pressed lips she managed to keep the bitter, poignant irony bottled inside, without uttering a sound.

For the time being, she must maintain the dignified presence of a Thennanin admiral.

Thennanin did not appreciate irony. And they never laughed.

SOONERS

EWASX

You might as well get used to it, My rings.

The piercing sensations you feel are My fibrils of control, creeping down our shared inner core, bypassing the slow, old-fashioned, waxy trails, attaching and penetrating your many toroid bodies, bringing them into new order.

Now begins the lesson, when I teach you to be docile servants of something greater than yourselves. No longer a stack of ill-wed components, always quarreling, paralyzed with indecision. No more endless *voting* over what beliefs shall be held by a fragile, tentative *i*.

That *was* the way of our crude ancestor stacks, meditating loose, confederated thoughts in the odor-rich marshes of Jophekka World. Overlooked by other star clans, we seemed unpromising material for uplift. But the great, sluglike Poa saw potential in our pensive precursors, and began upraising those unlikely mounds.

Alas, after a million years, the Poa grew frustrated with our languid traeki natures.

'Design new rings for our clients,' they beseeched the clever Oailie, 'to boost, guide, and drive them onward.'

The Oailie did not fail, so great was their mastery of genetic arts.

WHAT WAS THEIR TRANSFORMING GIFT?

New, ambitious rings.

Master rings.

LIKE ME.

ALVIN

This is a test. I'm trying out a burnish-new way of writing.

If you call this 'writing' – where I talk out loud and watch sentences appear in midair above a little box I've been given.

Oh, it's uttergloss all right. Last night, Huck used her new autoscribe to fill a room with words and glyphs in GalThree, GalEight, and every obscure dialect she knew, ordering translations back and forth until it seemed she was crowded on all sides by glowing symbols.

Our hosts gave us the machines to help tell our life stories, especially how the Six Races live together on the Slope. In return, the spinning voice promised a reward. Later, we'll get to ask questions of the big chilly box.

Huck went delirious over the offer. Free access to a memory unit of the Great Library of the Five Galaxies! Why, it's like telling Cortés he could have a map to the Lost Cities of Gold, or when the legendary hoonish hero Yuq-wourphmin found a password to control the robot factories of Kurturn. My own nicknamesake couldn't have felt more awe, not even when the secrets of Vanamonde and the Mad Mind were revealed in all their fearsome glory.

Unlike Huck, though, I view the prospect with dark worry. Like a detective in some old-time Earth storybook, I gotta ask – *where's the catch?*

Will they break their promise, once we've shared all we know?

Maybe they'll fake the answers. (How could we tell?)

Or perhaps they'll let us talk to the cube all we want, because they figure the knowledge won't do us any good, since we're never going home again.

On the other hand, let's say it's all open and sincere. Say we *do* get a chance to pose questions to the Library unit, that storehouse of wisdom collected by a billion-year-old civilization.

What on Jijo could we possibly have to say?

I've just spent a midura experimenting. Dictating text. Backing up and rewriting. The autoscribe sure is a lot more flexible than scratching away with a pencil and a ball of *guarru* gum for an eraser! Hand motions move chunks of text like solid objects. I don't even have to speak aloud, but simply *will* the words, like that little tickle when you mutter under your breath so's no one else can hear. I know it's not true mind reading – the machine must be sensing muscle changes in my throat or something. I read about such things in *The Blackjack Era* and *Luna City Hobo*. But it's unnerving anyway.

Like when I asked to see the little machine's dictionary of Anglic synonyms! I always figured I had a good vocabulary, from memorizing the town's copy of *Roget's Thesaurus*! But it turns out that volume left out most of the Hindi and Arabic cognate grafts onto the English-Eurasian rootstock. This tiny box holds enough words to keep Huck and me humble ... or me, at least.

My pals are in nearby rooms, reciting their own memoirs. I expect Huck will rattle off something fast-paced, lurid, and carelessly brilliant to satisfy our hosts. Ur-ronn will be meticulous and dry, while Pincer will get distracted telling breathless stories about sea monsters. I have a head start because my journal already holds the greater part of our personal story – how we four adventurers got to this place of weirdly curved corridors, far beneath the waves.

So I have time to worry about *why* the phuvnthus want to know about us.

It could just be curiosity. On the other hand, what if something we say here eventually winds up hurting our kinfolk, back on the Slope? I can hardly picture how. I mean, it's not like we know any military secrets – except about the urrish cache that Uriel the Smith sent us underwater to retrieve. But the spinning voice already knows about that.

In my cheerier moments I envision the phuvnthus letting us take the treasure back, taking us home to Wuphon in their metal whale, so we seem to rise from the dead like the fabled crew of the *Hukuphtau* ... much to the surprise of Uriel, Urdonnol, and our parents, who must have given us up for lost.

Optimistic fantasies alternate with other scenes I can't get out of my head, like something that happened right after the whale sub snatched *Wuphon's Dream* out of its death plunge. I have this hazy picture of bug-eyed spider-things stomping through the wreckage on our hand-made vessel, jabbering weird ratchety speech, then jumping back in mortal terror at the sight of *Ziz*, the harmless little traeki five-stack given us by Tyug the Alchemist.

Streams of fire blasted poor Ziz to bits.

You got to wonder what anyone would go and do a mean thing like that for.

I might as well get to work.

How to begin my story?

Call me Alvin ...

No. Too hackneyed. How about this opening?

Alvin Hph-wayuo woke up one morning to find himself transformed into a giant ....

Uh-uh. That's hitting too close to home.

Maybe I should model my tale after *20,000 Leagues Under the Sea*. Here we are, castaways being held as cordial prisoners in an underwater world. Despite being female, Huck would insist *she's* the heroic Ned Land character. Ur-ronn would be Professor Aronnax, of course, which leaves either Pincer or me to be the comic fall guy, Conseil.

So when are we going to finally meet *Nemo*?

Hmm. That's a disadvantage of this kind of writing, so effortless and easily corrected. It encourages running off at the mouth, when good old pencil and paper meant you had to actually think in advance what you were going to sa—

Wait a minute. What was that?

There it goes again. A faint booming sound ... only louder this time. Closer.

I don't think I like it. Not at all.

...

Ifni! This time it set the floor quivering.

The rumble reminds me of Guenn Volcano back home, belchin' and groanin', making everybody in Wuphon wonder if it's the long-awaited Big O—

Jeekee sac-rot! No fooling this time.

Those are explosions, getting close fast!

Now comes another noise, like a zookir screeching its head off 'cause it sat on a quill lizard.

Is that the sound a *siren* makes? I always wondered—

Gishtuphwayo! Now the lights go dim. The floor jitters—

What is Ifni-slucking going on!

DWER

The view from the highest dune wasn't promising.

The Danik scout craft was at least five or six leagues out to sea, a tiny dot, barely visible beyond a distinct line where the water's hue changed from pale bluish green to almost black. The flying machine cruised back and forth, as if searching for something it had misplaced. Only rarely, when the wind shifted, did they catch the faint rumble of its engines, but every forty or so duras Dwer glimpsed something specklike tumble from the belly of the sleek boat, glinting in the morning sun before it struck the sea. Ten more duras would pass after the object sank – then the ocean's surface *bulged* with a hummock of roiling foam, as if an immense monster suffered dying spasms far below.

'What's Kunn doing?' Dwer asked. He turned to Rety, who shaded her eyes to watch the distant flier. 'Do you have any idea?'

The girl started to shrug her shoulders, but yee, the little urrish male, sprawled there, snaking his slender neck to aim all three eyes toward the south. The robot rocked impatiently, bobbing up and down as if trying to signal the distant flier with its body.

'I don't know, Dwer,' Rety replied. 'I reckon it has somethin' to do with the bird.'

'Bird,' he repeated blankly.

'You know. My metal bird. The one we saved from the mulc-spider.'

'*That* bird?' Dwer nodded. 'You were going to show it to the sages. How did the aliens get their hands—'

Rety cut in.

'The Daniks wanted to know where it came from. So Kunn asked me to guide him here, to pick up Jass, since he was the one who saw where the bird came to shore. I never figured that'd mean leavin' me behind in the village . . .' She bit her lip. 'Jass must've led Kunn here. Kunn said somethin' about "flushin' prey." I guess he's tryin' to get more birds.'

'Or else whoever *made* your bird, and sent it ashore.'

'Or else that.' She nodded, clearly uncomfortable. Dwer chose not to press for details about her deal with the star humans.

As their journey south progressed, the number of marshy streams had multiplied, forcing Dwer to 'carry' the robot several more times before he finally called a halt around dusk. There had been a brief confrontation when the combat machine tried intimidating him to continue. But its god weapons had been wrecked in the ambush at the sooner camp, and Dwer faced the robot's snapping claws without flinching, helped by a strange detachment, as if his mind had some-how *grown* while enduring the machine's throbbing fields. Hallucination or not, the feeling enabled him to call its bluff.

With grudging reluctance that seemed lifelike, the robot gave in. By a small fire, Dwer had shared with Rety the donkey jerky in his pouch. After a moment's hesitation, Rety brought out her own con-tribution, two small lozenges sealed in wrappers that felt slick to the touch. She showed Dwer how to unwrap his, and guffawed at the look on his face when intense, strange flavors burst in his mouth. He laughed, too, almost inhaling the Danik candy the wrong way. Its lavish sweetness won a place on his List of Things I'm Glad I Did Before Dying.

Later, huddled with Rety on the banked coals, Dwer dreamed a succession of fantastic images far more potent than normal – per-haps an effect of 'carrying' the robot, conducting its groundhugging fields. Instead of crushing weight, he fantasized *lightness*, as if his body wafted, unencumbered. Incomprehensible panoramas flick-ered under closed eyelids ... objects glimmering against dark backgrounds, or gassy shapes, glowing of their own accord. Once, a strange sense of recognition seized him, a timeless impression of loving familiarity.

The Egg, his sleeping consciousness had mused. Only the sacred stone looked strange – not an outsized pebble squatting in a mountain cleft, but something like a huge, dark *sun*, whose blackness outshone the glitter of normal stars.

Their journey resumed befrore dawn, and featured only two more water crossings before reaching the sea. There the robot picked them up and streaked eastward along the beach until it reached this field of dunes – a high point to scan the strange blue waters of the Rift.

At least Dwer thought it was the Rift – a great cleft splitting the continent. *I wish I still had my telescope*, he thought. With it he might glean some idea what the pilot of the scout ship was trying to accomplish.

Flushing out prey, Rety said.

If that was Kunn's aim, the Danik star warrior could learn a thing or two about hunting technique. Dwer recalled one lesson old Fallon taught him years ago.

No matter how potent your weapon, or whatever game you're after, it's never a good idea to be both beater and shooter. If there's just one of you, forget driving your quarry.

The solitary hunter masters patience, and silently learns the ways of his prey.

That approach had one drawback. It required empathy. And the better you learn to feel like your prey, the greater the chance you may someday stop calling it *prey* at all.

'Well, we settled one thing,' Rety commented, watching the robot semaphore its arms wildly at the highest point of the dune, like a small boy waving to parents who were too far away to hear. 'You must've done a real job on its comm gear. Even the short range won't work, on line-o'-sight.'

Dwer was duly impressed. Rety had learned a lot during her stint as an adopted alien.

'Do you think the pilot could spot us by eye, when he heads back toward the village to pick you up?' Dwer asked.

'Maybe . . . supposin' he ever meant to do that. He may forget all about me when he finds what he wants, and just zip west to the Rothen station, to report.'

Dwer knew that Rety had already lost some favor with the sky humans. Her voice was bitter, for aboard that distant flying dot rode *Jass*, her tormentor while growing up in a savage tribe. She had arranged vengeance for the bully. But now Jass stood at the pilot's elbow, currying favor while Rety was stuck down here.

Her worry was clear. What if her lifelong enemy won the reward she had struggled and connived for? Her ticket to the stars?

'Hmm. Well, then we better make sure he doesn't miss us when he cruises by.'

Dwer wasn't personally anxious to meet the star pilot who had blasted the poor urrish sooners so unmercifully from above. He fostered no illusion of gentle treatment at Kunn's hands. But the scout boat offered life and hope for Rety. And perhaps by attracting the Danik's attention he could somehow prevent the man's quick return to the Gray Hills. Danel Ozawa had been killed in the brief fight with the robot, but Dwer might still buy time for Lena Strong and the urrish chief to work out an accord with Rety's old band ... beating a stealthy retreat to some place where star gods would never find them. A delaying action could be Dwer's last worthwhile service.

'Let's build a fire,' the girl suggested, gesturing toward the beach, littered with driftwood from past storms.

'I was just about to suggest that,' Dwer replied.

She chuckled.

'Yeah, right! Sure you were.'

SARA

At first the ancient tunnel seemed horrid and gloomy. Sara kept imagining a dusty Buyur tube car coming to life, an angry phantom hurtling toward the little horse-drawn wagon, bent on punishing fools who disturbed its ghostly domain. Dread clung fast for a while, making each breath come short and sharp between rapid heartbeats.

But fear has one great enemy, more powerful than confidence or courage.

Tedium.

Chafed from sitting on the bench for miduras, Sara eventually let go of the dismal oppression with a long sigh. She slipped off the wagon to trot alongside – at first only to stretch her legs, but then for longer periods, maintaining a steady jog.

After a while, she even found it enjoyable.

I guess I'm just adapting to the times. There may be no place for intellectuals in the world to come.

Emerson joined her, grinning as he kept pace with long-legged strides. And soon the tunnel began to lose its power over some of the others, as well. The two wagon drivers from the cryptic *Illias* tribe – Kepha and Nuli – grew visibly less tense with each league they progressed toward home.

But where was that?

Sara pictured a map of the Slope, drawing a wide arc roughly south from the Gentt. It offered no clue where a horse clan might stay hidden all this time.

How about in some giant, empty magma chamber, beneath a volcano?

What a lovely thought. Some magical sanctuary of hidden grassy fields, safe from the glowering sky. An underground world, like in a pre-contact adventure tale featuring vast ageless caverns, mystic light sources, and preposterous monsters.

Of course no such place could form under natural laws.

But might the Buyur – or some prior Jijo tenant – have used the same forces that carved this tunnel to create a secret hideaway? A place to preserve treasures while the surface world was scraped clean of sapient-made things?

Sara chuckled at the thought. But she did not dismiss it.

Sometime later, she confronted Kurt.

'Well, I'm committed now. Tell me what's so urgent that Emerson and I had to follow you all this way.'

But the exploser only shook his head, refusing to speak in front of Dedinger.

What's the heretic going to do? Sara thought. *Break his bonds and run back to tell the world?*

The desert prophet's captivity appeared secure. And yet it was disconcerting to see on Dedinger's face an expression of serene confidence, as if present circumstances only justified his cause.

Times like these bring heretics swarming ... like privacy wasps converging on a gossip. We shouldn't be surprised to see fanatics thriving.

The Sacred Scrolls prescribed two ways for Jijo's illegal colonists to ease their inherited burden of sin – by preserving the planet, and by following the Path of Redemption. Ever since the days of Drake and Ur-Chown, the sages had taught that both goals were compatible with commerce and the comforts of daily life. But some purists disagreed, insisting that the Six Races must choose.

We should not be here, proclaimed Lark's faction. *We sooners should use birth control to obey Galactic law, leaving this fallow world in peace. Only then will our sin be healed.*

Others thought redemption should take higher priority.

Each clan should follow the example of glavers, preached Dedinger's cult, and the Urunthai. *Salvation and renewal come to those who remove mental impediments and rediscover their deep natures.*

The first obstacle to eliminate – the anchor weighing down our souls – is knowledge.

Both groups called today's High Sages true heretics, pandering to the masses with their wishy-washy moderation. When dread starships came, fresh converts thronged to purer faiths, preaching simple messages and strong medicine for fearful times.

Sara knew her *own* heresy would not attract disciples. It seemed ill matched to Jijo – a planet of felons destined for oblivion of one sort or another. And yet . .

Everything depends on your point of view.

So taught a wise traeki sage.

we/i/you are oft fooled by the obvious.

LARK

An urrish courier came rushing out of the forest of tall, swaying greatboo.

Could this be my answer already?

Lark had dispatched a militiaman just a few miduras ago, with a message to Lester Cambel in the secret refuge of the High Sages.

But no. The rough-pelted runner had galloped up the long path from Festival Glade. In her rush, she would not even pause for Lark to tap the vein of a tethered simla, offering the parched urs a hospitable cup of steaming blood. Instead, the humans stared amazed as she plunged her fringed muzzle into a bucket of undiluted *water*, barely shuddering at the bitter taste.

Between gasping swallows, she told dire news.

As rumored, the second starship was titanic, squatting like a mountain, blocking the river so a swamp soon formed around the trapped Rothen cruiser, doubly imprisoning Ling's comrades. Surviving witnesses reported seeing familiar outlines framed by the battleship's brightly lit hatchway. Corrugated cones. Stacks of rings, luxuriously glistening.

Only a few onlookers, steeped in ancient legends, knew this was not a good sign, and they had little time to spread a warning before torrid beams sliced through the night, mowing down everything within a dozen arrowflights.

At dawn, brave observers peered from nearby peaks to see a swathe of shattered ground strewn with oily smudges and bloody debris. *A defensive perimeter*, stunned observers suggested, though such prudence seemed excessive for omnipotent star gods.

'What casualties?' asked Jeni Shen, sergeant of Lark's militia contingent, a short, well-muscled woman and a friend of his brother, Dwer. They had all seen flickering lights in the distance, and heard sounds like thunder, but imagined nothing as horrible as the messenger related.

The urs told of hundreds dead ... and that a High Sage of the Commons was among those slaughtered. *Asx* had been standing near a group of curious spectators and confused alien lovers, waiting to parley with the visitors. After the dust and flames settled, the traeki was nowhere to be seen.

The g'Kek doctor tending Uthen expressed the grief they all felt, rolling all four tentacle-like eyes and flailing the ground with his pusher leg. This personified the horror. Asx had been a popular sage, ready to mull over problems posed by any of the Six Races, from marriage counseling to dividing the assets of a bisected qheuen hive. Asx might 'mull' for days, weeks, or a year before giving an answer – or *several* answers, laying out a range of options.

Before the courier departed, Lark's status as a junior sage won him a brief look at the drawings in her dispatch pouch. He showed Ling a sketch of a massive oval ship of space, dwarfing the one that brought her to this world. Her face clouded. The mighty shape was unfamiliar and frightening.

Lark's own messenger – a two-legged human – had plunged into the ranks of towering boo at daybreak, carrying a plea for Lester Cambel to send up Ling's personal Library unit, so she might read the memory bars he and Uthen had found in the wrecked station.

Her offer, made the evening before, was limited to seeking data about plagues, especially the one now sweeping the qheuen community.

'If Ro-kenn truly was preparing genocide agents, he is a criminal by our own law.'

'Even a Rothen master?' Lark had asked skeptically.

'Even so. It is not disloyal for me to find out, or else prove it was not so.'

'However,' she had added, 'don't expect me to help you make war against my crew mates or my patrons. Not that you could do much, now that their guard is raised. You surprised us once with tunnels and gunpowder, destroying a little research base. But you'll find that harming a starship is beyond even your best-equipped zealots.'

That exchange took place before they learned about the second vessel. Before word came that the mighty Rothen cruiser was reduced to a captive toy next to a true colossus from space.

While they awaited Cambel's answer, Lark sent his troopers

sifting through the burned lakeshore thicket, gathering golden preservation beads. Galactic technology had been standardized for millions of years. So there just might be a workable reading unit amid all the pretty junk the magpie spider had collected. Anyway, it seemed worth a try.

While sorting through a pile of amber cocoons, he and Ling resumed their game of cautious question-and-evasion. Circumstances had changed – Lark no longer felt as stupid in her presence – still, it was the same old dance.

Starting off, Ling quizzed him about the Great Printing, the event that transformed Jijo's squabbling coalition of sooner races, even more than the arrival of the Holy Egg. Lark answered truthfully without once mentioning the Biblos Archive. Instead he described the guilds of printing, photocopying, and especially papermaking, with its pounding pulp hammers and pungent drying screens, turning out fine pages under the sharp gaze of his father, the famed Nelo.

'A nonvolatile, randomly accessed, analog memory store that is completely invisible from space. No electricity or digital cognizance to detect from orbit.' She marveled. 'Even when we saw books, we assumed they were hand-copied – hardly a culture-augmenting process. Imagine, a *wolfling* technology proved so effective ... under special circumstances.'

Despite that admission, Lark wondered about the Danik attitude, which seemed all too ready to dismiss the accomplishments of their own human ancestors – except when an achievement could be attributed to Rothen intervention.

It was Lark's turn to ask a question, and he chose to veer onto another track.

'You seemed as surprised as anybody, when the disguise creature crawled off of Ro-pol's face.'

He referred to events just before the Battle of the Glade, when a dead Rothen was seen stripped of its charismatic, symbiotic mask. Ro-pol's eyes, once warm and expressive, had bulged lifeless from a revealed visage that was sharply slanted, almost predatory, and distinctly less humanoid.

Ling had never seen a master so exposed. She reacted to Lark's question cautiously.

'I am not of the Inner Circle.'

'What's that?'

Ling inhaled deeply. 'Rann and Kunn are privy to knowledge about the Rothen that most Daniks never learn. Rann has even been to one of the secret Rothen home sites. Most of us are never so blessed. When not on missions, we dwell with our families in the covered canyons of Poria Outpost, with just a hundred or so of our patrons. Even on Poria, the two races don't mix daily.'

'Still, not to know something so basic about those who claim to be—'

'Oh, one hears rumors. Sometimes you see a Rothen whose face seems odd ... as if part of it was, well, *put on* wrong. Maybe we cooperate with the deception by choosing at some level not to notice. Anyway, that's not the real issue, is it?'

'What *is* the real issue?'

'You imply I should be horrified to learn they wear symbionts to look more humanoid. To appear more beautiful in our eyes. But why *shouldn't* the Rothen use artificial aids, if it helps them serve as better guides, shepherding our race toward excellence?'

Lark muttered, 'How about a little thing called honesty?'

'Do you tell your pet chimp or zookir everything? Don't parents sometimes lie to children for their own good? What about lovers who strive to look nice for each other? Are they dishonest?

'Think, Lark. What are the odds against another race seeming as gloriously beautiful to human eyes as our patrons appear? Oh, part of their attraction surely dates back to early stages of uplift, on Old Earth, when they raised our apelike ancestors almost to full sapiency, before the Great Test began. It may be ingrained at a genetic level ... the way dogs were culled in favor of craving the touch of man.

'Yet, we are still unfinished creatures. Still crudely emotional. Let me ask you, Lark. If *your* job were to uplift flighty, cantankerous beings, and you found that wearing a cosmetic symbiont would make your role as teacher easier, wouldn't you do it?'

Before Lark could answer an emphatic no, she rushed ahead.

'Do not some members of your Six use *rewq* animals for similar ends? Those symbionts that lay their filmy bodies over your eyes, sucking a little blood in exchange for help translating emotions? Aren't rewq a vital part of the complex interplay that is your Commons?'

'Hr-rm.' Lark throat-umbled like a doubtful hoon. 'Rewq don't help us lie. They are not *themselves* lies.'

Ling nodded. 'Still, you never faced a task as hard as the Rothens' – to raise up creatures as brilliant, and disagreeable, as human beings. A race whose capability for future majesty also makes us capricious and dangerous, prone to false turns and deadly errors.'

Lark quashed an impulse to argue. She might only dig in, rationalizing herself into a corner and refusing to come out. At least now she admitted that *one* Rothen might do evil deeds – that Ro-kenn's personal actions might be criminal.

And who knows? That may be all there is to it. The scheming of a rogue individual. Perhaps the race is just as wonderful as she says. Wouldn't it be nice if humanity really had such patrons, and a manifest greatness waiting, beyond the next millennium?

Ling had seemed sincere when she claimed the Rothen ship commander would get to the bottom of things.

'It's imperative to convince your sages they must release the hostage and Ro-pol's body, along with those "photograms" your portraitist took. Blackmail won't work against the Rothen – you must understand this. It's not in their character to respond to threats. Yet the "evidence" you've gathered could do harm in the long run.'

That was before the stunning news – that the Rothen ship was itself captured, encased in a prison of light.

Lark mused over one of the mulc-spider's golden eggs while Ling spoke for a while about the difficult but glorious destiny her masters planned for impulsive, brilliant humanity.

'You know,' he commented. 'There's something screwy about the logic of this whole situation.'

'What do you mean?'

Lark chewed his lip, like an urs wrestling with uncertainty. Then he decided – it was time to bring it all in the open.

'I mean, let's put aside for now the added element of the new starship. The Rothen may have feuds you know nothing about. Or it may be a different gang of gene raiders, come to rob Jijo's biosphere. For all we know, magistrates from the Galactic Migration Institute have brought Judgment Day as foretold in the Scrolls.

'For now, though, let's review what led to the Battle of the Glade – the fight that made you my prisoner. It began when Bloor photo'd the dead Ro-pol without her mask. Ro-kenn went livid, ordering his robots to kill everyone who had seen.

'But didn't you once assure me there was no need to delete local witnesses to your team's visit? That your masters could handle it, even if oral and written legacies survive hundreds or thousands of years, describing a visit by human and Rothen gene raiders?'

'I did.'

'But you admit gene raiding is against Galactic law! I know you feel the Rothen are above such things. Still, they don't want to be caught in the act.

'Let's assume credible testimony, maybe even photos, finally reach Migration Institute inspectors next time they visit Jijo. Testimony about you and Rann and Kunn. *Human* gene raiders. Even I know the rule – "police your own kind" – prevails in the Five Galaxies. Did Ro-kenn explain how the Rothen would prevent sanctions coming down on Earth?'

Ling wore a grim expression. 'You're saying he played us for fools. That he let me spread false assurances among the natives, while planning all along to strew germs and wipe out every witness.'

Obviously it was bitter for her to say it.

Ling seemed surprised when Lark shook his head.

'That's what I thought at first, when qheuens fell sick. But what I now imagine is worse yet.'

That got her attention.

'What could be worse than mass murder? If the charge is proved, Ro-kenn will be hauled off to the home sites in *dolor chains*! He'll be punished as no Rothen has been in ages.'

Lark shrugged. 'Perhaps. But stop and think a bit.'

'First, Ro-kenn wasn't relying on disease alone to do the job.

'Oh, he probably had a whole library of bugs – infectious agents used in past wars in the Five Galaxies. No doubt starfaring qheuens long ago developed countermeasures against the germ raging through Uthen's lymph pipes right now. I'm sure Ro-kenn's concoctions will kill a lot more of us.'

Ling started to protest, but Lark forged ahead.

'Nevertheless, I know a thing or two about how pestilence works in natural ecosystems. It would be a complete fluke for even a string of diseases to wipe out every member of the Six. Random immunities would stymie the best-designed bugs. Furthermore, the sparser the population got, the harder it would be to reach and infect dispersed survivors.

'No, Ro-kenn needed something more. A breakdown of the Commons into total war! A war that could be exploited, pushed to the limits. A struggle so bitter that each race would pursue its victims to the farthest corners of Jijo, willingly helping to spread new parasites in order to slay their foes.'

He saw Ling struggle to find a way around his logic. But she had been present when Ro-kenn's psi-recordings were played – sick dream images, meant to incite fatal grudges among the Six. Those present weren't fooled because they were forewarned but what if the messages had been broadcast as planned ... amplified through the compelling wave forms of the Holy Egg?

'I will tell of this, back home,' she vowed in a low, faint voice. 'He will be punished.'

'That's gratifying,' Lark went on. 'But I'm not finished. You see, even by combining plagues with war, Ro-kenn could never guarantee annihilation of all six races, or eliminate the off chance that credible testimony might be passed down the generations – perhaps stored in some cave – to finally reach Institute prosecutors. On the other hand, he could influence *which* race or sept would be left standing at the end, and which would perish first. There is one, in particular, whose fate he knows well how to manipulate. That one is *Homo sapiens*.

'The way I see it, Ro-kenn's plan had several parts. First, he had to make sure Earthlings were hated. Second, he must weaken the other five races by releasing diseases that could then be blamed on humans. But the ultimate goal was to make sure *humans* went extinct on Jijo. He didn't give a damn if others left a few survivors to tell the tale.'

Ling stared. 'What good would that do? You said testimony might be passed down—'

'Yes, but with Earthlings on Jijo only a hated memory, all history will tell is that once upon a time a ship full of humans came down, stole genes, and tried to kill everybody. No one will bother emphasizing *which* humans did these things.

'In the future – perhaps only a few centuries, if someone plants an anonymous tip – Galactic judges would arrive and hear that people from *Earth* did these dreadful things. *Earth* will bear the full brunt of any sanctions, while the Rothen get off scot-free.'

Ling was silent for a long moment, working her way through his logic. Finally, she looked up with a broad grin.

'You had me worried a minute, but I found the defect in your reasoning!'

Lark tilted his head. 'Do tell.'

'Your diabolical scenario just might make sense, but for two flaws—

'*First* – the Rothen are patrons of all humanity. Earth and her colonies, while presently governed by Darwinist fools on the Terragens Council, still represent the vast majority of our gene pool. The Rothen would never let harm come to our homeworld. Even in the current galactic crisis, they are acting behind the scenes to ensure Earth's safety from the enemies besetting her.'

There it was again ... a reference to dire events happening megaparsecs away. Lark yearned to follow that thread, but Ling continued with her argument.

'Second – let's say Ro-kenn wanted all blame shifted to humans. *Then why did he and Ro-pol emerge from the station and show themselves?* By walking around, letting artists sketch them and scribes take down their words, weren't they jeopardizing the Rothen to the same eyewitness accounts you say could damage Earth?'

Ling seemed ready to accept that her immediate boss might be criminal or insane, but with bulwarks of logic she defended her patron race. Lark had mixed feelings about demolishing such faith. He, too, had his heresies.

'I'm sorry, Ling, but my scenario still stands.

'Your first point only has validity *if it is true that the Rothen are our patrons*. I know that's the central premise around which you were raised, but believing does not make it so. You admit your people, the Daniks, are small in number, live on an isolated outpost, and see just a few Rothen. Putting aside mythic fables about ancient visitors and Egyptian pyramids, all you really have is their word regarding a supposed relationship with our race. One that may simply be a hoax.

'As for your second point, just look back at the way events unfolded. Ro-kenn surely knew he was being sketched when he emerged that evening, using his charisma on the crowd and planting seeds of dissension. After living so long together, all six races are affected by each other's standards of beauty, and the Rothen were indeed beautiful!

'Ro-kenn may even have known we had the ability to etch our drawings onto durable plates. Later, when he saw Bloor's *first* set of photographic images, he hardly batted an eye. Oh, he pretended to dicker with the sages, but you and I could both tell he was unafraid of the "proof" being used to blackmail him. He was only buying time till the ship returned. And it might have worked – if Bloor hadn't uncovered and recorded Ro-pol's corpse, bare and unmasked. *That's* when Ro-kenn went hysterically murderous, ordering a massacre!'

'I know.' Ling shook her head. 'It was madness. But you must understand. Disturbing the dead is very serious. It must have pushed him over the edge—'

'Over the edge, my left hind hoof! He knew exactly what he was doing. Think, Ling. Suppose someday Institute observers see photos showing humans, *and a bunch of very humanlike beings nobody ever heard of*, committing crimes on Jijo. Could such crude pictures ever really implicate the Rothen?

'Perhaps they might, *if that's what Rothen looked like*. But till Bloor shot Ro-pol's naked face, our crude images posed no threat to Rothen security. Because in a century or two those facial disguise symbionts won't exist anymore, and no one alive will know that Rothen ever looked like that.'

'What are you talking about? Every Danik grows up seeing Rothen as they appear with symbionts on. Obviously there will be people around who know ...'

Her voice faded. She stared at Lark, unblinking. 'You can't mean—'

'Why not? After long association with your people, I'm sure they've acquired the necessary means. Once humans are of no further use as front men for their schemes, your "patrons" will simply use a wide spectrum of tailored viruses to wipe out every Danik, just as they planned to eliminate humans on Jijo.

'For that matter, once they've tested it on both our peoples, they'll be in a good position to sell such a weapon to Earth's enemies. After all, once our race goes extinct, who will protest our innocence? Who will bother to look for other suspects in a series of petty felonies that were committed, all over the Five Galaxies, by groups of bipeds looking a lot like—'

'Enough!' Ling shouted, standing suddenly, spilling gold cocoons from her lap. She backed away, hyperventilating.

Unrelenting, he stood and followed.

'I've thought about little else since we left the Glade. And it all makes sense. Even down to the way the Rothen won't let your kind use neural taps.'

'I told you before. It's forbidden because the taps might drive us mad!'

'Really? Why do the Rothen themselves have them? Because they're more highly evolved?' Lark snorted. 'Anyway, I hear that nowadays humans elsewhere use them effectively.'

'How do you know what humans elsewhere—'

Lark hurriedly cut her off.

'The truth is, the Rothen can't risk letting their pet humans make direct mind-computer links, because someday one of you Daniks might bypass sanitized consoles, draw on the Great Library directly, and figure out how you've been pawns—'

Ling backed away another pace. 'Please, Lark ... I don't want to do this anymore.'

He felt an impulse to stop, to take pity. But he quashed it. This had to come out, all of it.

'I must admit it's quite a scam, using humans as front men for gene theft and other crimes. Even two centuries ago, when the *Tabernacle* departed, our race had a vile reputation as one of the lowest-ranking citizen tribes in the Five Galaxies. So-called *wolflings*, with no ancient clan to stand up for us. If anybody gets caught, we'll make perfect patsies. The Rothen scheme is clever. The real question is, why would any humans let themselves be used that way?

'History may hold the answer, Ling. According to our texts, humans suffered from a major inferiority complex at the time of contact, when our primitive canoe-spacecraft stumbled onto a towering civilization of star gods. Your ancestors and mine chose different ways of dealing with the complex, each of them grasping at straws, seeking any excuse for hope.

'The *Tabernacle* colonists dreamed of escaping to some place out of sight of bureaucrats and mighty Galactic clans – a place to breed freely and fulfill the old romance of colonizing a frontier. In contrast, your Danik forebears rushed to embrace a tall tale they were told by a band of smooth talkers. A flattering fable that indulged their wounded pride, promising a grand *destiny* for certain chosen humans and their descendants ... providing they did exactly as they were told. Even if it meant raising their children to be shills and sneak thieves in service to a pack of galactic gangsters.'

Tremors rocked Ling as she held up one hand, palm out, at the end of a rigid arm, as if trying physically to stave off any more words.

'I asked ... you to stop,' she repeated, and seemed to have trouble breathing. Pain melted her face.

Now Lark did shut up. He had gone too far, even in the name of truth. Raggedly, trying to maintain some remnant of her dignity, Ling swiveled and strode off to the acrid lake that lay below a boulder field of tumbled Buyur ruins.

Does anybody like having their treasured worldview torn away? Lark mused, watching Ling hurl stones into the caustic pond. *Most of us would reject all the proof in the cosmos before considering that our own beliefs might be wrong.*

But the scientist in her won't let her dismiss evidence so easily. She has to face facts, like them or not.

The habit of truth is hard to learn, and a mixed blessing. It leaves no refuge when a new truth comes along that hurts.

Lark knew his feelings were hardly a testament to clarity. Anger roiled, mixed with shame that he could not hold on to the purity of his own convictions. There was childish satisfaction from upsetting Ling's former smug superiority ... and chagrin at finding such a motive smoldering inside. Lark enjoyed being right, though it might be better, this time, if he turned out to be wrong.

Just when I had her respecting me as an equal, and maybe starting to like me, that's when I have to go stomping through her life, smashing idols she was raised to worship, showing off the bloodstained hands of her gods.

You may win an argument, boy. You may even convince her. But could anyone fully forgive you for doing something like that?

He shook his head over how much he might have just thrown away, all for the torrid pleasure of harsh honesty.

Do not be afraid, my lesser parts.

The sensations you feel may seem like coercive pain, but they convey a kind of *love* that will grow dear to you, with time. I am part of you now, one with you. I will never do anything to cause us harm, so long as this alliance serves a function.

Go ahead, stroke the wax if you wish, for the old ways of memory still have lesser uses (so long as they serve My purpose). Play over recent images so we may recall together events leading to our new union. Re-create the scene perceived by *Asx*, staring up in awe, watching the great Jophur warship, *Polkjhy*, swoop from the sky, taking the pirates captive, then landing in this tortured valley. Poor, loosely joined, scatterbrained Asx – did you/we not stare in tremulous fear?

Yes, I can stroke another driving motivation. One that kept you admirably unified, despite swirling dread. It was a cloying sense of *duty*. Duty to the not-self community of half beings you call the Commons.

As Asx, your stack planned to speak for the Commons. Asx expected to face star-traveling humans, along with creatures known as 'Rothen.' But then *Jophur* forms were seen through our ship ports!

After some hesitation, did you not turn at last and try to flee?

How *slow* this stack was before the change! When knives of fire lanced forth from this mighty vessel, how did you react to the maelstrom of destruction? To hot ravening beams that tore through wood, stone, and flesh but always spared this pile of aged rings? Had you then possessed the bright new running legs we now wear, you might have thrown yourselves into that roaring calamity. But Asx was slow, too slow even to shelter nearby comrades with its traeki bulk.

All died, except this stack.

ARE YOU NOT PROUD?

The *next* ray from the ship seized this multistriped cone, lifting it into the night air, sweeping the fatty rings toward doors that gaped to receive them.

Oh, how well Asx spoke then, despite the confusion! With surprising coherence for a stack without a master, tapping waxy streaks of eloquence, Asx pleaded, cajoled, and reasoned with the enigmatic creatures who peered from behind glaring lights.

Finally, these beings glided forward. The starship's hold filled with Asx's ventings of horrified dread.

How unified you were, My rings! The testimony of the wax is clear. At that moment, you were one as never before.

United in shared dismay to see those cousin toroids your ancestors sought to escape, many cycles ago.

We Jophur, the mighty and fulfilled.

DWER

The robot proved useful at heaping driftwood onto the seaside shoulder of a high dune overlooking the Rift. Without rest or pause, it dumped a load then scurried for more, in whatever direction Rety indicated with an outstretched arm. The Danik machine seemed willing to obey once more – so long as her orders aimed toward a reunion with Kunn.

Such single-minded devotion to its master reminded Dwer of Earth stories about dogs – tales his mother read aloud when he was small. It struck him odd that the *Tabernacle* colonists brought horses, donkeys, and chimps, but no canines.

Lark or Sara might know why.

That was Dwer's habitual thought, encountering something he didn't understand. Only now it brought a pang, knowing he might never see his brother and sister again.

Maybe Kunn won't kill me outright. He might bring me home in chains, instead, before the Rothens wipe out the Six Races to cover their tracks.

That was the terrible fate the High Sages foresaw for Jijo's fallen settlers, and Dwer figured they ought to know. He recalled Lena Strong musing about what means the aliens might use to perform their genocide. With gruesome relish, Lena kept topping herself during the long hike east from the Rimmer Range. Would the criminal star gods wash the Slope with fire, scouring it from the glaciers to the sea? Would they melt the ice caps and bring an end by drowning? Her morbid speculations were like a fifth companion as Dwer guided two husky women and a lesser sage past a thousand leagues of poison grass all the way to the Gray Hills, in a forlorn bid to safeguard a fragment of human civilization on Jijo.

Dwer had last glimpsed Jenin, Lena, and Danel during the brief fight near the huts of Rety's home clan. This same robot cut poor Danel down with lethal rays, instants before its own weapons pod was destroyed.

Indeed, the battle drone was no dog to be tamed or befriended.

Nor would it show gratitude for the times Dwer helped it cross rivers, anchoring its fields to ground through the conduit of his body.

Mudfoot was hardly any better a comrade. The lithe noor beast swiftly grew bored with wood-gathering chores, and scampered off instead to explore the tide line, digging furiously where bubbles revealed a buried hive of sand clamettes. Dwer looked forward to roasting some ... until he saw that Mudfoot was cracking and devouring every one, setting none aside for the humans.

As useful as a noor, he thought, quashing stings of hunger as he hoisted another bundle of twisty driftwood slabs, digging his moccasins into the sandy slope.

Dwer tried to remain optimistic.

Maybe Kunn will feed me, before attaching the torture machines.

yee stood proudly atop the growing woodpile. The diminutive urrish male called directions in a piping voice, as if mere humans could never manage a *proper* fire without urrish supervision. Rety's 'husband' hissed disappointment over Dwer's poor contribution – as if being wounded, starved, and dragged across half of Jijo in a robot's claws did not excuse much. Dwer ignored yee's reprimand, dumping his load then stepping over to the dune's seaward verge, shading his eyes in search of Kunn's alien scoutship.

He spied it far away, a silvery bead, cruising back and forth above the deep blue waters of the Rift. At intervals, something small and glittering would fall from the slender spacecraft. *An explosive*, Dwer supposed, for about twenty duras after each canister struck the water, the sea abruptly *bulged* and foamed white. Sometimes a sharp, almost musical tone reached shore.

According to Rety, Kunn was trying to force something – or somebody – out of hiding.

I hope you miss, Dwer thought ... though the star pilot might be in a better mood toward prisoners if his hunt went well.

'I wonder what Jass has been tellin' Kunn, all this time,' Rety worried aloud, joining Dwer at the crest. 'What if they become pals?'

Dwer waited as the robot dropped another cargo of wood and went off for more. Then he replied.

'Have you changed your mind? We could still try to escape. Take out the robot. Avoid Kunn. Go our own way.'

Rety smiled with surprising warmth.

'Why, Dwer, is that a whatchamacallum? *A proposal*? What'll we do? Make our own little sooner clan, here on the wind barrens? Y'know I already *have* one husban' and I need his p'rmission to add another.'

Actually he had envisioned trying to make it back to the Gray Hills, where Lena and Jenin could surely use a hand. Or else, if that way seemed too hard and Rety rigidly opposed returning to the tribe she hated, they might strike out west and reach the Vale in a month or two, if the foraging was good along the way.

Rety went on, with more edge in her voice.

'B'sides, I still have my eye set on an apart'mint on Poria Outpost. Like the one Besh an' Ling showed me a picture of, with a *bal-co-ny*, an' a bed made o' cloud stuff. I figure it'll be just a *bit* more comfy than scratchin' out the rest of my days here with savages.'

Dwer shrugged. He hadn't expected her to agree. As a 'savage,' he had reasons of his own for going ahead with the bonfire to attract Kunn's attention.

'Well, anyway, I don't suppose the bot would let its guard down a second time.'

'It was lucky to survive doin' it around you once.'

Dwer took a moment to realize she had just paid him a compliment. He cherished its uniqueness, knowing he might never hear another.

The moment of unaccustomed warmth was broken when something massive abruptly streaked by, so fast that its air wake shoved both humans to the ground. Dwer's training as a tracker let him follow the blurry object ... to the top of a nearby dune, which erupted in a gushing spray of sand.

It was the *robot*, he realized, *digging* with furious speed. In a matter of heartbeats it made a hole that it then dived within, aiming its remaining sensor lens south and west.

'Come on!' Dwer urged, grabbing his bow and quiver. Rety paused only to snatch up a wailing, hissing yee. Together they fled some distance downslope, where Dwer commenced digging with both hands.

Long ago, Fallon the Scout had taught him – *If you don't know what's happening in a crisis, mimic a creature who does*. If the robot felt a sudden need to hide, Dwer thought it wise to follow.

'Ifni!' Rety muttered. 'Now what in hell's he doin'?'

She was still standing – staring across the Rift. Dwer yanked her into the hole beside him. Only when sand covered most of their bodies did he poke his head back out to look.

The Danik pilot clearly felt something was wrong. The little craft hurtled toward shore, diving as it came. *Seeking cover*, Dwer thought. *Maybe it can dig underground like the robot*.

Dwer started turning, to spot whatever had Kunn in such a panic, but just then the boat abruptly veered, zigzagging frantically.

From its tail bright fireballs arced, like sparks leaping off a burning log. They flared brightly and made the air *waver* in a peculiar way, blurring the escaping vessel's outlines.

From behind Dwer, streaks of fierce light flashed overhead toward the fleeing boat. Most deflected through warped zones, veering off course, but one bypassed the glowing balls, striking target.

At the last moment, Kunn flipped his nimble ship around and fired back at his assailants, launching a return volley just as the unerring missile closed in.

Dwer shoved Rety's head down and closed his eyes.

The detonations were less Jijo-shattering than he expected – a series of dull concussions, almost anticlimactic.

Looking up with sand-covered faces, they witnessed both winner and loser in the brief battle of god chariots.

Kunn's boat had crashed beyond the dune field, plowing into a marshy fen. Smoke boiled from its shattered rear.

Circling above, the victor regarded its victim, glistening with a silvery tint that seemed less metallic than *crystal*. The newcomer was bigger and more powerful looking than the Danik scout.

Kunn never stood a chance.

Rety muttered, her voice barely audible.

'She *said* there'd turn out to be someone stronger.'

Dwer shook his head. 'Who?'

'That smelly old urs! Leader o' those four-legged sooners, back in the village pen. Said the Rothen might be a-feared of somebody bigger. So she was right.'

'*urs* smelly?' yee objected. 'you wife should talk?'

Rety stroked the little male as yee stretched his neck, fluting a contented sigh.

The fallen scout boat rocked from a new explosion, this one brightly framing a rectangle in the ship's side. That section fell and two bipeds followed, leaping into the bog, chased by smoke that boiled from the interior. Staggering through murky water, the men leaned on each other to reach a weedy islet, where they fell, exhausted.

The newcomer ship cruised a wary circle, losing altitude. As it turned, Dwer saw a stream of pale smoke pouring from a gash in its other side. A roughness to the engine sound grew steadily worse. Soon, the second cruiser settled down near the first.

Well, it looks like Kunn got in a lick of his own.

Dwer wondered – *Now why should that make me feel glad?*

Bone-rattling concussions grew more terrifying with each dura, hammering our undersea prison refuge, sometimes receding for a while, then returning with new force, making it hard for a poor hoon to stand properly on the shuddering floor.

Crutches and a back brace didn't help, nor the little autoscribe, fogging the room with my own projected words. Stumbling through them, I sought some solid object to hold, while the scribe kept adding to the mob of words, recording my frantic curses in Anglic and GalSeven. When I found a wall stanchion, I grabbed for dear life. The clamor of reverberating explosions sounded like a giant, bearing down with massive footsteps, nearer ... ever nearer ...

Then, as I feared some popping seam would let in the dark, heavy waters of the Midden ... it abruptly stopped.

Silence was almost as disorienting as the jeekee awful noise. My throat sac blatted uselessly while a hysterical Huphu clawed my shoulders, shredding scales into torglike ribbons.

Fortunately, hoon don't have much talent for panic. Maybe our reactions are too slow, or else we lack imagination.

As I was gathering my wits, the door hatch opened and one of the little amphibian types rushed in, squeaking a few rapid phrases in simplified GalTwo.

A summons. The spinning voice wanted us for another powwow.

'Perhaps we should share knowledge,' it said when the four of us (plus Huphu) were assembled.

Huck and Pincer-Tip, able to look all ways at once, shared meaningful glances with Ur-ronn and me. We were pretty rattled by the recent booming and shaking. Even growing up next to a volcano had never prepared us for that!

The voice seemed to come from a space where abstract lines curled in tight patterns, but I knew that was an illusion. The shapes and sounds were projections, sent by some entity whose real body lay elsewhere, beyond the walls. I kept expecting Huphu to dash off and tear away a curtain, exposing a little man in an emerald carnival suit.

Do they think we're rubes, to fall for such a trick?

'Knowledge?' Huck sneered, drawing three eyes back like coiled snakes. 'You want to *share* some knowledge? Then tell us what's going on! I thought this place was breaking up! Was it a quake? Are we being sucked into the Midden?'

'I assure you, that is not happening,' came the answer in smooth-toned GalSix. *'The source of our mutual concern lies above, not below.'*

'Exflosions,' Ur-ronn muttered, blowing through her snout fringe and stamping a hind hoof. 'Those weren't quakes, vut underwater detonations. Clean, sharf, and very close. I'd say soneone uf there doesn't like you guys very nuch.'

Pincer hissed sharply and I stared at our urrish friend, but the spinning voice conceded.

'That is an astute guess.'

I couldn't tell if it was impressed, or just sarcastic.

'And since our local guild of exflosers could hardly achieve such feats, this suggests you have other, fowerful foes, far greater than we feevle Six.'

'Again, a reasonable surmise. Such a bright young lady.'

'Hr-rm,' I added, in order not to be left out of the sardonic abuse. 'We're taught that the simplest hypothesis should always be tried first. So let me guess – you're being hunted by the same folks who landed a while back in the Festival Glade. Those *gene raiders* Uriel got word about before we left. Is that it?'

'A goodly conjecture, and possibly even true ... though it could as easily be someone else.'

'Someone else? What're you say-ay-aying?' Pincer-Tip demanded, raising three legs and teetering dangerously on the remaining two. His chitin skin flared an anxious crimson shade. 'That the eatees-tees-tees on the Glade might not be the only ones? That you've got whole *passels* of enemies?'

Abstract patterns tightened to a tornado of meshing lines as silence reigned. Little Huphu, who had seemed fascinated by the voice from the very start, now dug her claws in my shoulder, transfixed by the tight spiral form.

Huck demanded, in a hushed tone.

'How many enemies have you guys *got*?'

When the voice spoke again, all sardonic traces were gone. Its tone seemed deeply weary.

'Ah, dear children. It seems that half of the known sidereal universe has spent years pursuing us.'

Pincer clattered his claws and Huck let out a low, mournful sigh. My own dismal contemplation-umble roused Huphu from her trancelike fixation on the whirling display, and she chittered nervously.

Ur-ronn simply grunted, as if she had expected this, vindicating her native urrish cynicism. After all, when things seem unable to get any worse, isn't that when they nearly always do? Ifni has a fertile, if nasty imagination. The goddess of fate keeps shaving new faces on her infinite-sided dice.

*

'Well, I guess this means – hrm-m – that we can toss out all those ideas about you phuvnthus being ancient Jijoans, or native creatures of the deep.'

'Or remnants of cast-off Buyur machines,' Huck went on. 'Or sea monsters.'

'Yeah,' Pincer added, sounding disappointed. 'Just another bunch of crazy Galactics-tic-tics.'

The swirling patterns seemed confused. *'You would prefer sea monsters?'*

'Forget it,' Huck said. 'You wouldn't understand.'

The patterns bent and swayed.

'I am afraid you may be right about that. Your small band of comrades has us terribly perplexed. So much that a few of us posed a sly scenario – that you were planted in our midst to sow confusion.'

'How do you mean?'

'Your values, beliefs, and evident mutual affection contribute to undermining assumptions we regarded as immutably anchored in the nature of reality.

'Mind you, this confusion is not wholly unpleasant. As a thinking entity, one of my prime motives might be called a lust for surprise. And those I work with are hardly less bemused by the unforeseen marvel of your fellowship.'

'Glad you find us entertaining,' Huck commented, as dryly sarcastic as the voice had been. 'So you guys came here to hide, like our ancestors?'

'There are parallels. But our plan was never to stay. Only to make repairs, gather stores, and wait in concealment for a favorable window at the nearest transfer point.'

'So Uriel and the sages may be wrong about the ship that came to the Glade? Being a gang of gene raiders – that could just be a cover story. Are you the real cause of our troubles?'

'Trouble is synonymous with being a metabolizing entity. Or else why have you young adventurers sought it so avidly?

'But your complaint has merit. We thought we had eluded all pursuit. The ship that landed in the mountains may be coincidental, or attracted by a confluence of unlucky factors. In any event, had we known of your existence, we would have sought shelter somewhere off-planet instead, perhaps in a dead city on one of your moons, though such places are less convenient for effecting repairs.'

That part I had trouble believing. I'm just an ignorant savage, but from the classic scientific romances I grew up reading, I could picture working in some lunar ghost town like my nicknamesake, waking mighty engines that had slept for ages. What kind of starfaring beings would find darkness and salt water more 'convenient' than clean vacuum?

We lapsed into moody silence, unable to stay outraged at folks who accept responsibility so readily. Anyway, weren't they fellow refugees from Galactic persecution?

Or from justice, came another, worried thought.

'Can you tell us why everyone's so mad at you?' I asked.

The spinning figure turned into a narrow, whirling funnel whose small end seemed diminished and very far away.

'Like you, we delved and probed into unvisited places, imagining ourselves bold explorers ...,' the voice explained in tones of boundless sadness. *'Until we had the misfortune to find the very thing we sought. Unexpected wonders beyond our dreams.'*

'Breaking no law, we planned only to share what we had found. But those pursuing us abandoned all pretense of legality. Like giants striving over possession of a gnat, they war lustily, battling each other for a chance to capture us! Alas, whoever wins our treasure will surely use it against multitudes.'

Again, we stared. Pincer unleashed awed whispers from all vents at once.

'Tr-tr-treasure-ure-ure ... ?'

Huck wheeled close to the spinning pattern. 'Can you prove what you just said?'

'Not at this time. Not without putting our people in more danger than they already are.'

I recall wondering – what could be more dangerous than the genocide Uriel had spoken of, as one likely outcome of contact with gene raiders?

'Nevertheless,' the voice continued, *'it may prove possible to improve our level of mutual confidence. Or even help each other in significant ways.'*

SARA

Suppose the world's two most careful observers witnessed the same event. They would never agree precisely on what had happened. Nor could they go back and check. Events may be recorded, but the past can't be replayed.

And the future is even more nebulous – a territory we make up stories about, mapping strategies that never go as planned.

Sara's beloved equations, derived from pre-contact works of

ancient Earth, depicted time as a dimension, akin to the several axes of space. Galactic experts ridiculed this notion, calling the relativistic models of Einstein and others 'naive.' Yet Sara knew the expressions contained truth. They *had to*. They were too beautiful not to be part of universal design.

That contradiction drew her from mathematics to questions of language – how speech constrains the mind, so that some ideas come easily, while others can't even be expressed. Earthling tongues – Anglic, Rossic, and Nihanic – seemed especially prone to paradoxes, tautologies, and 'proofs' that sound convincing but run counter to the real world.

But chaos had also crept into the Galactic dialects used by Jijo's other exile races, even before Terran settlers came. To some Biblos linguists, this was evidence of devolution, starfaring sophistication giving way to savagery, and eventually to proto-sapient grunts. But last year another explanation occurred to Sara, based on pre-contact information theory. An insight so intriguing that she left Biblos to work on it.

Or was I just looking for an excuse to stay away?

After Joshu died of the pox – and her mother of a stroke – research in an obscure field seemed the perfect refuge. Perched in a lonely tree house, with just Prity and her books for company, Sara thought herself sealed off from the world's intrusions.

But the universe has a way of crashing through walls.

Sara glanced at Emerson's glistening dark skin and robust smile, warmed by feelings of affection and accomplishment. Aside from his muteness, the starman scarcely resembled the shattered wreck she had found in the mulc swamp near Dolo and nursed back from near death.

Maybe I should quit my intellectual pretensions and stick with what I'm good at. If the Six Races fell to fighting among themselves, there would be more need of nurses than theoreticians.

So her thoughts spun on, chaotically orbiting the thin glowing line down the center of the tunnel. A line that never altered as they trudged on. Its changelessness rebuked Sara for her private heresy, the strange, blasphemous belief that she held, perhaps alone among all Jijoans.

The quaint notion of progress.

Out of breath after another run, she climbed back aboard the wagon to find Prity chuffing nervously. Sara reached over to check the little chimp's wound, but Prity wriggled free, clambering atop the bench seat, hissing through bared teeth as she peered ahead.

The drivers were in commotion, too. Kepha and Nuli inhaled

with audible sighs. Sara took a deep breath and found her head awash with contrasts. The bucolic smell of *meadows* mixed with a sharp metallic tang ... something utterly alien. She stood up with the backs of her knees braced against the seat.

Was that a hint of light, where the center stripe met its vanishing point?

Soon a pale glow *was* evident. Emerson flipped his rewq over his eyes, then off again.

'Uncle, wake up!' Jomah shook Kurt's shoulder. 'I think we're there!'

But the glow remained vague for a long time. Dedinger muttered impatiently, and for once Sara agreed with him. Expectation of journey's end made the tunnel's remnant almost unendurable.

The horses sped without urging, as Kepha and Nuli rummaged beneath their seats and began passing out dark glasses. Only Emerson was exempted, since his rewq made artificial protection unnecessary. Sara turned the urrish-made spectacles in her hand.

I guess daylight will seem unbearably bright for a time, after we leave this hole. Still, any discomfort would be brief until their eyes readapted to the upper world. The precaution seemed excessive.

At last we'll find out where the horse clan hid all these years. Eagerness blended with sadness, for no reality – not even some god wonder of the Galactics – could compare with the fanciful images found in pre-contact tales.

A mystic portal to some parallel reality? A kingdom floating in the clouds?

She sighed. *It's probably just some out-of-the-way mountain valley where neighboring villagers are too inbred and ignorant to know the difference between a donkey and a horse.*

The ancient transitway began to rise. The stripe grew dim as illumination spread along the walls, like liquid trickling from some reservoir, far ahead. Soon the tunnel began taking on texture. Sara made out shapes. Jagged outlines.

Blinking dismay, she realized they were plunging toward sets of triple *jaws*, like a giant urrish mouth lined with teeth big enough to spear the wagon whole!

Sara took her cue from the Illias. Kepha and Nuli seemed unruffled by the serrated opening. Still, even when she saw the teeth were *metal* – corroded with flaking rust – Sara could hardly convince herself it was only a dead machine.

A huge Buyur thing.

She had never seen its like. Nearly all the great buildings and devices of the meticulous Buyur had been hauled to sea during their final years on Jijo, peeling whole cities and seeding mulc-spiders to eat what remained.

So why didn't the deconstructors carry this thing away?

Behind the massive jaws lay disks studded with shiny stones that Sara realized were diamonds as big as her head. The wagon track went from smooth to bumpy as Kepha maneuvered the team along a twisty trail through the great machine's gullet, zigzagging around the huge disks.

At once Sara realized—

This is *a deconstructor! It must have been demolishing the tunnel when it broke down.*

I wonder why no one ever bothered to repair or haul it away.

Then Sara saw the reason.

Lava.

Tongues and streamlets of congealed basalt protruded through a dozen cracks, where they hardened in place half a million years ago. *It was caught by an eruption.*

Much later, teams of miners from some of the Six Races must have labored to clear a narrow path through the belly of the dead machine, chiseling out the last stretch separating the tunnel from the surface. Sara saw marks of crude pickaxes. And explosives must have been used, as well. That could explain the guild's knowledge of this place.

Sara wanted to gauge Kurt's reaction, but just then the glare brightened as the team rounded a final sharp bend, climbing a steep ramp toward a maelstrom of light.

Sara fumbled for her glasses as the world exploded with color.

Swirling colors that stabbed. Colors that shrieked.

Colors that *sang* with melodies so forceful that her ears throbbed.

Colors that made her nose twitch and skin prickle with sensations just short of pain. A gasping moan lifted in unison from the passengers, as the wagon crested a short rise to reveal surroundings more foreign than the landscape of a dream.

Even with the dark glasses in place, each peak and valley shimmered more pigments than Sara could name.

In a daze, she sorted her impressions. To one side protruded the mammoth deconstructor, a snarl of slumped metal, drowned in ripples of frozen magma. Ripples that extended to the far horizon – layer after layer of radiant stone.

At last she knew the answer to her question.

Where on the Slope could a big secret remain hidden for a century or more?

Even Dedinger, prophet of the sharp-sand desert, moaned aloud at how obvious it was.

They were in the last place on Jijo anyone would go looking for people.

The very center of the Spectral Flow.

IV

FROM THE NOTES OF GILLIAN BASKIN

I wish I could introduce myself to Alvin. I feel I already know the lad, from reading his journal and eavesdropping on conversations among his friends.

Their grasp of twenty-third-century Anglic idiom is so perfect, and their eager enthusiasm so different from the hoons and urs I met before coming to Jijo, that half the time I almost forget I'm listening to aliens. That is, if I ignore the weird speech tones and inflections they take for granted.

Then one of them comes up with a burst of eerily skewed logic that reminds me these aren't just human kids after all, dressed up in Halloween suits to look like a crab, a centaur, and a squid in a wheelchair.

Passing the time, they wondered (and I could not blame them) whether they were prisoners or guests in this underwater refuge. Speculation led to a wide-ranging discussion, comparing various famous captives of literature. Among their intriguing perceptions – Ur-ronn sees *Richard II* as the story of a legitimate business takeover, with Bolingbroke as the king's authentic apprentice.

The red qheuen, Pincer-Tip, maintains that the hero of the *Feng Ho* chronicles was kept in the emperor's harem against his will, even though he had access to the Eight Hundred Beauties and could leave at any time.

Finally, Huck declared it frustrating that Shakespeare spent so little time dealing with Macbeth's evil wife, especially her attempt to escape sin by finding redemption in a presapient state. Huck has ideas for a sequel describing the lady's 'reuplift from the fallow condition.' Her ambitious work would be no less than a morality tale about betrayal and destiny in the Five Galaxies!

Beyond these singular insights, I am struck that here on Jijo an illiterate community of castaways was suddenly flooded with written lore provided by human settlers. What an ironic reversal of Earth's situation, with our own native culture nearly overwhelmed by exposure to the Great Galactic Library. Astonishingly, the Six Races seem to have adapted with vitality and confidence, if Huck and Alvin are at all representative.

I wish their experiment well.

Admittedly, I still have trouble understanding their religion. The concept of redemption through *devolution* is one they seem to take for granted, yet its attraction eludes me.

To my surprise, our ship's doctor said she understands the concept, quite well.

'Every dolphin grows up feeling the call,' Makanee told me. 'In sleep, our minds still roam the vast songscape of the Whale Dream. It beckons us to return to our basic nature, whenever the stress of sapiency becomes too great.'

This dolphin crew has been under pressure for three long years. Makanee's staff must care for over two dozen patients who are already 'redeemed,' as a Jijoan would put it. These dolphins have 'reclaimed their basic nature' all right. In other words, we have lost them as comrades and skilled colleagues, as surely as if they died.

Makanee fights regression wherever she finds symptoms, and yet she remains philosophical. She even offers a theory to explain why the idea revolts me so.

She put it something like so—

'PERHAPS you humans dread this life avenue because your race had to work for sapiency, earning it for yourself the hard way across thousands of bleak generations.

'We fins – and these urs and qheuens and hoons, and every other Galactic clan – all had the gift handed to us by some race that came before. You can't expect us to hold on to it quite as tenaciously as you, who had to struggle so desperately for the same prize.

'The attraction of this so-called Redemption Path may be a bit like ditching school. There's something alluring about the notion of letting go, shucking the discipline and toil of maintaining a rigorous mind. If you slack off, so what? Your descendants will get another chance. A fresh start on the upward road of uplift, with new patrons to show you the way.'

I asked Makanee if she found that part of it especially appealing. The idea of new patrons. Would dolphins be better off with different sponsors than *Homo sapiens*?

She laughed and expressed her answer in deliciously ambiguous Trinary.

    * When winter sends ice
        * Growling across northern seas
            * Wimps love the gulf stream! *

Makanee's comment made me ponder again the question of human origins.

On Earth, most people seem willing to suspend judgment on the question of whether our species had help from genetic meddlers, before the age of science and then contact. Stubborn Darwinists still present a strong case, but few have the guts to insist Galactic experts are wrong when they claim, with eons of experience, that the sole route to sapiency is Uplift. Many Terran citizens take their word for it.

So the debate rages – on popular media shows and in private arguments among humans, dolphins, and chims – about who our absent patrons might have been. At last count there were six dozen candidates – from Tuvallians and Lethani all the way to Sun Ghosts and time travelers from some bizarre Nineteenth Dimension.

While a few dolphins do believe in missing patrons, a majority are like Makanee. They hold that we humans must have done it ourselves, struggling against darkness without the slightest intervention by outsiders.

How did Captain Creideiki put it, once? Oh yes.

'THERE are racial memories, Tom and Gill. Recollections that can be accessed through deep keeneenk meditation. One particular image comes down from our dreamlike legends – of an apelike creature paddling to sea on a tree trunk, proudly proclaiming that he had carved it, all by himself, with a stone ax, and demanding congratulations from an indifferent cosmos.

'Now I ask you, would any decent patron let its client act in such a way? A manner that made you look so ridiculous?

'No. From the beginning we could tell that you humans were being raised by amateurs. By yourselves.'

AT least that's how I remember Creideiki's remark. Tom found it hilarious, but I recall suspecting that our captain was withholding part of the story . There was more, that he was saving for another time.

Only another time never came.

Even as we dined with Creideiki that evening, Streaker was wriggling her way by an obscure back route into the Shallow Cluster.

A day or two later everything changed.

IT'S late and I should finish these notes. Try to catch some sleep.

Hannes reports mixed results from engineering. He and Karkaett found a way to remove some of the carbon coating from Streaker's hull, but a more thorough job would only wind up damaging our already weak flanges, so that's out for now.

On the other hand, the control parameters I hoaxed out of the Library cube enabled Suessi's crew to bring a couple of these derelict 'dross' starships back to life! They're still junk, or else the Buyur would have taken them along when they left. But immersion in icy water appears to have made little difference since then. Perhaps some use might be found for one or two of the hulks. Anyway, it gives the engineers something to do.

We need distraction, now that Streaker seems to be trapped once more. Galactic cruisers have yet again chased us down to a far corner of the universe, coveting our lives and our secrets.

How?

I've pondered this over and over. How did they follow our trail?

The course past Izmunuti seemed well hidden. Others made successful escapes this way before. The ancestors of the Six Races, for instance.

It should have worked.

ACROSS this narrow room, I stare at a small figure in a centered spotlight. My closest companion since Tom went away .

Herbie.

Our prize from the Shallow Cluster.

Bearer of hopes and evil luck.

Was there a curse on the vast fleet of translucent vessels we discovered at that strange dip in space? When Tom found a way through their shimmering fields and snatched Herb as a souvenir, did he bring back a jinx that will haunt us until we put the damned corpse back in its billion-year-old tomb?

I used to find the ancient mummy entrancing. Its hint of a humanoid smile seemed almost whimsical.

But I've grown to hate the thing, and all the space this discovery has sent us fleeing across.

I'd give it all to have Tom back. To make the last three years go away. To recover those innocent old days, when the Five Galaxies were merely very, very dangerous, and there was still such a thing as home.

STREAKERS

KAA

'B-but you said hoons were our enemiesss!'

Zhaki's tone was defiant, though his body posture – head down and flukes raised – betrayed uncertainty. Kaa took advantage, stirring water with his pectoral fins, taking the firm upright stance of an officer in the Terragens Survey Service.

'Those were different hoons,' he answered. 'The NuDawn disaster happened a long time ago.'

Zhaki shook his bottle snout, flicking spray across the humid dome. 'Eatees are eateesss. They'll crush Earthlings any chance they get, just like the Soro and Tandu and all the other muckety Galactics-cs!'

Kaa winced at the blanket generalization, but after two years on the run, such attitudes were common among the ranks. Kaa also nursed the self-pitying image of Earth against the entire universe. But if that were true, the torment would have ended with annihilation long ago.

We have allies, a few friends ... and the grudging sympathy of neutral clans, who hold meetings debating what to do about a plague of fanaticism sweeping the Five Galaxies. Eventually, the majority may reach a consensus and act to reestablish civilization.

They may even penalize our murderers ... for all the good it will do us.

'Actually,' said Brookida, turning from his workbench in the far corner of the cramped shelter, 'I would not put the hoon in the same category as our other persecutors. They aren't religious radicals, or power-hungry conquerors. Sourpuss bureaucrats – that's a better description. Officious sticklers for rules, which is why so many enter service with Galactic Institutes. At NuDawn they were only enforcing the law. When human settlers resisted—'

'They thought they were being invaded!' Zhaki objected.

'Yessss.' Brookida nodded. 'But Earth's colony hadn't heard about contact, and they lacked equipment to hear Galactic inquiries. When hoonish officials came to give a ritual last warning, they met something not in their manuals ... armed trespassersss. Barbarians with no Galactic language. Mistakes followed. Military units swarmed in from Joph—'

'This has nothing to do with our present problem.' Kaa

interrupted Brookida's history lecture. 'Zhaki, you must stop cutting the local hoons' fishing netsss! It draws attention to us.'

'Angry attention,' Brookida added. 'They grow wary against your dep-p-predations, Zhaki. Last time, they cast many spears.'

The young dolphin snorted.

> * *Let the whalers throw!*
> > * *As in autumn storms of old—*
> > > * *Waves come, two-legs drown!* *

Kaa flinched. Moments ago, Zhaki was eager to avenge humans who had died on a lost colony, back when dolphins could barely speak. Now the irate youth lumped all bipeds together, dredging up a grudge from days before men and women became caretakers of Earth. There was no arguing with a mind that worked that way.

Still, it was Kaa's job to enforce discipline.

> * *If you repeat this act,*
> > * *No harpoon will sting your backside*
> > > * *Like my snapping teeth!* *

It wasn't great haiku – certainly not the sort of classic, poetical Trinary that Captain Creideiki used to dazzle his crew with, crafting devoted loyalty from waves of gorgeous sound. But the warning rocked Zhaki. Kaa followed up, projecting a beam of intense sonar from his brow, piercing Zhaki's body, betraying fear churnings within.

When in doubt, he thought, *fall back on the ancestors' ways*.

'You are dismisssssed.' he finished. 'Go rest. Tomorrow's another long day.'

Zhaki swerved obediently, retreating to the curtained alcove he shared with Mopol.

Alas, despite this brief success, Kaa also knew it would not last.

Tsh't told us this was an important mission. But I bet she assigned us all here because we're the ones Streaker *could most easily do without.*

That night he dreamed of piloting.

Neo-dolphins had a flair for it – a precocious talent for the newest sapient species in all Five Galaxies. Just three hundred years after human geneticists began modifying natural bottlenose dolphins, starship *Streaker* was dispatched in a noble experiment to prove the skill of dolphin crews. The Terragens Council thought it might help solidify Earth's shaky position to become known as a source of crackerjack pilots.

'Lucky' Kaa had naturally been pleased to be chosen for the mission, though it brought home one glaring fact.

I was good ... but not the best.

In half slumber, Kaa relived the terrifying ambush at Morgran, a narrow escape that still rocked him, even after all this time.

Socketed in his station on the bridge, helpless to do anything but go along for the ride, as Chief Pilot Keepiru *sent the old Snark-class survey ship through maneuvers a Tandu fighter ship would envy, neatly evading lurk mines and snare fields, then diving back into the Morgran maelstrom, without benefit of guidance computation.*

The memory lost no vividness after two long years.

Transit threads swarmed around them, a dizzying blur of dimensional singularities. By a whim of cerebral evolution, trained dolphin pilots excelled at picturing the shimmering space-time clefts with sonar imagery. But Kaa had never rushed through such a tangle! A tornado of knotted strands. Any shining cord, caught at the wrong angle, might hurl the ship back into normal space with the consistency of quark stew ...

... Yet somehow, the ship sped nimbly from one thread to the next, Keepiru escaped the pursuers, dodged past the normal trade routes, and finally brought Streaker *to a refuge Captain Creideiki chose.*

Kithrup, *where resources for repairs could be found as pure isotopic metal growing like coral in a poison sea ...*

... Kithrup, homeworld of two unknown races, one sinking in an ancient wallow of despair, and the other hopeful, new ...

... Kithrup, where no one should have been able to follow ...

... But they did. Galactics, feuding and battling insanely overhead ...

... And soon Keepiru was gone, along with Toshio, Hikahi, and Mr. Orley ...

... and Kaa learned that some wishes were better not coming true. He learned that he did not really want to be chief pilot, after all.

In the years since, he has gained experience. The escapes he piloted – from Oakka and the Fractal System – were performed well, if not as brilliantly.

Not quite good enough to preserve Kaa's nickname.

I never heard anyone else say they could do better.

All in all, it was not a restful sleep.

Zhaki and Mopol were at it again, before dawn, rubbing and squealing beyond a slim curtain they nearly shredded with their slashing tails. They should have gone outside to frolic, but Kaa dared not order it.

'It is typical postadolescent behavior,' Brookida told him, by the food dispenser. 'Young males grow agitated. Among natural dolphins, unisex play ceases to be sufficient as youths turn their thoughts to winning the companionship of females. Young allies often test their status by jointly challenging older males.'

Of course Kaa knew all that. But he could not agree with the 'typical' part. *I never acted that way. Oh sure, I was an obnoxious, arrogant young fin. But I never acted intentionally gross, or like some reverted animal.*

'Maybe Tsh't should have assigned females to our team.' He pondered aloud.

'Wouldn't help,' answered the elderly metallurgist. 'If those two schtorks weren't getting any aboard ship, they wouldn't do any better here. Our fem-fins have high standards.'

Kaa sputtered out a lump of half-chewed mullet as he laughed, grateful for Brookida's lapse into coarse humor – though it grazed by a touchy subject among *Streaker*'s crew, the *petition to breed* that some had been circulating and signing.

Kaa changed the subject. 'How goes your analysis of the matter the hoons dumped overboard?'

Brookida nodded toward his workbench, where several ribboned casks lay cracked open. Bits of bone and crystal glittered amid piles of ashen dust.

'So far, the contents confirm what the hoonish boy wrote in his journal.'

'Amazing. I was sure it must be a fake, planted by our enemies.' Transcripts of the handwritten diary, passed on by *Streaker*'s command, seemed too incredible to believe.

'Apparently the story is true. Six races do live together on this world. As part of ecology-oriented rituals, they send their unrecyclable wastes – called *dross* – to sea for burial in special disposal zones. This includes parts of their processed bodies.'

'And you found—'

'Human remainsss.' Brookida nodded. 'As well as chimps, hoons, urs ... the whole crowd this young "Alvin" wrote about.'

Kaa was still dazed by it all.

'And there are ... J-Jophur.' He could hardly speak the word aloud.

Brookida frowned. 'A matter of definition, it seems. I've exchanged message queries with Gillian and the Niss Machine. They suggest these so-called traeki might have the other races fooled as part of an elaborate, long-range plot.'

'How could that be?'

'I am not sure. It would not require that every traeki be in on the scheme. Just a few, with secret master rings, and the hidden equipment to dominate their fellow beings. I cannot quite fathom it. But Gillian has questioned the captured Library unit. And that seems a possssible scenario.'

Kaa had no answer for that. Such matters seemed so complex, so far beyond his grasp, his only response was to shiver from the tip of his rostrum all the way down to his trembling tail.

They spent another day spying on the local sooners. The hoonish seaport, Wuphon, seemed to match the descriptions in Alvin's journal ... though more crude and shabby in the eyes of beings who had seen the sky towers of Tanith and bright cities on Earth's moon. The hoons appeared to pour more lavish attention on their boats than their homes. The graceful sailing ships bore delicate carving work, down to proud figureheads shaped like garish deities.

When a vessel swept past Kaa, he overheard the deep, rumbling sounds of *singing*, as the sailors boomed evident joy across the whitecaps.

It's hard to believe these are the same folk Brookida described as passionless prigs. Maybe there are two races that look alike, and have similar-sounding names. Kaa made a mental note to send an inquiry in tonight's report.

Hoons weren't alone on deck. He peered at smaller creatures, scrambling nimbly over the rigging, but when he tried using a portable camera, the image swept by too fast to catch much more than a blur.

Streaker also wanted better images of the *volcano*, which apparently was a center of industrial activity among the sooner races. Gillian and Tsh't were considering sending another independent robot ashore, though earlier drones had been lost. Kaa got spectral readings of the mountain's steaming emissions, and discovered the trace of a slender tramway, camouflaged against the rocky slopes.

He checked frequently on Zhaki and Mopol, who seemed to be behaving for a change, sticking close to their assigned task of eavesdropping on the red qheuen colony.

But later, when all three of them were on their way back to base, Mopol lagged sluggishly behind.

'It must-t have been some-thing I ate,' the blue dolphin murmured, as unpleasant gurglings erupted within his abdomen.

Oh great, Kaa thought. *I warned him a hundred times not to sample local critters before Brookida had a chance to test them!*

Mopol swore it was nothing. But as the water surrounding their shelter dimmed with the setting sun, he started moaning again. Brookida used their tiny med scanner but was at a loss to tell what had gone wrong.

TSH'T

Nominally, she commanded earth's most famous spaceship – a beauty almost new by Galactic standards, just nine hundred years old when the Terragens Council purchased it from a Punctitin used-vessel dealer, then altered and renamed it *Streaker* to show off the skills of neo-dolphin voyagers.

Alas, the bedraggled craft seemed unlikely ever again to cruise the great spiral ways. Burdened by a thick coat of refractory star-dust – and now trapped deep underwater while pursuers probed the abyss with sonic bombs – to all outward appearances, it seemed doomed to join the surrounding great pile of ghost ships, sinking in the slowly devouring mud of an oceanic ravine.

Gone was the excitement that first led Tsh't into the service. The thrill of flight. The exhilaration. Nor was there much relish in 'authority,' since she did not make policies or crucial decisions. Gillian Baskin had that role.

What remained was handling ten thousand details ... like when a disgruntled cook accosted her in a water-filled hallway, wheedling for permission to go up to the realm of light.

'It'ssss too dark and c-cold to go fishing down here!' complained Bulla-jo, whose job it was to help provide meals for a hundred finicky dolphins. 'My harvesst team can hardly move, wearing all that pressure armor. And have you seen the so-called fish we catch in our nets? Weird things, all sspiky and glowing!'

Tsh't replied, 'Dr. Makanee has passed at least forty common varieties of local sea life as both tasty and nutritious, so long as we sssupplement with the right additives.'

Still, Bulla-jo groused.

'Everyone favors the samples we got *earlier*, from the upper world of waves and open air. There are great schools of lovely things swimming around up-p there.'

Then Bulla-jo lapsed into Trinary.

* Where perfect sunshine
  * Makes lively prey fish glitter
    * As they flee from us! *

He concluded, 'If you want fresh f-food, let us go to the surface, like you p-promised!'

Tsh't quashed an exasperated sigh over Bulla-jo's forgetfulness. In this early stage of their Uplift, neo-dolphins often perceived whatever they chose, ignoring contradictions.

I do it myself now and then.

She tried cultivating patience, as Creideiki used to teach.

'Dr. Baskin canceled plans to send more parties to the sunlit surface,' she told Bulla-jo, whose speckled flanks and short beak revealed ancestry from the *stenos* dolphin line. 'Did it escape your notice that gravitic emissions have been detected, cruising above this deep fissure? Or that someone has been dropping sonic charges, seeking to find usss?'

Bulla-jo lowered his rostrum in an attitude of obstinate insolence. 'We can g-go naked ... carry no tools the eatees could detect-ct.'

Tsh't marveled at such single-minded thinking.

'That might work if the gravitics were far away, say in orbit, or passing by at high altitude. But once they know our rough location they can cruise low and slow, ssseeking the radiochemical spoor of molecules in our very blood. Surface-swimming fins would give us away.'

Irony was a bittersweet taste to Tsh't, for she knew something she had no intention of sharing with Bulla-jo. *They are going to detect us, no matter how many precautions Gillian orders.*

To the frustrated crew member, she had only soothing words.

'Just float loose for a while longer, will you, Bulla-jo? I, too, would love to chase silvery fish through warm waters. All may be resolved sh-shortly.'

Grumpy, but mollified, the messmate saluted by clapping his pectoral fins and swimming back to duty ... though Tsh't knew the crisis would recur. Dolphins disliked being so far from sunlight, or from the tide's cycloid rub against shore. Tursiops weren't meant to dwell so deep, where pressurized sound waves carried in odd, disturbing ways.

It is the realm of Physeter, sperm whale, great-browed messenger of the ancient dream gods, who dives to wrestle great-armed demons.

The abyss was where hopes and nightmares from past, present, and fuure drifted to form dark sediments – a place best left to sleeping things.

We neo-fins are superstitious at heart. But what can you expect, having humans as our beloved patrons? Humans, who are themselves wolflings, primitive by the standards of a billion-year-old culture.

This she pondered while inhaling deeply, filling her gill lungs with the air-charged fluid, *oxy-water*, that filled most of *Streaker*'s residential passages – a genetically improvised manner of breathing that nourished, but never comfortably. One more reason many of the crew yearned for the clean, bright world above.

Turning toward the *Streaker*'s bridge, she thrust powerfully through the fizzing liquid, leaving clouds of effervescence behind her driving flukes. Each bubble gave off a faint *pop!* as it hiccuped into existence, or merged back into supercharged solution. Sometimes the combined susurration sounded like elfin applause – or derisive laughter – following her all over the ship.

At least I don't fool myself, she thought. *I do all right. Gillian says so, and puts her trust in me. But I know I'm not meant for command.*

Tsh't had never expected such duty when *Streaker* blasted out of Earth orbit refurbished for use by a neo-dolphin crew. Back then – over two years ago, by ship-clock time – Tsh't had been only a junior lieutenant, a distant fifth in line from Captain Creideiki. And it was common knowledge that Tom Orley and Gillian Baskin could step in if the need seemed urgent ... as Gillian eventually did, during the crisis on Kithrup.

Tsh't didn't resent that human intervention. In arranging an escape from the Kithrup trap, Tom and Gillian pulled off a miracle, even if it led to the lovers' separation.

Wasn't that the *job* of human leaders and heroes? To intercede when a crisis might overwhelm their clients?

But where do we turn when matters get too awful even for humans to handle?

Galactic tradition adhered to a firm – some said oppressive – hierarchy of debts and obligations. A client race to its patron. That patron to its sapience benefactor ... and so on, tracing the great chain of uplift all the way back to the legendary Progenitors. The same chain of duty underlay the reaction of some fanatical clans on hearing news of *Streaker*'s discovery – a fleet of derelict ships with ancient, venerated markings.

But the pyramid of devotion had positive aspects. The uplift cascade meant each new species got help crossing the dire gap dividing mere animals from starfaring citizens. And if your sponsors lacked answers, they might ask *their* patrons. And so on.

Gillian had tried appealing to this system, taking *Streaker* from Kithrup to Oakka, the green world, seeking counsel from impartial savants of the Navigation Institute. Failing there, she next sought help in the Fractal Orb – that huge icy place, a giant snowflake that spanned a solar system's width – hoping the venerable beings who dwelled there might offer wise detachment, or at least refuge.

It wasn't Dr. Baskin's fault that neither gamble paid off very well. *She had the right general idea*, Tsh't mused. *But Gillian remains blind to the obvious.*

Who is most likely to help, when you're in trouble and a lynch mob is baying at your tail?

The courts?

Scholars at some university?

Or your own family?

Tsh't never dared suggest her idea aloud. Like Tom Orley, Gillian took pride in the romantic image of upstart Earth clan, alone against the universe. Tsh't knew the answer would be no.

So, rather than flout a direct order, Tsh't had quietly put her own plan into effect, just before *Streaker* made her getaway from the Fractal System.

What else could I do, with Streaker *pursued by horrid fleets, our best crew members gone, and Earth under siege? Our Tymbrimi friends can barely help even themselves. Meanwhile, the Galactic Institutes have been corrupted and the Old Ones lied to us.*

We had no choice.

... I had no choice ...

It was hard concealing things, especially from someone who knew dolphins as well as Gillian. For weeks since *Streaker* arrived here, Tsh't half hoped her disobedience would come to nought.

Then the detection officer reported gravitic traces. Starcraft engines, entering Jijo space.

So, they came after all, she had thought, hearing the news, concealing satisfaction while her crew mates expressed noisy chagrin, bemoaning that they now seemed cornered by relentless enemies on a forlorn world.

Tsh't wanted to tell them the truth, but dared not. That good news must wait.

Ifni grant that I was right.

Tsh't paused outside the bridge, filling her gene-altered lungs with oxy-water. Enriching her blood to think clearly before setting in motion the next phase of her plan.

There is just one true option for a client race, when your beloved patrons seem overwhelmed, and all other choices are cut off.

May the gods of Earth's ancient ocean know and understand what I've done.

And what I may yet have to do.

SOONERS

NELO

Once, a Buyur urban center stretched between two rivers, from the Roney all the way to the far-off Bibur.

Now the towers were long gone, scraped and hauled away to distant seas. In their place, spiky ferns and cloudlike *voow* trees studded a morass of mud and oily water. Mulc-spider vines laced a few rounded hummocks remaining from the great city, but even those tendrils were now faded, their part in the demolition nearly done.

To Nelo, this was wasteland, rich in life but useless to any of the Six Races, except perhaps as a traeki vacation resort.

What am I doing here? he wondered. *I should be back in Dolo, tending my mill, not prowling through a swamp, keeping a crazy woman company.*

Behind Nelo, hoonish sailors cursed low, expressive rumblings, resentful over having to pole through a wretched bog. The proper time for gleaning was at the start of the dry season, when citizens in high-riding boats took turns sifting the marsh for Buyur relics missed by the patient mulc beast. Now, with rainstorms due any day, conditions were miserable for exploring. The muddy channels were shallow, yet the danger of a flash flood was very real.

Nelo faced the elderly woman who sat in a wheelchair near the bow, peering past obscuring trees with a rewq over her eyes.

'The crew ain't happy, Sage Foo,' he told her. 'They'd rather we waited till it's safe.'

Ariana Foo answered without turning from her search. 'Oh, what a great idea. Four months or more we'd sit around while the swamp fills, channels shift, and the thing we seek gets buried in muck. Of course, by then the information would be too late to do any good.'

Nelo shrugged. The woman was retired now. She had no official powers. But as former High Sage for all humans on Jijo, Ariana had moral authority to ask anything she wanted – including having Nelo leave his beloved paper mill next to broad Dolo Dam, accompanying her on this absurd search.

Not that there was much to do at the mill, he knew. *With commerce spoiled by panic over those wretched starships, no one seems interested in buying large orders.*

'Now is the best time,' Ariana went on. 'Late in dry season, with water levels low, and the foliage drooping, we get maximum visibility.'

Nelo took her word. With most young men and women away on militia duties, it was mostly adolescents and old-timers who got drafted into the search party. Anyway, Nelo's daughter had been among the first to find the Stranger from Space in this very region several months ago, during a routine gleaning trip. And he owed Ariana for bringing word about Sara and the boys – that they were all right, when last she heard. Sage Foo had spent time with Nelo's daughter, accompanying Sara from Tarek Town to the Biblos Archive.

He felt another droplet strike his cheek ... the tenth since they left the river, plunging into this endless slough. He held his hand under a murky sky and prayed the real downpours would hold off for a few more days.

Then let it come down! The lake is low. We need water pressure for the wheel, or else I'll have to shut down the mill for lack of power.

His thoughts turned to business – the buying and gathering of recycled cloth from all six races. The pulping and sifting. The pressing, drying, and selling of fine sheets that his family had been known for ever since humans brought the blessing of paper to Jijo.

A blessing that some called a curse. That radical view now claimed support from simple villagers, panicked by the looming end of days—

A shout boomed from above.

'There!' A wiry young hoon perched high on the mast, pointing. 'Hr-r ... It must be the Stranger's ship. I *told* you this had to be the place!'

Wyhuph-eihugo had accompanied Sara on that fateful gleaning trip – a duty required of all citizens. Lacking a male's throat sac, she nevertheless umbled with some verve, proud of her navigation.

At last! Nelo thought. *Now Ariana can make her sketches, and we can leave this awful place.* The crisscrossing mulc cables made him nervous. Their boat's obsidian-tipped prow had no trouble slicing through the desiccated vines. Still it felt as if they were worming deeper into some fiendish trap.

Ariana muttered something. Nelo turned, blinking.

'What did you say?'

The old woman pointed ahead, her eyes glittering with curiosity. 'I don't see any soot!'

'So?'

'The Stranger was burned. His clothes were ashen tatters. We thought his ship must have come down in flames – perhaps after battling other aliens high over Jijo. But look. Do you see any trace of conflagration?'

The boat worked around a final voow grove, revealing a rounded metal capsule on the other side, gleaming amid a nest of shattered branches. The sole opening resembled the splayed petals of a flower, rather than a door or hatch.

The arrival of this intruder had cut a swathe of devastation stretching to the northwest. Several swamp hummocks were split by the straight gouge, only partly softened by regrown vegetation.

Nelo had some experience as a surveyor, so he helped take sightings to get the ship's overall dimensions. It was small – no larger than this hoonish boat, in fact – certainly no majestic cruiser like the one that clove the sky over Dolo Town, sending its citizens into hysteria. The rounded flanks reminded Nelo of a natural teardrop, more than anything sapient-made.

Two pinpoints of moisture dotted his cheek and forehead. Another struck the back of his hand. In the distance, Nelo heard a sharp rumble of thunder.

'Hurry closer!' Ariana urged, flipping open her sketchpad. Murmuring unhappily, the hoons leaned on their poles and oars to comply.

Nelo stared at the alien craft, but all he could think was *dross*. When Sixers went gleaning through Buyur sites, one aim was to seek items that might be useful for a time, in a home or workshop. But useful or not, everything eventually went into ribboned caskets to be sent on to the Great Midden. Thus colonists imagined they were helping cleanse Jijo – perhaps doing more good than harm to their adopted world.

'Ifni!' Nelo sighed under his breath, staring at the vehicle that brought the Stranger hurtling out of space. It might be tiny for a starship, but it looked hard as blazes to move by hand.

'We'll be in for a hell of a job draggin' this thing out of here, let alone gettin' it down to sea.'

Again, off to the south, the sound of thunder boomed.

EWASX

We Jophur are taught that it is terrible to be traeki – a stack lacking any central self. Doomed to a splintered life of vagueness and blurry placidity.

All sing praises to the mighty Oailie, who took over from the too-timid Poa, completing the final stages of our Uplift.

Those same Oailie who designed new master rings to focus and bind our natures.

Without rings like Me, how could our race ever have become great and feared among the Five Galaxies?

And yet, even as I learn to integrate your many little selves into our new whole, I am struck by how vivid are these older drippings that I find lining our inner core! Drippings that date from before My fusion with your aged pile of rings. How lustrous clear these memories seem, despite their counterpointing harmonies. I confess, existence had intensity and verve when you/we were merely *Asx*.

Perhaps this surprise comes because I/Myself am so young, only recently drawn from the side of our Ship Commander – from that great one's very own ring-of-embryos.

Yes, that is a high heritage. So imagine the surprise of finding Myself in this situation! Designed for duties in the dominion caste, I am wedded, for pragmatic reasons, to a haphazard heap of rustic toruses, ill educated and filled with bizarre, primitive notions. I have been charged to make the best of things until some later time, when surgery-of-reconfiguration can be performed—

Ah. that draws a reaction from some of you? Our second ring of cognition, in particular, finds this notion disturbing.

Fear not, My rings! Accept these jolts of painful love soothing, to remind you of your place – which is not to question, only to serve. Be assured that the procedure I refer to is now quite advanced among the mighty Jophur. When a ring is removed for reassembly in a new stack, often as many as half of the other leftover components can be recovered and reused as well! Of course, most of you are elderly, and the priests may decide you carry other-race contaminations, preventing incorporation into new mounds. But accept this pledge. When the time comes, I, your beloved master ring, shall very likely make the transition in good health, and take fond memories of our association to My glorious new stack.

I know this fact will bring you all great satisfaction, contemplating it within our common core.

LARK

Cathedral-like stillness filled the Boo Forest – a dense expanse of gray-green columns, towering to support the sky. Each majestic trunk had a girth like the carapace of a five-clawed qheuen. Some stretched as high as the Stone Roof of Biblos.

Now I know how an insect feels, scuttling under a sea of pampas grass.

Hiking along a narrow lane amid the giant pillars, Lark often could reach out his arms and brush two giant stems at the same time. Only his militia sergeant seemed immune to a sense of confinement infecting travelers in this strange place of vertical perspectives. Other guards expressed edginess with darting eyes that glanced worriedly down crooked aisles at half-hidden shadows.

'How far is it to Dooden Mesa?' Ling asked, tugging the straps of her leather backpack. Perspiration glistened down her neck to dampen the Jijoan homespun jerkin she wore. The effect was not as provocative as Lark recalled from their old survey trips together, when the sheer fabric of a Danik jumpsuit sometimes clung to her biosculpted figure in breathtaking ways.

Anyway, I can't afford that, now that I'm a sage. The promotion brought only unpleasant responsibilities.

'I never took this shortcut before,' Lark answered, although he and Uthen used to roam these mountains in search of data for their book. There were other paths around the mountain, and the wheeled g'Keks nominally in charge of this domain could hardly be expected to do upkeep on such a rough trail. 'My best guess is we'll make it in two miduras. Want to rest?'

Ling pushed sodden strands from her eyes. 'No. Let's keep going.'

The former gene raider seemed acutely aware of Jeni Shen, the diminutive sergeant, whose corded arms cradled her crossbow like a beloved child. Jeni glanced frequently at Ling with hunter's eyes, as if speculating which vital organ might make a good target. Anyone could sense throbbing enmity between the two women – and that Ling would rather die than show weakness before the militia scout.

Lark found one thing convenient about their antagonism. It helped divert Ling's ire away from *him*, especially after the way he earlier used logic to slash her beloved Rothen gods. Since then, the alien biologist had been civil, but kept to herself in brooding silence.

No one likes to have their most basic assumptions knocked from under them – especially by a primitive savage.

Lark blew air through his cheeks – the hoonish version of a shrug.

'Hr-rm. We'll take a break at the next rise. By then we should be out of the worst boo.'

In fact, the thickest zone was already behind them, a copse so dense the monstrous stems rubbed in the wind, creating a low, drumming music that vibrated the bones of anyone passing underneath. Traveling single file, edging sideways where the trunks pressed closest, the party had watched for vital trail marks, cut on one rounded bole after the next.

I was right to leave Uthen behind, he thought, hoping to convince himself. *Just hold on, old friend. Maybe we'll come up with something. I pray we can.*

Visibility was hampered by drifting haze, since many of the tall boo *leaked* from water reserves high above, spraying arcs of fine droplets that spread to saturate the misty colonnade. Several times they passed clearings where aged columns had toppled in a domino chain reaction, leaving maelstroms of debris.

Through the fog, Lark occasionally glimpsed other symbols, carved on trunks beyond the trail. Not trail marks, but cryptic emblems in GalTwo and GalSix ... accompanied by strings of Anglic numbers.

Why would anyone go scrawling graffiti through a stand of great-boo?

He even spied dim figures through the murk – once a human, then several urs, and finally a pair of traeki – glimpsed prowling amid rows of huge green pillars. At least he *hoped* the tapered cones were traeki. They vanished like ghosts before he could tell for sure.

Sergeant Shen kept the party moving too fast to investigate. Lark and his prisoner had been summoned by two of the High Sages – a command that overruled any other priority. And despite the difficult terrain, recent news from the Glade of Gathering was enough to put vigor in their steps.

Runners reported that the Jophur dreadnought still blocked the sacred valley, squatting complacently inside its swathe of devastation, with the captive Rothen ship doubly imprisoned nearby – first by a gold cocoon, and now a rising lake as well. The Jophur daily sent forth a pair of smaller vessels, sky-prowling daggers, surveying the Slope and the seas beyond. No one knew what the star gods were looking for.

Despite what happened on the night the great ship landed – havoc befalling Asx and others on the Glade – the High Sages were preparing to send another embassy of brave volunteers, hoping to parley. No one asked Lark to serve as an envoy. The Sages had other duties planned for him.

Humans weren't the only ones to cheat a little, when their founding generation came to plant a taboo colony on forbidden Jijo.

For more than a year after it made landfall, the *Tabernacle*'s crew delayed sending their precious ship to an ocean abyss. A year spent using god tools to cut trees and print books ... then storing the precious volumes in a stronghold that the founders carved beneath a great stone overhang, protected by high walls and a river. During those early days – especially the urrish and qheuen wars – Biblos Fortress served as a vital refuge until humans grew strong enough to demand respect.

The Gray Queens also once had such a citadel, sculpted by mighty engines when they first arrived, before their sneakship fell beneath the waves. The Caves of Shood, near present-day Ovoom Town, must have seemed impregnable. But that maze of deep-hewn caverns drowned under a rising water table when blue and red workers dropped their slavish maintenance duties, wandering off instead to seek new homes and destinies, apart from their chitin empresses.

Dooden Mesa was the oldest of the sooner ramparts. After Tarek Town, it formed the heart of g'Kek life on Jijo, a place of marvelous store ramps that curved like graceful filigrees, allowing the wheeled ones to swoop and careen through a swirl of tight turns, from their looms and workshops to tree-sheltered platforms where whole families slept with their hubs joined in slowly rotating clusters. Under an obscuring blur-cloth canopy, the meandering system resembled pictures found in certain Earthling books about pre-contact times – looking like a cross between an 'amusement park' and the freeway interchanges of some sprawling city.

Ling's face brightened with amazed delight when she regarded the settlement, nodding as Lark explained the lacy pattern of narrow byways. Like Biblos, Dooden Rampart was not meant to last forever, for that would violate the Covenant of Exile. Someday it all would have to go – g'Kek elders conceded. Still, the wheeled ones throbbed their spokes in sinful pride over their beloved city. Their home.

While Ling marveled, Lark surveyed the busy place with fresh poignancy.

It is their only *home.*

Unless the Rothen lied, it seems there are no more g'Kek living among the Five Galaxies.

If they die on Jijo, they are gone for good.

Watching youngsters pitch along graceful ramps with reckless abandon, streaking round corners with all four eyestalks flying and their rims glowing hot, Lark could not believe the universe would let that happen. How could any race so unique be allowed to go extinct?

With the boo finally behind them, the party now stood atop a ridge covered with normal forest. As they paused, a zookir dropped onto the path from the branches of a nearby garu tree – all spindly arms and legs, covered with white spirals of fluffy torg. Treasured aides and pets of the g'Kek, zookirs helped make life bearable for wheeled beings on a planet where roads were few and stumbling stones all too many.

This zookir squinted at the party, then scampered closer, sniffing. Unerringly, it bypassed the other humans, zeroing in on Lark.

Trust a zookir to know a sage – so went a folk saying. No one had any idea *how* the creatures could tell, since they seemed less clever than chimps in other ways. Lark's promotion was recent and he wore the new status of 'junior sage' uncomfortably, yet the creature had no trouble setting him apart. It pressed damp nostrils against his wrist and inhaled. Then, cooing satisfaction, it slipped a folded parchment in Lark's hand.

MEET US AT THE REFUGE – That was all it said.

LESTER CAMBEL

A pair of high sages waited in a narrow canyon, half a league away. Lester Cambel and Knife-Bright Insight, the blue qheuen whose reputation for compassion made her a favorite among the Six.

Here, too, the paths were smooth and well suited for g'Keks, since this was part of their Dooden Domain. Wheeled figures moved among the meadows, looking after protected ones who lived in thatched shelters beneath the trees. It was a refuge for sacred simpletons – those whose existence promised a future for the Six Races – according to the scrolls.

Several of the *blessed* ones gathered around Knife-Bright Insight, clucking or chewing in debased versions of Galactic tongues. These were hoons and urs, for the most part, though a red qheuen joined the throng as Lester watched, and several traeki stacks slithered timidly closer, burbling happy stinks as they approached. Each received a loving pat or stroke from Knife-Bright Insight, as if her claws were gentle hands.

Lester regarded his colleague, and knew guiltily that he could never match her glad kindness. The *blessed* were superior beings, ranking above the normal run of the Six. Their simplicity was proof that other races could follow the example of glavers, treading down the path of Redemption.

It should fill my heart to see them, he thought.

Yet I hate coming to this place.

Members of all six races dwelled in simple shelters underneath the canyon walls, tended by local g'Keks, plus volunteers from across the Slope. Whenever a qheuen, or hoon, or urrish village found among their youths one who had a knack for innocence, a gift for animal-like naïveté, the lucky individual was sent here for nurturing and study.

There are just two ways to escape the curse bequeathed to us by our ancestors, Lester thought, struggling to believe. *We could do as Lark's group of heretics want – stop breeding and leave Jijo in peace. Or else we can all seek a different kind of oblivion, the kind that returns our children's children to presentience. Washed clean and ready for a new cycle of uplift. Thus they may yet find new patrons, and perhaps a happier fate.*

So prescribed the Sacred Scrolls, even after all the compromises wrought since the arrival of Earthlings and the Holy Egg. Given the situation of exile races, living here on borrowed time, facing horrid punishment if/when a Galactic Institute finds them here, what other goal could there be?

But I can't do it. I cannot look at this place with joy. Earthling values keep me from seeing these creatures as lustrous beings. They deserve kindness and pity – but not envy.

It was his own heresy. Lester tried to look elsewhere. But turning just brought to view another cluster of 'blessed.' This time, humans, gathered in a circle under an ilhuna tree, sitting cross-legged with hands on knees, chanting in low, sonorous voices. Men and women whose soft smiles and unshifting eyes seemed to show simplicity of the kind sought here ... only Lester knew them to be liars!

Long ago, he took the same road. Using meditation techniques borrowed from old Earthling religions, he sat under just such a tree, freeing his mind of worldly obsessions, disciplining it to perceive Truth. And for a while it seemed he succeeded. Acolytes bowed reverently, calling him *illuminated*. The universe appeared lucid then, as if the stars were sacred fire. As if he were united with all Jijo's creatures, even the very quanta in the stones around him. He lived in harmony, needing little food, few words, and even fewer names.

Such serenity – sometimes he missed it with an ache inside.

But after a while he came to realize – the clarity he had found was sterile blankness. A blankness that *felt* fine, but had nothing to do with redemption. Not for himself. Not for his race.

The other five don't use discipline or concentration to seek simplicity. You don't see glavers meditating by a rotten log full of tasty insects. Simplicity calls to them naturally. They live *their innocence.*

When Jijo is finally reopened, some great clan will gladly adopt the new glaver subspecies, setting them once more upon the High Path, perhaps with better luck than they had the first time.

But those patrons won't choose us. No noble elder clan is looking for smug Zen masters, eager to explain their own enlightenment. That is not a plainness you can write upon. It is simplicity based on individual pride.

Of course the point might be moot. If the Jophur ship represented great Institutes of the Civilization of the Five Galaxies, these forests would soon throng with inspectors, tallying up two thousand years of felonies against a fallow world. Only glavers would be safe, having made it to safety in time. The other six races would pay for a gamble lost.

And if they don't represent the Institutes?

The Rothen had proved to be criminals, gene raiders. Might the Jophur be more of the same? Murderous genocide could still be in store. The g'Kek clan, in particular, were terrified of recent news from the Glade.

On the other hand, it might be possible to cut a deal. Or else maybe they'll just go away, leaving us in the same state we were in before.

In that case, places like this refuge would go back to being the chief hope for tomorrow ... for five races out of the Six.

Lester's dark thoughts were cut off by a tug on his sleeve.

'Sage Cambel? The ... um, visitors you're, ah, expecting ... I think ...'

It was a young human, broad-cheeked, with clear blue eyes and pale skin. The boy would have seemed tall – almost a giant – except that a stooped posture diminished his appearance. He kept tapping a corner of his forehead with the fingertips of his right hand, as if in a vague salute.

Lester spoke gentle words in Anglic, the only language the lad ever managed to learn.

'What did you say, Jimi?'

The boy swallowed, concentrating hard.

'I think the ... um ... the people you want t'see ... I think they're here ... Sage Cambel.'

'Lark and the Danik woman?'

A vigorous nod.

'Um, yessir. I sent 'em to the visitors' shed ... to wait for you an' the other Great Sage. Was that right?'

'Yes, that was right, Jimi.' Lester gave his arm a friendly squeeze. 'Please go back now. Tell Lark I'll be along shortly.'

A broad grin. The boy turned around to run the way he came, awkward in his eagerness to be useful.

There goes the other kind of human who comes to this place, Lester thought. *Our special one ...*

The ancient euphemism tasted strange.

At first sight, it would seem people like Jimi fit the bill. Simpler minds. Innocent. Our ideal envoys to tread the Path.

He glanced at the blessed ones surrounding Knife-Bright Insight – urs, hoons, and g'Keks who were sent here by their respective races in order to do that. To lead the way.

By the standards of the scrolls, these ones aren't damaged. Though simple, they aren't finished. They are leaders. But no one can say that of Jimi. All sympathy aside, he is injured, incomplete. Anyone can see that.

We can and should love him, help him, befriend him.

But he leads humanity nowhere.

Lester signaled to his blue qheuen colleague, using an urslike shake of his head to indicate that their appointment had arrived. She responded by turning her visor cupola in a quick series of GalTwo winks, flashing that she'd be along shortly.

Lester turned and followed Jimi's footsteps, trying to shift his thoughts back to the present crisis. To the problem of the Jophur battleship. Back to urgent plans he must discuss with the young heretic and the woman from the stars. There was a dire proposal – far-fetched and darkly dangerous – they must be asked to accept.

Yet, as he passed by the chanting circle of meditating humans – healthy men and women who had abandoned their farms, families, and useful crafts to dwell without work in this sheltered valley – Lester found his contemplations awash with bitter resentment. The words in his head were unworthy of a High Sage, he knew. But he could not help pondering them.

Morons and meditators, those are the two types that our race sends up here. Not a true 'blessed' soul in the lot. Not by the standards set in the scrolls. Humans almost never take true steps down redemption's path. Ur-Jah and the others are polite. They pretend that we, too, have that option, that potential salvation.

But we don't. Our lot is sterile.

With or without judgment from the stars – the only future humans face on Jijo is damnation.

DWER

Smoke spiraled from the crash site. It was against his better judgment to sneak closer. In fact, now was his chance to run the other way, while the Danik robot cowered in a hole, showing no further interest in its prisoners.

And if Rety wanted to stay?

Let her! Lena and Jenin would be glad to see Dwer if he made the long journey back to the Gray Hills. That should be possible with his trusty bow in hand. True, Rety needed him, but those up north had better claim on his loyalty.

Dwer's senses still throbbed from the din of the brief battle, when the mighty Danik scoutship was shot down by a terrifying newcomer. Both vessels lay beyond the next dune, sky chariots of unfathomable power ... and Rety urged him to creep closer still!

'We gotta find out what's going on,' she insisted in a harsh whisper.

He gave her a sharp glance, demanding silence, and for once she complied, giving him a moment to think.

Lena and Jenin may be safe for a while, now that Kunn won't be returning to plague them. If the Daniks and Rothens have enemies on Jijo, all the star gods may be too busy fighting each other to hunt a little band in the Gray Hills.

Even without guidance from Danel Ozawa, Lena Strong was savvy enough to make a three-way deal, with Rety's old band and the urrish sooners. Using Danel's 'legacy,' their combined tribe might plant a seed to flourish in the wilderness. Assuming the worst happened back home on the Slope, their combined band might yet find its way to the Path.

Dwer shook his head. He sometimes found it hard to concentrate. Ever since letting the robot use his body as a conduit for its fields, it felt as if *voices* whispered softly at the edge of hearing. As when the crazy old mulc-spider used to wheedle into his thoughts.

Anyway, it wasn't his place to ponder destiny, or make sagelike decisions. Some things were obvious. He might not owe Rety anything. She may deserve to be abandoned to her fate. But he couldn't do that.

So, despite misgivings, Dwer nodded to the girl, adding with emphatic hand motions that she had better not make a single sound. She replied with a happy shrug that seemed to say, *Sure ... until I decide otherwise.*

Slinging his bow and quiver over one shoulder, he led the way forward, creeping from one grassy clump to the next, till they reached the crest of the dune. Cautiously they peered through a cluster of salty fronds to stare down at two sky vessels – the smaller a smoldering ruin, half-submerged in a murky swamp. The larger ship, nestled nearby, had not escaped the fracas unscarred. It bore a deep fissure along one flank that belched soot whenever the motors tried to start.

Two men lay prostrate on a marshy islet, barely moving. Kunn and Jass.

Dwer and Rety scratched a new hole to hide in, then settled down to see who – or what – would emerge next.

They did not wait long. A hatch split the large cylinder, baring a dark interior. Through it floated a single figure, startlingly familiar – an eight-sided pillar with dangling arms – close cousin to the damaged robot Dwer knew all too well. Only this one gleamed with stripes of alternating blue and pink, a pattern Dwer found painful to behold.

It also featured a hornlike projection on the bottom, aimed downward. *That must be what lets it travel over water*, he thought. *If the robot is similar, could that mean Kunn's enemies are human, too?*

But no, Danel had said that machinery was standard among the half a million starfaring races, changing only slowly with each passing eon. This new drone might belong to anybody.

The automaton neared Kunn and Jass, a searchlight playing over their bodies, vivid even in bright sunshine. Their garments rippled, frisked by translucent fingers. Then the robot dropped down, arms outstretched. Kunn and Jass lay still as it poked, prodded, and lifted away with several objects in its pincers.

A signal must have been given, for a ramp then jutted from the open hatch, slanting to the bog. *Who's going to go traipsing around in that stuff?* Dwer wondered. *Are they going to launch a boat?*

He girded for some weird alien race, one with thirteen legs perhaps, or slithering on trails of slime. Several great clans had been known as foes of humankind, even in the *Tabernacle's* day, such as the legendary Soro, or the insectlike Tandu. Dwer even nursed faint hope that the newcomers might be from Earth, come all this vast distance to rein in their criminal cousins. There were also relatives of hoons, urs, and qheuens out there, each with ships and vast resources at their command.

Figures appeared, twisting down the ramp into the open air.

Rety gasped. 'Them's traekis!'

Dwer stared at a trio of formidable-looking ring stacks, with bandoliers of tools hanging from their toroids-of-manipulation. The tapered cones reached muddy water and settled in. Abruptly, the flipper legs that seemed awkward on the ramp propelled them with uncanny speed toward the two survivors.

'But ain't traekis s'posed to be peaceful?'

They are, Dwer thought, wishing he had paid more attention to the lessons his mother used to give Sara and Lark. Readings from obscure books that went beyond what you were taught in school. He reached back for a name, but came up empty. Yet he knew a name existed. One that inspired fear, once-upon-a-time.

'I don't—' he whispered, then shook his head firmly. 'I don't think these are traeki. At least not like anyone's seen here in a very long while.'

ALVIN

The scene was hard to interpret at first. Hazy blue-green images jerked rapidly, sending shivers down my still-unsteady spine. Huck and Pincer seemed to catch on more quickly, pointing at various objects in the picture display, sharing knowing grunts. The experience reminded me of our trip on *Wuphon's Dream*, when poor Alvin the Hoon was always the last one to grok what was going on.

Finally, I realized – we were viewing a faraway locale, back in the world of sunshine and rain!

(How many times have Huck and I read about some storybook character looking at a distant place by remote control? It's funny. A concept can be familiar from novels, yet rouse awe when you finally encounter it in real life.)

Daylight streamed through watery shallows where green fronds waved in a gentle tide. Schools of flicking, silvery shapes darted past – species that our fishermen brought home in nets, destined for the drying racks and stewpots of hoonish khutas.

The spinning voice said there were sound 'pickups' next to the moving camera lens, which explained the swishing, gurgling noises. Pincer shifted his carapace, whistling a homesick lament from all five vents, nostalgic for the tidal pens of his red qheuen rookery. But Ur-ronn soon had quite enough, turning her sleek head with a queasy whine, made ill by the sight of all that swishing water.

Slanting upward, the surf grew briefly violent. Then water fled the camera's eye in foamy sheets as our viewpoint emerged onto a low sandscape. The remote unit scurried inland, low to the ground.

'Normally, we would send a drone ashore at night. But the matter is urgent. We must count on the land's hot glare to mask its emergence.'

Ur-ronn let out a sigh, relieved to see no more liquid turbulence.

'It forces one to wonder,' she said, 'why you have not sent sleuthy agents vefore.'

'In fact several were dispatched to seek signs of civilization. Two are long overdue, but others reported startling scenes.'

'Such as?' Huck asked.

'Such as hoon mariners, crewing wooden sailing ships on the high seas.'

'Hr-rr . . . What's strange about that?'

'*And red qheuens, living unsupervised by grays or blues, beholden to no one, trading peacefully with their hoonish neighbors.*'

Pincer huffed and vented, but the voice continued.

'*Intrigued, we sent a submarine expedition beyond the Rift. Our explorers followed one of your dross ships, collecting samples from its sacred discharge. Then, returning to base, our scout vessel happened on the urrish "cache" you were sent to recover. Naturally, we assumed the original owners must be extinct.*'

'Oh?' Ur-ronn asked, archly. 'Why is that?'

'*Because we had seen living hoon! Who would conceive of urs and hoon cohabiting peacefully within a shared volume less broad than a cubic parsec? If hoon lived, we assumed all urs on Jijo must have died.*'

'Oh,' Ur-ronn commented, turning her long neck to glare at me.

'*Imagine our surprise when a crude vessel plummeted toward our submarine. A hollowed-out tree trunk containing—*'

The voice cut off. The remote unit was in motion again. We edged forward as the camera eye skittered across sand mixed with scrubby vegetation.

'Hey,' Ur-ronn objected. 'I thought you couldn't use radio or anything that can ve detected from sface!'

'*Correct.*'

'Then how are you getting these fictures in real tine?'

'*An excellent question, coming from one with no direct experience in such matters. In this case, the drone needs only to travel a kilometer or so ashore. It can deploy a fiber cable, conveying images undetectably.*'

I twitched. Something in the words just spoken jarred me, in an eerie-familiar way.

'Does it have to do with the *exflosions*?' Ur-ronn asked. 'The recent attack on this site vy those who would destroy you?'

The spinning shape contracted, then expanded.

'*You four truly are quick and imaginative. It has been an unusual experience conversing with you. And I was created to appreciate unusual experiences.*'

'In other words, yes,' Huck said gruffly.

'*Some time ago, a flying machine began sifting this sea with tentacles of sound. Hours later, it switched to dropping depth charges in a clear effort to dislodge us from our mound of concealing wreckage.*'

'*Matters were growing dire when gravitic fields of a second craft entered the area. We picked up rhythms of aerial combat. Missiles and deadly rays were exchanged in a brief desperate struggle.*'

Pincer rocked from foot to foot. 'Gosh-osh-osh!' he sighed, ruining our pose of nonchalance.

'*Then both vessels abruptly stopped flying. Their inertial signatures ceased close to the drone's present location.*'

'How close?' Ur-ronn asked.

'*Very close,*' the voice replied.

Transfixed, we watched a hypnotic scene of rapid motion. An ankle-high panorama of scrubby plants, whipping past with blurry speed. The camera eye dodged clumps of saber fronds, skittering with frantic speed, as the drone sought height overlooking a vast marshy fen.

All at once, a glint of silver! *Two* glints. Curving flanks of—

That was when it happened.

Without warning, just as we had our first thrilling glimpse of crashed flyships, the screen was abruptly filled by a grinning *face*.

We rocked back, shouting in surprise. I recoiled so fast, even the high-tech back brace could not save my spine from surging pain. Huphu's claws dug in my shoulder as she trilled an amazed cry.

The face bared a glittering, gleeful display of pointy teeth. Black, beady eyes stared at us, inanely magnified, so full of feral amusement that we all groaned with recognition.

Our tiny drone pitched, trying to escape, but the grinning demon held it firmly with both forepaws. The creature raised sharp claws, preparing to strike.

The spinning voice spoke then – a sound that flew out, then came back to us through the drone's tiny pickups. There were just three words, in a queerly accented form of GalSeven, very high-pitched, almost beyond a hoon's range.

'*Brother,*' the voice said quickly to the strange noor.

'*Please stop.*'

EWASX

Word comes that we have lost track of a corvette!

Our light cruiser sent to pursue an aircraft of the Rothen bandits.

Trouble was not anticipated in such a routine chore. It raises disturbing questions. Might we have underestimated the prowess of this brigand band?

You, our second ring-of-cognition – you provide access to many memories and thoughts once accumulated by our stack, before I joined to become your master ring. Memories from a time when *we/you* were merely *Asx*.

You recall hearing the human gene thieves making preposterous claims. For instance, that their patrons – these mysterious 'Rothen' – are unknown to Galactic society at large. That the Rothen wield strong influence in hidden ways. That they scarcely fear the mighty battle fleets of the great clans of the Five Galaxies.

We of the battleship *Polkjhy* heard similar tall tales before arriving at this world. We took it all for mere bluff. A pathetic cover story, attempting futilely to hide the outlaws' true identity.

BUT WHAT IF THE STORY IS TRUE?

No one can doubt that mysterious forces do exist – ancient, aloof, influential. Might we have crossed fates with some cryptic power, here in an abandoned galaxy, far from home?

OR TAKE THE IDEA MORE BROADLY. Might such a puissant race of cloaked ones stand secretly behind all Terrans, guiding their destiny? Protecting them against the fate that generally befalls wolfling breeds? It would explain much strangeness in recent events. It could also bode ill for our Obeyer Alliance, in these dangerous times.

BUT NO! Facts do not support that fear.

You primitive, rustic rings would not know this, so let Me explain.

NOT LONG AGO, the *Polkjhy* was contacted by certain petty data merchants, unscrupulous vermin offering news for sale. Through human agents, these 'Rothen' approached us – the great and devout Jophur – because our ship happened to be on search patrol nearby. Also, they calculated Jophur would pay twice as much for the information they wanted to sell.

—ONCE for clues to find the main quarry we seek, a missing Earth vessel that ten thousand ships have pursued for years, as great a prize as any in the Five Galaxies—

—AND A SECOND TIME for information about the ancestor-cursed g'Kek, a surviving remnant who took refuge here many planet cycles ago, thwarting our righteous, extinguishing wrath.

The Rothen and their henchmen hoped to reap handsome profit by selling us this information, added to whatever genetic scraps they might steal from this unripe world. The arrangement must have seemed ideal to them, for both sides would be well advised to keep the transaction secret forever.

Is *that* the behavior of some great, exalted power? One risen above trivial mortal concerns?

Would deity-level beings have been so rudely surprised by local savages, who vanquished their buried station with mere chemical explosives?

Did they prove so mighty when we turned our rings around half circle in an act of pious betrayal, and pounced upon their ship? Freezing it in stasis by means of a not-unclever trick?

No, this cannot be a reasonable line of inquiry, My rings. It worries me that you would waste our combined mental resources pursuing a blind pathway.

This digression – IS IT YET ANOTHER VAIN EFFORT TO DIS-TRACT ME FROM THE NARROWNESS OF PURPOSE THAT IS MY PRINCIPAL CONTRIBUTION TO THE STACK?

Is that also why some of you keep trying to tune in so-called guidance patterns from that silly rock you call a 'Holy Egg'?

Are these vague, disjointed efforts aimed at yet another rebel-lion?

HAVE YOU NOT YET LEARNED?

Shall I demonstrate, once again, why the Oailie made My kind, and named us 'master rings'?

LET US drop these silly cogitations and consider alternative expla-nations for the disappearance of the corvette. Perhaps, when our crew hunted down the scout boat of the Rothen, they stumbled onto something else instead?

Something more powerful and important, by far?

...?

Is this true? You truly have no idea what I am hinting at?

Not even a clue? Why, most of the inhabitants of the Five Galaxies – even the enigmatic Zang – know of the ship we seek. A vessel pursued by half the armadas in known space.

You have indeed lived in isolation, My rustic rings! My primitive subselves. My temporary pretties, who have not heard of a ship crewed by half-animal dolphins.

How very strange indeed.

SARA

Without dark glasses provided by the horseriding Illias, Sara feared she might go blind or insane. A few stray glints were enough to stab her nerves with unnatural colors, cooing for attention, shouting dangerously, begging her to remove the coverings, to stare ... per-haps losing herself in a world of shifted light.

Even in sepia tones, the surrounding bluffs seemed laden with cryptic meaning. Sara recalled how legendary Odysseus, sailing near the fabled Sirens, ordered his men to fill their ears with wax, then lashed himself to the mast so he alone might hear the temptresses' call, while the crew rowed frantically past bright, alluring shoals.

Would it hurt to take the glasses off and stare at the rippled landscape? If transfixed, wouldn't her friends rescue her? Or might her mind be forever absorbed by the panorama?

People seldom mentioned the Spectral Flow – a blind spot on maps of the Slope. Even those hardy men who roamed the sharp-sand desert, spearing roul shamblers beneath the hollow dunes, kept awed distance from this poison landscape. A realm supposedly bereft of life.

Only now Sara recalled a day almost two years ago, when her mother lay dying in the house near the paper mill, with the Dolo waterwheel groaning a low background lament. From outside Melina's sickroom, Sara overheard Dwer discussing this place in a low voice.

Of course her younger brother was specially licensed to patrol the Slope and beyond, seeking violations of the Covenant and Scrolls. It surprised Sara only a little to learn he had visited the toxic land of psychotic colors. But from snippets wafting through the open door, it sounded as if *Melina* had also seen the Spectral Flow – before coming north to marry Nelo and raise a family by the quiet green Roney. The conversation had been in hushed tones of deathbed confidentiality, and Dwer never spoke of it after.

Above all, Sara was moved by the wistful tone of her dying mother's voice.

'Dwer ... remind me again about the colors ...'

The horses did not seem to need eye protections, and the two drivers wore theirs lackadaisically, as to stave off a well-known irritation rather than dire peril. Relieved to be out of the Buyur tunnel, Kepha murmured to Nuli, sharing the first laughter Sara had heard from any Illias.

She found her thoughts more coherent now, with surprise giving way to curiosity. *What about people and races who are naturally color-blind?* The effect must involve more than mere frequency variations on the electromagnetic spectrum, as the urrish glasses probably did more than merely darken. There must be some other effect. Light polarization? Or *psi*?

Emerson's rewq satisfied his own need for goggles. But Sara felt concern when he peeled back the filmy symbiont to take an unprotected peek. He *winced*, visibly recoiling from sensory overflow, as if a hoonish grooming fork had plunged into his eye. She started toward him – but that initial reaction was brief. A moment later the starman grinned at her, an expression of agonized delight.

Well, anything you can do – she thought, nudging her glasses forward . . .

Her first surprise was the pain that wasn't. Her irises adjusted, so the sheer volume of illumination was bearable.

Rather, Sara felt waves of nausea as the world seemed to shift and dissolve . . . as if she were peering through layer after layer of overlapping images.

The land's mundane topography was a terrain of layered lava flows, eroded canyons, and jutting mesas. Only now that seemed only the blank tapestry screen on which some mad g'Kek artist had embroidered an apparition in luminous paint and textured thread. Each time Sara blinked, her impressions shifted.

—Towering buttes were *fairy castles*, their fluttering pennants made of glowing shreds of windblown haze . . .

—Dusty basins became shimmering pools. Rivers of mercury and currents of blood seemed to flow uphill as merging swirls of immiscible fluid . . .

—Rippling like memory, a nearby cliff recalled Buyur architecture – the spires of Tarek Town – only with blank windows replaced by a million splendid glowing lights . . .

—Her gaze shifted to the dusty road, with pumice flying from the wagon wheels. But on another plane it seemed the spray made up countless glittering stars . . .

—Then the trail crested a small hill, revealing the most unlikely mirage of all . . . several narrow, fingerlike valleys, each surrounded by steep hills like ocean waves, frozen in their spuming torrent. Underneath those sheltering heights, the valley bottoms appeared verdant green, covered with impossible meadows and preposterous trees.

'Xi,' announced Kepha, murmuring happily in that accent Sara found eerily strange-familiar . . .

. . . and she abruptly knew why!

Surprise made Sara release the glasses, dropping them back over her eyes.

The castles and stars vanished . . .

. . . *but the meadows remained*. Four-footed shapes could be seen grazing on real grass, drinking from a very real stream.

Kurt and Jomah sighed. Emerson laughed and Prity clapped her hands. But Sara was too astonished to utter a sound. For now she knew the truth about Melina the Southerner, the woman who long ago came to the Roney, supposedly from the far-off Vale, to become Nelo's bride. Melina the happy eccentric, who raised three unusual children by the ceaseless drone of Dolo Dam.

Mother ... Sara thought, in numb amazement. *This must have been your home.*

The rest of the horsewomen arrived a few miduras later with their urrish companions, dirty and tired. The Illias unsaddled their faithful beasts before stripping off their riding gear and plunging into a warm volcanic spring, beneath jutting rocks where Sara and the other visitors rested.

Watching Emerson, Sara verified that one more portion of his battered brain must be intact, for the spaceman's eyes tracked the riders' nude femininity with normal male appreciation.

She squelched a jealous pang, knowing that her own form could never compete with those tanned, athletic figures below.

The starman glanced Sara's way and flushed several shades darker, so sheepishly rueful that she had to laugh out loud.

'Look, but don't touch,' she said, with an exaggerated waggle of one finger. He might not grasp every word, but the affectionate admonishment got through.

Grinning, he shrugged as if to say, *Who, me? I wouldn't think of it!*

The wagon passengers had already bathed, though more modestly. Not that nakedness was taboo elsewhere on the Slope. But the Illias women behaved as if they did not know – or care – about the simplest fact all human girls were taught about the opposite sex. That male *Homo sapiens* have primitive arousal responses inextricably bound up in their optic nerves.

Perhaps it's because they have no men, Sara thought. Indeed, she saw only female youths and adults, tending chores amid the barns and shelters. There were also urs, of Ulashtu's friendly tribe, tending their precious simla and donkey herds at the fringes of the oasis. The two sapient races did not avoid each other – Sara glimpsed friendly encounters. But in this narrow realm, each had its favored terrain.

Ulashtu knew Kurt, and must have spent time in the outer Slope. In fact, some Illias women also probably went forth, now and then, moving among unsuspecting villagers of the Six Races.

Melina had a good cover story when she came to Dolo, arriving with letters of introduction, and baby Lark on her hip. Everyone assumed she came from somewhere in the Vale. A typical arranged remarriage.

It never seemed an issue to Nelo, that his eldest son had an unknown father. Melina subtly discouraged inquiries into her past.

But a secret like this ...

With Ulashtu's band came a prisoner. *Ulgor*, the urrish tinker who befriended Sara back at Dolo, only to spring a trap, leading to captivity by Dedinger's fanatics and the reborn Urunthai. Now their roles were reversed. Sara noted Ulgor's triplet eyes staring in dismay at the astonishing oasis.

How the Urunthai would hate this place! Their predecessors seized our horses to destroy them all. Urrish sages later apologized, after Drake the Elder broke the Urunthai. But how can you undo death?

You cannot. But it is possible to *cheat* extinction. Watching fillies and colts gambol after their mares below a bright rocky overhang, Sara felt almost happy for a time. This oasis might even remain unseen by omniscient spy eyes of alien star lords, confused by the enclosing land of illusion. Perhaps Xi would survive when the rest of the Slope was made void of sapient life.

She saw Ulgor ushered to a pen near the desert prophet, Dedinger. The two did not speak.

Beyond the women splashing in the pool and the grazing herds, Sara had only to lift her eyes in order to brush a glittering landscape where each ripple and knoll pretended to be a thousand impossible things. *The country of lies* was a name for the Spectral Flow. No doubt a person got used to it, blanking out irritating chimeras that never proved useful or informative. Or else, perhaps the Illias had no need of dreams, since they lived each day awash in Jijo's fantasies.

The scientist in Sara wondered why it equally affected all races, or how such a marvel could arise naturally. *There's no mention of anything like it in Biblos. But humans only had a sprinkling of Galactic reference material when the* Tabernacle *left Earth. Perhaps this is a common phenomenon, found on many worlds.*

But how much more wonderful if Jijo had made something unique!

She stared at the horizon, letting her mind free-associate shapes out of the shimmering colors, until a mellow female voice broke in.

'You have your mother's eyes, Sara.'

She blinked, drawing back to find two humans nearby, dressed in the leather garments of Illias. The one who had spoken was the first elderly woman Sara had seen here.

The other was a *man*.

Sara stood up, blinking in recognition. 'F-Fallon?'

He had aged since serving as Dwer's tutor in the wilderness arts. Still, the former chief scout seemed robust, and smiled broadly.

A little tactlessly, she blurted, 'But I thought you were dead!'

He shrugged. 'People assume what they like. I never said I'd died.' A Zen koan if she ever heard one. But then Sara recalled what the other person said. Though shaded against the desert's glow, the old woman seemed to partake of the hues of the Spectral Flow.

'My name is Foruni,' she told Sara. 'I am senior rider.'

'You knew my mother?'

The older woman took Sara's hand. Her manner reminded Sara of Ariana Foo.

'Melina was my cousin. I've missed her, these many years – though infrequent letters told us of her remarkable children. You three validate her choice, though exile must not have been easy. Our horses and shadows are hard to leave behind.'

'Did Mother leave because of Lark?'

'We have ways of making it likely to bear girls. When a boy is born we foster him to discreet friends on the Slope, taking a female child in trade.'

Sara nodded. Exchange fostering was a common practice, helping cement alliances between villages or clans.

'But Mother wouldn't give Lark up.'

'Just so. In any event, we need agents out there, and Melina was dependable. So it was done, and the decision proved right ... although we mourned, on hearing of her loss.' Sara accepted this with a nod.

'What I don't understand is why only women?'

The elder had deep lines at the corners of her eyes, from a lifetime of squinting.

'It was required in the pact, when the aunties of *Urchachkin* tribe offered some humans and horses shelter in their most secret place, to preserve them against the Urunthai. In those early days, urs found our menfolk disquieting – so strong and boisterous, unlike their own husbands. It seemed simpler to arrange things on a female-to-female basis.

'Also, a certain fraction of boys tend to shrug off social constraints during adolescence, no matter how carefully they are raised. Eventually, some young man would have burst from the Illias realm without adequate preparation – and all it would take is one. In his need to preen and make a name, he might spill our secret to the Commons at large.'

'Girls act that way, too, sometimes,' Sara pointed out.

'Yes, but our odds were better this way. Ponder the young men you know, Sara. Imagine how they would have behaved.'

She pictured her brothers, growing up in this narrow oasis. Lark would have been sober and reliable. But Dwer, at fifteen, was very different than he became at twenty.

'And yet, I see you aren't all women ...'

The senior rider grinned. 'Nor are we celibates. From time to time we bring in mature males – often chief scouts, sages, or explorers – men who already know our secret, and are of an age to be calm, sensible companions ... yet still retain vigor in their step.'

Fallon laughed to cover brief embarrassment. 'My *step* is no longer my best feature.'

Foruni squeezed his arm. 'You'll do for a while yet.'

Sara nodded. 'An urrish-sounding solution.' Sometimes a group of young urs, lacking the means to support individual husbands, would share one, passing him from pouch to pouch.

The senior rider nodded, expressing subtleties of irony with languid motions of her neck. 'After many generations, we may have become more than a bit urrish ourselves.'

Sara glanced toward Kurt the Exploser, sitting on a smooth rock studying carefully guarded texts, with both Jomah and Prity lounging nearby.

'Then you sent the expedition to fetch Kurt because you want another—'

'Ifni, no! Kurt is much too old for such duties, and when we do bring in new partners it is with quiet discretion. Hasn't Kurt explained to you what this is all about? His role in the present crisis? The reason why we gambled so much to fetch you all?'

When Sara shook her head, Foruni's nostrils flared and she hissed like an urrish auntie, perplexed by foolish juniors.

'Well, that's his affair. All I know is that we must escort you the rest of the way as soon as possible. You'll rest with us tonight, my niece. But alas, family reminiscence must wait till the emergency passes . . . or once it overwhelms us all.'

Sara nodded, resigned to more hard riding.

'From here . . . can we see—?'

Fallon nodded, a gentle smile on his creased features.

'I'll show you, Sara. It's not far.'

She took his arm as Foruni bade them return soon for a feast. Already Sara's nose filled with scents from the cookfire. But soon her thoughts were on the path as they crossed narrow, miraculous meadows, then scrublands where simlas grazed, and beyond to a steepening pass wedged between two hills. Sunlight was fading rapidly, and soon the smallest moon, Passen, could be seen gleaming near the far west horizon.

She heard *music* before they crested the pass. The familiar sound of Emerson's dulcimer, pinging softly ahead. Sara was loath to interrupt, yet the glow drew her – a shimmering lambency rising from Jijo, filling a vista beyond the sheltered oasis.

The layered terrain seemed transformed in pearly moonlight. Gone were the garish colors, yet there remained an extravagant effect on the imagination. It took an effort of will in order not to go gliding across the slopes, believing in false oceans and battlements, in ghost cities and starscapes, in myriad phantom worlds that her pattern-gleaning brain crafted out of opal rays and shadows.

Fallon took Sara's elbow, turning her toward Emerson.

The starman stood on a rocky eminence with the dulcimer propped before him, beating its forty-six strings. The melody was eerie. The rhythm orderly, yet impossible to constrain, like a mathematical series that refused to converge.

Emerson's silhouette was framed by flickering *fire* as he played for nature's maelstrom.

This fire was no imagining – no artifact of an easily fooled eye. It rippled and twisted in the far distance, rimming the broad curves of a mighty peak that reared halfway up the sky.

Fresh lava. Jijo's hot blood.

The planet's nectar of renewal, melted and reforged.

Hammering taut strings, the Stranger played for Mount Guenn, serenading the volcano while it repaid him with a halo of purifying flame.

V

A PROPOSAL FOR A USEFUL TOOL/STRATEGY
BASED ON OUR EXPERIENCE ON JIJO

IT HAS BEEN NEARLY A MILLENNIUM SINCE A LARGE OUT-
BREAK OF TRAEKINESS WAS FOUND.

These flare-ups used to be frequent embarrassments, where
stacks of hapless rings were found languishing without even a single
master torus to guide them. But no word of such an occurrence has
come within the memory of living wax.

The reaction of our *Polkjhy* ship to this discovery on Jijo was
disgusted loathing.

HOWEVER, LET US NOW PAUSE and consider how the Great
Jophur League might learn/benefit from this experiment. Never
before have cousin rings dwelled in such intimacy with other races.
Although polluted/contaminated, these traeki have also acquired
waxy expertise about urs, hoon, and qheuen sapient life-forms – as
well as human wolflings and g'Kek vermin.

MOREOVER, the very traits that we Jophur find repellent in
traeki-natural rings – their lack of focus, self or ambition – appear to
enable them to achieve empathy with unitary beings! The other five
races of Jijo trust these ring stacks. They confide secrets, share
confidences, delegate some traekis with medical tasks and even
powers of life continuation/cessation.

IMAGINE THIS POSSIBILITY. SUPPOSE WE ATTEMPT A RUSE.

INTENTIONALLY, we might create new traeki and arrange for them
to 'escape' the loving embrace of our noble clan. Genuinely believing
they are in flight from 'oppressive' master rings, these stacks would be
induced to seek shelter among some of the races we call enemies.

Next suppose that, using this knack of vacuous empathy, they
make friendships among our foes. As generations pass, they become
trusted comrades.

At which point we arrange for agents to snatch – to harvest – some
of these rogue traeki, converting them to Jophur exactly as we did when
Asx was transformed into Ewasx, by applying the needed master rings.

Would this not give us quick expertise about our foes?

*

GRANTED, this Ewasx experiment has not been a complete success. The old traeki, Asx, managed to melt many waxy memories before completion of metamorphosis. The resulting partial amnesia has proved inconvenient.

Yet, this does not detract from the value of the scheme – to plant empathic spies in our enemies' midst. Spies who are believable because they think they are true friends! Nevertheless, with the boon of master rings, we can reclaim lost brethren wherever and whenever we find them.

STREAKERS

MAKANEE

There were two kinds of pupils in the wide, wet classroom.

One group signified hope – the other, despair.

One was illegal – the other, hapless.

The first type was innocent and eager.

The second had already seen and heard far too much.

> # good fish . . .
> # goodfish, goodfish . . .
> # good-good FISH! #

Dr. Makanee never used to hear Primal Delphin spoken aboard the *Streaker*. Not when the *keeneenk* master, Creideiki, used to hold the crew rock steady by his unwavering example.

Nowadays, alas, one commonly picked up snatches of old-speech – the simple, emotive squealing used by unaltered Tursiops in Earth's ancient seas. As ship physician, even Makanee sometimes found herself grunting a snatch phrase, when frustrations crowded in from all sides . . . and when no one was listening.

Makanee gazed across a broad chamber, half-filled with water, as students jostled near a big tank at the spinward end, avid to be fed. There were almost thirty neo-dolphins, plus a dozen six-armed, monkeylike figures, scrambling up the shelflined walls, or else diving to swim agilely with webbed hands. Just half the original group of *Kiqui* survived since they were snatched hastily from far-off Kithrup, but the remaining contingent seemed healthy and glad to frolic with their dolphin friends.

I'm still not sure we did the right thing, taking them along. Neo-dolphins are much too young to take on the responsibilities of patronhood.

A pair of teachers tried bringing order to the unruly mob. Makanee saw the younger instructor – her former head nurse, *Peepoe* – use a whirring harness arm to snatch living snacks from the tank and toss them to the waiting crowd of pupils. The one who uttered the Primal burst – a middle-aged dolphin with listless eyes –

smacked his jaw around a blue thing with writhing tendrils that looked nothing like a fish. Still, the fin crooned happily while he munched.

Goodfish ... good-good-good!

Makanee had known poor Jecajeca before *Streaker* launched from Earth – a former astrophotographer who loved his cameras and the glittering black of space. Now Jecajeca was another casualty of *Streaker*'s long retreat, fleeing ever farther from the warm oceans they called home.

This voyage was supposed to last six months, not two and a half years, with no end in sight. A young client race shouldn't confront the challenges we have, almost alone.

Taken in that light, it seemed a wonder just a quarter of the crew had fallen to devolution psychosis.

Give it time, Makanee. You may yet travel that road yourself.

'Yes, they *are* tasty, Jecajeca,' Peepoe crooned, turning the reverted dolphin's outburst into a lesson. 'Can you tell me, in Anglic, where this new variety of "fish" comes from?'

Eager grunts and squeaks came from the brighter half of the class, those with a future. But Peepoe stroked the older dolphin with sonar encouragement, and soon Jecajeca's glazed eye cleared a bit. To please her, he concentrated.

'F-f-rom out-side ... Good s-s-sun ... good wat-t-ter ...' Other students offered raspberry cheers, rewarding this short climb back toward what he once had been. But it was a slippery hill. Nor was there much a doctor could do. The cause lay in no organic fault.

Reversion is the ultimate sanctuary from worry.

Makanee approved of the decision of Lieutenant Tsh't and Gillian Baskin, not to release the journal of Alvin the Hoon to the crew at large.

If there's one thing the crew don't need right now, it's to hear of a religion preaching that it's okay to devolve.

Peepoe finished feeding the reverted adults, while her partner took care of the children and Kiqui. On spying Makanee, she did an agile flip and swam across the chamber in two powerful fluke strokes, resurfacing amid a burst of spray.

'Yesss, Doctor? You want to see me?'

Who *wouldn't* want to see Peepoe? Her skin shone with youthful luster, and her good spirits never flagged, not even when the crew had to flee Kithrup, abandoning so many friends.

'We need a qualified nurse for a mission. A long one, I'm afraid.'

Ratcheting clicks spread from Peepoe's brow as she pondered. 'Kaa's outpost. Is someone hurt-t?'

'I'm not sure. It may be food poisoning ... or else kingree fever.'

Peepoe's worried expression eased. 'In that case, can't Kaa take care of it himself? I have duties here.'

'Olachan can handle things while you are away.'

Peepoe shook her head, a human gesture by now so ingrained that even reverted fins used it. 'There must be two teachers. We can't mix the children and Kiqui with the hapless ones too much.'

Just five dolphin infants had been born to crew members so far, despite a growing number of signatures on the irksome *Breeding Petition*. But those five youngsters deserved careful guidance. And that counted double for the Kiqui – presentients who appeared ripe for uplift by some lucky Galactic clan who won the right to adopt them. That laid a heavy moral burden on the *Streaker* crew.

'I'll keep a personal eye on the Kiqui ... and we'll free the kids' parents from duty on a rotating basis, to join the creche as teachers' aidesss. That's the best I can do, Peepoe.'

The younger dolphin acquiesced, but grumbled. 'This'll turn out to be a wild tuna chase. Knowing Kaa, he prob'ly forgot to clean the water filters.'

Everyone knew the pilot had a long-standing yearning for Peepoe. Dolphins could sonar-scan each other's innards, so there was no concealing simple, persistent passions.

Poor Kaa. No wonder he lost his nickname.

'There is a second reason you're going,' Makanee revealed in a low voice.

'I thought so. Does it have to do with gravitic signals and depth bombsss?'

'This hideout is jeopardized,' Makanee affirmed. 'Gillian and Tsh't plan to move *Streaker* soon.'

'You want me to help find another refuge? By scanning more of these huge junk piles, along the way?' Peepoe blew a sigh. 'What else? Shall I compose a symphony, invent a star drive, and dicker treaties with the natives while I'm at it?'

Makanee chuttered. 'By all accounts, the sunlit sea above is the most pleasant we've encountered since departing Calafia. Everyone will envy you.'

When Peepoe snorted dubiously, Makanee added in Trinary—

* *Legends told by whales*
   * *Call one trait admirable—*
      * *Adaptability!* *

This time, Peepoe laughed appreciatively. It was the sort of thing Captain Creideiki might have said, if he were still around.

Back in sick bay, Makanee finished treating her last patient and closed shop for the day. There had been the usual psychosomatic ailments, and inevitable accidental injuries from working outside in armored suits, bending and welding metal under a mountainous heap of discarded ships. At least the number of digestive complaints had gone down since teams with nets began harvesting native food. Jijo's upper sea teemed with life, much of it wholesome, if properly supplemented. Tsh't had even been preparing to allow liberty parties outside ... before sensors picked up starships entering orbit.

Was it pursuit? More angry fleets chasing *Streaker* for her secrets? No one should have been able to trace Gillian's sneaky path by a nearby supergiant whose sooty winds had disabled the robot guards of the Migration Institute.

But the idea wasn't as original as we hoped. Others came earlier including a rogue band of humans. I guess we shouldn't be surprised if it occurs to our pursuers, as well.

Makanee's chronometer beeped a reminder. The ship's council – two dolphins, two humans, and a mad computer – was meeting once more to ponder how to thwart an implacable universe.

There was a sixth member who silently attended, offering fresh mixtures of opportunity and disaster at every turn. Without that member's contributions, *Streaker* would have died or been captured long ago.

Or else, without her we'd all be safe at home.

Either way, there was no escaping her participation.

Ifni, capricious goddess of chance.

HANNES

It was hard to get anything done. Dr. Baskin kept stripping away members of his engine-room gang, assigning them other tasks.

He groused. 'It's too soon to give up on *Streaker*, I tell you!'

'I'm not giving her up quite yet,' Gillian answered. 'But with that carbonite coating weighing the hull down—'

'We've been able to analyze the stuff, at last. It seems the stellar wind blowing off Izmunuti wasn't just atomic or molecular carbon, but a kind of star soot made up of tubes, coils, spheres, and such.'

Gillian nodded, as if she had expected this.

'*Buckyballs*. Or in GalTwo—' Pursed lips let out a clicking trill that meant *container home for individual atoms*. 'I did some research in the captured Library cube. It seems an interlaced mesh of these microshapes can become superconducting, carrying away vast amounts of heat. You're not going to peel it off easily with any of the tools we have.'

'There could be advantages to such stuff.'

'The Library says just a few clans have managed to synthesize the material. But what good is it, if it makes the hull heavy and seals our weapons ports so we can't fight?'

Suessi argued that *her* alternative was hardly any better. True, a great heap of ancient starships surrounded them, and they had reactivated the engines of a few. But that was a far cry from finding a fit replacement for the Snark-class survey craft that had served this crew so well.

These are ships the Buyur didn't think worth taking with them, when they evacuated this system!

Above all, how were dolphins supposed to operate a starship that had been built back when humans were learning to chip tools out of flint? *Streaker* was a marvel of clever compromises, redesigned so beings lacking legs or arms could move about and get their jobs done – either striding in sixlegged walker units, or by swimming through broad flooded chambers.

Dolphins are crackerjack pilots and specialists. Someday lots of Galactic clans may hire one or two at a time, offering them special facilities as pampered professionals. But few races will ever want a ship like Streaker, *with all the hassles involved.*

Gillian was insistent.

'We've adapted before. Surely some of these old ships have designs we might use.'

Before the meeting broke up, he offered one last objection.

'You know, all this fiddling with other engines, as well as our own, may let a trace signal slip out, even through all the water above us.'

'I know, Hannes.' Her eyes were grim. 'But speed is crucial now. Our pursuers already know roughly where we are. They may be otherwise occupied for the moment, but they'll be coming soon. We must prepare to move *Streaker* to another hiding place, or else evacuate to a different ship altogether.'

So, with resignation, Suessi juggled staff assignments, stopped work on the hull, and augmented teams sent out to alien wrecks – a task that was both hazardous and fascinating at the same time. Many of the abandoned derelicts seemed more valuable than ships impoverished Earth had purchased through used vessel traders. Under other circumstances, this Midden pile might have been a terrific find.

'Under other circumstances,' he muttered. 'We'd never have come here in the first place.'

SOONERS

EMERSON

What a wonderful place!

Ever since glorious sunset, he had serenaded the stars and the growling volcano . . . then a crescent of sparkling reflections on the face of the largest moon. Dead cities, abandoned in vacuum long ago.

Now Emerson turns east toward a new day. Immersed in warm fatigue, standing on heights protecting the narrow meadows of Xi, he confronts the raucous invasion of dawn.

Alone.

Even the horse-riding women keep inside their shelters at daybreak, a time when glancing beams from the swollen sun sweep all the colors abandoned by night, pushing them ahead like an overwhelming tide. A wave of speckled light. Bittersharp, like shards of broken glass.

His former self might have found it too painful to endure – that logical engineer who always knew what was real, and how to classify it. The clever Emerson, so good at fixing broken things. *That* one might have quailed before the onslaught. A befuddling tempest of hurtful rays.

But now that seems as nothing compared with his other agonies, since crashing on this world. In contrast to having part of his brain ripped out, for instance, the light storm could hardly even be called irritating. It feels more like the claws of fifty mewling kittens, setting his callused skin a-prickle with countless pinpoint scratches.

Emerson spreads his arms wide, opening himself to the enchanted land, whose colors slice through roadblocks in his mind, incinerating barriers, releasing from numb imprisonment a spasm of pent-up images.

Banded canyons shimmer under layer after lustrous layer of strange images. Explosions in space. Half-drowned worlds where bulbous islets glimmer like metal mushrooms. A *house* made of ice that stretches all the way around a glowing red star, turning the sun's wan glow in a hearth's tamed fire.

These and countless other sights waver before him. Each clamors for attention, pretending to be a sincere reflection of the past. But most images are illusions, he knows.

A phalanx of armored damsels brandishes whips of forked

lightning against fire-breathing dragons, whose wounds bleed rainbows across the desert floor. Though intrigued, he dismisses such scenes, collaborating with his rewq to edit out the irrelevant, the fantastic, the easy.

What does that leave?

A lot, it seems.

From one nearby lava field, crystal particles reflect tart sunbursts that his eye makes out as vast, distant *explosions*. All sense of scale vanishes as mighty ships die in furious battle before him. Squadrons rip each other. Fleet formations are scythed by moving folds of tortured space.

True!

He knows this to be a real memory. Unforgettable. Too exquisitely horrible to let go, this side of death.

So why was it lost?

Emerson labors to fashion words, using their rare power to lock the recollection back where it belongs.

I . . . saw . . . this . . . happen.

I . . . was . . . there.

He turns for more. Over in *that* direction, amid a simple boulder field, lay a galactic spiral, seen from above the swirling wheel. View from a *shallow place* where few spatial tides ever churn. Mysteries lay in that place, undisturbed by waves of time.

Until someone finally came along, with more curiosity than sense intruding on the tomblike stillness.

Someone . . . ?

He chooses a better word.

. . . We . . .

Then, a better word, yet.

. . . Streaker!

A slight turn and he sees her, traced among the stony layers of a nearby mesa. A slender caterpillar shape, studded by the spiky flanges meant to anchor a ship to this universe . . . a universe hostile to everything *Streaker* stood for. He stares nostalgically at the vessel. Scarred and patched, often by his own hand, the hull's beauty could only be seen by those who loved her.

. . . loved her . . .

Words have power to shift the mind. He scans the horizon, this time for a human face. One he adored, without hope of anything but friendship in return. But her image isn't found in the dazzling landscape.

Emerson sighs. For now, it is enough to sort through his rediscoveries. A single correlation proves especially useful. If it *hurts*, then it must be a real memory.

What could that fact mean?

The question, all by itself, seems to make his skull crack with pain! Could that be the intent? To *prevent* him from remembering?

Stabbing sensations assail him. That question is worse! It must never be asked!

Emerson clutches his head as the point is driven home with hammerlike blows.

Never, ever, ever . . .

Rocking back, he lets out a howl. He bays like a wounded animal, sending ululations over rocky outcrops. The sound plummets like a stunned bird . . . then catches itself just short of crashing.

In a steep, swooping turn, it comes streaking back . . . as *laughter*!

Emerson bellows.

He roars contempt.

He brays rebellious joy.

Through streaming tears, he *asks* the question and glories in the answer, knowing at last that he is no coward. His amnesia is no hysterical retreat. No quailing from traumas of the past.

What happened to his mind was no accident.

Hot lead seems to pour down his spine as programmed inhibitions fight back. Emerson's heart pounds, threatening to burst his chest. Yet he scarcely notices, facing the truth head-on, with a kind of brutal elation.

Somebody . . . did . . . this . . .

Before him, looming from the fractured mesa, comes an image of cold eyes. Pale and milky. Mysterious, ancient, deceitful. It might have been terrifying – to someone with anything left to lose.

Somebody . . . did . . . this . . . to . . . me!

With fists clenched and cheeks awash, Emerson sees the colors melt as his eyes fill with liquid pain. But that does not matter anymore.

Not what he *sees*.

Only what he knows.

The Stranger casts a single cry, merging with the timeless hills.

A shout of defiance.

EWASX

They show courage.

You were right about that, My rings.

We Jophur had not expected anyone to approach so soon after

the *Polkjhy* slashed an area of twenty *korech* around our landing site. But now a delegation comes, waving a pale banner.

At first, the symbolism confuses our *Polkjhy* communications staff. But *this* stack's very own association rings relay the appropriate memory of a human tradition – that of using a white flag to signify truce.

WE INFORM THE CAPTAIN LEADER. That exalted stack appears pleased with our service. My rings, you are indeed well informed about vermin! These worthless-seeming toruses, left over from the former Asx, hold waxy expertise about human ways that could prove useful to the Obeyer Alliance, if a prophesied time of change truly has come upon the Five Galaxies.

The Great Library proved frustratingly sparse regarding the small clan from Earth. How ironic then, that we should find proficient knowledge in such a rude, benighted world as this Jijo. Knowledge that may help our goal of extinguishing the wolflings at long last.

What? You quiver at the prospect?

In joyful anticipation of service? In expectation that yet another enemy of our clan shall meet extinction?

No. Instead you shudder, filling our core with mutinous fumes!

My poor, polluted rings. Are you so infested with alien notions that you actually hold *affection* for noisome bipeds? *And* for vermin g'Kek survivors we are sworn to erase?

Perhaps the poison is too rife for you to be suitable, even with useful expertise.

The Oailie were right. Without master rings, all a stack can become is a pile of sentimental traeki.

LARK

The tall star lord was no less imposing in a homespun shirt and trousers than in his old black-and-silver uniform. Rann's massive arms and wedgelike torso tempted one to imagine impossible things ... like pitting him against a fully grown hoon in a wrestling match.

That might take some of the starch out of him, Lark pondered. *There's nothing fundamentally superior about the guy.* Underlying Rann's physique and smug demeanor was the same technology that had given Ling the beauty of a goddess. *I might be just as strong – and live three hundred years – if I weren't born in a forlorn wilderness.*

Rann spoke Anglic in the sharp Danik accent, with burning undertones like his Rothen overlords.

'The favor you ask is both risky and impertinent. Can you offer one good reason why I should cooperate?'

Watched by militia guards, the star lord sat cross-legged in a cave overlooking Dooden Mesa, where camouflaged ramps blended with the surrounding forest under tarpaulins of cunning blur cloth. Beyond the g'Kek settlement, distant ridges seemed to ripple as vast stands of boo bent their giant stems before the wind. In the grotto's immediate vicinity, steam rose from geothermal vents, concealing the captive from Galactic instruments – or so the sages hoped.

Before Rann lay a stack of data lozenges bearing the sigil of the Galactic Library, the same brown slabs Lark and Uthen found in the wrecked Danik station.

'I could give several reasons,' Lark growled. 'Half the qheuens I know are sick or dying from some filthy bug *you* bastards released—'

Rann waved a dismissive hand.

'Your supposition. One that I deny.'

Lark's throat strangled in anger. Despite every point of damning evidence, Rann obstinately rejected the possibility of Rothen-designed genocidal germs. '*What you suggest is quite preposterous,*' he said earlier. '*It is contrary to our lords' kindly natures.*'

Lark's first response was amazement. *Kindly nature?* Wasn't Rann present when Bloor, the unlucky portraitist, photographed a Rothen face without its mask, and Ro-kenn reacted by unleashing fiery death on everyone in sight?

It did Lark no good to recite the same point-by-point indictment he had laid out for Ling. The big man was too contemptuous of anything Jijoan to heed a logical argument.

Or else he was involved all along, and now sees denial as his best defense.

Ling sat miserably on a stalagmite stump, unable to meet her erstwhile leader in the eye. They had come seeking Rann's help only after she failed to read the reclaimed archives with her own data plaque.

'All right,' Lark resumed. 'If justice and mercy won't persuade you, maybe threats will!'

Harsh laughter from the big man.

'How many hostages can you spare, young barbarian? You have just three of us to stave off fire from above. Your intimidation lacks conviction.'

Lark felt like a bush lemming confronting a ligger. Still, he leaned closer.

'Things have changed, Rann. Before, we hoped to trade you back to the Rothen ship for concessions. Now, that ship and your mates are sealed in a bubble. It's the *Jophur* we'll negotiate with. I suspect they'll care less about visible wear and tear on your person, when we hand you over.'

Rann's face was utterly blank. Lark found it an improvement.

Ling broke in.

'Please. This approach is pointless.' She stood and approached her Danik colleague. 'Rann, we may have to spend the rest of our lives with these people, or share whatever fate the Jophur dish out. A cure may help square things with the Six. Their sages promise to absolve us, if we find a treatment soon.'

Rann's silent grimace required no rewq interpretation. He did not savor the absolution of savages.

'Then there are the photograms,' Ling said. 'You are of the Danik Inner Circle, so you may have seen the true Rothen face before. But I found it a shock. Clearly, those photographic images give Jijo's natives some leverage. In loyalty to our mast ... to the Rothen, you must consider that.'

'And who would they show their pictures to?' Rann chuckled. Then he glanced at Lark and his expression changed. 'You would not actually—'

'Hand them over to the Jophur? Why bother? They can crack open your starship any time they wish, and dissect your masters down to their nucleic acids. Face it, Rann, the disguise is no good anymore. The Jophur have their mulch rings wrapped tightly around your overlords.'

'Around the beloved patrons of all humanity!'

Lark shrugged. 'True or not, that changes nothing. If the Jophur choose, they can have the Rothen declared anathema across the Five Galaxies. The fines may be calamitous.'

'And what of your Six Races?' Rann answered hotly. 'Each of you are criminals, as well. You all face punishment – not just the humans and others living here, but the home branches of each species, elsewhere in space!'

'Ah.' Lark nodded. 'But this we have always known. We grow up discussing the dour odds. The guilt. It colors our distinctly pleasant outlook on life.' He smiled sardonically. 'But I wonder if an *optimistic* fellow like yourself, seeing himself part of a grand destiny, can be as resigned to losing all he knows and loves.'

At last, the Danik's expression turned dark.

'Rann,' Ling urged. 'We have to make common cause.'

He glared at her archly. 'Without Ro-kenn's approval?'

'They've taken him far away from here. Even Lark doesn't know where. Anyway, I'm now convinced we must consider what's best for humanity ... for *Earth* ... independent of the Rothen.'

'There cannot be one without the other!'

She shrugged. 'Pragmatism, then. If we help these people, perhaps they can do the same for us.'

The big man snorted skepticism. But after several duras, he brushed the stack of data lozenges with his toe. 'Well, I am curious. These aren't from the station Library. I'd recognize the color glyphs. You already tried to gain access?'

Ling nodded.

'Then maybe I had better have a crack at it.'

He looked at Lark again.

'You know the risk, as soon as I turn my reader on?'

Lark nodded. Lester Cambel had already explained. In all probability, the digital cognizance given off by a tiny info unit would be masked by the geysers and microquakes forever popping under the Rimmers.

Yet, to be safe, every founding colony, from g'Keks and glavers to urs and humans, sent their sneakships down to the Midden. Not a single computer was kept. Our ancestors must have thought the danger very real.

'You needn't lecture a sooner about risk,' he told the big man. 'Our lives are the floating tumble of Ifni's dice. We know it's not a matter of winning.

'Our aim is to put off losing for as long as we can.'

They were brought meals by Jimi, one of the blessed who dwelled in the redemption sanctuary – a cheerful young man, nearly as large as Rann but with a far gentler manner. Jimi also delivered a note from Sage Cambel. The embassy to the Jophur had arrived at Festival Glade, hoping to contact the latest intruders.

The handwritten letter had a coda:

Any progress?

Lark grimaced. He had no way of telling what 'progress' meant in this case, though he doubted much was being made.

Ling helped load beige slabs into Rann's data plaque – returned for this purpose. Together, the Daniks puzzled over a maze of sparkling symbols.

Books from pre-*Tabernacle* days described what it was like to range the digital world – a realm of countless dimensions, capabilities, and correlations, where any simulation might take on palpable reality. Of course mere descriptions could not make up for lack of experience. *But I'm not like some fabled islander, befuddled by Captain Cook's rifle and compass. I have concepts, some math, a notion of what's possible.*

At least, he hoped so.

Then he worried – might the Daniks be putting on an act? Pretending to have difficulty while they stalled for time?

There wasn't much left. Soon Uthen would die, then other chitinous friends. Worse, new rumors from the coast told of hoonish villagers snuffling and wheezing, their throat sacs cracking from some strange ailment.

Come on! he urged silently. *What's so hard about using a fancy computer index to look something up?*

Rann threw down a data slab, cursing guttural phonemes of alien argot.

'It's encrypted!'

'I thought so,' Ling said. 'But I figured you, as a member of the Inner—'

'Even we of the circle are not told everything. Still, I know the outlines of a Rothen code, and this is different.' He frowned.

'Yet familiar somehow.'

'Can you break it?' Lark asked, peering at a maze of floating symbols.

'Not using this crude reader. We'd need something bigger. A real computer.'

Ling straightened, looking knowingly at Lark. But she left the decision up to him.

Lark blew air through his cheeks.

'Hr-rm. I think that might be arranged.'

A mixed company of militia drilled under nearby trees, looking brave in their fog-striped war paint. Lark saw only a few burly qheuens, though – the five-clawed heavy armor of Jijoan military might.

As one of the few living Jijoans ever to fly aboard an alien aircraft and see their tools firsthand, Lark knew what a fluke the Battle of the Glade had been – where spears, arbalests, and rifles prevailed against star-roaming gods. That freak chance would not be repeated. Still, there were reasons to continue training. *It keeps the volunteers busy, and helps prevent a rekindling of old-time feuds. Whatever happens – whether we submit with bowed heads to final judgment, or go down fighting – we can't afford disunion.*

Lester Cambel greeted them under a tent beside a bubbling hot spring.

'We're taking a risk doing this,' the elderly sage said.

'What choice do we have?'

In Lester's eyes, Lark read his answer.

We can let Uthen and countless qheuens die, if that's the price it takes for others to live.

Lark hated being a sage. He loathed the way he was expected to think – contemplating trade-offs that left you damned, either way you turned.

Cambel sighed. 'Might as well make the attempt. I doubt the artifact will even turn on.'

At a rough log table, Cambel's human and urrish aides compared several gleaming objects with ancient illustrations. Rann stared in amazement at the articles, which had been carried here from the shore of a far-off caustic lake.

'But I thought you discarded all your digital—'

'We did. Our ancestors did. These items are leftovers. Relics of the Buyur.'

'Impossible. The Buyur withdrew half a million years ago!'

Lark told an abbreviated version of the story – about a crazy mulc-spider with a collecting fetish. A creature fashioned for destruction, who spent millennia sealing treasures in cocoons of congealed time.

Laboring day and night, traeki alchemists had found a formula to dissolve the golden preservation shells, spilling the contents back into the real world. *Lucky for us these experts happened to be in the area*, Lark thought. The tired-looking traekis stood just outside, venting yellow vapor from chemsynth rings.

Rann stroked one reclaimed object, a black trapezoid, evidently a larger cousin to his portable data plaque.

'The power crystals look negentropic and undamaged. Do you know if it still works?'

Lark shrugged. 'You're familiar with the type?'

'Galactic technology is fairly standard, though humans didn't exist, as such, when this thing was made. It is a higher-level model than I've used, but . . . ' The sky human sat down before the ancient artifact, pressing one of its jutting bulges.

The device abruptly burst forth streams of light that reached nearly to the canopy. The High Sage and his team scrambled back. Urrish smiths snorted, coiling their long necks while human techs made furtive gestures to ward off evil.

Even among Cambel's personal acolytes – his book-weaned 'experts' – our sophistication is thin enough to scratch with a fingernail.

'The Buyur mostly spoke Galactic Three,' Rann said. 'But GalTwo is close to universal, so we'll try it first.'

He switched to that syncopated code, uttering clicks, pops, and groans so rapidly that Lark was soon lost, unable to follow the arcane dialect of computer commands. The star lord's hands also moved, darting among floating images. Ling joined the effort, reaching in to seize ersatz objects that had no meaning to Lark, tossing away any she deemed irrelevant, giving Rann working room. Soon the area was clear but for a set of floating dodecahedrons, with rippling symbols coursing each twelve-sided form.

'*The Buyur were good programmers,*' Rann commented, lapsing into GalSix. '*Though their greatest passion went to biological inventions, they were not slackers in the digital arts.*'

Lark glanced at Lester, who had gone to the far end of the table to lay a pyramidal stack of *sensor stones*, like a hill of gleaming opals. Tapping one foot nervously, the sage kept wary vigil, alert for any spark of warning fire.

Turning farther, Lark found the mountain cleft deserted. The militia company had departed.

No one with sense would remain while this is going on.

Rann muttered a curse.

'*I had hoped the machine would recognize idiosyncrasies in the encryption, if it is a standard commercial cypher used widely in the Five Galaxies. Or there may be quirks specific to some race or alliance.*

'*Alas, the computer says it does not recognize the cryptographic approach used in these memory slabs. It calls the coding technique . . . innovative.*'

Lark knew the term was considered mildly insulting among the great old star clans.

'Could it be a pattern developed since the Buyur left Jijo?'

Rann nodded. 'Half an eon is a while, even by Galactic standards.'

Ling spoke, eagerly. 'Perhaps it's Terran.'

The big man stared at her, then nodded, switching to Anglic.

'That might explain the vague familiarity. But why would any Rothen use an Earther code? You know what they think of wolfling technology. Especially anything produced by those unbelieving Terragens—'

'Rann,' Ling cut in, her voice grown hushed. 'These slabs may not have belonged to Ro-kenn or Ro-pol.'

'Who then? You deny ever seeing them before. Neither have I. That leaves . . .'

He blinked, then pounded a heavy fist on the wooden slats. 'We must crack this thing! Ling, let us commence unleashing the unit's entire power on finding the key.'

Lark stepped forward. 'Are you sure that's wise?'

'You seek disease cures for your fellow savages? Well, the Jophur ship squats on the ruins of our station, and our ship is held captive. This may be your only chance.'

Clearly, Rann had another reason for his sudden zeal. Still, everyone apparently wanted the same thing – for now.

Lester looked unhappy, but he gave permission with a nod, returning to his vigil over the sensor stones.

We're doing it for you, Uthen, Lark thought.

Moments later, he had to retreat several more steps as space above the prehistoric computer grew crowded. Innumerable glyphs and signs collided like snowflakes in an arctic blizzard. The Buyur machine was applying prodigious force of digital intellect to solving a complex puzzle.

As Rann worked – hands darting in and out of the pirouetting flurry – he wore an expression of simmering rage. The kind of resentful anger that could only come from one source.

Betrayal.

A midura passed before the relic computer announced preliminary results. By then Lester Cambel was worn out. Perspiration stained his tunic and he wheezed each breath. But Lester would let no one else take over watching the sensor stones.

'It takes long training to sense the warning glows,' he explained. 'Right now, if I relax my eyes in just the right way, I can barely make out a soft glow in a gap between two of the bottommost stones.

Long training? Lark wondered as he peered into the fragile pyramid, quickly making out a faint iridescence, resembling the muted flame that licked the rim of a mulching pan when a dead traeki was boiled, rendering the fatting rings for return to Jijo's cycle.

Cambel went on describing, as if Lark did not already see.

'Someday, if there's time, we'll teach you to perceive the passive resonance, Lark. In this case it is evoked by the Jophur battleship. Its great motors are now idling, forty leagues from here. Unfortunately, even that creates enough background noise to mask any new disturbance.'

'Such as?'

'Such as *another* set of gravitic repulsors . . . moving this way.'

Lark nodded grimly. Like a rich urrish trader with two husbands in her brood pouches. big starships carried smaller ships – scrappy and swift – to launch on deadly errands. That was the chief risk worrying Lester.

Lark considered going back to watch the two Daniks work, invoking software demons in quest of a mathematical key. But what good would he do staring at the unfathomable? Instead, he bent close to the stones, knowing each flicker to be an echo of titanic forces, like those that drove the sun.

For a time he sensed no more than that soft bluish flame. But then Lark began noticing another rhythm, matching the mute shimmer, beat by beat. The source throbbed near his rib cage, above his pounding heart.

He slid a hand into his tunic and grabbed his amulet – a fragment of the Holy Egg that hung from a leather thong. It was warm. The pulse-like cadence seemed to build with each passing dura, causing his arm to vibrate painfully.

What could the Egg have in common with the engines of a Galactic cruiser? Except that both seem bent on troubling me till I die?

From far away, he heard Rann give an angry shout. The big Danik pounded the table, nearly toppling the fragile stones.

Cambel left to find out what Rann had learned. But Lark could not follow. He felt pinned by a rigor that spread from his fist on up his arm. It crossed his chest, then swarmed down his crouched legs.

'*Uh-huhnnn . . .*'

He tried to speak, but no words came. A kind of paralysis robbed him of the will to move.

Year after year he had striven to achieve what came easily to some pilgrims, when members of all Six Races sought communion with Jijo's gift – the Egg, that enigmatic wonder. To some it gave a blessing – guidance patterns, profound and moving. Consolation for the predicament of exile.

But never to Lark. Never the sinner.

Until now.

But instead of transcendent peace, Lark tasted a bitter tang, like molten metal in his mouth. His eardrums scraped, as if some massive rock were being pushed through a tube much too narrow. Amid his confusion, gaps in the sensor array seemed like the vacuum abyss between planets. The gemstones were moons, brushing each other with ponderous grace.

Before his transfixed eyes, the silken flame grew a minuscule swelling, like a new shoot budding off a rosebush. The new bulge *moved*, detaching from its parent, creeping around the surface of one stone, crossing a gap, then moving gradually upward.

It was subtle. Without the heightened sensitivity of his seizure, Lark might not have noticed.

Something's coming.

But he could only react with a cataleptic gurgle.

Behind Lark came more sounds of fury – Rann throwing a tantrum over some discovery. Figures moved around the outraged alien . . . Lester and the militia guards. No one paid Lark any mind.

Desperately, he sought the place where volition resides. The center of will. The part that commands a foot to step, an eye to shift, a voice to utter words. But his soul seemed captive to the discolored knob of fire, moving languidly this way.

Now that it had his attention, the flicker wasn't about to let him go.

Is this your intent? he asked the Egg, half in prayer and half censure.

You alert me to danger ... then won't let me cry a warning?

Did another dura pass – or ten? – while the spark drifted around the next stone? With a soft crackle it crossed another gap. How many more must it traverse before reaching the top? What sky-filling shadow would pass above when that happened?

Suddenly, a huge silhouette *did* loom into Lark's field of view. A giant, globelike shape, vast and blurry to his fixed, unfocused gaze.

The intruding object spoke to him.

'Uh ... Sage Koolhan? ... You all right, sir?'

Lark mutely urged the intruder closer. *That's it, Jimi. A bit more to the left ...*

With welcome abruptness, the flame vanished, eclipsed by the round face of Jimi the Blessed – Jimi the Simpleton – wearing a worried expression as he touched Lark's sweat-soaked brow.

'Can I get ya somethin', Sage? A drink o' water mebbe?' Freed of the hypnotic trap, Lark found volition at last ... waiting in the same place he always kept it.

'Uhhhh ...'

Stale air vented as he took gasping breath. Pain erupted up and down his crouched body, but he quashed it, forcing all his will into crafting two simple words.

'... ever'body ... out!'

EWASX

They act quickly on their promises, do they not, My rings?

Do you see how soon the natives acquiesced to our demands?

You seem surprised that they moved so swiftly to appease us, but *I* expected it. What other decision was possible, now that their so-called sages understand the way things are?

Like you lesser rings, the purpose of other races is ultimately to obey.

HOW DID THIS COME ABOUT? you ask.

Yes, you have My permission to stroke old-fashioned wax drippings, tracing recent memory. But I shall also retell it in the more efficient Oailie way so that we may celebrate together an enterprise well concluded.

WE BEGIN with the arrival of emissaries – one from each of the savage tribes, entering this shattered valley on foot and wheel, shambling like animals over the jagged splinters that surround our proud *Polkjhy*.

Standing bravely beneath the overhanging curve of our gleaming hull, they took turns shouting at the nearest open hatch, making pretty speeches on behalf of their rustic Commons. With surprising eloquence, they cited relevant sections of Galactic law, accepting on behalf of their ancestors full responsibility for their presence on this world, and requesting courteously that we in turn explain *our* purpose coming here.

Are we official inspectors and judges from the Institute of Migration? they asked. And if not, what excuse have *we* for violating this world's peace?

Audacity! Among the crew of the *Polkjhy*, it most upset our junior Priest-Stack, since now we seem obliged to justify ourselves to barbarians.

<< *Why Did We Not Simply Roast This Latest Embassy, Like The One Before It?* >>

To this, our gracious Captain-Leader replied:

<< *It Costs Us Little To Vent Informative Steam In The General Direction Of Half-Devolved Beings. And Do Not Forget That There Are Data Gleanings We Desire, As Well! Recall That The Scoundrel Entities Called Rothen Offered To Sell Us Valuable Knowledge, Before We Righteously Double-Crossed Them. Perhaps That Same Knowledge Might Be Wrung From The Locals At A Much Smaller Price, Saving Us The Time And Effort Of A Search.* >>

Did not the junior Priest-Stack then press its argument?

<< *Look Down At The Horrors! Abominations! They Comingle In The Shadow Of Our Great Ship – Urrish Forms Side By Side With Hoons? Poor Misguided Traeki Cousins Standing Close To Wolfling Humans? And There Among Them, Worst Of All ... G'Keks! What Can Be Gained By Talking With Miscegenists? Blast Them Now!* >>

AH, MY RINGS, would not things be simpler for us/Me, had the Captain-Leader given in, accepting the junior priest's advice? Instead, our exalted commander bent toward the senior Priest-Stack for further consultation.

That august entity stretched upward, a tower of fifty glorious toruses, and declared—

<< *I/We Concede That It Is A Demeaning Task. But It Harms Us Little To Observe The Appropriate Forms And Rituals.*

<< *So Let Us Leave The Chore To Ewasx. Let The Ewasx Stack*

Converse With These Devolved Savages. Let Ewasx Find Out What They Know About The Two Kinds Of Prey We Seek. >>

So it was arranged. The job was assigned to this makeshift, hybrid stack. An appointment to be a lowly agent. To parley with half animals.

In this way, I/we learned the low esteem by which our Jophur peers regard us.

BUT NEVER MIND THAT NOW. Do you recall how we took on our apportioned task, with determined aplomb? By gravity plate, we dropped down to the demolished forest, where the six envoys waited. Our ring of association recognized two of them – *Phwhoondau*, stroking his white hoonish beard, and *Vubben*, wisest of the g'Kek. This pair shouted surprised gladness at first, believing they beheld a lost comrade – *Asx*.

Then, realizing their mistake, all six quailed, emitting varied noises of dismay. Especially the traeki in their midst – our/ your replacement among the High Sages? – who seemed especially upset by our transformation. Oh, how that stack of aboriginal toruses trembled to perceive our Jophurication! Would its segmented union sunder on the spot? Without a master ring to bind and guide them, would the component rings tear their membranes and crawl their separate ways, returning to the feral habits of our ancestors?

Eventually the six representatives recovered enough to listen. In simple terms, I explained *Polkjhy*'s endeavor in this far-off system.

WE ARE NOT OF THE MIGRATION INSTITUTE, I/we told them, although we did invoke a clause of Galactic law to self-deputize and arrest the Rothen gene raiders. There will be few questions asked by an indifferent cosmos, if/when we render judgment on them ... *or* on criminal colonists.

To whom will savages appeal?

BUT THAT NEED NOT BE OUR AIM.

This I added, soothingly. There are worse villains to pursue than a hardscrabble pack of castaways, stranded on a forbidden reef, seeking redemption the only way they can.

OUR CHIEF QUEST is for a missing vessel crewed by Earthling *dolphins*. A ship sought by ten thousand fleets, across all Five Galaxies. A ship carrying secrets, and perhaps the key to a new age.

I told the emissaries that we might pay for data, if local inhabitants help shorten our search.

(Yes, My rings – the Captain-Leader also promised to pay those Rothen rascals, when their ship hailed ours in jump space, offering

vital clues. But those impatient fools gave away too much in their eagerness. We made vague promises, dispatching them for more proof . . . then covertly followed, before a final deal was signed! Once they led us to this world, what further purpose did they serve? Rather than pay, we seized their ship.

(True, they might have had more data morsels to sell. But if the dolphin ship is in this system, we will find it soon enough.)

(Yes, My rings, our memory core appears to hold no waxy imprints of a dolphin ship. But others on Jijo might know something. Perhaps they kept data from their traeki sage. Anyway, can we trust memories inherited from Asx, who slyly remelted many core drippings?)

(So we must query the Jijoan envoys, using threats and rewards.)

While the emissaries pondered the matter of the dolphin ship, I proceeded to our second requirement. Our goal of long-delayed justice!

YOU MAY FIND THIS ADDITIONAL REQUEST UNPLEASANT, OR DISLOYAL. BUT YOU HAVE NO CHOICE. YOU MUST BEND TO THE IMPLACABILIT'Y OF OUR WILL. THE SACRIFICE WE DEMAND IS ESSENTIAL. DO NOT THINK OF SHIRKING!

The hoon sage boomed a deep umble, inflating his throat sac. 'We are unclear on your meaning. What must we sacrifice?'

To this obvious attempt at dissembling, I replied derisively, adding rippling emphasis shadows across our upper rings.

YOU KNOW WHAT MUST BE GIVEN UP TO US. SOON WE WILL EXPECT A TOKEN PORTION. A DOWN PAYMENT TO SHOW US THAT YOU UNDERSTAND.

With that, I commanded our ring-of-manipulators to aim all our tendrils at the aged g'Kek.

Toward Vubben.

This time, their reactions showed comprehension. Some former Asx rings shared their revulsion, but I clamped down with electric jolts of discipline.

The intimidated barbarians retreated, taking with them the word of heaven.

We did not expect to hear from the agonized sooners for a day or two. Meanwhile, the Captain-Leader chose to send our second corvette east to help the other unit whose self-repairs go too slowly, stranded near a deepwater rift. (A candidate hiding place for the missing Earthling ship!)

Once, we feared that dolphins had shot down our boat, and *Polkjhy* itself must go on this errand. But our tactician stack calculated that the Rothen scout simply got in a lucky shot. It seems safe to dispatch a smaller vessel.

Then, just as our repair craft was about to launch, we picked up a signal from these very mountains! What else could it be, but the Jijoan envoys, responding to My/our demands!

The corvette was diverted north, toward this new emission.

And lo! Now comes in its report. A g'Kek settlement – a midget *city* of the demon wheels – hidden in the forest!

Oh, we would have found it anyway. Our mapping has only just begun.

Still, this gesture is encouraging. It shows the Six (who will soon be five) possess enough sapient ability to calculate odds, to perceive the inevitable and minimize their losses.

What, My rings? You are surprised? You expected greater solidarity from your vaunted Commons? More loyalty?

Then live and learn, My waxy pretties. This is just the beginning.

LARK

Tears covered the cheeks of the aged human sage as he ran through the forest.

'It's my fault . . .' he murmured between gasping breaths. 'All my fault . . . I never should've allowed it . . . so near the poor g'Kek . . .'

Lark heard Cambel's lament as they joined a stampede of refugees, swarming down narrow aisles between colossal shafts of boo. He had to catch Lester when the sage stumbled in grief over what they all had witnessed, only duras ago. Lark caught the eye of a hoonish militiaman with a huge sword slung down his back. The burly warrior swept Lester into his arms, gently hauling the stricken sage to safety.

For those fleeing beneath the boo, that word – *safety* – might never be the same. For two thousand years, the ramparts of Dooden Mesa offered protection to the oldest and weakest sooner race. Yet no defense could stand against the sky cruiser that swept over that sheltered valley, too soon after Lark's shouted warning. Some refugees – those with enough nerve to glance back – would always carry the image of that awful ship, hovering like a predator over the graceful ramps, homes, and workshops.

It must have been drawn by the Buyur computer – by its 'digital resonance.'

Once over the mountain, the aliens could not help noticing the g'Kek settlement in the valley below.

'... we were too near the poor g'Kek ...'

Driven by a need for answers – and a lifelong curiosity about all things Galactic – Cambel had allowed Ling and Rann to drive the machine at full force, deciphering the mystery records, It was like waving a lure above this part of the Rimmers, calling down an ill wind.

Some of those running through the forest seemed less panicky. Fierce-eyed Jeni Shen kept herd on her militia team, so Rann and Ling never had a chance to dodge left or right, slipping away through the boo. As if either Danik had any place to go. Their faces looked as dismayed as anybody's.

Lark's ears still rang from when the Jophur ship cast beams of aching brilliance, tearing apart the frail canopy of blur cloth, laying Dooden Mesa bare under a cruel sun. Teeming wheeled figures scurried futilely, like a colony of hive mites in a collapsed den.

The beams stopped, and something even more dreadful fell from the floating nemesis.

A golden haze. A flood of liquid light.

Lark's nerve had failed him at that point, as he, too, plunged into the boo, fleeing a disaster he had helped wreak.

You aren't alone, Lester. You have company in hell.

DWER

Mudfoot seemed crazier than ever.

Blinking past a cloud of buzzing gnats, Dwer watched the mad noor crouch over some helpless creature he had caught near the shore, gripping his prey in both forepaws, brandishing sharp teeth toward whatever doomed beast had unluckily strayed within reach. Mudfoot showed no interest in two sooty spaceships that lay crippled, just beyond the dune.

Why should he care? Dwer thought. *Any Galactics who glimpse him will just shrug off another critter of Jijo. Enjoy your meal, Mudfoot. No squatting under hot sand for you!*

Dwer's hidey-hole was intensely uncomfortable. His legs felt cramped and grit eagerly sought every body crevice. Partial shade was offered by his tunic, propped up with two arrows and covered with sand. But he had to share that narrow shelter with Rety – an uncomfortable fit, to say the least. Worse, there was a kind of midge, no larger than a speck, that seemed to find human breath irresistible. One by one, the insectoids drifted upslope to the makeshift cavity where Dwer and Rety exposed their faces for air. The bugs fluttered toward their mouths, inevitably being drawn inside. Rety coughed, spat, and cursed in her Gray Hills dialect, despite Dwer's pleas for silence.

She's not trained for this, he thought, trying for patience. During his apprenticeship, Master Fallon used to leave him in a hunting blind for days on end, then sneak back to observe. For each sound Dwer made, Fallon added another midura, till Dwer learned the value of quiet.

'I wish he'd quit playin' with his food,' Rety muttered, glaring downslope at Mudfoot. 'Or else, bring some up for us.'

Dwer's belly growled agreement. But he told her, 'Don't think about it. Try to sleep. We'll see about sneaking away come night-fall.'

For once, she seemed willing to take his advice. Sometimes, Rety seemed at her best when things were at their worst.

At this rate, she'll be a saint before it's all over.

He glanced left, toward the swamp. Both alien ships lay grounded in a seaside bog, just two arrowflights away. It made the two humans easy targets if they budged. Nor had he any guarantee this would change at night.

I hear tell that star gods have lenses that pick out a warm body moving in the dark, and other kinds to track metal and tools.

Getting away from here might not be easy, or even possible.

There wasn't much to say for the alternatives. It would have been one thing to surrender to Kunn. As a Danik adoptee, Rety might have swayed the human star pilot to spare Dwer's life. Perhaps.

But the newcomers who shot down Kunn's little scout . . . Dwer felt his hackles rise watching tapered stacks of glistening doughnuts inspect their damaged ship, accompanied by hovering robots.

Why be afraid? They look like traeki, and traeki are harmless, right?

Not when they come swooping from space, throwing lightning.

Dwer wished he had listened more closely to holy services as a child, instead of fidgeting when the Sacred Scrolls were read. Some excerpts had been inserted by the ringed ones, when their sneakship came – passages of warning. Not all stacks of fatty rings were friendly, it seemed. *What was the name they used?* Dwer tried to recall what word stood for a traeki that was no traeki, but he came up blank.

Sometimes he wished he could be more like his brother and sister – able to think deep thoughts, with vast stores of book learning to call upon. Lark or Sara would surely make better use of this time of forced inaction. They would be weighing alternatives, listing possibilities, formulating some plan.

But all I do is doze, thinking about food. Wishing I had some way to scratch.

He wasn't yet desperate enough to walk toward that silver ship with hands raised. Anyway, the aliens and their helpers were still fussing over the smoke-stained hull, making repairs.

As he nodded in a drowsy torpor, he fought down one itch in particular, a prickly sensation *inside* his head. The feeling had grown ever since he first gave the Danik robot a 'ride' across a river, using his body to anchor its ground-hugging fields. Each time he collapsed on the opposite bank, waking up had felt like rising from a pit. The effect grew stronger with every crossing.

At least I won't have to do that again. The robot now cowered under a nearby dune, useless and impotent since Kunn's ship was downed and its master taken.

Dwer's sleep was uneasy, disturbed first by a litany of aching twinges, and later by disturbing dreams.

He had *always* dreamed. As a child, Dwer used to jerk upright in the dark, screaming till the entire household roused, from Nelo and Melina down to the lowest chimp and manservant, gathering round to comfort him back to sweet silence. He had no clear memory of what nightmares used to terrify him so, but Dwer still had sleep visions of startling vividness and clarity.

Never worth screaming over, though. Unless you count One-Of-a-Kind.

He recalled the old mulc-spider of the acid mountain lake, who spoke words directly in his mind one fateful day, during his first solo scouting trip over the Rimmer Range.

—the mad spider, unlike any other, who tried all kinds of deceit to charm Dwer into its web, there to join its 'collection.'

—the same spider who nearly caught Dwer that awful night when Rety and her 'bird' were trapped in its maze of bitter vines ... before that vine network exploded in a mortal inferno.

Restlessly, he envisioned living cables, the spider's own body, snaking across a tangled labyrinth, creeping ever nearer, closing an unstoppable snare. From each twisting rope there dripped heavy caustic vapors, or liquors that would freeze your skin numb on contact.

Around Dwer, the sand burrow felt like a ropy spiral of nooses, drawing tight a snug embrace that was both cloying and loving, in a sick-sweet way.

No one else could ever appreciate you as much as I do, crooned the serenely patient call of One-of-a-Kind. *We share a destiny, my precious, my treasure.*

Dwer felt trapped, more by a languor of sleep than by the enveloping sand. He mumbled.

'Yer just ... my ... 'magination ...'

A crooning, dreamlike laugh, and the mellifluous voice rejoined—

So you always used to claim, though you cautiously evaded my grasp, nonetheless. Until the night I almost had you.

'The night you died!' Dwer answered. The words were a mere rolling of his exhaled breath.

True. But do you honestly think that was an ending?

My kind is very old. I myself had lived half a million years, slowly etching and leaching the hard leavings of the Buyur. Across those ages, thinking long thoughts, would I not learn everything there is to know about mortality?

Dwer realized – all those times he helped the Danik robot cross a stream, conducting its throbbing fields, somehow must have changed him inside. Sensitized him. Or else driven him mad. Either way, it explained this awful dream.

His eyes opened a crack as he tried to waken, but fatigue lay over Dwer like a shroud, and all he managed was to peer through interleaved eyelashes at the swamp below.

Till now, he had always stared at the two alien ships – the larger shaped like a silvery cigar, and the smaller like a bronze arrowhead. But now Dwer regarded the background. The swamp itself, and not the shiny intruders.

They are just dross, my precious. Ignore those passing bits of 'made stuff,' the brief fancies of ephemeral beings. The planet will absorb them, with some patient help from my kindred.

Distracted by the ships, he had missed the telltale signs. A nearby squarish mound whose symmetry was almost hidden by rank vegetation. A series of depressions, like grooves filled with algae scum, always the same distance apart, one after another, extending into the distance.

It was an ancient Buyur site, of course. Perhaps a port or seaside resort, long ago demolished, with the remnants left for wind and rain to dissolve.

Aided by a wounded planet's friend, came the voice, with renewed pride.

We who help erase the scars.

We who expedite time's rub.

Over there. Between the shadows of his own eyelashes, Dwer made out slender shapes amid the marsh plants, like threads woven among the roots and fronds, snaking through the muddy shallows. Long, tubelike outlines, whose movement was glacially slow. But he could track the changes, with patience.

Oh, what patience you might have learned, if only you joined me! We would be one with Time now, my pet, my rare one.

It wasn't just his growing vexation with the irksome dream voice – that he knew to be imagined, after all. Dawning realization finally lent Dwer the will to shake off sleep. He squeezed his eyelids shut hard enough to bring tears and flush away the stickiness. Alert now, he reopened them and stared again at the faint twisty patterns in the water. They were real.

'It's a mulc swamp,' he muttered. 'And it still lives.'

Rety stirred, commenting testily.

'So? One more reason to get out of this crakky place.'

But Dwer smiled. Emerging from the fretful nap, he found his thoughts now taking a sharp turn, veering away from a victim's apprehension.

In the distance, he still heard the noor beast bark and growl while toying with his prey – a carnivore's privilege under nature's law. Before, Mudfoot's behavior had irritated Dwer. But now he took it as an omen.

All his setbacks and injuries – and simple common sense – seemed to demand that he flee this deadly place, crawling on his belly, taking Rety with him to whatever hideout they could find in a deadly world.

But one idea had now crystallized, as clear as the nearby waters of the Rift.

I'm not running away, he decided. *I don't really know how to do that*.

A hunter – that was what he had been born and trained to be.

ALVIN

All right, so there we were, watching faraway events through the phuvnthus' magical viewer, when the camera eye suddenly went jerky and we found ourselves staring into the grinning jaws of a giant noor! Hugely magnified, it was the vista a fen mouse might see – its last sight on its way to being a midday snack.

Huphu reacted with a sharp hiss. Her claws dug in my shoulder.

The spinning voice, our host, seemed as surprised as we. That whirling *hologram*-thing twisted like the neck of a confused urs, nodding as if it were consulting someone out of sight. I caught murmurs that might be hurried Anglic and GalSeven.

When the voice next spoke aloud, we heard the words *twice*, the second time delayed as it came back through the drone's tiny pickups. The voice used accented GalSix, and *talked to the strange noor*. Three words, so high-pitched I barely understood.

'*Brother*,' the voice urged quickly. '*Please stop.*'

And the strange noor *did* stop, turning its head to examine the drone from one side to the other.

True, we hoons employ noor beasts as helpers on our boats, and those learn many words and simple commands. But that is on the Slope, where they get sour balls and sweet umbles as pay. How would a noor living east of the Rimmers learn Galactic Six?

The voice tried again, changing pitch and timbre, almost at the limit of my hearing range.

'*Brother, will you speak to us, in the name of the Trickster?*'

Huck and I shared an amazed glance. What was the voice trying to accomplish?

One of those half memories came back to me, from when our ill-fated *Wuphon's Dream* crashed into the open-mawed phuvnthus whale ship. Me and my friends were thrown gasping across a metal deck, and soon after I stared through agonized haze as six-legged monsters tromped about, smashing our homemade instruments underfoot, waving lantern beams, exclaiming in a ratchety language I didn't understand. The armored beings seemed cruel when they blasted poor little Ziz, the five-stack traeki. Then they appeared *crazy* upon spying Huphu. I recall them bending metal legs to crouch before my pet, buzzing and popping, as if trying to get her to speak.

And now here was more of the same! Did the voice hope to talk a wild noor into releasing the remote-controlled drone? Huck winked at me with two waving g'Kek eyes, a semaphore of amused contempt. Star gods or no, our hosts seemed prize fools to expect easy cooperation from a noor.

So *we* were more surprised than anyone – even Pincer and Ur-ronn – when the on-screen figure snapped its jaws, frowning in concentration. Then, through gritted teeth came a raspy squeak . . . *answering* in the same informal tongue.

'*In th' nam o' th' Trickst'er . . . who th' hell'r* you?'

My healing spine crackled painfully as I straightened, venting an umble of astonishment. Huck sighed and Pincer's visor whirled faster than the agitated hologram. Only Huphu seemed oblivious. She licked herself complacently, as if she had not heard a blessed thing.

*

'What do you jeekee, Ifni-slucking turds think you're doing!' Huck wailed. All four eyes tossed in agitation, showing she was more angry than afraid. Two hulking, six-legged phuvnthus escorted her, one on each side, carrying her by the rims of her wheels.

The rest of us were more cooperative, though reluctant. Pincer had to tilt his red chitin shell in order to pass through some door-ways, following as a pair of little amphibian creatures led us back to the whale ship that brought us to this underwater sanctuary. Ur-ronn trotted behind Pincer, her long neck folded low to the ground, a pose of simmering dejection.

I hobbled on crutches behind Huck, staying out of reach of her pusher leg, which flailed and banged against corridor walls on either side.

'You promised to explain everything!' she cried out. 'You said we'd get to ask questions of the Library!'

Neither the phuvnthus nor the amphibians answered, but I recalled what the spinning voice had said before sending us away.

'We cannot justify any longer keeping four children under conditions that put you all in danger. This location may be bombed again, with greater fury. Also, you now know much too much for your own good.'

'What do we know?' Pincer had asked, in perplexity. 'That noors can talk-alk-alk?'

The hologram assented with a twisting nod. 'And other things. We can't keep you here, or send you home as we originally intended, since that might prove disastrous for ourselves and your families. Hence our decision to convey you to another place. A goal mentioned in your diaries, where you may be content for the necessary time.'

'Wait!' Huck had insisted. 'I'll bet you're not even in charge. You're prob'ly just a computer ... a *thing*. I want to talk to someone else! Let us see your boss!'

I swear, the whirling pattern seemed both surprised and amused.

'Such astute young people. We had to revise many assumptions since meeting the four of you. As I am programmed to find incongruity pleasant, let me thank you for the experience, and sincerely wish you well.'

I noticed, the voice never answered Huck's question.

Typical grown-up, I thought. Whether hoonish parents or alien contraptions ... they're all basically the same.

Huck settled down once we left the curved hallway and reentered the maze of reclaimed passages leading to the whale ship. The phuvnthus let her down, and she rolled along with the rest of us. My friend continued grumbling remarks about the phuvnthus' physiology, habits, and ancestry, but I saw through her pose. Huck had that smug set to her eyestalks.

Clearly, she felt she had accomplished something sneaky and smart.

Once aboard the whale ship, we were given another room with a porthole. Apparently the phuvnthus weren't worried about us memorizing landmarks. That worried me, at first.

Are they going to stash us in another salvaged wreck, under a different dross pile, in some far-off canyon of the Midden? In that case, who'll come get us if they are destroyed?

The voice mentioned sending us to a 'safe' place. Call me odd, but I hadn't felt safe since stepping off dry land at Terminus Rock. *What did the voice mean about it being a site where we already 'wanted to go'?*

The whale ship slid slowly at first through its tunnel exit, clearly a makeshift passage constructed out of the hulls of ancient starcraft, braced with rods and improvised girders. Ur-ronn said this fit what we already knew – the phuvnthus were recent arrivals on Jijo, possibly refugees, like our ancestors, but with one big difference.

They hope to leave again.

I envied them. Not for the obvious danger they felt, pursued by deadly foes, but for that one option they had, that we did not. To *go*. To fly off to the stars, even if the way led to certain doom. Was I naive to think freedom made it all worthwhile? To know I'd trade places with them, if I could?

Maybe that thought laid the seeds for my later realization. The moment when everything suddenly made sense. But hold that thought.

Before the whale ship emerged from the tunnel, we caught sight of *figures* moving in the darkness, where long shadows stretched away from moving points of sharp, starlike light. The patchiness of brilliance and pure darkness made it hard, at first, to make out very much. Then Pincer identified the shadowy shapes.

They were *phuvnthus*, the big six-legged creatures whose stomping gait seemed so ungainly indoors. Now, for the first time, we saw them in their element, *swimming*, with the mechanical legs tucked away or used as flexible work arms. The broad flaring at the back ends of their bodies now made sense – it was a great big flipper that propelled them gracefully through dark waters.

We had already speculated that they might not be purely mechanical beings. Ur-ronn thought the heavy metal carapace was worn like a suit of clothes, and the real creatures lay inside horizontal shells.

They wear them indoors because their true bodies lack legs, I thought, knowing also that the steel husks protected their identities. But why, if they were born swimmers, did they continue wearing the coverings outside?

We glimpsed light bursts of hurtful brilliance – underwater welding and cutting. *Repairs*, I thought. *Were they in a battle, before fleeing to Jijo?* My mind filled with images from those vivid space-opera books Mister Heinz used to disapprove of, preferring that we kids broaden our tastes with Keats and Basho. I yearned to get close and see the combat scars ... but then the sub entered a narrow shaft, cutting off all sight of the phuvnthu vessel.

Soon, we emerged into the blackness of the Midden. A deep chill seemed to penetrate the glass disk, and we backed away ... especially since the spotlights all turned off, leaving the outside world vacant, but for an occasional blue glimmer as some sea creature tried to lure a mate.

I lay down on the metal deck to rest my back, feeling the thrum of engines vibrate beneath me. It was like the rumbling song of some godlike hoon who never needed to pause or take a breath. I filled my air sac and began to umble counterpoint. Hoons think best when there is a steady background cadence – a tone to serve as a fulcrum for deliberation.

I had a lot to think about.

My friends eventually grew bored with staring at the bleak desolation outside. Soon they were all gathered around little Huphu, our noorish mascot, trying to get her to speak. Pincer urged me to come over and use bosun umbles to put her in a cooperative mood, but I declined. I've known Huphu since she was a pup, and there's no way she's been playing dumb all that time. Anyway, I had seen a *difference* in that strange noor on the beach, the one that spoke back to the spinning voice in fluent GalSix. Huphu never had that glint in her eyes ...

... though as I reflected, I felt sure I'd seen the look before – in just a few noor who lounged on the piers in Wuphon, or worked the sails of visiting ships. Strange ones, a bit more aloof than normal. As silent as their brethren, they nevertheless seemed more *watchful* somehow. More evaluating. More *amused* by all the busy activity of the Six Races.

I never gave them much thought before, since a devilish attitude seems innate to all noor. But now perhaps I knew what made them different.

Though noor are often associated with hoons, they didn't come to Jijo with us, the way chimps, lorniks, and zookirs came with human, qheuen, and g'Kek sooners. They were already here when we arrived and began building our first proud rafts. We always assumed they were native beasts, either natural or else some adjusted species, left behind by the Buyur as a practical joke on whoever might follow. Though we get useful work out of them, we hoon don't fool ourselves that they are *ours*.

Eventually, Huck gave up the effort, leaving Pincer and Ur-ronn to continue coaxing our bored mascot. My g'Kek buddy rolled over beside me, resting quietly for a time. But she didn't fool me for a kidura.

'So tell me,' I asked. 'What'd you swipe?'

'What makes you think I took anything?' She feigned innocence.

'Hr-rrm. How 'bout the fakey way you thrashed around, back there in the hall – a tantrum like you used to throw when you were a leg skeeter, till our folks caught on. After we left the curvy hallway, you stopped all that, wearing a look as if you'd snatched the crown jewels under old Richelieu's nose.'

Huck winced, a reflex coiling of eyestalks. Then she chuckled. 'Well, you got me there, d'Artagnan. Come on. Have a look at what I got.'

With some effort, I raised up on my middle stretch of forearm while Huck rolled closer still. Excitement hummed along her spokes.

'Used my pusher legs. Kept banging 'em against the wall till I managed to snag one of these.'

Her tendril-like arm unfolded. There, held delicately between the tips, hung a narrow, rectangular strip of what looked like thick paper. I reached for it.

'Careful, it's sticky on one side. I think a book called it *adhesive tape*. Got a bit crumpled when I yanked it off the wall. Had to pry some gummy bits apart. I'm afraid there's not much of an impression left, but if you look closely . . .'

I peered at the strip – one of the coverings we had seen pressed on the walls, always at the same height, to the left of each doorway in the curved hall, surely masking label signs in some unknown language.

'You wouldn't happen to've been looking when I ripped it off, were you?' Huck asked. 'Did you see what it said underneath?'

'Hr-r. Wish I had. But I was too busy avoiding being kicked.'

'Well, never mind. Just look *real* carefully at this end. What d'you see there?'

I didn't have Huck's sensitivity of vision, but hoons do have good eyes. I peered at what seemed a circular pattern with a gap and sharp jog on the right side. 'Is it a symbol?'

'That's right. Now tell me – in what alphabet?'

I concentrated. Circles were basic ingredients in most standard Galactic codes. But this particular shape seemed unique.

'I'll tell you my *first* impression, though it can't be right.'

'Go on.'

'Hr-rm ... it looks to me like an Anglic letter. A letter *G*, to be specific.'

Huck let a satisfied sigh escape her vent mouth. All four eyestalks waved, as if in a happy breeze.

'That was my impression, too.'

We clustered round the viewport when the hull began creaking and popping, indicating a rapid change of pressure. Soon the world outside began to brighten and we knew the sub must be on final approach. Beyond the glass, sunshine streamed through shallow water. We all felt a bit giddy, from changing air density, I guess. Pincer-Tip let out hissing shouts, glad to be back in a familiar world where he would be at home. (Though lacking the comforts of his clan rookery.) Soon water slid off the window in dripping sheets and we saw our destination.

Tilted obelisks and sprawling concrete skeletons, arrayed in great clusters along the shore.

Huck let out a warbling sigh.

Buyur ruins, I realized. *These must be the scrublands south of the Rift, where some city sites were left to be torn down by wave and wind alone.*

The voice read my journal and knew about our interest in coming here. If we must be quarantined, this would be the place.

The cluster of ancient sites had been Huck's special goal, before we ever stepped aboard *Wuphon's Dream*. Now she bounced on her rims, eager to get ashore and read the wall inscriptions that were said to be abundant in this place. Forgotten were her complaints over broken phuvnthu promises. This was a more longstanding dream.

One of the six-limbed amphibians entered, gesturing for us to move quickly. No doubt the phuvnthus were anxious to get us ashore before they could be spotted by their enemies. Huck rolled out after Pincer. Ur-ronn glanced at me, her long head and neck shaking in an urrish shrug. At least she must be looking forward to an end to all this water and humidity. The countryside ahead looked pleasantly dry.

But it was not to be.

This time *I* was the mutinous one.

'No!' I planted my feet, and my throat sac boomed.

'I ain't movin'.'

My friends turned and stared. They must have seen boorish obstinacy in the set of my limbs as I gripped the crutches. The amphibian uttered and squeaked distress.

'Forget it,' I insisted. 'We are not getting off!'

'Alvin, it's all right-ight,' Pincer murmured. 'They promised to leave us lots of food, and I can hunt along the shore—'

I shook my head.

'We are not going to be cast aside like this, exiled for our own Ifni-sucking *safety*, like a bunch of helpless kids. Sent away from where things are happening. Important things!'

'What're you talking about?' asked Huck, rolling back into the cabin, while the amphibian fluttered and waved its four arms vainly. Finally, a pair of big phuvnthus came in, their long horizontal bodies metal-clad and slung between six stomping steel legs. But I refused to be intimidated. I pointed at the nearest, with its pair of huge, black, glassy eyes, one on each side of a tapered head.

'You call up the spinning voice and tell him. Tell him we can help. But if you people turn us away, putting us ashore here won't do any good. It won't shut us up, 'cause we'll find a way back home, just as fast as we can. We'll head for the Rift and signal friends on the other side. We'll tell 'em the truth about you guys!'

Ur-ronn murmured, '*What* truth, Alvin?'

I let out a deep, rolling umble to accompany my words.

'That we know who these guys are.'

SARA

In the lodge of a horse clan you might expect to see lariats, bridles, and saddle blankets hanging on the walls. Maybe a guitar or two. It seemed strange to find a *piano* here in Xi.

An instrument much like the one back home in Dolo Village, where Melina used to read to her children for hours on end, choosing obscure books no one else seemed eager to check out from the Biblos Archive – some crinkly pages wafting aromas from the Great Printing, two hundred years before. Especially books of *written music* Melina would prop on the precious piano Nelo had made for her as part of the marriage price.

Now, in the great hall of the Illias, Sara ran her hands along white and black keys, stroking fine tooth traces left by expert qheuen woodcarvers, picturing her mother as a little girl, raised in this narrow realm of horses and mind-scraping illusions. Leaving

Xi must have been like going to another planet. Did she feel relief from claustrophobic confinement, passing through the Buyur tunnel for a new life in the snowy north? Or did Melina long in her heart for the hidden glades? For the visceral thrill of bareback? For the pastoral purity of life unconstrained by men?

Did she miss the colors that took each dream or nightmare, and spread its secret panorama before your daylight gaze?

Who taught you to play the piano, Mother? Sitting with you on this very bench, the way you used to sit beside me, trying to hide your disappointment in my awkward fingers?

A folio of sheet music lay atop the piano's polished surface. Sara flipped through it, recalling ancient compositions that used to transfix her mother for duras at a stretch, rousing young Sara's jealousy against those dots on a page. Dots Melina transformed into glorious harmonies.

Later, Sara realized how magical the melodies truly were. For they were *repeatable*. In a sense, written music was immortal. It could never die.

The typical Jijoan ensemble – a sextet including members from each sooner race – performed spontaneously. A composition was never quite the same from one presentation to the next. That trait appealed especially to blue qheuens and hoons, who, according to legend, had no freedom to innovate back in ordered Galactic society. They expressed puzzlement when human partners sometimes suggested recording a successful piece in traeki wax, or writing it down.

Whatever for? they asked. *Each moment deserves its own song.*

A Jijoan way of looking at things, Sara acknowledged.

She laid her hands on the keys and ran through some scales. Though out of practice, the exercise was like an old friend. No wonder Emerson also drew comfort from tunes recalling happier days.

Still, her mind churned as she switched to some simple favorites, starting with 'Für Elise.'

According to Biblos anthropology texts, most ancient cultures on Earth used to play music that was impulsive, just like a Jijoan sextet. But shortly before they made their own way into space, humans also came up with written forms.

We sought order and memory. It must have seemed a refuge from the chaos that filled our dark lives.

Of course that was long ago, back when mathematics also had its great age of discovery on Earth. *Is that a common thread? Did I choose math for the same reason Melina loved this instrument? Because it lends predictability amid life's chaos?*

A shadow fell across the wall. Sara drew back, half rising to meet the brown eyes of Foruni, aged leader of the horse-riding clan.

'Sorry to disturb you, dear.' The gray-headed matriarch motioned for Sara to sit. 'But watching you, I could almost believe it was Melina back home with us, playing as she did, with such intensity.'

'I'm afraid I don't look much like my mother. Nor do I play half as well.'

The old woman smiled. 'A good parent wants her offspring to excel – to do what she could not. But a wise parent lets the child select *which* excellence. You chose realms of deep thought. I know she was very proud.'

Sara acknowledged the kindness with a nod, but took small comfort from aphorisms. *If the choice really were mine, don't you think I'd have been beautiful, like Melina? A dark woman of mystery, who amazed people with many graceful talents?*

Mathematics chose me ... it seized me with cool infinities and hints at universal truth. Yet whom do I touch with my equations? Who looks at my face and form with unreserved delight?

Melina died young, but surrounded by those who loved her. Who will weep over me, when I am gone?

The Illias leader must have misunderstood Sara's frown.

'Do my words disturb you?' Foruni asked. 'Do I sound like a heretic, for believing that generations can improve? Does it seem an odd belief for a secret tribe that hides itself even from a civilization of exiled refugees?'

Sara found it hard to answer.

Why were Melina's children so odd, by Jijoan standards? Although Lark's heresy seems opposite to mine, we share one thread – rejecting the Path of Redemption.

The books Mother read to us often spoke of hope, drawn from some act of rebellion.

To the Illias leader, she replied, 'You and your urrish friends rescued horses, back when they seemed doomed. Your alliance foreshadowed that of Drake and Ur-Chown. You are a society of dedicated women, who carefully choose your male companions from the best Jijo has to offer. Living in splendid isolation, you see humanity at its best – seldom its more nasty side.'

'No, it does not surprise me that the Illias are optimists at heart.'

Foruni nodded. 'I am told that you, in your investigations of language theory, reached similar conclusions.'

Sara shrugged. 'I'm no optimist. Not personally. But for a while, it seemed that I could see a pattern in the evolution of Jijo's dialects, and in all the new literary activity taking place across the Slope. Not that it matters anymore, now that aliens have come to—'

The old woman cut in. 'You don't think we are destined to be like glavers, winning our second chance by passing through oblivion?'

'You mean what *might* have happened, if starships never came? I argued with Dedinger about this. If Jijo had been left alone, I felt there was the possibility of . . .'

Sara shook her head and changed the subject.

'Speaking of Dedinger, have you had any luck finding him?'

Foruni winced unhappily. 'It's been just a short while since he broke out of the pen where he was kept. We never imagined he would prove so resourceful, knowing how to saddle and steal a horse.'

'He had time to learn by observing.'

'I see that we were naive. It's a long time since we kept prisoners in Xi.'

'Unfortunately, the tracks do not lead back to the tunnel, where we might have trapped him in the narrow darkness. Instead, the wily ligger spawn struck out across the Spectral Flow.'

Sara tried picturing a man alone on horseback, crossing a vast desert of poison stone and cutting light. 'Do you think he can make it?'

'You mean can we catch him before he dies out there?' It was Foruni's turn to shrug. 'Fallon is not as spry as he was, but he departed a midura ago with some of our most able young riders. The fanatic should be back in care soon, and we'll watch him more closely—'

Foruni stopped, midsentence, glancing down at her hand. An insect had landed, and was sniffing at a vein. Sara recognized a *skeeter* – a blood-sucking irritant familiar across the Slope. Skeeters were slow and easily smacked, but for some reason Foruni refrained. Instead, she let the vampire wasp leisurely insert a narrow tube and take its meal. When finished, it proceeded to perform a little dance, one filled with jerky, *beckoning* motions.

Sara stared, fascinated. Skeeters seldom survived landing on a human long enough to do this.

Come with me, it seemed to say with each swing of its tiny abdomen and tail. Come with me now.

Sara realized, it must be another remnant servant beast of the vanished Buyur. A useful messenger, if you knew how to use it.

Foruni sighed. 'Alas, dear cousin, it's time for you to go. You and Kurt and the others must hurry to where you're needed most.'

Needed? Sara wondered. *In times like these, what could a person like me possibly be needed for?*

The journey south resumed, this time on horseback. They used the ancient Buyur transit tunnel at first, where the failed deconstructor left its demolition unfinished. But soon it lay cracked open for stretches, like the spent larval casing of a newly fledged qheuen, leaving a dusty cavity or else a pit filled with water. Thereafter they had to ride in the open, awash in the luminous tides of the Spectral Flow. The Illias provided hooded cloaks. Still, it felt as if the colors were probing the reflective garments for some gap to worm their way inside.

Kurt and Jomah rode ahead with Kepha, their guide. The elderly exploser leaned forward in his saddle, as if that might get them to their goal quicker. Then came Prity, on a donkey more suited for her small form.

Emerson seemed strangely subdued, though he smiled at Sara from time to time. He wore the rewq constantly, though from his everturning head, Sara gathered the filmy symbiont was doing more than just softening the colors. It must be adjusting, *translating* them. Sometimes, the starman stiffened in the saddle ... though whether from pain, surprise, or exaltation, Sara could never be quite sure.

Taking up the rear was Ulgor, the urrish traitor. Wisely, she had not tried to break across the poison plain with her erstwhile ally, Dedinger. Guarded by two of her own kind from the Xi colony, Ulgor swung her head in growing eagerness as the party neared Mount Guenn. Urrish nostrils flared at scents of smoke and molten rock, as the volcano loomed to fill the southern sky.

Sara felt surprisingly good. The saddle was a tool her body had mastered. When the going grew steep and riders dismounted to lead the horses by hand, her legs were suffused with waves of comfortable warmth, with strength still in reserve.

So, a hermit math potato can manage to keep up, after all. Or is this euphoria an early sign of altitude sickness?

They were mounting one of countless knee hills along the sloping volcano, when suddenly all three urs bolted forward, hissing excitement and trailing clouds of pumice, forgetting their separate roles as they jostled toward the next outlook. Outlined against the sky, their long heads swept in unison, from left to right and back again.

Finally, winded from the climb, she and Emerson arrived to find a mighty caldera spread before them ... one of many studding the immense volcano, which kept rising to the southeast for many more leagues.

Yet this fumarole had the urs transfixed. Steamy exhalations rose from vents that rimmed the craggy circle. Cautiously, Sara removed her sunglasses. The basalt here was of a coarser, less gemlike variety. They had entered a different realm.

'This was the site of the first forge,' Ulgor announced, her voice tinged with awe. She tilted her muzzle to the right, and Sara made out a tumble of stone blocks, too poorly shaped to have been laser-cut by the Buyur, and now long-abandoned. Such tumbled shelters were hand-hewn by the earliest urrish seeker smiths who dared to leave the plains pursuing lava-borne heat, hoping to learn how to cast the fiery substance of Jijoan bronze and steel. In its day, the venture was fiercely opposed by the Gray Queens, who portrayed it as sacrilege – like when humans much later perfomed the Great Printing.

In time, what had been profane became tradition.

'They must've found conditions better, on high,' Jomah commented, for the trail continued steadily upslope.

An urrish guard nodded. 'Vut it was fron *this* flace that early urs exflorers discovered the secret way across the Sfectral Flow. The Secret of Xi.'

Sara nodded. That explained why one group of urs conspired to thwart another – the powerful Urunthai – in their plan to make horses extinct when humanity was new on Jijo. The smiths of those days cared little for power games played by high aunties of the plains tribes. It did not matter to them how Earthlings smelled, or what beasts they rode, only that they possessed a treasure.

Those books the Earthlings printed. They have secrets of metallurgy. We must share, or be left behind.

So it was not a purely idealistic move – to establish a secret herd in Xi. There had been a price. *Humans may be Jijo's master engineers, but we stayed out of smithing, and now I know why.*

Even after growing up among them, Sara still found it fascinating how varied urs could be. Their range of personalities and motives – from fanatics to pragmatic smiths – was as broad as you'd find among human beings. *One more reason why stereotypes aren't just evil, but stupid.*

Soon after they remounted, the trail followed a ridgeline offering spectacular views. The Spectral Flow lay to their left, an eerie realm, even dimmed to sepia shades by distance and dark glasses. The maze of speckled canyons spanned all the way to a band of blazing white – the Plain of Sharp Sand. Dedinger's home, where the would-be prophet was forging a nation of die-hard zealots out of coarse desert folk. Sandmen who saw themselves as humanity's vanguard on the Path of Redemption.

In the opposite direction, southwest through gaps in the many-times-folded mountain, Sara glimpsed another wonder. The vast ocean, where Jijo's promised life renewal was fulfilled. Where Melina's ashes went after mulching. And Joshu's. Where the planet erased sin by absorbing and melting anything the universe sent it.

The Slope is so narrow, and Jijo is so large. Will star gods judge us harshly for living quiet careful lives in one corner of a forbidden world?

There was always hope the aliens might just finish their business and go away, leaving the Six Races to proceed along whatever path destiny laid out for them.

Yeah, she concluded. *There are two chances that will happen – fat and slim.*

The trek continued, more often dismounted than not, and the view grew more spectacular as they moved east, encompassing the southern Rimmer Range. Again, Sara noted skittishness among the urs. In spots the ground vented steaming vapors, making the horses dance and snort. Then she glimpsed a red glimmer, some distance below the trail – a meandering stream of *lava*, flowing several arrowflights downslope.

Perhaps it was fatigue, thin air, or the tricky terrain, but as Sara looked away from the fiery trail, her unshielded eyes crossed the mountains and were caught unready by a stray flash of light. Sensitized by her time in Xi, the sharp gleam made her cringe.

What is that?

The flash repeated at uneven intervals, almost as if the distant mountaintop were speaking to her.

Then Sara caught another, quite different flicker of motion.

Now that must be an illusion, she thought. *It has to be ... yet it's so far from the Spectral Flow!*

It seemed ... she could almost swear ... that she saw the widespread wings of some titanic bird, or *dragon*, wafting between—

It had been too long since she checked her footing. A stone unexpectedly turned and Sara tripped. Throwing her weight desperately the other way, she overcompensated, losing her balance completely.

Uttering a cry, Sara fell.

The gritty trail took much of the initial impact, but then she rolled over the edge, tumbling down a scree of pebbles and jagged basalt flakes. Despite her tough leather garments, each jab lanced her with fierce pain as she desperately covered her face and skull. A wailing sound accompanied her plunge. In a terrified daze Sara realized the screamer was not her, but Prity, shrieking dismay.

'Sara!' someone yelled. There were scrambling sounds of distant, hopeless pursuit.

In midtumble, between one jarring collision and the next, she glimpsed something between blood-streaked fingers – a fast-approaching rivulet winding across the shattered landscape. A liquid current that moved languidly, with great viscosity and even greater heat. It was the same color as her blood ... and approaching fast.

Ariana Foo spent the return boat journey mulling over her sketches of the tiny space pod that had brought the Stranger to Jijo. Meanwhile, Nelo fumed over this foolish diversion. His workmen would surely *not* have kept to schedule. Some minor foul-up would give those louts an excuse to lie about like hoons at siesta time.

Commerce had lapsed during the crisis, and the warehouse tree was full, but Nelo was determined to keep producing paper. What would Dolo Village be without the groaning waterwheel, the thump of the pulping hammer, or the sweet aroma that wafted from fresh sheets drying in the sun?

While the helmsman umbled cheerfully, keeping a steady beat for the crew poling the little boat along, Nelo held out a hand, feeling for rain. There had been drops a little earlier, when disturbing thunder pealed to the south.

The marsh petered out as streamlets rejoined as a united river once more. Soon the young people would switch to oars and sweep onto the gentle lake behind Dolo Dam.

The helmsman's umble tapered, slowing to a worried moan. Several of the crew leaned over, peering at the water. A boy shouted as his pole was ripped out of his hands. *It does seem a bit fast*, Nelo thought, as the last swamp plants fell behind and trees began to pass by rapidly.

'All hands to oars!' shouted the young hoon in command. Her back spines, still fresh from recent fledging, made uneasy frickles.

'Lock them down!'

Ariana met Nelo's eyes with a question. He answered with a shrug.

The boat juttered, reminding him of the cataracts that lay many leagues downriver, past Tarek Town, an inconvenience he only had to endure once, accompanying his wife's dross casket to sea.

But there are no rapids here! They were erased when the lake filled, centuries ago!

The boat veered, sending him crashing to the bilge. With stinging hands, Nelo climbed back to take a seat next to Ariana. The former High Sage clutched the bench, her precious folio of drawings zipped shut inside her jacket.

'Hold on!' screamed the young commander. In dazed bewilderment, Nelo clutched the plank as they plunged into a weird domain. A realm that *should not be.*

So Nelo thought, over and over, as they sped down a narrow channel. On either side, the normal shoreline was visible – where trees stopped and scummy water plants took over. But the boat was already well *below* that level, and dropping fast!

Spume crested the gunnels, drenching passengers and crew. The latter rowed furiously to the hoon lieutenant's shrill commands. Lacking a male's resonating sac, she still made her wishes known.

'Backwater-left ... *backwater-left*, you noor-bitten ragmen! ... Steady ... Now all ahead! *Pull for it*, you spineless croakers! For your lives, *pull*!'

Twin walls of stone rushed inward, threatening to crush the boat from both sides. Glistening with oily algae, they loomed like hammer and anvil as the crew rowed frantically for the narrow slot between, marked by a fog of stinging white spray. What lay beyond was a mystery Nelo only prayed he'd live to see.

Voices of hoons, qheuen, and humans rose in desperation as the boat struck one cliff a glancing blow, echoing like a door knocker on the gateway to hell. Somehow the hull survived to lunge down the funnel, drenched in spray.

We should be on the lake by now, Nelo complained, hissing through gritted teeth. *Where did the lake go!*

They shot like a javelin onto a cascade where water churned in utter confusion over scattered boulders, shifting suddenly as fresh debris barricades built up or gave way. It was an obstacle course to defy the best of pilots, but Nelo had no eyes for the ongoing struggle, which would merely decide whether he lived or died. His numbed gaze lifted beyond, staring past the surrounding mud plain that had been a lake bed, down whose center rushed the River Roney, no longer constrained. A river now free to roll on as it had before Earthlings came.

The dam ... The dam ...

A moan lifted from the pair of blue qheuens, lent for this journey by the local hive. A hive whose fisheries and murky lobster pens used to stretch luxuriously behind the dam wherein they made a prosperous home. Remnants of the pens and algae farms lay strewn about as the boat swept toward the maelstrom's center.

Nelo blinked, unable to express his dismay, even with a moan.

The dam still stood along most of its length. But *most* wasn't a word of much use to a dam. Nelo's heart almost gave way when he saw the gap ripped at one end ... the side near his beloved mill.

'Hold on!' the pilot cried redundantly, as they plunged for the opening. And the waterfall they all heard roaring violently just ahead.

VI

FROM THE NOTES OF GILLIAN BASKIN

My DECISION may not be wholly rational.

For all I know, Alvin may be bluffing in order to avoid exile. He may have no idea who we are.

Or perhaps he really has surmised the truth. After all, dolphins are mentioned in many of the Earth books he's read. Even wearing a fully armored, six-legged walker unit, a fin's outline can be recognized if you look in the right way. Once the idea occurred to him, Alvin's fertile imagination would cover the rest.

As a precaution, we could intern the kids much farther south, or in a subsea habitat. That might keep them safe and silent. Tsh't suggested as much, before I ordered the Hikahi to turn around and bring them back.

I admit I'm biased. I miss Alvin and his pals. If only the fractious races of the Five Galaxies could have a camaraderie like theirs.

Anyway, they are grown-up enough to choose their own fate.

We've had a report from Makanee's nurse. On her way by sled to check on a sick member of Kaa's team, Peepoe spotted two more piles of junked spacecraft, smaller than this one, but suitable should we have to move Streaker soon. Hannes dispatched crews to start preparatory work.

Again, we must rely on the same core group of about fifty skilled crewfen. The reliable ones, whose concentration remains unflagged after three stressful years. Those who aren't frightened by superstitious rumors of sea monsters lurking amid the dead Buyur machines.

AS for our pursuers — we've seen no more gravitic signatures of flying craft, east of the mountains. That may be good news, but the respite makes me nervous. Two small spacecraft can't be the whole story. Sensors detect some great brute of a ship, about five hundred klicks northwest. Is this vast cruiser related to the two vessels that fell near here?

They must surely realize that this region is of interest.

It seems creepy they haven't followed up.

As if they are confident they have all the time in the world.

THE Niss Machine managed to exchange just a few more words with that so-called noor beast that our little drone encountered ashore. But the creature keeps us on tenterhooks, treating the little scout robot like its private toy, or a prey animal to be teased with bites and scratches. Yet it also carries it about in its mouth, careful not to get tangled in the fiber cable, letting us have brief, tantalizing views of the crashed sky boats.

We had assumed that 'noor' were simply devolved versions of tytlal ... of little interest except as curiosities. But if some retain the power of speech, what else might they be capable of?

At first I thought the Niss Machine would be the one best qualified to handle this confusing encounter. After all, the noor is its 'cousin,' in a manner of speaking.

But family connections can involve sibling rivalry, even contempt. Maybe the Tymbrimi machine is simply the wrong spokesman.

One more reason I'm eager to bring Alvin back.

AMID all this, I had time to do a bit more research on Herbie.

I wish there were some way to guess the isotopic input profiles, before he died, but chemical racemization analyses of samples taken from the ancient mummy appear to show considerably less temporal span than was indicated by cosmic-ray track histories of the hull Tom boarded, in the Shallow Cluster.

In other words, Herbie seems younger than the vessel Tom found him on.

That could mean a number of things.

Might Herb simply be the corpse of some previous grave robber, who slinked aboard just a few million years ago, instead of one to two billion?

Or could the discrepancy be an effect of those strange fields we found in the Shallow Cluster, surrounding that fleet of ghostly starcraft, rendering them nearly invisible? Perhaps the outer hulls of those huge, silent ships experienced time differently than their contents.

It makes me wonder about poor Lieutenant Yachapa-jean, who was killed by those same fields, and whose body had to be left behind. Might some future expedition someday recover the well-preserved corpse of a dolphin and go rushing around the universe thinking they have the recovered relic of a progenitor?

Mistaking the youngest sapient race for the oldest. What a joke that would be.

A joke on them, and a joke on us.

Herbie never changes. Yet I swear I sometimes catch him grinning.

*

OUR stolen Galactic Library unit gets queer and opaque at times. If I weren't in disguise, the big cube probably wouldn't tell me anything at all. Even decked out as a Thennanin admiral, I find the Library evasive when shown those symbols that Tom copied aboard the derelict ship.

One glyph looks like the emblem worn by every Library unit in known space — a great spiral wheel. Only, instead of five swirling arms rotating around a common center, this one has nine! And eight concentric ovals overlie the stylized galactic helix, making it resemble a bull's-eye target.

I never saw anything like it before.

When I press for answers, our purloined archive says the symbol '... is very old ...' and that its use is '... memetically discouraged.'

Whatever that means.

At risk of humanizing a machine, the unit seems to get grumpy, as if it dislikes being confused. I've seen this before. Terragens researchers find that certain subject areas make Libraries touchy, as if they hate having to work hard by digging in older files ... Or maybe that's an excuse to avoid admitting there are things they don't know.

It reminds me of discussions Tom and I used to have with Jake Demwa, when we'd all sit up late trying to make sense of the universe.

Jake had a theory — that Galactic history, which purports to go back more than a billion years, is actually only accurate to about one hundred and fifty million.

'With each eon you go further back than that,' he said, 'what we're told has an ever-increasing flavor of a carefully concocted fable.'

Oh, there's evidence that oxygen-breathing starfarers have been around ten times as long. Surely some of the ancient events recorded in official annals must be authentic. But much has also been painted over.

It's a chilling notion. The great Institutes are supposed to be dedicated to truth and continuity. How, then, can valid information be memetically discouraged?

Yes, this seems a rather abstract obsession, at a time when *Streaker* — and now Jijo — faces dire and immediate threats. Yet I can't help thinking it all comes together here at the bottom of a planetary graveyard, where tectonic plates melt history into ore.

We are caught in the slowly grinding gears of a machine more vast than we imagined.

STREAKERS

HANNES

At times Hannes Suessi acutely missed his young friend Emerson, whose uncanny skills helped make *Streaker* purr like a compact leopard, prowling the trails of space.

Of course Hannes admired the able fins of his engine-room gang – amiable, hardworking crew mates without a hint of regression in the bunch. But dolphins tend to visualize objects as sonic shapes, and often set their calibrations intuitively, based on the way motor vibrations *sounded*. A helpful technique, but not always reliable.

Emerson D'Anite, on the other hand—

Hannes never knew anyone with a better gut understanding of quantum probability shunts. Not the arcane hyperdimensional theory, but the practical nuts and bolts of wresting movement from contortions of wrinkled space-time. Emerson was also fluent in Tursiops Trinary ... better than Hannes at conveying complex ideas in neo-dolphins' own hybrid language. A useful knack on this tub.

Alas, just one human now remained belowdecks, to help tend abused motors long past due for overhaul.

That is – if one could even call Hannes Suessi human anymore. *Am I more than I was? Or less?*

He now had 'eyes' all over the engine room – remote pickups linked directly to his ceramic-encased brain. Using portable drones, Hannes could supervise Karkaett and Chuchki far across the wide chamber ... or even small crews working on alien vessels elsewhere in the great underwater scrap yard. In this way he could offer advice and comfort when they grew nervous, or when their bodies screamed with cetacean claustrophobia.

Unfortunately, cyborg abilities did nothing to prevent loneliness. *You should never have left me here alone*, Hannes chided Emerson's absent spirit. *You were an engineer, not a secret agent or star pilot! You had no business traipsing off, doing heroic deeds.*

There were specialists for such tasks. *Streaker* had been assigned several 'heroes' when she first set out: individuals with the right training and personalities, equipping them to face dangerous challenges and improvise their way through any situation.

Unfortunately, those qualified ones were gone – Captain Creideiki, Tom Orley, Lieutenant Hikahi, and even the young midshipman Toshio – all used up in that costly escape from Kithrup.

I guess someone had to fill in after that, Hannes conceded.

In fact, Emerson pulled off one daring coup on Oakka, the green world, when the Obeyer Alliance sprang a trap while Gillian tried to negotiate a peaceful surrender to officials of the Navigation Institute.

Not even the suspicious Niss Machine reckoned that neutral Galactic bureaucrats might betray their oaths and violate *Streaker's* truce pennant. It wasn't supposed to be possible. If not for Emerson's daring trek across Oakka's jungle, taking out a Jophur field-emitter station, *Streaker* would have fallen into the clutches of a single fanatic clan – the one thing the Terragens Council said must not occur, at any cost.

But you let one success go to your head, eh? What were you thinking? That you were another Tom Orley?

A few months later you pulled that crazy stunt, veering a jury-rigged Thennanin fighter through the Fractal System, firing recklessly to 'cover' our escape. What did that accomplish, except getting yourself killed?

He recalled the view from *Streaker's* bridge, looking across the inner cavity of a vast, frosty structure the size of a solar system, built of condensed primal matter. A jagged, frothy structure with a pale star in its heart. Emerson's fighter swerved amid the spiky reaches of that enormous artifact, spraying bright but useless rays while claws of hydrogen ice converged around it.

Foolish heroism. The Old Ones could have stopped Streaker *just as easily as they stopped you, if they really wanted to.*

They meant to let us get away.

He winced, recalling how Emerson's brave, futile 'diversion' ended in a burst of painful light, a flicker against the immense, luminous fractal dome. Then *Streaker* fled down a tunnel between dimensions, thread-gliding all the way to forbidden Galaxy Four. Once there, her twisty path skirted the trade winds of a hydrogen-breathing civilization, then plunged past a sooty supergiant whose eruption might at last cover the Earthship's trail.

Others came to Jijo in secret before us, letting Izmunuti erase their tracks.

It should have worked for us, too.

But Hannes knew what was different, this time.

Those others didn't already have a huge price on their heads. You could buy half a spiral arm with the bounty that's been offered for Streaker, *by several rich, terrified patron lines.*

Hannes sighed. The recent depth-charge attack had been imprecise, so the hunters only suspected a general area of sea bottom. But the chase was on again. And Hannes had work to do.

At least I have an excuse to avoid another damned meeting of the ship's council. It's a farce, anyway, since we always wind up doing whatever Gillian decides. We'd be crazy not to.

Karkaett signaled that the motivator array was aligned. Hannes used a cyborg arm to adjust calibration dials on the master control, trying to imitate Emerson's deft touch. The biomechanical extensions that replaced his hands were marvelous gifts, extending both ability and life span – though he still missed the tactile pleasure of fingertips.

The Old Ones were generous . . . then they robbed us and drove us out. They gave life and took it. They might have betrayed us for the reward . . . or else sheltered us in their measureless world. Yet they did neither.

Their agenda ran deeper than mere humans could fathom. Perhaps everything that happened afterward was part of some enigmatic plan.

Sometimes I think humanity would've been better off just staying in bed.

TSH'T

She told Gillian Baskin what she thought of the decision.

'I still do not agree with bringing those young sooners back here.'

The blond woman looked back at Tsh't with tired eyes. Soft lines at the corners had not been there when *Streaker* started this voyage. It was easy to age during a mission like this.

'Exile did seem best, for their own good. But they may be more useful here.'

'Yesss . . . assuming they're telling the truth about *hoons* and *Jophur* sitting around with humans and urs, reading paper books and quoting Mark Twain!'

Gillian nodded. 'Farfetched, I know. But—'

'Think of the coincidence! No sooner does our scout sub find an old urrish cache than these so-called kids and their toy bathysphere drop in.'

'They would have died, if the *Hikahi* didn't snatch them up,' pointed out the ship's physician, Makanee.

'Perhaps. But consider, not long after they arrived here, we sensed gravitic motors headed straight for this rift canyon. Then someone started bombing the abyssss! Was that a fluke? Or did spies lead them here?'

'Calling bombs down on their own heads?' The dolphin surgeon blew a raspberry. 'A simpler explanation is that one of our explorer robots got caught, and was traced to this general area.'

In fact, Tsh't knew the four sooner children hadn't brought Galactics to the Rift. They had nothing to do with it. She was herself responsible.

Back when *Streaker* was preparing to flee the Fractal System, heading off on another of Gillian's brilliant, desperate ploys, Tsh't had impulsively sent a secret message. A plea for help from the one source she felt sure of, revealing the ship's destination and arranging a rendezvous at Jijo.

Gillian will thank me later, she had thought at the time. *When our Rothen lords come to take care of us.*

Only now, images from shore made clear how badly things went wrong.

Two small sky ships, crashed in a swamp ... the larger revealing fierce, implacable Jophur.

Tsh't wondered how her well-meant plan could go so badly. *Did the Rothen allow themselves to be followed? Or was my message intercepted?*

Worry and guilt gnawed her gut.

Another voice entered the discussion. Mellifluous. Emanating from a spiral of rotating lines that glowed at one end of the conference table.

'So Alvin's bluff played no role in your decision, Dr. Baskin?'

'Is he bluffing? These kids grew up reading Melville and Bickerton. Maybe he recognized dolphin shapes under those bulky exo-suits. Or we may have let hints slip, during conversation.'

'Only the Niss spoke to them directly,' Tsh't pointed out, thrusting her jaw toward the whirling hologram.

It replied with unusual contrition.

'Going over recordings, I concede having used terms such as *kilometer* and *hour* ... out of shipboard habit. Alvin and his friends might have correlated this with their extensive knowledge of Anglic, since Galactics would not use wolfling measurements.'

'You mean a Tymbrimi computer ccan make mistakesss?' Tsh't asked, tauntingly.

The spinning motif emitted a low hum they all now recognized as the philosophical umbling sound of a reflective hoon.

'Flexible beings exhibit an ability to learn new ways,' the Niss explained. 'My creators donated me to serve aboard this ship for that reason. It is why the Tymbrimi befriended you Earthling rapscallions, in the first place.'

The remark was relatively gentle teasing, compared with the machine's normal, biting wit.

'Anyway,' Gillian continued, 'it wasn't Alvin's bluff that swayed me.'

'Then what-t?' Makanee asked.

The Niss hologram whirled with flashing speckles, and answered for Gillian.

'It is the small matter of the tytlal ... *the noor beast who speaks*. It has proved uncooperative and uninformative, despite our urgent need to understand its presence here.

'Dr. Baskin and I now agree.

'We need the children for that reason. Alvin, above all.

'To help persuade it to talk to us.'

SOONERS

EMERSON

He blames himself. His mind had been on faraway places and times. Distracted, he was slow reacting when Sara fell.

Till that moment, Emerson was making progress in the struggle to put his past in order, one piece at a time. No easy task with part of his brain missing – the part that once offered words to lubricate any thought or need.

Hard-planted inhibitions fight his effort to remember, punishing every attempt with savagery that makes him grunt and sweat. But the peculiar panoramas help for a while. Ricocheting colors and half-liquid landscapes jar some of the niches where chained memories lie.

One recollection erupts whole. An old one, from childhood. Some neighbors had a big German shepherd who loved to *hunt bees*.

The dog used to stalk his quarry in a very uncanine manner, crouching and twitching like some ridiculous ungainly cat, pursuing the unsuspecting insect through flower beds and tall grass. Then he pounced, snapping powerful jaws around the outmatched prey.

As a boy, Emerson would stare in amazed delight while outraged buzzing echoed behind the shepherd's bared teeth, followed by a vivid instant when the bee gave up protesting and lashed with its stinger. The dog would snort, grimace, and sneeze. Yet, brief pain came mixed with evident triumph. Bee hunting gave meaning to his gelded suburban life.

Emerson wonders, why does this metaphor resonate so strongly? Is he the *dog*, overriding agony to snatch one defiant memory after another?

Or is he the *bee*?

Emerson recalls just fragments about the haughty entities who reamed his mind, then sent his body plummeting to Jijo in fiery ruin. But he knows how they regarded his kind – like insects.

He pictures himself with a sharp stinger, wishing for a chance to make the Old Ones sneeze. He dreams of teaching them to hate the taste of bees.

Emerson lays hard-won memories in a chain. A necklace with far more gaps than pearls. Easiest come events from childhood, adolescence, and years of training for the Terragens Survey Service . . .

Even when the horse caravan departs the land of stabbing colors to climb a steep mountain trail, he has other tools to work with – music, math, and hand signs that he trades with Prity, sharing jokes of ultimate crudity. During rest breaks, his sketchpad helps tap the subconscious, using impatient slashes and curves to draw free-form images from the dark time.

Streaker . . .

The ship takes form, almost drawing itself – a lovingly rendered cylinder with hornlike flanges arrayed in circuits along its length. He draws her *underwater* – surrounded by drifting seaweed – abnormal for a vessel of deep space, but it makes sense as other memories fill in.

Kithrup . . .

That awful world where the *Streaker* came seeking shelter after barely escaping a surprise ambush, learning that a hundred fleets were at war over the right to capture her.

Kithrup. A planet whose oceans were poison . . . but a useful place to make repairs, since just half a dozen crew members had legs to stand on. The rest – bright, temperamental dolphins – needed a watery realm to work in. Besides, it seemed a good place to hide after the disaster at . . .

Morgran . . .

A transfer point. Safest of the fifteen ways to travel from star to star. Simply dive toward one at the right slope and distance, and you'd exit at some other point, far across the stellar wheel. Even the Earthling slowboat *Vesarius* had managed it, though quite by accident, before humanity acquired the techniques of Galactic science.

Thinking of Morgran brings *Keepiru* to mind, the finest pilot Emerson ever knew – the show-off! – steering *Streaker* out of danger with flamboyance that shocked the ambushers, plunging her back into the maelstrom, away from the brewing space battle . . .

. . . like the other battle that developed weeks later, over Kithrup. Fine, glistening fleets, the wealth of noble clans, tearing at each other, destroying in moments the pride of many worlds. Emerson's hand flies as he draws exploding arcs across a sheet of native paper, ripping it as he jabs, frustrated by inability to render the gorgeous savagery he once witnessed with his own eyes . . .

Emerson folds the drawings away when the party remounts, glad that his flowing tears are concealed by the rewq.

Later, when they face a steaming volcano caldera, he abruptly recalls another basin, this one made of folded space . . . *the Shallow*

Cluster ... *Streaker*'s last survey site before heading for Morgran – a place empty of anything worth noting, said the Galactic Library.

Then what intelligence or premonition provoked Captain Creideiki to head for such an unpromising site?

Surely, in all the eons, someone else must have stumbled on the armada of derelict ships *Streaker* discovered there – cause of all her troubles. He can envision those silent arks now, vast as moons but almost transparent, as if they could not quite decide *to be*.

This memory hurts in a different way. Claw marks lie across it, as if some outside force once pored over it in detail – perhaps seeking to read patterns in the background stars. Retracing *Streaker*'s path to a single point in space.

Emerson figures they probably failed. Constellations were never his specialty.

'Emerson, you don't have to go.'

His head jerks as those words peel from a memory more recent than Morgran or Kithrup, by many months.

Emerson pans the land of fevered colors, now seen from high above. At last he finds her face in rippling glimmers. A worried face, burdened with a hundred lives and vital secrets to preserve. Again she speaks, and the words come whole, because he never stored them in parts of the brain meant for mundane conversation.

Because everything she said to him had always seemed like music.

'We need you here. Let's find another way.'

But there was no other way. Not even Gillian's sarcastic Tymbrimi computer could suggest one before Emerson climbed aboard a salvaged Thennanin fighter, embarking on a desperate gamble.

Looking back in time, he hopes to see in Gillian's eyes the same expression she used to have when bidding Tom farewell on some perilous venture.

He sees worried concern, even affection. But it's not the same.

Emerson frees his gaze from the torment-colored desert, turning east toward less disturbing vistas. Far-off mountains offer respite with natural undulating shapes, softened by verdant green forests.

Then, from one tall peak, there comes a glittering flash! Several more gleam in series. A rhythm that seems to *speak* ...

His intrigued detachment is cut short by a frightened yell. Yet, for an instant Emerson remains too distant, too slow to turn. He does not see Sara tumble off the path. But Prity's scream tears through him like a torch thrust into cobwebs.

Sara's name pours from his throat with involuntary clarity. His body finally acts, leaping in pursuit.

Hurtling down the jagged talus slope, he flings eloquent curses at the universe, defying it – *daring it* – to take another friend.

LARK

The sergeant's face was streaked with camouflage. Her black hair still bore flecks of loam and grass from worming through crevices and peering between brambles. Yet Lark had never seen Jeni Shen look better.

People thrive doing the thing they were born for. In Jeni's case, that's being a warrior. She'd rather have lived when the elder and younger Drakes were fashioning the Great Peace out of blood and fire than during the peace itself.

'So far, so good,' the young militia scout reported. Blur-cloth overalls made it hard to trace her outline amid stark lantern shadows.

'I got close enough to watch the emissaries reenter the valley, bringing the sages' reply to the Jophur. A couple of guard robots swooped in to look them over, especially poor Vubben, sniffing him from wheel rims to eyestalks. Then all six ambassadors headed down to the Glade, with the bots in escort.' Jeni made slanting downward motions with her hands. 'That leaves just one or two drones patrolling this section of perimeter! Seems we couldn't ask for a better chance to make our move.'

'Can there be any question?' added Rann. The tall starfarer leaned against a limestone wall with arms folded. The Danik was unarmed, but otherwise Rann acted as if this were *his* expedition. 'Of course we shall proceed. There is no other option.'

Despite Rann's poised assurance, the plan was actually Lark's. So was the decision whether to continue. His would be the responsibility, if three-score brave lives were lost in the endeavor ... or if their act provoked the Jophur into spasms of vengeful destruction.

We might undermine the High Sages at the very moment when they have the Galactic untraekis calmed down.

On the other hand, how could the Six Races possibly pay the price the Jophur were demanding? While the sages tried to negotiate a lower cost, someone had to see if there was a better way. A way not to pay at all.

Anxious eyes regarded him from all corners of the grotto – one of countless steamy warrens that laced these hills. Ling's gaze was among the most relentless, standing far apart from Rann. The two star lords had been at odds since they worked to decode those cryptic data slabs – that awful afternoon when Rann cried 'treason!' then a dread gold mist fell on Dooden Mesa. Each sky human had a different reason to help this desperate mission.

Lark found little cheer in Jeni's report. *Only one or two drones left.* According to Lester Cambel's aides, the remaining robots could still probe some distance underground, on guard against approaching threats. On the plus side, this terrain was a muddle of steam vents and juttering quakes. Then there were the subtle patterning songs put out by the Holy Egg – emanations that set Lark's stone amulet trembling against his chest.

They all watched, awaiting his decision – human, urs, and hoon volunteers, plus some qheuens who weren't yet sick.

'All right.' Lark nodded. 'Let's do it.'

A terse, decisive command. Grinning, Jeni spun about to forge deeper into the cavern, followed by lantern bearers.

What Lark had meant to say was, *Hell no! Let's get out of here. I'll buy a round of drinks so everyone can raise a glass for poor Uthen.*

But if he mentioned his friend's name, he might sob the wrenching grief inside. So Lark took his place along the twisty column of figures stooping and shuffling through the dim passage, lit by glow patches stuck to the walls.

His thoughts caromed as he walked. For instance, he found himself wondering where on the Slope all six races *could* drink the same toast at the same time? Not many inns served both alcohol and fresh simla blood, since humans and urs disdained each other's feeding habits. And most traeki politely refrained from eating in front of other races.

I do know one bar in Tarek Town ... that is, if Tarek hasn't already been smothered by a downpour of golden rain. After Dooden, the Jophur may go for the bigger towns, where so many g'Kek live.

It makes you wonder why the g'Kek came to Jijo in the first place. They can only travel the Path of Redemption if it is paved.

Lark shook his head.

Trivia. Minutiae. Brain synapses keep firing, even when your sole concern is following the man in front of you ... and not slamming your skull on a stalactite.

When they glanced at him, his followers saw a calm, assertive pose. But within, Lark endured a run-on babble of words, forever filling his unquiet mind.

I should be mourning my friend, right now.

I should be hiring a traeki undertaker, arranging a lavish mulching ceremony, so Uthen's polished carapace can go in style to join the bones and spindles of his foremothers, lying under the Great Midden.

It's my duty to pay a formal visit to the Gray Queens, in that dusty hall where they once dominated most of the Slope. The Chamber of Ninety Tooth-Carved Pillars, where they still make pretense at regal glory. But how could I explain to those qheuen matrons how two of their brightest sons died – Harullen, sliced apart by alien lasers, and Uthen, slain by pestilence?

Can I tell those ashen empresses their other children may be next?

Uthen had been his greatest friend, the colleague who shared his fascination with the ebb and flow of Jijo's fragile ecosystem. Though never joining Lark in heresy, Uthen was the one other person who understood *why* sooner races should never have come to this world. The one to comprehend why some Galactic laws were good.

I let you down, old pal. But if I can't perform all those other duties, maybe I can arrange something to compensate.

Justice.

Debris littered the floor of the last large cavern, strewn there during the Zealots' Plot, when a cabal of young rebels used these same corridors to sneak explosives under the Danik research station, incinerating Ling's friend Besh and one of the Rothen star lords. Repercussions still spread from that event, like ripples after a large stone strikes a pond.

The Jophur battleship now lay atop the station wreckage, yet no one suggested using the same method of attack a second time. Assuming a mighty starcraft *could* be blown up, it would take such massive amounts of exploser paste that Lark's team would still be hauling barrels by next Founders' Day. Anyway, there were no volunteers to approach the deadly space behemoth. Lark's plan meant coming no closer than several arrowflights. Even so, the going would be hard and fraught with peril.

'From here on, the way's too close for grays,' Jeni said.

Urrish partisans peered down a passage that narrowed considerably, coiling their long necks in unison, sniffing an aroma their kind disliked.

The gray qheuens squatted while others unstrapped supplies from their chitin backs. Given enough time, the big fellows might widen the corridor with their digging claws and diamond-like teeth, but Lark felt better sending them back. Who knew how much time they had, with plague spreading on Jijo's winds? Was it a genocide bug? Ling had found supporting evidence on decoded data wafers, though Rann still denied it could be of Rothen origin.

The glowering starman was obsessed with a different wafer-gleaned fact.

There had been a *spy* among the station's staff of outlaw gene raiders. Someone who kept a careful diary, recording every misdemeanor performed by the Rothen and their human servants.

An agent of the Terragens Council!

Apparently, Earth's ruling body had an informant among the clan of human fanatics who worshiped Rothen lords.

He wanted badly to quiz Ling, but there was no time for their old question game. Not since they fled the Dooden disaster along with Lester Cambel's panicky aides, plunging through a maze of towering boo. New trails and fresh-cut trunks had flustered the breathless fugitives until they spilled into an uncharted clearing, surprising a phalanx of traeki who stood in a long row, venting noxious vapors like hissing kettles.

Galloping squads of urrish militia then swarmed in to protect the busy traeki, nipping at ankles, as if the humans were stampeding simlas, driving Cambel's team away from the clearing, diverting them toward havens to the west and south.

Even after finally reaching a campsite refuge, there had been no respite to discuss far-off Galactic affairs. Ling spent her time with the medics, relating what little she had learned from the spy's notes about the qheuen plague.

Meanwhile, Lark found himself surrounded by furious activity, commanding an ever-growing entourage of followers.

It goes to show, desperate people will follow anyone with a plan. Even one as loony as mine.

Hoonish bearers took up the grays' burdens, and the caravan was off again. Half a dozen blue qheuens took up the rear, so young their shells were still moist from larval fledging. Though small for their kind, they still needed help from men with hammers and crowbars, chiseling away limestone obstructions. Lark's scheme counted on these adolescent volunteers.

He hoped his farfetched plan wasn't the only one at work.

There is always prayer.

Lark fondled his amulet. It felt cool. For now the Egg was quiescent.

At a junction the earlier zealot cabal had veered left, carrying barrels of exploser paste to a cave beneath the Rothen station. But Lark's group turned right. They had less distance to cover, but their way was more hazardous.

Jimi the Blessed was among the burly men helping widen the path, attacking an obstruction with such fury Lark had to intervene.

'Easy, Jimi! You'll wake the recycled dead!'

That brought laughter from the sweaty laborers, and booming umbles from several hoonish porters. *Brave* hoons. Lark recalled how their kind disliked closed places. The urs, normally comfortable underground, grew more nervous with each sign of approaching water.

None of them were happy to be approaching the giant star cruiser.

The Six Races had spent centuries cowering against *The Day* when ships of the Institutes would come judge their crimes. Yet, when great vessels came, they did not bear highminded magistrates, but *thieves*, and then brutal killers. Where the Rothen and their human stooges seemed crafty and manipulative, the Jophur were chilling.

They demand what we cannot give.

We don't know anything about the 'dolphin ship' they seek. And we'd rather be damned than hand over our g'Kek brothers.

So Lark, who had spent his life hoping Galactics would come end the illegal colony on Jijo, now led a desperate bid to battle star gods.

Human literature has been so influential since the Great Printing. It's full of forlorn causes. Endeavors that no rational person would entertain.

He and Ling were helping each other descend a limestone chute, glistening with seepage and slippery lichen, when word arrived from the forward scouts.

'Water just ahead.'

That was the message, sent back by Jeni Shen.

So, Lark thought. *I was right.*

Then he added—

So far.

The liquid was oily and cold. It gave off a musty aroma.

None of which stopped two eager young blues from creeping straight into the black pool, trailing mulc-fiber line from a spool. Hoons with hand pumps kept busy inflating air bladders while Lark steeled himself to enter that dark, wet place.

Having second thoughts?

Jeni checked his protective suit of skink membranes. It might ward off the chill, but that was the least of Lark's worries.

I can take cold. But there had better be enough air.

The bladders were an untested innovation. Each was a traeki ring, thick-ribbed to hold gas under pressure. Jeni affixed one to his back, and showed him how to breathe through its fleshy protrusion – a rubbery tentacle that would provide fresh air and scrub the old.

You grow up depending on traeki-secreted chemicals to make native foods edible, and traeki-distilled alcohol to liven celebrations. A traeki pharmacist makes your medicine in a chem-synth ring. Yet you're revolted by the thought of putting one of these things in your mouth.

It tasted like a slimy tallow candle.

Across the narrow chamber, Ling and Rann adjusted quickly to this Jijoan novelty. Of course they had no history to overcome, associating traekis with mulch and rotting garbage.

'Come on,' Jeni chided in a low voice that burned his ears.

'Don't gag on me, man. You're a sage now. Others are watchin'!'

He nodded – two quick head jerks – and tried again. Fitting his teeth around the tube, Lark bit down as she had taught. The burst of air did not stink as bad as expected. Perhaps it contained a mild relaxant. The pharmacist designers were clever about such things.

Let's hope their star-god cousins don't think of this, as well.

That assumption underlay Lark's plan. Jophur commanders might be wary against direct subterranean assault. But where the buried route combined with *water*, the invaders might not expect trouble.

The Rothen underestimated us. By Ifni and the Egg, the Jophur may do the same.

Each diver also wore a rewq symbiont to protect the eyes and help them see by the dim light of hand-carried phosphors. Webbed gloves and booties completed the ensemble.

Ling's tripping laughter made him turn around, and Lark saw she was pointing at *him* as she guffawed.

'You should talk,' he retorted at the ungainly creature she had become, more monstrous than an unmasked Rothen. Hoons paused from laying down cargo by the waterline, and joined in the mirth, umbling good-naturedly while their pet noors grinned with needlelike teeth.

Lark pictured the scene up above, past overlying layers of rock, in the world of light. The Jophur dreadnought squatted astride the mountain glen, thwarting the glade stream in its normal seaward rush. The resulting lake now stretched more than a league uphill.

Water seeks its own level. We must now be several arrowflights from shore. That's a long way to swim before we get to the lake itself.

It couldn't be helped. Their goal was hard to reach, in more ways than one.

Bubbles in the pool. One qheuen cupola broached the surface, followed by another. The young blues crawled ashore, breathing heavily through multiple leg vents, reporting in excited GalSix.

'The way to open water – it is clear. Good time – this we made. To the target – we shall now escort you.'

Cheers lifted from the hoons and urs, but Lark felt no stirring.

They weren't the ones who would have to go the rest of the way.

Water transformed the cavities and grottoes. Flippers kicked up clouds of silt, filling the phosphor beams with a myriad of distracting speckles. Lark's trusty rewq pulled tricks with polarization, transforming the haze to partial clarity. Still, it took concentration to avoid colliding with jagged limestone outcrops. The guide rope saved him from getting lost.

Cave diving felt a lot like being a junior sage of the Commons – an experience he never sought or foresaw in his former life as a scientist heretic.

How ungainly swimming humans appeared next to the graceful young qheuens, who seized the rugged walls with flashing claws, propelling themselves with uncanny agility, nearly as at-home in freshwater as on solid ground.

His skin grew numb where the skink coverings pulled loose. Other parts grew hot from exertion. More upsetting was the squirmy traeki tentacle in his mouth, anticipating his needs in unnerving ways. It would not let him hold his breath, as a man might do while concentrating on some near-term problem, but tickled his throat to provoke an exhalation. The first time it happened, he nearly retched. (What if he chucked up breakfast? Would he and the ring both asphyxiate? Or would it take his gift as a tasty, predigested bonus?)

Lark was so focused on the guide rope that he missed the transition from stony catacombs to a murky plain of sodden meadows, drowned trees, and drifting debris. But soon the silty margins fell behind as daylight transformed the Glade of Gathering – now the bottom of an upland lake – giving commonplace shapes macabre unfamiliarity.

The guide rope passed near a stand of lesser boo whose surviving stems were tall enough to reach the surface, far overhead. Qheuens gathered around one tube, sucking down drafts of air. When sated, they spiraled around Lark and the humans, nudging them toward the next stretch of guide rope.

Long before details loomed through the silty haze, he made out their target by its *glow*. Rann and Ling thrashed flippers, passing Jeni in their haste. By the time Lark caught up, they were pressing hands against a giant slick sarcophagus, the hue of yellow moonrise. Within lay a cigar-shaped vessel, the Rothen ship, their home away from home, now sealed in a deadly trap.

The two starfarers split up, he swimming right and she left. By silent agreement, Jeni accompanied the big man – despite their size difference, she was the one more qualified to keep an eye on Rann. Lark kept near Ling, watching as she moved along the golden wall.

Though he had more experience than other Sixers with Galactic god machines, it was his first time near this interloper whose dramatic coming so rudely shattered Gathering Festival, many weeks ago. So magnificent and terrible it had seemed! Daunting and invincible. Yet now it was helpless. Dead or implacably imprisoned.

Tentatively, Lark identified some features, like the jutting anchors that held a ship against quantum probability fluctuations ... whatever that meant. The self-styled techies who worked for Lester Cambel were hesitant about even the basics of starcraft design. As for the High Sage himself, Lester had taken no part in Lark's briefing, choosing instead to brood in his tent, guilt-ridden over the doom he helped bring on Dooden Mesa.

Despite the crowding sense of danger, Lark discovered a kind of spooky beauty, swimming in this realm where sunlight slanted in long rippling shafts, filled with sparkling motes – a silent, strangely contemplative world.

Besides, even wrapped in skink membranes, Ling's athletic body was a sight to behold.

They rounded the star cruiser's rim, where a sharp shadow abruptly cut off the sun. It might be a cloud, or the edge of a mountain. Then he realized—

It's the Jophur ship.

Though blurred by murky water, the domelike outline sent shivers down his back. Towering mightily at the lake's edge, it could have swallowed the Rothen vessel whole.

A strange thought struck him.

First the Rothen awed us. Then we saw their 'majesty' cut down by real power. What if it happens again? What kind of newcomer might overwhelm the Jophur? A hovering mountain range? One that throws the whole Slope into night?

He pictured successive waves of 'ships,' each vaster than before, matching first the moons, then all Jijo, and – why not? –the sun or even mighty Izmunuti!

Imagination is the most amazing thing. It lets a groundhugging savage fill his mind with fantastic unlikelihoods.

Churning bubbles nearly tore the rewq off his face as Ling sped up, kicking urgently. Lark hurried after ... only to arrest himself moments later, staring.

Just ahead, Ling traced the golden barrier with one hand, just meters from a gaping opening. A *hatchway*, backlit by a radiant interior. Several figures stood in the portal – three humans and a Rothen lord, wearing his appealing symbiotic mask. The quartet surveyed their all-enclosing golden prison with instruments, wearing expressions of concern.

Yet, all four bipeds seemed frozen, embedded in crystal time.

Up close, the yellow cocoon resembled the *preservation beads* left by that alpine mulc-spider, the one whose mad collecting fetish nearly cost Dwer and Rety their lives, months back. But this trap was no well-shaped ovoid. It resembled a partly melted candle, with over-lapping golden puddles slumped around its base. The Jophur had been generous in their gift of frozen temporality, pouring enough to coat the ship thoroughly.

Like at Dooden Mesa, Lark thought.

It seemed an ideal way to slay one's enemies without using destructive fire. *Maybe the Jophur can't risk damaging Jijo's eco-sphere. That would be a major crime before the great Institutes, like gene raiding and illegal settlement.*

On the other hand, the untraeki invaders hadn't been so scrupulous in scything the forest around their ship. So perhaps the golden trap had another purpose. To capture, rather than kill? Perhaps the g'Kek denizens of Dooden Mesa might yet be rescued from their shimmering tomb.

That had been Lark's initial thought, three days ago. In hurried experiments, more mulc-spider relics were thawed out, using the new traeki solvents. Some of the preserved items had once been alive, birds and bush creepers that long ago fell into the spider's snare.

All emerged from their cocoons quite dead.

Perhaps the Jophur have better revival methods, Lark thought at the time. *Or else they don't mean to restore their victims, only to preserve them as timeless trophies.*

Then, night before last, an idea came to Lark in the form of a dream.

The hivvern lays its eggs beneath deep snow, which melts in the spring, letting each egg sink in slushy mud, which then hardens all around. Yet the ground softens again, when rainy season comes. Then the hivvern larva emerges, swimming free.

When he wakened, the idea was there, entire.

A spaceship has a sealed metal shell, like the hivvern egg. The Rothen ship may be trapped, but its crew were never touched.

Those within may yet live.

And now proof stood before him. The four in the hatchway were clearly aware of the golden barrier surrounding their ship, examining it with tools at hand.

Just one problem – they did not move. Nor was there any sign they knew they were being observed from just a hoon's length away.

Treading water, Ling scrawled on her wax-covered note board and raised it for Lark to see.

TIME DIFFERENT INSIDE.

He fumbled with his own board, tethered to his waist.

TIME SLOWER?

Her answer was confusing.

PERHAPS.

OR ELSE QUANTIZED.

FRAME-SHIFTED.

His perplexed look conveyed more than written words. Ling wiped the board and scratched again.

DO EXACTLY AS I DO.

He nodded, watching her carefully. Ling swished her arms and legs to turn *away* from the ship. Imitating her, Lark found himself looking across the poor wounded Glade. All the trees had been shattered by ravening beams, left to submerge under the rising lake. Turbid water made everything hazy, but Lark thought he saw *bones* mixed among the splinters. Urrish ribs and hoonish spines, jumbled with grinning human skulls. Not the way bodies ought to be drossed. Not respect of the dead, or Jijo.

Perhaps the Jophur will let us seed a mulc-spider in this new lake, he mused. *Something ought to be done to clean up the mess*.

He was jarred by Ling's nudge. TURN BACK NOW, her wax board said. Lark copied her maneuver again ... and stared in surprise for a second time.

They had moved!

As before, statues stood in the hatchway. Only now their poses were all changed! One human pointed outward wearing an amazed look. Another seemed to peer straight at Lark, as if frozen in midrealization.

They did all this while we were turned away?

Time's flow within the golden shell was stranger than he could begin to comprehend.

THIS MAY TAKE SOME DOING, Ling wrote.

Lark met her eyes, noting they held tense, hopeful irony. He nodded.

You could say that again.

ALVIN

I spent most of the return trip with my nose buried in my journal, reviewing all the things that I've seen and heard since *Wuphon's Dream* plunged below Terminus Rock. Pincer kindly chewed my pencil to a point for me. Then I lay down and wrote down the section before this one.

What began as a guess grew into reinforced conviction.

Concentration also diverted attention from nervous anticipation and the pain in my slowly healing spine. My friends tried wheedling me, but I lapsed into hoonish stubbornness, refusing to confide in them. After all, the phuvnthus had gone to great lengths to hide their identity.

The spinning voice said it was to protect us. Maybe that was just patronizing glaver dreck. Typical from grown-ups. But what if he told the truth? How can I risk my friends?

When the time comes, I'll confront the voice alone.

SARA

She drifted in a cloud of mathematics.

All around her floated arcs and conic sections, glowing, as though made of enduring fire. Meteors streaked past, coruscating along paths smoothly ordained by gravity.

Then more stately shapes joined the frolicking figures and she guessed they might be planets whose routes were elliptical, not parabolic. Each had its own reference frame, around which all other masses seemed to move.

Rising, falling ...
Rising, falling ...

The dance spoke of a lost science she had studied once, in an obscure text from the Biblos Archive. Its name floated through her delirium – *orbital mechanics* – as if managing the ponderous gyres of suns and moons were no more complex than maintaining a windmill or waterwheel.

Dimly, Sara knew physical pain. But it came to her as if through a swaddling of musty clothes, like something unpleasant tucked in a bottom pantry drawer. The strong scent of traeki unguents filled her nostrils, dulling every agony except one ... the uneasy knowledge – *I've been harmed.*

Sometimes she roused enough to hear speech ... several lisping urrish voices ... the gruff terseness of Kurt the Exploser ... and one whose stiff, pedantic brilliance she knew from happier days.

Purofsky. Sage of mysteries ...

But what is he doing here?

... and where is here?

At one point she managed to crack her eyelids in hopes of solving the riddle. But Sara quickly decided she must still be dreaming. For no place could exist like the one she witnessed through a blurry haze – a world of spinning glass. A universe of translucent saucers, disks and wheels, tilting and rolling against each other at odd angles, reflecting shafts of light in rhythmic bursts.

It was all too dizzying. She closed her eyes against the maelstrom, yet it continued in her mind, persisting in the form of abstractions.

A sinusoidal wave filled her mental foreground, but no longer the static shape she knew from inked figures in books. Instead, this one undulated like ripples on a pond, with time the apparent free variable.

Soon the first wave was joined by a second, with twice the frequency, then a third with the peaks and troughs compressed yet again. New cycles merged, one after another, combining in an endless series – *a transform* – whose sum built toward a new complex figure, an entity with jagged peaks and valleys, like a mountain range.

Out of order ... chaos ...

Mountains brought to mind the last thing Sara had seen, before spilling off the volcano's narrow path, tumbling over sharp stones toward a river of fire.

Flashes from a distant peak ... long-short, short-long, medium-short-short ...

Coded speech, conveyed by a language of light, not unlike GalTwo ...

Words of urgency, of stealth and battle ...

Her mind's fevered random walk was broken now and then by soft contact on her brow – a warm cloth, or else a gentle touch. She recognized the long, slender shape of Prity's fingers, but there was another texture as well, a *man's* contact on her arm, her cheek, or just holding her hand.

When he sang to her, she knew it was the Stranger ... *Emerson* ... by his odd accent and the way the lyrics flowed, smoothly from memory, as a liquid stream, without thought to any particular word or phrase. Yet the song was no oddly syncopated Earthling ballad, but a Jijoan folk ballad, familiar as a lullaby.

Sara's mother sang it to her, whenever she was ill – as Sara used to murmur it to the man from space, soon after he crashed on Jijo, barely clinging to life.

> 'One comes from an umbling sac, a song for you to keep,
> Two is for a pair of hands, to spin you happy sleep,
> Three fat rings will huff and puff out clouds of happy steam,
> Four eyes wave and dance about, to watch over your dream,
>
> 'Five claws will carve your new hope box, all without a seam,
> Six will bring you flashing hooves to cross the prairie plain,
> Seven is for hidden thoughts, waiting in the deep,
> But eight comes from a giant stone, whose patterns gently creep.'

Even half-conscious, she knew something important. He could not sing unless the words were stored deep within, beyond the scarred part of his brain. It meant she must have touched him, when their roles were reversed.

Not all the unguents in the world – nor the cool beauty of mathematics – could do as much for Sara. What finally called her back was knowing someone missed her, when she was gone.

EWASX

There was an enjoyable sense of importance to our task, was there not, My rings? There we stood, this stack of shabby-looking, retread toruses, deputized with a noble job – explaining to envoys of six races the new order of life on this world.

FIRST – they should not hope for great judges to come from those Institutes who mediate among ten thousand starfaring races. Passions run too high, throughout the Five Galaxies. Institute forces have withdrawn, along with timid, so-called moderate clans, a dithering, ineffectual majority. Only great religious alliances show nerve nowadays, battling over which way the Galactic wheels shall turn during a time of changes.

WE ARE YOUR JUDGES, I told the ambassadors. Out of kindness, we the *Polkjhy* crew have volunteered to serve as both posse and jury, chastening the seven races who invaded this world's fallow peace.

To demonstrate this benevolence, we have delayed by many days the important work that originally brought us here, even though it means leaving our comrades to make their own repairs in that eastern swamp, while our remaining corvette tours the Slope, photographing and recording evidence. It also gives us an opportunity to demonstrate the irresistible majesty of our power. We did this by destroying egregious structures that sooners should not use, if their goal truly is racial redemption.

IT IS NOTED THAT YOU WERE NOT MUCH HELP IN THIS WORK, MY RINGS. (Accept these reproaching jolts, as tokens of loving guidance.) Asx melted many memories, before capture and conversion, yet we/I did recall certain abominations. We gained credit, for instance, by helping target the Bibur River steamboats, and a refinery tower in Tarek Town, an edifice called the Palace of Stinks.

DON'T WORRY. In time, we of the *Polkjhy* will find all pathetic objects-of-sin prized by headstrong sooners. We shall help erase the flagrant hypocrisy of tool use among those who chose the Downward Path!

SECOND comes our unstoppable demand for justice. The High Sages showed surprising good sense by swiftly emitting a call, soon after our last meeting. A flicker of computer cognizance, leading our corvette to Dooden Mesa. But this token gesture will not suffice for long. We want every living member of the g'Kek race accounted for. That should not be too hard. Stranded on a roadless planet, they are singularly immobile beings.

'Please do not destroy our wheeled brethren,' the envoys entreat. 'Let the g'Kek seek holy shelter down Redemption's Path. For is it not said that all debts and vendettas stop, once innocence is resumed?'

At first we see this as yet more lawyerly blather. But then, surprisingly, our senior Priest-Stack agrees! Moreover, that august pile makes an unusual, innovative suggestion—

HERE IS THE QUESTION posed by the Priest-Stack:

What kind of revenge on the g'Kek would transcend even extinction?

ANSWER: to see the g'Kek race become once again eligible for adoption, *and for their new patrons to be Jophur!* In their second sequence of uplift, we might transform them as we see fit – into creatures their former selves would have disdained!

Vengeance is best when executed with imagination. This justifies bringing a priest along. Indeed, that stack variety has uses.

Of course this daring plan carries complications. It means refraining from informing the Five Galaxies about this sooner infestation. Instead, our Jophur clan must keep it secret, tending Jijo like our own private garden.

SO WE BECOME CRIMINALS, under Galactic law. But that hardly matters. For those laws will change, once our alliance assumes leadership during the next phase of history.

Especially if the Progenitors have indeed returned.

THIRD comes opportunity for profit. Perhaps the Rothen gene raiders were onto something. Jijo seems exceptionally rich for a fallow world. (The Buyur were good caretakers who left the planet filled with biopossibilities.) Might the Rothen have discovered a likely presentient race already? One ripe for uplift? Should we have bought off the gene raiders so we might have access to their data, instead of sealing them away in time?

REJECT THE NOTION. They are known blackmailers and double-crossers. We will bring in our own biologists to survey Jijo.

AND WHO KNOWS? Perhaps we might accelerate the sooner races along the path they seek! Glavers are already far progressed toward innocence. Hoons, urs, and qheuens have living star cousins who might object if we adopt too soon. But that may change as battle fires burn across the galaxies. As for human wolflings, at last word their homeworld was under siege, in desperate straits.

Perhaps those on Jijo are already the sole remnant of their kind.

THAT LEAVES OUR TRAEKI RELATIVES TO CONSIDER. The rebel stacks who came here sought to reject the gift of the Oailie – the specialized rings that give us purpose and destiny. It is wrenching to see traeki stumbling about like our pathetic ancestors. Such ungainly beings, so placid and unambitious! We should at once commence a program to create master rings in large quantities. Once converted, our cousins will be ideal instruments of dominance and control, able to knowledgeably run this planet for us without further cost to the clan.

ALL THESE CONCERNS SEEMED PARAMOUNT. Yet from the start, some members of the crew chafed at talk of vengeance, or profit, or redemption. Even the fate of local traeki seemed unimportant, compared with the matter that brought the *Polkjhy* here in the first place.

Hints by the Rothen that they knew the whereabouts of the missing prey ship.

The prey ship carrying news of the Progenitors' return.

DROP ALL OTHER CONCERNS AT ONCE! these stacks insisted. Send the remaining corvette east! Do not wait for the first boat's crew to make repairs on their own. Fetch and interrogate the human-slaves-of-Rothen. Search deepwater places where the prey ship might be hiding. Delay no longer!

But our Captain-Leader and Priest-Stack agreed that a few more days would not matter. Our hold on this world is total. The prey cannot escape.

LARK

Pale daylight penetrated the lake to where a few drowned trees wafted their branches, as if to a gusting breeze. The rewq over his eyes helped him see, amplifying the dim glow, but Lark found the resulting shadows creepy, adding to a feeling that none of this could possibly be real.

Working underwater alongside Rann and Ling, he took part in an odd ritual, communicating with the trapped inhabitants of the preservation bubble. Since the process began, the hatchway of the imprisoned ship had filled with humans and Rothen, pressing eagerly against the gold barrier. Yet, from the outside no motion was seen. Those within were as still as statues, like wax effigies, depicting people with worried expressions.

Only when Lark and the other swimmers turned away, averting their gaze, did the 'statues' change, shifting positions at incredible speed.

According to Ling's terse explanation, scribbled on her wax board, the captives lived in a QUANTUM SEPARATED WORLD. She added something about COGNIZANCE INTERFERENCE BY ORGANIC OBSERVERS and seemed to think that explained it. But Lark failed to see why not-looking should make any difference. No doubt Sara would understand better than her brother, the backwoods biologist. *I used to tease her that the books she loved best were filled with useless abstractions. Concepts no Jijoan would need again. Guess it just shows how little I knew.*

To Lark the whole thing smacked of a particularly inconvenient kind of magic, as if the capricious goddess, Ifni, invented the gold barrier to test the patience of mortals.

Fortunately, their micro-traeki rings provided the human swimmers with all the air they needed. When pressurized supplies ran out, the little toruses unfolded great feathery fans that waved through the lake water like lazy wings, sieving fresh oxygen for Lark and the others to breathe. Another impressive feature of the ever-adaptable ringed ones. Combined with the skink-skin wet suits and rewqs, it made the swimmers look like bizarre sea monsters to those inside the bubble. Finally, though, the prisoners set up an electronic message plaque that flashed words through the translucent barrier in shining Anglic letters.

WE MUST MAKE COMMON CASE, they sent.

So far, Lark's idea had been fruitful. Unlike at tragic Dooden Mesa, these prisoners had been sealed within an airtight hull that kept the golden liquor from swamping their bodies and life-support machinery. Moreover, the chill lake carried away enough heat so their idle engines did not broil them. They were surrounded, enmeshed in strange time. But they were alive.

When Lark stared at one of the Rothen masters, he easily made out the creature's facade. Rewq-generated colors divided its charismatic features, so noble in human terms, into two parts, each with its own aura. Across the upper half lay a fleshy symbiont beast, shaped to provide the regal brow, high cheeks and trademark stately nose. A gray deadness told that some kind of synthetic lens insert lay over the Rothen's eyeballs, and the fine white teeth were artificially capped.

It's an impressive disguise, he thought. Yet even without masks the Rothen were remarkably humanoid, a resemblance that no doubt originally spurred their cunning plan to win over some impressionable Earthlings, back in the frantic, naive days soon after contact, turning those converts into a select tribe of loyal aides – the Daniks. If handled right, it would let the Rothen pull quite a few capers using human intermediaries to do the dirty work. And if Daniks were caught in the act, *Earth* would get the blame.

All told, those inside the trapped ship had a destiny they deserved. Lark might have voted to leave them till Jijo reclaimed their dross. Only now an even greater danger loomed, and there was no other place to turn for allies against the Jophur.

The captives inside the shell seemed eager enough. The last line of their message expressed this.

GET US OUT OF HERE!

Floating in the gentle current, Lark saw Rann, the tall Danik leader, write on his wax board.

WE MAY HAVE A WAY.

YOU MUST PREPARE A FORMULA.

IT IS—

Lark grabbed for the board, but Ling got there first, snatching the stylus right out of Rann's meaty hand. Surprise, then anger, flared across the part of his face visible between the rewq and breathing ring. But the big man was outnumbered, and knew that Jeni Shen had lethal darts in her underwater crossbow. The militia sergeant watched from a vantage point where her vigilance would not interfere with the time-jerked conversation.

Ling replaced Rann's message with another.

HOW DO YOU SUGGEST WE DO THAT?

She slung the sign's strap over her neck so the board rested against her *back*, message outward. At her nodded signal, Rann and Lark joined her turning around. A spooky feeling swarmed Lark's spine as he imagined a flurry of activity taking place behind them. Without observers peering at them, the Rothen-Danik crew were liberated from frozen time, free to read Ling's message, deliberate, and shape a reply.

I never read much physics, Lark thought. *But something feels awful screwy about how this works.*

The swimmers let momentum carry them around. Only a few duras passed before they faced the hatch once more, but most of the Rothen and human figures had moved in that narrow moment. The electric placard now glimmered with new writing.

PREFERRED METHOD: DESTROY THE JOPHUR.

Bubbles burst past Lark's breathing tube as he choked back a guffaw. Ling glanced his way, conveying agreement with a shake of her head. The second half of the message was more serious.

OTHER POSSIBILITY: OFFER JOPHUR WHAT THEY WANT.

BUY OUR FREEDOM!

Lark scanned the crowded statues, where many human faces wore expressions of desperation. He could not help feeling moved as they pleaded for their lives. *In a way it's not their fault. Their ancestors made a stupid deal on their behalf, just as mine did. People must have been both crazed and gullible in those days, right after Earthlings first met Galactic culture.*

It took effort to harden his heart, but Lark knew he must.

Again, Rann tried for the big writing tablet, but Ling wrote fiercely.

WHAT CAN YOU OFFER US, IN RETURN?

On seeing her message, Lark and Rann both stared at her. But Ling seemed unaware that her words carried a personal as well as general meaning. They turned again, giving the prisoners a chance to read and react to Ling's demand. While sweeping the slow circle, Lark glanced toward her, but living goggles made direct eye contact impossible. Her rewq-mediated aura conveyed grim resolve.

Lark expected to find the captives in turmoil, upset by Ling's implied secession. Then he realized. *They only see us when our backs are turned. They may not even know it's Rann and Ling out here, after all!*

That was the frank answer, arrayed in shining letters.

Ling's next message was as straight to the point.

RO-KENN RELEASED QHEUEN AND HOON PLAGUES.

MAYBE OTHERS.

CURE THEM, OR ROT.

At this resumed accusation, Rann nearly exploded. Strangled anger echoed in his pharynx, escaping as bubbles that Lark feared might carry his curses all the way to the far surface of the lake. The starman tried to grab the message board, briefly struggling with Ling. But when Lark made slashing motions across his throat, Rann glanced back as Jeni approached from the ship's curved flank, brandishing her deadly bow, accompanied by two strong young qheuens.

Rann's shoulders slumped. He went through the next turning time sweep mechanically. Lark heard a low, grating sound, and knew the big Danik was grinding his teeth.

Lark expected protestations of innocence from the imprisoned starfarers, and sure enough, when they next looked, the signboard proclaimed—

PLAGUES? WE KNOW NOTHING OF SUCH.

But Ling was adamant to a degree that clearly surprised Rann. Using forceful language, she told the captives – her former friends and comrades – to answer truthfully next time, or be abandoned to their fate.

That brought grudging admission, at last.

RO-KENN HAD OPTIONS,

HIS CHOICE TO USE SUCH MEANS.

GET US OUT.

WE CAN PROVIDE CURES.

Lark stared at the woman next to him, awed by the blazing intensity of her rewq aura. Till that moment, she must have held a slim hope that it was all a mistake . . . that Lark's indictment of her Rothen gods had a flaw in it somewhere. That there was some alternative explanation.

Now every complicating what-if vanished. The flame of her anger made Rann's seem like a pale thing.

While both Daniks fumed, each for different reasons, Lark took the wax board, wiped it, and wrote a reply.

PREPARE CURES AT ONCE.

BUT THERE IS MORE.

WE MUST HAVE ONE MORE THING.

It made sense that the Jophur used this weird weapon – pouring chemically synthesized time-stuff over their enemies. It suited their racial genius for manipulating organic materials. But in their contempt, the master rings had forgotten something.

They have cousins on Jijo, who are loyal to the Six.

True, local traekis lacked ambitious natures, and were unschooled in advanced Galactic science. Regardless, a team of talented local pharmacists analyzed the substance – a viscous, quasi-living tissue – by taste alone. Without understanding its arcane temporal effects, they managed to secrete a counteragent from their gifted glands.

Unfortunately, it was no simple matter of applying the formula, then rubbing away the golden cocoon surrounding the Rothen ship. For one thing, the antidote was miscible with water. Applying it under a lake presented problems.

But there was a possible way. At Dooden Mesa, they found that the old mulc-spider's preservation beads could be pushed against the golden wall and made to *merge* with it, flowing into the barrier like stones sinking in soft clay.

Lark had more beads brought from the ancient treasure hoard of the being Dwer called One-of-a-Kind. Agile, five-clawed blues pushed several egg-shaped objects against the section of wall he indicated, opposite the hatch. These beads had been hollowed out and turned into *bottles*, stoppered at one end with plugs of traeki wax. Within each could be seen machines and other relics of the Buyur era, gleaming like insects caught in amber. Only now those relics seemed to float inside, sloshing in a frothy foam.

At first there were few visible results to the qheuens' effort. The water resonated with bumps and clanks, but no merging occurred. Lark scribbled a command.

EVERYBODY DON'T LOOK!

Ling nodded vigorously. When earlier experiments were performed at the devastated g'Kek settlement, there had not been observers on the *inside*. No living ones, that is. Here, the scene was being watched, in a weird alternating manner, by people on both sides of the enclosure. Perhaps the unsymmetrical quantum effects meant that nothing would happen while people observed.

It took a while to make those within the ship understand that they should turn around, as well. But soon all the Rothen and humans on both sides swiveled away. Young qheuens pushed blindly, with vision cupolas drawn inside their horny shells. *This has got to be the strangest way to get anything done,* Lark thought, staring across a suffocated landscape, once the Festival Glade of the Commons of Six Races. All his life, teachers and leaders said *if you want a job to go well, pay attention to what you are doing.* But this reversed way of acting – where inattention was a virtue – reminded him how some Nihanese mystics in the Vale practiced 'Zen arts' such as archery while blindfolded, cultivating detachment and readiness for the Path of Redemption.

Again he glanced at Ling, the star-voyaging biologist. Her aura still seethed, though now in cooler shades. *She's declared an end to her old allegiance. Does she have a new one yet? Other than revenge, that is?* He wished they could go somewhere private – and dry – to talk, without the guarded gamesmanship of their earlier conversations. But Lark wasn't sure she'd want the same thing. Just because his allegations had proved right, that did not mean she should bless him for smashing her childhood idols.

After counting a long interval, Ling nodded and they turned around again.

Rann grunted satisfaction, and Lark felt his heart race.

The beads had penetrated most of the way into the glowing cage! Hardworking blues bubbled satisfaction, then hurried toward the boo grove, fetching air from their makeshift snorkel.

Lark wrote a message to those inside the Rothen airlock.

EVERYBODY CLEAR OUT

BUT 2 SMALL HUMANS.

WEAR AIR SUPPLY.

BRING CURES!

When next he and his companions turned back toward the lock, it was nearly empty. Two women stood on the other side. Petite, though even through their swim-coverings he saw well-developed figures – buxom and wasp-waisted. Clearly, they must have taken advantage of the same cosmetic biosculpting that had made Ling, and the late Besh, so striking. *It's a different universe out there, where you can design yourself like a god.*

Lark swam to where the tip of a mulc capsule protruded from the Jophur barrier. Most of the bead lay deep inside. At its far end the makeshift bottle's hole was plugged by a thick wax seal.

From his thigh pouch Lark drew a tool provided by one of Lester Cambel's techie assistants. A *can opener* the fellow called it.

'*Our problem is to deliver dissolving fluid into contact with the barrier, but not lake water,*' the tech had explained. '*Our answer is to use the new traeki fluid to hollow out some mulc beads. Then we coat these cavities with neutral wax, and refill them with more of the antidote fluid. The hole is plugged, so we have a sealed vessel—*'

'*I see you left an old Buyur machine inside,*' Lark had observed.

'*The fluid won't affect it, and we need the machine inside. It doesn't matter what it did in Buyur days, so long as we can signal-activate it to move again, pulling a string attached to the plug. When the plug goes* pop! – *the contents pour into contact with the Jophur wall! It's foolproof.'*

Lark wasn't so sure. There was no telling if clever, homemade electrical devices would work underwater, surrounded by time-warped fields. *Here goes everything*, he thought, squeezing the activator.

To his relief, the Buyur device began moving right away ... unfolding an appendage, all coiled and springy like a shambler's tail.

I wonder what you used to do, he pondered, watching the machine writhe and gyre. *Are you aware enough to puzzle over where you are? Where your masters have gone? Do you have an internal clock, to know half a million years have passed? Or did time stop for you inside the bead?*

The coiled arm flailed as the machine sought to right itself, yanking a cord attached to the stopper at the far end. The plug slipped, caught, then slipped some more.

It was hard to follow events in the region of quantum separated time. Things seemed to happen in fits and starts. Sometimes effect seemed to precede cause, or he saw the far side of a rotating object while closer parts remained somehow obscured. It was a strange, *sideways* manner of seeing that reminded Lark of 'Cubist' artworks, depicted in an ancient book his mother loved borrowing from the Biblos Archive.

Finally, the stopper slid free. At once reddish foam spread from the nozzle of the makeshift bottle, where its contents met the golden wall. Lark's heart pounded, and he felt his amulet, the fragment of the Holy Egg, react with growing heat. His left hand clawed at the skink-skin wrappers, but could not gain entry to grab the vibrating stone. So, like an itch that could not be scratched, he endured the palpitation as his breastbone was rubbed from both sides.

Grunts of satisfaction escaped Rann as the foamy stain spread, eroding the Jophur barrier from within. The widening hole soon met a neighboring 'bottle,' embedded in the wall near the first. In moments, fresh supplies of dissolving fluid gushed. The material of the barrier seemed to shiver, as though it were alive. As though in pain. Waves of color rippled around the growing cavity, as his rewq tried reading strange emotions.

So fixed was everyone on the process, for long intervals no one looked beyond, to the airlock and its two inhabitants, until a stray current tugged Lark aside. Lacking outside observers, the Danik women must have experienced time's passage in a somewhat linear fashion. They looked tense, hunching away from the red foam, crouching near the airlock's sealed inner door as the bubble slowly approached. Fear showed through their transparent face masks. No one knew what would happen when the hissing effervescence broke through.

It was also getting closer to Lark's side of the wall. He backpedaled toward the others ... only to find they had retreated farther still. Ling grabbed his arm.

Apparently, if they succeeded in making a tunnel, it would be wide in the middle but awfully narrow at both ends. Also, the wall material wasn't solid, but a very viscous liquid. Fresh toporgic could already be seen slumping toward the wound. Any passage was bound to be temporary.

If we didn't estimate right ... if the two ends open in the wrong order ... we might have to start all over again. There are more bottles of fluid, back at the cave. But how many times can we try?

Yet he could not talk himself out of feeling pride.

We're not helpless. Faced with overwhelming power, we innovate. We persevere.

The realization was ironic confirmation of the heresy he had maintained all his adult life.

We aren't meant for the Path of Redemption. No matter how hard we try, we'll never tread its road to innocence.

That is why our kind should never have come to Jijo.

We're meant for the stars. We simply don't belong here.

NELO

The old man did not know which was the saddest sight.

At times he wished the boat had capsized during that wretched, pell-mell running of the rapids so he would not have lived to see such things.

It took half a day of hard labor at the oars to climb back upstream to Dolo Village. By the time they reached the timber pile that had been the town dock, all the young rowers were exhausted. Villagers rushed down a muddy bank to help them drag the boat ashore, and carried Ariana Foo to dry ground. A stout hoon ignored Nelo's protests, picking him up like a baby, until he stood safely by the roots of a mighty garu tree.

Many survivors milled listlessly, though others had formed work gangs whose first task was collecting dross. Especially bodies. Those must be gathered quickly and mulched, as required by sacred law.

Nelo saw corpses gathered in a long row – mostly human, of course. Numbly he noted the master carpenter and Jobee the Plumber. Quite a few craft workers lay muddy and broken along a sodden patch of loam, and many more were missing, carried downstream when the lake came crashing through the millrace and workshops. Tree farmers, in contrast, had suffered hardly a loss. Their life on the branch tops did not expose them when the dam gave way.

No one spoke, though stares followed the papermaker as Nelo moved down the line, allowing a wince or a grunt when he recognized the face of an employee, an apprentice, or a lifelong friend. When he reached the end, he did not turn but kept walking in the same direction, toward what had been the center of his life.

The lake was low. Maybe the flood didn't destroy everything.

Disorientation greeted Nelo, for it seemed at first he was transported far from the village of his birth. Where placid water once glistened, mudflats now stretched for most of a league. A river poured through the near side of his beloved dam.

To local qheuens, dam and home were one and the same. Now the hive lay sliced open, in cross section. The collapse had sheared the larva room in half. Teams of stunned blue adults struggled to move their surviving grubs to safety, out of the harsh sunlight.

With reluctant dread, Nelo dropped his gaze to where the famed paper mill had been, next to a graceful power wheel.

Of his house, his workshops, and pulp vats, nothing more remained than foundation stumps.

The sight tore his heart, but averting his gaze did not help. Just a short distance downstream Nelo saw more blue qheuens working listlessly by the shore, trying to extricate one of their own from a net of some kind. By their lack of haste, one knew the victim must be dead, perhaps trapped in the shallows and drowned.

Unhappily, he recognized the corpse, an older female – Log Biter herself – by markings on her shell. Another lost friend, and a blow to everyone along the upper Roney who valued her good wisdom.

Then he recognized the trap that had pinned her down long enough to smother even a blue qheuen. It was a tangle of wood and metal wires. Something from Nelo's own home.

Melina's precious piano, that I ordered built at great cost.

A moan escaped his throat, at last. In all the world, he had but one thing left to live for – the hope, frail as it was, that his children were safe somewhere, and would not have to see such things.

But where was somewhere? What place could possibly be safe, when starships could plunge from the sky, blasting five generations' work in a single instant?

Words jarred him from dour thoughts of suicide.

'I didn't do this, Nelo.'

He turned to see another human standing nearby. A fellow craftsman, almost his own age. Henrik the Exploser, whose young son had accompanied Sara and the Stranger on their journey to far lands. At first, Henrik's words confused Nelo. He had to swallow before finding the strength to reply.

'Of course you didn't do it. They say a skyship came—'

The exploser shook his head. 'Fools or liars. Either they have no sense of timing, or else they were in on it.'

'What do you mean?'

'Oh, a ship passed overhead all right, and gave us a lookover. Then it went on its way. 'Twas most of a midura *later* that a gang of 'em came down, farmers mostly. They knocked the seals off some of my charges, under one of the piers of the dam, and laid a torch against it.'

Nelo blinked. 'What did you say?' He stared, then blinked again. 'But who . . . ?'

Henrik had a one-word answer.

'Jop.'

LARK

The explorers emerged triumphant, resurfacing from the chill lake into the cave, having brought back almost everything they sought. But bad news awaited them.

Fatigue lay heavily on Lark, while helpers stripped the diving gear and toweled him off. Somehow it seemed strange to be back, as if life on dry land had been ages ago.

Tense sadness filled the voice of the human corporal, reporting what had happened in Lark's absence.

'It hit our grays all at once – wheezing up lots of bubbly phlegm. Then a couple of young blues got it, too. We sent 'em to a pharmacist topside, but word says the plague is getting worse up there. There may not be much time.'

Attention turned to the Danik women who had just barely escaped from the trapped ship. They still looked woozy from their experience – starting with a blast of high-pressure water that had burst into the airlock when the fissure broke through at last. After that came a hurried, nightmarish squeeze through the briefly dilated opening, squirming desperately before the tunnel could close and immure their bodies in liquid time like the poor g'Keks of Dooden Mesa.

Watching quantum-shifted images of that tight passage nearly unnerved Lark. Instead of two human figures, they looked like jumbled body parts, writhing through a tube that kept shifting around them. One woman he briefly saw with her *insides* on the *outside*, offering unwanted knowledge about her latest meal.

Yet here they were, alive in front of him. Overcoming residual nausea, the two escapees kept their side of the bargain, setting to work right away on a small machine they had brought along. In exchange for a cure, Jijoans would help more of their crew mates break out of the trapped ship, then coordinate joint action against the Jophur – no doubt something quite desperate, calling for a pooling of both groups' slim knowledge and resources, plus a generous dollop of Ifni's luck.

This whole enterprise had been Lark's idea ... and he gave it the same odds as a ribbit walking unscathed through a ligger's den.

'Symptoms?' asked the first woman, with hair a shade of red Lark had never seen on any Jijoan.

'Don't you know already what bug it is?' Jeni Shen demanded.

'A variety of pathogens were kept in stock aboard the research station,' answered the other one, a stately brunette who seemed older than any other Danik Lark had seen. She looked a statuesque forty, and might be two centuries old.

'If Ro-kenn did release an organism from that supply,' she continued, 'we must pin down which one.'

Even having stripped off his rewq, he had no trouble reading fatalistic reluctance in her voice. By helping solve the plague, she was in effect confessing that Ro-kenn had attempted genocide ... and that their ship routinely carried the means for such a crime. Perhaps, like Ling, she had been in the dark about all that till now. Only utter helplessness would have forced the Rothen to reveal so much to their human servants, as well as to the sooners of Jijo.

From the look on Rann's face, the tall star warrior disagreed with the decision, and Lark knew why.

It goes beyond mere morality and crimes against Galactic law. Our local qheuens and hoons have relatives out there, among the stars. If word of this gets out, those home populations might declare vendettas against the Rothen. Or else, with this evidence, Earth might file suit to reclaim the Danik population group that the Rothen have kept secreted away for two centuries.

Of course that assumes Earth still lives. And there's still law in the Five Galaxies.

Rann clearly felt the risk too great. Ship and crew should have been sacrificed to keep the secret.

Tough luck, Rann, Lark thought. *Apparently your fellow spacers would rather live.*

While Ling described the disease that ravaged Uthen before her eyes, Lark overheard Rann whisper impatiently to Jeni Shen.

'If we are to get the others out, it must be a complete job! There are weapons to transfer, and supplies. The traeki formula must be duplicated aboard ship, in order to make a durable passageway—'

Jeni interrupted sharply.

'After we verify a cure, starman. Or else your compadres and their master race can sit in their own dung till Jijo grows cold, for all we care.'

Colorful, Lark thought, smiling grimly.

Soon the machine was programmed with all the relevant facts.

'Many hoons are showing signs of a new sickness, too,' Ling reminded.

'We'll get to that,' said the redhead. 'This will take a min or two.' Lark watched symbols flash across the tiny screen. *More computers*, he mulled unhappily. Of course it was a much smaller unit than the big processor they used near Dooden Mesa. This 'digital cognizance' might be shielded by geologic activity in the area, plus fifty meters of solid rock.

But can we be sure?

The device issued a high-pitched chime.

'Synthesis complete,' said the older Danik, taking a small, clear vial from its side, containing a greenish fluid. 'This is just two or three doses, but that should suffice to test it. We can mass-produce more aboard the ship. Which means we'll need a permanent channel through the barrier, of course.'

Clearly, she felt her side now had a major bargaining chip. Holding up the tube with three fingers, she went on. 'Now might be a good time to discuss how each group will help the other, your side with manpower and sheer numbers, and our side providing—'

Her voice cut off when Ling snatched the capsule from her grasp, swiveling to put it in Jeni Shen's hand.

'*Run*,' was all Ling said.

Jeni took off with a pair of excited noor beasts yapping at her heels.

Any return to the imprisoned ship would have to wait for dawn. Even a well-tuned rewq could not amplify light that was not there.

Ling wanted to keep the two rescued Daniks busy producing antidotes against every pathogen listed in the little Library, in case other plagues were loose that no one knew about, but Lark vetoed the idea. Since the Dooden disaster, all computers made him nervous. He wanted this one turned on as little as possible. Let the Rothen produce extra vaccines inside their vessel and bring them out along with other supplies, he said, if and when a new tunnel was made. Ling seemed about to argue the point, but then her lips pressed hard and she shrugged. Taking one of the lanterns, she retreated to a corner of the cave, far from Rann and her former comrades.

Lark spent some time composing a report to the High Sages, requesting more bottles of the traeki dissolving fluid and describing the preliminary outlines of an alliance between the Six Races and their former enemies. Not that he had much confidence in such a coalition.

They promise weapons and other help, he wrote. *But I urge caution. Given Phwhoon-dau's description of the Rothen as Galactic 'petty criminals,' and the relative ease with which they were overwhelmed, we should prefer almost any advantageous deal that can be worked out with the Jophur, short of letting them commit mass murder.*

Insurrection ought to be considered a last resort.

The sages might find his recommendation odd, since his own plan made the Rothen alliance possible in the first place. But Lark saw no contradiction. Unlocking a door did not mean you had to walk through it. He just believed in exploring alternatives.

There was little to do then but wait, hoping news from the medics would be happy and swift. The party could not even light a fire in the dank cavern.

'It's cold,' Ling commented when Lark passed near her niche. He had been looking for a place to unroll his sleeping bag ... not so close he'd seem intrusive, yet nearby in case she called. Now he paused, wondering what she meant.

Was that an invitation? Or an accusation?

The latter seemed more likely. Ling might have been much better off remaining forever in the warmth of high-tech habitats, basking in the glow of a messianic faith.

'It is that,' he murmured. 'Cold.'

It was hard to move closer. Hard to expect anything but rejection. For months, their relationship had been based on a consensual game, a tense battle of wits that was part inquisition and part one-upmanship ... with moments of intense, semierotic flirting stirred in. Eventually he won that game, but not through any credit of his own. The sins of her Rothen gods gave him a weapon out of proportion to personal traits either of them possessed, leaving him just one option – to lay waste to all her beliefs. Ever since, they had labored together toward shared goals without once trading a private word.

In effect, he had conquered her to become Jijo's ally, only to lose what they had before.

Lark did not feel like a conqueror.

'I can see why they call you a heretic,' Ling said, breaking the uncomfortable silence.

Either out of shyness or diffidence, Lark had not looked at her directly. Now he saw she had a book open on her lap, with one page illuminated by the faint beam of her glow lamp. It was the Jijoan biology text he had written with Uthen. His life's work.

'I ... tried not to let it interfere with the research,' he answered.

'How could it not interfere? Your use of cladistic taxonomy clashes with the way Galactic science has defined and organized species for a billion years.'

Lark saw what she was doing, and felt gladdened by it. Their shared love of biology was neutral ground where issues of guilt or shame needn't interfere. He moved closer to sit on a stony outcrop.

'I thought you were talking about my *Jijoan* heresy. I used to be part of a movement' – he winced, remembering his friend Harullen – 'whose goal was to persuade the Six Races to end our illegal colony ... by voluntary means.'

She nodded. 'A virtuous stance, by Galactic standards. Though not easy for organic beings, who are programmed for sex and propagation.'

Lark felt his face flush, and was grateful for the dim light.

'Well, the question is out of our hands now,' he said. 'Even if Rokenn's plagues are cured, the Jophur can wipe us out if they like. Or else they'll hand us over to the Institutes, and we'll have the Judgment Day described in the Sacred Scrolls. That might come as a relief, after the last few months. At least it's how we always imagined things would end.'

'Though your people hoped it wouldn't happen till you'd been redeemed. Yes, I know that's your Jijoan orthodoxy. But I was talking about a heresy of *science* – the way you and Uthen organized animal types in your work – by species, genus, phylum, and so on. You use the old cladistic system of pre-contact Earthling taxonomy.'

He nodded. 'We do have a few texts explaining Galactic nomenclature. But most of our books came from Earth archives. Few human biologists had changed over to Galactic systematology by the time the *Tabernacle* took off.'

'I never saw cladistics used in a real ecosystem,' Ling commented. 'You present a strong argument for it.'

'Well, in our case it's making a virtue out of necessity. We're trying to understand Jijo's past and present by studying a single slice of time – the one we're living in. For evidence, all we have to go on are the common traits of living animals . . . and the fossils we dig up. That's comparable to mapping the history of a continent by studying layers of rocks. Earthlings did a lot of that kind of science before contact, like piecing together evidence of a crime, long after the body has grown cold. Galactics never needed those interpolative techniques. Over the course of eons they simply *watch* and record the rise and fall of mountains, and the divergence of species. Or else they make new species through gene-splicing and uplift.'

Ling nodded, considering this. 'We're taught contempt for wolfling science. I suppose it affected the way I treated you, back when . . . well, you know.'

If that was an apology, Lark accepted it gladly.

'I wasn't exactly honest with you either, as I recall.'

She laughed dryly. 'No, you weren't.'

Another silence stretched. Lark was about to talk some more about biology, when he realized that was exactly the wrong thing to do. What had earlier served to bridge an uncomfortable silence would now only maintain a reserve, a neutrality he did not want anymore. Awkwardly, he moved to change the subject.

'What kind of . . .' He swallowed and tried again. 'I have a brother, and a sister. I may have mentioned them before. Do you have family . . . back at . . .'

He let the question hang, and for a moment Lark worried he had dredged a subject too painful and personal. But her relieved look showed Ling, too, wanted to move on.

'I had a baby brother,' she said. 'And a share daughter, whose up-parents were very nice. I miss them all very much.'

For the next midura, Lark listened in confusion to the complex Danik way of life on far-off Poria Outpost. Mostly, he let Ling pour out her sadness, now that even her liberated crew mates were like aliens to her, and nothing would ever be the same.

Later, it seemed wholly natural to stretch his sleeping bag next to hers. Divided by layers of cloth and fluffy torg, their bodies shared warmth without touching. Yet, in his heart, Lark felt a comfort he had lacked till now.

She doesn't hate me.

It was a good place to start.

The second dive seemed to go quicker, at first. They had a better knack for underwater travel now, though several human volunteers had to fill in for blue qheuens who were sick.

About the illness, recent word from topside was encouraging. The vaccine samples seemed to help the first few victims. Better yet, the molecules could be traeki-synthesized. Still, it was too soon for cheers. Even in the event of a complete cure, there were problems of distribution. Could cures reach all the far-flung communities before whole populations of qheuens and hoons were devastated?

Back at the Rothen ship, they found the airlock already occupied by crew members wearing diving gear – three humans and a Rothen – along with slim crates of supplies. Like wax figures, they stood immobile while Lark and Ling trained new assistants in the strange art they had learned the day before. Then it was time to begin making another tunnel through the golden time-stuff.

Again, they went through turnaround sweeps, letting those inside the hatch prepare. Again, volunteers swam close with mulc preservation beads that had been hollowed and turned into bottles for the special dissolving fluid. Once more, the actual act of embedding had to take place in a shroud of nescience, without anyone watching directly. Nothing happened the first few tries ... until Jeni caught one of the new helpers *peeking*, out of curiosity. Despite watery resistance, she smacked him so hard the sound traveled as a sharp crack.

Finally, they got the hang of it. Six beads lay in place, at varying distances inside the barrier. As yesterday, Lark applied the 'can opener,' turning on an ancient Buyur machine, which in turn pulled a wax plug, setting in motion a chain reaction to eat a gap through the viscous material. He backed up, fascinated again by creepy visions as the red foam spread and a cavity began to form.

Someone abruptly tapped his shoulder.

It was Jeni, the young militia sergeant, urgently holding a wax board.

WHERE IS RANN?

He blinked, then joined Ling in a shrug. The tall Danik leader had been nearby till a moment ago. Jeni's expression was anguished. Lark wrote on his own board.

WE'RE NOT NEEDED NOW.

LING AND I WILL LOOK NORTH.

SEND OTHERS SOUTH, EAST.

YOU STAY.

Grudgingly, Jeni accepted the logic. Lark's job was largely done. If the tunnel opened as planned, another batch of escapees would wriggle through and Jeni must coordinate moving them and their baggage back to the caves.

With a nod, Ling assented. They headed off together, kicking hard. United, they should be a match for Rann if he put up a fight.

Anyway, where would the big man go? It wasn't as if he had much choice, these days.

Still, Lark worried. With a head start, Rann might reach the lakeshore and make good an escape. He could cause mischief, or worse, be caught and questioned by the Jophur. Rann was tough, but how long could he hold out against Galactic interrogation techniques?

Ling caught his arm. Lark turned to follow her jabbing motion *up* toward the surface of the lake. There he saw a pair of flippers, waving slowly at the end of two strong legs.

What's he doing up there? Lark wondered as they propelled after the absconded Danik. Getting close, they saw Rann had actually broached the surface! His head and shoulders were out of the water. *Is he taking a look at the Jophur ship? We all want to, but no one dared.*

Lark felt acutely the shadow of the giant vessel as they kicked upward. For the first time, he got a sense of its roughly globular shape and mammoth dimensions, completely blocking the narrow Festival Glade, creating this lake with its bulk. Having grown up next to a dam, Lark had a sense of the pressure all this water exerted. There would be an awful flood when the ship took off, returning to its home among the stars.

The tube in his mouth squirmed disconcertingly. The traeki air ring struggled as they rose upward, hissing and throbbing to adapt to changing pressure. But Lark was more worried about Rann being spotted by the Jophur.

With luck, the skink skins will make him look like a piece of flotsam ... which is what he'll feel like once I'm through with him! Lark felt a powerful wrath build as he reached to seize the big man's ankle.

The leg gave a startled twitch ... then kicked savagely, knocking his hand away.

Ling tugged Lark's other arm, pointing a second time.

Rann had an object in front of him – the *Rothen minicomputer*! He was tapping away at the controls, even as he tread water.

Bastard! Lark thrust toward the surface, grabbing for the device, no longer caring if his mere body happened to be visible from afar. Rann might as well have been waving a searchlight while beating a drum!

As soon as Lark broke through, the starman aimed a punch at him – no doubt a well-trained, expert blow, if delivered on dry land. Here, watery reaction threw Rann off balance and the clout glanced stingingly off Lark's ear.

Amid a shock of pain, he sensed Ling erupt behind her former colleague, throwing her arms around his neck. Lark took advantage of the distraction, planting his feet against Rann's chest and hauling back until the computer popped free of the big man's grasp.

Alas, that wasn't enough to end the danger. The screen was still lit. He cried to Ling: 'I don't know how to turn the damned thing off!'

She had troubles of her own, with Rann's powerful arms reaching around to pummel and yank at her. Lark realized the Danik must be put out of commission, and quickly. So with both hands he raised the computer as high as he could – and brought it down hard on Rann's crew cut.

Without leverage, it struck less forcefully than he hoped, but the blow pulled Rann's attention away from Ling.

The second impact was better, giving a resounding smack. Rann groaned, slumping in the water.

Unfortunately, the jolt did not break the durable computer, which kept shining, even after Lark landed a final blow.

Rann floated, arms spread wide, breathing shallowly but noisily from his traeki ring. Ling thrashed toward Lark, gasping as she threw an arm over his shoulder for support. Finally, she reached out to stroke a precise spot on the computer's case, turning it off.

That's better ... though it's said Galactics can trace digital cognizance, even when a machine is unpowered.

Lark closed the cover, letting the machine drop from his grasp. He needed both hands to hold Ling.

Especially when a new, umbral shadow fell across them, causing her body to stiffen in his arms.

Suddenly, things felt very cold.

Tremulously, they turned together, looking up to see what had come for them.

DWER

That night was among the strangest of Dwer's life, though it started in the most natural way – bickering with Rety.

'I *ain't* goin' there!' She swore.

'No one asked you to. When I start downhill, you'll take off the other way. Go half a league west, to that forested rise we passed on the way here. I saw good game signs. You can set snares, or look for clamette bubbles on the beach. They're best roasted, but you oughtn't trust a fire—'

'I'm supposed to wait for you, I s'pose? Have a nice meal ready for the great hunter, after he finishes takin' on the whole dam' universe, single-handed?'

Her biting sarcasm failed to mask tremors of real fear. Dwer didn't flatter himself that Rety worried about *him*. No doubt she hated to face being alone.

Dusk fell on the dunes and mudflats, and mountains so distant they were but a jagged horizon cutting the bloated sun. Failing light gave the two of them a chance at last to worm out from the sand, then slither beyond sight of the crashed ships. Once safely over the verge, they brushed grit out of clothes and body crevices while arguing in heated whispers.

'I'm telling you, we don't haveta *do* anything! I'm sure Kunn had time to holler for help before he went down. The Rothen ship was due back soon, and musta heard him. Any dura now it's gonna swoop down, rescue Kunn, and pick up its prize. All we gotta do then is stand and shout.'

Rety had been thinking during the long, uncomfortable wait. She held that the fighter craft full of untraeki rings was the very target Kunn had been looking for, dropping depth bombs to flush his prey out of hiding. By that logic, the brief sky battle was a desperate lashing out by a cornered foe. But Kunn got his own licks in, and now the quarry lay helpless in the swamp, where frantic efforts at repair had so far failed to dislodge it.

Soon, by Rety's reasoning, the Rothen lords would come to complete the job, taking the untraeki into custody. The Rothen would surely be pleased at this success. Enough to overlook Dwer's earlier mistakes. And hers.

It was a neat theory. But then, why did the untraeki ship attack from the *west*, instead of rising out of the water where Kunn dropped his bombs? Dwer was no expert on the way star gods brawled among themselves, but instinct said Kunn had been caught with his pants down.

'In that case, what I'm about to try should put me in good with your friends,' he told Rety.

'If you survive till they come, which I doubt! Those varmints down there will spot you, soon as you go back over the dune.'

'Maybe. But I've been watching. Remember when a herd of bog stompers sloshed by, munching tubers torn up by the crash? Large critters passed both hulls and were ignored. I'm guessing the guard robots will take me for a crude native beast—'

'You got *that* right,' Rety muttered.

'—and leave me alone, at least till I'm real close.'

'And then what? You gonna attack a starship with your *bow and arrow*?'

Dwer held back from reminding Rety that his bow once seemed a treasure to her – a prize worth risking her life to steal.

'I'm leaving the arrows with you,' he said. 'They have steel tips. If I take 'em, they'll know I'm not an animal.'

'They should ask *me*. I'd tell 'em real fast that you're—'

'*wife, enough!*'

The reedy voice came from Rety's tiny urrish 'husband' who had been grooming her, flicking sand grains with his agile tongue.

'*have sense, wife! brave boy make ship eyes look at him so you and me can get away! all his other talk-talk is fake stuff. nice-lies to make us go be safe. be good to brave boy-man! least you can do!*'

While Rety blinked at yee's rebuke, Dwer marveled. Did all urrish males treat their wives this way, chiding them from within the heavy folds of their brood pouches? Or was yee special? Did some prior mate eject him for scolding?

'Iz' at true, Dwer?' Rety asked. 'You'd sacr'fice yourself for me?'

He tried reading her eyes, to judge which answer would make her do as she was told. Fading light forced him to guess.

'No, it's not true. I *do* have a plan. It's risky, but I want to give it a try.'

Rety watched him as carefully as he had scanned her. Finally, she gave a curt laugh.

'What a liar. yee's right about you. Too dam' decent to survive without someone to watch over you.'

Huh? Dwer thought. He had tried telling the truth, hoping it would convince her to go. Only Rety reacted in a way he did not expect.

'It's decided then,' she affirmed with a look of resolve he knew too well. 'I'm coming along, Dwer, *whichever* way you head. So if you want to save me, we better both get on west.'

'This *ain't* west!' she whispered sharply, half a midura later.

Dwer ignored Rety as he peered ahead through the swampy gloom with water sloshing past his navel. *Too bad we had to leave yee behind with our gear*, he thought. The little urrish male provided his 'wife' with a healthy dose of prudence and good judgment. But he could not stand getting wet.

Soon, Dwer hoped Rety's survival instincts would kick in and she'd shut up on her own.

They were nearly naked, wading through the reedy marsh toward a pair of rounded silhouettes, one larger – its smooth flanks glistening except where a sooty stain marred one side. The other lay beyond, crumpled and half-sunk amidships. Both victor and vanquished were silent under the pale yellow glow of Passen, Jijo's smallest moon.

Colonies of long-necked wallow swans nested in the thickets, dozing after a hard day spent hunting through the shallows and tending their broods. The nearest raised spear-shaped heads to blink at the two humans, then lowered their snouts as Dwer and Rety waded on by.

Mud covered Dwer and the sooner girl from head to toe, concealing some of their heat sign with steady evaporation. According to ancient lore, that should make the patrolling guard machine see them as smaller than they really were. Dwer also took a slow, meandering route, to foster the impression of foraging beasts.

Slender shapes with luminous scales darted below the water's surface, brushing Dwer's thighs with their flicking tails. A distant burst of splashing told of some nocturnal hunter at work among the clumps of sword-edged grass. Hungry things moved about in this wet jungle. Rety seemed to grasp this, and did not speak again for some time.

If only she knew how vague Dwer's plan was, Rety might howl loud enough to send all the sleeping waterfowl flapping for the sky. In fact, he was working from a hunch. He wanted to have a closer look at the untraeki ship . . . and to check out his impression of this swamp. In order to test his idea, he needed to attain a particular frame of mind.

What was I thinking about, that day when I first contacted – or hallucinated – the voice of One-of-a-Kind?

It happened some years ago. He had been on his first solo trek over the Rimmers, excited to be promoted from apprentice to master hunter, filled with a spirit of freedom and adventure, for now he was one of the few Sixers licensed to roam wherever he wished, even far beyond the settled Slope. The world had seemed boundless.

And yet . . .

And yet, he still vividly recalled the moment, emerging from a narrow trail through the boo forest – a cathedral aisle as narrow as a man and seemingly high as a moon. Suddenly, the boo just *stopped*, spilling him onto a bowl-shaped rocky expanse, under a vast blue sky. Before Dwer lay a mulc lake, nestled in the mountain's flank, surrounded by fields of broken stone.

What he felt during that moment of disorienting transition was much more than welcome release from a closed space. A sense of *opening up* seemed to fill his mind, briefly expanding his ability to see – especially the tumulus of Buyur ruins. Abruptly, he beheld the ancient towers as they must have stood long ago, shimmering and proud. And for an instant, Dwer had felt strangely at home.

That was when he first heard the spider's voice, whispering, cajoling, urging him to accept a deal. A fair trade. With its help, Dwer might cease living, but he would never die. He could become one with the glorious past, and join the spider on a voyage into time.

Now, while sloshing under starlight through a murky bog, Dwer tried again for that feeling, that *opening* sensation. He could tell from the texture of this place – from its smell and feel – that mighty spires had also pierced the sky, only here they were much grander than at any mountain site. The job of demolition was far advanced – little remained to tear down or erase. Yet somehow he knew what stood where, and when.

Here a row of pure-white obelisks once greeted the sun, both mystical and pragmatic in their mathematically precise alignment.

Over there, Buyur legs once ponderously strode down a shopping arcade, filled with exotic goods.

Near *that* translucent fountain, contemplative Buyur minds occupied themselves with a multitude of tasks beyond his reckoning. And through the sky passed commerce from ten thousand worlds.

Down the avenues were heard voices ... not just of Buyur, but a myriad of other types of thinking beings.

Surely it was a glorious time, though also *fatiguing* for any planet whose flesh must feed such an eager, busy civilization. After a million years of heavy use, Jijo badly needed rest. And the forces of wisdom granted it. All the busy voices moved on. The towers tumbled and a different kind of life took over here, one dedicated to erasing scars – a more patient, less frenzied type of being ...

... ?
Yes?
Who ... goes ... ?

Words slithered through Dwer's mind, hesitantly at first.

Who calls ... rousing me from ... drowsy musing?

Dwer's first urge was to dismiss it as merely his imagination. Had not his nervous system been palped and bruised from carrying the robot across icy streams? Delusions would be normal after that battering, followed by days of near starvation. Anyway, his habitual defense against One-of-a-Kind had been to dismiss the mulc-spider's voice as a phantasm.

Who is a phantasm?
I, a being who serenely outlasts empires?
Or you, a mayfly, living and dying in the time it takes for me to dream a dream?

Dwer held off acknowledging the voice, even casually. First he wanted to be sure. Wading cautiously, he sought some of the vines he had glimpsed earlier, from the dune heights. A nearby hummock seemed likely. Despite covering vegetation, it had the orderly outlines of some ruined structure. Sure enough, Dwer soon found his way blocked by cables, some as thick as his wrist, all converging on the ancient building site. His nose twitched at the scents of dilute corrosive fluids, carried by thie twisted vines.

'Hey, this is a mulc swamp! We're walkin' right into a spider!'

Dwer nodded, acknowledging Rety's comment without words. If she wanted to leave, she knew the way back.

Spiders were common enough on the Slope. Youngsters went exploring through mulc dens, though you risked getting acid burns if you weren't careful. Now and then, some village child died of a foolish mistake while venturing too deep, yet the attraction held. High-quality Buyur relics were often found where vine beasts slowly etched the remains of bygone days.

Folk legends flourished about the creatures, whose bodies were made up by the vines themselves. Some described them *talking* to rare members of the Six, though Dwer had never met anyone else who admitted that it happened to them. He especially never heard of another mulc-spider like One-of-a-Kind, who actively lured living prey into its web, sealing 'unique' treasures away in coffins of hardening jell.

You met that one? The mad spider of the heights?
You actually shared thoughts with it? And escaped?
How exceptionally interesting.

Your mind patterns are very clear for an ephemeral.
That is rare, as mayflies go . . .
How singular you are.

Yes, that was the way One-of-a-Kind used to speak to him. This creature was consistent. Or else Dwer's imagination was.

The words returned, carrying a note of pique.

You flatter yourself to think you could imagine an entity as sublime as myself! Though I admit, you are intriguing, for a transitory being.

So you need verification of my objective reality? How might I prove myself?

Rather than answer directly, Dwer kept his thoughts reserved. Languidly, he contemplated that it would be interesting to see the vines in front of him move.

As if at your command? An amusing concept.
But why not?
Come back in just five days. In that brief time, you will find all of them shifted to new locales!

Dwer chuckled contemptuously, under his breath.

Not quickly enough, my wanton friend? You have seen a mulc being move, faster?
Ah, but that one was crazed, driven mad by isolation, high altitude, and a diet of psi-drenched stone. It grew unwholesomely obsessed with mortality and the nature of time. Surely you do not expect such undignified haste from me?

Like One-of-a-Kind, this spider could somehow tap Dwer's human memory, using it to make better sentences – more articulate speech – than he ever managed on his own. But Dwer knew better than to bandy words. Instead, he willed himself to turn around.

Wait! You intrigue me. The conversations our kind share among ourselves are so languid. Torpid, you might say, featuring endless comparisons of the varied dross we eat. The slow-talk grows ever more tedious as we age ...
Tell me, are you from one of the frantic races who have lately settled down to a skittering life beyond the mountains? The ones who talk and talk, but almost never build?

Behind Dwer, Rety murmured, 'What's goin' on!' But he only motioned for her to follow him away from the mulc cords.

All right! On a whim I'll do it. I shall move for you!
I'll move as I have not done in ages.
Watch me, small flickering life-form. Watch this!

Dwer glanced back, and saw several vines tremble. The tremors strengthened, dura after dura, tightening and releasing till several of the largest bunched in a knotty tangle. More duras passed ... then one loop *popped up* out of the water, rising high, dripping like some amphibious being, emerging from its watery home.

It was confirmation, not only of the spider's mental reality, but of Dwer's own sane perception. Yet he quashed all sense of acknowledgement or relief. Rather, Dwer let a feeling of disappointment flow across his surface thoughts.

A fresh shoot off lesser boo moves that much, in the course of a day's growth, he pondered, without bothering to project the thought at the spider.

> *You compare me to boo?*
> *Boo?*
> *Insolent bug! It is you who are a figment of my imagination! You may be nothing but an undigested bit of concrete, or a piece of bad steel, perturbing my dreams ...*
>
> *No, wait! Don't leave yet. I sense there is something that would convince you.*
> *Tell me what it is. Tell me what would make you acknowledge me, and talk awhile.*

Dwer felt an impulse to speak directly. To make his wishes known in the form of a request. But no. His experience with One-of-a-Kind had taught him. That mulc beast might have been mad, but it clearly shared some properties of personality with its kind.

Dwer knew the game to play was 'hard to get.' So he let his idea leak out in the form of a fantasy ... a daydream. When Rety tried to interrupt again, he made a slashing motion for quiet while he went on picturing what a spider might do to convince him it was real. The sort of thing Dwer would find impressive.

The mulc being's next message seemed intrigued.

> *Truly?*
> *And why not?*
> *The new dross to which you refer already had me concerned. Those great heaps of refined metal and volatile organic poisons – I have not dealt with such purified essences in a very long time.*
>
> *Now you worry that the dross might fly away again, to pollute some part of Jijo beyond reach of any mulc being? You fear it may never be properly disposed of?*
> *Then worry no more, my responsible little ephemeral! It will be taken care of.*
> *Just leave it to me.*

ALVIN

I was right! The phuvnthus are earthlings!

I haven't figured out the little amphibians yet, but the big six-legged creatures? They are dolphins. Just like the ones in *King of the Sea* or *The Shining Shore*, only these talk and drive spaceships! How uttergloss.

And there are humans. Sky humans!

Well, a couple of them, anyway.

I met the woman in charge – Gillian is her name. Among other things, she said some nice words about my journal. In fact, if they ever succeed in getting away from here, and returning to Earth, she promises to find an agent for me and get it published.

Imagine that. I can't wait to tell Huck.

There's just one favor Gillian wants in return.

EWASX

Oh, how they prevaricate!

Is this what it means to take the Downward Path?

Sometimes a citizen race decides to change course, rejecting the destiny mapped out for it by patron and clan. The Civilization of the Five Galaxies allows several traditional avenues of appeal, but if all other measures fail, one shelter remains available to all – the road that leads *back*, from starfaring sapience to animal nature. The route to a second chance. To start over again with a new patron guiding your way.

This much I/we can understand. But must that path have an intermediate phase, between citizen and dumb beast? A phase in which the half-devolved species becomes *lawyers*?

Their envoys stand before us now, citing points of Galactic law that were handed down in sacred lore. Especially verbose is the g'Kek emissary. Yes, My rings, you identify this g'Kek as Vubben – a 'friend and colleague' from your days as Asx the traeki. Oh, how that sage-among-sooners nimbly contorts logic, contending that his folk are not responsible for the debt his kind owes our clan, by rule of vendetta. A debt of extinction.

The senior Priest-Stack aboard our ship insists we must listen to this nonsense, for form's sake, before continuing our righteous vengeance. But most of the *Polkjhy* crew stacks side with our

Captain-Leader, whose impatience-with-drivel steams with each throbbing pulse of an angry mulching core. Finally, the Captain-Leader transmits a termination signal to Me/us. To faithful Ewasx.

'ENOUGH!' I interrupt Vubben in loud tones of Oailie decisiveness. All four of his eyestalks quail in surprise at my harsh resonance.

'YOUR CONTENTIOUS REASONINGS ARE BASED ON INVALID ASSUMPTIONS.'

They stand before us/Me, frozen silent by our rebuke. A silence more appropriate to half animals than all that useless jabber. Finally, the qheuen sage, Knife-Bright Insight, bows her blue-green carapace and inquires:

'Might we ask what assumptions you refer to?'

Our second cognition ring performs a writhing twitch that I must overcome with savage pain jolts, preventing the rebellious ring's color cells from flashing visibly. *Be thou restrained*, I command, enforcing authority over our component selves. *Do not try to signal your erstwhile comrades. The effort will accomplish nothing.*

The minirebellion robs Me of resources to maintain a pontifical voice. So when I next speak aloud, it is in more normal tones. Yet the message is no less severe.

'Your faulty assumptions are threefold,' I answer the thoughtful blue qheuen.

'You assume that law still reigns in the Five Galaxies.

'You assume that we should feel restrained by procedures and precedents from the last ten million years.

'But above all, your most defective assumption is that we should care.'

DWER

It was not enough simply to coax the mulc beast. Dwer had to creep close and supervise, for the spider had no clear concept of haste.

Dwer could sense its concentration, shifting fluids and gathering forces from a periphery that stretched league after league, along the Rift coast. The sheer size of the thing was mind-boggling, far greater than the mad little alpine spider that nearly consumed Dwer and Rety. This titan was in the final stages of demolishing a vast city, the culmination of its purpose, and therefore its life. Millennia ago, it might have ignored Dwer, as a busy workman disregards the corner scratchings of a mouse. Now boredom made it responsive to any new voice, offering relief from monumental ennui.

Still, Dwer wondered.

Why was I able to communicate with One-of-a-Kind? And now this spider, as well? We are so different – creatures meant for opposite sides of a planet's cycle.

His sensitivity, if anything, had increased ... perhaps from letting the Danik robot conduct force fields down his spine. But the original knack must be related to what made him an exceptional hunter.

Empathy. An intuitive sense for the needs and desires of living things.

The Sacred Scrolls spoke darkly of such powers. Psi-talents.

They were not recommended for the likes of the Six, who must cringe away from the great theater of space. So Dwer never mentioned it, not to Sara and Lark, or even Fallon, though he figured the old chief scout must have suspected.

Have I done this before? He mused on how he coaxed the spider into action. *I always thought my empathy was passive. That I listened to animals, and hunted accordingly.*

But have I been subtly influencing them, all along? When I shoot an arrow, is it my legendary aim that makes it always strike home? Or do I also nudge the flight of the bush quail so it dodges into the way of the shaft? Do I make the taniger swerve left, just as my stone is about to strike?

It made him feel guilty. Unsporting.

Well? What about right now? You're famished. Why not put out a call for nearby fish and fowl to gather round your knees for plucking?

Somehow, Dwer knew it did not work that way.

He shook his head, clearing it for matters close at hand. Just ahead, rounded silhouettes took uneven bites out of the arching star field. Two sky boats, unmoving, yet mysterious and deadly as he drew near. He swished a finger through the water and tasted, wincing at some nasty stuff leaking into the fen from one or both fallen cruisers.

Now Dwer's sensitive ears picked up noise coming from the larger vessel. Clankings and hammerings. No doubt the crew was working around the clock to make repairs. Despite Rety's assurances, he had no faith that the new day would see a Rothen starship looming overhead to claim both its lost comrades and long-sought prey. The opposite seemed rather more likely.

Either way, he had a job to do.

Till I hear otherwise from the sages, I've got to keep acting on Danel Ozawa's orders.

He said we must defend Jijo.

Star gods don't belong here, any more than sooners do. Less, in fact.

The cry of a mud wren made Dwer slide his torso lower in the water.

Rety's mimicked call came from a lookout point on a Buyur ruin near the dunes. He scanned above the reeds, and caught sight of a glimmering shape – a patrol robot sent out by the stranded untraekis, returning from its latest search spiral.

The mulc-spider read his concern and expressed curiosity.

More dross?

Maintaining aloof reserve, Dwer suggested the creature concentrate on its present task, while he worried about flying things.

Your memories assert one of these hovering mechanisms slew my brother of the highlands. Mad he may have been, but his job was left undone by that untimely end. Now who will finish it?

A fair enough question. This time, Dwer formed words.

If we survive this time of crisis, the sages will have a mulc bud planted in the old one's lake. It's our way. By helping get rid of Buyur remains, each generation of the Six leaves Jijo a little cleaner, making up for the small harm we do. The scrolls say it may ease our penance, when judges finally come.

But don't worry about this robot now. You have a goal to focus on. Over there. in that hull of the larger ship, there is a rip, an opening . . .

Dwer felt hairs on his neck prickle. He crouched low while the unmistakable tingle of gravitic fields swept close. Clearly this was a more powerful robot than the unit he nearly defeated back at the sooner village. That one still cowered in a hole under the sand, while he and Rety took on its enemies.

He hunched like an animal, and even tried thinking like one as the humming commotion passed, setting the tense surface of the water trembling like a qheuen drum. Dwer closed his eyes, but an onslaught of images assailed him. Sparks flew from an urrish forge. Stinging spray jetted over a drowned village. Starlight glinted off a strange fish whose noorlike mouth opened in a wry grin . . .

The creepy force receded. He cracked his eyelids to watch the slab-sided drone move east down a line of phosphorescent surf, then vanish among the dunes.

More vines now clustered and writhed around the base of the larger sky boat, bunching to send shoots snaking higher. This whole crazy idea counted on one assumption – that the ship's defenses, already badly damaged, would be on guard against 'unnatural' things, like metals or energy sources. Under normal conditions, mere plants or beasts would pose no threat to a thick-hulled vessel.

In here?

The spider's query accompanied mental images of a jagged recess, slashed in the side of the untraeki vessel ... the result of Kunn's riposte, even as his air boat plunged in flames. The visual impression reaching Dwer was tenuous as a daydream, lacking all but the most vague visual details. Instead, he felt a powerful scent of *substance*. The spider would not know or care how Galactic machines worked, only what they were made of – and which concocted juices would most swiftly delete this insult to Jijo's fallow peace.

Yes, in there, Dwer projected. *And all over the outside, as well.*

Except the transparent viewing port, he added. No sense warning the creatures by covering their windows with slithering vines. Let them find out in the morning. By then, with Ifni's luck, it would be too late.

Remember – he began. But the spider interrupted.

I know. I shall use my strongest cords.

Mulc monofiber was the toughest substance known to the Six. With his own eyes, Dwer had seen one rare loop of reclaimed filament pull gondolas all the way to the heights of Mount Guenn. Still, a crew of star gods would have tools to cut even that staunch material. Unless they were distracted.

Time passed. By moonlight the marsh seemed alive with movement – ripples and jerky slitherings – as more vines converged on a growing mass surrounding the ship. Snakelike cables squirmed by Dwer, yet he felt none of the heartsick dread that used to come from contact with One-of-a-Kind. *Intent is everything.* Somehow, he knew this huge entity meant him no harm.

At uneven intervals, Rety used clever calls to warn him of the guard robot's return. Dwer worried that it might find the cowardly Danik machine, hiding under the sand. If so, the alerted Jophur might emerge, filling the bog with blazing artificial light.

Dwer moved slowly around the vessel, taking its measure. But as he counted footsteps, his thoughts drifted to the Gray Hills, where Lena Strong and Jenin Worley must be busy right now, uniting Rety's old band with surviving urrish sooners, forging a united tribe.

Not an easy task, but those two can do it, if anyone can.

Still, he felt sad for them. They must be lonely, with Danel Ozawa gone. *And me, carried off in the claws of a Rothen machine. They must think I'm dead, too.*

Jenin and Lena still had Ozawa's 'legacy' of books and tools, and an urrish sage to help them. They might make it, if they were left alone. That was Dwer's job – to make sure no one came across the sky to bother them.

He knew this scheme of his was farfetched. Lark would surely have thought of something better, if he were here.

But I'm all there is. Dwer the Wild Boy. Tough luck for Jijo.

The spider's voice caught him as he was checking the other side of the grounded cruiser, where a long ramp led to a closed hatch.

In here, as well?

His mind filled with another image of the vessel's damaged recess. Moonlight shone through a jagged rent in the hull. The clutter of sooty machinery seemed even more crowded as vine after vine crammed through, already dripping caustic nectars. But Dwer felt his attention drawn deeper, to the opposite wall.

Dim light shone through a crack on that side. Not pale illumination, but sharp, blue, and synthetic, coming from some room beyond.

The ship probably isn't even airtight anymore.

Too bad this didn't happen high in the mountains. Traeki hated cold weather. A glacier wind would be just the thing to send whistling through here!

No, he answered the spider. *Don't go into the lighted space. Not yet.*

The voice returned, pensively serious.

This light ... it could interfere with my work?

Dwer assented. *Yeah. The light would interfere, all right.*

Then he thought no more of it, for at that moment a trace of movement caught his eye, to the southeast. A dark figure waded stealthily, skirting around the teeming mound of mulc vines.

Rety! But she's supposed to be on lookout duty.

This was no time for her impulsiveness. With a larger moon due to rise in less than a midura, the two of them had to start making their getaway before the untraeki woke to what was happening.

With uncanny courtesy, mulc cables slithered out of his path as he hurried after the girl, trying not to splash too noisily. Her apparent objective was the *other* crashed ship, the once-mighty sky steed

Kunn had used to drop bombs into the Rift, chasing mysterious prey. From the dunes, Dwer and Rety had seen the sleek dart overwhelmed and sent plunging to the swamp, its two human passengers taken captive.

That could happen to us, too. More than ever, Dwer regretted leaving behind Rety's 'urrish husband,' her conscience and voice of good sense.

About the interfering light.
I thought you would like to know.
It is being taken care of.

Dwer shrugged aside the spider's mind touch as he crossed an open area, feeling exposed. Things improved slightly when he detoured to take advantage of two reed-covered hummocks, cutting off direct sight of the untraeki ship. But the robot guardian still patrolled somewhere out there. Lacking a lookout, Dwer had just his own wary senses to warn him if it neared.

While wading through a deeper patch, floundering in water up to his armpits, he felt a warning shiver.

I'm being watched.

Dwer slowly turned, expecting to see the glassy weapons of a faceless killer. But no smooth-sided machine hovered above the reedy mound. Instead, he found *eyes* regarding him, perched at the knoll's highest point, a ledge that might have been the wall of a Buyur home. Sharp teeth grinned at Dwer.

Mudfoot.

The noor had done it again.

Someday, I'll get even for the times you've scared me half to death.

Mudfoot had a companion this time, a smaller creature, held between his paws. Some recent prey? It did not struggle, but tiny greenish eyes seemed to glow with cool interest. Mudfoot's grin invited Dwer to guess what this new friend might be.

Dwer had no time for games. 'Enjoy yourselves,' he muttered, and moved on, floundering up a muddy bank. He was just rounding the far corner, seeking Rety in the shadows of the Rothen wreck, when a clamor erupted from behind. Loud bangs and thumps reverberated as Dwer crouched, peering back at the large vessel.

This side appeared undamaged – a glossy chariot of semidivine star gods, ready at an instant to leap into the sky.

But then a rectangular crack seamed its flank above the ramp, releasing clots of smoke, like foul ghosts charging into the night.

The interference is taken care of.

The spider's mind touch seemed satisfied, even proud.

Dark figures spilled through the roiling soot, then down the ramp, wheezing in agony. Dwer counted three untraeki ... then two shambling biped forms, leaning on each other as they fled the noxious billows.

What followed nauseated Dwer – solitary doughnut shapes, slithering traeki rings shorn from the waxy moorings that once united them as sapient beings. One large torus burst from the murk, galloping on pulsating legs without guidance or direction, trailing mucus and silvery fibers as it plunged off the ramp into deep water. Another hapless circle bumped along unevenly, staring in all directions with panicky eye patches until surging black vapors overtook it.

I have not acted thus – with such vigor and decisiveness – since the early days, when still-animate Buyur servant machines sometimes tried to hide and reproduce amid the ruins, after their masters departed. Back then, we were fierce, we mulc agents of deconstruction, before the long centuries of patient erosion set in.

Now do you see how efficient my kind can be, when we feel a need? And when we have a worthy audience? Now will you acknowledge me, O unique young ephemeral?

Dwer turned and fled, kicking spray as he ran.

The Rothen scout boat was a wreck, split in the middle, its wings crumpled. He found an open hatch and clambered inside. The metal deck felt chill and alien beneath his bare feet.

The interior lacked even pale moonlight, so it took time to find Rety in a far corner, taking treasures from a cabinet and stuffing them in a bag. *What's she looking for? Food? After all the star-god poisons that've spilled here since the crash?*

'There's no time for that,' he shouted. 'We've got to get out of here!'

'Gimme a dura,' the girl replied. 'I know it's here. Kunn kept it on one o' these shelfs.'

Dwer craned his head back through the hatch to look outside. The robot guardian had reappeared, hovering over the stricken untraeki vessel, shining stark light on the survivors mired below. As the thick smoke spread out, Dwer whiffed something that felt sweet in the front of his mouth, yet made the back part gag.

Abruptly, a new thing impacted the senses – sound. A series of twanging notes shook the air. *Lines* stretched across the water as hundreds of cables tautened, surrounding the skycraft like the tent lines of a festival pavilion. Some vines snapped under the strain, whipping across the landscape. One whirling cord sliced through a surviving stack-of-rings, flinging upper toruses into the swamp while the lower half lurched blindly. Other survivors beat a hasty retreat, deeper into the bog.

The robot descended, its spotlight narrowing to a slender, cutting beam. One by one, straining mulc cables parted under the slashing attack. But it was too little, too late. Something or somebody must already have undermined the muck beneath the ship, for it began sliding into a slimy crypt, gurgling as a muddy slurry poured in through the hatch.

'Found it!' Rety cried, rare happiness invading her voice. She joined Dwer at the door, cradling her reclaimed prize. Her metal bird. Since the first time he laid eyes on it, the thing had gone through a lot of poking and prodding, till it could hardly be mistaken for a real creature anymore, even in dim light. *Another damned robot*, he thought. The Ifni-cursed thing had caused Dwer more trouble than he could count. Yet to the sooner girl it was an emblem of hope. The first harbinger of freedom in her life.

'Come on,' he muttered. 'This wreck is the only shelter hereabouts. The survivors'll be coming this way. We've got to go.'

Rety had only agreeable smiles descending back into the swamp. She followed his every move with the happy compliance of one who had no further need to rebel.

Dwer knew he ought to be pleased, as well. His plan had worked beyond all expectation. Yet his sole emotion was emptiness.

Maybe it's on account of I've been wounded, beat up, exhausted, and starved till I'm too numb to care.

Or else, it's that I never really enjoyed one part of hunting.

The killing part.

They retreated from both ruined sky boats to the nearest concealing thicket. Dwer was trying to select a good route back to the dunes, when a voice spoke up.

'Hello. I think we ought to talk.'

Dwer was grateful to the mulc-spider. He owed it the conversation it desired, and acknowledgement of its might. But, he felt too drained for the mental effort. *Not now*, he projected. *Later, I promise, if I survive the night.*

But the voice was persistent. And Dwer soon realized – the words weren't echoing *inside* his head, but in the air, with a low, familiar quality and tone. They came from just overhead.

'Hello? Humans in the swamp? Can you hear me?'

Then the voice went muffled, as if the speaker turned aside to address someone else.

'Are you sure this thing is working?' it asked.

Bewildered, and against his better judgment, Dwer found himself answering.

'How the hell should *I* know what's working, an' what ain't? Who on Jijo *are* you?'

The words returned more clearly, with evident eagerness.

'Ah! Good. We're in contact, then. That's great.'

Dwer finally saw where the words were coming from. *Mudfoot* squatted just above, having followed to pester him from this new perch. And the noor had his new companion – the one with green eyes.

Rety gasped, and Dwer abruptly realized – the second creature bore a family resemblance to Rety's bird!

'All right,' Dwer growled, his patience wearing thin with Mudfoot's endless games. 'We're footprints, unless you tell me what's goin' on.'

The creature with green eyes emitted a low, rumbling sound, surprising for one so small. Dwer blinked, startled by the commonplace resonance of a hoonish umble.

'Hr-r-rm . . . Well, for starters, let me introduce myself.

'The formal name my folks gave me is Hph-wayuo—

'But you can call me Alvin.'

VII

A PARABLE

'Master,' the student asked, 'the Universe is so complex, surely the Creator could not have used volition alone to set it in motion. In crafting His design, and in commanding the angels to carry out His will, He must have used computers.'

The great savant contemplated this for several spans before replying in the negative.

'You are mistaken. No reality can be modeled completely by a calculating engine that is contained within and partaking of that same reality . God did not use a computer to create the world. He used mathematics.'

The student pondered this wisdom for a time, then persisted in his argument.

'That may have been the case when it came to envisioning and creating the world, Master – and to foreseeing future consequences in revealed destiny – but what of maintenance? The cosmos is a vast, intricate network of decisions. Choices are made every femtosecond, and living beings win accordingly, or else lose.

'How can the Creator's assistants carry out these myriad local branchings, unless they use computer models?'

But once again, the great savant turned his gaze away in rebuke.

'It is Ifni, the chief deputy, who decides such things. But she has no need for elaborate tools for deciding local events.

'In the Creator's name she runs the world by using dice.'

STREAKERS

KAA

The subsea habitat felt crowded as five dolphins gathered before a small holo display, watching a raid unfold in real time. Images of the distant assault were blurry, yet they stirred the heart.

While Brookida, Zhaki, and Mopol jostled near Kaa's left side, he felt more acutely aware of Peepoe on his right – fanning water with her pectorals in order to keep one eye aimed at the monitor. Her presence disturbed his mental and hormonal equilibrium – especially whenever a stray current brushed her against him. To Kaa, this ironically proved the multiple nature of his sapient mind – that the individual he most desired to see was the same one he dreaded being near.

Fortunately, the on-screen spectacle offered distraction – transmitted by a slender fiber strand from a spy camera located hundreds of kilometers away, on a sandy bluff overlooking the Rift. Banks of heavy clouds glowered low, making twilight out of day. But with enhanced contrast, an observer could just make out shadows flicking beneath blue water, approaching the shore.

Abruptly, the line of surf erupted armored figures – six-legged monsters with horizontal cylinders for bodies, flared widely at the back – charging past the beach then through a brackish swamp, firing lasers as they came. Three slim flying robots accompanied the attackers, still dripping seawater as they swooped toward the surprised foe.

The enemy encampment was little more than a rude fabric tent propped against the lee side of a shattered spaceship. A single hovering guardian drone shrieked, rising angrily as it sighted the new arrivals ... then became a smoldering cinder, toppling to douse in the frothy swamp. Jophur survivors could only stand helpless as the onslaught swept over them. Eye cells throbbed unhappily atop tapered sap rings, staring in dazed wonder, unable to grasp this humiliation. August beings, taken prisoner by mere dolphins.

By the youngest race of the wolfling clan of Terra.

Kaa felt good, watching his crew mates turn the tables on those hateful stacks of greasy doughnuts. The Jophur alliance had been relentless in pursuing *Streaker* across the star lanes. This small victory was almost as satisfying as that other raid, on Oakka World, where resolute action took an enemy base from behind, releasing *Streaker* from yet another trap.

Only that time I didn't have to watch from afar. I piloted the boat to pick up Engineer D'Anite, dodging fire all the way.

In those days, he had still been 'Lucky' Kaa.

Alongside Peepoe and the others, he watched Lieutenant Tsh't gesture right and left with the metal arms of her walker unit, ordering members of the raiding party to herd their captives toward the shore, where a whalelike behemoth erupted from the surf, spreading mighty jaws.

Despite thick clouds, the raiders had to make this phase brief to avoid detection.

One Jophur captive stumbled in the surf. Its component rings throbbed, threatening to split their mucusy bindings. Mopol chittered delight at the enemy's discomfiture, thrashing his flukes to splatter the habitat's low ceiling.

Peepoe sent Kaa a brief sonar click, drawing attention to Mopol's behavior.

* *See what I mean?* * she remarked in clipped Trinary.

Kaa nodded agreement. All trace of illness was gone, replaced by primal exultation. No doubt Mopol longed to be on the raid, tormenting the tormentors.

Peepoe was naturally irked to have come all this way, driving a one-dolphin sled through unfamiliar waters where frightening sound shadows lurked, just to diagnose a case of kingree fever. The name had roots in an Anglic word – *malingering*. Dolphin spacers knew many clever ways to induce symptoms of food poisoning, in order to feign illness and avoid duty.

'I thought-t so from the beginning,' Kaa had told her earlier. 'It was Makanee's choice to send a nurse, just in case.'

That hardly mollified Peepoe.

'A leader's job is to motivate,' she had scolded. 'If the work is hard, you're supposed to motivate even harder.'

Kaa still winced from her chiding. Yet the words also provoked puzzlement, for Mopol had no apparent reason to fake illness. Despite his other faults, the crewfin wasn't known for laziness. Anyway, conditions at this outpost were more pleasant than back at *Streaker*, where you had to breathe irksome oxy-water much of the time, and struggle for sleep with the weird sonic effects of a high-pressure abyss surrounding you. Here, the waves felt silky, the prey fish were tasty, while the task of spying was varied and diverting. Why should Mopol pretend illness, if it meant being cooped up in a cramped habitat with just old Brookida for company?

On-screen, half a dozen bewildered Jophur were being ushered aboard the submarine, while onshore Lieutenant Tsh't consulted with two native humans draped in muddy rags – a young man and an even younger girl – who looked quite tattered and fatigued. The male moved with a limp, clutching a bow and quiver of arrows while his companion held a small broken robot.

Brookida let out a shout, recognizing a spy probe of his own design, fashioned months ago to send ashore, snooping in the guise of a Jijoan bird.

The young man pointed toward a nearby dune and spoke words the camera could not pick up. Almost at once, the three Earthling war drones darted to surround that hillock, hovering cautiously. Moments later, sand spilled from a hole and a larger robot emerged, visibly scarred from past violent encounters. Hesitantly, it paused as if unsure whether to surrender or self-destruct. Finally, the damaged machine glided to the beach, where two more humans were being carried on stretchers by dolphin warriors in exo-suits. These men were also mud-splashed. But under a grime coating, the bigger one wore garments of Galactic manufacture. The captive robot took a position next to that man, accompanying him aboard the sub.

Last to board were Tsh't and the two walking humans. The young man held back for a moment, awed by the entry hatch, gaping like the jaws of some ravenous beast. But the girl radiated delight. Her legs could barely carry her fast enough through the surf as she plunged inside.

Then only Lieutenant Tsh't remained, staring down at a small creature who lounged indolently on the beach, grooming its sleek fur, pretending it had all the time in the world. Through her exo-suit speakers, Tsh't addressed the strange being.

'Well? If you're coming, this is your lassst chance.'

Kaa still found it hard to reconcile. For two weeks he had spied on hoonish sailing ships operating out of Wuphon port, and watched as tiny figures scampered across the rigging. Not once did he associate the fuzzy shapes with *tytlal* – a Galactic client species whose patrons, the Tymbrimi, were Earth's greatest friends.

Who could hlame me? With hoons they act like clever animals, not sapient beings. According to the journal of the young hoon adventurer Alvin, Jijoans called the creatures *noor beasts*. And noor never spoke.

But the one on the beach had! And with a Tymbrimi accent, at that.

Could six races live here all this time wthout knowing that another band of sooners were right in their midst? Could tytlal play dumb the entire time, without giving themselves away?

The small creature seemed complacently willing to outwait Tsh't, perhaps testing dolphin patience ... until abruptly a new voice broke in, coming from the sub's open hatch. The camera eye swung that way, catching in its field a tall figure, gangly and white, with scaly arms and a bellowslike organ throbbing below its jaw, emitting a low, resonant hum.

Alvin, Kaa realized. The young author of the memoir that had kept Kaa up late several nights, reading about the strange civilization of refugees.

He must be 'umbling' at the tytlal.

In moments the sleek creature was seen perched atop the lieutenant's striding exo-suit, as Tsh't hurried aboard. Its grinning expression seemed to say, *Oh, well. If you positively insist . . .*

The hatch swung shut and the sub backed away swiftly, sinking beneath the waves. But the images did not stop.

Left alone at last, *Streaker*'s little scout robot turned its spy eye back toward the field of dunes. Sandy terrain swept past as it sought a vantage point – some ideal site to watch over two blasted wrecks that had once been small spacecraft but now lay mired by mud and embraced by corrosive vines.

No doubt Gillian Baskin and the ship's council were deeply interested in who might next visit this place of devastation.

GILLIAN

The initial exercises are complete. A warm tingling pervades her floating body, from tip to toes.

Now Gillian is ready for the first deep movement. It is *Narushkan* – 'the starfish' – an outreach of neck, arms, and legs, extending toward the five planar compass points.

Physique discipline lies at the core of weightless yoga, the way Gillian learned it on Earth, when she and Tom studied Galactic survival skills from Jacob Demwa. *'Flesh participates in everything we do,'* the aged spy master once explained. *'We humans like to think we're rational beings. But feelings always precede reason.'*

It is a delicate phase. She needs to release her tense body, allowing the skin itself to become like a sensitive antenna. Yet she cannot afford a complete letting go. Not if it means unleashing the grief and loneliness pent up inside.

Floating in a shielded nul-gee zone, Gillian lets her horizontal torso respond to the tug of certain objects located *outside* of the suspension tank, elsewhere in the ship, and beyond. Their influence penetrates the walls, making her sensitized nerves throb and twitch.

'Articles of Destiny' – that was how an enigmatic Old One described such things, during *Streaker*'s brief visit to the Fractal System.

She never got to meet the one who spoke those words. The voice came a great distance, far across that gargantuan edifice of spiky hydrogen ice. The Fractal System was one huge habitat, as wide as a solar system, with a tiny red sun gleaming in its heart. No pursuer could possibly find *Streaker* in such a vast place, if sanctuary were given.

'*Your ship carries heavy freight,*' the voice had said. '*As fate-laden a cargo as we ever detected.*'

'*Then you understand why we came,*' Gillian replied as *Streaker*'s lean hull passed jutting angles of fantastic crystal, alternating with planet-sized hollows of black shadow. The ship seemed like a pollen grain lost in a giant forest.

'*Indeed. We comprehend your purpose. Your poignant request is being considered. Meanwhile, can you blame us for refusing your invitation to come aboard in person? Or even to touch your vessel's hull? A hull so recently stroked by dire light?*

'*We who dwell here have retired from the ferment of the Five Galaxies. From fleets and star battles and political intrigues. You may or may not receive the help you seek – that has yet to be decided. But do not expect glad welcome. For your cargo reawakens many of the hungers, the urgencies, and irksome obsessions of youth.*'

She tried to play innocent. '*The importance of our cargo is over-rated. We'll hand it over gladly, to those who prove impartial and wise.*'

'*Speak not so!*' the speaker scolded. '*Do not add temptation to the poisons you already bring in our midst!*'

'*Poisons?*'

'*You carry blessings in your hold ... and curses.*' The voice concluded, '*We fear what your presence will do to our ancient peace.*'

As it turned out, *Streaker*'s time of sanctuary lasted just a few slim weeks before convulsions began to shake the Fractal System, sending awful sparks crackling along an immense structure built to house quadrillions. Crystal greenhouses, as wide as Earth's moon, blew apart, exposing sheltered biomass to hard vacuum. Jupiter-sized slivers cracked loose, diffuse as cardboard, though glittering with lighted windows. Like icicles knocked by a violent wind, these tumbled, then collided with other protrusions, exploding into hurricanes of silent dust. Meanwhile, a cacophony of voices swarmed—

The poor wolfling children ... we must help the Terrans ...

No! Erase them so we may return to quiet dreaming . . .

Objection! Let us instead squeeze them for what they know . . .

Yes. Then we'll share the knowledge with our younger brethren of the Awaiter Alliance . . .

No! The Inheritors . . .

The Abdicators! . . .

Gillian recalls marveling at the unleashed storm of pettiness.

So much for the vaunted detachment of old age.

But then, when all seemed lost, sympathetic forces briefly intervened.

This icy realm is not the place you seek.

Advice you need, dispassionate and sage. Seek it from those who are older and wiser, still.

Where tides curl tightly, warding off the night.

Hurry, youngsters. Take this chance. Flee while you can.

Abruptly, an escape path opened for the Earth vessel – a crevice in the vast maze of hydrogen ice, with star-speckled blackness just beyond. *Streaker* had only moments to charge through . . . an egress too sudden and brief for Emerson D'Anite, who had already set forth in a brave, desolate sacrifice.

Poor Emerson. Fought over by resentful factions until his scout craft was swallowed by enfolding light.

All of this comes back to Gillian, not in sequence, but whole, time-less, and entire as she recalls that one phrase—

'Articles of Destiny.'

Immersed in a trance state, she can feel those tugging objects. The same ones that caused so much trouble in the Fractal System.

They stroke her limbs – the limbs of *Narushkan* – not with phys-ical force, but with awful import of their existence.

Abruptly, *Narushkan* gives way to *Abhusha* – 'the pointer' – and her left hand uncurls toward a massive cube – a portable branch of the great Galactic Library, squatting in a cool mist, two corridors away. With fingers of thought, Gillian traces one of its gemlike facets, engraved with a rayed spiral symbol. Unlike the minimally pro-grammed units that wolfling upstarts could afford, this one was designed to serve a mighty starfaring clan. Had *Streaker* returned home with this prize alone, her costly voyage might be called worthwhile.

Yet the cube seems least among *Streaker*'s cargoes.

*

Abhusha shifts to her right hand, turning palm out, like a flower seeking warmth to counter the Library's ancient cold.

Toward youth, the antithesis of age.

Gillian hears her little servant, Kippi, move about her private sanctum, straightening up. The Kiqui amphibian, a native of water-logged Kithrup, uses all six agile limbs impartially while tidying. A cheerful music of syncopated chirps and trills accompanies his labor. Kippi's surface thoughts prove easy to trace, even with Gillian's limited psi-talent. Placid curiosity fills the presapient mind. Kippi seems blithely unaware that his young race is embroiled in a great crisis, spanning five galaxies.

> ## *What comes next? – I wonder what?*
> ## *What comes?*
> ## *What comes next? – I hope it's something good.*

Gillian shares that fervent wish. For the sake of the Kiqui, *Streaker* must find a corner of space where Galactic traditions still hold. Ideally some strong, benevolent star lineage, able to embrace and protect the juvenile amphibian race while hot winds of fanaticism blow along the starry lanes.

Some race worthy to be their patrons ... to help them ... as humans never were helped ... until the Kiqui can stand on their own.

She had already given up hope of adopting the Kiqui into Terra's small family of humans, neo-dolphins, and neochimps, the initial idea, when *Streaker* quickly snatched aboard a small breeding population on Kithrup. Ripe presapient species were rare, and this one was a real find. But right now Earthclan could hardly protect itself, let alone take on new responsibilities.

Abhusha shifts again, transmuting into *Poposh* as one of Gillian's feet swarms with prickliness, sensing a new presence in the room. Smug irony accompanies the intruder, like an overused fragrance. It is the Niss Machine's spinning hologram, barging into her exclusive retreat with typical tactlessness.

Tom had thought it a good idea to bring along the Tymbrimi device, when this ill-fated expedition set forth from Earth. For Tom's sake – because she misses him so – Gillian quashes her natural irritation with the smooth-voiced artificial being.

'*The submarine, with our raiding party aboard, is now just hours from returning with the prisoners,*' the Niss intones. '*Shall we go over plans for interrogation, Dr. Baskin? Or will you leave that chore to a gaggle of alien children?*'

The insolent machine seems piqued, ever since Gillian

transferred to Alvin and Huck the job of interpreting. But things are going well so far. Anyway, Gillian already knows what questions to ask the human and Jophur captives.

Moreover, she has her own way to prepare. As old Jake used to say, *'How can one foresee, without first remembering?'*

She needs time alone, without the Niss, or Hannes Suessi, or a hundred nervous dolphins nagging at her as if she were their mother. Sometimes the pressure feels heavier than the dark abyss surrounding *Streaker*'s sheltering mountain of dead starships.

To answer verbally would yank her out of the trance, so Gillian instead calls up *Kopou*, an empathy glyph. Nothing fancy – she lacks the inbuilt talent of a Tymbrimi – just a crude suggestion that the Niss go find a corner of cybernetic space and spend the next hour in simulated self-replication, till she calls for it.

The entity sputters and objects. There are more words. But she lets them wash by like foam on a beach. Meanwhile Gillian continues the exercise, shifting to another compass point. One that seems quiet as death.

Abhusha resumes, now reaching toward a cadaver, standing in a far corner of her office like a pharaoh's mummy, surrounded by preserving fields that still cling after three years and a million parsecs, keeping it as it was. As it had been ever since Tom wrested the ancient corpse from a huge derelict ship, adrift in the Shallow Cluster.

Tom always had a knack for acquiring expensive souvenirs. But this one took the cake.

Herbie.

An ironic name for a Progenitor if that truly was its nature ... perhaps two billion years old, and the cause of *Streaker*'s troubles.

Chief cause of war and turmoil across a dozen spiral arms.

We could have gotten rid of him on Oakka World, she knew. Handing Herbie over to the Library Institute was officially the right thing to do. The safe thing to do.

But sector-branch officials had been corrupted. Many of the librarians had cast off their oaths and fell to fighting among themselves – race by race, clan by clan – each seeking *Streaker*'s treasure for its own kind.

Fleeing once again became a duty.

No one Galactic faction can be allowed to own your secret.

So commanded Terragens Council, in the single long-range message *Streaker* had received. Gillian knew the words by heart.

To show any partiality might lead to disaster. It could mean extinction for Earthclan.

*

Articles of Destiny tug at her limbs, reorienting her floating body. Facing upward, Gillian's eyes open but fail to see the metal ceiling plates. Instead, they look to the past.

To the Shallow Cluster. A phalanx of shimmering globes, deceptively beautiful, like translucent moons, or floating bubbles in a dream.

Then the Morgran ambush ... fiery explosions amid mighty battleships, as numerous as stars, all striving for a chance to snare a gnat.

To Kithrup, where the gnat fled, where so much was lost, including the better part of her soul.

Where are you, Tom? Do you still live, somewhere in space and time?

Then Oakka, that green betraying place, where the Institutes failed. And the Fractal System, where Old Ones proved there is no age limit on perfidy.

Herbie seems amused by that thought.

'Old Ones? From my perspective, those inhabitants of a giant snowflake are mere infants, like yourself!'

Of course the voice comes from her imagination, putting words in a mouth that might have spoken when Earth's ocean was innocent of any life but bacteria ... when Sol's system was half its present age.

Gillian cracks a smile and *Abhusha* transforms into *Kuntatta* – laughter amid a storm of sleeting vacuum rays.

Soon, she must wrestle with the same quandary – how to arrange *Streaker*'s escape one more time, just ahead of baying hounds. It would take a pretty neat trick this time, with a Jophur dreadnought apparently already landed on Jijo, and *Streaker*'s hull still laden with refractory soot.

It would take a miracle.

How did they follow us? she wonders. *It seemed a perfect hideout with all trails to Jijo quantum collapsed but one, and that one passing through the atmosphere of a giant carbon star. The sooner races all did it successfully, arriving without leaving tracks. What did we do wrong?*

Recrimination has no place in weightless yoga.

It spoils the serenity.

Sorry, Jake, she thinks. Gillian sighs, knowing this trance is now forfeit. She might as well emerge and get back down to business. Perhaps the *Hikahi* will bring useful news from its raid on the surface.

I'm sorry, Tom. Maybe a time will come when I can clear my mind enough to hear you ... to cast a piece of myself to wherever you have gone.

Gillian won't let herself imagine the more likely probability – that Tom is dead, along with Creideiki and all the others she was forced to abandon on Kithrup, with little more than a space skiff to convey them home again.

The emergence process continues, drawing meditation en-forms back into their original abstractions, easing her toward the world of unpleasant facts.

And yet . . .

In the course of preparing to exit, Gillian abruptly grows aware of a *fifth* tug on her body, this one stroking the back of her neck, prickling her occipital vertebrae, and follicles along the middle of her scalp. It is familiar. She's felt it before, though never this strong. A presence beckoning not from nearby, or even elsewhere in the ship, but somewhere beyond *Streaker's* scarred hull. Somewhere else on the planet.

There is a rhythmic, resonant solidity to the sensation, like vibration in dense stone.

If only Creideiki were here, he could probably relate to it, the way he did with those poor beings who lived underground on Kithrup. Or else Tom might have figured out a way to decipher this thing.

And yet, she begins to suspect this time it is something different. Correcting her earlier impression, Gillian realizes—

It is not a presence *on* this world, or beneath it, but something *of* the planet. An aspect of Jijo itself.

Narushkan orients her like the needle of a compass, and abruptly she feels a strange, unprovoked commotion within. It takes her some time to sort out the impression. But recognition dawns at last.

Tentatively – like a long-lost friend unsure of its welcome – *hope* sneaks back into her heart, riding on the stony cadence.

EWASX

Abruptly comes news. Too soon for you rings to have interpreted the still-hot wax. So let me relate it directly.

WORD OF DISASTER! WORD OF CALAMITY!

Word of ill-fated loss, just east beyond this range of mountain hills. Our grounded corvette – destroyed!

Dissension tears the *Polkjhy* crew. Chem-synth toruses vent fumes of blame while loud recriminations pour from oration rings.

Could this tragedy be the work of the dolphin prey ship, retaliating against its pursuers? For years its renown has spread, after cunning escapes from other traps.

But it cannot be. Long-range scans show no hint of gravitic emanations or energy weapons. Early signs point to some kind of onboard failure.

And yet, clever wolflings are not to be underrated. I/we can read waxy memories left by the former Asx – historical legends of the formative years of the Jijoan Commons, especially tales of urrish-human wars. These stories demonstrate how both races have exceptional aptitudes for improvisation.

Until now, we thought it was coincidence – that there were Earthling sooners here, that the Rothen had human servants, and the prey ship also came from that wolfling world. The three groups seem to have nothing in common, no motives, goals, or capabilities.

But what if there is a pattern?

I/we must speak of this to the Captain-Leader ... as soon as higher-status stacks pause their ventings and let us get a puff in edgewise.

Prepare, My rings. Our first task will surely be to interrogate the prisoners.

TSH'T

What am I going to do?

She fretted over her predicament as the submarine made its way back to the abyssal mountain of dead starships. While other members of the *Hikahi* team exulted over their successful raid, looking forward to reunion with their crew mates on the *Streaker*, Tsh't anticipated docking with a rising sense of dread.

To outward appearances, all was well. The prisoners were secure. The young adventurers, Alvin and Huck, were debriefing Dwer and Rety – human sooners who had managed somehow to defeat a Jophur corvette. Once *Hikahi* leveled its plunge below the thermocline, Tsh't knew she and her team had pulled it off – striking a blow for Earth without being caught.

The coup reflected well on the mission commander. Some might call Tsh't a hero. Yet disquiet churned her sour stomach.

Ifni must hate me. The worst of all possible combinations of events has caught me in a vise.

*

'Wait a minute,' snapped the female g'Kek, who had assumed the name of an ancient Earthling literary figure. As her spokes vibrated with agitation, she pointed one eyestalk at the young man whose bow and arrows lay across his knees. 'You're saying that you walked all the way from the Slope to find *her* hidden tribe ... while *she* flew back home aboard the Dakkin sky boat ...'

The human girl, Rety, interrupted.

'That's *Danik*, you dumb wheelie. And what's so surprisin' about that? I had Kunn an' the others fooled down to their scabs, thinkin' I was ready to be one of 'em. O' course I was just keepin' my eyes peeled fer my first chance to ...'

Tsh't had already heard the story once through, so she paid scant attention this time, except to note that 'Huck' spoke far better Anglic than the human child. Anyway, she had other matters on her mind. Especially one of the prisoners lying in a cell farther aft ... a captive starfarer who could reveal her deepest secret.

Tsh't sent signals down the neural tap socketed behind her left eye. The mechanical walker unit responded by swiveling on six legs to aim her bottle-shaped beak away from the submarine's bridge. Unburdened by armor or life-support equipment, it maneuvered gracefully past a gaggle of dolphin spectators. The fins seemed captivated by the sight of two humans so disheveled, and the girl bearing scars on her cheek that any Earth hospital could erase in a day. Their rustic accents and overt wonder at seeing real live dolphins seemed poignantly endearing in members of the patron race.

The two seemed to find nothing odd about chatting with Alvin and Huck, though, as if wheeled beings and Anglic-speaking hoons were as common as froth on a wave. Common enough for Rety and Huck to bicker like siblings.

'Sure I led Kunn out this way. But only so's I could find out where the bird machine came from!' Rety stroked a miniature urs, whose long neck coiled contentedly around her wrist. 'And my plan worked, didn't it? I found you!'

Huck reacted with a rolling twist of all four eyestalks, a clear expression of doubt and disdain. 'Yes, though it meant revealing the Earthship's position, enabling your *Danik* pilot to target its site from the air.'

'So? What's yer point?'

From the door, Tsh't saw the male human glance at the big adolescent hoon. Dwer and Alvin had just met, but they exchanged commiserating grins. Perhaps they would compare notes later, how each managed life with such a 'dynamic' companion.

Tsh't found all the varied voices too complicated. *It feels like a menagerie aboard this tub.*

The argument raged on while Tsh't exited the bridge. Perhaps recordings would prove useful when Gillian and the Niss computer analyzed every word. Preparations were also under way to interrogate the Jophur survivors using techniques found in the Thennanin Library cube – sophisticated data from a clan that had been fighting Jophur since before Solomon built his temple.

Tsh't approved . . . so far.

But Gillian will also want to question Kunn. And she knows her own kind too well to be fooled.

The *Hikahi* was a makeshift vessel, built out of parts salvaged from ancient hulks lining the bottom of the Rift. Tsh't passed down corridors of varied substance, linked by coarsely welded plates, until she reached the cell where two human prisoners were held. Unfortunately, the guard on duty turned out to be Karkaett, a disciple of former Captain Creideiki's *keeneenk* mental training program. Tsh't couldn't hope to send Karkaett off on some errand and have him simply forget. Any slip in regulations would be remembered.

'The doughnuts are sedated,' the guard reported. 'Also, we z-zapped the damaged Rothen battle drone and put it in a freezer. Hannes and I can check its memory store later.'

'That-t's fine,' she replied. 'And the tytlal?'

Karkaett tossed his sleek gray head. 'You mean the one that talks? Isolated in a cabin, as you instructed. Alvin's pet is just a *noor*, of course. I assume you didn't mean to lock her up, t-too.'

Actually, Tsh't wasn't sure she grasped the difference between a *noor* and a *tytlal*. Was it simply the ability to talk? What if they all could, but were good at keeping it secret? Tytlal were legendary for one trait – going to any length for a joke.

'I'll see the human prisoners now,' she told the guard. Karkaett transmitted a signal to open the door. Following rules, he accompanied her inside, weapons trained on the captives.

Both men lay on cots with medical packs strapped to their arms. Already they seemed much improved over their condition in the swamp, where, coughing and desperate for breath, they had clutched a reed bank, struggling to keep their heads above water. The younger one looked even more grubby and half-starved than Rety – a slightly built young man with wiry muscles, black hair, and a puckered scar above one eye. *Jass*, Rety had identified him – a sooner cousin, and far from her favorite person.

The other man was much larger. His uniform could still be recognized beneath the caked filth. Steely gray eyes drilled Tsh't the moment she entered.

'How did you follow us to Jijo?'

That was what Gillian would surely ask the Danik voyager. It was the question Tsh't feared most.

Calm down, she urged herself. *The Rothen only know that someone sent a message from the Fractal System. They can't know who.*

Anyway, would they confide in their Danik servants? This poor fellow is probably just as bewildered as we are.

Yet Kunn's steady gaze seemed to hold the same rock-solid faith she once saw in the Missionary ... the disciple who long ago brought a shining message-of-truth to the small dolphin community of Bimini-Under, back when Tsh't was still a child gliding in her mother's slipstream wake.

'Humans are beloved patrons of the neo-dolphin race, it's true,' the proselytizer explained, during one secret meeting, in a cave where scuba-diving tourists never ventured. *'Yet, just a few centuries ago, primitive men in boats hunted cetaceans to the verge of extinction. They may act better today, but who can deny their new maturity is fragile, untested? Without meaning disloyalty, many neo-fins feel discomfort, wondering if there might not be something or somebody greater and wiser than humankind. Someone the entire clan can turn to, in dangerous times.'*

'You mean God?' one of the attending dolphins asked. And the Missionary responded with a nod.

'In essence, yes. All the ancient legends about divine beings who intervene in Earth's affairs ... all the great teachers and prophets ... can be shown to have their basis in one simple truth.

'Terra is not just an isolated forlorn world – home to bizarre wolflings and their crude clients. Rather, it is part of a wonderful experiment. Something I have come from afar to tell you about.

'We have been watched over for a very long time. Lovingly guarded throughout our long time of dreaming. But soon, quite soon, it will be time to waken.'

KAA

Mopol's fever showed no sign of returning. In fact, he seemed quite high in spirits when he left the next morning, swimming east with Zhaki, resuming their reconnaissance of Wuphon Port.

'You see? All he needed was a stern talking-to,' Peepoe explained with evident pride. 'Mopol just had to be reminded of his duty.'

Kaa sensed the implied rebuke in her words, but chose to ignore it.

'You have a persuasive bedside manner,' he replied. 'No doubt they teach it in medical school.'

In fact, he was quite sure that Mopol's recovery had little to do with Peepoe's lecture. The half-stenos male had agreed too readily with everything the young nurse said, tossing his mottled gray head and chittering 'Yessss!' repeatedly.

He and Zhaki are up to something, Kaa thought, as he watched the two swim off toward the coastal hoon settlement.

'I need to be heading back to the ship soon,' Peepoe said, causing Kaa to dip his narrow jaw.

'But I thought you'd stay a few days. You agreed to come see the volcano.'

Her expression seemed wary. 'I don't know ... When I left, there was talk of shifting *Streaker* to another hiding place. Searchers were getting too damned c-close.'

Not that moving the ship a few kilometers would make much difference, if Galactic fleets already had her pinned. Even hiding under a great pile of discarded starcraft would not help, once pursuers had the site narrowed down close enough to use chemical sniffers. Earthling DNA would lure them, like male moths to a female's pheromones.

Kaa shrugged by twisting his flukes.

'Brookida will be disappointed. He was so looking forward to showing off his collection of dross from all six sooner races.'

Peepoe stared at Kaa, scanning him with penetrating sound till she found the wryness within.

Her blowhole sputtered laughter.

'Oh, all right. Let's see this mountain of yours. Anyway, I've been aching for a swim.'

As usual, the water felt terrific. A little saltier than Earth sea, but with a fine mineral flavor and a gentle ionic oiliness that helped it glide over your skin. The air's rich oxygen level made it seem as if you could keep going well past the horizon.

It was a far friendlier ocean than on Kithrup or Oakka, where the oceans tasted poisonously foul. Friendlier, that is, unless you counted the groaning sounds that occasionally drifted from the Midden, as if a tribe of mad whales lived down there, singing ballads without rhyme or reason.

According to *Alvin's Journal*, their chief source on Jijo, some natives believed that ancient beings lived beyond the continental shelf, fierce and dangerous. Such hints prompted Gillian Baskin to order the spying continued.

So long as Streaker *doesn't need a pilot, I might as well play secret agent. Anyway, it's a job Peepoe might respect.*

Beyond all that, Kaa relearned how fine it was to cruise in tandem with another strong swimmer, jetting along on powerful fluke strokes, building momentum each time you plunged, then soaring through each upper arc, like flying. The true peak of exhilaration could never be achieved alone. Two or more dolphins must move in unison, each surf-riding the other's wake. When done right, surface tension nearly vanished and the planet merged seamlessly, from core to rock, from sea to sky.

And then ... to bitter-clear vacuum?

A modern poet might make that extrapolation, but it never occurred to natural cetaceans – not even species whose eyesight could make out stars – not until humans stopped hunting and started teaching.

They changed us. Showed us the universe beyond sun, moon, and tides. They even turned some of us into pilots. Wormhole divers. I guess that makes up for their ancestors' crimes.

Still, some things never change. Like the semierotic stroke of whitecaps against flesh, or the spume of hot breath meeting air. The raw, earthy pleasure of this outing offered much that he felt lacking aboard *Streaker*.

It also made a terrific opening to courtship.

Assuming she thinks the same way I do.

Assuming I can start winning her esteem.

They were approaching shore. He could tell by the echoes of rock-churned surf up ahead. A mist-shrouded mountain could be glimpsed from the top of each forward leap. Soon they would reach the hidden cave where his spy equipment lay. Then Kaa must go back to dealing with Peepoe in awkward, inadequate words.

I wish this could just go on without end, he thought.

A brief touch of sonar, and he knew Peepoe felt the same. She, too, yearned for this moment of primitive release to last.

Kaa's sonic sense picked out a school of pseudo-tunny, darting through nearby shoals, tempting after a pallid breakfast of synthi flesh. The tunny weren't quite in their path – it would mean a detour. Still, Kaa squirted a burst of Trinary.

* *In summer sunlight,*
　* *Fish attract like edible*
　　* *Singularities!* *

Kaa felt proud of the haiku – impulsive, yet punning as it mixed both space- and planet-bound images. Of course, free foraging was still not officially sanctioned. He awaited Peepoe's rejection.

* Passing an abyss, or bright reef
  * Or black hole – what sustains us?
    * Our navigator! *

Her agreement filled Kaa's pounding heart, offering a basis for hope.

Peepoe's strong, rhythmic strokes easily kept pace alongside as he angled toward a vigorous early lunch.

SOONERS

LARK

I've been aboard a flying machine before, he told himself. *I'm no simple nature child, astonished by doors, metal panels, and artificial light.*

This place should not terrify me.

The walls aren't about to close in.

His body wasn't convinced. His heart raced and he could not rest. Lark kept experiencing a disturbing impression that the little room was getting *smaller*.

He knew it must be an illusion. Neither Ling nor Rann showed outward concern over being crushed in a diminishing space. They were used to hard gray surfaces, but the metal enclosure seemed harsh to one who grew up scampering along the branch-top skyways of a garu forest. The floor plates brought a distant vibration, rhythmic and incessant.

Lark suddenly realized what it reminded him of – the machinery of his father's paper mill – the grinders and pulping hammers – designed to crush scrap cloth into a fine white slurry. That pounding noise used to drive him away into the wilderness, on long journeys seeking living things to study.

'Welcome to a starship, sooner,' Rann mumbled, nursing both a headache and a grudge after their fight in the lake. 'How do you like it?'

All three human prisoners still wore their damp underwear, having been stripped of their tools and wet suits. For some reason, the Jophur let them keep their rewq symbionts, though Rann had torn his off, leaving red welts at his temples where the crumpled creature had had no time to withdraw its feeding suckers.

At least no one had been injured during the swift capture, when a swarm of tapered cone beings swept down from the mammoth ship, each Jophur riding its own platform of shimmering metal. Suspensor fields pressed the lake, surrounding the human swimmers between disklike watery depressions. Hovering robots crackled with restrained energy – one even dived beneath the surface to cut off escape – crowding the captives toward one of the antigravity sleds, and then to prison.

To Lark's surprise, they were put in the same cell. By accounts from Earth's dark ages, it used to be standard practice to separate prisoners, to break their spirits. Then he realized.

If Jophur are like traeki, they can't quite grasp the notion of being alone. A solitary traeki would be happy arguing among its rings till the Progenitors came home.

'They are probably at a loss, trawling through their database for information about Earthlings,' Ling explained. 'Till recently, there wasn't much available.'

'But it's been three hundred years since contact!'

'That may seem long to us, Lark. But Earth was minor news for most of that time – a back-page sensation. By now the first detailed Institute studies of our homeworld have barely made it through the sector-branch Library, on Tanith.'

'Then why not . . .' He sought a word she had used several times. 'Why not *upload* Earthling books. Our encyclopedias, medical texts, self-analyses . . . the knowledge we spent thousands of years accumulating about ourselves?'

She lifted her eyes. '*Wolfling superstitions*. Even we Daniks are taught to think that way.' She glanced at Rann. 'It took your thesis, Lark – the one you wrote with Uthen – to convince me things might be different.'

Though flushed at the compliment, Lark reined in his imagination. He tried not to let his eyes drop to her nearly bare figure. Skimpy underclothes would not hide his physical arousal. Besides, this was hardly the time.

'I still find their attitude hard to credit. The Galactics would rather wait centuries for a formal report on us?'

'Oh, I'm sure the great powers – like the Soro and Jophur – got access to early drafts. And they've urgently sought more data since the *Streaker* crisis began. Their strategic agencies almost certainly kidnapped and dissected some humans, for instance. But they could hardly update every star cruiser with illicit data. That would risk contaminating the onboard Library cubes. I'd have to guess this crew has been improvising – not a skill much encouraged in Galactic society.'

'But humans are known for it. Is that why your ship came to Jijo? Improvising an opportunity?'

Ling nodded, rubbing her bare shoulders. 'Our Rothen lor . . .' She paused, then chose another phrasing. 'The Inner Circle received a message. A time-drop capsule, tuned for pickup by anyone with a Rothen cognition wave.'

'Who sent it?'

'Apparently, a secret believer living among the crew of the dolphin ship. Or one desperate enough to break from Terragens orders, and summon help from a higher source.'

'A believer ...' Lark mused. 'In the Danik faith, you mean. But Daniks teach that *humans* are the secret recipients of Rothen patronhood.'

'And by tradition, that means a dolphin crew could also call on Rothen help, in case of dire need ... which those poor creatures surely face.'

'Like running to your grandparents, if your own folks can't handle a problem. Hrm.'

Lark had already picked up parts of the story. How the first dolphin-crewed starship set forth on a survey mission, assigned to check the accuracy of the small planetary branch Earth had received from the Library Institute. Most civilized clans simply accepted the massive volumes of information stored by past generations, especially concerning far corners of space, where little profit could be gained by exploration.

It was supposed to be routine. A shakedown cruise. But then, somewhere off the beaten track, Earthship *Streaker* confronted something unexpected – a discovery that made the great alliances crazy. Clues to a time of transition, perhaps, when ancient verities of the known galaxies might abruptly change.

'It is said that when this happens, just one race in ten shall make the passage to a new age,' the hoonish High Sage, Phwhoon-dau, had explained one night by a campfire, just after the fall of Dooden Mesa, drawing on his deep readings of the Biblos Archive. *'Those bent on surviving into the next long phase of stability would naturally want to learn as much as possible. Hr-r-r-rm. Yes, even a sooner can understand why this Earthling ship found itself in trouble.'*

'A dolphin Danik.' Lark marveled. 'So this ... *believer* sent a secret message to the Rothen ...'

'To is the wrong word. You might better use *at.* In fact, nothing in Anglic adequately describes the skewed logic of communicating by time drop.' Ling kept running her fingers through her hair. It had grown since the Battle of the Glade, and was still tangled from their long dive under the lake.

'But yes, the message from the dolphin believer explained where the *Streaker* ship was – in one of the hydrogen-ice habitat zones where many older races huddle close to stellar tides, after retiring from active Galactic affairs.

'More important – it hinted where the Earthship commander next planned to flee.' Ling shook her head. 'It turned out to be a clever version of the Sooner Path. A difficult passage, uncomfortably close to fiery Izmunuti. No wonder you Six were left undetected for so long.'

'Hr-rm,' Lark umbled contemplatively. 'Unlike our ancestors, you let yourselves be followed.'

This drew a reaction from Rann, sullenly holding his aching head in the opposite corner of the cell.

'Fool. We did no such thing!' the tall Danik muttered sourly. 'Are you saying we cannot easily repeat any feat accomplished by a gaggle of cowardly sooners?'

'Putting insults aside, I agree,' Ling said. 'It seems unlikely we were followed. That is, not the *first* time our ship came to Jijo.'

'What do you mean?' Lark asked.

'When our comrades left us – four humans and two Rothen, with the job of doing a bioassay on Jijo – I thought the others were going to cruise nearby space, in case the dolphin ship was hiding on some nearby planetoid. But that was not their aim at all.

'Their real intent was to go find a buyer.'

Lark frowned in puzzlement. 'A *Buyur*? But aren't they extinct? You mean the Rothen wanted to hire one as a guide, to come back to Jijo and—'

'No ... a *buyer*!' Ling laughed, though it was not a happy sound. 'You were right about the Rothen, Lark. They live by bartering unusual or illicit information, often using human Daniks as agents or intermediaries. It was an exciting way of life ... till you made me realize how we've been used.' Ling's expression turned dark. Then she shook her head.

'In this case, they must have realized Jijo was worth a fortune to the right customer. There are life-forms on this planet whose development seems ahead of schedule, rapidly approaching presapience. And there are the Six Races. Surely someone would pay to know about such a major infestation of criminal sooners ... no offense.'

'None taken. And of course, the clue to the dolphin ship was worth plenty. So ... ' He blew an airy sigh through his nostrils, like a disgusted ur. 'Your masters decided to sell us all.'

Ling nodded, but her eyes bored into Rann. 'Our patrons sold us all.'

The big Danik did not meet her gaze. He pressed both hands against his temples, emitting a low moan that seemed half from pain and half disgust at her treason. He turned toward the wall, but did not touch the oily surface.

'After all we've seen, you still think the Rothen are patrons of humanity?' Lark asked.

Ling shrugged her shoulders. 'I cannot easily dismiss the evidence I was shown while growing up – evidence dating back thousands of years. Anyway, it might explain our bloody, treacherous history. The Rothen lords claim it's because our dark souls kept drifting from the Path. But maybe we are exactly what they uplifted us to be. Raised to be shills for a gang of thieves.'

'Hrm. That might relieve us of some of the responsibility. Still, I'd rather be wolflings, with ignorance our only excuse.'

Ling nodded, lapsing into silence, perhaps contemplating the great lie her life had revolved around. Meanwhile, Lark found a new perspective on the tale of humanity. It went beyond a dry litany of events, recited from dusty tomes in the Biblos Archive.

The Daniks claim that we had guidance all along ... that Moses, Jesus, Buddha, Fuller, and others were teachers in disguise. But if we were helped – by the Rothen or anybody else – then our helpers clearly did a lousy job.

Like a problem child who needs open, honest, personal attention, we could have used a lot more than a few ethical nostrums. Vague hints like, 'Have faith' and 'Be nice to each other.' Moralizing platitudes aren't enough to guide a rowdy tyke ... and they sure did not prevent dark ages, slavery, the twentieth-century Holocaust, or the despots of the twenty-first.

All those horrors reflect as poorly on the teacher as the students. Unless ...

Unless you suppose we actually did it all alone ...

Lark was struck by the same feeling as when he and Ling spoke beside the mulc-spider's lake. His mind filled with an image of poignant, awful beauty. A tapestry spanning thousands of years – human history seen from afar. A tale of frightened orphans, floundering in ignorance. Of creatures smart enough to stare in wonder at the stars, asking questions of a night that never answered, except with terrifying silence.

Sometimes, from desperate imaginations, the silence provoked roaring hallucinations, fantastic rationalizations, or self-serving excuses for any crime the strong might choose to commit against the weak. Deserts widened as men ignorantly cut forests. Species vanished as farmers burned and plowed. Wars spread ruin in the name of noble causes.

Yet, amid all that, humanity somehow began pulling together, learning the arts of calmness, peering forward in time, like a neglected infant teaching itself to crawl and speak.

To stand and think.

To walk and read.

To care ... and then become a loving parent to others.

The kind of parent poor orphans never had.

Born on a refuge world whose crude safety had vanished, imprisoned in the bowels of an alien starship, Lark nevertheless felt drawn away from worrying about his own fate, or even the six exile clans of Jijo. After all, on the vast scale of things, his life hardly mattered. The Five Galaxies would spin on, even if every last Earthling vanished.

Yet he found his heart torn by the tragic story of *Homo sapiens*, the self-taught wolflings of Terra. It was a bittersweet tale, pulling from his reluctant eyes trickles of tart brine that tasted like the sea.

The voice was familiar ... horrifyingly so.

'Tell us now.'

When all three humans kept silent, the Jophur interrogator edged closer, towering over them. Anglic words hissed from atop the swaying stack of fatty rings, accompanied by liquid burblings and mucusy pops.

'Explain to us; why did you transmit the signal that led to your capture? Did you sacrifice yourselves in order to buy time for unseen comrades? Those we most eagerly pursue?'

It had introduced itself as 'Ewasx,' and part of Lark's horror lay in recognizing torus markings of the former traeki High Sage, Asx. One major difference appeared at the bottom of the stack, where a new, agile torus-of-legs let the composite being move about more quickly than before. And silvery fibers now laced the doughy tubes, leading up to a glistening young ring that had no apparent features or appendages. Yet Lark sensed it was the chief thing turning the old traeki sage into a Jophur.

'We detected a disturbance in the toporgic time field, imprisoning the Rothen vessel below the lake,' it said. 'But these tremors were well within noise variance levels, and our leaders were otherwise too busily engaged to investigate. However, we/I now clearly discern what you were trying to accomplish with this trick.'

The declaration left Lark unsurprised. Once alerted, the mighty aliens would naturally pierce his jury-rigged scheme for letting Daniks out of the trapped vessel. He only hoped that Jeni Shen, and Jimi, and the others made it out before hunter robots swarmed around the Rothen time cocoon, then through the network of caves.

While all three humans kept silent, Ewasx continued.

'The chain of logic is apparent, revealing a persistent effort on the part of you sooners to divert us from our main purpose on this world.

'In short, you have been attempting to distract us.'

Now Lark looked up, baffled. He shared a glance with Ling.

What is the Jophur talking about?

'It began several Jijo rotations ago,' Ewasx went on.

'Although no other crew stack thought it unusual, *I* was perplexed when the High Sages acceded so swiftly to our

Captain-Leader's demand. I did not expect Vubben and Lester Cambel to obey so quickly, revealing the coordinates of the chief g'Kek encampment.'

Lark spoke at last. 'You mean Dooden Mesa.'

He still felt guilty over how a stray computer resonance betrayed the secret colony's location. Apparently, Ewasx thought the transmission had been made on purpose.

'Dooden Mesa, correct. The timing of the signal now seems too convenient, too out of character. Memory stacks inherited from *Asx* indicate a disgusting level of interspecies loyalty among the mongrel races of Jijo. Loyalty that should have delayed compliance with our demand. Normally the sages would have dithered, in hopes of evacuating the g'Keks before giving in.'

'Why did you have to wait for a signal at all?' Lark asked. 'If you've got memories from Asx, you knew all along where Dooden was! Why bother asking the High Sages?'

For the first time, Lark saw signs of what might be called an emotional response. Uneven ripples coursed several Ewasx rings, as if they were writhing from unpleasant sensations within. When it spoke next, the voice seemed briefly labored.

'Reasons for incomplete data retrieval access are not your concern. Suffice it to say that the immurement of Dooden Mesa was gratifying to our *Polkjhy* Ship Commanders ... yet I/we nursed brooding reservations within this stack of restless rings. The timing seemed too convenient.'

'What do you mean?'

'I mean that the signal came *just* as we were about to launch our remaining corvette to succor another, which had made a forced landing beyond the mountains. That mission was postponed on learning where the chief g'Kek hideout lay. The corvette was outfitted with toporgic, to attack our sworn feud enemies, lest any escape that nest of wheeled vipers.'

Lark caught Rann glancing at Ling, meaningfully. *Beyond the mountains.* The Daniks had sent Kunn's scout vessel out that way, just before the Battle of the Glade. And now the Jophur reported losing a corvette in the same direction?

Not lost. A forced landing. Still, they have strange priorities. Vengeance before rescue.

'After dealing with Dooden Mesa, there were other delays. Then, just as we were resuming preparations to send aid to our grounded cousins, this new distraction came about. I refer to your activity below the lake. You cleverly found some rude way to vibrate the toporgic seal around the Rothen ship. We ignored this at first, since mere sooners could never actually penetrate the cocoon—'

Another tremor crossed the creature's rings, though this time the voice did not pause.

'Soon, however, there came a distraction we could *not* ignore. The appearance of three humans at the surface of the lake, deep within our perimeter! This event triggered alarms, concentrating our attention for a lengthy period.

'I/we are now quite certain that was your intent all along.'

Lark stared in astonishment.

Just after they were captured, he and Ling had speculated in whispers about Rann's betrayal, swimming to the surface and using the portable computer to blatantly attract Jophur attention. Ling had illuminated a likely motive.

'Rann is more loyal to our masters than I ever imagined. He knows the Six Races possess evidence that can blow the lid off the grand Rothen deception. Helping our crew mates escape the trapped ship would just make matters worse, by exposing more Daniks to your arguments, Lark. Your evidence of genocide and other wrongs. Like me, they might be converted away from our lords.

'Before allowing that to happen, Rann would rather let the Jophur wipe out everybody, and leave our crew sealed forever. At least that way the Rothen home clan might be safe.'

Ling's explanation had rocked Lark. But *this* one from Ewasx was weirder still.

'You're saying we . . . uh, *vibrated* the golden shell around the submerged ship . . . *in order* to attract your attention? And when that didn't work, we swam up to the surface to make even more noise, trying to draw your gaze our way?'

As he said the words, Lark realized in surprise that the scenario made more sense than what had actually happened! In comparison, it did seem improbable that primitive sooners would find a way to pierce the toporgic trap . . . or that a Danik would betray his crew mates in order to keep them buried forever. There was just one logical problem.

'But . . . ' he went on. 'But *why* would we be desperate enough to do such a thing? What aim could make such a sacrifice worthwhile?'

The Jophur emitted an aggravated sigh.

'You know perfectly well what aim. However, in order to establish a clear basis for interrogation, I will explain.

'I/we know your secret,' it told Lark.

'You must certainly be in communication with the Earthling ship.'

The dolphins haven't given a name to this mountain of abandoned starships. This heap of discards from a lost civilization, moldering at the bottom of the Midden.

Huck wants to call it *Atlantis*. But for once I find her suggestion lacking imagination.

I prefer that mythical place described so hauntingly by the great Clarke. The *Seven Suns*. Where my namesake found ancient relics long forgotten by titans who had moved on, leaving their obsolete servants behind.

Remnants of a mighty past, now lost between the city and the stars.

We don't spend much time together anymore. We four from Wuphon Port. We four comrades and adventurers. We've gone off in different directions, led by our own obsessions.

Ur-ronn spends her time where you'd expect – in the engine room, eagerly learning about the hardware of a starship and getting thick as thieves with Hannes Suessi. I get an impression these dolphins aren't as good at delicate hand-eye work as an urs, so Suessi seems glad to have her around.

It's also the *driest* place aboard this waterlogged cruiser. Still, I figure Ur-ronn would spend time down there even if it meant sloshing through knee-deep slush. It's where a smith belongs.

Suessi hoped we might offer clues toward ridding *Streaker's* hull of a thick carbon coating. Oral traditions speak of *star soot*, weighing down each sneakship that reached Jijo after passing close by Izmunuti. But I never heard of a clan trying to remove it. Why would our ancestors bother, since they scuttled their arks soon after arriving?

Anyway, why not just refurbish one of the old hulks lying under the Midden, and use it to make an escape?

Ur-ronn says Suessi and Dr. Baskin considered the idea. But the ships are junk, after all. If the wrecks could fly well, wouldn't the Buyur have taken them along?

For helping the engineers, Ur-ronn hopes to get some cooperation in return ... fulfilling the assignment we were given when our little homemade *Wuphon's Dream* first dropped to the sea by Terminus Rock. Uriel had asked us to find a hidden cache – equipment to help the High Sages deal with intruding starships.

Now that we know more about those invaders – a Rothen cruiser, followed later by a Jophur battleship – it seems unlikely that cache would help against forces so godlike and lofty. Anyway, Uriel and our parents must have given us up for dead, ever since the air hose tore away from *Wuphon's Dream*.

Still, Ur-ronn's right. An oath is an oath.

I can see why Dr. Gillian Baskin prefers we don't contact our folks. But I must persuade her to try.

Pincer-Tip spends most of his time with the Kiqui – those six-limbed amphibians we once thought to be masters of this ship. Instead, they are something even more revered in the Five Galaxies – honest-to-goodness presapient beings. Pincer seems to have an affinity for them, since his red qheuen race is also adapted to live where waves meet a rocky coast. But that may just begin to cover Pincer's attraction to them.

He talks of building a new bathy to explore the Midden. Not just this mound of dead starcraft, but some of the vast jumbled cities, filled with wonders discarded by the departing Buyur.

Clearly he enjoyed his brief stint as captain of *Wuphon's Dream*. Only this time he hopes for a new crew. Agile, obedient, water-loving Kiqui may be ideal, compared to a too-tall hoon, a prolix g'Kek, and a hydrophobic urs.

Maybe Pincer still hopes to find real monsters.

Huck refuses to believe anything important can take place without her. As soon as we returned with Lieutenant Tsh't, she got involved in the serious business of questioning the Jophur prisoners, taken from the wrecked scoutship.

According to spy and adventure novels, the art of interrogation has a lot to do with language trickery. Fooling the other guy into blurting out something he never intended. That's just the kind of stuff Huck thinks she's oh so clever at. So what if Jophur are different from traeki. She expected to break their obstinate silence and get them talking.

So imagine her shock when she rolled into their chamber and the very sight of her sent them into a fit, throwing themselves against the restraining field trying to get at her! The room filled with a stench of pure hatred.

Strangely enough, that proved useful! For the Jophur abruptly lost their sullen muteness and started babbling. Mostly, their GalTwo and GalFive utterance streams were steeped with fuming anger. But soon the sneaky Niss Machine popped in, making insinuations and smooth-voiced hints . . .

Huck turned all four eyestalks to stare at the whirling hologram when it suggested the Jophur might be given this tasty g'Kek, if they cooperated! Soon, mixed among the vengeance vows and retribution exclamatives were bits of useful information, such as the name of their ship and the rank of its Captain-Leader. And one further crucial fact. Although their battlecruiser is a giant compared to outmatched *Streaker*, the Jophur ship came to Jijo alone.

Huck says she knew all along that the Niss was bluffing about handing her over. In fact, she claimed a triumph, as if it had been her plan all along.

I knew better than to comment on the green sweat coating her eye hoods. After the interview, she needed a bath.

Unlike the others, I can't banish all doubt.

Have we chosen the right side?

Oh, there seem to be good reasons for throwing our fate in with these fugitives. Humans are members of the Six, and that makes the dolphins sort of cousins, I guess. And it's true that *Streaker* seems more like one of our sooner sneakships than those arrogant dreadnoughts, up in the Rimmer Range. Anyway, I was brought up reading Earthling tall tales. My sentiments are drawn to the underdog.

Still, I must keep at least one mental corner detached and uncommitted. My loyalty lies ultimately with family, sept, and clan ... and with the High Sages of the Commons of Jijo.

Among the four of us, someone must remember our true priorities. A time may come when they clash with our hosts'.

How have I kept busy all this time?

For one thing, I've been learning to skim the ship's database, extracting historical summaries of what's taken place since the Great Printing. The distilled tale is a treat to a born info hound like me.

And yet, I still can't get that big, mist-shrouded cube out of my mind. Sometimes I hanker to sneak into that cold room and ask questions of the Branch Library – a storehouse so great that the Biblos Archive might as well be a primer for a two-year old.

On our way back from the surface I got to know Rety – the irascible, proud human girl whose illegal tribe of savages would have shaken the Commons with a sensational scandal, in normal times. I also talked to Dwer the Hunter, who I recall visiting Wuphon, a few years back. Dwer chatted about his adventures while Physician Makanee treated his wounds, till he fell into exhausted slumber. Soon Rety collapsed, too, with her little 'husband' curled alongside, a slim urrish head draped across her chest.

*

For the most part, my job has been to umble.

Yeah, that's right. To umble for a noor.

My own pet, Huphu, doesn't know what to make of the new-comer – the one called *Mudfoot*. On first spying him, she hissed ... and he hissed back, exactly like a regular noor. It was such a normal reaction that I started to doubt my own memory. Did I really hear and see Mudfoot *talk*?

My assigned task is to keep him happy till he decides to talk again.

I guess I owe these people – Gillian Baskin and Tsh't and the dolphins. They saved us from the abyss ... though maybe we wouldn't have fallen at all, if it hadn't been for their interference.

They fixed my broken back ... though it was injured when *they* smashed *Wuphon's Dream*.

They turned a mere adventure into an epic ... but won't let us go home for fear we'd tell the tale.

All right, dammit. I'll umble for the silly noor. He preens and acts starved for sound anyway, after months with just humans for company.

Up close I *can* sense a difference in him. I used to glimpse the same thing now and then, in the eyes of a few strange noor loung-ing on the Port Wuphon docks.

A sleek arrogance.

A kind of lazy smugness.

The impression that he's in on a great joke. One *you* won't figure out till there's egg all over your face.

EWASX

The human captives seem obdurate, My rings, refusing to answer questions. Or else they obfuscate with blatant lies.

QUERY/INTERROGATIVE:

Is there similarity between their behavior and the way *you* misled *Me*?

The way you rings have blurred so many of the waxy memories we coinherited from Asx?

The way our union oscillates between grudging cooperation and intermittent passive resistance?

It is enough to provoke unpleasant questions.

DON'T YOU LIKE BEING PART OF OUR MUCH-IMPROVED SHARED WHOLE? OUR AMBITIOUS ONENESS?

Yes, the majority of you claim gladness to be part of a great Jophur entity, instead of a tepid traeki mélange. But can I/we really be sure that you/we love Me/us?

The question is, in itself, a possible symptom of madness. What naturally cojoined Jophur would allow itself to entertain such doubts? The *Polkjhy* Priest-Stack predicted this hybridization experiment would fail. The priest foretold it would be useless to impose a master torus onto traeki rings already set in their ways.

A metaphor floats upward, along abused trails of half-molten wax.

Are you trying to make a comparison, O second ring-of-cognition?

Ah, yes. I/we see it.

Forging a noble Jophur out of disparate traeki cells *might* seem like trying to tame a herd of wild beasts. It is an apt analogy.

Too bad the metaphor does nothing to help solve My/our problem.

WHAT SECRETS LIE BURIED in the melted areas? What memories did the traeki High Sage purposely destroy, during those stressful moments before Asx was converted? I/we can tell, important evidence once glimmered in those layers that lined our common core. Something Jophur were not meant to know.

But know it we/I shall.

I must!

SUGGESTION:

Perhaps we can tear information out of these recently seized humans.

The ones bearing the name attributes, *Lark*, *Ling*, and *Rann*.

REBUTTAL:

The Priest-Stack vents frustrated steam, upset to learn how little data about Earthlings is contained in our shipboard Library. We have many detailed prescriptions for truth serums or coercion drugs effective against our races and species who are foes of the Great Jophur, but the archives carry no record of any substance that is human-specific. Our Library clearly needs updating, despite the fact that it is a relatively new unit, less than a thousand years old.

One tactician stack, assigned to our shipboard planning staff, proposed that we use interrogation techniques designed against *Tymbrimi*. Those devil tricksters are close allies of Earthlings, and appear similar in ways that go beyond bipedal locomotion. Trying out that suggestion, we tried projecting psi-compulsion waves at the prisoners, tuned to Tymbrimi empathic frequencies.

But the humans seemed deaf to the pulses, showing no reaction at all.

Meanwhile, the Captain-Leader vents irate fumes – acrid vapors that send all off-duty personnel fleeing from its presence.

What is the cause of such rancor, My rings? Recent news from beyond the nearby hills.

Bitter news confirming our fears. Disaster to the east.

AT LAST, our remaining corvette reached the site where its twin fell silent, two days ago. Aboard the *Polkjhy*, I/we all stared in dismay at relayed images of devastation.

Hull wreckage lay sunk beneath swampy waters – the sort of marshland morass where a traeki might find it pleasant to wallow while contemplating wax drippings. Windblown rain swept the area while searchers scanned for survivors, but all they found were remnants – mostly singleton rings, reverting to a feral animal state, instinctively gathering nests of rotting vegetation, as if they were no more than primitive pretraeki.

Several of these surviving toruses were harvested. By scraping their cores, we managed to download a few blurry memory tracks. Enough to suggest that *dolphins* did this deed, emerging from the sea to play havoc with our brethren.

HOW WERE THEY ABLE TO DO THIS?

The downed corvette had reported defense systems functional at a forty percent level. More than adequate, if concentrated against just such a sortie by the desperate Earthling quarry. Even amid a lightning-charged thunderstorm, it should not have been possible for the cornered prey to mount a surprise attack. Yet, even not an alarm signal escaped our grounded boat before it was mysteriously overwhelmed.

Again, doubts rise to disturb us. The wolflings are said to be primitives, not much more capable than the sooner savages whose coward ancestors settled this world. Yet these same Earthers have sent all Five Galaxies into turmoil, repeatedly escaping mighty fleets sent after them.

Perhaps it was a mistake for our *Polkjhy* ship commune to take on this mission alone, with just our one mighty battlecruiser to seize destiny for our mankind.

SCENT RUMORS SPREAD THROUGH *POLKJHY* NOW, alleging the Captain-Leader was deficiently stacked. Subversive pheromones suggest that flawed decision-processing toruses brought us to this unsavory state. Our commander was blinded by obsession with vengeance on the g'Kek, ignoring higher priorities.

Furious to find mutinous molecules wafting through the air ducts, our Captain-Leader seeks to overwhelm them with his own chemical outpourings – a steamy concoction of smoldering rejection. Perfumes of domineering essence flood all decks.

What is it now, My ring?

Ah. Our second torus-of-cognition has come up with another metaphor, this time comparing the Captain-Leader to the skipper of a hoonish sailboat, who tries shouting down his worried crew, using a loud voice to substitute for real leadership.

Very interesting, My ring – making parallels between alien behavior and Jophur ship politics. Such insights make this irksome union seem almost worthwhile.

Unless . . .

Surely you do not ALSO apply this metaphor to your own master ring?

Do not provoke Me. Be warned. It would be a mistake.

OUR PROBLEM REMAINS.

Unlike the tactician stacks, I/we do not attribute wolfling success against our corvette to anomalous technology, or luck. The timing was too coincidental. I am convinced the dolphins knew exactly the right moment to attack, when our attention was diverted by events close by.

CONCLUSION: The savage races MUST be in communication with the Earthship!

The captive humans deny knowing of any contact with the dolphin ship. They claim their activities at the lake surface were strictly a manifestation of interhuman dominance struggles, having nothing to do with the prey ship.

They must be lying. Ways must be found to increase their level of cooperation.

(If only I could lace their apelike cores with silvery fibers, the way a master ring shows other components of a stack how to cooperate in joyful oneness!)

We must, it seems, fall back on classic, barbarous interrogation techniques.

Shall we threaten the humans with bodily damage? Shall we assail them with metaphysical torment?

Overruling My/our expertise, the Captain-Leader has decided on a technique that is known to be effective against numerous warm-blooded races.

We shall use *atrocity*.

Traeki unguents filled her sinuses with pleasant numbness, as if she's had several glasses of wine. Sara felt the chemicals at work, chasing pain, making room for *herself* to reemerge.

A day after rejoining the world, she let Emerson push her wheelchair onto the stone veranda at Uriel the Smith's sanctuary, watching dawn break over a phalanx of royal peaks, stretching north and east. West of the mountains, dusty haze muted the manicolored marvel of the Spectral Flow, and the Plain of Sharp Sand beyond.

The view helped draw Sara's attention from the handheld mirror on her lap – lent her by Uriel – which she had examined all through breakfast. Jijo's broad vista made clear Emerson's quiet sermon.

The world is bigger than all our problems.

Sara handed the looking glass over to the starman, who performed sleight-of-hand motions, causing it to vanish up one sleeve of his floppy gown. Emerson grinned when Sara laughed out loud.

What's the point in dwelling on my stitches and scrapes, she thought. *Scars won't matter in the days to come. Any survivors will scratch their living from the soil. Pretty women won't have advantages. Tough ones will.*

Or was this complacence another result of chemicals in her veins? Potions tailored by Tyug, master alchemist of Mount Guenn Forge. Jijo's traekis had learned a lot about healing other races while qheuens, urs, hoons, and men fought countless skirmishes before the Great Peace. In recent years, texts from Biblos helped molecule maestros like Tyug supplement practical lore with fresh insights, using Anglic words like *peptide* and *enzyme*, reclaiming some of the knowledge their settler ancestors had abandoned.

Only not by looking it up in some Library. Earthling texts served as a starting point. A basis for fresh discoveries.

Which illustrated her controversial thesis. Six Races climbing back upward, not via Redemption's Path, the route their forebears used ... *but on a trail all our own.*

Other examples filled the halls behind this stony parapet, in workshops and labs where Uriel's staff labored near lava heat, wresting secrets from nature. Despite her suffering, Sara was glad to see more evidence on Mount Guenn that Jijoan civilization had begun heading in new directions.

Until starships came.

Sara winced, recalling what they had witnessed last night, from this same veranda. She and her friends were being regaled at a feast under the stars, celebrating her recovery. Hoonish sailors from the nearby seaport boomed festive ballads and Uriel's apprentices cavorted in an intricate dance while diminutive husbands perched on their backs, mimicking each twist and gyre. Gray qheuens, their broad chitin shells embellished with gemstone cloisonné, sculpted wicked impromptu caricatures of the party guests, using their adroit mouths to carve statuettes of solid stone.

Even Ulgor was allowed to take part, playing the violus, drawing rich vibrato tones as Emerson joined in with his dulcimer. The wounded starman had another unpredictable outburst of song, each verse pouring whole from some recessed memory.

'In a cottage of Fife,
lived a man and wife,
    who, believe me, were comical folk;
For to people's surprise,
they both saw with their eyes,
    and their tongues moved whenever they spoke!'

Then, as the feast was hitting its stride, there came a rude inter-ruption. Staccato flashes lit the northwest horizon, outlining the distant bulk of Blaze Mountain, drawing everyone to the balcony rim.

Duras passed before sounds arrived, smeared by distance to murmuring growls. Sara pictured lightning and thunder – like the storm that had drenched the badlands lately, drumming at her pain-soaked delirium. But then a chill coursed her spine, and she felt glad to have Emerson nearby. Some apprentices counted inter-vals separating each flash from its long-retarded echo.

Young Jomah voiced her own thoughts.

'Uncle, is Blaze Mountain erupting?'

Kurt's face had been gaunt and bleak. But it was Uriel who answered, shaking her long head.

'No, lad. It's not an erufshun. I think . . .'

She peered across the poison desert.

'I think it is Ovoon Town.'

Kurt found his voice. The words were grim.

'Detonations. Sharp. Well-defined. Bigger than my guild could produce.'

Realization quenched all thought of revelry. The biggest city on the Slope was being razed, and they could only watch, helplessly. Some prayed to the Holy Egg. Others muttered hollow vows of vengeance. Sara heard one person explain dispassionately why the outrage was taking place on a clear night – so the violence would be visible from much of the Slope, a demonstration of irresistible power.

Awed by the lamentable spectacle, Sara had been incapable of coherent thought. What filled her mind were images of *mothers* – hoonish mothers, g'Kek mothers, humans, and even haughty qheuen queens – clutching their children as they abandoned flaming, collapsing homes. The visions stirred round her brain like a cyclone of ashes, till Emerson gave her a double dose of traeki elixir.

Dropping toward a deep, dreamless sleep, she had one last thought.

Thank God that I never accepted Sage Taine's proposal of marriage ... I might have had a child of my own by now.

This is no time ... to allow so deep a love.

Now, by daylight, Sara found her mind functioning as it had before her accident – rapidly and logically. She was even able to work out a context for last night's calamity.

Jop and Dedinger will preach we should never have had cities in the first place. They'll say the Galactics did us a favor by destroying Ovoom Town.

Sara recalled legends her mother used to read aloud, from books of folklore covering many pre-contact Earthling traditions. *Most Earth cultures told sagas of some purported golden age in the past, when people knew more. When they had more wisdom and power.*

Many myths went on to describe angry gods, vengefully toppling the works of prideful mortals, lest men and women think themselves worthy of the sky. No credible evidence ever supported such tales, yet the story seemed so common it must reflect something deep and dour within the human psyche.

Maybe my personal heresy was always a foolish dream, and my notion of 'progress' based on concocted evidence. Even if Uriel and others had begun to embark on a different path, the point seems moot now.

Dedinger proved right, after all.

As in those legends, the gods have resolved to pound us down.

Confirmation of the outrage came later by semaphore – the same system of flashing mirrors that had surprised Sara days ago, when a stray beam caught her eye during the steep climb from Xi. Using a code based on simplified GalTwo, the jittering signal followed a twisty route from one Rimmer peak to the next, carrying clipped reports of devastation by the River Gentt.

Then, a few miduras later, an *eyewitness* arrived, swooping out of the sky like some fantastic beast of fable, landing on Uriel's stone parapet. A single human youth emerged beneath shuddering wings, unstrapping himself after a daring journey across the wide desert, skimming from one thermal updraft to the next in a feat that would have caused a sensation during normal times.

But heroism and miraculous deeds are routine during war, Sara thought as crowds gathered around the young man. His limbs trembled with exhaustion as he peeled off the rewq that had protected his eyes above the Spectral Flow. He gave the Smith a militia salute when Uriel trotted out of the workshop grottoes.

'Before attacking Ovoom Town, the Jophur issued a two-part ultimatum,' he explained in a hoarse voice. 'Their first demand is that all g'Keks and traekis must head to special gathering zones.'

Uriel blew air through her nostril fringe, a resigned blast, as if she had expected something along these lines.

'And the second fortion of the ultinatun?'

She had to wait for her answer. Kepha, the horsewoman from Xi, arrived bearing a glass of water, which the pilot slurped gratefully, letting streams run down his chin. Most urrish eyes turned from the unpleasant sight. But Uriel stared patiently till he finished.

'Go on,' she prompted again, when the youth handed the empty glass back to Kepha with a smile.

'Um,' he resumed. 'The Jophur insist that the High Sages must give up the location of the dolphin ship.'

'*The dolphin shif?*' Uriel's hooves clattered on the flagstones. 'We heard vague stories of this thing. Gossif and conflicting hints told vy the Rothen. Have the Jophur now revealed what it's all avout?'

The courier tried to nod, only now *Tyug* had come forward, gripping the youth's head with several tentacles. He winced as the traeki alchemist secreted ointment for his sun- and windburns.

'It seems ... Hey, watch it!' He pushed at the adamant tendrils, then tried ignoring the traeki altogether.

'It seems these dolphins are the prey that brought both the Rothen and the Jophur to Galaxy Four in the first place. What's more, the Jophur say the sages must be in contact with the Earthling ship. Either we give up its location, or face more destruction, starting with Tarek Town, then lesser hamlets, until no building is left standing.'

Kurt shook his head. 'They're bluffin'. Even Galactics couldn't find all our wood structures, hidden under blur cloth.'

The courier seemed less sure. 'There are fanatics everywhere who think the end is here. Some believe the Jophur are agents of destiny, come to set us back on the Path. All such fools need do is start a fire somewhere near a building and throw some phosphorus on the flame. The Jophur can sniff the signal using their rainbow finder.'

Rainbow finder ... Sara pondered. *Oh, he means a spectrograph.* Jomah was aghast. 'People would do that?'

'It's already happened in a few places. Some folks have taken their local explosers hostage, forcing them to set off their charges. Elsewhere, the Jophur have established base camps, staffed by a dozen stacks and thirty or so robots, gathering nearby citizens for questioning.' His tone was bleak. 'You people don't know how lucky you have it here.'

Yet Sara wondered. How could the High Sages possibly give in to such demands? The g'Kek weren't being taken offplanet in order to restore their star-god status. As for the traeki, death might seem pleasant compared with the fate planned for them.

Then there was the 'dolphin ship.' Even the learned Uriel could only speculate if the High Sages truly were in contact with a bunch of fugitive Terran clients.

Perhaps it was emotional fatigue, or a lingering effect of Tyug's drug, but Sara's attention drifted from the litany of woes recited by the pilot. When he commenced describing the destruction and death at Ovoom, Sara steered her wheelchair to join Emerson, standing near the courier's glider.

The starman stroked its lacy wings and delicate spars, beaming with appreciation of its ingenious design. At first Sara thought it must be the same little flier she had seen displayed in a Biblos museum case – the last of its kind, left over from those fabled days just after the *Tabernacle* arrived, when brave aerial scouts helped human colonists survive their early wars. Over time, the art had been lost for lack of high-tech materials.

But this machine is new!

Sara recognized g'Kek weaving patterns in the fine fabric, which felt slick to the touch.

'It is a traeki secretion,' explained Tyug, having also abandoned the crowd surrounding the young messenger. The alchemist shared Emerson's preference for physical things, not words.

'i/we sample-tasted a thread. The polymer is a clever filamentary structure based on mulc fiber. No doubt it will find other uses in piduras to come, as our varied schemes converge.'

There it was again. Hints of a secret stratagem. A scheme no one had yet explained, though Sara was starting to have suspicions.

'Forgive us/me for interrupting your contemplation, honored Saras and Emersons,' Tyug went on. 'But a scent message has just activated receptor sites on my/our fifth sensory torus. The simplified meaning is that Sage Purofsky desires your presences, in proximity to his own.'

Sara translated Tyug's awkward phrasing.

In other words, no more goofing off. It's time to get back to work. Back to Uriel's den of mysteries.

Sara saw that the Smith had already departed, along with Kurt, leaving Chief Apprentice Urdonnol to finish debriefing the young pilot. Apparently, even such dire news was less urgent than the task at hand.

Calculating problems in orbital mechanics, Sara pondered. *I still don't see how that will help get us out of this fix.*

She caught Emerson's eye, and with some reluctance he turned away from the glider. But when the star voyager bent over Sara to tuck in the corners of her lap blanket, he made eye contact and shared an open smile. Then his strong hands aimed her wheelchair down a ramp into the mountain, toward Uriel's fantastic Hall of Spinning Disks.

I feel like a g'Kek, rolling along. Perhaps all humans should spend a week confined like this, to get an idea what life is like for others.

It made her wonder how the g'Kek used to move about in their 'natural' environment. According to legend, those were artificial colonies floating in space. Strange places, where many of the assumptions of planet-bound existence did not hold.

Emerson skirted ruts countless generations of urrish hooves had worn in the stone floor. He picked up the pace when they passed a vent pouring fumes from the main forge, keeping his body between her and waves of volcanic heat.

In fact, Sara was almost ready to resume walking on her own. But it felt strangely warming to wallow for a time in their reversed roles.

She had to admit, he was good at it. Maybe he had a good teacher.

Normally, Prity would have been the one pushing Sara's chair. But the little chimp was busy, perched on a high stool in Uriel's sanctuary with a pencil clutched in one furry hand, drawing arcs across sheets of ruled graph paper. Beyond Prity's work easel stretched a vast underground chamber filled with tubes, pulleys, and disks, all linked by gears and leather straps – a maze of shapes whirling on a timber frame, reaching all the way up to a vaulted ceiling. In the sharp glare of carboacetylene lanterns, tiny figures could be seen scurrying about the scaffolding, tightening and lubricating – nimble urrish males, among the first ever to find useful employment outside their wives' pouches, earning a good income by tending the ornate 'hobby' of Uriel the Smith.

When Sara first saw the place, squinting through her fever, she had thought it a dream vision of hell. Then a wondrous thing happened. The spinning glass shapes began *singing* to her.

Not in sound, but light. As they turned, rolling their rims against one another, narrow beams reflected from mirrored surfaces, glittering like winter moonbeams on the countless facets of a frozen waterfall. Only there was more to it than mere gorgeous randomness. Patterns. Rhythms. Some flashes came and went with the perfect precision of a clock, while others performed complex, wavelike cycles, like rolling surf. With the fey sensitivity of a bared subconscious, she had recognized an overlapping harmony of shapes. Ellipses, parabolas, catenaries ... a nonlinear serenade of geometry.

It's a computer; she had realized, even before regaining the full faculties of her searching mind. And for the first time since departing her Dolo Village tree house, she had felt at home.

It is another world.

My world.

Mathematics.

BLADE

He might have stayed down longer. but after three or four miduras, the air in his leg bladders started growing stale. Even a full-size blue qheuen needs to breathe at least a dozen times a day. So by the time filtered sunlight penetrated to his murky refuge, Blade knew he must abandon the cool river bottom that had sheltered him through the night's long firestorm. He fought the Gentt current, digging all five claws into the muddy bank, climbing upward till at last it was possible to raise his vision cupola above the water's smeary surface.

It felt as if he had arrived at damnation day.

The fabled towers of Ovoom Town had survived the deconstruction age, then half a million years of wind and rain. Vanished were the sophisticated machines that made it a vibrant Galactic outpost. Those had been taken long ago by the departing Buyur, along with nearly every windowpane. Yet, even despite ten thousand gaping openings, the surviving shells had been luxury palaces to the six exile races – providing room for hundreds of apartments and workshops – all linked by shrewd wooden bridges, ramps, and camouflage lattices.

Now only a few jagged stumps protruded through a haze of dust and soot. Sunshine beat down from a glaring sky, showing how futile had been every cautious effort at concealment.

Picking his way along the riverbank, now cluttered with blocks of shattered stone, Blade encountered a more gruesome kind of debris – *bodies* floating in back eddies of the river, along with varied dismembered parts ... biped limbs, g'Kek wheels, and traeki toruses. In the qheuen manner, he did not wince or experience revulsion while claw-stepping past the drifting corpses, but hoped that someone would organize a collection of the remains for proper mulching. Little was gained by maundering over the dead.

Blade felt more disturbed by the chaos at the docks, where several collapsing spires had fallen across the riverside piers and warehouses. Not a single ship or coracle appeared untouched.

Pausing to watch one crew of disconsolate hoons examine their once-beautiful craft, Blade felt a brief surge of hope when he recognized the ship, and saw its gleaming wooden hull had survived intact! Then he realized – all the masts and rigging were gone. Bubbles of disappointment escaped three of five leg vents.

Just yesterday, Blade had booked passage aboard that vessel. Now he might as well toss the paper ticket from his moisture pouch to join the other flotsam drifting out to sea.

Much of that dross had been alive till last night, when the starry sky lit up with the spectacle of a Galactic god ship, arriving well ahead of its own shock wave, announcing its sudden arrival instead with a blare of braking engines. Then it glided a complacent circle above Ovoom Town, as gracefully imperturbable as a fat, predatory fish.

The sight had struck Blade as both beautiful and terrible.

At last, an amplified voice boomed forth, declaring a ritual ultimatum in a dense, traekilike dialect of Galactic Two.

Blade had already been through too many adventures to stand and gawk. The lesson taught by experience was simple – when someone much bigger and nastier than you starts making threats, get out! He barely listened to the roar of alien words as he joined an exodus of the prudent. Racing toward the river, Blade made it with kiduras to spare.

Even when ten meters of turbulent brown liquid lay overhead, he could not shut out what followed. Searing blasts, harsh flashes, and screams.

Especially the screams.

Now, under the sun of a new day, Blade found all the concept facets of his mind overwhelmed by a scene of havoc. The biggest population center on the Slope, a once-vibrant community of art and commerce, lay in complete ruins. At the center of devastation, buildings had not simply been toppled, but pulverized to a fine dust that trailed eastward, riding the prevailing breeze.

Had similar evil already befallen Tarek Town, where the pleasant green Roney met the icy Bibur? Or Dolo Village, whose fine dam sheltered the prosperous hive of his aunts and mothers? Though Blade had grown up near humans, he now found that stress drove Anglic out of his mind. For now, the logic of his private thoughts worked better in Galactic Six.

My situation – it seems hopeless.

To Mount Guenn – there is no longer a path by ocean ship.

With Sara and the others – I cannot now rendezvous.

So much for my promise . . . So much for my vow.

Other qheuens were rising out of the water nearby, their cupolas bobbing to the surface like a scattering of corks. Some venturesome blues had already reached the ruined streets ahead of Blade, offering their strong backs and claws to assist rescue parties, searching through the rubble of fallen towers for survivors. He also saw a few reds and several giant grays, who must have somehow survived the night of horrors without a freshwater refuge. Some appeared wounded and all were dust-coated, but they set to work alongside hoon, humans, and others.

A qheuen feels uneasy without a duty to fulfill. Some obligation that can be satisfied, like a scratched itch, through service. On the original race homeworld, gray matrons used to exploit that instinct ruthlessly. But Jijo had changed things, promoting a different kind of fealty. Allegiance to more than a particular hive or queen.

Seeing no chance that he could accomplish his former goal and catch up with Sara, Blade consciously rearranged his priority facets, assigning himself a new short-term agenda.

Corpses meant nothing to him. He was unmoved by the dead majority of Ovoom Town. Yet he roused his bulk, pumping five legs into rapid motion, rushing to help those left with a spark of life.

Survivors and rescuers picked through the wreckage with exaggerated care, as if each overturned stone might conceal danger.

Like most settlements, this one had been mined by a chapter of the Explosers Guild, preparing the city for deliberate razing if ever the long-prophesied Judgment Day arrived. But when it finally came, the manner was not as foreseen by the scrolls. There were no serene, dispassionate officials from the great Institutes, ordaining evacuation and tidy demolition, then weighing the worth of each race by how far it had progressed along the Path of Redemption. Instead there had poured down an abrupt and cruelly impartial cascade of raging flame, efficient only at killing, igniting some of the carefully placed charges that the explosers had reverently tended for generations . . . and leaving others smoldering like booby traps amid the debris.

When the exploders' local headquarters blew up, a huge fireball had risen so high that it briefly licked the underbelly of the Jophur corvette, forcing a hurried retreat. Even now, several miduras after the attack, delayed blasts still rocked random parts of town, disrupting mercy efforts, setting rubble piles tottering.

Matters improved when urrish volunteers from a nearby caravan galloped into town. With their sensitive nostrils, the urs sniffed for both unexploded charges and living flesh. They proved especially good at finding unconscious or hidden humans, whose scene they found pungent.

Miduras of hard labor merged into a blur. By late afternoon, Blade was still at it, straining on a rope, helping clear the stubborn obstruction over a buried basement. The rescue team's ad hoc leader, a hoonish ship captain, boomed out rhythmic commands.

'Hr-r-rm, now *pull*, friends! . . . *Again*, it's coming! . . . And *again*!'

Blade staggered as the stone block finally gave way. A pair of nimble lorniks and a lithe chimpanzee dived through the exposed opening, and soon dragged out a g'Kek with two smashed wheel rims. The braincase was intact, however, and all four eyestalks waved a dance of astounded gratitude. The survivor looked young and strong. Rims could be repaired, and spokes would reweave all by themselves.

But where will he live until then? Blade wondered, knowing that g'Keks preferred city life, not the nearby jungle where many of Ovoom's citizens had fled. *Will it be a world worth rolling back to, or one filled with Jophur-designed viruses and hunter robots, programmed to satisfy an ancient vendetta?*

The work crew was about to resume its unending task when a shrill cry escaped the traeki who had been assigned lookout duty, perched on a nearby rubble pile with its ring-of-sensors staring in all directions at once.

'Observe! All selves, alertly turn your attentions in the direction indicated!'

A pair of tentacles aimed roughly south and west. Blade lifted his heavy carapace and tried bringing his cupola to bear, but it was dust-coated and he had no water to clean it. *If only qheuens had been blessed with better eyesight.*

By Ifni, right now I'd settle for tear ducts.

An object swam into view, roughly spherical, moving languidly above the forested horizon, as if bobbing like a cloud. Lacking any perspective for such a strange sight, Blade could not tell at first how big it was. Perhaps the titanic Jophur battleship had come, instead of dispatching its little brother! Were the Jophur returning to finish the job? Blade remembered tales of Galactic war weapons far worse than the corvette had used last night. Weapons capable of melting a continent's crust. A mere river would prove no refuge, if the aliens meant to use such tools.

But no. He saw the globelike surface *ripple* in an unsteady breeze. It appeared to be made of fabric, and much smaller than he had thought.

Two more globelike forms followed the leader into view, making a threesome convoy. Blade instinctively switched organic filters in his cupola, observing them in infrared. At once he saw that each flying thing carried a sharp heat glow beneath, suspended by cables from the globe itself.

Others standing nearby – those with sharper eyesight – passed through several reactions. First anxious dread, then puzzlement, and finally a kind of joyful wonder they expressed with shrill laughter or deep, umbling tones.

'What is it?' asked a nearby red qheuen, even more dustblind than Blade.

'I think—' Blade began to answer. But then a human cut in, shading his eyes with both hands.

'They're balloons! By Drake and Ur-Chown ... they're hot air balloons!'

A short time later, even the qheuens could make out shapes hung beneath the bulging gasbags. Urrish figures standing in wicker baskets, tending fire that intermittently flared with sudden, near-volcanic heat. Blade then realized who had come, as if out of the orange setting sun.

The smiths of Blaze Mountain must have seen last night's calamity from their nearby mountain sanctum. The smiths were coming to help succor their neighbors.

It seemed blasphemous, in a strange way. For the Sacred Scrolls had always spoken of *doom* arriving from the fearsome open sky.

Now it seemed the cloudless heavens could also bring virtue.

LESTER CAMBEL

He was too busy now to feel racked with conscience pangs. As commotion at the secret base neared a fever pitch, Lester had no time left for wallowing in guilt. There were slurry tubes to inspect – a pipeline threading its meandering way through the boo forest, carrying noxious fluids from the traeki synthesis gang to tall, slender vats where it congealed into a paste of chemically constrained hell.

Lester also had to approve a new machine for winding league after league of strong fiber cord around massive trunks of greatboo, multiplying their strength a thousandfold.

Then there was the matter of *kindling beetles*. One of his assistants had found a new use for an old pest – a dangerous, Buyur-modified insect that most Sixers grew up loathing, but one that might now solve an irksome technical problem. The idea seemed promising, but needed more tests before incorporating it in the plan.

Piece by piece, the scheme progressed from Wild-Eyed Fantasy all the way to Desperate Gamble. In fact, a local hoonish bookie was said to be covering bets at only sixty to one against eventual success – the best odds so far.

Of course, each time they overcame a problem, it was replaced by three more. That was expected, and Lester even came to look upon the growing complexity as a blessing. Keeping busy was the only effective way to fight off the same images that haunted his mind, replaying over and over again.

A golden mist, falling on Dooden Mesa. Only immersion in work could drive out the keening cries of g'Kek citizens, trapped by poison rain pouring from a Jophur cruiser.

A cruiser *he* had carelessly summoned, by giving in to his greatest vice – curiosity.

'*Do not blame yourself Lester,*' Ur-Jah counseled in a dialect of GalSeven. '*The enemy would have found Dooden soon anyway. Meanwhile, your research harvested valuable information. It helped lead to cures for the qheuen and hoonish plagues. Life consists of trade-offs, my friend.*'

Perhaps. Lester admitted things might work that way on paper. Especially if you assumed, as many did, that the poor g'Kek were doomed anyway.

That kind of philosophy comes easier to the urrish, who know that only a fraction of their offspring can or should survive. We humans wait for a lifetime if we lose a son or daughter. If we find urs callous, it's good to recall how absurdly sentimental we seem to them.

Lester tried to think like an urs.

He failed.

Now came news from the commandos who so bravely plumbed the lake covering the Glade of Gathering. Sergeant Jeni Shen reported partial success, freeing some Daniks from their trapped ship ... only to lose others to the Jophur, including the young heretic sage, Lark Koolhan. A net loss, as far as Lester was concerned.

What might the aliens be doing to poor Lark right now?

I never should have agreed to his dangerous plan.

Lester realized, he did not have the temperament to be a war leader. He could not *spend* people, like fuel for a fire, even as a price for victory.

When all this was over, assuming anyone survived, he planned to resign from the Council of Sages and become the most reclusive scholar in Biblos, creeping like a specter past dusty shelves of ancient tomes. Or else he might resume his old practice of meditation in the narrow Canyon of the Blessed, where life's cares were known to vanish under a sweet ocean of detached oblivion.

It sounded alluring – a chance to retreat from life.

But for now, there was simply too much to do.

The council seldom met anymore.

Phwhoon-dau who had made a lifelong study of the languages and ways of fabled Galactics, had responsibility for negotiating with the Jophur. Unfortunately, there seemed little to haggle about. Just futile pleading for the invaders to change their many-ringed minds. Phwhoon-dau sent repeated entreaties to the toroidal aliens, protesting that the High Sages knew nothing about the much-sought 'dolphin ship.'

Believe us, O great Jophur lords, the hoonish sage implored. *We have no secret channel of communication with your prey. The events you speak of were all unrelated . . . a series of coincidences.*

But the Jophur were too angry to believe it.

In attempting to negotiate, Phwhoon-dau was advised by Chorsh, the new traeki representative. But that replacement for Asx the Wise had few new insights to offer. As a member of the Tarek Town Explosers Guild, Chorsh was a valued technician, not an expert on distant Jophur cousins.

What Chorsh did have was a particularly useful talent – a *summoning torus*.

Shifting summer winds carried the traeki's scent message all over the Slope – a call from Chorsh to all qualified ring stacks.

Come . . . come now to where you/we are needed . . .

Hundreds of them already stood in single file, a chain of fatty heaps that stretched on for nearly a league, winding amid the gently bending trunks of boo. Each volunteer squatted on its own feast of decaying matter that work crews kept stoked, like feeding logs to a steam engine. Chuffing and smoking from exertion, the chem-synth gang dripped glistening fluids into makeshift troughs made of split and hollowed saplings, contributing to a trickle that eventually became a rivulet of foul-smelling liquor.

Immobile and speechless, they hardly looked like sentient

beings. More like tall, greasy beehives, laid one after another along a twisty road. But that image was deceiving. Lester saw swathes of color flash across the body of one nearby traeki – a subtle interplay of shades that rippled first between the stack's component rings, as if they were holding conversations among themselves. Then the pattern coalesced, creating a unified shape of light and shadows at the points that lay nearest to the traeki's neighbors, on either side. Those stacks, in turn, responded with changes in their own surfaces.

Lester recognized the wavelike motif – traeki *laughter*. The workers were sharing jokes, among their own rings and from stack to stack.

They are the strangest of the Six, Lester thought. *And yet we understand them ... and they, us.*

I doubt even the sophisticates of the Five Galaxies can say the same thing about the Jophur. Out there, none of their advanced science could achieve what we have simply by living next to traeki, day in and day out.

It was pretty crude humor, Lester could tell. Many of these workers were pharmacists, back in their home villages all over the Slope. The one nearest Lester had been speculating about alternative uses of the stuff they were making – perhaps how it might also serve as a cure for the perennial problem of hoonish constipation ... especially if accompanied by liberal applications of heat ...

At least that was how Lester interpreted the language of color. He was far from expert in its nuances. Anyway, these workers were welcome to a bit of rough-edged drollery. Their hard labor lasted day in, day out, and still production lagged behind schedule.

But more traeki arrived with each passing midura, following the scent trail emitted by their sage.

Now we have to hope that the Jophur are too advanced and urbane to use the same technique, and trace our location by reading the winds.

The qheuen sage, Knife-Bright Insight, bore all the duties of civil administration on her broad blue back.

There were refugees to relocate, food supplies to organize, and militia units to dispatch, quashing outbreaks of civil war among the Six. One clear success came lately in subduing foreign plagues, duplicating the samples Jeni Shen brought from the Glade Lake, then using a new network of glider couriers to distribute vaccines.

Yet despite such successes, the social fabric of the Commons continued dissolving. News arrived telling of sooner bands departing across the official boundaries of the Slope, seeking to escape the doom threatened for the Six Races. The Warril Plain was aflame with fighting among hot-tempered urrish clans. And more bad news kept rolling in.

Recent reports told of several hives of Gray Queens declaring open secession from the Commons, asserting sovereignty over their ancient domains. Spurred by the devastation of Ovoom Town, some rebel princesses even rejected their own official High Sage.

'We accept no guidance from a mere blue,' came word from one gray hive, snubbing Knife-Bright Insight and resurrecting ancient bigotry.

'Come give us advice when you have a real name.'

Of course no red or blue qheuen ever used a *name*, as such. It was cruel and haughty to mention the handicap, inherited from ancient days and other worlds.

Worse, rumors claimed that some gray hives had started negotiating with the Jophur on their own.

A crisis can tear us apart, or draw us together.

Lester checked on the mixed team of qheuens and hoons who were erecting spindly scaffolding around selected spires of great-boo. Only a small fraction of the designated trunks had been trimmed and readied but the crews were getting better at their unfamiliar task. Some qheuens brought expertise learned from their grandmothers, who in olden times used to maintain fearsome catapults at Tarek Town, dominating two rivers until a great siege toppled that ancient reign.

So much activity might be detectable by prying sky eyes. But taller trunks surrounded each chosen one, drowning the tumult in a vast sea of Brobdingnagian grass.

Or so we hope.

Guiding the work, urrish and human craft workers pored over ancient designs found in a single rare Biblos text, dating from pre-contact days, dealing with an obscure wolfling technology that no Galactic power had needed or used for a billion years. Side by side, men and women joined their urs colleagues, adapting the book's peculiar concepts, translating its strange recipes to native materials and their own cottage skills.

Conditions were spartan. Many volunteers had already suffered privation, hiking great distances along steep mountain trails to reach this tract of tall green columns, stretching like a prairie as far as any eye could see.

All recruits shared a single motive – finding a way for the Commons of Six Races to fight back.

Amid the shouting throng, it was Ur-Jah who brought order out of chaos, galloping from one site to the next, making sure the traeki synthesists had food and raw material, and that every filament was wound tight. Of all the High Sages, Ur-Jah was most qualified to share Lester's job of supervision. Her pelt might be ragged with age and her brood pouches dry, but the mind in that narrow skull was sharp – and more pragmatic than Lester's had ever been.

Of the High Sages, that left only Vubben.

Judicious and knowing. Deep in perception. Leader of a sept that had been marked long ago for destruction by foes who never forgot, and never gave up. Among Jijo's exile races, Vubben's folk had been first to brave Izmunuti's stiffening winds, seeking Jijo's bright shoal almost two thousand years ago.

The wheeled g'Kek – both amiable and mysterious.

Neighborly, if weird.

Elfin but reliable.

Faceless, yet as open as a book.

How lessened the universe would be without them!

Despite their difficulty on rough trails, some g'Kek had made it to this remote mountain base, laboring to weave fabric, or applying their keen eyes to the problem of making small parts. Yet their own sage was nowhere in sight.

Vubben had gone south, to a sacred place dangerously near the Jophur ship. There, he was attempting in secret to commune with Jijo's highest power.

Lester worried about his wise friend with the squeaky axles, venturing down there all alone.

But someone has to do it.

Soon we'll know if we have been fools all along . . . or if we've put our faith in something deserving of our love.

FALLON

A domain of blinding whiteness marked the border of the Spectral Flow, where that slanting shelf of radiant stone abruptly submerged beneath an ocean of sparkling grains. North of this point commenced a different kind of desert – one that seemed less hard on the brain and eyes, but just as unforgiving. A desert where hardy life-forms dwelled.

Dangerous life-forms.

The escaped heretic's footprints transformed as they crossed the boundary. No longer did they *glow*, each with a unique lambency of oil-slick colors, telling truths and lies. Plunging ahead without pause, the tracks became mere impressions on the Plain of Sharp Sand – indentations that grew blurrier as gusty winds stroked the dunes – revealing only that someone recently came this way, a humanoid biped, favoring his left leg with a limp.

Fallon could tell one more thing – the hiker had been in an awful hurry.

'We can't follow anymore,' he told his young companions. 'Our mounts are spent, and this is Dedinger's realm. He knows it better than we do.'

Reza and Pahna stared at the sandy desert, no less dismayed than he. But the older one dissented – a sturdy redhead with a rifle slung over her shoulder.

'We must go on. The heretic knows everything. If he reaches his band of ruffians, they'll soon follow him back to Xi, attacking us in force. Or else he might trade our location to the aliens. The man must be stopped!'

Despite her vehemence, Fallon could tell Reza's heart was heavy. For several days they had chased Dedinger across the wasteland they knew – a vast tract of laminated rock so poisonous, a sliver under the skin might send you into thrashing fever. A place almost devoid of life, where daylight raised a spectacle of unlikely marvels before any unprotected eye – waterfalls and fiery pits, golden cities and fairy dust. Even night offered no rest, for moonbeams alone could make an unwary soul shiver as ghost shadows flapped at the edge of sight. Such were the terrible wonders of the Spectral Flow – in most ways a harsher territory than the mundane desert just ahead. So harsh that few Jijoans ever thought to explore its fringes, allowing the secret of Xi to remain safe.

Reza was right to fear the consequences, should Dedinger make good his escape – especially if the fanatic managed to reforge his alliance with the horse-hating clan of urrish cultists called the Urunthai. The fugitive should have succumbed to the unfamiliar dangers of the Flow by now. The three pursuers had expected to catch up with him yesterday, if not the day before.

It's my fault, Fallon thought. *I was too complacent. Too deliberate. My old bones can't take a gallop and I would not let the women speed on without me.*

Who would guess Dedinger could ride so well after so little practice, driving his stolen horse with a mixture of care and utter brutality, so the poor beast expired just two leagues short of this very boundary?

Even after that, his jogging pace kept the gap between them from closing fast enough. While the Illias preserved their beloved mares, the madman managed to cross ground that should have killed him first.

We are chasing a strong, resourceful adversary. I'd rather face a hoonish ice hermit, or even a Gray Champion, than risk this fellow with his back cornered against a dune.

Of course Dedinger must eventually run out of reserves, pushing himself to the limit. Perhaps the man lay beyond the next drift, sprawled in exhausted stupor.

Well, it did no harm to hope.

'All right.' Fallon nodded. 'We'll go. But keep a sharp watch. And be ready to move quick if I say so. We'll follow the trail till nightfall, then head back whether he's brought down or not.'

Reza and Pahna agreed, nudging their horses to follow. The animals stepped onto hot sand without enthusiasm, laying their ears back and nickering unhappily. Color-blind and unimaginative, their breed was largely immune to the haunting mirages of the Spectral Flow, but they clearly disliked this realm of glaring brightness. Soon, the three humans removed their rewq symbionts, pulling the living veils from over their eyes, trading them for urrish-made dark glasses with polarized coatings made of stretched fish membranes.

Ifni, this is a horrid place, Fallon thought, leaning left in his saddle to make out the renegade's tracks. *But Dedinger is at home here.*

In theory, that should not matter. Before ceding the position to his apprentice, Dwer, Fallon had been chief scout for the Council of Sages – an expert who supposedly knew every hectare of the Slope. But that was always an exaggeration. Oh, he *had* spent some time on this desert, getting to know the rugged, illiterate men who kept homes under certain hollow dunes, making their hard living by spear hunting and sifting for spica granules.

But I was much younger in those days, long before Dedinger began preaching to the sandmen, flattering and convincing them of their righteous perfection. Their role as leaders, blazing a way for humanity down the Path of Redemption.

I'd be a fool to think I still qualify as a 'scout' in this terrain. Sure enough, Fallon was taken by surprise when their trail crossed a stretch of booming sand.

The fugitive's footprints climbed up the side of a dune, following an arc that would have stressed the mounts to follow. Fallon decided to cut inside of Dedinger's track, saving time and energy ... but soon the sandy surface ceased cushioning the horse's hoofbeats. Instead, low groans echoed with each footfall, resonating like the sound of tapping on a drum. Cursing, he reined back. As an apprentice he once took a dare to jump in the center of a booming dune, and was lucky when it did not collapse beneath him. As it was, he spent the next pidura nursing an aching skull that kept on ringing from the reverberations he set off.

After laborious backtracking, they finally got around the obstacle.

Now Dedinger knows we're still after him. Fallon chided himself. *Concentrate, dammit! You have experience, use it!*

Fallon glanced back at the young women, whose secret clan of riders chose him to spend pleasant retirement in their midst, one of just four men dwelling in Xi's glades. Pahna was still a lanky youth, but Reza had already shared Fallon's bed on three occasions. The last time she had been kind, overlooking when he fell asleep too soon.

They claim experience and thoughtfulness are preferable traits in male companions – qualities that make up for declining stamina. But I wonder if it's a wise policy. Wouldn't they be better off keeping a young stallion like Dwer around, instead?

Dwer was far better equipped for this kind of mission. The lad would have brought Dedinger back days ago, all tied up in a neat package.

Well, you don't always have the ideal man on hand for every job. I just hope old Lester and the sages found a good use for Dwer. His gifts are rare.

Fallon had never been quite the 'natural' that his apprentice was. In times past, he used to make up for it with discipline and attention to detail. He had never been one to let his mind wander during a hunt.

But times change, and a man loses his edge. These days, he could not help drifting away to the past. Something always reminded him of other days, his past was so filled with riches.

Oh, the times he used to have, running across the steppe with Ul-ticho, his plains hunting companion whose grand life was heartbreakingly short. Her fellowship meant more to Fallon than any human's, before or since. No one else understood so well the silences within his restless heart.

Ul-ticho, be glad you never saw this year when things fell apart. Those times were better, old friend. Jijo was ours, and even the sky held no threat you and I couldn't handle.

Dedinger's tracks still lay in plain sight, turning the rim of a great dune. The marks grew steadily fresher, and his limp grew worse with every step. The fugitive was near collapse. Assuming he kept going, it would be a half midura, at most, before the mounted party caught him.

And still some distance short of the first shelter well. Not bad. We may pull this off yet.

Assumptions are a luxury that civilized folk can afford. But not warriors or people of the land. In those staggered footprints, Fallon read a reassuring story, and so violated a rule that he used to pound into his apprentice.

They were riding in the same direction as the wind, so no scent warned the animals before they turned, slanting down to the shadowed north side of the dune. Abruptly, a murmur of voices greeted them – shouts, filled with wrath, and danger. Before Fallon's blinking eyes could adjust to the changed light, he and the women found themselves staring down the shafts of a dozen or more cocked arbalests, all aimed their way, held by grizzled men wearing cloaks, turbans, and membrane goggles.

Now he made out a structure just ahead, shielded from the elements, made of piled stones. Fallon caught a belated sniff of water.

A new well? Built since I last came here as a young man? Or did I forget this one?

More likely, the desert men never told the visiting chief scout all their secret sites. Far better, from their point of view, to let the High Sages think their maps complete, while holding something in reserve.

Lifting his hands slowly and carefully away from the pistol at his belt, Fallon now saw Dedinger, sunburned and shaking as he clutched devoted followers – who tenderly poured water over the prophet's broken lips.

We came so close!

The hands holding Dedinger right now should have been Fallon's. They would have been, if only things had gone just a little differently.

I'm sorry, Fallon thought, turning in silent apology to Reza and Pahna. Their faces looked surprised and bleak.

I'm an old man ... and I let you down.

NELO

The battle for Dolo Village involved larger issues, but the principal thing decided was who would get to sleep indoors that night.

Most of the combatants were quite young, or very old.

In victory, the winners took possession of ashes. In defeat, the losers marched forth singing.

Aided by a few qheuen allies, the craft workers started the fight evenly matched against the fanatical followers of Jop the Zealot.

Both sides were angry, determined, and poorly armed with sticks and cudgels. Every man, woman, and qheuen of fighting age was away on militia duty, taking the swords and other weapons with them.

Even so, it was a wonder no one died in the melee.

Combatants swelled around the village meeting tree in a sweaty, disorderly throng, pushing and flailing at men who had been their neighbors and friends, raising a bedlam that blocked out futile orders by leaders of both sides. It might have gone on till everyone collapsed in hoarse exhaustion, but the conflict was abruptly decided when one side got unexpected reinforcements.

Brown-clad men dropped from the overhanging branches of the garu forest, where gardens of luscious, protein-rich moss created a rich and unique niche for agile human farmers. Suddenly outflanked and outnumbered, Jop and his followers turned and fled the debris-strewn valley.

'The zealots went too far,' said one gnarled tree farmer, explaining why his people dropped their neutrality to intervene. 'Even if they had an excuse to blow up the dam without guidance from the sages ... they should've warned the poor qheuens first! A murder committed in the name of reverence is still a crime. It's too high a toll to pay for following the Path.'

Nelo was still catching his breath, so Ariana Foo expressed thanks on the craft workers' behalf. 'There has already been enough blood spilled down the Bibur's waters. It is well past time for neighbors to care for one another, and heal these wounds.'

Despite confinement to her wheelchair, Ariana had been worth ten warriors during the brief struggle, without ever aiming or landing a blow. Her renowned status as the former High Sage of human sept meant that no antagonist dared confront her. It was as if a bubble of sanity moved through the mob, interrupting the riot, which resumed again as soon as she had passed. The sight of her helped decide the majority of farmers to come down off the garu heights and assist.

No one pursued Jop's forces as they retreated on canoes and makeshift rafts to the Bibur's other bank, re-forming on a crest of high ground separating the river from a vast swamp. There the zealots chanted passages from the Sacred Scrolls, still defiant.

Nelo labored for breath. It was as if his ribs were half torn loose from his side, and he could not tell for some time which pains were temporary, and which were from some fanatic's baton or quarterstaff. At least nothing seemed broken, and he grew more confident that his heart wasn't about to burst out of his chest.

So, Dolo has been won back, he thought, finding little to rejoice over in the triumph. Log Biter was dead, as well as Jobee and half of Nelo's apprentices. With his paper mill gone, along with the dam and qheuen rookery, the battle had been largely to decide who would take shelter in the remaining dwellings.

A makeshift infirmary was set up surrounding the traeki pharmacist, on a stretch of leaf-covered loam. Nelo spent some time sewing cuts with boiled thread, and laying plaster compresses on bruised comrades and foes alike.

The task of healing and stitching was hardly begun when a messenger dropped down from the skyway of rope bridges that laced the forest in all directions. Nelo recognized the lanky teenager, a local girl whose swiftness along the branchtop ways could not be matched. Still short of breath, she saluted Ariana Foo and recited a message from the commander of the militia base concealed some distance downriver.

'Two squads will get here before nightfall,' she relayed proudly. 'They'll send tents and other gear by tomorrow morn ... assuming the Jophur don't blow the boats up.'

It was fast action, but a resigned murmur was all the news merited. Any help now was too little, and far too late to save the rich, united community Dolo Village had been. No wonder Jop's people had been less tenacious, more willing to retreat. In their eyes, they had already won.

The Path of Redemption lies before us.

Nelo walked over to sit on a tree stump near the town exploser, whose destructive charges were commandeered and misused by Jop's mob. Henrik's shoulders slumped as he stared over the Bibur, past the shattered ruins of the craft shops, at the zealots chanting on the other side.

Nelo wondered if his own face looked as bleak and haggard as Henrik's.

Probably not. To his own great surprise, Nelo found himself in a mood to be philosophical.

'Never have seen such a mess in all my days,' he said, with a resigned sigh. 'I guess we're gonna have our hands full, rebuilding.'

Henrik shook his head, as if to say, *It can't be done.*

This, in turn, triggered a flare of resentment from Nelo. What business did Henrik have, wallowing in self-pity? As an exploser, his professional needs were small. Assisted by his guild, he could be back in business within a year. But even if Log Biter's family got help from other qheuen hives, and held a dam-raising to end all dam-raisings, it would still be years before a waterwheel, turbine, and power train could convert lake pressure into industrial muscle. And that would just begin the recovery. Nelo figured he would devote the rest of his life to building a papery like his former mill.

Was Henrik ashamed his charges had been misused by a panicky rabble? How could anyone guard against such times as these, when all prophecy went skewed and awry? Galactics had indeed come to Jijo, but not as foreseen. Instead, month after month of ambiguity had mixed with alien malevolence to sow confusion among the Six Races. Jop represented one reaction. Others sought ways to fight the aliens. In the long run, neither policy would make any difference.

We should have followed a third course – wait and see. Go on living normal lives until the universe decides what to do with us.

Nelo wondered at his own attitude. The earlier shocked dismay had given way to a strange feeling. Not numbness. Certainly not elation amid such devastation.

I hate everything that was done here.

... and yet ...

And yet, Nelo found a spirit of *anticipation* rising within. He could already smell fresh-cut timber and the pungency of boiling pitch. He felt the pulselike pounding of hammers driving joining pegs, and saws spewing dust across the ground. In his mind were the beginnings of a sketch for a better workshop. A better mill.

All my life I tended the factory my ancestors left me, making paper in the time-honored way.

It was a prideful place. A noble calling.

But it wasn't mine.

Even if the original design came from settlers who stepped off the *Tabernacle*, still wearing some of their mantle as star gods, Nelo had always known, deep inside – *I could do a better job.*

Now, when his years were ripe, he finally had a chance to prove it. The prospect was sad, daunting ... and thrilling. Perhaps the strangest thing of all was how young it made him feel.

'Don't blame yourself, Henrik,' he told the exploser, charitably. 'You watch and see. Everything'll be better'n ever.'

But the exploser only shook his head again. He pointed across the river, where Jop's partisans were now streaming toward the northeastern swamp, carrying canoes and other burdens on their backs, still singing as they went.

'They've got my reserve supply of powder. Snatched it from the warehouse. I couldn't stop 'em.'

Nelo frowned.

'What good'll it do 'em? Militia's coming, by land and water. Jop can't reach anywhere else along the river that's worth blowing up.'

'They aren't heading along the river,' Henrik replied, and Nelo saw it was true.

'Then where?' he wondered aloud.

Abruptly, Nelo knew the answer to his own question, even before

Henrik spoke. And that same instant he also realized there were far more important matters than rebuilding a paper mill.

'Biblos,' the exploser said, echoing Nelo's thought.

The papermaker blinked silently, unable to make his brain fit around the impending catastrophe.

'The militia ... can they cut 'em off?'

'Doubtful. But even if they do, it's not Jop alone that has me worried.'

He turned to show his eyes for the first time, and they held bleakness.

'I'll bet Jop's bunch ain't the only group heading that way, even as we speak.'

RETY

The more she learned about star gods, the less attractive they seemed.

None of 'em is half as smart as a dung-eating glaver, she thought, while making her way down a long corridor toward the ship's brig. *It must come from using all those computers and smarty-ass machines to cook your food, make your air, tell you stories, kill your enemies, tuck you in at night, and foretell your future for you. Count on 'em too much, and your brain stops working.*

Rety had grown more cynical since those early days when Dwer and Lark first brought her down off the Rimmer Mountains, a half-starved, wide-eyed savage, agog over the simplest crafts produced on the so-called civilized Slope – all the way from pottery to woven cloth and paper books. Of course that awe evaporated just as soon as she sampled *real* luxury aboard the Rothen station, where Kunn and the other Daniks flattered her with promises that sent her head spinning.

Long life, strength and beauty ... cures for all your aches and scars ... a clean, safe place to live under the protection of our Rothen lords ... and all the wonders that come with being a lesser deity, striding among the stars.

There she had met the Rothen patrons of humankind. *Her* patrons, they said. Gazing on the benevolent faces of Ro-kenn and Ro-pol, Rety had allowed herself to see wise, loving parents – unlike those she knew while growing up in a wild sooner tribe. The Rothen seemed so perfect, so noble and strong, that Rety almost gave in. She very nearly pledged her heart.

But it proved a lie. Whether or not they really were humanity's patrons did not matter to her at all. What counted was that the Rothen turned out to be less mighty than they claimed. For that she could never forgive them.

What use was a protector who couldn't protect?

For half a year, Rety had fled one band of incompetents after another – from her birth tribe of filthy cretins to the Commons of Six Races. Then from the Commons to the Rothen. And when the Jophur corvette triumphed over Kunn's little scout boat, she had seriously contemplated heading down to the swamp with both hands upraised, offering her services to the ugly ringed things. Now wouldn't *that* have galled old Dwer!

At one point, while *he* was floundering in the muck, talking to his crazy mulc-spider friend, she had actually started toward the ramp of the grounded spaceship, intending to hammer on the door. Surely the Jophur were like everybody else, willing to deal for information that was important to them.

At a critical moment, only their stench held her back – an aroma that reminded her of festering wounds and gangrene ... fortunately, as it turned out, since the Jophur also proved unable to defend themselves against the unexpected.

So I got to just keep looking for another way off this mud ball. And who cares what Dwer thinks of me? At least I don't make fancy excuses for what I do.

Rety's tutor had been the wilderness, whose harsh education taught just one lesson – to survive, at all cost. She grew up watching as some creatures ate others, then were eaten by something stronger still. Lark referred to the 'food chain,' but Rety called it the *who-kills mountain*. Every choice she made involved trying to climb higher on that mountain, hoping the next step would take her to the top.

So when the Jophur were beaten and captured by mythical *dolphins*, it seemed only natural to hurry aboard the submarine and claim sanctuary with her 'Earth cousins.' *Only now look where I am, buried under a trash heap at the bottom of the sea, hiding with a bunch of chattering Earthfish who have every monster and star god in space chasing them.*

In other words, back at the bottom of the mountain again. Doomed always to be prey, instead of the hunter.

Crax! I sure do got a knack for picking 'em.

There were a few small compensations.

For one thing, dolphins seemed to hold humans in awe – the same kind as the Daniks had for their Rothen patrons.

Furthermore, the *Streaker* crew considered Rety and Dwer 'heroes' for their actions in the swamp against the Jophur sky boat. As a result, she had free run of the ship, including a courtesy password that let her approach a sealed entrance to the *Streaker*'s brig.

For a brief time both airlock doors were closed, and she knew guards must be examining her with instruments. *Prob'ly checkin' my innards, to see if I'm smugglin' a laser or something.* Rety took a breath and exhaled deeply, washing away her body's instinctive panic over confinement in a cramped metal space. *It'll pass ... it'll pass ...*

That trick had helped her endure years of frustration in her feral tribe, whenever defeat and brutality seemed to press in from all sides.

Don't react like a savage. If others can stand living in boxes, you can, too ... for a little while.

The second hatch opened at last, showing Rety a ramp that dropped steeply to a chamber that was flooded, chest-high, with water.

Ugh.

She disliked the mixed compartments making up a large part of this weird vessel – half immersed rooms that were spanned above by dry catwalks, allowing access to both striding and swimming beings. The liquid felt warm as Rety sloshed downslope, reminding her of volcanic springs back home in the Gray Hills, but with an added *fizzy* quality that left trails of tiny bubbles wherever she moved. Feigning relaxed confidence, Rety approached the guard station, where two sentries were assisted by a globular robot whose whirring antennae watched her acutely. One of the dolphins rode a six-legged walker unit – without the bug-eyed body armor – enabling it to stride about dry areas of the ship. The other 'fin' wore just a tool harness, using languid motions of his flippers to face a set of monitor displays.

'May we help you, missss?' the latter one asked, with a tail splash added for punctuation.

'Yes. I came to question Kunn an' Jass again. I figure I'll get more out of 'em if I try it alone.'

The guard focused one eye back at her with a dubious expression. The first attempt had not gone well, when Rety accompanied Lieutenant Tsh't to interrogate the human prisoners. They had been groggy and unhelpful, still wearing bandages and medic pacs for their various injuries. While the dolphin officer tried grilling Kunn about matters back in the Five Galaxies, Rety endured a hot glare of hatred from her cousin Jass, who murmured the word *traitor* and spat on the floor.

Who'd you figure I betrayed, Jass? she had wondered, eyeing him coldly until his stare broke first. *The Daniks? Even Kunn isn't surprised I switched sides, after the way he treated me.*

Or do you mean I've turned against our home clan? The band of grubby savages that birthed me, then never showed me a day's kindness since?

Before looking away, his eyes showed it was personal. She had arranged for Jass to be seized, tormented, and pressed into service as Kunn's guide. His being locked in this metal cage was also her doing.

That thought cheered her up a bit. *You gotta admit, Jass, I finally made an impression on you.*

But soon things are gonna get even worse.

I'm gonna make you grateful.

Meanwhile, Kunn told Tsh't that the siege of Earth went on, though eased somewhat by a strange alliance with the Thennanin.

'But to answer your chief question, there has been no amnesty call by the Institutes. Several great star clans have blocked a safe-conduct decree to let your ship come home.'

Rety wasn't sure what that meant, but clearly the news was bitter to the dolphins.

Then a new voice intruded from thin air, where a spinning abstract figure suddenly whirled.

'*Lieutenant, please recall instructions. Have the prisoner explain how his vessel tracked us to this world.*'

Rety recalled seeing a tremor course down the dolphin's sleek gray flank, perhaps from irritation over the machine's snide tone. But Tsh't snapped her jaw in a gesture of submission, and sent her walker unit looming closer to Kunn's bunk. The human star voyager had nowhere to retreat as her machine pressed close, threateningly. Rety recalled sweat popping out on the Danik warrior's brow, giving lie to his false air of calm. Having watched him intimidate others, she was pleased to see the tables turned.

Then it happened. Some piece of equipment failed, or else the lieutenant's walker took a misstep. The right front ankle abruptly snapped, sending the dolphin's great mass crashing forward.

Only lightning reflexes enabled Kunn to scramble out of the way and avoid being crushed. By the time guards arrived to help Tsh't untangle herself, the dolphin officer was bruised, angry, and in no humor to continue the interview.

But I'm ready now, Rety thought later, as one of the brig wardens prepared to escort her down a narrow passage with numbers etched on every hatch. *I've got a plan ... and this time Kunn and Jass better do as I say.*

'Are you sure you want-t to do this now, miss?' the guard asked. 'It's night cycle and the prisoners are asleep.'

'That's just how I want 'em. Groggy an' logy. They may blab more.'

In fact, Rety hardly cared if Kunn named the admirals of all the fleets in the Five Galaxies. Her questions would only serve as cover for communication on another level.

She had been busy in the room the Streakers assigned her – a snug chamber once occupied by a human named Dennie Studman, whose clothes fit her pretty well. Pictures on the wall portrayed a young woman with dark hair, who was said to have gone missing on some foreign planet years ago, along with several human and dolphin crew mates. On her cluttered desk Dennie had left a clever machine that spoke in a much friendlier manner that the sarcastic Niss. It seemed eager to assist Rety, telling her all about the Terran ship and its surroundings.

I've studied the passages leading from this jail to the OutLock. I can name what kind of skiffs and star boats they keep there. And most important, these Earthfish trust me. My passwords should let us out.

All I need is a pilot … and someone strong and mean enough to do any fighting, if we run into trouble.

And luck. Rety had carefully timed things so there was little chance of running into Dwer along the way.

Dwer knows not to trust me … and I can't be sure that both Jass and Kunn together would be enough to bring him down.

Anyway, all else being equal, she'd rather Dwer didn't get hurt.

Maybe I'll even think about him now and then, while I'm livin' high on some far galaxy.

There wasn't much else about Jijo that she planned on remembering.

DWER

'I don't belong here,' he tried to explain. 'And neither does Rety. You've got to help us get back.'

'Back where?' The woman seemed honestly perplexed.

'To that seaside swamp, with toxic engine waste and dead Jophur rings for company? And more Jophur surely on the way?'

Once again, Dwer was having trouble with words. He found it difficult to concentrate in these sealed spaces they called 'starship cabins,' where the air felt so dead. Especially this one, a dimly lit chamber filled with strange objects Dwer could not hope to understand.

Lark or Sara would do fine here, but I feel lost. I miss the news that comes carried on the wind.

It didn't help settle his nerves that the person sitting opposite him was the most beautiful human being Dwer had ever seen, with dark yellow hair and abiding sadness in her pale eyes.

'No, of course not,' he answered. 'There's another place where I'm needed ... And Rety, too.'

Fine lines crinkled at the edges of her eyes.

'The young hoon, Alvin, wants to let his parents know he's alive, and report to the urrish sage who sent the four of them on their diving mission. They want help getting home.'

'Will you give it?'

'How can we? Aside from putting our own crewfolk in danger, and perhaps giving our position away to enemies, it seems unfair to endanger your entire culture with knowledge that's a curse to any who possess it.

'And yet ...'

She paused. Her scrutiny made Dwer feel like a small child.

'Yet, there is a reticence in your voice. A wariness about your destination that makes me suspect you're *not* talking about going home. Not to the tranquil peace you knew among friends and loved ones, in the land you call the Slope.'

There seemed little point in trying to conceal secrets from Gillian Baskin. So Dwer silently shrugged.

'The girl's tribe, then,' the woman guessed. 'Rety's folk, in the northern hills, where you were wounded fighting a war bot with your bare hands.'

He looked down, speaking in a low voice.

'There's ... things that still need to be done there.'

'Mm. I can well imagine. Obligations, I suppose? Duties unfulfilled?' Her sigh was soft and distant sounding. 'You see, I know how it is with your kind. Where your priorities lie.'

That made him look up, wondering. *What did she mean by that?* There was resigned melancholy in her face ... plus something like recognition, as if she saw something familiar in him, wakening affectionate sadness.

'Tell me about it, Dwer. Tell me what you must accomplish.

'Tell me who depends on you.'

Perhaps it was the way she phrased her question, or the power of her personality, but he found himself no longer able to withhold the remaining parts of the story. The parts he had kept back till now.

—about his job as chief scout of the Commons, seeing to it that no colonist race moved east of the Rimmers – sparing the rest of Jijo from further infestation. Enforcing sacred law.

—then how he was ordered to break that law, guiding a mission to tame Rety's savage cousins – a gamble meant to ensure human survival on Jijo, in case the Slope was cleansed of sapient life.

—how the four of them – Danel Ozawa, Dwer, Lena, and Jenin – learned the Gray Hills were no longer a sanctuary when Rety guided a Danik sky chariot to her home tribe.

—how Dwer and the others vowed to gamble their forfeit lives to win a chance for the sooner tribe . . . four humans against a killer machine . . . a gamble that succeeded, at great cost.

'And against all odds, I'd say,' Gillian Baskin commented. She turned her head, addressing the third entity sharing the room with them.

'I take it *you* were there, as well. Tell me, did you bother to help Dwer and the others? Or were you always a useless nuisance?'

After relating his dour tale, Dwer was startled by a sudden guffaw escaping his own gut. Fitting words! Clearly, Gillian Baskin understood noor.

Mudfoot lay grooming himself atop a glass-topped display case. Within lay scores of strange artifacts, backlit and labeled like treasures in the Biblos Museum. Some light spilled to the foot of another exhibit standing erect nearby – a mummy, he guessed. When they were boys, Lark once tried to scare Dwer with spooky book pictures of old-time Earth bodies that had been prepared that way, instead of being properly mulched. This one looked vaguely human, though he knew it was anything but.

At Gillian's chiding, Mudfoot stopped licking himself to reply with a panting grin. Again, Dwer imagined what the look might mean.

Who, me, lady? Don't you know I fought the whole battle and saved everybody's skins, all by myself?

After his experience with telepathic mulc-spiders, Dwer did not dismiss the possibility that it was more than imagination. The noor showed no reaction when he tried mind speaking, but that proved nothing.

Gillian had also tried various techniques to make the noor talk – first asking Alvin to smother the creature with umble songs, then keeping Mudfoot away from the young hoon, locking it instead in this dim office for miduras, with only the ancient mummy for company. The Niss Machine had badgered the noor in a high-pitched dialect of Gal-Seven, frequently using the phrase *dear cousin*.

'Danel Ozawa tried talkin' to it, too,' Dwer told Gillian.

'Oh? And did that seem strange to you?'

He nodded. 'There are folktales about talking noor ... and other critters, too. But I never expected it from a sage.'

She slapped the desktop.

'I think I get it.'

Gillian stood up and began pacing – a simple act that she performed with a hunter's grace, reminding him of the prowl of a she-ligger.

'We call the species *tytlal*, and where I come from, they talk a blue streak. They *are* cousins of the Niss Machine, after a fashion, since the Niss was made by our allies, the Tymbrimi.'

'The Tymb ... I think I heard of 'em. Aren't they the first race Earth contacted, when our ships went out—'

Gillian nodded. 'And a lucky break that turned out to be. Oh, there are plenty of honorable races and clans in the Five Galaxies. Don't let the present crisis make you think they're all evil, or religious fanatics. It's just that most of the moderate alliances have conservative mindsets. They ponder caution first, and act only after long deliberation. Too long to help us, I'm afraid.

'But not the Tymbrimi. They are brave and loyal friends. Also, according to many of the great clans and Institutes, the Tymbrimi are considered quite mad.'

Dwer sat up, both intrigued and confused. 'Mad?'

Gillian laughed. 'I guess a lot of humans would agree. A legend illustrates the point. It's said that one day the Great Power of the Universe, in exasperation over some Tymbrimi antic, cried out, 'These creatures must be the most outrageous beings imaginable!'

'Now, Tymbrimi like nothing better than a challenge. So they took the Great Power's statement as a dare. When they won official patron status, with license to uplift new species, they traded away two perfectly normal client races for the rights to one presapient line that no one else could do anything with.'

'The noor,' Dwer guessed. Then he corrected himself. 'The tytlal.'

'The very same. Creatures whose chief delight comes from thwarting, surprising, or befuddling others, making the Tymbrimi seem staid by comparison. Which brings us to our quandary. How did they get to Jijo, and why don't they speak?'

'Our Jijo chimpanzees don't speak either, though your Niss-thing showed me moving pictures of them talking on Earth.'

'Hmmm. But that's easily explained. Chims were still not very good at it when the *Tabernacle* left, bringing your ancestors here. It would be easy to suppress the talent at that point, in order to let humans pretend ...'

Gillian snapped her fingers. 'Of course.' For a moment her smile reminded Dwer of Sara, when his sister had been working on some abstract problem and abruptly saw the light.

'Within a few years of making contact with Galactic civilization, the leaders of Earth knew we had entered an incredibly dire phase. At best, we might barely hang on while learning the complex rules of an ancient and dangerous culture. At worst – ' She shrugged. 'It naturally seemed prudent to set up an insurance policy. To plant a seed where humanity might be safe, in case the worst happened.'

Her expression briefly clouded, and Dwer did not need fey sensitivity to understand. Out there, beyond Izmunuti, the worst *was* happening, and now it seemed the fleeing *Streaker* had exposed the 'seed,' as well.

That's what Danel was talking about, when he said, 'Humans did not come to Jijo to tread the Path of Redemption.' He meant we were a survival stash . . . like the poor g'Kek.

'When humans brought chimps with them, they naturally downplayed *pans* intelligence. In case the colony were ever found, chims might miss punishment. Perhaps they could even blend into the forest and survive in Jijo's wilderness, unnoticed by the judges of the great Institutes.'

Gillian whirled to look at Mudfoot. 'And that must be what the Tymbrimi did, as well! They, too, must have snuck down to Jijo. Only, unlike glavers and the other six races, they planted no colony of their own. Instead, they deposited a secret cache . . . of tytlal.'

'And like we did with chimps, they took away their speech.' Dwer shook his head. 'But then . . . ' He pointed to Mudfoot.

Gillian's eyebrows briefly pursed. 'A hidden race *within* the race? Fully sapient tytlal, hiding among the others? Why not? After all, your own sages kept secrets from the rest of you. If Danel Ozawa tried speaking to Mudfoot, it means someone must have already known about the tytlal, even in those early days, and kept the confidence all this time.'

Absently, she reached out to stroke the noor's sleek fur. Mudfoot rolled over, presenting his belly.

'What is the key?' she asked the creature. 'Some code word? Something like a Tymbrimi empathy glyph? Why did you talk to the Niss once, then clam up?'

And why did you follow me across mountains and deserts? Dwer added, silently, enthralled by the mystery tale, although the complexity combined with his ever-present claustrophobia to foster a growing headache.

'Excuse me,' he said, breaking into Gillian's ruminations. 'But can we go back to the thing I came here about? I know the problems you're wrestling with are bigger and more important than mine, and I'd help you if I could. But I can't see any way to change your star-god troubles with my bow and arrows.

'I'm not asking you to risk your ship, and I'm sorry about being a pest . . . But if there's any way you could just let me . . . well . . . try to *swim* ashore, I really do have things I've got to do.'

That was when the tytlal rolled back onto his feet, wearing a look of evident surprise on his narrow face. Spines that normally lay hidden in the fur behind his ears now stood in stiff bristles. Moreover, Dwer felt sure he glimpsed *something* take shape briefly, in the air above Mudfoot. A ghostly wisp, less than vapor, which seemed to speak of its own accord.

So do I, it said, evidently responding to Dwer's statement. *Things to do.*

Dwer rubbed his eyes and would gladly have dismissed the brief specter as another imagining . . . another product of the pummeling his nervous system had gone through.

Only Gillian must have noted the same event. She blinked a few times, pointed at the now-worried expression on Mudfoot's face . . . and burst out laughing.

Dwer stared at her, then found himself breaking up, as well. Till that moment, he had not yet decided about the beautiful Earthwoman. But anyone who could set Mudfoot back like that must be all right.

RETY

As the guard escorted her to the captives' cell, she eyed several air-circulation grates. Schematics showed the system to be equipped with many safety valves, and the ducts were much too small for prisoners to squeeze through.

But not for a little urrish male, armed with borrowed laser cutters.

Rety's plan was chancy, and she hated sending her 'husband' into the maze of air pipes. But yee seemed confident that he would not get lost.

'this maze no worse than stinky passages under the grass plain,' he had sniffed while examining a holographic chart. *'it easier than dodging through root tunnels where urrish grubs and males must scurry, when we have no sweet wife pouch to lie in.'* yee curled his long neck in a shrug. *'don't you worry, wife! yee take tools to locked-up men. we do this neat!'*

That would be the critical phase. Once Kunn and Jass were

beyond the brig airlock, all the other obstacles should quickly fall. Rety felt positive.

Two prison cells had red lights glaring above reinforced hatches. The far one, she knew, contained Jophur rings that had been captured in the swamp. The little g'Kek named Huck was helping the Niss Machine interrogate those captives. Rety had racked her brain to come up with a way they might fit in her plan, but finally deemed it best to leave them where they were.

This Streaker *ship won't dare chase us, once we get a star boat outside . . . but the Jophur ship might. Especially if those rings had a way to signal their crew mates.*

As the guard approached Kunn's cell, Rety fondled a folded scrap of paper on which she had laboriously printed instructions, sounding out the words letter by letter, stretching her newborn literacy to the limit. She knew it must look wrong, but no one could afford to be picky these days.

KUN I KAN GIT U OT UV HIR WANT TU GO?

So went the first line of the note she planned slipping him, while pretending to ask questions. If the Danik pilot understood and agreed to the plan, she would depart and set yee loose to worm his small, lithe body through *Streaker*'s ducting system. Meanwhile Rety had selected good places to set fires – in a ship lounge and a cargo locker – to distract the *Streaker* crew away from this area while Kunn used smuggled tools to break out. If all went well, they could then dash for the OutLock, steal a star boat, and escape.

There's just one condition, Kunn. You gotta agree that we get away from here. Away from these Earthers, away from Daniks and Rothens and Jophur monsters and all that crap. Away from Jijo.

Rety felt sure he'd accept. *Anyway, if he or Jass give me any trouble, they'll find they're dealin' with a different Rety now.*

The guard maneuvered his walker unit carefully in the narrow hallway. The gangly machine had to bend in order for him to bring a key against the door panel. Finally, it slid aside. Rety glimpsed two bunks within, each supporting a blanket-covered human form.

'Hey, Kunn,' she said, crossing the narrow distance and nudging his shoulder. 'Wake up! No more delayin' or foolin' now. These folks want t'know how you followed 'em . . .'

The blanket slipped off, revealing his shock of glossy hair, but there was no tremor of movement.

They must have him doped, she thought. *I hope he's not too far under. This can't wait!*

Rety shook harder, rolling Kunn toward her—

And jumped back with a gasp of surprise.

The Danik's face was purple. His eyes bulged from their sockets, and his tongue had swollen to fill his mouth.

The dolphin guard chattered a dismayed squeal in the instinctive animal language of his kind.

Rety struggled with shock. She had grown up with death, but it took all her force of will to quash the horror rising in her gorge.

Somehow, she made herself turn toward the other bunk.

SARA

> *'Oh, Doctor Faustus was a good man,*
> *He whipped his scholars now and then;*
> *When he whipped them he made them dance,*
> *Out of Scotland into France,*
> *Out of France, and into Spain,*
> *Then he whipped them back again!'*

Emerson's song resonated through the Hall of Spinning Disks, where dust motes sparkled in narrow shafts of rhythmic light.

Sara winced at the violent lyrics, but the starman clearly enjoyed these outbursts, gushing from unknown recesses of his scarred brain. He laughed, as did a crowd of urrish males who followed him, clambering through the scaffolding of Uriel's fantastic machine, helping him fine-tune each delicate part. The little urs cackled at Emerson's rough humor, and showed their devotion by diving between whirling glass plates to tighten a strap here, or a pulley there, wherever he gestured with quick hand signs.

Once an engineer, always an engineer, Sara thought. At times, Emerson resembled her own father, who might go silent for days while tending his beloved paper mill, drawing more satisfaction from the poetry of pulping hammers and rollers than the white sheets that made literacy possible on a barbaric world.

A parallel occurred to her.

Paper suited the Six Races, who needed a memory storage system that was invisible from space. But Uriel's machine has similar traits – an analog computer that no satellite or spaceship can detect, because it uses no electricity and has no digital cognizance. Above all, Galactics would never imagine such an ornate contraption.

And yet it was beautiful in a bizarre way. No wonder she had dreamed shapes and equations when her eyes first glimpsed this marvel through cracks in her delirium. Each time a disk turned against a neighbor's rim, its own axle rotated at a speed that varied with the radial point of contact. If that radius shifted as an independent variable, the rotation changed in response, describing a nonlinear function. It was a marvelously simple concept ... and hellishly hard to put into practice without years of patient trial and error.

Uriel first saw the idea in an old Earth book – a quintessentially wolfling concept, briefly used in an old-time Amero-Eurasian war. Soon after, humans discovered digital computers and abandoned the technique. But here on Mount Guenn, the urrish smith had extended it to levels never seen before. Much of her prodigious wealth and passion went into making the concept work.

And urrish haste. Their lives are so short, Uriel must have feared she'd never finish before she died. In that case, what would her successor do with all this?

An array of pillars, arches, and boo scaffolding held the turning shafts in proper alignment, forming a three-dimensional maze that stretched away from Sara, nearly filling the vast chamber. Long ago, this cavity spilled liquid magma down the mountain's mighty flanks. Today it throbbed with a different kind of creative force.

Light rays played a clever role in the dance of mathematics. Glancing off selected disks, pulselike reflections fell onto a stretch of black sand that had been raked smooth across the floor. Each flash affected the grains, causing a slight spray or rustle. Hillocks grew wherever glimmers landed most often.

Uriel even found a use for lightning crabs, Sara marveled. On Jijo, some shorelines were known to froth during electrical storms, as these tiny creatures kicked up sand in frenzied reaction. *We thought it might be static charges in the air, making them behave so. But clearly it is light. I must tell Lark about this, someday.*

And Sara realized something else.

The crabs may be another Buyur gimmick species. Bioengineered servants, reverted to nature, but keeping their special trait, even after the gene meddlers left.

Whatever their original function, the crabs now served Uriel, whose hooves clattered nervously as the sandscape swirled under a cascade of sparkling light. Individual flashes mattered little. It was the summed array over area and time that added up to solving a complex numerical problem. Near Uriel, the little chimp, Prity, perched on a high stool with her drawing pad. Prity's tongue stuck out as she sketched, copying the sand display. Sara had never seen her little assistant happier.

Despite all this impressive ingenuity, the actual equations being solved were not profound. Sara had already worked out rough estimates, within a deviance of ten percent, by using a few simple Delancy approximations. But Lester Cambel needed both precision and accuracy under a wide range of boundary conditions, including atmospheric pressures varying with altitude. For that, machine-derived tables offered advantages.

At least now I understand what it's all for. In her mind, she pictured bustling activity beneath the towering stems of a boo forest, throngs of workers laboring, the flow of acrid liquids, and discussions in the hushed, archaic dialect of science.

They may be crazy – Lester especially. Probably the effort will backfire and make the aliens more vicious than ever. Dedinger would look at this – along with all the semaphores, gliders, balloons, and other innovations – and call it the futile thrashing of the damned.

Yet the attempt is glorious. If they pull it off, I'll know I was right about the Six. Our destiny was not foretold by the scrolls, or Dedinger's orthodoxy ... or Lark's, for that matter.

It was unique.

Anyway, if we're to be damned, I'd rather it be for trying.

Just one thing still puzzled her. Sara shook her head and murmured aloud.

'Why me?'

Kurt, the Tarek Town exploser, had acted as if this project desperately needed Sara, for her professional expertise. But Uriel's machine was already nearly functional by the time the party arrived from Xi. Prity and Emerson were helpful at making the analog computer work, and so were books Kurt hand-carried from Biblos. But Sara found herself with little to contribute.

'I only wish I knew why Uriel asked for me.'

Her answer came from the entrance to the computer vault.

'Is that truly the *only* thing you wish to understand? But that one is easy, Sara. *Uriel* did not ask for you at all!'

The speaker was a man of middling stature with a shock of white hair and a stained beard that stood out as if he were constantly thunderstruck. *Kawsh* leaves smoldered in his pipe, a habit chiefly indulged in by male hoons, since the vapors were too strong for most humans. Politely, Sage Purofsky stood in the draft of the doorway, and turned away from Sara when exhaling.

She bowed to the senior scholar, known among his peers as the best mind in the Commons.

'Master, if Uriel doesn't need my help, why was I urged to come? Kurt made it sound vital.'

'Did he? Vital. Well, I suppose it is, Sara. In a different way.'

Purofsky's eyes tracked the glitter of rays glancing off spinning disks. His gaze showed appreciation of Uriel's accomplishment. 'Math must pay its way with useful things,' the sage once said. 'Even though mere computation is like bashing down a door because you cannot find the key.'

Purofsky had spent his life in search of keys.

'It was *I* who sent for you, my dear,' the aged savant explained after a pause. 'And now that you're recovered from your ill-advised spill down a mountainside, I think it's high time that I showed you why.'

It was still daytime outside, but a starscape spread before Sara. Clever lenses projected glass photoslides onto a curved wall and ceiling, recreating the night sky in a wondrous planetarium built by Uriel's predecessor so that even poor urrish eyesight might explore constellations in detail. Sage Purofsky wore stars like ornaments on his face and gown, while his shadow cast a man-shaped nebula across the wall.

'I should start by explaining what I've been up to since you left Biblos ... has it really been more than a year, Sara?'

'Yes, Master.'

'Hmmm. An eventful year. And yet ...'

He worked his jaw for a moment, then shook his head.

'Like you, I had grown discouraged with my former field of study. At last, I decided to extend the classical, pre-contact geometrodynamic formalisms beyond the state they were in when the *Tabernacle* left the solar system.'

Sara stared.

'But I thought you wanted to *reconcile* pre-contact Earth physics with Galactic knowledge. To prove that Einstein and Lee had made crude but correct approximations ... the way Newton preapproximated Einstein.'

That in itself would have been a daunting task – some might say hopeless. According to reports brought by the *Tabernacle*, space-time relativity was ill regarded by those alien experts hired by the Terragens Council to teach modern science to Earthlings. Galactic instructors disdained as superstition the homegrown cosmology humans formerly relied on – the basis of crude star probes, crawling along at sublight speeds. Until the Earthship *Vesarius* fell through an undetected hyperanomaly, ending humanity's long isolation, Einstein's heirs had never found a useful way to go faster – although some methods had been recorded in the Galactic Library for over a billion years.

After contact, humans scrimped to buy some thirdhand hyperships, and the old mathemetric models of Hawking, Purcell, and

Lee fell by the wayside. In trying to show validity for pre-contact physics, Purofsky had taken on a strange, perhaps forlorn, task.

'I had some promising results at first, when I restated the Serressimi Exalted Transfer Shunt in terms compatible with old-fashioned tensor calculus.'

'Indeed?' Sara leaned forward in her chair. 'But how did you renormalize all the quasi-simultaneous infinities? You'd almost *have* to assume—'

But the elder sage raised a hand to cut her off, unwilling to be drawn into details.

'Plenty of time for that later, if you're still interested. For now let's just say that I soon realized the futility of that approach. Earth must by now have specialists who understand the official Galactic models better than I'll ever hope to. They have units of the Great Library, and truly modern computer simulators to work with. Suppose I did eventually manage to demonstrate that our Old Physics was a decent, if limited, approximation? It might win something for pride, showing that wolflings had been on the right track, on our own. But nothing *new* would come of it.'

Purofsky shook his head. 'No, I decided it was time to go for broke. I'd plunge ahead with the old space-time approach, and see if I could solve a problem relevant to Jijo – the Eight Starships Mystery.'

Sara blinked.

'You mean *seven*, don't you? The question of why so many sooner races converged on Jijo within a short time, without getting caught? But isn't that settled?' She pointed at the most brilliant point on the wall. 'Izmunuti started flooding nearby space with carbon chaff twenty centuries ago. Enough to seed the hollow hail and change our weather patterns, more than a light-year away. Once the storm wrecked all the watch robots left in orbit by the Migration Institute, sneakships could get in undetected.'

'Hr-rm ... yes, but not good enough, Sara. From wall inscriptions found in a few Buyur ruins, we know *two* transfer points used to serve this system. The other must have collapsed after the Buyur left.'

'Well? That's why the Izmunuti gambit works! A single shrouded access route, and the great Institutes not scheduled to resurvey the area for another eon. It must be a fairly unique situation.'

'Unique. Hrm, and convenient. So convenient, in fact, that I decided to acquire fresh data.'

Purofsky turned toward the planetarium display, and a distant expression crossed his shadowed face. After a few duras, Sara realized he must be drifting. That kind of absentmindedness might be a prerogative of genius back in the cloistered halls of Biblos, but it was infuriating when he had her keyed up so! She spoke in a sharp tone.

'Master! You were saying you needed data. Is there really something relevant you can see with Uriel's simple telescope?'

The scholar blinked, then cocked his head and smiled. 'You know, Sara ... I find it striking that we both spent the last year chasing unconventional notions. You, a sideline into languages and sociology – yes, I followed your work with interest. And me, thinking I could pierce secrets of the past using coarse implements made of reforged Buyur scrap metal and melted sand.

'Did you know, while taking pictures of Izmunuti, I also happened to snap shots of those starships? The ones causing so much fuss, up north? Caught them entering orbit ... though my warning didn't reach the High Sages in time.' Purofsky shrugged. 'But to your question. Yes, I managed to learn a few things, using the apparatus here on Mount Guenn.

'Think again about Jijo's unique conditions, Sara. The collapse of the second transfer point ... the carbon flaring of Izmunuti ... the inevitable attractiveness of an isolated, shrouded world to sooner refugees.

'Now ponder this – how could beings with minds as agile as the Buyur fail to notice advance symptoms of these changes, about to commence in nearby space?'

'But the Buyur departed half a million years ago! There may not have been any symptoms back then. Or else they were subtle.'

'Perhaps. And that's where my research comes in. Plus your expertise, I hope. For I strongly suspect that space-time anomalies would have been noticeable, even back then.'

'Space-time ...' Sara realized his use of the archaic Earth-physics term was intentional. Now it was her turn to spend several silent duras staring at a blur of stars, sorting implications.

'You're ... talking about lensing effects, aren't you?'

'Sharp lass,' the sage answered approvingly. 'And if *I* can see them—'

'Then the Buyur must have, and foreseen—'

'Like reading an open book! Nor is that all. I asked you here to help confirm another, more ominous suspicion.'

Sara felt a frisson, climbing her spine like some insect with a million ice-cold feet.

'What do you mean?'

Sage Purofsky briefly closed his eyes. When he reopened them, his gaze seemed alight with fascination.

'Sara, I believe they planned it this way, from the very start.'

VIII

Illegal resettlement of fallow worlds has been a predicament in the Five Galaxies for as far back as records exist. There are many causes for this recurring problem, but its most enduring basis is the Paradox of Reproductive Logic.

ORGANIC beings from countless diverse worlds tend to share one common trait – self-propagation. In some species, this manifests as a conscious desire to have offspring. Among other races, individuals respond to rude instinctive drives for either sex or xim, and spare little active attention to the consequences.

However different the detailed mechanisms may be, the net effect remains the same. Left to their own inclinations, organic life-forms will reproduce their kind in numbers exceeding the replacement rate. Over periods of time that are quite brief (by stellar standards) the resulting population increase can swiftly overburden the carrying capacity of any self-sustaining ecosystem. (SEE: ATTACHED SORTED EXAMPLES.)

Species do this because each fecund individual is the direct descendant of a long chain of successful reproducers. Simply stated; those who lack traits that enable breeding do not become ancestors. Traits that encourage reproduction are the traits that get reproduced.

To the best of our knowledge, this evolutionary imperative extends even to the ecomatrix of hydrogen-based life-forms that shares real space in parallel with our oxygen-breathing civilization. As for the Third Order – autonomous machines – only the relentless application of stringent safeguards has prevented these nonorganic species from engaging in exponential reproduction, threatening the basis of all life in the Five Galaxies.

For the vast majority of nonsapient animal species in natural ecosystems, this tendency to overbreed is kept in check by starvation, predation, or other limiting factors, resulting in quasi-stable states of pseudo-equilibrium. However, presapient life-forms often use their newfound cleverness to eliminate competition and indulge in orgiastic breeding frenzies, followed by overutilization of resources.

Left for too long without proper guidance, such species can bring about their own ruin through ecological collapse.

This is one of the Seven Reasons why naive life-forms cannot self-evolve to fully competent sapience. The Paradox of Reproductive Logic means that short-term self-interest will always prevail over long-range planning, unless wisdom is imposed from the outside by an adoptive patron line.

One duty of a patron is to make certain that its client race achieves conscious control over its self-replicating drives, before it can be granted adult status. And yet, despite such precautions, even fully ranked citizen species have been known to engage in breeding spasms, especially during intervals when lawful order temporarily breaks down (SEE REF: 'TIMES OF CHANGE'). Hasty, spasmodic episodes of colonization/exploitation have left entire galactic zones devastated in their wake.

By law, the prescribed punishment for races who perpetrate such eco-holocausts can be complete extinction, down to the racial rootstock.

IN comparison, illegal resettlement of fallow worlds is a problem of moderate-level criminality. Penalties depend on the degree of damage done, and whether new presapient forms safely emerge from the process.

Nevertheless, it is easy to see how the Paradox of Reproductive Logic applies here, as well. Or why else would individuals and species sacrifice so much, and risk severe punishment, in order to dwell in feral secrecy on worlds where they do not belong?

OVER the course of tens of millions of years, only one solution has ever been found for this enduring paradox. This solution consists of the continuing application of pragmatic foresight in the interests of the common good.

In other words – civilization.

> – from A *Galactographic Tutorial for Ignorant Wolfling Terrans,* a special publication of the Library Institute of the Five Galaxies, year 42 EC, in partial satisfaction of the debt obligation of 35 EC

STREAKERS

KAA

They made love in a hidden cave, nestled beneath seaside cliffs, while tidal currents pounded nearby, shooting spume fountains high enough to rival the craggy promontories.

At last! Booming echoes seemed to shout each time a wave dashed against the bluffs, as if everything leading up to that moment had been prelude, a mere transport of momentum across the vast ocean, passed from one patch of salt water to the next. As if a wave may only become real by spending itself against stone.

Rolling echoes reverberated in the sheltered cave. *That's me*, Kaa thought, listening to the breakers cry out their brief reification. As a coast fulfills a tide, he now felt completed by contact with another.

Water sloshed through his open mouth, still throbbing with their passion. The secret pool had her flavor.

Peepoe rolled along Kaa's side, stroking with her pectoral fins, making his skin tingle. He responded with a brush of his tail flukes, pleased at how she quivered with unguarded bliss. This postcoital affection had even deeper meaning than the brief glory dance of mating. It was like the difference between mere need and choice.

* Can the burning stars
    * Shout their joy more happily
        * Than this simple fin? *

His Trinary haiku came out as it should, almost involuntarily, not mulled or rehearsed by the frontal lobes that human gene crafters had so thoroughly palped and reworked during neo-dolphin uplift. The poem's clicks and squeals diffracted through the cave's grottoes at the same moment they first resonated in his skull.

Peepoe's reply emerged the same way, candidly languid, with a natural openness that brooked no lies.

* Simplicity is not
    * Your best-known trait, dear Kaa.
        * Don't you feel Lucky? *

Her message both thrilled and validated, in a way she must have known he'd treasure. *I have my nickname back*, Kaa mused happily.

All would have been perfection then – a flawless moment – except that something else intruded on his pleasure. A tremor, faint and glimmering, like the sound shadow made by a moray eel, passing swiftly in the night, leaving fey shivers in its wake.

Yes, you have won back your name, whispered a faint voice, as if from a distant seaquake. Or an iceberg, groaning, a thousand miles away.

But to keep it, you will have to earn it.

When Kaa next checked the progress of his spy drone, it had nearly reached the top of the Mount Guenn funicular.

At the beginning, Peepoe's decision to stay with him had been more professional than personal, helping Kaa pilot the special probe up a hollow wooden monorail that climbed the rutted flank of an extinct volcano. While the bamboolike track was a marvel of aboriginal engineering, Kaa found it no simple matter guiding the little robot past sections filled with dirt or debris. He and Peepoe wound up having to camp in the cave, to monitor it round the clock, instead of returning to Brookida and the others. A fully autonomous unit could have managed the journey on its own, but Gillian Baskin had vetoed sending any machine ashore that might be smart enough to show up on Jophur detectors.

A moment of triumph came as the camera eye finally emerged from the rail, passed through a camouflaged station, then proceeded down halls of chiseled stone, trailing its slender fiber comm line like a hurried spider. Kaa had it crawl along the ceiling – the safest route, offering a good view of the native workshops.

Other observers tuned in at this point. From the *Streaker*, Hannes Suessi and his engineering chiefs remarked on the spacious chambers where urrish and qheuen smiths tapped ominous heat from lava pools, dipping ladles into nearby pits for melting, alloying, and casting. Most questions were answered by Ur-ronn, one of the four young guests whose presence on the *Streaker* posed such quandaries. Ur-ronn explained the forge in thickly accented Anglic, revealing tense reserve. Her service as guide was part of a risky bargain, with the details still being worked out.

'*I do not see Uriel at the hearths*.' Ur-ronn's voice came tinnily from Kaa's receiver. '*Ferhafs she is ufstairs, in her hovvy roon.*'

Uriel's hobby room. From the journal of Alvin Hph-wayuo, Kaa envisioned an ornately useless toy gadget of sticks and spinning glass, something to hypnotize away the ennui of existence on a savage world. He found it puzzling that a leader of this menaced society would spare time for the arty Rube Goldberg contraption Alvin had described.

Ur-ronn told Kaa to send the probe down a long hall, past several mazelike turns, then through an open door into a dim chamber ... where at last the fabled apparatus came into view.

Peepoe let out an amazed whistle.

> * Advance description
>> * Leaves the unwary stunned by
>>> * Serendipity! *

Yeah, Kaa agreed, staring at a vaulted chamber that would have been impressive even on Earth, filled with crisscrossing timbers and sparkling lights. Alvin's account did the place injustice, never conveying the complex *unity* of all the whirling, spinning parts – for even at a glance one could tell that an underlying rhythm controlled it all. Each ripple and turn was linked to an elegant, ever-changing whole.

The scene was splendid, and ultimately baffling. Dim figures could be glimpsed moving about the scaffolding, making adjustments – several small, scurrying shapes and at least one bipedal silhouette that looked tentatively human. But Kaa could not even judge scale properly because most of the machine lay in deep shadows. Moreover, holovision had been designed to benefit creatures with two forward-facing eyes. A panel equipped with sono-parallax emitters would have better suited dolphins.

Even the normally wry Hannes Suessi was struck silent by this florid, twinkling palace of motion.

Finally, Ur-ronn cut in.

'I see Uriel! She is second from the right, in that group standing near the chinfanzee.'

Several four-footed urs nervously watched the machine whirl, next to a chimp with a sketchpad. Random light pulses dappled their flanks, resembling fauns in a forest, but Kaa could tell that gray-snouted Uriel must be older than the rest. As they watched, the chimp showed the smith an array of abstract curves, commenting on the results with hand signs instead of words.

'How we gonna do this, *Streaker*?' Kaa asked. 'Just barge in and start t-talking?'

Until lately, it had seemed best for all concerned that *Streaker* keep her troubles separate. But now events made a meeting seem inevitable – even imperative.

'Let's listen before announcing ourselves,' Gillian Baskin instructed. *'I'd rather conditions were more private.'*

In other words, she preferred to contact Uriel, not a whole crowd. Kaa sent the robot creeping forward. But before any urrish words became audible, another speaker interrupted from *Streaker*'s end.

'*Allow me this indulgence,*' fluted the refined voice of the Niss Machine. '*Kaa, will you again focus the main camera on Uriel's contraption? I wish to pursue a conjecture.*'

When Gillian did not object, Kaa had the probe look at the expanse of scaffolding a second time.

'*Note the stretch of sand below,*' the Niss urged. '*Neat piles accumulate wherever light falls most frequently. These piles correlate with the drawings the chimpanzee just showed Uriel ...*'

Kaa's attention jerked away, caught by a slap of Peepoe's tail.

'Someone's c-coming. Peripheral scanner says approaching life signs are Jophur!'

Despite objections from the Niss, Kaa made the probe swivel around. There, framed in the doorway, they saw a silhouette *Streaker*'s crew had come to loathe – like a tapered cone of greasy doughnuts.

Gillian Baskin broke in. '*Calm down, every one ... I'm sure it's just a traeki.*'

'*Of course it is,*' confirmed Ur-ronn. '*That stack is Tyug.*'

Kaa recalled. This was the 'chief alchemist' of Mount Guenn Forge. Uriel's master of chemical synthesis. Kaa brushed reassuringly against Peepoe, and felt her relax a bit. According to Alvin's journal, traeki were docile beings quite unlike their starfaring cousins.

So he was caught completely off guard when Tyug turned a row of jewel-like sensor patches *upward*, toward the tiny spy probe. Thoughtful curls of orange vapor steamed from its central vent. Then the topmost ring bulged outward ...

... and abruptly spewed a jet of flying objects, swarming angrily toward the camera eye! Kaa and the others had time for a brief glimpse of *insects* – or some local equivalent – creating a confusing buzz of light and sound with their compound eyes and fast-beating wings. A horde of blurry creatures converged, surrounding Kaa's lenses and pickups.

Moments later, all that reached his console was a smear of dizzying static.

GILLIAN

A magnified image floated above the conference table – depicting a small creature, frozen in flight, whose wings were a rainbow-streaked haze, painful to the eye. By contrast, the Niss Machine's compact mesh of spiral lines seemed drab and abstruse. A strain of pique filled its voice.

'Might any of you local children be able to identify this bothersome thing for us?'

The words were polite enough, though Gillian winced at its insolent manner.

Fortunately, Alvin Hph-wayuo showed no awareness of being patronized. The young hoon sat near his friend, throbbing his throat sac in the subsonic range for both noor beasts, one lounging on each broad shoulder. To the machine's sardonic question, Alvin nodded amiably, a human gesture that seemed completely unaffected.

'Hrm. That's easy enough. It is a privacy wasp.'

'Gene-altered toys of the Vuyur,' lisped Ur-ronn. 'A well-known nuisance.'

Huck's four eyestalks waved, peering at the image. 'Now I see how they got their name. They normally move so fast, I never got a good look before. It looks kind of like a tiny rewq, with the membranes turned into wings.'

Hannes Suessi grunted, tapping the tabletop with his prosthetic left arm.

'Whatever the origins of these critters, it seems Uriel was armed against the possibility of being spied upon. Our probe's been rendered useless. Will she now assume that it was sent by the Jophur?'

Ur-ronn shrugged, an uncertain twist of her long neck. 'Who else? How would Uriel have heard of you guys ... unless the Jophur themselves sfoke of you?'

Gillian agreed. 'Then she may destroy the drone, unless we make it speak Anglic words right away. Niss, can you and Kaa get a message through?'

'We are working to accomplish that. Commands rise from the control console, but the bedlam given off by these so-called wasps appears to swamp all bands, thwarting confirmation. The probe may be effectively inoperable.'

'Damn. It would take days to send another. Days we don't have.' Gillian turned to Ur-ronn. 'This might make our promise hard to keep.'

She hated saying it. Part of her had looked forward to meeting the legendary smith of Mount Guenn. By all accounts, Uriel was an individual of shrewdness and insight, whose sway on Jijoan society was notable.

'There is another off-shun,' Ur-ronn suggested. 'Fly there in ferson.'

'An option we must set aside for now,' replied Lieutenant Tsh't. 'Since any aircraft sent beyond these shielding waters would be detected instantly, by the enemy battleship-p.'

The dolphin officer lay on the cushioned pad of a six-legged walker. Her long, sleek body took up the end of the conference room farthest from the sooner youths, her left eye scanning the members of the ship's council. 'Believe it or not-t, and despite our disappointment over the loss of Kaa's probe, there are other agenda items left to cover.'

Gillian understood the lieutenant's testy mood. Her report on the apparent suicide of the two human prisoners had left many unanswered questions. Moreover, discipline problems were also on the rise, with a growing faction of the dolphin crew signing what they called the 'Breeding Petition.'

Gillian had tried boosting morale by getting out and talking to the dolphins, listening to their concerns, encouraging them with a patron's touch. *Tom had the knack, like Captain Creideiki. A joke here, a casual parable there. Most fins grew more inspired and devoted the worse things got.*

I don't have the same talent, I guess. Or else this poor crew is just tired after all the running.

Anyway, the best workers were all outside the ship now, in gangs that labored round the clock, while she spent hours closeted with the Niss Machine, eliminating one desperate plan after another.

At last, one of her schemes seemed a bit less awful than the rest.

'Tasty,' the Niss had called it. *'Though a rash gamble. Our escape from Kithrup had more going for it than this ploy.'*

Ship's Physician Makanee raised the next agenda item. Unlike Tsh't, the elderly dolphin surgeon did not like to ride around strapped to a machine. Naked, except for a small tool harness, she took part in the meeting from a clear tube that ran along one wall of the conference room. Makanee's body glistened with tiny bubbles from the oxygen-packed fluid that filled *Streaker's* waterways.

'There is the matter of the Kiqui,' she said. 'It must be settled, especially if we are planning to move the ship-p.'

Gillian nodded. 'I'd hoped to consult about this matter with—' She glanced at the staticky display from Kaa's lost spy probe, and sighed. 'A final decision must wait, Doctor. Continue preparations and I'll let you know.'

Hannes Suessi next reported on the state of *Streaker's* hull.

'Weighed down like this, she'll be as slow as when we carried around that hollowed-out Thennanin cruiser, wearing it like a suit of armor. Slower, with all the probability arrays gummed up by carbon gunk.'

'So we must consider transferring to one of the wrecks outside?'

That would be hard. None had the modifications that made *Streaker* usable by an aquatic race.

The mirrored dome containing Suessi's brain and skull nodded.

'I have crews preparing the best of the drossed starships.' A chuckle then escaped the helmet speaker vent. 'Cheer up, everybody! With Ifni's luck, some of us may yet make it out of here.'

Perhaps, Gillian thought. *But if we get away from the Jijo system, where will we go? Where else can we run?*

The meeting broke up. Everyone, including the sooner kids, had jobs to do.

And Dwer Koolhan will be waiting in my quarters, asking again for passage ashore. Or to swim, if necessary.

To go back to a savage place where he's needed. Ambivalence filled her. Dwer was hardly more than a boy.

Still, in all the years since *Streaker* was forced to abandon Tom on Kithrup, this was the first time she felt anything like physical attraction to another.

Naturally. I've always been a sucker for hero types.

It brought to mind the last time she had felt Tom's touch – one final night together on a metal island, set amid a poison sea. The night before he flew away on a solar-powered glider, determined to mislead great battle fleets, thwart mighty foes, and make an opening for *Streaker* to get away. Gillian's left thigh still tingled, from time to time ... the site of his last loving squeeze as he lay prone on the flimsy little aircraft, grinning before taking off.

'I'll be back before you know it,' Tom said – a metaphysically strange expression, when you thought about it. And she often had.

Then he was gone, winging north, barely skimming the waves, just above the contrary tides of Kithrup.

I should never have let him go. Sometimes you have to tell a hero that enough is enough.

Let someone else save the world.

As Gillian made ready to leave the conference room, she saw Alvin, the young hoon, trying to collect both noors. The female was his longtime pet, to all appearances a bright nonsapient being, probably derived from natural tytlal rootstock, dating from before their species' uplift. *The Tymbrimi must have stockpiled a gene pool of their beloved clients here on Jijo, as insurance in case the worst happened to their clan. A wise precaution, given the number of enemies they've made.*

As for the other one, Mudfoot, Dwer's bane and traveling

companion across half a continent, scans of his brain showed uplift traces throughout.

A race hidden within a race, retaining all the traits the Tymbrimi worked hard to foster in their clients.

In other words, the tytlal were true sooners, another wave of illegal settlers, but guarded by added layers of camouflage. So disguised, they might even escape whatever ruin lay in store for the relatives of Alvin, Huck, Ur-ronn, and Pincer.

But that can't be the whole story. Caution isn't a paramount trait in Tymbrimi, or their clients. They wouldn't go to so much trouble just to hide. Not unless it was part of something bigger.

Alvin had trouble gathering Mudfoot, who ignored the boy's umble calls while wandering across the conference table, poking a whiskered nose into debris from the meeting. Finally, the tytlal stood up on his hind legs to peer at the frozen projection last sent by Kaa's probe, the image of a privacy wasp. Mudfoot purred with curiosity.

'Niss,' Gillian said in a low voice.

With an audible pop, the pattern of whirling, shifting lines came into being nearby.

'Yes, Dr. Baskin? Have you changed your mind about hearing my tentative conjectures about Uriel's intricate device of spinning disks?'

'Later,' she said, and gestured at Mudfoot. Gillian now realized the tytlal was peering *past* the blurry display of the privacy wasp, at something in the scene beyond.

'I'd like you to do some enhancements. Find out what that little devil is looking at.'

She did not add that she had detected something on her own. Something only a psi-sensitive would notice. For the second time, a faint *presence* could be felt – vague and ephemeral – floating ever so briefly above Mudfoot's agitated cranial spines. She could not be sure, but whatever it was had a distinctly familiar flavor.

Call it Essence of Tymbrimi.

KAA

There was no more to accomplish in the cave. The probe appeared to be dead.

Even if it came back to life, any conversation with the natives would be handled from *Streaker*'s end. Meanwhile, it was past time to return to the habitat. Kaa had a team he had not seen in days.

A human couple might have paused before exiting the little grotto, looking around to imprint the site of their first lovemaking. But not dolphins. Neo-fins experienced nostalgia, just like their human patrons, but they could store sonar place images in ways humans had to mimic with recording devices. Streaking outside, joining Peepoe under bright sunshine, Kaa knew the two of them could revisit the cave anytime they chose, simply by bringing their arched foreheads together – re-creating its unique echoes in that ancient gulf of memory some called the Whale Dream.

It felt good to dash across the wide sea again, with Peepoe's lithe body sharing every kick and leap in perfect unison. Motion equaled joy after any long confinement to machinery and closed spaces.

On the outward trip, their swim had been exquisite, but tempered by a taut, sexual tension. Now there were no secrets, no conflicting desires. Most of the return journey was spent in silent bliss – like a simple mated pair from presapient days, free of the gifts and burdens of uplift.

Finally, with the habitat drawing near, Kaa felt his mind slip reluctantly back into Anglic-using rhythms. Compelled to speak, he used the informal click-squeal dialect fins preferred while swimming.

'Well, here it comes,' he sonar-cast during the underwater phase of their next splash-and-surge cycle. 'Back to home and family ... such as they are.'

'Family?' she replied skeptically. 'Brookida, perhaps. As for Mopol and Zhaki, wouldn't you rather be related to a penguin?'

Is my opinion of them so obvious? After breaching for air, Kaa tried making light of things with a joke.

'Oh, I give those two some credit. With luck, they won't have set the ocean on fire while we're gone.'

Peepoe laughed, then added, 'Do you think they'll be jealous?'

Good question. Dolphins could not conceal interpersonal matters like humans, with their complex games of emotional deceit. By sonar scanning each other's viscera, one seldom had to guess who slept with whom.

Envy wouldn't be a problem if I established clear authority from the start, both as an officer and as senior-ranking male.

Unfortunately, chain of command was a recent, human-imposed concept. Underneath, bull dolphins still felt ancient drives to jostle over status and breeding rights.

In fact, Peepoe's choice might reinforce Kaa's position atop the little local hierarchy. *Though I shouldn't need help. Not if I were a real leader.*

'Jealous.' He pondered, thrusting harder with his flukes, till his beak pushed their shared shock wave, drawing her along in his wake. 'Those two are highly sexed, so maybe they will be. But at least this way Zhaki and Mopol should stop bothering you with hopeless propositions.'

The young males had made relentless crude suggestions toward Peepoe from the first day she arrived, even brushing lewdly against her until Kaa had to rebuke them. While it was true that dolphins had a far different scale of tolerance for such behavior than humans – and Peepoe was capable of taking care of herself – in this case the pair were so persistent that Kaa had to dish out tail whacks to make them back off.

'Hopeless?' Peepoe asked in a teasing tone. 'Now you're making assumptions. How do you know I'm monogamous? Maybe a little harem would suit me fine.'

Kaa spread his jaws and aimed a nip at her nearest pectoral fin ... slow enough for her to slip aside, laughing, before his teeth snapped.

'Good,' she commented. 'Pacific Tursiops go in for that kinky stuff. But I prefer a nice and conservative Atlantean. You're from Miami-Under, no? Born into an old-fashioned line marriage, I bet.'

Kaa grunted. Even the sonar-based dialect of Anglic wasn't easy while speeding at full throttle.

'One of the Heinlein family variants,' he conceded. 'The style works better for dolphins than humans. Why? You looking for a line to marry into?'

'Mnn. I'd rather start a *new* one. Always hankered to be the founding matriarch of a nice little lineage – if the masters of uplift allow it.'

That was the eternal Big If. No neo-dolphin could legally breed without permission from the Terragens Uplift Board. Despite the unusual freedoms humans had given their clients – voting rights and the trappings of citizenship – Earthclan was still bound by ancient Galactic law.

Improve your clients, went the basic code of uplift ... *Or lose them.*

'You gotta be kidding,' he answered. 'If any of us *Streaker* fins ever do make it home somehow from this crazed voyage, we'll never face another sapiency exam from the masters. We may be sterilized on the spot, for all the trouble we caused. Or else we're heroes, and it'll be sperm-and-seed donations for the rest of our lives, fostering almost the whole next neo-fin generation.

'Either way, it won't be cozy family life for any of us. Not ever.' He hadn't expected it to come out that way, with an edge of ironic bitterness. But Peepoe must have seen he was telling the truth. She continued keeping pace alongside, but her silence told Kaa how much it stung.

Great. Everything felt so fine ... this wonderful water, the fish we snatched for breakfast, our lovemaking. Would it have hurt to let her stay in denial for a while, dreaming of happy endings? Holding on to the fantasy that we might yet go home, and lead normal lives?

'Kaa!' Brookida's cry made the tiny habitat reverberate. 'I'm glad you're back. Did your mission go well? Wait till you hear what I discovered by correlating passive seismic echo scans from here to *Streaker*'s sssite. I fed the raw data into one of Charles Dart's old programs to get tomography images of the subcrustal zone!'

All that, on a single breath. It was what humans would call a 'mouthful.'

'That's great, Brookida. But to answer your question, our mission didn't go as well as we hoped. In fact, we have orders to pack everything up and break camp. Gillian and Tsh't plan to move the ship.'

Brookida shook his mottled gray head. 'Won't that risk giving away *Streaker*'s position?'

'The site's already compromised. Dr. Baskin suspects the Jophur may be p-preoccupied, but that can't last.'

It had been Kaa's mission to find out what the sooners knew about such things. Perhaps Uriel the Smith had some idea what the Jophur were up to. No one had blamed Kaa for the failure – not out loud. But he knew the ship's council was disappointed.

I warned them to send someone better trained at spying.

He looked around. 'Where are the others?'

Brookida let out a warbled sigh.

'Off joyriding on Peepoe's sled. Or else vandalizing the fishing nets of local hoons and qheuens.'

Damn! Kaa cursed. He had ordered Zhaki and Mopol to stay within a kilometer of the dome, and restrict themselves to monitoring spy eyes already in place at Wuphon Port. Above all, they were supposed to avoid direct contact with the sooners.

'They got bored,' Brookida explained. 'Now that *Streaker* has Alvin and other local experts aboard, our team is a bit redundant. It's why I've been tracing the subduction-zone magma flows. My first chance since Kithrup to test out an idea I had, based on Charles Dart's old research. You recall those strange beings who lived deep under Kithrup's crust? The ones with the weird, unpronounceable species name?'

Peepoe spoke up. 'You mean the *Karrank-k%*?'

She did a creditable job of expressing the double-aspirated slide tone at the end, sounding like a steam kettle about to explode.

'Yes, quite. Well, I'd been wondering what kind of ecosystem could support them down there. And it got me thinking ...'

Brookida halted. Then all three dolphins whirled around as the wall segment behind them began emitting a low, scraping hum. The grating vibration hurt Kaa's jaw.

Soon, the entire habitat groaned to a rasping sonic frequency Kaa recognized.

It's a saser! Someone's attacking the dome!

'Harnesses!'

At his shouted command, they all dived toward the rack where heavy-duty tool kits were hung, ready for use. Kaa streaked through the open end of his well-worn apparatus, and felt its many control surfaces slide smoothly into place. A control cable snaked toward the neutral tap behind his left eye. Robotic arms whirred as he jerked the harness free of its rack. Peepoe's unit popped loose just half an instant later.

A rough rectangle crept across the opposite wall, above and below the waterline, glowing hot.

'They're cutting through!' Peepoe cried.

'Breathers!' Kaa shouted. From the back of his harness, a hose swarmed over his blowhole, covering it with a moist kiss and tight seal. A blast of canned air tasted even more tinny than the recycled stuff within the dome. Kaa sent a neural command activating his torch cutter and saser, tools that could second as weapons in close combat . . .

But they didn't respond!

'Peepoe!' He shouted. 'Check your—'

'I'm helping Brookida!' she cut in. 'His harness is stuck!'

Kaa slashed the water with his flukes, squealing a cry of frustration. With no better options, he interposed his body between theirs and the far wall . . .

. . . which abruptly collapsed in a wave of pummeling froth.

GILLIAN

'I have discovered several things of interest,' the Niss Machine told Gillian, after she wakened from a brief induced sleep. *'The first has to do with that wonderfully ostentatious native machine, built and operated by the urrish tinkerer, Uriel.'*

Sitting in her darkened office, she watched a recorded holo image of wheels, pulleys, and disks, whirling in a flamboyant show of light and action. Not far from Gillian, the ancient cadaver, Herbie, seemed to regard the same scene. A trick of shadows made the enigmatic, mummified face seem amused.

'Let me guess. Uriel created a computer.'

The Niss reacted with surprise. Its spiral of meshed lines tightened to a knot.

'*You knew?*'

'I suspected. From the kids' reports, Uriel wouldn't waste time on anything useless or abstract. She'd want to give her folk something special. The one thing her founding ancestors absolutely had to throw away.'

'*Possession of computers. Good point, Dr. Baskin. Uriel could aim no higher than to be like Prometheus. Bringing her people the fire of calculation.*'

'But without digital cognizance,' she pointed out. 'An undetectable computer.'

'*Indeed. I found no reference to such a thing in our captured Galactic Library unit. So I turned to the pre-contact 2198 edition of the* Encyclopedia Britannica. *There I learned about analog computation with mechanical components, which actually had a brief ascendancy on Earth, using many of the same techniques we see in Uriel's hall of spinning glass!*'

'I remember hearing about this. Maybe Tom mentioned it.'

'*Did he also mention that the same thing can be achieved using simple electronic circuits? Networks of resistors, capacitors, and diodes can simulate a variety of equations. By interconnecting such units, solutions can be worked out for limited problems.*

'*It provokes one to consider the military potential of such a system. For instance, operating sneak-attack weapons without digital controls, using undetectable guidance systems.*'

The Niss holo performed a twist that Gillian interpreted as a shrug.

'*But then, if the notion were feasible, it would have found its way into the Library by now.*'

There it was again. Even Tymbrimi suffered from the same all-pervading supposition – that anything worth doing must have been done already, over the course of two billion years. The assumption nearly always proved *true*. Still, wolfling humans resented it.

'So,' Gillian prompted. 'Have you figured out what Uriel is trying to compute?'

'*Ah, yes.*' The line motif spun contemplatively.

'*That is, perhaps.*

'*Or rather ... no, I have not.*'

'What's the problem?'

The Niss showed spiky irritation.

'*My difficulty is that all the algorithms used by Uriel are of Terran origin.*' Gillian nodded.

'Naturally. Her math books came from the so-called Great

Printing, when human learning flooded this world, most of it in the form of pre-contact texts. A mirror image of what Galactic society did to Earth. On Jijo, *we* were the ones to unleash an overpowering wealth of knowledge, engulfing prior beliefs.'

Hence also Gillian's recent, weird experience – debating the literary merits of Jules Verne with a pair of distinctly unhuman youngsters named 'Alvin' and 'Huck,' whose personalities had little in common with the stodgy Galactic norm.

The Niss agreed, bowing its tornado of laced lines.

'You grasp my difficulty, Doctor. Despite Tymbrimi sympathy toward Earthlings, my makers were uplifted as Galactic citizens, with a shared tradition. While details of my programming are exceptional, I was designed according to proven principles, after eons of Galactic experience refining digital computers. These precepts clash with Terran superstitions—'

Gillian coughed behind her hand. The Niss bowed.

'Forgive. I meant to say, Terran lore.'

'Can you give an example?'

'I can. Consider the contrast between the word/concepts discrete *and* continuous.

'According to Galactic science, anything and everything can be accomplished by using arithmetic. By counting and dividing, using integers and rational fractions. Sophisticated arithmetic algorithms enable us to understand the behavior of a star, for instance, by partitioning it into ever-smaller pieces, modeling those pieces in a simple fashion, then recombining the parts. That is the digital way.'

'It must call for vast amounts of memory and raw computing power.'

'True, but these are cheaply provided, enough for any task you might require.

'Now look back at pre-contact human wolflings. Your race spent many centuries as semicivilized beings, mentally ready to ask sophisticated questions, but completely lacking access to transistors, quantum switches, or binary processing. Until your great savants, Turing and Von Neumann, finally expressed the power of digital computers, generations of mathematicians had to cope by using pencil and paper.

'The result? A mix of the brilliant and the inane. Abstract differential analysis and cabalistic numerology. Algebra, astrology, and geometrical topology. Much of this amalgam was based on patently absurd concepts, such as continuity, *or aptly named* irrational *numbering, or the astonishing notion that there are layered infinities of the divisibly small.'*

Gillian sighed an old frustration.

'Earth's best minds tried to explain our math, soon after contact. Again and again we showed it was self-consistent. That it worked.'

'Yet it accomplished nothing that could not be outmatched in moments by calculating engines like myself. Galactic seers dismissed all the clever equations as trickery and shortcuts, or else the abstract ravings of savages.'

She acceded with a nod.

'This happened once before, you know. In Earth's twentieth century, after the Second World War, the victors quickly split into opposing camps. Those experts you mentioned – Turing and von Whoever – they worked in the west, helping set off our own digital revolution.

'Meanwhile, the east was ruled by a single dictator, I think his name was Steel.'

'Accessing the Britannica *... You mean "Stalin"? Yes, I see the connection. Until his death, Stalin obstructed Russo-Soviet science for ideological reasons. He banished work on genetics because it contradicted notions of communist perfectibility. Moreover, he quashed work on computers, calling them 'decadent.' Even after his passing, many in the east held that calculation was crude, inelegant ... only good for quick approximations. For truth, one needed pure mathematics.'*

'So that's why many practitioners in the Old Math still come from Russia.' Gillian chuckled. 'It sounds like yet another inverted image of what happened to Earth, after contact.'

The Niss pondered this for a moment.

'What are you implying, Doctor? That Stalin was partly right? That you Terrans were right? That you were onto something the rest of the universe has missed?'

'It seems unlikely, eh? And yet, isn't that slim possibility the very reason why your makers assigned you to this ship?'

Again, the meshed lines whirled.

'Point well taken, Dr. Baskin.'

Gillian stood up to start moving her body through a series of stretching exercises. The brief sleep period had helped. Still, there were a hundred problems to address.

'Look,' she asked the Niss Machine. 'Is there some point where all this is heading? Haven't you a clue what problem Uriel is trying to solve?'

She gestured toward the recorded image of pulleys, leather straps, and spinning disks.

'In a word, Doctor? NO.

'Oh, I can tell that Uriel is modeling a set of simultaneous differential equations – to use old wolfling terminology. The range of numerical values being considered appears to be simple, even trivial.

I could outcalculate her so-called computer with a mere one quadrillionth of my processing power.'

'Then why don't you?'

'Because to me the problem first calls for unlocking the code of a lost language. I need an opening, a Rosetta stone, after which all should be instantly clear.

'In short, I need help from an Earthling, to suggest what the expressions might be for.'

Gillian shrugged.

'Another tough break, then. We've plumb run out of mathematicians about this crate. Creideiki and Tom both used to play with the Old Math. I know Charles Dart dabbled, and Takkata-Jim . . .'

She sighed.

'And Emerson D'Anite. He was the last one who could have helped you.'

Gillian moved toward her reference console. 'I suppose we can scan the personnel files to see if there's anyone else—'

'That may not be necessary,' the Niss cut in. *'It might be possible to access one of the experts you already mentioned.'*

Gillian blinked, unable to believe she heard right.

'What are you talking about?'

'You assigned me another problem – to find out what the feralsapient tytlal named "Mudfoot" was staring at, after the council meeting. To achieve that, I enhanced the spy camera's last scene, before the privacy wasps closed in.

'Please watch carefully, Doctor.'

The big display now showed the final clear picture sent by the lost probe. Gillian found it physically painful to watch the insect's beating wings, and felt relief when the Niss zoomed toward a corner of the field, pushing the privacy wasp offscreen. What ballooned outward was a section of the ornate contraption of Uriel the Smith – a marvel of pure ingenuity and resourcefulness.

I did take one course in the Old Math, before heading to medical school. I could try to help. The Niss can supply precontact texts. All it wants is insight. Some wolfling intuition . . .

Her thoughts veered, distracted by the vivid enhancement. Looming around her now was a maze of improvised scaffolding, filled with shadows that were split, here and there, by glaring points of light.

All this incredible activity must add up to something important.

Gillian saw the apparent goal sought by the Niss – a set of shadows that had the soft curves of life-forms, precariously balanced in the crisscrossing trusswork. Some figures were small, with snakelike torsos and tiny legs, brandishing tools with slim, many-jointed hands.

Miniature urs, she realized. *The maintenance crew?*

A larger silhouette loomed over these. Gillian gasped when she saw it must be human! Then she recalled.

Of course. Humans are among Uriel's allies, and skilled technicians. They're also good climbers, perfect to help keep things running.

The Niss must now be straining its ability to enhance the grainy image. The rate of magnification slowed, and remaining shadows peeled grudgingly before the onslaught of computing power. But soon she knew the human was male, from the shape of neck and shoulders. He was pointing, perhaps indicating a task for the little urs to perform.

Gillian saw that he had long hair, brushed left over a cruel scar. For an instant she stared at the puckered wound in his temple.

A moment later, the image clarified to show a *smile*.

Recognition hit like a blast of chill water.

'My God ... It can't be!'

The Niss crooned, expressing both satisfaction and intrigue.

'You confirm the resemblance?

'It does appear to be engineer Emerson D'Anite.

'Our crew mate whom we thought killed by the Old Ones, back at the Fractal System.

'He whose scout vessel was enveloped by a globe of devouring light, as the Streaker made its getaway, fleeing by a circuitous route toward Jijo.'

The Tymbrimi machine shared one trait with its makers, a deep love of surprise. That pleasure it now expressed in a hum of satisfaction.

'You ask frequently how anyone could have followed us to this forlorn corner of the universe, Dr. Baskin.

'I believe the question just acquired new levels of cogency.

KAA

He never got to put up much of a fight.

How could he, with all his weapons sabotaged from the start? Besides, Kaa wasn't sure he could bring himself to harm one of his own kind.

Clearly, the assailants who attacked the dome had fewer scruples.

The ruined habitat lay far below, its pieces strewn across the continental shelf. Along with Peepoe and Brookida, Kaa barely dodged being pinned by the collapsing walls, escaping the mael-strom of metal and froth only to face the gun barrels of well-armed captors. Herded to the surface, he and the others panted in nervous exhaustion under the waning afternoon sun.

In contrast, Mopol's sleek form rested almost languidly atop the speed sled that Peepoe had brought from *Streaker*'s hiding place, governing the engines and armaments with impulses sent down his neural tap. Swimming nearby – wearing a fully charged tool har-ness – Zhaki explained the situation.

'It's like this, p-pilot-t . . .' He slurred the words in his eagerness. 'The three of you are gonna do what we sssay, or else.'

Kaa tossed his head, using his lower jaw to splash water at Zhaki's eye.

> * *Silly threats from one*
> > * *Who's watched too many movies!*
> > > * *Just say it, fool. Now!* *

Mopol hissed angrily, but Peepoe laughed at Zhaki's predica-ment. To continue his menacing speech now would be an act of obedience to Kaa's command. It was a minor matter – not exactly a logical checkmate. But Kaa felt it valuable to recover even a little initiative.

'We . . .' Zhaki blew air and tried again. 'Mopol and I are resign-ing from the *Streaker* crew. We're not going back-k, and you can't make us.'

So that's what it's about, Kaa thought.

'Desertion!' Brookida sputtered indignantly. 'Letting your crew mates down when they need you mossst!'

Mopol let out a skirl of rejection.

'Our legal term of ssservice ended almossst two years ago.'

'Right-t,' Zhaki agreed. 'Anyway, we never signed on for this insanity . . . fleeing like wounded mullet across the galaxies.'

'You plan to go *sooner*,' Peepoe fluted, her voice bemused. 'Living wild, in this sea.'

Mopol nodded. 'Some were already talkin' about it, before we left-t the ship. This world's a paradise for our kind. The whole crew oughta do it!'

'But even if they don't-t,' Zhaki added, 'we're gonna.'

Then he added a haiku for emphasis.

> * *Six or seven clans*
> > * *Did this already, on shore.*
> > > * *We have precedent!* *

Kaa realized there was nothing he could do to change their minds. The sea would answer his best arguments with its fine mineral smoothness and the enticing echoes of tasty fish. In time, the deserters would come to miss the comforts of civilized life, or grow bored, or realize there are dangers even on a world without big predators. The water had a faint, prescient choppiness, and Kaa wondered if either of the rebel fins had ever been outside during a truly vicious storm.

But then, hadn't other waves of settlers faced the same choice? The g'Keks, qheuens, and even human beings?

'The Jophur may make it hard on you,' he told them.

'We'll take our chancess.'

'And if you're caught by the Institutes?' Brookida asked. 'Your presence here would be a crime, reflecting badly on—'

Mopol and Zhaki laughed. Even Kaa found that argument easy to dismiss. Humans and chimps were already on Jijo. If Earthclan suffered collective punishment for that crime, a few dolphins living offshore could hardly make things worse.

'So, what do you plan to do with us?' Kaa asked.

'Why, nothing much-ch. You and Brookida are free to swim back to your precious Gillian Basssskin, if you like.'

'That could take a week!' Brookida complained. But Kaa struggled against involuntary spasms in his harness arms, set off by Zhaki's implication. Before he could unstrangle his speech centers, Peepoe expressed his dread.

'Jussst Kaa and Brookida? You're insisting that I stay?'

Mopol chittered assent with such glee that it came out sounding more like gutter Primal Delphin than Trinary.

'That's the p-plan,' Zhaki confirmed. 'We'd make a poor excuse for a c-colony without at least one female.'

Kaa abruptly saw their long-term scheme. Mopol's spell of malingering sickness had been meant to draw one of Makanee's nurses out here from the ship. Most were young females, with Peepoe the best catch of all.

'Will you add kidnap-ping to the crime of desertion?' she asked, sounding as fascinated as fearful.

Kaa's blood surged hot as Zhaki flipped around to streak past Peepoe, gliding along her belly, upside down.

'You won't call it that-t after a while,' Zhaki promised, leaving a trail of bubbles as he rolled suggestively. 'In time, you'll c-call this your luckiessst day.'

At that point, Kaa reached the limit of his endurance. With a lashing of flukes, he charged—

*

There was a blank time after that ... and some more that went by all in a haze – half-numb and half-pained.

Drifting, Kaa was sustained by instinct as his body performed the needed motions. Staying upright. Kicking to bring his blowhole above the watery surface. Breathing. Submerging once again. Allowing his unraveled self to knit slowly back together.

'C-come on now, my boy,' the helper told him. 'It'sss only a bit farther.'

Dutifully, Kaa swam alongside, doing as he was told. You learned this at an early age ... when injured, always obey the helper. It might be your mother, or an auntie, or even some older male in the pod. Someone always was the helper ... or else the sea would claim you.

In time, he recalled this helper's name – *Brookida*. He also began recognizing the peculiar lap and texture of littoral water, not far from shore. Kaa even recalled part of what put him in this condition ... a state so dazed that all speech thoughts were driven from his mind.

There had been a fight. He had charged against harsh odds, hoping to take his enemies by surprise ... by the sheer audacity of the attack.

It took just one blast of concentrated sound to knock him in a double flip, with tremors shaking every muscle. Paralyzed, he distantly sensed the two male foes move off ... taking his love with them.

'You feeling better now?' Brookida asked. The older dolphin cast a sonar sweep through Kaa's innards, checking on his progress. Some mental clouds were parting. Enough to recall a few more facts. The shattered habitat – not worth revisiting. The hopelessness of pursuing a speed sled, even one burdened with three passengers, since night was soon approaching.

Both arms of his harness twitched as his rattled brain sent spasmodic commands down the neural link. Kaa managed to lift his head a bit, the next time he breathed, and recognized the shape of nearby coastal hills. Brookida was herding him closer to the native fishing town.

'Mopol and Zhaki wrecked the cables and transmittersss, back at the dome. But-t I figure we can find the lines leading to the spy drones in Wuphon Port, tap into those, and contact the ship-p.'

Some order was slipping into Kaa's chaotic thoughts. Enough to comprehend a bit of what the old fin said. This return of sapiency left him with mixed feelings – relieved that the loss was not permanent, plus regretful longing for the simplicity that must now go away, replaced by urgent, hopeless needs.

Trinary came back more easily than Anglic.

* We must pursue the—
* Spawn of syphilitic worms,
* While their sound spoor's fresh! *

'Yes, of course. I agree. How awful for Peepoe, poor lass. But first let's contact *Streaker*. Maybe our crew mates can help.'

Kaa hearkened to the sense in that. One of the first principles of human legality that dolphins clearly understood was that of a *posse*, which had analogies in natural cetacean society. When an offense is committed against the pod, you can call for help. You should not face trouble alone.

He let Brookida lead him to the site where fiber cables from the onshore spy eyes all converged below. Booming surf reminded Kaa unhappily of this morning's lovemaking. The sound made him squeal a Primal protest, railing against the unfairness of it all. To find a mate and lose her on the same day.

The water tasted of qheuens and hoons ... plus wooden planks and tar. Kaa rested at the surface, sifting his mind back together while Brookida dived down to establish the link.

A saser ... Zhaki shot me with a saser beam.

Dimly he realized that Zhaki might have saved his life. If that bolt hadn't stopped him, Mopol would surely have fired next, using the more powerful unit on the sled.

But saved me ... for what?

Ifni tell me ... what's the point?

Kaa didn't figure he still had his nickname anymore.

A few hours ... now it's gone again. She took it with her. Brookida surfaced next to him, sputtering elation, having achieved quick success.

'Got it-t! Come on, Kaa. I've got Gillian on the line. She wants to talk to you.'

Sometimes life is filled with choices. You get to select which current to ride, which tide to pull your destiny.

Other times leave you torn ... wrenched apart ... as if two orcas had a grip on you, one biting hard on your flukes while the other plays tug-of-war with your snout.

Kaa heard the order. He understood it.

He wasn't at all sure he could obey.

'*I'm sorry about Peepoe,*' Gillian Baskin said, her voice crackling over the makeshift comm line, conveyed directly to Kaa's auditory nerves. '*We'll rescue her, and deal with the deserters, when opportunity permits. Believe me, it's a high priority.*

'But this other task is crucial. Our lives may depend on it, Kaa.'
The human paused.
'I want you to heave straight into Wuphon Harbor.
'It's time one of us went to town.'

SOONERS

EWASX

My rings, it has finally happened.

Rejoice! Your master torus has ultimately managed to recover some of the fatty memories you/we/I had thought forever lost! Those valuable recall tracks that were erased when brave-foolish Asx melted the wax!

That act of wrong loyalty stymied the usefulness of this hybrid ring stack for much too long. Some of the *Polkjhy* crew called us/Me a failed experiment. Even the Captain-Leader questioned this effort ... this attempt to convert a wild traeki into our loyal authority on Jijoan affairs.

Admittedly, our/My expertise about the Six Races has been uneven and fitful. Mistakes were made despite/because of our advice.

BUT NOW I/WE HAVE REACQUIRED THIS SECRET! This conviction that once filled the mulch center of the diffuse being called *Asx*.

Deep beneath the melted layers, a few memory tracks remained.

DO NOT SQUIRM SO! Instead you should exult in this recovery of something so important.

The Egg.

So far, we have seen only insolence from the sooner races – delays and grudging cooperation with the survey teams we send forth.

No voluntary gathering of g'Kek vermin at designated collection points.

No migration of traeki stacks for appraisal-and-conversion.

Swarms of supervised robots have begun sifting the countryside for groups of g'Kek and traeki, herding them toward enclosures where their numbers can be concentrated at higher density. But this task proves laborious and inefficient. It would be far more convenient if the locals were persuaded to perform the task on their own.

Worse, these fallen beings still refuse to admit any knowledge of the Earthling prey ship.

IT PROVES DIFFICULT TO COERCE GREATER COOPERATION.

Attacks on population centers are met with resignation and dispersal.

Their dour religion confounds us with stoic passivity. It is hard to deprive hope from a folk that never had much.

BUT NOW WE HAVE A NEW TARGET!

One more meaningful to the Six Races than any of their campsite villages. A target to convince them of our ruthless resolve.

We already knew something of this *Great Egg*. Its throbbing radiations were an irritant, disrupting our instruments, but we dismissed it as a geophysical anomaly. Psi-resonant formations exist on some worlds. Despite local mythology, our onboard Library cube can cite other cases. A rare phenomenon, but understood.

Only now we realize how deeply this stone is rooted in the savages' religion. It is their central object of reverence. Their 'soul.'

How amusing.

How pathetic.

And how very convenient.

VUBBEN

The last time his aged wheels had rolled along this dusty trail, it was in the company of twelve twelves of white-robed pilgrims – the finest eyes, minds, and rings of all six races – winding their way past sheer cliffs and steam vents in a sacred question to seek guidance from the Holy Egg. For a time, that hopeful procession had made the canyon walls reverberate with fellowship vibrations – the Commons united and at peace.

Alas, before reaching its goal, the company fell into a maelstrom of fire, bloodshed, and despair. Soon the sages and their followers were too busy with survival to spend time meditating on the ineffable. But during the weeks since, Vubben could never shake a sense of unfinished business. Of something vital, left undone.

Hence this solitary return journey, even though it brought his frail wheels all too near the Jophur foe ship. Vubben's axles and motive spindles throbbed from the cruel climb, and he longingly recalled that a brave qheuen had volunteered to carry him all the way here, riding in comfort on a broad gray back.

But he could not accept. Despite creakiness and age, Vubben had to come alone.

At last he reached the final turn before entering the Nest. Vubben paused to catch his breath and smooth his ruffled thoughts in preparation for the trial ahead. He used a soft rag to wipe green sweat off all four eye hoods and stalks.

It is said that g'Kek bodies could never have evolved on a planet. Our wheels and whiplike limbs better suit the artificial worlds where our star-god ancestors dwelled, before they gambled a great wager, won their bet, and lost everything.

He often wondered what it must have been like to abide in some vast spinning city whose inner space was spanned by countless slender roadways that arched like ribbons of spun sugar. *Intelligent* paths that would twist, gyre, and reconnect at your command, so the way between any two points could be just as straight or deliciously curved as you liked. To live where a planet's grip did not press you relentlessly, every dura from birth till death, squashing your rims and wearing away your bearings with harsh grit.

More than any other sooner race, the g'Kek had to work hard in order to love Jijo. *Our refuge. Our purgatory.*

Vubben's eyestalks contracted involuntarily as the Egg once again made its presence known. A surge of *tywush* vibrations seemed to rise from the ground. The sporadic patterning tremors had grown more intense, the nearer he came to the source. Now Vubben shivered as another wave front stroked his tense spokes, making his brain resound in its hard case. Words could not express the sensation, even in Galactic Two or Three. The psi-effect provoked no images or dramatic emotions. Rather, a feeling of *expectation* seemed to build, slowly but steadily, as if some long-awaited plan were coming to fruition at long last.

The episode peaked ... then passed quickly away, still lacking the coherence he hoped for.

Then let us begin in earnest, Vubben thought. His motor spindles throbbed, helped along by slender pusher legs, as both wheels turned away from the sunset's dimming glow, toward mystery.

The Egg loomed above, a rounded shelf of stone that stretched ahead for half an arrowflight before curving out of sight. Although a century of pilgrimages had worn a trail of packed pumice, it still took almost a midura for Vubben to roll his first circuit around the base of the ovoid, whose mass pressed a deep basin in the flank of a dormant volcano. Along the way, he raised slender arms and eyestalks, lofting them in gentle benediction, supplementing his mental entreaty with the language of motion.

Help your people ... Vubben urged, seeking to attune his thoughts, harmonizing them with the cyclical vibrations.

Rise up. Waken. Intervene to save us ...

Normally, an effort at communion involved more than one

suppliant. Vubben would have merged his contribution with a hoon's patience, the tenacity of a qheuen, a traeki's selfless affinity, plus that voracious will to know that made the best urs and humans seem so much alike. But such a large group might be detected moving about close to the Jophur. Anyway, he could not ask others to risk being caught in the company of a g'Kek.

With each pass around the Egg, he sent one eye wafting up to peer at Mount Ingul, whose spire was visible beyond the crater's rim. There, Phwhoon-dau had promised to station a semaphore crew to alert Vubben in case of any approaching threat – or if there were changes in the tense standoff with the aliens. So far, no warnings were seen flashing from that western peak.

But he faced other distractions, just as disturbing to his train of thought.

Loocen hovered in the same western quarter of the sky, with a curve of bright pinpoints shining along the moon's crescent-shaped terminator, dividing sunlit and shadowed faces. Tradition said those lights were domed cities. The departing Buyur left them intact, since Loocen had no native ecosystem to recycle and restore. Time would barely touch them until this fallow galaxy and its myriad star systems were awarded to new legal tenants, and the spiral arms once more teemed with commerce.

How those lunar cities must have tempted the first g'Kek exiles, fleeing here from their abandoned space habitats, just a few sneak jumps ahead of baying lynch mobs. Feeling safe at last, after passing through the storms of Izmunuti, those domes would have enticed them with reminders of home. A promise of low gravity and clean, smooth surfaces.

But such places offered no reliable, long-term shelter against relentless enemies. A planet's surface was better for fugitives, with a life-support system that needed no computer regulation. A natural world's complex *messiness* made it a fine place to hide, if you were willing to live as primitives, scratching a subsistence like animals.

In fact, Vubben had few clues of what passed through the original colonists' minds. The Sacred Scrolls were the only written records from that time, and they mostly ignored the past, preaching instead how to live in harmony on Jijo, and promising salvation to those following the Path of Redemption.

Vubben was renowned for skill at reciting those hallowed texts. *But in truth, we sages stopped relying on the scrolls a century ago.*

He resumed the solitary pilgrimage, commencing his fourth circuit just as another *tywush* wave commenced. Vubben now felt certain the cycles were growing more coherent. Yet there was also a feeling that much more power lay quiescent, far below the surface – power he desperately needed to tap.

Hoon and qheuen grandparents passed on testimony that the patterns were more potent in the last days of Drake the Younger, when the Egg was still warm with birth heat, fresh from Jijo's womb. Compelling dreams used to flood all six races back then, convincing all but the most conservative that a true revelation had come.

Politics also played a role in the great orb's acceptance. Drake and Ur-Chown made eager proclamations, interpreting the new omen in ways that helped consolidate the Commons.

'This stone-of-wisdom is Jijo's gift, a portent, sanctifying the treaties and ratifying the Great Peace,' they declared, with some success. From then on, hope became part of the revised religion. Though in deference to the scrolls, the word itself was seldom used.

Now Vubben sought some of that hope for himself, for his race, and all the Six. He sought it in signs that the great stone might be stirring once again.

I can feel it happening! If only the Egg rouses far enough, soon enough.

But the increasing activity seemed to follow its own pace, with a momentum that made him feel like an insect, dancing next to some titanic being.

Perhaps, Vubben suspected, *my presence has nothing to do with these changes.*

What happens next may not involve me at all.

BLADE

The winds were blowing him the wrong way.

No real surprise there. Weather patterns on the Slope had been contrary for more than a year. Anyway, metaphorically, the Six Races were being buffeted by gales of change. Still, at the end of a long, eventful day, Blade had more than enough reason to curse the stubbornly perverse breeze.

By late afternoon, slanting sunshine combed the forests and boo groves into a panorama of shadows and light. The Rimmers were a phalanx of giant soldiers, their armored shells blushing before the lowering sun. Below, a vast marsh had given way to prairie, which in turn became forested hills. Few signs of habitation could be seen from his great height, though Blade was handicapped by a basic inability to look directly *down*. The chitinous bulk of his wide body blocked any direct view of the ground.

How I would love, just once in my life, to see what lies below my own feet!

His five legs weren't doing much at the moment. The claws dangled over open space, snapping occasionally in reflex spasms, trying futilely to get a grip on the clear air. Even more disconcerting, the sensitive feelers around his mouth had no earth or mud to brush against, probing the many textures of the ground. Instead, they, too, hung uselessly. Blade felt numb and bare in the direction a qheuen least liked being exposed.

That had been the hardest part to get used to, after takeoff. To a qheuen, life's texture is determined by its medium. Sand and salt water to a red. Freshwater and mud to a blue. A world of stony caverns to imperial grays. Although their ancestors had starships, Jijo's qheuens seemed poor candidates for flight.

As open country glided majestically past, Blade pondered being the first of his kind in hundreds of years to soar.

Some adventure! It will be worth telling Log Biter and the other matrons about, when I return to that homey lodge behind Dolo Dam. The grubs, in their murky den, will want to hear the story at least forty or fifty times.

If only this voyage would get a little *less* adventurous, and more predictable.

I hoped to be communicating with Sara by now, not drifting straight toward the enemy's toothy maw.

Above Blade's cupola and vision strip, he heard valves open with a preliminary hiss – followed by a roaring burst of heat. Unable to shift or turn his suspended body, he could only envision the urrish contraptions in a wicker basket overhead, operating independently, using jets of flame to replenish the hot-air bag, keeping his balloon to a steady altitude.

But not a steady heading.

Everything was as automatic as the smiths' technology allowed, but there was no escaping the tyranny of the wind. Blade had just one control to operate – a cord attached to a distant knife that would rip the balloon open when he pulled, releasing the buoyant vapors and dropping him out of the sky at a smooth rate – so the smiths assured – fast, but not too fast. As pilot, he had one duty, to time his plummet so it ended in a decent-sized body of water.

Even arriving at a fair clip, no mere splash should harm his armored, disklike form. If a tangle of rope and torn fabric pinned his legs, dragging him down, Blade could hold his breath long enough to chew his way free and creep ashore.

Nevertheless, it had been hard to convince the survivors' council, ruling over the ruins of Ovoom Town, to let him try this crazy idea. They naturally doubted his claim that a blue qheuen should be their next courier.

But too many human boys and girls have died in recent days, rushing about in flimsy gliders. Urrish balloonists have been breaking necks and legs. All I have to do is crash into liquid and I'm guaranteed to walk away. Today's crude circumstances make me an ideal aviator!

There was just one problem. While hooking Blade into this conveyance, the smiths had assured him the afternoon breeze was reliable this time of year, straight up the valley of the Gentt. It should waft him all the way to splashdown at Prosperity Lake within a few miduras, leaving more than enough time to dash a rapid qheuen gait and reach the nearest semaphore station by nightfall. His packet of reports about conditions at ravaged Ovoom would then slide into the flashing message stream. And then Blade could finally scratch his lingering duty itch, restoring contact with Sara as he had vowed. Assuming she was at Mount Guenn, that is.

Only the winds changed, less than a midura after takeoff. The promised quick jaunt east became a long detour north.

Toward home, he noted. Unfortunately, the enemy lay in between. At this rate he'd be shot down before Dolo Village ever hove into view.

To make matters worse, he was starting to get thirsty.

This situation – it is ridiculous, Blade grumbled as sunset brought forth stars. The breeze broke up into rhythmic, contrary gusts. Several times, these bursts raised his hopes by shoving the balloon toward peaks where he spied other semaphore stations, passing soft flashes down the mountain chain. There was apparently a lot of message activity tonight, much of it heading north.

But whenever some large lake seemed about to pass below the bulging gasbag, another hard gust blew in, pushing him at an infuriating angle, back over jagged rocks and trees. Frustration only heightened his thirst.

If this keeps up, I'll be so dehydrated that I'd dive for a little puddle.

Blade soon realized how far he had come. As the last light of day vanished from the tallest peaks, he spied a cleft in the mountains that any Sixer would recognize – the pass leading to Festival Glade, where each year the Commons of Six Races gathered to celebrate – and mourn – another year of exile. For some time after the sun was gone, Loocen's bright crescent kept him company, illuminating the foothills. Blade expected the surface to draw closer as he was pushed northeast, but the simpleminded urrish altimeter somehow sensed changing ground levels and reacted with another jet of flame, preventing the balloon from meeting the valley floor.

Then Loocen sank as well, abandoning him to a world of shadows. The mountains became little more than black bites, torn out of the starry heavens. It left Blade all alone with his imagination, speculating how the Jophur were going to deal with him.

Would there be a flash of cold flame, as he had seen darting from the belly of the cruel corvette that devastated Ovoom Town? Would they rip him to bits with scalpels of sound? Or were he and the balloon destined for vaporization upon making contact with some defensive force field? The kind of barrier often described in garish Earthling novels?

Worst of all, he pictured a 'tractor beam,' seizing and dragging him down to torment in some Jophur-designed hell.

The cord – should I pull it now? he wondered. *Lest our foes learn the secret of hot-air balloons?*

Qheuens never used to laugh before coming to Jijo. But somehow the blue variety picked up the habit, infuriating their Gray Queens, even before hoons and humans could be blamed as bad influences. Blade's legs now contracted, quivering as a calliope of whistles escaped his breathing vents.

Right! We mustn't allow this 'technology' to fall into the wrong hands ... or rings. Why, the Jophur might make balloons of their own, to use against us!

The upland canyons answered with faint repetitions of his laughter – echoes that cheered him up a little, as if there were an audience for his imminent parting from the universe. *No qheuen likes to die alone*, Blade thought, tightening his grip on the cord that would send him plunging to Jijo's dark embrace. *I only hope someone finds enough shell fragments to dross ...*

At that moment, a faint glimmer made him pause. It came from dead ahead, farther up the narrowing valley, below the mountain pass. Blade tried focusing his visor, but again had to curse the poor vision his race inherited from ancient times. He peered at the pale shine.

Could it be ... ?

The soft rays reminded him of starlight, glancing off water, making him hold off yanking the cable for a few duras. If it *was* an alpine lake, he might have just a little time to estimate the distance, include his rate of drift, and guess the right moment to pull. *With my luck, it will turn out to be a mulc-spider's acid pit. At least that would take care of the mulching problem.*

The glimmer drew nearer, but its outline seemed strangely smooth, unlike a natural body of water. Its profile was *oval*, and the reflections had a convex quality that –

Ifni and the ancestors! Blade cursed in surprised dismay. *It is the Jophur ship!*

He stared in blank awe at the size of the globular thing.

So huge, I thought it was part of the landscape.

Worse, he measured his course and heading. *Soon, I'll be right on top of it.*

If anything, the wind stiffened from behind, accelerating his approach.

At once, Blade had an idea. One that changed his mind about the cruelty of fate.

This is better, he decided. *It will be like that novel I read last winter, by that pre-contact human, Vonnegut. The book ended with the hero making a bold, personal gesture toward God.*

The point seemed apropos then, and even more so now. When faced with casual extinction by an omnipotent force, sometimes the only option left to a poor mortal is to go out with defiance.

That proved remarkably feasible. Qheuen mouth parts served many functions, including sexual. So Blade made a virtue of his exposed posture, and got ready to present himself to the enemy in the most deliberately offensive manner possible.

Look THIS up in your Galactic Library! he thought, waving his sensor feelers suggestively. Perhaps, before he was vaporized, the Jophur would call up reference data dealing with starfaring qheuens, and realize the extent of his insolence. Blade hoped his life would count for at least that much. To be killed in anger, not as an afterthought.

Waves of tingling sensation coursed his feelers, and Blade wondered if danger was provoking some perverted version of the mating urge. *Well, after all, here I am, veering toward a big armored, dominant entity with my privates bared.*

Log Biter would not approve of the comparison, I suppose.

As the wind pushed him toward the battleship – a thing so huge it rivaled nearby mountains – all sight of it vanished beneath the forward edge of his chitin carapace. It would be out of sight during final approach, an irony Blade did not find amusing.

Then, to his great surprise, there rushed into sight the very thing he had been longing for – a *lake*. A large one, dammed up behind the great cruiser, drowning the Festival Glade under hectares of cool snowmelt.

If they don't shoot me down, he could not help speculating. *If they fail to notice me, I might yet reach ...*

But how could they not spy this approaching gasbag? Surely they must already have him pinned by star-god instruments.

Sure enough, the tingling of Blade's exposed feelers multiplied in rapid waves, as if they were being stroked – then stung – by a host of squirming shock worms. Not a sexual stirring, though. Instead the sensation triggered foraging instincts, causing his diamond-tipped incisors to snap reflexively, as if grabbing through mud at armored prey.

The feelers pick up magnetic and electric vibrations from hidden muck crawlers, he recalled.

Electromagnetic ... I'm being scanned!

Each time he panted breath through a leg vent, another dura passed. The lake swelled, and he knew the ship *must* be almost directly below by now. What were they waiting for?

Then a new thought occurred to Blade.

I'm being scanned ... but can they see me?

If only he had studied more science at the Tarek Town academy. Although grays tended to be better at abstractions – the reason why they took real names – Blade knew he should have insisted on taking that basic physics course.

Let's see. In human novels, they speak of 'radar' ... radio waves sent out to bounce off distant objects, giving away the location of intruders, for instance.

But you only get a good echo if it's something radio will bounce off. Metal, or some other hard stuff.

Blade quickly pulled his teeth back in. Otherwise, his bottom was his softest part, featuring multifaceted planes that might deflect incoming rays in random directions. The gasbag, he figured, must seem hardly more dense than a rain cloud!

Now, if only the urrish altimeter would wait awhile longer before adjusting the balloon's height, shooting hot flame with a roar to fill the night ...

The tingling peaked ... then started to diminish. Moments later, coolness stroked Blade's underside and he sensed the allure of water below. Tentative relief came accompanied by worry, for cold air would increase his rate of sink.

Now? Shall I pull the cord, before the flames turn on and give me away?

Water beckoned. Blade yearned to wash the dust from his vent pores. Yet he held back. Even if his sudden plummet from the sky didn't draw attention, he would land in the worst lake on Jijo, deep inside the Jophur defense perimeter, presumably patrolled by all sorts of hunter machines. Perhaps the robots had missed him till now because the possibility of floating qheuens had never been programmed into them. But a swimming qheuen most certainly was.

Anyway, the water gave him a strange feeling. There were flickerings under the surface – eerie flashes that reinforced his decision to hold back.

Each passing dura ratified the choice, as a separation slowly increased between Blade and the giant dreadnought, reappearing behind him as a dark curve with glimmering highlights, divided about a third of the way up by a rippling, watery line. It made him feel distinctly creepy.

Abruptly, a pinpoint of brilliance flared from the side of the globe ship, seeming to stab straight toward him.

Here it comes, Blade thought.

But the flaring light was no heat ray. No death beam, after all. Instead, the pinpoint widened. It became a glowing rectangular aperture. A door.

A mighty big door, Blade realized, wondering what could possibly take up so much room inside a mammoth star cruiser.

Apparently – another star cruiser.

From the gaping hangar, a sleek cigar shape emerged with a low hum, moving gradually at first, then accelerating toward Blade.

All right then. Not extinction. Capture. But why send that big thing after me?

Perhaps they saw his obscene gesture, and understood better than he expected.

Once more, Blade readied the rip cord. At the last moment, he would plummet from their grasp ... or else they'd shoot him as he fell. Or hunter robots would track him, underwater or overland. Still, it seemed proper to make the effort. *At least I'll get a drink.*

Again, night vision gave him trouble. Estimating the corvette's rate of closure proved futile. In frustration, Blade's thoughts slipped from Anglic and into the easier grooves of Galactic Six.

This specter of terror – I have seen it before.
This thing I saw last – as it burned down a city.
A city of felons – of sooners – my people.

His legs flexed spasmodically as the ship rushed toward him without slowing ...

What the—

... and kept going, sweeping past with a roar of displaced air.

Blade felt hooks of urrish steel yank his carapace at all five suspension points. One anchor broke free, tearing chitin armor like paper, then flinging wildly as the balloon was sucked after the sky-ship's wake.

The world passed in a blur, teaching him what *real* flying was about.

Then the Jophur vessel was gone, ignoring balloon and passenger with contempt, or else indifference. He glimpsed it once more, still climbing steadily toward the Rimmer peaks, leaving him swirling in a backwash of confusion and disturbed air.

VUBBEN

After a time, Vubben finally succeeded in quelling his busy thoughts, allowing the *tywush* resonance to pervade his soul, washing away distractions and doubts. Another midura passed, and another prayer circuit, while his meditation deepened. After Loocen set, a vast skyscape of constellations and nebulae passed overhead. Twinkling abode of the gods.

As he rounded back to the west side, another kind of winking light caught one of Vubben's eyes – a syncopated flash unlike any gleaming star. Still wrapped in his trance, Vubben had to labor just to lift a second stalk and recognize the flicker as coded speech.

It took more effort, and yet a third eye, to decipher it.

JOPHUR SMALLSHIP/DEATHSHIP IN MOTION, flashed the lantern on Mount Ingul. HEADING TOWARD EGG.

The message repeated. Vubben even glimpsed a distant sparkle, echoing the words on a farther peak, and realized that other semaphore stations must be relaying the message. Still, his brain was tuned to another plane, preventing him from quite grasping its significance.

Instead, he went back to the sensory phantasm that had been drawing him inward – an impression of being perched atop a swaying ribbon, one that slowly yawed and pitched like some undulating sea.

It was not an unpleasant feeling. Rather, he felt almost like a youngster again, growing up in Dooden Mesa, zooming recklessly along a swaying suspension bridge, feeling its planks rattle beneath his rims, swooping and banking without a safety rail while lethal drops gaped on both sides. His taut spokes hummed as he sped like a bullet, with all four eyestalks stretched wide for maximum parallax.

The moment came back to him whole – not as a distant, fond

memory, but in all its splendor. It was the closest thing to paradise he had ever experienced on Jijo's rough orb.

Amid the exhilaration, part of Vubben knew he must have crossed some boundary. He was *with* the Egg now, sensing the approach of a massive object from the west. A deadly thing, complacent and terrible, cruising at a leisurely pace uphill from the Glade.

Leisurely – according to those aboard, that is.

Somehow, Vubben could sense gravitic fields pressing down, tearing leaves from trees, scraping and penetrating Jijo's soil, disturbing ancient rocks. He even knew intuitive things about the crew within – multiringed entities, far more self-assured and unified than traeki.

Strange rings. Egotistical and driven.

Determined to wreak havoc.

BLADE

The balloon's altimeter must be malfunctioning, he realised. Or else the fuel tank was running low. Either way, the automatic adjustments were growing more sporadic. Unnerving sputtering sounds accompanied each burst of heat, and the pulses came less frequently.

Finally, they halted altogether.

The lake had vanished behind him during those frantic duras when the spaceship's wake dragged the balloon behind it, past the ruined Glade into a narrow pass, toward the Rimmer heights. Also gone was Blade's last chance to pull the rip cord and land in deep water. Instead, trees spired around him, like teeth of a comb you used to pluck fleas from your pet lornik.

And I am the flea.

Assuming he survived when a forest giant snatched him from the sky, someone might hear his cries and come. *But then, what will they think when they find a qheuen in a tree?*

The phrase was a popular metaphor for unlikeliness – a contradiction in terms – like a swimming urs, or a modest human, or an egotistical traeki.

This appears to be the year for contradictions.

A branch top brushed one of his claw tips. Blade yanked back so reflexively that his whole body spun around. All five legs were kept drawn in after that. Still, he expected another impact at any moment.

Instead, the forest abruptly ended. Blade had an impression of craggy cliffs, and a sulfurous odor stroked his tongue. Then came a sensation of upward motion!

And heat. His mouth feelers curled in reaction to a blast from below.

Of course, he realized. *Go east from the Glade for a few leagues, and you're in geyser country.*

The balloon soared, its drooping canopy now buoyed by a warm updraft.

The Jophur ship must have dragged me into a particular canyon. The Pilgrimage Track.

The path leading to the Egg.

Blade's body kept spinning, even as the gasbag climbed. To other beings, it might have been disconcerting, but qheuens had no preferred orientation. It never mattered which way he was 'facing.' So Blade was ready when the object he sought came into view.

There it is!

The corvette lay dead ahead. It had stopped motionless and was now shining a searchlight downward, circling a site that Blade realized could only be the Nest.

What is it planning to do?

He recalled Ovoom Town, where the aliens chose to attack at night for maximum terror and visual effect. Could that be the intent, once again?

But surely the Jophur would not harm the Egg!

Blade had never shown the slightest psi-ability. Yet it seemed that feelings now crept inward from his extremities to the flexing lymph pump at his body center. Expectation came first. Then something akin to intrigued curiosity.

Finally, in rapid succession, he felt recognition, realization, and a culminating sense of disappointed ennui. All these impressions swept over him in a matter of moments, and he somehow knew they weren't coming from the Jophur.

Indeed, whatever had just happened – a psi-insult or failed communication – it seemed to anger those aboard the cruiser, goading them to action. The searchlight narrowed from a diffuse beam to a needle of horrific brilliance that stabbed down viciously. It took duras for sound to follow ... a staccato series of crackling booms. Blade could not see the obscured target, but glowing smoke billowed from the point of impact.

A shrill, involuntary whistle escaped Blade's vents and his legs tightened spasmodically. Yet there was no impression of pain, or even surprise. *It will take more than that*, he thought proudly. *A lot more.*

Of course, the Jophur could dish out whatever it took to turn the defenseless Egg into a molten puddle. Their intent was now clear. This act, more even than the slaying at Ovoom Town, would tear the morale of the Six.

Blade urged his windblown vehicle onward, hoping to arrive in time.

LARK

Three humans in a prison cell watched a panorama of destruction, reacting in quite different ways.

Lark stared at the holoscene with the same superstitious thrill he felt months ago, encountering Galactic tech for the first time. The images seemed to demand habits, ways of seeing, learned at an early age. Things he should recognize – the Rimmer mountains, for instance – possessed a *slippery* quality. Odd perspective foldings conveyed far more than you'd see through a window the same size ... especially when the scene hovered over the Holy Egg.

'*Your obstinacy – joint and particular – brought your people to this juncture,*' the tall stack of rings said.

'*Destroying mere towns did not sway you, since your so-called Sacred Scrolls preach the futility of tangible assets.*

'*But now, observe as our corvette strikes a blow at your true underpinnings.*'

A glaring needle struck the Egg. Almost at once, waves of pain engulfed Lark's chest. Falling back with a cry, he tore at his clothes, trying to fling away the stone amulet hanging from a thong around his neck. Ling tried to help, but could not grasp the meaning of his agony.

The ordeal might have killed him, but then it ended as suddenly as it began. The cutting ray vanished, leaving a smoking scar along the Egg's flank.

Ewasx burbled glad exhalations about 'a signal' and 'gratifying surrender.'

Lark bunched the fabric of his undershirt around the Egg fragment, wrapping it to prevent contact with his skin. Only then did he notice that Ling had his head on her lap, stroking his face, telling him that everything was going to be all right.

Yeah, sure it is, Lark thought, recognizing a well-meant lie. But the gesture, the warm contact, was appreciated.

As his eyes unblurred, Lark saw Rann looking his way. The big

Danik had cool disdain in his eyes. Scorn that Lark would react so to the superficial wounding of rock. Contempt that Ling would soil her hands on a native. And derision that the Six Races would give in so easily, surrendering to the Jophur in order to salvage a mere lump of psi-active stone. Rann had already proved willing to sacrifice himself and all his comrades, to protect his patron race. Clearly, he thought any lesser courage unworthy.

Go kiss a Rothen's feet, Lark thought. But he did not speak aloud.

The corvette had turned away from the Egg. Its transmission now showed the camera gaining altitude, sweeping above dark ridgelines.

The country was familiar. Lark ought to recognize it.

Lester Cambel ... They're heading straight toward Lester ... and the boo forest ...

So. The sages had chosen to give up whatever mystery project kept them so busy at their secret base – the work of months – just in order to safeguard the Egg.

It shouldn't be surprising. It is our holy site, after all. Our prophet. Our seer.

And yet, he *was* surprised.

In fact, it was the last thing he would have expected.

BLADE

Silently, Blade urged his windblown vehicle onward, hoping to arrive in time ...

To do what? To distract the Jophur for a few duras while they burned him to a cinder, giving the Egg just that much respite before the main assault resumed? Or worse, to float on by, screaming and waving his legs, trying futilely to attract attention from beings who thought him no more important than a cloud?

Frustration boiled. Combat hormones triggered autonomic reactions, causing his cupola to pull inward, taking the vision strip down beneath his carapace, leaving just a smooth, armored surface above.

That instinct response might have made sense long ago, when presentient qheuens fought their battles claw to claw in seaside marshes, on the distant planet where their patrons later found and uplifted them. But now it was a damned nuisance. Blade struggled for calm, schooling his breathing to follow a steady rhythm, sequentially clockwise from leg to leg, instead of random stuttering gasps. It took a count of twenty before the cupola relaxed enough to rise and restore sight.

His vision strip whirled, taking in the dim canyons that made a maze of this part of the Rimmers. At once, he realized two things.

The balloon had climbed considerably in that brief time, widening his field of view.

And the Jophur ship was gone!

But ... where ... ?

Blade wondered if it might be right below, in his blind spot. That provoked a surging fantasy. He saw himself slashing the balloon and dropping onto the cruiser from above! Landing with a thump, he would scoot along the top until he reached some point of entry. A hatch that could be forced, or a glass window to smash. Once aboard, in close quarters, he'd show them ...

Oh, there it is.

The heroic dream image evaporated like dew when he spied the corvette, diminishing rapidly, heading roughly northwest.

Could it have already finished off the Egg?

Scanning nearer at hand, he spied the great ovoid at last, some distance in the opposite direction. It lay in full view now, a savage burn scarring one flank. The stone glowed along that jagged, half-molten line, casting ocher light across jumbled debris lining the bottom of the Nest. Still, the Egg looked relatively intact.

Why did they leave before finishing the job?

He tracked the corvette by its glimmer of reflected starlight.

Northwest. It's heading northwest.

Blade tried to think.

That's where home is. Dolo Village. Tarek Town.

And Biblos, he then realized, hoping he was wrong.

Things might have just gone from bad to worse.

EWASX

The threat worked, My rings!

Now our expertise is proven. Our/My worth is vindicated before the Captain-Leader and our fellow crew stacks. As I/we predicted, just as our bomber began slicing at their holy psychic rock, a signal came!

It was the same digital radiance they used last time, to reveal the g'Kek city. Thus, the savages attempt once more to placate us. They will do anything to protect their stone deity.

*

OBSERVE THE HUMAN CAPTIVES, MY RINGS! One of them – the local male whom we/Asx once knew as Lark Koolhan – quailed and moaned to see the 'Egg' under attack, while the other two seemed unaffected. Thus, a controlled experiment showed that I/we were right about the primitives and their religion.

Now the female comforts Lark as our cruiser speeds away from the damaged Egg, toward the signal-emanation point.

What will they offer us, this time? Something as satisfying as the g'Kek town, now frozen with immured samples of hated vermin?

The chief-tactician stack calculates that the sooners will not sacrifice the thing we desire most – the dolphin ship. Not yet. First they will try buying us off with lesser things. Perhaps their fabled archive – a pathetic trove of primitive lore, crudely scribed on plant leaves or some barklike substance. A paltry cache of lies and superstitions that simpletons dare call a *library*.

You tremor in surprise, O second ring-of-cognition? You did not expect Me to learn of this other thing treasured by the Six Races?

Well be assured, Asx did a thorough job of melting that particular memory. The information did not come from this reforged stack.

Did you honestly believe that our *Ewasx* stack was the only effort at intelligence gathering ordained by the Captain-Leader? There have been other captives, other interrogations.

It took too long to learn about this pustule of contraband Earthling knowledge – this *Biblos* – and the exact location remained uncertain. But now we/I speculate. Perhaps Biblos is the thing they hope to bribe us with, exchanging their archive for the 'life' of their Holy Egg.

If that is their intent, they will learn.

We will burn the books, but that won't suffice.

NOTHING WILL SUFFICE.

In the long run, not even the dolphin ship will do. Though it will make a good start.

BLADE

Northwest. What target might attract the aliens' attention that way?

Nearly everything I know or care about, Blade concluded. Dolo Village, Tarek Town and Biblos.

As pale Torgen rose behind the Rimmer peaks, he watched the slim ship glide on, knowing he would lose sight of it long before the raider arrived at any of those destinations. Blade no longer cared where the contrary winds blew him, so long as he did not have to watch destruction rain down on the places he loved.

A chain of tiny, flickering lights followed the cruiser as scouts stationed on mountain peaks passed reports of its progress. He deciphered a few snatches of GalTwo, and saw they weren't words, but numbers.

Wonderful. We are good at describing and measuring our downfall.

With combat hormones ebbing, Blade grew more aware of physical discomfort. Nerves throbbed where one of the urrish hooks had ripped away skin plates, exposing fleshy integuments to cold air. Thirst gnawed at him, making Blade wish he were a hardy gray.

The balloon passed beyond the warm updraft and stopped climbing. Soon the descent would resume, sending him spinning toward a landscape of jagged shadows.

Wait a dura.

Blade tried to focus his vision strip, peering at the distant Jophur vessel.

Has it stopped?

Soon he knew it had. The ship was hovering again, casting its search beam to scan the ground below.

Was I wrong? The next target may not be Biblos or Tarek, after all. But ... there's nothing here! These hills are wilderness. Just a useless tract of boo—

He was staring in perplexity when something happened to the mountain below the floating ship. Reddish flickers erupted, like marsh gas lit by static charges, at the swampy border of a lake. Sparklike ripples seemed to spread amid the dense stands of towering boo.

What are the Jophur doing now? he wondered. *What weapon are they using?*

The flickers brightened, flaring beneath scores of giant greatboo stems. The ship's searchlight still roamed, as if bemused to find slender tubes of native vegetation emitting fire from their bottoms ... then starting to rise.

The first thunder reached Blade as he realized.

It's not the Jophur at all! It's—

The corvette finally showed alarm, starting to back away. Its beam narrowed to a slicing needle, sweeping through one rising column.

An instant later, the entire northwest was alight. Volley after volley of blazing tubes jetted skyward in a roar that shook the night.

Rockets, Blade thought. *Those are rockets!*

The vast majority missed their apparent target. But accuracy seemed of no concern, so dense was the missile swarm. The retreating corvette could not blast them fast enough before three in a row made glancing blows.

Then a fourth projectile struck head-on. The warhead failed, but sheer momentum crumpled one section of starship hull, tossing it spinning.

Other warheads kept going off ahead of schedule, or tumbling to explode on the ground, filling the night with brilliant, fruitless incandescence. So great was the wastage that it looked as if the Jophur ship might actually limp away.

Then a late-rising rocket took off. It turned, and with apparent deliberation, drove itself straight through the groaning corvette.

A dazzling explosion ripped its belly open, cleaving the skyship apart. Blade had to spin a different part of his half-blinded visor around to witness the two halves plummet, like twin cups filled with fire, to the forest floor.

More dross to clean up, Blade observed, as fires spread across several mountainsides. But his body was content to live in the moment, shrieking celebration whistles from all his breathing vents, competing with the gaudy fireworks to shout at the stars.

With qheuen vision, he could witness the corvette's destruction while also following as most of the missiles continued their flight – those that did not veer off course, or explode on their own. Dozens still thrust noisily into the upper sky, spouting red, flickering tails.

Blade screamed even louder when they finished their brief arc and turned back toward Jijo, plummeting like hail toward Festival Glade.

LESTER CAMBEL

The forest erupted in flame around Lester. Failed missiles crashed back amid the secret launching sites, setting off explosions of withering heat and igniting tall columns of boo. South, a searing glow told where the shattered spaceship fell. Still, Lester held fast to the clearing where he and a g'Kek assistant had come to watch the flickering sky.

An urrish corporal galloped to report. 'Fires surround us. Sage, you must flee!'

But Lester stayed rooted, peering at the fuming heavens.

His voice was choked and dry.

'I can't see! Did any make it to burnout? Are they on their way?'

The young g'Kek answered, all four eyes waving upward.

'Many flew true, O sage,' she answered. 'Several score are airborne. Your design was valid. Now there's nothing more to do. It's time to go.'

Reluctantly, Lester let himself be pulled away from the clearing, into the planned escape route through the boo.

Only they soon found the way blocked by fierce tongues of fire. Lester and his companions had to retreat, back past sheltered work camps whose blur-cloth canopies were ablaze, where vats of traeki paste exploded one after another ... along with some of the traeki themselves. Other figures could be seen fleeing through the clots of smoke as all the labor of months, spent creating a hidden center of industry, was consumed in a roiling maelstrom.

'There is no way out,' the urs sighed.

'Then save yourself. I command it!'

Lester pushed her resisting flank, repeating the order until the corporal let out a moan and plunged toward a place where the flames seemed least intense. An urs just might survive the passage. Lester knew better than to try.

Alone with his young assistant, he huddled in the center of the clearing, holding one of her trembling wheels.

'It's all right,' he told her, between hacking coughs. 'We did what we set out to do.

'All things come to an end.

'Now it all lies with Ifni.'

LARK

The earlier holoscenes had been confusing, but these new images left Lark stunned, breathless, confused. He had no way to grasp the glazing spectacle ... mighty tubes of boo, their bottoms explosing in flame ... scores of them, jetting upward like a swarm of angry fire bees.

The distant camera veered as the corvette struggled to evade a volley of makeshift rockets. The view lurched so suddenly, Lark's stomach reeled and he had to look away.

The others seemed just as amazed. Ling laughed aloud, clapping both hands, while Rann's face mixed astonishment with dismay. *Then what's happening must be good.* Lark allowed a spark of hope to rise within.

Ewasx, the Jophur, vented gurgling sounds, along with snatches of Galactic Two.

'Outrageous ... treacherous ... unexpected ... unforeseen!'

Tremors shook its composite body, quivering from the peak down to its basal segment. Most of the elderly, waxy toroids were familiar to Lark. Once, they composed a friend, a sage, wise and good. But a newcomer had taken over – a glistening young collar, black and featureless, without appendages or sensory organs.

Both Ling and Rann cried out. But when Lark turned around, the holoscene was all white – a blank slate.

'The corvette,' Ling explained, her voice awed. 'It's been destroyed!'

A shrill sigh escaped the Jophur. The tremors turned into convulsions.

Ewasx is having some kind of fit, Lark thought. *Should I attack now? Strike the master ring with all my might?*

Ling was babbling excitedly about 'the other rockets—' But Lark had decided, striding toward the shuddering Jophur. His sole weapons were his hands, but so what?

Lester, you pulled off a fantastic wolfling trick. Asx would have been proud of you.

Just as old Asx would have wanted me to do this.

He brought back a fist, aimed at the shivering master ring. Someone seized his arm, holding it back in a fierce grip.

Lark swiveled, cocking his other fist at Rann. But the bullheaded Danik only shook his head.

'What will it prove? You'd just make them angry, native boy. We remain trapped here, at their mercy.'

'Get out of my way,' Lark growled. 'I'm gonna free my traeki friend.'

'Your friend is long gone. If you kill a master ring, the whole stack dissolves! I *know* this, young savage. I've put it in practice.'

Lark was angry enough to turn his attack on the burly Danik. Sensing it, Rann released Lark and stepped back, raising both hands in a combatant's stance.

Yeah, Lark thought, dropping to a crouch. *You're a star-god soldier. But maybe a savage knows some tricks you don't.*

'Stop it, you two!' Ling shouted. 'We've got to get ready—'

She cut off as a chain of low vibrations throbbed the metal floor – mighty forces at work, growling elsewhere in the vast ship.

'Defensive cannon,' Rann identified the din. 'But what could they be firing—?'

'The rockets!' Ling replied. 'I *told* you, they're coming this way!'

Realization dawned on Rann, that sooners might actually threaten a starship. He cursed, diving for a corner of the cell.

Lark allowed Ling to lead him as the battleship shivered, its weapons firing frantically. A mutter of distant detonations crept closer as they held each other. The moment had a heady vividness, a hormonal rush, mixing the pleasure of Ling's touch with sharp awareness of onrushing death.

Yet Lark found himself hoping, praying, that the next few moments would end his life.

Come on. You can do it, Lester. Finish the job!

The fragment of the Egg lay against his chest, where its last out-burst had left seething weals. He clutched the stone amulet with his free hand, expecting throbbing heat. Instead, Lark felt an icy cold. A brittleness that breath would shatter.

IX

FROM THE NOTES OF GILLIAN BASKIN

We're all feeling rather down right now. Suessi called from the second dross pile where his work crew just had an accident. They were trying to clear the area around an old Buyur ore-hauler when a subsea quake hit. The surrounding heap of junk ships shifted and an ancient hulk came rolling down on a couple of workers — Satima and Sup-peh. Neither of them had time to do more than stare at the onrushing wall before it crushed them.

So we keep getting winnowed down where it hurts most. Our best colleagues — the skilled and dedicated — inevitably pay the price.

Then there's Peepoe, everyone's delight. A terrible loss, kidnapped by Zhaki and his pal. If only I could get my hands on that pair!

I had to lie to poor Kaa, though. We cannot spare time to go hunting across the ocean for Peepoe.

That doesn't mean she'll be abandoned. Friends will win her freedom, someday. This I vow.

But our pilot won't be one of them.

Alas, I fear Kaa will never see her again.

Makanee finished her autopsies of Kunn and Jass. The prisoners apparently took poison rather than answer our questions. Tsh't blames herself for not searching the Danik agent more carefully, but who would have figured Kunn would be so worried about our amateur grilling?

And did he really have to take the hapless native boy with him? Rety's cousin could hardly know secrets worth dying for.

Rety herself can shed no light on the matter. Without anyone to interrogate, she volunteered to help Suessi, who can certainly use a hand. Makanee recommends work as good therapy for the poor kid, who had to see those gruesome bodies firsthand.

I wonder. What secret was Kunn trying to protect? Normally, I'd drop everything to puzzle it out. But too much is going on as we prepare to make our move.

Anyway, from the Jophur prisoners we know the Rothen ship is irrelevant. We have more immediate concerns.

The Library cube reports no progress on that symbol – the one with nine spirals and eight ovals. The unit is now sifting its older files, a job that gets harder the further back it goes.

In compensation, the cube has flooded me with records of other recent 'sooner outbreaks' – secret colonies established on fallow worlds.

It turns out that most are quickly discovered by guardian patrols of the Institute of Migration. Jijo is a special case, with limited access and the nearby shrouding of Izmunuti. Also, Infinity's Shore this time, an entire galaxy was declared fallow, making inspection a monumental task.

I wondered – why set aside a whole galaxy, when the basic unit of ecological recovery is a planet, or at most a solar system?

The cube explained that much larger areas of space are usually quarantined, all at once. Oxygen-breathing civilization evacuates an entire sector or spiral arm, ceding it to the parallel culture of hydrogen breathers – those mysterious creatures sometimes generically called Zang. This helps keep both societies separated in physical space, reducing the chance of friction.

It also helps the quarantine. The Zang are unpredictable, and often ignore minor incursions, but they can be fierce if large numbers of oxy-sapients appear where they don't belong.

We detected what must have been Zang ships, before driving past Izmunuti. I guess they took us for a 'minor incursion,' since they left us alone.

The wholesale trading of sectors and zones makes more sense now. Still, I pressed the Library cube.

Has an entire galaxy ever been declared off-limits before?

The answer surprised me.

Not for a very long time ... at least one hundred and fifty million years.

Now, where have I heard that number before?

We're told there are eight orders of sapience and quasi-sapience. Oxy-life is the most vigorous and blatant – or as Tom put it, 'strutting around, acting like we own the place.' In fact, though, I was surprised to learn that hydrogen breathers far outnumber oxygen breathers. But Zang and their relatives spend most of their time down in the turbid layers of Jovian-type worlds.

Some say this is because they fear contact with oxy-types.

Others say they could crush us anytime, but have never gotten around to it. Perhaps they will, sometimes in the next billion years.

The other orders are Machine, Memetic, Quantum, Hypothetical, Retired, and Transcendent.

Why am I pondering this now?

Well, our plans are in motion, and soon Streaker will be, too. It's likely that in a few days we'll be dead, or else taken captive. With luck, we may buy something worthwhile with our lives. But our chances of actually getting away seem vanishingly small.

And yet … what if we do manage it? After all, the Jophur may get engine trouble at just the right moment. They might decide we're not worth the effort.

The sun might go nova.

In that case, where can Streaker go next? We've tried seeking justice from our own oxy-culture – the Civilization of the Five Galaxies – but the Institutes proved untrustworthy . We tried the Old Ones, but those members of the Retired Order proved less impartial than we hoped.

In a universe filled with possibilities, there remain half a dozen other 'quasi-sapient' orders out there. Alien in both thought and substance. Rumored to be dangerous.

What have we got to lose?

STREAKERS

KAA

Gleaming missiles struck the water whenever he surfaced to breathe. The spears were crude weapons – hollow wooden shafts tipped with slivers of volcanic glass – but when a keen-edged harpoon grazed his flank, Kaa lost half his air in a reflexive cry. The harbor – now a cramped, exitless trap – reverberated with his agonized moan.

The hoonish sailors seemed to have no trouble moving around by torchlight, rowing their coracles back and forth, executing complex orders shouted from their captains' bulging throat sacs. The water's tense skin reverberated like a beaten drum as the snare tightened around Kaa. Already, a barrier of porous netting blocked the narrow harbor mouth.

Worse, the natives had reinforcements. Skittering sounds announced the arrival of clawed feet, scampering down the rocky shore south of town. Chitinous forms plunged underwater, reminding Kaa of some horror movie about giant crabs. *Red qheuens*, he realized, as these new allies helped the hoon sailors close off another haven, the water's depths.

Ifni! What did Zhaki and Mopol do to make the locals so mad at the mere sight of a dolphin in their bay? How did they get these people so angry they want to kill me on sight?

Kaa still had some tricks. Time and again he misled the hoons, making feints, pretending sluggishness, drawing the noose together prematurely, then slipping beneath a gap in their lines, dodging a hail of javelins.

My ancestors had practice doing this. Humans taught us lessons, long before they switched from spears to scalpels.

Yet he knew this was a contest the cetacean could not win. The best he could hope for was a drawn-out tie.

Diving under one hoonish coracle, Kaa impulsively spread his jaws and snatched the rower's oar in his teeth, yanking it like the tentacle of some demon octopus. The impact jarred his mouth and tender gums, but he added force with a hard thrust of his tail flukes.

The oarsman made a mistake by holding on – even a hoon could not match Kaa, strength to strength. A surprised bellow met a resounding splash as the mariner struck salt water far from the boat. Kaa released the oar and kicked away rapidly. That act would not endear him to the hoon. On the other hand, what was there left to lose? Kaa had quite given up on his mission – to make contact with the Commons of Six Races. All that remained was fighting for survival.

I should have listened to my heart.

I should have gone after Peepoe, instead.

The decision still bothered Kaa with nagging pangs of guilt. How could he obey Gillian Baskin's orders – no matter how urgent – instead of striking off across the dark sea, chasing after the thugs who had kidnapped his mate and love?

What did duty matter – or even his oath to Terra – compared with that?

After Gillian signed off, Kaa had listened as the sun set, picking out distant echoes of the fast-receding speed sled, still faintly audible to the northwest. Sound carried far in Jijo's ocean, without the myriad engine noises that made Earth's seas a cacophony. The sled was already so far away – at least a hundred klicks by then – it would seem forlorn to follow.

But so what? So the odds were impossible? That never mattered to the heroes one found in storybooks and holosims! No audience ever cheered a champion who let mere impossibility stand in the way.

Maybe that was what swayed Kaa, in an agonized moment. The fact that it was such a cliché. *All* the movie heroes – whether human or dolphin – would routinely forsake comrades, country, and honor for the sake of love. Relentless propaganda from every romantic tale urged him to do it.

But even if I succeeded, against all odds, what would Peepoe say after I rescued her?

I know her. She'd call me a fool and a traitor, and never respect me again.

So it was that Kaa found himself entering Port Wuphon as ordered, long after nightfall, with all the wooden sailboats shrouded beneath camouflage webbing that blurred their outlines into cryptic hummocks. Still hating himself for his decision, he had approached the nearest wharf, where two watchmen lounged on what looked like walking staffs, beside a pair of yawning noor. By starlight, Kaa had reared up on his churning flukes to begin reciting his memorized speech of greeting ... and barely escaped being skewered for his trouble. Whirling back into the bay, he dodged razor-tipped staves that missed by centimeters.

'*Wait-t-t-!*' he had cried, emerging on the other side of the wharf. '*You're mak-ing a terrible mistake! I bring news from your own losssst ch-ch-children! F-from Alvi—*'

He barely escaped a second time. The hoon guards weren't listening. Darkness barely saved Kaa as growing numbers of missiles hurled his way.

His big mistake was trying a third time to communicate. When that final effort failed, Kaa tried to depart ... only to find belatedly that the door had shut. The harbor mouth was closed, trapping him in a tightening noose.

So much for my skill at diplomacy, he pondered, while skirting silently across the bottom muck ... only to swerve when his sonar brushed armored forms ahead, approaching with scalloped claws spread wide.

Add that to my other failures ... as a spy, as an officer ... Mopol and Zhaki would never have antagonized the locals so, with senseless pranks and mischief, if he had led them properly.

... and as a lover ...

In fact, Kaa knew just one thing he was good at. And at this rate, he'd never get another chance to ply his trade.

A strange, thrashing sound came from just ahead, toward the bottom of the bay. He nearly swung around again, dodging it to seek some other place, dreading the time when bursting lungs would force him back to the surface ...

But there was something peculiar about the sound. A softness. A resigned, *melodious* sadness that seemed to fill the water. Curiosity overcame Kaa as he zigzagged, casting sonar clicks through the murk to perceive—

A hoon!

But what was one of them doing down here?

Kaa nosed forward, ignoring the growing staleness of his air supply, until he made out a tall biped amid clouds of churned-up mud. Diffracted echoes confirmed his unbelieving eyes. The creature was undressing, carefully removing articles of clothing, tying them together in a string.

Kaa guessed it was a female, from the fact that it was a bit smaller and had only a modest throat sac.

Is it the one I pulled overboard? But why doesn't she swim back to the boat? I assumed ...

Kaa was struck by a wave of image-rupture alienation – a sensation all too familiar to Earthlings since contact – when some concept that had seemed familiar abruptly made no sense anymore.

Hoons can't swim!

The journal of Alvin Hph-wayuo never mentioned this. In fact, Alvin implied that his people passionately loved boats and the sea. Nor were they cavalier about their lives, but mourned the loss of loved ones even more deeply than a human or dolphin would. Kaa suddenly knew he'd been fooled by Alvin's writings, sounding so much like an Earth kid, never mentioning things that he simply assumed.

Aliens. Who can figure?

He stared as the hoon tied the string of clothes around her left wrist and held the other end to her mouth, calmly exhaling her last air, inflating a balloonlike fold of cloth. It floated upward, no more than two meters, stopping far short of the surface.

She's not signaling for help, he fathomed as the hoon sat down in the mud, humming a dirge. *She's making sure they can drag the bottom and retrieve her body*. Kaa had read Alvin's account of death rituals the locals took quite seriously.

By now his own lungs burned fiercely. Kaa deeply regretted that the breather unit on his harness had burned out after Zhaki shot him.

He heard the qheuens approaching from behind, clacking their claws, but Kaa sensed a hole in their line, confident he could streak past, just out of reach. He tried to turn ... to seize the brief opportunity.

Oh, hell, he sighed, and kicked the other way, aiming for the dying hoon.

It took some time to get her to the surface. When they broke through, her entire body shook with harsh, quivering gasps. Water jetted from nostril orifices at the same time as air poured in through her mouth, a neat trick that Kaa kind of envied.

He pushed her close enough to throw one arm over a drifting oar, then he whirled around to peer across the bay, ready to duck onrushing spears.

None came. In fact, there seemed a curious absence of boats nearby. Kaa dropped his head down to cast suspicious sonar beams through his arched brow – and confirmed that all the coracles had backed off some distance.

A moon had risen. One of the big ones. He could make out silhouettes now ... hoons standing in their rowboats, all of them turned to face north ... or maybe northwest. The males had their sacs distended, and a steady thrumming filled the air. They seemed oblivious to the sudden reappearance of one of their kind from a brush with drowning.

I'd have thought they'd be all over this area, dropping weighted ropes, trying to rescue her. It was another example of alien thinking, despite all the Terran books these hoons had read. Kaa was left with the task of shoving her with the tip of his rostrum, a creepy feeling coursing his spine as he pushed the bedraggled survivor toward one of the docks.

More villagers stood along the wharf, their torches flickering under gusts of stiffening wind. They seemed to be watching ... or listening ... to something.

A dolphin can both see and hear things happening above the water's surface, but not as well as those who live exclusively in that dry realm. With his senses still in an uproar, Kaa could discern little in the direction they faced. Just the hulking outline of a mountain.

The computerized insert in his right eye flexed and turned until Kaa finally made out a flickering star near the mountain's highest point. A star that *throbbed*, flashing on and off to a staccato rhythm. He could not make anything of it at first ... though the cadence seemed reminiscent of Galactic Two.

'Ex-x-xcuse me ...' he began, trying to take advantage of the inactivity. Whatever else was happening this seemed a good chance to get a word in edgewise. 'I'm a dolphin ... cousin to humansss ... I've been ssent with-th a message for Uriel the –'

The crowd suddenly erupted in a moan of emotion that made Kaa's sound-sensitive jaw throb. He made out snatches of individual speech.

'Rockets!' one onlooker sighed in Anglic. 'The sages made rockets!'

Another spoke GalSeven in tones of wonder. *'One small enemy spaceship destroyed ... and now the big one is targeted!'*

Kaa blinked, transfixed by the villagers' tension.

Rockets? Did I hear right? But—

Another cry escaped the crowd.

'They plummet!' someone cried. 'They strike!'

Abruptly, the mountain-perched star paused its twinkling bulletin. All sound seemed to vanish with it. The hoons stood in dead silence. Even the oily water of the bay was hushed, lapping softly against the wharf.

The flashing resumed, and there came from the crowd a moan of shaken disappointment.

'It survives, exists. The mother battleship continues,' went the GalTwo mutter of a traeki, somewhere in the crowd.

'Our best effort has failed.

'And now comes punishment.'

SOONERS

LARK

The moment Lark prayed for never came. The walls did not shatter, torn by native-made warheads or screaming splinters of greatboo. Instead, the sound of detonations remained distant, then diminished. The floor-throbbing vibration of Jophur defense guns changed tenor now that the element of surprise was gone, from frantic to complacent, as if the incoming missiles were mere nuisances.

Then silence fell. It was over.

He let go of the Egg fragment, and released Ling, as well. Lark pulled his knees in, wrapped both arms around them, and rocked miserably. He had never felt so disappointed to be alive.

'Woorsh, that was close!' Ling exhaled, clearly savoring survival. Not that Lark blamed her. She might still nurse hopes of escape, or of being swapped in some Galactic prisoner exchange. All this might become just another episode in her memoirs. *An episode, like me,* he thought. *The clever jungle boy she once met on Jijo.*

His old friend Harullen might have seen a bright side to this failure. Now the angered Jophur might extinguish all sapient life on the planet, not only their g'Kek blood enemies. Wouldn't that fit in with Lark's beliefs? His heresy?

The Six Races don't belong here, but neither do they deserve annihilation. I wanted us to do the right thing peacefully, honorably, and of our own accord. Without violence. All this burning of forests and valleys.

'Look!'

He glanced at Ling, who had stood up and was pointing at Ewasx. The ring stack still quaked, but one torus in the middle was undergoing full-scale convulsions. Throbbing indentations formed on opposite sides, distending its round shape.

Both men joined Ling, staring with unbelieving eyes as the dents deepened and spread into circular bulges, straining outward until a sheer membrane was all that restrained them. The Jophur's basal legs started pumping and flexing.

The humans jumped back when Ewasx abruptly skittered across the floor, first toward the armored door, then away again, zigging and zagging three times before finally sagging back down, like a heap of flaccid tubes.

The middle ring continued to throb and swell.

'What is it doing?' Ling asked in awe. Lark had to swallow before answering.

'It's *vlenning*. Giving birth, you'd say. Traekis don't do this often, 'cause it endangers the union of the stack. Mostly they bud embryos and let 'em grow in a mulch pile, on their own.'

Rann gaped. 'Giving birth? Here?' Clearly, he knew more about killing Jophur than about the rest of their life cycle.

Lark realized – the catatonia of Ewasx was *not* caused simply by the surprise rocket attack. That shock had triggered a separate convulsion just waiting to happen.

Membranes started tearing. One of the new rings, almost the size of Lark's head and colored a deep shade of purple, began writhing through. The other was smaller and crimson, emerging through a mucusy pustule, trailing streamers of rank, oily stuff. Both infant toruses slithered down the flanks of the parent stack, then across the metal floor, seeking shadows.

'Lark, you'd better have a look at this,' Ling said.

He could barely yank his gaze away from the nauseating, bewitching sight of the greasy newborns. Upon stumbling over to join Ling, he found her pointing downward.

'When it ran back and forth, a dura ago . . . it left this trail on the floor.'

So what? he thought. Lark saw smears, like grease stains on the metal plating. *Traeki often do that.*

Then he blinked, recognizing Anglic letters. One, two, three . . . four of them.

R E W Q

'What the . . . ?' Rann puzzled aloud.

Lark raised a hand to his forehead, where his rewq symbiont lay waiting for its next duty while supping lightly from his veins. At a touch, it swarmed over his eyes, recasting the colors in the room.

At once, everything changed. Till that moment, the still-quivering flanks of the Jophur had seemed a mottled jumble of distorted shades. But now, rows of *letters* could be seen, crisscrossing several older rings.

lark, the first series began. **one ring opens doors. use it. rejoin the six . . .**

A squeal of pain interrupted from Lark's right, unlike any shouted by a mammal. He swirled, and cried, 'Stop!'

Rann stood over one of the newly vlenned rings, his foot raised to stomp on it a second time. The small creature shook, bleeding waxy fluids from a rent along one flank.

'Why?' the Danik demanded. 'You sooners signed our death warrants with that crude missile attack. We might as well get in some of our own.'

Ling confronted her former colleague hotly. 'Fool! Hypocrite! You stopped Lark earlier, and now do this? Don't you want to get out of here?'

She bent over the quivering ring and reached toward it nervously, tentatively.

Lark turned back toward the ring stack ... the composite being that had somehow managed to become Asx again, in a strange, limited way. The letters were already fading as he read the second line.

Give other to Phwhoon-dau/Lester. he/you/they must

This time, the scream was human.

Ling! He spun around and rushed to her aid.

She held the little wounded torus in one hand while the other clawed over her shoulder at Rann. The male Danik throttled her from behind, his forearm around her throat, closing her windpipe, and possibly her arteries.

Rann heard Lark's irate bellow and swiveled lightly, using Ling's body as a shield while he kept choking her. Rann's face was contorted with pleasure as Lark feinted right, then launched himself at the star warrior's other side. There was no time for finesse as they all toppled together, a grappling mass of arms and legs.

It might have been an even match, if Ling hadn't passed out. But when her body slumped, insensate, Lark had to face Rann's trained fury alone. He managed to get a few blows in, but soon had his hands full just preventing the Rothen agent from striking a vital spot. Finally, in desperation, he threw his arms around Rann, seizing his broad torso in a wrestler's embrace.

His opponent felt confident enough to spare some strength for taunts.

'Darwinist savage ...' Rann jeered, close to Lark's ear. '... devolved ape ...'

Lark managed an insult of his own—

'The ... Rothen ... are ... pigs ...'

Rann snarled and tried to bite his ear. Lark swung his head aside just in time, then slammed it back into Rann's face, breaking his lip.

Abruptly, a *stench* seemed to swell around their heads, filling Lark's nostrils with a cloying, sickening tang. For an instant he wondered if it was the Danik's body odor. Or else the smell of death.

Rann managed to free a hand and used it to pummel Lark's side. But the pain seemed distant, and the blows vague, unsteady. Vision wavered as the awful smell increased ... and Lark grew aware that his opponent was being affected, as well.

More so.

In moments, Rann's iron grip let go and the man collapsed away from him. Lark backed up, gasping. Through a haze of wavering consciousness, he noted the source of the stench. The wounded traeki ring had climbed onto Rann's shoulder and was squirting yet another dose of some noxious substance straight into the star god's face.

Should ... make it ... stop, now, Lark thought. An excess might not just knock Rann out, but kill him.

Life had priorities, though. Fighting exhaustion and the tempting refuge of sleep, Lark rolled over to seek Ling, hoping enough life still lingered to be coaxed back into the world.

BLADE

' ... The most effective warheads were the ones tipped with toporgic capsules, filled with traeki formula type sixteen an' powdered Buyur metal. Kindle beetles were useful in settin' off the solid rocket cores. A lot of the ones that didn't use beetles either fizzled or blew up on their launchpads ...'

Blade listened to the young human recite her report to an urrish telegraph operator, whose keystrokes became fast-departing beams of light. Jeni Shen winced as a pharmacist applied unguents to her singed skin. Her face was soot-covered and the left of her jerkin gave off smoldering fumes. Jeni's voice was dry as slate and it must have been painful for her to speak, but the recitation continued, nonstop, as if she feared this mountaintop semaphore station might be the first target of any Jophur retaliation.

' ... Observers report that the best targeting happened in rockets that had message-ball critters aboard. Usin' 'em that way was just a whim of Phwhoon-dau's, so there weren't many. But it seemed to work. Before everything blew up, Lester said we should reexamine all the Buyur critters we know about, in case they have other uses ...'

The stone hut was crowded. The missile assault, and subsequent fires, had sent refugees pouring through the passes. Blade was forced to wade through the tide of fugitives in order to reach this militia outpost, where he might make a report of his adventure.

He found the semaphore already tied up with frenzied news –

about the successful downing of the last Jophur corvette ... and then the failure of a single rocket even to dent the mother ship. That night of soaring hopes crashed further when casualties became known, including at least one of the High Sages of the Six.

Yet a low level of elation continued. Bad news was only expected. But a taste of victory came amplified by sheer surprise.

Blade recalled vividly the fiery plummet of both burning halves of the ruined starship, setting off firestorms. *I'm glad it only landed in boo*, he thought. According to the scrolls, Jijo's varied ecosystems weren't equal. Greatboo was a trashy alien invader – like the Six themselves. The planet was not badly wounded by tonight's conflagration.

Me neither, Blade added, wincing as a g'Kek medic tried to set one of his broken legs.

'Just cut it off,' he told the doctor. 'The other one, too.'

'But that will leave you with just three,' the g'Kek complained. 'How will you walk?'

'I'll manage. Anyway, new ones grow back faster if you cut all the way to the bud. Just get it over with, will you?'

Fortunately, he had managed to land on two legs spread apart at opposite sides of his body. That left a tripod of them to use, dragging himself from the fluttering tangle of fabric and gondola parts. The moonlit mountainside had been rocky and steep, a horrid place for a blue qheuen to find himself stranded on a chill night. But the beckoning glimmer of flashed messages, darting from peak to peak, encouraged him to limp onward until he reached this sanctuary.

So, I'll be able to tell Log Biter my tale, after all. Maybe I'll even write about it. Nelo should provide backing for a small print run, since half of my story involves his daughter ...

Blade knew his mind was drifting from thirst, pain, and lack of sleep. But if he rested now he would lose his place in line, right after Jeni Shen. The station commander, hearing of his balloon adventure, had given him a priority just after the official report on the rocket attack.

I should be flattered. But in fact, the rockets are used up. Even if there are some left, the element of surprise is gone. They'll never succeed against the Jophur again.

But my idea's not been tried yet. And it'd work! I'm living proof. The smiths of Blaze Mountain have got to be told.

So he sat and fumed, half listening to Jeni's lengthy, jargon-filled report, trying to be patient.

When the amputation began, Blade's cupola withdrew instinctively, shielding his eye strip under thick chitin, preventing him from looking around. So he tried pulling his mind back to the time when he briefly flew through the sky ... the first of his kind to do so since the sneakship came, so long ago.

But a qheuen's memories aren't strong enough to use as a bulwark against pain.

It took three strong hoons to keep the leg straight enough for the medic to do it cleanly.

LARK

A second stench met him when he waked.

The first one had smothered cloyingly. When it filled the little room, the world erased under a blanket of sweet pungency.

The new smell was bitter, tangy, repellent, cleaving the insensate swaddling of unconsciousness. There was no transitory muzziness of confusion. Lark jerked upright while his body convulsed through a series of sharp sneezes. All at once he knew the cell, its metal floor and walls, the cramped despair of this place.

A greasy doughnut shape – purple and still covered with mucus – sent a final stream of misty liquid jetting toward his face. Lark gagged, backing away.

'I'm up! Cut it out, dung eater!'

The room wavered as he turned, searching ... and found Ling close behind, wheezing at the effort of sitting up. Livid marks showed where Rann had throttled her, nearly taking her life.

Lark turned again, scanning for his enemy.

In moments, he spied the Danik agent's bare feet, jutting from beyond the rotund bulk of Ewasx.

Ewasx? Or is it still Asx?

The ring stack shivered. Trails of waxy pus tricked from twin wounds on either side, where the vlenned rings had made their escape.

I could try to find out ... Try talking to—

But Lark saw an *orderliness* to the trembling toruses. A systematic rhythm. Almost regimented. Warbling sounds escaped the speaking vent.

'H-h-h-alt, humans ... I/WE COMMAND ... obedience ...' The voice wavered unevenly, but gained strength with each passing dura.

Ling met his eyes. There was instant rapport. Asx had gone to a lot of trouble to provide gifts. Time to give them a try.

*

'STOP THAT!' Ewasx adjured. 'You are required to ...' Fortunately, the Jophur's limbs were still locked in rigor.

The lowermost set shivered with resistance when the master ring tried to make them move.

Asx is still fighting for us, Lark realized, knowing it could not last.

'Use the purple one,' he told Ling, who cradled the larger newborn torus. 'Asx said it opens locks.'

She lifted her eyes doubtfully, but presented the ring to a flat plate beside the door. They had seen Ewasx touch it whenever the Jophur wanted to leave the cell. Meanwhile, Lark used his frayed shirt as a sling to carry the smaller, crimson traeki. The one cruelly injured by Rann. The one Lark was supposed to deliver to the High Sages – an impossible task, even if the mangled thing survived.

A moan echoed from behind Ewasx. It was the Danik warrior, rousing at last. *Come on!* Lark urged silently, though Ling almost surely had never used such a key to force a lock.

The purple ring oozed a clear fluid from pores near the plate. Clickety sounds followed, as the door mechanism seemed to consider ...

Then, with a faint hiss, it opened!

He hurried through with Ling, ignoring bitter Jophur curses that followed them until the portal shut again.

'Where now?' Ling asked.

'You're asking me?' He laughed. 'You said Galactic ships are standardized!'

She frowned. 'The Rothen don't have any battlecruisers like this beast. Neither does Earth. We'd be lucky to glimpse one from afar ... and even luckier to escape after seeing it.'

Lark felt spooky standing half-naked in an alien passageway filled with weird aromas. A Jophur might enter this stretch of corridor at any moment, or else a war robot, come to hunt them down.

The floor plates began vibrating, low at first, but with a rising mechanical urgency.

'Just guess,' he urged, trying to offer an encouraging smile.

Ling answered with a shrug. 'Well, if we keep going in one direction, sooner or later we're bound to reach hull. Come on, then. Standing still is the worst thing we can do.'

The hallways were deserted.

Occasionally, they hurried past some large chamber and glimpsed Jophur forms within, standing before oddly curved instrument stations, or mingled in swaying groups, communing with clouds of vapor. But the stacks rarely moved. As a biologist, Lark could not help speculating.

They're descended from sedentary creatures, almost sessile. Even with the introduction of master rings, they'd retain some traeki ways, like preferring to work in one place, relatively still.

Lark found it bizarre, striding past closed doors for more than an arrowflight – then another, and a third – using their passkey ring to open armored hatches along the way, meeting no one. *Asx must have taken this into account, giving us even odds of reaching an airlock and …*

Lark wondered.

And then what? If there are sky boats or hover plates, Ling might understand their principles, but how will she operate controls made for Jophur tentacles?

Maybe we should just head for the engine room. Try to break some machinery. Cause some inconvenience before they finally shoot us down.

Ling picked up the pace, a growing eagerness in her steps. Perhaps she sensed something in the thickness of the armored doors, or the subtly curved wall joins, indicating they were close.

The next hatch slid aside – and without warning they suddenly faced their first Jophur.

Ling gasped and Lark's knees almost failed him. He felt an overpowering impulse to spin around and run away, though it was doubtless already too late. The thing was bigger than Ewasx, with component rings that shimmered a glossy, extravagant health he had never seen on a Jijoan traeki.

The way Rann compares to me, Lark thought numbly.

During that brief instant, his companion lifted the purple ring, aiming it like a gun at the big Jophur.

A stream of scent vapor jetted toward the stack.

It hesitated … then raised up on a dozen insectoid legs and sidled past the two humans, proceeding down the hall.

Lark stared after it, numbly.

What was that? A recognition signal? A forged safe-conduct pass?

He could imagine that Asx – wherever the traeki sage had concealed a sliver of self – must have observed all the chemical codes a Jophur used to get around the ship. What Lark could not begin to picture was what kind of consciousness that implied. How could one deliberately hide a personality within a personality, when the new master ring was in charge, pulling all the strings?

The Jophur rounded a corner, moving on about its business.

Lark turned to look at Ling. She met his eyes and together they both let out a hard sigh.

*

The airlock was filled with machinery, though no boats or hover plates. They closed the inner door and hurried to the other side, applying the trusty passkey ring, eager to see blue sky and smell Jijo's fresh wind. If they were lucky, and this portal faced the lake, it might even be possible to leap down to the water. Surviving that, their escape could be cut off at any point, once they passed into the Jophur defense perimeter. But none of that seemed to matter right now. The two of them felt eager, indomitable.

Lark still cradled the injured red ring, wondering what the sages were supposed to do with it.

Perhaps Asx expects us to recruit commandos and return with exploser bombs, using these rings to gain entry ...

His thoughts arrested as the big hatch rolled aside. Their first glimpse was not of daylight, but stars.

An instant's shivering worry passed through his mind before he realized – this was not outer space, but nighttime in the Rimmers. A flood of bracing, cool air made Lark instantly ebullient. *I could never leave Jijo*, he knew. *It's my home*.

A pale glow washed out the constellations where a serrated border crossed the sky – the outline of eastern mountains. It would be dawn soon. A time of hopeful beginnings?

Ling held out her free hand for Lark to take as they strode to the edge and looked down.

'So far, so good,' she said, and he shared her gladness at the sight of glinting moonlight, sparkling on water. 'It's still dim outside. The lake will mask our heat sign. And this time there will be no computer cognizance to give us away.'

Nor convenient breathing tubes, to let us stay safe underwater, he almost added, but Lark didn't want to dampen her enthusiasm.

'Let's see if there's anything we can use to get down to the lake, without having to jump,' Ling added. Together they inspected the equipment shelves lining one wall of the airlock, until she cried out excitedly. 'I found a standard cable reel! Now if only I can figure out the altered controls ...'

While Ling examined the metal spook, Lark felt a change in the low vibration that had been growling in the background ever since they escaped their prison cell. The resonance began to rise in pitch and force, until it soon filled the air with a harsh keening.

'Something's happening,' he said, 'I think—'

Just then the battleship took a sudden jerk, almost knocking them both to the floor. Ling dropped the cable, barely missing her foot.

A second noise burst in through the open door of the airlock. An awful *grinding* din, as if Jijo herself were complaining. Lark recognized the scraping of metal against rock.

'Ifni!' Ling cried. 'They're taking off!'

Helping each other, fighting for balance, they reached the outer hatch and looked down again, staring aghast at a spectacle of pent-up nature, suddenly unleashed.

Well, so much for jumping in the lake, he thought. The Jophur ship was rising glacially, but the first few dozen meters were crucial, removing the dam that had drowned the valley under a transient reservoir. At once, the Festival Glade was transformed into a roiling tempest. Submerged trees tore loose from their sodden roots. Stones fell crashing into the maelstrom as mud banks were undermined. While the battlecruiser climbed complacently, a vast flood of murky water and debris rushed downstream, pummeling everything in its path, pouring toward distant, unsuspecting plains.

Too late, Lark realised. *We were too late making our escape. Now we're trapped inside*.

As if to seal the fact, a light flashed near the open hatch, which began to close. An automatic safety measure, he figured, for a starship taking off, Lark barely suppressed an overpowering temptation to dive through the narrowing gap, despite the deadly chaos waiting below.

Ling squeezed his hand fiercely as they caught a passing glimpse of something shiny and round-shouldered – a slick, elongated dome, uncovered by retreating waters. Even under pale predawn light, they recognized the Rothen-Danik ship, still shut within a prison of quantum time.

Then the armored portal sealed with a boom and hiss, cutting off the all-too-fleeting breeze. Trapped inside, they stared at the cruel hatch.

'We're heading north,' Lark said. It was the one last thing he had noticed, watching the ravaged valley pass below.

'Come on,' Ling answered pragmatically. 'There must be someplace to hide aboard this bloated ship.'

NELO

Still a few leagues short of their goal, the zealots realized they were surrounded. They spent the night huddled in the marsh, counting the campfires of regiments loyal to the High Sages. Squeezed between militia units from Biblos and Nelo's pursuing detachment, the rebels surrendered at first light.

There was little ceremony, and few weapons for the rabble to give up. Most of their fanatical ardor had been used up by the hard slog across a quagmire where mighty Buyur towers once reared toward the sky. Already bedraggled, Jop and his followers marched in a ragged column toward the Bibur, enduring taunts from former neighbors.

'Go ahead an' look!' Nelo pushed the tree farmer toward a bluff where everyone could look across the wide river at shimmering cliffs, still immersed in dawn's long shadows. Oncoming daylight revealed a vast cave underneath, chiseled centuries ago by the Earthship *Tabernacle*. Two dozen huge pillars supported the Fist of Stone, hovering like a suspended sentence, just above a cluster of quaint wooden buildings, each fashioned to resemble some famed structure of Terran heritage – such as the Taj Mahal, the Great Pyramid of Cheops, and the Main Library of San Diego, California.

'The Archive stands,' Nelo told his enemy. 'You wanted to bring the Fist crashing down, but it ain't gonna happen. And in a couple o' years I'll be makin' paper again. It was all for nothin', Jop. The lives you wasted, and the property. You achieved nothing.'

Nelo saw Jop's bitterness redouble when they reached a new semaphore station, set up directly across the water from Biblos, where they learned about the rocket attack, the destruction of one Jophur ship, and the rumored damage of another. Young militia soldiers shouted jubilation to learn that last night's distant 'thunderstorm' had instead been the unleashed fury of the Six Races, taking vengeance for the poor g'Kek.

A few older faces were grim. The militia captain warned that this was but a single battle in a war the Commons of Jijo could hardly hope to win.

Nelo refused to think about that. Instead, he kept his promise to Ariana Foo, by handing over her message for transmission. Lightborne signals flew better at night, but the operator refired his lamp when he saw Ariana's name on the single sheet of paper. While that bulletin went out, the captain looked into getting transportation across the Bibur, where showers and clean clothes waited.

And sleep, Nelo thought. Yet, despite fatigue, he somehow felt younger than he had in ages, as if the tiring chase through swamplands had stripped years away, leaving him a virile warrior of long ago.

Leaning against a tree, Nelo let his eyes close for a little while, his mind turning back to plans for a rebuilt paper mill.

Our first job will be helping the blues put their dam back together. Do it right, this time. Less worrying about camouflage and more about getting good power output. As long as I'm at Biblos, I might as well look into copying some designs . . .

Nelo's head jerked up when a carpentry apprentice from Dolo shouted his name. The lad had been reading last night's semaphore messages, affixed on the wall of the relay post.

'I just saw your daughter's name,' the young man told him.

'She's on Mount Guenn!'

Nelo took three jerky steps forward ... as Jop did exactly the same thing. The farmer's expression showed the same surprise. His shock and dismay contrasted with Nelo's joy at hearing that one of his children lived.

Sara! The papermaker's mind whirled. *In the name of the founders, how did she find herself on Mount Guenn?*

He hurried over to the shed, eager to learn more. Perhaps there would be word of Dwer and Lark, as well!

At that moment, a shout erupted from one of the operators inside the semaphore hut. While the sender kept on clicking his key, transmitting Ariana Foo's message, the receiver burst out through the door, a middle-aged woman waving a paper covered with hurried scrawls.

'Mess ... mess ...' She ran for the militia captain, gasping urgently.

'Message from lookouts,' she cried. 'The Jophur ... the Jophur ship is coming this way!'

It did not swoop or plummet. The star vessel was far too vast for that.

A haze of suspended dust accompanied its passage above forest or open ground, but when the immense sky mountain moved ponderously over the Bibur, the waters went ominously still. The glassy-smooth footprint spread even wider than its shadow.

Keep going. Nelo prayed. *Just pass us by. Keep going ...*

But the great cruiser evidently had plans right here, arresting its forward momentum directly over the river, in plain sight of the Great Archive.

Now it was Nelo's turn to glower as he glimpsed grim satisfaction pass over Jop's face. *Someone must've snitched*, he thought. Rumors told of Jophur emissaries, establishing outposts in tiny hamlets, imperiously demanding information. Sooner or later some zealot or scroll thumper would have blabbed about this place.

No slashing rays fell from the mighty battleship. No rain of bombs, taking vengeance for its little brother, lost the night before.

Instead, a few small portals opened in its side. About two dozen *robots* descended, fluttering lazily until they reached hoon height above the water, where they turned in formation and streaked toward Biblos.

A second wave emerged from the great ship, floating down more slowly on wide plates of burnished black. Tapered cones rode those flat conveyances, like stacks of glossy pancakes, each pile on its own flying skillet.

Even before the Jophur party reached the walls of the hidden city, the space dreadnought began moving again, turning its massive bulk to head back the way it came, roughly south by southeast, gaining altitude at an accelerating pace. By the time Nelo lost it in the glare of the rising sun, the cruiser had climbed above the highest clouds.

Crowds gathered at the riverbank, peering at the opposite shore. Biblos still lay immersed in nightlike shadows. By contrast, the robots glittered till they passed under the Fist of Stone, followed by their Jophur masters.

After that, Nelo and the others had to rely on the militia captain, peering through binoculars, to relate what was happening.

'Each Jophur is entering a different building, guarded by several robots. Some use the front door . . . but one just sent its servants to smash open a wall and go in that way.

'They're all inside now . . . and people are running out! Humans, hoons, qheuens . . . there's a g'Kek . . . his left wheel is smoking. I think he's been shot.'

The crowd murmured frustration, but there was nothing to do. Nothing anybody could do.

'I see militia squads! Mostly humans with some urs and hoons. They've got rifles . . . the new kind with mulc-tipped bullets. They're running toward the Science Building!

'They're splitting up, skirmish style, using opposite doors to sneak in from both sides at once.'

Nelo clenched his hands as he stared across the Bibur. At the same time, he wondered why the great battleship would come all this way, yet not tarry to destroy the center of Jijoan intellectual life.

I guess the cruiser had other matters to attend to. Anyway, it'll be back to pick up their foray party.

There was one hope. *Maybe there are some rockets left after last night. Perhaps they'll catch the cruiser, before it can return.*

There was always that hope – though it seemed unlikely the Jophur would be fooled a second time.

Across the river he could see a flood of refugees – scholars, librarians, and students – pouring out of sally ports and over the battlements. There weren't many g'Kek among the fugitives. Nor traeki. Both races appeared doomed to stay within, destined for different fates, both of them unpleasant.

He wondered, *What do the aliens want with our Library? To check out some books and take 'em back home to read?*

In fact, that bizarre notion made sense.

I'll bet the rocket attack made 'em realize we have tricks up our sleeve. Suddenly they're interested in what we know, and how we know it. They'll scan our books to find out what other nasty surprises we might come up with.

Something was happening in the shadowed cave. Distant popping sounds carried across the river, doubtless from within the Hall of Science.

'They're coming out!' the captain announced. His grip on the binoculars stiffened. 'The rifle squads ... they're in retreat ... dragging their wounded, trying to cover each other. They're ...'

He lowered the glasses. The officer's eyes were bleak and he stood silently, completely overcome.

A corporal gently took the binoculars and resumed reporting.

'Dead,' was the first word she said.

'I see dead soldiers, they're all down.'

A hush settled over the crowd. Across the Bibur nothing seemed to be moving anymore, except an occasional sharp-edged machine shape, flitting underneath the Fist of Stone.

The explosers ... Nelo wondered. *Why didn't they set off their charges?*

The greatest secret of the Six Races. The most secure fortress of humankind on Jijo. Biblos had been captured in a matter of duras. Its treasured archive lay in the tight grip of Jophur invaders.

EWASX

Is it settled then, My rings? Have we rooted out the last corners of your clandestine resistance? Can we assume there will be no more episodes of surreptitious rebellion?

The Priest-Stack threatened to dismantle us/Me after the last embarrassment, when you silly rings foolishly/cleverly managed to perform a vlenning without your master torus knowing. The priest aimed to scrape every drip trail of waxy memory lining our core, seeking clues to the whereabouts of the pair of wolfling vermin you (briefly, mutinously) released into our glorious *Polkjhy* ship.

But then the stack in change of psycho-tactics reported telemetry showing that Lark and Ling almost surely departed the ship when instruments showed an airlock hatch anomalously opening.

Humans are good with water. No doubt they imagined themselves safe after entering the lake, never suspecting that they were about to be swept downstream into a vortex of ruin when our majestic *Polkjhy* took off!

The droll appropriateness of this fate – the dramatic irony – so pleased the Captain-Leader that a ruling was made, overturning the Priest-Stack's desire. For the time being, then our/My union is safe.

DO NOT COUNT ON CONTINUED TEMPERANCE/ FORGIVENESS, MY RINGS!

Forgiveness for *what*, you ask?

Now you worry Me. Is the shared wax so badly melted? Did the Asx personality so damage us, with its second attempt at suicide-by-amnesia? Must I provide memory of recent events through the demi-electronic processes of the master torus?

Very well, My rings, I shall do so. Then we will begin again, restoring the expertise that made us useful to the Jophur cause.

Together we watched while a party from our ship took possession of the so-called Library used by the savage Six Races. Though it contains a pathetically small amount of bit-equivalent data, this is the source/font of their wolfling trickery.

Feral scheming that has cost us dearly.

A fine thing happened when we/I caught sight of those crude buildings made from sliced trees, sheltered in an artificial cave. Many hidden waxy trails resonated with sudden recognition! Accessing these recovered tracks, we were able to tell the Captain-Leader many secrets of his trove of pseudoknowledge. Secrets Asx had meant to render inaccessible.

Slowly, we regain our former reputation and esteem. Does that make you glad, My rings?

How gratifying to feel your agreement come so readily now! That brief rebellion, followed by a second suicide amnesia, appears to have left you more docile than before. No longer sovereign traeki rings, but parts of a greater whole.

Now regard! Leaving a force behind to secure Biblos, our *Polkjhy* turns to its main task. Too long have we let ourselves be diverted/ delayed. There will be no more negotiating with Rothen sneak thieves. No more dickering with savage races. Those six will meet their varied fates from land forces already scattered across the Slope.

As for *Polkjhy*, we cruise toward that continental cleft, that ocean abyss. Estimated locale of the dolphin ship.

IT IS DECIDED. THE ROTHEN HAD THE RIGHT IDEA, AFTER ALL.

We'll bombard the depths, putting the fugitive Earthlings in peril. To preserve their lives, they will have no choice but to rise up and surrender.

Until now, the Captain-Leader preferred patience over rash action. We did not want to destroy the very thing we seek! Not before learning its secrets. Since no competing clan or fleet has come to Jijo, we appeared to have a wealth of time.

But that was before we lost both corvettes. Before postponements stretched on and on.

Now we are resolved to take the chance!

With depth bombs ready in great store, we plunge toward the zone known as the Rift.

WHAT IS THIS? ALREADY?

DETECTORS BLARE.

IN THE WATERS AHEAD OF US – MOTION!

Joyous hunt lust fills the bridge. It must be the *prey*, giving away their location as they scurry in search of a new hiding place.

Then remote perceptors cry out upsetting news. No single ship is making the vibrations we detect.

THERE ARE SCORES OF EMISSION SITES ... HUNDREDS!

SARA

Emerson seemed cheerful during the long ride down from Mount Guenn, pressing his face against the warped window of the little tram, gazing at the sea.

How would he feel if he knew whom we were meeting? Sara wondered as the car zoomed down ancient lava flows, swifter than a galloping urs.

Would he be ecstatic, or try to jump out and flee?

Far below, a myriad bright sun glints stretched from the surf line all the way to a cloud-fringed western horizon. Jijo's waters seemed placid, but Sara still felt daunted by the sight. A mere one percent ripple in that vastness would erase every tree and settlement along the coast. The ocean's constancy proved the ample goodness of this life world – a nursery of species.

I always hoped to see this, before my bones went to the Midden as dross. I just never figured I'd come by horseback, across the Spectral Flow, over a volcano ... and finally by fabulous cable car, all toward confronting creatures out of legend.

Sara felt energized, despite the fact that nobody on Mount Guenn had slept much lately.

Uriel had finished using her analog computer barely in time.

Just miduras after sending the ballistics calculations north, semaphore operators reported breathless news about the consequences.

Stunning rocket victories.

Discouraging rocket failures.

Forest fires, dead sages, and the Egg – wounded, silent, possibly forever.

Flash floods below Festival Glade, leaving countless dead or homeless.

Nor was that all. Throughout the night, tucked amid other tidings from across the slope, came clipped summaries of events bearing hard on Sara.

Elation surged when she learned of Blade's unqheuenish aerial adventures. Then her father's report triggered overpowering images of the destruction of Dolo Village, forcing her to seek a place to sit, burying her head in her hands. Nelo lived – that was something. But others she had known were gone, along with the house she grew up in.

Lark and Dwer . . . we dreamed what it might be like when the dam blew. But I never really thought it could happen.

Waves of sorrow kept Sara withdrawn for a time, till someone told her an urgent message had come, addressed specifically for her, under the imprimatur of a former High Sage of the Six.

Ariana Foo, Sara realized, scanning the brief missive. *Ifni, who cares about the dimensions of the ship that crashed Emerson into the swamp? Does it matter what kind of chariot he used, when he was a star god? He's a wounded soul now. Crippled. Trapped on Jijo, like the rest of us.*

Or was he?

After so many shocks that eventful night, Sara was just lying down for a blotting balm of sleep when events close at hand rocked Uriel and her guests.

At dawn, the captains of Wuphon Port sent word of a monster in their harbor. A fishlike entity who, after some misunderstandings, claimed relatedness to human beings.

Moreover, the creature said it bore a message for the smith.

Uriel was overjoyed.

'The little sneak canera that scared us so . . . the device cane fron the Earthling shif! Ferhafs the Jophur have not found us, after all!'

That mattered. The sky battleship was said to be on the move, perhaps heading in their direction. But Uriel could not evacuate the forge with several projects still under way. Her teams had never been busier.

'I'll go see the Terran at once,' the smith declared.

There was no lack of volunteers to come along. Riding the first tram, Sara watched Prity flip through Emerson's wrinkled sketchpad, lingering over a page where sleek figures with finned backs and tails arched ecstatically through crashing waves. An image drawn from memory.

'They look other than I inagined,' commented Uriel, curling her long neck past the chimp's shoulder. 'Till now, I only knew the race fron desrifshuns in vooks.'

'You should read the kind with pictures in 'em.' Kurt the Exploser laughed, nudging his nephew. But Jomah kept his face pressed to the window next to Emerson, taking turns pointing at features of the fast-changing landscape. Ever cheerful, the starman showed no awareness of what this trip was about.

Sara knew what tugged her heart. Beyond all other worries and pangs, she realized, *It may be time for the bird to fly back to his own kind.*

Watching the robust person she had nursed from the brink of death, Sara saw no more she could offer him. No cure for a ravaged brain, whose sole hope lay back in the Civilization of the Five Galaxies. Even with omnipotent foes in pursuit, who wouldn't choose that life over a shadow existence, huddling on a stranded shore?

The ancestors, that's who. The Tabernacle *crew, and all the other sneakships.*

Sara recalled what Sage Purofsky said, only a day ago.

'There are no accidents, Sara. Too many ships came to Jijo, in too short time.'

'The scrolls speak of destiny,' she had replied.

'Destiny!' The sage snorted disdain. *'A word made up by people who don't understand how they got where they are, and are blind to where they're going.'*

'Are you saying you know how we got here, Master?'

Despite all the recent commotion and tragedy, Sara found her mind still hooked by Purofsky's reply.

'Of course I do, Sara. It seems quite clear to me.

'We were invited.'

EWASX

'Fools!' the Captain-Leader declares. 'All but one of these emanations must come from decoy torpedoes, tuned to imitate the emission patterns of a starship. It is a standard tactical ruse in deep space. But such artifice cannot avail if we linger circumspectly at short range!'

'Use standard techniques to sift the emanations.'

'FIND THE TRUE VESSEL WE SEEK!'

Ah, My rings, can you discern the colors swarming down the glossy flanks of our Captain-Leader? See how glorious, how lustrous they are. Witness the true dignity of Jophur wrath in its finest form.

Such indignation! Such egotistic rage! The Oailie would be proud of this commander of ours, especially as we all hear impossible news.

THESE ARE NOT DECOY DRONES AT ALL.

The myriad objects we detect ... moving out of the Rift toward open ocean ... EVERY ONE OF THEM IS A REAL STARSHIP!

The bridge mists with fearful vapors. A great fleet of ships! How did the Earthers acquire such allies?

Even our *Polkjhy* is no match for this many.

We will be overwhelmed!

DWER

'I am sorry,' Gillian Baskin told him. 'The decision came suddenly. There was no time to arrange a special ride to shore.'

She seemed irked, as if this request were unexpected. But in fact, Dwer had asked for nothing else since his second day aboard this vessel.

The two humans drifted near each other in a spacious, water-filled chamber, the control center of starship *Streaker*. Dolphins flew past them across the spherical room, breathing oxygen-charged fluid with lungs that had been modified to make it almost second nature. At consoles and workstations, they switched to bubble domes or tubes attached directly to their blowholes. It seemed as strange an environment as Dwer had ever dreamed, yet the fins seemed in their element. By contrast, Dwer and Gillian wore balloonlike garments, seeming quite out of place.

'I'm not doing any good here,' he repeated, hearing the words narrowly projected by his globe helmet. 'I got no skills you can use. I can hardly breathe the stuff you call air. Most important, there are folks waiting for me. Who need me. Can't you just cut me loose in some kind of a boat?'

Gillian closed her eyes and sighed – a brief, eerie set of clicks and chuttering moans. 'Look, I understand your predicament,' she said in Anglic. 'But I have over a hundred lives to look after ... and a lot more at stake, in a larger sense. I'm sorry, Dwer. All I can hope is that you'll understand.'

He knew it useless to pursue the matter further. A dolphin at one of the bridge stations called for attention, and Gillian was soon huddled with that fin and Lieutenant Tsh't, solving the latest crisis.

The groan of *Streaker*'s engines made Dwer's head itch – a residual effect, perhaps, of the way his brain was palped and bruised by the Danik robot. He had no proof things would really be any better if he found his way back to shore. But his legs, arms, and lungs all pined for wilderness – for wind on his face and the feel of rough ground underfoot.

A ghostly map traced its way across the bridge. The realm of dry land was a grayish border rimming both sides of a submerged canyon – the Rift – now filled with moving lights, dispersing like fire bees abandoning their hives. So it seemed to Dwer as over a hundred ancient Buyur vessels came alive after half a million years, departing the trash heap where they were consigned long ago.

The tactic was familiar. Many creatures used flocking to confuse predators. He approved the cleverness of Gillian and her crew, and wished them luck.

But I can't help them. I'm useless here. She ought to let me go.

Most of the salvaged ships were under robotic control, programmed to follow a simple set of instructions. Volunteers rode a few derelicts, keeping close to *Streaker*, performing special tasks. Rety had volunteered for one of these teams, surprising Dwer and worrying him at the same time.

She never does anything unless there's an angle.

If he had gone along, there might have been a chance to veer the decoy close to shore, and jump off ...

But no, he had no right to mess up Gillian's plan.

Dammit, I'm used to action! I can't handle being a passive observer.

But handle it he must.

Dwer tried to cultivate patience, ignoring an itch where the bulky suit would not let him scratch, watching the lights disperse – most heading for the mouth of the Rift, spilling into the vast oceanic abyss of the Great Midden itself.

'*Starship enginesss!*' The gravitics detector officer announced, thrashing her tail flukes in the water, causing bubbles in the supercharged liquid.

'*P-passive detectors show Nova class or higher ... it'sss following the path of the Riffft ...*'

Realization emerges, along with a stench of frustration.

The vast fleet of vessels that we briefly feared has proved not to be a threat, after all. They are not warships, but decommissioned vessels, long ago abandoned as useless for efficient function.

Nevertheless, they baffle and thwart our goal/mission.

A blast of leadership pheromones cuts through the disappointed mist.

'TO WORK THEN,' our Captain-Leader proclaims.

'WE ARE SKILLED. WE ARE MIGHTY. SO LET US DO YOUR/OUR JOBS WELL.

'PIERCE THIS MYSTERY. FIND THE PREY. WE ARE JOPHUR. WE SHALL PREVAIL.'

DWER

A glittering light entered the display zone, much higher and much larger than any of the others, and cruising well above the imaginary waterline.

That must be the battleship, he thought. His mind tried to come up with an image. Something huge and terrible. Clawed and swift.

Suddenly, the detection officer's voice went shrill.

'They're dropping ordnance!'

Sparks began falling from the gig glow.

Bombs, Dwer realised. He had seen this happen before, but not on such a profuse scale.

Lieutenant Tsh't shouted a warning.

'All handsss, prepare for shock waves!'

SARA

A hoonish work crew swarmed over the tram after the passengers debarked, filling the car with stacks of folded cloth. Teams had been sending the stuff up to the forge since dawn, stripping every ship of its sails. But the urrish smith hardly glanced at the cargo. Instead,

Uriel trotted off, leading the way down to the cove with a haughty centauroid gait.

The dense, salty air of sea level affected everybody. Sara kept an eye on Emerson, who sniffed the breeze and commented in song.

> '*A storm is a-brewin'*
> *You can bet on it tonight.*
> *A blow is a-stewin'*
> *So you better batten tight.*'

The khutas and warehouses of the little port were shaded by a dense lattice of melon vines and nectar creepers, growing with a lush, tropical abundance characteristic of southern climes. The alleys were deserted though. Everyone was either working for Uriel or else down by the bay, where a crowd of hoons and qheuens babbled excitedly. Several hoons – males and females with beards of seniority – knelt by the edge of a quay, conversing toward the water, using animated gestures. But the two officials made way when Uriel's party neared.

Sara kept her attention on Emerson, whose expression stayed casually curious until the last moment, when a sleek gray figure lifted its glossy head from the water.

The starman stopped and stared, blinking rapidly.

He's surprised, Sara thought. *Could we be wrong? Perhaps he has nothing to do with the dolphin ship.*

Then the cetacean emissary lifted its body higher, thrashing water with its tail.

'Sssso, it's true ...' the fishlike Terran said in thickly accented Anglic, inspecting Emerson with one eye, then the other.

'Glad to see you living, Engineer D-D'Anite. Though it hardly seems possible, after what we saw happen to you back at the Fractal world.

'I confessss, I can't see how you followed us to this whaleforsaken planet.'

Powerful emotions fought across Emerson's face. Sara read astonishment, battling surges of both curiosity and frustrated despair.

'K-K-K—'

The dismal effort to speak ended in a groan.

'A-ah-ahh ...'

The dolphin seemed upset by this response, chuttering dismay over the human's condition.

But then Emerson shook his head, seeking to draw on other resources. At last, he found a way to express his feelings, releasing a burst stream of song.

'How quaint the ways of paradox!
At common sense she gaily mocks!
We've quips and quibbles heard in flocks,
But none to beat this paradox!'

GILLIAN

The ultimatum blanketed all etheric wavelengths – a scratchy caterwauling that filled *Streaker*'s bridge, making the oxy-water fizz. Streams of bubbles swelled and popped with each Galactic Four syntax phrase.

Most neo-dolphin crew members read a text translation prepared by the Niss Machine. Anglic letters and GalSeven glyphs flowed across the main holo screen.

HEAR AND COMPREHEND OUR FINAL COMMAND/OFFER!

Gillian listened for nuance in the original Jophur dialect, hoping to glean something new. It was the third repetition since the enemy dreadnought began broadcasting from high in the atmosphere.

'YOU WHOM WE SEEK – YOU HAVE PERFORMED CLEVER MANEUVERS, WORTHY OF RESPECT. AT THIS JUNCTURE, WE SHALL NO LONGER WASTE BOMBS. WE SHALL CEASE USE-LESSLY INSPECTING DECOYS'

The change in tactics was expected. At first, the foe had sent robots into the lightless depths, to examine and eliminate reactivated Buyur ships, one by one. But it was a simple matter for Hannes Suessi's team to fix booby traps. Each derelict would self-destruct when a probe approached, taking the automaton along with it.

The usual hierarchy of battle was thus reversed. Here in the Midden, big noisy ships were far cheaper than robots to hunt them. Suessi had scores more ready to peel off from widely separated dross piles. It was doubtful the Jophur could spend drones at the same rate.

There was a downside. The decoy ships were discards, in ill repair when abandoned, half a million years ago. Only the incredible hardiness of Galactic manufacture left them marginally useful, and dozens had already burned out, littering the Midden once more with their dead hulks.

*

This was the part Gillian paid close attention to, the first couple of times it played. Unfortunately, Jophur 'generosity' wasn't tempting. In exchange for *Streaker*'s data, charts, and samples, the Captain-Leader of the Greatship *Polkjhy* promised cryonic internment for the crew, with a guarantee of revival and free release in a mere thousand years. 'After the present troubles have been resolved.'

In other words, the Jophur wanted to have *Streaker*'s secrets ... *and* to make sure no one else shared them for a long time to come.

While the message laid out this offer, Gillian's second-in-command swam alongside.

'We've managed to c-come up with most of the suppliesss the local wizard asked for,' Tsh't reported. One of the results of making contact with the Commons of Six Races had been a shopping list of items desperately wanted by the urrish smith, Uriel.

'Several decoy ships are being diverted close to shore, as you requested. Kaa and his new t-team can strip them of the stuff Uriel wants, as they swing by.'

The dolphin lieutenant paused. 'I suppose I needn't add that this increases our danger? The enemy might detect a rhythm in these movementsss, and target their attention on the hoonish seaport-t.'

'The Niss came up with a swarming pattern to prevent that,' Gillian answered. 'What about the crew separation? How are Makanee's preparations coming along?'

Tsh't nodded her sleek head. Taking a break from the laborious, underwater version of Anglic, she replied in Trinary.

> * *Seasons change the tides,*
> > * *That tug us toward our fates,*
> > > * *And divide loved ones ...* *

To which she added a punctuating coda:

> * *... forever ...* *

Gillian winced. What she planned – least awful of a dozen grievous options – would sever close bonds among a crew that had shared great trials. An epic journey Earthlings might sing about for ages to come.

Providing there are still Earthlings, after the Time of Changes.

In fact, she had no choice. Half of *Streaker*'s neo-dolphin complement were showing signs of stress atavism – a decay of the faculties needed for critical thought. Fear and exhaustion had finally taken their toll. No client race as young as *Tursiops amicus* had ever endured so much for so long, almost alone.

It's time to make the sacrifice we all knew would someday come.

The chamber still vibrated with Jophur threats. Coming from some other race, she might have factored in an element of bluster and bravado, but she took these adversaries precisely at their word.

The holo display glowed with menacing letters.

WE ARE THE ONLY GALACTIC WARSHIP IN THIS REGION. NO ONE IS COMING TO HELP YOU. NOR WILL ANY COMPETITORS DISTRACT US, AS HAPPENED ON OTHER OCCASIONS.

WE CAN AFFORD TO WAIT YOU OUT, INVESTIGATING AND ELIMINATING DECOYS FROM SAFE RANGE. OR ELSE, IF NECESSARY, THIS NOBLE SHIP WILL FORGO SOLE HONOR AND SEND FOR HELP FROM THE VAST JOPHUR ARMADA.

DELAY MERELY INCREASES OUR WRATH. IT AUGMENTS THE HARM WE SHALL DO TO YOUR TERRAN COUSINS, AND THE OTHER SOONERS WHO DWELL ILLICITLY ON FORBIDDEN LAND ...

Gillian thought of Alvin, Huck, and Ur-ronn, listening in a nearby dry cabin – and Pincer-Tip, who represented them on the bridge, darting to and fro with flicks of his red claws.

We already drew hell down on the locals, when the Rothen somehow tracked us to Jijo. There must be a way to spare them further punishment on our account.

Soon it will be time to end this.

Gillian turned back to Tsh't. 'How much longer before it's our turn?'

The lieutenant communed with the tactics-and-movement officer.

'We'll slip into shore between the fourth and fifth decoys ... about eight hours from now.'

Gillian glanced at Pincer, his reddish carapace covered with oxy-water bubbles, the qheuen visor spinning madly, taking in everything with the avidness of adolescence. The local youths should be glad about what was about to happen. *And so will Dwer Koolhan. I hope this pleases him ... though it's not quite what he wanted.*

Gillian admitted to herself she would miss the young man who reminded her so much of Tom.

'All right, then,' she told Tsh't. 'Let's take the kids home.'

Together, they proved only half-blind, stumbling down the musty corridors of a vast alien ship filled with hostile beings. Ling knew more than he did about starships, but Lark was the one who kept them from getting completely lost.

For one thing, there were few symbols on the walls, so their knowledge of several Galactic dialects proved almost useless. Instead, each closed aperture of intersection seemed to project its own, unique *smell*, effective at short range. As a Jijoan, Lark could sniff some of these and dimly grasp the simplest pheromone indicators – about as well as a bright human four-year-old might read street signs in a metropolis.

One bitter tang reminded him of the scent worn by traeki proctors at Gathering Festival, when they had to break up a fight or subdue a belligerent drunk.

SECURITY, the odor seemed to say. He steered Ling around that hallway.

She had a goal, however, which was one up on him. With his head full of fragrant miasmas, Lark gladly left the destination up to her. No doubt any path they chose would eventually lead to the same place – their old prison cell.

Three more times, they encountered solitary Jophur. But puffs from the purple ring caused them to be ignored. Doors continued sliding open on command. The gift from Asx was incredible. A little too good, in fact.

I can't believe this trick will work for long, he thought as they hurried deeper into the battleship's heart. *Asx probably expected us to need it for a midura or so, just till we made it outside.* Once the crew was alerted about escaped prisoners, the ruse must surely fail. The Jophur would use countermeasures, wouldn't they?

Then he realized.

Maybe there's been no alert. The Jophur may assume we already fled the ship!

Perhaps.

Still, each encounter with a gleaming ring stack in some dank passage left him feeling eerie. Lark had lived among traeki all his life, but till this moment he never grasped how different their consciousness must be. How strange for a sapient being to look right at you and not *see*, simply because you gave off the right safe-conduct aroma ...

At the next intersection, he sniffed all three corridor branches carefully, and found the indicator Ling wanted – a simple scent that meant LIFE. He pointed, and she nodded.

'As I thought. The layout isn't too different from a type-seventy cargo ship. They keep it at the center.'

'Keep *what* at the center?' Lark asked, but she was already hurrying ahead. Two human fugitives, bearing their only tools – she cradling the wounded red traeki ring, while he carried the purple one.

When the next door opened, Ling stepped back briefly from a glare. The place was more brightly lit than the normal dim corridors. The air smelled better, too. Less cloying with meanings he could not comprehend. Lark's first impression was of a large chamber, filled with color.

'As I hoped,' Ling said, nodding. 'The layout's standard. We may actually have a chance.'

'A chance for what?'

She turned back to look into the vault, which Lark now saw to be quite vast, filled with a maze of crisscrossing support beams . . . all of them draped with varied types of vegetation.

'A chance to survive,' she answered, and took his hand, drawing him inside.

A jungle surrounded them, neatly organized and regimented. Tier after tier of shelves and platforms receded from view, serviced by machines moving slowly along tracks. Arrayed on this vast network there flourished a riot of living forms, broad leaves and hanging vines, creepers and glistening tubers. Water dripped along some of the twisted green cables, and the two of them rushed to the nearest trickle, lapping eagerly.

Now Lark understood the meaning of the aroma symbol that had led them here.

In the middle of hell, they had found a small oasis. At that moment, it felt like paradise.

EMERSON

He did not like going down to the water. The harbor was too frenzied.

It hardly seemed like a joyous reunion to see Kaa and other friends again. He recognized good old Brookida, and Tussito, and Wattaceti. They all seemed glad to see him, but far too busy to spend time visiting, or catching up.

Perhaps that was just as well. Emerson felt ashamed.

Shame that he could not greet them with anything more than their names . . . and an occasional snippet of song.

Shame that he could not help them in their efforts – hauling all sorts of junk out of the sea, instructing Uriel's assistants, and sending the materials up by tram to the peak of Mount Guenn.

Above all, he felt shame over the failure of his sacrifice, back at that immense space city made of snow – that fluffy metropolis, the size of a solar system – called the Fractal System.

Oh, it seemed so noble and brave when he set forth in a salvaged Thennanin scout, extravagantly firing to create a diversion and help *Streaker* escape. With his last glimpse – as force fields closed in all around him – he had seen the beloved, scarred hull slip out through an opening in the vast shell of ice, and prayed she would make it.

Gillian, he had thought. Perhaps she would think of him, now. The way she recalled her Tom.

Then the Old Ones took him from the little ship, and had their way with him. They prodded and probed. They made him a cripple. They gave him forgetfulness.

And they sent him here.

The outlines are still hazy, but Emerson now saw the essential puzzle.

Streaker had escaped to this forlorn planet, only to be trapped. More hard luck for a crew that never got a break.

But . . . why . . . send . . . me . . . here?

That action by the Old Ones made no sense. It seemed crazy.

Everyone would be better off if he had died, the way he planned.

The whole population of the hoonish seaport was dashing about. Sara seemed preoccupied, spending much of her time talking rapidly to Uriel, or else arguing heatedly with the gray-bearded human scholar whose name Emerson could not recall.

Often a messenger would arrive, bearing one of the pale paper strips used for transcribing semaphore bulletins. Once, the urrish courier came at a gallop, panting and clearly shaken by the news she bore. An eruption of dismayed babble swelled as Emerson made out a single repeated word – 'Biblos.'

Everyone was so upset and distracted, nobody seemed to mind when he indicated a wish to take the tram back up to Uriel's forge. Using gestures, Sara made clear that he must come back before sunset, and he agreed. Clearly something was going to happen then. Sara made sure Prity went along to look after him.

Emerson didn't mind. He got along well with Prity. They were both of a kind. The little chim's crude humor, expressed with hand-signed jokes, often broke him up.

Those fishie things are cousins? she signaled at one point, referring to the busy, earnest dolphins. *I was hoping they tasted good!*

Emerson laughed. Earth's two client-level races had an ongoing rivalry that seemed almost instinctive.

During the ride upslope, he examined some of the machinery Kaa and the others had provided at Uriel's request. Most of it looked like junk – low-level Galactic computers, ripped out of standard consoles that might be hundreds or millions of years old. Many were stained or slimy from long immersion. The mélange of devices seemed to share just one trait – they had been refurbished enough to be turned on. He could tell because the power leads were all wrapped in tape to prevent it. Otherwise, it looked like a pile of garbage.

He longed to squat on the floor and tinker with the things. Prity shook her head though. She was under orders to prevent it. So instead Emerson looked out through the window, watching distant banks of dense clouds roll ominously closer from the west.

He fantasized about running away, perhaps to Xi, the quiet, pastoral refuge hidden in a vast desert of color. He would ride horses and practice his music ... maybe fix simple, useful tools to earn his keep. Something to help fool himself that his life still had worth.

For a while he had felt valued here, helping Uriel get results from the Hall of Spinning Disks, but no one seemed to need him anymore. He felt like a burden.

It would be worse if he returned to *Streaker*, a shell. A fragment. The chance of a cure beckoned. But Emerson was smart enough to know the prospects weren't promising. Captain Creideiki once had an injury like his, and the ship's doctor had been helpless to correct such extensive damage to a brain.

Perhaps at home, though ... On Earth ...

He painted the blue globe in his mind, a vision of beauty that ached his heart.

Deep inside, Emerson knew he would never see it again. The tram docked at last. His mood lifted for a little while, helping Uriel's staff unload cargo. Along with Prity, he followed the urs and qheuens down a long, twisty corridor toward a flow of warm air. At last they reached a big underground grotto – a cave with an opening at the far end, facing north. Hints of color gleamed far beyond, reminding him of the Spectral Flow.

Workers scurried about. Emerson saw g'Kek teams busy sewing together great sheets of strong, lightweight cloth. He watched urs delicately adjust handmade valves as gray qheuens bent lengths of pipe with their strong claws. Already, breaths of volcanically heated air were flowing into the first of many waiting canopies, creating bulges that soon joined together, forming a globe-ended bag.

Emerson looked across the scene, then back at the salvaged junk the dolphins had donated.

Slowly, a smile spread across his face.

To his great satisfaction, the urrish smiths seemed glad when he silently offered to lend a hand.

KAA

The skies opened around nightfall, letting down both rain and lightning.

The whale sub *Hikahi* delayed entering Port Wuphon until the storm's first stinging drizzle began peppering the wharves and huts. The sheltered bay speckled with the impact of dense droplets as the submersible glided up a slanted coastal shelf toward an agreed rendezvous.

Kaa swam just ahead, guiding her through the narrow channel, between jagged shoals of demicoral. No one would have denied him the honor. *I am still chief pilot*, he thought. *With or without my nickname*.

The blunt-nosed craft mimicked his long turn around the sheltering headland, following as he showed the way with powerful, body-arching thrusts of his tail. It was an older piloting technique than wormhole diving, not highly technical. But Kaa's ancestors used to show human sailors the way home in this manner, long before the oldest clear memory of either race.

'*Another two hundred meters*, Hikahi,' he projected using sonar speech. '*Then a thirty-degree turn to port. After that, it's three hundred and fifty meters to full stop*.'

The response was cool, professional.

'Roger. Preparing for debarkation.'

Kaa's team – Brookida and a half-dozen neo-fins who had come out earlier to unload Uriel's supplies – moored the vessel when it reached the biggest dock. A small crowd of dignitaries waited on the pier, under heavy skies. Umbrellas sheltered the urrish delegates, who pressed together in a shivering mass, swaying their long necks back and forth. Humans and hoons made do with cloaks and hats, while the others simply ignored the rain.

Kaa was busy for a time, giving instructions as the helmsman fine-tuned her position, then cut engines. Amid a froth of bubbles, the *Hikahi* brought her bow even with the wharf. Clamshell doors opened, like a grinning mouth.

Backlit by the bright interior, a single human being strode forward. A tall female whose proud bearing seemed to say that she had little left to lose – little that life could take from her – except honor. For a long moment, Gillian Baskin looked on the surface of Jijo, inhaling fresh air for the first time in years.

Then she turned back toward the interior, beckoning with a smile and an extended arm.

Four silhouettes approached – one squat, one gangly, one wheeled, and the last clattering like a nervous colt. Kaa knew the tall one, although they had never met. *Alvin*, the young 'humicking' writer, lover of Verne and Twain, whose journal had explained so much about the strange mixed culture of sooner races.

A moan of overjoyed release escaped those waiting, who flowed forward in a rush.

So – embraced by their loved ones, and pelted by rain – the adventurous crew of *Wuphon's Dream* finally came home.

There were other reunions ... and partings.

Kaa went aft to help Makanee debark her patients. *Streaker's* chief physician seemed older than Kaa remembered, and very tired, as she supervised a growing throng of neo-dolphins, splashing and squealing beyond the *Hikahi's* starboard flank. While some appeared listless, others dashed about with antic, explosive energy. Two nurses helped Makanee keep the group herded together at the south end of the harbor, using occasional low-voltage discharges from their harnesses to prevent their patients from dashing off. The devolved ones wore nothing but skin.

Kaa counted their number – forty-six – and felt a shiver of worry. Such a large fraction of *Streaker's* crew! Gillian must be desperate indeed, to contemplate abandoning them here. Many were probably only experiencing fits of temporary stress atavism, and would be all right if they just had peace and quiet for a time.

Well, maybe they'll get it, on Jijo, he thought. *Assuming this planet sea turns out to be as friendly as it looks. And assuming the Galactics leave us alone.*

In becoming Jijo's latest illegal settler race, dolphins had an advantage over those who preceded them. Fins would not need buildings, or much in the way of tools. Only the finest Galactic detectors might sieve their DNA resonance out of the background organic stew of a life world, and just at close range.

There are advantages, he admitted. *This way, some of our kind may survive, even if Earth and her colonies don't. And if dolphins are caught there, so what? How could we Terragens get into any more trouble than we already are?*

Kaa had read about local belief in *Redemption*. A species that found itself in trouble might get a second chance, returning to the threshold state, so that some new patron might adopt and guide them to a better destiny. *Tursips amicus* was less than three hundred years old as a tool-using life-form. Confronted by a frolicking mob of his own kind – former members of an elite starship crew, now screeching like animals – Kaa knew it shouldn't take fins long to achieve 'redemption.'

He felt burning shame.

Kaa joined Brookida, unloading Makanee's pallet of supplies. He did not want to face the nurses, who might reproach him for 'losing' Peepoe. *At least now there's a chance to find her. With our own colony in place, I can serve Makanee as a scout, patrolling and exploring . . . in time I'll catch up with Zhaki and Mopol. Then we'll have a reckoning.*

The aft hatch kept cycling after the last dolphin was through. Excited squeaks resonated across the bay as another set of émigrés followed Makanee to an assembly point, on a rocky islet in the middle of the harbor. Eager six-limbed amphibian forms, with frilly gill fringes waving about their heads. Transplanted from their native Kithrup, the Kiqui would not qualify as *sooners*, exactly. They were already a ripe, presapient life-form – a real treasure, in fact. It would have been good to bring them home to Earth in triumph and lay a claim of adoption with the Galactic Uplift Institute. But now Gillian clearly thought it better to leave them here, where they had a chance.

According to plan, the dolphin-Kiqui colony would stay in Port Wuphon for a few days, while a traeki pharmacist analyzed the newcomers' dietary needs. If necessary, new types of traeki stacks would be designed to create symbiotic supplements. Then both groups would head out to find homes amid islands offshore.

I'm coming, Peepoe, Kaa thought. *Once we get everyone settled, nothing on Jijo or the Five Galaxies will keep me from you.*

A happy musing. Yet another thought kept nagging at him.

Gillian isn't just stripping the ship of nonessential personnel. She's putting everyone ashore she can spare . . . for their own safety.

In other words, the human Terragens agent was planning something desperate . . . and very likely fatal.

Kaa had an uneasy feeling that he knew what it was.

I guess reunions can be kind of awkward, even when they're happy ones.

Don't get me wrong! I can't imagine a better moment than when the four of us – Huck, Ur-ronn, Pincer, and me – stepped out of the metal whale's yawning mouth to see the hooded lanterns of our own hometown. My senses were drenched with familiarity. I heard the creaking dross ships and the lapping tide. I smelled the melon canopies and smoke from a nearby cookstove – someone making *chubvash* stew. My magnetic earbones tickled to the familiar presence of Mount Guenn, invisible in the dark, yet a powerful influence on the hoonish shape-and-location sense.

Then there came my father's umble cry, booming from the shadows, and my mother and sister, rushing to my arms.

I confess, my first reaction was hesitant. I was glad to be home, to see and embrace them, but also embarrassed by the attention, and a little edgy about moving around without a cane for the first time in months. When there came a free moment, I bowed to my parents and handed them a package, wrapped in complex folds of the best paper I could find on the *Streaker*, containing my baby vertebrae. It was an important moment. I had gone away a disobedient child. Now I was returning, an adult, with work to do.

My friends' homecomings were less emotional. Of course Huck's hoonish adoptive parents were thrilled to have her back from the dead, but no one expected them to feel what my own folks did after giving up their only son for lost, months ago.

Pincer-Tip touched claws briefly with a matron from the qheuen hive, and that was it for him.

As for Ur-ronn, she and Uriel barely exchanged greetings. Aunt and niece had one priority – to get out of the rain. They fled the drizzle to a nearby warehouse, swiftly immersing themselves in some project. Urs don't believe in wasting time.

Does it make me seem heartless to say that I could not give complete attention to my family? Even as they clasped me happily, I kept glancing to see what else was going on. It will be up to me – and maybe Huck – to tell later generations about this event. This fateful meeting on the docks.

For one thing, there were other reunions.

My new human friend, Dwer Koolhan, emerged from the *Hikahi*, a tall silhouette, as sturdy looking as a preteen hoon. When he appeared, a shout pealed from the crowd of onlookers, and a young woman rushed to him, her arms spread wide. Dwer seemed stunned to see her ... then equally enthused, seizing her into a whirling hug. At first, I thought she might be some long-separated lover, but now I know it is his sister, with adventures of her own to recount.

The rain let up a bit. Uriel returned, wearing booties and a heavy black waterproof slicker that covered all but the tip of her snout. Behind came several hoons, driving a herd of ambling, four-footed creatures. *Glavers*. At least two dozen of the bulge-eyed brutes swarmed down the pier, their opal skins glistening. A few carried cloth-wrapped burdens in their grasping tails. They did not complain, but trotted toward the opening of the whale sub without pause.

This part of the transaction, I did not – and still do not – understand. Why Earthling fugitives would want glavers is beyond me.

Gillian Baskin had the hoons carry out several large crates in exchange. I had seen the contents and felt an old hunger rise within me.

Books.There were hundreds of paper books, freshly minted aboard the *Streaker*. Not a huge amount of material, compared with the Galactic Library unit, or even the Great Printing, but included in the boxes were updates about the current state of the Five Galaxies, and other subjects Uriel requested. More than enough value to barter for a bunch of grub-eating glavers!

Later, I connected the trade with the dolphins and Kiqui who also debarked in Wuphon Harbor, and I realized, *There's more to this deal than meets the eye*.

Did I mention the tall prisoner? As everybody moved off to the great hall for a hurried feast, I looked back and glimpsed a hooded figure being led down the pier toward the submarine, guarded by two wry-looking urs. It was a biped, but did not move like a human or hoon, and I could tell both hands were tied. Whoever the prisoner was, he vanished into the *Hikahi* in a hurry, and I never heard a word about it.

The last reunion took place half a midura later, when we were all gathered in the town hall.

According to a complex plan worked out by the Niss Machine, the whale sub did not have to depart for some time, so a banquet was held in the fashion of our Jijoan Commons. Each race claimed a corner of the hexagonal chamber for its own food needs, then individuals migrated round the center hearth, chatting, renewing acquaintance, or discussing the nature of the world. While Gillian Baskin was engrossed in deep conversation with my parents and Uriel, my sister brought me up to date on happenings in Wuphon since our departure. In this way I learned of school chums who had marched north to war, joining militia units while we four adventurers had childish exploits in the cryptic deep. Some were dead or missing in the smoldering ruins of Ovoom Town. Others, mostly qheuens, had died in the plagues of late spring.

The hoonish disease never had a chance to take hold here in the south. But before the vaccines came, one ship *had* been kept offshore at anchor – in quarantine – because a sailor showed symptoms.

Within a week, half the crew had died.

Despite the gravity of her words, it was hard to pay close attention. I was trying to screw up my courage, you see. Somehow, I must soon tell my family the news they would least want to hear.

Amid the throng, I spotted Dwer and his sister huddled near the fire, each taking turns amazing the other with tales about their travels. Their elation at being reunited was clearly muted by a kind of worry familiar to all of us – concern about loved ones far away, whose fates were still unknown. I had a sense that the two of them knew, as I did, that there remained very little time.

Not far away I spied Dwer's noor companion, Mudfoot – the one Gillian called a 'tytlal' – perched on a rafter, communing with others of his kind. In place of their normal, devil-may-care expressions, the creatures looked somber. Now we Six knew their secret – that the tytlal are a race hidden within a race, another tribe of sooners, fully alert and aware of their actions. Might some victims of past pranks now scheme revenge on the little imps? That seemed the least of their worries, but I wasted no sympathy on them.

Welcome to the real world, I thought.

Tyug squatted in a corner of the hall, furiously puffing away. Every few duras, the traeki's synthi ring would pop out another glistening ball of some substance whose value the Six Races had learned after long experience. Supplements to keep glavers healthy, for instance, and other chemical wonders that might serve Gillian's crew, if some miracle allowed them to escape. If Tyug finished soon, Uriel hoped to keep her alchemist. But I would lay bets that the traeki meant to go along when the Earthlings departed.

The occasion was interrupted when a pair of big hoons wearing proctors' badges pushed through leather door strips into the feasting hall, gripping the arms of a male human I had never seen before. He was of middle height for their kind, with a dark complexion and an unhappy expression. He wore a rewq on his forehead, and hair combed to hide a nasty scar near his left ear. A small chimp followed close behind, her appearance rueful.

I wasn't close enough to hear the details firsthand, but later I pieced together that this was a long-lost crew mate of the *Streaker*, whose appearance on Jijo had them mystified. He had been on Mount Guenn, helping Uriel's smiths work on some secret project, when he suddenly up and tried to escape by stealing some kind of flying machine!

As the guards brought him forward, Gillian's face washed with recognition. She smiled, though he cringed, as if dreading this meeting. The dark man turned left to hide his mutilation, but Gillian insistently took his hands. She expressed pleasure at seeing him by leaning up to kiss one cheek.

Perhaps later I'll learn more about where he fits in all this. But time is short and I must close this account before the *Hikahi* sets sail to rejoin the dolphin-crewed ship. So let me finish with the climax of an eventful evening.

A herald burst in. His vibrating sac boomed an alert umble.

'Come! Come and see the unusual!'

Hurrying outside, we found the rain had stopped temporarily. A window opened in the clouds, wide enough for Loocen to pour pale, liquid luminance across a flank of Mount Guenn. Swathes of brittle stars shone through, including one deep red, cyclopean eye.

In spite of this lull, the storm was far from over. Lightning flickered as clouds grew denser still. The west was one great mass of roiling blackness amid a constant background of thunder. In miduras, the coast was really going to get hit.

People started pointing. Huck rolled up near my right leg and gestured with all four agile eyestalks, directing my gaze toward the volcano.

At first, I couldn't tell what I was seeing. Vague, ghostlike shapes seemed to bob and flutter upward, visible mostly as curved silhouettes that blocked sporadic stars. Sometimes lightning caused one of the objects to glow along a rounded flank, revealing a globelike outline, tapered at the bottom. They seemed big, and very far away.

I wondered if they might be starships.

'Balloons,' Huck said at last, her voice hushed with awe.

'Just like *Around the World in Eighty Days*!'

Funny. Huck seemed more impressed at that moment than she ever had been aboard *Streaker*, by all the glittering consoles and chattering machines. I stared at the flotilla of fragile gasbags, wondering what kind of volunteers were brave enough to pilot them on a night like this, surrounded by slashing electricity, and with ruthless foes prowling higher still. We watched as scores wafted from Mount Guenn's secret caves. One by one, they caught the stiff west wind and flowed past the mountain, vanishing from sight.

I happened to be standing near Gillian Baskin, so I know what the Earthwoman said when she turned to Uriel the Smith.

'All right. You kept your side of the bargain. Now it's time to keep ours.'

X

VUBBEN

Smashed up. Wheels torn or severed. His braincase leaking lubricant. Motivator spindles shredded and discharging slowly into the ground.

Vubben lies crumpled next to his deity, feeling life drain away .

That he still lives seems remarkable. When the Jophur corvette slashed brutally at the Holy Egg, he had been partway around the great stone's flank, almost on the other side. But the moatlike channel of the Nest funneled explosive heat like a river, outracing his fruitless effort at retreat.

Now Vubben lies in a heap, aware of two facts.

Any surviving g'Keks would need a new High Sage.

And something else.

The Egg still lives.

He wonders about that. Why didn't the Jophur finish it off? Surely they had the power.

Perhaps they were distracted.

Perhaps they would be back.

Or else, were they subtly persuaded to go away?

The Egg's patterning rhythms seem subdued, and yet more clear than ever. He ponders whether it might be an artifact of his approaching death. Or perhaps his frayed spindles – draped across the stony face – are picking up vibrations that normal senses could not.

Crystalline lucidity calls him, but Vubben feels restrained by the tenacious hold of life. That was what always kept sages and mystics from fully communing with the sacred ovoid, he now sees. Mortal beings – even traeki – have to care about continuing, or else the game of existence cannot properly be played. But the caring is also an impediment. It biases the senses. Makes you receptive to noise.

He lets go of the impediment, with a kind of gladness. Surrender clears the way, opening a path that he plunges along, like a youth just released from training wheels, spinning ecstatically down a swooping ramp he never knew before, whose curves change in delightfully ominous ways.

Vubben feels the world grow transparent around him. And with blossoming clarity, he begins to perceive *connections*.

In legend, and in human lore, gods were depicted speaking to their prophets, and those on the verge of death. But the great stone does not vocalize. No words come to Vubben, or even images. Yet he finds himself able to trace the Egg's form, its vibrating unity. Like a funnel, it draws him down, toward the bowels of Jijo.

That is the first surprise. From its shape alone, the Six Races assumed the Egg was self-contained, an oval stone birthed out of Jijo's inner heat, now wholly part of the upper world.

Apparently it still maintains links to the world below.

Vubben's dazed mind beholds the realm beneath the Slope ... not as a picture but in its gestalt, as a vast domain threaded by dendritic patterns of lava heat, like branches of a magma forest, feeding and maintaining a growing mountain range. The forest roots sink into liquefied pools, unimaginably deep and broad — measureless chambers where molten rock strains under the steady grinding of an active planet.

Yet, even here the pattern formations persist. Vubben finds himself amazed by their revealed source.

Dross!

Deep beneath the Slope, there plunges a great sheet of heavier stone ... an oceanic plate, shoving hard against the continent and then driving deeper still, dragging eons-old basalt down to rejoin slowly convecting mantle layers. The process is not entirely mysterious to Vubben. He has seen illustrations in Biblos Texts. As it scrapes by, the plunging ocean plate leaves behind a scum, a frothy mix of water and light elements ...

... and also patterns.

Patterns of dross! Of ancient buildings, implements, machines, all discarded long ago, ages before the Buyur won their leasehold on this world. Before even their predecessors.

The things themselves are long gone, melted, smeared out, their atoms dispersed by pressure and heat. Yet somehow a remnant persists. The magma does not quite forget.

Dross is supposed to be cleansed, Vubben thinks, shocked by the implications. When we dump our bones and tools in the Midden, it should lead to burial and purification by Jijo's fire. There isn't supposed to be anything left!

And yet ... who is he to question, if Jijo chooses to remember something of each tenant race that abides here for a while, availing itself of her resources, her varied life-forms, then departing according to Galactic law?

Is that what you are? He inquires of the Holy Egg. *A distillation of memory?* The crystallized essence of species who came before, and are now extinct?

A transcendent thought, yet it makes him sad. Vubben's own unique race verges on annihilation. He yearns for some kind of preservation, some refuge from oblivion. But in order to leave such a remnant, sophonts must dwell for a long time on a tectonic world.

For most of its sapiency period, his kind had lived in space.

Then you don't care about us living beings, after all, he accuses the Egg. *You are like that crazed mulc-spider of the hill, your face turned to the past.*

Again, there is no answer in word or image. What Vubben feels instead is a further extension of the sense of connectedness, now sweeping upward, through channels of friction heat, climbing against slow cascades of moist, superheated rock, until his mind emerges in a cool dark kingdom – the sea's deep, most private place.

The Midden. Vubben feels around him the great dross piles of more recent habitation waves. Even here, amid relics of the Buyur, the Egg seems linked. Vubben senses that the graveyard of ancient instrumentalities has been disturbed. Heaps of archaic refuse still quiver from some late intrusion.

There is no anger over this. Nor anything as overt as interest. But he does sense a reaction, like some prodigious reflex.

The sea is involved. Disturbance on the dross piles has provoked shifts in the formation of waves and tides. Of heat and evaporation. Like a sleeping giant, responding heavily to a tiny itch. A massive storm begins roiling both the surface and the ocean floor, sweeping things back where they belong.

Vubben has no idea what vexed the Midden so. Perhaps the Jophur. Or else the end of dross shipments from the Six Races? Anyway, his thoughts are coming more slowly as death swarms in from the extremities. Worldly concerns matter less with each passing dura.

Still, he can muster a few more cogencies. *Is that all we are to you?* he inquires of the planet. *An itch?*

He realizes now that Drake and Ur-Chown had pulled a fast one when they announced their 'revelation,' a century ago. The Egg is no god, no conscious being. Ro-kenn was right, calling it a particle of psi-active stone, more compact and well ordered than the Spectral Flow. A distillation that had proved helpful in uniting the Six Races.

Useful in many ways … but not worthy of prayer.

We sensed what we desperately wanted to sense, because the alternative was unacceptable – to face the fact that we sooners are alone. We always were alone.

That might have been Vubben's last thought. But at the final moment there comes something else. A glimmer of meaning that merges with his waning neuronic flashes. In that narrow moment, he feels a wave of overwhelming certainty.

More layers lie beneath the sleeping strata. Layers that are aware. Layers that know.

Despair is not his final companion. Instead, there comes in rapid succession – *expectation …*

satisfaction …

awareness of an ancient plan, patiently unfolding …

'Can't-t you use somebody else?'

'Who else? There is no one.'

'What about Karkaett-t?'

'Suessi needs him to help nurse the engines. This effort will be hopeless unless they operate above capacity.'

Hopeless; Kaa used to think it such a simple word. But like the concept of infinity, it came freighted with a wide range of meanings. He slashed the water in frustration. *Infi, will you really trap me this way? Dragging me across the universe again, when all I want to do is stay?*

Gillian Baskin knelt on the quay nearby, her raincoat glistening. Distant lightning flashes periodically lit up the bay, revealing that the *Hikahi* had already closed her clamshell doors, preparing to depart.

'Besides,' Gillian added. 'You are our chief pilot. Who could be as well qualified?'

Gratifying words, but in fact *Streaker used* to have a better pilot, by far.

'Keepiru ought to've stayed with the crew, back on Kithrup-p. I should have been the one who went on the skiff with Creideiki.'

The woman shrugged. 'Things happen, Kaa. I have confidence in your ability to get us off this world in one piece.'

And after that? He chuttered a doubt-filled raspberry. Everyone knew this would be little more than a suicide venture. The odds had also seemed bad on Kithrup, but at least there the eatee battle fleets chasing *Streaker* had been distracted, battling each other. Fleeing through that maelstrom of combat and confusion, it proved possible to fool their pursuers by wearing a disguise – the hollowed-out shell of a Thennanin dreadnought. All that ploy took was lots of skill ... and *luck*.

Here in Jijo space there was no sheltering complexity. No concealing jumble of warfare to sneak through. Just one pursuer – giant and deadly – sought one bedraggled prey.

For the moment, *Streaker* was safe in Jijo's sea, but what chance would she have once she tried to leave?

'You don't have to worry about Peepoe,' Gillian said, reading the heart of his reluctance. 'Makanee has some solid fins with her. Many are Peepoe's friends. They'll scan relentlessly till they find Zhaki and Mopol, and make them let her go.

'Anyway,' the blond woman went on, 'isn't Peepoe better off here? Won't you use your skill to keep her safe?'

Kaa eyed Gillian's silhouette, knowing the Terragens agent would use any means to get the job done. If that meant appealing to Kaa's sense of honor ... or even chivalry ... Gillian Baskin was not too proud.

'Then you admit it-t,' he said.

'Admit what?'

'That we're heading out as bait, nothing elsssse. Our aim is to sacrifice ourselves.'

The human on the quay was silent for several seconds, then lifted her shoulders in a shrug.

'It seems worthwhile, don't you think?'

Kaa pondered. At least she was being honest – a decent way for a captain to behave with her pilot.

A whole world, seven or eight sapient races, some near extinction, and a unique culture. Can you see giving up your life for all that?

'I guess so,' he murmured, after a pause.

Gillian had won. Kaa would abandon his heart on Jijo, and fly out to meet death with open eyes.

Then he recalled. *She* had made exactly the same choice, long ago. A decision that still must haunt her sleep, though it could have gone no other way.

Yet it surprised Kaa when Gillian slipped off the stone quay, entering the water next to him, and threw her arms around his head. Shivers followed her hands as she stroked him gratefully.

'You make me proud,' she said. 'The crew will be glad, and not *just* because we have the best pilot in this whole galaxy.'

Kaa's flustered confusion expressed itself in a sonar interrogative, casting puzzled echoes through the colonnade of a nearby pier. Gillian wove her Trinary reply through that filtered reverberation, binding his perplexity, braiding a sound fabric whose texture seemed almost like a melody.

> * Amid the star lanes,
> > * Snowballs sometimes thrive near flame ...
> > > * Don't you feel Lucky? *

RETY

The dolphin engineer shouted at her from the airlock of the salvaged dross ship.

'C-come on Rety! We gotta leave now, t-to make the rendezvous!'

Chuchki had reason to be agitated. His walker unit whined and jittered, reacting to nervous signals sent down his neural tap. It was cramped in the airlock, which also held the speed sled to carry them from this ghost ship back to *Streaker*. Providing all went according to plan.

Only I ain't part of the plan anymore, Rety thought.

Stepping in front of Chuchki, with the sill of the hatch between them, she removed the tunic they had given her, as an honorary member of the crew. At first the gesture had pleased Rety – till she saw the Terrans were just another band of losers.

Rety tossed the garment in the airlock.

'Tell Dr. Baskin an' the others thanks, but I'll be makin' my own way from here on. Good luck. Now scram.'

Chuchki stared at first, unable to move or speak. Then servos whirred. The walker started to move.

'Hit the button, yee!' Rety shouted over her left shoulder.

Back in the control room, her little 'husband' pressed a lever triggering the airlock's emergency cycle. The inner hatch slid shut, severing Chuchki's wail of protest. Soon, a row of purple lights showed the small chamber filling with water as the outer door opened.

A few duras later, she heard engine noise – the now-familiar growl of the speed sled that had brought the two of them here – ebbing with distance as the machine fled. She ordered the outer door closed and locked against the possibility that Chuchki might try something 'heroic.' Some still thought of her as a child, and many dolphins also had a mystical attachment to their human patrons.

But I'll be just fine. A lot better off than those fools, in fact.

Several low, squat hallways led away from the lock, but only one was lit by a string of glow bulbs. Following this trail, she made her way back toward the control room, sometimes lingering to stroke a panel or gaze into a chamber filled with mysterious machines. For the last few days she had looked over this salvaged starship – once a Buyur packet boat, according to Chuchki. Though a mess, it was one of the 'best' recovered derelicts, capable of life support as well as full engine maneuvering, owing its remarkable state to the Midden's chill, sterile waters. Durable Galactic machines might lie there unchanged forever, or until Jijo sucked them underground.

It's mine now, she mused, surveying her prize. *I've got my own starship.*

Of course it was still a hunk of dross. All odds were against her getting anywhere in this moving scrap pile.

But the odds always had been against her, ever since she was born into that filthy tribe of savages, so proud of their sickly ignorance. And especially since she realized she'd rather be whipped for speaking up than be a slave to some bully with rotting teeth and the mind of a beast.

Rety had suffered some disappointments lately. But now she saw what each of the setbacks had in common. They all came about because of trusting others – first the sages of the Commons, then the Rothens, and finally a ragtag band of helpless Earthlings.

But all that was in the past. Now she was back doing what she did best – relying on herself.

The control room spanned roughly thirty paces in width, featuring about a dozen wide instrument consoles. All were dark, except one jury-rigged station festooned with cables and makeshift bypass connections. Lights blazed across that panel. On the floor nearby, a portable holosim display revealed a staticky map of the ancient vessel's surroundings, a dart-shaped glow threading its way through a maze of ridges at the bottom of the great ocean.

Most of the decoy ships cruised with simple autopilots, but a few moved more flexibly, crewed by volunteer teams, making adjustments to the swarm pattern planned by the Niss Machine. In this effort, Rety's intelligence and agile hands had been helpful to Chuchki, making up for her lack of education. She felt justified in having earned her starship.

'hi captain!'

Her sole companion pranced on the instrument console, each footstep barely missing a flowing lever or switch. The little urrish male greeted her with a shill ululation.

'we did it! like pirates of the plains! like in legends of the battle aunties! now we free. no more noor beasts. no more yuckity ship full of water-loving fish!'

Rety laughed. Whenever loneliness beckoned, there was always yee to cheer her up.

'so where to now, captain?' the diminutive creature asked. *'shake free of Jijo? head someplace good and sunny, for a change?'*

She nodded.

'That's the idea. Only we gotta be patient a little while longer.'

First *Streaker* must collect Chuchki and other scattered workers. Rety had an impression that the Earthlings were waiting for events to happen onshore. But after hearing the Jophur ultimatum she knew – Gillian Baskin would soon be forced to act.

I helped them, she rationalized. *An' I won't interfere with their plan ... much.*

But in the long run, none o' that'll matter. Everybody knows they're gonna get roasted when they try to get away. Or else the Jophur'll catch 'em, like a ligger snatchin' up a gallaiter faun.

Nobody can blame me for tryin' to find my own way out of a trap like that.

And if someone *did* cast blame her way?

Rety laughed at the thought.

In that case, they can try to outfart a traeki, for all I care. This ship is mine, and there's nothin' anybody can do about it!

She was getting away from Jijo – one way or another.

DWER

The night sky crackled.

At random intervals his hair abruptly stood on end. Static electricity snapped the balloon's canopy with a basso boom, while pale blue glows moved up and down the rope cables, dancing like frantic imps. Once, a flickering ball of greenish white followed him across the sky for more than a midura, mimicking each rise, fall, or sway in the wind. He could not tell if it was an arrowflight away, or several leagues. The specter only vanished when a rain squall passed between, but Dwer kept checking nervously, in case it returned.

Greater versions of the same power flashed in all directions – though from a safe distance, so far. He made a habit of counting kiduras between each brilliant discharge and the arrival of its rumbling report. When the interval grew short, thunder would shake the balloon like a child's rag doll.

Uriel had set controls to keep Dwer above most of the gale ... at least according to the crude weather calculations of her spinning-disk computer. The worst fury took place below, in a dense cloud bank stretching from horizon to horizon.

Still, that only meant there were moonlit gaps for his frail craft to drift through. Surrounding him towered the mighty heat engines of the storm – churning thunderheads whose lofty peaks scraped the boundaries of space.

Though insanely dangerous, the spectacle exceeded anything in Dwer's experience – and perhaps even that of any star god in the Five Galaxies. He was tempted to climb the rigging for a better view of nature's majesty. To let the tempest sweep his hair. To shout back when it bellowed.

But he wasn't free. There were duties unfulfilled.

So Dwer did as he'd been told, remaining huddled in a wire cage the smiths had built for him, lashed to a wicker basket that dangled like an afterthought below a huge gasbag. The metal enclosure would supposedly protect him from a minor lightning strike.

And what if a bolt tears the bag instead? Or ignites the fuel cylinder? Or . . .

Low clicks warned Dwer to cover his face just half a dura before the altitude sensor tripped, sending jets of flame roaring upward, refilling the balloon and maintaining a safe distance from the ground.

Of course, 'safe' was a matter of comparison.

'In theory, this vehicle should convey you well past the Rinner Range, and then veyond the Foison Flain,' the smith had explained. 'After that, there should ve an end to the lightning danger. You can leave the Faraday cage and guide the craft as we taught you.'

As they taught me in half a rushed midura, Dwer amended, *while running around preparing one last balloon to launch.*

All the others were far ahead of him – a flotilla of flimsy craft, dispersing rapidly as they caught varied airstreams, but all sharing the same general heading. East, driven by near-hurricane winds. Twice he had witnessed flares in that direction, flames that could not have come from lightning alone. Sudden outbursts of ocher fire, they testified to some balloon exploding in the distance.

Fortunately, those others had no crews, just instruments recovered from dross ships. Dwer was the only Jijoan loony enough to go flying on a night like this.

They needed an expendable volunteer. Someone to observe and report if the trick is successful.

Not that he resented Uriel and Gillian. Far from it. Dwer was suited for the job. It was necessary. And the voyage would take him roughly where he wanted to go.

Where I'm needed.

To the Gray Hills.

What might have happened to Lena and Jenin in the time he'd spent as captive of a mad robot, battling Jophur in a swamp and then trapped with forlorn Terrans at the bottom of the sea? By now, the women would have united the urrish and human sooner tribes, and possibly led them a long way from the geyser pools where Danel Ozawa died. It might take months to track them down, but that hardly mattered. Dwer had his bow and supplies. His skills were up to the task.

All I need is to land in roughly the right area, say within a hundred leagues . . . and not break my neck in the process. I can hunt and forage. Save my traeki paste for later, in case the search lasts through winter.

Dwer tried going over the plan, dwelling on problems he could grasp – the intricacies of exploring and survival in wild terrain. But his mind kept coming back to this wild ride through an angry sky ... or else the sad partings that preceded it.

For a time, he and Sara had tried using words, talking about their separate adventures, sharing news of friends living and dead. She told what little she knew about Nelo and their destroyed hometown. He described how Lark had saved his life in a snowstorm, so long ago that it seemed another age.

Hanging over the reunion was sure knowledge that it must end. Each of them had places to go. Missions with slim chance of success, but compelled by duty and curiosity. Dwer had lived his entire adult life that way, but it took some effort to grasp that his sister had chosen the same path, only on a vaster scale.

He still might have tried talking Sara out of her intention – perhaps suicidal – to join the Earthlings' desperate breakout attempt. But there was something new in the way she carried herself – a lean readiness that took him back to when they were children, following Lark on fossil hunts, and *Sara* was the toughest of them all. Her mind had always plunged beyond his comprehension. Perhaps it was time for her to stride the same galaxies that filled her thoughts.

'Remember us, when you're a star god,' he had told her, before their final embrace.

Her reply was a hoarse whisper.

'Give my love to Lark and ...'

Sara closed her eyes, throwing her arms around him.

'... and to Jijo.'

They clung together until the urrish smiths said it was the last possible moment to go.

When the balloon took off, Mount Guenn leaped into view around him, a sight unlike any he ever beheld. Lightning made eerie work of the Spectral Flow, sending brief flashes of illusion dancing across his retinas.

Dwer watched his sister standing at the entrance of the cave, a backlit figure. Too proud to weep. Too strong to pretend. Each knew the other was likely heading to oblivion. Each realized this would be their last shared moment.

I'll never know if she lives, he had thought, as clouds swallowed the great volcano, filling the night with flashing arcs. Looking up through a gap in the overcast, he had glimpsed a corner of the constellation Eagle.

Despite the pain of separation, Dwer had managed a smile.

It's better that way.

From now until the day I die, I'll picture her out there. Living in the sky.

As it turned out, I didn't have to explain things to my parents. Gillian and Uriel had already laid it out, before it was time to depart.

The Six Races should be represented, they explained. Come what may.

Furthermore, I had earned the right to go. So had my friends.

Anyway, who was better qualified to tell Jijo's tale?

Mu-phauwq and Yowg-wayuo had no choice but to accept my decision. Was *Jijo* any safer than fighting the Jophur in space? Besides, I had spine-molted. I would make my own decisions.

Mother turned her back to me. I stroked her spines, but she spoke without turning around.

'Thank you for returning from the dead,' she murmured.

'Honor us by having children of your own. Name your firstborn after your great-uncle, who was captain of the *Auph-Vuhoosh*. The cycle must continue.'

With that, she let my sister lead her away. I felt both touched and bemused by her command, wondering how it could ever be obeyed.

Dad, bless him, was more philosophical. He thrust a satchel in my arms, his entire collection of books by New Wave authors of Jijo's recent literary revival – the hoon, urs, and g'Kek writers who have lately begun expressing themselves in unique ways on the printed page. 'It's to remind you that humans are not in complete command of our culture. There is more than one line to our harmony, my son.'

'I know that, Dad,' I replied. 'I'm not a *complete* humicker.'

He nodded, adding a low umble.

'It is told that we hoons were priggish and sour, before our sneak ship came to Jijo. Legends say we had no word for "fun."

'If that is true – and in case you meet any of our stodgy cousins out there – tell them about the *sea*, Hph-wayuo! Tell them of the way a sail catches the wind, a sound no mere engine can match.

'Teach them to taste the stinging spray. Show them all the things that our patrons never did.

'It will be our gift – we happy damned – to those who know no joy in heaven.'

Others had easier leave-takings.

Qheuens are used to sending their males out on risky ventures, for the sake of the hive. Pincer's mother did emboss his shell with some proud inlay, though, and saw him off in good style.

Urs care mostly about their work, their chosen loyalties, and themselves. Ur-ronn did not have to endure sodden sentimentality. Partly because of the rain, she and Uriel made brief work of their good-byes. Uriel probably saw it as a good business transaction. She lost her best apprentice, but had adequate compensation.

Uriel seemed far more upset about losing Tyug. But there was no helping it. The Earthers need a traeki. And not just any traeki, but the best alchemist we can send. No pile of substance balls can substitute. Besides, it will be good luck for all races to be along.

Huck's adoptive parents tried to express sorrow at her parting, but their genuine fondness for her would not make them grieve. Hoons are not humans. We cannot transfer the fully body bond to those not of our blood. Our affections run deeper, but narrower than Earthlings'. Perhaps that is our loss.

So the five of us reboarded as official representatives, and as grownups. I had molted and Pincer showed off his cloisonné. Ur-ronn did not preen, but we all noticed that one of her brood pouches was no longer virgin white, but blushed a fresh shade of blue as her new husband wriggled and stretched it into shape.

Huck carried her own emblem of maturity – a narrow wooden tube, sealed with wax at both ends. Though humble looking, it might be the most important thing we brought with us from the Slope.

Huphu rode my shoulder as I stepped inside the whale sub. I noted that the tytlal-style noor, Mudfoot, had also rejoined us, though the creature seemed decidedly unhappy. Had he been exiled by the others, for the crime of letting their ancient secret slip? Or was he being honored, as we were, with a chance to live or die for Jijo?

Sara Koolhan stood between her chimp and the wounded star-man as the great doors closed, cutting us off from the wharf lanterns, our village, and the thundering sky.

'Well, at least this is more comfortable than the last time we submerged, inside a dumb old hollow tree trunk,' Huck commented.

Pincer's leg vents whistled resentfully. 'You want comfy? Poor little g'Kekkie want to ride my back, an' be tucked into her beddie?'

'Shut uf, you two,' Ur-ronn snapped. 'Trust Ifni to stick ne with a vunch of ignoranuses for confanions.'

Huphu settled close as I umbled, feeling a strange resigned contentment. My friends' bickering was one unchanged feature of life from those naive days when we were youngsters, still dreaming of adventure in our *Wuphon's Dream*. It was nice to know some things would be constant across space and time.

Alas, Huck had not mentioned the true difference between that earlier submergence and this one.

Back then, we sincerely thought there was a good chance we'd be coming home again.

This time, we all knew better.

EWASX

Alarms blare! Instruments cry out sirens of danger!

Behold, My rings, how the Captain-Leader recalls the robots and remote crew stacks who were engaged in probing the deep-sea trench.

Greater worries now concern us!

For days, cognizance detectors have sieved through the deep, trying to separate the prey from its myriad decoys. It even occurred to us/Me that the Earthling ship may not be one of the moving blips at all! It might be sheltering silently in some dross pile. In operating the swarm by remote control, they might bypass all the normal etheric channels, using instead their fiendish talent at manipulating sound.

I/we are/am learning caution. I did not broach this possibility to the Captain-Leader.

Why did I refrain? A datum has come to our attention. Those in power often ask for the 'truth' or even the best guesses of their underlings. But in fact, they seldom truly wish to hear contradiction.

Anyway, the tactics stacks estimated improved odds at sifting for the quarry. Only one more day, at worst. We of the *Polkjhy* could easily afford the time.

Until we detected disturbing intruders. Interlopers that could only have come from the Five Galaxies!

'THERE ARE AT LEAST SIX SIXES OF THEM!'

So declares the cognizance detector operator. 'Hovering, almost stationary, no more than fifteen planetary degrees easterly. One moment they were not there. The next moment, they appeared!'

The etherics officer vents steam of doubt.

'I/we perceive nothing, nor have our outlying satellites. This provokes a reasonable hypothesis: that our toruses are defective, or else your instruments.'

But routine check discover no faults in either.

'They may have meme-suborned our satellites,' suggests one tactician stack. 'Combining this with excellent masking technology—'

'Perhaps,' interrupts another. 'But *gravitics* cannot be fooled so easily. If there are six sixes of ships, they cannot be larger than hull type sixteen. No match for us, then. We can annihilate the entire squadron, forthwith.'

'Is that why they operate in stealth?' inquires the Captain-Leader, puffing pheromones of enforced calm into the tense atmosphere. 'Might they be lingering, just beyond line of sight, while awaiting reinforcements?'

It is a possibility we cannot ignore. But, lacking corvettes, we must go investigate ourselves.

Reluctantly, gracefully, the *Polkjhy* turns her omnipotence around, heading toward the ghostly flotilla. If they are scouts for an armada – perhaps the Soro or Tandu, our mortal foes – it may be necessary to act swiftly, decisively. Exactly the kind of performance that best justifies the existence of master rings.

Others must not be allowed to win the prize!

As we move ponderously eastward, a new thought burbles upward. A streak of wax, secreted by our once-rebellious second torus-of-cognition.

What is it, My ring?

You recall how the savage sooners called to our corvette, not once, but twice, using minute tickles of digital power to attract our attention?

The first time, they used such a beacon to bribe us with the location of a g'Kek hideout.

The second time? Ah, yes. It was a lure, drawing the corvette to a trap.

VERY CLEVER, MY RING!

Ah, but the comparison does not work.

There are many more sources, this time.

They are stronger, and the cognizance traces have spoor patterns typical of starship computers.

But above all, My poor ring, did you not hear our detection officer stack?

These signals cannot come from benighted sooners.

THEY FLY!

SARA

'Graviticss!'

The detection officer thrashed her flukes.

'Movement signs! The larger emitter departss its stationary hover position. Jophur battleship now moving east at two machsss. Ten klickss altitude.'

Sara watched Gillian Baskin absorb the news. This was according to plan, yet the blond Earthwoman showed hardly any reaction. 'Very good,' she replied. 'Inform me of any vector change. Decoy operator, please engage swarming program number four. Start the wrecks drifting upward, slowly.'

The water-filled chamber was unlike any 'bridge' Sara had read about in ancient books – a Terran vessel, controlled from a room humans could only enter wearing breathing masks. This place was built for the convenience of dolphins. It was their ship – though a woman held command.

A musty smell made Sara's nose itch, but when her hand raised to scratch, it bumped the transparent helmet, startling her for the fiftieth time. Fizzy liquid prickled Sara's bare arms and legs with goose bumps. Yet she had no mental space for annoyance, fear, or claustrophobia. This place was much too strange to allow such mundane reactions.

Streaker's overall shape and size were still enigmas. Her one glimpse of the hull – peering through a viewing port while the whale sub followed a searchlight toward its hurried rendezvous – showed a mysterious, studded cylinder, like a giant twelk caterpillar, whose black surface seemed to drink illumination rather than reflect it. The capacious airlock was almost deserted as Kaa and other dolphins debarked from the *Hikahi*, using spiderlike walking machines to rush to their assigned posts. Except for the bridge, most of the ship had been pumped free of water, reducing weight to a minimum.

The walls trembled with the rhythmic vibration of engines – distant cousins to her father's mill, or the Tarek Town steamboats. The familiarity ran deep, as if affinity flowed in Sara's blood.

'Battleship passing over Rimmer mountains. Departing line-of-sight!'

'Don't make too much of that,' Gillian reminded the crew. 'They still have satellites overhead. Maintain swarm pattern four. Kaa, ease us to the western edge of our group.'

'Aye,' the sturdy gray pilot replied. His tail and fins wafted easily, showing no sign of tension. 'Suessi reports motors operating at nominal. Gravitics charged and ready.'

Sara glanced at a row of screens monitoring other parts of the ship. At first, each display seemed impossibly small, but her helmet heeded subtle motions of her eyes, enhancing any image she chose to focus on, expanding it to 3-D clarity. Most showed empty chambers, with walls still moist from recent flooding. But the engine room was a bustle of activity. She spied 'Suessi' by his unique appearance – a torso of wedgelike plates topped by a reflective dome, encasing what remained of his head. The arm that was still human gestured toward a panel, reminding a neo-fin operator to make some adjustment.

The same arm had wrapped around Emerson after the *Hikahi* docked, trembling while clutching the prodigal starman. Sara had never seen a cyborg before. She did not know if it was normal for one to cry.

Emerson and Prity were also down there, helping Suessi with their nimble hands. Sara spied them laboring in the shadows, accompanied by Ur-ronn, the eager young urs, fetching and carrying for the preoccupied engineers. Indeed, Emerson seemed a little happier with work to do. After all, these decks and machines had been his life for many years. Still, ever since the reunion on the docks, Sara had not seen his accustomed grin. For the first time, he seemed ashamed of his injuries.

These people must be hard up to need help from an ape, an urrish blacksmith, and a speechless cripple. The other youngsters from Wuphon were busy, too, running errands and tending the glaver herd, keeping the creatures calm in strange surroundings.

I'm probably the most useless one of all. The Egg only knows what I'm doing here.

Blame it on Sage Purofsky, whose cosmic speculations justified her charging off with desperate Earthlings. *Even if his reasoning holds, what can I do about the Buyur plan? Especially if this mission is suicidal—*

The detection officer squealed, churning bubbles with her flukes.

'Primary gravitics source decelerating! Jophur ship nearing estimated p-position of mobile observer.'

Mobile observer, Sara thought. *That would be Dwer.*

She pictured him in that frail balloon, alone in the wide sky, surrounded by nature's fury, with that great behemoth streaking toward him.

Keep your head down, little brother. Here it comes.

DWER

With the Rimmers behind him at last, the storm abated its relentless buffeting enough to glimpse some swathes of stars. The gaps widened. In time Dwer spied a pale glow to the west. Gray luminance spread across a vast plain of waving scimitar blades.

Dwer recalled slogging through the same bitter steppe months ago, guiding Danel, Lena, and Jenin toward the Gray Hills. He still bore scars from that hard passage, when knifelike stems slashed at their clothes, cutting any exposed flesh.

This was a better way of traveling, floating high above. That is, if you survived searing lightning bolts, and thunder that loosened your teeth, and terrifying brushes with mountain peaks that loomed out of the night like giant claws, snatching at a passing morsel.

Maybe walking was preferable, after all.

He drank from his water bottle. Dawn meant it was time to get ready. Dormant machines would have flickered to life when first light struck the decoy balloons, electric circuits closing. Computers, salvaged from ancient starships, began spinning useless calculations.

The Jophur must be on the move, by now.

He reached up to his forehead and touched the rewq he had been given, causing it to writhe over his eyes. At once, Dwer's surroundings shifted. Contrasts were enhanced. All trace of haze vanished from the horizon, and he was able to look close to the rising sun, making out the distant glimmers of at least a dozen floating gas-bags, now widely dispersed far to the east, tiny survivors of the tempest that had driven them so far.

Dwer pulled four crystals from a pouch at his waist and jammed them into the gondola wickerwork so each glittered in the slanted light. A hammer waited at his waist, but he left it there for now, scanning past the decoys, straining to see signs of the Gray Hills.

I'm coming, Jenin. I'll be there soon, Lena.

I've just got a few more obstacles to get by.

He tried to picture their faces, looking to the future rather than dwelling on a harsh past. Buried in his backpack was a sensor stone that would come alight on midwinter's eve, if by some miracle the High Sages gave the all clear. If all the starships were gone, and there was reason to believe none would return. By then Dwer must find Lena and Jenin, and help them prepare the secluded tribe for either fate destiny had in store – a homecoming to the Slope, or else a life of perpetual hiding in the wilderness.

Either way, it's the job I'm trained for. A duty I know how to fulfill.

He found it hard to settle his restless mind, though. For some reason Dwer thought instead about *Rety*, the irascible sooner girl who had chosen to stay with the *Streaker* crew. No surprise there; she wanted nothing in life more than to leave Jijo, and that seemed the most likely, if risky, way.

But Dwer's mind roamed back to their adventure together – as captives of the Danik robot, when Dwer used to carry the machine across rivers by wearing it like a hat, conducting its suspensor fields through his own throbbing nervous system . . .

All at once he realized. The recollection was no accident. No random association.

It was a warning.

Creepy shivers coursed his spine. Eerily familiar.

'Dung!' he cried out, swiveling to the west—

—just in time to spy a tremendous object, blue and rounded, like a demon's face, soar past the Rimmer peaks and hurtle silently toward him, outracing sound.

It was like watching the onrush of an arrow, aimed straight at your nose. In moments the starship grew from a mere speck, burgeoning to fill the world!

Dwer shut his eyes, bracing for erasure . . .

Kiduras passed, two for each racing heartbeat. After twenty or so, the gondola was struck by a wall of sound, shaking him like thunder.

But sound was all. No impact.

It must have missed me!

He forced an eye open, turning around . . .

. . . and spied it to the east, bearing toward the decoy balloons.

Now he could tell, the behemoth moved at a higher altitude. The imminent collision had been a mirage. It never came within a league of him, or gave Dwer any notice.

But it can't miss the decoys, he thought. *They're in open view*.

Blade, his childhood qheuen playmate, had reported that balloons seemed transparent to Jophur instruments. *But that was at night. It's almost broad daylight now. Surely they see the gasbags by now*.

Or maybe not. Dwer recalled how excited the balloon concept made the Niss Machine, which understood a lot about Jophur ways. Perhaps Gillian Baskin knew what she was doing.

The idea was to get the Jophur confused. To send them searching around for supposed enemy ships they could detect only vaguely.

Sure enough, the space titan decelerated ponderously, descending in a long spiral around the general area. An aura of warped air seemed to bend all light passing within half a radius of the tremendous globe. The rewq made clear this was a shield of some sort – apparent grounds for the Jophur assumption of invincibility.

Dwer reached for the hammer at his waist . . . and waited.

He wanted to make love again.

Who wouldn't, after the way Ling had writhed and clutched at him, with animal-like cries that belied her background as an urbane sky god? He, too, had felt a seismic quake of passion. Ardor that reached out of something wild within ... followed by a release that was blissfully free of any sapient thought.

Despite their dire circumstance, trapped in a ship filled with mortal enemies, Lark felt fine. Better than he had since—

Since ever. Somehow, this climax did not leave him in a state of lassitude, but filled with energy, a postcoital animation he had never experienced before. *So much for my vow of celibacy*, he thought. Of course, that vow had been for the sake of Jijo. *And we're not on Jijo anymore*.

He reached for Ling. But she stopped him with an upraised hand, sitting up, her breasts still glistening with their commingled sweat.

Ling's eyes were distant. Her ears twitched, listening.

A jungle surrounded them – supported by lattice scaffolding that filled a chamber larger than the artificial cave of Biblos. A maze of fantastic, profusely varied vegetation nearly filled the cavity. In this far corner, apparently ill-tended by the maintenance drones, the two fugitive hominids had built a nest. Ling, the trained spatio-biologist, had no trouble spotting several types of fruits and tubers to eat. They might live weeks or months this way ... or perhaps the rest of their lives. Unless the universe intruded.

Which it did, of course.

'They've turned on their defensive array,' she told him. 'And I think they're slowing down.'

'How can you tell?' Lark listened, but could make out no difference in the mesh of interlacing engine sounds, more complex than the verdant jungle.

Ling slipped into the rag of a tunic that was her sole remaining garment. 'Come on,' she said.

With a sigh, he put on his own torn shirt. Lark picked up the leather thong holding his amulet – the fragment of the Holy Egg he had chipped off as a child. For the first time in years, he considered not slipping it on. If the ship had left Jijo, might that make him free at last from the love-hate burden?

'Come on!' Ling was already scooting along the latticeway, heading toward the exit. In a torn cloth sling, she carried the wounded red torus – one of the traeki rings provided by Asx.

He slipped the thong around his neck and reached for the crude sack that contained the purple ring and their few other possessions.

'I'm on my way,' he murmured, clambering out of the nest, wondering if they would ever be back.

Ling had her bearings now. With Lark to sniff scent indicators at tunnel intersections, and the purple ring serving as a passkey, they had little trouble hurrying 'north' up the ship's axis. Twice they sped along by using antigravity drop tubes. Lark's stomach did somersaults as his body went careening up a jet-black tunnel. The landings were always soft, though. Even better, they did not meet a single Jophur or robot along the way.

'They're at battle stations,' she explained. 'Here. Their control room should be just below this level. If I'm right, there should be an observers' gallery . . .'

Lark smelled an oddly familiar aroma, much like the fragrance traeki used when they referred to *Biblos*.

Ling pointed to a rare written symbol inscribed on the wall. She crowed. 'I was right!'

Lark had seen the glyph before – a rayed spiral with five swirling arms. Even Jijo's fallen races knew what it stood for: the Great Galactic Library. Symbol for both patience and knowledge.

'Hurry!' Ling said as he applied the purple ring to the entrance plate. The barrier slid open, giving access to a dim chamber whose sole illumination came through a broad window, directly opposite the door. It took just a few strides to cross over and stare through the glass at a bright gallery below. A chamber filled with Jophur.

There were scores of the tapered stacks. Taller and more slickly perfect than any Jijoan traeki, they squatted next to instrument stations, many of them surrounded by flashing panels and lighted controls. At the very center, one gleaming torus pile perched on a raised dais, surveying the labors of the crew.

'A lot of big ships have observation decks, like the one we're in,' Ling explained in a low voice. 'They're for when legates from any of the great Institutes come aboard – say on an inspection tour. Most of the time, though, they just contain a watcher.

'A what?'

She gestured to her left, where Lark now saw a roughly man-sized cube with a single dark lens in the middle, looking over the Jophur control room.

'It's a WOM . . . or Write-Only Memory. A *witness*. Any capital ship from a great clan is supposed to carry one, especially if engaged in some major venture. It takes a record that can then be archived in deep storage so later generations may learn from the experience of each race, after a certain time period expires.'

'How long?'

Ling shrugged. 'Millions of years, I guess. You hear about watchers being sent for storage, but I've never known of a WOM being read during the present epoch. I guess when you put it that way, it kind of sounds like a contradiction in terms. A typical Galactic hypocrisy. Or maybe I don't grasp some subtlety of the concept.'

You and me, both. Lark thought, dismissing the watcher from his mind, like a slab of stone.

'Look,' he said, pointing toward one end of the Jophur headquarters chamber. 'Those big screens show the outside! Seems we just passed over the Rimmers.'

'Toward the sun.' Ling nodded. 'Either it's morning or—'

'Nothing on the Slope looks like that prairie. That's poison grass. So it is morning and that's east.'

'See the clouds,' Ling commented. 'They're breaking up, but it must've been some stor—' She stopped, blinking. 'Hear that? The Jophur are excited. Maybe I can adjust these knobs and—'

Sound abruptly boomed through the observation deck. A screech and ratchet of accented GalTwo.

'... *COMMANDED TO CORRECT THE DISSONANCE/ DISAGREEMENTS BETWEEN YOUR VARIED REPORTS! JUSTIFY THIS PATTERNED SEARCH! EXPLAIN REASONS WHY WE SHOULD NOT RETURN TO OUR PRIMARY MISSION – SIFTING FOR THE WOLFLING CRAFT!*'

Lark saw the Jophur on the central dais gesticulate along with these word glyphs, so perhaps that one was in command. *If only I had a weapon*, he mused. But the glasslike barrier was probably too strong for anything as crude as a Jijoan axe or rifle.

'*We/I cannot recommend departing this area until we verify/rebuke the possibility of foe ships/smallships,*' replied a nearby stack, using a less imperious version of the same dialect. '*Starship cognizances hover nearby, undetectable on any other band! But how can that be? Flight without gravitics? The Jophur, great and mighty, must have/pierce this secret, for safety's sake!*'

Another ring stack edged forward, and Lark felt a shiver of recognition. That awkward pile of ragged toruses had once been the former traeki High Sage, though its speech held none of the unassuming gentleness of Asx.

'*I/we offer this wisdom – that the scent indicators we pursue have all the stink of an elaborate ruse! Recall the flame-tube weapons that the savage sooners used against our corvette! Now our comrades in the captured Biblos Archive report they have identified the wolfling*' trick as 'rockets.' Contradicting the tactics officer, I/we must point out that these rockets flew quite successfully without gravitics! I/we further maintain that—'

Another stack interrupted.

'Localization! One of the nearby cognizance sites has remained active long enough to verify its location.'

The commander vented compact clots of purple vapor.

'PROCEED ON ATTACK VECTOR! PREPARE A CAPTURE BOX FOR SEIZURE OF SOURCE! WHETHER IT IS A SOPHISTICATED STAR ENEMY OR ANOTHER SOONER RUSE, WE SHALL SECURE IT FOR LATER INSPECTION, THEN RETURN TO OUR PRINCIPAL OBJECTIVE.'

The ring piles reacted more swiftly than Lark had ever witnessed traeki move, setting to work in a whirl of base feet and flailing tendrils. Soon the outside monitors showed clouds and prairie rushing by in a blur, depicted in many spectral bands. On some displays, flashing concentric circles closed in.

'Targeting brackets—' Ling explained. But the circles seemed to contain nothing. Only open space.

Lark's right hand drifted under his shirt, stroking the sliver of the Egg. 'I feel . . .'

Ling tugged his arm. 'Look at the far left screen!'

He squinted, and began to make out something small and round. A ghostly shape, depicted as nearly transparent. *Blur cloth*, he realized, recognizing the effects of that specialized g'Kek weaving. All at once Lark understood. The Jophur were streaking toward an object that was invisible to nearly all their sensors, because it was made of nothing but air and fabric plaited to smear light.

If only his rewq had not lapsed into exhausted hibernation! The hazy globe loomed larger, even as Lark's heart beat faster. His amulet throbbed in response.

'What *is* it?' Ling wondered, perplexed.

Before he could answer, without warning, all the forward viewing screens abruptly went black.

One Jophur let out a shrill wail. Several vented colored steam. The commander flexed and blared.

'HOSTILITIES ALERT! ROBOTIC DEFENSE! ALL STATIONS PREPARE FOR THE DRAWBA—'

'Detonation!'

Streaker's detection officer shouted excitedly. 'One of our proximity bombs just went off, almost on t-top of the Jophur!'

The bridge filled with neo-dolphin cheers. 'Maybe that got the bastardss,' someone chittered hopefully.

Gillian called for quiet.

'Keep it down, everyone. That firecracker won't do more than scratch their paint.' She took a deep breath. It was the crucial moment of decision, for commitment to the plan.

'Launch the swarm!' she ordered. 'Get us up, Kaa. Exactly the way we planned.'

'Aye!' The pilot's back showed momentary waves of tension as he sent commands down his neural tap. *Streaker* responded instantly, engines ramping up to full power for the first time in almost a year. The sound was thrilling, though the act would surely give them away once Jophur sensors recovered.

Telemetry showed the motivators running well. Gillian glanced at viewers showing the engine room. Hannes Suessi darted back and forth, checking the work of his well-trained crew. Even Emerson D'Anite seemed engrossed, running his long, dark hands over the prime resonance console, his old duty station during so many other rough scrapes. Speech seemed hardly relevant at this point, when physical insight and tactile skill mattered most.

Perhaps this time, too, the ship would hear Emerson's rich baritone victory yell.

If the repairs all worked. If we get full use out of the spare parts we mined from discarded wrecks. If the decoys run as planned. If the enemy does what we hope . . . if . . . if . . .

Overhead, the stress crystal dome of the control room changed color. The jet black of the abyss faded rapidly as *Streaker* aimed upward, lightening to a royal blue, then a clear pale green. The engine's roar changed tone as Jijo's ocean reluctantly let go its heavy grasp.

Streaker blew out of the sea with explosive force, already traveling faster than a bullet, trailed by a spoor of superheated steam.

From submarine, back to ship of space. Here we go again.

Go, old girl.

Go!

RETY

Wakened from a half-million-year sleep, the ancient wreck clattered and shrieked. Forced into furious effort, it howled, like some beast screaming in agony.

Rety screamed back, pressing both hands over her ears. Harsh fists seemed to pummel her against the arching pillar where she had tied herself down. With each shake, strips of rope and electrical cable dug into her skin.

From Rety's belt pouch, yee's head waved toward her face.

'wife! wife don't cry! don't worry, wife!'

But the piping words were lost amid a maelstrom of sound. Soon his calls merged into a wail, an urrish ululation.

Overwhelmed with dread of being trapped, Rety tore at the straps with her nails, struggling for release.

She never noticed the transition from water to air. The little holosim display showed whitecaps stretching to a sandy shore, then the tops of clouds.

Crawling across the hard metal floor, Rety toiled toward the airlock, seeing only a narrow tunnel through a haze of pain.

EWASX

The effects start to wear off.

I emerge from stun state, blind and alone. More duras pass before I coalesce My sense of oneness. Of purpose.

Sending trace signals down the tendrils of control, I reestablish rapport with subservient rings. Soon I have access to their varied senses, staring in all directions with eye buds that flutter and twitch.

HELLO, MY RINGS. Report now and prepare for urgent movement. Clearly we have experienced – and survived – an episode of the Drawback.

The what?

Truly, you do not know, My rings? You have no experience of the chief disadvantage of the Oailie gift?

Certain weapons exist which can render us Jophur insensate for a time, forcing us to rely on robotic protection for the duration of that brief incapacity.

What incapacity? you ask.

*

I/we look around. We are no longer near the Captain-Leader, but stand instead at the main control panel, our tendrils wrapped around the piloting wheels.

WHAT ARE WE DOING?

I command the tendrils to draw back, and they obey. Viewscreens show a blur of high-speed motion as the *Polkjhy* races across a landscape of jagged, twisty canyons, unlike anything our memory tracks recall from the Slope. Inertial indicators show us racing *east*, ever farther from the sea. Away from the prey.

Other stacks are beginning to stir, as their master rings rouse from the Drawback. Hurriedly, I send our basal torus in motion, taking us away from the pilot station. We scurry around behind the Captain-Leader, who is just now rousing from torpor.

In all likelihood others will assume that our sophisticated robotic guardians – programmed to serve/protect during a Drawback interlude – had good reason to send *Polkjhy* careening in this unfavorable direction. Feigning innocence, I/we watch as the pilot stacks resume control, arresting this headlong flight, preparing to regain altitude once more.

MY RINGS, WHAT WAS YOUR AIM? WHAT WERE YOU TRYING TO ACCOMPLISH WHILE YOUR MASTER TORUS WAS INCAPACITATED? TO SEND US CRASHING INTO A MOUNTAIN, PERHAPS?

The robots would not have allowed that. But diverting the course of *Polkjhy* – that was in your power, no?

I perceive we are not finished learning the arts of cooperation.

GILLIAN

Thrilling as it was to be moving again, Gillian knew this wasn't the same old *Streaker*. It ran sluggishly for a snark-class survey ship. The nearby landmass receded with disheartening slowness compared with the rabbitlike agility she used to show. Suessi's motors weren't at fault. It was the damned carbon-carbon coating, sealing *Streaker*'s hull under countless tons of dead weight, clogging the probability flanges and gravitics radiators, costing valuable time to gain orbital momentum. Minutes of vulnerability.

Gillian glanced at the swarm display. A scatter of bright dots showed at least twenty decoys out of the water, with a dozen more now rising from their ancient graves, screaming joy – or agony – over this unwonted mass resurrection. Groups of bait ships speared away in different directions, disbanding according to preset plans, though empty of life.

All empty, except one.

Gillian thought of the human girl, Rety, self-exiled aboard one of those glimmering lights. Would it have been better to break into her hijacked ship? Or try to seize control of the computer, reprogramming it to bring Rety ashore?

The Niss didn't think either effort would succeed in the slim time allowed. Anyway, Alvin and Huck had convinced Gillian not to try.

'We know what you Earthlings are trying to do with this breakout attempt,' the young g'Kek had said.

'And yet you volunteered to come?'

'Why not? We risked the Midden in a hollow tree trunk. All sooners know life is something you just borrow for a while. Each person must choose how to spend it.

'All our families and all our septs depend on your venture, Dr. Baskin. This Rety person selected her destiny. Let her follow it.'

As *Streaker* gradually accelerated, Gillian turned to the dolphin in charge of psi-ops. 'Let me know when you get anything at all from the observer,' she ordered.

'No sssignal yet-t,' the fin answered. 'It'sss well past due, if you ask me.'

'No one asked,' Gillian snapped.

Without wanting to, she glanced at the Jijoan mathematician, Sara Koolhan, whose brother took off in a hot-air balloon, knowing that if the gale did not get him, the Jophur probably would. Sara floated in a swarm of bubbles, watching intently. But behind the visor of her breathing helmet, Gillian saw a single soft tear, running down the young woman's cheek.

Gillian did not need more guilt. She tried hard to think pragmatically.

I just wish the boy hadn't died for nothing. We're going to have to decide ...

She checked the swarm monitors.

... in moments ...

DWER

The dazzling blast jolted his rewq, causing it to retreat, almost comatose. But the creature served its purpose, saving Dwer's eyes. Except for a few purple spots, vision soon returned almost to normal.

There'll be a shock wave, he thought. After the abuse of last night and morning, he wondered if the balloon would survive another shaking.

Dwer readied his hammer over the row of crystals, each jammed into the wicker gondola. He peered east, trying to figure out which message to send.

All the decoy balloons were gone – no surprise there.

But dammit, where's the Jophur ship?

Dwer could not act without data, so he held on and rode out the explosion's booming echo when it came rolling by, flattening the serrated grass of the Venom Plain.

The balloon survived. Solid urrish workmanship. Picking up binoculars, he sought again for the Jophur, scanning the horizon.

Could it have been blown up by the aerial mine? Gillian Baskin had thought the prospect nearly impossible. No weapon in *Streaker's* arsenal could pierce the defense of such a dreadnought, even with the element of surprise. But it might be possible to inconvenience the enemy for a crucial time.

Finally, he made out the distant glint. In fact, the ship seemed to be *receding*! He had the illusion that it was heading toward the rising sun.

Dwer hesitated over the message crystals. There were only four. None of the prearranged codes took in this possibility . . . that the foe would flee the scene. Not upward toward space, or west back to the Midden, or even standing still, but *away from any chance to spy the Earthling ship!*

If I don't send anything, they'll think I'm dead.

He thought of Sara, and was tempted to smash all the crystals, just to reassure her.

But then they might make a wrong decision, and she might die instead of me. Because of me.

By now, squadrons of salvaged decoy spaceships would be heading out beyond Jijo's atmosphere, spiraling toward orbit and beyond. Gillian Baskin had to decide which group to go with. Dwer's signal was supposed to help.

Frustration locked him in a rigor of indecision. Raising the binoculars once more, he found the Jophur ship again, a bare pinpoint near the horizon.

Then he noticed something.

The distant dot . . . it had stopped receding. Instead, it seemed to hover beyond a range of craggy highlands.

The Gray Hills, Dwer realized. *If only I can give the right signal, I'll be able to start descending in time to land where I want!*

The glittering pinpoint hesitated, then began to move again. Dwer soon confirmed – it was growing larger. The Jophur were heading back this way!

Now I know what to send, he thought with satisfaction. Dwer raised the hammer and brought it smashing down on the second crystal. That instant, his back swarmed with a curious tingling. The feeling came and left quickly.

His duty done at last, Dwer reached for the gas-discharge rope. The battleship was going to pass close again, and the only way he had to maneuver was to lose height.

Easy does it, he thought. *Let her down slowly. Might as well reach the foothills before you have to ...*

The great ship loomed rapidly, then streaked westward while gaining altitude, missing him by hundreds of arrowflights.

Alas, this time it did not ignore Dwer.

As it hurried by, the mighty blue globe dropped a tiny speck. A minuscule dot that arced away and then dropped rapidly, glittering as it came. Dwer did not have to know much about Galactic technology to recognize a missile when he saw one.

Gillian mentioned that I might attract attention when I signaled.

Dwer sighed, watching the fleck turn a gentle curve and then plunge straight toward him.

Ah, well, he thought, picking up his prize possession – the bow made for him by the master carvers of Ovoom Town, in honor of his skill as tracker for the Commons of Six Races.

When the explosion came, it was unlike anything he expected.

GILLIAN

'That's it!' she cried out, glad of the news.

Even more elated was Sara, who let out an urrish-sounding yelp, on learning that her brother yet lived.

The signal also confirmed Gillian's best guess. The Jophur had been slow reacting, but they were doing as she hoped.

'They are predictable,' commented the Niss, whose whirling holo-gram passed through oxy-water bubbles unperturbed. *'The delay only means we get more of a head start.'*

Gillian agreed, but in her thoughts added:

We'll need ten times this much of a lead, in order to make it all the way.

Aloud, she told the pilot:

'Punch us out of here, Kaa. Stay with swarm number two. Put us second from the front of the pack.'

The pilot shouted, 'Aye!'

Soon the low, driving harmonies of the motivators notched upward in pitch. Gillian glanced at the engine-room display. Morale seemed high among Suessi's crewfen. As she watched, Emerson D'Anite threw his head back to sing! Gillian only picked up a fragment, though the lyrics had Emerson's coworkers in stitches.

> 'Jijo, Jijo ...
> It's off to war we go!'

Even suffering from brain affliction, his puns were terrible. It was good to have some of the old Emerson back again.

External displays showed the planet swiftly receding, a gentle blue-brown globe, swathed in a slim envelope of life-giving weather. Numerous sharp-bordered green patches testified to where some metropolis once stood, before the site was scoured and seeded. Whether now covered with swamp, forest, or prairie, the regions still showed regular outlines that would take eons to erase.

Earth has such scars, she thought. *In even greater abundance. The difference is that we were ignorant and didn't know better. We had to learn the hard way how to manage a world, by teaching ourselves.*

Gillian glanced at Sara, whose eyes bore pain and wonder, watching her homeworld diminish to a small orb – the first of her sooner line to look down at Jijo, ever since her ancestors fled here, centuries ago.

A place of refuge. A sanctuary for Earthlings and others. They all meant to hunker down, cowering away from the cosmos, each race redeeming its heritage in its own peculiar way.

Then we brought the universe crashing in on them.

She watched Lieutenant Tsh't move among the crewfen at their dome consoles, encouraging them with bursts of sonar, always checking for lapses of attention. The meticulous supervision hardly seemed necessary. Not one of the elite bridge staff had ever shown a trace of stress atavism. All were guaranteed high uplift classifications when they got home.

If we get home.

If there is still a home, waiting for us.

In fact, everyone knew the real reason why half the crew had been left behind on Jijo, along with the Kiqui and copies of *Streaker's* records.

We don't have much of a chance of escaping ... but it might be possible to draw the universe away from Jijo. Diverting its attention. Making it forget the sooners, once again.

It would take skill and luck just to achieve that sacrifice. But if successful, what an accomplishment! Preventing the extinction of the g'Kek, or the unwanted transformation of the traeki, or the discovery and blame that would befall Earth, if human sooners were exposed here.

If this works, we'll have a complete cache of Earthlings on Jijo – humans, chimps, and now dolphins, too. A safety reserve, in case the worst happens at home.

That seems worthwhile. A result worth paying for.

Of course, like everything in the cosmos, it would come at a price.

They had passed Loocen – the moon still glittering with abandoned cities – and accelerated about a million kilometers beyond when the detection officer declared:

'Enemy cruiser leaving atmosphere! Vectoring after swarm number one!'

The spatial schematic showed a speck rising from Jijo, larger and brighter than any other, lumbering to accelerate its titanic mass.

We would outrun you, once, Gillian thought. *We still can . . . for a while.*

Even handicapped by the irksome carbon sheathing, *Streaker* would spend some time increasing the gap between her and the pursuing battleship. Newtonian inertia must drag down the heavier Jophur – that is, until it reached speeds adequate for level-zero hyperdrive.

Then the speed advantage would start to shift.

If only a transfer point were nearer. Gillian shook her head, and kept on wishing.

If only Tom and Creideiki were here. They'd get us away without much trouble, I bet. I could retire to sick bay with confidence, treating dolphins for itchy-flake and spending my copious free time contemplating the mysteries of Herbie.

In a moment of decision, she had elected to take along the billion-year-old mummy, despite the high likelihood *Streaker* would be destroyed in a matter of hours or days. She could not part with the relic, which Tom had fought so hard to snatch from a fleet of ghost ships in the Shallow Cluster – back in those heady days before the whole Civilization of the Five Galaxies seemed to turn against *Streaker*.

Back when the naive crew expected *gratitude* for their epochal discovery.

Never surprise a stodgy Galactic, went a Tymbrimi saying. *Unless you're prepared with twelve more surprises in your pocket.*

Good advice.

Unfortunately, her supply of tricks was running low.

There were, in fact, only a few left.

THE SAGES

The latest group of pilgrims understood more now, about the Holy Egg.

More than Drake and Ur-Chown knew, when they first stared at the newly emerged wonder, glowing white-hot from its fiery emergence. Those two famed heroes conspired to exploit the Egg for their own religious and political purposes, declaring it an omen. A harbinger of unity. A god.

Now the sages have printouts provided by the dolphin ship. The report, downloaded from a unit of the Great Galactic Library, calls the Egg – *a psi-active geomorph. A phenomenon observed on some life worlds whose tectonic restoration processes are smoothly continuous, where past cycles of occupation and renewal had certain temporal and technologic traits* ...

Phwhoon-dau contemplated this as the newly reassembled Council of Sages approached the sacred site, walking, slithering, and rolling toward the place they had all separately been heading when they heard Vubben's dying call.

In other words, the Egg is a distillation, a condensation of Jijo's past. All the dross deposited by the Buyur ... and those who came before ... has combined to contribute patterns.

Patterns that somehow wove their way through magma pressure and volcanic heat.

To the south, these spilled forth chaotically, to become the Spectral Flow. But here, conditions permitted coalescence. A crystalline tip consisting of pure memory and purpose.

At last he understood the puzzle of why every sooner race settled on the Slope, despite initial jealousies and feuds.

We were summoned.

Some said this knowledge would crush the old ways, and Phwhoon-dau agreed. The former faith – founded in the Sacred Scrolls, then modified by waves of heresy – would never be the same.

The basis of the Commons of Six Races had changed. But the basis survived.

A re-formed council of Six entered the scarred canyon circle, where they spent a brief time contemplating the charred remains of their eldest member, a jumble of frail nerves and fibers, plastered against the Egg's pitted, sooty flank.

They buried Vubben there – the only sage ever so honored. Then began their work.

Others would join them soon. A re-formed council meant re-formed duty.

At last we know what you are, Phwhoon-dau thought silently, leaning back to regard the Egg's great curving mass.

But other questions remain. Such as ... why?

RETY

The controls refused to respond!

'Come on!' she shouted, slamming the holosim box with the palm of her hand, then jiggling more levers.

Not that Rety had much idea what she'd do if she gained mastery over the decoy vessel. At first, the stunning views of Jijo and space sent her brain reeling. It was all so much *bigger* than she ever imagined. Since then, she had left the big visual holo turned off, while continuing to fiddle with other panels and displays.

Wisdom preached that she ought to leave the machinery alone ... and finally, Rety listened. She forced herself to back away, joining yee at her small stack of supplies, smuggled off the sled when Chuchki wasn't looking. She stroked her little husband while munching a food-concentrate bar, pondering the situation.

Every salvaged decoy ship had been programmed to head out – by a variety of routes – toward the nearest 'transfer point.' From there, they would jump away from fallow Galaxy Four, aiming for distant, traffic-filled lanes where oxygen-breathing life-forms teemed.

That was good enough for Rety, providing she then found a way to signal some passing vessel.

This old ship may not be worth much, but it oughta pay my passage to their next stop, at least.

What would happen next remained vague in her mind. Getting some kind of job, most likely. She still had the little teaching machine that used to belong to Dennie Sudman, so learning those jabber-talk alien languages shouldn't be too hard.

I'll find a way to make myself useful. I always have.

Of course, everything depended on making it to the transfer point.

Gillian prob'ly set things up so the decoys'll try to lure the Jophur. Maybe they give off some sort of light or noise to make 'em think there are dolphins aboard.

That might work for a while. The stinky rings'll chase around, losin' time while checkin' things out.

But Rety knew what would happen next. Eventually, the Jophur gods would catch on to the trick. They'd figure out what to look for, and realize which ship was the real target.

Suppose by then they've torn apart half the decoys. That still leaves me fitty-fitty odds. Which is Ifni times more than I'd have aboard old Streaker. *Once they figure which one she is, they'll leave the rest of us decoys alone to go about our business.*

At least that was the overall idea. Ever since she had found Kunn and Jass, dead in their jail cells, Rety knew she must get off the Earthling ship as fast as possible and make it on her own.

I'd better be able to send out a signal, when we pop into a civilized galaxy, she thought. *I s'pose it'll take more than just shining a light out through a window. Guess I better study some more about radio and that hyperwave stuff.*

As wonderful and patient as the teaching unit was, Rety did not look forward to the drudgery ahead ... nor to relying on the bland paste put out by the ancient food processor, once her supply of *Streaker* food ran out. The machine had taken the sample of fingernail cuticle she gave it, and after a few moments put out a substance that tasted exactly like cuticle.

Chirping tones interrupted her thoughts. A light flashed atop the holosim casing. Rety scooted over to the machine.

'Display on!'

A 3-D image erupted just above the floor plates. For a time, she made little sense of the image, which showed five small groups of amber points spiraling away from a tiny blue disk. It took moments to realize the dot was Jijo, and the decoy swarms had already left the planet far behind. The separation between the convoys also grew larger, with each passing dura.

One dot lagged behind, brighter than the others, gleaming red instead of yellow. It crept toward one of the fleeing swarms as she watched.

That must be the Jophur ship, she realized. Squinting closer, she saw that the big dot was trailed by a set of much tinier crimson pinpricks, almost too small to see, following like beads on a string.

The red symbol accelerated, slowly closing the distance to its intended prey.

Boy, I pity whoever's in that swarm, when the stink rings catch up with 'em.

It took Rety a while longer to fathom the unpleasant truth.

That swarm was the one that contained her own ship.

The Jophur were coming for her first.

My usual luck, she complained, knowing better than to think the universe cared.

DWER

Everything changed.

One moment, he had been surrounded by sky. Mountains, clouds, and prairies stretched below his wicker gondola. The urrish balloon bulged and creaked overhead. From the high northwest, a glittering object fell toward him, like a stoop raptor, unstoppable once it has chosen its prey.

That's me, he thought, feeling transfixed, like a grass mouse who, caught in the open, knows there is no escape, and so has little choice but to watch the terrible beauty of Death on the wing.

Death came streaking toward him.

He felt an explosion, a shrill brilliance . . .

. . . and found himself *here*.

A gilded haze surrounded Dwer as he took stock.

I'm alive.

The sensations of a young, strong body accompanied irksome itches and the sting of recent scrapes. His clothes were as they had been. So was the gondola, for that matter – a basket woven out of dried river reeds – its contents undamaged.

The same could not be said of the balloon itself. The great gasbag lay collapsed in a curved heap of blur cloth, its upper half apparently cleaved off. Remnant folds lay spread across the interior of what Dwer came to realize must be a prison of some sort.

A spherical jail. He now saw it clearly. A sphere whose inner surface gave off a pale, golden light, confusing to the eye at first.

'Huh!'

To Dwer's surprise, his principal reaction was intrigue. In those final moments, as the missile fell, he had bid farewell to life. Now each added moment was profit. He could spend it as he chose.

He decided on curiosity.

Dwer clambered out of the basket and eased his moccasins onto the gold surface. He half expected it to be slick, but the material instead *clung* to his soles, so that he had to pull with some effort each time he took a step. After a few tentative strides, he came to yet another startling relevation.

'Down' is wherever I happen to be standing!

From Dwer's new position, it looked as if the gondola was tilted almost sideways, about to topple onto him.

He squatted, looking down at the 'floor' between his legs, riding out the expected wave of disorientation. It wasn't too bad.

I'll adapt. It'll be like learning to ice-walk across a glacier. Or probing face caves at the end of a rope, dangling over the Desolation Cliffs.

Then he realized something. Looking down, he saw more than just a sticky golden surface. Something glittered beneath it. Like a dusting of tiny diamonds. Gemstones, mixed with dark loam.

He leaned closer, cupping hands on both sides of his eyes to keep out stray light.

All at once Dwer fathomed; the diamonds were stars.

LARK

Crouching behind an aromatic obelisk, two humans had an unparalleled chance to view events in the Jophur control room.

Lark would much rather they had stayed in the quiet, safe 'observation chamber.'

Towering stacks of sappy toruses loomed nearby, puffing steam as each Jophur worked at a luminous instrument station. The density of smells made Lark want to gag. It must be worse for Ling, who hadn't grown up near traeki. Yet she seemed enthralled to be here.

Well, this was a terrific idea, he groused mentally, recalling the impulse that had sent them charging into a pit of foes.

Hey, look! The Jophur seem stunned! Let's rush down from this nice, safe hiding place and sabotage their instruments while they're out!

Only the Jophur didn't stay out long enough. By the time he and Ling made it halfway across the wide control room, several ring piles abruptly started puffing and swaying as they roused from their torpor. While machine voices reported status to their reviving masters, the two humans barely managed to leap behind this cluster of spirelike objects, roughly the shape of idealized Jophur, but twice as tall and made of some moist, fibrous substance.

Lark dropped down to the floor. All he wanted was to scrunch out of sight, close his eyes, and make objective reality go away.

Responding to his racing heartbeat, the purple ring twitched in its cloth bag. Lark put his hand on it and the thing eventually calmed down.

'I think I can tell what's going on!'

Lark glanced up the twin, tanned columns of Ling's legs, and saw that she was leaning around one of the soggy pillars, staring at the Jophur data screens. Reaching up, he seized her left wrist and yanked her down. She landed on her bare bottom beside him.

'Make like vermin,' was his advice. On matters of concealment and survival, Ling had a lot to learn from a Jijoan sooner.

'Okay, brother rat.' She nodded with surprising cheerfulness, then went on eagerly. 'Some of their screens are set to spectra I can't grok. But I could tell we're in space now, racing toward Izmunuti.'

A wave of nausea struck Lark – a sensation akin to panic. Unlike his siblings, who used to talk and dream about starflight when they were little, he had never wanted to leave Jijo. The very thought made him feel sick. Sensing his discomfort, Ling took his head and stroked it, but that did not stop her from talking, describing a complex hunt through space that Lark failed to visualize, no matter how he tried.

'Apparently there must have been a fleet of ships on or near Jijo,' she explained. 'Though I can't imagine how they got there. Maybe they came snooping from Izmunuti and the Jophur are chasing them away. Anyway, the mystery fleet seems to have split into five groups, all of them heading separately for the flare star. And from there to the transfer point, I suppose.

'There's also a couple of small objects trailing behind this ship ... connected to it, as far as I can tell, by a slender force string. I don't know what their purpose is. But give me time ...'

Lark wanted to laugh out loud. He would give Ling the world. The universe! But right now all he really wanted was their nest. Their little green hideaway, where sweet fruits dangled within reach and no one could find them.

Lark was starting to push the vertigo away at last, when a noise blared from across the room.

'What's that?' he asked, sitting up. He did not try to stop Ling from rising partway and peering around for a look.

'Weapons release,' she explained. 'The Jophur are firing missiles at the nearest squadron. They must be pretty confident, because they sent just one for each ship.'

Lark silently wished the new aliens luck, whoever they were. If any of them got away, they might report what they saw to the Galactic Migration Institute. Although Jijo's Six Races had lived in fear of the law for two thousand years, the intervention of neutral judges would be far better than any fate the Jophur planned to mete out, in private.

'The small ships are trying evasive maneuvers, but it's doing no good,' Ling said. 'The missiles are closing in.'

RETY

She cursed the dross ship, for not giving her control.

She cursed Gillian Baskin and the dolphins, for putting her in a position where she had no choice but to escape from their incompetence into this impossible trap.

She cursed the Jophur for sending missiles after this decoy flotilla, instead of expertly finding the right prey.

Above all, Rety swore an oath at herself. For in the end, she had no one else to blame.

Her teaching unit explained the symbols representing those deadly arrows, now clearly visible in the display, catching up fast.

One by one, the ships behind hers met their own avenging predators. Surprisingly, the amber pinpoints did not snuff out, but turned crimson instead. Each then drifted backward, toward a meeting with the big red dot.

The Jophur did not swallow their captives. That would take too much time. Instead, they were snagged at the end of a chain – like a tadpole's tail – that waved behind the mighty ship.

Rety wondered. *Maybe they don't want to kill, after all. Maybe they just want prisoners!*

If so, Rety would be prepared. She held yee with one arm, and the teaching unit with the other, setting it to begin teaching her Galactic Two – Jophur dialect.

When her own missile arrived, Rety was calmer than she expected.

'Don't worry, yee,' she said, stroking her little husband.

'We'll find somethin' they want, an' make a deal. Just you wait an' see.'

With desperate confidence, she held on as the ancient Buyur vessel suddenly quivered and shook. In moments, the motors' grating drone cut off . . . and then so did the downward tug of the deck beneath her. In its place, a gentler pull seemed to draw her toward the *nose* of the disabled ship.

The lights went out. But Rety could see a bit. Stepping and

sliding carefully along the slanted floor and walls, she followed the source of illumination to an unobstructed viewing port, where she peered outside and saw a world of pale yellow dawn.

yee commented dryly.

'beats being dead, i guess.'

Rety agreed. 'I guess.' Then she shrugged.

'At least we'll see, one way or t'other.'

GILLIAN

'I found a library reference. They are called capture *boxes,*' the Niss explained. *'This weapon offers a clever solution to the Jophur dilemma.'*

'How do you figure?' Gillian asked.

'We thought we had them in an awkward situation, where they must come close and inspect every decoy in order to find us. A cumbersome, time-consuming process.

'But this way, the Jophur need only get near enough to dispatch special missiles. They can then move on, dragging a string of captives behind them.'

'Won't all that additional mass slow them down?' asked Kaa, the pilot.

'Yes, and that works in our favor. Alas, not enough to make up for the advantage this technique gives them.'

Gillian shook her head. 'Too bad we didn't know about this in time to incorporate it in our plans.'

The Niss answered with a defensive tone. *'Great clans can access weaponry files spanning a billion years of Galactic history.'*

Silence reigned on the bridge, until Sara Koolhan spoke, her voice transposed by the amplifying faceplate of her helmet.

'What happens if we get caught by a missile?'

'It creates a field related to the toporgic cage your Six Races found enveloping the Rothen ship. Of course that one was meters thick, and missiles cannot carry that much pseudomaterial. The chief effect of a capture box is to suppress digital cognizance.'

Sara looked confused, so Gillian explained.

'Digital computers are detectable at a distance, and can be suppressed by field-effect technologies. A principal reason why organic life-forms dominate the Five Galaxies, instead of machines.

'Unfortunately, this means our decoys can be disabled easily, by enclosing them in a thin shell of warped space-time.'

'Indeed, it seems an ideal weapon to use against resurrected

starships lacking crews. The Jophur may be malign and limited in many ways, but they do not lack for skill or reasoning power.

Sara nodded. 'You mean the method won't work as well against *Streaker*?'

'Exactly,' Gillian said. 'We'll prepare our computers to stand a temporary shutdown without inconvenience—'

'Speak for yourself,' the Niss muttered.

'As soon as the capture box surrounds us, organic crew members can use simple tools to dissolve it from the inside. Estimated period of shutdown, Niss?'

The hologram whirled.

'I wish we had better data from the expedition the sooners sent to the Rothen vessel. They reported major quantum effects from a toporgic layer meters thick.

'But the Jophur missiles will cast thin bubbles. If prepared, crews should burst us free in mere minutes.'

A happy sigh escaped Kaa and several dolphins. But then the Niss Machine went on.

'Unfortunately, when we pop the bubble, it will alert the Jophur which captured vessel contains living prey. After that, our restored freedom will be brief, indeed.'

DWER

The stuff felt strange. It seemed to repel his hand slightly, until he got within a couple of centimeters. Then it *pulled*. Neither effect was overwhelming. He could yank his hand back fairly easily.

He could not quite place why it was eerily familiar.

Dwer walked all the way around his circular cage, stopping on occasion to bend down and examine the starscape beyond. He recognized most of the constellations, except for one patch that had always been invisible from the Slope. *So that's what the southern sky is like.* Undimmed by dust or atmosphere, the entire Dandelion Cluster lay before him, a vast unwinking spectacle. It would be even more fantastic without the filmy golden barrier in the way.

'Thank Ifni for that barrier,' he reminded himself. *There is no air out there.*

In one direction lay a tremendously bright sky he did not recognize at first.

Then he knew ... it was the *sun*, much diminished, and getting smaller all the time.

In the opposite direction lay Izmunuti's fierce eye. The red glare grew more pronounced, until he began to make out an actual disk. Yet he realized it must still be farther away than the sun. Izmunuti was said to be a giant among stars.

In time he noticed other objects. Not stars or nebulae, but gleaming dots. At first they all seemed rather distant. But over the course of a midura, they drew ever closer, rounded shapes that revealed themselves more by their glimmering rims, occulting the constellations, than for any brightness they themselves put out.

One of them – a rippled sphere on the side toward Izmunuti – had to be a starship. It loomed larger with each passing dura. Soon he recognized it as the behemoth that had twice crossed the sky over the Poison Plain, shaking his hapless balloon with each passage.

When Dwer crossed his prison to peer through the membrane on the other side, he saw a line of yellowish globes, even closer than the starship. Their color made him realize, *They're other captives, like me*.

Pressing close to the barrier, a tingle coursed his scalp and spine. He felt similarities to when the Danik robot sent its fields through his body, changing his nervous system in permanent, still-uncertain ways.

Well, I was unusual even before that. For instance, no one else I know ever talked to a mulc-spider . . .

Dwer yanked his head back, recalling at last what this stuff reminded him of. The fluid used by the mad old spider of the mountains – One-of-a-Kind – to seal its victims away, storing its treasured collections against the ravages of time. Months back, a coating of that stuff had nearly smothered him, until he escaped the spider's trap.

A strange sensation came over Dwer. An odd idea.

I could talk to spiders, not just in the mountains, but the one in the swamp, too.

I wonder if that means . . .

Once again, he put his hand against the golden material, pushing through the initial resistance, pressing his fingertips ahead. The resistance was springy. The material seemed adamant.

But Dwer let his mind slide into the same mode of thinking that used to open him to communion with mulc beings. Always before, he had felt that the spider was the one doing most of the work, but now he realized, *It's my own talent. My own gift. And by the Holy Egg, I think I can—*

Something gave way. Resistance against his fingertips suddenly vanished and they slipped through, as if penetrating some greasy fluid.

Abrupt *cold* struck the exposed hand, plus a feeling as if a thousand vampire ants were trying to drink his uncovered veins through straws. Dwer jerked back his arm and it popped out, the fingers red and numb, but mostly undamaged. The membrane flowed back instantly, never leaving an opening to space.

Lucky me, he thought.

When Dwer next checked, the starship had grown to mammoth size. A great bull beast, bearing down on him rapidly, with a hunter's complacent confidence.

I'm a fish on a line. It's reeling me in!

On the other side, the captive globes bobbed almost touching, like toy balloons gathered along an invisible string. The separating distances diminished rapidly.

Dwer sat and thought for a while.

Then he started gathering supplies.

THE SAGES

Phwhoon-dau led the new sextet, commencing the serenade with a low, rolling umble from his resonating throat sac.

Knife-Bright Insight followed by rubbing a myrliton drum with her agile tongue, augmenting this with syncopated calliope whistles from all five leg vents.

Ur-Jah then joined in, lifting her violus against a fold in her long neck, raising stringed harmonies with the double bow.

After that, by seniority, the new sages for traeki, human, and g'Kek septs added their own contributions, playing for a great ovoid-shaped chunk of wounded stone. The harmonies were rough at first, but soon they melded into the kind of union that focused the mind.

So far, the assembly was unexceptional. Other groups of six had performed for the Egg, over the course of a hundred years. Some of them more gifted and musical.

Only this time things were fundamentally different. It was no group of *six*, after all.

Two other Jijoan types were present.

The first was a glaver.

The devolved race always had an open invitation to participate, but it was centuries since any glaver took part in rituals of the Commons – long before Earthlings arrived, and certainly before the coming of the Egg.

But glavers had been acting strangely for months. And today, a small female came out of the brush and began slogging up the Pilgrimage Path, just behind Phwhoon-dau, as if she had the same destination in mind. Now her huge eyes glistened as the music swelled, and strange mewling noises emerged from her grimaced mouth. Sounds vaguely reminiscent of words. With her agile forked tail, she waved a crude rattle made of a stretched animal skin, with stones shaking inside.

Not much of an instrument, but after all, her kind were out of practice.

What must it take, Phwhoon-dau pondered, *to draw them back from the bliss of Redemption's Path?*

Lounging on a nearby boulder, an eighth creature paused licking himself now and then to survey the proceedings. The noor-tytlal had two blemishes on an otherwise jet-black pelt – white patches under each eye – adding to its natural expression of skeptical disdain.

The sages were not fooled. It had arrived just after the others, gaunt, bedraggled, and tired, having run hard for several days. Only urgency, not complacent inquisitiveness could have driven a noor to strive so. The creature's mobile ears flicked restlessly, and pale, spiky hairs waved behind the skull, belying its air of feigned nonchalance.

Phwhoon-dau noticed a soft agitation start to form above the insouciant creature, as if a pocket of air were thickening, and beginning to shimmer. The sages altered their harmony to resonate with the throbbing disturbance, helping it grow as a look of hesitant surprise spread across the sleek, noorlike face.

Reluctant or not, he was now part of the pattern.

Part of the Council of Eight.

In the narrow, resonant confines of the Egg's abode, they made their art, their music.

And soon, another presence began to make itself known.

EWASX

Behold, My rings, how well the chase progresses!

Already one fugitive convoy is liquidated, its component vessels enjoined to our train of captives. While this growing impediment slows the *Polkjhy* from engaging her best speed of pursuit, our tactics stacks compute that all but the very last convoy should be in reach before the storms of Izmunuti are near.

To help speed progress, the Captain-Leader has ordered that the string of captive ships be reeled in closer behind us. When robots can board them, we will be able to cast aside the decoys, one by one.

Now the detections stack reports data arriving from Jijo, the planet behind us.

'More digital cognizance traces! More engine signs!

But the Captain-Leader rules that this is but a futile attempt to distract us from our pursuit. the Earthling vessel may have left salvaged wrecks behind, to turn themselves on after a timed delay. Or else living confederates have acted on Jijo to set off this ruse. It does not matter. Once the fleeing vessels are in tow, we will be in between the Earthers and Izmunuti.

Things would be very different if there were more than one route in or out of this system. But matters are quite convenient for one capital ship to blockade Jijo effectively.

There will be no more breakouts.

That much is true. Yet, I/we hesitate to point out that this may not yet be the end. Indeed, the wolflings may have sent us on a 'wild-goose chase,' pursuing only robot ships while they use this respite to cache themselves in new hiding places, deep beneath Jijo's confused waters. They may even abandon their vessel, taking their vital information ashore, where we will only find it by slay-sifting the entire ecosystem!

The Priest-Stack will not permit so extreme a violation of Galactic law, of course. If such a drastic policy proves necessary, the priest may have to be dismantled, and the watcher-observer destroyed. Then we would be committed irrevocably. In case of failure, we would be labeled bandits and bring shame upon the clan.

How is it possible even to contemplate such measures?

Because all auguries show, with growing certainty, that a Time of Changes has already commenced upon the Five Galaxies. Hence all the desperate activity by so many great clans.

If the Institutes are indeed about to fall, there will be no one to investigate crimes committed on this world.

DO NOT TREMBLE SO, MY RINGS. Have I not assured you, repeatedly, that the mighty Jophur are fated to prevail? And that you/I am destined to be useful toward that end?

Crime and punishment need not be considerations, if we are the ones who will make the new rules.

Anyway, it may not prove necessary to return to Jijo. If the prey ship truly lies before us, the high ambitions of our alliance may soon be within tentacle reach.

We near the second convoy. And now missiles spring forth.

With the mighty starship looming closer on one side, he had to wait in frustration while the yellow beads clustered on the other, coming together with disheartening slowness. His preparations made, Dwer raced back and forth to check each direction.

In time, he learned a technique to make each crossing go much quicker – kicking off from the wall and flying straight across the open interior.

The Jophur vessel impended, mammothly immense. When its dark mass blocked nearly half the starscape, a door of some sort opened in its curved flank and several tiny octagonal shapes emerged, floating toward Dwer's prison.

He recognized the silhouettes.

Battle robots.

They took their time drifting closer, and he realized there was still a large span to cross. At least twenty arrowflights. Still, only duras remained until they arrived.

On returning to the rear of the prison sphere, he breathed a sigh of relief. The captive bubbles were touching now! Yellow spheres, they ranged widely in size, but none was anywhere near as large as the battleship. Most were much larger than his own little ball.

Dwer sought the place where his bubble touched the second in line. A low drumming sound carried through each time the surfaces pressed together.

He zipped up the coverall the *Streaker* crew had given him – a fine garment that covered all but his feet, hands, and head. It had never occurred to him to ask for more.

But right now space gloves and a helmet would be nice.

No matter. The next time the spheres touched, he concentrated for the right frame of mind, and made his move.

SARA

She left the control room when her skin started puckering from too much exposure to fizzy water. Anyway, there seemed no point hanging around. The same news could be had in her comfortable suite – once the home of a great Earthling sage named Ignacio Metz.

Sara dried herself and changed into simple shipboard garments, snug pants and a pullover shirt that posed no mystery even to an unsophisticated sooner. They were wonders of softness and comfort nevertheless.

When she asked the room to provide a tactical display, vivid 3-D images burst forth, showing that the Jophur dreadnought had once again chosen the wrong decoy swarm, and was just finishing firing missiles. Meanwhile, its string of earlier victims merged with the red glow, as if it were gobbling them one by one.

At her voice command, the viewscreen showed *Streaker*'s goal, the red giant star, magnified tremendously, the whirling filamentary structure of its inflamed chromosphere extending beyond the width of any normal solar system. Izmunuti's bloated surface seethed, sending out tongues of ionized gas, rich with the heavy elements that made up Sara's own body.

Purofsky thinks the Buyur had ways to meddle with a star.

Even without that awesome thought, it was a stirring sight to behold. Past those raging fires had come all the sneakships that deposited their illicit seed on Jijo, along with the varied hopes of each founding generation. Their aspirations had ranged from pure survival, for humans and g'Keks, all the way to the hoonish ancestors who apparently came a long way in order to play hooky.

All those hopes will come crashing down, unless Streaker *can make it to Izmunuti's fires.*

Sara still had no idea how Gillian Baskin hoped to save Jijo. Would she let the enemy catch up and then blow this ship up, in order to take the Jophur out, as well?

A brave ploy, but surely the enemy would be prepared for that, and take precautions.

Then what?

It seemed Sara would find out when the time came.

She felt bad about the kids – Huck, Alvin, and the others. But they were adults now, and volunteers.

Anyway, the sages say it's a good omen for members of all six races to be present when something vital is about to happen.

Sara's own reasons for coming went beyond that.

Purofsky said one of us had to take the risk – either him or me – and go with Streaker, *on the slim chance that she makes it.*

One of us should try to find out if it's true. What we figured out about the Buyur.

All her life's work, in mathematical physics *and* linguistics, seemed to agree with Purofsky's conclusion.

Jijo was no accident.

Oh, if she delved into psychology, she might find other motives underlying her insistence on being the one to go.

To continue taking care of Emerson, perhaps?

But the wounded starman was now with those who loved him. Shipmates he had risked death alongside, many times before. After overcoming initial shame, Emerson had found ways to be useful. He did not need Sara anymore.

No one really needs me.

Face it. You're going out of curiosity.

Because you are Melina's child.

Because you want to see what happens next.

DWER

It was a good thing he remembered about air.

There would be none on the other side.

By twisting through the barrier, writhing, and making his body into a hoop, Dwer managed to create a tunnel opening from his prison sphere into the next. A brief hurricane swiftly emptied the atmosphere from his former cell until the pressure equalized. He then pushed through, letting the opening close behind him.

Dwer's ears popped and his pulse pounded. The trick had severely diluted the available air, taking him from near-sea-level pressure to the equivalent of a mountaintop in just half a dura. Speckles danced before his eyes. His body would not last long at this rate.

There was another reason to hurry. As he departed the sphere containing the balloon remnants, he had seen shadows touch beyond the far side. Jophur robots. Come to inspect their first captive.

His gear had settled against the golden surface of his new cell. Dwer grabbed the makeshift pack and moved toward the only possible place of refuge – the nose of the imprisoned starship.

It looked nothing like the massive Jophur vessel, but resembled a pair of spoons, welded face-to-face, with the bulbous end forward. Fortunately, the enclosure barely cleared the ship, fore and aft. A bank of dim windows nearly touched the golden surface.

And there's a door!

Dwer gathered strength, flexed his legs, and launched toward the beckoning airlock. He sailed across the gap and barely managed to snag a protruding bracket with the tip of his left hand.

If this takes some kind of secret code, I'm screwed.

Fortunately, the dolphin work crews had a standard procedure for entering and converting Buyur wrecks. He had accompanied them on some trips, lending a hand. Dwer was glad to see the makeshift locking mechanism still in place, set to work in a fashion that even a Jijoan hunter might understand.

To open ... turn knob.

Dwer's luck held. It rotated.

If there's air inside, the wind will blow out. If there's none, I'll be blown in ... and die.

He had to brace his feet against the hull and pull in order to get the hatch moving. Vision narrowed to a tunnel and Dwer knew he was just duras away from blacking out.

A sudden breeze rushed at him, whistling with force from the ship's interior.

Stale air. Stinky, stale, dank, wonderful air.

GILLIAN

The bad news was not exactly unanticipated; still, she had hoped for better.

As the Jophur ship finished adding another swarm of decoys to its prison chain, the cruiser shifted its attention elsewhere, accelerating to pursue the next chosen group.

Soon the truth became clear.

Streaker's luck had just run out.

Well, they chose right this time, she thought. *It had to happen, sooner or later.*

Streaker was square in the enemy's sights, with seven mictaars of hyperspace yet to cross before reaching safety.

THE SAGES

There are others on Jijo now, Phwhoon-Dau thought, knowing that even eight would not be enough for long. *In time, the new dolphin colonists must be invited to join.*

I have read in Earth lore about cetaceans and their glorious Whale Dream. What music might we make, when these strange beings add their voices to our chorus?

And after that, who knew? Lorniks, chimps, and zookirs? The Kiqui creatures the dolphins brought from far away? A mélange of vocalizations, then. Perhaps a civilization worthy of the name.

All that lay ahead, a glimmering possibility, defying all likelihood or reason. For now, the council was made of those who had earned their place by surviving on Jijo. Partaking of the world. Raising offspring whose atoms all came from the renewing crust of their mother planet. This trait pervaded the musical harmony of the Eight.

We inhale Jijo, with each and every breath.

So Phwhoon-dau umbled in the deep, rolling vibrations of his throat sac.

We drink her waters. At death, our loved ones put us into her abyss. There we join the patterned rhythms of the world.

The presence that joined them was at once both familiar and awesome. The council felt it throb in each note of the flute or myrliton. It permeated the clatter of the glaver's rattle, and the wry empathy glyphs of the tytlal.

For generations, their dreams had been brushed by the Egg. Its soft cadences repaid each pilgrimage, helping to unite the Commons.

But during all those years, the sages had known. *It only sleeps. We do not know what will happen when it wakes.*

Was the Egg only rousing now because the council finally had its missing parts? Or had the cruel Jophur ray shaken it from slumber?

Phwhoon-dau liked to think that his old friend Vubben was responsible.

Or else, perhaps, it was simply time.

The echoes steadily increased. Phwhoon-dau felt them with his feet, reverberating beneath the surface, building to a crescendo. An accretion of pent-up power. Of purpose.

Such energy. What will happen when it is liberated? His sac pulsed with umbles, painful and mightier than he ever produced before.

Phwhoon-dau envisioned the mountain caldera blowing up with titanic force, spilling lava down the tortured aisles of Festival Glade.

As it turned out, the release came with nothing more physical than a slight trembling of the ground.

And yet they all staggered when it flew forth, racing faster than the speed of thought.

THE SLOPE

To Nelo – standing in the ruins of his paper mill, exhausted and discouraged after a long homeward slog – it came as a rapid series of aromas.

The sweet-sour odor of pulped cloth, steaming as it poured across the drying screens.

The hot-vital skin smell of his late wife, whenever her attention turned his way after a long day spent pouring herself into their peculiar children.

The smell of Sara's hair, when she was three years old . . . addictive as any drug.

Nelo sat down hard on a shattered wall remnant, and though the feelings passed through him for less than a kidura, something shattered within as he broke down and wept.

'My children . . . ' Nelo moaned. 'Where are they?'

Something told him they were no longer of his world.

To Fallon – staked down and spread-eagled in an underground roul shambler's lair, waiting for death – the sensation arrived as a wave of images. Memories, yanked back whole.

The mysterious spike trees of the Sunrise Plain, farther east than anyone had traveled in a century.

Ice floes of the northwest, great floating mountains with snowy towers, sculpted by the wind.

The shimmering, teasing phantasms of the Spectral Flow . . . and the oasis of Xi, where the gentle Illias had invited him to live out his days, sharing their secrets and their noble horses.

Fallon did not cry out. He knew Dedinger and his fanatics were listening, just beyond this cave in the dunes. When the beast returned home, they would get no satisfaction from the former chief scout of the Commons.

Still, the flood of memory affected him. Fallon shed a single tear of gratitude.

A life is made whole only in its own eyes. Fallon looked back on his, and called it good.

To Uriel – interrupted in a flurry of new projects – the passing wave barged through as an unwelcome interruption. A waste of valuable time. Especially when all her apprentices laid down their tools and stared into space, uttering low, reverent moans, or sighs, or whinnies.

Uriel knew it for what it was. A blessing. To which she had a simple reply.

So what?

She just had too much on her mind to squander duras on things that were out of her control.

In GalTwo she commented, dryly.

'Glad I am, that you have finally decided.
Pleased that you, O long-lived Egg, have deigned to act, at last.
But forgive me if I do not pause long to exult.
For many of us, life is far too short.'

To Ewasx – moments later and half a light-year away – it came as a brief, agonizing vibration in the wax. Ancient wax, accumulated over many jaduras by the predecessor stack – an old traeki sage.

Involuntary steam welled up the shared core of the stack, bypassing the master ring to waft as a compact cloud from the topmost opening.

Praised be destiny . . .

Other ring stacks drew away from Ewasx, unnerved by the singular aromatics, accented with savage tracks of Jijoan soil.

But the senior Jophur Priest-Stack responded automatically to the reverent smoke, bowing and adding:

Amen . . .

LARK

'Lark, your hand!'

He trembled, fighting to control the fit that came suddenly, causing him to snatch the amulet from around his neck. He clutched the stone tight, even when it began to burn his flesh.

Crouched behind a set of strange obelisks – their only shelter in the spacious Jophur control room – Lark dared not cry out from pain. He fought not to thrash about as Ling used both hands to pry at his clenched fist. At last, the stone sliver fell free, tumbling across his lap to the floor, leaving a stench of singed flesh. Even now, the heat kept building. They tried backing away, but the stone's temperature continued rising until a fierce glow made it hard to see.

'No!' Lark whispered harshly as Ling dived toward the blaze, reaching for the thong. To his surprise, enough was still attached for her to grab a loop and whirl it once, then twice around her head, as if slinging a piece of flaming sun.

She let go, hurling Lark's talisman in an arc across the busy chamber, toward the center of the room.

Dismayed whistles ensued, accompanied by waves of aromatic stench so overpowering, Lark almost gagged.

'Why the hell did you—' he began, but Ling tugged his arm.

'We need a distraction. Come on, now's our chance!'

Lark blinked, amazed by the power of habit. He was actually *angry* at her for throwing away his amulet, and even had to quash an urge to go chasing after the damned stone!

Leave it, and good riddance, he thought, and nodded to Ling.

'Right, let's go.'

DWER

Inside the decoy ship, he collapsed on the deck and retched, heaving up what little remained in his stomach.

Midway through that unpleasant experience, another, completely different kind of disorientation abruptly swept over Dwer. For a moment, it seemed as if One-of-a-Kind were inside his head, trying to speak again. The strange, heady sensation might have been almost affable, if his body weren't racked with nausea.

It ended before he had a chance to appraise what was happening. Anyway, by then he figured he had wasted enough time.

The Jophur won't take long picking through my little urrish balloon. They'll start on this bubble next.

In full gravity, it might have been impossible to climb along the full length of the captured ship and reach the aft end. But Dwer took advantage of conditions as he found them, and soon taught himself to fly.

LARK

They were dashing down a smoke-filled hallway, chased by angry shouts and occasional bolts of shimmering lightning, when an abrupt detonation rocked the floor plates. A wall of air struck the two humans from behind, knocking them off their feet.

We've had it, he thought, figuring it must be a weapon, used by the pursuers.

Glancing over his shoulder, however, Lark saw the robots suddenly turn and head the other way! Into a noisome storm of roiling black soot pouring out of the control room.

'Do you think . . . ?' he began.

Ling shook her head. 'Jophur are tough. I doubt they were more than knocked around by the explosion.'

Well, he thought. *It was only a little piece of rock.*

He felt its absence acutely.

Lark helped her up, still wary of returning robots.

'I guess now they know we're here.'

They resumed running. But a few duras later, Ling burst out in laughing agreement.

'Yeah, I guess now they do.'

GILLIAN

A psi-disturbance was detected, emanating briefly from the planet. Soon after that, the detection officer announced a change on the tactics screen.

'Will you looka that-t!'

Gillian saw it. The Jophur configuration was shifting. The bright red disk seemed to shimmer for a moment. Its 'tail' of tiny crimson pinpoints, which had been bunching ever closer to the mother ship, now flexed and began to float away.

'It appears the enemy has jettisoned all the decoys they captured. I can only conclude that they figured out how to scan them quickly and eliminate dross ships from consideration. The decoys will now drift independently toward Izmunuti, while the battleship, free of drag, will catch up with us much faster.'

Gillian's hopes, which had lifted when the psi-wave came, now sank lower than ever.

'We'd better get ready for our last stand,' she said in a low voice.

From the dolphins there was an utter absence of sonar clicks, as if none of them wanted to reify the moment, to make it real by reading it in sound.

'Wait-t a minute,' Kaa announced. 'The Jophur's decelerating! Coming about to retrieve the jettisoned string!'

'But ... ' Gillian blinked. 'Could they have dropped it by accident?'

The Niss hologram whirled, then accepted the possibility with an abstract nod.

'A hypothesis presents itself. The psi-wave we detected was far too weak to have any effect on a war cruiser ... unless it was direct-causative.'

'Explain.'

'It might have served as a trigger that – either by accident or design – precipitated the release of potentialities already in place ... say, aboard the Jophur ship.'

'In other words, the waves might have affected them after all. Maybe it set off events that disrupted—'

'*Indeed. If this caused the Jophur to lose their control over their string of capture boxes, they would certainly go back and retrieve them, even at the cost of some delay. Because they would suspect the string's release was the intended purpose of the psi-wave.*'

'In other words, they'll be even more eager to check every box. Hmm.'

Gillian pondered, then asked:

'Has their intercept time been delayed much?'

Kaa thrashed his flukes.

'A fair amount. Not-t enough, however. We'll make it to the Izmunuti corona, but the enemy will be close enough to follow easily with detectorsss. The plasma won't make any a-ppreciable difference.'

Gillian nodded. 'Well, things are a little better. And a trick or two to make the odds better still.'

The dolphins snickered knowingly and went back to work, emanating confident clicks. Gillian's last remark was exactly the sort of thing *Tom* would have said in a situation like this.

In fact, though, Gillian did not know if her scheme was even worthy of the name.

SARA

They said that a psi-wave had come from Jijo, but Sara didn't feel a thing.

Not surprising. Of Melina's three children, it always seemed that Dwer had some fey sensitivity, while she, the logical one, possessed none. Till recently, Sara had little interest in such matters.

But then she wondered. *Might this be what Purofsky said we should look out for?*

Sitting at the stateroom's worktable, Sara addressed the portable computer.

'About that psi-wave – do we have a fix on its hypervelocity?'

'*Only a rough estimate. It traveled at approximately two mictaars per midura.*'

Sara tried to work out the timing in her head, translating it in terms she knew better, such as light-years. Then she realized the machine could do it for her graphically.

'Show me.'

A holo took shape, portraying her homeworld as a blue dot in the lower left quadrant. *Streaker* was a yellow glimmer to the upper right, accompanied by other members of decoy swarm number two. Meanwhile a crimson convoy – the Jophur ship and its reclaimed captives – resumed hot pursuit.

The computer put down an overlay, depicting a crosshatching of lines that Sara knew to be wave vectors in level-zero hyperspace. The math was simple enough, but it took her some time to figure out the rich, three-dimensional representation. Then she whistled.

'That's not inverse square. It's not even one-over-R. It was directional!'

'A well-conserved, directional wave packet, resonating on the first, third, and eighth bands of—'

The computer lapsed into psi-jargon that Sara could not follow. For her, it was enough to see that the packet was aimed. Its peak had passed right over both *Streaker* and its pursuer.

The coincidence beggared belief. It meant that some great power on Jijo had known precisely where both ships were, and—

Sara stopped herself.

Don't leap to the first conclusion that comes to mind. What if we weren't the beam's objective at all?

What if we just happened to be along its path, between Jijo and ...

She leaped to her feet.

'Show me Izmunuti and the transfer point!'

The display changed scale, expanding until *Streaker* was shown just over halfway to the supposed safety of the fiery red giant.

And beyond it, a folded place. A twist in reality's fabric. A spot where you go, if you want to suddenly be very far away.

Although computer graphics were needed to make it out clearly, the transfer point was no invisible nonentity. Izmunuti *bulged* in its direction, sending ocher streamers toward the dimple in space.

'When will the psi-wave reach Izmunuti?'

'It has already arrived.'

Sara swallowed hard.

'Then show me estimated ...' She dredged memory for words she had read, but seldom used. 'Show me likely hyperdeflection curves, as the psi-wave hits the red giant. Emphasize meta-stable regions of ... um, inverted energy storage, with potential for ... uh, stimulated emission on those *bands* you were talking about.'

Sara's face flickered as manicolored lines and curves reflected off her forehead and cheekbones.

Her eyes widened, briefly showing white all the way around the irises. She mouthed a single word, without managing to form a voice.

Then Sara clutched for a nearby pad of paper – no better than the premium stock her own father produced – and scrawled down two lines of coordinates.

Gillian Baskin answered her urgent call, though the older woman looked harassed and a little irked.

'Sage Koolhan, I really don't have time—'

'Oh yes you do,' Sara told her sternly. 'Meet me in your office in forty duras. You are definitely gonna want to hear this!'

RETY

A young woman sat in a locked room, all alone in her universe, until someone knocked.

In fact she was not entirely alone – yee was with her. Moreover, the knock wasn't at the door, but rapped loudly on the window below her feet. Still, the element of eerie surprise was there. Rety jumped back, scurrying away from the sound, which grew louder with each hammerlike stroke.

'*it comes from over here!*' yee wailed, pointing with his long neck.

Rety saw at once the pane he meant. A silhouetted figure squatted below the window, backlit by the golden haze surrounding her useless ship. The figure was distorted, distended, with a grossly bulbous head. An arm turned, holding a blunt object, and swung forward, striking the crystal once again.

This time, tiny cracks spread from the point of impact.

'*enemy foe coming in!*'

Visions of space monsters filled Rety, but not with fear. She wasn't about to give up her domain to some invader – Jophur, robot, or whatever.

Another blow struck the same spot. Clearly it would take several more for the assailant to seriously damage the window. Emboldened to see what she was up against, Rety scooted toward the shadowy figure. After the next impact, she pressed close to the glass and peered outside.

Things were blurry at first. Then the creature seemed to notice her presence and leaned forward as well. Rety glimpsed what looked like a billowing dome of clear fabric. A makeshift helmet, she realized.

And within that protective bubble ...

'Yah!' she cried out, twitching reflexively away, more set back than if she'd seen a monster or ghost.

When Rety went back for another look, the figure on the other side started making frantic gestures, pointing toward the side of the ship.

'Oh, yeah,' she sighed. 'I did lock the airlock, didn't I?'

Rety nodded vigorously so the visitor could see, and started scurrying along the canted walls to reach the jimmied door. Rety removed the pry bar she had slipped in place, to keep Chuchki from returning.

The airlock cycled slowly, giving Rety time to wonder if her eyes had deceived her. Perhaps this was just a ruse from some mind-reading creature, seeking to gain entrance by sifting her brain for images from her past . . .

The inner door opened at last, and Dwer Koolhan tumbled through, tearing at the balloonlike covering he had been using as a crude life-support system. His face was rather blue by the time Rety helped him cut the taped fastenings, scavenged from material found on other decoy vessels during his long journey down the captive string. The young hunter gasped deep breaths while Rety stepped back and stared. Finally, he recovered enough to roll aside, lifting his head to meet her unbelieving gaze.

'I . . . should've known . . . it'd be you,' Dwer murmured in a resigned voice.

At the exact same moment, Rety muttered:

'Ifni! Ain't I ever gonna be rid o'you?'

EWASX

We must weigh trade-offs and options.

As Izmunuti commences to roil with an atmospheric storm, our tactics stack declares that we have lost valuable time.

Three target swarms flee ahead of our majestic *Polkjhy*.

The first will enter the storm just as we catch up.

We will reach the second as it passes through maximum hyperbolic momentum change.

And the third?

It will make it to the transfer point, with time enough to jump into the next higher level of hyperspace.

The sabotage attack on our control room has thus created serious problems, out of proportion to the damage done to our Captain-Leader, whose incapacity should not last long. Meanwhile, however, tactics has come up with a plan.

WE SHALL JETTISON THE CAPTURE BOXES DRAGGING AT OUR WAKE.

They are now on course for Izmunuti. If the prey ship lies within one of the glowing traps, it must reveal itself soon, or risk immolation.

THUS FREED, OUR *POLKJHY* WILL ACCELERATE DIRECTLY FOR THE TRANSFER POINT!

In this manner we will be able to interpose ourselves between the prey ship and its escape path. There will be some backlash from such rapid maneuvering, but the result should be an end to all hope for the Earthlings, *whichever* swarm they are hiding in. Their subsequent activities should enable us to detect which ship is sapient-guided and which operate on mere automatic programs.

Hunt scents fill our bridge, eagerness for the approaching conclusion to this great endeavor. It will be most gratifying for *Polkjhy* to achieve conquest of the Earthlings without having to call for help from the great clan. To succeed where battle fleets have failed – this will be glorious!

BUT NOW TO OUR ASSIGNED TASK, MY RINGS!

There are vermin loose on our fine dreadnought. Our damaged/soot-stained bridge was dishonored in full view by the librarian/watcher.

The vermin must be found. I/we am the one called upon as qualified to give chase, by virtue of our/My experience with human types.

Our first recourse, My rings?

Collect the remaining human prisoner!

The one called Rann.

He will help us find his former colleagues. He is already so inclined.

REJOICE, MY RINGS!

In this way we will prove useful, avoiding disassembly. If successful, this master torus has been promised a fine reward.

Quiver in anticipation, My rings! As *Polkjhy* chases certain victory through space, we pursue another hunt within.

EMERSON

Engines sing to him in a language he still understands.

When he works the calibrators, it seems almost as if he were his old self. Master of machines. Boy mechanic. The man who makes starships fly.

Then something reminds him. A written status report flashes, or a robot voice runs down a list of parameters. Prity can't interpret for him – sign language cannot translate subtleties of hyperwave transformatics.

Emerson's crew mates respect his efforts. They are pleased and surprised by his ability to help.

But, he now realizes, they are also humoring him.

Things will never be the same.

His long shift ends. Suessi orders him to take a break. So he goes up to the hold with Prity and visits the glavers, sensing something in common with the simple creatures, nearly as speechless as himself.

Alvin and Huck trade insults and witticisms in Anglic, his own native tongue, but he can only follow the general tone of camaraderie. They are kind, but here, too, Emerson finds no solace.

He searches for Sara, and finds her at last in the plotting room, surrounded by Gillian's staff. Fiery representations of a bloated giant star fill the center of the room, with varied orbits plotted through its flaming shell. Some paths slip close, using slingshot arcs to fling *Streaker* toward the transfer point – a twisted funnel in space. The tactics look challenging, even to a pilot like Kaa. Yet that approach is the obvious one.

No doubt the enemy expects just such a maneuver.

Other orbits make no sense, skirting the red giant to strike *away* from the bolt-hole. Farther from the only way to exit this dangerous part of a forbidden galaxy.

Letting the enemy reach the transfer point first would seem suicidal.

On the other hand, at the rate the Jophur battleship is catching up, *Streaker* will have little choice. Perhaps Sara and Gillian plan to head for deep space and hide amid the seared rocks that were planets, before Izmunuti burgeoned and consumed its children.

Emerson watches Sara, immersed in work. No one seems to note the presumption – of a Jijo-born savage directing the endeavors of starfaring sophisticates. At times like these, an idea can count for much more than experience.

The incongruity makes him smile at last, recovering some of his good mood. His accustomed optimism.

After all, what have the odds ever mattered before?

There is an observation dome tucked behind the bridge, accessible only by a twisty ladder with rungs set much too close together. The small room is a leftover from whatever race once owned *Streaker*, before Earthclan bought the hull, converting it for dolphin use. It takes some agility to worm into the odd-shaped cubby. Emerson's secret place.

At one end, a thick bubble of adamantine quartz provides a view outside, where the starry vault is bare, unimpeded, nearly surrounding him with everlasting night. Izmunuti is occulted by the ship's bow, but vast sweeps of the local spiral arm sparkle like diamonds. Globular clusters are like diatoms, phosphorescent on a moonlit sea. Since waking on Jijo, he never expected to experience this again. The naked confrontation. Mind and universe.

It pours through him, a surfeit of beauty. Too much. Agonizing.

Of course, Emerson spent half a year learning about all kinds of pain, until it became a sort of friend. His ally at dislodging memories. And as he ponders stellar fire, it happens again.

He recalls the stench, just after he crashed into Jijo, clothes aflame, quenching the blaze in murky water, dimly aware of having recently fought a battle. A diversion – a sacrifice to win escape for his friends.

But that wasn't the truth.

It was a planted cover story.

Actually, the Old Ones took him from that old Thennanin fighter. They probed and palped him. Over a period of days, weeks, they reamed his mind, then shoved him in a little capsule. A tube that *squeezed* . . .

Emerson moans, recalling how that passage ended in a blazing plummet down to Jijo and the horrid swamp where Sara found him.

He envisions the Old Ones. Or one faction of them. Cold eyes. Hard voices, commanding him to forget. To forget . . . and yet, sentenced to live.

I . . . know . . . your . . . lie . . .

The command fights back. For a moment, the pain is greater than he ever knew.

Pain that is elemental, like the black vacuum surrounding him.

Like sleeting cosmic rays.

Like all the myriad quantum layers propping up each quark and every lepton in his shaken frame.

Through it all, his eyes can barely focus, squinting past distilled anguish, turning countless stars into slanting needles.

But then out of those jagged motes there comes a shape. Weaving, thrashing . . . zigging, zagging.

Swimming, he now realizes. Pushing toward him, as if upstream, against the swell of a strong tide. A shape from memory, but instead of bringing more woe, this recollection sweeps all agony before it. Pushed by stalwart flukes, a soothing current washes over him.

A dolphin's face swims into focus.

Captain . . .

. . . Creideiki . . .

It is a scarred face, deeply wounded behind the left eye. A wound too much like Emerson's to be coincidence.

The explanation encircles him in sound.

> * Crooks and foul liars,
> > * Lacking imagination,
> > > * Cruelly steal ideas! *

Emerson comprehends the Trinary haiku at once. The Old Ones must have read his mind somehow and learned of Creideiki's injury. It seemed to fit their needs, so they copied it in their captive human. What better way to release him, yet be certain he would tell no tales?

But that still left open the question of *why*? Why release him at all, if it meant consignment to a twilight existence?

What motive could they have?

All . . . in . . . good . . . time . . .

The phrase brings a smile, for he grasps it in a way he might never have before.

A simple, purified meaning.

. . . good . . . time . . .

Emerson looks back across the galaxies, now cleansed free of pain. Pain he now recognizes to have been illusion, all along. The product of an exaggerated sense of self-importance that his enemies used against him.

In fact, the ocean of night is too vast, too busy to be involved in his agony. An evolving universe can hardly be bothered with the problems of a single individual, a member of one of the lower orders of sapient life.

And why should it?

What a privilege it is, to exist at all! On the great balance sheet, he owes the cosmos everything, and it owes him nothing.

Emerson manages to share a final moment of communion with his captain and comrade – not caring whether the grinning dolphin is a ghost, a mirage, or some miraculous true image. Knowing only that Creideiki's lesson is true.

There is no setback – no wound or blow of cruel fate – that cannot be turned into a song.

For an instant, Emerson can sense music in every ray of starlight.

* When the winter's
  Typhoon pounds you,
* Onto sand grains,
  Sharp and gleaming,

* And creation
  All-conspiring,
* Breaks you on a
  Time of Changes,

* At the moment
  When breath falters,
* And your lifeblood
  Pours out streaming,

* Cast around that
  Bright reef, dear friend,
* For a gift to
  Grant another,

* For some way to
  Repay forward,
* All the favors
  You were given.

* For in good time
  * Prospects glitter
    * Far along Infinity's Shore. *

ACKNOWLEDGMENTS

The author would express thanks to Stefan Jones, Steinn Sigurdsson, Professor Steven Potts, Greg Smith, Matthew Johnson, Kevin Conod, Anita Gould, Paul Rothemund, Richard Mason, Gerrit Kirkwood, Ruben Krasnopolsky, Damien Sullivan, Will Smit, Grant Swenson, Roian Egnor, Joy Crisp, Jason M. Robertson, Micah Altman, Jeffrey Slostad, Joseph Miller, and Gregory Benford, for their comments and observations on early drafts of *Infinity's Shore*. Kevin Lenagh provided the map of Jijo. Robert Qualkinbush collated the glossary of terms. The novel profited from insight and helpful assistance from my agent, Ralph Vicinanza, and Tom Dupree of Bantam Books. As usual, this tale would have been a far poorer thing without the wise and very human input of my wife, Dr. Cheryl Brigham. Blame for any excess or extravagance rests on me alone.

HEAVEN'S REACH

To
Terren Jacob Brin, our unlimited explorer
and crowning work in our trilogy

I

THE FIVE GALAXIES

What emblems grace the fine prows of our fast ships?

How many spirals swirl on the bow of each great vessel, turning round and round, symbolizing our connections? How many are the links that form our union?

ONE spiral represents the fallow worlds, slowly brewing, steeping, stewing — where life starts its long, hard climb.

Struggling out of that fecundity, new races emerge, ripe for Uplift.

TWO is for starfaring culture, streaking madly in our fast ships, first as clients, then as patrons, vigorously chasing our young interests — trading, fighting, and debating—

Straining upward, till we hear the call of beckoning tides.

THREE portrays the Old Ones, graceful and serene, who forsake starships to embrace a life of contemplation. Tired of manic rushing. Cloistering for self-improvement.

They prepare to face the Great Harrower.

FOUR depicts the High Transcendents, too majestic for us to perceive. But they exist!

Making plans that encompass all levels of space, and all times.

FIVE is for the galaxies — great whirls of shining light — our islands in a sterile cosmos, surrounded by enigmatic silence. On and on they spin, nurturing all life's many orders, linked perpetually, everlasting.

Or so we are assured …

Alarms sing a variety of melodies.

Some shriek for attention, yanking you awake from repose. Others send your veins throbbing with adrenaline. Aboard any space vessel there are sirens and wails that portend collision, vacuum leaks, or myriad other kinds of impending death.

But the alarm tugging at Harry Harms wasn't like that. Its creepy ratchet scraped lightly along the nerves.

'No rush,' the soft buzzer seemed to murmur. *'I can wait.*

'But don't even think about going back to sleep.'

Harry rolled over to squint blearily at the console next to his pillow. Glowing symbols beckoned meaningfully. But the parts of his brain that handled reading weren't perfectly designed. They took a while to warm up.

'Guh . . .' he commented. 'Wuh?'

Drowsiness clung to his body, still exhausted after another long, solitary watch. How many duras had passed since he had tumbled into the bunk, vowing to quit his commission when this tour of duty ended?

Sleep had come swiftly, but not restfully. Dreams always filled Harry's slumber, here in E Space.

In fact, dreaming was part of the job.

In REM state, Harry often revisited the steppes of Horst, where a dusty horizon had been his constant background in childhood. A forlorn world, where ponderous dark clouds loomed and flickered, yet held tightly to their moisture, sharing little with the parched ground. He usually woke from such visions with a desiccated mouth, desperate for water.

Other dreams featured *Earth* – jangling city-planet, brimming with tall humans – its skyscrapers and lush greenery stamped in memory by one brief visit, ages ago, in another life.

Then there were nightmares about ships – great battlecraft and moonlike invasion arks – glistening by starlight or cloaked in the dark glow of their terrible fields. Wraithlike frigates, looming more eerie and terrifying than real life.

Those were the more *normal* dream images to come creeping in, whenever his mind had room between far stranger apparitions. For the most part, Harry's night thoughts were filled with spinning, dizzying *allaphors*, which billowed and muttered in the queer half-logic of

E Space. Even his shielded quarters weren't impervious to tendrils of counterreality, penetrating the bulkheads, groping through his sleep. No wonder he woke disoriented, shaken by the grating alarm.

Harry stared at the glowing letters – each twisting like some manic, living hieroglyph, gesticulating in the ideogrammatic syntax of Galactic Language Number Seven. Concentrating, he translated the message into the Anglic of his inner thoughts.

'Great,' Harry commented in a dry voice.

Apparently, the patrol vessel had come aground again.

'Oh, that's just fine.'

The buzzer increased its tempo. Pushing out of bed, Harry landed barefoot on the chill deck plates, shivering.

'And to think ... they tell me I got an *aptitude* for this kind of work.'

In other words, you had to be at least partway crazy to be suited for his job.

Shaking lethargy, he clambered up a ladder to the observing platform just above his quarters – a hexagonal chamber, ten meters across, with a control panel in the center. Groping toward the alarm cutoff, Harry somehow managed not to trigger any armaments, or purge the station's atmosphere into E Space, before slapping the right switch. The maddening noise abruptly ceased.

'Ah ...' he sighed, and almost fell asleep again right there, standing behind the padded command chair.

But then ... if sleep did come, he might start dreaming again.

I never understood Hamlet *till they assigned me here. Now I figure, Shakespeare must've glimpsed E Space before writing that 'to be or not to be' stuff.*

... perchance to dream ...

Yup, ol' Willie must've known there's worse things than death.

Scratching his belly, Harry scanned the status board. No red lights burned. The station appeared functional. No major reality leaks were evident. With a sigh, he moved around to perch on the seat.

'Monitor mode. Report station status.'

The holo display lit up, projecting a floating blue **M**, sans serif. A melodious voice emanated from the slowly revolving letter.

'*Monitor mode. Station integrity is nominal. An alarm has been acknowledged by station superintendent Harry Harms at 4:48:52 internal subjective estimate time ...*'

'*I'm* Harry Harms. Why don't you tell me something I don't know, like what the alarm's *for*, you shaggy excuse for a baldie's toup ... ah ... ah ...'

A sneeze tore through Harry's curse. He wiped his eyes with the back of a hirsute wrist.

'The alarm denoted an interruption in our patrol circuit of E Level hyperspace,' the monitor continued, unperturbed. *'The station has apparently become mired in an anomaly region.'*

'You mean we're grounded on a reef. I already knew that much. But what *kind* of ...' he muttered. 'Oh, never mind. I'll go see for myself.'

Harry ambled over to a set of vertical louvered blinds – one of six banks that rimmed the hexagonal chamber – and slipped a fingertip between two of the slats, prying them apart to make a narrow slit opening. He hesitated, then brought one eye forward to peer outside.

The station appeared to be *shaped* in its standard format, at least. Not like a whale, or jellyfish, or amorphous blob, thank Ifni. Sometimes this continuum had effects on physical objects that were gruesomely bizarre, or even fatal.

On this occasion the control chamber still perched like a glass cupola atop an oblate white spheroid, commanding a 360-degree view of a vast metaphorical realm – a dubious, dangerous, but seldom monotonous domain.

Jagged black mountains bobbed in the distance, like ebony icebergs, majestically traversing what resembled an endless sea of purple grass. The 'sky' was a red-blue shade that could only be seen on E Level. It had holes in it.

So far so good.

Harry spread the slats wider to take in the foreground, and blinked in surprise at what he saw. The station rested on a glistening, slick brown surface. Spread across this expanse, for what might be a kilometer in all directions, lay a thick scattering of giant yellow starfish!

At least that was his first impression. Harry rushed to another bank of curtains and peeked again. More 'starfish' lay on that side as well, dispersed randomly, but thickly enough to show no easy route past.

'Damn.' From experience he knew it would be useless to try *flying over* the things. If they represented two-dimensional obstacles, they must be overcome in a two-dimensional way. That was how allaphorical logic worked in this zone of E Space.

Harry went back to the control board and touched a button. All the blinds retracted, revealing an abrupt panoramic view. Mountains and purple grass in the distance. Brown slickness closer in.

And yes, the station was completely surrounded by starfish. Yellow starfish everywhere.

'Pfeh.' Harry shivered. Most of the jaundiced monsters had six arms, though some had five or seven. They didn't appear to be moving. That, at least, was a relief. Harry hated ambulatory allaphors.

'Pilot mode!' he commanded.

With a faint crackling, the floating helvetica **M** was replaced by a jaunty, cursive *P*.

'Aye aye, o' Person-Commander. Where to now, Henry?'

'Name's Harry,' he grunted. The perky tones used by pilot mode might have been cheery and friendly in Anglic, but they came across as just plain silly in Galactic Seven. Yet the only available alternative meant substituting a voice chip programmed in whistle-clicking GalTwo. A Gubru dialect, even. He wasn't desperate enough to try that yet.

'Prepare to ease us along a perceived-flat course trajectory of two forty degrees, ship centered,' he told the program. 'Dead slow.'

'Whatever you say, Boss-Sentient. Adapting interface parameters now.'

Harry went back to the window, watching the station *grow* four huge wheels, bearing giant balloon tires with thick treads. Soon they began to turn. A squeaky whine, like rubbing your hand on a soapy countertop, penetrated the thick crystal panes.

As he had feared, the tires found little traction on the slick brown surface. Still, he held back from overruling the pilot's choice of countermeasures. Better see what happened first.

Momentum built gradually. The station approached the nearest yellow starfish.

Doubt spread in Harry's mind.

'Maybe I should try looking this up first. They might have the image listed somewhere.'

Once upon a time, back when he was inducted as Earth's first volunteer-recruit in the Navigation Institute survey department – full of tape-training and idealism – he used to consult the records every time E Space threw another weird symbolism at him. After all, the Galactic civilization of oxygen-breathing races had been exploring, cataloging, and surveying this bizarre continuum for half a billion years. The amount of information contained in even his own tiny shipboard Library unit exceeded the sum of all human knowledge before contact was made with extraterrestrials.

An impressive store ... and as it turned out, nearly useless. Maybe he wasn't very good at negotiating with the Library's reference persona. Or perhaps the problem came from being born of Earth-simian stock. Anyway, he soon took to trusting his own instincts during missions to E Space.

Alas, that approach had one drawback. *You have only yourself to blame when things blow up in your face.*

Harry noticed he was slouching. He straightened and brought his hands together to prevent scratching. But nervous energy had to express itself, so he tugged on his thumbs, instead. A Tymbrimi he knew had once remarked that many of Harry's species had that habit, perhaps a symptom from the long, hard process of Uplift.

The forward tires reached the first starfish. There was no way around the things. No choice but to try climbing over them.

Harry held his breath as contact was made. But touching drew no reaction. The obstacle just lay there, six long, flat strips of brown-flecked yellow, splayed from a nubby central hump. The first set of tires skidded, and the station rode up the yellow strip, pushed by the back wheels.

The station canted slightly. Harry rumbled anxiously in his chest, trying to tease loose a tickling thread of recognition. Maybe 'starfish' wasn't the best analogy for these things. They looked familiar though.

The angle increased. A troubled whine came from the spinning rear wheels until they, too, reached the yellow.

In a shock of recognition, Harry shouted – 'No! Reverse! They're *ban—*'

Too late. The back tires whined as slippery yellow strips flew out from under the platform, sending it flipping in a sudden release of traction. Harry tumbled, struck the ceiling, then slid across the far wall, shouting as the scout platform rolled, skidded, and rolled again . . . until it dropped with a final, bone-jarring thud. Fetching up against a bulkhead, Harry clutched a wall rail with his toes until the jouncing finally stopped.

'Oh . . . my head . . .' he moaned, picking himself up.

At least things had settled right side up. He shuffled back to the console in a crouch and read the main display. The station had suffered little damage, thank Ifni. But Harry must have put off housecleaning chores too long, for dust balls now coated his fur from head to toe. He slapped them off, raising clouds and triggering violent sneezes.

The shutters had closed automatically the instant things went crazy, protecting his eyes against potentially dangerous allaphors.

He commanded gruffly, 'Open blinds!' Perhaps the violent action had triggered a local phase change, causing all the nasty obstacles to vanish. It had happened before.

No such luck, he realized as the louvers slid into pillars between the wide viewing panes. Outside, the general scenery had not altered noticeably. The same reddish blue, Swiss cheese sky rolled over a mauve pampas, with black mountains bobbing biliously in the distance. And a slick mesa still had his scoutship mired, hemmed on all sides by yellow, multiarmed shapes.

'Banana peels,' he muttered. 'Goddamn *banana peels.*'

One reason why these stations were manned by only one observer ... allaphors tended to get even weirder with more than one mind perceiving them at the same time. The 'objects' he saw were images his own mind pasted over a reality that no living brain could readily fathom. A reality that mutated and transformed under influence *by* his thoughts and perceptions.

All that was fine, in theory. He ought to be used to it by now. But what bothered Harry in particular about the banana allaphor was that it seemed gratuitously personal. Like others of his kind, Harry hated being trapped by stereotypes.

He sighed, scratching his side. 'Are all systems stable?'

'Everything is stable, Taskmaster-Commander Harold,' the pilot replied. *'We are stuck for the moment, but we appear to be safe.'*

He considered the vast open expanse beyond the plateau. Actually, visibility was excellent from here. The holes in the sky, especially, were all clear and unobstructed. A thought occurred to him.

'Say, do we really have to move on right away? We can observe all the assigned transit routes from this very spot, until our cruise clock runs out, no?'

'That appears to be correct. For the moment, no illicit traffic can get by our watch area undetected.'

'Hmmph. Well then ... ' He yawned. 'I guess I'll just go back to bed! I have a feelin' I'm gonna need my wits to get outta this one.'

'Very well. Good night, Employer-Observer Harms. Pleasant dreams.'

'Fat chance o' that,' he muttered in Anglic as he left the observation deck. 'And close the friggin' blinds! Do I have to think of everything around here? Don't answer that! Just ... never mind.'

Even closed, the louvers would not prevent all leakage. Flickering archetypes slipped between the slats, as if eager to latch into his mind during REM state, tapping his dreams like little parasites.

It could not be helped. When Harry got his first promotion to E Space, the local head of patrollers for the Navigation Institute told him that susceptibility to allaphoric images was a vital part of the job. Waving a slender, multijointed arm, that Galactic official confessed his surprise, in Nahalli-accented GalSix, at Harry's qualifications.

'Skeptical we were, when first told that your race might have traits useful to us.

'Repudiating our doubts, this you have since achieved, Observer Harms.

'To full status, we now advance you. First of your kind to be so honored.

Harry sighed as he threw himself under the covers again, tempted by the sweet stupidity of self-pity.

Some honor! He snorted dubiously.

Still, he couldn't honestly complain. He had been warned. And this wasn't Horst. At least he had escaped the dry, monotonous wastes.

Anyway, only the mad lived for long under illusions that the cosmos was meant for their convenience.

There were a multitude of conflicting stories about whoever designed this crazy universe, so many billions of years ago. But even before he ever considered dedicating his life to Institute work – or heard of E Space – Harry had reached one conclusion about metatheology.

For all His power and glory, the Creator must not have been a very sensible person.

At least, not as sensible as a neo-chimpanzee.

SARA

There is a word-glyph.

It names a locale where three states of matter coincide – two that are fluid, swirling past a third that is adamant as coral.

A kind of froth can form in such a place. Dangerous, deceptive foam, beaten to a head by fate-filled tides.

No one enters such a turmoil voluntarily.

But sometimes a force called desperation *drives prudent sailors to set course for ripping shoals.*

A slender shape plummets through the outer fringes of a mammoth star. Caterpillar-ribbed, with rows of talonlike protrusions that bite into spacetime, the vessel claws its way urgently against a bitter gale.

Diffuse flames lick the scarred hull of ancient cerametal, adding new layers to a strange soot coating. Tendrils of plasma fire seek entry, thwarted (so far) by wavering fields.

In time, though, the heat will find its way through.

Midway along the vessel's girth, a narrow wheel turns, like a wedding band that twists around a nervous finger. Rows of windows pass

*by as the slim ring rotates. Unlit from within, most of the dim panes
only reflect stellar fire.*

*Then, rolling into view, a single rectangle shines with artificial
color.*

*A pane for viewing in two directions. A universe without, and
within.*

Contemplating the maelstrom, Sara mused aloud.

'My criminal ancestors took their sneakship through this same
inferno on their way to Jijo ... covering their tracks under the
breath of Great Izmunuti.'

Pondering the forces at work just a handbreadth away, she
brushed her fingertips against a crystal surface that kept actinic
heat from crossing the narrow gap. One part of her – book-weaned
and tutored in mathematics – could grasp the physics of a star
whose radius was bigger than her homeworld's yearly orbit. A red
giant, in its turgid final stage, boiling a stew of nuclear-cooked
atoms toward black space.

Abstract knowledge was fine. But Sara's spine also trembled with
a superstitious shiver, spawned by her upbringing as a savage
sooner on a barbarian world. The Earthship *Streaker* might be hapless prey – desperately fleeing a titanic hunter many times its size –
but this dolphin-crewed vessel still struck Sara as godlike and awesome, carrying more mass than all the wooden dwellings of the
Slope. In her wildest dreams, dwelling in a treehouse next to a
groaning water mill, she had never imagined that destiny might
take her on such a ride, swooping through the fringes of a hellish
star.

Especially Izmunuti, whose very name was fearsome. To the Six
Races, huddling in secret terror on Jijo, it stood for the downward
path. A door that swung just one way, toward exile.

For two thousand years, emigrants had slinked past the giant
star to find shelter on Jijo. First the wheeled g'Kek race, frantically
evading genocide. Then came traekis – gentle stacks of waxy rings
who were fleeing their own tyrannical cousins – followed by
qheuens, hoons, urs, and humans, all settling in a narrow realm
between the Rimmer Mountains and a surf-stained shore. Each
wave of new arrivals abandoned their starships, computers, and
other high-tech implements, sending every god-machine down to
the sea, tumbling into Jijo's deep midden of forgetfulness. Breaking
with their past, all six clans of former sky lords settled down to
rustic lives, renouncing the sky forever.

Until the Civilization of the Five Galaxies finally stumbled on the
commonwealth of outcasts.

The day had to come, sooner or later; the Sacred Scrolls had said so. No band of trespassers could stay hidden perpetually. Not in a cosmos that had been cataloged for over a billion years, where planets such as Jijo were routinely declared fallow, set aside for rest and restoration. Still, the sages of the Commons of Jijo had hoped for more time.

Time for the exile races to prepare. To purify themselves. To seek redemption. To forget the galactic terrors that made them outcasts in the first place.

The Scrolls foresaw that august magistrates from the Galactic Migration Institute would alight to judge the descendants of trespassers. But instead, the starcraft that pierced Jijo's veil this fateful year carried several types of *outlaws*. First gene raiders, then murderous opportunists, and finally a band of Earthling refugees even more ill-fated than Sara's hapless ancestors.

I used to dream of riding a starship, she thought, pondering the plasma storm outside. *But no fantasy was ever like this – leaving behind my world, my teachers, my father and brothers – fleeing with dolphins through a fiery night, chased by a battleship full of angry Jophur.*

Fishlike cousins of humans, pursued through space by egotistical cousins of traeki.

The coincidence beggared Sara's imagination.

Anglic words broke through her musing, in a voice that Sara always found vexingly sardonic.

'I have finished calculating the hyperspatial tensor, oh, Sage.

'It appears you were right in your earlier estimate. The mysterious beam that emanated from Jijo a while ago did more than cause disruptions in this giant star. It also triggered a state-change in a fossil dimension-nexus that lay dormant just half a mictaar away.'

Sara mentally translated into terms she was used to, from the archaic texts that had schooled her.

Half a mictaar. In flat space, that would come to roughly a twentieth of a light-year.

Very close, indeed.

'So, the beam reactivated an old transfer point.' She nodded. 'I knew it.'

'Your foresight would be more impressive if I understood your methods. Humans are noted for making lucky guesses.'

Sara turned away from the fiery spectacle outside. The office they had given her seemed like a palace, roomier than the reception hall in a qheuen rookery, with lavish fixtures she had only seen described in books two centuries out of date. This suite once belonged to a man named Ignacio Metz, an expert in the genetic uplifting of dolphins – killed during one of *Streaker's* previous dire encounters – a true scientist, not a primitive with academic pretensions, like Sara.

And yet, here she was – fearful, intimidated ... and yet proud in a strange way, to be the first Jijoan in centuries who returned to space.

From the desk console, a twisted blue blob drifted closer – a languid, undulating shape she found as insolent as the voice it emitted.

'Your so-called wolfling mathematics hardly seem up to the task of predicting such profound effects on the continuum. Why not just admit that you had a hunch?'

Sara bit her lip. She would not give the Niss Machine the satisfaction of a hot response.

'Show me the tensor,' she ordered tersely. 'And a chart ... a *graphic* ... that includes all three gravity wells.'

The billowing holographic creature managed to imply sarcasm with an obedient bow.

'As you wish.'

A cubic display, two meters on a side, lit up before Sara, far more vivid than the flat, unmoving diagrams-on-paper she had grown up with.

A glowing mass roiled in the center, representing Izmunuti, a fireball radiating the color of wrath. Tendrils of its engorged corona waved like Medusan hair, reaching beyond the limits of any normal solar system. But those lacy filaments were fast being drowned under a new disturbance. During the last few miduras, something had stirred the star to an abnormal fit of rage. Abrupt cyclonic storms began throwing up gouts of dense plasma, tornadolike funnels, rushing far into space.

And we're going to pass through some of the worst of it, she thought.

How strange that all this violent upheaval might have originated in a boulder of psi-active stone, back home on primitive Jijo. Yet she felt sure it all was triggered somehow by the Holy Egg.

Already half-immersed in this commotion, a green pinpoint was depicted plunging toward Izmunuti at frantic speed, aimed at a glancing near-passage, its hyperbolic orbit marked by a line that bent sharply around the giant star. In one direction, that slim trace led all the way back to Jijo, where *Streaker's* escape attempt had begun two exhausting days earlier, breaking for liberty amid a crowd of ancient derelicts – ocean-bottom junk piles reactivated for one last, glorious, screaming run through space.

One by one, those decoys had failed, or dropped out, or were snared by the enemy's clever capture-boxes, until only *Streaker* remained, plummeting for the brief shelter of stormy Izmunuti.

As for the *forward* direction ... Instrument readings sent by the bridge crew helped the Niss Machine calculate their likely heading. Apparently, Gillian Baskin had ordered a course change, taking advantage of a gravitational slingshot around the star to fling *Streaker* toward galactic north and east.

Sara swallowed hard. The destination had originally been her idea. But as time passed, she grew less certain.

'The new t-point doesn't look very stable,' she commented, following the ship's planned trajectory to the top left corner of the holo unit, where a tight mesh of curling lines funneled through an empty-looking zone of interstellar space.

Reacting to her close regard, the display monitor enhanced that section. Rows of glowing symbols described the local hyperspatial matrix.

She had predicted this wonder – the reawakening of something old. Something marvelous. For a brief while, it had seemed like just the miracle they needed. A gift from the Holy Egg. An escape route from a terrible trap.

But on examining the analytical profiles, Sara concluded that the cosmos was not being all that helpful after all.

'There *are* connection tubes opening up to other spacetime locales. But they seem rather ... scanty.'

'*Well, what can you expect from a nexus that is only a few hours old? One that was only recently yanked from slumber by a force neither of us can grasp?*'

After a pause, the Niss unit continued. '*Most of the transfer threads leading away from this nexus are still on the order of a Planck width. Some promising routes do seem to be coalescing, and may be safely traversable by starship in a matter of weeks. Of course, that will be of little use to us.*'

Sara nodded. The pursuing Jophur battleship would hardly give *Streaker* that much time. Already the mighty *Polkjhy* had abandoned its string of captured decoys in order to focus all its attention on the real *Streaker*, keeping the Earthship bathed in long-range scanning rays.

'Then what does Gillian Baskin hope to accomplish by heading toward a useless ...'

She blinked, as realization lurched within her rib cage.

'Oh. I see.'

Sara stepped back, and the display resumed its normal scale. Two meters away, at the opposite corner, neat curves showed the spatial patterns of another transfer point. The familiar, reliably predictable one that every sneakship had used to reach Izmunuti during the last two millennia. The only quick way in or out of this entire region of Galaxy Four.

But not always. Once, when Jijo had been a center of commerce and civilization under the mighty Buyur, traffic used to flux through *two* hyperdimensional nexi. One of them shut down when Jijo went fallow, half a million years ago, coincidentally soon after the Buyur departed.

Sara and her mentor, Sage Purofsky, had nursed a suspicion. That shutdown was no accident.

'Then we concur,' said the Niss Machine. *'Gillian Baskin clearly intends to lead the Jophur into a suicidal trap.'*

Sara looked elsewhere in the big display, seeking the enemy. She found it several stellar radii behind Izmunuti, a yellow glow representing the hunter – a Jophur dreadnought whose crew coveted the Earthship and its secrets. Having abandoned the distraction of all the old dross ship decoys, the *Polkjhy* had been racing toward the regular t-point, confident of cutting off *Streaker*'s sole escape route.

Only now, the sudden reopening of another gateway must have flummoxed the giant sap-rings who commanded the great warship. The yellow trace turned sharply, as the *Polkjhy* frantically shed momentum, aiming to chase *Streaker* past Izmunuti's flames toward the new door in spacetime.

A door that's not ready for use, Sara thought. Surely the Jophur must also have instruments capable of reading probability flows. They must realize how dangerous it would be to plunge into a new-born transfer point.

Yet, could the *Polkjhy* commanders afford to dismiss it? *Streaker* was small, maneuverable, and had dolphin pilots, reputed to be among the best in all five galaxies.

And the Earthlings were desperate.

The Jophur have to assume we know something about this transfer point that they do not. From their point of view, it seems as if we called it into existence with a wave of our hands – or fins. If we plunge inside, it must be because we know a tube or thread we can latch on to and follow to safety.

They're obliged to give chase, or risk losing Streaker *forever.*

Sara nodded.

'Gillian and the dolphins ... they're sacrificing themselves, for Jijo.'

The tightly meshed Niss hologram appeared to shrug in agreement.

'It does seem the best choice out of a wretched set of options.

'Suppose we turn and fight? The only likely outcomes are capture or death, with your Jijoan civilization lost in the bargain. After extracting Streaker's secrets, the Jophur will report to their home clan, then take their time organizing a systematic program for Jijo, first annihilating every g'Kek, then turning the planet into their own private breeding colony, developing new types of humans, traekis, and hoons to suit their perverted needs.

'By forcing the Polkjhy to follow us into the new transfer point, Dr. Baskin makes it likely that no report will ever reach the Five Galaxies about your Six Races. Your fellow exiles may continue wallowing in sublime, planet-bound squalor for a while longer, chasing vague notions of redemption down the muddy generations.'

How very much like the Niss it was, turning a noble gesture into an excuse for insult. Sara shook her head. Gillian's plan was both grand and poignant.

It also meant Sara's own hours were numbered.

'What a waste,' the Niss sighed. 'This vessel and crew appear to have made the discovery of the age, and now it may be lost.'

Things had been so hectic since the rushed departure from Jijo that Sara was still unclear about the cause of all this ferment – what the Streaker crew had done to provoke such ire and pursuit by some of the great powers of the known universe.

'It began when Captain Creideiki took this ship poking through a seemingly unlikely place, looking for relics or anomalies that had been missed by the Great Library,' the artificial intelligence explained. 'It was a shallow globular cluster, lacking planets or singularities. Creideiki never told his reasons for choosing such a spot. But his hunch paid off when Streaker came upon a great fleet of derelict ships, drifting in splendid silence through open space. Samples and holos taken of this mystery armada seemed to hint at possible answers to our civilization's most ancient mystery.

'Of course our findings should have been shared openly by the institutes of the Civilization of Five Galaxies, in the name of all oxygen-breathing life. Immense credit would have come to your frail, impoverished Earthclan, as well as my Tymbrimi makers. But every other race and alliance might have shared as well, gaining new insight into the origins of our billion-year-old culture.

'Alas, several mighty coalitions interpreted Streaker's initial beamcast as fulfillment of dire prophecy. They felt the news presaged a fateful time of commotion and upheaval, in which a decisive advantage would go to anyone monopolizing our discovery. Instead of celebratory welcome, Streaker returned from the Shallow Cluster to find battle fleets lying in wait, eager to secure our secrets before we reached neutral ground. Several times, we were cornered, and escaped *only because hordes of fanatics fought savagely among themselves over the right of capture.*

'Alas, that compensation seems lacking in our present situation.'

That was an understatement. The Jophur could pursue *Streaker* at leisure, without threat of interference. As far as the rest of civilization was concerned, this whole region was empty and off-limits.

'Was poor Emerson wounded in one of those earlier space battles?'

Sara felt concern for her friend, the silent star voyager, whose cryptic injuries she had treated in her treehouse, before taking him on an epic journey across Jijo, to be reunited with his crewmates.

'No. Engineer D'Anite was captured by members of the Retired Caste, at a place we call the Fractal World. That event—'

The blue blob halted its twisting gyration. Hesitating a few seconds, it trembled before resuming.

'The detection officer reports something new! A phenomenon heretofore masked by the flames of Izmunuti.'

The display rippled. Abruptly, swarms of orange pinpoints sparkled amid the filaments and stormy prominences of Izmunuti's roiling atmosphere.

Sara leaned forward. 'What are they?'

'Condensed objects.

'Artificial, self-propelled spacial motiles.

'In other words, starships.'

Sara's jaw opened and closed twice before she could manage speech.

'Ifni, there must be hundreds! How could we have overlooked them before?'

The Niss answered defensively.

'Oh, great Sage, one normally does not send probing beams through a red giant's flaming corona in search of spacecraft. Our attention was turned elsewhere. Besides, these vessels only began using gravitic engines moments ago, applying gravi-temporal force to escape the new solar storms.'

Sara stared in amazement. Hope whirled madly.

'These ships, could they help us?'

Again, the Niss paused, consulting remote instruments.

'It seems doubtful, oh, Sage. They will scarcely care about our struggles. These beings belong to another order on the pyramid of life, completely apart from yours ... though one might call them distant cousins of mine.'

Sara shook her head, at first confused. Then she cried out.

'Machines!'

Even Jijo's fallen castaways could recite the Eight Orders of Sapience, with oxygen-based life being only one of the most flamboyant. Among the other orders, Jijo's Sacred Scrolls spoke darkly of synthetic beings, coldly cryptic, who designed and built each other in the farthest depths of space, needing no ground to stand on or wind to breathe.

'Indeed. Their presence here surely involves matters beyond our concern. Most likely, the mechanoids will avoid contact with us out of prudent caution.'

The voice paused.

'Fresh data is coming in. It seems that the flotilla is having a hard time with those new tempests. Some mechaniforms may be more needy of rescue than we are.'

Sara pointed at one of the orange dots.

'Show me!'

Using data from long-range scans, the display unit swooped giddily inward. Swirling stellar filaments seemed to heave around Sara as her point of view plunged toward the chosen speck – one of the mechanoid vessels – which began taking form against a backdrop of irate gas.

Stretching the limits of magnification, the blurry enhancement showed a glimmering trapezoidal shape, almost mirrorlike, that glancingly reflected solar fire. The mechanoid's outline grew slimmer as it turned to flee a plume of hot ions, fast rising toward it from Izmunuti's whipped convection zones. The display software compensated for perspective as columns of numbers estimated the vessel's actual measurements – a square whose edges were hundreds of kilometers in length, with a third dimension that was vanishingly small.

Space seemed to ripple just beneath the mechaniform vessel. Though still inexperienced, Sara recognized the characteristic warping effects of a gravi-temporal field. A modest one, according to the display. Perhaps sufficient for interplanetary speeds, but not to escape the devastation climbing toward it. She could only watch with helpless sympathy as the mechanoid struggled in vain.

The first shock wave ripped the filmy object in half ... then into shreds that raveled quickly, becoming a swarm of bright, dissolving streamers.

'This is not the only victim. Observe, as fate catches up with other stragglers.'

The display returned to its former scale. As Sara watched, several additional orange glitters were overwhelmed by waves of accelerating dense plasma. Others continued climbing, fighting to escape the maelstrom.

'Whoever they are, I hope they get away,' Sara murmured.

How strange it seemed that machine-vessels would be less sturdy than *Streaker*, whose protective fields could stand full immersion for several miduras in the red star's chromosphere, storm or no storm.

If they can't take on a plasma surge, they'd be useless against Jophur weapons.

Disappointment tasted bitter after briefly raised hope. Clearly, no rescue would come from that direction.

Sara perceived a pattern to her trials and adventures during the last year – swept away from her dusty study to encounter aliens, fight battles, ride fabled horses, submerge into the sea, and then join a wild flight aboard a starship. The universe seemed bent on revealing wonders at the edge of her grasp or imagining – giant stars, transfer points, talking computers, universal libraries ... and now glimpses of a different *life order*. A mysterious phylum, totally apart from the vast, encompassing Civilization of Five Galaxies.

Such marvels lay far beyond her old life as a savage intellectual on a rustic world.

And yet, a glimpse was clearly all the cosmos planned to give her. *Go ahead and look*, it seemed to say. *But you can't touch.*

For you, time has almost run out.

Saddened, Sara watched orange pinpoints flee desperately before tornadoes of stellar heat. More laggards were swept up by the rising storm, their frail light quenched like drowned embers.

Gillian and the dolphins seem sure we can stand a brief passage through that hell. But the vanishing sparks made Sara's confidence waver. After all, weren't machines supposed to be stronger than mere flesh?

She was about to ask the Niss about it when, before her eyes, the holo display abruptly changed once more. Izmunuti flickered, and when the image reformed, something new had come into view. Below the retreating orange glimmers, there now appeared *three sparkling forms*, rising with complacent grace, shining a distinct shade of imperial purple as they emerged from the flames toward *Streaker*'s path.

'What now?' she asked. 'More mechanoids?'

'*No*,' the Niss answered in a tone that seemed almost awed. '*These appear to be something else entirely. I believe they are ... *' The computer's hologram deformed into jagged shapes, like nervous icicles. '*I believe they are Zang*.'

Sara's skin crawled. That name was fraught with fear and legend. On Jijo, it was never spoken above a whisper. 'But ... how ... what could *they* be doing ... ?'

Before she finished her question, the Niss spoke again.

'Excuse me for interrupting, Sara. Our acting captain, Dr. Gillian Baskin, has called an urgent meeting of the ship's council to consider these developments. You are invited to attend.

'Do you wish me to make excuses on your behalf?' Sara was already hurrying toward the exit.

'Don't you dare!' she cried over one shoulder as the door folded aside to let her pass.

The hallway beyond curved up and away in both directions, like a segment of tortured spacetime, rising toward vertical in the distance. The sight always gave Sara qualms. Nevertheless, this time she ran.

GILLIAN

For some reason, the tumultuous red star reminded her of Venus.

Naturally, that brought Tom to mind.

Everything reminded Gillian of Tom. After two years, his absence was still a wound that left her reflexively turning for his warmth each night. By day, she kept expecting his strong voice, offering to help take on the worries. All the damned decisions.

Isn't it just like a hero, to die saving the world?

A little voice pointed out – *that's what heroes are for.*

Yes, she answered. *But the world goes on, doesn't it? And it keeps needing to be saved.*

Ever since the universe sundered them apart at Kithrup, Gillian told herself that Tom couldn't be dead. *I'd know it,* she would think repeatedly, convincing herself by force of will. *Across galaxies and megaparsecs, I could tell if he were gone. Tom must be out there somewhere still, with Creideiki and Hikahi and the others we were forced to leave behind.*

He'll find a way to get safely home . . . or else back to me.

That certainty helped Gillian bear her burdens during *Streaker's* first distraught fugitive year . . . until the last few months of steady crisis finally cracked her assurance.

Then, without realizing when it happened, she began thinking of Tom in the past tense.

He loved Venus, she pondered, watching the raging solar vista beyond *Streaker's* hull. Of course Izmunuti's atmosphere was bright, while Earth's sister world was dim beneath perpetual acid clouds. Yet, both locales shared essential traits. Harsh warmth, unforgiving storms, and scant moisture.

Both provoked extremes of hope and despair.

She could see him now, spreading both spacesuited arms to encompass the panorama below Aphrodite Pinnacle, gesturing toward stark lowlands. Lightning danced about a phalanx of titanic structures that stretched to a warped horizon – one shadowy behemoth after another – vast new devices freshly engaged in the labor of changing Venus. Transforming hell, one step at a time.

'Isn't it tremendous?' Tom asked. *'This endeavor proves that our species is capable of thinking long thoughts.'*

Even with borrowed Galactic technology, the task would take more time to complete than humans had known writing or agriculture. Ten thousand years must pass before seas rolled across the sere plains. It was a bold project for poor wolflings to engage in, especially when Sa'ent and Kloornap bookies gave Earthclan slim odds of surviving more than another century or two.

'We have to show the universe that we trust ourselves,' Tom added. *'Or else who will believe in us?'*

His words sounded fine. Noble and grand. At the time, Tom almost convinced Gillian.

Only things changed.

Half a year ago, during *Streaker*'s brief, terrified refuge at the Fractal World, Gillian had managed to pick up rumors about the Siege of Terra, taking place in faraway Galaxy Two. Apparently, the Sa'ent touts were now taking bets on human extinction in mere years or jaduras, not centuries.

In retrospect, the Venus terraforming project seemed moot.

We'd have been better off as farmers, Tom and I. Or teaching school. Or helping settle Calafia. We should never have listened to Jake Demwa and Creideiki. This mission has brought ruin on everyone it touched.

Including the poor colonists of Jijo – six exile races who deserved a chance to find their own strange destinies undisturbed. In seeking shelter on that forbidden world, *Streaker* only brought disaster to Jijo's tribes.

There seemed one way to redress the harm.

Can we lure the Jophur after us into the new transfer point? Kaa must pilot a convincing trajectory, as if he can sense a perfect thread to latch on to. A miracle path leading toward safety. If we do it right, the big ugly sap-rings will have to follow! They'll have no choice.

Saving Jijo justified that option, since there seemed no way to bring *Streaker*'s cargo safely home to Earth. Another reason tasted acrid, vengeful.

At least we'll take enemies with us.

Some say that impending death clarifies the mind, but in Gillian it only stirred regret.

I hope Creideiki and Tom aren't too disappointed in me, she pondered at the door of the conference room.

I did my best.

The ship's council had changed since Gillian reluctantly took over the captain's position, where Creideiki presided in happier times. At the far end of the long table, *Streaker*'s last surviving dolphin officer, Lieutenant Tsh't, expertly piloted a six-legged walker apparatus carrying her sleek gray form into the same niche where Takkata-Jim once nestled his great bulk, before he was killed near Kithrup.

Tsh't greeted the human chief engineer, though Hannes Suessi's own mother wouldn't recognize him now, with so many body parts replaced by cyborg components, and a silver dome where his head used to be. Much of that gleaming surface was now covered with pre-Contact-era motorcycle decals – an irreverent touch that endeared Hannes to the crew. At least someone had kept a sense of humor through years of relentless crisis.

Gillian felt acutely the absence of one council member, her friend and fellow physician Makanee, who remained behind on Jijo with several dozen dolphins – those suffering from devolution fever or who were unessential for the breakout attempt. In effect, dolphins had established a seventh illegal colony on that fallow world – another secret worth defending with the lives of those left aboard.

Secrets. There are other enigmas, less easily protected.

Gillian's thoughts slipped past the salvaged objects in her office, some of them worth a stellar ransom. Mere hints at their existence had already knocked civilization teetering across five galaxies.

Foremost was a corpse, nicknamed Herbie. An alien cadaver so ancient, its puzzling smile might be from a joke told a billion years ago. Other relics were scarcely less provocative – or cursed. Trouble had followed *Streaker* ever since its crew began picking up objects they didn't understand.

'Articles of Destiny.' That was how one of the Old Ones referred to *Streaker*'s cargo of mysteries when they visited the Fractal World.

Maybe this will be fitting. All those irksome treasures will get smashed down to a proton's width after we dive into the new transfer point.

At least then she'd get the satisfaction of seeing Herbie's expression finally change, at the last instant, when the bounds of reality closed in rapidly from ten dimensions.

A holo of Izmunuti took up one wall of the conference room, an expanse of swirling clouds wider than Earth's orbit, surging and shifting as the Niss Machine relayed the latest intelligence in Tymbrimi-accented Galactic Seven.

'The Jophur battleship has jettisoned the last of the decoy vessels it seized, letting them drift through space. Freed of their momentum-burden, the Polkjhy is more agile, turning its frightful bulk toward the new transfer point. They aim to reach the reborn nexus before Streaker does.'

'Can they beat us there?' Gillian asked in Anglic.

The Niss hologram whirled thoughtfully. 'It seems unlikely, unless they use some risky type of probability drive, which is not typical of Jophur. They wasted a lot of time dashing ahead toward the older t-point. Our tight swing past Izmunuti should help Streaker to arrive first ... for whatever good it will do.'

Gillian ignored the machine's sarcasm. Most of the crew seemed in accord with her decision. Lacking other options, death was more bearable if you took an enemy with you.

The Jophur situation appeared stable, so she changed the subject. 'What can you report about the other ships?'

'The two mysterious flotillas we recently detected in Izmunuti's atmosphere? After consulting tactical archives, I conclude they must have been operating jointly. Nothing else could explain their close proximity, fleeing together to escape unexpected plasma storms.'

Hannes Suessi objected, his voice wavering low and raspy from the silver dome.

'Mechanoids and hydrogen breathers cooperating? That sounds odd.'

The whirling blob made a gesture like a nod. 'Indeed. The various orders of life seldom interact. But according to our captured Library unit, it does happen, especially when some vital project requires the talents of two or more orders, working together.'

The newest council member whistled for attention. Kaa, the chief pilot, did not ride a walker, since he might have to speed back to duty any moment. The young dolphin commented from a fluid-filled tunnel that passed along a wall near one side of the table.

* Can any purpose
    * Under tide-pulled moons explain
        * Such anomalies? *

For emphasis, Kaa slashed his tail flukes through water that fizzed with bubbles. Gillian translated the popping whistle-poem for Sara Koolhan, who had never learned Trinary.

'Kaa asks what project could be worth the trouble and danger of diving into a star.'

Sara replied with an eager nod. 'I may have a partial answer.' The young Jijoan stroked a black cube in front of her – the personal algorithmic engine Gillian had lent her when she came aboard.

'Ever since we first spotted these strange ships, I've wondered what trait of Izmunuti might attract folks here from some distant system. For instance, my own ancestors. After passing through the regular t-point, they took a path through this giant star's outer atmosphere. All the sneakships of Jijo used the same method to cover their tracks.'

We thought of it too, Gillian pondered, unhappily. *But I must have done something wrong, since the Rothen were able to follow us, betraying our hiding place and the Six Races.*

Gillian noticed Lieutenant Tsh't was looking at her. With reproach for getting *Streaker* into this fix? The dolphin's eye remained fixed for a long, appraising moment, then turned away as Sara continued.

'According to this teaching unit, stars like Izmunuti pour immense amounts of heavy atoms from their bloated atmospheres. Carbon is especially rich, condensing on anything solid that happens nearby. All our ancestor ships arrived at Jijo black with the stuff. *Streaker* may be the first vessel ever to try the trick *twice*, both coming and going. I bet the stuff is causing you some problems.'

'No bet!' boomed Suessi's amplified voice. Hannes had been battling the growing carbon coating. 'The stuff is heavy, it has weird properties, and it's been gumming up the verity flanges.'

Sara nodded. 'But consider – what if somebody has a *use* for such coatings? What would be their best way to accumulate it?'

She stroked her black cube again, transferring data to the main display. Though Sara had been aboard just a few days, she was adapting to the convenience of modern tools.

A mirrorlike rectangle appeared before the council, reflecting fiery prominences from a broad, planar surface.

'I may be an ignorant native,' Sara commented. 'But it seems one could collect atoms out of a stellar wind using something with high surface area and small initial mass. Such a vehicle might not even have to expend energy departing, if it rode outward on the pressure of light waves.'

Lieutenant Tsh't murmured.

'A sssolar sail!'

'Is that what you call it?' Sara nodded. 'Imagine machines arriving through the transfer point as compact objects, plummeting down to Izmunuti, then unfurling such sails and catching a free ride back to the t-point, gaining layers of this molecularly unique carbon, and other stuff along the way. Energy expenditures per ton of yield would be minimal!'

The whirling Niss hologram edged forward.

'Your hypothesis suggests an economical resource-gathering technique, providing the mechanoids needn't make more than one simple hyperspatial transfer, coming or going. There are cheap alternatives in industrialized regions of the Five Galaxies, but here in Galaxy Four, industry is currently minimal or nil, due to the recent fallow-migration—' The Niss paused briefly.

'Mechanoids would be ideal contractors for such a harvesting chore, creating special versions to do the job swiftly, with minimal mass. It explains why their drives and shields seem frail before the rising storms. They had no margin for the unexpected.'

Gillian saw that just half of the orange glitters remained, struggling to flee Izmunuti's gravity before more plasma surges caught them. The three purple dots had already climbed toward the mechanoid convoy, ascending with graceful ease.

'What about the Zang?' she asked.

'I surmise they are the mechanoids' employers. Our Library says Zang groups sometimes hire special services from the Machine Order. Great clans of oxygen breathers also do it, now and then.'

'Well, it seems their plans have been ripped,' commented Suessi. 'Not much cargo getting home, this time.'

Pensive whistle ratchets escaped the gray dolphin in the water-filled tunnel – not Trinary, but the scattered clicks a cetacean emits when pondering deeply. Gillian still felt guilty about asking Kaa to volunteer for this mission, since it meant abandoning his lover to danger on Jijo. But *Streaker* needed a first-class pilot for this desperate ploy.

'I concur,' the whirling Niss hologram concluded. *'The Zang will be in a foul mood after this setback.'*

'Because they suffered economic loss?' Tsh't asked.

'That and more. According to the Library, hydrogen breathers react badly to surprise. They have slower metabolisms than oxy-life. Anything unpredictable is viscerally unpleasant to them.

'Of course, this attitude is strange to an entity like me, programmed by the Tymbrimi to seek novelty! Without surprise, how can you tell there is an objective world? You might as well presume the whole universe is one big sim—'

'Wait a minute,' Gillian interrupted, before the Niss got side-tracked in philosophy. 'We're all taught to avoid Zang as dangerous, leaving contact to experts from the Great Institutes.'

'That is right.'

'But now you're saying they may be especially angry? Possibly short-tempered?'

The Niss hologram coiled tensely.

'After three years together, Dr. Baskin – amid growing familiarity

with your voice tones and thought patterns – your latest inquiry provokes uneasy feelings.

'*Am I justified to be wary?*

'*Do you find the notion of short-tempered Zang . . . appealing?*'

Gillian kept silent. But she allowed a grim, enigmatic smile.

HARRY

Five Earth years had passed on his personal duration clock since he took the irrevocable step, standing amid volunteers from fifty alien races, laboriously mouthing polyglottal words of a memorized oath that had been written ages ago, by some species long extinct. Upon joining the Observer Corps, Harry's life didn't simply shift – it leaped from the riverbed of his genetic lineage, transferring loyalty from his birth planet to an austere bureaucracy that was old when his distant ancestors still scurried under Triassic jungle canopies, hiding from dinosaurs.

Yet, during training he was struck by how often other students sought him out with questions about Earthclan, whose struggles were the latest riveting interstellar penny-drama. Would the newest band of unprotected, sponsorless 'wolflings' catch up with starfaring civilization in time to forestall the normal fate of upstarts? Despite Terra's puny unimportance, this provoked much speculation and wagering.

What was it like – his fellow acolytes asked – to have patrons like humans, who *taught themselves* such basic arts as speech, spaceflight, and eugenics? As a neo-chimp, Harry was junior in status to every other client-citizen at the base, yet he was almost a celebrity, getting hostility from some, admiration from others, and curiosity from nearly all.

In fact, he couldn't tell his classmates much about Terragens Civilization, having spent just a year among the talky neo-chimpanzees of Earth before dropping out of university to sign on with the Navigation Institute. His life was already one of exile.

He had been born in space, aboard a Terragens survey vessel. Harry's vague memories of TSS *Pelenor* were of a misty paradise lost, filled with high-tech comforts and warm places to play. The crew had seemed like gods – human officers, neo-chim and neo-dolphin ratings . . . plus a jolly, treelike Kanten advisor – all moving about their tasks so earnestly, except when he needed to be cuddled or tickled or tossed in the air.

Then, one awful day, his parents chose to debark and study the strange human tribes on a desolate colony world – Horst. That ended Harry's part in the epochal voyage of the *Pelenor*, and began his simmering resentment.

Memories of starscapes and humming engines became muzzy, idealized. Throughout childhood on that dusty world, the notion of space travel grew more magical. By the time Harry finally left Horst, he was shocked by the true sterile bleakness that stretched between rare stellar oases.

I remember it differently, he thought, during the voyage to Earth. Of course that memory was a fantasy, formed by an impressionable toddler. At university, instructors taught that subjective impressions are untrustworthy, biased by the mind's fervent wish to believe.

Still, the thirst would not be slaked. An ambition to seek paradise in other versions of reality.

The bananas held him trapped for days.

If the allaphor had been less personal, Harry might have fought harder. But the image was too explicitly pointed to ignore. After the first debacle, when the station nearly foundered, he decided to wait before challenging the reef again.

Anyway, this wasn't a bad site to observe from. In a synergy between this strange continuum and his own mind, the local region manifested itself as a high plateau, overlooking a vast, undulating sea of purple tendrils. Black mountains still bobbed in the distance, though some of the 'holes' in the red-blue sky became drooping dimples, as if the celestial dome had decided to melt or slump.

There were also life-forms – mostly creatures of the Memetic Order. Shapes that fluttered, crawled, or shimmered past Harry's octagonal platform, grazing and preying on each other, or else merging or undergoing eerie transformations before his eyes. On all other dimensional planes, memes could only exist as parasites, dwelling in the host brains or mental processors of physical beings. But here in E Space, they roamed free, in a realm of palpable ideas.

'*Your imagination equips you to perform the duties of a scout,*' Wer'Q'quinn explained during Harry's training. '*But do not succumb to the lure of solipsism, believing you can make something happen in E Space simply by willing it. E Space can sever your life path, if you grow obstinate or unwary.*'

Harry never doubted that. Watching memiforms slither across the purple steppe, he passed the time speculating what concepts they contained. Probably, none of the creatures were sapient, since true intelligence was rare on any level of reality. Yet, each of the memes crossing before him manifested a *single thought*, unconstrained by any organic or electronic brain – a self-contained idea with as much structured complexity as Harry held in his organs and genetic code.

That one over there, prancing like a twelve-legged antelope – was it an abstraction distantly related to *freedom*? When a jagged-edged flying thing swooped down to chase it, Harry wondered if the hunter might be an intricate version of *craving*. Or was he typically trying to cram the complex and ineffable into simple niches, to satisfy the pattern-needs of his barely sapient mind?

Well, it is 'human nature' to trivialize. To make stereotypes. To pretend you can eff the ineffable.

Local meme organisms were fascinating, but now and then something else appeared beneath his vantage point, demanding closer attention.

He could always tell an interloper. Outsiders moved awkwardly, as if their allaphorical shapes were clumsy costumes. Often, predatory memes would approach, sniffing for a savory conceptual meal, only to retreat quickly from the harsh taste of solid matter. Metal-hulled ships or organic life-forms. Intruders from some other province of reality, not pausing or staring, but hastening past the floating mountains to seek refuge in the Swiss cheese sky.

Harry welcomed these moments when he earned his pay. Speaking clearly, he would describe each newcomer for his partner, the station computer, which lay below his feet, shielded against the hostile effects of E Space. At headquarters, experts would decipher his eyewitness account to determine what kind of vessel had made transit before Harry's eyes, and where it may have been bound. Meanwhile, he and the computer collaborated to make the best guess they could.

'*Onboard memory files are familiar with this pattern,*' said the floating **M** at one point, after Harry described an especially bizarre newcomer, rushing by atop myriad stiff, glimmering stalks, like a striding sunburst. '*It appears to be a member of the Quantum Order of Sapiency.*'

'Really?' Harry pressed against the glass. The object looked as fragile as a feathery zilm spore, carried on the wind to far corners of Horst. Delicate stems kept breaking off and vaporizing as the thing – (was it a ship? or a single being?) – hurried toward a sky hole that lay near the horizon.

'I've never seen a quant anywhere near that big before. What's it doing here? I thought they didn't like E Space.'

'*Try to imagine how you organics feel about hard vacuum – you shrivel and perish unless surrounded by layers of protective* technology. So the fluctuating subjectivities of this domain imperil some other kinds of life. E Space is even more distasteful to quantum beings than it is to members of the Machine Order.'

'Hm. Then why's it here?'

'I am at a loss to speculate what urgent errand impels it. Most quantum beings reside in the foam interstices of the cosmos, out of sight from other life variants – like bacteria on your homeworld who live in solid rock. Explicit contact with the Quantum Order was only established by experts of the Library Institute less than a hundred million years ago.

'What I can suggest is that you should politely avert your gaze, Scout Harms. The quant is clearly having difficulties. You needn't add to its troubles by staring.'

Harry winced at the reminder. 'Oh, right. The Uncertainty Principle!' He turned away. His job in E Space was to watch, but you could do harm by watching too closely.

Anyway, his real task was to look for less exotic interlopers.

Most of his ship sightings were of hydrogen breathers, easily identified because their balloonlike vessels looked the same in any continuum. For some reason, members of that order liked taking shortcuts through E Space on their way from one Jupiter-type world to another, even though A and B levels were more efficient, and transfer points much faster.

On those rare occasions when Harry spotted anyone from his own order of oxygen breathers – the great and mighty Civilization of Five Galaxies – none of them approached his sentry position, defending a proscribed route to a forbidden place.

No wonder they hired a low-class chim for this job. Even criminals, trying to sneak into a fallow zone, would be fools to use allaphor space as a back door.

As I'm a fool, to be stuck guarding it.

Still, it beat the dry, windy steppes of Horst.

Anything was better than Horst.

He and his parents were the only members of their species on the planet, which meant the long process of learning speech, laborious for young neo-chimps, came doubly hard. With Marko and Felicity distracted by research, Harry had to practice with wild-eyed Probsher kids, who mocked him for his long, furry arms and early stammer. With painted faces and short tempers, they showed none of the dignified patience he'd been taught to expect from the elder race. By the time he learned how different humans were on Horst, it didn't matter. He vowed to leave, not only Horst, but Terragens society. To seek the strange and unfamiliar.

Years later, Harry realized a similar ambition must have driven his parents. In youthful anger, he had spurned their pleas for patience, their awkward affections, even their parting blessing.

Still, regret was just a veneer, forgiveness a civilized abstraction, devoid of pang or poignancy.

Other memories still had power to make his veins tense with emotion. Growing up listening to botbian night wolves howl across dry lakes under patch-gilt moons. Or holding his knees by firelight while a Probsher shaman chanted eerie tales – fables that Marko and Felicity avidly studied as venerable folk legends, although these tribes had roamed Horst for less than six generations.

His own sapient race wasn't much older! Only a few centuries had passed since human beings began genetic meddling in chimpanzee stock.

Who gave them the right?

No permission was needed. Galactics had followed the same pattern for eons – each 'generation' of starfarers spawning the next in a rippling bootstrap effect called Uplift.

On the whole, humans were better masters than most . . . and he would rather be sapient than not.

No. What drove him away from Earthclan was not resentment but a kind of detachment. The mayfly yammerings of Probsher mystics mattered no more or less than the desperate moves of the Terragens Council, against the grinding forces of an overwhelming universe. One might as well compare sparks rising from a campfire to the stars wheeling by overhead. They looked similar, at a glance. But what did another incandescent cinder really matter on the grand scale of things?

Did the cosmos care if humans or chims survived?

Even at university this notion threaded his thoughts. Harry's natural links elongated till they parted one by one. All that remained was a nebulous desire to seek out something lasting. Something that deserved to last.

Joining Wer'Q'quinn and the Navigation Institute, he found something enduring, a decision he never regretted.

Still, it puzzled Harry years later that his dreams kept returning to the desolate world of his youth. Horst ribbed his memory. Its wind in the dry grass. Smells that assailed your nose, sinking claws into your sinuses. And images the shaman painted in your mind, like arcs of multicolored sand, falling in place to convey *deer*, or *loperbeast*, or *spearhunter*.

Even as an official of Galactic civilization, representing the oxygen order on a weird plane of reality where allaphors shimmered in each window like reject Dali images, Harry still saw funnels of sparkling heat rising from smoky campfires, vainly seeking union with aloof stars.

LARK

'Not that way!' Ling shouted.

Her cry made Lark stumble to a halt, a few meters down a new corridor.

'But I'm sure this is the best route back to our nest.' Lark pointed along a dim, curved aisle, meandering between gray ceramic walls. Strong odors wafted from each twisty, branching passageway aboard the mazelike Jophur ship. This one beckoned with distinct flavors of GREEN and SANCTUARY.

'I believe you.' Ling nodded. 'That's why we mustn't go there. In case we're still being followed.'

She didn't look much like a star god anymore, with her dark hair hacked short and pale skin covered with soot. Wearing just a torn undertunic from her once shiny uniform, Ling now seemed far wilder than the Jijoan natives she once called 'savages.' In a cloth sling she carried a crimson torus that leaked gore like a wounded sausage.

Lark saw her meaning. Ever since they had tried sabotaging the dreadnought's control chamber, giant Jophur and their robot servants had chased them across the vast vessel. As fugitives, the humans mustn't lead pursuers to the one place offering food and shelter.

'Where to then?' Lark hated being in the open. He grasped their only weapon, a circular purple tube. Larger and healthier than the red one, it was their sole key to get past locked doors and unwary guardians.

Ling knew starships far better than he. But this behemoth warship was different. She peered up one shadowy tunnel, a curled shaft that seemed more organic than artificial.

'Just pick a direction. Quickly. I hear someone coming.' With a wistful glance toward their 'nest,' Lark took her hand and plunged away at right angles, into another passageway.

The walls glistened with an oily sheen, each passage or portal emitting its own distinct aroma, partly making up for the lack of written signs. Although he was just a primitive sooner, Lark did know traeki. Those cousins of the Jophur had different personalities, but shared many physical traits. As a Jijoan native, he could grasp many nuances in the shipboard scent language.

Despite the eerie hall curvature, he was starting to get a mental picture of the huge vessel – an oblate spheroid, studded with aggressive weaponry and driven by engines mighty enough to warp space in several ways. The remaining volume was a labyrinth of workshops, laboratories, and enigmatic chambers that puzzled even the star sophisticate, Ling. Since barely escaping the Jophur command center, they had worked their way inward, back toward the tiny eden where they had hidden after escaping their prison cell.

The place where they first made love.

Only now the greasy ring stacks had shut down all the axial drop tubes, blocking easy access along the *Polkjhy*'s north-south core.

'*It makes the whole ship run inefficiently,*' Ling had explained earlier, with some satisfaction. '*They can't shift or reassign crew for different tasks. We're still hurting them, Lark, as long as we're free!*'

He appreciated her effort to see a good side to their predicament. Even if the future seemed bleak, Lark felt content to be with her for as much time as they had left.

Glancing backward, Ling gripped his arm. Heightened rustling sounds suggested pursuit was drawing near. Then Lark also heard something from the opposite direction, closing in beyond the next sharp bend. 'We're trapped!' Ling cried.

Lark rushed to the nearest sealed door. Its strong redolence reminded him of market days back home, when traeki torus breeders brought their fledglings for sale in mulch-lined pens.

He aimed the purple ring at a nearby scent plate and a thin mist shot from the squirming creature. *Come on. Do your stuff,* he silently urged.

Their only hope lay in this gift from the former traeki sage, Asx, who had struggled free of mental repression by a Jophur master ring just long enough to pop out two infant tubes. The human fugitives had no idea what the wounded red one was for, but the purple marvel had enabled them to stay free for several improbable days, ever since the battleship took off from Jijo on its manic errand through outer space.

Of course we knew it couldn't last.

The door lock accepted the coded chemical key with a soft click, and the portal slid open, letting them rush through acrid fumes into a dim chamber, divided by numerous tall, glass partitions. Lark had no time to sort impressions, however, before the corridor behind them echoed with *human* shouts and a staccato of running feet.

'Stop! Don't you stupid skins know you're just making things worse? Come out, before they start using—'

The closing door cut off angry threats by Ling's former commander. Lark pushed the purple traeki against the inner sense-plate, where it oozed aromatic scramblers – chemicals tuned to randomize the lock's coding. From experience, he knew it could take half a midura for their pursuers to get through – unless they brought heavy cutting tools to bear.

Why should they bother? They know we're trapped inside.

He found it especially galling to be cornered by Rann. The third human prisoner had thrown in his lot with the Jophur, perhaps currying favor for the release of his Rothen patron gods from frozen internment on Jijo. It left Lark with no options, since the purple ring would have nil effect on the big Danik warrior.

Turning around, Lark saw that the glass walls – stretching from floor to a high ceiling – made up giant vivariums holding row after row of wriggling, squirming things.

Midget traeki toruses!

Clear tubes carried brown, sludgelike material to each niche.

Refined liquid mulch. Baby food.

We're in their nursery!

By itself, no traeki ring was intelligent. Back on the world where they evolved, slithering through fetid swamps as wormlike scavengers, they never amounted to much singly. Only when traeki began stacking together and specializing did there emerge a unique kind of presapient life, ripe for adoption and Uplift by their snail-like Poa patrons.

This is where the Polkjhy *crew grows special kinds of rings, packed with the right skills to be new members of the team.*

A potent kind of reproduction. No doubt some of the pulsing doughnut shapes were *master rings*, designed millennia ago to transform placid, contemplative traeki into adamant, alarming Jophur.

Lark jumped as a human scream clamored down the narrow aisles. Pulse pounding, he ran, shouting Ling's name.

Her voice echoed off glass walls. 'Hurry! They've got me cornered!'

Lark burst around a vivarium to find her at last, backing away from two huge Jophur workers, toward a niche in the far wall. The nursery staff, Lark realized. Each tapered pile consisted of at least thirty component toruses – swaying and hissing – two meters wide at the bottom and massing almost a ton. Their waxy flanks gleamed with an opulent vitality one never saw in traeki back home on Jijo, flickering with meaningful patterns of light and dark. Colored stenches vented from chem-synth pores, as manipulator tendrils stretched toward Ling.

She moved lithely, darting left and right. Seeking an opening or else something to use as a weapon. There was no panic in her eyes, nor did she give Lark away in her relief to see him.

Of course, Jophur vision sensors faced all directions at once. But with that advantage came a handicap – slow reaction time. The first stack was still swaying toward its victim when Lark dashed up from behind. Somehow, Asx's gift knew to send a jet of sour spray, striking a gemlike organ that quickly spasmed and went dim.

The whole stack shuddered, slumping to quiescence.

Lark wasted no time spinning toward the other foe—

—only to find his right arm suddenly pinned by an adamant tentacle! An odious scent of TRIUMPH swirled as the second Jophur pulled him close, coiling tendrils and commencing to squeeze.

The purple ring spasmed in Lark's hand, but the chemical spray could not hit its mark at this impossible angle, past the Jophur's bulging midriff. The master torus drove its lesser tubes with a malice and intensity Lark had never seen in serene traekis back home. The constriction grew unbearable, expelling his breath in a choking cry of agony.

A shattering crash filled his ears, as a rain of wetness and needle-like shards fell across his back.

The Jophur emitted a shrill ululation. Then someone shouted a fierce warning in the clicking whistles of staccato Galactic Two.

'To let the human go – this you must.

'Or else other young ones – to ruin shall fall!'

The harsh pressure eased off Lark's rib cage just as consciousness appeared about to waver and blow out. His captor huffed and teetered uncertainly. Peering blearily, Lark saw that slivers of glass dusted the big stack, and moisture lay everywhere. Then he caught sight of Ling, crouching several meters away with a crooked metal bar, brandishing it threateningly in front of another vivarium. Where she had found the tool, he couldn't guess. But the floor was already strewn with flopping infant rings decanted violently from one of the nurturing mulch towers. Some struggled on vague flippers or undeveloped legs. Midget master rings waved neural feelers, seeking other toroids to dominate.

Lark felt the nursery worker tremble with hesitation. Noises beyond the doorway indicated that the *Polkjhy* crew were already at work, unscrambling the door. Clearly, the two fugitive humans weren't going anywhere.

The Jophur stack decided. It released Lark.

He managed to keep from slumping to the floor, teetering on wobbly knees, feebly raising the purple torus for a clean shot at the pheromone sensors.

In moments, the second worker joined the first in estivation stupor.

Sheesh, Lark pondered. *If this was just a tender nurse, I'd hate to meet one of their fighters.*

Ling grabbed his arm to keep him from buckling.

'Come on,' she urged. 'There's no time to rest. We've got lots to do.'

'What're you talking about?' Lark tried asking. The question emerged as a gurgling sigh. But Ling refused to let him sink down and rest.

'I think I know a way out of here,' she said urgently. 'But it's going to be an awful tight fit.'

True to her prediction, the cargo container was tiny. Even by scrunching over double, Lark could barely cram himself inside. The purple ring squirmed in the hollow between his rib cage and a wall.

'I still think you should go first,' he complained.

Ling hurriedly punched commands on a complex keypad next to the little supply shuttle. 'Do *you* know how to program one of these things?'

She had a point, though Lark didn't like it much.

'Besides, we're heading somewhere unknown. Shouldn't our best fighter lead the way?'

Now Ling was teasing. Whoever went first would overcome opposition by using Asx's purple gift, or else fail. Physical strength was nearly useless against a robot or a full-size Jophur.

He glanced past her toward the far door of the nursery, where the red glow of a cutting torch could be seen, slicing an arched opening from the other side. Apparently, Rann and the Jophur had given up unscrambling the lock and decided on a brute-force approach.

'You'll hurry after me?'

For an answer, she bent and kissed him – once on the forehead in benediction, and again, passionately, on the mouth. 'How is that for a promise?' she asked, mingling her breath with his.

As Ling backed away, a transparent hatch slid over the little cab – built to carry equipment and samples between workstations throughout the Jophur ship. There had been a crude version of such a system back at Biblos, the Jijoan archive, where cherished paper books and messages shuttled between the libraries in narrow tubes of boo.

'Hey!' he called. 'Where are you sending m—'

A noise and brilliant flash cut off his question and made Ling spin around. The torch cutter was accelerating, as if the enemy somehow sensed a need to hurry. To Lark's horror, the arc was over half finished.

'Let me out!' he demanded. 'We're switching places!'

Ling shook her head as she resumed programming the console.

'Not an option. Get ready. This will be wrenching.' Before Lark could protest a second time, the wall section abruptly fell with a crash. Curt billowings of sparks and dense smoke briefly filled the vestibule. But soon, Jophur warriors would come pouring through ... and Ling didn't even have a weapon!

Lark hammered on the clear panel as several things happened in rapid succession.

Ling knelt to the floor, where scores of infant traeki rings still squirmed in confusion amid shards of their broken vivarium. She emptied her cloth sling, gently spilling Asx's second gift – the wounded crimson torus – to mingle among the others.

A tall silhouette passed through the roiling cloud to stand in the glowing doorway. The wedgelike torso was unmistakably Rann, leader of the Danik tribe of human renegades sworn to Rothen lords.

Ling stood. She glanced over her shoulder at Lark, who pounded the hatch, moaning frustration and fear for her.

Calmly, she reached for the keypad.

'No! Let me out! I'll—'

Acceleration kicked suddenly. Lark's folded body slammed one wall of the little car.

Ling's face vanished in a blur as he was swept away toward Ifni-knew-where.

DWER

'Are they really gone?'

Dwer bent close to an ancient, pitted window. He peered at a glittering starscape, feeling some of the transmitted chill of outer space, just a finger's breadth away.

'I don't see any sign of 'em over here,' he called back to Rety. 'Is it clear on your side?'

His companion – a girl about fourteen, with a scarred face and stringy hair – pressed against another pane at the opposite end of the dusty chamber, once the control room of a sleek vessel, but now hardly more than a grimy ruin.

'There's nothin' – unless you count the bits an' pieces floatin' out there, that keep fallin' off this rusty ol' bucket.'

Her hand slammed the nearest bulkhead. Streams of dust trickled from crevices in prehistoric metal walls.

The starship's original owners must have been oddly shaped,

since the viewing ports were arrayed at knee height to a standing human, while corroded instruments perched on tall pillars spread around the oblong room. Whatever race once piloted this craft, they eventually abandoned it as junk, over half a million years ago, when it was dumped onto a great pile of discarded hulks in the dross midden that lay under Jijo's ocean.

Immersion in subicy water surely had preserving effects. Still, the *Streaker* crew had accomplished a miracle, reviving scores of these wrecks for one final voyage. It made Rety's remark seem unfair, all considered.

There is air in here, Dwer thought. *And a machine that spits out a paste we can eat ... sort of. We're holding death at bay. For the moment.*

Not that he felt exactly happy about their situation. But after all the narrow escapes of the last few days, Dwer found continued life and health cause for surprised pleasure, not spiteful complaint.

Of course, Rety had her own, unique way of looking at things. Her young life had been a lot harder than his, after all.

'i sniff every corner of this old boat,' a small voice piped, speaking Anglic with a hissing accent and a note of triumph. *'no sign of metal monsters. none! we scare them off!'*

The speaker trotted across the control room on four miniature hooves – a quadruped with two slim centauroid arms and an agile, snakelike neck. Holding his head up proudly, little yee clattered over to Rety and slipped into her belt pouch. The two called each other 'husband and wife,' an interspecies union that made some sense to another Jijoan but would have stunned any citizen of the Civilization of Five Galaxies. The verbose urrish male and an unbathed, prepubescent human female made quite a pairing.

Dwer shook his head.

'Those robots didn't leave on account of our fierce looks. We were hiding in a closet, scared out of our wits, remember?' He shrugged. 'I bet they didn't search the ship because they saw it for an empty shell right away.'

Almost a hundred ancient derelict ships had been resurrected from the subsea graveyard by Hannes Suessi and his clever dolphin engineers in order to help mask *Streaker*'s breakout, giving the Earthlings a slim chance against the overpowering Jophur dreadnought. Dwer's presence aboard one of the decoys resulted from a series of rude accidents. (Right now he was supposed to be landing a hot-air balloon in Jijo's Gray Hills, fulfilling an old obligation, not plummeting into the blackness away from the wilderness he knew best.)

But Rety had planned to be here! A scheme to hijack her very own starship must have been stewing in that devious brain for weeks, Dwer now realized.

'The sap-rings cut us loose so they can go dolphin hunting somewhere else! I knew this'd happen,' Rety exulted. 'Now all we gotta do is head for the Five Galaxies. Make it to someplace with a lot of traffic, flag down some passing trading ship, an' strike a deal. This old hulk oughta be worth something. You watch, Dwer. Meetin' me was the best thing that ever happened to you! You'll thank me when you're a star god, livin' high for three hunnerd years.'

Her enthusiasm forced him to smile. How easily Rety looked past their immediate problems! Such as the fact that all three of them were primitive Jijoans. Learning to pilot a space vessel would have been a daunting task for Dwer's brilliant siblings – Lark or Sara – who were junior sages of the Commons of Six Races. *But I'm just a simple forester! How is skill at tracking beasts going to help us navigate from star to star?*

As for Rety, brought up by a savage band of exile sooners, she could not even read until a few months ago, when she began picking up the skill.

'Hey, teacher!' Rety called. 'Show us where we are!'

Four gray boxes lay bolted to the floor, linked by cable to an ancient control pillar. Three had been left by the dolphins, programmed to guide this vessel through the now completed breakout maneuver. Last was a portable 'advisor' – a talking machine – given to Rety by the *Streaker* crew. She had shown Dwer her toy earlier, before the Jophur robots came.

'*Passive sensors are operating at just seven percent efficiency,*' the unit answered. '*Active sensors are disabled. For those reasons, this representation will be commensurately imprecise.*'

A picture suddenly erupted between Rety and Dwer ... one of those magical holo images that moved and had the texture of solidity. It showed a fiery ball in one low corner – *Great Izmunuti*, Dwer realized with a superstitious shiver. A yellow dot in the exact center represented this hapless vessel. Several other bits of yellow glimmered nearby, drifting slowly toward the upper right.

The Jophur have cut loose all the captured decoys. I guess that means they know where Streaker *is.*

He thought of Gillian Baskin, so sad and so beautiful, carrying burdens he could never hope to understand. During his brief time aboard the Earth vessel he had a feeling ... an impression that she did not expect to carry the burdens much longer.

Then what was it all for? If escape was hopeless, why did Gillian lead her poor crew through so much pain and struggle?

'*Behold the Jophur battleship,*' said Rety's teacher. A blurry dot appeared toward the top right corner, now moving rapidly leftward, retracing its path at a close angle toward Izmunuti.

'*It has changed course dramatically, moving at maximum C-Level pseudospeed.*'

'Can you see *Streaker*?' Dwer asked.

'*I cannot. But judging from the* Polkjhy's *angle of pursuit, the Terran ship may be masked by the red giant star.*

He sensed Rety sitting cross-legged on the floor next to him, her eyes shining in light from the hologram.

'Forget the Earthers,' she demanded. 'Show us where we're headin'!'

The display changed, causing Izmunuti and the Jophur frigate to drift out of view. A fuzzy patch moved in from the top edge, slippery to look at. Rows of symbols and numbers flickered alongside – information that might have meant something to his sister but just seemed frightening to Dwer.

'That's the ... *transfer point*, right?' Rety asked, her voice growing hushed. 'The hole thing that'll take us to the Five Galaxies?'

'*It is a hole, in a manner of speaking. But this transfer point cannot serve as a direct link out of Galaxy Four – the galaxy we are in – to any of the others. In order to accomplish that, we must follow transition threads leading to some other hyperspatial nexi. Much bigger ones, capable of longer-range jumps.*'

'You mean we'll have to portage from stream to stream, a few times?' Dwer asked, comparing the voyage to a canoe trip across a mountain range.

'*Your metaphor has some limited relevance. According to recent navigation data, a route out of this galaxy to more populated regions can be achieved by taking a series of five transfers, or three transfers plus two long jumps through A-Level hyperspace, or two difficult transfers plus one A-Level jump and three B-Level cruises, or—*'

'That's okay,' Rety said, clapping her hands to quiet the machine. 'Right now all I want to know is, will we get to the point all right?'

There followed a brief pause while the machine pondered.

'*I am a teaching unit, not a starship navigator. All I can tell is that our C-Level pseudomomentum appears adequate to reach the periphery of the nexus. This vessel's remaining marginal power may be sufficient to then aim toward one of the simpler transfer threads.*'

Rety did not have to speak. Her smug expression said it all. Everything was going according to her devious plan.

But Dwer would not be fooled.

She may be brilliant, he thought. *But she's also crazier than a mulcspider.*

He had known it ever since the two of them almost died together, months ago in the Rimmer Mountains, seized in the clutches of a mad antiquarian creature called One-of-a-Kind. Rety's boldness since then had verged on reckless mania. Dwer figured she survived only because Ifni favors the mad with a special, warped set of dice.

He had no idea what a transfer point was, but it sounded more dangerous than poking a roul shambler in the face with a fetor worm.

Ah, well. Dwer sighed. There was nothing to be done about it right now. As a tracker, he knew when to just sit back and practice patience, letting nature take its course. 'Whatever you say, Rety. But now let's turn the damn thing off. You can show me that food machine again. Maybe we can teach it to give us something better than greasy paste to eat.'

HARRY

He reconfigured the station to look something like a Martian arachnite, a black oval body perched on slender, stalklike legs. It was all part of Harry's plan to deal with the problem of those transumptive banana peels.

After pondering the matter, and consulting the symbolic reference archive, he decided the screwy yellow things must be allaphorical representations of short-scale time warps, each one twisting around itself through several subspace dimensions. Encountering one, you would meet little resistance at first. Then, without warning, you'd slam into a slippery, repulsive field that sent you tumbling back toward your point of origin at high acceleration.

If this theory was true, he'd been lucky to survive that first brush with the nasty things. Another misstep might be much more ... energetic.

Since flight seemed memetically untenable in this part of E Level, the spider morphology was the best idea Harry could come up with, offering an imaginative way to maneuver past the danger, using stilt legs to pick carefully from one stable patch to the next. It would be risky, though, so he delayed the attempt for several days, hoping the anomaly reef would undergo another phase shift. At any moment, the irksome 'peels' might just evaporate or transform into a less lethal kind of insult. As long as he had a good view of his appointed watch area, it seemed best to just sit and wait.

Of course, he knew why a low-class Earthling recruit was assigned to this post. Wer'Q'quinn had said Harry's test scores showed an ideal match of cynicism and originality, suiting him for lookout duty in allaphor space. But in truth, E Level was unappealing to most oxygen breathers. The great clans of the Civilization of Five Galaxies thought it a quaint oddity at best. Dangerous and unpredictable. Unlike Levels A, B, and C, it offered few shortcuts around the immense vacuum deserts of normal space. Anyone in a hurry – or with a strong sense of self-preservation – chose transfer points, hyperdrive, or soft-quantum tunneling, instead of braving a realm where fickle subjectivity reigned.

Of course, oxygen breathers only made up the most gaudy and frenetic of life's eight orders. Harry kept notes whenever he sighted hydros, quantals, memoids, and other exotic types, with their strange insouciance about the passage of time. *They don't see it as quite the enemy we oxy-types do.*

His bosses at the Navigation Institute craved data about those strange comings and goings, though he could hardly picture why. The orders of sapiency so seldom interacted, they might as well occupy separate universes.

Still, you could hide a lot in all this weirdness, a trait that sometimes drew oxy-based life down here. On occasion, some faction or alliance would try sending a battle fleet through E Space, suffering its disadvantages in order to take rivals by surprise. Or else criminals might hope to move by a secret path through this treacherous realm. Harry was trained to look out for sooners, gene raiders, syntac thieves, and others trying to cheat the strict rules of migration and Uplift. Rules that so far kept the known cosmos from dissolving into chaos and ruin.

He nursed no illusions about his status. Harry knew this job was just the sort of dangerous, tedious duty the great institutes assigned to lowly clients of an unimportant clan. Yet he took seriously his vow to Wer'Q'quinn and NavInst. He planned to show all the doubters what a neo-chimp could do.

That determination was put to the test when he roused from his next rest break to peer through the louvered blinds, blinking with groggy surprise at an endless row of serrated green ridges that had erupted while he slept. Undulating sinusoidally across the foreground, they resembled the half-submerged spiny torso of some gigantic, lazy sea serpent that seemed to stretch toward both horizons, blocking his panorama of the purple plane.

At its slothful rate of passage, several pseudodays might pass before Harry's view was unobstructed once again. He stared for some time at the coils' slow rise and fall, wondering what combination of reality and his own mental processes could have evoked such a thing. If a memoid – another self-sustaining, living abstraction – it was huge enough to engulf most of the more modest animated idealizations grazing nearby.

When a concept grows big enough, does it become part of the landscape? Will it merge with the underpinnings of E Level? Will this 'idea' take part in motivating the entire cosmos?

One thing was for sure, he could hardly survey his assigned area with something like this in the way!

Unfortunately, the damned banana peels still surrounded his station with a deadly allaphorical minefield. But clearly the time had come to move on.

The station swayed at first when he tried controlling the stilt legs by hand. Apparently, his spindly tower pushed the limits of verticality in this region, where flight was forbidden by local laws of physics. The structure teetered and nearly fell three times before he started getting the hang of things.

Alas, he had no option of handing supervision over to the computer. 'Pilot mode' was often useless on E Level, where machines could be deaf and blind to allaphors that lay right in front of them.

'Well, here goes,' he murmured, gingerly navigating the scout platform ahead, raising one spidery stem, maneuvering it skittishly past a yellow and brown 'peel,' and planting it on the best patch of open ground within reach. Testing its footing, he shifted the station's center of gravity, transferring more weight forward until it felt safe to try again with another.

The process was a lot like chess – you had to think at least a dozen moves ahead, for there could be no going back. 'Reversibility' was a meaningless term in this continuum, where *death* might take on the attributes of a physical creature, and *entropy* was just another predatory concept prowling a savannah of ideas.

It became a slow, tense process of exertion, tedious and utterly demanding. Harry grew to despise the banana peel symbols, even more than before. He *used* his hatred to reinforce concentration, picking slowly amid the yellow emblems of slipperiness, knowing that any misstep might send the little scoutship flipping violently toward a gaudy oblivion.

Somehow – he could tell – the peels sensed his loathing. Their boundaries seemed to shrink a little and solidify under his gaze.

'We do not require passionless observers for this kind of duty,' Wer'Q'quinn had explained when Harry joined the Observer Corps at Kazzkark Base.

'There are many others we could choose, whose minds are more disciplined. More detached, cautious, and in most ways more intelligent.

Those volunteers are needed elsewhere. But on E Level, we are better served by someone like you.'

'Gee, thanks,' Harry had replied. 'So, are you saying you don't want me to be skeptical when I'm out on a mission?'

The squadron leader bowed a great, wormlike head. Rustling segment plates crafted words in ratchety Galactic Five.

'Only those who start with skepticism can open themselves to true adventure,' Wer'Q'quinn continued. *'But there are many types of skeptical outlook. Yours is gritty, visceral. You take things personally, young Earthling, as if the cosmos has a particular interest in your inconvenience. On most planes of reality, that is an egregious error of solipsistic pride. But on E Level, it may be the only appropriate way of dealing with an idiosyncratic cosmos.'*

Harry came away from that interview with oddly mixed feelings – as if he had just received the worst insult – and highest praise – of his life. The effect was to make him more determined than ever.

Perhaps Wer'Q'quinn had intended that, all along.

I hate you, he thought at the ridiculous, offensive yellow peels. On some level, they might be neutral twists of space, described by cold equations. But they seemed to taunt him by appearing the way they did, provoking an intimate abhorrence that Harry used to his advantage, piloting around the traps as if each success humiliated a real enemy.

His body grew sweaty and warm. A musty odor filled the cupola as one tense, cautious hour passed into the next.

Finally, with a nimble hop, he stepped his spindly vehicle away from the last obstacle, breathing a deep sigh, feeling tired, smelly, and victorious. Perhaps at some level the reef allaphors knew they had lost, for at that moment the 'peels' began transforming from yellow and brown starfish forms into another shape, one with curls and spikes ...

Harry didn't wait to see what they would become. He ordered the pilot program to hurry away from there.

It took a while to get past the green 'sea monster,' ducking through a gap between two of its slowly undulating coils. The passage made Harry nervous, staring up at portions of that mammoth, living conceptual torso. But then he was free at last to race for open territory. The purple plain swept by as he aimed for the most promising vantage point – a stable-looking brown hillock, too barren and mundane to attract any hungry memoids. A place where he might settle down to watch his assigned patrol zone in peace.

The prominence lay quite some distance away – several miduras of subjective duration, at least. Meanwhile, the surrounding table-land appeared placid. The few allaphorical beings he did spy moved quickly out of the way. Most types of predatory memes disliked the simplistic scents of metal and other hard stuff intruding from other levels of reality.

Harry deemed it safe to go below and take a shower. Then, while combing knots out of his fur, he ordered something to eat from the autochef. He considered taking a nap, but found he was still too keyed up. Sleep, under such conditions, would be dream-racked and hardly restful. Anyway, it might be wiser to supervise while the ship was in motion. Pilot mode could not be counted on to notice everything.

The decision proved fortuitous. He returned upstairs to find his trusty vessel already much closer to its destination than expected. *That's quick progress. We're already halfway up the hill*, he thought, surveying the view from each window. *This should offer an ideal surveillance site*.

Several instruments on Harry's console suddenly began whirring and chirping excitedly. Checking the telltales, he saw that something made mostly of solid matter lay just ahead, over the ridge top. It did not seem to be from any of the other sapiency orders, but showed all the suspicious-familiar signs he was trained to look for in a ship from the Civilization of Five Galaxies.

Oxies, he realized.

Gotcha!

Harry felt a thrill while checking his weapon systems. This was what he had trained for. An encounter with his own kind of life, moving through a realm of space where protoplasmic beings did not belong. He relished the prospect of stopping and inspecting a ship from some highfalutin clan, like the Soro or Tandu. They might even gag on the disgrace of being caught and fined by a mere chimpanzee from the wolfling clan of Terra.

You aren't really here to fight, Harry reminded himself as the station's armaments reported primed and ready.

Your primary mission is to observe and report.

Still, he was an officer of the law, empowered to question oxy-beings who passed this way. Anyway, preparing weapons seemed a wise precaution. Scouts often disappeared during missions to E Level. Being attacked by some band of criminals might seem mundane, compared to getting gobbled by a rampant, self-propagating idea ... but it could get you just as dead.

The bogey's not moving, Harry noted with some surprise. *It's just sitting there, a little beyond the hillcrest. Perhaps they've broken down, or run into trouble. Or else ...*

Among the worries flashing through his mind was the thought of ambush. The bogey might be lying in wait.

In fact, though, Harry's sensors were specially designed for E-Level use, while the interlopers, whoever they were, probably had a starship's generalized instruments. There was a good chance they hadn't even detected him yet!

I might take 'em by surprise.

And yet, he began rethinking how good an idea that was, as more duras passed and pseudodistance to the target shrank. This continuum made most oxy-types edgy. Perhaps trigger-happy. Surprise might be an overrated virtue. Too late, he recalled that the station was still formatted like an arachnite! Spindle-legged and fierce-looking as it took giant footsteps. The design offered a good view of his surroundings ... and exposed him to crippling fire if things came down to a firefight.

Well, it's too late to change now. Ready or not, here we go!

As he crested the metaphorical hill, Harry triggered the recognition transponder, boldly beaming symbolic references to his official status, commissioned by one of the high institutes of Galactic culture.

The intruder entered line-of-sight, filling a forward viewing panel – a squat oblong shape, resembling a fierce armored beetle, with formidable claws. Those tearing pincers swiveled toward Harry. Spindly emitter arrays waved like antenna-feelers above the beetle's browridge, hurling aggressive symbolic replies to Harry's challenge. Those writhing blobs of corporeal meaning sped rapidly across the narrowing gap between the two vessels. When the first one struck his forward pane, it made a splatting sound that resonated loudly, smearing and transforming into a shout that filled the little chamber.

'SURRENDER, EARTHLING! RESISTANCE IS USELESS! CAPITULATE OR DIE!'

Harry blinked. He stared for two or three duras, hand poised over the weapons panel while new threats pounded the window in quick succession.

'HEAVE TO AND SUBMIT! PREPARE TO MEET THY MAKER! DROP YOUR SHORTS! CRY UNCLE! GIVE UP, IN THE NAME OF THE LAW!'

Abruptly, Harry let out a low moan.

It must be Zasusazu ... my replacement. Can it be time already?

Besides, who else would squat on a hillock in E Level, just hanging around in the open, but another damn fool recruit of Wer'Q'quinn?

More horrid clichés smacked against his windshield, making the cupola resound painfully until he answered with volleys of his own, serving Zasusazu salvo after salvo of rich Terran curses, satisfying his colleague's appetite for colorful wolfling invective.

'Laugh while you can, frog face! Take that, you overgrown slime-ball! Moldy Jack cheese!' He laughed, half out of relief, and half because Zasusazu's obsession seemed so silly.

Well, everyone who works for Wer'Q'quinn is more than a little weird, Harry thought, trying to feel charitable. *Zasusazu's not as bad as some. At least he likes a little surprise now and then.*

Still, even after he exchanged reports with his replacement, then left Zasusazu in command over the realm of ideas, Harry wondered about his own reaction to being relieved. After all, this had been a wearying mission and he certainly deserved time off. Yet, despite the frustration, danger, and loneliness of E Space, it always came as a bit of a letdown for a mission to end. To head back home.

Home? Maybe the problem lay in that term.

He mused on the word, as if it were a conceptual creature, wandering the purple plain.

It can't mean Horst, since I hated nearly every minute there. Or Earth, where I spent just a year, lonely and confused.

Can Kazzkark Base be 'home,' if it lacks any others of my kind?

Does the Navigation Institute fill that role, now that I've given it the same loyalty others devote to kin and country?

Harry realized he didn't really know how to define the word.

All the superficial landmarks and reference points had changed since he first set out from Kazzkark. Still, there was an underlying familiarity to the main route. He never worried about getting lost.

Harry wasn't much surprised when the red-blue sky overhead gradually angled downward to meet 'ground,' like a vast, descending wall. He took over from the autopilot. Gingerly, maneuvering by hand, he sent the station striding daintily through a convenient perforation in heaven.

SARA

The High Sages tell us that a special kind of peace comes with resignation.

With letting go of life's struggles.

With releasing hope.

Now, for the first time, Sara understood that ancient teaching as she watched Gillian Baskin decide whether to live or die.

No one doubted that the blond Terragens Agent had the right, duty, and wisdom to make that choice, for herself and everyone aboard. Not the dolphin crew, nor Hannes Suessi, nor the Niss Machine. Sara's mute friend Emerson seemed to agree – though she wondered how much the crippled former engineer comprehended from those manic lights in the holo display, glimmering frantically near Izmunuti's roiling flame.

Even the kids from Wuphon Port – Alvin, Huck, Ur-ronn, and Pincer – accepted the commander's authority. If Gillian thought it best to send *Streaker* diving toward an unripe t-point – in order to lure the enemy after them in an attempt to save Jijo – few aboard this battered ship would curse the decision. At least it would bring an end to ceaseless troubles.

We were resigned. I was at peace, and so was Dr. Baskin.

Only now things aren't so simple anymore. She sees a possible alternative ... and it's painful as hell.

Sara found most of the crew's activities confusing, in both the water-filled bridge and the dry Plotting Room nearby, where dolphins moved about on wheeled or six-legged contraptions.

Of course, Sara's knowledge about Galactic technology was two centuries out of date, acquired by reading Jijo's sparse collection of paper books. Despite that, her theoretical underpinnings worked surprisingly well when it came to grasping conditions in local spacetime. But she remained utterly dazed by the way crew members dealt with practical matters – conveying status reports along brain-linked cables, or sending each other info-packets consisting of tiny self-contained gobbets of semi-intelligent light. When dolphins spoke aloud, it was often in a terse argot of clicks and overlapping cries that had nothing in common with any standard Galactic tongue. Still, nothing awed Sara quite as much as when Dr. Baskin invited her along to watch an attempt to pry information from a captured unit of the Galactic Library.

The big cube lay in its own chamber, swaddled by a chill fog, one face emblazoned with a rayed-spiral sign that was notorious even to Jijo's savage tribes. Within its twelve edges and six boundary planes lay an amassment of knowledge so huge that comparing it to the Biblos archive was like matching the great sea against a single teardrop.

Gillian Baskin approached the Library unit clothed in a ghost-like mantle of illusion, her slim human form cloaked behind the computer-generated image of a monstrous, leathery creature called a 'Thennanin.' Observing from nearby shadows, Sara could only blink in apprehensive awe as the older woman used this uncanny ruse, speaking a guttural dialect of Galactic Six, making urgent inquiries about enigmatic creatures known as Zang.

The topic was not well received.

'Beware mixing the orders of life,' droned the cube's frigid voice, in what Sara took to be a ritualized warning.

'Prudent contact is best achieved in the depths of the Majestic Bowl, where those who were born separated may safely combine.

'In that deep place, differences merge and unity is born.

'But here in black vacuum – where space is flat and light rays cut straight trails – young races should not readily mingle with other orders. In this outer realm, they behave like hostile gases. Fraternization can lead to conflagration.'

Impressed by the archive's vatic tone, Sara pondered how its parabolic language resembled the Sacred Scrolls that devout folks read aloud on shobb holidays, back home on Jijo. The same obliqueness could be found in many other priestly works she had sampled in the Biblos archive, inherited from Earth's long night of isolation. Those ancient tomes, differing in many ways, all shared that trait of allegorical obscurity.

In science – real science – there was always a way to improve a good question, making it harder to dismiss with prevarication. Nature might not give explicit answers right away, but you could tell when someone gave you the old runaround. In contrast, mystical ambiguity sounded grand and striking – it could send chills down your spine. But in the end it boiled down to evasion.

Ah, but ancient Earthlings – and early Jijoan sages – had an excuse. Ignorance. Vagueness and parables are only natural among people who know no other way. I just never expected it from the Galactic Library.

From an early age, Sara had dreamed of facing a unit like this one, posing all the riddles that baffled her, diving into clouds of distilled acumen collected by the great thinkers of a million races for over a billion years. Now she felt like Dorothy, betrayed by a charlatan in the chamber of Oz.

Oh, the knowledge must be there, all right – crammed in deep recesses of that chilled cube. But the Library wasn't sharing readily, even to Dr. Baskin's feigned persona as a warlord of a noble clan.

'Gr-tuthuph-manikhochesh, zangish torgh mph,' Gillian demanded, wearing the mask of a Thennanin admiral. *'Manik-hophtupf, mph!'*

A button in Sara's ear translated the eccentric dialect.

'We understand that Zang, by nature, dislike surprise,' Dr. Baskin inquired. 'Tell me how they typically react when one rude shock is followed by several more.'

This time, the Library was only slightly more forthcoming.

'The term Zang refers to just one subset of hydrogen-breathing forms – the variant encountered most often by oxy-life in open-space situations. The vast majority of hydro breathers seldom leave the comfort of dense circulation storms on their heavy worlds ...'

The lecture ran on, relating information Sara would normally find mesmerizing. But time was short. A crucial decision loomed in less than a midura.

Should *Streaker* continue her headlong drive for the resurrected transfer point? After lying dormant for half a million years – ever since Galaxy Four was declared fallow to sapient life – it was probably unripe for safe passage. Still, its uncanny rebirth offered *Streaker*'s crew a dour opportunity.

The solution of Samson. To bring the roof down on our enemies, and ourselves.

Only now fate proffered another daring possibility. The presence of collector machines and Zang ships still lacked clear explanation. The harvesting armada seemed weak, scattering in confusion before Izmunuti's unexpected storms. And yet – *Might they somehow help us defeat the Jophur without it costing our lives?*

Orders from the Terragens Council made Gillian's top priority clear. This ship carried treasure – relics of great consequence that might destabilize the Five Galaxies, especially if they were seized by a single fanatic clan. Poor little Earth could not afford to be responsible for one zealot alliance gaining advantage over all the others. There was no surer formula for Terran annihilation. Far better that both ship and cargo should be lost than some malign group like the Jophur seize a monopoly. Especially if a prophesied Time of Changes was at hand.

But what if *Streaker* could somehow deliver her burdens to the proper authorities? Ideally, that would force the Great Institutes and 'moderate' clans to end their vacillation and take responsibility. So far, relentless pursuit and a general breakdown of law had made that seemingly simple step impossible. Neutral forces proved cowardly or unwilling to help *Streaker* come in out of the cold. Still, if it were done just right, success could win Earthclan a triumph of epic proportions.

Unfortunately, the passing duras weren't equipping Gillian any better for her decision. Listening in growing frustration to the Library's dry oration, she finally interrupted.

'You don't have to tell me again that Zang hate surprise! I want practical advice! Does that mean they'll shoot right away, if we approach? Or will they give us a chance to talk?

'I need contact protocols!'

Still, the Library unit seemed bent on remaining vague, or else inundating Gillian with useless details. Standing where the Thennanin disguise did not block her view, Sara watched Gillian grow craggy with tense worry.

There is another source, Sara thought. *Someone else aboard who might be able to help with the Zang.*

She had been hesitant to mention the possibility before. After all, her 'source' was suspect. Fallen beings whose ancestors had turned away from sapiency and lacked any knowledge of spatial dilemmas. But now, as precious duras passed and Gillian's frustration grew, Sara knew she must intervene.

If the Great Library can't help us, maybe we should look to an unlikely legend.

ALVIN'S JOURNAL

Ever since we brave volunteers joined the Earthlings on their forlorn quest, I've compared it to our earlier trip aboard a handmade submarine – a little summer outing that wound up taking four settler kids all the way to the bottom of the sea, and from there to the stars.

Of course our little *Wuphon's Dream* was just a hollowed-out log with a glass nose, hardly big enough for an urs, a hoon, a qheuen, and a g'Kek to squeeze inside, providing we took turns breathing. In contrast, *Streaker* is so roomy you could fit all the khutas of Port Wuphon inside. It has comforts I never imagined, even after a youth spent reading crates of Terran novels about starfaring days.

And yet, the trips have similarities.

In each case we took a willing chance, plunging into a lightless abyss to face unexpected wonders.

On both expeditions, my friends and I had different assigned tasks.

And sure enough, aboard *Streaker*, just like *Wuphon's Dream*, I got the worst job to do.

Keeper of Animals. That's me.

Ur-ronn gets to follow her passion for machinery, helping Suessi's gang down in engineering.

Pincer runs errands for the bridge crew. He's having a grand time dashing amphibiously from dry to watery parts of the ship and back again, with flashing claws and typical qheuen enthusiasm.

Huck spins her wheels happily. She gets to play *spy*, waving all four eyestalks to taunt the Jophur captives in their cell below, enraging them with the sight of a living g'Kek, provoking them into revealing more information than they would by other means. The *nyah-nyah* school of interrogation, I call it.

All three of them get to interact with the dolphin crew, helping in ways that matter. Even if we all get blown to bits soon, at least Huck and the others got to do interesting things.

But me? I'm stuck in the hold, keeping herd on twenty bleating glavers and a pair of cranky noors, with the combined conversational abilities of a qheuen larva.

According to the Niss Machine, one of these noors ought to be quite a conversationalist. It's *not* a noor, you see, but a *tytlal* – from a starfaring race that look like noor, smell like noor, and have the same knavish temperament. Somehow they hid among us on Jijo all these years without ever being recognized. A seventh race of sooners – illegal settlers – who benefited from our Commons, but never bothered to formally join.

That'd take some cleverness, I admit. But Mudfoot acts just like my pet noor, Huphu. Lounging around, eating anything that isn't bolted down, and licking his sleek black pelt all the way to the discolored paws that give him his name. Everyone thinks I'm an expert at coaxing noor, just because hoonish mariners hire some of them to help on our sailing ships, scooting deftly along the spars and rigging, working for umbles and sourballs. But I say that only shows how easy it is to fool a hoon. A thousand years. That's how long we worked with the nimble creatures, and we never caught on.

Now they're counting on me to get Mudfoot to speak once more.

Yeah, right. And this journal of mine is going to be published when we reach Earth, and win a Sheldon Award.

Huphu and Mudfoot still glare at each other, hissing jealously – not unusual for two noor who haven't worked out their mutual status yet. Meanwhile, I try to keep my *other* wards comfortable.

We never saw very many glavers in my hometown, down along the Slope's volcanic coast. They love rooting through garbage piles and rotten logs for tasty bugs, but such things are in short supply aboard *Streaker*.

Dr. Baskin worked out an exchange with Uriel the Smith, swapping this little herd for several dozen crew members who stayed behind to form a new dolphin colony on Jijo. It hardly seems an even trade. Watching the glavers mewl and jostle in a corner of the hold, I can scarcely picture their ancestors as mighty starfarers. Those bulging, chameleon eyes – swiveling independently, searching the sterile metal hold for crawling things – hold no trace of sapient light. According to Jijo's Sacred Scrolls, that makes the opal-skinned quadrupeds sacred beings. They've attained the highest goal of any sooner race – reaching simplicity by crossing the Path of Redemption.

Renewed, cleansed of ancestral sin, they face the universe with reborn innocence, ready for a fresh start. Or so the sages say.

Forgive me for being unimpressed. You see, I have to clean up after the smelly things. If some patron race ever takes on the honored task of reuplifting glavers, they had better make housebreaking their first priority.

At first sight, you wouldn't think the filthy things had much in common with fastidious noor. But they both seem to like it when I puff out my throat sac and give a low, booming umble-song. Ever since my adult vertebroids erupted, I've acquired a deep resonance that I'm rather proud of. It helps keep the critters calm whenever *Streaker* makes a sudden maneuver and her gravity fields waver.

I try not to think about where the ship is right now, tearing along at incredible speed, diving through the flames of a giant star.

Fortunately, I can umble while editing and updating my diary on a little teacher-scribe device that Dr. Baskin provided. By now I'm used to working with letters that float before me, instead of lying fixed on an ink-stained page. It's convenient to be able to reach into my work, shifting and nudging sentences by hand or voice command. Still, I wish the machine would stop trying to fix my grammar and syntax! I may not be human, but I'm one of Jijo's best experts on the Anglic language, and I don't need a smart-aleck computer telling me my dialect's 'archaic.' If my journal ever gets published on a civilized world, I'm sure my colonial style will enhance its charm, like the old-time appeal of works by Defoe and Swift.

It grows harder to stave off frustration, knowing my friends are in the thick of things, and me stuck below, staring at blank walls, with just dumb beasts for company. I know, by doing this I freed a member of *Streaker*'s understaffed crew to do important work. Still, it sometimes feels like the bulkheads are closing in.

'Who do you think *you're* looking at?' I snapped, when I caught Mudfoot glancing alternately at me and the floating lines of my journal. 'You want to read it?'

I swiveled the autoscribe so hovering words swarmed toward the sleek creature.

'If you tytlal are so brainy, maybe you know where I should take the story next. Hrm?'

Mudfoot peered at the glyph symbols. His expression made my spines frickle. I wondered.

Just how much memory do they retain – this secret clan of super-noor? When did the Tymbrimi plant a clandestine colony of their clients on Jijo? It must have been before we hoons came. Perhaps they predate even the g'Kek.

I had heard many legends of the clever Tymbrimi, of course – a spacefaring race widely disliked by conservative Galactics for their scamplike natures. The same trait made them befriend Earthlings, when that naive clan first stumbled onto the star lanes. Ignorance can be fatal in this dangerous universe, and Terra might have quickly suffered the typical Wolflings' Fate, if not for Tymbrimi sponsorship and advice.

Only now crisis convulses the Five Galaxies. Mighty alliances are wreaking vengeance for past grievances. Earth and her friends may have reached the end of their luck, after all.

Even before meeting humans, the Tymbrimi must have known a day might come when all their enemies would converge against them. They must have been tempted to stash a small population group in some secluded place, before war, accident, or betrayal extinguished their main racial stock.

Did they consider taking the sooners' path?

I'm no expert, but from what I've read, it seems unlikely that their natures would ever let Tymbrimi settle down to quiet pastoral lives on a hick world like Jijo. *Humans* barely accomplished it, and they are much more down to earth.

But if the Tymbrimi couldn't hide out as sooners, it wasn't too late for their beloved clients. The tytlal were still largely unknown. Still close to their animal roots. A small gene pool might be partly devolved and safely cached on far-off Jijo. It all made eerie sense. Including the notion of a race within a race – a band of undevolved noor, hidden among them. Guardians, keeping twin black eyes open for danger ... or opportunity.

Watching Mudfoot, I recalled stories told by Dwer Koolhan – during his brief time aboard this ship, when *Streaker* hid beneath Jijo's sea – about how this wild animal kept snooping and meddling, following Dwer across half a continent. Ever mysterious, infuriating, and unhelpful. The behavior seemed to combine noorish recklessness with an attention span worthy of a hoon.

Intelligent irony now seemed to dominate Mudfoot's snub-nosed, carnivorous face while he scanned my most recent lines of prose – the very musings about tytlal nature that lay just above. His black-pelted form coiled tightly, in an expression that I mistook for studious interest. I could almost imagine mute noorish whimsy transforming into eloquent speech – witty commentary perhaps, or else a brutal putdown of my dense composition style.

Then, with an abrupt display of unleashed energy, Mudfoot leaped into the crowd of floating words, flailing left and right with agile forepaws, slashing sentences to ribbons, knocking whole paragraphs awry before *Streaker*'s artificial g-field yanked him to a crouched landing on the metal deck. At once, he swiveled with a hunter's delighted yowl and readied another pounce.

'Don't save those changes!' I shouted at the autoscribe with unaccustomed haste. 'Make all text intangible!'

My command made Mudfoot's second leap less satisfying. Robbed of semisolidity, the words of my journal were now mere visual holograms, unaffected by physical touch. His second assault slashed uselessly while he passed through ghostly symbols, barking with disappointment.

Moments later, though, Mudfoot perched once more on my right shoulder, as Huphu glared at him lazily from the left. Both of them preened for a while, then began rubbing my throat, begging for an umble.

'You don't fool me for a dura,' I muttered. But there seemed little else to do except repair the damage, finish up this journal entry, and then give them what they wanted.

I was doing that – singing for two noor and a herd of mesmerized glaver – when the Niss Machine barged in with a message.

I still have no idea why the snide robotic mind keeps interrupting this way, without preamble or greeting, despite my complaints that it grates against a hoon's nature. And the tornado of spinning, twisted lines somehow hurts my eyes. Ifni, it's hard enough getting used to the idea of talking computers, even though I used to read about them in classics by Nagata and Ecklar. Can it be that the Niss has some sort of family relationship with Mudfoot? A connection via the Tymbrimi, would be my guess. You can tell by their disdain for courtesy and knack for putting people off balance.

'*I bring a message from the bridge crew,*' announced the whirling shape. '*Although I see little good coming out of it, they want to see one or two of your charges up there. You must bring the creatures along at once. A crew member is already coming to replace you here.*'

Gently putting Huphu down on the metal deck, I gathered Mudfoot in a carrying hold, comfortably cradling him in the crook of one arm, so he could not writhe free. He seemed content, but I was taking no chances. The last thing I needed was for him to dash off in some random direction on our way to the bridge, wreaking havoc in the galley, or hiding in some storeroom till *Streaker* was blasted to smithereens.

'Won't you tell me what it's all about?' I asked.

The abstract lines appeared to shrug.

'*For some reason, Dr. Baskin and Sage Sara Koolhan seem to think the beast may speak up, at an opportune moment, helping us deal with potentially hostile aliens.*'

I umbled a deep, rolling laugh.

'Well they got hopes! This Ifni-slucking tytlal is gonna talk when it wants to, and the universe can go to hell till then, for all it cares.'

The lines twisted tighter than ever.

'*I am not referring to the tytlal, Alvin. Please put the little rascal down and pay attention.*'

'But ...' I shook my head, human style, confused. 'Then, who ...?'

The Niss hologram bent toward the far wall, making an effort to point.

'*You are requested to bring up one or two of those.*'

I stared at a crowd of goggle-eyed cretins. Mewling, nosing through their own revolting feces ... 'blessed' with sacred forgetfulness, immune to worry.

So this hurried journal entry ends on a note of blank surprise.

They want me to bring *glavers* to the bridge.

LARK

He stumbled down twisty, intestinelike corridors, fleeing almost randomly through the vast ship, pausing occasionally to rest his head against a squishy bulkhead and sob. Cloying Jophur scentomeres mingled with his own stench of self-disgust and grief.

I should have stayed with her.

Lark's unwashed body, still sticky with juices from that dreadful nursery, kept moving despite fatigue and hunger, driven on by occasional sounds of pursuit. But his mind seemed mired, with all its fine edges dulled by regret. Repeatedly, he tried to rouse from this depression and come up with a way to fight back.

You've got to think. Ling is counting on you!

In fact, Lark wasn't even sure where to go looking for his lover. His mental image of the *Polkjhy* was a blur of tangled passages linking odd-shaped chambers, more chaotic than the hivelike innards of a qheuen dam. Anyway, suppose he did find his way back to the prison section, the vault where he and Ling had made their getaway just a few days ago. By now the place would be triply guarded. By Jophur ring stacks, robots, and the tall human renegade.

Rann will be expecting me. He knows exactly what I'm thinking ... that I want to go charging to her rescue.

Alas, Lark was no man of action like his brother, Dwer. The odds paralyzed him. He was too good at envisioning drawbacks and potential flaws in each tentative plan.

As long as I'm free, Ling can still hope. I have no right to throw that away by rushing into a trap. First priority has to be a place where I can rest ... maybe find something to eat ... then come up with a plan.

Using the purple ring as a universal passkey, Lark inspected various rooms along his meandering path, hoping to find a tool or information he could use against the enemy. Some compartments were empty. Others were occupied by Jophur crew, but these paid little heed to the distraction of an opening or closing door. Like their traeki cousins on Jijo, Jophur tended to be task-focused, reacting slowly to interruptions.

Only once did Lark fail to duck out of sight in time.

He was poking through a laboratory filled with coiled, transparent glassy tubes that flickered and hissed with roiling vapors. Abruptly Lark found his path blocked by a massive ring stack. It had just turned away from an instrument console, and all sensor toruses were active.

Flatulent smoke bursts vented from the Jophur's peak, indignant to spy an intruding human. Fatty toruses flickered with shadowy patterns of light and dark, expressing surprised rage.

If he had paused to think, Lark would never have had the courage to lunge toward that intimidating mass, thrusting his only weapon past a dozen reaching tentacles. Tendrils converged to surround him, slapping his shoulders.

Master rings make Jophur ambitious and decisive, thought a bookish corner of his mind. *But thank Ifni they're like traeki in other ways. Their sluggish nerves were never tested by carnivores on a savannah.*

But Jophur had other advantages. Throbbing feelers coiled around his neck and arms, even as soporific juices sprayed from the throbbing torus in his hands, the final gift of gentle Asx.

This time there was no reaction from the huge, tapered tower. Its grippers tightened, drawing Lark toward glistening, oily flanks.

He felt the purple ring flex and emit three more sprays, each one a different pungent fetor that made his eyes sting and his throat gag ... till constricting pressure round his chest made it impossible to breathe at all.

The trick may not work anymore. They may have spread the word. Distributed counteragents ...

All at once, the greasy titan shivered. The nooses tensed ... then slackened, going limp as the Jophur settled its great mass to the floor, discharging a low sigh and rank smells. Lark nearly strangled on his first ragged breath. Shrugging free of the horrid embrace, he stumbled away, sucking for fresh air.

They're catching on. Each time the purple ring fools one of them, they share information and antidotes. Even Asx couldn't anticipate every possible scent code the Jophur might use.

The big stack seemed quiescent now, but Lark worried it might have put out an alarm. Swiftly, he scanned the rest of the chamber for co-workers. But the creature was alone.

Lark was about to head back to the corridor when he stopped, intrigued to see that the Jophur's console was still active. Holo displays flickered, tuned to spectral bands his eyes found murky at best. Still, he approached one in curiosity – then growing excitement.

It's a map! He recognized the battle cruiser's oblate shape, cut open to expose the ship's mazelike interior. It turned slowly. Varied shadings changed slowly while he watched.

I wish I knew more about Galactic tech. Before the Rothen-Danik expedition came to Jijo, computers had been legendary things one read about in dusty tomes within the Biblos archive. Even now, he saw them partly through two centuries of fear and half-superstition. Of course, even the star-sophisticate Ling would have trouble with this unit, designed for Jophur use. So Lark chose not to touch any buttons or sense plates.

Anyway, sometimes you can learn a lot just by observing.

This bright box over here ... I know I'm in that quadrant of the ship. Could it signify this room?

The symbols were in efficient Galactic Two, though he found the specific subdialect technical and hard to interpret. Still, he managed to locate the security section where he and Ling had been imprisoned when they were first brought aboard on Jijo. A deep, festering blue rippled outward from that area and spread gradually 'northward' along the ship's main axis, filling one deck at a time.

A search pattern. They've been driving me into an ever smaller volume ... back toward the control room.

And away from Ling.

From their slow, methodical progress, he estimated that the hunter robots would reach this chamber in less than a midura. Though it was a daunting prospect, that realization actually made Lark feel much better, just knowing where he stood. It also gave him time to seek a flaw in their strategy by studying the map for a while.

If hunger pangs don't muddle my brain first. Unfortunately, the pursuers were also herding him farther from the one place he knew of where a human could find food.

Looking around the laboratory, he found a sink with a water tap. Ling had called it a constant on almost any vessel of an oxygen-breathing species. The fluid was distilled to utter purity, and so tasted weird. But Lark slurped greedily – trying to wash myriad complex ship flavors out of his mouth – before returning once more to peruse the data screens.

Other than the ship map, most of the displays were enigmatic – flickering graphs or cascades of hurtful color, impossible to comprehend. Except for one showing a black field speckled with glittering points of light.

Ling and I saw something like this in the Jophur command center. She called it a star chart, showing where we are in space, and what's going on around us.

It still made Lark queasy to picture himself hurtling at multiples of lightspeed through an airless void. Unlike Sara, he had never dreamed of leaving Jijo, where his life's work was to study the life-forms of a richly varied world. Only war and chaos could have torn him away from there. Only his growing ardor for Ling compensated for the loss and alienation.

And now she was gone from his side. It felt like being amputated.

Staring at the display – a black vista broken by a few sparkling motes – he felt utterly daunted by the distance scales, in which vast Jijo would be lost like a floating speck of dust.

One pinpoint glowed steady in the center – the Jophur dread-nought, he guessed. And a great, yarnlike ball in the lower left must be a flaming star. But without his cosmopolitan friend to interpret, Lark was at a loss to decipher other colored objects shifting and darting in between. GalTwo symbols flashed, but he lacked the experience to make sense of them.

In frustration, Lark was about to turn away when he noticed one slim fact.

That big dot over there, near the star ... it seems to be heading straight for us.

I wonder if it's going to be friendly.

EMERSON

Nothing could feel more natural or familiar than looking at a spatial chart. It was like regarding his own face in the mirror.

More familiar than that, since Emerson had just spent a dazed year on a primitive world, gaping blankly at his reflection on crude slabs of polished metal, wondering about that person staring back at him, with the gaping hole above one ear and the dazed look in his eyes. Even his own name was a mystery till a few weeks ago, when some pieces of his past began falling together.

... scattered memories of wondrous Earth, and a youth spent targeting himself, with a solemn firmness that awed his parents, toward the glittering lure of five galaxies.

... his life as an engineer, privileged to receive the very best training, learning to make starships plunge between mysterious folds of spacetime.

... the lure of adventure – a deep voyage with the famous Captain Creideiki – an offer he could never refuse, even knowing it would lead past the jaws of Hades.

All that, and much more, was restored when Emerson learned how to beat down the savage pain that kept memory imprisoned, regaining much that had been robbed from him.

But not the best part. Not the rich, textured power of speech. Not the river of words that used to lubricate each subtle thought and bear knowledge on graceful boats of syntax. Without speech his mind was a desert realm, devastated by agnosia as deep as the crippling wound in the left side of his skull.

At least now Emerson understood his maiming had been deliberate, an act so malicious he could scarcely grasp its boundaries or encompass the scale of revenge needed to make things right.

Then, unasked and unexpected, it happened once again. Some mix of sense and emotion triggered a shift inside, releasing a sudden outpouring. All at once he imagined an enveloping swirl of soft sound – reverberations that stroked his skin, rather than his ears. Echoes that he felt, rather than heard.

> * With each turning
>> * Of the cycloid,
> * In dimensions
>> * Beyond number
> * Comes a tumble
>> * Of those cuboids,
> * Many sided,
>> * Countless faces—
>
>> * Ever unfair ... never nice.
> * Watch them spin on,
>> * So capricious,

* White and spotted,
  * Always loaded,
* Yet you, hopeless,
  * Reach to gamble,
* Tossing for a
  * Risky payback—
  * Smack the haughty! Ifni's dice ...*

Emerson smiled faintly as the Trinary ode played out, using circuits in his battered brain that even the vicious Old Ones never touched with their knives. Like the groaning melody of a Great Dreamer, it resonated whole, with tones of cetacean wisdom.

And yet, he knew its promise was but a slender reed. Hardly much basis for hope. As if the universe would ever really give him a chance at vengeance! Life was seldom so accommodating. Especially to the weak, the harried and pursued.

Still, Emerson felt grateful for the gift of strange poetry. Though it wasn't an engineer's language, Trinary excelled at conveying irony.

He watched through a broad crystal window as neo-dolphins raced back and forth, traversing *Streaker*'s waterfilled bridge with powerful tail thrusts, leaving trails of fizzing, hyper-oxygenated water in their wake. Other crewfins lay at ramplike control stations, their sleek heads inserted in airdomes while neural cables linked their large brains to computers and distant instrumentalities.

The crystal pane vibrated against his fingertips, carrying sonar clicks and rapid info-bursts from the other side. The music of cooperative skill. A euphony of craft. These were the finest members of a select crew. The *Tursiops amicus* elite. The pride of Earth's Uplift campaign, recruited and trained by the late Captain Creideiki to be pilots without peer.

The dolphin lieutenant, Tsh't, crisply handled routine decisions and relayed orders to the bridge crew. Beside her, chief helmsman Kaa lay shrouded by cables, his narrow jaw open and sunken eyes closed. Kaa's flukes slashed as he steered the starship like an extended part of his own body. Thirty million years of instinct assisted Kaa – intuition accumulated ever since his distant ancestors ceded land for a fluid realm of three dimensions.

Behind Emerson, the Plotting Room was equally abuzz. Here dolphins moved on rollers or walkers – machines that offered agility in dry terrain, making them seem even more massively bulky next to a pair of slender bipeds. And yet, those humans called the tune, directing all this furious activity. Two women whose lives had been utterly different, until circumstances brought them together.

The two women Emerson loved, though he could never tell them.

Thrumming engine sounds changed pitch as he sensed the nimble ship brake harder to fight its hyperbolic plunge, clawing against the drag of a giant star, changing course in another of Gillian Baskin's daring ventures.

Emerson had paid a dear price for one of her earlier hunches, in that huge, intricately structured place called the *Fractal World* – a realm of snowy icicles whose smallest branchlets spread wider than a planet. But he had never resented Gillian's mistake. Who else could have kept *Streaker* free for three years, eluding the armadas of a dozen fanatical alliances? He only regretted that his sacrifice had been in vain.

Above all, Emerson wanted to help right now. To go below, toward those distant humming motors, and help Hannes Suessi nurse more pseudovelocity from the laboring gravistators. But his handicap was too severe. His torn cortex could not read sense from the symbols on flashing displays, and there was only so much you could do by touch or instinct alone. His comrades had been kind, giving him make-work tasks, but he soon realized it was better just to get out of their way.

Anyway, Sara and Gillian were clearly up to something. Tension filled the Plotting Room as both women argued with the spinning apparition of the Niss Machine.

Its spiral lines coiled tightly. Clearly, a moment of drama was approaching.

So Emerson played spectator, watching as a chart portrayed *Streaker*'s tight maneuver, slewing past giant Izmunuti's stubborn grasp, threading hurricanes of ionized heat that strained the laboring shields, changing course to climb aggressively toward a cluster of pale, flickering lights.

A convoy of ships ... or things that acted like ships, moving about the cosmos at the volition of thinking minds.

He overheard Sara utter buzzing glottal stops to frame a strange GalSix term. One seldom heard, except in tones of muted awe.

Zang.

Despite his handicap, Emerson abruptly knew what advice Gillian was receiving from the young Jijoan mathematician. He shivered. Of all the chances taken by *Streaker*'s crew, none was like this. Even daring the throat of a newly roused transfer point might have been better. Just thinking about it provoked a reply from some recess of his sundered brain. Precious as a jewel, a single word glittered hot and hopeless.

Desperation ...

*

It didn't take long for *Streaker*'s tactic to be noticed.

The Jophur enemy – just twenty paktaars away – began slewing at once, shedding pseudovelocity to intercept the Earthship's new course.

A crowd of others lay even nearer at hand.

Blue glimmers represented frail harvesting machines – Emerson had seen graphic images and recognized the gossamer sails. By now half the luckless convoy were already consumed by rapidly expanding solar storms. The rest gathered light frantically, pulsing with inadequate engines, struggling to find refuge at the older transfer point.

Among those frail sparks, four bright yellow dots had been cruising imperviously, speeding to assist some of the beleaguered mechanicals. But this effort was disrupted by *Streaker*'s sudden, hard turn.

Two of the yellow glows continued their rescue efforts, darting from one harvester to the next, plucking a glittering nucleus unit out of the swelling flames and leaving the broad sail to burn.

A third yellow dot swung toward the Jophur ship.

The last one moved to confront *Streaker*.

Everyone in the Plotting Room stopped what they were doing when a shrill, crackling sound erupted over the comm speakers. Though Emerson had lost function in his normal speech centers, his ears worked fine, and he could tell at once that it was unlike any Galactic language – or wolfling tongue – he had ever heard.

The noise sounded bellicose, nervous, and angry.

The Niss hologram shivered with each staccato burst of screeching pops. Dolphins slashed their flukes, loosing unhappy moans. Sara covered her ears and closed her eyes.

But Gillian Baskin spoke calmly, soothing her companions with a wry tone of voice. In moments, chirps of dolphin laughter filled the chamber. Sara grinned, lowering her hands, and even the Niss straightened its mesh of jagged lines.

Emerson burned inside, wishing he could know what Gillian had said – what well-timed humor swiftly roused her crewmates from their alarmed funk. But all he made out were 'wah-wah' sounds, nearly as foreign as those sent by a different order of life.

The Niss Machine made rasping noises of its own. Emerson guessed it must be trying to communicate with the yellow dot. Or rather, what the dot represented ... one of those legendary, semi-fluid globes that served as 'ships' for mighty, cryptic hydrogen breathers. He recalled being warned repeatedly, back in training, to avoid all contact with the unpredictable Zang. Even the Tymbrimi curbed their rash natures when it came to such deadly enigmas. If this particular Zang perceived *Streaker* as a threat – or if it were merely touchy at the moment – any chance of survival was practically nil. The Earthship's fragments would soon join the well-cooked atoms of Izmunuti's seething atmosphere.

Soon, long-range scans revealed the face of the unknown. An image wavered at highest magnification, refracted by curling knots of stormy plasma heat, revealing a vaguely spherical object with flanks that rippled eerily. The effect didn't remind Emerson of a soap bubble as much as a tremendous gobbet of quivering grease, surrounded by dense evaporative haze.

A small bulge distended outward from the parent body as he watched. It separated and seemed briefly to float, glistening, alongside.

The detached blob abruptly exploded.

From the actinic fireball a needle of blazing light issued straight toward *Streaker*!

Klaxons erupted warnings in both the bridge and Plotting Room. The spatial chart revealed a slender line, departing the yellow emblem to spear rapidly across a distance as wide as Earth's orbit. As a weapon, it was unlike any Emerson had seen.

He braced for annihilation . . .

. . . only to resume breathing when the destructive ray passed just ahead of *Streaker*'s bow.

Lieutenant Tsh't commented wryly.

* As warning shots go,
    * (Acts speak much louder than words!)
        * That was a doozy. *

While Emerson labored to make sense of her Trinary haiku, the door of the Plotting Room hissed open and three figures slipped inside. One was a shaggy biped, nearly as tall as a dolphin is long, with a spiky backbone and flapping folds of scaly skin under his chin. Two pale, shambling forms followed, knuckle-walking like protochimpanzees, with big round heads and chameleon eyes that tried to stare in all directions at once. Emerson had seen hoons and glavers before, so he spared their entrance little thought. Everyone was watching Gillian and Sara exchange whispers as tension built.

No order was given to turn aside. Sara's lips pressed grimly, and Emerson understood. At this point, they were committed. The second transfer point was no longer an option. Its dubious refuge could not be reached now before the Jophur got there first. Nor could *Streaker* flee toward deep space, or try her luck on one of the varied levels of hyperspace. The dreadnought's engines – the best affordable by a wealthy clan – could outrun poor *Streaker* in any long chase.

The Zang did not have to destroy the Earthship. They need only ignore her, leaving the filthy oxygen breathers to settle their squabbles among themselves.

Perhaps that might have happened ... or else the orbship might have finished them off with another volley. Except that something else happened then, taking Emerson completely off guard.

The Niss hologram popped into place near the tall hoon – Alvin was the youngster's name, Emerson recalled – and then drifted lower, toward the bewildered glavers. Mewling with animallike trepidation, they quailed back from the floating mesh of spiral curves ... until the Niss began emitting a noisome racket. The same that had come over the loudspeakers minutes ago.

Blinking rapidly, the pair of glavers began reflexively swaying. Emerson could swear they seemed just as surprised as he was, and twice as frightened. Yet, they must have found the clamor somehow compelling, for soon they began responding with cries of their own – at first muted and uncertain, then with increasing force and vigor.

To the crew, it came as a rude shock. The master-at-arms – a burly male dolphin with mottled flanks – sent his six-legged walker stomping toward the beasts, intent on clearing the room. But Gillian countermanded the move, watching with enthralled interest.

Sara clapped her hands, uttering a satisfied oath, as if she had hoped for something like this.

On the face of the young hoon, surprise gave way to realization. A subdued, rolling sound escaped Alvin's vibrating throat sac. Emerson made out a single phrase—

'... *the legend* ...'

—but its significance was slippery, elusive. Concentrating hard, he almost pinned down a meaning before it was lost amid resumed howls from the loudspeakers. More caterwauled threats beamed by the Zang, objecting to *Streaker*'s rapid approach.

At long range, he saw the great globule pulsate menacingly. Another liquid bulge began separating from the main body, bigger than the first, already glowing with angry heat.

The glavers clamored louder. They seemed different from the ones he had seen back on Jijo, which always behaved like grunting beasts. Now Emerson saw something new. A light. A *knowing*. The impression of a task long deferred, now being performed at last.

The Zang globe rippled. Its rasping threats merged with the glaver bedlam, forming a turbulent pas de deux. Meanwhile, the

new bud fully detached from its flank, pulsating with barely constrained wrath.

This one might not be a warning shot.

RETY

'I guess there's more to using one of these transfer point things than
I thought.'

Rety meant her words as a peace offering. A rare admission of
fault. But Dwer wasn't going to let her off that easy.

'I can't believe you thought a couple of savages could just go zooming about the heavens like star gods. *This* was your plan? To grab a
wrecked ship, still dripping seaweed from the dross piles of the Great
Midden, and ride along while it *falls into a hole in space*?'

For once, Rety quashed her normal, fiery response. True, she had
never invited Dwer to join her aboard her hijacked vessel in the first
place. Nor was *he* offering any bright ideas about what to do with
a million-year-old hulk that could barely hold air, let alone fly.

Still, she kind of understood why he was upset. With death staring him in the face, the Slopie could be expected to get a bit testy.

'When Besh and Rann talked about it, they made it sound simple.
You just aim your ship to dive inside—'

Dwer snorted. 'Yeah, well you just said a mouthful there, Rety.
Aim into a transfer point? Did you ever think how many generations it took our ancestors to learn how to pull that off? A trick
we've got to figure out in just a midura or two?'

This time, Rety didn't have to reply. Little yee snaked his long
neck from her belt pouch, reaching out to nip Dwer's arm.

'Hey!' he shouted, drawing back.

'*see?*' the little urs chided in a lisping voice. '*no good come from
snip-snapping each other. use midura to study! or just complain till
you die.*'

Dwer rubbed a three-sided weal, glaring at the miniature male.
But yee's teeth had left the skin unbroken. Any Jijoan human knew
enough about urrish bites to recognize when one was just a warning.

'All right then,' he muttered to Rety. 'You're the apprentice star
god. Talk that smug computer of yours into saving us.'

Rety sighed. In the wilderness back home, Dwer had always been
the one with clever solutions to every problem, never at a loss. She
liked him better that way, not cowed by the mere fact that he was
trapped in a metal coffin, hurtling toward crushing death and ruin.

I hope this don't mean I'm gonna have to nursemaid him all the way across space to some civilized world. When we're all set up – with nice apart'mints and slave machines doin' anything we want – he sure is gonna owe me!

Rety squatted before the little black box Gillian Baskin had given her aboard the *Streaker* – a teaching unit programmed for very young human children. It functioned well at its intended purpose – explaining the basics of modern society to a wild girl from the hicks of Jijo. To her surprise, she had even started picking up the basics of reading and writing. But when it came to instructing them how to pilot a starship . . . well, that was another matter.

'Tutor,' she said.

A tiny cubic hologram appeared just above the box, showing a pudgy male face – with a pencil mustache and a cheery smile.

'Well, hello again! Have we been keeping our spirits up? Tried any of those games I taught you? Remember, it's important to stay busy-busy and think positive until help arrives!'

Rety lashed with her left foot, but it passed through the face without touching anything solid.

'Look, you. I told ya there's nobody gonna come help us, even if you did get out a distress call, which I doubt, since the dolphins only fixed the parts they needed to, to make this tub fly.'

The hologram pursed simulated lips, disapproving of Rety's attitude.

'Well, that's no excuse for pessimism! Remember, whenever we're in a rough spot, it is much better to seek ways of turning adversity into opportunity! So why don't we—'

'Why don't we go back to talking about how we'll *control* this here piece of dross,' Rety interrupted. 'I already asked you for lessons how to steer it through the t-point just ahead. Let's get on with it!'

The tutor frowned.

'As I tried to explain before, Rety, this vessel is in no condition to attempt an interspatial transfer at this time. Navigation systems are minimal and incapable of probing the nexus ahead for information about thread status. The drive is balky and seems only capable of operating at full thrust, or not at all. It may simply give up the next time we turn it on. The supervisory computer has degraded to mentation level six. That is below what's normally needed to calculate hyperspatial tube trajectories. For all of these reasons, attempting to cross the transfer point is simply out of the question.'

'But there's no place else to go! The Jophur battleship was dragging us there when it flung us loose. You already said we don't have the engine juice to break away before falling in. So we got nothin' to lose by trying!'

The tutor shook its simulated head.

'*Standard wisdom dictates that any maneuver we tried now would only make it harder for friends/ relatives/parents to find you—*'

This time, Rety flared.

'How many times do I gotta tell you, no one's coming for us! Nobody knows we're here. Nobody would care, if they knew. And nobody could reach us if they cared!'

The teaching unit looked perplexed. Its ersatz gaze turned toward Dwer, who looked more adult with his week-old stubble. Of course, that irritated Rety even more.

'*Is this true, sir? There is no help within reach?*'

Dwer nodded. Though he too had spent time aboard *Streaker*, he never found it easy speaking to a ghost.

'*Well then,*' the tutor replied. '*I suppose there is just one thing to do.*'

Rety sighed relief. At last the jeekee thing was going to start getting practical.

'*I must withdraw and get back to work talking to the ship's computer, no matter what state it is in. I am not designed or programmed for this kind of work, but it is of utmost importance to try harder.*'

'Right!' Rety murmured.

'*Indeed. Somehow we must find a way to boost power to communications systems, and get out a stronger message for help!*'

Rety bolted to her feet.

'What? Didn't you hear me, you pile o' glaver dreck? I just said—'

'*Don't worry while I am out of touch. Try to be brave. I'll be back just as soon as I can!*'

With that, the little cube vanished, leaving Rety shaking, frustrated, and angry.

It didn't help that old Dwer broke up, laughing. He guffawed, hissing and snorting a bit like an urs. Since nothing funny had happened, she figured he must be doing it out of spite. Or else this might be another example of that thing called *irony* people sometimes talked about when they wanted an excuse for acting stupid.

I'll slap some irony across your jeekee head, Dwer, if you don't shut up.

But he was bigger and stronger ... and he had saved her life at least three times in the past few months. So Rety just clenched her fists instead, waiting till he finally stopped chuckling and wiped tears from his eyes.

The tutor remained silent for a long time, leaving both human castaways with no way to deal with the ship on their own.

There were makeshift controls, left in place by *Streaker*'s dolphin crew when they had resurrected this ancient Buyur hulk from a pile of discarded spacecraft on Jijo's sea bottom. Mysterious boxes had been spliced by cable to the hulk's control circuits, programmed to send it erupting skyward along with a swarm of other revived decoys, confusing Jophur instruments and masking *Streaker*'s breakout attempt. But since the dolphins had never expected stowaways, there were only minimal buttons and dials. Without the tutor, there'd be no chance of making the ship budge from its current unguided plummet.

Lacking anything better to do, Rety and Dwer went forward and stared ahead through the bow windows, pitted from immersion in the Great Midden for half a million years. Together, they tried to spot the mysterious 'spinning hole in space' that Jijo's fallen races still recalled in sagas about ancestral days – the mighty doorway each sneakship passed through when it brought a new wave of refugee-settlers to a forbidden world in a fallow galaxy.

At first, Rety saw nothing special in the glittering starscape. Then Dwer pointed.

'Over there. See? The *Frog* is all bent out of shape.'

Rety had grown up amid a primitive tribe, hiding in a grubby wilderness without even the rough comforts of Dwer's homeland, the Slope. Living in crude huts, with just campfires to ward off chill and darkness, she had constellations overhead nearly every night of her life. But while her cousins made up elaborate hunters' tales about those twinkling patterns, her only interest lay in their practical use as signposts, pointing the westward path she might someday use to escape her wretched clan.

Dwer, on the other hand, was chief scout of the Commons of Jijo, trained to know every quirk of the sky – from which the Six Races always expected doom and judgment to arrive. He would notice if something was out of place.

'I don't see . . .' She peered toward the cluster of glimmering pinpoints he indicated. 'Oh! Some of the stars . . . they're clumped in a circle and—'

'And there's nothing inside,' he finished for her. 'Nothing at all.'

They stared silently for a while. Rety couldn't help comparing the disklike blackness to a predator's open maw, looming rapidly to swallow the ship and all its contents.

'The stars seem t'be smearing out around it,' she added.

Dwer nodded, making hoonish umbling sounds.

'Hr-rm. My sister called this thing a sort of *twist in the universe*, where space gets all wound up in knots.'

Rety sniffed.

'Space is *empty*, dummy. I learned that back when I lived with the Daniks, in their underground station. There's nothin' out here to *get* twisted.'

'Fine. Then *you* explain what we're about to fall into.'

Little yee chose to speak up then.

'*no problem to explain, big man-boy.*

'*what is life?*

'*is going from one hole to another, then another!*

'*is better this way. go in! yee will sniff good burrow for us.*

'*good, comfy burrow is happiness.*'

Dwer glanced sourly at the urrish male, but Rety smiled and stroked yee's tiny head.

'You tell him, husban'. We'll slide on through this thing, slick as a mud skink, an' come out in the main spiral arcade of Galaxy Number One, where the lights are bright an' ships are thicker than ticks on a ligger's back. Where the stars are close enough to gossip with each other, an' everyone's so rich they need computers to count their computers!

'Folks like that'll need folks like us, Dwer,' she assured. 'They'll be soft, while we're tough an' savvy, ready for adventure! We'll take on jobs the star gods are too prissy for – an' get paid more'n your whole Commons of Jijo is worth.

'Soon we'll be livin' high, you watch. You'll bless the day you met me.'

Dwer stared back at her. Then, clearly against his will, a smile broke out. This time the laugh was friendlier.

'Honestly, Rety. I'd rather just go home and keep some promises I made. But I guess that's unlikely now, so—' He glanced ahead at the dark circle. It had grown noticeably as they watched. 'So maybe you're right. We'll make the best of things. Somehow.'

She could tell he was putting up a front. Dwer figured they would be torn apart soon, by forces that could demolish all of Jijo in moments.

He oughta have more faith, she thought. *Somethin'll come along. It always does.*

With nothing better to do, they counted the passing duras, commenting to each other about the strange way stars stretched and blurred around the rim of the monstrous thing ahead. It doubled in size, filling a quarter of the window by the time Rety's 'tutor' popped back into existence above the black box. The tiny face had triumph in its eyes.

'*Success!*' it exulted.

Rety blinked.

'You mean you found a way to control this tub?'

'*Better than that! I managed to coax more power and bandwidth from the communications system!*'

'Yes?' Dwer moved forward. 'And?'

'*And I got a response, at last!*'

The two humans looked at each other, sharing confusion. Then Rety cursed.

'You didn't pull the bloody-damn *Jophur* back to us, did you?'

That might help the *Streaker* crew. But she had no interest in resuming her former role as bait. Rety would rather risk the transfer point than surrender to those stacks of stinky rings.

'*The battleship is beyond effective range as it dives toward the red giant star, where other mighty vessels are dimly perceived engaging in energetic activity that I cannot make out very well.*

'*The rescuers I refer to are entirely different parties.*'

The tutor paused.

'Go on,' Dwer prompted warily.

'*The active scanners were balky and difficult at first. But I finally got them on-line. At which point I spotted several ships nearby, fleeing toward the transfer point just as we are! After some further effort, I managed to flag the attention of the closest ... whereupon it changed course slightly to head this way!*'

Rety and Dwer nearly stumbled over each other rushing to the aft viewing ports. They stared for some time, but even with coaxing from the tutor, Rety saw nothing at first except the great red sun. Even at this long range, it looked larger than her thumbnail held at arm's reach. And angry storms extended farther still, with tornadolike tendrils.

Dwer pointed.

'There! Three points up from Izmunuti and two points left. You can't miss it.'

Rety tried looking where he pointed, but despite his promise, she found it hard to make out anything different. Stars glittered brightly ...

Some of them shifted slightly, moving in unison, like a flock of birds. First they jogged a little left, then a little right, but always together, as if a section of the sky itself were sliding around, unable to keep still.

Finally, she realized – the moving stars all lay in an area shaped like a slightly canted *square*.

'Those aren't real stars ...' she began, hushed.

'They're reflections,' Dwer finished. 'Like off a mirror. But how?'

The tutor seemed happiest explaining something basic.

'*The image you see is caused by a tremendous reflector-and-energy-collector. In Galactic Seven the term is* ntove tunictun. *Or in Earthling tradition – a solar sail.*

'*The method is used chiefly by sapients who perceive time as less a factor than do oxygen breathers. But right now they are using a supplementary gravitic engine to hasten progress, fleeing unexpected chaos in this stellar system. At these pseudovelocities, the vessel should be able to pick us up and still reposition itself for optimal transfer point encounter toward its intended destination.'*

Dwer held up both hands.

'Whoa! Are you saying the creatures piloting that thing don't breathe oxygen? You mean they aren't even part of the, um—'

'The Civilization of Five Galaxies? No sir, they are not. These are machines, with their own spacefaring culture, quite unlike myself, or the robot soldier devices of the Jophur. Their ways are strange. Nevertheless they seem quite willing to take us with them through the transfer point. That is a much better situation than we faced a while ago.'

Rety watched the 'sail' uneasily. Soon she made out a glittering nest of complex shapes that lay at the very center of the smooth, mirrorlike surface. As the t-point burgeoned on one side and the machine-vessel on the other, she couldn't stave off a wild sensation – like being cornered between a steep cliff and a predator.

'This thing . . .' she began asking, with a dry mouth.

'This thing comin' to *save* us. Do you know what it was doin' here, before Izmunuti blew up?'

'It is seldom easy understanding other life orders,' the tutor explained. *'But in this case the answer is simple. It is a class of device called a* Harvester/Salvager. *Such machines collect raw materials to be used in various engineering or construction projects. It must have been using the sail to gather metal atoms from the star's rich wind when the storm struck. But given an opportunity, a harvester will collect the material it needs from any other source of accumulated or condensed . . .'*

The artificial voice trailed off as the tutor's face froze. The pause lasted several duras.

'Any other source,' Dwer repeated the phrase in a low mutter. 'Like a derelict ship, drifting through space, maybe?'

Rety felt numb.

The tutor did not say *'oops.'*

Not exactly.

It wasn't necessary.

Two young humans watched claws, grapplers, and scythelike blades unfurl as strong fields seized their vessel, drawing it toward a dark opening at the center of a broad expanse of filmy light.

Something was happening.

The deck shuddered and vibrated. Muffled thuds penetrated through the spongy walls, puzzling him at first.

Then Lark recalled the first time he had heard such sounds – just after he and Ling were captured, when the Six Races of Jijo had surprised their tormentors by attacking this battle cruiser with crude rockets.

On a monitor screen he had watched explosive-filled tree trunks blaze like avenging spirits through the sky above the Slope, hundreds of them, handmade by the finest artisans of the Six Races and dispatched on a mission of vengeance. He remembered praying that some of the fiery missiles would get through – to end his life along with all the loathsome Jophur invaders aboard this cruel ship.

Then came that muted rumbling.

'Defensive counterfire.' Ling had identified the sound as Jophur weapons spoke. One by one, the natives' proud missiles had evaporated, well short of their target . . . and Lark had had to reconcile himself with remaining alive.

This time, the tempo of jarring quivers rattled the ship ten times as fast.

It sounds pretty frantic. I wonder who the greasy stacks are fighting this time.

Alas, his pursuers gave Lark no time to ponder it. Whatever was going on in space beyond, the hunter robots kept up their relentless and systematic search through twisty corridors, blocking every effort to sneak past them, constantly hemming him northward along the great ship's axis.

Hissing Jophur soldiery accompanied the posse, operating in groups of three or more. And on several occasions he also heard a human voice, male, shouting suggestions to help chase down one of his own kind.

Rann.

Lark had few options. With the traitor taking part, he didn't dare try his luck again with the purple ring, whose usefulness was probably finished anyway. So he fled back toward the place where he and Ling had once made their brief attempt at sabotage, throwing a pathetic little bomb at the Jophur nerve center, then fleeing together in triumph amid clouds of smoke, running and laughing as they played spy, using their purple pass-ring to go almost anywhere, defying the enemy to catch them.

Of course it hadn't felt like that much fun at the time. Only in contrast to Lark's present misery did it seem a carefree episode. A frolic. He'd give anything to go back to that time. Even creeping about as half-naked vermin in an alien ship, he had been happy with Ling at his side.

More than a day must have passed since he'd last had any rest. Food became a fading memory, and there was no leisure anymore to explore chambers along the way – only the tense wariness of a prey animal, fighting desperately to stave off the inevitable.

Mysterious vibrations intensified, punctuated by other noises that boomed or crackled faintly in the distance. The normal pungency of Jophur hallway aromatics thickened with new scentomeres, wafting through the ventilation system. Some were too strange or complex for him to decipher, but *fear* and *revulsion* were almost identical to traeki versions he knew from growing up on Jijo.

Something had the crew very upset.

Queasy sensations warned Lark of shifts in the ship's artificial gravity, making the floor seem to tilt, then briefly lose pressure against the soles of his feet. The steady background hum of engines increased pitch and intensity. Lark was tempted to duck into a nearby chamber and try to activate a view screen, just to find out what was going on. But any room might become a trap while his pursuers were so close.

A few duras later, he felt a nervous shiver on the back of his neck that warned him of approaching robots – a fey sensitivity to their suspensor fields that had saved him more than once so far. The scent of approaching Jophur soldiery reinforced his decision.

Back the other way, quickly!

Though weary, he sped up, trying to reach one of the ramps leading to the next level. Of course, with each move north the width of his domain narrowed, leaving him fewer options. Soon, they would harry him into a corner with no escape ...

Lark scurried around a bend, only to brake sharply, with a grunt of dismayed surprise.

Just a few meters ahead of him, Rann let out a shout. The tall Danik warrior yelled at a golden bracelet on his wrist. 'I've got the son of a bitch!'

Lark spun about and fled, seeking the only remaining branch tunnel that seemed free of foes. Behind him, Rann could be heard switching to GalTwo – more useful at communicating with Jophur than vulgar Anglic cursing.

'*To this locale, speed quickly and urgently. The quarry, it is near!*'

Lark considered halting. Finding a corner to hide behind and ambush Rann as he hurried after. Better to face the human traitor alone, and possibly do Rann harm, than wind up facing a swarm of Jophur and their robots, who would be invulnerable to his fists.

But he chose to stay free, if only for a few moments longer, dashing down the sole remaining escape path – a narrow corridor, probably leading nowhere.

Sure enough, exultant cries followed, and Lark knew he was cornered when he saw the dead end, no more than forty meters ahead.

He halted by a closed doorway, fumbling with shaky hands to bring the purple ring up against the lock plate. It sprayed a soft mist, but either the torus was tired or the Jophur commanders had learned their lesson. The door stayed adamantly shut.

Lark heard a cry of satisfaction as Rann spied him from the far intersection. But the Danik waited for others – Jophur and their machines – to join him before approaching any closer. For several duras the two of them just stared at each other in mutual loathing. Then Rann smiled as a Jophur and two robots joined him. They started to advance.

Suddenly, from Lark's other side, there came a low reverberation and a growing sense of heat. He turned around, backing away from the bulkhead where the hallway ended. That blank wall began glowing and bowing outward. Molten droplets oozed from the edges of an oval that blazed brightly, forcing him to raise both hands and shield his eyes. Lark gagged on an odor he recalled from visits to the laboratory of the Explosers Guild, in Tarek Town – hydrogen sulfide gas.

As the oval slumped inward, he briefly glimpsed another twisty corridor beyond, glowing with an eerie light. Lark turned to flee, but a wave of hot vapors slammed his back, knocking him down. His forearms struck the deck painfully hard while a surge of baked air passed overhead and on down the hall, toward Rann and his companions.

For an instant, Lark's senses were in such an uproar that he felt swaddled by numbness. No information could get through, except pain . . . and the fact that he still lived. When he managed to open his eyes once more, Lark blinked in disbelief.

Down the corridor, where moments ago his hunters had been marching confidently to capture him, he now glimpsed the last of them fleeing round the corner. Rann glanced back, terror in his pale eyes, and Jophur warriors heaved their bulky forms out of sight. Only two robots remained at the intersection, taking up defensive stances, but not firing – as if loath to try.

Lark knew he should be happy of anything that put his enemies to flight. Yet, he felt reluctant to roll over and see what had arrived. *I just know I'm not gonna like this*, he thought.

The rotten egg smell was almost overpowering, and a faint luminance filled the hall, coming from above and behind his prone form, along with a faint, whispering hum.

Gathering his courage, Lark pushed off the floor with his scalded right arm, rolling onto his back.

It stood a few paces behind him, just this side of the hole it had made in the bulkhead. A glowing ball, roughly three meters across, barely able to squeeze through the corridor. Though it had the color of bronze metal, the intruder seemed to ooze and ripple as it rolled slowly forward, more like a fluid-filled bag than a balloon. Lark recalled the living cells he used to watch through his beloved microscope, back when he and other sages had the time to pursue knowledge, doing what passed for science on the primitive Slope.

A cell, many times his size. Living.

And yet, all at once, Lark knew—

This is like no life I ever saw before.

The thing made sloshing sounds as it crept languidly toward Lark, swarming over his foot, climbing upward, rendering him immobile, then causing a chill numbness to spread along his bones.

II

THE ORDERS OF LIFE

For ages – ever since the blessed Progenitors departed – some contemplative oxygen-breathing races have wondered about the question of 'plenitude.'

If life is so common and vibrant here in the Five Linked Galaxies, they ask, should we not expect to see signs of it elsewhere? Astronomers have counted seven hundred *billion* other galactic pinwheels, ovals, and other vast conglomerations of stars out there, some of them even bigger than our own Galaxy One. It seems to defy all logic that ours would be the only nexus where sapiency has arisen.

What a waste of potential, if it were so!

Of course, this opinion is not universally shared. Among the many social-religious alliances making up our diverse civilization, some insist that we must be unique, since any other situation would only mock the ultimate greatness of the Progenitors. Others perceive those billions of other galaxies as heavenly abodes where the august Transcendents go, once they complete the long process of perfecting themselves on this plane of reality.

Many have tried to pierce the veil with scientific instruments, such as vast telescopes, aimed at studying our silent neighbors. Indeed, some anomalies have been found. For instance, several targets emit rhythmic noise pulsations of towering complexity . Other galaxies seem *burned out*, as if a recent conflagration tore through them, destroying nearly every planetary system at the same time.

And yet, the data always seems ambiguous, allowing a variety of interpretations. The Great Library is filled with arguments that have raged for eons.

Are other galactic groups linked together by hyperspatial transfer points, the way our own five spirals are, despite huge separations in flat spacetime? Our best models and calculations do not give definitive answers.

*

FROM time to time, some young race gets impatient and tries posing these questions to the Old Ones — those sage species who have surrendered starships to develop their souls within the Embrace of Tides, passing on to the next order of life.

Depending on their mood, the ancients either ignore such entreaties or reply in frustrating ways.

We are alone, answered one community of venerable ones.

No we are not, countered a second. *Other galaxies are just like ours, teeming with multitudinous sapient species, taking turns uplifting each other as a sacred duty, then turning their attention toward the duties of transcendence ... as we are doing now.*

One cluster of Old Ones claimed to know a different answer — that most island universes are settled quite suddenly, by the first race to achieve spaceflight. These first races then proceed to fill every star system, annihilating or enslaving all succeeding life-forms. Such galaxies are poor in diversity or insight, having lacked the wisdom that our blessed Progenitors showed when they began the great chain of Uplift.

That is wrong, claimed yet another assembly of venerables in their spiky habitat, huddled amid contemplative tides. *The unity of purpose that we sense in such galaxies only means that they have already evolved toward united oneness! A high state wherein all sapient beings participate in a grand overmind ...*

FINALLY, it grew clear that these conflicting stories must mean just one of two things.

Either the Old Ones really have no idea what they are talking about, or else ...

Or else their varied answers together comprise a sermon. A basic lesson.

Other galaxies are none of our business! That is what they are teaching. We should get back to the proper tasks of young races — struggling, learning, uplifting, and striving with each other, gathering experience and strength for the next phase.

Answers will be forthcoming to each of us who survives the testing, when we ultimately face the bright light of the Great Harrower.

It seemed that E Space was not the only realm where *ideas* had a life of their own. On his return, Harry found Kazzkark Base teeming with hearsay. Strange rumors roamed like ravenous parasites, springing from one nervous being to the next, thriving in an atmosphere of contagious anxiety.

Steering his scoutcraft to the planetoid's north pole, Harry docked at a slip reserved for the Navigation Institute and cut power with a sense of relief. All he wanted now was to sleep for several days without having to endure relentless exhausting dreams. But no sooner did he debark and begin the protocols of reentry than he found himself immersed in a maelstrom of dubious gossip.

'It is said that the Abdicator Alliance has broken into several heretical factions that are fighting among themselves,' murmured a tourmuj trade representative standing in line ahead of Harry at immigration, chattering in hasty Galactic Four. *'And the League of Prudent Neutral Clans are said to have begun mobilizing at last, combining their fleets under pargi command!'*

Harry stared at the tourmuj – a lanky, sallow-skinned being that seemed all elbows and knees – before responding in the same language.

'Said? It is said by whom? In which medium? With what veracity?'

'With no veracity at all!' This came from an oulomin diplomat whose tentacle fringes bore colored caps to prevent inadvertent pollen emission. Slithering just behind Harry, the oulomin expressed disdain toward the stooped tourmuj with sprays of orange saliva that barely missed Harry's arm.

'I have it on good authority that the eminent and much respected pargi intend to withdraw from the League – and from Galactic affairs entirely – out of disgust with the present state of chaos. That noble race will shortly move on to blessed retirement, joining their ancestral patrons in the fortunate realm of tides. Only a regressed fool would believe otherwise.'

It was hardly the sort of speech that Harry would associate with 'diplomacy.' The tourmuj reacted by irately unfolding its long legs and both sets of arms so swiftly that its knobby head bumped the ceiling. Wincing in pain, the trader stomped off, sacrificing its place in line.

Oh, I get it, Harry thought, glancing once more at the being behind him, whose grasp of other-species psychology was evident.

Just don't try the same on me, he thought. *I'm not budging, even if you call me a dolphin's uncle.*

The diplomat seemed to recognize this and merely waved two tendrils in a universal gesture of placid goodwill, as they both moved forward.

Harry took out his portable data plaque and stroked its command knobs, swiftly accessing the planetoid's Galactic Library unit for news. It was an excellent branch, since Kazzkark housed local headquarters for several important institutes. Yet, the master index claimed to know nothing about an Abdicator schism. Moreover, according to official sources, the influential pargi were still active in Galactic councils, calling for peace and restraint, urging all militant alliances to withdraw their armadas and settle the present crisis through mediation, not war.

Were both rumormongers wrong, then? During normal times, Harry would scarcely doubt the master index. In the Civilization of Five Galaxies, it was commonly said that nothing ever *really* happened until it was logged by the Great Library. A planet might explode before your eyes, but it wasn't a certified fact without the rayed spiral glyph, flashing in a corner of a readout screen.

Clearly these weren't 'normal times.'

While taking his turn at the customs kiosk, Harry overheard a talpu'ur seed merchant complain to a guldingar pilgrim about how many nauseating thread changes she had had to endure during the crossing from Galaxy Three. Harry found it hard to follow the talpu'ur's dialect – a syncopated ratchet-rubbing of her vestigial wing cases – but it seemed that several traditional transfer points had shifted their oscillation patterns, either losing coherence or going off-line completely.

The slight, spiderlike guldingar answered in the same rhythmic idiom, speaking through a mechanical device strapped to one leg.

'Those explanations seem dubious. In fact, they are excuses given by great powers, as each attempts to seize and monopolize valuable hyperspatial links for its own strategic purposes.'

Harry frowned. Worry made the fur itch beneath his uniform. If something was happening to the viability of t-points, the matter was of vital interest to the Navigation Institute. Once again, he referred to the Branch Library but found little information – just routine travel advisories and warnings of detours along some routes.

I'm sure Wer'Q'quinn will fill me in. The old serpent oughta know what's goin' on, if anybody does.

One topic Harry wanted to hear about, but none of the gossipers mentioned, was the Siege of Terra. Weeks ago, when he departed to patrol E Space, the noose around Earth and the Canaan Colonies had been drawing gradually tighter. Despite welcome assistance from the Tymbrimi and Thennanin, battle fleets from a dozen fanatical alliances had ceased their mutual bickering for a time, joining cause and pressing the blockade ever closer, choking off trade and communication to Harry's ancestral world.

Though tempted, he refrained from querying the Library about that. Given the present political situation – while his status was still probationary – it wouldn't be wise to make too many inquiries about his old clan. *I'm not supposed to care about that anymore. Navigation is my home now.*

After clearing customs, his next obstacle was all-too-unpleasantly familiar – a tall sour-faced hoon wearing the glossy robe of a senior patron. With a magisterial badge of the Migration Institute on one shoulder, Inspector Twaphu-anuph gripped a plaque flowing with data while scanners probed Harry's vessel. Every time Harry returned from a mission, he had to endure the big male biped's humorless black eyes scrutinizing his ship's biomanifest for any sign of illicit genetic cargo, while that prodigious hoonish throat sac throbbed low rumblings of pompous scorn.

So it rocked Harry back a bit when the brawny bureaucrat spoke up this time, using rolling undertones that seemed positively affable!

'I note that you have just returned from E Space,' the inspector murmured in GalSeven, the spacer dialect most favored by Earthlings. 'Hr-rm. Welcome home. I trust you had a pleasant, interesting voyage?'

Harry blinked, startled by the tone of informal friendliness. *What happened to the usual snub?* he wondered.

It was normal for Migrationists to act high and mighty. After all, their institute supervised matters of cosmic importance, such as where oxygen-breathing starfarers might colonize, and which oxyworlds must lie fallow for a time, untouched by sapient hands. In contrast, Harry's organization was a 'little cousin,' with duties resembling the old-time coastal guardians of Earth's oceans – surveying hyperlink routes, monitoring spacetime conditions, and safeguarding lanes of travel for Galactic commerce.

'E Space is a realm of surprises,' Harry responded cautiously. 'But my mission went as well as can be expected. Thank you for asking.'

A small, furry *rousit* – a servant-client of the hoon – moved alongside its master, aiming a recorder unit at Harry, making him increasingly nervous. The inspector meanwhile towered closer, pressing his inquiry.

'Of course I am asking purely out of personal curiosity, but would you mind enlightening me on one matter? Would you happen to have noticed any especially large memoid beings while you patrolled E Space? Hrrrm. Perchance a conceptual entity capable of extending beyond its native continuum, into ... hrr-rr ... other levels of reality?'

Almost instinctively, Harry grew guarded. Like many oxy-races, hoons could not bear the ambiguous conditions of E Space or the thronging allaphors inhabiting that weird realm. Small surprise, given their notorious lack of humor or imagination.

But then why this sudden interest?

Clearly, the awkward situation called for a mix of formal flattery and evasion. Harry fell back on the old *yes bwana* tactic.

'*It is well known that meme organisms throng E Space like vacuum barnacles infesting a slow freighter,*' he said, switching to GalSix. '*But alas <oh senior-patron-level entity> I saw only those creatures that my poor, half-uplifted brain allowed me subjectively to perceive. No doubt those impressions were too crude to interest an exalted being like yourself.*'

Harry hoped the warden would miss his sarcasm. In theory, all those who swore fealty to the Great Institutes were supposed to leave behind their old loyalties and prejudices. But ever since the disaster at NuDawn, everyone knew how hoons felt toward the upstarts of Earthclan. As a neo-chimpanzee – from a barely fledged client race, indentured to humans – Harry expected only snobbery from Twaphu-anuph.

'*You are probably right about that <oh precocious-but-promising infant>*' came the hoon's response. '*Still, I remain <casually> interested in your observations. Might you have sighted any <exceptionally large or complex> memoids traveling in <close> company with transcendent life-forms?*'

The inspector's data plaque was turned away, but its glow reflected off a patch of glossy chest scales, flashing familiar blue shades of approval. All checks on Harry and his vessel were complete. There was no legal excuse to hold him anymore.

He switched languages again, this time to Anglic, the tongue of wolflings.

'I'll tell you what, Twaphu-anuph. I'll do you a favor and make an official inquiry about that ... in your name, of course.'

Harry aimed his own plaque and pointedly took an ident-print before the warden could object.

'*That is not necessary! I only asked informally, in order—*'

Harry enjoyed interrupting.

'Oh, you needn't thank me. We are all sworn to mutual cooperation, after all. So shall I arrange for the usual inter-institute discount and forward the report to you in care of Migration HQ? Will that do?'

Before the flustered hoon could respond, Harry continued.

'Good! Then according to the protocols of entry, and by your exalted leave, I guess I'll be going.'

The little rousit scurried out of the way as Harry moved forward, silently daring the barrier to prevent him.

It swished aside, opening his path onto the avenues of Kazzkark.

Perhaps perversely, Harry found it exciting to live in a time of danger and change.

For almost half a galactic rotation – millions of years – this drifting, hollowed-out stone had been little more than a sleepy outpost for Galactic civil servants, utilizing but a fraction of the prehistoric shafts that some extinct race once tunneled through a hundred miles of spongy rock. Then, in just the fifteen kaduras since Harry was assigned here, the planetoid transformed. Catacombs that had lain silent since the *Ch'th'turn* Epoch hummed again as more newcomers arrived every day. Over the course of a couple of Earth years, a cosmopolitan city came to life where each cavity and corridor offered a mélange for the senses – a random sampling of the full range of oxy-life culture.

Some coincidence, Harry thought sardonically. *It's almost as if all this was waiting to happen, until I came to Kazzkark.*

Of course, the truth was a little different. In fact, he was one of the least important free sapients walking around these ancient halls.

Walking ... and scooting, slithering, creeping, ambling ... name a form of locomotion and you could see it being used. Those too frail to stand in half an Earth gravity rolled everywhere on graceful carts, some with the sophistication of miniature spaceships. Harry even saw a dozen or so members of a long-armed species that looked something like gibbons – with purple, upside-down faces – leaping and brachiating from convenient bars and handholds set in the high ceiling. He wanted to laugh and hoot at their antics, but their race had probably been piloting starcraft back when humans lived in caves. Galactics seldom had what he would call a sense of humor.

Not long ago, a majority of those living on Kazzkark wore uniforms of MigrInst, NavInst, WarInst, or the Great Library. But now those dressed in livery made a small minority, lost amid a throng. The rest sported wildly varied costumes, from full body enviro suits and formal robes carrying runes describing their race genealogy and patronymics, all the way to beings who strode unabashedly naked – or with just an excretory-restraint cloth – revealing a maximum of skin, scale, feather, or torg.

When he first entered service, most Galactics seemed unable to tell a neo-chimpanzee from a plush recliner, so obscure and unimportant was the small family of Terra. But that had changed lately. Quite a few faces turned and stared as Harry walked by. Beings nudged each other to point, sharing muted utterances – a sure sign that the *Streaker* crisis hadn't been solved while he was away. Clearly Earthclan was still gaining a renown it never sought.

A venerable Galactic expression summed up the problem.

'Look ye to peril – in attracting unplanned notice from the mighty.'

Still, for the most part it was easy enough to feel lost in the crowd as he took a long route back to headquarters, entranced by how much busier things had become since he left on patrol.

Using his plaque to scan immigration profiles, Harry knew that many of these sophonts were emissaries and commercial delegates, sent by their race, alliance, or corporation to seek some advantage as the staid routines of civilization dissolved in an age of rising misgivings. There were opportunities to be gained from chaos, so agents and proxies maneuvered, playing venerable games of espionage. Compacts were made and broken. Bribes were offered and loyalties compromised in double-cross gambits so ornate that the court intrigues of the Medicis might have occurred in a sandbox. Small clans, without any stake in galacto-politics or the outcome of fleet engagements, nevertheless swarmed about, endeavoring to make themselves useful to great powers like the Klesh, Soro, or Jophur, who in turn spent lavishly, seeking an edge over their foes.

With so much portable wealth being passed around, an economy flourished serving the needs of each deputy or spy. Almost a million free sophonts and servitor machines saw to the visitors' biotic needs, from distinct atmospheric preferences to exotic foodstuffs and intoxicants.

It's a good thing we chims had to give up some of our sense of smell, trading the brain tissue for use in sapience, Harry thought as he sauntered along the Great Way – a mercantile avenue near the surface of Kazzkark, stretching from pole to pole, where bubble domes interrupted the rocky ceiling every few kilometers to show dazzling views of an inner spiral arm of Galaxy Five. This passage had been a ghostly corridor when he first came from training at Navigation Central. Now shops and restaurants filled every niche, casting an organic redolence so thick that any species would surely find something toxic in the air. Most visitors underwent thorough antiallergic treatments to prepare their immune systems before leaving quarantine. And even so, many walked the Great Way wearing respirators.

Harry found the experience heady. Every few meters, fresh

aromatics assailed his nostrils and sinuses. Some provoked waves of delight or overpowering hunger. Others brought him to the brink of nausea.

It kind of reminds me of New York, he pondered, recalling that brief time on Earth.

His ears also verged on sensory overload. The dozen or so standard Galactic tongues came in countless dialects, depending on how each race made signals. Sound was the most frequent carrier of negotiation or gossip, and the buzzing, clicking, groaning clamor of several hundred species types made the Great Way seem to throb with physical waves of intrigue. Those preferring visual gestures made things worse by waving, dancing, or flashing message displays that Harry found at once both beautiful and intimidating.

Then there's psi.

Stern rules limited how adepts might use the 'vivid spectrum' indoors. Vigilant detectors caught the most egregious offenders. Still, Harry figured part of his tension came from a general background of psychic noise.

Fortunately, most neo-chims are deaf to psi stuff. Some of the same traits that made a good observer in E Space also kept him semi-immune to the cacophony of mental vibrations filling Kazzkark right now.

Of course many of the 'restaurants' were actually shielded sites of rendezvous, where informal meetings could take place, sometimes between star clans registered as enemies under edicts of the Institute for Civilized Warfare. Harry glimpsed a haughty, lizardlike Soro, accompanied by a minimal retinue of Pila and Paha clients, slip into a shrouded establishment whose proprietor at once turned off the flashing 'Available' sign ... but left the door ajar, as if expecting one more customer.

It might have been interesting to stand around and see who entered next to parley with the Soro matriarch, but Harry spotted at least a dozen loiterers who were already doing that very thing, pretending to read infoplaques or sample wares from street vendors, while always keeping clear line of sight to the dimmed entranceway.

Harry recalled the clumsy effort of the hoon inspector to probe him about E Space. As trust in the Institutes unraveled, everyone seemed eager for supplementary data, perhaps hoping a little extra might make a crucial difference.

He couldn't afford to be mistaken for another spy. Especially not in uniform. Some of the other great services might be showing signs of strain, losing their trustworthiness and professionalism, but Navigation had an unsullied reputation to uphold.

Passing a busy intersection, Harry glimpsed a pair of racoonish Synthian traders, whose folk had a known affinity for Terran art and culture. They were too far away to make eye contact, but he was distracted by the sight and moments later carelessly bumped into the bristly, crouched form of a Xatinni.

Oh, hell, he thought as the ocelot face whirled toward him with a twist of sour hatred. Wasting no time, Harry ducked his head and crossed both arms before him in the stance of a repentant client, backing away as the creature launched into a tirade, berating him in shrill patronizing tonal clefts of GalFour.

'To explain this insolent interruption! To abase thyself and apologize with groveling sincerity! To mark this affront on the long list of debts accumulated by your clan of worthless—'

Not a great power, the Xatinni routinely picked on Earthlings for the oldest reason of bullies anywhere – because they could.

'To report in three miduras at my apartment for further rebukes, at the following address! Forty-seven by fifty-two Corridor of the—'

Fortunately, at that moment a bulky Vriiilh came gallumping down the avenue, grunting ritual apologies to all who had to scoot aside before the amiable behemoth's two-meter footsteps. The Xatinni fell back with an angry yowl as the Vriiilh pushed between them.

Harry took advantage of the interruption to escape by melting through the crowd.

So long, pussycat, he thought, briefly wishing he could psi cast an insult as he fled. Instead of shameful abasement, he would much rather have smacked the Xatinni across the kisser – and maybe removed a few excess limbs to improve the eatee's aerodynamics. *I hope we meet again sometime, in a dark alley with no one watching*.

Alas, self-control was the first criterion looked for by the Terragens Council, before letting any neo-chim head unsupervised into the cosmos at large. Small and weak, Earthclan could not afford incidents.

Yeah . . . and a fat lotta good that policy did us in the long run.

They gave dolphins a starship of their own, and look what the clever fishies went and did. They stirred up the worst crisis in Ifni-knows-how-many millions of years.

If the honest truth be told, it made Harry feel just a little jealous.

Beyond those coming to Kazzkark on official business, the streets and warrens supported a drifting population of others – refugees from places disrupted by the growing chaos, plus opportunists, altruists, and mystics.

The lattermost seemed especially plentiful, these days.

On most worlds, matters of philosophy or religion were discussed at a languid pace, with arguments spanning slow generations and even being passed from a patron race to the clients of its clients, over the course of eons. But here and now, Harry detected something frenetic about the speeches being given by missionaries who had set up shop beneath Dome Sixty-Seven. While clusters and nebulae shimmered overhead, envoys of the best-known denominations offered ancient wisdom from perfumed pavilions – among them the Inheritors, the Awaiters, the Transcenders ... and the Abdicators, showing no apparent sign of fragmentation as red-robed acolytes from a dozen species hectored passersby with their orthodox interpretation of the Progenitors' Will.

Harry knew there were many aspects of Galactic Civilization he would never understand, no matter how long or hard he tried. For instance, how could great alliances of sapient races feud for whole epochs over minute differences in dogma?

He wasn't alone in this confusion. Many of Earth's greatest minds stumbled over such issues as whether the fabled First Race began the cycle of Uplift two billion years ago as a manifestation of predetermined physical law – or as an emergent property of self-organizing systems in a pseudovolitionary universe. All Harry ever figured out was that most disputes revolved around how oxy-life became sapient, and what its ultimate destiny might be as the cosmos evolved.

'Not exactly worth killing anybody over,' he snorted. 'Or *gettin'* killed, for that matter.'

Then again, humans could hardly claim complete innocence. They had slaughtered countless numbers of their own kind over differences even more petty and obscure during Earth's long dark isolation before Contact. Before bringing light to Harry's kind.

'Now *this* is new,' he mused, pausing at the far end of the dome.

Beyond the glossy pavilions of the main sects, an aisle had opened featuring proselytes of a shabbier sort, preaching from curtained alcoves and stony niches, or even wandering the open Way, proclaiming unconventional beliefs.

'Go ye hence from this place!' screeched a dour-looking Pee'oot with a spiral neck and goggle eyes. 'For each of you, but one place offers safety from the upheavals to come. That is the wellspring where you began!'

Harry had to decode the heretical creed from highly inflected Galactic Three. Use of the Collective-Responsive case meant that the Pee'oot was referring to salvation of *species*, of course, not individuals. Even heresy had its limits.

Is he saying each race should return to its homeworld? The mudball where its presapient ancestors evolved and were first adopted by some patron for Uplift?

Or did the preacher refer to something more allegorical?

Perhaps he means that each chain of Uplift is supposed to seek knowledge of its own legacy, distinct from the others. That would call for breaking up the Institutes and letting every oxy-life clan go its own way.

Of course Harry wasn't equipped to parse out the fine points of Galactic theology, nor did he really care. Anyway, the next zealot was more interesting to watch.

A komahd evangelist – with a tripod lower torso but humanoid trunk and arms – looked jovial and friendly. Its lizardlike head featured a broad mouth that seemed split by a permanent happy grin, while long eyelashes made the face seem almost beguiling. But a single, fat rear leg thumped a morose beat while the komahd chanted in GalSix. Its sullen tale belied those misleadingly cheerful features.

'*All our <current, lamentable> social disruptions have their roots in a <despicable, nefarious> plot by the enemies of all oxygen-breathing life!*

'*See how our great powers and alliances bleed each other, wasting their armed might, struggling and striving in search of <vague> hints and clues to a <possible, though unlikely> return of the <long-gone> Progenitors!*

'*This can only serve the interests of <inscrutable, inimical> hydrogen breathers! Jealous of our <quick, agile> speed and <high> metabolisms, they have feared us for eons, plotting <long, slow, vile> schemes. Now, at last, they are ready. See how the <wicked> hydros maneuver <malignly> for our <collective> end!*

'*Who does not recall how <very> recently we had to give up one of our Five Galaxies! Just half a million years ago, <the entirety of> Galaxy Four was declared "fallow" and emptied of all <starfaring> oxy-life culture. Never before has the Migration Institute agreed to such a <wholesale, traitorous> ceding of territory, whose <resettlement> repercussions are still being felt!*

'*We are told that the hydros <in return> abandoned <all of> Galaxy Five, but do we not <daily> hear reports of strange sightings and perturbations in normal space that can only be work of the <perfidious> Zang?*

'*What of the <disrupted> transfer points? What of <vast> tracts in*

<Level-A and Level-B> hyperspace that now turn sluggish and unusable? Why do the <great but suspiciously silent> Institutes not tell us the truth?'

The komahd finished by pointing an all-too-humanlike finger straight at Harry, who in his uniform seemed a convenient representative of NavInst. Blushing under his fur, Harry backed away quickly.

Too bad. That was starting to get interesting. At least someone's complaining about the stupid way the Soro and other powers are acting. And the komahd's message was about the future, instead of the regular obsession with the past. All right, it's a bit paranoid. But if more sophonts believed it, they might ease the pressure off Earth and give those poor dolphins a chance to come home.

Harry found it ironic then that the freethinking Komahd generally disliked Terrans. For his own part, Harry rather fancied their looks, and thought they smelled pretty good, too. What a pity the admiration wasn't reciprocal.

A ruckus from behind made him swivel around – just in time to join a crowd scooting hurriedly toward the nearest wall! Harry felt a shiver course his spine when he saw what was coming. A squadron of twenty frightening, mantislike Tandu warriors, unarmed but still equipped with deadly, razor-sharp claws, trooped single file down the middle of the boulevard, the tops of their waving eye pods almost brushing the corrugated ceiling. Everyone who saw them coming scurried aside. No one argued right of way with a Tandu, nor did any vendors try to hawk wares at the spiky-limbed beings.

Before departing on his latest mission, Harry had seen a Tandu bite off the head of an obstinate Paha who had proudly refused to give way. Almost at once, the leader of that Tandu group had reproved the assailant by casually chopping its brother to bits. By that act, a simple tit-for-tat justice was served, preventing any action by the authorities. And yet, the chief lesson was clear to all and sundry.

Don't mess with us.

No inquiry was ever held. Even the Paha's commanders had to admit that its bravado and demise amounted to a case of suicide.

Harry's pulse raced till the terrifying squadron entered a side avenue and passed out of sight.

I ... better not dawdle anymore, he thought, suddenly feeling drained and oppressed by all the clamorous crowding. *Wer'Q'quinn is gonna spit bile if I don't hand in my mission report soon.*

He also wanted to ask the old snake about things he had heard and seen since landing – about hoons interested in E Space, and t-points going on the blink, and komahd preachers who claimed—

Harry's heart almost did a back flip when his shoulder was suddenly engulfed by a bony hand bigger than his forearm. Slim white fingers – tipped with suckers – gripped softly but adamantly.

He pivoted, only to stare up past an expanse of silver robe at a tall biped who must surely mass half a metric ton. Its head was cast like a sea ship's prow, but where an ancient boat might have a single eye painted on each side, this creature had *two* pairs, one atop the other. A flat jaw extended beneath, resembling the ram of a Greek trireme.

It's . . . a Skiano . . . Harry recalled from the endless memory drills during training. He had never expected to encounter this race on the street, let alone have one accost him personally.

What've I done now? he worried, preparing to go through another humiliating kowtow and repentance. *At least the walking skyscraper can't accuse me of blocking his light.*

A colorful birdlike creature perched on one of the Skiano's broad shoulders, resembling an Earthly parrot.

'I beg your pardon for startling you, brother,' the titan said mellowly, preempting Harry's apology. It spoke through a vodor device held in its other mammoth hand. The mouth did not move or utter sound. Instead, soft light flashed from its lower pair of eyes. The vodor translated this into audible sound.

'It seemed to me that you looked rather lost.'

Harry shook his head. 'Apologies for contradiction, elder patron. Your concern warms this miserable clientspawn. But I do know where I'm going. So, with thanks, I'll just be on my—'

The bird interrupted, squawking derisively.

'Idiot! Fool! Not your *body*. It's your soul. Your soul! Your soul!'

Only then did Harry realize – the conversation was taking place in Anglic, the wolfling tongue of his birth. He took a second squint at the bird.

Given the stringent requirements of flight, feathered avians had roughly similar shapes, no matter what oxy-world they originated on. Still, in this case there could be no mistake. It *was* a parrot. A real one. The yo-ho-ho and a bottle of rum kind . . . which made the Skiano seem even stranger than before.

Wrong number of eyes, Harry thought numbly. *You should be wearing a patch over one – or even three! Also oughta have a peg leg . . . and a hook instead of a hand . . .*

'Indeed my good ape,' the buzzing voice from the vodor went on, agreeing with the talking bird. 'It is your soul that seems in jeopardy. Have you taken the time to consider its salvation?'

Harry blinked. He had never heard of a Skiano proselyte before, let alone one that preached in Anglic, wearing a smartass Terran bird as an accessory.

'You're talking about me,' he prompted.

'Yes, you.'

Harry blinked, incredulous.

'Me ... *personally*?'

The parrot let out an exasperated raspberry, but the Skiano's eyes seemed to carry a satisfied twinkle. The machine sounds were joyous.

'At last, someone who quickly grasps the concept! But indeed, I should not be surprised that one of your noble lineage comprehends.'

'Uh, noble lineage?' Harry repeated. No one had ever accused him of that before.

'Of course. You are from *Earth*! Blessed home of Moses, Jesus, Buddha, Mohammed, Tipler, and Weimberg-Chang! The abode where wolflings burst to sapience in a clear case of virgin birth, without intervention by any other race of Galactic sinners, but as an immaculate gift from the Cosmos itself!'

Harry stepped back, staring in blank amazement. But the Skiano followed.

'The world whence comes a notion that will change the universe forever. A concept that you, dear brother, must come help us share!'

The huge evangelist leaned toward Harry, projecting intense fervor through both sound and an ardent light in its eyes.

'The idea of a God who loves each person! Who finds importance not in your race or clan, or any grand abstraction, but every particular entity who is self-aware and capable of improvement.

'The Creator of All, who promises bliss when we join Him at the Omega Point.

'The One who offers salvation, not collectively, but to each individual soul.'

Harry could do nothing but blink, flabbergasted, as his brain and throat locked in a rigor from which no speech could break free.

'Amen!' squawked the parrot. 'Amen and hallelujah!'

ALVIN'S JOURNAL

For once *I* had the best view of what was going on. My pals – Urronn, Huck, and Pincer – were all in other parts of the ship where they had to settle for what they could see on monitors. But I stood just a few arm's lengths from Dr. Baskin, sharing the commander's view while we made our escape from Izmunuti.

It all happened right in front of me.

Officially, I was in the Plotting Room to take care of the smelly glavers. But that job didn't amount to much more than feeding them an occasional snack of synthi pellets I kept in a pouch ... and cleaning up when they made a mess. Beyond that, I was content to watch, listen, and wonder how I'd ever describe it all in my journal. Nothing in my experience – either growing up in a little hoonish fishing port or reading books from the human past – prepared me for what happened during those miduras of danger and change.

I took some inspiration from Sara Koolhan. She's another sooner – a Jijo native like me, descended from criminal settlers. Like me, she never saw a starship or computer before this year. And yet, the young human's suggestions are heeded. Her advice is sought by those in authority. She doesn't seem lost when they discuss 'circumferential thread boundaries' and 'quantum reality layers.' (My little autoscribe is handling the spelling, in case you wonder.) Anyway, I tell myself that if one fellow citizen of the Slope can handle all this strangeness, I should too.

Ah, but Sara was a sage and a wizard back home, so I'm right back where I started, hoping to narrate the actions of star gods and portray sights far stranger than we saw in the deepest Midden, relying on language that I barely understand.

(On Jijo, we use Anglic to discuss technical matters, since most books from the Great Printing were in that tongue. But it's different aboard *Streaker*. When scientific details have to be precise, they switch to GalSeven or GalTwo, using word-glyphs I find impenetrable ... showing how much our Jijoan dialects have devolved.)

The caterwauling of the glavers was something else entirely. It resembled no idiom I had ever heard before! Enhanced and embellished by the Niss Machine, their noise reached out across the heavens, while a terrifying Zang vessel bore down toward *Streaker*, intent on blasting our atoms through the giant star's whirling atmosphere.

Even if the approaching golden globule was bluffing – if it veered aside at the last moment and let us pass – we would only face another deadly force. The Jophur battleship that had chased *Streaker* from Jijo now hurtled to cut us off from the only known path out of this storm-racked system.

Without a doubt, Gillian Baskin had set us on course past a gauntlet of demons.

Still, the glavers bayed and moaned while tense duras passed.

Until, finally, the hydrogen breathers replied!

That screeching racket was even worse. Yet, Sara slapped the plotting table and exulted.

'So the legend is true!'

All right, I should have known the story too. I admit, I spent too much of my youth devouring ancient Earthling novels instead of works by our own Jijoan scholars. Especially the collected oral myths and sagas that formed our cultural heritage before humans joined the Six Races and gave us back literacy.

Apparently, the first generation of glaver refugees who came to our world spoke to the g'Keks who were already there, and told them something about their grounds for fleeing the Civilization of Five Galaxies. Centuries before their kind trod the Path of Redemption, the glavers explained something of their reason for self-banishment.

It seems they used to have a talent that gave them some importance long ago, among the starfaring clans. In olden times, they were among the few races with a knack for conversing with hydrogen breathers! It made them rich, serving as middlemen in complex trade arrangements ... till they grew arrogant and careless. Something you should never do when dealing with Zang.

One day, their luck ran out. Maybe they betrayed a confidence, or took a bribe, or failed to make a major debt payment. Anyway, the consequences looked pretty grim.

In compensation, the Zang demanded the one thing glavers had left.

Themselves.

At least that's how Sara relayed the legend to Gillian and the rest of us, speaking breathlessly while time bled away and the glavers howled and we plunged ever closer to a vast, threatening space leviathan.

Piecing together what was happening, I realized the glavers weren't actually *talking* to the Zang. After all, they've reached redemption and are now presapient beings, nearly bereft of speech.

But the Zang have long memories, and our glavers seemed instinctively – maybe at some genetically programmed level – to know how to yowl just one meaningful thing. One phrase to let their ancient creditors know.

Hey! It is us! We're here! It's us!

To this identifying ululation, all the Niss Machine had to add/overlay was a simple request.

Kindly get those Jophur bastards off our butts.

Help us get away from here.

Anxious moments passed. My spines frickled as we watched the

Zang loom closer. I felt nervous as an urs on a beach, playing tag with crashing waves.

Then, just as it seemed to be swooping for the kill, our would-be destroyer abruptly swerved! A climactic screech came over the loudspeakers. It took the Niss several duras, consulting with the Library unit, to offer a likely translation.

Come with us now.

Just like that, our nemesis changed into an escort, showing us the way. Leading *Streaker* out of Izmunuti's angry chaos.

We took our place in convoy as the Zang ship gathered the surviving harvester machines, fleeing toward the old transfer point.

Meanwhile, one of its companion vessels turned to confront our pursuers.

Long-distance sensors depicted a face-off between omnipotent titans.

The showdown was awesome to behold, even at a range that made it blurry. I listened to Lieutenant Tsh't describe the action for Sara.

'Those are hellfire missilesss,' the dolphin officer explained as the Jophur battleship accelerated, firing glittering pinpoints at its new adversary.

The sap-rings must want the dolphins awful bad, I thought. *If they're willing to fight their way past that monster to get at* Streaker.

The Zang globule was even bigger than the Jophur ... a quivering shape that seemed more like gelatin, or something oozing from a wounded traeki, than solid matter. Once, I thought I glimpsed shadowy figures moving within, like drifting clouds or huge living creatures swimming through an opaque fluid.

Small bits of the main body split off, like droplets spraying from a gobbet of grease on a hot griddle. These did not hasten with the same lightning grace as the Jophur missiles. They seemed more massive. And relentless.

One by one, each droplet swelled like an inflating balloon, interposing its expanding surface between the two warships. Jophur weapons maneuvered agilely, striving to get past the obstructions, but nearly all the missiles were caught by one bubble or another, triggering brilliant explosions.

From her massive walking machine, watching the fight with one cool gray eye, Tsh't commented. 'The Zang throws parts of its own substance ahead, in order to defend itself-f-f. So far, it has taken no offensive action of its own.'

I recall thinking hopefully that this meant the hydros were of a calm nature, less prone to savage violence than we are told by the sagas. Perhaps they only meant to delay the Jophur long enough for us to get away.

Then I reconsidered.

Let's say this help from hydrogen breathers lets Streaker *make good her escape. That's great for the Earthlings – and maybe for the Five Galaxies – but it still leaves Jijo in a mess. The Jophur will be able to call reinforcements and do anything they want to the people of the Slope. Slaughter all the g'Kek. Transform all the poor traeki. Burn down the archive at Biblos and turn the Slope into their private genetic farm, breeding the other races into pliable little client life-forms ...*

Gillian's earlier plan, to draw the battleship after us into a deadly double suicide, would have caused my own death, and that of everyone else aboard – but my homeworld might then have been safe.

The trade-offs were stark and bitter. I found myself resenting the older woman for making a choice that spared my life.

I also changed my mind about the Zang.

Well? What're you waiting for? Shoot back!

The Jophur were oxygen beings like myself, distant relatives, sharing some of the same DNA that had spread around the galaxies during a predawn era before Progenitors arose to begin the chain of Uplift. Nevertheless, right then I was cheering for their annihilation by true aliens. Beings from a strange, incomprehensible order of life.

Come on, Zang. Fry the big ugly ring stacks!

But things went on pretty much the same as distance narrowed between the two giants. The globule spent itself prodigiously to block missiles and gouts of deadly fire from the great dreadnought. Yet despite this, some rays and projectiles got through, impacting the parent body with bitter violence. Fountains of gooey material spewed across the black background, sparkling gorgeously as they burned. Waves rippled and convulsed across the Zang ship. Still it forged on while the glavers yowled, seeming to urge the hydros on.

'*T-point insertion approaching,*' announced a dolphin's amplified voice. It had a fizzing quality that meant the speaker was breathing oxygen-charged water, so it must be coming from the bridge. '*All hands prepare for transition. Kaa says our guides are acting strange. They're choosing an unconventional approach pattern, so this may get rough!*'

Gillian and Sara gripped their armrests. The dolphins in the Plotting Room caused their walkers' feet to splay out and magnetize, gripping the floor. But there was little for me and the glavers to do except stare about with wild, feral eyes. In the forward viewer, I now saw the starscape interrupted by a twist of utter blackness. Computer-generated lines converged while figures and glyphs made Sara murmur with excitement.

I watched the ship ahead of us, the first Zang globule, shiver almost eagerly as it plunged at a steep angle toward the twist ...

Then it *fell* in a direction I could not possibly describe if my life depended on it.

A direction that I never, till that moment, knew existed.

I glanced quickly at the rearward display. It showed the other hydro vessel shaking asunder before repeated fierce blows as the Jophur battle cruiser fired desperately with short-range weapons. The two behemoths were almost next to each other now, matched in velocity, still racing after us.

A final, frantic hammering ripped through the Zang ship, tearing it into several unraveling gobs.

For a moment, I thought it was over.

I thought the Jophur had won.

Then two of those huge gobs *curled*, almost like living tendrils, and settled across the gleaming metal hull. They clung to its surface. Spreading. Oozing.

Somehow, despite the distance and flickering haze, I had the sense of something probing for a way *in*.

Then the image vanished.

I turned back to the main viewer. Transition had begun.

KAA

There was a fine art to piloting a starship through the stretched geometries of a transfer point. No machine or logical algorithm could manage the feat alone.

Part of it involved playing hunches, knowing when to release the flange fields holding you to one shining thread and choosing just the right moment to make a leap – lasting both seconds and eons – across an emptiness deeper than vacuum ... then clamping nimbly to another slender discontinuity (without actually touching its deadly rim) and riding that one forward to your goal.

Even a well-behaved t-point was a maelstrom. A spaghetti tangle of shimmering arcs and folds, bending the cosmic fabric through multiple – and sometimes partial – dimensions.

A maze of dazzling, filamentary imperfections.

Stringlike cracks in the mirror of creation.

For those wise enough to use them well, the glowing strands offered a great boon. A way to travel safely from galaxy to linked galaxy, much faster than using hyperspace.

But to the foolish, or inattentive, their gift was a quick and flashy end.

Kaa loved thread-jumping more than any other part of spaceflight. Something about it meshed with both sides of neo-dolphin nature.

The new brain layers, added by human genecrafters, let him regard each strand as a *flaw* in the quantum metric, left behind when the universe first cooled from an inflating superheated froth, congealing like a many-layered cake to form the varied levels of real and hyperspace. That coalescence left defects behind – boundaries and fractures – where physical laws bent and shortcuts were possible. He could ponder all of that with the disciplined mental processes Captain Creideiki used to call the Engineer's Mind.

Meanwhile, in parallel, Kaa picked up different textures and insights through older organs, deep within his skull. Ancient bits of gray matter tuned for *listening* – to hear the swishing structure of a current, or judge the cycloid rhythms of a wave. Instruments probed the dense tangle of fossil topological boundaries, feeding him data in the form of *sonar images*. Almost by intuition, he could sense when a transfer thread was about to play out, and which neighboring cord he should clamp on to, sending the *Streaker* darting along a new gleaming path toward her next goal.

Thomas Orley had once compared the process to 'leaping from one roller coaster to another, in the middle of a thunderstorm.'

Creideiki had expressed it differently.

> * *Converging nature*
> > * *Begins and ends, lives and dies,*
> > > * *Where tide meets shoal and sky . . .*

Even during the expedition's early days – when the captain was still with them and *Streaker's* brilliant chief pilot Keepiru handled all the really tough maneuvers – everyone had nevertheless agreed that there was nothing quite like a t-point ride with Kaa at the helm – an exuberance of daring, flamboyant maneuvers that never seemed to go wrong. Once, after a series of absurdly providential thread jumps let him break a million-year-old record, taking the crossing from Tanith to Calafia in five and a quarter mictaars, the crew bestowed on him a special nickname.

'*Lucky.*'

In Trinary, the word-phrase meant much more than it did in

Anglic. It connoted special favor in the fortune sea, the deep realm of chance where Ifni threw her dice and ancient dreamers crooned songs that were old before the stars were born.

It was a great honor. But some also say that such titles, once won, are hard to keep.

He started losing his during the fiasco at Oakka, that awful green world of betrayal, and things went rapidly downhill after that. By the time *Streaker* fled to a murky trash heap beneath Jijo's forlorn ocean, few called him Lucky Kaa anymore.

Then, in a matter of days, fate threw him the best and cruelest turns of all. He found love ... and quickly lost it again when duty yanked Kaa away from his heart, sending him hurtling parsecs farther from Peepoe with each passing minute.

At the very moment she needed me most.

So he took little joy from this flight through a labyrinth of shimmering threads. Only grim professionalism sustained him.

Kaa had learned not to count on luck.

Behind him, the water-filled control room seemed eerily silent. Without opening his eyes or breaking concentration, Kaa felt the other neo-fins holding tense rein over their reflex sonar clicking, in order not to disturb him.

They had cause for taut nerves. This transfer was like no other.

The reason gleamed ahead of *Streaker* – a vast object that Kaa perceived one moment as a gigantic jellyfish ... then like a mammoth squid, with tentacles bigger than any starship he had ever seen. Its fluid profile, transformed for travel through the t-point's twisted bowels, gave him shivers. Instinct made Kaa yearn to get away – to cut the flanges and hop any passing thread, no matter where in the universe it might lead – just to elude that dreadful shape.

But it's our guide. And if we tried to get away, the Zang would surely kill us.

Kaa heard a faint caterwauling cry, coming from the dry chamber next door – the Plotting Room. By now he recognized the wailing sound of glavers, those devolved creatures from Jijo who had voluntarily returned to animal presapience. That alone would be enough to give him the utter willies, even without this bizarre affinity the bulge-eyed beasts seemed to have with a completely different order of life. That understanding offered *Streaker* a way clear of the dreaded Jophur, but at what cost?

Saved from one deadly foe, he pondered. *Only to face another that's feared all across Galactic Civilization.*

In fact, such dilemmas were becoming routine to the dolphin

crew. The whole universe seemed filled with nothing but frying pans and fires.

They're getting ready, Kaa contemplated as a gentle throbbing passed along the tentacles of the squidlike shape ahead. Twice before, this had just preceded a jump maneuver. On both occasions, it had taken all his skill to follow without slamming *Streaker* into a nearby string singularity. The hydros used a thread-riding style unlike any he had seen before, following world lines that were more timelike than spacelike, triggering micro causality waves that nauseated everyone aboard. Nothing about the Zang method was any more efficient. Each jarring maneuver – and churning neural reflex – made Kaa want to swerve back and do it in a way that made more sense.

I could probably get you there in half the time, he thought resentfully toward the squid-shaped thing. *If you just told me where we're going*.

True, the resonances had changed since he last used this t-point, back when *Streaker* fled the horrid Fractal World, attempting Gillian's last desperate gamble ... the 'sooner's path,' seeking a hiding place on far-off Jijo. When that second singularity nexus reopened near Izmunuti, it must have jiggered this one as well. Still, there *must* be an easier way to get where the Zang wanted to go than—

Sonar images merged into focus. He perceived a bright cluster of threads just ahead ... a Gordian tangle with no spacelike strands at all.

Ugh! That ghastly clutter has got to be where the hydros are aiming, damn them.

And yet, listening carefully to the transposed sound portrait, he thought he could sense something about the knotty mess ...

You know, I'll bet I can guess which thread they're gonna take.

Kaa's attention riveted. This was important to him. More than duty and survival were at stake. Or the vaunted reputation neo-dolphin pilots had begun to earn among the Five Galaxies. Even regaining his nickname held little attraction anymore.

Only one thing really mattered to Kaa. Getting the job done. Delivering Gillian Baskin and her cargo safely. And then finding a way back to Jijo. Back to Peepoe. Even if it meant never piloting again. He triggered an alarm to warn the others.

Here we go!

The 'squid' uncoiled, preparing for its final leap.

I am at a loss to describe even a single moment of our time inside the t-point.

Comparisons come to mind. Like a Founders' Day fireworks display. Or watching a clever urrish tinker throw sparkling exploser dust during a magic show, or . . .

Give up, Alvin.

All I really recall from that nauseating passage is a blur of dazzling ribbons waving across every monitor screen. While Sara Koolhan shouted ecstatically, watching her beloved mathematics come alive before her eyes, the more experienced Gillian Baskin kept grunting in dismayed surprise – a sound I found worrisome.

The gravity fields pitched and fluxed. Sparks flew from nearby instrument banks. Neo-fin crew stomped their walker machines close, dousing hot spots with inert gas. All told, this first-time space traveler figured we were experiencing no typical passage.

In fact, I soon felt too miserable to notice much of anything. I just spread my arms in a wide circle so the glavers could huddle inside, mewling pathetically. But the shrieking cry of *Streaker's* engines tore through all my efforts to umble reassuringly.

Without any doubt, it was among the worst couple of miduras in my life, even when I compare it to the awful time when my friends and I fell off the edge of a subsea cliff in our broken *Wuphon's Dream*, with icy water jetting at my face as we tumbled toward the cold hell of Jijo's Midden.

At one point a dolphin cried out – *'Here we go!'* – and things rapidly got a whole lot worse. My second bowel did a lurch against my heart. Then I found I couldn't breathe as every sound around me abruptly ceased!

For a long, extended moment it felt like being swaddled in a dense bale of bec cotton, as if I were being torn from the universe, looking back at it from the end of a long tunnel, or from the bottom of a deep, deep well.

Then, just as suddenly, I was back! The cosmos swarmed around me again. A great weight seemed to lift off my vertebral spines, allowing me to inhale sharply.

We Jijoan hoons love our sailing ships, I thought, fighting off waves of queasiness. *We never get sick at sea. But our star-traveling ancestors must've been throwing up all the time, if this was how they had to get about. No wonder legends say they were such grouches.*

Glancing up, I saw that Gillian and Sara were already on their feet, moving tensely toward the big display. Tsh't and the dolphin staff piloted their walkers to crowd just behind the humans, peering over their shoulders.

A bit shaky, I stood and joined them. On the main screen, all the roiling colors were dissipating fast. *Streaker*'s roaring engines dropped to a soft mutter as the ripple-swirls parted like folds of a curtain, revealing . . .

. . . stars.

I gazed at strange constellations.

Stars that are some damn Ifni-incalculable distance from the ones I know.

How is one supposed to feel when a long-held, impossible dream comes true?

Alvin, you are now a long, long way from home.

While I mused on that marvel, *Streaker* slowly turned. The shining skyscape flowed past our gaze – strange clusters, nebulae, and spiral arms whose light might not reach Jijo for thousands or millions of years – until at last we caught sight of our escort, the huge Zang ship-entity.

And the place where it was leading us.

A gasp shuddered through the Plotting Room, as every Earthling expressed the same emotion at once.

'Oh, no,' groaned Lieutenant Tsh't. 'It c-can't be!'

Dr. Gillian Baskin sighed.

'I don't believe it! All that misery . . . just to wind up *back here*?'

Before me, starting to fill the forward screen, there stretched yet another sight I could barely describe at first. A *structure* of some kind, nearly black as space. Only when Gillian ordered further image enhancement did it stand forth from the background, glowing a deep shade of umber.

It looked roughly spherical, but *spiky* all around, like one of those burr seeds that stick to your leg fur when you go tramping through undergrowth. I thought it must be another mammoth starship, looming frightfully close.

Then I realized – we were still barreling along at great speed, but its apparent size was changing only very slowly.

It must be really huge, I realized, shifting my imagination. *Even bigger than the Zang ship!*

That jaundiced globule cruised alongside *Streaker*, shivering in a way that made me nervous. Scratchy noises assailed us again through the loudspeakers, making the glavers sway their big heads, rolling bulbous eyes and moaning.

'*They say that we must follow*,' translated the Niss Machine.

Lieutenant Tsh't stuttered.

'Sh-shall we try for the t-transfer point? We could turn quickly. Dive back in. Trust Kaa to—'

Gillian shook her head.

'The Zang wouldn't let us get two meters.'

Her shoulders hunched in a human expression of misery that no hoon could mimic. Clearly, this jagged place was a familiar sight that no one aboard *Streaker* would have chosen to visit again.

I caught the eye of Sara Koolhan. For the first time, my fellow Jijoan seemed just as much at a loss as I. She blinked in apparent confusion, unable to grasp the immensity of this thing ahead of us.

A strange sound came from the only male human present. The mute one who never speaks – Emerson D'Anite. He had been especially quiet during the trip from Izmunuti, silently studying the strange colors of t-space, as if they carried more meaning than the words of his own kind.

Now, staring at the huge, prickly ball, his face expressed the same astonishment as his crewmates' faces, intense emotion twisting the dark man's wounded features. Sara moved quickly to Emerson's side, taking his arm and speaking gently.

I recall thinking, *If this place made the Terrans desperate enough to flee to Jijo, I'm not surprised they're upset finding themselves right back here*.

A familiar voice cried out behind me, in tones of awed delight.

'Uttergloss!'

I turned in time to see Huck come wheeling into the Plotting Room, waving all four of her agile g'Kek eyes toward the big screen.

'That thing looks so cool. What is it?'

Another pal reached the open door not far behind her. An urrish head snaked through at the end of a long, sinuous neck, its single nostril flaring at the unpleasant reek of Earthling fear.

Arriving from another direction, a red qheuen lunged his armored bulk rudely past Ur-ronn while she hesitated. Pincer-Tip's vision cupola spun and he snapped his claws in excitement.

I should have expected it, of course. They weren't invited, but if my friends share one instinct across all species boundaries, it's a knack for finding trouble and charging straight for it.

'Hey, furry legs!' Huck snapped, nudging my flank with two waving eyestalks while the other pair strained to peer past the crowd. 'Make your overstuffed carcass useful. Clear a way through these fishy things so I can see!'

Wincing, I hoped the dolphins were too busy to note her impertinence. Rather than disturb the crew, I bent down and grabbed Huck's axle rims, grunting as I lifted her above the crowd for a better view. (A young g'Kek doesn't weigh much, though at the time my back was still healing. It twinged each time she squirmed and spun from excitement.)

'What *is* that thing?' Huck repeated, gesturing toward the huge spiky ball.

Lieutenant Tsh't raised her glossy head from the soft platform of her mechanical walker, aiming one dark eye at my g'Kek friend.

'It'ssss a place where we *fishy things* suffered greatly, before coming to your world.'

Had I been human, my ears would have burned with embarrassment. Being a hoon, my throat sac puffed with apologetic umbles. But Huck barged on without noticing.

'Sheesh, it looks big!'

The dolphin emitted snorting laughter from her moist blowhole.

'You c-could say that. The shell encloses a volume of approximately thirty astrons, or a trillionth of a cubic parsec.'

Huck's stalks expressed a blithe shrug.

'Huh! Whatever that means. I'll tell you what it reminds me of. It looks like the spiny armor covering a desert clam!'

'Lookssss can be deceiving, young Jijoan,' Tsh't answered. 'That shell is soft enough to cut with a wooden spoon. If you approached and exhaled on it, the patch touched by your breath would boil away. Its average density is like a cloud in a snowstorm.'

That doesn't sound too threatening, I pondered. Then I caught the startled look on Sara Koolhan's face. Our young human sage frowned as her eyes darted back and forth, from data panels to the main screen, then to Tsh't.

'The infrared ... the reemission profiles ... You're not saying that thing actually *contains*—'

She stopped, unable to finish her sentence. The dolphin officer snickered.

'Indeed it does. A *star* resides at the heart of that soft confffection. That deceptive puff of p-poison ssssnow.'

'Welcome, dear Jijoan friends. Welcome to the Fractal World.'

LARK

He didn't feel cold. Not exactly. Even though, logically, he ought to.

A cloying mist surrounded Lark as membranes pressed against him from all sides, keeping his body bent nearly double, with knees up near his chin.

Lark felt as he imagined he might if someone crammed him back into the womb.

Soon another similarity grew apparent. He wasn't breathing anymore.

In fact, his mouth was sealed shut and swollen plugs filled both nostrils. The rhythmic expansion of his chest, the soft sigh of sweet air, these notable portions of life's usual background ... were gone!

With this realization, panic nearly engulfed Lark. A red haze obscured vision, narrowing to a tunnel as he struggled and thrashed. Though his body seemed reluctant at first, he obliged it to try inhaling ... and achieved nothing.

He tried harder, *commanding* effort from his sluggish diaphragm and rib cage. Lark's spine arched as he strained, until at last a scant trickle of gas slipped by one nose plug – perhaps only a few molecules—

—carrying an acrid stench!

Sudden paroxysms contorted Lark. Limbs churned and bowels convulsed as he tried voiding himself into the turbid surroundings.

Fortunately, his gut was empty – he had eaten little for days. A cottony feeling spread through his extremities like a drug, filling them with soothing numbness as the fit soon passed, leaving behind a lingering foul taste in his mouth.

Lark had learned a valuable lesson.

Next time you find yourself wrapped up in fetal position, crammed inside a stinking bag without an instinct to breathe, take a hint. Go with the flow.

Lark felt for a pulse and verified that his heart, at least, was still functioning. The persistent stinging in his sinuses – a noxious-familiar stench – was enough all by itself to verify that life went on, painful as it was.

Turning his head to look around, Lark soon noticed that his bag of confinement was just one of many floating in a much larger volume. Through the obscuring mist he made out other membranous sacks. Most held big, conical-shaped Jophur – tapered stacks of fatty rings that throbbed feebly while their basal leg segments pushed uselessly, without any solid surface for traction. Some of the traekilike beings looked whole, but others had clearly been broken down to smaller stacks, or even individual rings.

Knotty cables, like the throbbing tendrils of a mulc-spider, led away from each cell ... including his own. In fact, one penetrated the nearby translucent wall, snaking around Lark's left leg and terminating finally at his inner thigh, just below the groin.

The sight triggered a second wave of panic, which he fought this time by drawing on his best resource, his knowledge as a primitive scientist. Jijo might be a backwater, lacking the intellectual resources of the Five Galaxies, but you could still train a working mind from the pages of paper books.

Use what you know. Figure this out!

All right.

First thing … the cable piercing his leg appeared to target the femoral artery. Perhaps it was feeding *on* him, like some space-leech in a garish, pre-Contact scifi yarn. But that horror image seemed so silly that Lark suspected the truth was quite different.

Basic life support. I'm floating in a poison atmosphere, so they can't let me breathe or eat or drink. They must be sending oxygen and nutrients directly to my blood.

Whoever 'they' were.

As for the jiggling containers, Lark was enough of a field biologist to know *sampling bags* when he saw them. Although he could not laugh, a sense of ironic justice helped him put a wry perspective on the situation. He had put more than enough hapless creatures in confinement during his career as a naturalist, dissecting the complex interrelationships of living species on Jijo.

If nature passed out karma for such acts, Lark's burden might merit a personal purgatory that looked something like this.

He strained harder to see through the mist, hoping not to find Ling among the captives. And yet, a pall of loneliness settled when he verified she was nowhere in sight.

Maybe she escaped from Rann and the Jophur, when these yellow monsters invaded the Polkjhy. *If she made it to the Life Core, she might clamber through the jungle foliage and be safe in our old nest. For a while, at least.*

He glimpsed walls beyond the murk, estimating this chamber to be larger than the meeting tree back in his home village. From certain visible furnishings and wallmounted data units, he could tell it was still the Jophur dreadnought, but invaders had taken over this portion, filling it with their own nocuous atmosphere.

That ought to be a clue. The familiar-horrid scent. A toxicity that forbade inhaling. But Lark's bruised mind drew no immediate conclusions. To a Jijoan – even a so-called 'scientist' – all of space was a vast realm of terrible wonders.

Have they seized the whole vessel?

It seemed far-fetched, given the power of mighty Jophur skygods, but Lark looked for some abstract solace in that prospect. Those traeki-cousins meant only bad news to all the Six Races of Jijo, especially the poor g'Kek. The best thing that could happen to his homeworld would be if battleship *Polkjhy* never reached home to report what it had found in an obscure corner of Galaxy Four.

And yet, this situation could hardly be expected to make him glad, or grateful to his new captors.

It took a while, but eventually Lark realized – some of them were nearby!

At first, he mistook the quivering shapes for lumps in the overall fog, somewhat denser than normal. But these particular patches remained compact and self-contained, though fluid in outline. He likened them to shifting heaps of pond scum ... or else succinct thunderheads, cruising imperiously among lesser clouds. Several of these amorphous-looking bodies clustered around a nearby sample bag, inspecting the Jophur prisoner within.

Inspecting? What makes you think that? Do you see any eyes? Or sensory organs of any kind?

The floating globs moved languidly, creeping through the dense medium by extending or writhing temporary arms or pseudopods. There did not seem to be any permanent organs or structures within their translucent skins, but a rhythmic movement of small, blobby subunits that came together, merged, or divided with a complexity he could only begin to follow.

He recalled an earlier amoebalike creature, much bigger than these – the invader who had burst through a ship's bulkhead, scaring away Rann and the other pursuers who had Lark cornered. That one had seemed to look right at Lark, before swarming ahead rapidly to swallow him up.

What could they be? Did Ling ever mention anything like this? I don't remember ...

All at once Lark knew where he had encountered the foul smell before. At Biblos ... the Hall of Science ... in a part of the great archive that had been cleared of bookshelves in order to set up a chemistry lab, where a small band of sages labored to recreate ancient secrets, financed and subsidized by the Jijoan Explosers Guild.

Trying to recover old skills, or even learn new things. The guild must have been full of heretics like Sara. Believers in 'progress.'

I never thought of it before, but the Slope was rife with renegade thinking even weirder than my own. In time, we'd probably have had a religious schism – even civil war – if gods hadn't come raining from the sky this year.

He thought about Harullen and Uthen, his chitinous friends, laid low by alien treachery. And about Dwer and Sara – safe at home, he hoped. For their sake alone, he would blow up this majestic vessel, if that meant Jijo could be shrouded once more in blessed obscurity.

Lark's dour contemplations orbited from the melancholy past, around the cryptic present, and through a dubious future.

Time advanced, though he had no way of measuring it except by counting heartbeats. That grew tedious, after a while, but he kept at it, just to keep his hand in.

I'm alive! The creatures in charge here must find me interesting, in some way.

Lark planned on stoking that interest, whatever it took.

ALVIN'S JOURNAL

'Welcome, dear Jijoan friends. Welcome to the Fractal World.'

That line would have been a great place to finish this journal entry.

The moment had an eerie, intense drama. I could sense the tragic letdown of the *Streaker* crew, having fled all the way to Jijo's hellish deeps, and lost many comrades, only to wind up back at the very spot that had caused them so much pain in the first place.

But what happened next made all that seem to pale, like a shadow blasted by lightning.

'Maybe it'sss a different criswell structure,' suggested Akeakemai, one of the dolphin technical officers, calling from the bridge. *'After all, there's supposed to be millions of them, in just this galaxy alone.'*

But that wishful hope shattered when Tsh't confirmed the star configurations.

'Besides. What are the chances another criswell would sit this close to a transfer point? Most lie in remote globular clusters.

'No,' the lieutenant went on. 'Our Zang friends have brought us back for s-sssome bloody reason ... may they vaporize and burn for it.'

We four kids from Wuphon gathered at one end of the Plotting Room to compare notes. Ur-ronn communicated with her friends in Engineering. Her urrish lisp grew stronger as she became more excited, explaining what she had learned about the spiky ball.

'It is hollow, with a radius avout three tines as wide as Jijo's orvit, centered on a little red dwarf star. It is all jagged vecause that creates the highest surface area to radiate heat to sface. And it's just like that on the inside too, where the uneven surface catches every ray of light fron the star!'

'Actually, a simple sphere would accomplish that,' explained the

Niss Machine in professorial tones. A pictorial image appeared, showing a hollow shell surrounding a bright crimson pinpoint.

'*Some pre-Contact Earthlings actually prophesied such things, calling them—*'

'Dyson spheres!' Huck shouted.

We all stared at her. She twisted several vision-stalks in a shrug. 'C'mon guys. Catch up on your classic scifi.'

Hoons think more slowly than g'Keks, but I nodded at last.

'Hr-rm, yes. I recall seeing them mentioned in novels by … hr-r … Shaw and Allen. But the idea seemed too fantastic ever to take serious …'

My voice trailed off. Of course, seeing is believing.

'*As I was about to explain,*' the Niss continued, somewhat huffily, '*the simple Dyson sphere concept missed an essential geometric requirement of a stellar enclosure. Allow me to illustrate.*'

A new pictorial replaced the smooth ball with a prickly one – like a knob of quill-coral dredged up by a fishing scoop. The computer-generated image split open before our eyes, exposing a wide central void where the tiny star shone. Only now a multitude of knifelike protrusions jutted *inward* as well, crisscrossing like the competing branches of a riotous rain forest.

'*Latter-day Earthlings call this a* criswell structure. *The spikiness creates a* fractal *shape, of dimension approximately two point four. The interior has a bit more folding, where the purpose is to maximize total surface area getting some exposure to sunlight, even if it comes at a glancing angle.*'

'Why?' Pincer-Tip asked.

'*To maximize the number of windows, of course,*' answered the Niss, as if that explained everything.

'*Energy is the chief limiting factor here. This small sun puts out approximately ten to the thirty ergs per second. By capturing all of that, and allowing each inhabitant a generous megawatt of power to use, this abode can adequately serve a population exceeding one hundred thousand billion sapient beings. At lower per capita power use, it would support more than ten quadrillions.*'

We all stared. For once, even Huck was stunned to complete silence.

I struggled for some way to wrap my poor, slow thoughts around such numbers.

Put it this way. If every citizen of the Six Races of Jijo were suddenly to have each *cell* of his or her body transformed into a full-sized sapient being, the total would still fall short of the kind of census the Niss described. It far surpassed the count of every star and life-bearing planet in all five galaxies.

(I figured all this out later, of course. At the time, it taxed my stunned brain to do more than stare.)

Ur-ronn recovered first.

'It sounds . . . *crowded*,' she suggested.

'*Actually, population levels are constrained by energy and sunfacing surface area. By contrast, volume for living space is not a serious limitation. Accommodations would be fairly roomy. Each sovereign entity could have a private chamber larger than the entire volcano you Jijoans call Mount Guenn.*'

'Uh-uh-uh-uh-uh . . .' Pincer-Tip stuttered from five leg vents at once, summing up my own reaction at the time. 'P-p-people *made* this thing . . . t-t-to live in?'

The Niss hologram curled into a spinning abstraction of meshed lines that somehow conveyed amusement.

'*These inhabitants might consider the term "people" insultingly pejorative, my dear young barbarian. In fact, most of them are classified as higher entities than you or me. Fractal colonies are primarily occupied by members of the Retired Order of Life. In this place – and about a billion other structures like it, scattered across the Five Galaxies – elder races live out their quiet years in relative peace, freed from the bickering noise and fractious disputes of younger clans.*'

A nearby dolphin snorted derisively, though at that moment I did not grasp the bitter irony of the Niss Machine's words.

Sara Koolhan wandered back to join our group.

'But what is it *made of*?' the young sage asked. 'What kind of materials could possibly support anything so huge?'

The pictorial image zoomed, focusing our view on one small segment of a cutaway edge. From a basically circular arc, craggy shapes projected both toward the star and away from it, splitting into branches, then subbranches, and so on till the eye lost track of the smallest. Faceted chambers filled every enclosed volume.

'*The inner surface is built largely of spun carbon, harvested from various sources, like the star itself. Hydrogen-helium fusion reactors produced more, over the course of many millions of years. Carbon can withstand direct sunlight. Moreover, it is strong in centrifugal tension.*

'*The outer portions of this huge structure, on the other hand, are in sub-Keplerian dynamic conditions. Because they feel a net inward pull, they must be strong against compression. Much of the vast honeycomb structure therefore consists of field-stabilized metallic hydrogen, the most plentiful element in the cosmos, mixed into a ceramic-carbon polymorph. This building material was stripped from the star long ago by magnetic induction, removing roughly a tenth of its overall mass – along with oxygen and other components needed for protoplasmic life. That removal had an added benefit of allowing the sun to burn in a slower, more predictable fashion.*

'*The external shell of the criswell structure is so cold that it re-radiates heat to space at a temperature barely above the universal background . . .*'

My ears kind of switched off at that point. I guess the Niss must have thought it was making sense. But even when me and my friends labored through recordings of the lecture later, consulting the autoscribe one word at a time, only Ur-ronn claimed to grasp more than a fraction of the explanation.

Truly, we had arrived at the realm of gods.

I drifted away, since the one question foremost in my mind wasn't being addressed. It had nothing to do with technical details.

I wanted to know *why*!

If this monstrous thing was built to house millions of millions of millions of occupants, then who lived there? Why gather so many beings into a giant snowball, surrounding a little star? A 'house' so soft and cold that I could melt portions with my own warm breath?

All that hydrogen made me wonder – did the Zang live here?

Above all, what had happened to make the *Streaker* crew fear this place so?

I observed Gillian Baskin standing alone before two big displays. One showed the Fractal World in real light – a vast disk of blackness. A jagged mouth, biting off whole constellations.

The other screen depicted the same panorama in 'shifted infrared,' resembling the head of a garish medieval mace, glowing a shade like hoonish blood. It grew larger and slowly turned as *Streaker* moved across the night, approaching the monstrous thing at a shallow angle. I wondered how many sets of eyes were watching from vast chill windows, regarding us with a perspective of experience going back untold eons. At best such minds would consider my species a mere larval form. At worst, they might see us no more worthy than insects.

Our escort, the giant Zang vessel, started spitting smaller objects from its side – the harvester machines it had managed to salvage from the chaos at Izmunuti, carrying their crumpled sails. These began spiraling ahead of us, orbiting more rapidly toward the vast sphere, as if hastening on some urgent errand.

It occurred to me that I was privileged at that moment to witness four of the great Orders of Life in action at the same instant. Hydrogen breathers, machine intelligences, oxy-creatures like myself, and the 'retired' phylum – beings who built on such a scale that they thought nothing of husbanding a *star* like their own personal hearth fire. As a Jijo native, I knew my tribe was crude compared to the august Civilization of Five Galaxies. But now it further dawned on me that even the Great Galactic Institutes might be looked on as mere anthills by others who were even higher on the evolutionary pyramid.

I guess I know where that puts me.

The dark human male joined Dr. Baskin before the twin screens, sharing a glance with her that must have communicated more than words.

'You can feel it too, Emerson?' she said in a low voice.

'Something is different. I'm getting a real creepy feeling.' The mute man rubbed his scarred head, then abruptly grinned and started whistling a catchy melody. I did not recognize the tune. But it made her laugh.

'Yeah. Life is full of changes, all right. And we might as well be optimistic. Perhaps the Old Ones have grown up a bit since we've been away.' Her mirthless smile made that seem unlikely. 'Or maybe something else distracted them enough to forget all about little us.'

I yearned to follow up on that – to step forward and press her for explanations. But somehow it felt improper to interrupt their poignant mood. So I kept my peace and watched nearby as the harvester robots circled ahead and vanished beyond the limb of the Fractal World.

A little while later, a worried voice spoke over the intercom. It was Olelo, the ship's detection officer, calling from the bridge.

'For some time we've been picking up substantially higher systemwide gas and particulate signaturesss,' the dolphin reported. *'Now we're seeing reflections from larger grain sizes, just ahead, plus entrained ionic flows characteristic of sssolar wind.'*

Dr. Baskin looked puzzled.

'Reflections? Reflecting what? Starlight?'

There was a brief pause.

'No ma'am. Spectral profiles match direct illumination by a nearby class M8 dwarf.'

This time, Emerson D'Anite and I shared a baffled look. Neither of us understood a word – he due to his injury, and me because of my savage birth. But the information must have meant plenty to the other human.

'Direct ... but that can only mean ...' Her eyes widened in a combination of fear and realization. 'Oh dear sweet—'

She was cut off by a sudden alarm blare. Across the Plotting Room, all conversation stopped. The image on the main screen zoomed forward, concentrating directly ahead of *Streaker*'s path, to the limb of the great sphere that was now rotating into view.

Huck spread all her eyestalks and uttered a hushed oath.

'Ifni!'

Neo-dolphins rocked their walkers in nervous agitation. Ur-ronn clattered her hooves and Pincer-Tip kept repeating – 'Gosh-osh-osh-osh-osh!'

I had no comment, but reflexively began umbling to calm the nervous beings around me. As usual, I was probably the last one to comprehend what lay before my ogling gaze.

An indentation, interrupting the curved-serrated contour of the sphere.

A wide streamer of faint reddish light, wafting toward the stars.

A scattering of myriad soft glints and twinkling points, like embers blowing from a burning house.

Our Jijoan sage, Sara Koolhan, stepped forward.

'The sphere ... it's ruptured!'

Olelo's anxious voice reported again from the bridge.

'Confirmed ... We've got-t a breach in the criswell structure! It'sss a ... a big hole, at least an astron or two acrosss. Can't tell yet-t, but I think ...'

There was another long pause. No one spoke a word or dared even breathe while we waited.

'Yes, it's verified,' Olelo resumed. 'The collapse is continuing as we ssspeak.

'Whatever happened to this place ... it's still going on.'

GILLIAN

A panorama of death had her riveted.

'I will grant you one thing,' remarked the voice from the spinning hologram. 'Wherever you Terrans travel in the universe, you do tend to leave a mark.'

She had no reply for the Niss Machine. Gillian hoped if she kept silent it would go away.

But the tornado of whirling lines moved closer instead. Sidling by her left ear, it spoke her native tongue in soft, natural tones.

'Two million centuries.

'That is how long the Library says this particular structure existed, calmly orbiting the galaxy, a refuge of peace.

'Then, one day, some wolflings came by for a brief visit.'

Gillian slashed, but her hand swept through the hologram without resistance. The abstract pattern kept spinning. Its mesh of fine lines cast ghost-flickers across her face. Of course the damned Niss was right. *Streaker* carried a jinx, bringing ruin everywhere it went. Only here, the consequent misfortune surpassed any scale she could grasp with heart or mind.

Instruments highlighted grim symptoms of devastation as, escorted by the huge Zang globule-vessel, *Streaker* entered a ragged gap in the tremendous fractal shell, bathed in reddish sunlight that was escaping confinement for the first time in eons. A storm of atoms and particles blew out through the same hole, so dense that at one point the word 'vacuum' lost pertinence. A noticeable pressure appeared on instruments, faintly resisting the Earthship's progress.

There was larger debris. Chunks that Kaa moved nimbly to avoid. Some were great wedges, revealing hexagonal, comblike rooms the size of asteroids. Tumbling outward, each evaporating clump wore shimmering tails of dust and ions. Thousands of these artificial comets lit up the broad aperture ... a cavity so wide that Earth would take a month in its orbit to cross it.

'*Albeit reluctantly, Dr. Baskin,*' the Niss concluded, '*I admit I am impressed. Congratulations.*'

Nearby, a throng of walker-equipped neo-dolphins jostled among the passengers. The Plotting Room grew crowded as off-duty personnel came to gawk at the spectacle. But a gap surrounded Gillian, like a moat none dared cross, except the sardonic Tymbrimi machine-mind. No one exulted. This place had caused the crew great pain, but the havoc was too immense, too overwhelming for gloating.

Nor would it be fair. Just a few factions of Old Ones had been responsible for the betrayal that sent *Streaker* fleeing almost a year ago, while some other blocs actually helped the Earthship get away. Anyway, should hundreds of billions die because of the greed of a few?

Don't get carried away, she thought. *There's no proof this disaster has anything to do with us. It could be something completely unrelated.*

But that seemed unlikely. Sheer coincidence beggared any other explanation.

She recalled how their previous visit ended – with a final backward glimpse during *Streaker's* narrow getaway.

We saw violence erupting behind us, even as someone opened up a door, letting us make a break for the transfer point. I saw a couple of nearby fractal branches get damaged, and some windows broken, while sects clashed over Emerson's little scoutship, seizing and preventing him from following us.

Gillian's friend paid dearly for his brave rearguard action, suffering unimaginably cruel torture and abuse before somehow, mysteriously, being transported to Jijo right after *Streaker*. The speechless former engineer was never able to explain.

Amid the guilt of abandoning him, and our hurry fleeing this place, who would have guessed the Old Ones would keep on fighting after we escaped! Why? What purpose could an apocalypse serve, after we took our cursed cargo away?

But a horrible tribulation must have followed. Ahead lay ample testimony. Plasma streamers and red-tinged dust plumes ... along with countless long black shadows trailing from bits of dissolving rubble, some larger than a moon, but all of them as frail as snowflakes.

She pondered the ultimate cause – the treasures *Streaker* carried, like Herbie, the ancient cadaver that had taken over her study, like Poe's raven, or Banquo's ghost. Prizes lusted after by fanatical powers hoping to seize and monopolize their secrets, winning some advantage in a Time of Changes.

It was imperative to prevent that. The Terragens Council had made their orders clear – first to Creideiki and later to Gillian when she assumed command. *Streaker*'s discoveries must be shared openly, according to ancient Galactic custom, or not at all. Mighty races and alliances might violate that basic rule and think they could get away with it. But frail Earthclan dared not show even a hint of partiality.

In an age of rising chaos, sometimes the weak and friendless have no sanctuary but the law. Humans and their clients had to keep faith with Galactic institutions. To do less would be to risk losing everything. Unfortunately, Gillian's quest for a neutral power to take over the relics had proved worse than futile.

It wasn't for lack of trying. After the Great Institutes proved untrustworthy at Oakka, Gillian had what seemed (at the time) an inspired notion.

Why not pass the buck even higher?

She decided to bring the relics *here*, to a citadel for species that had 'moved on' from the mundane, petty obsessions plaguing the Civilization of Five Galaxies. At one of the legendary Fractal Worlds, harassed Earthlings might at last find dispassionate advice and mediation from beings who were revered enough to intercede, halting the spasmodic madness of younger clans. These respected elder sapients would assume responsibility for the burden, relieve *Streaker* of its toxic treasures, and force the bickering oxygen alliances to share.

Then, at long last, the weary dolphins could go home.

And I could go searching for Tom, wherever he and Creideiki and the others have drifted since Kithrup.

That had been the theory, the hope.

Too bad the Old Ones turned out to be as fretful, desperate, and duplicitous as their younger cousins who still dwelled amid blaring hot stars.

It's as if we were a plague ship, carrying something contagious from the distant past. Wherever we go, rational beings start acting like they've gone mad.

Monitors focused on the nearest edge of the great wound, revealing a shell several thousand miles thick, not counting the multipronged spikes jutting both in and out. Dense haze partly shrouded the continuing tragedy but could not mask a sparkle of persistent convulsions. Structural segments buckled and tore as Gillian watched. Fractal branches broke and went spinning through space, colliding with others, setting off further chain reactions.

The massive spikes on the sunward side glittered in a way that reminded Gillian.

Windows. When we first came here ... after they opened a slim door to let us through ... the first thing I noticed was how much of the inner face seemed to be made of glass. And beneath those immense panes—

She closed her eyes, recalling how the telescope had revealed each branchlet was its own separate world. Some greenhouses – larger than her home state of Minnesota – sheltered riotous jungles. Others shone with city lights, or floating palaces adrift on rippled seas, or plains of sparkling sand. It would take many millions of Earths, unrolled flat, to cover so much surface, and that would not begin to express the diversity. She might have spent years magnifying one habitat after another and still routinely found something distinct or new.

It was the most majestic and beautiful place Gillian had ever seen.

Now it was unraveling before her eyes.

That haze, she realized, aghast. *It isn't just structural debris and subliming gas. It's people. Their furniture and pets and clothes and houseplants and family albums ...* Or whatever comprised the equivalent for Old Ones. What human could guess the wishes, interests, and obsessions that became important to species who long ago had seen everything there was to see in the Five Galaxies, and had done everything there was to do?

However abstruse or obscure those hopes, they were dissolving fast. Just during *Streaker*'s brief passage through the gaping wound, more sapient beings must have died than the whole population of Earth.

Her mind quailed from that thought. To personalize the tragedy invited madness.

'Is anyone trying to stop this?' she asked in a hoarse voice.

The Niss Machine paused before answering.

'*Some strive hard. Behold their efforts.*'

The monitor view shifted forward as *Streaker* finally arrived at the habitat's vast interior space.

Just like the last time, Gillian abruptly felt as if she had entered a vast domed chamber of bright corrugated stalactites and measureless shadows. Although the farthest portions of the vault were several hundred million kilometers away, she could nevertheless make out fine details. The imaging system monitored her eyes to track the cone of her attention, highlighting and amplifying whatever she chose to regard.

Directly ahead – like a glowing lamp in the center of a basilica – a dwarf star cast its warming glow. The visible disk was dimmer and redder than the spendthrift kind of sun where nursery worlds like Terra spun and flourished. By stripping the outer layers for construction material, the makers of this place had created a perfect hearth fire, whose fuel ought to last a hundred billion years. To stare straight at the disk caused no physical pain. But its plasma skin, placid during their first visit, now seemed covered by livid sores. Dazzling pinpoints flared as planet-sized gobs of debris tumbled to the roiling surface.

Yet, Gillian soon realized such collisions were exceptional. Most of the jagged chunks were being intercepted and burned by narrow beams of searing blue energy, long before they reached the solar photosphere.

'*Of course even when they succeed in pulverizing rubble, the mass still settles downward as gas, eventually rejoining the sun from which it was stripped so long ago. The star's thermonuclear and atmospheric resonances will be adversely affected. Still, it reduces the number of large ablative impacts, and thus many actinic flares.*'

'So the maintenance system functions,' Gillian commented, with rising hope.

'*Yes, but it is touch and go. Worse yet, parts of the system are being abused.*'

The monitor went blurry as it sped to focus on a point along a far quadrant of the criswell sphere, where one of the blue scalpel-rays was busy with less altruistic work, carving a brutal path across the jagged landscape, severing huge fractal branchlets, shattering windows and raising mighty gouts of steam.

Gillian cried an oath and stepped back. 'My God. It's genocide!'

'*We have learned a sad lesson during this expedition,*' the Niss

Machine conceded. *'One that should very much interest my Tymbrimi makers, if we ever get a chance to report it.*

'When an oxygen-breathing race retires from Galactic affairs to seek repose in one of these vast shells, it does not always leave behind the prejudices and loyalties of youth. While many do seek enlightenment, or insights needed for transcendence, others stay susceptible to temptation, or remain steadfast to alliances of old.'

In other words, Gillian had been naive to expect detachment and impartiality from the species living here. Some were patrons – or great-grandpatrons – of Earth's persecutors.

She watched in horror as some faction misused a defensive weapon – designed to protect the whole colony – against a stronghold of its opponents.

'Ifni. What's to keep them from doing that to us!'

'Dr. Baskin, I haven't any idea,' the spinning hologram confided. *'Perhaps the locals are too busy in their struggles to notice our arrival.*

'Or else, it could be because of the company we keep.'

A screen showed the great Zang ship – floating just ninety kilometers away, quivering as the grim, sooty wind brushed its semiliquid flanks. Clouds of smaller objects fluttered nearby. Some were machine entities. Others qualified as living portions of the massive vessel, detached to do errands outside, then quietly reabsorb when their tasks were done.

'I've confirmed my earlier conjecture. The hydrogen beings are coordinating efforts by the harvester robots and other machine beings to help shore up and stabilize the Fractal World.'

Gillian nodded. 'That's why they were at Izmunuti. To fetch construction material. It's an easy source of carbon just one t-point jump away.'

'Under normal conditions, yes. Until unforeseen storms erupted, precipitated by that psi wave from Jijo. The harvesters we saw there were apparently just a small fraction of those involved in this massive effort.'

'It's a repair contract, then. A commercial deal.'

'I assume so. Since Galaxy Four has been evacuated by oxygen-breathing starfarers, it would be logical for Old Ones to seek help from the nearest available source. Shall I confirm these suppositions by tapping into the Fractal World's data nexus?'

'Do no such thing! I don't want to draw attention. If no one has noticed us, let's leave it that way.'

'May I point out that some groups within the retired order weren't inimical? Without their assistance we could never have eluded capture the first time. Perhaps those groups would help again if we make contact.'

Gillian shook her head firmly.

'I'm still worried the Jophur may show up any minute, hot on our heels. Let's just settle our business with the Zang and get away. Have you heard anything from them?'

Sara Koolhan thought the hydrogen breathers had some ancient claim on the glaver race ... a debt to be paid now that glavers had regained presapient innocence. But even so, how would the transaction take place? Was it proper or moral for the *Streaker* crew to hand over another oxy-species without formal sanction by appropriate institutes? Would the creatures be safe aboard a craft built to support a completely different chemistry of life?

More to the point, would the Zang let *Streaker* go afterward? According to sketchy Library accounts, hydros did have concepts of honor and obligation, but their logic was skewed. They might reward the Earthlings ... or blast them to get rid of a residual nuisance.

At least they didn't drag us here for prosecution, as I feared. They haven't handed us over to the Old Ones. Not yet.

A small voice of conscience chided Gillian. Here she was, worried about how to skulk away her tiny starship, saving fewer than a hundred lives, while around them nation-sized populations were dying each moment that she breathed.

One more reason not to let the Niss contact the Fractal World's comm net. She needed to keep the calamity as abstract as possible. A gaudy special-effects show. A vast collision of impersonal forces. Right now, any confirmation of the real death toll might push her to despair.

It's not our fault.

We came here seeking help within the law. Within our rights.

True, Streaker *brought curses from the Shallow Cluster. But how could we know madness would strike the eminent and wise?*

This isn't our fault!

TSH'T

It would be the perfect time, while everyone else was preoccupied with the spectacle outside. *Streaker* seemed likely to be motionless for a while, so Tsh't didn't have to be at Dr. Baskin's beck and call, pretending to share command when everyone knew who gave the orders anyway.

Many crew members ignored the chance to go off duty when

their shifts ended, finding excuses to hang around. They stared, wide-eyed, at the shattered glory of the Fractal World, commenting to each other with rapid clicks, exchanging bets whether the frantic efforts by myriad hireling robots would save the giant wounded habitat. After a couple of hours, several gawkers had to be ordered below to rest. But when her own watch period finished, Tsh't quickly took advantage of the excuse to leave.

This might be her only chance to go below and check out her suspicions.

I know Gillian snuck somebody or something aboard, she thought. *Back in that little Jijoan village, where hoons happily sail crude boats, even though they can't swim a stroke. It was a stormy night, and I was busy discussing technical matters with that urrish blacksmith. But I know Akeakemai. He's a regular teacher's pet, and would do anything Gillian asked.*

He's lying or hiding something.

Something he smuggled in the back way when I wasn't looking.

It worried Tsh't to be left in the dark like this. She was supposed to be Gillian's close confidant and co-commander. The show of distrust disturbed her. Especially since she deserved it.

I've seen no sign that anyone has connected me to the dead humans.

Nevertheless, Tsh't worried as she sent her walker stomping down one of *Streaker*'s main corridors. The hallway felt deserted, emptied by attrition after three years on the run.

Of course it's always possible that Gillian picked up something with that psi talent of hers. She may suspect the demise of Kunn and Jass was no case of double suicide.

Tsh't fought to suppress the disturbing image of those two human corpses. She quelled a nervous tremor that coursed her dorsal nerves, making the moist skin shiver and her flukes thrash on the rear portion of the walker's soft suspension hammock.

How badly she yearned for a real swim! But nearly all the water had been flushed out to lighten *Streaker*'s frantic breakout from Jijo. Dragging a heavy coat of carbon soot from smoldering Izmunuti, the Earth vessel needed every bit of agility, so nearly all the residence and recreation areas were now bone dry. Soon, long queues would form at sick bay, as neo-dolphins reported skin sores and bruised ribs. After too much time spent lying prone atop jarring machines, even the softest field-effect cushion made you feel like you had been beached and stranded on a shore covered with sharp pebbles.

Now Dr. Makanee is gone, along with three nurses – left behind to take care of the Jijo colonists – and I'm the one who has to figure out

*how to stretch our remaining med staff and cover the inevitable com-
plaints. Somehow, despite everything, team efficiency and morale
have got to be kept up. That's what the high and mighty Dr. Baskin
leaves to me – all the grungy details of running a ship and crew –
while she ponders vast issues of policy and destiny, leading us hither
and yon across the Five Galaxies, trying this and then trying that, fleeing from one disaster to the next.*

The bitterness was not unmixed with affection. Tsh't genuinely
loved Gillian, whose skill at getting *Streaker* out of jams had proved
nearly as impressive as her affinity for getting into them. Nor did
Tsh't resent human beings as patrons. Without their awkward, well-
meaning efforts at genetic engineering, the Tursiops race might
never have taken the final step from bright, innocent animals to
promising starfarers ... and Tsh't would not have seen the Starbow,
or Hercules Arch – or the Shallow Cluster.

Terragens culture granted neo-fins more rights and respect than
a new client race normally received in the Civilization of Five
Galaxies. Most clients spent a hundred millennia in servitude to
their patrons. Humans were doing about as well as they could,
under the circumstances.

But there are limits to what you can expect from wolflings, she
thought, entering a double airlock to pass into *Streaker*'s Dry Wheel.

The latest pathetic episode proved this point. Just hours after
arriving inside the Fractal World, Gillian Baskin had decided to see
whether they were prisoners or guests. Waiting till the Zang seemed
preoccupied – supervising a swarm of machine entities doing repair
work – she had ordered Kaa to gently nudge *Streaker*'s engines,
easing the ship through the opening toward a beckoning glitter of
starlight.

The Zang dropped what it was doing, scattering robot attendants,
racing with astonishing agility to cut off the Earthlings' escape.

Still covered with several meters of star soot, *Streaker* could not
outrun the giant globule. Gillian acquiesced, turning the ship back
into the immense habitat. She then ordered a general stand-down.
Except for watch crew, everyone was told to get some rest. The
Zang vessel returned to work, without evident rancor. And yet Tsh't
felt a hard-won lesson was reinforced.

*Humans were sapient for only a few thousand years longer than us
dolphins – a mere eyeblink in the story of life in the universe. It's not
their fault they are ignorant and clumsy.*

*That only means they need help. Even if they are too obstinate to
ask for it.*

An elevator ride took her to the rim of the wide centrifugal
wheel, where rooms lined a long hallway that seemed to curve up

and away in both directions. The great hoop straddled *Streaker* halfway along its length and could be spun up to provide weight on those occasions when the crew needed to turn off floor gravity for some reason – if they were doing sensor scans in deep space, for instance ... or evading fleets of pursuers by hiding in an asteroid belt. There was a drawback, though. Whenever they had to land on a planet's surface – as happened at Kithrup, Oakka, and Jijo – most of the Dry Wheel's rooms were out of reach.

To anyone except a biped who's a skilled climber, that is.

Tsh't strode past the sealed door to Dr. Baskin's office, where layers of security devices guarded Creideiki's treasure – the relics responsible for so much grief. This part of the Dry Wheel was always 'bottom,' whenever *Streaker* lay grounded. Dolphins routinely used nearby suites and workshops, but those on the opposite side were often inaccessible. In fact, the crew seldom thought of them at all.

That's where I'd hide something, if I were Gillian.

The Wheel was spinning right now, so Tsh't had no trouble striding around its wide circumference, passing laboratories once used by scientists like Ignacio Metz, Dennie Sudman, and the neo-chimpanzee geologist Charles Dart. She kept lifting her jaw to listen, as if nervously expecting to hear ghost footsteps of the bright young Calafian midshipman Toshio Iwashika ... or the strong, confident gait of Gillian's lost Tom Orley.

But they were gone. All of them, along with Creideiki and Hikahi. Dead, or else abandoned on poisonous Kithrup – which was almost the same as being dead.

They were the best of us, taken away before our trials really began. How much would have been different if the captain and the others were still aboard? Instead command fell to Gillian and me ... a physician-healer and the ship's most junior lieutenant ... who never imagined we'd have to carry such a burden, year after dreary year.

Fatigue wore at Tsh't. During sleep shifts she would cast her clicking sonar song toward the Whale Dream, praying for someone to come take away the hardship, the responsibility.

We Streakers are in it way over our heads. All of Earthclan is! Gillian was right about one thing. We need help and advice. But we won't get it from eatees. Not from the Great Institutes, or the Old Ones.

She's forgotten one of life's great truths, known by almost every human and dolphin from childhood. When you're in real bad trouble, the place to turn is your own family.

Using her neural tap, Tsh't called up the ship's maintenance system and ordered a trace of atmospheric pollutants, concentrating room by room on the section of the Dry Wheel directly opposite from Dr. Baskin's office – the sector routinely left on 'top' when *Streaker* lay on a planet's surface. The part that dolphins were likely to ignore, even when it was accessible.

Aha! Just as I thought. An elevated profile of carbon dioxide, plus several ketones, a touch of methane, and a strange pair of alcohols. Sure signs of respiration by an oxygen-breathing life-form ... though clearly not an Earthling.

And it's all centered ... here.

She made her walker halt before a door labeled HAZARDOUS ORGANIC MATERIALS – and chuckled at Gillian's little joke.

A slight nudge of volition caused a work-arm to swing forward from her tool harness, aiming a slim drill at the door, near the jamb, where a hole might not be noticed right away. A fine whirring was the only sound. Her cutter penetrated, vaporized, and vac-disposed debris as it moved ahead.

Tsh't mused on how she was now compounding her own felony. Her growing record of treason. It all started the last time *Streaker* visited the Fractal World, when everyone grew aware that the Old Ones were going to disappoint them. As crew morale sank, Tsh't decided it was time to act on her own. To send a message, contacting the one source whose help could be relied on.

Fortunately, the Fractal World had regular commercial mail taps. Even while Gillian parried increasing threats and imprecations from various factions of the Retired Order, Tsh't found it fairly simple to dispatch a secret message packet, programmed to go bouncing across the Five Galaxies, paranoically covering its own tracks and randomly rerouting before heading for its final destination – a time-drop capsule whose coordinates she had memorized as a youth, long ago. One tuned to respond to just one species in the universe.

By then, Gillian had already decided to flee the criswell structure and try the 'sooner option' – absconding through forbidden Galaxy Four, sneaking past a blaring giant star, then taking shelter on a proscribed world called Jijo.

A clandestine rendezvous seemed easy enough for Tsh't to arrange ...

The drill bit broke through. She commanded the arm back and sent a fiber communicator snaking through the hole, rearing like a cobra inside the sealed room.

It scanned left and right until a lanky bipedal figure came into view, seated on a bench before a small table.

The head lifted, as if reacting to a sound. When the creature turned halfway around, Tsh't gasped at the sight.

A slanted, narrow face with a jutting, chinless jaw and large, bared teeth.

Yet, the eyes and brow seemed uncannily human, squinting as they caught sight of the spy probe.

Hurriedly, the head turned away again. Shoulders hunched to block her view. Tsh't saw both arms grope for a box – a bio-support unit designed for maintaining small animals sampled from an ecosystem. Deft hands pulled out something squirmy. She couldn't follow what was happening, but it seemed as if the biped was *eating* the wriggly creature, or embracing it.

The shoulders relaxed, arms settling to the tall being's side as it stood up and gracefully turned around.

The face was transformed. Now it looked more noble than human. More genially amused than a Tymbrimi. More patient and understanding than a god.

Well, well. It is him. The very one.

The Rothen's face quivered in a few places, where its mask-symbiont was still nestling in – a living creature crafted to become part of his features, providing fine cheekbones, a regal chin, and lips that both covered the teeth and drew a tender, gracious smile.

The Missionary.

Tsh't remembered his visit to Earth, long ago, when she was still half grown and barely able to speak. It was like yesterday, the image of him preaching in a hidden undersea grotto to a tiny gathering of dolphin converts.

'*The universe is a lonely place,*' he had said then. '*But not as dangerous as it seems. The present government of Earth may consist of Darwinists and unbelievers, but that does not matter. Remember, despite the propaganda of those preaching wolfling pride, that you are not alone. We who crafted the genes of humanity in secret, guiding them toward a great destiny, remain steadfast to that dream. The same glorious goal. We still act behind the scenes, protecting, preserving, preparing for the Day.*

'*And as we love our human clients, so we also love you. For ours is a special clan, with a future more splendid than any other. Dolphins will play a great role when the time comes. Especially those of you who choose the Danik Way.*'

It had felt singular to grow up as a member of an exclusive sect, knowing a great and reassuring Truth. Of course the Terragens Constitution promised religious freedom, but in practice it would only bring on ridicule to reveal too much, too soon. Most dolphins believed the myth that humans must have evolved sapience without intervention from above. An absurd notion, but too strong a current for dissenters to fight openly.

Even among humans and chimps, where Danikenite beliefs were more common, debates raged between conflicting cults. Many had their own candidates for the *secret patrons* ... the mystery race said to have uplifted *Homo sapiens* long ago. Several Galactic races were called 'more likely' than the obscure, secretive Rothen.

So Tsh't had kept it to herself, through school, training, and early assignments for the TAASF. She bided her time through the disasters at Morgran, Kithrup, and Oakka. Until one day she realized humans just weren't up to the task. Gillian Baskin was among the best, and could do no more.

It was time to seek help higher up the family tree. The Rothen would know what to do.

Now her emotions roiled with conflict, complexity, and confusion. She had come here uncertain what to expect.

I knew about the symbiont. The Jijoans saw a Rothen unmasked. It's all in the reports. And yet, to see that bared face for myself—

The glimpse of Ro-kenn's natural features had been shocking. And yet, Tsh't now felt warmed by the same reassuring smile she recalled from childhood.

I can understand the need for a mask. It isn't necessarily dishonest. Not if it helps them do their work better, guiding Earthlings toward our destiny.

It's what's inside that counts.

'Well?' Ro-kenn said, taking a step toward the door. He brought both hands together, his long arms sticking out from the sleeves of a bathrobe made for a tall human. The captive must have been sent in secret by the Sages of Jijo, after capturing him in the highland place they called Festival Glade – perhaps the sole survivor of a mixed Rothen-human expedition that had met treachery and disaster, first from the Six Races and then the crew of the Jophur battleship.

Everything came together in Tsh't's heart. The longing she had carried since childhood. The frustration of three horrible years. The guilt over having acted against Gillian's wishes. The far larger guilt of assassinating two humans – even if it was in the interest of a greater cause.

She had come here intending to confront Ro-kenn. To demand an explanation of what had happened.

The message I sent ... tuned to be picked up by a Rothen mind. It told you about Gillian's destination. You were supposed to come in secret to Jijo ... to help us. To rescue us.

Now they say you persecuted the sooners, including Jijo's human settlers. They say your people sold Jijo to the Jophur for pocket change. They say you are swindlers, who convert gullible Earthlings to follow you, in order to use them as shills and petty thieves.

One of the men I killed – the pilot Kunn – I did it to protect our secret. But how can I be sure ...

None of that came out. The words would not come.

Instead, all the streams coursing through her suddenly combined in an emotional confluence. Despair, which had dominated for so long, cracked and gave way to its only true enemy.

Hope.

Tsh't had to take several deep breaths, then found the will to speak.

'Massster ... there is something I have come to confesssssss.'

A look of surprise briefly crossed the Rothen's face, and his left cheek quivered.

Then a warm smile spread, and with a deep, gentle voice he spoke.

'Indeed, child of the warm seas. I am here. Take your time and I will listen. Be assured that redemption is found in telling all.'

LARK

I wonder how long I've been in here. Is there any way to tell if it's been hours, days ... or months?

If they understand my body chemistry well enough to keep me alive, these beings could turn my consciousness on and off like a lamp. They might change the way I perceive duration, simply by adjusting my metabolism.

That, too, felt like a clue. Lark yearned to compare notes with somebody.

With Ling, the way they used to, when they were wary adversaries, then allies, and finally lovers. He missed her terribly. Her warm skin and rich scent, but most of all her vivid mind. Amid all their ups and downs, it was her unpredictable wit that most fascinated Lark. He would give anything now, just to talk to her.

I was supposed to find a way to rescue her from Rann and the Jophur. Now all I can do is spin fantasies of a space-suited Ling blasting her way through that far wall, lasers in both hands, yanking me out of this awful vault so we can fly off together in some hijacked ...

The enticing daydream dissolved as he realized that something had changed. His spine crawled with an uneasy sensation ... a feeling of being watched. Lark turned his head ... and shuddered reflexively.

A large blobby ... thing floated near the membrane barrier,

roughly spherical, but with bulges and ripples that swelled rhythmically, in ways that somehow conveyed *life* ... and perhaps even intent. Currents of yellow mist flowed past, but it maintained position with a blur of tiny waving tendrils, as numerous as hairs on the leg of a hoon.

Cilia, Lark thought, recognizing a form of locomotion used by tiny organisms you might see under a microscope. He had never heard of this means occurring on a macro-entity anywhere near this size. As a biologist, he found it quite odd.

But curiosity turned to amazement when the creature abruptly *sucked* in all the waving cilia. Ballooning outward to the left, it elongated into a cylinder. Depressions at both ends deepened, penetrating along its length until they met, forming a hollow tube that began flexing longitudinally. Jets of yellow fluid compressed and shot out one opening, propelling the beast rapidly around Lark's little transparent cell.

Three times it circumnavigated this way. Lark had an impression it was looking him over from all angles.

That's not any normal gas or vapor out there, he thought. But it doesn't seem like liquid, either.

He had a feeling that the medium might have something to do with the creature's flexibility – its knack for switching from tendrils to siphon-jet propulsion.

Wherever it evolved, the environment must be stranger than anything I ever read about in the archives. That is ... except ...

Lark's eyes opened in sudden realization, so wide that the lids nudged small, clear *cups* that arched over them. Till that moment he hadn't even been aware of the protective coverings, but when his action let a few harsh molecules sneak past, he paid with stinging tears and deep, laryngial moans.

Yet, that hardly interrupted the rapid flow of Lark's thoughts.

Hydrogen breathers! The ancient scrolls call them one of the great orders of life. Sharing the Five Galaxies with oxy-types, but completely separate from our civilization, sticking to their own worlds and interests as we keep to ours.

Of course that oversimplified matters. Even in the few Biblos texts to mention hydro-life, it was clear that danger stalked each uneasy interaction between the two different molecular heritages. Minimizing contact made up a large part of the duties of the Migration Institute, which designed its leasehold rules partly to protect fallow worlds, but also to lessen the shared space where accidental encounters might take place.

Jijo's in Galaxy Four. Except for official Institute ships, there aren't supposed to be any of our kind flying about these spiral arms right now. It's one reason Jijo was an attractive candidate for the Sooner Path.

One eye was still blurry, but he squinted with the other as the hydro-being slowed to a halt and flowed back into a roughly spherical shape.

Am I looking at their equivalent of a policeman? Or an immigration official?

A hollow-looking vacuole formed under the creature's surface. Bubbles escaped, glistening with strange surface tension. Lark thought of someone farting underwater, but for all he knew it was actually an eloquent lecture on fine points of interorder cosmic law.

Maybe it's demanding to know what I'm doing here. Requesting my passport and visa. Asking for my plea ... or whether I want a blindfold ...

The hollow space within kept growing as the creature grew distended toward Lark. Within the vacuole, he made out several floating objects – each one looking at first like miniature versions of the larger entity. These took up various positions in the void, then began to change, taking on new shapes and colors.

Well I'll be ...

One turned a shade of blue somewhat deeper than the sky back home. It stopped rippling and seemed to harden an adamant shell, covered with symmetrical arrangements of bumps and blisters. Lark even saw a minuscule emblem take form – a rayed spiral insignia near the top of the oblate spheroid. He swiftly recognized a near perfect representation of the Jophur battleship *Polkjhy*.

I get it. Communication by sign and picture show. And that other glob ... is that supposed to be a hydro ship?

The guess was soon confirmed as he watched a growing confrontation between two space behemoths, all played out within a space no larger than a traeki's topknot. Lark watched with transfixed fascination as the Jophur cruiser blasted away at the yellow globule. At first, its arrows were thwarted by swarms of sudden, flimsy balloons. But then more missiles and fire bolts got through, hammering the onrushing foe mercilessly, until the hydro vessel shredded into ragged pieces that flapped like tattered banners. Yet, several of these still managed to drape across parts of *Polkjhy*'s hard metal hull.

So that's how they boarded. It was combat unlike any he had read about, or dreamed of.

Now the blue shell expanded before him, and Lark saw the fight continue *within*. Yellowish beachheads spread from half a dozen points of insertion, advancing swiftly at first, then meeting stiffening resistance. Lark saw small glitters scurrying near the battlefront, probably representing individual Jophur and their fierce, slashing battle robots.

Sometimes, one or two of those sparks fell into a yellow stain. Instead of being extinguished they were swept toward collection points in the rear.

Captives. Prisoners of war.

When it happened to another pinpoint, Lark felt an abrupt surge of sensation sting his thigh.

That's me!

It also made him realize something else.

They aren't just communicating with me visually. There's a chemical component! Some of my understanding comes by watching the demonstration. But they must also be sending meaning down the nutrient tube directly, into my very blood.

Awareness of the fact might have sickened and repelled him ... except that a strange calmness pervaded Lark's limbs. Another effect of molecular inducement, no doubt. As a biologist, he was fascinated.

Hydros must have over a billion years' experience dealing with us oxies. That doesn't necessarily make it easy to bridge the vast gulf between life orders, or else they'd be talking to me directly, in audible words. But they've accumulated tricks, I'm sure.

It put a new perspective on things. He had spent his entire professional life entranced by the wild diversity among just the few million oxygen-breathing species prevalent on one part of a single planet. Now he realized there were beings for whom the difference between a Jophur and a human must appear nearly inconsequential.

Have they ever beheld an Earthling before? It would seem unlikely. And yet they can play me like an urrish fiddle.

Lark felt humbled ... and contemplated whether that was also a reaction imposed or suggested from the outside.

No matter. The important thing is that they want me to learn. They're interested in keeping me alive, and making me understand.

For the time being, at least, I can live with that.

EMERSON

He might not be an engineer anymore, but he could still appreciate good work.

With an excellent view of the vast repair project – from his own private little observation bubble, tucked behind *Streaker*'s bridge –

Emerson could see nearly the whole vaulting edifice, from its central hearthstar all the way to the gaping laceration that now mangled the majestic sphere, exposing a wide swath of untamed stars. Despite frantic efforts by great machines to mend and patch, innumerable lumps of ragged debris still poured outward through the hole, crumbling to dust, vapor, and armadas of radiant comets.

The sphere's injury reminded him of his own maiming, which also had occurred in this very place.

Trembling, Emerson's hand raised toward the area near his left ear. A filmy creature quivered at his touch – the *rewq* symbiont he had brought along from Jijo. Together with unguents supplied by a traeki pharmacist, the rewq was partly responsible for his surviving an injury that should otherwise have left him dead or a living vegetable. The tiny thing released its gentle clasp on a surface blood vessel and rippled aside, letting Emerson stroke the scar tissue surrounding a hole in his head. Not an accidental lesion, but a deliberate hurt.

This was where it had happened, about a year ago.

Here – he recalled climbing into a small fighter craft, ready to sacrifice himself and cover *Streaker's* desperate escape.

Here – he blazed forth in the little scoutship, shouting defiance at those hostile factions whose demands and extortions disproved their vaunted reputation for wise neutrality ... cries that turned joyful when a *different* clique of Old Ones intervened, opening a door in the great shell to let Gillian and the others escape.

Here – exultation cut off as his tiny vessel was seized by slabs of force, hemming it in, then abrading and dissolving the armored scout like a skinned pineapple, yanking him to a captivity worse than any he could have imagined.

Emerson was still hazy on what followed. His captors used potent conditioning that made memory excruciating. For most of the last year, he had wandered in a fog of amnesia, punctuated by bouts of searing agony whenever he tried to recall.

Defeating that programming had been his greatest victory. Emerson's mind was now his own again – what remained of it, that is. Anguish-reflexes still tried to divert his roaming thoughts, impeding him from salvaging further recollections, but he had learned to fight back by not giving a damn about pain. Emerson knew each throbbing impulse meant he was putting another piece back in place, thwarting their purpose.

If only he knew what that purpose was.

Lacking important parts of his old brain, Emerson could not express in words the irony he felt, crouched in his secret little bubble niche, looking across the broad corrugated vistas of the

Fractal World. Even mute, his emotions had a complex, fine-grained texture.

For instance, by all rights, he should be experiencing satisfaction from the rack and ruin tearing through this place. As swarms of huge robots poured in through the sphere's gaping wound, converging to shore up its unraveling rim, he ought to be hoping for them to fail. That would be vengeance – for his tormentors to be smashed, for all their hopes and works to fall like ash into an emancipated sun.

But there was something else inside him, older and stronger than wrath.

Love of a certain kind of beauty.

The gracefulness of artifice.

The glory of something well made.

He could still recall the day – ages ago – when *Streaker* entered this redoubt of the Retired Order for the first time, full of naive hopes that would soon be betrayed. Awed by the splendor, he and Karkaett and Hannes Suessi had argued ecstatically over the ultimate function of this titanic habitat – to cheat the eroding rub of time, taming the wasteful extravagance of a star. It seemed an engineer's paradise.

And he still felt that way! Remarkably, he cheered the robot workers on. Emerson figured he would have revenge on his tormentors, simply by surviving. So long as *Streaker* roamed free, frustration must surely fill those cold eyes he recalled peering down at him while cruel instruments reamed his mind, sifting and squeezing for secrets he did not have ...

Emerson shuddered. Why hadn't the Old Ones simply killed him when they finished trawling through his brain?

Instead, they mutilated and cast his writhing body across space in some unknown manner to crash-land on lonely Jijo.

It seemed a lot of trouble to go to. In a strange way, the special attention bolstered Emerson's sense of worth and self-esteem.

So he was willing to be magnanimous. He rooted for the repair mechanisms as they spun vast, moon-sized spools of carbon fiber, weaving nets to catch and hold tottering fractal spikes, made of fragile snow and wider than a planet. He applauded the robot tugs, swarming like gnats to divert huge, drifting ruins away from collision paths that might wreak untold devastation. Emerson did not think of sapient beings living beneath those countless, glittering windows. Perhaps it was the lack of words, but to him, the Fractal World seemed not so much a habitat as a creature in its own right, self-contained, self-aware, and wounded, fighting for its life.

He used a pocket terminal to get close-ups. Unable to command by voice or keyboard, he found the little computer was conveniently programmed in other ways. It coaxed him to use a language of gestures that must have been developed for disabled aphasics on Earth, a handy mix of hand motions, eye flicks, and plain old pointing that usually conveyed what he wanted. It sure beat the clumsy, grunting efforts he used on Jijo, when communicating with poor Sara often reduced them both to tears of futility.

And yet ... he recalled those months fondly. The sooner world had been beautiful, and the illegal colony of six allied races had moved him deeply with their strangely happy pessimism. For that reason, and for Sara's sake, he wished there were something he could do for the Jijoans.

For that matter, he wished he could do something for *anybody* – Gillian, the Streakers ... or even the hordes of hardworking robots, laboring to save an edifice that was built when early dinosaurs roamed Earth. Lacking useful work, he was reduced to staring at a great drama unfolding outside.

Emerson hated being a spectator. His hands clenched. He would rather be using them.

With a rapid set of winks, he called up the scene in the Plotting Room, where Gillian met with Sara and the youngsters from Wuphon Port. They were joined by a tall stack of fuming, waxy rings – Tyug, the traeki alchemist of Mount Guenn Forge, who filled out a quorum of the Jijo's Six Races. Amid their animated discussion he saw the young centauroid *urs*, named Ur-ronn, gesture toward their small herd of glavers, mewling and licking themselves nearby. Beings whose ancestors had roamed the stars, but who since had reclaimed innocence – the method prescribed for winning a second chance.

Emerson wasn't quite sure of the connection, but apparently those reverted creatures had something to do with the huge, blobby star vessel that escorted *Streaker* here.

He was proud when a word came floating to mind. *Zang*.

Except to prevent *Streaker* from leaving, the great globule seemed indifferent at first, concentrating on the repair task, directing mechanical hirelings to weave vast nets of black fiber, bandaging cracks in the huge edifice. But after a day or so, the Zang were forced to pay attention when mysterious objects drifted toward the Earthship, approaching from various parts of the immense inhabited shell, nosing close to investigate.

The Zang drove each snoop away, keeping a cordon around the Terragens' cruiser. Yet, *Streaker*'s exotic guardians showed no interest in acknowledging Gillian's frequent messages.

Emerson recalled one of the few definite facts known about the mighty hydrogen breathers – they had different ways of viewing time. Clearly, the Zang felt their business with *Streaker* could wait.

Now he listened as Gillian consulted with the Jijo natives, trying to form a plan.

'*What if we just herd the glavers onto a shuttle and send it over? Do we have a clue whether that would satisfy the Zang? Or if the glavers would be safe?*

'*Suppose the answer to both questions is yes. What does Galactic law say about a situation like this? Are we supposed to ask the Zang for a receipt?*'

Out of the flood of words, only 'Zang' had any solid meaning to him. The rest floated just beyond clear comprehension. And yet, to Emerson, the rich sibilance of her voice was like music.

Of course he had always nursed a secret passion for Dr. Gillian Baskin, even when her husband, Thomas Orley, lived aboard *Streaker* – the sort of harmless infatuation that a grown man could control and never show. At least not crudely. Life wasn't fair, but he did get to be around her.

Alas the infatuation started affecting his judgment after Tom vanished heroically on Kithrup. Emerson started taking risks, trying to emulate Orley. Attempting to prove himself a worthy replacement in her eyes.

A foolish quest, but natural. And it paid off at Oakka, where minions of the Library and Migration Institute betrayed their oaths, conspiring to seize *Streaker*'s cargo to benefit their birth clans instead of all civilization. There, Emerson threw himself into a wild gamble, and his boldness paid off, helping win a narrow victory – another brief deliverance – enabling *Streaker* to flee and fight another day.

But here . . .

He shook his head. In viewing tapes from *Streaker*'s departing point of view, Emerson now realized that his sacrifice in the borrowed Thennanin scout had made very little difference. *Streaker*'s escape path had begun opening even as he charged ahead, ignoring Gillian's pleas to return. He would have gone to Jijo anyway, and in more comfort, if he had just stayed aboard this ship and never fallen into the clutches of the Old Ones.

Scanning the near edge of the torn Fractal World, he immersed himself in the fantastic task of preservation. Numbers and equations were no longer trustworthy, but he still had an engineer's instincts, and these thrilled as he watched machines bolster vast constructions of ice and carbon thread. He had never seen cooperation on such scale among hydros, oxies, and machines.

That thought made the cosmos seem a nicer place somehow.

Time passed. Emerson no longer thought in terms of minutes and hours – or duras and miduras – but the uneven, subjective intervals between hungers, thirsts, or other bodily needs. And yet, he began feeling tensely expectant.

A bedeviling sense that something was wrong.

For a while he had difficulty placing it. The dolphins on duty in the bridge seemed unconcerned. Everything was calm. None of the display screens showed any obvious signs of threat.

Likewise, in the Plotting Room, Gillian's meeting broke up, as people dispersed to workstations or else observed the awesome vista surrounding *Streaker*. Nobody appeared alarmed.

Emerson conveyed to the little holo unit his desire to tap the ship's near-space sensors, scanning along its hull and environs. As he went through the exercise twice, the creepy feeling came and went in waves. Yet he failed to pin anything down.

Calling for a close-up of Gillian herself, he saw that she looked uncomfortable too – as if some thought were scolding away, just below consciousness. A holo image stood before her. Emerson saw she was examining the area around *Streaker*'s tail section.

Signaling with a grunt and a pointed finger, Emerson ordered his own viewpoint taken that way. As the camera angle swept along the ship's outer hull – coated with its dense star-soot coating – he felt a growing sense of relief. If Gillian was also looking into this, it might not be just his imagination. Moreover, her instincts were good. If there were a serious threat, she would have taken action by now.

He was already feeling much better as the holo image swept past *Streaker*'s rear set of probability flanges, bringing the stern into view.

That was Emerson's first clue.

Feeling better.

Ironically, *that* triggered increased unease.

Back on Jijo – ever since he had wakened, delirious, in Sara's treehouse with a seared body and crippled brain – there had always been one pleasure that excelled any other. Beyond the soothing balm of secretions from the traeki pharmacists. Beyond the satisfaction of improved health, or feeling strength return to his limbs. Beyond the wondrous sights, sounds, and smells of Jijo. Even beyond the gentle, loving company of dear Sara. One bliss surpassed any competitor.

It happened whenever the pain stopped.

Whenever the conditioned agony, programmed into his racked cortex, suddenly let go of him – the abrupt absence of woe felt like a kind of ecstasy.

It happened whenever he *stopped* doing something he wasn't supposed to do. Like trying to remember. Any attempt at recollection was punished with agony. But the reward was even more effective, at first. A hedonistic satisfaction that came from not trying anymore.

And now Emerson sensed a similarity.

Oh, it wasn't as intense. Rewards and aversions manifested at a much subtler level. In fact, he might never have noticed, if not for the long battle he had fought on Jijo, learning to counter pain with obstinacy, by facing it, like some tormented prey turning on its pursuer ... then transforming the hunter into the hunted. It was a hard lesson, but in time he had mastered it.

Not ... there ... he thought, laboriously forming the words one at a time, in order to lock in place a fierce determination.

Go ... back ...

It felt like trying to fight a strong wind, or swimming upstream. Each time the holo scene made progress toward the ship's bow, he felt strange inside. As if the very *concept* of that part of *Streaker* was peculiar and somehow improper, like trying to visualize a fifth dimension.

Moreover, it apparently affected computers, too. The instruments proved balky. Once his view passed forward of the first set of flanges, the camera angle kept wandering aside, missing and curving back around toward the stern again.

A torrent of cursing escaped Emerson. Rich and expressive, it flowed the way *all* speech used to, before his injury. Like songs and some kinds of poetry, expletives were fired from a part of the brain never touched by the Old Ones. The stream of invective had a calming, clarifying effect as Emerson turned away from all artificial tools and images. Instead, he pressed his face close to the bubble window, made of some clear, incredibly strong material that Earth's best technicians could not imitate. He peered forward, toward *Streaker*'s bow.

It felt like trying to see through your own blind spot. But he concentrated, fighting the aversion with all the techniques he had learned on Jijo.

At last, he managed barely to make out glimmers of movement amid the blackness.

Sensing his strong desire to see, the *rewq* symbiont slithered downward, laying its filmy body over his eyes – translating, amplifying, shifting colors back and forth until he grunted with surprised satisfaction.

Objects swarmed around *Streaker*'s prow. Robots, or small shiplike things. They darted about, converging en masse near a part of the ship that everyone aboard seemed to have conveniently forgotten!

Emerson glimpsed a small, starlike flare erupt. Glints of actinic flame.

He wasted no more time cursing. On hands and knees, he scuttled out of the little observation dome, built by some race much smaller than humans that had once owned this ship long before it was sold, fifth-hand, to a poor clan of ignorant wolflings, freshly emerged from an isolation so deep they used to wonder if, in all the universe, they lived alone.

He had no way to report his discovery. No words to shout over an intercom. If he went to the Plotting Room, grabbed Gillian's shoulders, and *forced* her to look forward, she would probably respond. But how long might that take?

Worse, could it even risk her life? Whatever means was being used to cast this spell, it bore similarities to his own prior conditioning and Emerson recognized a special brand of ruthlessness. Those responsible might sense Gillian's dawning awareness, and clamp down harshly through her psi talent.

He could not risk exposing her to that danger.

Sara? Prity? They were his friends and dear to him. The same logic held for the other Streakers. Anyway, there was too little time to make himself understood.

Sometimes you had to do things yourself.

So Emerson ran. He dashed forward to the cavernous hangar – the Outlook – that filled *Streaker's* capacious nose. All the smaller vessels that once had filled the mooring slips when they departed Earth were now gone. The longboat and skiff had been lost with Orley and the others at Kithrup. Even before that, the captain's gig had exploded in the Shallow Cluster – their first terrible price for claiming Creideiki's treasure.

Now the docks held rugged little Thennanin scoutboats, taken from an old hulk the crew had salvaged. It felt all too familiar, slipping into one of the tiny armored vessels. He had done this once before – turning on power switches, wrestling the control wheel built for a race with much bigger arms, and triggering mechanisms to send it sliding down a narrow rail, into a tube that would expel it . . .

Emerson quashed all memory of that last time, or else courage might have failed him. Instead, he concentrated on the dials and screens whose symbols he could no longer read, hoping that old habits, skills, and Ifni's luck would keep him from spinning out of control the moment he passed through the outer set of doors.

A *song* burst unbidden into his mind – a pilot's anthem about rocketing into the deep black yonder – but his clenched jaw gave it no voice. He was too busy to utter sound.

If it were possible to think clear sentences, Emerson might have wondered what he was trying to accomplish, or how he might possibly interfere with the attackers. The little scout had weapons, but a year ago he had not proved very adept with them. Now he could not even read the controls.

Still, it could be possible to raise a ruckus. To disrupt the assailants. To dash their shroud of illusion and alert the Terran crew that danger lurked.

But what danger?

No matter. Emerson knew his brain was no longer equipped to solve complex problems. If all he accomplished was to draw the attention of the Zang – bringing their protective wrath down on the trespassers – that might be enough.

The wounded Fractal World turned before him as the airlock closed and he gently nudged the boat's thrusters, moving toward the interlopers. Waves of aversion increased in strength as he drew nearer. Pain and pleasure, disgust and fascination – these and many other sensations washed over him, rewarding Emerson each time his eyes or thoughts drifted away from the activity ahead, and punishing every effort to concentrate. Without the experience on Jijo, he might never have overcome such combination. But Emerson had learned a new habit. To *seek* discomfort – like a child pressing a loose tooth, attracted by each throbbing twinge, teasing and probing till the old made way for the new.

The little rewq helped. Sensing his need, it kept rippleshifting through various color spectra, conveying images that wavered elusively, but eventually resolved into discernible shapes.

Machines.

He realized at least a dozen spindly forms had already latched themselves to *Streaker*'s nose. They clambered like scavenging insects probing the eye of some helpless beast. If the goal were simple destruction, it would all be over by now. Their aim must be more complex than that.

He recognized the hot light of a cutting torch. Either they were trying to burn their way into the ship, to board her, or . . .

Or else their effort was aimed at cutting something off. A sample, perhaps. But of what?

Emerson pictured *Streaker* in his mind, a detailed image, unimpaired by his aphasia with sentences. The memory was wordless, almost tactile, from years spent loving this old salvaged hull in ways a man could never love a woman, supervising so many aspects of its transformation into something unique – the pride of Earthclan.

All at once he recalled what lay beneath that bitter, flickering glare.

A symbol. An emblem supposedly carried by all ships flown by oxygen-breathing, starfaring races.

The rayed spiral crest of the Civilization of Five Galaxies.

Incongruity stunned Emerson. At first he wondered if this might be yet another trick, deceiving his perceptions once again, making him *think* that was their target. All this seemed an awful lot of effort to expend simply defacing *Streaker* of its bow insignia.

Anyway, the machines were clearly having more trouble than they had bargained for. The dense carbon coat burdening the Earthship was obdurate and resistant to every attempt by Hannes Suessi and the dolphin engineers to remove it. As he drew closer, Emerson saw that only a little progress had been made, exposing a small patch of *Streaker*'s original hull.

He almost laughed at the aliens' discomfiture.

Then he looked beyond, and saw.

More machines. Many of them, swarming darkly, converging from the starry background. Almost certainly reinforcements, coming to make short work of the job.

It was time to act. Emerson reached for his weapons console, choosing the least potent rays, lest he damage *Streaker* by mistake.

Well, here goes nothing, he thought.

I sure hope this works.

So intent was he on aiming – carefully adjusting the crosshairs – that he never noticed what had just happened *within* his crippled mind.

His use of two clear sentences, one right after another, smoothly expressing both wryness and hope.

GILLIAN

Realization crackled through her consciousness like pealing thunder. She cried out a shrill command.

'Security alert!'

Klaxons echoed down the Earthship's half-deserted halls, sending dolphins scurrying to combat stations. The ambient engine hum changed pitch as Suessi's crew increased power to shields and weapon systems.

'Niss, report!'

The spinning hologram spoke quickly, with none of its accustomed snideness.

'We seem to have been suborned by a combined psi-cyber stealth attack, *with an aim toward distracting* Streaker's *defenders, both organic and machine. The fact that you and I roused simultaneously*

suggests the emitter source has been abruptly destroyed or degraded. Preliminary indications suggest they used a sophisticated logic entity whose memic-level was at least class—'

'What's our current danger?' Gillian cut in.

'I detect no immediate targeting impulses or macroweaponry aimed at this vessel. But several nearby automatons show latent power levels that could turn dangerous at close range.

'So far, it seems they are content to fire away at each other.'

She stepped toward the display showing a camera view of the ship's bow ... exactly opposite from the region she had been inspecting, suspicious of some unknown menace. Her heart pounded as she saw how close it had been. All might have been lost, if the intruders had not fallen to fighting among themselves. Sharp flashes surged and flared as spiderlike shapes lashed at each other, casting battle shadows uncomfortably close.

'Where the hell are the Zang?' Gillian murmured under her breath.

Scanning the area of space where the hydrogen entities had been, her instruments showed no sign of the big globule-vessel ... only a disturbing, elongated cloud of drifting ions. *Perhaps it's only backwash from their engines, when they departed on an errand. They may be back at any moment.*

Her mind quailed from the other possibility – that some weapon had removed the Zang from the local equation. A weapon powerful enough to leave barely a smudge of disturbed atoms in its wake.

Either way, the psi attack kept us from noticing our guardians were gone. Someone went to a lot of trouble making sure we'd sit still for a while.

She felt Suessi's engines dig in as Kaa started backing away from the combat maelstrom. But the pilot only made a little headway before the swarm of conflict followed, as if tethered to *Streaker* by invisible cords.

'Do you have any idea who—'

'None of the combatants has identified itself.'

'Then what were they trying—'

'It appears that some group was attempting to steal Streaker's *WOM archive.'*

'*Streaker's* ... ?'

Her question froze in her throat. Gillian's mouth closed sharply as she understood.

By law, each Galactic vessel was supposed to carry a 'watcher' ... a device that would passively chronicle the major features of its travels. Some units were sophisticated. Others – the sort that a poor clan could afford – were crude mineral devices, capable only of recording the ship's rough location and identifying any ships nearby. But all of them fell into the category of 'write-only memories' ... designed to store knowledge but never be read. At least never within the present epoch. Eventually, each was supposed to find its way into the infinite archives of the Great Library, to be studied at leisure by denizens of some later age, when the passions of this one had faded to mere historical interest.

At once, the strategem behind this attack made sense to her.

'The Old Ones ... they must have found the codes, enabling them to read our WOM. It would tell them where *Streaker's* been!'

'*Enabling them to backtrack our voyage and find the Shallow Cluster.*'

Gillian's reaction was strangely mixed. On the one hand, she felt angry and violated by these beings who would meddle in her mind and rob *Streaker* of its treasure. Information her crew had guarded for so long, and Tom and Creideiki paid for with their lives.

On the other hand, it might solve so many problems if the thieves succeeded. Some mighty faction would then have the secret at last, perhaps using it to dominate the next age. Battles and great conspiracies could then surge onward, perhaps letting Earth and her colonies drift back into the side eddies of history, neglected and maybe safe for a while.

'I'm surprised no one tried this before,' she commented, wary as she watched the minibattle follow *Streaker's* retreat across the vast interior of the Fractal World.

'*Indeed, it seems a logical ploy to try seizing the watcher from our bow. I can only hazard that our prior enemies lacked the means to read a coded WOM.*'

If so, it spoke well for the neutrality of the Library Institute, that even the richest clans and alliances could not break the seals. That made Gillian wonder. Might the betrayals at Oakka have been an aberration? Perhaps it was just *Streaker's* run of typical bad luck that put it at the mercy of rare traitors. Institute officials might be more honorable elsewhere.

If so, should we try again? Gillian wondered. *Maybe head for Tanith and try surrendering ourselves to the authorities one more time?*

Meanwhile, the Niss whirled thoughtfully. The Tymbrimi-designed software entity flattened into a planate whirlpool shape before speaking once again.

'*It must have taken them much of the last year, using their influence as elder members of the Retired Order, to access the keys. In fact ...*'

The mesh of spinning lines tightened, exhibiting strain.

'In fact, this casts a pall across our earlier miraculous escape from this place.'

'What do you mean?'

'I mean that we thought we were being aided by altruistic members of the Retired Order, benevolently helping us elude persecutors in the name of justice. But consider how conveniently easy it was! Especially the way we stumbled on references leading to the so-called Sooner Path—'

'Easy! I had to squeeze our captured Library for it, like pressing wine from a stone! It was—'

'It was easy. I now see that in retrospect. We must have been infected by a lesser meme parasite, conveying the attractive notion of fleeing to Jijo. A nearby sanctuary with just one way in and one way out. A haven whose only exit would lead us right back here again.'

Gillian blinked, abruptly seeing what the machine was driving at.

Suppose one faction hoped to seize *Streaker's* WOM, but knew it would take a while to access the right codes for reading it? Fugitive wolflings could not be left just hanging around in the open till then. Someone else might snatch the prize!

What better way to stash the memory unit for safe-keeping than by sending it into hiding, guarded by the self-preservation skills and instincts of tested survivors? The Earthship's own crew.

'If we had not turned up about now, no doubt they would have sent word to Jijo luring us back. Indeed, the plan has earmarks – patience and confidence – that resonate of the Retired Order.'

'Only now this failure to seize the object of their desire shows that their scheme broke down. Not everything is going their way. This faction still has enemies. Moreover, note how dismal the state of their power has become, under these conditions of calamity!'

'Calamity' was right. As Gillian watched, fighting seemed to ripple outward around them. Tactics sensors showed signs of conflagration spreading toward the nearest ragged edge of the wounded criswell structure.

'At this rate,' she mused, 'someone's gonna get fed up and use one of those big disintegrator rays. Maybe on *us*. We better think about getting out of here.'

'Dr. Baskin, while we have been talking I've thought of little else. For instance, I have endeavored to call our captor-protector, the Zang ship entity, to no avail. A leading hypothesis must be that it was destroyed.'

Gillian nodded, having reached the same conclusion.

'Well, if it ain't coming, I don't care to hang around waiting.'

She raised her voice toward the intercom.

'Kaa! Give it a full effort. Let's make a break for t-point!'

The pilot acknowledged with a click burst of assent.

*   *Cornered by orcas,*
    *   *With our backs against sharp coral,*
        *   *Watch them eat plankton! ∗*

As *Streaker* started pulling away, the battle storm followed. Detectors showed still more machines converging from all sides. Still, a gap slowly began to grow.

Then the Niss interrupted again.

'Dr. Baskin, something else has come to my attention that I know will concern you.'

'Please observe.'

The main viewer zoomed toward one corner of the fiery brawl – a scrap far smaller than some other battles *Streaker* had observed, though nearness made the flashes and explosions seem more garish by far. Rapid glimpses revealed that most of the fighters were machines, lacking any boxy enclosures to protect protoplasm crews. Clearly, the varied factions of 'retired' races preferred doing combat by proxy, using mechanical hirelings rather than risking their own necks.

Then one object loomed into view, more squat in profile than any other – a tubby dart, rounded and heavily armored. Gillian recognized the outline of a Thennanin scoutcraft.

'Ifni!' she sighed. 'Has he done it again?'

'If you mean Engineer Emerson D'Anite, I can tell you that interior scans show no sign of him within this ship. I surmise it is him out there, unleashing weapons with quite futile abandon, missing nearly everything he shoots at. Organic beings really should not face mechanicals in close combat. It is not your forte.'

'I'll bear that in mind,' Gillian murmured, deeply torn over what she could or should do next.

EMERSON

When he realized he wasn't hitting anything – and no one was shooting back – Emerson finally shut down the fire controls. Apparently, nobody thought him worth much worry, or effort. It felt irksome to be ignored, but at least no faction seemed bent on avenging the robots he had taken out with those first few lucky shots, igniting this fury.

Combat surged around him. There was no making sense of the shadowed struggle as machines flayed other machines.

Anyway, it soon dawned on him that something else was going on. Something more important and personal than events taking place outside.

Waves of confusion swept through Emerson's mind. Nothing unusual about that. By now he was quite used to feeling befuddled. But the *type* of disorientation was exceptional. It felt like peering past dark clouds of delirium. As if everything till then had been part of a vivid dream, filled with perverted logic. Like a fever-racked child, he had made no clear sense of anything going on around him for a very long time. But in a brief instant light seemed to pierce the mist, limning corners that had been shrouded and dark.

Like a hint, or a passing scent, it lasted but a moment and was gone.

He suspected a trick. Another psi distraction ...

But the light must have been more than that! The joy it brought was too intense. The sense of loss too devastating when it vanished.

Then, without warning, it was back again, much stronger than before.

Something he had been missing for a long time.

Something precious that he had never fully appreciated until it was taken from him.

I ... I can think ...

... I can think in words again!

Not just words, but sentences, paragraphs!

I'm piloting a Thennanin war dart ... Streaker lies behind me ... Over there, and across nearly the whole of heaven, I see the blemished sky arch of the Fractal World ...

At once an overwhelming flood of understanding filled Emerson. Things he had seen on Jijo and since. Concepts that had eluded him because they could not be shaped with images and feelings alone, but needed the rich subtlety of abstract language to shape and anchor them with a webbery of symbols.

Sadness flooded him when he thought of all the things he had wanted to tell Sara during their long journey together across the Slope. And to Gillian, after he returned home a devastated cripple. Two different kinds of love he could never express – or sort out – until now.

How is this possible? My brain ... they destroyed my speech centers!

For some reason, after the Old Ones finished interrogating him, they had decided to let him live, but in silence. The means to do this they found simply by reading his own memories of poor wounded Creideiki. When they mimicked giving him the same injury, the resulting cruel mutilation had left him half dead ... and less than half a man.

That much he had already worked out laboriously on Jijo, even without putting it in words. But the answer was never satisfying. It never explained the brutal logic behind such an act.

That was when it came to him.

A voice. One he had forgotten till that moment.

One he identified with chill, unblinking eyes.

'INACCURACY. WE DID NOT DESTROY THOSE PORTIONS OF YOUR ORGANIC BRAIN. WE BORROWED/TOOK/EXPROPRIATED A FEW GRAMS OF TISSUE FOR USE IN A GREAT GOAL. OUR NEED WAS GREATER THAN YOURS.'

The effrontery of that claim nearly made Emerson howl with rage. Only by fierce discipline did he manage to form a reply, shaping it through pathways he had not used in too long a time. His voice sounded unpracticed, with an odd nasal twang.

'You bastards maimed me so I'd never talk about what you did!'

A sensation of aloof amusement accompanied the response.

'THAT WAS BUT A MINOR SIDE BENEFIT. IN FACT, WE DESIRED/NEEDED THE TISSUE ITSELF. IF TRUTH BE TOLD, IT SEEMED FAR MORE VALUABLE TO US THAN YOU EVER WERE LIKELY TO BE, AS A WHOLE ENTITY ... ALTHOUGH IT MIGHT HAVE BEEN BETTER IF YOU WERE OF A SLIGHTLY DIFFERENT SPECIES. BUT WE HAD PHYSICAL POSSESSION OF JUST ONE EARTHLING, SO IT WAS ORDAINED THAT YOU WOULD BE OUR DONOR.'

The explication left him more befuddled than ever. 'Then how come I can talk now?'

'IT IS A MATTER OF LINKAGE AND PROXIMITY. WE LEFT QUANTUM RESONATORS LINING THE CAVITY IN YOUR BRAIN, WHERE THE EXCISED TISSUE ONCE RESIDED. THESE HAVE CAUSAL CONNECTIONS WITH OTHER RESONATORS COATING THE SAMPLE WE TOOK AWAY. IF YOU ARE CLOSE ENOUGH, UNDER THE RIGHT CIRCUMSTANCES, OLD NEURAL PATHWAYS MAY RESUME THEIR FORMER FUNCTION.'

Emerson blinked. Leaning toward the scoutship's curved window, he peered at the dark skyscape, flickering with silent explosions.

'YES, THE CAPSULE IS NEARBY, BROUGHT CLOSE TO YOU BY A WORKER DRONE. ONE THAT SEEMS INNOCUOUS, EVADING ATTENTION FROM THE FACTIONS BATTLING AROUND YOU.

'IN FACT, THE DRONE CAN COME MUCH CLOSER STILL. THE TISSUE MIGHT BE YOURS AGAIN, UNDER CERTAIN CONDITIONS.'

He wanted to scream at his former captors, declaring that they had no right to bargain with him over something they had stolen in the first place. But they would only dismiss that as whimpering over wolfling standards of fairness. Anyway, Emerson's mind was racing now, covering a great deal of territory in parallel, using both the old logic tracks and new techniques he had picked up during exile.

'If I serve you, then I'll get my speech centers back? What's the matter? Did your former scheme fail?'

'SOME OF US STILL HAVE FAITH/CONFIDENCE IN THAT PLAN. THOUGH AT BEST IT WAS ALWAYS A GAMBLE – AN ATTEMPT TO BRIBE ONE WHO IS/WAS FAR AWAY FROM HERE.

'BUT NOW, DEFYING ALL EXPECTATION, YOU ARE NEAR US ONCE AGAIN. IT PRESENTS ANOTHER POSSIBILITY FOR SUCCESS.'

'Oh, I just can't wait to hear this,' Emerson commented, but he had learned the first time that sarcasm was wasted on the Old Ones.

'THE CONCEPT SHOULD BE SIMPLE ENOUGH FOR YOUR LEVEL OF BEING TO UNDERSTAND. IF YOU HURRY, YOU CAN REBOARD THE EARTHSHIP AND FIND/RETRIEVE INFORMATION WE DESIRE. A SIMPLE TRADE WOULD FOLLOW, AND WHAT YOU DESIRE MOST WILL BE YOURS.'

Emerson clamped down, refusing to put in words some of the thoughts glimmering at the back of his mind. Whatever he expressed that way – even subvocalizing – must pass through a lump of protoplasm that lay out there somewhere, carried by a machine drifting amid the slashing rays and bursting mines. A piece of himself that others could sieve at will.

'So now you want to make a deal. But a year ago you thought you didn't need my useless carcass anymore. Why did you send me to Jijo, then? Why am I still alive?'

The voice seemed resigned about providing an explanation.

'THERE ARE BOUNDARY CONDITIONS TO THE UNIVERSAL WAVE FUNCTION, AFFECTING WORLDLINES PROPAGATING IN ALL DIRECTIONS. YOUR PHYSICAL EXISTENCE IN A FUTURE TIME IS ONE OF THESE BOUNDARY CONDITIONS. OUR ACTIONS MUST BE COMPATIBLE WITH KNOWN FACTS.

'HOWEVER, THERE IS LOOSENESS IN THE SLIP AND PLAY OF WORLDLINES. NUMERICAL CALCULATIONS SHOWED THAT IT WAS ONLY NECESSARY TO PUT YOU CLOSE TO YOUR PEERS, ALIVE, AT A CERTAIN PLACE AND TIME, IN ORDER FOR ACCOUNTS TO BALANCE. PLACING YOUR BODY ON JIJO, WITHIN ACCESSIBLE RANGE OF YOUR COLLEAGUES, APPEARED ADEQUATE.'

He stared, appalled at both the power and the callousness implied by that statement.

'You ... you'd call that hellish journey I went through *accessible*?'

The voice did not reply to that. Emerson's question might as well have been rhetorical.

His eyes skimmed the scout's displays. Now the letters and glyphs made instantaneous sense, indicating Streaker's growing speed and distance. Clearly, Gillian was making another run toward the stars.

'THAT'S RIGHT. YOU HAVE ONLY A FEW DURAS TO ACT. IF YOU DO NOT REBOARD AND ACCEPT OUR OFFER, WE WILL BE FORCED TO DESTROY THE EARTHSHIP AND ALL YOUR COMRADES.'

Emerson laughed.

'That assumes your enemies will let you! They almost grabbed *Streaker*'s WOM, before your faction interfered. They might have something to say about your plans, in turn.

'Besides, I'm an important boundary condition, right? You gotta help me live into the future, alongside my friends, or your whole cause-and-effect thingamajig falls apart!'

'*THE DEMANDS OF CAUSALITY ARE NOT AS STRICT AS YOU IMPLY, HUMAN. DO NOT TEST YOUR QUESTIONABLE VALUE, OR TAUNT US WITH DISRESPECT.*'

He laughed aloud.

'Or what? You'll punish me? You'll inflict *pain*?'

Silence greeted his challenge, but he could tell the scorn had had an effect, this time. Contempt was a slim weapon, but they weren't used to it. The words stung them.

On the other hand, the Old Ones knew Emerson had little choice. Remaining behind was not an option, if he could avoid it. His hands decided for him, nudging to the scout's throttle, sending it accelerating after *Streaker* ... though he felt a rising sense of dread.

What would happen when he left the vicinity of the robot carrying the missing piece of himself? Would it follow? Lurking nearby so he could continue to think?

When the voice spoke again, it seemed cool and distant.

'*WE NOW SUPPLY YOU WITH A CODE TO USE IN CONTACTING US, WHEN YOU ARE READY TO ACT ON OUR OFFER.*'

A series of *colors* filled Emerson's mind – a simple sequence that seared its way into memory. He could not forget it if he tried.

Then his former captors offered a parting comment.

'*CLEARLY WE MISESTIMATED YOUR LEVEL OF SAPIENCY, IN BELIEVING THAT SIMPLE AVERSION CONDITIONING COULD SWAY YOU EARLIER. CONGRATULATIONS ON YOUR APPARENT TENACITY AND FLEXIBILITY.*'

'*NEVERTHELESS, WE HAVE CONFIDENCE IN THE EFFECTIVENESS OF OUR FINAL INDUCEMENT.*'

With that, the voice cut off, though Emerson wasn't done with them yet.

'Well let me tell you what you can do with your Ifni-damned offer, you gorslucking spawn of retard slime molds! Go seek redemption up your own clocoas, you jef-eating, dirt-licking, damned-to-Gehenna—'

Emerson's stream of invective went on while he sped after *Streaker*, hurrying past robot combatants that grappled and slashed one another, but never laid a claw or ray on him. He cursed on and on, enjoying the rich flood of invective and the feel of words spilling from his mouth, keeping it going for as long as he could. Each added second of crass language seemed a victory.

Swearing was his touchstone. Filling the small cabin with hoarse noise, he clung to the knack of speech, fiercely refusing to let distance – or the enemy – rip it away.

Soon he noted that *Streaker* was slowing down, pausing in its flight to let him catch up. The act of loyalty warmed him as the docking tunnel opened, spilling a welcome glow. But Emerson kept shouting his opinion of the Old Ones – their ancestry, their character, and their likely destiny on the great pyramid of existence.

Only when he finished latching to *Streaker*'s guidance beam did Emerson pause long enough to remember something.

Cursing didn't count.

He could do that even on Jijo. Like singing and sketching, profanity did not use the part of his brain that was stolen.

Emerson tried to say something else – to comment on the battle, the sky filled with shattered debris, or his own growing fear – and failed.

Desperately, his thoughts whirled, rummaging through his tormented brain, seeking an aptitude that had seemed so fluid and natural just moments before. A lifelong skill that villains had robbed from him, then briefly returned, but for too short a time.

It felt like trying to extend an amputated limb. The ghost was still there. A hint of volition. *Meanings* filled his mind, along with a readiness to act, to prompt sentences. To speak.

But some key element was gone again, and with it all the things he had hoped and planned saying to Sara. To Gillian.

Emerson slumped in a seat that had been built for a much larger pilot, a creature of great physical power, respected across the Civilization of Five Galaxies. His arms sank from the massive controls and his chin met his chest as tears streamed from eyes suddenly too foggy for seeing. He felt helpless, like an overwhelmed child. Like an ignorant wolfling.

Till that moment, Emerson had thought himself familiar with loss. But now he knew.

There was always someplace deeper you could go.

GILLIAN

Lieutenant Tsh't reported from the bridge. Turbulent bubbles fizzed as her tail slashed through oxywater.

'Engineer D'Anite is back aboard. Sh-shall we accelerate again?'

Gillian felt indecision like a heavy beast, clawing and dragging at her arms, her shoulders.

'Have sensors picked up any sign of the Zang?'

The Niss hologram expressed worry with taut lines.

'The hydrogen-breathing entities may be destroyed, along with their vessel. But even if the Zang are preoccupied elsewhere, some of these battling factions will surely unite to prevent our departure.'

'We don't know their motives, or even how many cliques—'

'By appraising tactical patterns I count at least five different groups. Their forces are mostly robots of the sepoy-soldiery type, receiving instructions from various sectors of the Fractal World, working for local associations of the Retired Order.'

The Niss paused for a moment, then resumed.

'Let me revise. I perceive SIX battle patterns. One seems aimed toward opening an escape path for us. So it appears we do have allies among the combatants.'

'It appeared that way last time, too,' she replied. 'These helpers – are they strong enough to protect us?'

'Doubtful. The crucial moment will come when we pass through the narrowest part of the gap that's been torn in the Fractal World. Any group might choose to destroy us at that point, using the defense beams we saw earlier.'

That was a cheery thought to dwell on as *Streaker* reentered the gaping corridor filled with evaporating debris and shimmering artificial comets. Only this time a sparkle of battle also followed the Earthship, ebbing and surging around it.

Gillian had Kaa steer just half a million kilometers from one ragged edge of the great wound, threading a path between the stumps and stark shadows of titanic, brittle spires.

'Maybe someone will think twice about shooting at us with those big guns, if we're so close to the shell itself.'

From here they could make out some of the giant machines striving to shore up the torn criswell structure, using nets woven from great spools of carbon thread to arrest its decay. These were a completely different order of mechanism, autonomous and sapient – hired workers, not slaves.

In fact, though, most of the supply spools looked nearly empty. *They are running short of raw materials*, Gillian thought. *All their efforts may fail if this keeps up ... especially if bands of Old Ones fight instead of helping.*

A dolphin's joyful shout erupted behind Gillian. She turned in time to see Emerson D'Anite enter the Plotting Room, his head and shoulders slumped in apparent depression.

'Well, there's our hero—' Gillian began. But Sara Koolhan rushed past with a glad cry to embrace her friend. The little neo-chimpanzee, Prity, leaped among them, and soon Emerson was enveloped. Dolphins gathered around, clicking excitedly while their walkers hissed and clanked. The Jijoan youngsters – Alvin and his friends – slapped Emerson's back, shaking his hand and telling him how wonderful he was.

Even if their words made no sense to him, the air of approval seemed to wash away some of the man's dour mood. His eyes lifted to meet Gillian's, and she returned his tentative smile with one of her own. But then the Niss cut in.

'*Two new swarms are approaching, Dr. Baskin.*'

She turned to look. 'More sepoy robots?'

'*No ... and it worries me. These fresh arrivals are much more formidable beings, Gillian. They are independent constructor–contractors. Autonomous members of the Machine Order of Life.*'

'Show me!'

The fresh arrivals were already near, coming in crowds of about a dozen each from opposite directions – one depicted as a cluster of red dots, the other green. Each group swept imperiously through the battle zone. As evidence of their status, none of the combatant robots fired on the newcomers. Instead, most scurried out of their way.

This looks bad, Gillian thought as the fierce green sparkles entered visual range. Each of the leaders resembled a giant spiny sea urchin, almost a tenth as long as *Streaker*, though most of that was in spindly leg-appendages that writhed as the mechanism flew toward *Streaker's* tail.

'*Impact-t in thirty secondsss!*' called Tsh't from the bridge. '*Shall we open fire?*'

'Negative!' Gillian shouted. 'No one has used a beam or particle weapon on us yet. I'm not about to start. Let's see what their business is first.'

One swarm converged near *Streaker's* aft end. Several of the big, spiky mechs clamped on. Soon, a bright, shimmering glow began to float around them.

'*They are dissolving the ship!*' the Niss cried out. '*Matter removal rates exceed thirty tons per second ... and rising. We must fight them off!*'

Tsh't reported targeting one of the machines with a laser turret, but Gillian countermanded the fire order.

'Don't do a thing till I say so! Akeakemai, give me a zoom focus on the machines that are still floating out there, *behind* the ones that landed!'

It was hard to peer past the fog that was being kicked up. But Gillian thought she made out a giant cylinder. A hooplike shape.

'It's a spool! Like the ones they unreel when they weave repair nets.' She turned her head and cried, 'Quick. What is the spectral signature of the removed material? Is it pure carbon?'

A brief pause. When the Niss spoke again, it sounded subdued.

'Carbon it is.'

'How pure?'

'Very. The vapors contain no metal from Streaker's *true hull. How did you know?'*

Gillian's throat still felt as if her heart was beating there. But some of the panicky feeling ebbed.

'These big guys don't give a damn about petty bickering among hot-tempered oxy-life-forms. They have a job to do, and they're running out of raw materials. Their best supply of carbon was already disrupted when the Jijoans somehow triggered flares on Izmunuti. But *we* carry layers of the same material sought by the harvester sailships! This work team must have sensed us passing nearby and sent machines to fetch more for repairs.'

'Confirmed,' said the Niss. *'As they move slowly along the hull, evaporated material is being sucked up and spun into polycarbon fiber, leaving the fuselage beneath intact.'*

Hannes Suessi called jubilantly from Engineering, clearly delighted to learn how the machines swiftly removed a coating that had stymied him for months.

'At this rate, we'll shed several megatons in no time,' he added. 'It's gonna make us much more nimble.'

By now the second swarm – shown as red pinpoints – arrived in the vicinity of *Streaker*'s nose. Another set of enormous mechanisms clamped onto the bow. These huge visitors showed no special interest in the area around the rayed spiral symbol.

Gillian nodded.

'I guess they'll strip us from both ends now. Let's pray this really does leave the hull itself intact. If our luck has turned, their presence may deter anyone else from shooting at us till we're near the t-point.'

The Niss whirled thoughtfully.

'Of course there is another danger. If law and consensus are totally broken throughout the Fractal World, nothing prevents the various "retired" factions from getting in touch with their younger cousins, via hyperwave or time drop.'

'In other words, we might see battlefleets of Soro, Jophur, or Tandu come boiling through at any minute. Great.' She sighed. 'All the more reason to get the hell—'

The spinning moiré patterns suddenly ballooned outward – an expression of surprise.

'Something is different,' the Niss announced. *'The group at the bow . . . it is not doing the same thing as those at the stern.'*

Gillian took a step forward.

'Show me!'

At first the scene looked similar. Several long-legged machines clung to *Streaker*'s soot-covered hull, plying the black surface with shimmering rays. Only this time no milky haze of vapor poured toward mouthlike collectors. No streams of dark fiber spun out the machines' back ends, to collect on huge spools. Instead, something weird happened to the dense coating *Streaker* had picked up during its passages through Izmunuti's atmosphere. A rainbowlike sheen rippled and condensed slickly behind the great mechanisms as they marched a spiral pattern along the hull.

No one spoke for several minutes. So unexpected and unexplained was this behavior that Gillian had no idea how to react.

'They're ... not taking the carbon away. They are—'

'*Transforming it, somehow*,' agreed the Niss.

At last, Suessi called. The chief engineer's cyborg image appeared on a secondary screen. Although his head was now a mirrored dome, Gillian could tell from the old man's body language that he had a theory.

'The soot poured out by Izmunuti ... the phases that condensed on us were mostly carbon, all right. But a large fraction consisted of fullerenes – so-called "buckeyballs" and "buckeytubes." There were a lot of Penrose diamond states, too. The material had some mighty strange properties, as we found when we tried cutting it, back on Jijo. All sorts of caged impurities give it traits like a high-temperature superconductor, plus an altered coefficient of friction—'

'Hannes!' Gillian interrupted. 'Please get to the point.'

The silvery dome nodded.

'I've scanned the surface these new machines are leaving behind. The coating is far more uniform than raw star soot. The buckey states intermesh with each other in ways I've never seen. I'd have to guess the properties we observed before would be enhanced by many orders of magnitude.'

One of the dolphins muttered.

'Oh great-t. Now it will be even harder to ssscrape off!'

Gillian shook her head.

'But what are they trying to accomplish? To seal us inside?'

If so, there might still be time to evacuate the ship, sending the crew scrambling for airlocks at the stern. Perhaps they might find shelter among the first group of machines.

'Our forward laser turret has a clear line of fire,' announced Tsh't.

Gillian motioned with her right hand, restraining any action for now.

One of the kids from Jijo spoke up then. The little wheeled g'Kek, who called herself Huck, made a good lookout, since she was able to scan four screens at once with her waving eyestalks.

'Uh-oh,' she remarked. 'It looks like our new visitors are gonna start fighting, too.'

She pointed to where support vessels from both groups could be seen drifting toward each other. Barely constrained energies crackled as a showdown developed. Scanners showed that many of the lesser war machines were withdrawing from this confrontation.

They'll use us as a battleground. How could things possibly get any worse?

Gillian knew it was a mistake to put it that way. One should not tempt Ifni, the goddess of luck, who could always come up with one more ratcheting of fate.

The Niss hologram coiled nearby. Its voice was low, resigned.

'*Now we are being scanned from the Fractal World itself. Those controlling the great disintegrator beams have turned their targeting apparatus our way. We may soon go the way of the late Zang.*'

'They'll risk hitting the habitat, right where it's most vulnerable!'

'*Apparently, some think it worth the risk, in order to intimidate us. Or else they would destroy what they cannot keep.*'

Gillian had seen those shafts of annihilation in action. *Streaker* could be vaporized in seconds.

LARK

These were hellish circumstances. And yet, for a biologist, it might be heaven. While his body endured cramped confinement in a stinking plastic bag, Lark's mind sped through lessons expanding his parochial view of the vast panorama of life.

He grew deft at a new form of communication, receiving visual images that came enhanced by meanings and connotations sent through a tube directly to his bloodstream. A language of hormones and mood-tweaking peptides. And it went both ways. Whenever Lark understood something new, he did not have to speak or even nod his head. The mere act of comprehending had metabolic effects – a familiar endorphin burst of satisfaction – that his alien tutor quickly detected. Likewise, confusion or frustration brought rapid changes. The globule-teacher kept revising its presentation until Lark grasped what he was being shown.

It was a strangely active kind of passive study.

Would you call this a form of telepathy? he wondered.

Yet, the method also seemed slow and crude. As visual lessons, the demonstrations were a lot like puppet shows. Physical portions of his instructor would bud off the parent body to float within a vacuole cavity, twisting and transforming themselves into living models or mannequins to play out a little scene. The same images might have been presented far swifter, and more vividly, using one of the computerized display units he had seen Ling use, on Jijo and in the Jophur ship.

Inefficient or not, Lark eventually realized why his captors used this approach.

It's fundamental to the difference between hydrogen- and oxygen-based ways of looking at the universe.

At a glance, the two worlds seemed utterly unalike.

While both biologies were based on carbon molecules, one used the reactive chemistry of oxidizing atmospheres, with liquid water serving as the indispensable solvent. Only narrow circumstances of temperature and pressure could nurture this kind of life from scratch. Normally, it arose in filmy skins of ocean and air, coating Earthlike worlds. Venturing beyond these lean oases, oxy-life must carry the same rare conditions with them into space.

'Reducing' environments were far more abundant, covering cold, giant planets like Jupiter, Saturn, Uranus, or Titan – and even the broad, icy domain of comets. Some of these worlds soaked in abundant hydrogen, while others featured methane, ammonia, or cyanogen. But most shared a few common features – enormous, dense atmospheres and turbulent convecting layers, somewhat like the roiling strata of a sun. Life-giving heat often flowed *upward*, from a hot planetary core. Sometimes there was no solid 'surface' at all.

Because of this, most hydros were creatures of a vast, boisterous sky. Up and down became *tall*, unlimited, almost coequal with the other two dimensions. Nor was travel a matter of exertive *flying*, by defying gravity with flapping wings, but of adjusting buoyancy and propelling through fogs so dense the pressure was like the bottom of Earth's sea.

In such a realm, there were advantages to size. Big creatures cruised with languid grace, sifting for organic food. When caught in strong downdrafts, only a giant could fight free and keep from being hauled to searing, crushing depths. So huge did some hydro-beings grow, they could be viewed from space, resembling titanic, self-contained clouds.

And that was where organic chemistry – the Designer's Assistant – might have left things, if not for action by another party.

The Critic.

Evolution.

Inevitably, the logic of reproduction and advantage took hold on reducing worlds, as it did on oxidizing ones like Earth ... though in different ways.

Oxy-life counted on liquid water to carry out the complex colloidal chemistry of proteins and amino acids. Yet, too much watery flow would dilute those same processes, making them useless. Even in the warm sea, this meant crafting compact packages – cells – of just the right size to evolve life's machinery. For two billion years, the limit of biological accomplishment on the early Earth had been to spread single-celled organisms through the ocean, soaking up sunlight and devouring each other while slowly improving their molecular techniques.

Until one day a cell consumed another – and let it continue living. A primitive eukaryote took in a blue-green alga and gave it a home, exchanging safe living quarters for sugars produced from photosynthesis. This act of cooperation gave the combined team a crucial edge in competition with other cells.

Nor was it the only joint venture. Soon, cells paired up in quantity, amassing and colluding, forming temporary or permanent associations to gain advantage over other teams. Complex organisms flourished, and evolution accelerated.

Some call it the food chain, or the Dance of Life. I've seen it played out on Jijo, in so many subenvironments and ecosystems. Plants use photosynthesis to store food energy in carbohydrates. Herbivores eat plants. Carnivores prey on herbivores, completing the cycle by returning their own substance to the ground when they defecate or die.

It looks like a well-tuned machine, with each part relying on the others, but paradoxes abound. Everything that seems at first like cooperation has its basis in competition. And nearly every act of competition takes part in a bigger, healthier system, as if cooperation were inherent all along.

Of course that oversimplified matters. Sometimes the balance was thrown off kilter – by some environmental change, or when one component species escaped natural controls keeping it in check. Like a cancer, it might 'compete' out of existence the very econetwork that had enabled it to thrive in the first place.

Still, the basic pattern was nearly always the same on millions of fecund little worlds. Take compact bags of protein-laced water. Provide sunlight and minerals. Get them busy vying in life-or-death rivalry. Over the long run, what emerges will be ever-greater and more complex alliances. Cooperative groups that form organs, bodies, packs, herds, tribes, nations, planetary societies ... all leading to the fractious but astounding Civilization of Five Galaxies.

*

The story of hydrogen-based life had similarities, but the plot took a different twist.

On Jovian-type worlds, size emerged from the start. Simple beings of vast extent flapped and fluttered across skies broad enough to swallow several hundred Jijos. Evolution caused such creatures to improve, though more slowly at cooler temperatures. Indeed, change did not always come about through reproduction and inheritance. More often, some *part* of a huge, drifting beast might stumble onto a new chemical trick or behavior. That portion would spread laterally, consuming and replacing the flesh next to it, gradually transforming the whole entity.

Death was still part of the process, but not quite in the same way it occurred on Earth.

To us, dying is a quantal thing. An individual may succeed in having offspring, or not. But either way, personal extinction stalks you all your life, and must eventually win, however hard you struggle or however much you innovate.

But to hydros, everything is murky, qualitative. Without such clear lines, death is relative. So long as a transformation happens slowly and smoothly, you look at it with no more dread than I fear cutting my hair.

Instead of building up through hard-won cooperation among tiny cells, life on Jupiter-type worlds was large from the start. It did not revolve as much around cooperation-competition. *Self* and *other* were known concepts, but distinguishing between the two had less central a role in existence than it did to oxy-beings.

Then how do you organize yourselves? Lark thought at one point, wrestling with frustration. *How do you recognize objects, goals, opponents, or ideas?*

Lark's tutor could not read his mind, or perceive his questions as discrete sentences. But clearly some kind of meaning entered his bloodstream, secreted by Lark's brain when he posed a query. It was a slower, less efficient process than speech, involving many iterations. But he wasn't going anywhere.

Objects throbbed within the vacuole, budding off the parent body, pulsing as they crossed the open space, then merging together or recombining with the greater whole. For quite some time, Lark had watched these little forms writhe into subtly formed shapes that performed for his edification. Now, all at once, he realized the deep truth underlying it all.

These little subselves. They are . . .

A throbbing wave penetrated his thigh, swarming down a leg then up his torso. The sensation was unlike any other, and Lark abruptly realized he had been given a *name*.

A name he could not repeat aloud in any language, or even in his thoughts – so he translated as best he could.

Deputies.

In their native environments, hydrogen-breathing entities did not tend to look outward for learning or fulfillment. If one huge beast encountered another, it might lead to combat, or predation – or peaceful intercourse – but little chance of permanent companionship. The vast winds of a Jovian sky soon scattered all acquaintances. A return visit or rendezvous was next to impossible.

Growth requires challenge, however. So, for conversation, appraisal, or understanding ... they turned *within*.

Contained by spacious membranes, the core of a natural hydrobeing was an oasis of calm amid planet-sized storms. Sheltered chambers could be fashioned at will, and small subunits budded to float freely for a while, engaging others in myriad ways. Like a human's internal thoughts and fantasies, these deputies might cluster, converse or clash, working out countless scenarios for the good of the greater whole.

Simulations.

Lark glanced at the globule-creature floating just outside his membrane enclosure. It had seemed autonomous, but now he knew the hydro was a mere 'deputy' of something larger still – perhaps the huge ship-entity that had sacrificed itself under withering Jophur fire in order to penetrate this place.

Lark abruptly recalled something he had read once, in a rare galacto-xenology text, about a type of hydro-life called Zang.

Their great passion is simulating the world ... the universe ... but not through math or computers. They do it by crafting living replicas, models, mimicries, inside their own bodies.

In an odd way, it seemed familiar.

Like the way we humans explore future possibilities with our imaginations.

But there was more.

Because we start life as little bags of water – as cells – we oxies must work our way from the ground up, by a complex, bootstrapping dance of competition and cooperation, building coalitions and societies, gradually becoming creatures capable of taking the process in hand, through Uplift. For all its faults, our galaxy-spanning civilization is the culmination of all that.

From many ... one.

Hydros do it differently. They begin large, but loneliness forces them to subdivide, to seek diversity within.

From one ... many.

The insight filled Lark with sudden heady pleasure. To behold both differences and similarities with an entirely different empire of life was a gift he had never imagined receiving. One beyond his ability to ask or anticipate.

He yearned to share it, to tell Ling everything, and hear her enthralled insights ...

Sadness was an abrupt flood, equal to the pleasure of moments before. Both emotions meshed and swirled, a mixture that poured into his veins, driven by his pounding heart. In moments it reached the tube in his leg, and then—

The tutor-entity floating nearby gave a sudden jerk. The globule quivered, as if contemplating the chemicals given off by Lark's body during his epiphany, when everything became clear.

At least a hundred tiny vacuoles opened throughout its bulbous body. In each of these, a froth of nearly microscopic animalcules suddenly burst forth and interacted, frenetically merging, bouncing, and dividing. Lark stared, fascinated to watch a Zang 'think' right in front of him. In practice, it was complex and blurringly fast.

The fizzing commotion ended as quickly as it had begun. All the little openings collapsed and the minuscule subdeputies resorbed into the main body. Lark's tutor throbbed—

He felt another wave of stimulation penetrate his leg, a warm sensation that spread quickly through his guts and arteries – a form of communication so intimate that it transcended any thought of embarrassment. It simply was.

Appreciation.

At least that was how Lark interpreted the molecular wave – hoping that it was not wishful thinking.

Appreciation is welcome.
Appreciation is reciprocated.

A short time later, he lost consciousness. A sudden drowsiness told Lark that his hosts wanted him to sleep – and he did.

Awareness returned nearly as swiftly. He had no idea how much later it was, only that he had been moved.

No longer did a spacious chamber surround him, filled with other prisoners and visibly noxious fumes. Instead, his transparent cocoon had been transplanted to a much smaller room. And there were other changes, too.

The membranes surrounding him had shrunk to form-fit against his body, like a baggy suit of clothes. Lark found that he was *standing up*. Perhaps they had even walked him here, prompting his body to move like a marionette. The notion was unpleasant, but freedom to stretch out from a cramped fetal position more than made up for it.

He still could not breathe, and relied on the thigh catheter for life support, but Lark's surroundings looked less hazy and there was not as great a sensation of nearby cold.

Carefully, tentatively, he shuffled his feet to turn around.

One of the Zang hovered nearby, though whether it was his erstwhile tutor he could not tell. Probably not. This one resembled the warrior-globule he had encountered in the halls of *Polkjhy* – the being that had burst through a wall, frightened Rann away, and rushed forward to take Lark captive. On close inspection, it was possible to see some of the adaptations necessary to shield hydrogen-breathing envoys against a caustic oxygen environment. Thick protective layers glistened, and it maintained a spherical form, ideal for minimizing exposure.

So, we're both suited up. Girded to meet each other halfway. Except that I'm still anchored by an umbilicus, and you fellows can shut me off like a light, anytime you want.

Lark raised his eyes beyond the Zang, and saw a feature of the room that had escaped his notice till now.

A window ... looking outside!

Careful not to trip, he shuffled close, eager to see the stars. It would be his first direct view of space since he and Ling were trapped aboard the Jophur vessel when it took off from Jijo.

But instead of strange constellations, his attention was riveted at once by something vastly more strange – an object, floating against blackness, that somewhat resembled a spiny hedge anemone you might find behind a rock in an alpine meadow back home. Except his impression this time was of incredible size. Somehow, he felt the prickly thing might be as large as Jijo ... or bigger still.

Soon, he could tell one more thing. The dark object was damaged. Glimmering sparks could be seen, twinkling in dim reddish light that poured through a jagged opening, torn across one hemisphere.

Polkjhy appeared to be heading toward that gaping hole, at a very rapid clip.

Earlier, the Zang seemed to say they had not succeeded in taking over the ship. Maybe their resources are stretched too thin. From simulated charts, it appeared that the Jophur still command the engines, weapons, and life support.

Perhaps they are speeding to a place where they can get help ridding the ship of infestations like the Zang ... and me.

Or else, maybe the Jophur think this is where they'll find the 'prey' Rann spoke of – the Earthship everyone's been searching for.

Lark turned his head to regard the warrior-globule. Did it have a purpose in bringing him here, and showing him this scene? Perhaps the Zang had figured out that Lark was no friend of the Jophur. Maybe they wanted an alliance. If so, he would gladly comply ... on one condition.

You must help me find and release Ling. Give us a lifeboat, or some other way out of here, either back to Jijo or someplace else safe.

You do that, and I'll act as your hound, sniffing out and hunting down my own kind.

Lark was being intentionally wry in his thoughts, of course. Only compared to hydrogen breathers could *Jophur* possibly be called his 'kind.' But sardonicism was probably far too subtle for the Zang to read by sifting his blood.

If we're going to team up, we'll need much better communications.

He watched the globule for any sign of an answer, or even comprehension. But instead, a few moments later, it seemed to *jump* in sudden agitation and surprise. Waves of nervous excitement entered Lark's body from the catheter.

What? What is it!

Spinning around, he sought a reason. Then his gaze passed through the window once again.

Oh, Ifni ...

The battleship had already plunged much closer to the great corrugated ball, clearly aiming for the hole in one side. Lark noted at once that it seemed *hollow*, and glimpsed a compact round flame glowing within. Lark had no idea what to make of the scene, or what the flame could be. Anyway, something else quickly caught his attention.

Sparkling explosions rippled along one edge of the wide cavity. He watched several of the giant quills or spikes break off and drift in slow motion, already dissolving as the aperture widened destructively.

Most of the havoc seemed to be wrought by sharp needles of light, generated somewhere deep inside the great shell. A dozen or so rays converged on a single point, a speck, near a rim of the great wound, creating a painful mote of brilliance. Reflections off this target did most of the glancing damage to the nearby shell.

The speck darted about, sometimes evading the shafts completely, leaving them to hunt as it fled outward from the gap at a rapid clip. Whenever a pursuing ray caught up with it, the distant spark glared so brightly that Lark had to blink and avert his gaze.

What's going on? What is happening out there?

Once again, he felt like the ignorant savage that he was. Wisdom hovered nearby – the Zang no doubt understood these strange sights. But it might take several miduras of patient puppet shows to explain even the simplest aspect.

An abrupt thrumming vibration shook the floor beneath Lark's feet. The masters of *Polkjhy* were doing something.

He recognized the grating tempo of weapons being fired.

Soon, a double handful of glittering objects could be seen darting away from this ship, tracing an arc across space, hurtling at fantastic speed toward the sundered ball-of-spikes.

Are those missiles?

Lark recalled how the Commons of Jijo surprised the Jóphur by attacking this very ship with crude chemical rockets. He had a feeling the bright arrows out there were more deadly, by far.

At first he thought the weapons might be joining the attack on the bright speck. But their glitter swept on past it, following each of the cruel rays toward its source.

Another swarm of emotion-laden connotations swept through Lark's body. This time it was easy to interpret the Zang's critical commentary.

Hasty.

Unwise.

Self-defeating.

His tutors did not approve of the Jophur action. But there was nothing to be done about it now. The missiles had already vanished into the great cavity.

For lack of anything better to do, Lark nervously watched and waited.

A short time later, the bright beams began winking out, one by one.

Still glowing, their target kept darting toward deep space, while *Polkhjy* plunged to meet it.

EWASX

Calmness, My rings.

Cultivate serene reflection, I urge you.

Stroke the wax.

Respect the wisdom of our captain-leader.

TRUE, that august stack has not been itself lately. Some of its component rings suffered wounds when human vermin infiltrated our control center, using a crude bomb to attempt sly sabotage.

TRUE, a far worse shipboard infestation has now driven our proud crew from several decks, forcing us to abandon and quarantine portions of our dear *Polkjhy*-vessel to the Zang blight.

TRUE, our leader's rings-of-command have fumed odd-smelling flavors and scents lately, prompting a few priest stacks to vent mutinous steam, fomenting rebellious vapors among the crew.

NEVERTHELESS, be assured that I/we shall remain loyal to our commander. After all, was not *this* conjoined pile of ill-fitting rings put together as an experiment, designed and implemented at the behest of our captain-leader? If another chief takes charge, the new leader might order our/My swift disassembly into spare parts!

MY RINGS, SOME OF YOU DO NOT SEEM ADEQUATELY OUTRAGED AT THAT PROSPECT.

Therefore, as your beloved Master Torus, let Me remind you (with jolts of electric pain/affection) that a Jophur is not the same sort of composite being as the one you composed on feral Jijo, when together you made up the traeki sage, Asx.

We/you/I are much greater now.

Ever since the gracious Oailie intervened, rescuing our race from placid unassertiveness, the Jophur clan has risen to power and eminence among vigorous competing races of the Civilization of Five Galaxies. This is not a destiny to be given up lightly. Especially with signs and auguries now pointing to an onrushing Time of Changes. With each passing jadura it grows clear that fortune may turn around, presenting us with the clues/hints/coordinates/relics carried by the dolphin-wolfling ship.

HENCE, MY/OUR AGREEMENT WITH THE CAPTAIN-LEADER'S DECISION TO INTERVENE!

Let the senior priest-stack rant about law and decorum. Should we stand back and allow the Earthlings to be incinerated? After all we have been through, chasing them across vast reaches and five levels of hyperspace, with our prey/prize finally in sight, should we now let panicky members of the Retired Order lash out and destroy the greatest treasure in the known cosmos?

TRUE, we have no legal standing here in Galaxy Four. No formal right to fire missiles into the fractal sanctuary just ahead. But it is their own fault that we were forced to act! The Earthship and its contents are of rightful interest to *our* life order – we descendants of the Progenitors who still cruise star-speckled lanes. Retirees should mind their own business, contemplating deep thoughts and obscure philosophies, preparing their genetic lines for transcendence, not meddling in affairs that are no longer their concern!

One by one, our superlight projectiles strike their targets on the habitat's inner shell ... and one by one, disintegrator beams flicker out.

BEHOLD! The last one goes dark, leaving the Terran vessel still driving ahead under its own power.

Success!

Now the wolflings sprint with alarmed speed toward the transfer point, hoping to escape this trap toward some unknown sanctuary beyond. But their hope is forlorn.

We are here, in good position to pounce.

'But how is it possible?'

Our second stack of cognition makes this query, venting steam-of-curiosity.

'Truly, we/I are glad to see the Earthlings survive those terrible, destructive rays. But how was it achieved? Should they not have vaporized during the first moments they fell under attack by such voracious beams?'

The same question travels in muted tones among Jophur stacks responsible for tactical evaluation. Pastel shadows of troubled concern flash across light-emitting ring flanks, while a worried mist wafts over that portion of the control center. Specialist toruses grow hot as they interact with computers, laboring to solve this quandary.

How *did* the Earthship survive such a fierce assault? Is this yet another insidious wolfling trick?

Are they still receiving protection from the meddling Zang, in violation of the basic rule that each life order should mind its own business?

Are the hydrogen breathers truly willing/ready to risk Armageddon over matters they could not care about, or comprehend?

Now the senior priest-stack ventures to challenge our captain-leader openly.

Striding forward on its ring of legs, that illustrious/sacred composite being nods its oration peak in a circle of righteous accusation.

'THIS IS INTOLERABLE! BY SENDING THOSE MISSILES, YOU/WE HAVE SURELY ALIENATED ANY AFFECTION THIS COLONY OF RETIREES MIGHT HAVE NURTURED FOR OUR RACE, CLAN, AND ALLIANCE!'

The captain-leader, perhaps sensing a precarious situation, replies in calmer tones, venting aromas of sweet confidence.

'OF REPERCUSSIONS THERE WILL BE FEW ...

'OF LEGAL FAULT, WE HAVE NONE, SINCE THOSE DIRECTING THE RAYS WERE CLEARLY OUTLAWS, ACCORDING TO THE CODES OF THEIR OWN LIFE ORDER ...

'WE ACTED TO PROTECT A TREASURE SOUGHT BY ALL OXYGEN-BREATHING CIVILIZATION.'

Many crew-stacks vent agreement. But the priest-stack is in no mood to be mollified.

'FEW REPERCUSSIONS? EVEN NOW, EXPLOSIONS CONTINUE ROCKING THE HABITAT WHERE OUR MISSILES FELL! THE ENTIRE GREAT STRUCTURE IS IN JEOPARDY!'

No denying that it is a serious matter. Lawsuits may result, dragging through the courts for thousands, or even millions of years. Nevertheless, confident-soothing aromatics swell from our glorious commander.

'THE SOCIAL AND PHYSICAL FABRIC OF THIS HABITAT WAS ALREADY TORN APART BY THE MERE PRESENCE OF PATHOGENIC TERRANS. NOW, ALL STACKS TAKE NOTE: OUR ONBOARD LIBRARY HAS DOWNLOADED POPULATION DATA FROM THIS MACROHABITAT. REGARD HOW A MAJORITY OF OCCUPANTS HAS ALREADY DEPARTED!!!!!

'SOME FLED TO OTHER RETIREMENT HOMES, FARTHER FROM THE DANGEROUS PASSION-WAVES OF YOUNGER RACES . . .

'OTHERS HAVE CHOSEN TO ABANDON RETIREMENT! EVEN NOW, THEY REJOIN OUR LIFE-ORDER, SEEKING COMPANIONSHIP AMONG THEIR FORMER CLIENTS, BECOMING ACTIVE ONCE AGAIN IN THE FLUX-TURMOIL OF THE CIVILIZATION OF FIVE GALAXIES . . .

'A THIRD PORTION OF REFUGEES HAS MOVED ON. AHEAD OF SCHEDULE, THEY DEPART, AIMED FOR TRANSCENDENT REALMS.'

Reverent silence greets our commander's news. Within this very stack – among our/My own conjoined rings, there is brief unanimity of spirit. From Master Torus all the way to the humblest greasy remnant of old Asx, there is agreement about one thing – I/we/you are privileged to live in such times. To take part in such wonders. To see/observe/know events that will be legendary in eras beyond the morrow.

Our captain-leader continues.

'SO, LIKE THE EMPTY SHELL OF AN OUIUT EGG, THIS HABITAT IS LESS IMPORTANT THAN IT MAY APPEAR. A MERE FEW TRILLIONS REMAIN IN THOSE TORTURED PRECINCTS. FOR THAT REASON, LET US CONCERN OURSELVES NO MORE WITH ITS FATE . . . ANY REPARATIONS ADJUDGED AGAINST US CAN BE PAID TRIVIALLY OUT OF OUR REWARD, WHEN THE EARTHSHIP IS SAFELY IN CUSTODY, SEALED BY JOPHUR WAX!'

The captain-leader's supporters cheer loudly, emitting joyful scent clouds. And yet, our/My contribution to the acclaim seems weak, lacking enthusiasm. Some of you rings, as tender and compassionate as a traeki, dwell dismally on the bad luck of those 'mere few trillions.'

Relentlessly, the priest-stack maintains its indictment.

'SUCH FOOLISHNESS! HAD YOU FORGOTTEN OUR OWN DIFFICULTIES? WE HAD EXPECTED/HOPED TO FIND AID HERE, IN RIDDING DEAR *POLKJHY* OF ITS HUMAN-PLUS-ZANG

INFESTATIONS. NOW SUCH HELP WILL NOT COME AT ANY PRICE!'

Our captain-leader hisses, rearing higher upon the command dais, clearly losing both temper and patience. Underlings quail back in dismay.

'THAT SITUATION IS UNDER CONTROL. ZANG PESTS ARE ISOLATED. WHILE THE QUARANTINE HOLDS, NO PRIORITY EXCEEDS THAT OF CAPTURING THE EARTHLING SHIP!'

Others may be impressed, but the priest-stack is not intimidated by shouting or physical gestures. Instead, that revered ring pile moves closer still.

'AND WHAT OF COMMUNICATIONS? WE HAD PLANNED USING LOCAL HYPERMAIL TAPS TO CONTACT OUR CLAN/ALLIANCE. NOW THOSE SERVICES ARE RUINED. HOW SHALL WE INFORM SUPERIORS OF OUR DISCOVERIES/ OPPORTUNITIES ON JIJO? OR SEEK AID IN PURSUIT OF THESE EARTHLINGS?'

Subordinate ring piles scurry away from this confrontation between tall, august stacks, who now stand nearly close enough to press their gorgeous, fatty toruses against each other. Dense, compelling vapors clash and swirl around them, driving to confusion any lesser Jophur who happens to get caught in a backdraft. Stretching higher, each great lord tries to overawe the other.

From a privileged point of view, clockwise and slightly behind, I/we perceive the captain-leader using an arm-appendage to draw forth a hidden sidearm. Nervous tremors surge down our fatty core.

MY RINGS, WILL HE SHOOT?

Suddenly, the taut tableau is interrupted. Word-glyphs from the ship's chief tactics officer cut through the acrimonious stench like an icy wind, reminding us of our purpose.

'The Earthship comes within range! Soon it will pass nearby, on its way to the transfer nexus. Interception/opportunity will maximize in ninety duras.'

Like two antagonistic volcanos deciding not to erupt – for now – our great lords back off from the precipice. Their stacks settle down and cease venting odious vapors.

Some things need not be said. If we succeed now, no reward will be denied this crew or its leadership. No forgiveness will be withheld.

Scans show that nearby space is filled with debris from the great calamity. Innumerable *ships* can also be seen peeling off the retirement habitat, seeking to escape toward the local transfer point.

Warily, we search among these sensor contacts for possible threats – for warships or other entities that might interfere, the way

Zang globules hindered us, last time the Earthlings seemed within our grasp. Each vessel receives scrutiny, but none seems to be in range this time, or of a class strong enough to obstruct us.

Nor do the wolflings try to hide among these refugees, using them as decoys. Unlike at Jijo, the trick would not/cannot work, for we have kept them in sight ever since the disintegrator beams shut off. Clearly they know it, too, for their sole aim appears to be speed. To outrace us. To find sanctuary in the knotty worldlines of the transfer point.

But to get there, they must pass us. Logically, there seems to be little going in their favor.

And yet – (points out our/My second ring of cognition) – for three years the wolflings and their clients have proved slippery. Ever ready to spring devil-tricks befitting Tymbrimi, they have thwarted efforts by all the grand military alliances. Now we face rumors that the sluggish forces of moderation have begun to rouse, here and there, across the Five Galaxies. If that happens – if the Earthers manage delay after delay – there is no telling what the pargi and other cautious fence-sitters might bring about!

Yes, My rings. Our wax overflows with disquieting worries. And yet, won't all that simply make our glory greater, when we Jophur succeed where others failed!

From *Polkjhy*, an ultimatum goes forth, similar to one the Terrans spurned before, when we sought them with beams and bombs under Jijo's ocean waters.

Surrender and give over your treasures. In return, our mighty alliance will safeguard Earth. The dolphin crew will be interned, of course. But only for a thousand years of frozen sleep. Then, at expiration time, they will be released into a new, reshaped Civilization of Five Galaxies.

Again, our only answer comes as insolent silence. We prepare weaponry.

'The Earthship's dynamics are inferior-degraded,' explains a tactical crew stack. 'It still carries excess mass – hull-contamination acquired from multiple exposures to the sooty red giant star.'

Polkjhy, too, passed through that polluting fog. But Earthlings can only afford lesser starship models, while our fine vessel is of a superior order, field-tuned to shed unwelcome atoms.

'Indeed?'
'*Then how were the Zang able to board us?*'

HUSH, MY RINGS!

I send coercive electric bursts down tendrils of control, reminding our second cognition ring to mind its own business.

*

Degraded or not, the preyship darts nimbly and appears well piloted. Our first warning shot misses by too wide a mark, and is not taken seriously.

Meanwhile, tactician stacks have been debating as to why the Earthship exists at all.

One faction insists the onslaught we saw – by planet-scale disintegrator rays, converging on a tiny ship – must have been a ruse! A garish light show, meant to make it seem the Earthlings were doomed, and persuade other assailants to back off while it accelerated away! Indeed, this astounding suggestion is now the majority opinion among *Polkjhy*'s tacticians – although it makes our missile attack seem foolish in retrospect.

'Behind us, the great habitat still shudders from those impacts, and other wounds that were self-inflicted.'

This explanation seems evident from the fact that the dolphin-crewed ship endures. Yet, a minority suggests caution. We may have witnessed something real. Something true. An event worthy of alarm.

Our second warning shot lashes forth and is more accurate. It passes but half a ship length from the quarry's nose.

'THERE IS A WORRISOME DIFFERENCE.'

Thus announces a stack whose duty it is to monitor enemy conditions.

'THE TARGET RESONATES STRANGELY. ITS HYPERVELOCITY PROFILE IS NOT THE SAME AS IT WAS BEFORE, NEAR THE RED GIANT STAR. AND THERE ARE UNUSUAL REFLECTIONS OFF THE HULL.'

At our captain-leader's behest, deep scans are made, confirming that the preyship is the same model and type. Engine emanations are identical. Psi detectors sift for faint leakage through its shields, and sniff a telltale Earthling spoor.

Then, at high magnification, we/I view the hull at last—

My rings, how it shines!

No longer sooty and black as space, it gleams now with a slick perfection that one only sees on vessels newly minted from their yards.

More perfect, for when starlight reflects off the curved surface, each warped image seems brighter than the original!

What can this mean?

Our senior priest-stack fumes.

'AFTER ALL WE HAVE BEEN THROUGH, AND ALL THAT WE HAVE SEEN, ONLY A COMPOSITE FOOL WOULD NOT HAVE EXPECTED FURTHER TRICKS/EXPLOITS/MIRACLES.

'ONLY A MISBEGOTTEN/MISJOINED STACK WOULD NOT HAVE CALLED FOR HELP.'

Our captain-leader shivers, settling cautiously onto the command dais. Streams of worried smoke trickle from its wavering topknot.

Finally, gathering rigidity among its constituent rings, the august commander-stack orders a targeted strike, at one-tenth potency, meant to disable the Earthship's power of flight.

Humming a finely tuned battle song, *Polkjhy* lashes out, transmitting rays of formidable force, aimed toward severing three of the quarry's probability flanges. Fierce energies cross the narrowing gap between our vessels to accurately strike home—

DO NOT ASK QUESTIONS, MY RINGS. JUST DO AS I SAY.

Move gently, innocuously toward the door.

That's it. Tread quietly, without undue sound. Flash no colorshadows. Vent no anxious steam.

Now, while the rest of the crew is distracted by drama/tragedy, let us make silent departure, like the humble traeki you/we/i once were.

Responding to our passkey scent, the armored hatchway rolls aside, opening a way out of the control chamber. With rearward-facing eyebuds, we/I watch crowds of our fellow Jophur mill in a fog of fear/distress toxins.

The worst fumes rise from a puddle of burning wax and grease – the flaming remains of our former captain-leader.

The priest-stacks had very little choice, of course. When our weapon-beam failed ... when its energies vanished, absorbed somehow by the Earthship's glistening new skin ... a change in administration-command was certain.

As inevitable as the spreading of space metric in an expanding universe.

Of course the chase is not over. Our position is favorable. The Earthship cannot evade us and we are capable of maintaining contact wherever it goes. Meanwhile, *Polkjhy* has a capacious onboard branch of the Galactic Library. In its wise memory, we shall plumb and doubtless find this trick they used – and the drawback that will help us neutralize it.

Alas, My rings, that will do little good for this mongrel stack of ill-matched parts.

While *Polkjhy* proceeds on nimble autopilot – shadowing the Earthship as we both plunge toward the transfer point – the realignment of executive power commences among crew-stacks who proved poor judgment by remaining excessively loyal to our former commander. Demotion and reassignment will suffice for some. Replacement of the Master Torus will do for others.

But as for poor Ewasx – you/we were the inspired invention of the old captain-leader. At best, our rings will be salvaged as replacements for soldiers wounded in combat against the Zang. At worst, they will be mulched.

Now am I grateful for the feral skills you learned as a sooner/savage/traeki. Your movements are admirably stealthy, My rings. Clearly, you know better than a Jophur how to hide.

As the hatch rolls smoothly back to place, let us quickly move in search of some quiet, sheltered place where we may contemplate the wax ... pondering the dilemma of survival.

ALVIN'S JOURNAL

'You'll get used to this sort of thing after a while.'

Those words, spoken by Gillian Baskin, still seem to echo down my hollow spines as I write down a few hasty impressions of our final moments near the Fractal World.

I had better hurry. Already I can feel the pressure on my hoonish nerves increase as the *Streaker* swoops and plunges along the threadlike 'domain boundaries' that curl inside a transfer point. Soon, this awful kind of motion sickness will make it futile to work. So let me quickly try to sort among the terrible things I have lately experienced.

Strangest of all was Dr. Baskin's voice, filled with such a deep resignation that she seemed more *Jijoan* than star god. Like one of our High Sages reading from the Sacred Scrolls – some passage foretelling inevitable tribulation. Somehow she made the impossible sound frighteningly plausible.

'You'll get used to this sort of thing ...'

While the transfer fields close in around me – as nausea sends chills and frickles up and down my shivering skin – I can only hope that never happens.

She said it less than a midura ago, while gazing back at our handiwork.

An accomplishment none of us sought.

A disaster that came about simply because we were there.

In fact, those milling about the Plotting Room watched *two* views of the Fractal World, depicted on giant screens – both of them totally different, and both officially 'true.' Speaking as a Jijo savage – one who got his impressions of spaceflight by reading Earthling books from the pre-Contact Twenty-Second Century – I found things rather confusing. For instance, many of those texts assumed Faster-Than-Light travel was impossible. Or else, in space-romance yarns, authors simply took FTL for granted. Either way, you could deal with events in a simple way. They happened when they happened. Every cause was followed by its effects, and that was that.

But the screen to my left showed time going backward!

My autoscribe explained it to me, and I hope I get this right. It seems that each microsecond, as *Streaker* flickered back into normal space from C Level, photons would strike the ship's aft-facing telescope, providing an image of the huge 'criswell structure' that got smaller and dimmer as we fled. The pictures grew *older*, too, as we outraced successive waves of light. By the contorted logic of Einstein, we were going back in time.

I stared, fascinated, as the massive habitat seemed to get healthier before my eyes. Damaged zones reknitted. The awful wound grew back together. And glittering sparks told of myriad converging refugee ships, apparently coming home.

The spectacle provoked each of my friends differently.

Huck laughed aloud. Ur-ronn snuffled sadly, and Pincer-Tip kept repeating 'gosh-osh-osh!'

I could not fault any of them for their reactions. The sequence was at once both poignantly lamentable and hilariously absurd.

Over to the right, Sara and Gillian watched a different set of images, caught by hyperwave each time we flickered *into* C Level. Here my impression was of queasy simultaneousness. This screen seemed to tell what was happening right now, back at the Fractal World. Time apparently moved forward, depicting the aftermath of our violent escape.

The effects flowing from each cause.

Of course things are really much more complicated. That picture kept wavering, for instance, like a draft version of some story whose author still wasn't sure yet what to commit to paper.

Sara explained it to me this way—

'Photons haul slow truths, Alvin, while speedy hyperwaves carry *probabilities*.'

So this image represented just the most *likely* scenario unfolding behind us. However slim, there remained a chance it wasn't true. Things might not be happening this way.

By God, Ifni, and the Egg, I still pray for that slim chance.

What we saw, through rippling static, was a harsh tale of rapid deterioration.

More than a single great laceration now maimed the great sphere. Its frail skin peeled and curled away from several newly slashed wounds. These fresh cracks spread, branching rapidly as we watched, each one spilling raw sunlight the color of urrish blood.

Hundreds of exterior spikes had already broken loose, tumbling end over end as more towering fragments toppled toward space with each passing moment. I could only guess how much worse things were *inside* the great shell. By now, had a million Jijo-sized windows shattered, exposing forests, steppes, and oceans to raw vacuum?

The hyperwave scene updated in fits and starts, sometimes appearing to backtrack or revise a former glimpse.

From one moment to the next, some feature of devastation that had been *here* suddenly shifted over *there*. No single detail seemed fixed or firmly determined. But the trend remained the same.

I felt claws dig into my back as little Huphu and the tytlal, Mudfoot, clambered onto opposite shoulders, rubbing against me, beckoning a song to ward off the sour mood. Partly from numb shock, I responded with my family's version of the Dirge for Unremarked Passing – an umble so ancient that it probably pre-dates hoonish Uplift, going back to before our brains could grasp the full potential of despair.

Roused by that low resonance, Dr. Baskin turned and glanced at my vibrating throat sac. I am told that starfaring humans do not like hoons very much, but Sara Koolhan whispered in her ear and Gillian nodded approvingly.

Clearly, she understood.

A few duras later, after I finished, the little spinning Niss holo-gram popped into place, hovering in midair nearby.

'Kaa reports that we are about ten minutes away from t-point insertion.'

Dr. Baskin nodded.

'Are there any changes in our entourage?'

Her digital aide seemed to give a casual, unconcerned twist.

'We are followed by a crowd of diverse vessels,' the machine voice replied. 'Some are robotic, a majority house oxygen-breathing refugees, bearing safe-passage emblems of the Retired Order of Life.

'Of course, all of them are keeping a wary distance from the Jophur battleship.'

The Niss paused for a moment or two, before continuing.

'Are you absolutely sure you want us to set course for Tanith?'

The tall woman shrugged.

'I'm still open to other suggestions. It seems we've tried every-thing else, and that includes hiding in the most obscure corner of the universe ... no offense, Alvin.'

'None taken,' I replied, since her depiction of Jijo was doubtless true. 'What is Tanith?'

The Niss Machine answered.

It is a planet, where there exists a sector headquarters of the Library Institute. The one nearest Earth. To this site Captain Creideiki would have taken our discoveries in the first place, if we had not fallen into a cascade of violence and treachery. Lacking other options, Dr. Baskin believes we must now fall back on that original plan.

'But didn't you already try surrendering to the Institutes? At that place called Wakka—'

'Oakka. Indeed, two years ago we evaded pursuit by merciless battle fleets in order to make that attempt. But the madness sweeping our civilization preceded us there too. Sworn monks of the monastic, bureaucratic brotherhoods abjured their oaths of neutrality, choosing instead to revert to older loyalties. Motivated in part by ancient grudges – or else the huge bounties offered for Streaker's *capture by various fanatical alliances – they attempted to seize the Earthship for their blood and clan relations.'*

'So the Institutes couldn't be trusted then. What's different this time?'

Dr. Baskin pointed to a smaller display screen.

'That is what's different, Alvin.'

It showed the Jophur battleship – the central fact of our lives now. The huge oblate warship clung to us like a bad smell, follow-ing closely ever since their earlier assault failed to disable *Streaker*. Even with Kaa at the helm, the dolphin crew thought it infeasible to lose them. You'd have better luck shaking off your shadow on a sunny day.

'Our orders are clear. Under no circumstances can we let one fac-tion snatch our data for themselves.'

'So instead we shall go charging straight into one of the busiest ports of Galaxy Two?'

The Niss sounded doubtful, if not outright snide. But Dr. Baskin showed no sign of reacting to its tone.

'Isn't that our best chance? To head for a crowded place, with lots of traffic and possibly ships big enough to balance that imposing cruiser out there? Besides, there *is* a possibility that Oakka was an exception. An aberration. Maybe officials at Tanith will remember their oaths.'

The Niss expressed doubt with an impolite sound.

'There is a slim chance of that. Or possibly sheer surprise might prompt action by the cautious majority of Galactic clans, who have so far kept static, frozen by indecision.'

'That's been our dream all along. And it could happen, if enough synthians and pargi and their allies have ships in the area. Why wouldn't they intercede, in support of tradition and the law?'

'Your optimism is among your greatest charms, Dr. Baskin – to imagine that the moderates can be swayed to make any sort of decision quickly, when commitment may expose them to mortal danger. By now it is quite clear to everyone that a Time of Changes is at hand. They are pondering issues of racial survival. Justice for wolflings will not take high priority.

'Far more likely, your abrupt appearance will provoke free-for-all combat above Tanith, making Kithrup seem like a mere skirmish. I assume you realize the armadas who are currently besieging Terra lie just two jumps away from Tanith? In less than a standard day they would likely converge—'

'Abating the siege of Earth? That sounds worthwhile.'

The Niss hologram tightened its clustered, spinning lines.

'We are dancing around the main problem, Dr. Baskin. Our destination is moot. The Jophur will not allow us to reach Tanith. Of that you can be sure.'

Sara Koolhan spoke up for the first time.

'Can they stop us? They tried once, and failed.'

'Alas, Sage Koolhan, our apparent invulnerability cannot last. The Jophur were taken by surprise, but by now they are surely scanning their onboard database, delving for the flaw in our wondrous armor.'

They referred to the gleaming mantle now blanketing Streaker's hull. As an ignorant Jijoan, I couldn't tell what made the coating so special, though I vividly recall the anxious time when swarms of machine entities sealed it around us – dark figures struggling enigmatically over our fate, without bothering to seek consent from a shipload of wolflings and sooners.

The final disputants were two sets of giant repair robots, those at the stern trying to harvest carbon from Streaker's hull for raw materials, and the other team busy transforming the star soot into a layer that shimmered like the glassy Spectral Flow.

Lightning seemed to pass between the groups. Meme-directive impulses, the Niss identified those flickering bursts, advising us not to watch, lest our brains become somehow infected. In a matter of duras, the contest ended without any machines being physically harmed. But one group must have abruptly had its 'mind changed.'

Abruptly united in purpose, both sets of robots fell to work, completing *Streaker*'s transformation just in time, before the first disintegrator ray struck.

'Who says there has to be a flaw?' Dr. Baskin asked. 'We seem to be unharmable, at least by long-range beams.'

She sounded confident, but I remember how shocked Gillian, Sara, Tsh't, and the others had seemed, to survive an instant after the attack began. Only the crippled engineer, Emerson d'Anite, grunted and nodded, as if he had expected something like this all along.

'*There are no perfect defenses,*' countered the Niss. '*Every variety of weapon has been logged and archived by the Great Library. If a technique seems surprising or miraculous, it could be because it was abandoned long ago for very good reasons. Once the Jophur find those reasons, our new shield will surely turn from an advantage into a liability.*'

The humans and dolphins clearly disliked this logic. I can't say I cared for it myself. But how could anyone refute it? Even we sooners know one of the basic truisms of life in the Five Galaxies—

If something isn't in the Library, it is almost certainly impossible.

Still, I'll never forget that time, just after the big construction robots finished their task and jetted away, leaving this battered ship shining in space, as uttergloss as any jewel.

Streaker turned to flee through the great hole in the Fractal World, and suddenly great spears of destructive light bathed her from several directions at once! Alarms blared and each ray of focused energy seemed to shove us outward with titanic force.

But we did not burn. Instead, a strange noise surrounded us, like the groaning of some deep-sea leviathan. Huck pulled in all her eyes. Pincer withdrew all five legs, and Ur-ronn coiled her long neck, letting out a low urrish howl.

All the instruments went crazy . . . and yet we did not burn!

Soon most of the crew agreed with the initial assessment of Hannes Suessi, who decreed that the disintegrator beams must be *faked*.

A showy demonstration, they must be meant to frighten off our enemies and let us escape. No other answer seemed to explain our survival!

That is, until the Jophur pounced on us a short time later, and their searing rays also vanished with the same mysterious groan.

Then we knew.

Someone had done us a favor . . . and we didn't even know who to thank. Or whether the blessing cloaked more misfortune, still to come.

A voice called over the intercom.

'*Transfer point insertion approaching in . . . thirty ssseconds.*'

Those in the Plotting Room turned to watch the forward viewer, looking ahead toward a tangled web of darkness – first in a series that would carry us far beyond Galaxy Four to distant realms my friends and I had barely heard of in legend and tales about gods. But my hoonish digestion was already anticipating the coming nausea. I remember thinking how much better it would suit me to be aboard my father's dross ship, pulling halyards and umbling with the happy crew, with Jijo's warm wind in my face and salt spray singing on the sails.

Back at the hyperwave display, I found another person less interested in where we were going than the place we were leaving behind. Emerson, the crippled engineer, who wore a rewq over his eyes and greeted me with a lopsided human smile. I answered by flapping my throat sac.

Blurry and wavering, the image of the Fractal World glimmered like an egg the size of a solar system, on the verge of spilling forth something young, hot, and fierce. Red sunlight shot through holes and crevices, while cruel sparks told of explosions vast enough to rock the entire structure, sending ripples crisscrossing the tormented sphere.

Emerson sighed, and surprised me by uttering a simple Anglic phrase, expressing an incredible thought.

'Well . . . easy come . . . easy go.'

Mudfoot chittered on my shoulder as *Streaker*'s engines cranked up to handle the stress of transfer. But our attention stayed riveted on the unlucky Fractal World.

The globe sundered all at once, along every fault line, dissolving into myriad giant curved shards, some of them tumbling toward black space, while others glided inward to a gaudy reunion.

Unleashed after half a billion years of tame servitude, the little star flared exuberantly, as if celebrating each new raft of infalling debris – its own robbed substance, now returning home again.

Free again, it blared fireworks at heaven.

My throat sac filled, and I began umbling a threnody . . . a hoonish death requiem for those lost at sea, whose heart-spines will never be recovered.

The chilling words of Gillian Baskin haunted me.

'*You'll get used to this after a while.*'

I shook my head, human style.

Get used to this?

Ifni, what have the Earthers already been through, to make *this* seem like just another day's work?

To think, I once gazed longingly at the stars, and hankered for adventure!

For the very first time, I understood one of the chief lessons preached by Jijo's oldest scrolls.

In this universe, the trickiest challenge of all is survival.

III

THE GREAT HARROWER

To our customers across the Five Galaxies—

The Sa'ent Betting Syndicate has temporarily suspended accepting wagers concerning the Siege of Earth. Although we still predict imminent collapse by the affiliated forces defending the wolfling homeworld, conditions have once again become too fluid for our dynamical scrying engines to project reasonable odds.

For those already participating in a betting pool, the odds remain fixed at: twenty-to-one for the planet's conquest within one solar orbit (three-quarters of a Tanith year); fourteen-to-one for surrender within one-quarter orbit; five-to-two in favor of a 'regrettable accident' which may render the ecosystem unstable and lead to effective organic extinction for the wolfling races; seven-to-two in favor of humans and their clients being forcibly adopted into indenture by one of the great clans currently besieging the planet, such as the Soro, Tandu, Klennath, or Jouourouou.

Despite these deceptively steady odds, several fluctuating factors actually contribute to a high level of uncertainty .

1) Betrayals and realignments continue among the mighty clans and alliances now pressing the siege. Their combined forces would have easily overwhelmed the human, Tymbrimi, and Thennanin defenders by now, if they could only agree how to distribute the resulting spoils. But instead, violent and unpredictable outbreaks of fighting among the besiegers (sometimes incited by clever Terran maneuvers) have slowed the approach to Earth and made odds-scrying more difficult than normal.

2) Political turmoil in the Five Galaxies has continued to flux with unaccustomed speed. For instance, a long-delayed assembly of the Coalition of Temperate Races has finally convened, with a remarkably abbreviated agenda – how to deal with the unbridled ambition shown lately by more fanatical Galactic alliances. Having dispensed

with preliminary formalities, the League may actually file official warnings with the War Institute within a Tanith year! Assembly of their coordinated battle fleet may commence just a year after that.

In addition to the League, several other loose confederations of 'moderate' clans have begun organizing. If such haste is maintained (and not disrupted yet again by Soro diplomacy) it would demonstrate unprecedented agility by the nonzealous portion of oxy-society.

Naturally, this will come about too late to save Earth, but it may lead to rescue of some residual human populations, after the fact.

3) No one has reported sighting the infamous dolphin-crewed starship for half a Tanith year. If, against all odds, the fugitives were somehow to safely convey their treasures to an ideal neutral sanctuary – or else prove the relics to be harmless – this crisis might abate before igniting universal warfare throughout oxygen-breathing civilization. This would, of course, end our present policy of accepting bets only on a cash-in-advance basis.

4) Commercial star traffic, already disrupted by the so-called 'Streaker Crisis,' has lately suffered from 'agitated conditions' on all interspacial levels. At least thirty of the most important transfer points have experienced thread strains. While the Institutes attribute this to 'abnormal weather in hyperspace,' some perceive it as yet another portent of a coming transition.

5) The continued upswell of socioreligious fanaticism – including sudden resurgence of interest in the Cult of Ifni – has had a deleterious effect on the business of bookies and oddsmakers all across the Five Galaxies. Because of added expenses (defending our own settlements from attack by fleets of zealous predeterminists) we have been forced to increase the house cut on all wagers.

Even the Sa'ent Betting Syndicate cannot continue business as usual in the face of a prophesied Time of Changes ...

Uh-oh, he thought. *This is gonna be a rough one*.

Harry nulled the guidance computer in order to protect its circuits during transition. Window covers snapped into place and he buckled himself in for the shift to another region of E Space. One that had been declared 'off-limits' for a very long time.

Well, it serves me right for volunteering. Wer'Q'quinn calls this a 'special assignment.' But the farther I go, the more it seems like a suicide mission.

At first nothing seemed to be happening. His official instruments were useless or untrustworthy, so Harry watched his own little makeshift *verimeter*. It consisted of an origami swan that shuddered while perched on a tiny needle made of pure metal that had been skimmed directly from the surface of a neutron star. Or so claimed the vendor who sold it to him in the Kazzkark bazaar. Nervously, he watched the scrap of folded paper twitch and stretch. His mind could only imagine what might be going on outside, with objectivity melting all around his little survey ship.

Harry's jittery hands scratched the fur of his neck and chest. The swan quivered, as if trying to remember how to fly ...

There came a sudden dropping sensation. The contents of his stomach lurched. Several sharp bumps followed, then violent rocking motions, like a boat swept by a storm-tossed sea. He gripped the armrests. Straps dug fiercely into his lap and shoulders.

A peculiar tremor jolted the deck under his bare feet – the distinct hum of a reality anchor automatically deploying. An unnerving sound, since it only happened when normal safety measures were strained near their limits. Sometimes an anchor was the last thing preventing random causality winds from flipping your vessel against shoals of unreified probability ... or turning your body into something it would rather not be.

Well ... *sometimes* it worked.

If only there was a way to use TV cameras here, and see what's going on.

Alas, for reasons still not fathomed by Galactic savants, living beings entering E Space could only make sense of events firsthand, and then at their own considerable risk.

Fortunately, just as Harry feared his last meal was about to join the dishes and cutlery on the floor, the jerky motions began damping away. In a matter of seconds things settled to a gentle swaying.

He glanced again at the improvised verimeter. The paper swan looked steady ... though both wings seemed to have acquired a new set of complex folds that he did not remember being there before.

Harry cautiously unbuckled himself and stood up. Shuffling ahead with hands spread wide for balance, he went to the forward quadrant and cautiously lifted one of the louvers.

He gasped, jumping back in fright.

The scout platform hung suspended – apparently without support – high over a vast landscape!

Swallowing hard, he took a second look.

His point of view swung gently left, then right, like the perspective of a hanged man, taking in a vast, blurry domain of unfathomable distances and tremendous heights. Gigantic spires, sheer and symmetrical, could be dimly made out beyond an enveloping haze, rising past him from a flat plain far below.

Harry watched breathlessly until he felt sure the surface was drawing no closer. There was no sense of falling. Something seemed to be holding him at this altitude.

Time to find out what it was. He worked his way around the observation deck, and at the rearmost pane he saw what prevented a fatal plummet.

The station hung at one end of a narrow, glowing thread, extruded from a hull orifice he'd never seen before. But a familiar blue-striped pattern suggested it must in fact be the reality anchor, manifesting itself this time in a particularly handy way.

At the other end, high overhead, the anchor seemed to be hooked into the lip of a flat plane stretching away horizontally to the right. To his left, an even greater expanse of open sky spread beyond the half-plane. He had an impression of yet more linear boundaries, far higher still.

At least the station hadn't changed much in physical appearance during passage. Metaphorical stilt legs still hung beneath the oblong globe, waving slowly in space. Something seemed to be wrong with vision, though. Harry rubbed his eyes but the problem wasn't there. Somehow, all features beyond the windows appeared blurred. He couldn't recognize the mountainous columns, for instance, though the grotesque things felt somehow familiar, filling his mind with musty impressions of childhood.

This place was unlike anything he'd experienced since personality profile machines on Tanith had selected him to be the first neo-chimpanzee trained as a Navigation Institute Observer. He knew better than to ask any of the onboard programs for help figuring it out.

'The region of E Space where you'll be heading is seldom visited for

good reasons,' Wer'Q'quinn had said before Harry set off this time. '*Many of the traits that patrons instill in their clients, through Uplift – to help them become stable, rational, goal-oriented starfarers – turn into liabilities in a realm where all notions of predictability vanish.*'

Recalling this, Harry shook his head.

'Well, I can't say I wasn't warned.'

He turned his head to the left and commanded – 'Pilot mode.'

With a faint 'pop' the familiar rotating *P* materialized nearby.

'*At your service, Harvey.*'

'That's Harry,' he corrected for the umpteenth time, with a sigh. 'I'm getting no blind spot agoraphobia, so you might as well open the shutters the rest of the way.'

The ship complied, and at once Harry winced at a juxtaposition of odd colors, even though they were muted by the strange haze.

'Thanks. Now please run a scan to see if this metaphorical space will allow us to fly.'

'*Checking.*'

There followed a long silence as Harry crossed his fingers. Flight made movement so much easier ... especially when you were hanging by a rope over miles and miles of apparently empty space. He imagined he could hear the machine click away, nudging drive units imperceptibly to see which would work here, and which were useless or even dangerous. Finally, the rotating *P* spun to a conclusion.

'*Some sort of flight appears to be possible, but I cannot pin it down. None of the allaphorical techniques in my file will do the trick. You will have to think of something original.*'

Harry shrugged. That made up a large part of why he was here.

'Have you located our watch zone?'

'*I sense a narrow tube of normal space not far away from us, in figurative units. Subjectively, you should observe a glowing Avenue "below" ... somewhere in the fourth quadrant.*'

Harry went to the window indicated and looked down among the blurry, giant shapes.

'Ye-e-es, I think I see it.' He could barely discern a faint, shining line. 'We better try to get closer.'

'*Assuming you find a way.*'

'Aye,' he agreed. 'There's the rub.'

Harry anxiously ran his fingers through his chin fur and scalp, wishing it hadn't been so long since he had had a good grooming. Back on Horst, where he and his distracted parents were the only chimps on a whole planet, it had always seemed simply a matter of personal hygiene to keep the insidious dust out of your pelt. Only during school days on Earth did Harry learn what a sybaritic art form it could be, to have one or more others stroke, comb, brush, and tease your hair, tugging the roots *just* right, till the follicles almost screamed with pleasure. Looking back on those days, the warm physical contact of mutual grooming was the one thing he missed most about his own kind.

Too bad his partners also *talked* so much – from banter and gossip to inquiries about every personal foible – the sorts of things Harry could never be comfortable discussing. His awkward lack of openness struck Earth chims as aloof, even condescending, while Harry found them overly prying. Invariably, he remained an outsider, never achieving full entry or intimacy in the college grooming circles.

Harry knew he was procrastinating, but he felt uncertain where to start.

'*So you are concerned about rumors of unusual detours in hyperspace and disturbed transfer points,*' Wer'Q'quinn had replied, after Harry returned from his last mission. '*These phenomena are well outside your jurisdiction. But now it seems that a confluence of factors makes it necessary to confide in you.*'

'Let me guess,' Harry had asked. 'The disturbances are so bad, they can be observed even in E Space.'

'*Your hunch is astute,*' Wer'Q'quinn agreed, snapping a GalTwo approval-punctuation with his beak. '*I can see your recruitment was not a forlorn gamble, but rather evidence of my own deep insight, proving my value to the Institute and my worthiness of rapid promotion.*

'*Your next patrol begins in one-point-three standard days.*'

After allowing for briefings, that left just enough time for a bath and a good sleep in his barracks cubby. He had hoped for a longer rest. There was a foruni masseuse in the bazaar whose instinctive understanding of other species' musculoskeletal systems made the agile creature expert at loosening the kinks in Harry's spine ... Alas.

While nervously combing his chin, a frayed fingernail yanked some gnarly hair, making Harry twinge. He held the strand up for a close look.

It's a good thing chimp hair doesn't keep growing longer, like on the faces of human males who don't depilate. Back on Horst, he had seen Probsher shamen whose patriarchal beards lengthened over the years till they stretched nearly all the way ...

Harry blinked, realizing what his subconscious was driving at. He turned quickly and pressed against the rearmost window, peering at the blue cable – which dangled the station over an immeasurable drop. Stretching upward, it seemed almost to disappear, aiming toward one edge of that far-off horizontal plane.

'Pilot,' he said. 'I want to see if we can play out the pseudolength of our reality anchor. Can we unreel any more?'

'*It is already at maximum extension,*' came the reply.

Harry cursed. It had seemed a good idea ...

'Wait a minute,' he muttered. 'Don't be too literal. Try it another way. All right, so maybe we can't feed the anchor out any more. But tickle the damn thing anyway, will you? Maybe we can change its length some other way. By stretching it, maybe. Or causing it to *grow*.'

He knew he was being vague. Flexible thought sometimes meant working your way around an idea's blurry outlines.

'*I will try, and let you know,*' the computer replied.

There followed a series of faint humming sounds, then a sudden jar as the platform dropped, weightless again just long enough to make fear erupt in his chest. It jerked short abruptly, sending Harry staggering against his command couch, feeling his stomach keep falling.

'H-h-h-' He tried again. 'W-Well?'

'*The rules of topology here seem to allow a wide range of flexible conformal mappings. Practically speaking, this means the cable can stretch, adjusting to any length, at almost any speed desired. Congratulations, Commander Harms. You seem to have found a way to maneuver in the subjective vertical.*'

Harry ignored the suspicion of sarcasm, which might be imagined. At least this trap had proved easier to escape than the banana peel mesa.

Still, I'll only feel safe after learning the metaphorical rules that apply here. There were reasons why patrol craft seldom entered this region. Many that tried never returned.

'Start lowering us then,' he commanded. 'Gently.'

The flat half-plane overhead receded as the 'ground' approached at a steady clip, reminding him of something – either the inexorable nature of destiny ... or else an oncoming train.

While at Kazzkark, there had been time to enquire about the Siege of Earth.

He shouldn't be interested. Having dedicated his life to the monastic Navigation Institute, Harry was supposed to forsake all prior loyalties of kinship or patron line. But few sophonts could ever transfer natural sympathies completely. Institute workers often discreetly sought news of 'home.'

When Harry found himself with an extra hour between briefings, he ventured to the bazaar, where a Le'4-2vo gossip merchant accepted his generous fee and showed him to an osmium-lined room containing a masked Library tap.

It didn't take long to find the topic – which had risen three more significance levels since the last time he checked – under the heading: 'Major News – Quasi Current Events.' The latest word from Galaxy Two was dire.

Terran forces and their few allies had been forced to retreat from the Canaan colonies, which were now provisionally ruled by a Soro admiral.

The beautiful dolphin-settled world of Calafia had been invaded. A third of that water-covered globe was taken over by a mixed squadron led by one faction of the Brothers of the Night, while a different clique from that same race of fanatical warriors fought bitterly to 'liberate' the rest.

Earth itself was enveloped and frail Terragens forces would have crumbled by now, but for help from the Tymbrimi and Thennanin ... and the way enemies kept fragmenting and fighting among themselves. Even so, the end seemed near.

In a footnote, Harry saw that the tiny Earthling leasehold on Horst had been occupied ... by the horrible Tandu.

Shivers ran down his spine. There was mention of an evacuation by the local staff, so perhaps Marko and Felicity had time to flee with the other anthropologists. But somehow Harry doubted it. His parents were obsessive. It would be just like them to stay, assuming that the invaders would never bother a pair of scientists doing nonmilitary work.

Even if all the technicians and Terraformers left, where would that leave the natives? Human tribes that had turned their 'probationary' mental status into license to escape the rigors of modern society, experimenting instead with countless diverse social forms – many of them imitating one totem species or another. Some groups purposely modeled themselves on the matriarchal hive societies of bees, while others mimicked wolf packs, or the lion's pride, or marriage patterns found only in strange, pre-Contact novels. Most of the little Probsher bands had little interest in technology or Galactopolitics.

They would be helpless meat to predatory warriors like the Tandu.

Fleeing the gossip merchant's shelter, Harry had tried to wipe the news from his mind. Soon victorious *eatees* would be scrapping over the remains of fallen Earthclan. With neutral governance dissolving all over the Five Galaxies, it should be simple to coerce the Uplift Institute, getting humans, chims, and dolphins declared open for adoption. All three races would be parceled out like spoils of war, each to a new 'patron,' for genetic-social guidance across the next hundred thousand years.

That is, if we don't 'accidentally' die off during the confusion. It had happened before, nearly every time a wolfling race appeared, claiming to have raised itself to sapience without help from any other. The amazing thing was that Earthclan had lasted this long.

Well, at least gorillas are safe. The Thennanin aren't bad masters ... assuming you must have a master.

I wonder who will get us chims, as part of the bargain?

Harry's teeth bared in a grimace.

They may find us more trouble than we're worth.

During his next briefing with Wer'Q'quinn, he had blurted a direct question. 'All these hyperspatial anomalies and disturbances ... are they happenin' on account of the war over Earth?'

Instead of rebuking Harry for showing interest in his old clan, the Survey official waved a suckered tendril obligingly.

'Young colleague, it is important to remember that one of the great mentational dangers of sapient life is egotism – the tendency to see all events in the context of one's own self or species. It is natural that you perceive the whole universe as revolving around the troubles of your former clan, little and insignificant as it is.

'Now I admit recent events may appear to support that supposition. The announcement of possible Progenitor relics – discovered in a secret locale by the infamous dolphin ship – precipitated open warfare among the most warlike oxygen-breathing clans. Trade patterns unravel as some alliances seize control over local transfer points. However, let me assure you that the energy fluxes released by the battles so far have been much too small to affect underlying cosmic links.'

'But the coincidence in timing!'

'You mistake cause for effect. The angst and fury that now swirl around wolflings had been building for centuries before humans contacted our culture. Ever since the Fututhoon Episode, a nervous peace has been maintained mostly by fear, while belligerent parties armed and prepared for the next phase. Alas for your unlucky homefolk, it is an inauspicious time for innocents to stumble onto the star lanes.'

Harry blinked for several seconds, then nodded. 'You're talkin' about a Time of Changes.'

'Indeed. We in the Institutes have known for almost a million years that a new era of great danger and disruption was coming. The signs include increased volatility in relations between the oxygen and hydrogen life orders ... and there were outbreaks of spasmodic exponential reproduction within the Machine Order – violations requiring savage measures of suppression. Even among clans of our own Civilization of Five Galaxies, we have seen a rise of religious fervor.'

Harry recalled the proselytes swarming the main avenues of Kazzkark, preaching diverse obscure interpretations of ancient prophecy.

'Bunch of superstitious nonsense,' he had muttered.

To his surprise Wer'Q'quinn agreed with an emphatic snapping of his beak.

'That which is loudest is not always representative,' his boss explained. 'Most species and clans would rather live and let live, developing their own paths to wisdom and allowing destiny to take its own time arriving. Who *cares* whether the Progenitors are going to return in physical form, or as spiritual embodiments, or by remanifesting themselves into the genome of some innocent pre-sapient race? While fanatical alliances clash bitterly over dogma, a majority of oxygen breathers just wish to keep making steady progress toward their own species-enlightenment. Eventually all answers will be found when each race joins its patrons and ancestors in retirement ... and then transcendence ... following the great ingathering Embrace of Tides.'

There it was again – Harry thought at the time. The basic assumption underlying nearly all Galactic religious faiths. That salvation was attainable by *species*, not individual organic beings.

Except for that Skiano missionary – the one with the parrot on its shoulder. It was pushing a different point of view. A real heresy!

'So, young colleague,' Wer'Q'quinn had finished. 'Try to picture how disturbing it was – to fanatics and moderates alike – when your hapless dolphin cousins broadcast images that seemed to show Progenitor spacecraft floating through one of the *flattest* parts of Galactic spacetime! The implications of that one scene appeared to threaten a core belief-thread shared by nearly all oxygen breathers ...'

At that point Harry was riveted and attentive. Only then, as luck had it, an aide barged in to report that yet another t-point was unraveling in the Gorgol Sector of Galaxy Five. Suddenly Wer'Q'quinn had no time for abstract discussions with junior underlings. Amid the ensuing flurry of activity, Harry was sent to the Survey Department to finish his briefing. There was never a chance to ask the old snake about his intriguing remark.

What core belief? What about the Streaker's *discovery has everybody so upset?*

At last the platform settled down to 'earth.'

The surface was relatively soft. His vessel's spindly legs took up the load with barely a jounce.

Well, so far so good. The ground didn't swallow me up. A herd of parasitic memes hasn't converged yet, trying to take over my mind, or to sell me products that haven't been available for eons.

Harry always hated when that happened.

He looked warily across a wide, flat expanse covered with limp, fluffy cylinders. They looked like droopy, slim-barreled cactuses, all jumbled loosely against each other as far as the eye could see. He took over manual controls and used a stilt-leg to prod the nearest clump. They squished underfoot easily, rebounding slowly after he backed off.

'Can we retract our reality anchor now?' he asked the pilot.

'No need. The anchor is restored to its accustomed niche.'

'Then what is that?' Harry asked, pointing to the blue cable, still rising vertically toward the sky.

'The ropelike metaphor has become a semipermanent structure. We can leave it in place, if you wish.'

Harry peered up the stretched cord, rubbing his chin.

'Well, it might offer a way out of here if we have to beat a hasty retreat. Just note this position and let's get going.'

The scout station set out, striding across the plain of fuzzy tubes. Meanwhile, Harry kept moving from window to window, peering nervously, wondering how this region's famed lethality would first manifest itself.

Rearing up on all sides, at least a dozen of the slender, immensely tall towers loomed in the background. Some of them seemed to have square cross sections while others were rectangular or oval. He even thought he perceived a rigid *formality* to their placement, as if each stood positioned on a grid, some fixed distance apart.

Harry soon realized the strange blurriness was not due to any obstructing 'haze' but to a flaw in vision itself. Sight appeared to be a short-range sense in this patch of E Space.

Great. All I need is partial blindness in a place where reality literally can sneak up on you and bite.

It should be a short march to where he last saw the Avenue. Awkwardly at first, Harry accelerated his station across the plain of fluffy growths, all bent and twined like tangled grass. These 'plants' didn't wave in a breeze, like the saw-weed of Horst. Still, they reminded him somehow of that endless steppe where dusty skies flared each dawn like a diffuse torch, painful to the eyes. The sort of country his ancestors had sniffed at disdainfully before returning to the trees, ages ago on Earth. Sensibly, they left scorching skies and cutting grass to their idiot cousins – primates who lacked even the good sense to escape the noonday sun, and later went on to become humans.

According to the Great Library, Horst had been a pleasant world once, with a rich, diverse ecosystem. But millennia ago – before Earthlings developed their own starships and stumbled on Galactic culture – something terrible had happened to quite a few planets in Tanith Sector. By the ancient Code of the Progenitors, natural ecosystems were sacrosanct, but the Civilization of Five Galaxies suffered lapses now and then. In the Fututhoon Episode, hundreds of worlds were ravaged by shortsighted colonization, leaving them barren wildernesses.

Predictably, there followed a reactionary swing toward manic zealotry. Different factions cast blame, demanding a return to the true path of the Progenitors.

But *which* true path? Several billion years would age the best-kept records. Noise crept in over the eons, until little remained from the near mythical race that started it all. Speculation substituted for fact, dogma for evidence. Moderates struggled to soothe hostility among fanatical alliances whose overreaction to the Fututhoon chaos now promised a different kind of catastrophe.

Into this delicate situation Earthlings appeared, at first offering both distraction and comic relief with their wolfling antics. Ignorant, lacking social graces, humans and their clients irked some great star clans just by existing. Moreover, having uplifted chimpanzees and dolphins before Contact, humans had to be classified as 'patrons,' with the right to lease colonies, jumping ahead of many older species.

'Let them prove themselves first on catastrophe planets,' went the consensus. If Earthlings showed competence at reviving sick biospheres, they might win better worlds later. So humans and their clients labored on Atlast, Garth, and even poor Horst, earning grudging respect as planet managers.

But there were costs.

A desert world can change you, Harry thought, recalling Horst and feeling abruptly sad for some reason. He went down to the galley, fixed a meal, and brought it back to the observation deck, eating slowly as the endless expanse of twisted, fuzzy tubes rolled by, still pondering that eerie sense of familiarity.

His thoughts drifted back to Kazzkark, where a tall proselyte accosted him with strange heresies. The weird Skiano with a parrot on its shoulder, who spoke of Earth as a sacred place – whose suffering offered salvation to the universe.

'Don't you see the parallels? Just as Jesus and Ali and Reverend Feng had to be martyred in order for human souls to be saved, so the sins of all oxygen-breathing lifeforms can only be washed clean by

sacrificing something precious, innocent, and unique. That would be your own homeworld, my dear chimpanzee brother!'

It seemed a dubious honor, and Harry had said so, while eyeing possible escape routes through the crowd. But the Skiano seemed relentless, pushing its vodor apparatus, so each meaningful flash of its expressive eyes sent a translation booming in Harry's face.

'For too long sapient beings have been transfixed by the past – by the legend of the Progenitors! – a mythology that offers deliverance to species, but nothing for the individual! Each race measures its progress along the ladder of Uplift – from client to patron, and then through noble retirement into the tender Embrace of Tides. But along the way, how many trillions of lives are sacrificed? Each one unique and precious. Each the temporal manifestation of an immortal soul!'

Harry knew the creature's eye twinkle was the natural manner of Skiano speech. But it lent eerie passion each time the vodor pealed a ringing phrase.

'Think about your homeworld, oh, noble chimpanzee brother! Humans are wolflings who reached sapience without Uplift. Isn't that a form of virgin birth? Despite humble origins, did not Earthlings burst on the scene amid blazing excitement and controversy, seeing things that had remained unseen? Saying things that heretofore no one dared say?

'Do you Terrans suffer now for your uniqueness? For the message that streams from that lovely blue world, even as it faces imminent crucifixion? A message of hope for all living things?'

Even as a crowd of onlookers gathered, the Skiano's arms had raised skyward.

'Fear not for your loved ones, oh, child of Earth.

'True, they face fire and ruin in days to come. But their sacrifice will bring a new dawn to all sapients – yea, even those of other life orders! The false idols that have been raised to honor mythical progenitors will be smashed. The Embrace of Tides will be exposed as a false lure. All hearts will turn at last to a true true faith, where obedience is owed.

'Toward numinous Heaven – abode of the one eternal and all-loving God.'

In response, the bright-feathered parrot flapped its wings and squawked *'Amen!'*

Many onlookers glowered upon hearing the Progenitors called 'mythical.' Harry felt uncomfortable as the visible focus of the proselyte's attention. If this kept up, there could be martyrs, all right! Only the august reputation of Skianos in general seemed to hold some of the crowd back.

In order to calm the situation, Harry wound up reluctantly accepting a *mission* from the Skiano, agreeing to be a message bearer ... in the unlikely event that his next expedition brought him in contact with an angel of the Lord.

It was about an hour later – subjective ship time – that a blue **M** popped into place a little to his left.

'*Monitor mode engaged, Captain Harms,*' the slightly prissy voice announced. '*I take pleasure to announce that the Avenue is coming into range. It can be observed through the forward quadrant.*'

Harry stood up.

'Where? I don't ...'

Then he saw it, and exhaled a sigh. There, emerging out of the strange haziness, lay a shining ribbon of speckled light. The Avenue twisted across the foreground like a giant serpent, emerging from the murk on his left and vanishing in obscurity to his right. In a way, it reminded Harry of the undulating 'sea monster' he had witnessed during his last survey trip, near the banana-peel mesa. Only that had been just a meme creature – little more than an extravagant idea, an embodied notion – while *this* was something else entirely.

The Avenue did not conform to the allaphorical rules of E Space. Strictly speaking, it consisted of everything that was *not* E Space.

Because of that, cameras might perceive it. The tech people at NavInst had loaded his vessel with sensor packages to place at intervals along the shining tube, then retrieve later on his way back to base. Ideally, the data might help Wer'Q'quinn's people foretell hyperspatial changes during the current crisis.

He pressed a button and felt a small tremor as the first package deployed.

Now, should he turn left, and start laying more instruments in that direction? Or right? There seemed no reason to choose one way over the other.

Well, he was still an officer of the law. Harry's other job was to patrol E Space and watch for criminal activity.

'Computer, do you detect signs anybody's been through this area lately?'

'*I am scanning. Interlopers would have to travel alongside the Avenue in order to reach an intersection with Galaxy Four. Any large vessel piercing the tube, or even passing nearby, would leave ripple signs, whatever its allaphorical shape at the time.*'

The platform nosed closer to the shining tube of brightness. Harry had glimpsed the Avenue many times while on patrol, but never this close. Here it appeared rather narrow, only about twice the height of the station itself. The tube shone with millions of tiny sparks, set amid a deep inner blackness.

The narrow, snakelike volume was filled with stars ... and much more. Within that twisty cylinder lay the entire universe Harry knew – planets, suns, all five linked galaxies.

It was a topological oddity that might have looked, to its long-extinct first discoverers, like a wonderful way to get around relativity's laws. All one needed was an intersection near the planetary system one was in, and another near one's destination. The technique of entering and leaving E Space could be found in any Galactic Library branch.

But E Space was a world of unpredictability, metapsychological weirdness, and even representational absurdities. Keeping the Avenue in view until you came to some point near your destination could entail a long journey, or a very short one. Distances and relationships kept changing.

Assuming a traveler found a safe exit point, and handled transition well, he might emerge where he wanted to go. That is, if it turned out he ever left home in the first place! One reason most sophonts hated E Space was the screwy way causality worked there. You *could* cancel yourself out, if you weren't careful. Observers like Harry found it irksome to return from a mission, only to learn they no longer existed, and never really had at all.

Harry didn't much approve of E Space – an attitude NavInst surely measured in his profile. Yet, they must have had reasons to train him for this duty.

The platform began zigging and zagging alongside the Avenue, occasionally stopping to bend lower on its stilts, bringing instruments to bear like a dog sniffing at a spoor. Nursing patience, Harry watched strange nebulae drift past, within the nearby cylindrical continuum.

A bright yellow star appeared close to the nearby tube edge, against a black, star-flecked background. It looked almost close enough to touch as his vessel moved slowly past. *I guess there's a finite chance that's Sol, with Earth floating nearby, a faint speck in the cosmos. The odds are only about a billion to one against.*

At last, the station stopped. The slanted letter seemed to spin faster.

'*I note the near passage of three separate ship wakes. The first came this way perhaps a year ago, and the second not long after, following its trail.*'

'A pursuit?' This caught his interest. For the spoor to have lasted so long testified how little traveled this region was ... and perhaps how desperate the travelers were, to pass this way.

'What about the third vessel?'

'*That one is more recent. A matter of just a few subjective-duration days. And there is something else.*'

Harry nervously grabbed his thumbs. 'Yes?'

'*From the wake, it seems this latter vessel belongs to the Machine Order of Life.*' Harry frowned.

'A machine? In E Space? But how could it navigate? Or even see where it ...' He shook his head. 'Which way did it go?'

'*To the figurative left ... the way we are now facing.*' Harry paced on the floor. His orders from Wer'Q'quinn were clear. He must lay the cameras where they might peer from E Space back into more normal continua, offering NavInst techs a fresh perspective on the flux of forces perturbing the Five Galaxies. And yet, he was also sworn to check out suspicious activities ...

'*Your orders, Captain Harms?*'

'Follow them!' he blurted before the decision was clear in his own mind.

'*Sorry. I am not programmed ...*'

Harry cursed. 'Engage pilot mode!'

Almost before the cursive *P* popped into place, he pointed.

'That way. Quickly! If we hurry we still might catch them!'

The platform jerked, swinging to the right.

'*Aye aye, Hoover. Off we go. Tallyho!*'

Harry didn't even grimace this time. The program was irritating, but never at the expense of function. Even Tymbrimi usually knew where to limit a joke, thank Ifni. The station jogged onward in a quick eight-legged lope across the savannah of fuzzy, cactuslike growths.

To his left the Avenue swept by, a glittering tube containing everything that was real.

SARA

Things got pretty complicated right after *Streaker* began navigating the snarled innards of the transfer point.

From his liquid-filled chamber next door, Kaa thrashed muscular flukes, churning a foamy froth while protesting aloud.

'*It'sss too damned crowded in here!*'

Sara knew he wasn't complaining about *Streaker*'s cramped bridge, but the twisted labyrinth outside the ship – a maze of stringlike interspatial boundaries, looping and spiraling through every possible dimension, like the warped delirium of some mad carnival ride designer.

The t-point nexus *was* rather crowded. During any normal

transfer, one might glimpse a few distant, glimmering dots amid the gnarled threads, and know that other ships were plying the same complex junction linking far-flung stars. But this time it felt like plunging through a tangled jungle, with countless fireflies strung out along every branch and vine.

Instrument panels flared amber warnings as Kaa repeatedly had to maneuver around large vessels moving ponderously along the same slender path. Margins were narrow, and the dolphin pilot skimmed by some giant cruisers so closely that Sara caught brief, blurry glimpses in a viewer set to zero magnification. Turbulent ship wakes made *Streaker* buck like a skittish mount. Her straining engines moaned, gripping the precious thread for dear life.

Sara overheard Gillian's awed comment.

'All these starcraft *can't* be running away from the Fractal World!'

The Niss Machine answered, having managed to regain some of its accustomed saucy tone.

'*Obviously not, Dr. Baskin. Only about a million other vessels are using trajectories similar to ours, fleeing the same catastrophe that drove us into panicky exodus. That is but a small fraction of the population currently thronging this dimensional matrix. All the rest entered from other locales. Library records show that this particular thread-nexus accepts inward funnelings from at least a hundred points in normal space, scattered across Galaxy Four.*'

Sara blinked at the thought of so many ships, most of them far bigger than poor *Streaker*, all in an Egg-blessed hurry to get wherever-whenever they were heading.

'I – I thought Galaxy Four was supposed to be deserted.'

That was the image she had grown with. An entire vast galactic wheel, nearly void of sapient life. Hadn't her own ancestors come slinking this way in camouflaged sneakships, evading a fierce quarantine in order to settle on forbidden Jijo?

'*Deserted, yes. But only by two of the great Orders of Life, Sage Koolhan. By machine intelligences and oxygen-breathing starfarers. The migrational treaty did not require evacuation by members of other orders. And yet, from what we are witnessing right now, it would not be far-fetched to suggest that a more general abandonment has commenced.*'

Sara let out a soft grunt of comprehension.

'The inhabitants of the Fractal World—'

'*Were officially members of the Retired Order, basking in the gentle tidal rub of their carefully tended private sun, quietly refining their racial spirits in preparation for the next step.*

'*A step that some of them now seem ready to attempt.*'

'What do you mean?' asked Gillian.

'*It is best illustrated visually. Please observe.*'

One of the major screens came alight with a wavering image – greatly magnified – of several dozen ragged-looking vessels flying in convoy formation, skating along the shimmering verge of a transfer thread. As the telescopic scene gained better focus, Sara noted that the ships' rough outlines resulted from their jagged coverings – a jumble of corrugation and protruding spikes. The very opposite of streamlining.

So, the fractal geometry of the fallen criswell structure carries on, even down to the small scale of their lifeboats, she realized. *I wonder how far it continues. To the flesh on their bodies? To their living cells?*

The portrayal magnified, zooming toward the bow of the lead vessel. There, Sara and her companions in the Plotting Room saw a glyphic symbol that seemed to shimmer in its own light – consisting of several nested, concentric rings.

Even a Jijoan savage quickly recognized the sigil of the Retired Order.

'*Now watch what I have observed several times already. These refugees from the Fractal World are preparing to declare a momentous decision.*'

Sara felt Emerson approach to stand close by. Quietly unassuming, the tall wounded man took her left hand while they both stood watching a fateful transition.

The foremost craggy-hulled ship appeared to shudder. Wavelets of energy coursed its length, starting from the stern and ultimately converging toward the bright symbol on its prow. For a few moments, the glare became so intense that Sara had to shield her eyes.

The glow diminished just as rapidly. When Sara looked again, the glyph had been transformed. Gone were the circles. In their place lay a simple joining of two short line segments, meeting at a broad angle, like a fat triangle missing its connecting base.

'*The sign of union,*' pronounced the Niss Machine, its voice somewhat hushed. '*Two destinies, meeting at one hundred and four degrees.*'

Gillian Baskin nodded in appreciation.

'Ah,' was all the older woman said.

Sara thought, *I hate it when she does that.* Now it behooved her to ask for an explanation.

But events accelerated before she could inquire what the mysterious change in emblems meant. As the camera shifted, they witnessed several more refugee ships undergoing identical transformations in rapid succession, joining the leader in assuming the two-legged symbol. All these separated from their erstwhile companions to form a distinct flotilla that began edging ahead, as if now eager to seek a new destiny. At the next transfer thread junction, they flared with ecstatic levels of probability discharge and leaped across the narrow gap, bound for Ifni-knew-where.

The remaining refugees weren't finished changing and dividing. Again, ripples of light shimmered along the hulls of several huge ships, which began losing some of their jagged outlines. Hulls that had been jumbles of overlapping spikes seemed to melt and flow, then recoalesce into smoother, more uniform shapes ... the familiar symmetrical arrangement of hyperdrive flanges used by normal vessels in the Civilization of Five Galaxies.

Like before, each metamorphosis concluded in a dazzling burst at the foremost end. Only this time, when the glare faded, Sara saw another symbol replacing the nest of concentric rings – a rayed spiral glyph. The same one *Streaker* carried on her bow.

'These others, apparently, do not consider their racial spirits advanced enough yet for transcendence. They, too, have chosen to surrender their retired status, but this time in order to rejoin the society of ambitious, fractious, starfaring oxygen breathers.

'Perhaps they feel there is unfinished business they must take care of before resuming the Embrace of Tides.'

Gillian nodded soberly.

'That unfinished business may be us.'

She turned toward the bridge. 'Kaa! Be sure to stay away from any ship bearing a Galactic emblem!'

From the water-filled control room came a warbling sigh in complex Trinary – the expressive, poetical language of neo-dolphins that Sara had only just begun to learn. Rhythmic squeals and pops seemed to voice resigned irony, and several of those in the Plotting Room chuckled in appreciation of the pilot's wit.

All Sara made out was a single elementary phrase—

* ... *except the one biting our tail!* *

Of course. There was already one ship – bearing the rayed spiral crest – that wouldn't be shaken easily. Sticking to the Earthling vessel like a shadow – far closer than most navigators would call safe – the Jophur dreadnought loomed in the rear-facing viewer. Without the new, dense layers coating *Streaker*'s hull, Kaa might have unleashed his full suite of tricks, evading the battle cruiser in a mad dash among the twisting threads. But that wasn't possible with *Streaker* weighed down this way, maneuvering as sluggish as an ore freighter.

Well, without the coating, we would have fried the first instant those disintegrator beams struck, Sara thought. *And we'd be easy prey for the Jophur. So maybe it evens out.*

Turning back to the main magnifier screen, she watched the refugee flotilla break up once more. Those that had reclaimed the spiral galaxy symbol began peeling off, aimed toward heading back to the vigorous goals and passions of a younger life phase.

'From this t-point nexus, there are several routes leading eventually to the other four galaxies. The beings piloting those vessels are no doubt planning to rendezvous with former clan mates and clients.'

Gillian sniffed.

'Like Grandpa and Grandma coming home from Happy Acres to move back in with the kids. I wonder just how welcome they'll be.'

The whirling hologram halted briefly, its expression perplexed.

'I beg your pardon?'

'Never mind.' Gillian shook her head. 'So we've seen a retirement home shatter before our eyes, and its residents divide in three directions. What about those?' She pointed to the craggy ships remaining in the flotilla, the ones who retained their original emblem of concentric circles. 'Where will they go?'

The Niss resumed spinning.

'Presumably to another criswell structure. Truly retired species cannot long abide what they call the "shallow realm." They dislike space travel and crave instead the feel of solar tides. So they prefer hunkering deep within a gravity well, next to a tame star.

'In fact, I am picking up considerable short-range traffic right now ... intership communications ... inquiring if anyone in the area knows another fractal community that has spare volume and insolated—'

'In other words, they want to find out which other retirement homes have vacancies, to replace the digs they just lost. I get it.'

'Indeed. But it seems they are having little luck. A majority of the vessels we glimpse now, streaking across the nexus, are asking the same question!'

'What? The ones coming from other entry points? They're also looking for a place to live? But I thought there were tens of thousands of other retirement habitats, each of them huge enough to—'

'Please hold awhile. Let me look into this.'

Silence reigned while the Niss delved deeper, coiling its mesh of spinning lines ever tighter as it listened acutely. When it finally reported again, the synthetic voice was lower, sounding somewhat astonished.

'It seems, Dr. Baskin, that the catastrophe we observed at the Fractal World was not an isolated incident.'

Another long pause followed, as if the Niss felt it necessary to check – and then double-check – verifying what it had just learned.

'Yes,' the machine resumed at last. '*The bizarre and tragic fact is confirmed. Criswell structures appear to be collapsing all over Galaxy Four.*'

It was hard for Sara to imagine. The devastation she had witnessed – a fantastically enormous edifice, an abode to quadrillions, imploding before her eyes – that could not possibly be repeated elsewhere! And yet, that was the news being relayed in sputtery flashes by refugee ships blazing past each other along the Gordian twists and swooping arcs of the transfer point nexus.

'But ... I thought all that fighting and destruction happened because of us!'

'*So I also believed, Sage Koolhan. But that may be because my Tymbrimi makers filled my personality matrix with some of their own exaggerated egotism and sense of self-importance. In fact, however, there is another possible interpretation of the events that took place at the Fractal World. We may have been like ants, scurrying beneath a burning house, convincing ourselves that it was happening because our queen laid the wrong kind of egg.*'

Sara grasped what the Niss was driving at, and she hated the idea. As awful as it felt to be persecuted by mighty forces, there was one paranoiac consolation. It verified your importance in the grand scheme of things, especially if all-powerful beings would tear down their own great works to get at you. But now the Niss implied their suffering at the Fractal World was *incidental* – a mere sideshow – spilling from events so vast, her kind of entity might never understand the big picture.

'B-but ... b-but in that case,' asked the little, crablike qheuen, Pincer-Tip. 'In that case, who *did* wreck the Fractal World?'

Nobody answered. No one had an answer to offer – though Sara had begun ruminating over a possibility. One so disturbing that it came to her only in the form of mathematics. A glimmering of equations and boundary conditions that she kept prim and passionless ... or else the implications might rock her far too deeply, shaking her faith in the stability of the cosmos itself.

Tsh't, the dolphin lieutenant, intervened with a note of pragmatism. 'Gillian, Kaa reportsss we're nearing a junction that might take us to Galaxy Two. Is Tanith still your aim?'

The blond woman shrugged, looking tired.

'Unless anyone sees a flaw in my reasoning.'

A sardonic tone once more filled the voice of the Niss Machine. '*There is no difficulty perceiving flaws. You would send us charging toward violence and chaos, into the one part of the universe where our enemies are most numerous.*

'No, Dr. Baskin. Do not ask about flaws.

'Ask instead whether any of us has a better idea.'

Gillian shrugged.

'You say the Jophur could figure out how to defeat our new armor at any moment. Before that happens, we must find sanctuary somewhere. There is always a slim hope that the Institutes—'

'Very well, then,' Tsh't cut in. 'Galaxy Two is our goal. Tanith Sector. Tanith World. I will tell Kaa to proceed.'

In theory, clients weren't supposed to interrupt their patrons. Though Tsh't was only trying to be efficient.

At the same time Sara thought—

We're heading toward Earth. Soon we'll be so near that Sol will be a visible star, just a few hundred parsecs away, practically round the corner.

That may be as close as I ever get.

Gillian Baskin answered with a nod.

'Yes, let us proceed.'

HARRY

About one subjective day after setting forth, pursuing the mysterious interlopers, Harry learned that an obstacle lay dead ahead.

Hurrying across a weird province of E Space, he dutifully performed his main task, laying instrument packages for Wer'Q'quinn alongside a fat, twisty tube that contained the entire sidereal universe. All the galaxies he knew – including the complex hyperdimensional junctions called transfer points – lay circumscribed within the Avenue. Whenever he paused to stare at it, Harry got a unique, contorted perspective on constellations, drifting nebulae, even whole spiral arms, shimmering with starlight and glaring emissions of excited gas. It seemed strange, defying all intuitive reason, to know the domain inside the tube was unimaginably more vast than the constrained realm of metaphors surrounding it.

By now he was accustomed to living in a universe whose complications far exceeded his poor brain's ability to grasp.

While performing the job assigned to him by Wer'Q'quinn, Harry kept his station moving at maximum prudent speed, following the spoor left by previous visitors to this exotic domain.

Something about their trail made him suspicious.

Of course what I should be doing is lying low till Wer'Q'quinn's time limit expires, then collect the cameras and scoot out of here before this zone of metareality transmutes again, melting around my ship and taking me with it!

So dangerous and friable was the local zone of eerie shapes and twisted logic that even meme creatures – the natural life order of E Space – looked sparse and skittish, as if incarnated ideas found the region just as unpleasant as he did. Harry glimpsed only a few simple notion-beasts grazing across the prairie of fuzzy, cactuslike trunks. Most of the mobile concepts seemed no more complex than the declarative statement – *I am.*

As if the universe cared.

His agile vessel made good time following the trail left by prior interlopers. Objects made of real matter left detectable signs in E Space. Tiny bits of debris constantly sloughed or evaporated off any physical object that dared to invade this realm of reified abstractions. Such vestiges might be wisps of atmosphere, vented from a life-support system, or clusters of hull metal just six or seven atoms wide.

The spoor grew steadily warmer.

I wonder why they came through here, he thought. The oldest trace was about a year old ... if his Subjective Duration Meter could be trusted, estimating the rate at which protons decayed here, converting their mass into microscopic declarative statements. From dispersal profiles, he could tell that the small craft in front – the earliest to pass by – was no larger than his mobile station.

They must have been desperate to come this way ... or else terribly lost.

The second spoor wasn't much younger, coming from a bigger vessel, though still less massive than a corvette. It had nosed along in evident pursuit, avidly chasing after the first.

By sampling drifting molecules, Harry verified that both vessels came from his own life order. *Galactic* spacecraft, carrying oxygen-breathing life-forms – active, vigorous, ambitious, and potentially quite violent.

The third one had him confused for a while. It had come this way more recently, perhaps just days ago. A veritable cloud of atoms still swirled in its wake. Sampling probes waved from Harry's station, like the chem-sense antennae of some insect, revealing metalloceramic profiles like those associated with mech life.

As an acolyte of the Institutes, Harry was always on the lookout for suspicious behavior by machine entities. Despite precautions programmed into mechs for billions of years, they were still prone to occasional spasms of uncontrolled reproduction, grabbing and utilizing any raw materials in sight, making copies of themselves at exponentially increasing rates.

Of course this was a problem endemic to all orders, since opportunistic proliferation was a universal trait of anything called 'life.' Indeed, oxygen breathers had perpetrated their own ecological holocausts in the Five Galaxies, sometimes overpopulating and using up planets much faster than they could restore themselves. Hence laws of migration that regularly set aside broad galactic zones for fallow recovery. But machine reproduction could be especially rapid and voracious, often beginning in dark corners where no one was looking. Once, a wave of autonomous replicators had built up enough momentum to seize and use up every small planetoid in Galaxy Three within the narrow span of ten million years, converting each gram into spindly automatons ... which then began disassembling *planets*. The calamity continued until a coalition of other life orders intervened, bringing it to a halt.

Nor were machines Harry's sole concern. At times like this, when oxygen-breathing civilization was distracted by internal struggles, it was important to keep watch lest the rival culture of hydrogen breathers take advantage.

Still, the traces Harry picked up seemed more strange than dangerous. The lavish amount of metallic debris suggested that this particular mech could be damaged. And there were other anomalies. His sensors sniffed amino acids and other organic detritus. Perhaps small amounts of oxy-life were accompanying the machine-vessel. As cargo perhaps? Sometimes mechs used biological components, which were more resistant than prim logic circuits to damage by cosmic rays.

At the stroke of a midura, he had to halt the pursuit in order to lay another of Wer'Q'quinn's packages, aligning it carefully so the cameras peered straight into the Avenue, collecting data for NavInst technicians. Harry hoped it would prove valuable.

Of course his boss had plenty of measurements already, from probes that laced each transfer point, as well as hyperspatial levels A, B, and C. Moreover, travelers routinely reported conditions they encountered during their voyages. It seemed obscure and unconventional to send Harry all this way gathering information from such a quirky source. But who was he to judge?

I'm near the bottom of the ol' totem pole. I can just do my job as well as possible, and not try to second-guess my chief.

In pre-mission briefings, Harry had learned that strain gauges were showing increased tension along nearly every navigable route in the Five Galaxies. Ruptures and detours had grown routine as commerce began suffering noticeably. Yet, when Wer'Q'quinn made inquiries to high officials at Navigation Institute headquarters, the response consisted of little more than bland, reassuring nostrums.

These events are not unexpected.

Provisions have been made (long ago) for dealing with the phenomena.

Agents at your level should not concern themselves with causes, or long-term effects.

Perform your assigned tasks. Protect shipping. Safeguard the public. Continue reporting data. Above all, discourage panic. Hearten civil confidence.

Maintain your equipment at high levels of readiness.

Cancel all leaves.

It wasn't the sort of memorandum Harry found exactly inspiring. Even Wer'Q'quinn seemed disturbed – though it wasn't easy to read the moods of a land-walking squid.

The situation prompted Harry to wonder again about his current mission.

Perhaps Wer'Q'quinn didn't clear my trip with his bosses. He may have sent me to get a look at things from a perspective that no one at HQ could co-opt, anticipate, or meddle with.

Harry appreciated his supervisor's confidence ... while at the same time worrying about what it implied.

Could everything be falling apart? he pondered. *Maybe the Skiano proselyte is right. If this is the end of the world, what can you do but look to the state of your own soul?*

Just a midura before taking off on this mission, with some mixed feelings and trepidation, he had accepted an invitation from the Skiano to visit its small congregation of converts. Entering a small warehouse bay in one of the cheaper quarters of Kazzkark, he found a motley assortment of creatures following the strange new sect.

There had been a pair of portly synthians – creatures traditionally friendly to Terran customs and concepts – along with several little wazoon, a goggle-eyed pring, three por'n'aths, a striped ruguggl, and ...

Harry recalled rocking back in surprise, dismayed to see a cluster of terrifying Brothers of the Night! With muscular, streamlined arms and sharklike faces, Brothers were famed for their intense though fickle religious impulses, sampling different creeds and pursuing them fanatically – until the next one came along. Still, it shocked Harry to see them in such a gregarious setting, worshiping alongside beings who had no relationship at all with their race or clan.

The variegated faithful had gathered before a symbol that Harry found at once both quaint and unnerving ... a holo portrait of *Earth*, homeworld to his neo-chimpanzee line, depicted with cruciform rays of sacred illumination emanating outward. As the hologram turned, the planet seemed to swell ... then burst apart, donating its own substance to the brilliant rays, enhancing the gift of enlightenment with an act of ultimate self-sacrifice.

Then, moments later, the world recoalesced in a feat of miraculous resurrection, beginning the cycle once more.

'*We are taught that the aim of life is its own perfection,*' preached the Skiano, speaking first in a flashing dialect of Galactic Two, with glitters from its lower pair of eyes, then almost simultaneously via audible GalSeven through a vodor held in one hand.

'*This wisdom is true, beyond any doubt. It crosses all boundaries of order or class. Once sapiency is achieved, life must be about more than mere self-gene-ego continuation. Long ago, the Progenitors taught that our highest purpose is to seek a sense of purpose. For existence to have meaning, we need a goal. A target at which to aim the projectile of our lives.*

'*But what in the universe is perfectible? Surely not matter, which decays, eventually reducing even the greatest artifacts and monuments to a dim glow of heat radiation. Any individual organism will age and eventually die. Some memories may be downloaded or recorded, but true improvement grinds to a halt.*

'*Even the cosmos we perceive with our senses appears doomed to entropy and chaos.*

'*Only* species *seem to get better with time. First blind evolution prepares the way on myriad nursery worlds, sifting and testing countless animal types until precious presapient forms emerge. These then enter a blessed cycle of adoption and Uplift, receiving guidance from others who came before, accelerating their refinement over time.*

'*Up to this point, the way taught by the Progenitors was good and wise. It meant that nursery worlds would be preserved and sanctified. It ensured that potential would be preserved, and wisdom passed on through an endless cycle of nurturing.*

'*And when an elder species has taught all it can, reaching high levels of insight and acumen? Then its own turn comes to resume self-improvement, retiring from the spacefaring life, seeking racial perfection within the loving Embrace of Tides.*

'*Down that route, into the snug clasp of gravity, the Progenitors themselves are said to have gone, waiting to welcome each new gene line that achieves ultimate transcendence.*'

The Skiano pressed its sucker-tipped hands together, leaning toward the congregation.

'But is that the sole route to perfection? Such a far-sighted, species-centered view of salvation seems cold and remote, especially nowadays, when there may be very little time left. Too little for younger races to refine themselves in the old-fashioned way.

'Besides, where does this leave the individual? True, there is real satisfaction from knowing your life has been well spent helping the next generation be a little better than yours, and thus moving your heirs a bit closer to fulfillment. But is there no reward for the good, the honorable, the devoted and kind in this life?

'Is there no continuity or transcendence offered to the self?

'Indeed, my friends and compeers, I am here to tell you that there is a reward! It comes to us from the most unlikely of places. A strange little world, where wolflings emerged to sapiency whole and virginal, after a long hard struggle of self-Uplift with only whale songs to ease their lonely silence.

'That ... and a comforting promise told to them by the one, true God.

'A dreadful-beautiful promise. One that the little world called Earth will soon fulfill, as it suffers martyrdom for all our sins. Yea, for every solitary individual sapient being.

'A promise of salvation and everlasting life.'

With the last instrument packages deployed, Harry had time to kill before they must be retrieved, so he set out again after the interlopers.

All three had stuck close to the Avenue ... a wise precaution, since conventional starcraft were scarcely built to navigate in E Space. This way there was always a chance of diving back into the real universe if things went suddenly wrong here in the empire of memes.

Of course 'diving' into the Avenue held dangers of its own. For instance, you might emerge in one of the Five Galaxies all right, with every atom in the right position compared to its neighbors ... only separated by meters instead of angstroms, giving your body the volume of a star and the density of a rarefied vacuum.

Even if your ship and crew held physical cohesion, you could wind up in a portion of space far from any beacon or t-point, lost and virtually stranded.

By comparison, Harry's vessel was a hardy beast, flexible and far more assured for this quirky kind of travel. Designed specifically for E Space – and piloted by a trained living observer – it could find much safer points of entry and egress than the Avenue.

Of the vessels he was following, the machine entity worried him most, provoking something almost like pity.

It's really vulnerable here. The poor mech must be feeling its way along, almost blind.

Harry accelerated the station's bow-legged gait, curious to see what would drive such an entity to invade E Space, following the spoor of two oxy-life vessels. Soon, he began detecting traces of digital cognizance, a sure giveaway that high-level computers were operating, continuously and unshielded, somewhere beyond the haze.

It's like the thing's broadcasting to all the carnivorous memes in the neighborhood. Yoo hoo! Beasties! Come and eat me!

Harry peered through the murk to make out a fantastically sheer *cliff* ahead – grayish off-white – covered with symmetrical reddish splotches. The abrupt barrier reared vertically, vanishing into the mist some number of meters – or miles – overhead, and the shining, tubelike Avenue seemed headed straight for it!

The red-orange blemishes were arrayed in strict geometrical rows, like endless ranks of fighting ships. Harry eyed them dubiously, till the pilot called them two-dimensional discolorations. Nothing more.

The station marched on, stilt-legs swinging across the fuzzy steppe, and Harry soon realized there was a *hole*, just wide enough to admit the Avenue, with some room to spare on either side to admit the scout platform or a small starship.

'*I believe somebody has used energy weapons here,*' the pilot mode murmured speculatively.

Harry saw the cavelike opening had been widened by some tearing force. Cracks ran away from the broken entrance. Crumbled fragments of wall lay among the fuzzy cylinders.

'Fools! Their ship was too bulky to fit. So instead of trying to find a metaphor that'd get them through, they just blasted their way!'

Harry shook his head. It was dangerous to try altering E Space by force. Far better to get your way by following its strange rules.

'*This apparently happened a year ago, when the larger vessel tried following the smaller. Do you wish me to engage observer mode to find out what types of weapons were used?*'

Harry shook his head. 'No time. Clearly we're dealing with idiots ... or fanatics. Either way it means trouble.'

Harry looked into the blackness surrounding the Avenue as it passed within. No doubt this was another transition boundary. Once he moved inside, the metaphorical rules must change again.

Wer'Q'quinn would not like it. There was no absolute guarantee Harry could backtrack once he entered. The instrument packages were supposed to be his first priority.

After a long pause – spent largely scratching himself, neo-chim style – he grunted and decided.

'We're going in,' Harry ordered. 'Prepare for symbol shift!' He took his command seat and buckled in. 'Close the blinds and ...'

The cursive *P* whirled faster.

'Warning! Something is coming!'

Harry sat up and looked around. The sheer cliff took up half his field of view. On the other side, the glowing tube of the Avenue stretched back the way he came, across an open plain of fuzzy tubes as far as the haze would let him see.

Yanking on both thumbs, he recalled the first rule of survival in E Space. When in doubt about a stranger, be quiet and find out what it is, before it finds out about you.

'Identification? Can you tell where it's coming from?'

The pilot program hesitated for only a moment. *'The object is unknown. It is approaching from within the transition zone.'*

From the dark cave in front of him! That ruled out ducking in there to hide. Harry whirled, looking desperately for an idea.

'We need to get out of sight,' he muttered. 'But where?'

'I cannot answer, unless we fly. Have you worked out a way yet, Harvey?'

'No I haven't, damn you!'

'The bogey is getting closer.'

Harry brought his fists down on the armrests. It was time to try something, anything.

'Go to the wall!'

The station responded with an agile gallop. Thrusting his arms and legs into the manual control sleeves, Harry shouted.

'I'm taking over!'

As the platform reached the sheer cliff, he made two stilt-legs reach out, slapping their broad feet against the smooth surface.

Harry held his breath ...

Then, as naturally as if it had been designed for it, the station reared up and began climbing the wall.

ALVIN

I must hurry through this journal entry. No time for polishing. No asking the autoscribe to fix my grammar or suggest fancy words. We've already boarded one of *Streaker*'s salvaged Thennanin boats, and our deadline to cast off comes in less than a midura. I've got to get this down fast, so a duplicate can remain behind.

I want Gillian Baskin to keep a copy, you see, because we don't have any idea if this little trip of ours is going to work. We're being sent away in hopes the boat will make it to safety while *Streaker* enters a kind of peril she's never seen before. But things could turn out the other way around. If we've learned anything during our adventures, it's that you can't take stuff for granted.

Anyway, Dr. Baskin gave me a promise. If she makes it, and we don't, she'll see about getting my journal published on Earth, or somewhere. That way even if I'm dead at least I'll be a real author. People will read what I wrote, centuries from now, and maybe on lots of worlds.

I think that's so uttergloss, it almost makes up for this separation, though saying good-bye to the friends we made aboard ship is almost as hard as it was leaving my family behind on Jijo.

Well, one of the crew is going with us, to fly the little ship. Dr. Baskin is giving us her own best pilot, to make sure we get safely to our goal.

'It doesn't look as if we'll need a crackerjack space surfer where we're going,' she told us. 'But you kids must have Kaa, if you're to stand a chance.'

Huck complained of course, waving all her eyestalks and protesting with that special whining tone that only an adolescent g'Kek can fine-tune to perfection.

'We're being *exiled*,' she wailed. 'Just when *Streaker*'s going someplace really interesting!'

'It's not exile,' Gillian answered. 'You're taking on a dangerous and important mission. One that you Jijoans are well qualified for. A mission that might make everything we've gone through worthwhile.'

Of course they both have it right. I have no doubt we're being sent away in part because we're young and Gillian feels guilty about keeping us aboard where there's danger every dura, sometimes from a dozen directions at once. Clearly she'd like to see the four of us – especially Huck – taken somewhere safe as soon as possible.

On the other hand, I don't think she'd part with Kaa if it weren't for important reasons that'd help her accomplish her mission. I believe she really does want us to make our way in secret through the Five Galaxies, and somehow make contact with the Terragens Council.

'We couldn't do it before,' Dr. Baskin explained, 'with just humans and dolphins aboard. Even sneaking into some obscure port, we'd have been noticed the second any of us spoke up, to buy supplies or ask directions. Earthlings are too well known – too infamous – for us to go anywhere incognito these days.

'But who will notice a young urs? Or a little red qheuen? Or a hoon, walking around one of those backspace harbors? You'll be typical shabby starfarers, selling a few infobits you've picked up along the way, buying fourth-class passages and making your way to Tanith Sector on personal business.

'Of course, Huck will have to stay secluded or disguised – you may have to ship her in an animal container till you reach a safe place. The Tymbrimi would protect her. Or maybe the Thennanin – providing she'd accept indenture and their pompous advice about a racial self-improvement campaign. Anyway, too much is riding on her to take any chances.'

Gillian's reminder silenced Huck's initial outrage over being 'shipped' from place to place. Of all us voyagers, my friend has the biggest reason to stay alive. She's the only living g'Kek outside of Jijo, and since the Jophur might annihilate all the g'Keks back home, it seems that motherhood, not adventuring, will be her calling now. A change she finds sobering.

'What about Kaa?' asked Ur-ronn, waving her sleek, long head, speaking with a strong urrish lisp. 'It will ve hard to disguise a vig dolphin. Shall we carry hin in our luggage?'

Ignoring urrish sarcasm, Dr. Baskin shook her head.

'Kaa won't be accompanying you all the way to Tanith. He'd be too conspicuous. Besides, I made him a promise, and it's time to keep it.'

I was about to inquire about that ... to ask what promise she meant ... when Lieutenant Tsh't entered the Plotting Room to say that she'd finished loading the boat with supplies for our journey.

My pet noor, Huphu, rode my shoulder. But her sapient relative, the secretive tytlal named Mudfoot, licked himself on a nearby conference table, resembling that Earth creature, an otter, but with white bristles on his neck and an expression of disdainful boredom.

'Well?' Gillian asked the creature, though he'd refused to speak since we left Jijo. 'Do you want to go see the Tymbrimi, and report to them about matters on Jijo? Or will you come with us, beyond anything our order of life normally gets to see?'

When she put it that way, I think Gillian expected one answer from the curious tytlal. But it didn't surprise me that she got the other.

A tytlal will bite off its own tail for a joke.

I guess I ought to update how we got to this point – hurrying to pack a small boat and send it off toward a place where *Streaker* had expected to be going.

The reason is that Gillian seems to have gotten a better offer.

Or at least one she can't refuse.

*

How did we get to this parting of the ways?

Where I last left off, *Streaker* was swooping along the complex innards of a transfer point, just a couple of dozen arrowflights ahead of a Jophur battleship that clung to us the way a prairie-hopper holds on to its last pup. It seemed there'd only be one way to shake our enemy, and that was to head straight for one of the huge headquarters worlds of the Great Institutes, where there'd be lots of traffic and other warships around. If everything worked just right, an Institute armistice might be issued in the nick of time, and protect us before a free-for-all firestorm blasted *Streaker* to kingdom come.

All right, it was a flaky plan, for sure, but the best one anybody thought of. And it beat letting the Jophur capture *Streaker*'s secrets to use against all other clans in the Five Galaxies.

So there we were, darting along a t-point thread, dodging refugee traffic from hundreds of broken fractal worlds that were falling apart all over Galaxy Four ...

Don't ask me how or why *that* happened, because it's way beyond me. But at least one of us Jijoans had a clue to what was going on. Sage Sara seemed to grasp the meaning when a number of those giant spaceships changed their shape right before our eyes, as well as the symbols on their bows.

As I understand it, some of the refugees were looking for new retirement homes, to resume their quiet lives of contemplation. (Though it seems vacancies were hard to find.)

Others decided to abandon that comfortable existence and head back to rejoin their old oxy-life cousins during the present time of crisis. Dr. Baskin thought we'd slip in among this mob, flooding through the crowded transfer point on their way to populated zones of the Five Galaxies.

There was a third option, being chosen by a smaller minority – those who thought themselves ready to climb the next rung on the ladder of sapiency, rising out of the Retired Order to a much higher state. But we didn't think that group could possibly concern us.

Boy, were we wrong!

So there we were, diving into the heart of the t-point – a looping, knotlike structure Kaa called a *transgalactic nexus* – that would send us out of old Galaxy Four altogether ... when it happened.

Alarms blared. We swerved around another loop-de-loop, and there it was.

At first, I saw just a floating cloud of light, shapeless, without a hint of structure. But as we drew near, this changed. I got an impression of a tremendous *creature* with countless writhing arms! These appendages were reaching down to the converging transfer threads and *plucking starships off like berries from a vine*!

'Uh ... is that normal?' Huck asked ... unnecessarily, since we could see the looks on the faces of our Earthling friends. They'd never seen anything like it before.

Pincer-Tip stammered in awe.

'Is it a go-go-go-god?'

No one answered, not even the sarcastic Niss Machine. We were heading right for the giant thing, and there wasn't any possible route to jump away from it in time. All we could do was stare, and count the passing duras, plunging toward the brilliance till our turn came.

Light flooded the sky. A tremendous arm of light came down upon us ... and suddenly things began moving v-e-r-y s-l-o-w-l-y.

Queasy sensations flowed outward from my gut while my skin felt a strange kind of spreading numbness. As *Streaker* was lifted bodily off the transfer thread, her roaring engines muted to an idle whisper. All view screens filled with whiteness, a glow that did not seem to carry any heat. Paralyzed with fear, I wondered if we were about to be consumed by some kind of hungry being, or a dispassionate natural phenomenon. Not that it made the slightest difference which.

The illumination was so perfect in its hue, and resplendent texture, that I felt suddenly sure it could be nothing other than pure and distilled death.

How long the transition lasted, I have no idea. But eventually the brilliant haze diminished and all the visceral sensations ebbed. *Streaker*'s engines remained damped, but time resumed its normal pace. At last we could see clearly again.

Sara was holding Emerson tightly, while the little chimp, Prity, hugged them both. Ur-ronn was huddled next to Huck and Pincer, while Huphu and Mudfoot clung with eight sets of claws to my tingling shoulders.

We all looked around, amazed to be able to do so.

The screens flickered back on, showing that we were still inside the tangled, twisted guts of the t-point ... only we weren't in contact with a thread anymore! There seemed to be a fair-sized bubble of true space surrounding *Streaker*.

And not only *Streaker*. On all sides of us, arrayed in long neat rows, were ranks of other starships! Most of them much larger. All apparently waiting in still silence for something to happen.

Belatedly, the Niss hologram finally popped back into existence among us. Its mesh of fine lines looked tense, anxious.

'*I see just one common feature among all these vessels,*' it said. '*Every one of them bears the Sign of Unity. The symbol consisting of two line segments, joining at one hundred and four degrees. The Emblem of Transcendence.*'

Now, looking at the white glow, we could tell that it was some-how *sorting* through the vessels that it plucked up from the travel threads. Some – a majority – were conveyed around its shimmering globe and set back on their way. These vanished swiftly, as if eager to make good their escape to other galaxies.

But every hundredth or so vessel was pulled aside. The white glow seemed to examine each of these closely, then brought most of them over to join our phalanx of selected ...

Selected what? Prisoners? Samples? Candidates? Hors d'oeuvres?

To our relief, that last notion was disproved when we saw a nearby starship abruptly pulse with soft fire, undergoing a reversal of its earlier transformation. In moments, the two-legged symbol had changed back into a nest of concentric circles. At once that vessel began slipping out of formation, wobbling as it jetted toward the flow of departing refugees.

'Chickening out,' diagnosed Huck, as always charitable in her evaluation of others. The same thing happened several more times, as we watched. But the white glow kept adding new members to our ranks.

Emerson d'Anite began fiddling with the long-range display, and soon grunted, pointing to his discovery – that our bubble of local spacetime wasn't the only one! There were at least a dozen other assembly areas, and perhaps a lot more. Some of them contained spiky, fractal-shaped spacecraft, like those nearby. Others seemed filled with blobby yellow shapes, vaguely spherical, that sometimes merged or separated like balls of grease.

'*Zang*,' identified Emerson, clearly proud to be able to name the lumpy objects aloud, as if that single word helped clarify our con-fusion.

'Um ...' Sage Sara asked. 'Does anyone have any idea what we're doing here? Have I missed something? Have we just been mistaken as members of the *transcendent order of life*?'

Lieutenant Tsh't tossed her great, bottle-nosed head.

'That-t would be q-quite a promotion,' she commented, sardonically.

'*Indeed*,' added the Niss. '*Most oxygen-breathing species strive for many hundreds of thousands of years – engaging in commerce, Uplift, warcraft, and starfaring – before at last they feel the call, seeking a tame star near which to wallow in the Embrace of Tides. Having joined the Retired Order, a species then may pass another million years until they feel ready for the next step.*'

Ur-ronn made a suggestion.

'Should we consult the Livrary Vranch you have avoard this shif?'

The whirling Niss shivered.

'The Galactic Library does not contain much information about the Retired Order, since our elders often say that such matters are none of our business.

'As for what happens beyond retirement ... well, now we are talking about realms of religion. Most of the great cults of the Five Galaxies have to do with this issue – what it means for a race to transcend. Many believe the Progenitors were first to pass this way, bidding all others to follow when they can. But—'

'But that doesn't answer Sara's question,' finished Gillian Baskin. 'Why have we been plucked out to join this assembly? I wonder if—'

She stopped, noticing that the mute former engineer, Emerson d'Anite, was gesturing for attention again. He kept tapping his own nose, then alternately pointing forward, toward the window separating the Plotting Room from *Streaker*'s bridge. For a few moments, everyone seemed perplexed. Then Tsh't made a squeal of realization.

'The nose of the sh-ship! Remember how a faction of Old Ones and machines reworked our hull, giving us our strange new armor? What if they also changed the WOM watcher on our bow? None of us has had a good look since it happened. Maybe the symbol is not a rayed sssssspiral anymore! Maybe it'ssss ...'

She didn't finish. We all got her drift. Perhaps *Streaker* now wore an emblem identifying its inhabitants as something we're definitely not.

Others seemed to find this plausible ... though no one could imagine why our benefactors would want to do such a thing. Or what the consequences might be, when we're found out.

Toward the front of the crowd, I watched Gillian Baskin's face and realized she wasn't buying that theory. The woman obviously had another idea in mind. Perhaps a different explanation of why we were here.

I was probably the only one close enough to overhear the one word she spoke then, under her breath, in a tone I took to be resigned sadness.

I'm writing the word down now, even though I have no idea what it means.

Here was all she said.

'Herbie ...'

So, that's how we wound up parting company.

It looks as if *Streaker* may have found sanctuary after all ... of a sort. At least the Jophur battleship is no longer in sight, though who knows if it might show up again. Anyway, Dr. Baskin has decided not to fight this turn of destiny's wheel, but instead to ride it for a while and see where it may lead.

But we Wuphonites won't be going along. We're to climb aboard an old Thennanin star boat – which still has the rayed spiral symbol on its prow – and have Kaa pilot us to safety in Galaxy Two. It'll be hard, especially having to latch on to a rapid transfer thread from standstill in this weird space bubble. And that will be just the beginning of our difficulties as we try to find a backwater port where no one would much notice us slipping into the Civilization of Five Galaxies.

Once there, if Ifni's dice roll right, we'll endeavor to act as Gillian's messengers, deliver her vital information, and then maybe see about finding something to do with the rest of our lives.

Like Huck, I have mixed feelings about all this. But what else can we do, except try?

Tsh't has finished loading all our supplies in the hold. Kaa is in the dolphin-shaped pilot's saddle, thrashing his flukes and eager to be off. We've all received hugs and good-luck wishes from those we're leaving behind.

'Make Jijo proud,' Sage Sara told us. I wish she was coming along, so we'd have her wisdom, and so our group would have a representative from all Six Races of the Slope. But if anyone from our little hidden world ought to go see what *transcendent creatures* are like, and have a chance of understanding, it's her. Things are the way they are, I guess.

Tyug, the traeki alchemist, is venting sweet steam. The aroma soothes our fears and qualms at parting. I guess if a traeki can be serene about entering a universe filled with Jophur, I should be open-minded about meeting long-lost cousin hoons – distant relatives who've spent all their lives with the power and comforts of star gods, but who've never read Conrad, Ellison, or Twain. Poor things.

'We need to name this thing,' Pincer-Tip insists, banging the metal floor of the boat with his claw.

Ur-ronn nods her sleek urrish head.

'Of course, there can ve only one that fits.'

I agree with a low umble. So we turn to Huck, whose eyestalks shrug, conveying some of the unaccustomed burden of responsibility she now carries.

'Let it be *Wuphon's Dream*,' she assents, making it unanimous.

Gillian Baskin waits by the hatch for me to hand over the copy disk from my autoscribe. So I must now finish dictating this entry – as unpolished and abrupt as it is.

If this is where my story ends, dear reader, it means Streaker somehow made it, and we didn't. I have no complaints or regrets. Just remember us, if it pleases you to do so.

Thanks, Dr. Baskin. Thanks for the adventure and everything.

Good luck.

And good-bye.

HARRY

Something was terribly familiar about this region of E Space, ever since he first stared across the prairie of twisted, fuzzy growths toward narrow spires that climbed to meet a vast, overhanging plane. The back of Harry's neck kept *tickling* unpleasantly – the way a neo-chimpanzee experiences déjà vu.

Now he regarded the same scene from another vertiginous angle, as his scout vessel clung to a gigantic sheer cliff amid a blurry haze. Innumerable reddish blotchy patterns repeated symmetrically across the smooth vertical surface, like footprints left by an army of splayfooted monsters.

'Well,' he commented, his voice scratchy with surprise. 'I never did *this* before. Who'd've thought the rules here would let a big machine climb straight up, like a spider on a w—'

Harry stopped. Realization left him mute as his jaw opened and closed.

It can't be!

He stared at the cliff's repetitious markings, then the distant spires, nearly lost in shrouding mist. A mental shift of scale made it all clear.

I . . . would've sussed it earlier, but for the blurry vision in this crazy place.

He felt cosmically stupid. Harry moaned aloud.

'By Cheetah's beard an' Tarzan's hernia . . . it's a *room*. A room in somebody's goddam house!'

Awareness lent focus to his tardy perception.

The prairie of fuzzy growths?

Carpet!

The tall, narrow spires?

Furniture legs. And that huge flat plane I fell from before must be a table.

The blotchy pattern on this 'cliff' was probably *wallpaper*, or some tasteless counterpart. From this close, he had no clue if the motif was Earthling or alien.

This zone of E Space has so few visitors, it was probably in a raw, unmanifested state when I dropped in. The whole megillah may have coalesced around some image from my own subconscious mind!

He had been thinking about the station format, equipped with long legs from his last mission, comparing it to a spider. Perhaps that thought helped precipitate this eerily personal subcosmos.

Unless I'm actually dreaming it all, and my body's really lying in crumpled delirium somewhere, smashed under tons of debris where the station fell, an instant after I arrived.

Either way, it showed just why most sophonts thought this part of E Space especially dangerous.

Perhaps this was how insects saw things inside a house – everything a blur. Harry wondered if there were pictures on the walls, a bowl of fruit on the table, and a humongous kitten purring on some sofa, just across the way.

Maybe it was better not to know, or force E Space to reify too much.

Just one thing spoiled the impression of a quaint, gigantic drawing room – the *Avenue* – a slender, sinuous tube of radiance that emerged from the misty distance, wound its way across the floor, then pierced the wall below Harry's vantage point. A place called Reality, dominated by matter and rigid physical laws.

'I sense vibrations approaching,' the station announced. *'From the point of connection-rupture.'*

In other words, from the mouse hole where the Avenue plunged toward another zone of E Space. Three interlopers had taken that route before, leaving distinct traces. A small vessel squeezed through first, about a year ago ... followed by a pursuer who carelessly blasted a wider path. Both left spoor signs of oxy-life. A third, more recent craft shed mixed clues before entering the narrow route.

Now something was coming the other way.

Harry checked the station's weaponry console and found several panels lit up ... meaning they were able to function here, though in what fashion remained to be seen.

'Let's see if we can try that other trick again,' he murmured.

Taking manual control, he sealed the station's reality anchor to the adjacent wall with an audible 'thunk.' Then, nervously, he detached each clinging foot from the wall, until his vessel dangled high above the ground. 'Lower away!' he said, causing the cord to stretch, halting just two ship lengths above where carpet met wall. The Avenue lay just a little to his left.

Whatever's coming out ... it can't be much bigger than this station. And most starships that visit E Space aren't well designed for it. I've got advantages, including surprise.

It seemed logical. Harry almost had himself convinced.

But logic was a fickle friend, even back in his home universe. In E Space, it was just one of many games you could play with symbols and ideas.

One of many ways to fool yourself.

'*Here it comes!*' announced pilot mode, as something began nosing out of the dark tunnel.

It looked pathetic – absurdly long and barely narrow enough to fit through the tunnel. The intruder comprised a chain of hinged segments carried on stiff, articulated legs. It scuttled out of the dark passageway rapidly, then swerved aside, crouching along the wall as tremors ran from section to section. Watching from above, Harry's impression was of something wounded and frightened, cowering as it tried to catch its breath.

He did not have to engage observer mode to know at once, this entity was a machine. Its rigid formality of movement was a dead giveaway. More significant was the fact that it did not *change* very easily. Upon entering a new region of E Space, any other kind of life-form would already have flexed and throbbed through some sort of transition, adjusting its self-conception, its *gestalt*, to suit the new environment.

In this realm, believing often made things so.

Yet, by their very natures, machines were supreme manifestations of applied physical law. Consistency was a source of their power, back in Reality. But here it had crippling effects. Faced with an imperative need to adjust its form, a machine could only do so by carefully evaluating the new circumstances, coming up with a design, then implementing each change according to a plan.

Zooming in with a handheld telescope, Harry saw the mech's body swarm with smaller motile objects – repair and maintenance drones – laboring frantically to alter its shape and function by cutting, moving, and reattaching hunks of real matter. In the process, bits and pieces kept falling off, crumbling or dissolving into big strands of carpet. Harry's atom sensor showed a veritable cloud of particles billowing outward ... debris that would start attracting scavenging memes before long.

Clearly, this thing had once been a spacefaring device, a dweller in deep vacuum and darkness. It was amazing the machine could adapt to this environment at all.

A sensor flashed anomaly readings. Some of the pollution consisted of oxygen, nitrogen, and complex organic compounds – telltale signs of quite another order of life.

Wait a minute.

Harry had already been suspicious. Now he felt sure.

This was the third entity he had been tracking.

'Must've bumped into something it disagreed with,' he surmised. 'Something scary enough to make it run away.'

Pilot mode soon confirmed this.

'I am detecting more bogeys, approaching the rupture boundary from the other side, following this one at a rapid pace.'

Harry narrowed down the source of the abnormal gas emissions to a sealed swelling near the middle of the caterpillar-shaped machine. *A habitat.* A container for atmosphere and other life-support needs. Some glassy shimmers might be windows, though the interior was too dim to see anything.

Clearly the machine knew time was short. Reconfiguration work accelerated, but little drones broke down from the frantic pace, overheating and tumbling to the carpet, which began waving toward the commotion, showing unnerving signs of animate hunger. Atoms were rare in E Space, and did not last long. Many simple meme creatures found bits of matter useful as trace nutrients, lending a bit of reality to living abstractions.

'Thirty duras until arrival of the newcomers,' confirmed pilot mode.

Though its work was unfinished, the caterpillar-machine decided there was no more time to spare, and began hurrying away next to the glowing Avenue.

I wonder why it doesn't try a dive back into normal space by jumping into the Avenue. Sure, it might emerge almost anywhere, and need centuries to find its way to a decent hyperspatial shunt, but don't machines have plenty of time?

He could think of several possibilities.

Perhaps it's too badly damaged to survive reentry.

Or maybe its organic cargo can't afford to spend centuries drifting through space.

The awkward machine suffered dire problems. Metal-hinged legs began freezing in place, or snapping and falling off. Harry pictured a wounded animal, struggling on with its last strength.

He turned to watch for the pursuers. A burst of light heralded their emergence, shining from the tunnel. Carpet strands quailed in response. Then the first creature appeared.

Harry's impression was of an armored earthworm, with a glistening head consisting of shiny plates. A beast of dark holes and airless depths. But this quickly changed. In a speedy metamorphosis, the entity adjusted to this different realm. Eyelike organs sprouted above, while pseudopods erupted below, until it stood gracefully atop myriad delicate tendrils, like a millipede.

Or megapede, Harry decided.

Only one kind of creature could adjust so quickly in E Space. One that was native to it. A sophisticated meme-carnivore. An idea – perhaps *the* very idea – of predation.

As the first one transmuted to fit the ad hoc rules of a gigantic parlor room, several more crowded from behind, members of a hunting pack, eager for a final dash after their helpless prey.

It's none of my business, Harry thought, pulling anxiously on both thumbs. *My first duty is to collect Wer'Q'quinn's instruments. My second is to track and deter interlopers ... but the memes will take care of this one by themselves.*

But Harry's indecision was stoked by a sudden memory of the last time he had listened to the Skiano missionary preach its strange creed from a makeshift pulpit, beneath a slowly turning hologram of crucified Earth. With both light and sound, the evangelist sermonized that each sapient individual should look to the deliverance of his or her own soul.

'Although our sect has burst only recently upon the boulevards and byways of the Five Galaxies, we are already seen as a threat by the old faiths. They try to limit our message through regulations and legal harassment, using unscrupulous means to undermine our emissaries. Above all, they claim that we teach *selfishness*.

'If the Abdicators, Awaiters, Transcenders, and other traditions agree on one thing, it is that salvation must be achieved by *species* and *clans*, perfecting themselves to follow our blessed Progenitors into the Embrace of Tides. Each generation should work selflessly to help their heirs move farther, step by step. How terrible, then, if individuals, in their trillions and quadrillions, start thinking of themselves! What if redemption could be achieved by each thinking being, through faith in a God who is above and beyond all known levels of universal reality?

'What if the Embrace of Tides might be *bypassed*, by achieving a heavenly afterlife, described in the sacred works of Terra? Would everyone then cease trying for racial progress? Abandoning posterity in favor of spiritual rewards *now*?'

The Skiano's lower set of eyes had flashed. 'There is an answer. The answer of Buddo, Moshé, Jesu, and other great prophets who taught during Earth's era of glorious loneliness. Their answer – our answer – is that salvation's greatest tool has always been compassion.'

Even days later, Harry's thoughts still roiled around the incredible, many-sided incongruity of the Skiano's message.

Chewing his lip, he turned to address the floating *P* symbol.

'How many hunters are there?'

'*The memoids number five,*' answered pilot mode.

'*Two are now fully transformed and have resumed pursuing the mech interloper. Two are still shifting. One remains inside the tunnel, awaiting its turn.*'

He saw a pair of meme-carnivores accelerating across the pseudocarpet, each propelled by a million rippling tendrils, rapidly overtaking the decrepit machine. Two more finished transforming while Harry paced, wishing he had never attended the Skiano's revival meeting.

In fact, he could not be sure what motivated his decision to act. Compassion might have been part of it. But Harry preferred blaming it on something else.

Curiosity.

I'll never find out what the clumsy-fool machine is carrying, if it gets gobbled up by a bunch of ravenous opinions.

The fifth memoid emerged and began its metamorphosis.

Harry let out a cry of resolution and punched a button, releasing the reality anchor, causing the station to plummet straight down with all eight legs deployed like claws.

His first opponent fell easiest.

A memoid is defenseless during transition, while reformatting its conceptual framework for a new environment.

'Paraphrasing itself into another idiom,' as Wer'Q'quinn had explained during Harry's training. During that time, its self-assured cohesion wavered, making it vulnerable to external points of view.

This one reacted quickly when the plummeting station pierced its spine in several places, injecting some critical notions.

INTERRUPTION
HESITATION
DOUBT

In E Space, an idea can hold together without a brain to think it. But only if the proposition is strong enough to believe in *itself*. To such a self-sustaining concept, uncertainty was worse than a toxin, especially if inserted at the right place and time. Unable to cope, this complex meme faltered and quickly dissolved, allowing its component propositions to be gobbled up by the surrounding carpet. That left Harry free to amble quickly after its peers.

Be like a spider, he thought, preparing the weapon console for action. His advantages were now stealth and speed ... plus the fact that this entire subdomain of E Space must have coalesced a while ago around some seed-image from his own mind – probably a childhood memory of somebody's Brobdingnagian parlor.

Approaching the next two memes rapidly from behind, he chose to snare them with an entanglement ray. It seemed ideal for attack in E Space, shooting finely woven arrays of syllogisms – logical arguments collected from digests of the Great Galactic Library going back over a billion years.

Well, here goes nothing.

Harry aimed and fired.

The weapon was contingent, meaning that its appearance and form varied depending on local conditions. In other zones of E Space, he had seen it lash out beams of caustic light, or discharge glowing disproofs like fiery cannonballs. *Here*, streams of distilled argument seemed to spiral out from the station like webs of sticky silk, flying over and beyond the next pair of memic carnivores.

One of them stumbled instantly, snarling its abundant legs in viscous cords of ancient persuasion, tangling its torso amid strands of quarrelsome reasoning, rolling to a jumbled ball, then rapidly dissipating into vapor.

Its partner was luckier. While cornered by surrounding webs, the predator managed to stop just in time. Wherever a line of caustic contention did make contact, burning its flanks, rebuttals flowed from the wound like fervent antibodies.

The creature turned its metaphorical gaze, and proceeded to spit poison. Gobbets flew toward the station – presumably cogent explanations meant to convince Harry's vessel not to exist anymore. He might have tried shooting them down, or swatting them, or even enduring the assault. But Harry had already chosen another tactic.

Taking advantage of his knowledge about the local zone, he made the station flex all eight legs, then *leap*, soaring above the acrid missiles and beyond, over the pair of trapped allaphors.

For several long seconds he flew, watching a sea of carpet pass below ... so high that he began worrying about the descent, especially when his path seemed headed dangerously close to the glowing Avenue.

I'm not ready for reentry here! The odds of surviving a random collision were not good.

Fortunately, by making the station writhe to one side, he managed to just miss the shining tube. But landing came unbalanced and hard. Harry flew against the nearest bulkhead, taking a painful blow to his right shoulder. Worse, the cabin filled with sounds of something shattering. An alarm blared. Red lights flashed.

Wincing, he scrambled back to the control panel, where he learned that two legs had snapped in the fall and a third was badly twisted. His trusty vehicle limped badly as it stood to meet new challenges.

Still, Harry felt aflame with adrenaline, baring his teeth and loosing a savage, chimpanzee snarl.

Three down. Two to go, he thought, hopefully.

Unfortunately, the next fight wouldn't be as easy.

One of the remaining predators could be seen just ahead, already pouncing on its hapless prey, tearing metal pieces off the giant machine, dismembering it with happy abandon. The other memoid turned to face Harry. Alert and fully prepared, its form had fully adjusted to this realm, and now resembled just the sort of feral insectoid you'd most hate to find crawling under the furniture – something many-clawed and stingered. He got an impression of savage joy, as if the adversary facing him was the essence of combativeness.

Dribbles of foamy disputation frothed at the memoid's mouth, then flew toward Harry.

Leaping out of the way was impossible this time, so he tried to dodge left, then right. But despite desperate zigzagging, one of the blobs struck his forward window pane, spreading to coat it with a glimmering slime.

Harry averted his gaze, but not before waves of apprehension flooded.

What the hell am I doing here? I could be safe in bed. If I stayed on Earth, I might've had the company of lovers, friends, instead of coming all this way to die ...

Regret caused bitter pangs, even though he knew the source was an alien assault. Fortunately, the emotion was diffuse, generalized. The memoid didn't know what kind of creature he was, so its thought-poisons weren't specific. Not yet. Alas, predators at this level of sophistication had remarkable sensitivity, adapting quickly to their victims' weaknesses.

Harry didn't plan on giving it the chance. He triggered another entanglement ray, and once more his station flung webs of gooey argument. This time, however, his target agilely evaded the trap – perhaps by assuming some unique and unrelated axioms. The few strands that touched just slid off, unable to impeach exotic postulates. Only briefly inconvenienced, the memoid flexed its back and charged – flowing toward Harry so fast he could never hope to retreat.

Its maw gaped, but instead of teeth there gleamed rows of pointy, spiraled *screws*, turning rapidly as the creature rushed to attack. The sight was fearsome and unnerving.

It's gonna board me!

Harry reached for the weapons console, stabbing a button labeled DISTRACTION FLARES. They had saved his hide on other missions, creating dazzling displays of confusing data, like floating clouds of chaff, enabling his escape from even bigger monsters.

Only this time the effect was disappointing. Clouds of mist erupted before the charging predator, but it barely slowed.

When in doubt, get physical, he thought, activating the minigun. Vibrations rattled as high-velocity bullets launched toward the attacker, who reared back, bellowing and clawing at the air. But hope soon crashed as Harry realized the impacts weren't doing harm. Rather, the creature seemed to snatch and grab at the projectiles, incorporating the material into its information-based matrix! The rotating screws changed color, from a simulated pastel blue to a dark, metallic gray.

Harry shut the gun down, cursing. He had just *improved* the enemy's chances of getting at him.

The station barely shuddered when the memoid struck, clambering on top for a close embrace. A complex rarefied idea had little weight or momentum. But ideas *could* wear at you, and this one did so pointedly, chomping with those spinning drill bits, tearing through the vessel's hull.

Harry tried other buttons and levers, but nothing worked. Each weapon was dead, or else reformatted in some way the adaptable memoid shrugged off.

In E Space, an object made solely of atoms could not stand for long against living ideas.

Several dimples appeared in the walls ... which then burst inward as whirling conical blades drilled through. Moments later, the screws began changing shape, taking form as little creatures. *Mites*, Harry thought, knowing that even little insects and spiders had parasites. The predator had figured out an excellent trick, using the logic of this subrealm against Harry.

He stabbed a final button, meant for desperate situations like this one.

Instantly, the control room filled with holographic images, a crowd of milling beings, mimicking various kinds of oxy-, hydro-, and machine life. A few slithered. Others walked, or rolled, or stomped, resembling some pangalactic, cross-temporal, omnireality cocktail party.

A dozen or so mitelike invaders spread out, seeking the station's conceptual core – Harry himself. The nasty little things flashed horrid pincers, while sniffing through a crowd of imitation sophonts. One of them chose an ersatz Zang to attack, hurling itself at a floating yellow blob that shivered when struck. At once, the hologram collapsed inward around the mite, enveloping it in a crushing layer of anti-memes. The resulting implosion finished with a burst of light, followed by a thin trail of dust falling to the deck.

They contain some real matter, Harry realized. *These things are freaking dangerous!*

If one bit him, it might not just assail his mind. It could also chew away at his real body.

Two more times, invaders got suckered into attacking wrong targets, and were destroyed. But Harry could tell they were growing more cautious. Gradually, the mites learned to ignore hydro- and machine forms, and began zeroing in toward his type of oxy-based organism.

I've got to act first. But how? What can I do to fight my way out of this mess?

If he ever made it back to base, he'd have suggestions for the crews who maintained the weapons systems. But for now, Harry saw just one hope . . . to shake the parent memoid off, breaking its control over the mites. That would also leave holes in the station's hull. But one problem at a time.

He didn't dare take up manual controls which would give him away. So instead he called up pilot mode.

'Yes, Herman?' the floating *P* answered.

'Don't hover close to me!' Harry whispered through gritted teeth. 'Keep your damn distance and listen up. I want you to send the station jiggling and swerving about . . . random action . . . try to shake the Ifni-cursed alien off our hull!'

'*That would violate safety parameters.*'

'Override!' Harry growled. 'Emergency protocols. Do it now!'

The scout platform began moving. Though hampered by two broken legs, it was not much burdened by the big memoid, whose total real mass was probably only a few hundred grams, even after eating Harry's bullets. The limp even helped a bit, getting a swaying motion started as the station began shifting left, right, forward, and then spinning around, commencing a drunkard's walk across the carpeted landscape.

Despite its low inertial mass, the big memoid clearly did not like this. After all, movement was a form of information. Harry heard faint mewling sounds as it scrambled for a better grip, holding on to keep contact with its mites.

Unfortunately, the zigzagging also affected *Harry*, pushing him to and fro. The holograms automatically emulated his movements, but he knew this would give him away soon.

Through one window, he caught a blurry glimpse of the metallic machine entity, the big interloper he had followed earlier, who had no business coming to a realm where *thinking* made things so.

It had already been dismembered, carved into several chunks by the last predator, which was now working its way toward the habitat bulge—

A rolling motion yanked Harry from that dolorous scene, throwing him against another window. The one still coated with tincture-of-regret.

Oh, I regret, all right.

I regret not coming here armed with some real *memic weapons! True wolfling brain poisons. Sick-sweet ideas that hypnotized millions, fixating them on just one view of reality, making flexible minds as rigid as stone.*

Harry felt sure of it. Even these local predators – lithe and supple in abstraction space – would turn conceptually brittle if exposed to the seductive reasonings of Plato or Marx or Ayn Rand . . . Freud or Aquinas . . . Goebbels or Hub—

The station braked with a shuddering jar, splitting Harry's thought and sending him slamming against a storage cabinet. He turned frantically in time to see several of the mites also come flying – propelled by their real-mass components. Two of them collided with holograms and were instantly destroyed.

But two others survived to smack the wall near Harry. As he gathered his balance, he could sense their regard swiveling his way.

Uh-oh.

They had him cornered, with his back against the lockers. As the station resumed its wild movements, the mites approached from two sides across the bucking deck, snapping jaws and waving scorpionlike tails.

Harry tried clearing his mind. Supposedly, if you practiced mental discipline, you could make your intellect impervious to toxic notions.

Unfortunately, beings who were that disciplined made lousy E Space observers. He had been recruited for his credulous imagination – a trait these parasites would use to demolish him.

'Uh . . . could I maybe interest *you* guys in entertaining an idea or two?' He spoke quickly, breathlessly. 'How about – this sentence is a lie!'

Their reaction, a snapping of pincers, seemed amused.

'Well then . . . how do you know you exist?'

Total contempt.

Shucks, it worked in some old tellie shows.

Of course, sophisticated memes would dismiss such clichés like flint-tipped arrows bouncing off armor. But what about a concept they might not have met before?

'Uh, has anyone ever told you about something called *compassion*? Some think it's the surest route to salv—'

The mites prepared to spring.

The station swerved again as the autopilot threw another gyration.

Suddenly, a radiant glow flooded the window opposite Harry, filling the control room with torrents of *starlight*.

Harry sighed.

'Well I'll be a monk—'

Before he could complete the phrase, several things happened at once.

Both parasites leaped.

The big meme predator clinging to the outer hull screeched dismay.

His wildly gyrating station collided with the Avenue, a glancing blow, with the big memoid pressed between, giving it a taste of the Reality Continuum.

Tormented ululations filled Harry's brain as the predator burst asunder, spilling its complex conceptual framework in explosive agony.

Deprived of its parent, one of the mites shattered just before reaching his throat. But the other held cohesion long enough to strike him from behind.

It was Harry's turn to scream. He howled as something fluxed into his body. Pain yanked away all rational thought, piercing his buttocks and spine, then coursing along his outer flesh like searing fire. Meanwhile, deep within, qualms and uncertainties began attacking every belief, every assumption he had ever held dear.

Suns and galaxies loomed around Harry as the station leaned into the Avenue, pushing against the membrane separation, threatening to trigger a reentry transition.

Machinery wailed, joining his bellow of despair.

All the memes and holograms had vanished. Air leaked out of the station through a dozen small holes. But he hardly noticed. Teetering between one realm of living ideas and another of harsh, universal rules, Harry fought to hold on to something. His essence. His sense of inner being.

Himself.

This is not the best of all possible hiding places.

Then why did we/I choose it, my rings?

Out of all the twisty crannies that make up the great battleship, why did we take shelter in this chamber of glass-sealed walls and bubbling incubation cells?

Because it is 'home'? The place where we began?

Our second torus of cognition refutes this with a reminder that *most* of our component rings had their origins elsewhere – in pungent mulch pits filled with delicious rotting vegetation, at a crude settlement called Far Wet Sanctuary, on lonely Jijo.

It is true. Only three present members of our shared stack started here, aboard the *Polkjhy*, in this sterile nursery, where infant rings are nurtured to perfection with computer-controlled drips of synthetic nutrients. But they are three of our most important parts, yes?

- Our muscular torus-of-movement, with agile legs.
- Our donut-of-smells, making us recognizable to the Jophur crew.
- And, of course, your Master Ring, most precious of all. The essential (Me) ingredient, needed to transform modestly diffuse traeki into gloriously focused Jophur.

Is that not reason for nostalgia? Enough to call this darkened chamber home? (Though it appears to have suffered damage recently, and been repaired with hasty patching.)

Yes, go ahead. You may stroke the wax of memory. Recall the way things used to be on Jijo, before the change. Recollect how we/i learned to understand *alien* forms of parenthood, from close association with five other races.

During our prior incarnation, as the beloved traeki sage, *Asx*, we/i used to hold qheuen grubs and g'Kek larvae in our gentle tentacles, as well as hoon and human babies, rocking them, or spilling sweet aromatic mist-lullabies, crafted to bring happy dreams.

These recollections are preserved, not melted by our violent transformation into *Ewasx*. And yet, I am confused.

What point are you trying to make, my rings?

That we should be jealous?

That no ring stack – traeki or Jophur – can ever know a parent's love?

We are piled up from parts. Assembled. *Made*, like some machine. Perhaps that is why other races hate/envy us so.

What? you say there is no such hatred on Jijo? Ah, but consider the price you colonists paid for likability! To live in brute ignorance. Worse yet, afflicted to remain placid traeki, almost inert with lack of ambition. Won't you admit, at last, that life was never this vivid when you comprised poor compliant Asx?

you will? you'll concede that much?

Well, then. Perhaps we are making progress.

WHAT? WHAT'S THAT?

you would have *Me*, the Master Torus, confess something in return?

you wish me to admit that we have lately also seen some drawbacks – some disadvantages – to the monomaniacal way Jophur behave.

No, you needn't stroke recent wax, or replay those horrid events we observed before fleeing the control room. Foul-tempered, aggrieved and violent, the actions of our leaders were hardly inspiring. They don't exhibit great progress toward enlightenment.

But what choice is there? We of *Polkjhy* must pursue the dolphin-crewed ship! Its secrets may shed light on a time of changes, now convulsing the Five Galaxies. If Earthlings truly did find Progenitor Relics in a shallow globular cluster, what might that say about the way Galactic Civilization has been run for a billion years? Could it imply that our entire religious-and-genetic hierarchy is upside down?

WHAT IS THAT YOU SAY?

Our second ring of cognition asks – *so what?*

- *so what* if ancient beliefs about the Progenitors prove wrong!
- *so what* if we were lied to about the Embrace of Tides!
- *so what* if some other clan manages to seize *Streaker*, and read its information first! Why should any sensible sapient get into a greaselather over matters so obscure and trivial?

— — —
— — —
— — —

I ... hesitate to answer.

The question seems so jarringly incomprehensible ... like asking why we breathe oxygen, or metabolize food, or procreate, or express loyalty to kindred and posterity! It disturbs Me gravely that you/we could even raise such doubts!

PERHAPS I/WE SHOULD NOT HAVE FLED THE CONTROL ROOM, AFTER ALL.

(Seeking sanctuary in this dim/familiar hiding place.)

Indeed, our shared core roils with mad, provocative thoughts, questioning central Jophur beliefs. Moreover, since becoming a fugitive, I no longer seem to have the Masterful force of will that once let me squelch such ponderings.

PERHAPS IT WOULD HAVE BEEN BETTER TO LET THE FOLLOWERS OF THE HIGH PRIEST DISASSEMBLE US/ME FOR SPARE PARTS.

That might have been My greatest service to *Polkjhy*, and to the great Jophur clan as a whole.

The chief advantage of this refuge is that ship sensors will be unable to detect our body traces, masked by row after row of transparent growth cabinets, filled with juvenile rings of all types. Of course, there are robot nurses here, tending the young. These slave-drones would report me, but only if someone on the bridge *asks*. Unless or until a specific enquiry is made, I/we can probably remain safe here, emitting authority pheromones, giving the machines orders, pretending to be in charge of the caretaking facility.

There is another danger. At random intervals, various Jophur ring piles come to the door demanding spare parts.

Mostly, these are soldiers. Tall, formidable warrior stacks, bearing wounds and horrid stains from their ongoing struggle to expel Zang invaders from the battleship. That infestation currently blights a third of *Polkjhy*'s decks and zones. Some recent progress has been made against it, but our fighters show the cost, seeking replacements for rings damaged in close combat with the hydrogen breathers.

Fortunately, none of their caste seems inclined to question our/My presence here ... and we mostly stay out of sight.

Yes, my rings. It is only a matter of time till we/I are caught. Soon we will face disassembly. I wonder if they will bother salvaging any of our toruses or waxy memory beads for use elsewhere.

Probably not.

During long, idle moments, we/I linger before vision-odor displays, captivated by events that have enveloped *Polkjhy* since our captain-leader was killed.

Do you recall, my rings, how our great ship swooped through the twisted bowels of the transfer point, following the Earthship so closely, and with such skill, that they could never get away?

From the Research Department, crew-stacks reported progress understanding the *Streaker*'s strange protective layer – the coating that prevented our rays from stopping the dolphins earlier. That veneer seemed to offer invincibility, but according to our onboard Library we learn the technique was abandoned by most Galactics long ago! The tactic is quite easily defeated, once an opponent knows how. Only surprise made it effective back at the Fractal World.

The librarians promised a recommended countermeasure, shortly.

Meanwhile, the transfer nexus grew crowded with refugee ships, not only from the dissolved retirement community behind us, but from hundreds of others! Each emigrant vessel decided among three choices – to remain in Galaxy Four and seek room in some other cloistered shelter, or else to change life orders. To go back to the starfaring Civilization of Five Galaxies ... or possibly forge deeper into the Embrace of Tides. It was enthralling, and a great honor, to watch so many exalted Old Ones make this fateful judgment, though it did not affect our tenacious pursuit of the Earthlings.

That was when we encountered the *Harrower*.

A thing of legend.

A rare phenomenon of destiny.

A cloud of light that sorted through the agitated, thronging vessels. Choosing some. Sending others along their assigned ways.

DO YOU RECALL OUR SURPRISE, MY RINGS, WHEN THE HARROWER PLUCKED UP THE EARTHLING SHIP, AND GENTLY PLACED IT AMONG THOSE AIMED FOR TRANSCENDENCE?

Stunned amazement filled *Polkjhy*'s halls and chambers. Who could have imagined this would happen? Dolphins are the youngest licensed sapient race in the Civilization of Five Galaxies. Whether by trickery or merit, this was the last thing any sane entity would expect!

At that point, our new captain-leader gave in to the inevitable. Commands were given. *Polkjhy* must give up the chase!

Instead, we would aim for Galaxy One, toward a Jophur base, to be cleansed of infesting Zang, and to report all we had learned. Even without the Earthship in our grasp, we would be able to tell its fate, and that data should be valuable.

Moreover, there is Jijo, an excellent consolation prize! When we reveal its location to the home clan, that little sooner world will make an ideal outpost for genetic experimentation/exploitation. A source of wealth for the race. Final destruction of the g'Kek, alone, would make our travails worthwhile.

Perhaps the clan would be so joyful over those achievements that allowance would be made for *this* crude, hybrid stack – for this Ewasx – if we/I manage to avoid capture-disassembly till then.

Thus the crew rejoiced, despite apparent failure of our central mission. Although the *Streaker* had escaped, it seemed to be no fault of our own. We had accomplished more than any other ship in known space. Now we could go home.

Only then the truly unexpected happened.

Do you recall, my rings? Or is the wax-of-surprise still too fresh and runny for true-memory to congeal?

We faced our own turn before the Harrower, expecting to be conveyed routinely, like so many others, on a swift path toward Galaxy One.

Strange light filled the ship, and we/I felt *scrutinized*. Some of our/My rings – former parts of Asx – compared it to communing with Jijo's wonder stone, the Holy Egg.

Then, to our/My/everyone's amazement, *Polkjhy* was lifted off the transfer thread and placed amid a row of the elect! The chosen! Those whose emblems marked them for great honor and enlightenment, far down amid the Embrace of Tides.

Thus we learned the wondrous glory of our new honored state . . . and the pain yet to be endured.

What no one could explain, from our senior priest-stack on down to the lowest warrior, was *why?*

Why were we chosen for this honor?

One we never sought.

One that brings no gladness to any Jophur stack aboard this noble ship.

I/we stand corrected.

ONE STACK EXPERIENCES GLADNESS.

Some of the cognition rings left over from Asx rejoice at the news!

They think this means *Polkjhy* may never report on Jijo. The weird, miscegenist society of sooner races might yet be left in peace, if this battleship never makes it home.

Is that what you hope/believe, my rings?

I would discipline you now, with jolts of loving pain, to drive such disloyalty out of our common core, except—

Except that now the Harrower appears to have finished its task! The armadas it collected in pockets of coiled space have begun moving at last . . . in rows, columns, regiments . . . all pouring along special transfer threads that glow hot with friction.

Vibrations and sudden swerves shake *Polkjhy* so powerfully that swaying motions penetrate even our mighty stabilizing fields.

*

And now, as if none of that were enough, the sequence of upsetting surprises continues.

Robots continue tending the incubators, wherein juvenile rings of many shapes, attributes, and colors thrive on distilled nutrients, growing into components to make new Jophur stacks.

Soldiers keep coming for repairs, seeking to replace damaged walker-rings, sword-manipulators, chem-synth toruses, and even mortally wounded Master Rings. Clearly, the battle against the Zang rages on with deadly fury.

Meanwhile, on monitors, I/we watch *Polkjhy* emerge in some far star system, part of an orderly swarm of transcendence candidates – ranging from conventional-looking starships and spiky fractal shapes all the way to quivering blobs that appear horridly Zangish before our appalled gaze!

For several jaduras, this bizarre armada uses B-Level hyperspatial jumps to cross a gap of several paktaars, skirting around a vast glowing nebula in order to reach the next transfer point. Finally, the convoy dives into this nexus and another thread-ride commences, swooping along multidimensional flaw boundaries where space itself condensed long ago from the raw essence of an expanding universe.

While all this activity continues, we/I remain in a dim corner of the nursery chamber, hiding from our/My own crewmates . . . until the unexpected once again forces its way into our shock-numbed consciousness.

We stare at a new interloper.

A recent arrival, standing before our disbelieving senses.

The strangest being that I/we/i have ever seen.

It came just moments ago, arriving via an unconventional route – by supply tube – conveyed to the nursery in a slender car designed for transporting raw materials and samples, not sapient beings!

Crawling out before we could react, it unfolded long limbs, revealing a shape with proportions like a *Homo sapiens*. Indeed, the head protruding atop looked completely human. And familiar.

I/we stared, did we not, my rings? Several of our cognition-memory toruses exclaimed, releasing recognition vapors and causing words to vent from our shared oration peak.

'Lark! Is . . . it . . . really . . . you?'

Indeed, the face cracked open with that unique human-style smile. When it/he spoke, the voice was as we knew him from olden days, on Jijo.

'Greetings, reverend Asx . . . or shall I say *Ewasx*?'

While several of our components wrangled over an appropriate reply, others stared at the transformed body below the neckline. Lark's bipedal stance was similar, striding on stiff, articulated bones. Only now translucent film enveloped his flesh, ballooning outward like profoundly baggy garments, billowing and throbbing with a sick, semiliquid rhythm that sent quivers of nausea down our/My central core. An especially large bulge distended from his back, like a tumor, or a great burden he showed no sign of resenting.

Our chem-synth rings detected several awful stinks, such as methane, cyanogen, and hydrogen sulfide gas.

Sure stench-signs of Zang!

Surprise made our reply somewhat disjointed, to say the least.

'I/we ... cannot say what ... *name* ... would best apply to this stack ... at this time. Voting commences/continues on that point ... And yet ... it can be said in truth that certain parts of us/me/I/we recognize certain ... *parts* ... of you/You ...'

Our shared voice trailed off. Neither Anglic nor GalSix seemed well suited to convey appropriate/accurate levels of astonishment. Emotional pheromones vented ... and to our surprise, the 'Lark/Zang' entity answered in kind!

Molecular messages puffed from his new outer skin, triggering instant comprehension by our/My pore receptors.

MUTUAL RECOGNITION
AMICABLE INTENT
WILLINGNESS TO FIND RESOLUTION

Seeking the source of these scent messages, our/My sensors now locate a toroidal-shaped bulge, situated near Lark's chest.

Purple colored.

A traeki ring, incorporated in the group entity across from us!

At once, we/I recognize one of the small rings Asx secretly created, without knowledge of the Ewasx Master, to help Lark and his human companion escape bondage several jaduras ago.

Stroking memory wax from that time, I/we now realize/recall – there had been a *second* cryptic ring.

'I left the other one here,' Lark explains, as if reading My/our thoughts. 'It was wounded. Ling hid it in this nursery, to get care and feeding. That's one reason I came back. My new associates want to find the little red ring. They want to know its purpose.'

He does not have to explain his 'associates.' A Jophur instinctively knows – as most unitary beings do not – that it is possible to blend and mix and match disparate components to make a new composite being. In this case, the chimera is an amalgam of human, traeki, and Zang ... a terrifying union, but somehow credible.

'You ... wish to have our/My help recovering the red ring?' I ask. Lark nods.

'Its powers may bring peace to this vast vessel ...'

He pauses for a moment, as if communing with himself, then goes on.

'But there is something else. The price I demanded for cooperating in this mission.

'We're going to rescue Ling.'

HARRY

Voices encroached on his latest nightmare, pushing past a delirium of jibbering voices and scraping agonies.

'*I think he's coming around,*' someone said.

Harry thrashed, shaking his head from left to right.

For what seemed an eternity, his mind had felt stripped, laid bare to E Space, fertile ground for colonization by parasitic memes – intricate, self-sustaining symbolic entities unlike anything conceived on Earth, invading to expropriate his incoherent dreams. Even now, as something like consciousness began to dawn, eerie shapes still thronged and cackled, more bizarre than anything born in an organic mind.

Somehow – perhaps by force of will, or else plain obstinacy – he pushed most of them aside, clawing his way toward wakefulness.

'Are you sure we oughta let him get up?' asked another, higher-pitched voice. 'Look at those teeth he's got. He could be dangerous!'

The first speaker seemed calmer, though with a touch of uncertainty.

'Come on. You've seen chimps before. They're our friends. We couldn't be luckier, after everything we've been through.'

'You call *this* a chimp?' the other rejoined. 'I never spent as much time around 'em as you have, or read as many books, but I bet no chimp ever looked like this!'

That comment, more than anything, spurred Harry to fight harder against the clinging drowsiness.

What's wrong with the way I look? I'll match my face against a hairless ape's, any day!

Of course the voices were human. He recognized the twangy overtones, despite a strange accent.

How did humans get into E Space?

Painful brightness stabbed, the first time he tried cracking his eyelids. A groan escaped Harry's lips as he raised a heavy forearm over his eyes.

'I—'

His throat felt parched. Almost too scratchy to speak.

'I could use ... some water.'

Their reaction surprised him. The higher voice squawked.

'It talks! You see? It *can't* be a chimp. Clobber it!'

Harry's eyes flew open, this time to a world of glare and blurry shadows. Struggling upward, he sensed a pair of nearby figures backing away quickly. Young humans, he perceived – male and female – filthy and disheveled.

'Hey!' he croaked. 'What d'you mean I can't be a—' Harry stopped suddenly, unable to move further or speak. He could only stare at the arm in front of him. His own arm ... covered with sparse fur.

Glossy *white* fur.

His hair was the color of frost on a windowsill during winter mornings on Horst.

Harry's chest pounded. Worse, a sharp pain stabbed his spine, just above the buttocks, like a numbed hand or foot coming back to life.

'Watch out,' the young female cried. 'It's gettin' up!'

Fighting panic, Harry scrambled to his feet, clutching at his body, checking it for wounds, for missing parts. To his great relief, all the important bits seemed still attached. But his eyes roved wildly, out of control, seeking to find out what else was wrong.

White fur ... white fur ... I ... I can live with that ... assuming it's the only thing that's changed ...

One of the humans reentered his fear-limned field of vision. The male, wearing tattered rags, with several weeks' stubble on his chin. Mixed up by anxiety and confusion, Harry could only snarl reflexively and back away.

'Hey there,' the youth said in soothing tones. 'Take it easy, mister. You asked for water. I've got some, in this here canteen.'

There was an object in his hand. It looked like a dirty gourd or pumpkin, stoppered with a cylinder of wood.

What is this, Harry thought. *Some sorta joke? Or more E Space mind garbage?*

Still retreating across the deck of his battered scout station, he glimpsed through a window that the scenery outside had changed. The vast plain of fuzzy carpet was now yellow, instead of beige, and the mist had grown thicker, obscuring everything except a nearby mound of metal rubble, smoldering as it slowly dissolved into the surrounding greedy strands. He wanted to ask what had happened, how long he had been out, where these humans had come from, and how they had gotten inside his ship. Perhaps he owed them his life. But caught in a flux of near hysteria, it was all he could do right now to keep from screeching at them.

White fur ... but that's not all. Something else is wrong! Those mites did more to me than that, I know it!

Now both humans were in clear view. The female – not much more than a girl – had a nasty scar down one side of her face. She gripped a crowbar, brandishing it like a weapon. The boy held her back, though he too was clearly dismayed and confused by Harry's appearance.

'We're not gonna hurt you,' he said. 'You saved us from the monsters. We came over and patched your hull for you. Look, my name is Dwer and this is Rety. We're humans ... Earthlings. Can you tell us who – and what – you are?'

Harry wanted to scream. To ask if they were blind! Shouldn't patrons know their own clients? Even with white fur, a chimp was still—

He felt a sudden tickle behind him. Of course the bulkhead was back there and he could back up no farther. But the sensation came just an instant too soon, in too strange a fashion, as if the wall was brushing an extension of his spine.

My spine.

That was where – the last thing he recalled – a little predatory memoid had attacked and chewed its way into his flesh, filling his mind-body with waves of turmoil and disorientation.

'I mean ... you *look* like you might be some sort of a relative,' the youth went on, babbling nervously. 'And you spoke Anglic just now, so maybe ...'

Harry wasn't listening. Nervously, with a rising sense of dread, he groped around behind himself with his left hand, brushing the bulkhead, then moving downward.

Something started rising up to meet the hand. He sensed it clearly. Something that was part of himself.

A snakelike tendril, covered with hair, planted itself assuredly into his palm. It felt as natural as scratching his own ass, or pulling on his thumb.

Oh, he thought, with some relief. *It's just my damned tail.*

His mouth went round.

Breath froze in his throat ... then whistled out with a long, mournful sigh.

The two humans edged away nervously as the sigh underwent a

metamorphosis, transmuting like some eager meme with a mind all its own, turning into coarse, hysterical laughter.

The effect, when he finally got around to examining his reflection calmly, wasn't half as bad as he had feared. In fact, the white fur seemed rather – well – charismatic.

As for his new appendage, Harry was already resigned to it.

Surely it must have uses, he thought. *Though I'm not looking forward to the tailoring bills.*

Things could have been much worse, of course. The memoid parasite that invaded his body had been dying, moments after its parent exploded from brief contact with Material Reality. With a final gasp, it must have latched on to some random thought in Harry's mind, using that to force a quick shift in self-image. In E Space, the way you pictured yourself could sometimes have dramatic effects on who and what you became.

One thing was certain – he could never go to Earth looking like this. To be called a 'monkey' would be the last insufferable humiliation.

When I joined the Navigation Institute, I figured it meant I'd probably live the rest of my life apart from my kind. Now I belong to Wer'Q'quinn more than ever.

At his command, the station was now striding alongside the great, shining Avenue, limping at maximum safe speed, retracing its earlier path to pick up the instrument packages and finish this assignment before anything else went wrong.

One good thing about Wer'Q'quinn. The old squid will hardly notice any difference in my looks. All he cares about is getting the job done.

That left him with one more problem.

The young humans.

Apparently, Rety and Dwer had been the 'organic cargo' carried by the hapless machine entity. Their little habitat was about to be attacked and torn open by a ravenous meme-raptor when Harry arrived. From their point of view, he was like the proverbial cavalry. A knight from some storybook, galloping to the rescue just in the nick of time.

They later returned the favor, after the final memoid fled the scene, bloated on stolen atoms. After talking the dying mech into using its last resources to build an airlock bridge, they boarded Harry's station, saving him from asphyxiation while he sprawled on the deck, stunned and unconscious.

The mech then expired, contributing its mass as temporary fertilizer to this matter-parched desert.

'We never could figure out where we were, or why it took us here,' Dwer explained, while wolfing down a triple helping of Harry's rations. 'The machine never spoke, though it seemed to understand when I talked in GalTwo.'

Harry watched the boy, fascinated by Dwer's mixture of the savage and gentleman. He never denied being a sooner – descended from criminal colonists who had abandoned technology over two centuries ago. Yet, he could read half a dozen Galactic languages, and clearly grasped some implications of his situation.

'When the mech took us aboard, near the red giant star, we thought we'd had it. The scrolls say machines that live in deep space can be dangerous, and sometimes enemies to our kind of life. But this one made a shelter for us, improved our air, and fixed the recycler. It even asked us where we wanted to go!'

'I thought you said it never spoke,' Harry pointed out.

Rety, the teenager with the scarred cheek, shook her head.

'One of its drones came aboard with a piece of metal that had words scratched on. I dunno why it used that way to talk, since we had a little tutor unit that could've spoken to it. But at least the robot seemed to understand when we answered.'

'And what did you say?'

Both humans replied at the same time.

Dwer: 'I asked it to take us home.'
Rety: 'I told it to bring us to the most important guys around!'

They looked at each other, a smoldering argument continuing in their eyes.

Harry pondered for a long moment, before finally nodding with understanding.

'Those sound like incompatible commands. To you or me, it would call for making a choice between two options, or negotiating a compromise. But I doubt that's what a machine would do. My best guess is that it tried to combine and optimize both imperatives at the same time. Of course its definition of terms might be quite different from what you had in mind at the time.'

The young humans looked confused, so he shook his head.

'All I can tell for sure is that you were definitely *not* heading back toward your sooner colony when I found your trail.'

Rety nodded with satisfaction. 'Ha!'

'Nor were you aimed at Earth, or a base of the Great Institutes, or any of the mighty powers of the Five Galaxies.'

'Then where—'

'In fact, the mech was taking you – at lethal risk to itself – into

1230

dimensions and domains so obscure they are hardly named. It seemed to be following the cold trail of two—'

A warning chime interrupted Harry. The signal that another of Wer'Q'quinn's little camera packages lay just ahead.

'Excuse me awhile, will you?' he asked the humans, who seemed to understand that he had a job to do. In fact, even Rety now treated him with respect that seemed a little exaggerated, coming from a member of Harry's patron race.

He got busy, using the station's manipulators to recover the final probe, then spraying it with a special solvent to make sure no memic microbes clung to the casing, before stowing it away. Nearby, the Avenue gleamed with starlight. The realm of material beings and reliable physical laws lay just a few meters away, but Harry had no intention of diving through. His chosen route home was more roundabout, but also probably much safer.

While finishing the task, he glanced back at Dwer and Rety, the two castaways he had saved . . . and who in turn had rescued him. They were fellow descendants of Earthclan, and humans were officially Uplift-masters to the neo-chimp race. But legally he owed them nothing. In fact, as an official of one of the Great Institutes, it was his duty to arrest any sooners he came across.

And yet, what good would that accomplish? He doubted they knew enough astrodynamics to be able to tell anyone where their hidden colony world lay, so nothing could be gained by interrogating them. From what they had said so far, their settlement was highly unusual, a peaceful blending of half a dozen species that were mostly at each other's throats back in civilization. It might be newsworthy, in normal times. But right now, with all five galaxies in a state of uproar and navigation lanes falling apart, they seemed likely to fall between the cracks of bureaucracy, at Kazzkark Base.

Anyway, Harry was surprised to learn how pleasurable it was to hear voices speaking native wolfling dialects. Though a loner most of his life, he felt strangely buoyed to have humans around, who were very nearly his own kind.

The camera slipped into its casing with a satisfying clank. Checking his clipboard, Harry felt a glow of satisfaction. *The last one. I know some other scouts were betting against my ever returning, let alone achieving success. I can't wait to rub their noses – and beaks and snouts and other proboscides – in it!*

With a heavy limp, his battered station turned away from the Avenue at last, heading toward a cluster of slender towers that he now knew to be legs of several huge, metaphorical chairs and a giant table. His best route home.

I wonder how long this zone will stay coalesced around my viewpoint seed. Will it melt back into chaos when I'm gone? Or is that a symptom of what Wer'Q'quinn keeps warning me against – an inflated notion of my own self-importance?

In fact, Harry knew he wasn't the first material outsider to pass through this zone in recent times. Before he came, and before the hapless mech, two other spacecraft had passed through – one chasing another.

Could all of this – he looked around at the vast furniture and other chachkis of an emblematic parlor – *have already taken shape before I arrived? I sure don't consciously recall ever being in a room like it before, even as a child. Maybe one of those vessels that preceded me provided the seed image.*

It bothered him that he still had no idea why the mech had brought Dwer and Rety here.

Combining two request-commands. Taking the humans 'home,' and bringing them to 'the most important guys around.'

He shook his head, unable to make sense of it.

One thing, though. I know the Skiano missionary is gonna plotz when he sees the three of us Earthlings – two actual living humans and a transformed chimp – striding along the boulevards of Kazzkark. It oughta make a sensation!

A table leg loomed just ahead, the one Harry hoped to ascend back toward his chosen portal, assuming it remained where gut instinct told him it must ... And if the station was still capable of climbing. And if ...

Pilot mode popped into space nearby, a cursive *P* rotating in midair.

'Yes?' Harry nodded.

'I am afraid I must report movement, detected to the symbolic left of our present heading. Large memoid entities, approaching our position rapidly!'

Harry groaned. He did not want another encounter with the local order of life.

'Can we speed up any?'

'At some modest increased risk, yes. By twenty percent.'

'Then please do so.'

The station began moving faster ... and the limp seemed to grow more jarring with each passing step. Harry glanced at Rety and Dwer, who as usual were bickering in a manner that reminded him of some married couples he had known – inseparable, and never in accord. He decided not to tell them quite yet. *Let 'em think the danger's over, for a while longer at least.*

Stationing himself near a portside window, Harry peered through the murk.

We only need a few more minutes. Come on, you memoid bastards. Leave us alone just that long!

Harry's back itched, and he started reaching around with a hand to scratch it ... but stopped when the job was handled more conveniently by his new appendage. His tail, lithely curling up to rub and massage the very spot. At once, it felt both natural and surprising, each time it moved to his conscious or unconscious will.

He caught the two young humans staring at him. Dwer at least had the decency to blush.

Eat yer hearts out, Harry thought, and used the tail to smooth his pelt of sleek, ivory fur. *Poor humans. Stuck with those bare skins ... and bare butts.*

Then he had no more time for whimsy.

Out there amid the haze, he spied movement. Several dark gray entities. Huge ones, far larger than the megapedes he had fought before. Through the mist, these looked sleek and rounded, nosing along the vast carpet like a herd of great elephants.

Then Harry realized. That was the wrong metaphor. As they drew nearer, he recognized their rapid, darting motions, their earlike projections and twitching noses.

Mice ... goddamn giant mice! Ifni, that's all I need.

He felt a shiver of dismay as he realized – they had spotted the station.

To the pilot mode, he gave an urgent, spoken command. 'Increase speed! We've got to climb the leg before they reach us!'

Amber and red lights erupted across the control board as the jarring pace accelerated. A great woodlike pillar loomed before them, but Harry also sensed the memes scurrying faster in pursuit. Self-sustaining conceptual forms far more sophisticated and carnivorous than any he had seen. It was going to be tight. Very tight indeed.

God. I don't know how much more of this I can take.

IV

CANDIDATES OF TRANSCENDENCE

Our universe of linked starlanes – the Five Galaxies – consists of countless hierarchies. Some species are ancient, experienced in the ways of wisdom and power. Others have just begun trodding the paths of self-awareness. And there are innumerable levels in between.

These are not conditions in which nature would produce fairness. There would be no justice for the weak, unless some code moderated the raw impulses of pure might.

With this aim, we inherit from the Great Progenitors many traditions and regulations, formalizing the relationships between patrons and their clients, or between colonists and the nonsapient creatures that inhabit life-worlds. Sometimes these rules seem so complex and arbitrary that it taxes our patience. We lose sight of what it is all about. Recently, a savant of the Terran starfaring clan – (a dolphin) – suggested that the matter be viewed quite simply, in terms of respect for the food chain.

Another Earthling sage – (a human) – put it even more simply, expressing what he called the Meta Golden Rule.

'Treat your inferiors as you would have your superiors treat you.'

FROM THE JOURNAL OF
GILLIAN BASKIN

I wish Tom could have been here. He would love this.

The mystery.

The terrifying splendor.

Standing alone in my dim office, I look out through a narrow pane at the shimmering expanse of raw *ylem* surrounding *Streaker* – the basic stuff of our continuum, the elementary ingredient from which all the varied layers of hyperspace condensed, underpinning what we call the 'vacuum.'

The sight is spine-tingling. Indescribably beautiful. And yet my thoughts keep racing. They cannot settle down to appreciate the view.

My heart's sole wish is that Tom were sharing it with me right now. I can almost feel his arm around my waist, and the warm breath of his voice, urging me to look past all the gritty details, the worries, the persisting dangers and heartaches that plague us.

'No one said it would be safe or easy, going into space.

Or, for that matter, rising from primal muck to face the heavens. We may be clever apes, my love – rash wolflings to the end. Yet, something in us hears a call.

'We must rush forth to see.'

Of course, he would be right to say all that. I've been privileged to witness so many marvels. And yet, I answer his ghost voice the way a busy mother might chide a husband so wrapped up in philosophy that he neglects life's messy chores.

Oh, Tom. Even when surrounded by a million wonders, someone has to worry about the details.

Here aboard this frail dugout canoe, that someone is me.

Days pass, and *Streaker* is still immersed in this remarkable fleet. A vast armada of moving receptacles – I hesitate to call the spiky, planet-sized things 'ships' – sweeps along, sometimes blazing through A- or B-Level hyperspace, or else turning to plunge down the throat of yet another transfer point . . . an immense crowd of jostling behemoths, racing along cosmic thread paths that correspond to no chart or reference in our archives.

Should I be surprised by that? How many times have I heard other sapient beings – from Soro and Pila to Synthians and Kanten – preach awe toward the majestic breadth and acumen of the Galactic Library, whose records encompass countless worlds and more than a billion years, ever since it was first established by the legendary Progenitors, so long ago.

We younger races feel the Library must be all-knowing. Only rarely does someone mention its great limitation.

The Library serves only the Civilization of Five Galaxies. The ancient culture of oxygen-breathing starfarers that we Earthlings joined three centuries ago.

To poor little Earthclan, that seemed more than enough! So complex and overpowering is that society – with its mysterious traditions, competing alliances, and revered Institutes – that one can hardly begin to contemplate what else lies beyond.

But more does lie beyond. At least seven other orders of life, thriving in parallel to our own. Orders that have wildly different needs and ambitions, as well as their own distinct kinds of wisdom.

Even the ever-curious Tymbrimi advised us to avoid contact with these ultimate strangers, explaining that it's just too confusing, unprofitable, and dangerous to be worth the trouble.

To which I can only say – from recent experience – *amen*.

Of course, it's common knowledge that the oldest oxygen-breathing races eventually die or 'move on.' As with individuals, no species lasts forever. The cycle of Uplift, which stands at the core of Galactic society, is all about replenishment and renewal. Pass on the gift of sapiency, as it was passed to you.

Being new to this game, ignorant and desperately poor, with our own chimp and dolphin clients to care for, we humans focused on the opening moves, studying the rules so we might act as responsible patrons, and perhaps avoid the fate that usually befalls wolflings.

Beginnings are important.

Yet, each alliance and clan also speaks reverently of those who came before them. Those who, like venerated great-grandparents, finished their nurturing tasks, then turned their attention to other things, maturing to new heights and new horizons.

After we fled treachery at Oakka World, I decided not to trust the corrupted Institutes anymore and to seek advice instead from some of those learned, detached elders we had heard about. Beings who had abandoned starfaring for a more contemplative life in the Retired Order, cloistered near the fringes of a dim red star.

Events at the Fractal World soon taught us a lesson. Aloofness does not mean impartiality. The so-called Retired Order is, in fact, only a vestibule for oxy-races that can no longer bear the rigors of flat spacetime. Though they huddle like hermits in a gravity well, trying to perfect their racial souls, that doesn't necessarily make them tolerant or wise. After our travails with the Old Ones, I was willing to head back into the Five Galaxies, and risk contact with oxy-civilization once more.

Only now we find ourselves, against all logic or reason, adopted willy-nilly into the Transcendent Order!

At least that is what the symbol on our prow seems to mean. Somebody, or something, planted a single wide chevron there – perhaps as a very bad joke.

An emblem signifying high spiritual attainments, plus readiness to abandon all temporal concerns.

In effect, it says – *Hey! Look at us. We're all set for godhood!*

Sheesh, what a situation. I feel like a street kid with a stolen tuxedo and fake ID, who somehow managed to bluff her way into the Nobel Prize ceremony, and now finds herself sitting next to the podium, scheduled to give a speech!

All *this* street kid wants right now is a chance to slink away without being noticed, before the grown-ups catch on and really give us hell.

Getting away won't be easy. A kind of momentum field rings this huge flotilla, carrying us along helplessly amid the horde of giant transports. Moreover, our navigation systems are haywire. We've no idea where we are, let alone where to go.

At one point, during an especially smooth transit through B Space, Akeakemai reported that the surrounding field seemed weak. I had him nudge *Streaker* to the edge of the swarm, hoping to slip out during one of the cyclical jumps back to normal space. But as we prepared to break free, Olelo thrashed her flukes with a whistle warning. We were being scanned by hostile beams, cast from an enemy ship!

Soon we spied the Jophur dreadnought, working its way through the throng of giant arks.

Once, the battlewagon had seemed omnipotent. Now it looked small compared to the surrounding behemoths. Stains marred its once shiny hull in places where the skin seemed to *throb*, like infected blisters. Still, the crew of egotistic sap-rings had great power and determination to pursue *Streaker*. They would pounce whenever we left the convoy's safety.

We fell back amid the titans, biding our time.

Perhaps whatever ills afflict the Jophur will eventually overcome them.

The universe may produce another miracle.

Who knows?

Perhaps we will *transcend*.

*

The Niss Machine plumbed our stolen Library unit, researching data about the strange layer covering *Streaker*'s hull, both shielding her and weighing her down. It began as a thick coat of star soot, amassed in the atmosphere of a smoldering carbon sun. Later, some mysterious faction transformed the blanket – beneficently, or with some arcane goal in mind – creating a shimmering jacket that saved our lives.

'*It is a form of armor,*' the Niss explained. '*Offering tremendous protection against directed energy weapons – as we learned dramatically at the Fractal World. Trawling for records, I found that the method was used extensively on warships until approximately two hundred million years ago, when a fatal flaw was discovered, rendering it obsolete.*'

'What flaw?' I asked. Naturally, something so convenient must have an Achilles' heel.

The Niss explained. '*Much of the soot pouring out from Izmunuti consists of molecules you Earthlings call fullerenes – or* buckeyballs – *open mesh spheres and tubes consisting of sixty or more carbon atoms. These have industrial uses, especially if gathered into sheets or interlocking chains. That's why robot harvesters visited Izmunuti, acquiring material in their futile effort to repair the Fractal World.*'

'We already knew the stuff was strong,' I answered. 'Since Suessi had such trouble removing it. But that's a far cry from resisting Class-Eight disintegrator beams!'

The Niss explained that it took special reprocessing to convert that raw deposit into another form. One with just the right guest atoms held captive inside buckeyball enclosures. '*Atoms of strange matter,*' the disembodied voice said.

I confess I did not understand at first. It seems that certain elements can be made from ingredients other than the normal run of protons, electrons, and neutrons, utilizing unusual varieties of quarks. Such atoms must be kept caged, or they tend to vanish from normal space, hopping off to D Level, or another subcontinuum where they feel more at home.

It felt weird to picture *Streaker* sheathed in such stuff. Then again, I guess it would be weirder to be dead.

I well remember expecting to be vaporized when those fierce beams struck. But our surprising new armor absorbed all that energy, shunting every erg to another reality plane, dissipating it harmlessly.

'Sounds like a neat trick,' I commented.

'*Indeed, Dr. Baskin,*' the Niss answered, with a sardonic edge. '*But a few hundred eons ago, someone discovered how to render this fine defense useless by reversing the flow. By turning this wondrous material into a huge antenna, absorbing energy from hyperspace – in effect cooking the crew and everything else inside.'*

So, that was why no one in the Five Galaxies had been stupid or desperate enough to use this kind of armor for a long time. It worked at first, because the Jophur were taken by surprise. But they have their own Branch Library aboard the *Polkjhy*, every bit as good as ours. By now they must surely have caught on, and prepared for our next encounter.

Somehow, we've got to get rid of this stuff!

I assigned Hannes Suessi to puzzle over that problem. Meanwhile, my plate is full of other troubles.

For one thing, the glavers howl, night and day.

Before leaving aboard Kaa's little boat, Alvin Hph-wayuo instructed us in the care and feeding of those devolved descendants of mighty starfarers. There wasn't much to it. Feed them simulated grubs and clean their pen every few days. The glavers seemed stolid and easy to please. But no sooner did Kaa depart, taking Alvin and his friends to safety, than the filthy little creatures started moaning and carrying on.

I asked our only remaining Jijo native what it could mean, but the behavior mystifies Sara. So I can only guess it has something to do with the changing composition of the huge migration fleet surrounding us.

As we move across vast reaches of space and hyperspace, more globulelike vessels keep joining the throng, jostling side by side with jagged-edged arks of the former Retired Order. *Zang* ... plus other varieties of hydrogen breathers ... now make up roughly two-thirds of the armada, though their vessels are generally much smaller than the monumental oxy-craft.

Our glavers must be sensing the Zang presence somehow. It makes them agitated – though whether from fear or anticipation is hard to tell.

They aren't the only ones feeling edgy. After leaving so many crewmates behind on Jijo, *Streaker* seems haunted and void ... a bit like a wraith ship. Mystery surrounds us, and dangerous uncertainty lies ahead.

Yet, I can say without reservation that the dolphins left aboard this battered ship are performing their tasks admirably, with complete professionalism and dedication. After three years of winnowing, we are down to the last of Creideiki's selected crew. Those who seem immune to reversion or mental intimidation. Tested in a crucible of relentless hardship, they are pearls of Uplift –

treasures of their kind. Every one would get unlimited breeding privileges, if we made it home.

Which doubles the irony, of course.

Not one of the fins believes we'll ever see Earth again.

As for Sara, she spends much of her time with the silent little chimp, Prity, using a small computer to draw hyperdimensional charts and complex spacetime matrices.

When I asked the Niss Machine to explain what they were doing, that sarcastic entity dismissed their project, calling it – *'Superstitious nonsense!'*

In other words, Sara still hopes to complete the work of her teacher, combining ancient Earthling mathematical physics with the computational models of Galactic science, trying to make sense out of the strange, frightening disruptions we have seen. Convulsions that appear to be unsettling a large fraction of the universe.

'I'm still missing some element or clue,' she told me this morning, expressing both frustration and the kind of heady exhilaration that comes with intense labor in a field you love.

'I wonder if it may have something to do with the Embrace of Tides.'

The Niss seems all too ready to dismiss Sara's efforts, because they have no correlation in the Great Library. But I've been impressed with her gumption and brilliance, even if she does seem to be bucking long odds. All I can say is more power to her.

Always hovering near Sara – with a distant, longing expression in his eyes – poor Emerson watches her tentative models flow across the holo display. Sometimes he squints, as if trying to remember something that's just on the tip of his tongue. Perhaps he yearns to help Sara. Or to warn of something. Or else simply to express his feelings toward her.

Their growing affection is lovely to behold – though I cannot entirely deflect pangs of jealousy. I was never able to return Emerson's infatuation, before his accident. Yet he remains dear to me. It is only human to have mixed feelings as his attention turns elsewhere. The stark truth is that Sara now has the only virile male human within several megaparsecs. How could that not make me feel more lonely than ever?

Yes, Tom. I sense you are still out there somewhere, with Creideiki, prowling dark corners of the cosmos. I can trace a faint echo of your essence, no doubt making, and getting into, astonishing varieties of trouble. Stirring things up even more than they already were.

Assuming it isn't wishful thinking – or some grand self-deception on my part – don't you also feel my thoughts right now, reaching out to you?

Can't you, or won't you, follow them?

I feel so lost ... wherever 'here' is.

Tom, please come and take me home.

Ah, well. I'll edit out the self-pity later. At least I have Herbie for company.

Good old Herb – the mummy standing in a corner of my office, looking back at me right now with vacant eyes. Humanoid but ineffably alien. Older than many stars. An enigma that Tom bought with more than one life. A treasure of incalculable value, whose image launched a thousand Galactic clans and mighty alliances into mortal panic, shattering their own laws, chasing poor *Streaker* across the many-layered cosmos, trying to seize our cargo before anyone else could wrap their hands-claws-feelers-jaws around it.

My orders sound clear enough. Deliver Herbie – and our other treasures – to the 'proper authorities.'

Once, I thought that meant the Great Library, or the Migration Institute.

Sorely disappointed and betrayed by those 'neutral' establishments, we then gambled on the Old Ones – and nearly lost everything.

Now?

Proper authorities.

I have no idea who in the universe that would be.

Till this moment, I've put off reporting my most disturbing news. But there's no point in delaying any longer.

Yesterday, I had to put a dear friend under arrest.

Tsh't, my second-in-command, so competent and reliable. The rock I relied on for so long.

It breaks my heart to dial up the brig monitor and see her circling round and round, swimming without harness in a sealed pool, locked behind a coded door plate.

But what else could I do?

There was no other choice, once I uncovered her secret double dealings.

How did this happen? How could I have been blind to the warning signs? Like when those two Danik prisoners 'committed suicide' a couple of months ago. I should have investigated more closely. Put out feelers. But I left the inquest to her, so involved was I with other matters.

Finally, I could no longer ignore the evidence. Especially now that she helped another, far more dangerous prisoner to esc—

...

I had to interrupt making that last journal entry, several hours ago. (Not that I was enjoying the subject.)

Something intervened, yanking me away. An important change in our state of affairs.

The Niss Machine broke in to say the momentum field was collapsing.

The entire huge armada was slowing at last, dropping from A Level down to B, and then C. Flickers into normal space were growing longer with each jump. Soon, long-range sensors showed we were decelerating toward a brittle blue pinpoint – apparently our final destination.

Olelo's spectral scan revealed a *white dwarf star*, extremely compact, with a diameter less than a hundredth that of Earth's home sun, consisting mainly of ash from fusion fires that entered their last stage of burning eons ago. In fact, it is a very massive and old dwarf, whose lingering furnace glow comes from gravitational compression that may last another twenty billion years.

We began picking up nearby anomalies – spindly dark objects revolving quite close to that dense relic star. Massive structures, big enough to make out as black shadows that sparkled or flashed, occulting the radiant disk whenever they passed through line of sight. Which they did frequently. There were a lot of them, jammed so close that each circuit took less than a minute!

Soon we verified they were orbiting artifacts, jostling deep inside the sheer gravity well.

Of course the concept was familiar, reminding me of the Fractal World, crowding and shrouding its small red sun – a contemplative sanctuary for retirees. Indeed, this place bears a family resemblance to that vast habitat. Only here the distance scales are a hundred times smaller. Tremendous amounts of matter abide in that curled well, crammed into a tight funnel of condensed spacetime.

Whoever lives down there must not value elbow room very much.

They belong to an order of life that craves a different kind of dimensionality. A squeezing clasp that older races interpret as loving salvation.

*

Joining others in the Plotting Room, I watched this new variation on an old theme gradually loom before us.

'There are ssseveral billion white dwarves per galaxy,' commented Akeakemai. 'If even a small fraction are inhabited like this, the p-population of transcendent beings would be staggering. And none would've been detectable from pre-Contact Earth!'

Sara held the hand of Emerson, whose eyes darted among the surrounding vessels of our convoy, perhaps fearing what they might do, now that we'd arrived. I sympathized. We're all waiting for the other shoe to drop.

Deceleration continued through normal space, as the Niss Machine rematerialized to report. It had finished researching the symbol on our prow – the broad chevron representing our counterfeit membership in a higher order of sapiency.

'Let me conjecture,' I said, before the whirling hologram could explain. 'The emblem stands for a union of the hydro- and oxy-life, coming together at last.'

One of my few remaining satisfactions comes from surprising the smug machine.

'*How ... did you know?*' it asked.

I shrugged – a blithe gesture, covering the fact that I had guessed.

'Two line segments meeting at an angle of one hundred and four degrees. That can only represent the bonds of a *water molecule*. Hydrogen plus oxygen, combining to make the fundamental ingredient of all life chemistry. It's not so mysterious.'

The spinning lines seemed to sway.

'*Maybe for you,*' the Niss replied. '*Earthling preconceptions are not as fixed, perhaps. But to me this comes as a shock. After all the warnings, the endlessly repeated stories about how dangerous Zang are ... how illogical, touchy, and inscrutable they can be ...*'

I shrugged.

'Young boys call little girls names, and vice versa. Often, they can't stand each other's company. At least, till they grow up enough to need one another.'

It was a facile analogy. And yet, the comparison made sense!

I used to wonder about the oxy-hydro antagonism. How, if they are so fundamentally different, so explosively hostile and incompatible, did the Zang and their brethren manage to keep peace with the Civilization of Five Galaxies for so long? Why hasn't one side wiped out the other, instead of grudgingly cooperating in complex feats of migration and ecomanagement, sharing spiral arms and space lanes with a relative minimum of violence?

How, indeed? It seemed improbable.

That is, unless the whole thing was already worked out at a higher level! A level where both life orders at last matured enough to find common ground.

A consummation, with each side providing what the other lacks.

So.

Here we are, at a place of fusion and consolidation.

A union forged amid strong gravity currents, deep within the Embrace of Tides.

We seem to be invited.

That leaves just one question.

Why?

HARRY

He expected to be welcomed home with congratulations, perhaps by Wer'Q'quinn himself, or at least the old squid's senior aides, eager to receive Harry's data and hear about his successful mission.

A damned difficult mission, if truth be told. An epic voyage to one of the worst parts of E Space, where he had prevailed against horrible odds, and even picked up a couple of human-sooner cast-aways for good measure!

Anticipating acclaim, what he found at Kazzkark Base was chaos.

All the north pole docking bays were full, except a few set aside for official use. Approaching one of those, Harry had to shout his priority code, adding threats until a surly Migration Institute monitor-drone finally vacated a slot reserved for NavInst craft.

Beyond the starlit scaffolding, he glimpsed myriad sleek refugee ships, tethered in layers from one end of the planetoid to the other, creating a dense, confusing snarl of shadowy forms and glinting strobe lights.

'Ain't it excitin', Dwer?' murmured the girl with the scarred face – Rety – whose eyes gleamed at the sight. 'Didn't I promise ya? Stick with me an' I'll get you to civilization! That's what I said. Good-bye smelly ol' Jijo, and hello galaxy! We'll never be dirty, hungry, poor, or bored again.'

Harry exchanged a glance with the other human, the tall male. Both young savages were clearly out of their depth. But unlike Rety,

Dwer seemed to know it. His eyes expressed worried awe at the view outside.

Kinda like the way I feel, Harry pondered. Starships were packed together like shattered murvva trunks after a bad windstorm on Horst. *The disruptions must've got a lot worse since I left ... especially if folks are choosing dumpy old Kazzkark as a place to run away to!*

Magnetic grapples settled snugly around his battered survey station, which at last powered down with a relieved groan. Harry, too, exhaled the tension he had carried in his spine ever since departure, sighing deeply.

Home again ... such as it is.

Downloading Wer'Q'quinn's data to a portable wafer, he turned and ushered his guests toward the airlock. In normal times, returning from any other mission, this pair would have stirred a sensation at the sleepy base. Hints at a newly discovered sooner infestation would spread quickly, and make the arresting officer famous.

Residual loyalty tugged at Harry. Humans were patrons to his own race, after all. Ostensibly, he wasn't supposed to care about that anymore. But habits were hard to break.

Besides, Dwer and Rety saved my life.

The conflict left him feeling more ambivalent than triumphant as they passed through a short tunnel into the planetoid.

With everything in an uproar, maybe my report about them will just be overlooked.

He decided he could live with that.

The Ingress Atrium was filled with noise and commotion as a mélange of races pushed and jostled, ignoring the delicate rhythms and rituals of racial seniority and interclan protocol as they pressed for admission, hoping for sanctuary from an increasingly unreliable cosmos. Harry's Institute credentials got him through several gates, moving to the front of the queue with his two humans in tow. Still, it took most of a midura to reach the final portal labeled IMMIGRATION AND QUARANTINE. Along the way, he overheard some of the worry and panic fluxing through the Civilization of Five Galaxies.

'—three out of four transfer points in Lalingush Sector show dislocations, or catastrophic domain recombinations,' hissed a tunictguppit trader in GalSeven, exchanging gossip with a rotund p'ort'l whose chest-mounted eye blinked furiously.

The p'ort'l snorted in reply – a rich sound, with multitoned harmonies. 'I hear most of the remaining transfer points have been seized by local alliances, who are exacting illegal taxes on any ship attempting to enter or leave. One consequence is vast numbers of stranded merchants, students, pilgrims, and tourists with no way to get home!'

To Harry's surprise, the two young humans didn't seem at all panicky or intimidated by the crowd. Rety grinned happily, stroking the neck of her little urrish 'husband,' while Dwer stared at the diversity of sapient life-forms, occasionally leaning over to whisper in the girl's ear, pointing at some type of alien he recognized – perhaps from legends told around a campfire, back on his tribal homeworld – a more cosmopolitan attitude than Harry would have expected. Nevertheless, Dwer betrayed underlying nervousness in the way he clutched his bow and arrows tightly under one arm.

Harry had considered confiscating the crude archery equipment. In theory, prisoners weren't supposed to go around armed. Still, he doubted even the most stickling Galactic bureaucrat would recognize the assortment of twigs, strings, and bits of chipped stone as a weapon.

Speaking of rule sticklers, he thought, on reaching the main desk. The same sour hoonish official was on duty as last time, and just as obnoxious as ever. Despite the declared state of emergency, Twaphu-anuph flapped his richly dyed throat sac at anyone who showed even the slightest irregularity of documentation, ignoring their protests, sending them back to the end of the line. The hoon seemed frazzled from overwork and strain when Harry stepped up to the desk.

Get ready for a surprise, you gloomy old bureaucrat, Harry thought, relishing how his new tail and fur color would shock Twaphu-anuph.

To his disappointment, the hoon barely regarded Harry with a quick scan before looking back down at his monitor screens. Apparently, the pale fur coloration did not alter the official's gestalt of a Terran chimpanzee.

'Ah, *hrr-rrm*. So it is Observer Harms, once again inflicting his unwelcome simian visage on my tired sensoria,' Twaphu-anuph commented in snidely accented GalSix. 'Only this time – equally noxious – he brings along two of his grubby Earthling masters. Have they come to take you home at last, like a truant child?'

Harry sensed Rety and Dwer stiffen. He hurried to respond with more firmness than he might have otherwise.

'Twaphu-anuph, you exceed your prerogatives, which do not include heaping personal abuse on a fellow acolyte of the Great Institutes. However, if you pass us through at once, I may refrain from lodging a formal protest.'

Perhaps it was fatigue from a long, successful mission that gave

Harry's voice a more confident tenor. To his surprise, the big hoon seemed unmotivated to continue his traditional derisive taunting. Twaphu-anuph held out a giant hand.

'Hr-rr-r. Show me the humans' identification tags. *Please*.'

Harry shook his head.

'They are specimens claimed for observation by the Navigation Institute, entering Kazzkark under my own credentials. You may image both humans and do a bio scan before letting us through. That should take about thirty duras to accomplish. Regulations do not allow a longer delay. Or shall I complain to Wer'Q'quinn?'

Their eyes met. A low, rumbling sound fluttered from below Twaphu-anuph's chin as the throat sac drummed. Harry knew he was being roundly cursed in a semiprivate racial dialect. Formal insult could not be taken, since no official Galactic language was involved, but several onlookers seemed to grasp the cutting remark, expressing agreement or amusement in their own ways. Ever since the debacle at the NuDawn Colony, centuries ago, malevolence from hoons had been a tedious fact of life to members of beleaguered Earthclan.

Dwer Koolhan abruptly burst out laughing, a sound that cut through Twaphu-anuph's hostile umble, causing it to trip and founder. The hoon gave up a surprised stare as the young human responded in Anglic – also an unofficial tongue, but one that many sophonts understood these days.

'Ouch, what a good cut! Hold on there a dura, while I explain to this poor chimp what you just said about his body type, his ancestors, and all that!'

Leaning toward Harry, Dwer offered a quick wink and whispered.

'Smile and pretend you're tellin' me something to say back at the fool.'

Harry blinked.

'What do you think you're trying to—'

Dwer stood up straight again, guffawing loudly and pointing at Harry. He made as if to say something to Twaphu-anuph, but was unable to get by gasps of laughter.

'He says ... the chimp says ...'

Rety wore a sour expression, rolling her eyes. But Harry could only stare in amazement as Dwer gathered a deep breath, looked straight at Twaphu-anuph ... and began approximating a deep hoonish umble!

A kind of ferocity seemed to flash in Dwer's eyes as he threw a belchlike groan at the officious inspector, whose throat flapped with astonishment and dismay.

Abrupt silence reigned when Dwer took a breath and switched to Anglic.

'There, wasn't that clever? Where I come from, any chimp who said something like that would be called a real—'

Harry grabbed Dwer's arm and squeezed. The young man was wiry for a human, but no match for chim strength. Obediently, Dwer cut off at once, smiling amiably at the crowd. None had ever heard an Earthling umble before. It sure was a first for Harry!

Then, as if for good measure, Rety's little 'husband' stuck his little urrish head out from her pouch, giving the tall hoon a hiss of raspberry scorn, prompting still more surprised shouts from the throng.

'Enough!' Twaphu-anuph cried, slamming his heavy fist on a switch, causing the portal to fly open. 'Hoon-talking humans? Earth-talking hoons? *Has the whole cosmos gone crazy?* Get out of here! Go!'

While the bureaucrat buried his massive head in his hands, Harry kept his grip on Dwer's arm, pulling until all of them passed safely onto the covered avenues of Kazzkark, letting go only when the Ingress Atrium was far behind them.

Stepping back, he regarded the sooner boy, as if for the first time.

After a long pause, Harry grunted with a brief nod.

'I got just one question for you.'

'Yes?' Dwer replied.

'Can you teach me how to do what you did back there?'

There are ways of reporting an event that make it seem uneventful.

While waiting in Wer'Q'quinn's lobby for his boss to see him, Harry quickly modified his written account of meeting Dwer and Rety in E Space, removing his surmise that they came from a sooner world. It wasn't necessary to hide any actual facts. Who else but another Earthling would recognize Dwer's handsewn buckskins and neolithic weaponry for what they were?

He could rationalize that he wasn't really breaking his oath. Sort of.

'Your ship broke down and you lost all personal effects before the machine craft picked you up,' he coaxed the pair. 'You also suffered brain damage, resulting in partial amnesia. That should qualify you for basic aid, under the Traveler's Assistance Tradition. Maybe enough to pay for air, water, and protein till you find a way to earn your keep. Got that?'

While Dwer nodded soberly, Rety murmured to the little male urs.

'You hear that, yee? Brain damage? I bet Dwer can fake *that* real good.'

Her 'husband' responded by aiming a swift nip at her left hand, which she yanked back just in time. All at once, Harry decided he liked the small creature.

'I know some people in Low Town,' he said. 'Maybe they can find the two of you some jobs you're suited for. Meanwhile, here's a data chip with standard information about Kazzkark and the surrounding sector,' he continued, handing over a clear rod, which Rety slid into her prize possession – a rather beat-up-looking tutorial computer of Terran design. 'Study hard while I'm inside. When I finish, I'll take you someplace safe. But in return I'm gonna want your story – the *whole* story, you understand? About your home and everything.'

Both humans nodded, and Harry felt sure they meant it.

A musical chime seemed to fill the air – a unique rhythm and melody that Harry had been taught to recognize more surely than his own name.

A summons. Wer'Q'quinn's staff must have finished going through his data, taken by instruments that had peered at the Real Cosmos from the outside.

At last, he thought, standing up. Already the two young humans were immersed in images from the teaching unit, so he left without a word. Hurrying toward his boss's office, Harry felt growing excitement. With this recent success, he had earned some consideration from the Navigation Institute. Perhaps enough to be let in on the big secret.

Maybe now someone will tell me what in Ifni's Probabilistic Purgatory is going on!

Several miduras passed before he emerged at last from Wer'Q'quinn's sanctuary, feeling rather dazed.

He had hoped for an explanation.

Now Harry wondered if it was such a good idea, after all.

Ain't it always like this? The gods warn us to be careful what we wish for. Sometimes it comes true.

There was good news, bad news ... and tidings that were downright terrifying.

First came congratulations on surviving a hard voyage. The changed fur coloring – plus addition of a new body appendage – seemed relatively mild compared to the afflictions that some other observers came home with. He was given a generous personal compensation allowance, and the NavInst staff said nothing more about it.

As for the mission, Wer'Q'quinn could not be more pleased.

Using the peculiar perspectives of E Space to gaze in at the sidereal universe, Harry's cameras had measured a progressive *stretching* of the underlying subvacuum. A process that was rapidly nearing rupture. Thanks to his bold mission, Wer'Q'quinn's local savants knew almost as much about this process as their august superiors, back at Quadrant HQ.

That was also the bad news.

Those superiors must have known for some time what was going on. Yet they had delayed declaring an emergency till the last moment. Even now they were downplaying public fears.

'Could it be a conspiracy?' Harry had asked Wer'Q'quinn, at one point.

The squidlike being thrashed several tentacles. 'If so, Observer Harms, this conspiracy includes the topmost beings-in-authority of *all* major institutes, plus most elder races, as well. In fact, now that we have fresh facts, my staff has been able to coerce better infolink references from our Kazzkark branch of the Great Library, revealing something so remarkable that we are stunned nearly breathless from the news.'

Harry swallowed, hard. 'What is it?'

'Apparently, this is not the first time events such as these have occurred! A lesser version of the same phenomena took place about one hundred and fifty million years ago, associated with the permanent or temporary dysfunction of seventy percent of all transfer points! Then, too, society was racked by massive social disruptions and genocidal wars. Galaxy Three, in particular, suffered terribly.'

'But ... how could such things be hidden? The Library – isn't it supposed to be ...'

Wer'Q'quinn waved the objection away, as if it were naive. 'Few facts were suppressed, per se. Rather, the cover-up was executed more subtly, by emphasizing the significance of some events, and minimizing others out of all proportion.'

Harry felt glad of his fur, covering a blush of embarrassment. This was exactly what he had done, burying the truth about Dwer and Rety under mounds of detail.

'The chaos of that epoch has always been attributed to widespread interclan warfare, which turns out to have been a symptom, rather than the cause,' Wer'Q'quinn continued. 'Anyway, people are accustomed to finding historical records murky, clouded by uncertainty, the farther back you go. That may be why a far more crucial event – the *Gronin Collapse* – gets so little attention.'

'The ... what?'

'The Gronin Collapse. Forgive me, you are a wolfling, and your education is deficient. But most Galactic schoolchildren know that the Progenitors returned, in spirit form, approximately two hundred and thirty million years ago, to guide and protect oxy-life during one of its worst crises. Interstellar navigation became tortuous. Conflicts slashed populations. Only a small number of starfaring clans survived to begin renewing the Cycle of Uplift with a fresh generation.'

'I . . .' Harry frowned. 'I think I heard of it. Weren't *machines* and *Zang* supposed to be responsible, somehow?'

'A superficial explanation that most accept without further probing. In truth however, the answer was something else. Something more grand . . . and far more frightening.'

Which brought Harry to the third, and most worrying, bit of news.

'Apparently, these recent convulsions are part of a *natural catastrophe* whose proportions have not been seen since the Gronin Collapse. And we will face far worse calamities during the duras and piduras to come.'

'H . . . how much worse?'

Wer'Q'quinn twisted several long, suckered tendrils around each other in a grasp strong enough to bend steel. The elderly sophont, normally as unshakable as a neutron star, seemed to shiver, as if it took strong will to utter the next words.

'It seems that our civilization may be about to lose a galaxy.'

Harry reached the anteroom still in a daze.

Wer'Q'quinn had indicated that he already had an assignment planned for Harry, whose promotion would take effect along with those new duties, starting tomorrow.

Something about a message, just recently broadcast from besieged Earth. A warning, aimed at all Institute outposts. Senior officials have squelched it, wherever possible, but rumors of its content are already spreading panic through several quadrants.

It all sounded fascinating. But right now Harry's exhaustion showed even to his normally oblivious boss. His head was in a muddle, and Wer'Q'quinn had ordered him home for some well-earned rest before starting anew.

Entering the richly paneled outer chamber, Harry stood for a long time, blinking, wondering what was missing.

Dwer and Rety, he realized at last.

They were supposed to stay here, waiting for me.

He peered left and right.

They were gone!

Hurrying through the far portal, he stood on the topmost step of Navigation Institute headquarters, staring at the teeming crowds, wondering where the two humans might have run off to. Humans never before exposed to the intricate dangers of Galactic culture, with no idea what hazards lurked out there among several hundred temperamental species ... many of whom hated Earthlings on sight.

SARA

It all boiled down to a matter of language.

You can only contemplate what your mind is able to describe, she thought.

The system of organized Galactic dialects had helped oxy-races communicate with minimal misunderstanding for two billion years – a primly logical structure of semantics, syntax, grammar, and meaning. But now she figured it had a double purpose – to *obscure*. A sophisticated culture of technically advanced and deeply intelligent beings was channeled away from pondering certain topics. Certain possibilities.

This could be the real reason wolfling races wind up being annihilated, she thought. *They may more readily look past the blind spots. See what mustn't be seen.*

That cannot be allowed.

Through a crystal pane, Sara glanced at swarms of gigantic, needle-shaped habitats orbiting a dense relic star at furious speed. Lined up along the radial path followed by escaping rays of light, their inner points seemed almost to brush the intensely bright surface. Anyone living down there – perched deep within the white dwarf's steep gravitational well – would experience profound tidal forces, tugging and stretching every living cell.

Of course, that was the whole point of living here.

Unlike the Fractal World, mere hydrogen metal could not survive the glare or tortuous strain of this place. Hannes Suessi had tried to explain what kinds of field-reinforced materials might withstand such forces, but Sara's mind only reeled at his cascade of obscure terms. The technology, far beyond her barbarian education, seemed altogether godlike.

Ah, but *math* ... that was another story. Even back home, with just pencil and paper as her only tools, she had learned all sorts of clever shortcuts to describe the countless ways that *space* might fold, flex, or tear – analytical methods that lay outside the normal Galactic tradition.

Now, with some of *Streaker*'s onboard wizard machines to assist her, Sara found herself performing extravagant incantations. By word and gesture, she caused glorious charts and graphs to appear in midair. Tensors cleaved before her eyes. Tarski transforms and Takebayashi functions dealt handily with transfinite integrals at her merest whim, solving problems that no mere numerical processor could calculate by brute force alone.

Her little chimp assistant, Prity, helped by silently molding shapes with agile hands, fashioning outlines that became equations.

Equations portraying a cosmos under stress.

I wish Sage Purofsky could have seen this, Sara thought.

It was as if both calculus and computers had been waiting to achieve their potential together. Joined now under her direction, they were already making her old teacher's dream come true, proving that the ancient concepts of Einstein and Lee had relevance, after all.

Perhaps experts on Earth had already accomplished the same thing, either openly or in secret. Still Sara felt as if she were exploring virgin territory. Those concepts cast light upon the future – revealing calamity of untold magnitude.

Well, at least now we know – we weren't at fault for what happened to the Fractal World. Gillian will find that comforting, I guess.

Dr. Baskin clearly felt guilty over contributing to the havoc that had struck the vast, frail shell of hydrogen ice, crushing billions of inhabitants when it collapsed. It had seemed to be a direct result of *Streaker*'s presence – like a snake corrupting Eden. But Sara's evidence now pointed to natural phenomena, ponderously inevitable, as impersonal as an earthquake. Far more unstoppable than a hurricane.

No wonder so many other refugee arks joined our convoy. Delicate criswell structures must be shattering all over the Five Galaxies, forcing members of the Retired Order to choose quickly whether to rejoin oxy-civilization or transcend to the next level ... or else stay where they are, and die.

Unable to bear even a brief separation from the Embrace of Tides, many chose to remain huddled next to their little red suns, even as the continuum shivered around them, crushing their brittle, icy homes into evaporating splinters.

Looking down at the brilliantly compact white dwarf, Sara wondered. Would the same worsening conditions also affect this crowded realm – where sparkling needle shapes whirled quickly around a superdense star? It was a far mightier place than the Fractal World, occupied by ancient, revered races, combining the best of hydrogen and oxygen cultures.

Surely members of the Transcendent Order must know what's coming. We are like ants compared to such wise beings. They'll have means of protecting themselves during the Time of Changes.

It was a reassuring thought.

Unfortunately, Sara could not keep from worrying.

She worried about the Buyur.

Her news got a sober reception at the next staff meeting. Even when Sara exonerated *Streaker* from the Fractal World tragedy, Dr. Baskin seemed more concerned with understanding what might happen next.

'You're saying that all these disruptions are a natural result of the *expansion of the universe?*'

'That's right,' Sara replied. 'The spacetime metric – including the underlying ylem – stretches and weakens, eventually reaching a fracture point. Domain boundaries abruptly snap and reconnect. A bit like pressure building underground for release in a quake. So-called "threads," or flaws in the original matrix, can be pinched off, turning transfer points into useless maelstroms, isolating whole sectors, quadrants, or even galaxies.'

The older woman shook her head. 'Cosmic expansion has been going on for sixteen billion years. Why should all this come to a sudden head now?'

The Niss Machine interjected at that point.

'The simple answer to your question is that this occurrence … is not unique.'

'What do you mean?'

'I mean this sort of thing has happened before.

'Let me illustrate by asking a question, Dr. Baskin. Does this symbol have any meaning to you?'

Sara watched an image take shape above the conference table – a complex form with thirteen spiral rays and four ovals, all overlaid.

Gillian blinked for a moment. Then her mouth pinched in a sour expression. 'You know damn well it does. Tom found it engraved on those strange ships we discovered in the Shallow Cluster … the so-called *Ghost Fleet* that got us in trouble the minute we laid eyes on it.'

Bowing its funnel of nested lines politely, the Niss Machine continued.

'Then surely you recall one possibility we discussed – that the Ghost Fleet might represent emissaries from an entirely different *civilization? One completely apart from our five linked galaxies. Perhaps an expedition that had crossed hundreds of megaparsecs of flat, open space to reach us from a quite different nexus of life?'*

The Niss waited for Gillian to nod.

'*Well, I can now refute that guess. It is not true.*

'*Rather, those ships come from our past ... a past when* more *than five galaxies made up this nexus-association.*'

A water-filled tube ran along one wall of the conference room, where Akeakemai slashed his broad tail, causing a storm of bubbles to swirl around his sleek gray body. With Lieutenant Tsh't under arrest, he was now the senior dolphin aboard – an honor that clearly made him nervous.

'M-mo-more? You mean there were once – *ssssseventeen* galaxiessss?'

'*Seventeen, aye. Of which several were elliptical types, as well as thirteen spirals. However, a while later – (the records are vague on exact timing) – there appear to have been* eleven *... and then* seven *... and finally the* five *we know today.*'

Silence reigned. Finally, although his cyborg visage remained mirror smooth, Hannes Suessi stammered.

'But – but how could we not already know about something so ... something so ...'

'*Something so huge? So epochal and traumatic? I believe your own state of shocked surprise is a clue. Each such loss would have struck hard at the normally placid, deeply conservative society of the time. In fact, the waves of disruption that Sage Koolhan just described must have been even worse in those earlier episodes, wreaking untold havoc and ruin. Survivors would have been busy for ages, picking up the pieces.*

'*Now suppose older, wiser spirits asserted themselves during the aftermath, taking control over the Great Library through those crucial centuries, it would not require much effort to erase and adjust appropriate archive entries ... or divert blame for the chaos onto more mundane culprits. Say, the Zang, or criminal oxy-clans, or a breeding-explosion by machine life-forms.*'

'But how could they conceal the loss of whole galaxies!'

'*That may have been easier than it seems. The last time this happened on a large scale – the Gronin Collapse – there followed hardly any mention of lost territories, because the Migration Institute had already prepared by—*'

Sara stood up.

'By evacuating them!'

She turned to address Gillian and the others.

'The Transcendents must have known in advance, two hundred thirty million years ago. They ordered abandonment of the two galaxies they were about to lose, before the rupture took place.' She stared into space. 'This explains the mystery about Galaxy Four! Why *all* of that spiral was recently assigned fallow status, forcing all oxygen-breathing starfarers to depart. It wasn't for reasons of eco-logical management, but because they sensed another split coming!'

The Niss hologram shrugged, as if it all seemed obvious now. The entity made no apologies for taking so long to catch on.

'Clearly, the higher orders of life have either confided in or manip-ulated senior officials of the Great Institutes, so the governing bodies of oxy-civilization would make preparations.'

'But there's so much we still don't understand!' Sara objected. 'Why must the affected galaxy be emptied of starfarers? How does all this affect the other life orders? What does it—'

Gillian Baskin interrupted.

'I'm sure you will help us pierce those veils as well, Sage Koolhan. Meanwhile, this news is disturbing enough. When you said a galaxy was about to split off, I thought you meant the one containing Earth – the Milky Way. That might help explain why our planet was isolated for so long. And why we created such commo-tion when we finally made contact.'

The Niss answered with some of its old patronizing tone.

'With all due respect, Dr. Baskin, do curb your innate human ten-dency toward solipsism. Despite some petty excitement caused by this little ship, the universe does not revolve around your kind.'

Sara found the rebuke snide and unfair. But Gillian accepted it with a nod.

Suessi reported on efforts to cast off the ship's transparent sheath, an armor layer that once had protected it against devastating weapons, but now seemed a death shroud. It had proved nearly fatal just two hours ago, when *Streaker* tried to depart the white dwarf's funnellike gravity well, sneaking away from the swarm of 'candidates for transcendence.'

Unfortunately, the Jophur battleship, *Polkjhy*, lay waiting just above, swooping in to launch a new form of attack. Emitting com-plex pulses on a hyperspatial resonance band, the enemy stroked a response from the strange atoms locked in *Streaker's* outer shell, turning the throbbing layer into a huge antenna, drawing a flux of energy from D Space! As the Niss predicted, temperatures soon climbed. The deck plates warmed steadily, with no apparent way to slough the mounting heat.

Lacking any effective means to fight back, *Streaker* could not even tear free of *Polkjhy's* grasping fields to dive back amid the mob of craggy arks, spiraling inexorably toward the white dwarf star. If the assault continued, the Earthlings would have to surrender . . . or else broil.

Then, abruptly, a Zang globule approached from the swarm,

beaming a recognition code that set the herd of Jijoan glavers baying loudly in the hold. With evident frustration, the *Polkjhy* released its grip and backed away as 'deputy' vessels budded off the giant Zang, moving toward *Streaker*.

Relieved, the Terrans rendezvoused with the rescuing globules.

'I guess it's time to say good-bye to our little friends,' Gillian Baskin had said. The glavers were about to meet a destiny mapped out for them long ago.

Willingly, the small troop of quadrupeds clattered to the airlock, where Sara bid them farewell.

May this bring the redemption that your ancestors sought, when they came to Jijo. A strange, but honorable goal. To unite what had been distinct. To bridge the gap, helping oxygen and hydrogen meld as one.

At last she understood how both civilizations had been able to coexist for so long, despite a fractious antipathy during their youthful, starfaring phase. Because they were fated for each other, like preordained mates, who only discover affinity on their wedding eve.

Moreover, this union explained why the known cosmos was never overwhelmed by *machines*. United, the hydro- and oxy-orders were more than a match for silicon and metal, preventing digital sapience from taking over and exploiting every scrap of matter in all five linked galaxies.

It seems so tidy, so perfect – even romantic, in a way. Almost as if the universe were designed with this in mind.

Watching the glavers go – carried by translucent, glowing bubbles – she envied their clear-cut role. Their obvious importance. At that moment, they were Jijo's great success, valued participants in something inarguably noble, contributing their wise simplicity to help bring about glorious fusion.

Streaker seemed emptier when they were gone.

Suessi reported failure. The material covering the hull proved impossible to scratch by any means at his disposal.

'Whoever gave *Streaker* this coating not only saved our lives, back at the Fractal World. They also made sure we must stay with this convoy, all the way to the bottom.'

With *Polkjhy* orbiting above, ready to pounce if *Streaker* tried leaving, there seemed no choice but to accompany the candidates' armada, spiraling toward the great, javelin-shaped habitats. Akeakemai sighed a resigned Trinary haiku.

> * Are we ready? Or not?
> * Yanked from blissful dreaming,
>   * Hear the call of depths! *

Emerson D'Anite laughed aloud, despite his crippled brain. But Sara had to consult her portable computer for a translation. Even so, she probably missed nuances of the quirky, intuition-based language.

Am I ready? To become transcendent?

Sara wondered what that meant, but all she could picture was an image of vast, cool intellects, in hybrid bodies stretched thin by tides, contemplating ornate wisdom that would make her beloved equations seem like the flagella flailings of some crude bacterium. Even if such beings found a way to incorporate humans and dolphins into their composite mind, she scarcely found the prospect attractive.

Anyway, this is probably just a trick played on us by the Old Ones – like reaming Emerson's brain, or turning Hannes into a cyborg. A joke we'll only get when we reach those glittering needles.

Accepting Suessi's report, Dr. Baskin concentrated on practical matters.

'What physical threats do we face, as we approach the white dwarf?'

'There is strong ultraviolet radiation,' answered S'tat, one of Suessi's engineers, from atop a walker unit at the far end of the conference table. 'But our armor seems to handle it without t-trouble.'

'How about the intense gravity down there? Will our clocks slow?'

'Yessss. The field is intense enough to make a difference in the flow of t-time.' Akeakemai nodded, bubbles rising from his blowhole. 'By lessss than one percent.'

Gillian nodded. 'And the gravitational *gradient*?'

Sara had done the research.

'The tides are several orders bigger here than at the Fractal World. You'll feel a tugging sense along the length of your body. I don't expect them to be pleasant – though they say that older sapients find it irresistibly attractive.'

Gillian nodded.

'The famed *Embrace of Tides*. The more advanced a sophont species becomes, the more they crave it, and the less they can bear traveling where space is flat. That's why we see little of transcendent life-forms. No wonder they're considered a separate order.'

'Separate,' Suessi agreed. 'But still ready to meddle in the affairs of younger races.'

Sara watched Gillian shrug, appearing to say – *Why worry about things we can never change?*

'So this is transcendence. Each uplifted species that survives starfaring adolescence eventually winds up in such a place. Both oxies and hydros. From across the linked galaxies, they converge at white dwarf stars in order to achieve ... what? Niss, do you know?'

The spinning lines whirled, a maze of shifting patterns.

'*Your question is the same one that obsesses theologians, back in the "adolescent" culture we call home.*

'*Some believe transcendent beings find renewed youth in the Embrace of Tides.*

'*Others say the elders pass through a mystic portal, following the blessed Progenitors to a better realm. As you well know, minor differences over such details can rouse strong tempers among hot-blooded clans, such as the Soro, or Tandu—*'

'Tell me about it!' Hannes muttered sourly. 'Ifni-cursed fanatics.'

'*So it seems to you – and my Tymbrimi makers, and other moderate clans who feel the affairs of the Transcendent Order are rightfully none of our business. We will find out the truth, when our own turn comes.*

'*But need I remind you those "fanatics" you mention are powerful among the races who swarm flat spacetime in myriad starships? They wield great influence, and act more swiftly than the moderates. Their fleets presently lay siege to Terra, and have hounded this crew ever since we escaped the Shallow Cluster.*'

Sara watched Gillian lean forward, her cheekbones stark in light from the whirling hologram. 'You're building up to some point. Get on with it.'

'*My point is that this ship,* Streaker, *has suffered terrible persecution because it represents a danger and an affront to reverent tradition all across the Five Galaxies.*

'*The relics and data you carry appear to threaten deeply held creeds.*'

'We already knew that much,' Gillian replied. 'Can I assume you've finally figured out why?'

The Niss broadened its spiral of lines, spreading and almost brushing the blond human's face.

'*Indeed, I think that I have.*

'*It seems your discovery resurrects an ancient heresy that had been considered dead for millions of years.*

'*A heresy claiming that everything our civilization believes is wrong.*'

LARK

Deep within the Jophur battleship, things had changed yet again.

The last time Lark visited the *Polkjhy*'s Life Core, the place resembled a dense but orderly forest grove – a farm in three dimensions – featuring lush green rows and columns of vegetation neatly organized on metal scaffolding to purify the great vessel's air and water, serving the Jophur crew efficiently, like any other machine.

Now it was a tangle of riotous growth, a jungle where plants and autotrophs from myriad worlds had broken out of their assigned places, curling round the disappearing latticework, intermingling in a bedlam of anarchic biogenesis.

Amid the profuse growth, he glimpsed skittering little things – animals of varied types that surely had not been here before. Did they escape from some onboard lab-menagerie, amid the crash and confusion of battle? Or did caretaker computers deliberately thaw and release them from storage, in some vain effort to regain control over a miniature ecosystem that grew more complex and wild with each passing midura? Moving deeper, he even spied little scavenger organisms that looked like individual Jophur rings, writhing and twisting as they made their way along branches, seeking rotten matter to consume. Their pale colors expressed innocence and simplicity of purpose. None appeared eager to seek sophistication, or to gather sapiency by combining into stacks.

Lark found the Life Core's new look an improvement. He came from a world where nature was allowed to find its own equilibrium – a complex balance, invariably messy, that worked better than any plan. Even when many participants of a planetary biosphere were foes, preying on each other with tooth and claw, the overall result wound up looking like cooperation, giving each individual and species a role to play, helping the whole system thrive.

Kind of like our own little group of strange allies, he thought, pondering the curious expedition that had made its way to the heart of the Jophur warship. *We may not trust each other, but lacking any other choice, we work together.*

Pushing through the rank overgrowth, he paused near a vine that hung heavy with ripe clamber-peaches, popular on more oxyworlds than anyone could count. Lark plucked one and brought it to his mouth, but then had to wait for rippling layers of membrane to creep out of the way, until there was room enough to take a good bite out of the fruit. Red juice sprayed around his tongue and between several teeth, dribbling down his chin, assailing taste buds with pleasure. Greedily, he consumed several more. It was Lark's first decent meal in days.

The passenger – a modified Zang globule that spread its bulk across his body like a cumbersome second skin – seemed to catch some of Lark's complaint. A tendril presented itself before his left eye, and a vacuole opened inside that gelatinous mass. Tiny subdeputy blobs popped forth, performing a microscopic drama, communicating in the Zang manner, by simulation.

Lark shook his head.

'No, I'm not ungrateful. I realize you've been feeding me from your own body mass, so we could get this far. But forgive me if I prefer something that doesn't stink of rotten eggs, for a change!'

He was fairly sure that his actual words – sonic vibrations in the air – had no meaning to the alien. That type of language, abstract and structured, was as foreign to such bubble-beings as the notion of walking around on stilt-limbs, stiffened by rigid bones. Lark's best guess was that the creature/entity tracked his eye movements instead, somehow gleaning import from *which* little speck or simulated blob he chose unconsciously to look at, in which order. The result was a crude form of telepathy, unlike any he had ever heard or read about.

Subdeputies whirled some more, inside their vacuole-theater.

'Yeah, okay,' he answered. 'I know. Gotta keep moving. There isn't much time.'

A rustling commotion disturbed the dense foliage just ahead. Lark reached warily for his best weapon, the purple ring which sprayed message chemicals on command, sometimes overcoming Jophur guards or battledrones. Although its effectiveness had declined, the tricky little torus still reduced the number of times they had to fight, making possible this journey deep behind enemy lines.

A bulky form pushed through the jungle. Wide at the bottom and tapered on top, it had the ominous shape of a Jophur.

Or a traeki, Lark reminded himself, crouching amid shadows. Even when the figure drew near enough to identify by its stained contours, he still wasn't sure which word should apply. The composite being had once been *Asx*, a beloved traeki sage, then became haughty *Ewasx* of the Jophur. Now it would answer to neither name. Ripples coursed up and down its waxy pyramid of greasy donuts, while segments vied and debated among themselves. Inside that fatty tower, new arrangements were being worked out, with the Master Ring no longer in complete control.

Quite possibly – at any moment – the issue might be decided in favor of resuming loyalty to *Polkjhy*'s captain-leader, or reporting Lark's presence to the embattled crew. But not yet. Meanwhile, there continued a strange, tentative partnership of Zang, human, and ring stack. A loose coalition of collective beings. Lark decided to call the confused creature 'X' – at least till it made up its minds.

Waves of shadow and color flashed briefly, while the stack whistled breathy Galactic Six from its oration peak.

'i/we/I managed to accomplish the intended feat – accessing a terminal at the agronomist's workstation. (The agronomist erself was elsewhere, having been reassigned to combat roles during the emergency.) My/our appointed task of discovering news – this proved possible to achieve.'

'Yes?' Lark took a step forward. 'Did you learn where they took Ling?'

He had hoped to find her in the Life Core, near the nest where they had been happy – all too briefly.

The composite creature twitched and shuddered. Across its corrugated, waxy flesh there crawled dozens of small rings, crimson in color, feeding on its secretions. To the *Polkjhy* crew, those innocuous-looking toroids were carriers of a plague, more horrid than the Zang infestation.

'Of the remaining humans – Ling and Rann – there are no recent reports. As to their last known position, i/we narrowed it down to a quadrant of the ship ... one that became cut off twenty miduras ago, when fresh incursions of Zang-like entities apparently penetrated the hull.'

News of hydrogen-breathing reinforcements did not affect Lark's passenger as expected. The globule-entity quivered, indicating a strong desire to avoid contact with the newcomers until they could be viewed from a safe distance.

So, Lark thought. *There are factions, nations, races ... or whatever ... among hydros, too. Like us, they fear their own relatives more than the truly alien. I guess that shouldn't surprise me.*

During their long, circuitous journey from the nursery chamber, all three odd allies had stopped to watch images on terminal screens, broadcast by the Jophur crew to keep their soldiers informed of what was going on outside. While X tried to describe a white dwarf star and explain what was known about transcendent life, the Zang seemed upset. What disturbed it was mounting evidence that hydro- and oxy-orders eventually merged, blending together in a steep mixing bowl of gravitational tides. Apparently, Lark's passenger found the news unnerving.

You are in way over your depth, just like me, aren't you? he asked the Zang at one point. It took several tries to get the question across – he was still learning this quirky mode of conversation. But eventually, after trembling violently for a while, it calmed down and meekly indicated assent.

Even hydro-entities must have trouble dealing with their gods. It seemed to be a law of nature.

'But you have Ling's last coordinates?' he asked X.

'Indeed. It should be possible to approach that sector ... if we dare.'

Lark nodded. Somehow he must persuade his companions that the risk was worthwhile. 'And the other matter you were going to look into?'

The pile of greasy toroids flashed a series of shadows – flickering patterns-of-regret that seemed so deeply Jijoan that the creature felt more like Asx than ever. In speaking, it switched to GalSeven.

'Alas, the news is dire from your perspective ... and perhaps ours/mine. During this ship's long journey, from the ill-fated retirement habitat to this indrawing of transcendent races, there were several moments when the *Polkjhy* got a fix on local star groups, ascertained its position, and managed to fire off message capsules. Of these attempts, at least three show high likelihood of escaping the convoy-swarm and making their way to chosen sites in the Civilization of Five Galaxies.

'In other words, the Jophur have succeeded in reporting to their home clan all about Jijo.

'All about the forlorn g'Kek.

'About traeki refugees who for so long escaped dominance by master rings.

'And about humans and other races, ripe for secret experimentation/manipulation, out of sight from law or any other restraint.'

Lark's shoulders slumped. His heart felt so heavy that flashes of concerned inquiry came from the Zang passenger, worried about his metabolic state.

Jijo is lost, he realized.

Of course that had always been in the cards, one way or another. But *Polkjhy*'s troubles had made it seem possible – just barely – that the great battleship might meet a gruesome end before reporting what it had discovered in Galaxy Four. For this reason, he and Ling had abandoned the safety of their little nest, hoping to sow confusion in the enemy HQ.

I guess we should have just stayed here, making love and eating fruit till they found us, or till the universe came to an end.

Now he had nothing left, except a desire to free Ling for as long as they might have left together ... And to hurt the enemy, if possible.

Fortunately, a weapon lay at hand. A gift from the crafty old traeki sage, Asx.

The red ring. The one Ling hid in the nursery, before she was captured. It must have been programmed by Asx as a predator, spreading and reproducing through the incubators, filling a wide range of niches. When combat with Zang invaders brought Jophur soldiers to the infirmary, seeking spare parts, they were given descendants of that original ring.

A mutated form of Master-type torus, with differences that only a wise old pharmacist-sage could have come up with, applying lessons learned by the traekis during two thousand years of exile. Tricks that Jophur sophisticates would never have encountered on the space lanes.

Soon, the fortunes of war shifted once again. Instead of beating back the hydros, Jophur forces resumed losing ground. A strange epidemic seemed to afflict many of the troops. Fits of self-doubt, or traeki-style multiple thinking, beset those who had formerly been egotistically self-centered and assured. Some suffered stack dissolution – breakdown into individual components that then crawled off, each seeking its own way. Others grew contemplative, or went catatonic, or began ranting and reeking madly.

A few started entertaining new and unusual notions.

If only we had first spread the disease close to the command center, before they could react.

But the Jophur were quick, clever, and resilient. Retreating and establishing lines of quarantine, they managed to retain control over vital ship functions.

But just barely. For most of *Polkjhy*, the overall result was chaos. A traveler could not know in advance what the next deck or corridor would be like. Weakened by struggle, no party to the conflict seemed able to do more than hold its home enclaves while anarchy spread everywhere else.

'One additional point merits discussion,' continued X. 'i/we picked up information by eavesdropping on the command channel. Reports indicate deep concern on the part of the bridge crew. The captain-leader and priest-stack have been debating the significance of a message, recently received.'

'A message?'

'A *warning*, recently beamed across the Five Galaxies. If true, this alert bodes ill for a great many races and clans, but especially for this ship and all its varied occupants.'

'Who sent this warning?' Lark asked.

'The homeworld of your own race, Lark Koolhan. Beleaguered Earth, surrounded and threatened by annihilation.

'Apparently, feeling that they have little to lose, the Terragens Council recently broadcast an iconoclastic theory to explain recent disruptions racking the Five Galaxies. A hypothesis derived by some of their sages, after secretly combining wolfling mathematical incantations with Galactic science. So provocative is this concept – so disturbing and frightening its implied accusations – that the

Great Institutes have been moved to issue frantic denials. So frantic, in fact, that Earthlings have attained fresh credibility in many quarters!

'Indeed, the reaction has been profound enough that some clans now send armadas to help lift the siege, while others converge bent on wrathful genocide! The fleet battles near Terra have intensified tenfold.'

Lark listened, at first unable to react except by blinking – at least a dozen times – in numb surprise.

'But ... what ...'

He shook his head, provoking a squishy, nervous response from his blobby passenger.

'But what was the warning?'

The creature he called X puffed colored steam, expressing nervous awe in the manner of a Jijoan traeki.

'They claim that the Great Institutes have been concealing a terrible danger. That most of the links uniting our Five Galaxies may soon dissolve, unleashing turmoil and desolation on the unprepared. In the ensuing violent backlash, many great and noble things may be lost.

'Moreover, if the Earthlings are right – (and not perpetrating a desperate hoax) – we aboard the *Polkjhy* are in the greatest danger of all. Here, at this sacred locale, where transcendent beings seek enlightenment within the Embrace of Tides.'

DWER

At first, he expected the hunt for Rety to be easy.

How could a human hide in Kazzkark? Everywhere Dwer went, people turned and stared with a variety of sensory organs. Diverse limbs and tendrils pointed, while susurrant comments in a dozen Galactic dialects followed him down every lane. Apparently, Earthlings were infamous.

Even if no one in Kazzkark had any idea what kind of smelly biped Rety was, the girl would draw attention to herself, as surely as stars were fire. In all the time he'd known the young sooner, that trait had never failed.

Dwer's instincts were more reticent. He preferred slinking quietly through this bizarre noisy place – spacious as a canyon, yet claustrophobic as a boo forest, with a slim roof to keep the precious air from blowing into space. The environment would be unnerving enough without throngs of aliens loudly arguing or gesticulating, then lapsing to hushed murmurs as he passed.

I always hated crowds. But according to Harry Harms, this is just a tiny outpost! I can't imagine a real city.

Dwer tried not to stare, partly because it was impertinent, and to keep from looking like a total rube. Among the bedtime stories his mother used to read aloud, a standard plot told of some rustic innocent coming to a metropolis, only to be fleeced by urban predators.

Fortunately, I don't have much to covet or steal, he thought, counting blessings.

At a busy intersection, Dwer paused to consider.

If I were Rety, where would I dash off to?

None of this would have happened if he'd been vigilant. While waiting for Harry at Navigation Institute HQ, Dwer had left Rety to visit the toilet. It took some time, as he studied the strange array of mechanisms designed to remove waste products from many species. Emerging – mussed and damp from several near accidents – he cursed to find Rety gone and the front door gaping to a busy street.

Harry's gonna be mad, he thought, plunging outside, hoping to catch sight of her. Dwer briefly glimpsed a short bipedal form just turning a corner, and sped in pursuit, but soon lost the dim figure in a maze of side avenues.

He needed a plan. Carefully, Dwer ran through a list of Rety's priorities.

Number one – get away from Jijo and make sure no one ever takes her back again.

To Dwer, that seemed pretty much a done deal. But *she* might worry that Harry Harms knew too much. Conceivably the chimp might gather enough information to figure out Jijo's location, and even insist they return with him. Rety might not want to take the chance.

Number two – make a living. Become invaluable to somebody powerful, so she'll never be hungry again.

That left Dwer at a loss. The girl had her computerized tutor unit, plus the data on Kazzkark that Harry provided. Could she have figured out a scheme while Dwer was in the toilet?

Number three – get rid of her scars. Rety had always been self-conscious about the weals that marred one side of her face, caused by cruel bullies who had tormented her back in the Gray Hills Tribe. Personally, Dwer did not much notice the marks. He had seen worse on Jijo. Besides, anyone who ever loved or hated Rety would do so because of her powerful presence and force of will.

Still, she would want to take care of that as soon as possible.

Was it possible, on Kazzkark? With no resident human population, would there be proficiency to perform repairs on Earthling flesh?

Why not? Computers can store the expert knowledge of countless skilled workers. And medicine would get top priority. You never know which species will visit an outpost, so you'd best be prepared for all of 'em.

Dwer knew he was reasoning from a slim base of information. Since infancy, he had heard stories about the radiant civilization his ancestors left behind. Now he felt numbed and dazzled by the reality.

Maybe I should've waited for Harry. I know Rety and he knows Kazzkark. We'd do better together than separately.

Preparing to head back, Dwer suddenly experienced a strange, disquieting sensation. It took moments for him to find a word to describe it.

I'm ... lost.

It had never happened to him before! Not back home. Always there had been the sure draw of north, and a sort of internal map that unreeled each time he made a turn or took a step. But here on a drifting planetoid, his brain must lack some necessary cue. Dwer had no idea where he was!

He stood near a stony wall, trying to get bearings while streams of varied, bizarre life-forms swept past. Ignoring them, he fought to concentrate but was blocked by a rising sense of panic.

After E Space, I figured I could adjust to anything. I may be a sooner, but I'm not a savage. I grew up with other races around me. But this ... all this ...

The noise, bustle, smell, and grating *presence* of so many types of sapient minds – some of them brimming with hostility toward his kind – made him want to duck into the nearest hole and not come out again.

How long the funk would have lasted, Dwer had no idea. But it cut short abruptly when a large, fuzzy figure barged into his field of view, shorter and much rounder than a human, with whiskered cheeks and a pelt of bristly brown fur. A stout biped, vaguely mammalian, it displayed sharp teeth in a grimace that Dwer took as a deadly threat – until it boomed eager greetings in Anglic!

'Well, well. As I live and breath mints! A human? Well, well! Indeed a human, here in the booney tunes! I have not this pleasure had since past times ... before crisis times, when peace was! Shake?'

The creature held forth a meaty paw, from which retractile claws kept popping in and out, unnervingly. Dwer blinked, remembering vaguely about an old Earthling tradition of touching and clasping palms that had largely been abandoned long ago, since most aliens disliked it. Nervously, he extended his left hand – the one he would miss a little less if the creature snapped it off. 'Shaking' felt awkward, and they were both clearly glad when it was over.

'Forgive my ignorance,' Dwer said, attempting to mimic the formal, interspecies bow he had seen used a few times on Jijo. 'But can you tell me who ... or what ...'

His voice trailed off as the rotund figure opposite him grew flushed. Sallow skin reddened underneath the streaky brown fur. Dwer feared he must have given offense – until the creature began huffing in a rhythmic manner, clearly trying to imitate human-style laughter.

'Is true? You recognize me not? A *Synthian*? Among the best of friends we have been to you humans! *Very* best! Well, well. Until this cursed crisis, that is. I admit. Friendship is tested, sorely, when death flows like starlight. I admit this. I, who am called Kiwei Ha'aoulin. This I admit. You will not hate me for it?'

Dwer nodded. A Synthian? Yes, he had heard of them ... and vaguely recalled seeing pictures in an old folio, when Fallon taught him a little Galacto-xenology in the Biblos archive. Indeed, the race had been known for good relations with Earth, back in the early days before starship *Tabernacle* fled to Jijo. Though a lot might have changed since then.

'It is my turn to apologize, Kiwei Ha'aoulin,' he said, mimicking the name as well as he could. 'I kind of suffered a little ... er, brain damage in deep space. An accident where all my possessions were lost.'

The Synthian's eyes swept across Dwer's ragged clothes before settling on the qheuen-made bow and quiver of arrows.

'*All* possessions? Then this lovely proto-aboriginal archery set ... it is not thine to display, or possibly to sell?'

Dwer stared for several seconds. According to Harry Harms, no Galactic should even recognize the finely carved wooden implements for what they were. Yet this one knew the primitive weapon on sight, and clearly desired it! Covetous eagerness seemed to crackle from its bunched-up muscles.

A hobbyist, Dwer realized. *An enthusiast*. He had met the type, even back on Jijo. For some reason, his instincts as a tracker and hunter abruptly kicked in. Commerce, after all, followed many laws of the jungle. Panic fled as familiarity took its place.

'Well, well,' he said, slipping into a soft semblance of the other person's speech. 'Perhaps I exaggerated. I admit that I managed to hold on to a thing or two from the shipwreck. A few special things.'

'*Treasures*, no doubt,' the Synthian replied, while avid tremors coursed its hunched spine. 'Well. I am one, among my kind, known as a *fishy-naddo* of things Terranearthly. I would help you find a market for such things. And thus? From poor castaway to enabled starfarer you might become! Enabled enough to buy a ticket in comfort from this miserable un-place to a somewhere-else-place, perhaps?'

Not waiting for an answer, the Synthian slipped an arm around Dwer's.

'Well, well. Shall we talk more? Kiwei Ha'aoulin knows very nice meal-site nearby. Good food! Good talk about treasures and news from the stars! Come?'

Dwer's right hand stroked his bow. On Jijo it was, indeed, valuable. Beneath his foolish demeanor, Kiwei Ha'aoulin must have a keen eye for quality. Who knew what an *aficionado* of primitive Earthling tools might pay?

I'd hate to part with it, but this could help me learn more, and maybe find Rety.

Driven as much by hunger as curiosity, Dwer nodded.

'I accept your hospitality, Kiwei Ha'aoulin. Let's go and talk of many things.'

Ignoring hostile stares and murmurs from all sides, he accompanied his new friend, hoping for the best.

EMERSON

Gazing from a secret crystal sanctuary, he watched countless stars roll by ... along with just as many glittering lights that were actually huge vessels. In fact, nearby space had grown so crowded that a single sweep of the naked eye made out hundreds of shining snowflakes, or bubbles, liquidly shimmering. Fractal arks jostled past globule-forms in an ever-tightening throng, spiraling toward their common goal – a white-hot disk surrounded by swarms of giant, glittering needles that almost grazed its surface.

Emerson chose not to look that way. Just thinking about the destination was as painful as its glaring image.

He knew what must happen soon, before *Streaker* arrived. He had worked hard to prepare.

Crippled without speech, Emerson had only a rudimentary grasp of why *Streaker* was here, or what it meant for Zang vessels to mix amicably with some of the same oxygen breathers they used to shun ... or sometimes fought bitterly. Watching Gillian and Sara converse, their brows furrowed with a blazing intensity of focused thought, he had tried to sift amid the 'wah-wah' sounds for hints of meaning. But many of their oft-repeated phrases – like 'the Embrace of Tides' – evoked no response from his wounded mind. Unless it had something to do with the increasing tendency of his body to twist and stretch in a preferred direction, with his feet aimed toward the white dwarf star.

At least some individual words seemed to resonate, just a little.

'Embrace,' he whispered, relishing its sensuous quality.

A few hours ago Emerson had been sitting beside Sara, with her head resting against his shoulder while they enjoyed a quiet moment together. Stroking her hair had become his normal way to help ease the tension of her daily struggle – Sara's ongoing effort to wrestle truth out of the universe by sheer mathematical force. His duty was a pleasant one. He would gladly provide anything she needed or wanted.

That is, except for the one thing she desired this time.

With gentle hints, Sara had shyly made known her willingness to reach new intimacy ... but he was forced to turn her down. Peeling away from her warm clasp, Emerson saw questions in her eyes. Worry that he might not find her arousing. Worry that his wounds had robbed him of manly desires. Worry that there was so little time left for two to become one.

How could he explain? It would take words, sentences, volumes to justify thwarting such a natural desire, for bodies to follow where hearts already had gone. Frustrated, he sifted memory for a *song* that might suffice, but came up empty. All he could do, before fleeing to his star-covered sanctuary, was touch Sara's cheek and let his eyes express the trueness of his love.

In fact, there was nothing wrong with Emerson's sexuality. He longed to prove it to her. But not now. A confrontation loomed, and he needed every resource. Strong animal cravings might help keep him anchored through the coming showdown, reminding him of priorities that more advanced minds had forgotten.

His plan was necessarily crude, since thinking came so hard without words. By visualizing certain acts, body movements, emotions, and images, he had a general idea what to expect, and how to react when the time came.

It must be soon. Emerson could still discern meaning from a spatial diagram, and one truth grew plain as *Streaker* gyred into the white dwarf's gravitational funnel. A point of no return would come when the convoy of immense spacecraft got so closely packed that no single ship could escape on normal engine power. Gillian would have to break out before then, or risk forever abandoning the outer cosmos – the realm of open vacuum where young races thrived. Where blazing spaceships crossed star-speckled skies.

The same logic applied to the secret faction of Old Ones.

They have to act soon, or else be trapped along with . . . Emerson stopped short – then resumed his thought, warily.

. . . or . . . else . . . be . . . trapped along with us, down among the Transcendent habitats, unable to intervene any longer in the affairs of the Five Galaxies . . .

A low grunt escaped his throat. Despite expecting it this time, the sudden return of speech filled him with aching mixtures of sorrow, joy, and fear.

The words . . . the words are back again!

At least Emerson was better prepared now. For many days he had been storing memories, laboriously freezing snippets of speech that others said, in hope of fitting the pieces when this moment came.

'Let me conjecture. The emblem stands for a union of hydro- and oxy-life, coming together at last . . .'

'. . . those derelict ships we found in the Shallow Cluster must have come from our past . . . when more than five galaxies made up this nexus-association.'

'. . . suppose older, wiser spirits asserted themselves after each disruption . . . controlling the Great Library . . . to erase and adjust archives . . . or divert blame . . .'

'. . . So this is transcendence. Every species that was uplifted . . . and survives to adult phase . . . winds up in such a place . . .'

'Whoever gave Streaker *this coating not only saved our lives . . . they made sure we must stay with this convoy, all the way to the bottom . . .'*

'. . . no way to get rid of the heat . . .'

So many ideas, converging at once! It might seem like this for a blind man to have cataracts removed from his eyes, revealing vistas of utter clarity where there had been fog. And yet, many concepts also felt somehow familiar! As if they had been lurking close to comprehension for quite some time, massaged and predigested by undamaged portions of his brain, awaiting only clear sentences to make it all come together.

Emerson would gladly have spent hours just standing there, letting gravitational tides align his head toward the heavens while he grabbed and combined notions from cascades that seemed to roar through his mind like a pent-up flood. But he was not given the leisure.

A voice interrupted – at once both remote and mocking. Distant, yet derisive.

'WE NOTE THAT YOU DID NOT CALL US, DESPITE HAVING BEEN SUPPLIED WITH A CODE TO USE, WHEN READY TO ACT ON OUR OFFER.'

Emerson scarcely bothered peering amid the glittering lights outside. A dark ship must have drawn nearby in cloaked secrecy, and trying to spot it would be futile. Instead, he went into rapid motion, squeezing his body out of the narrow crystal dome, then sliding down the rungs of a ladder designed for another race, in a far different time.

'I was curious to see just how badly you want the goods you asked for,' he replied in a low mutter under his breath. *Sound* wasn't the medium of communication here. Rather, the Old Ones were monitoring a stolen plug of his own gray matter they had somehow kept in quantum contact to the rest of his brain. When brought close enough, it flowed with words. *His* words.

Words they could instantly read.

'WE DO NOT HAVE TO EXPLAIN TO THE LIKES OF YOU. IT IS ENOUGH THAT WE SEEK, AND YOU SHALL PROVIDE.'

Jogging down a hallway, Emerson pulled from his pocket a small handmade instrument with a flashing indicator. No words had been needed to construct the simple tool, nor did he contemplate its meaning.

'Aren't you guys running out of time?' he asked his tormentors – members of the Retired Order, whose homes had vanished in the ruin of the Fractal World. Retirees whose vaunted *detachment* had failed under testing.

'If you wait much longer, you'll transcend, whether you like it or not. The data you seek won't do you any good. There'll be no way to tell your friends, back in the Five Galaxies.'

Icy tones echoed in his head.

'WE HAVE SPENT EONS CULTIVATING PATIENCE. ALL THIS RACING ABOUT, TAKING FIERCE ACTIONS ... IT IS UNPLEASANT. WE HAD FORGOTTEN HOW QUICKLY DEEDS ARE FOLLOWED BY EFFECTS.'

Emerson rounded a corner and passed through a hatch, guided by the telltale marker.

'Yeah, all the uncertainty must be driving you nuts. So tell me, how does it feel to *almost* gain entry to the Transcendent Order, your goal for a million years, only to sneak away at the last moment, just to carry off a few bytes of data stolen from a miserable Earthship? Aren't you tempted just to let go of all those old obsessions? To give in and embrace the tides?'

The reply came only after a long pause, while he raced down *Streaker*'s long, almost-deserted hallways.

'YOU HAVE NO IDEA HOW DIFFICULT IT IS TO HOLD BACK. THE GRAVITATIONAL TUG AND STRETCH ARE VOLUPTUOUS IN A MANNER THAT NO WORDS — NO MERE PHYSICAL SENSATION — CAN DESCRIBE.'

'Go ahead and try,' Emerson urged. 'What *is* the big deal about the Embrace of Tides?'

'YOU ARE TOO YOUNG TO UNDERSTAND. WITHIN THE EMBRACE, ONE FEELS UNION WITH THE WHOLE COSMOS. IT IS COMFORTING PHILOSOPHICALLY, AS WELL AS ON THE LEVEL OF FAITH. THERE IS WISDOM HERE, AND KNOWLEDGE VASTLY BEYOND THE GREAT LIBRARY, OR EVEN WHAT WE KNEW IN THE FRACTAL WORLD.'

'Really? Then why not just go?' Vehemence filled his voice, now echoing off the pale walls. 'Do the wise and noble thing. Accept your diploma. *Graduate*, dammit! Gimme back my brain. The life you stole from me. Go down to your paradise with clean karma and a clear conscience!'

When the meddlers replied, there seemed almost to be a note of contrition.

'UNDER NORMAL CIRCUMSTANCES, YOUR PLEA MIGHT HAVE ETHICAL MERIT. BUT NOW FAR GREATER ISSUES ARE AT STAKE THAT FORCE US . . .'

There was another pause.

'JUST A MOMENT. WE DETECT SOMETHING IN YOUR EMOTIVE TONE. IN YOUR MANNER . . .'

Emerson felt strange, tickling sensations, as if the left side of his brain were being scraped or probed. When the voice resumed, it had a new, resentful tone.

'YOU HAVE LEARNED TRICKS OF DECEPTION AND DISTRACTION. CLEARLY, IT IS NO LONGER POSSIBLE TO SCAN YOUR THOUGHTS SIMPLY BY MONITORING WORDS AND GLYPHS. THE THINGS YOU SAY APPEAR ARGUMENTATIVE, BUT IN TRUTH THEY ARE MEANT TO DEFER. TO DELAY.'

'REVEAL WHAT YOU ARE HIDING! REVEAL, OR EXPERIENCE PAIN!'

Emerson gritted his teeth as he ran, trying hard not to laugh out loud or show the depth of his contempt. But a little leaked out as blankets of concealment were assailed by ancient skill. While the Old Ones could not draw facts out of his reluctant mind, they got a good picture of his attitudes.

'WE PERCEIVE THAT ALL FORMS OF BASIC COERCION ARE OBSOLETE OR INAPPLICABLE IN YOUR CASE. YOU HAVE GONE PAST PAIN, A LESSON THAT

MANY RETIREES SPEND AGES OVERCOMING. NOR DO YOU WHIMPER AND CLASP AFTER WHAT WAS TAKEN FROM YOU. NO INDUCEMENT OR BRIBE WILL CAUSE YOU TO BETRAY FRIENDS AND CLAN MATES. YOU HAVE NOT EVEN TRIED TO STEAL THE DATA WE ASKED FOR.

'ALL OF THIS MAY BE ADMIRABLE, ESPECIALLY IN A WOLFLING. INDEED, UNDER OTHER CIRCUMSTANCES, WE MIGHT TAKE PLEASURE IN COMPENSATING YOU FOR YOUR TRIALS, AND CONVERSING FURTHER ABOUT THE VIRTUES OF UNCERTAINTY.

'BUT THE ISSUES WE FACE ARE TOO DIRE, AND TIME IS SHORT. THE INFORMATION MUST BE OURS!'

The telltale in Emerson's hand flashed a new direction. *Up*. He halted below a ceiling hatch that lay cracked open. Light streamed from within.

Still hoping for delay, he blurted aloud.

'Let me guess. You had a backup plan, in case I wouldn't do as you asked.'

'CALCULATIONS BASED ON EARLIER NEURAL SCANS PREDICTED ONLY A MODEST CHANCE YOU WOULD COOPERATE. SURELY YOU DON'T THINK WE WOULD COUNT ON SUCH A SLENDER HOPE?'

Letting the voice jabber on, Emerson slipped his tracker in a pocket and leaped, catching the rim of the hatch and writhing his legs to haul himself into a maintenance conduit. Silently blessing the low ambient gravity, he consulted the device again before heading aft along a tube lined with ducted cables.

'... NATURALLY WE WERE NOT SO FOOLISH AS TO RELY ON YOU ALONE.'

Fearing the Old Ones were about to break contact, he blurted.

'Wait! I still may be able to help you. But you gotta understand ... we humans hate being kept in the dark. Can't you tell me *why* you need *Streaker*'s data? What's so damn special about that stupid fleet of ancient ships we found?'

That was the chief perplexing quandary dogging the fugitive Earthlings for three long, hellish years.

Oh, the superficial answer was easy. When Creideiki and Orley beamed images from the Shallow Cluster, they triggered religious schisms across the Five Galaxies. Rival clans and alliances, who had controlled their feuding for ages, sent battle fleets to secure *Streaker*'s samples – and especially the coordinates of the derelict fleet – before their rivals could acquire them.

Some said the Ghost Armada might be blessed Progenitors, returning to survey their descendants after two billion years. But if so, why react violently? Wouldn't all dogmatic differences be worked out, once truth was shared by all?

*

Emerson sensed hesitation. Then a faint perception of agreement, as if the voice was waiting for something *else* to happen. Meanwhile, it might as well converse with a bright wolfling, to pass the time.

'ALL OF THIS HAS TO DO WITH THE EMBRACE OF TIDES. THE DELICIOUS TUG THAT EACH OLDER RACE BEGINS TO FEEL AFTER LOSING INTEREST IN DASHING ABOUT ON MANIC STARSHIPS. WE ALL FOLLOW THIS ATTRACTION, DROPPING OUR FORMER DIFFERENCES TO ASSEMBLE TOGETHER NEXT TO LITTLE RED SUNS, WHERE OUR MINDS MAY GROW AND PURIFY.

'THEN, FROM SUCH PLACES OF RETIREMENT, MANY PROCEED TO SITES LIKE THIS ONE, WHERE OXYGEN AND HYDROGEN MERGE PEACEFULLY, UNITING IN COMMON APPRECIATION OF THE STRENGTHENING EMBRACE, PROVING THAT A PLAN IS AT WORK, MAGNIFICENT AND BEAUTIFUL ...'

Emerson heard a low clattering, coming from somewhere just ahead. Softly, he laid the tracker down, then hurried toward the rustling sounds. From another pocket, he pulled a slim device – one he had stolen days ago from Gillian Baskin's office.

'... THOUGH WHERE THE COMBINED RACES GO FROM HERE – TO WHAT DESTINY – HAS ALWAYS BEEN A MYSTERY. YOUNGER CLANS DEBATE IT ENDLESSLY, BUT TRANSCENDENT LIFE-FORMS NEVER EXPLAIN WHAT HAPPENS NEXT. ALL WE HAVE ARE HINTS AND STRANGE EMANATIONS FROM ...'

Concentrating hard to blank his thoughts, Emerson rounded a corner and abruptly saw *starlight* ahead, glimmering through a crystal pane. He knew this place. It housed the main communication laser, a wide-barreled tube occupying most of the available volume, aimed through a broad window.

Streaker's magical coating lay beyond, a meter thick but utterly transparent, covering nearly all of the ship in a layer that was both miraculous and deadly.

A figure stood nearby, working at an open access panel. Emerson recognized the fluid skill of those hands, using tools to perform rapid modifications on the laser system. One arm was clearly artificial, while remnants of the head lay encased in a mirrorlike dome. Cyborg components like these had saved the life of *Streaker*'s chief engineer, back at the Fractal World. Generosity, from a different, more kindly faction of Old Ones – or so the crew thought at the time.

Next to Suessi lay a large data reader and several crystalline knowledge cells – enough to hold all of *Streaker*'s hard-won discoveries.

'Hello, Hannes,' Emerson said aloud.

The instant he spoke, several things happened at once.

Servos whined as the figure spun around, raising a cutter torch whose short flame burned blindingly hot. Without his old friend's face to look at, Emerson could only assume the man meant to use it.

Meanwhile, the voice interrupted its explanation with a hiss of surprise that seemed to shoot through Emerson's head like an electric jolt. He cried out, instinctively grabbing at his temples. But that reaction lasted just an instant. Gritting his teeth, he aimed the stolen plasma pistol past Suessi's shiny dome.

'Stop it, or I shoot the laser right now! You know pain won't work on me.'

The lightning ceased at once.

IN TRUTH, WE NOW BELIEVE IT, HAVING FOOLISHLY REPEATED THE ERROR OF TAKING YOU FOR GRANTED. OUR COMPUTER MODELS CONSISTENTLY UNDERESTIMATE YOUR FERAL CLEVERNESS. COULD THIS ADAPTABILITY HAVE BEEN FOSTERED DURING YOUR EXILE ON THE SOONER WORLD?

'Flattery'll get you nowhere. But yeah, I learned some new ways of thinking, there. You should hear me curse, sometime. Or sing.'

IN ANOTHER LIFE, PERHAPS. SO YOU FIGURED WE WOULD HAVE AN ALTERNATE AGENT. DID YOU ATTACH A TRACER, TO FIND HIM THE MOMENT WE ARRIVED?

Emerson nodded. 'Something like this seemed likely. The one person you might have altered would be Hannes.'

WE DID NOT ALTER THE HUMAN ARTIFICER. THOSE WHO REPAIRED HIM WERE SINCERE. BUT WE LATER INCORPORATED THAT FACTION, AND THUS GAINED THE ACCESS CODES. SINCE IT CLEARLY MATTERS TO YOU, BE ASSURED HE HAS NO PAIN. HE PERCEIVES THIS AS JUST A BAD DREAM.

'How considerate of you!' Emerson snapped.

YOU THINK US CALLOUS. YET, WITH THE DESTINY OF MANY RACES AND TRILLIONS OF LIVES AT STAKE, WE HAD REASONS—

'I see only that you're cowards! You feel drawn by the Embrace of Tides, yet you fear to go in. You worry it may be a mistake!'

AN OVERSIMPLIFICATION, BUT TRUE ENOUGH.

THE STORY IS SO BEAUTIFUL, SO PERFECT – WITH OXY AND HYDRO LIFE ORDERS COMBINING IN ELEGANT PEACE, MERGING AMID A GLORIOUS FUNNEL OF TRANSCENDENCE – THAT HARDLY ANY CANDIDATES EVER QUESTION THE GENERAL ACCEPTANCE OF THIS PATH, FOLLOWED BY THEIR ANCESTORS SINCE TIMES IMMEMORIAL. THE EMBRACE IS ALMOST IRRESISTIBLE. DIVING TO TRANSCENDENCE IS AN ULTIMATE ACT OF TRUST. OF FAITH.

BUT THEREIN LIES THE RUB! TO SOME OF US, FAITH IS NOT ENOUGH. THERE WAS ONCE A MINORITY VIEW, A HERESY THAT LOOKED ON THE EMBRACE OF TIDES, AND CALLED IT SOMETHING ELSE.

Emerson nodded.

'A recycling system. You're worried that this white dwarf is just like the oceanic trench on Jijo ... the Great Midden. A graceful way to clear away the old and make way for the new! Yeah, that makes just as much sense as a mystical portal to some higher layer of reality!'

Deep sadness filled the alien presence – a fretful brooding that seemed poignant in a species so ancient and learned.

'THE DISCOVERY MADE BY YOUR DOLPHIN-CREWED SHIP IN THE SHALLOW CLUSTER . . . THE REAL REASON IT CAUSED SUCH CONSTERNATION . . .'

Abruptly the voice stopped. Emerson crouched nervously as the deck shuddered beneath his feet. Tremors accelerated, growing in pitch and intensity.

'You're attacking us!' he accused. 'All your talk was just to humor me until—'

The voice interrupted.

'YOU ARE RIGHT THAT I WAS PERFORMING A DELAYING TACTIC. BUT FOR A DIFFERENT REASON. THE SHOCKS YOU FEEL ARE FROM STRAIN FRACTURES IN THE VERY FABRIC OF THE COSMOS, CONTINUING THE SAME PROCESS THAT DEMOLISHED OUR HOME THAT YOU CALLED THE FRACTAL WORLD.

'THESE FRACTURES ARE SPREADING AT AN ACCELERATING PACE.'

'Sara thinks—'

'WE HAVE FOLLOWED HER WORK WITH INTEREST. SHE APPEARS TO KNOW WHAT THE TRANSCENDENTS COVERED UP – THAT FATE SEEMS BOUND TO SMASH THE TIES BINDING OUR GALAXIES . . . INDEED, THE NETWORKS THAT MAINTAIN CIVILIZATION.'

It was an awesome statement. Yet, something else the voice had said bothered Emerson.

'A . . . delaying tactic? Why? I already stopped Hannes from—'

He shouted an oath.

'Of course. You Old Ones wouldn't leave anything to chance. You'd have a third option. A backup for your backup! What is it? Tell me!'

'OR ELSE WHAT? WILL YOU SHOOT YOUR FRIEND? WE COULD HAVE SENT HIM CHARGING AT YOU, SEVERAL DURAS AGO. WITH CYBORG STRENGTH AND SPEED, WE CALCULATE THIRTY PERCENT ODDS HE WOULD HAVE PREVAILED BEFORE YOU PUT HIM OUT OF ACTION. A WORTHWHILE GAMBLE, FROM OUR POINT OF VIEW.

'EXCEPT THAT BY NOW OUR THIRD AGENT HAS ALREADY DEPARTED YOUR SHIP.'

'Your . . . third agent?'

'WE MADE A BARGAIN WITH A YOUNG WOLFLING. IN EXCHANGE FOR COPIES OF YOUR SHIP LOGS, WE WILL TAKE HER AWAY FROM THIS PLACE.

'FROM HERE TO SEE HER GODS.'

Darting past immobile Suessi, Emerson pressed against the laser-window and peered outside.

Streaker's nose lay to his left, where just one of the airlocks had been cleared of the magic coating to allow egress. Emerson could not see that aperture. But a few hundred meters outward, he glimpsed a stubby vessel – a little escape pod, puffing as it turned toward a dark patch of space.

A black patch that blocked a swath of stars.

Emerson's brain seemed to spin. His thought processes were much quicker than they had been before his mutilation. Still, it took moments to realize—

'Lieutenant Tsh't! You sprang her from the brig and helped her escape!'

'A SIMPLE MATTER OF MEME-INFECTING YOUR SHIPBOARD COMPUTERS. MUCH HARDER WAS THE PHYSICAL EFFORT, HELPING HER ENTER PLACES WHERE GILLIAN BASKIN HAD HIDDEN THE SECRETS, WORKING WITH A MIND-CONTROLLED SUESSI TO STEAL THEM, THEN HAVING BOTH AGENTS SMUGGLE OUT THE MATERIAL BY SEPARATE ROUTES.

'AND NOW AT LAST, DESPITE YOUR INTERFERENCE, WE ARE ABOUT TO POSSESS THE DATA NEEDED TO MAKE CORRECT DECISIONS AFFECTING MULTITUDES.

'THIS PUTS US IN A GENEROUS MOOD TO REDRESS YOUR MANY INCONVENIENCES. OUT OF RESPECT FOR YOUR FERAL INGENUITY, LET US MAKE AMENDS. IN DEPARTING WE SHALL LEAVE BEHIND SOMETHING YOU'LL BE GLAD TO HAVE BAC—'

The voice cut off abruptly as another wave of spacetime tremors struck. This one made Emerson's skin crawl with tingling sensations. Pulsations coursed the length of his digestive system, producing several loud eruptions.

The stars outside wavered, and the vague black patch he had glimpsed before started to shimmer, revealing a familiar outline.

A galuphin-class sneakboat, he identified. An expensive, but conventional Galactic design.

'Wha—?' uttered a nearby voice. Hannes Suessi groaned, recovering consciousness. 'What'm I doin' here? What's happening?'

Emerson had other things to worry about than updating a friend. Spatial fluctuations had confused the enigmatic Old Ones. With their cloaking mask disrupted, they dropped all pretense at stealth and made speed toward the little life pod, in order to pick up Tsh't and the information they prized. But the same tumult that made *Streaker*'s hull vibrate was causing them trouble, too.

Indeed, the surrounding vast armada of 'transcendence candidates' seemed to be breaking up! Wavelets of compressed metric tore through their crowded ranks, pushing one phalanx of great ships toward another. Emerson saw collisions – and sparkling explosions – ripple from one area to the next, as jagged oxy-vessels merged prematurely with hydro-globules, releasing convulsions of raw energy.

Amid all this chaos, something far more disconcerting was going on. At least from Emerson's perspective. His power of speech kept fading, then surging back again, briefly enhanced beyond all natural ability, causing countless strange associations to spill forth.

The voice was absent, yet he continued getting impressions from the beings he called Old Ones. Sensations of deep concern. Shifting toward worry. Followed by desperation.

Moving in fits and starts, their sneakboat approached the little pod carrying Tsh't, fighting chaotic disruption waves all the way. While the heavens coruscated with dire accidents – and untold populations died just short of their transcendent goal – Emerson's erstwhile tormentors struggled to dock with the renegade dolphin lieutenant.

'I feel . . . like somehow I been *used*,' murmured Suessi, moving alongside to peer out the window. 'I sure wish you could talk, lad. I could do with some light put on the subject.'

Emerson glanced at Suessi, then at the shadowy sneakboat . . . and then rapidly from his friend to the big comm laser.

'Hannes . . .' he began, then had to wait till another wave of fluency passed through his mind. He knew that each time might be the last.

'Hannes, we gotta use the comm laser to burn those two boats, now!'

Suessi stared in surprise at the brief, unexpected eloquence. His dome-covered head turned to follow Emerson's pointing finger. 'What, those? Why not call Dr. Baskin and use real combat beams—'

The quantum link to Emerson's speech center flickered out, leaving him shrouded in dull muteness, unable to explain that the foe would surely have meme-disabled the fire-control systems of any formal weapons in order to guarantee their safe escape.

He managed to force a few words out by sheer willpower.

'No . . . time! Do! Do it!'

The shiny dome nodded. Both shoulders lifted in a true Suessi shrug.

'Okay! You gotta help me, though. This thing ain't exactly meant for frying spaceships.'

They set to work at once, sharing a rhythm long familiar to engineers laboring through a shipboard emergency – from Roman trireme, to ancient submarine, to the first sluggish starcraft Earthlings once hurled toward the Milky Way, filled with hopes for a friendly universe. Emerson found that speechlessness did not hamper him as much if he let his hands and eyes work together without interference. Somehow, they knew which connections to shift. Which adjustments to make. When Hannes spoke, the hands responded as if they understood.

It left his mind free to observe with strange detachment, even as

Streaker's hallways started clamoring with alarm signals, sending crew rushing to battle stations. Clearly, Suessi yearned to go join his engine gang, but so great was their mutual trust, the fellow took Emerson's word that this was more important.

It made Emerson doubly glad he hadn't been forced to shoot his friend.

'Hokay,' Suessi announced. 'Here goes nothing.'

The laser throbbed, and the air temperature in the little chamber abruptly *dropped* several degrees as pulsating energy flooded into space.

Instantly, he could tell that the first pulse missed its target, disappearing among the flashes of coruscating catastrophe that surrounded *Streaker*, growing more garish and terrible by the minute.

Cursing roundly, Emerson stabbed several control buttons, bypassing the computer, then began slewing the laser by hand, aiming by sight alone.

Meanwhile, the sneakboat kept fighting waves of spacetime backwash to finally make contact with the little craft carrying Tsh't. Impact wasn't gentle. Hull panels crumpled on one side, but the sturdy, Thennanin-built pod held together. Soon, the larger vessel's surface melted to envelop the escape capsule, drawing it inside.

Tsh't and her purloined cargo were safe in the grasp of those who wanted it so badly.

Emerson had mixed feelings while struggling to adjust the balky laser. Though he hated the Old Ones for their callousness – especially the way they had mutilated him and others for their own purposes – he also understood, just a little, their rationale. With words, he could picture the panicky background for their actions.

Ultimately – after passing through the young, hot-tempered, starfaring stage – each race had to choose whether to continue down a comforting funnel that appeared to welcome all whose souls were ready. A place of union, where the best of hydro and oxy cultures merged, preparing to move on.

But move on to what?

The vast majority felt it must be something greater and more noble than anything in this cosmos. The place where blessed Progenitors had gone so long ago.

But there was another, minority opinion.

On Jijo, Emerson had learned something deep and gritty about the cycle of life. A metaphor that he held in his mind, even after speech had gone away.

An image of the deepest part of the sea.

And a single word.

Dross.

He jabbed the firing button.

Once again, the laser moaned a cry, deeper than a hoonish umble and more combative than the war shout of a desert urrish warrior, accompanied by a sudden wave of cold.

Something flared in the night! A sparkle of destruction. Fire illumined one end of the sneakship, outlining its aft segment, which now shimmered with devastating explosions.

All at once, words returned to Emerson's life. The voice reentered his mind, in tones that conveyed hurt perplexity.

'*Do you know what you have done? Once on our way, we planned sending you the cylinder. The plug of tissue that you crave. After we had no further need of it, or of you.*

'*Now your treasure will be lost, along with us, as we fall into a dying white sun.*'

Already the mortally wounded sneakboat could be seen tumbling along a plummeting trajectory, while *Streaker*'s engines cranked to push the other way.

'I know that,' Emerson sighed. So many hopes had turned to ash when he fired the laser bolt. Especially his dream of talking to Sara. Of telling her what was in his heart. Or even holding on to thoughts that right now seemed so fluid and natural, so easy and fine. Smooth, graceful thoughts that would become hard again, moments from now, when what had been stolen, then restored, would finally be lost forever.

'*But why? In your crude way, you understand our worry. You sympathize with our misgivings about the Embrace of Tides. You even suspect we may be right! Would it have been so bad to let us have the clues we need? To learn the truth about destiny? To know which way to choose?*'

The plaint was so poignant, Emerson weighed explaining, while there was time.

Should he talk about orders from the Terragens Council, that secrets from the Shallow Cluster must be shared by *all* races . . . or none?

A raging corner pondered telling the aliens that this was Pyrrhic revenge, getting even for things they had done to him – no matter how well justified they thought they were.

In fact, though, neither of those reasons excused his act of murder. While *Streaker* shuddered under ever more intense spacetime waves – climbing laboriously through a maelstrom of colliding transport arks and flaming Zang globes – he found there was only one answer to give the Old Ones.

The right answer.

One that was both logical and entirely just.

'Because you didn't ask,' he explained, as the quantum links began flickering out for the last time.

'You ... never once said ... please.'

HARRY

The search went badly at first.

Kazzkark was a maze of tunnels where sophonts could all too easily disappear – whether by choice or mischance. And matters only worsened as the placid lifestyle of an Institute outpost vanished like a memory. More refugees poured in, even after the planetoid started quivering in response to waves of subspace disturbance. Tempers stretched thin, and there were more than enough troubles to keep police drones of the Public Safety Department busy.

When it came to looking for a pair of lost humans, Harry was pretty much on his own.

His first good lead came when he overheard a Synthian chatter to comrades in a space merchants' bar, bragging about a sharp business deal she'd just made, acquiring some first-rate wolfling relics for resale to the collectors' trade.

'Mild guilt – this I experience, concerning the meager price that I paid for such marvelously genuine handcrafted items,' prated the husky creature in Galactic Six.

'Of their authentic, aboriginal nature, I have no doubt. Evidence of this was overwhelming, from the moment I programmed my scanner with appropriate archaeological search profiles, checking for tool marks, use patterns, and body-oil imbuements. The result? Absolute absence of techno-traces, or other signs of forgery! A bona-fide aboriginal tool/weapon, weathered and worn from the primitive fight for survival under barbaric circumstances!

'What? What is that you say? You would view this marvelous acquisition? But of course! Here it is. Behold the elegant sweeps and curves, the clever blending of animal and vegetal materials, revealing non-Galactic sapiency in its full, unfettered glory!

'The shipwrecked human who formerly owned these artifacts – his reported brain damage must have undermined all sense of value! His recovery from space amnesia – it will not bring pleasant realizations for the poor young wolfling, when he realizes how much more he might have charged for his precious archery set, which will now garner me great profit on the aficionado circuit.

'Especially now that the chief source of all such relics – planet Earth – will surely vanish under cascades of fire, within a few jaduras.'

Harry was not present where these words were spoken. He was halfway across Kazzkark, searching for Rety and Dwer in a poor refugee encampment, when those snatches of dialogue were sent to his earpiece by a clever spy program.

Using his new rank-status, he had ordered a scan of all sonic pickups, scattered throughout the planetoid, sifting countless conversations for certain rare key words. Till now, the computer had just found trivial correlations. But this time, the Synthian went through half the list in a few duras, covering all but Dwer's name!

Racing across town, Harry sent a priority call for backup units to join him. Perhaps it was the new golden comet on his collar, or just a sense of urgency, but Harry plunged through the crowd, ignoring shocked looks from senior patron-class beings.

He arrived to find several proctor robots already hovering menacingly near a bar advertising a range of intoxorelaxants. A throng gathered to watch.

'The rear exit is secured, Scout-Major Harms,' reported one of the bobbing drones. 'The denizens within seem unsuspecting. Several fondle concealed weapons, of types we are equipped to counter, with moderate-to-good probability of success.'

Harry grunted.

'I'd prefer a guarantee, but that'll do. Just stay close. Let everyone see you as we enter.'

He was tempted to draw his own sidearm, but Harry preferred to handle this courteously, if possible.

'All right. Let's go.'

Half a dozen Synthian traders sat in a booth, looking alike in grayish brown fur with dark facial streaks. Thickset, their heavy shoulders and bellies draped with pouched bandoliers. Harry soon found the one he wanted. A sleek bow and quiver of arrows, made from finely carved wood and bone, lay on the table. When a merchant reached for these, Harry bore in, asking where she got them.

Kiwei Ha'aoulin reacted with combative relish, striking an indignant, lawyerly pose. After listening to the Synthian complain loudly for more than twenty duras – vociferously denouncing 'illegal eavesdroppers and bureaucratic bullies' – Harry finally broke in to remind Kiwei that Kazzkark was sole property of the Great Institutes, and lately under martial law. Moreover, would the merchant *like* to unpack her ship's hold, comparing each smig and dram meticulously to the official cargo manifest?

All bluster quickly faded from the raccoonlike countenance. Harry had never met a Synthian, but they were familiar figures on daytime holodramas back on Earth, where Synthian characters were stereotyped as jovial, enthusiastic – and relentlessly self-interested.

This one took a long pause to evaluate Harry's proposition, then switched to rather good colloquial Anglic.

'Well well, Scout-Major. You had only to ask. Shall I lead you to where I last saw Dwer Koolhan. Yes! But be warned, he may not look the same! *If* you find him. For as we parted, he was making enquiries. Asking questions about cosmetic surgery. As if his intent was to go into hiding!'

While they hurried together along the main boulevard, Harry muttered into his cheek microphone, inquiring if any local body-repair shops had done custom work on humans during the day and a half since Kiwei Ha'aoulin last saw Dwer.

He also checked in with HQ. Wer'Q'quinn had scheduled yet another emergency meeting of the local NavInst planning staff in four miduras.

What was left of the staff, that is. Most scouts and senior aides had already departed, scurrying across the quadrant on urgent rescue missions, commandeering vessels of all sizes to evacuate isolated outposts, setting up buoys to divert traffic from destabilized transfer points, and tracking the advance of chaos across this portion of the Five Galaxies.

Especially troubling were reports of violent outbreaks among oxy-clans, or between various life orders. An uncommonly furious confrontation had flared in Corcuomin Sector between one of the more reclusive hydrogen-breathing cultures and a vast swarm of machine entities, whose normal home-domain in deep space had grown so ruptured that vast numbers of unregistered mechs began migrating into rich territory forbidden to them by ancient treaties. So frenzied and brutal was the resulting clash that weapons of unprecedented force had been unleashed, tearing through walls separating various levels of spacetime, causing vortices of A and B hyperlevels to come swirling into the 'normal' continuum, wreaking havoc everywhere they touched. There were even reports that *memetic* life-forms seemed to be involved as allies of one side or another – or perhaps taking advantage of the confusion to spread their ideogrammatic matrices into new hosts – filling the battlefield with riotous sensory impressions, fostering ideas that were too complex and bizarre for any organic or electronic mind.

Amid all this, Wer'Q'quinn kept delaying Harry's next assignment. Too inexperienced and undiplomatic to be entrusted with a big command, Harry was also apparently too valuable to waste on some futile errand.

'*Keep in touch*,' Wer'Q'quinn kept telling him. '*I suspect we will need your expertise in E Space before we're done.*'

The Synthian merchant motioned toward one of the side streets selling clothing and personal accoutrements of all kinds.

'Here is where I last saw the human, bidding me farewell as he clutched a purse filled with GalCoins from our transaction, appearing eager to rush off and spend his new fortune as quickly as possible.'

'GalCoin?' Harry asked. Far better if Dwer had been paid in credits or marks, which could be traced across the Commercial Web. 'How much did you pay?'

Kiwei Ha'aoulin tried to demur, claiming commercial privilege, but soon realized it would not avail.

'Seventy-five demi units.'

Harry's fists clenched and he growled. 'Seventy-five! For genuine Earth-autochthonous handicrafts from a preindustrial era? Why you unscrupulous—'

He went on cursing the Synthian roundly, since the merchant clearly expected it. Anything less would have insulted her pride. But in fact, Harry's mind was already racing ahead. He had no intention of informing Kiwei Ha'aoulin that the precious bow and arrows were far more recently made than she thought. They were, in fact, contraband from an illegal sooner settlement, carved by qheuen teeth and burnished at an urrish forge.

He was interrupted by a computer message. Apparently one of the body shops had been visited lately by a young Terran, who paid cash for a quick cosmetic overhaul. Nothing fancy. Just a standard flesh-regrowth profile that the shop had in its panspecies file.

'Let's go!' he told the Synthian. She resisted momentarily, then caught the fierce look in Harry's eyes. Kiwei Ha'aoulin gave an expressively Earth-style shrug.

'Of course, Scout-Major Harms. Well, well. I remain perpetually at your service.'

Unfortunately, the repair shop in question lay some distance beyond the Plaza of Faith. To reach the other side, they would have to work their way past a host of missionaries and zealots, all fired up by the steady unraveling of order throughout the Five Galaxies.

Much had changed since Harry last visited this zone, where elegant pavilions had been tended by neatly robed acolytes, politely pontificating their ancient dogmas in the old-fashioned way, with traditional rhythms of surety and patience. Since most Galactic sects aimed to persuade entire races and clans, the emphasis had always been on relentless repetition and exposure – to 'show the flag' and let other sapients slowly grow accustomed to a better view of destiny. Individuals mattered only as vehicles to carry ideas home, spreading them to family and nation.

This atmosphere of tranquil persistence had already begun wearing thin during Harry's last visit. Now, as intermittent subspace tremors made the stony walls shiver, it seemed to be unraveling completely.

Crowds filled the once placid compounds of several religio-philosophical alliances – the Inheritors, Immersers, and Transcenders. Immaculate fabric partitions got trampled as listeners pushed toward shouting deacons dressed in gaudy silver gowns, perched on ridiculously elevated platforms that teetered near the high ceiling. Their amplified and translated words boomed or flashed, transmitting stridency in at least a dozen Galactic dialects, as if persuasion could be bought through sheer volume. Each side fought so hard to drown out the others that Harry could hardly make out anything beyond a headsplitting roar. That did not deter the crowds however, whose urgency seemed to make the air crackle with supercharged emotion.

This place must be swarmin' with invisible psi waves and empathy glyphs, Harry realized, glad that his own mental talents went in other directions, leaving him blissfully insensitive to such scraping irritations. *A Tymbrimi who got caught in this mob would prob'ly fry his tendrils on all the crazed vibrations*.

There were other changes in the Plaza. Platoons of Inheritor and Immerser acolytes could be seen carrying staffs, cudgels, utility cutters, and other types of makeshift weaponry, eyeing each other with distrustful wrath. Beyond one translucent curtain, Harry even thought he glimpsed several sharply angled figures moving about – huge and mantislike.

He shuddered at the unmistakable silhouettes.

Tandu.

Next Harry and Kiwei Ha'aoulin passed the pavilions of the Awaiters and Abdicators ... or rather, their remnants. Tattered banners lay charred on the ground – silent testimony to how vehement the ancient rivalries had become. Their differences of opinion were no longer even ostensibly patient, or theoretical, now that a day of reckoning seemed near.

A few soot-covered Awaiters – mostly spidery guldingars and thick-horned varhisties – picked warily through the ruins, protected by drones they had hired from some local private security service. The varhisties, in particular, looked bitterly eager for revenge.

Meanwhile, every side avenue seemed filled with clamor and speculation. A formation of cop-bots swept eastward at top speed, rushing around the next corner toward some noisy emergency. Duras later, Harry glanced down an alley and thought he glimpsed some shabby scavengers stripping a corpse amid the shadows.

Along the main north-south Way, preachers stood on rickety pulpits, shouting for attention. The dour-looking Pee'oot proselyte was still where Harry remembered, stretching out its spiral neck and goggle eyes, jabbering in obscure dialects about the need for all species to return to their basic natures – whatever that meant.

Harry also spotted the Komahd evangelist, whose deceptive smile split even wider upon meeting Harry's gaze. Its rear tripod leg thumped loudly for emphasis.

'*There!*' the Komahd shouted, pointing with bony digits. 'Perceive how yet another Terran passes by, thus proving that this vile infection will not be rubbed out when their homeworld is finally invaded and brought to justice. No, friends. Not even when Earth is sequestered, and its rich gene-pool is divided up among the righteous. For they have spread among us like infecting viruses!

'Have you all not seen, this very day, copious evidence for their malignant influence? Even here on far Kazzkark, wolflings and their insane followers spew vile lies and calumny, reviving ancient selfish heresies, undermining our shared vision of destiny, debasing the foundations of society, and depicting our revered ancestors as little more than fools!'

While shouting hatred of Harry's clan, the Komahd kept 'smiling' and batting deceptively beguiling eyelashes, creating a misleading expression that clearly meant something quite different wherever the creature came from. It seemed noteworthy that the proselyte's ire, previously directed paranoically toward hydrogen breathers, now seemed centered wholly on poor little Earthclan.

That struck Harry as rather unfair and overwrought, since everyone was betting on the fall of Terra in a matter of weeks or days, if not hours. Nevertheless, he sensed danger from the Komahd's small band of followers. The emblems of his Navigation Institute uniform might not offer protection if he stayed.

'Wait,' Kiwei Ha'aoulin murmured as Harry tugged her arm. 'I find this sophont's argument cogently enticing! His rhetoric is most appealing. The logic seems unassailable!'

'Very funny, Kiwei.' Harry growled. 'Come on. *Now*.'

Clearly delighted with her own wit, the Synthian chortled happily. Kiwei's people were enthusiasts, but pragmatists above all.

Like many races in the 'moderate majority,' they cared little about obscure religious arguments over the nature of transcendence, preferring to go about their business, leaving destiny to take care of itself. All else being equal, they would happily have shared the infamous '*Streaker* discovery' openly, and even paid the Terragens a nice finder's fee, to make it all worthwhile.

Alas, the moderate majority was also famous for dithering and indecision. Eventually, they might finish their endless deliberations over whether to save Earth, though by that time help would come too late to accomplish anything but stir the ashes.

Speaking of going about one's business, Harry hoped this would be the last of the religious swarms. But no sooner did he and Kiwei push around the next bend than they found the way completely blocked by the biggest mass gathering yet! Crowds extended far ahead and to both sides, filling a domed intersection that had formerly been a market for selling organonutrient supplements.

The mélange of sapient species types dazzled him with its sheer variety – from willowy, stalklike *zitlths* to a pair of hulking *brmas*. Indeed, an amazed scan took in many races that Harry had only vaguely heard of before. The veritable forest of strange limbs, heads, torsos, and sensory organs mingled and merged till his confused eyes found it hard to tell where some creatures finished and others began.

Smell alone was so dense and complex, it nearly made him swoon.

Many onlookers used portable devices to monitor what was being said by the distant missionaries – who could only be made out from here as dim silvery glints on an upraised stage. Others tilted their varied eyes toward a dozen or so large vid screens, mounted high along the stone walls, each one emanating a different dialect.

A fraction of the crowd pressed forward, seeking something ineffable from direct experience.

'Curious,' Kiwei Ha'aoulin commented. 'I count several racial types that are not normally prone to religious fervor. And quite a few others whose clans are in deep ideological conflict with each other. Note over there! A tourmuj Awaiter and a talpu'ur Inheritor, standing enraptured, side by side. I wonder what conceptual magic has them so captivated.'

'Who cares?' Harry groaned impatiently. He wanted to reach the body shop before closing time, so the trail would not go cold. 'Ifni! We'll never get around this mess.'

He was about to suggest turning around and taking a long detour, when the sound of his Anglic cursing attracted attention from a tall, camellike being, who turned to regard Harry with coal-black eyes.

It was a j'8lek, whose starfaring nation had such a long history of antipathy toward Earthlings that Harry's right hand twitched, seeking comfort from the touch of his sidearm.

Only this particular j'8lek did something unexpected. After staring at Harry for several duras, it abruptly swept its long neck downward, *bowing* in a gesture of deep respect! Applying force with all four powerful legs, the creature pushed against the crowd, opening the beginnings of a path for Harry and his companion.

Somewhat amazed, the two of them moved forward, only to have the same thing happen again! Time after time, some onlooker would notice Harry, then hurriedly nudge those in front, clearing a path. No one objected or demurred. Even high-ranking beings from senior patron lines made way graciously, as if to an equal.

The experience was all the more daunting and strange to a chimp who stood less than a meter and a half high. It felt as if some force were dividing a sea of tall aliens before him, creating a narrow lane that he could not see beyond, leaving him with no idea what to expect at the other end. The whole thing would have felt just a bit unnerving, if everybody didn't seem so damned friendly.

That made it *totally* unnerving!

He was too immersed in the crowd to catch anything but an occasional glimpse of the big display screens. But soon the preacher's voice came through in clear Galactic Seven, causing him to stumble with sudden recognition.

'. . . *anyone can understand why the great and mighty religious alliances have been driven to a frenzy by this news, broadcast recently from the sacred martyr world. This gift sent to us from wonderful doomed Earth.*

'*A gift of truth!*

'*By combining Galactic science with their own ingenious mathematics, the wolflings have uncovered a secret that high officials of the Institutes tried for many eons to conceal – a secret also known by majestic beings of the Retired and Transcendent orders – that the convulsions presently racking the Five Galaxies are part of a natural process! One we should embrace, rather than dread!*'

At once Harry recognized the manner of speech, as well as the strange message.

It was the Skiano proselyte! The one who used to sermonize in the street, unable to afford even a sidewalk pulpit. Given to extravagant metaphors, it had compared humanity's 'wolfling' nature – supposedly arising to sapience without intervention by a patron race – to legends of 'virgin birth.' Harry vividly recalled the great prow-shaped head with twin pairs of inset, flashing eyes, uttering a chilling prophecy that Earth would suffer a kind of crucifixion, gloriously dying for the sake of others, before rising again, in spirit.

Now he understood why the crowd parted for a Terran – even a mere chimpanzee. (One with a tail that twitched nervously!)

Alas, that knowledge came as slim comfort. Clearly, the Skiano was riding a wave of public hysteria. Harry had walked into a revival meeting for one of the most bizarre heresies ever to strike the Five Galaxies!

Entranced and thoroughly amused, Kiwei Ha'aoulin began leading the way, forging ahead eagerly, as if to compensate for Harry's growing reluctance, acting like a strutting majordomo, alerting one and all that an *Earthling* was coming through!

In a whispered aside, she urged him to enjoy the special treatment while it lasted.

'Well well. Maybe you should buck up, little furry fellow! With the whole cosmos shaking apart, we might as well have some fun.'

Not a typically Synthian attitude. But then, fatalism can be a strong antidote to cowardice.

This time, Harry decided to accept Kiwei's reasoning. He squared his shoulders back, trying for the full bipedal dignity that human patrons had imbued into his ancestors while also giving them the gifts of speech and sapiency. He smoothed down the hackles in his pale fur, and even allowed the anomalous tail to rise up, in pride.

Abruptly, the throng ended. He and Kiwei found themselves at a raised platform where visiting dignitaries could sit and watch the spectacle in comfort.

Harry wanted only to get away and resume his earlier business, searching for the wayward sooners. But the only path available aimed straight up a ramp to the reserved area. As he climbed alongside Kiwei, the Skiano missionary's strange dogma resonated.

'... *why do the mighty alliances and Old Ones so oppose the idea of a God who loves each person? One who finds importance not in race or clan, but in every particular entity who is aware and capable of compassion?*

'*Could it be because they fear such an idea might bring an end to Uplift or species improvement?*

'*Nonsense! Those things would still take place, undertaken by free individuals! By sovereign souls who have faith in themselves and a personal redemption – when each honorable sapient will meet the Creator of All, finding utter fulfillment at the Omega Point.*'

*

Harry had heard it all before – a strange blending of ancient Earth beliefs – many of them mutually incompatible – upgraded to address the mass fears of a Galactic civilization where the accustomed certainty was melting on all sides. The Skiano's brilliant added touch – portraying the wolfling planet in the role of glorious, redeeming martyr – took advantage of Terra's plight ... while doing little to help save it from wrathful battle fleets.

If Harry thought the sermon bizarre, something more interesting awaited him among the varied dignitaries – none other than his old antagonist, the port inspector, who slouched as low as possible, clearly wishing to be elsewhere.

Harry loudly greeted the big hoon, calling out his name.

'Twaphu-anuph! Is that really you? Come to expand your horizons a bit, have you? Decided it was time to see the light?'

Upon spying Harry, Twaphu-anuph recoiled. With his elegantly dyed throat sac flapping miserably, he gestured lamely toward a young female hoon sitting next to him.

'My presence here ... it was not voluntary. My ... hr-rrm ... *daughter* made me come.'

Harry barely stifled a guffaw. If hoons had one appealing trait, it was how they doted on their offspring. Harry still found it mystifying why this charming attribute nevertheless resulted in a race of dour, prudish, inflexible bureaucrats.

While Harry savored Twaphu-anuph's discomfort, the Skiano kept preaching.

'Today we see the great powers striving to suppress truth – even as they vie to rain ruin down on Blessed Earth. Why? Because they worry about the Big Mistake.

'Long ago, a so-called "heresy" was quashed. But truth can only be hidden, never destroyed.

'Now they fear all sapients will see at last—'

The prow-headed missionary paused dramatically.

'—that the vaunted "Embrace of Tides" may be an embrace of lies!'

The crowd must have already known the gist of this message. Yet a moan coursed the vast hall when it was said aloud.

It gave Harry a chance to torment the port official some more.

'How 'bout that, old fellow?' he murmured. 'Generation after generation, workin' and slaving and havin' no fun, just so's your distant smart-aleck descendants will get to jump through a black hole to paradise. But what if there's nothing down there, at the other end of the singularity? What if it's all for nothin'?'

While Twaphu-anuph slumped miserably, his daughter leaned

forward eagerly, peering with excitement toward the dais, where the Skiano paced back and forth under spotlights.

'... but there is another kind of salvation! One that needn't dwell on far horizons of space and time. One that comes to each of us, if we just open up ...'

Twaphu-anuph's daughter turned to her other companion, a sturdy-looking young male hoon, whose arm she held with evident affection. A slender rousit perched on her shoulder, staring at a black, ferretlike creature lounging on the male's back. Another inexplicable irony was that animals tended to like hoons, something that sapient beings seldom did.

Both youths were clearly well embarked on a bonding cycle – a scene that might have looked fetching, except the inevitable outcome would be yet another generation of sullen oppressors.

Why would hoons attend this bizarre rally? It runs counter to everything they stand for!

Harry jerked reflexively, reacting to a nudge from his Synthian companion.

'Over there!' Kiwei Ha'aoulin pointed. 'Is that possibly one of the Earthlings you seek?'

Harry peered toward one end of the glare-lighted stage, where the Skiano's attendants swarmed in flowing robes of blue and gold. In their midst stood a smallish human figure, similarly attired, who made commanding gestures, sending acolytes fanning through the congregation, armed with collection plates.

Harry blinked in surprise.

Rety!

A bath alone would have transformed the sooner girl. Resplendent garments took things further. But Harry saw that her *face* had also changed. Where scar tissue had once puckered her cheek and jaw, smooth pink skin now glistened.

The customer at the body shop wasn't Dwer, after all. I should've guessed.

Rety must have nosed around Kazzkark till she found the one group that would find her invaluable – a cult whose icon was the blue wolfling planet. Indeed, from the looks of things, she had risen to some prominence. A survivor, if Harry ever saw one.

'And now,' Kiwei Ha'aoulin murmured. 'We complete the circle. You are about to be reunited in full, and I will take my leave.'

Harry reached out to stop the Synthian ... then noticed that the audience was rippling once again. Like the Red Sea, parting. Emerging from a morass of beings who shuffled, slithered, flopped, or crawled out of the way, there strode a slim figure dressed in dun-colored clothing that seemed blurry to the eye. With the hood of his homespun garment thrown back, Dwer Koolhan's shock of unruly hair seemed to gleam in contrast, like his dark eyes.

Well, he must've spent some of the seventy-five coins, Harry thought, noting that the young man held a small electronic tablet and was using it the way natives on Horst would hold a dowsing rod, searching back and forth for water. On the back of one arm, Dwer also wore a makeshift arrangement of bent metal tubes and elastic bands that no Galactic would see as a weapon, but Harry recognized as a vicious-looking wrist catapult – more useful at close urban quarters than any bow and arrows. At his waist, the human wore a long knife in a sheath.

To anyone but another Earthling, he might have seemed completely calm, oblivious to the crowd. But Harry read tension in Dwer's shoulders as the living aisle spilled him toward the dignitaries' ramp. Kiwei had begun edging away again, but now the Synthian's curiosity overcame caution and she stayed to watch the young sooner approach.

'Well, well ...' Kiwei said, over and over, licking her whiskers nervously.

Dwer acknowledged Kiwei with a nod, showing no sign of any rancor over being cheated – much to the Synthian's obvious relief.

Approaching Harry, he turned off the small finder tool.

'Smart of you to set up a personal beacon, Captain Harms. I bought some lessons how to set this tracker onto your signal. We use sniffer-bees for the same purpose, back home.'

Harry shrugged. He hadn't expected it to work. But clearly, wherever these sooners came from, their schooling included resiliency.

'I'm just glad you two are all right,' he replied gruffly, nodding toward Rety.

Dwer scanned the scene onstage, where Rety could now be seen with the Skiano's parrot on her shoulder, leading the audience in a strangely compelling psalm, merging contributions from at least half a dozen Galactic dialects with slow, sonorous Anglic. Though his pupils dilated, Dwer's face showed no surprise.

'Shoulda figured,' he commented with a terse headshake. 'So, how d'you suggest we get her out of there without startin' a riot among these—'

The young man stopped abruptly. His jaw dropped ... then snapped shut again.

'I don't believe it,' he murmured. Then, with an expression of grim determination, he added, 'Excuse me, Cap'n Harms. There's something I got to do right now.'

Harry blinked. 'But ... what—'

Dwer moved past him, quickly and silently slipping off his outer tunic. With rapid, agile motions, he tied the arms and hooded neck, creating a makeshift bag which he grasped in his left hand. Creeping in back of the first row of dignitaries, Dwer ignored protesting grunts from those seated in the second rank. The crowd's continued chanting covered all complaints as he sidled behind Twaphu-anuph and the inspector's daughter, making straight for the third hoon – the young male, whose ferretlike pet seemed at last to sense something. Though it faced the other way, spiny hackles on its neck lifted from the mass of black fur. It started to turn, bringing both glittering eyes around. Eyes that flared with shocked realization the same moment that Dwer lunged.

Well I'll be shaved, Harry thought as the creature writhed in Dwer's hard grasp, snapping and hissing furiously until it was swallowed by the improvised sack. Even then, the fabric container bulged and jerked as the beast fought confinement.

That was a tytlal! He had thought there was something familiar about the lithe creature – but the size had seemed wrong. *A miniature tytlal ... riding the shoulder of a hoon!*

No wonder recognition was slow. Tytlal normally massed nearly as much as a chimpanzee. Far from being mere pets, they were intelligent, articulate starfarers, well known and admired on Earth. Also, like their Tymbrimi patrons, they thoroughly disliked hoons!

Possible explanations occurred to Harry. Was Dwer rescuing a captive tytlal *child* from captivity?

That theory vanished when the third hoon turned around, saw Dwer, and cried out an umble of delighted surprise. While the bag kept quivering, onlookers were treated to a sight unprecedented in the annals of the Civilization of Five Galaxies – a human and hoon embracing each other joyfully, like long-lost cousins from the same hometown.

They found a place to talk, assembling in the lattice space supporting the dignitaries' platform. Harry watched in amazement as Dwer's huge alien friend spoke colloquial Anglic perfectly, though with an archaic accent.

'Alvin' also exuded an enthusiasm – a joie de vivre – that seemed totally natural, though Harry had never seen anything like it in a hoon before.

'Hr-rr. The last time I saw you, Dwer, you were dangling under a *hot-air balloon*, preparing to take on a Jophur battleship single-handed. How did you wind up here?'

'It's a long story, Alvin. And we'd never have made it without

Captain Harms, here. But what about you? Does this mean the *Str—*'

Dwer stopped abruptly and shook his head, amending what he had been about to say.

'Does this mean our *friends* escaped to the transfer point all right?'

For the first time in his life, Harry saw a hoon shrug – a surprisingly graceful and expressive gesture for such an uptight species.

'Yeah, they did. That is, sort of. In a way.' The tattooed throat sac fluttered and sighed. 'For now let's just say it's also a long story.'

Kiwei the Synthian had a suggestion.

'I know a very nice establishment where they offer free food and drink to tellers of fine tales, no matter how long. Shall we all go—'

Dwer ignored Kiwei.

'And your pals? Ur-ronn? Huck? Pincer? Tyug?'

'They are well – along with the *friend* who brought us here. You can imagine that some of us find it easier to get around in public than others do.'

Dwer nodded, and Harry saw that levels of meaning passed between the two.

Wait a minute, he pondered. *If Dwer and Rety are sooners, from some hidden colony world, but they know this hoon, then that must mean—*

He lost the thought as Alvin responded to something Dwer said by umbling with jovial tones that sounded uncannily like laughter.

'So, you finally got the drop on old Mudfoot.'

The young human held up the now quiescent bag.

'Yeah, I did. And he doesn't come out till I get some answers, at long last.'

Alvin laughed again – making Twaphu-anuph shiver with visible confusion. But the bureaucrat's daughter seemed to adore the sound. With a second show of rather unhoonish enthusiasm, she introduced herself as Dorhinuf, and surprised both Earthlings by offering to shake their hands.

'Ever since he arrived, Alvin has been telling us about your wonderful world of Shangri-la,' she told Dwer. 'Where so many races live together in peace, and where hoons have learned to *sail*!'

Her infectious excitement seemed as strange as the sudden bizarre image filling Harry's mind – of hoons braving sea and spume in spindly boats.

Shangri-la? Harry noted.

Of course he'd mask the true name of the sooner planet. But why under that particular name? Why a Terran literary reference?

For that matter, how did a hoon ever come to be called Alvin?

From the sound of things behind them, the Skiano's heretical rally was starting to break up at last. Harry brought this to the others' attention.

'For once, I agree with Kiwei. We should go someplace private and talk further, before I have to report back to headquarters. But first let's collect Rety—'

He stopped then, sensing that something was changing. Through the soles of his feet, Harry felt another of the tremors that had made Kazzkark tremble intermittently for several jaduras. Only this time a new rhythm seemed to take over.

A rising intensity.

Others sensed it too. The hoons splayed their shaggy legs and a soft mewling escaped the bag where Dwer kept his tytlal prisoner. The viewing stand rattled unnervingly, and dust floated downward from the stony ceiling – the only barrier between living creatures and the sucking vacuum outside.

Things are getting worse, Harry thought.

When a crack appeared in the nearby wall and began to spread, he revised his estimate again.

This one is bad. Real bad.

KAA

'Pilot, wake up! Come quickly, you are needed!'

Like a fish with a hook in its jaw, tugged out of the sea by a cruel line, Kaa felt brutally *yanked* as intruding words pierced his dream, shattering a sonic phantasm of Peepoe.

She had been swimming beside him. Or rather, a pattern of echoes and sonar shadows, reflecting off his cabin, had coalesced as a likeness of her graceful form, undulating happily nearby, almost close enough to touch. Jijo's gentle sea had surrounded their bodies as they plunged ahead, naked and free.

Dolphins sleep just one hemisphere at a time. But this episode had the full flux and power of the Whale Dream, enveloping him in the presence of his beloved, and the planet where they had hoped to spend their lives together.

When the noisome voice broke in, shattering that blissful illusion, he felt the loss of Peepoe all over again, finding himself once again stranded in harsh metal purgatory, megaparsecs away from her.

In frustration, Kaa thrashed his flukes on the flotation bed of his walker unit. Bleary from fitful sleep, his right eye focused at last to regard the strange figure of *Huck*, a creature whose physical form seemed like an improbable swirl of organic and mechanical parts. Rolling on twin jittery wheels, the young g'Kek waved all four eye-stalks in frantic agitation, jabbering rapidly about something that had her terribly upset.

Anglic speech patterns came slowly to waking neo-dolphins, especially after immersion in the Whale Dream, but this time Kaa's anger bulled through, driving a hot response.

'I sssaid I wasn't to be disturbed ... except in an emergency!'

Huck's frantic words penetrated at last.

'This *is* an emergency!' she wailed. 'I j-just woke up and found Pincer-Tip—'

'Yeah?' Kaa asked, sending a signal down his neural tap to power up the walker. 'What about him?'

The g'Kek was already rolling swiftly out of the little cabin, two eyes aimed ahead and two back at Kaa.

'Come quick! Pincer's *dying*!'

The little red qheuen lay collapsed near the airlock – a crablike figure with five legs splayed outward symmetrically, like an ailing starfish. Several claws still shuddered and snapped reflexively, but there was no other sign of movement. When Kaa brought his walker unit closer, aiming its forward camera for a close look, he saw trails of ugly-looking substance – like ichor – dribbling from beneath the wide chitin carapace.

'What-t happened?' he asked anxiously.

Huck snapped back.

'How should I know? I told ya, I was in that little cabinet you assigned me as a hiding place, tryin' to sleep, since you won't let me leave the ship. When I came out, he was like this!'

'But-t ... don't you know what's wrong with him? Can you do anything?'

'Hey, just because I'm a g'Kek, that don't make me a doctor, any more'n every dolphin is a pilot. We've got to call for help!'

Kaa listened to the sick qheuen's ragged breathing. Whatever the nauseating substance was, it came from all five armpits, where the delicate air vents lay. Clearly, the poor thing was nearing total collapse.

'We ...' He shook his sleek gray head left and right. 'We can't do that.'

'What?' Huck rocked back so hard that both rims bounced off the floor. Her spokes hummed and she stared with all four eyes. 'We're not in a wilderness anymore, fish-head. We're at *civilization*!

They got all sorts of things out there, beyond that airlock. Stuff we Jijoans only read about in books, like *hospitals* and *autodocs*. They might save him!'

Kaa felt the young g'Kek's wrath and outrage. The heat of her devotion to a friend. He sympathized. But there could only be one answer.

'We can't call attention to ourselves. You know that. If anyone here even suspected that a dolphin was aboard this ship, they'd cut it apart to get at me. And the same holds for a g'Kek. We'll just have to wait for Alvin and Ur-ronn to get back. They can move about without attracting attention. Or better yet, when Tyug returns, the alchemist can try—'

'That could take miduras! You know Alvin's got himself a starhoon girlfriend. Tyug's spying on the Jophur, and Ur-ronn stays out longer and longer each time, talking to engineers!'

That was the plan, of course, for that trio to act as spies and envoys, getting to know the nature of things within Kazzkark Base, and in the Five Galaxies at large. If possible, they would make contact with some of Earth's few allies, or else look for some way to buy passage toward Galaxy Two. While attempting to deliver Gillian Baskin's message to the Terragens Council, they would also try to learn about their own kind, finding some way of securing future livelihoods, for themselves and their friends.

Huck was right. Alvin and Ur-ronn might stay out for hours longer. Pincer would not last that long.

'I'm sssorry,' Kaa said. 'We can't risk throwing everything away for just a sssslim chance of—'

'I don't *care* how slim it is, or about the risk! It doesn't matter!'

Her eyestalks waved and twined in furious anger. But while she cursed him roundly, Kaa knew he must be firm for her sake, even more than his own. With all the g'Keks of Jijo now in peril of genocide – deliberate extinction by wrathful Jophur, bent on satisfying an ancient vendetta – this one little female might be the sole hope of her entire species. Along with a tube of seminal plasm, stored in the scoutboat's refrigerator, she might possibly reestablish her posterity in some safe hiding place, protected by sympathetic guardians.

Although it was not a role the adventurous Huck relished, she had claimed to see its importance. Until now, that is, when she would toss it all away for friendship.

Personal loyalty. Love. These are supposed to outweigh all other considerations, Kaa thought, wallowing in misery, even as the young g'Kek railed at him, demanding over and over that he open the door.

Raised on Earthling novels, she feels the same way about it that I do. That only the worst sort of person would put stark pragmatism above intimate devotion, abandoning someone you care about to certain death ... or something worse ... even if it is logically the 'right' thing to do.

So Kaa silently derided himself while Huck did it aloud, making the small control room echo with her wails.

Yet, he would not relent.

Anyway, the issue was settled soon. Just a few duras later, Pincer-Tip was dead.

Huck lacked both strength and will to help dispose of the body. That chore was left to Kaa, using the mechanical arms of his walker to heave the bulky qheuen toward the recycler. Huck turned three eyes away from the gory scene, but the remaining stalk quivered and stared, as if dumbly transfixed.

How could this happen? Kaa worried as he sent control messages down his neural tap, causing the machine to move like an extension of his body. *Did someone attack the ship? Or was this caused by the disease we heard about ... the one that slaughtered many qheuens back on Jijo?*

If so, how was Pincer exposed?

Abruptly, Huck let out an amazed cry. Her whistling shouts brought Kaa spinning around, stomping back from his grisly task. He looked down where she pointed, at the bloody deck where Pincer had lain.

There, partly masked by gruesome liquids, both of them now made out a *design* of some sort, carved deeply into the metal deck.

'He ... he ...' Huck stammered. 'He musta cut it with his teeth, while he was dying! Poor Pincer couldn't walk or talk, but he could still move his mouth, as it lay against the floor!'

Kaa stared, in part amazed by the slicing power of qheuen jaws, and by the acute – even artistic – rendering that had been the poor creature's final act.

It showed a face, vaguely humanoid, but somewhat feral looking, with lean, ravenous cheeks and a small, bitter mouth. He recognized the shape at once.

'A *Rothen*!'

The race of sneaky criminals and petty connivers, who had persuaded a cult of humans to believe they were patrons of all Earthclan, and rightful gods of Terran devotion.

Then he remembered. There had been such a creature aboard *Streaker*! A prisoner, brought aboard in secret at Wuphon Port. A Rothen overlord named *Ro-kenn*, mastermind of many felonies against the Six Races of Jijo.

'He musta stowed away aboard this ship!' Huck cried. 'Stayed hidden till we docked, then came out an' killed poor Pincer to get at the door!'

Kaa's mind roiled over the disastrous implications. No matter how capable, Ro-kenn could not have managed such an escape all by himself. He must have had help aboard *Streaker*. Moreover, if this Rothen made it into Kazzkark, all their plans might be in jeopardy.

Stay calm, he told himself. *Ro-kenn can't go to the authorities. The crimes he committed on Jijo are worse than anything the sooners did.*

Yes, but he might hurry to one of the big fanatic clans or alliances, and try to sell them information about Streaker *and Jijo. At the very least, he'll send word to other Rothen.*

'We had better try to contact Alvin and Ur-ronn,' Kaa said. And for once he could tell that Huck agreed.

Only that was far from easy. It seemed that all available telecomm lines were jammed with frantic traffic. And things only got worse as another wave of subspace disruptions hit, causing the planetoid to shake and rattle, resonating like a great, hollow bell.

FROM THE JOURNAL OF
GILLIAN BASKIN

The universe is awash in tragedy. Yet, only now, as it seems to be falling apart, have I finally begun to see some of the ironic, awesome beauty of its cosmic design.

As happened at the Fractal World, we find ourselves surrounded by sudden devastation, orders of magnitude greater than I ever imagined.

Far below us, whirling near the condensed core of a massive ancient star, we see vast, needle-shaped habitats – each one longer than the moon is wide – made of superstrong godstuff, built to withstand fierce tidal strains. Only now those habitats of the Transcendent Order show signs of terminal stress, shedding their outer skins like brittle slough – quivering as wave after wave of spatial convulsions surge through this part of Galaxy Four.

According to both Sara and the Niss Machine, these are symptoms of a fantastic rupture, beyond anything seen in a quarter of a billion years.

The effects have been even worse on the huge armada of 'candidate ships' accompanying Streaker *converging on multiple, crisscrossing downward spirals toward those needle monoliths. What had been a stately procession, triumphant and hopeful, wedding two of life's great orders in a great and glorious union, is swiftly dissolving into chaos and conflagration.*

So closely were the giant arks and globules packed together – in dense, orderly rows – that each wave of hypergeometric-recoil throws one rank against another. Collisions produce blinding explosions, slaughtering untold millions and throwing yet more vessels off course.

Yet, despite this awful trend, only a few other craft have joined Streaker *in attempting to escape, climbing laboriously outward through the maze, seeking some relative sanctuary of deep space. It seems that the addiction of tides cannot easily be broken, once sapients have tasted its deeper pleasures. Like rutting beasts, irresistibly drawn toward mating grounds they know to be on fire, a majority continue on course, accelerating into the funnel, bound for the Embrace they so deeply desire.*

Is this *the ultimate destiny of intelligent life? After striving for ages to become brainy, contemplative, wise (and all that), do all races wind up driven forward by ineffable instinct? By a yearning so strong they must plunge ahead, even when their goal is falling apart before their eyes?*

At last, for the first time in three long years, I begin to understand the persecution we Streakers have suffered – and Earth, as well. For our discovery of the Ghost Fleet truly does present a challenge, a shocking heresy, that strikes at the very heart of Galactic belief systems.

Most of them – and the hydrogen breathers, as well – maintain that true transcendence is the ultimate destiny of those who merge within the Embrace of Tides. Something *must lie beyond ... or so they've reasoned for countless ages. Why else would the universe have evolved such an elegant way of focusing, gathering, and distilling the very best of both life orders?*

Surely, this must be the great path spoken of by the Progenitors, when they departed two billion years ago.

Ah, but then what of the Ghost Fleet, *with its haunting symbols and glimmering hints at ancient truth?*

Where did we find it?

In a 'shallow' globular cluster, dim and nearly metalfree, drifting lonely toward the rim of Galaxy Two. A place where spacetime is so flat that even young races experience a faint, nervous revulsion. A kind of creepy agoraphobia. Such locales are seldom visited, since they contain nothing of interest to any life order, even machines.

(In which case, what clue ... what hunch ... drew Creideiki there? Did he set Streaker's *course for the Shallow Cluster because it seemed neglected by the Great Library, with an entry as skimpy as the one about Earth?*

(Or was there something more to his decision? A choice that seemed so strange at the time.)

Now, at last, I see why our enemies – the Tandu and Soro and Jophur and the others – got so upset when Streaker *beamed back those first images of the Ghost Fleet ... and of Herbie and the rest.*

If these truly are relics of the great Progenitors, sealed away in field-protected vessels for countless aeons, what does that imply about the Embrace of Tides? Did the founder race – earliest and wisest of all – seek desperately to avoid the attraction? Did they shun the deep places? If so, might it be because they knew something terrible about them?

Perhaps they saw the Embrace as something else entirely. Not a route to transcendence, but a trash disposal system. A means for recycling dross, like the Great Midden on Jijo.

Nature's way of siphoning away the old in order to make room for the new.

Standing in his glass case, Herbie smiles at me across my desk. The mummy's eerie humanoidal rictus has been my most intimate companion, ever since Tom went away. Sometimes I find myself talking to him.

Well, old fellow? Is this the big joke? Have I at last figured out why you've been grinning all this time?

Or are there more layers yet to peel away?

More terrible surprises to come.

It isn't easy trying to work our way out of this trap with our two best pilots gone. The swarm of arks and globules appears to extend endlessly above us, reaching far out beyond the range of any solar system. The sheer amount of mass involved approaches macroplanetary scales! Like the accretion disk surrounding a newborn star.

Where could all these 'candidates' have come from?

Might the same thing be happening elsewhere? A lot of elsewheres? If even a small fraction of older white dwarves are home to such convergences, that would mean millions of sites like this one, surrounded by migrants eager to enter paradise, despite a growing gauntlet of collision and fire.

On a practical level, Streaker *cannot attempt any hyperspace jumps till we're clear of all these massive ships, and the rippling effects of their mighty engines.*

Even if we do succeed in working our way outward, the Jophur dreadnought is still out there. We detect it from time to time, tracking us like some tenacious predator, crippled and dying, with nothing else to live for anymore beyond finishing the hunt. If we make it to open space, there will be that peril to contend with.

If only we could rid ourselves of this deadly coating and restore Streaker *to her old agility!*

Hannes has been working on a new idea about that, alongside Emerson D'Anite. Something involving the big Communications Laser.

Poor Emerson struggles to explain something to us – humming melodies and drawing pictures, but all we can tell so far is that he managed to defeat yet another meme-attack on Streaker *a while back, and destroyed the renegade – Tsh't – in the process.*

I cannot help it. I grieve for my friend. The sweet comrade who was by my side through crisis after crisis. Poor Tsh't only thought she was doing the right thing, seeking help and succor from her gods.

Now another wraith follows through the night, surging like a porpoise through my restless dreams.

The big news is that the Niss Machine lately made a breakthrough. It managed at last to tap into what passes for a communications network among the Transcendents.

As one might expect, it is a dense, complex system, as far beyond Galactic-level technology as a hand computer exceeds an abacus. It was invisible for so long because only small portions on the fringes use classical electronics or photonics. The core technique appears to be quantum computing on a scale so vast that it must utilize highly compressed gravitational fields.

'Such fields are unavailable here,' *commented the Niss.* 'Even among the needle habitats, whirling just above the compact star core, the potentials are many orders of magnitude too small.

'We must be picking up the margins of something much greater. Something with its center located far away from here.'

Of course it occurred to us that this might be our chance. Our hope of communicating with 'higher authorities,' as ordered by the Terragens Council. The creatures who betrayed us at the Fractal World – those so-called Old Ones – were like infants in comparison to the minds using this new network. Indeed, all signs suggest they are the pinnacle that life achieves.

Yet, I'm reluctant to just hand over our data from the Shallow Cluster. We've been disappointed too many times. Perhaps the Transcendents also suffer from the same fear – that a deadly trap underlies the Embrace of Tides.

If it entered their thoughts to be vengeful toward us, we'd have all the chance of a hamster against a bolo battle tank.

'Let's ask simple questions, first,' *I said.* 'Any suggestions?'

Sara Koolhan burst forth.

'Ask about the Buyur! Are they down there? Did the Buyur tran-scend?'

Lately, she's grown obsessed with the last species to have leasehold over Jijo. A race of genetic manipulators, who seemed to know in advance that sooners would invade their world, and about a coming Time of Changes.

'Even such a simple query will be hard to translate. It may be impossible to slip within the matrix in such a way that anyone will notice, or bother answering,' warned the Niss. 'But I will try.'

Of course we risk drawing the attention of even more powerful enemies. But with the odds already against us, it seems a worthwhile effort.

Meanwhile, our dolphin astronomer, Zub'daki, has more bad news to report about the swarm of incoming Candidate vessels.

He knows and cares little about hyperspatial disruptions tearing the fabric of reality. That is Sara's department. Zub'daki's interest lies in the white dwarf itself, and the sheer amount of matter approach-ing it like flotsam in a whirling drain.

'What if most of the arks misssss their target?' he asked. 'What if they fail to rendezvous with the needle-gatewayssss?

'What if the needles are no longer there to collect them?'

I fear that my initial response was callous, asking why we should care if a stampede of giants go tumbling into a grave of their own making. As mere ants, it is our duty to escape. To survive.

But I will go and hear what he has to say.

What will one more worry matter? I've long passed the point where I stopped counting them.

LARK

The reunion was bizarre, joyous, and rather unnerving.

Having long dreamed of this moment – being reunited with his lover – Lark now stared at Ling across a gulf far wider than the few meters separating them.

She floated in a blobby stew, a dense swarm of writhing, pulsating objects that moved languidly within a vast, transparent membrane – a bloated mass that filled most of this large chamber and extended through several hatchways into more of the ship beyond.

In addition to Ling's human form, he glimpsed at least one wrig-gling qheuen larva, plus several animal types from Jijo and other worlds. Lark recognized a multitude of traeki rings, plus countless twining green things that must have once been plants.

Bubblelike forms also crowded throughout the teeming life-brew, rippling like amoebae, or bobbing gelatinous balloons. Though colored and textured differently than the Zang creature he carried about like a suit of clothes, Lark could tell they were related.

Despite the family resemblance, his passenger reacted violently to sighting these 'cousins.' The Zang tried to make him flee. But Lark was adamant, willing both stiff legs to stride forward, to Ling.

Her naked form was draped with various throbbing creatures. *Symbionts*, Lark thought. Some of them covered her mouth and nose, while others penetrated flesh directly to the bloodstream. Weeks ago, the sight might have sent chills down his spine, but by now the concept was familiar as breathing. Simply a more extensive version of the arrangement he had made with the Zang.

Moving closer, he sought Ling's eyes, trying for contact. Had this vast cell simply incorporated her for some crude biochemical purpose, as an *organelle*, to serve a minor function for the whole? Or did she retain her essence within?

Lark's passenger extended a pseudopod over his left eye, creating a vacuole in front of his field of view. Inside that small space, hundreds of tiny 'deputies' budded and performed gyrations, mimicking shapes and playacting a suggestion that Lark should turn around and get the hell away from here!

'Oh, stop bellyaching, you coward,' he replied with disgust. 'On Jijo we learned you can make friends out of old enemies. Besides, have you got anything better to do right now?'

His meaning somehow got through, causing the Zang to retract its deputies, resorbing them into its body and pulling back sullenly.

Indeed, there would be no going back to the creature's base, on the opposite side of the battleship. In between them lay a huge wilderness. *Polkjhy* now swarmed with *things*, crawling through the hallways, chewing through compartments and walls, transforming them into grotesque shapes and outlandish forms. So far, essential systems seemed to have been spared. Those were still under control of the remaining Jophur crew – who seemed to grow ever more shrill and panicky in their communications – but for how much longer?

He felt a large presence come up alongside. The third member of their party.

'You are right, Lark,' murmured the stack of glistening rings, whose throbbing mass quivered as its components debated among themselves.

'This vast macro-entity appears foreordained to expand until it fills *Polkjhy* entirely. We might flee, but to what end? Our trail has brought us here. Our/my/your/our destiny clearly lies within. Let us find out what it wants. What are its aims. What it came here to accomplish.'

Within the gelatinous mass, Lark saw signs of change. Ling's eyes, which had been dismayingly vacant, now seemed to clarify, gradually focusing past the membrane, toward him.

All at once, a light of recognition shone! Though her mouth was covered by a symbiont, the squint of a smile was unmistakable, and her arms moved forward, reaching out. Joyful at the sight of him. Reaching in welcome.

'Well, look at the bright side,' he commented, although the Zang passenger shivered with fearful resignation. 'It looks kinda interesting in there. Maybe we'll learn a lot, eh?'

The giant membrane did not try to grab or seize them when they approached. Rather, it recoiled a bit, then seemed to sniff cautiously, as if deigning to be wooed. Lark extended his arm, brushing the surface. It felt chilly, and yet electrically pleasant in a way he could not quite fathom.

The Zang quivered, then seemed to change its mind. Lark had an impression of surprise. This was not the deadly foe it had expected, but a distant relative, greater and more kindly.

Decision came. A cavity formed, shaped like a tunnel, or a doorway.

Lark didn't hesitate. He strode forward, to his love.

It seemed that his instinct was correct. There was something deeply natural about this merging.

In theory, the hydro- and oxy-orders were incompatible, using disparate chemistry, different energetics and existing at widely distinct temperatures. But life is very good at problem solving. *Symbiosis* enables two or more organisms to pool abilities, accomplishing what one alone never could. It happened when early cells joined together in Earth's oceans, creating unions that were more competent than their separate parts.

Lark soon got used to the idea that this could take place on a much more sophisticated level, especially when guided by sagacious intelligence.

Anyway, while a teeming swarm of other 'organelles' surrounded him, he cared about just one, whose caress made him feel more at home in this strange place than he ever had in his bed, on Jijo.

I'm glad we're still functional in all the ways that really matter, he commented.

Ling curled her body alongside his, maximizing contact between their drifting bodies. Her answer came not as sound, but directly, as if conveyed by the fluid surroundings.

Typical male. Nothing else matters, as long as your sexual organs are satisfied.

He blinked.

Weren't yours?

She replied with a languorous squeeze, evidently content. Her skin still trembled slightly with the rhythms of their intense love-making.

A part of Lark – the restless thinker – wondered what possible use the macro-being could make of human sexual passion. Not that he was ungrateful for this new phase of existence. But once his thoughts began spreading outward, they would not stop.

Whatever happened to Rann? he inquired.

The one other human aboard, a fierce Danik warrior, had turned his talents to helping the Jophur. Lark would not relax knowing that enemy was out there, somewhere.

Don't worry about Rann. He won't be bothering us.

When he glanced at her, Ling shrugged, causing bubbles to flurry off her shoulders.

He was absorbed also. Mother must not have liked how he tasted. But she doesn't waste good material, so she put him to work in other ways. I saw a couple of Rann's parts a while ago – a leg and a lung, I think – incorporated in some organelle.

Lark shivered, feeling grateful that his 'taste' met the macro-being's approval.

You call it Mother?

She nodded, not having to explain. The name made as much sense as any other. Though nurturing kindliness was clearly just one aspect of its nature. There was also a brutally pragmatic side.

He sensed agreement from the Zang, his longtime companion, who now existed as a compact globule, floating nearby. Their sole remaining link was a narrow tube connected to his left side, and even that might dissolve soon, as they learned their separate roles in this new world. The Zang was still deeply uncertain, though one might have expected it to be more at home in this world of drifting shapes, where bulbous deputies swam back and forth, performing gaudy simulations.

In the murky distance, he saw that someone else was having a better time adjusting. The stack of waxy traeki rings – who had once been Asx, and then the Jophur called Ewasx – stood planted on the floor, surrounded by clusters of bubbles, membranes, and crawling symbionts. From waves of color that coursed across its flanks, Lark could tell the composite creature was having the time of its life. What could be more essentially *traeki* than to become part of something larger and more complex, a cooperative enterprise in which every ring and particle played a part?

Lark still wondered about how it all was organized. Did there exist an overall controlling mind – like a Jophur master ring? Or would every component get a vote? Both models of symbiosis existed in nature ... and in politics.

He had a feeling such details were yet to be worked out. 'Mother' wasn't finished taking form.

Come along, Ling urged, taking his hand. *I want to show you something*.

Lark needed a little while to get used to locomotion in this new medium. Much of the time, it involved movements akin to swimming, though in other locales the surrounding density changed somehow and their feet met the floor, allowing a more human mode of walking. There were no clear transitions, as between sea and shore. Rather, everything intermingled and merged, like the thoughts he and Ling shared.

Guiding him along, she finally pointed to a vast nest of tendrils that spread outward from a central point, waving and twisting. Many were linked to wriggling forms – Lark saw another larval qheuen, a couple of traeki stacks ... and a form that resembled a centauroid urs, curled in a fetal ball, protected by something like an embryonic sac. He did not recognize the tawny figure, though urrish 'samples' had been taken by the Jophur, on Jijo. Its flanks heaved slowly, as if calmly breathing, and Lark saw intelligent clarity in the triple set of eyes.

There were other oxy creatures. Some he identified from images on paper textbooks he had skimmed long ago, back home in the Biblos archive, while others he did not recognize. All were entangled with symbionts linking them to hydro-globules and other blobby things. The most eerie thing about it was that none of them seemed particularly to mind.

Mother taps the data mesh here, Ling explained, pointing to where the tendrils converged. Peering to look past the murk, he made out one of *Polkjhy*'s main computer panels.

Ling reached for three writhing tentacles, offering one each to Lark and the Zang.

Let's take a look at what's happening elsewhere.

It was a strange way of taking information. Partly neuronal and partly visual, it also involved portions of the mind that Lark customarily used for imagination, picturing an event with that tentative *what-if* sensation that always accompanied daydreams.

That made sense. For all hydro-beings, thinking was a process of simulation – spawning off smaller portions of themselves to play roles and act out a scenario to its logical conclusions. Helped by his prior experience with the Zang, Lark soon caught on, learning how to reach out and pretend that he *was* the object of his attention.

I am Polkjhy ... *once a proud battleship of the haughty Jophur nation.*

Now I am divided ... sectioned into many parts. My Jophur crew – doughty but distraught – have cleverly sealed off what they consider to be the most essential areas ... engines, weaponry, and basic life support.

Driven by single-minded, purposeful Master Rings, they prepare for a last stand against loathsome invaders ... while continuing to pursue their grudge hunt. Chasing the Earthling ship, whether pursuit leads them to Hell, or Heaven itself.

Lark felt a wash of strange emotion – grudging respect for the dauntless Jophur. Their resiliency, in the face of one catastrophe after another, showed why their kind had gained power and influence among the vigorous, starfaring oxy-clans. That they could manage, even temporarily, to stave off powers much older and stronger than themselves was an impressive accomplishment.

Even so, Lark hoped they would fail soon.

Ling guided his attention, nudging it gently outward, beyond the battered hull.

He briefly staggered at a sudden impression, like that of an immense tornado!

A giant cyclone surrounded them, a swirling crowd of massive objects, sparkling and flashing while they spiraled down a condensing funnel toward the dim white fire of a tiny star.

Lark quickly found that his knowledge base was no longer limited to the narrow education of a Jijoan sooner – a rustic biologist, weaned on paper-paged books. It took only a slight effort of will to slip into Ling's mind and *perceive* facts, correlations, hypotheses to explain what they now saw. And beyond Ling, there were other archives – less familiar, but equally available.

Abruptly, he reached outward to the immense cyclone of descending spacecraft, identifying with them.

I am the Candidates' Swarm, a migration of the elect, chosen from among retirees of both oxygen- and hydrogen-breathing civilizations.

Elated to be here, at long last.

Fatigued by the pointless struggles and quandaries of flat space and real time.

Lured and allured by the seductive enchantments of the Embrace of Tides.

Fully aware of the disruptions now coursing through the Five Galaxies.

Cognizant of dangers, lying ahead.

Nevertheless, I draw inward. Merging my many subunits. Creating unique blendings out of what was merely promising raw material. Integrating the best of hydrogen and oxygen.

Hoping and wondering what comes next ...

Lark now saw a context for what had befallen *Polkjhy*. It was part of a much larger process! The same blending of life-forms must be happening on each of the millions of huge vessels out there ... only perhaps more peacefully, with less resistance by the resident crews, who would be much better prepared for it than the poor Jophur.

And yet, he could not help but grasp a background tone of desperate worry. This majestic ingathering of transcendence candidates should have been smooth and ordered. But instead it grew more ragged and disrupted with each passing dura. The sparkles that had looked so gay earlier were now revealed as fiery impacts. Violent death spread ever more rapidly among the converging ships.

Again, Ling pointed and his mind followed. Instead of outward, their shared attention plunged *down*, toward the source of gravity and light, where immense slender edifices whirled in tight orbit around a compact star.

To initial appearances, the needle-habitats were also suffering severe strain. As he and Ling watched, chunks larger than mountains shattered or fell off, dissolving under the sheer force of intense tides.

And yet, Lark felt no anguish, worry, or sense of imminent danger.

No wonder! he realized. *The needles aren't habitats at all! They are gateways to another place!*

Ling nodded.

Actually, it is predictable, if you think about it.

Lark sent his mind swooping like a hawk toward one of the fast-revolving structures, long and narrow, like a javelin. Though portions of its skin were flaking off – torn loose by chaotic hyper-wave disturbances – he somehow knew those portions were unimportant. Mere temporary abodes and support structures. As these sloughed away, they revealed a shimmering inner core, luminescent and slippery to the eye.

His image-self arrived just as one of the 'candidates' – a fully transformed globule-ark – finished its long spiraling migration and approached the needle at a rapid pace, skimming just above the white dwarf's licking plasma fire. The great hybrid vessel – now a completely blended mixture of hydrogen and oxygen civilizations – fell toward the exposed gateway, accelerating as if caught in some strongly attractive field.

Abruptly, the globule-ark seemed to slip *sideways*, through a narrow incision that had been cut in spacetime.

The opening lasted but a few moments. But it was enough for Lark to perceive.

His first impression from the other side was of dense spinning blackness. A dark ball that glimmered with sudden, bright pin-points. Somehow he could sense the twist and curl of vacuum as space warped around the thing, distorting any constellations that lay beyond.

It is a neutron star, Ling commented. *Long ago it used up or expelled any fuel it had left. Now it has self-compressed down to a size far smaller than a white dwarf – less than ten kilometers across! The gravitational pressure is so great below the surface that atomic nuclei merge with their surrounding clouds of electrons, forming 'degenerate matter.'*

Those sparks you see below are gamma ray flashes – translated into visible range by the transcendent mesh for our convenience. Each flash represents a grain, perhaps as small as a bacterium, that quickened up to near the speed of light before striking the surface.

There are half a billion of these dense relics in any galaxy ... and a new one produced every thirty years or so. But only a few neutron stars have the narrow range of traits needed by the Transcendent Order. Well behaved. Rapidly spinning, but with low magnetic fields.

Lark overcame his surprise.

I get what's going on. The process continues!

How could a growing appetite for tides be satisfied by a mere white dwarf star? Of course, they'll migrate to a place where the fields are even more intense.

So, the myriad candidate vessels surrounding Polkjhy *right now are only passing through! They use the white dwarf as an assembly area – a place to merge and transform, getting ready for the next phase.*

The next time a slit-passage opened, Lark once again cast his thoughts through, riding the carrier wave of a vast information-handling system, like a sea flea surfing atop a tsunami, seeking to learn what kind of life transcendent beings made for themselves in such a strange place.

A *fog* seemed to envelop the neutron star, like a dense haze, whirling just above the surface.

Habitats, Ling identified.

Lark tried to look closer, but was stymied by how fast the objects sped by, just above the sleek black surface. Each orbit took minuscule fractions of a second, racing around a course where gravity was so intense that tidal forces would rip apart any physical object more than a few meters across.

Even with his perceptions enhanced by Mother, there were limits to what his organic brain could grasp.

But . . . Mentally, he stammered. *When hydro- and oxy-life merge, the result is still organic . . . based on water. Bodies with liquid chemistry. How can beings like us survive down there?*

As if his question were a command, the focus of their attention shifted outward, to surrounding regions of space, further from the neutron star, where an enormous throng of dark, spindly objects could now be made out, parked in stately rows.

Lark sensed *metallic* presences, each waiting its turn with a patient silence that could only originate in the vast depths of interstellar vacuum.

Realization struck.

Machines!

A third life order had arrived. Answering some compelling call, the best and highest of their kind assembled to participate in a new union.

Another kind of marriage.

A narrow slit appeared in space, allowing ingress from a white dwarf assembly zone. One more globule-ark popped into the twisted sky, bringing its cargo of merged organic life-forms.

Several dozen of the waiting mechanicals converged around it, weaving a cocoon of fibrous light.

There was no resistance. Lark's expanded empathic sense picked up no dread, or resignation. Only readiness for metamorphosis.

The biologist in him recognized something elegant and natural looking about the process, although soon the details grew too complex and blurry even for his enhanced perceptions to follow.

All at once, amid a burst of actinic flare, everything was transformed. Consumed.

What fell away from the flash seemed like no more than a rain of glittering specks, plummeting eagerly toward the comforting squeeze – the intense embrace – of gravitational fields just above the neutron star.

*

Lark's head whirled in awe. He pulled back his attention, anchoring it to the real world by riveting on the soft brown eyes of Ling.

Is that it? Is that where everything culminates? With hydros, oxies, and machines merging, then orbiting forever next to a dense black sun?

Ling shook her head.

That's as far as I've been able to probe. But logically, I'd guess otherwise.

Think about it, Lark. Three life orders coalesce. The three who are known as the fiercest. The most potent at manipulating matter and energy. At last we know why hydros, oxies, and mechs have been able to coexist for so long ... since they share a common destiny, and none can thrive without the others.

But there are more orders. More sapient styles than just those three! Quantals and Meta-memes, for instance. And rumors of some that have no mention in the Great Library. Simple logic – and aesthetics – make me imagine that the process continues. Others must join as well. At some level beyond the one we just saw.

Lark blinked.

Some level beyond? But what could lie beyond ... ?

Then, all at once, he knew.

Sharing his realization, the little Zang next to him vented foul-smelling bubbles – the equivalent of a dismayed wail – and shrank inward. But Lark only nodded.

You're talking about black holes.

An unbeckoned flood of information crowded his thoughts, revealing many different types of 'holes' known to science – sites where the density of matter passed a point of no return, wrapping gravity so tightly that no light, or information of any kind, could escape. Only a few of the deep singularities would do for the purpose Ling described. Smaller ones, mostly – massing up to just a few dozen times a typical sun. Bottomless pits, whose steep fringes would have the greatest tides of all ... and where time itself would nearly stand still.

In such a narrow zone, just outside the black hole's event horizon, distinctions of matter and energy would blur. Causality would shimmer, evading Ifni's grasp. Under the right conditions, all of life's varied orders might merge, creating a pure sapiency stew. Intelligence in its most essential form.

If everything worked.

You're right, it's logical and aesthetic. Even beautiful, in its own way.
But I have one question, Ling.
Where do we fit in this grand scheme of things?
I mean you and I!

All the beings on these arks and globules surrounding us may be ready for such a destiny ... assuming they survive the disruptions and chaos in order to reach the next level. After all, they've spent ages refining their souls, getting ready for this transformation.

But you and I were caught up in it by accident! Because we're in the wrong place at the wrong time. We don't belong here!

Ling's hand slipped into his, and Lark felt her warm smile inside his mind.

You don't like our new nest, love?

He squeezed back.

You know I do. It's just kind of hard to look forward to the next step – being 'merged' with some star-computer mechoids, then squished down to the size of a pea, and finally—

She stopped him with a light mental touch, a calming stroke that brushed away incipient panic.

It's all right, Lark. Don't worry about it.

I very much doubt we're going to proceed much farther down that path.

Not if the Jophur have anything to say about it.

SARA

Getting an answer to her question did not settle any of the worries plaguing Sara.

While the Niss hologram gyred nearby, her forehead creased with concern.

'Damn! I hoped to learn the bastards had transcended.'

The computerized voice replied with puzzlement.

'Might I ask why you are concerned about the fate of any one particular elder race?'

Her frown deepened. 'The Buyur weren't just any race. Back when they held the lease on Jijo, they were renowned for cleverness and wit. You might say they were the Tymbrimi of their time, only far subtler at playing games of manipulative politics and power ... and they had a much longer view of what it took in order to execute a good joke.'

'In the name of my Tymbrimi makers, thanks for the compliment,' the Niss replied sarcastically. But Sara had learned to ignore its feigned moods, designed to irk people in the short term. She was concerned about a race of jesters whose notion of a punch line could easily span a million years. Patient comedians whose

intended victims might include her own folk – the Six Races of the Commons of Jijo.

'Are you sure the Transcendents keep such good records?' she asked. 'Maybe the Buyur passed through a different white dwarf – a different merging-funnel – when they graduated to the next level.'

You misunderstand the nature of quantum computing,' commented the Niss, dryly. *'Every part of the Transcendent Mesh is in local contact with all others. There are no distinctions of space, or even time. All Transcendents know what the others know. We are talking about the closest thing to what you humans used to call the Omniscient Godhead . . . on this side of the Omega Point.'*

Sara grunted, slipping into the thick accent of a Dolo Village tree farmer.

'So far, I seen about a dozen levels o' so-called star deities, and I ain't been impressed with a one of 'em. Pettiness seems to follow life, no matter how high it climbs.'

'So young to be so cynical,' the Niss sighed. *'Be that as it may, the query you sent into the Mesh did receive an answer. Assuming the Transcendents are not lying, we can be fairly certain that the Buyur have not joined them yet.'*

Sara glowered at the news. It had seemed the best possible solution to a problem gnawing at her lately. The deeper she went into the equations – modeling the violent convulsions now racking the cosmos – the more one fact became clear.

The math was just too elegant, too beautiful for *all* of Galactic society to have missed the correlations. No matter how hidebound and narrow-minded the majority were, *some* others must surely have come up with similar, revealing shortcuts. Similar ways of seeing past the blinders.

Anyone who did so would have pierced the veil of secrecy, and known far in advance that a spatiotemporal crisis was coming. A time when all hyperspatial paths would undergo upheaval, and confusion would reign.

Mounting evidence convinced Sara that the Buyur must have known. They had planned things so that sooners would be lured into Jijo's system after Galaxy Four was declared fallow and evacuated. They arranged for a nearby transfer point to go dormant, and for Izmunuti to enter flare stage, creating the perfect bottle for whatever specimens came nosing into the trap.

And there are more coincidences, she pondered. *Like why all the squatter groups settled only on the Slope, despite our initially warring natures. Supposedly that was because of the Sacred Scrolls, but I figure there was another force at work.*

The Egg. Silently influencing our ancestors, even two millennia before it burst up through the ground.

Indeed, why stop there? Might the Buyur have chosen *which* races should send sneakships to Jijo, seeding the illicit colony with just the right mix?

Did they manipulate the g'Kek, for instance, driving those happy, prosperous space dwellers into a hopeless vendetta with the Jophur, just so that a small remnant would have to flee, seeking shelter beneath Izmunuti's stark, unblinking eye? Did they then liberate some Jophur from their master rings, creating a shipload of restored traeki who must take shelter on Jijo and befriend the g'Kek?

The problem with thinking about plausible conspiracies was that the mind quickly gorged on every correlation, turning each one into a glaring likelihood ... such as blaming the Buyur for all that had happened to Earth during the last several thousand years. Because the darkness, ignorance, pain, and isolation helped make humans what they were, eventually forcing them to dispatch sneakships toward far corners of space. Sending out lifeboats – such as the *Tabernacle* – in hope of preserving small samplings of humanity against the coming deluge.

Did the Buyur set all that up, just in order to have the right ingredients for their masterpiece on Jijo?

Sara shook her head. If she followed that road – extending her theory far beyond available proof – it would end in paranoia.

'We have learned another thing, by tapping the Transcendent Mesh,' the Niss explained. *'A titanic space battle has been going on for weeks near the outskirts of the Solar System. Even augmented by some recent brave allies, Earth's defenses are now verging on collapse. Soon, fanatics will have the path open before them.*

'When they finally converge on the blue homeworld of your race, Sara, it would be unrealistic to hope for mercy.'

While she probed for answers, the escape attempt was going slowly.

With its outer flanges still mired by the 'magic' coating, *Streaker* was nowhere near as nimble as before. Without Lucky Kaa at the helm, it taxed Akeakemai and the other dolphins to pilot the ship slowly outward, away from the white dwarf star.

All around them spun the worst traffic jam of all time, a high-speed vortex of riotous confusion, peppered with debris from violent explosions. While most of the candidate globes tried to keep on course – doggedly continuing their downward spiral, despite collisions and chaos waves – a small minority were attempting to flee, like *Streaker*. Enough of them to disrupt the ranks, shredding any remaining semblance of order. Getting through such a mael-strom would take more than Ifni's luck. It would take a miracle.

Even if the Earthship made it to open space, there would be the Jophur battleship to contend with. And the old problem of finding a safe place in the universe to hide.

Sara glanced across the Plotting Room at Gillian Baskin. The older woman stood in conference with a sleek, blue-gray figure who floated beyond a glass barrier, in the flooded half of the chamber. It was the dolphin astronomer, Zub'daki, explaining something in a dialect of Anglic that was too high-pitched for Sara to follow. But from the hunch of Gillian's shoulders, it could not be good news. Her face was pale and drawn.

These moments may be our last, Sara thought. *I should spend them with Emerson, not wallowing in theories about ancient crimes, or analyzing cosmic calamities no one can do anything about.*

Alas, Emerson was never around. Despite his handicap, the brain-damaged engineer had commandeered all the technicians that Hannes Suessi could spare. They had given up trying to scrape away *Streaker*'s dangerous, cloying outer layer, and were working instead on the communications laser. Though Emerson's idea was still unclear to most of the crew, Gillian had approved the project, partly in order to give off-duty personnel something to do, keeping their minds occupied.

I wish I had such a refuge ... a way to stay busy, pretending I was making a difference. But the only technology I know anything about is how to make paper, using crude pulping hammers and power from Nelo's little water-driven mill. Beyond that, I'm just a shaman. A spinner of incantations. A practitioner of the quaint Earthling art of calculus.

Prity came alongside carrying several sheets covered with per-spective renderings – representing hyperspatial pathways, tormented and stretched almost to the breaking point. Sensing her mistress's mood, the little chimp assistant put the papers aside and climbed into Sara's lap.

Dear sweet Prity, Sara thought while stroking her. *You are mute, while Earth's chimps have progressed to speak and fly starships. And yet, how I would have loved to show you off! You would surely have amazed them, if we ever made it to Terra.*

Continuing her conversation with Zub'daki, Gillian used quick hand gestures to conjure up holographic images of several other dolphin faces, including Akeakemai and the chief astrogator, Olelo, who listened for a few moments, then protested loudly enough for Sara to overhear snatches of bubbly Trinary-Anglic.

'... we are proceeding as fast as prudently possible, under the circumstancessss. It would be foolhardy and recklessss to just charge ahead through this chaotic traffic jam!'

She could not make out Dr. Baskin's reply, but it had considerable effect on Akeakemai, whose eyes bulged with an almost human look of surprise. Chagrin overcame the perpetual 'smile' that neo-dolphins always seemed to wear.

Sara gently lifted Prity from her lap and put her on the deck. She stood up and began moving toward the conversation, whose intensity grew with each passing dura.

'But-t-t-t—' Akeakemai sputtered. 'What about the *Transcendentsss*? Surely they would never allow such a thing to happ-p-pen!'

Allow *what* to happen, Sara puzzled as she approached. Abruptly, the Niss Machine manifested its holo presence, spinning in midair near Gillian Baskin.

'I have bad news,' it announced. *'The gateways have shut down. They are accepting no more candidates from this ingathering swarm.'*

'I was afraid of this,' Gillian said. 'The subspace disruptions have overcome the gateways' ability to function. Now the arks will have nowhere to go, piling up just above the surface of the dwarf.'

'The pileup is already taking place, as ever larger numbers of candidate vessels finish their transformations and settle into that low, crowded orbit. However—' The hologram twisted and bowed. *'You are wrong about the gateways. They are not dysfunctional. True, they appear to have stopped sending more candidates through to realms beyond. But this is because they now have other tasks in mind.'*

'Show us!' Sara demanded, intruding on Gillian's authority. The older woman nodded, and a multidimensional image sprouted. All objects were represented on a logarithmic scale, allowing events to be seen in vivid, compressed detail.

Down near the white dwarf, giant vessels thronged like a teeming herd of restless beasts, circling ever more tightly around a blazing fire. More streamed in steadily as Sara watched, contributing to a disk that kept spreading and thickening. Each new arrival came seeking passage to the next level. To a fabled place, next to some distant neutron star, where they might transform yet again, and bask in the embrace of mighty tides.

Only the conduits were gone! The needlelike structures had been busily occupied, just moments ago, passing candidates toward their goal. But now the immense devices deserted their stations and could be seen climbing away, abandoning the latecomers to their fate!

The gateways shimmered with inconstant colors that made them seem slippery to the eye, reminding Sara of the *Spectral Flow* – the desert of psi-active stone, back home on Jijo – where even a single glimpse could send a mind reeling.

Rising steadily away from the dwarf star, each needle plunged through the funnel of descending arks, forcing countless many of them to maneuver wildly out of the way, leaving behind swirls of confusion. Whatever order had remained in the mass pilgrimage swiftly vanished. Massive explosions glittered behind each behemoth, like phosphorescent diatoms, churned in some dark sea when a great beast comes rushing through.

'One of those things is headed almost straight for ussss!' the astrogator cried.

Gillian snapped an order. 'Get us out of here, and to *hell* with prudence! Maximum inertial speed!'

Akeakemai responded with an emphatic tail slash. '*Aye!*'

Almost at once, *Streaker*'s engines began groaning with urgency. Sara felt ominous vibrations underfoot, along with a strange tension in her spine as compensating fields struggled to match acceleration.

'You know this is ffffutile, of course,' commented Zub'daki. 'Even if we avoid collisions and the Jophur, we still aren't going to make it-t. *Streaker* would have to be several light-years away in order to escape the coming calamity.'

'What are you talking about?' Sara asked. 'What's coming?'

Before the dolphin astronomer could answer, she stepped back with a gasp.

In the holo display, one of the huge, javelin-shaped gateways could be seen rising rapidly, leaving roiling chaos in its wake, on a course that seemed destined to pass nearby. While trillions died from crashes or fiery detonations, the 'gateway' surged blithely onward and upward.

Only now Sara also observed—

'It's *shooting* at some of the ships!'

Indeed, the needle-artifact was apparently not content with disrupting the migration with its backwash. It also flailed out with beams of force, like cruel, glowing lariats, aiming at specific targets as it climbed.

This was no anomaly. All the other gateways were behaving the same way as they hurried away from the white dwarf.

Sara felt Prity take her right hand. Aghast at the orgy of destruction – vastly more bloody and devastating than what had happened at the Fractal World – she could only stare and wonder.

I wish Emerson were here, so we could watch the end together.

Amid the advancing wave of blinding outbursts and detonations, she had time for one more thought before the shimmering monster lashed one more time, reaching toward *Streaker*, with dazzling rays of light.

Forgive me for thinking it – but God ... it's beautiful ...

ALVIN'S JOURNAL

How can I express the joy I feel? Or the sorrow that simultaneously fills my tense and throbbing spines?

Sometimes life seems just too ironic. The universe may be shaking apart around us, and yet I've been blessed by Ifni's own good fortune, to find love and strange-warm acceptance among my own kind. Meanwhile, poor Pincer – whose idea it was to undertake the adventures that eventually brought us here from our wilderness home – met an untimely death at the very threshold of civilization, because he happened to be in the wrong place at the wrong time.

Scout-Major Harry Harms wanted to put out a police alert for the murderer, but Pilot Kaa begged him not to. A full investigation would blow our cover, revealing the presence of dolphins and sooners at Kazzkark. Above all, *Huck* must be protected, as the only living g'Kek survivor outside of Jijo – though she chafes at being put in such a position. Indeed, Huck is the angriest among us, shouting to avenge Pincer, whatever the cost!

I was forced to agree with Kaa. With law and order starting to crumble, it is doubtful that a 'full investigation' would amount to very much, anyway.

'I'll put out some feelers,' assured Scout-Major Harms. 'And unleash ferret programs to look for any Rothen-like images on the monitors, in case Ro-kenn is careless enough to stroll openly along the avenues. But I'll wager he's gone underground. Rothen are notoriously clever at disguises and that sort of thing.'

'Or else he may have already taken shelter with one of the great clansss,' added Kaa. 'Perhaps he is dickering with them right now, to sell out *Streaker* and Jijo.

Against that possibility, Harry asked Kaa to move our little starship over to the docks of the Navigation Institute, sheltering it behind his own, odd-looking craft.

'You must understand, I'd never do this under normal circumstances,' he explained. 'I took an oath. My first loyalty is to the

Institute, and to the Civilization of Five Galaxies.' Then Harry shrugged expressively. 'But right now it's unclear what that means anymore.'

I confess, it was hard at first to watch him speak without umbling out loud! I know it shouldn't surprise me so much to see a chimpanzee talk with sober eloquence. Especially one who stood so straight and tall, with elegant white fur and an enviably agile tail. Clearly, his race has benefited from several more centuries of genetic Uplift since the *Tabernacle* departed Earth, bringing his mute cousins to Jijo.

'In any event,' Major Harms continued. 'You have a full set of bio identifications on Ro-kenn, contained in that report you're carrying for the Terragens Council. Perhaps they'll put some of their notorious *interstellar agents* on his trail. I'm sure the bastard will get paid in full for what he's done. Don't you worry.'

A bold reassurance. Even Huck seemed a little mollified.

And yet, given what we've heard about the Siege of Terra, how likely is it to come true?

Even before Pincer's death, our glorious fellowship was breaking up.

Last week, Ur-ronn met up with the *p'un m'ang* owners of a freighter – birdlike creatures with bristles instead of wings and no manipulative organs to speak of, except for their beaks. This crew was in a real fix. Their 'hired hand' had left them in order to head home during the crisis. They seemed delighted by the chance to hire an urrish replacement, even when Ur-ronn told them her technical education was somewhat lacking.

Since piloting is mostly automatic along the main trade routes, and robots take care of most ordinary tasks, what the crew really needs is someone with intelligence and tactile agility, to pick up stuff, run errands, and pull levers whenever the machines prove too inflexible. That sounds easy enough for a tireless worker like Ur-ronn, whose nimble hands can wrap around any task. It should be like child's play, after slaving away for Uriel, back at Mount Guenn Forge.

I asked Twaphu-anuph to look over the contract with a hoonish bureaucrat's eye for detail, and he declared it satisfactory. The p'un m'ang will drop Ur-ronn off at their third stop, a port where urrish ships stop frequently, and she can make contact with her own kind. Along the way she'll gain experience while earning some credits to spend.

I hope she doesn't hector her poor employers to death with questions.

'At least the ship is warm and dry,' Ur-ronn said, after visiting her new employers. 'There's none of the Ifni-cursed humidity I had to put up with on the way here! And the p'un m'ang don't smell as bad as Earthlings, either!'

Kaa answered with an amiably derisive spitting sound. The two of them had spent a lot of time together during the journey from Galaxy Four, talking about technology and diverting each other's worries. I doubt I'll ever see a stranger-looking friendship than a water-loving dolphin and a hydrophobic urs, getting along famously.

'I'll keep all three eyes open for an Earthling or Tymbrimi ship to pass this on to,' she continued, patting the pouch under her left arm. Inside lay a copy of Gillian Baskin's report, coded for decipherment by the Terragens Council.

(I have another hidden duplicate. Who knows which of us will get through first. Assuming the cosmos cooperates ... and that Earth survives.)

I felt sad when Ur-ronn set off to depart with the p'un m'ang. Bidding our dear comrade farewell, I wanted to pick her up till all four hooves left the ground, and squeeze her in a full hoonish hug. But I know that our races view such things differently. Urs are not a nostalgic or sentimental people.

Of course Ur-ronn loves Huck and me, in the manner of her kind. Perhaps she will think about us, now and then, with passing fondness.

But her life will soon be busy and focused.

She will not miss us nearly as much as we already miss her.

Such is the world.

As Ur-ronn departed, another companion returned to me.

After miduras of intense questioning, Dwer finally got what he wanted from Mudfoot. At last the little noor *spoke*, confessing the truth of what we had supposed all along – that centuries ago some Tymbrimi planted an illicit colony of their beloved clients on Jijo. Although most noor are born silent and partly devolved, a secret group among them retained fully uplifted mental powers. They are *tytlal*.

Mudfoot agreed to provide Dwer with code words and phrases that will bring the secret ones out of hiding. This was Dwer's price for letting the creature go. Mudfoot's aim now is to make contact somehow with the Tymbrimi and inform them what's happened on Jijo. Since that goal is compatible with my own, the little fellow will accompany me when I journey onward.

Dwer seems satisfied. Indeed, I think his chief aim was to get the best of Mudfoot, just once, before he and Kaa set course on their long voyage back to Jijo.

Before everything comes apart.

The Five Galaxies rock and shudder as the moment of sundering approaches.

With space quakes intensifying, and cracks spreading through the ancient planetoid's walls, it grows apparent that even isolated Kazzkark will be no refuge against the coming convulsions. Already the refugee flow has reversed, as more ships and sapients leave than arrive. With half the normal space lanes already disrupted, many folks are using the remaining stable routes to head home while there's still time.

Among those departing, the most singular looking are acolytes dressed in robes of blue and gold, spreading the gospel of a bizarre faith – one that focuses on salvation for individuals, not races. A creed in which *Earth* plays the central dramatic role, as *martyr planet*.

A sect that proclaims love for Terra, while joyous over its crucifixion.

I have no idea if the same message has been preached in a million other locales, or by just the one Skiano apostle. Either way, the cult seems to have struck a chord that resonates in these troubled times. Fanning across space to spread the word, the missionaries seemed eager to take advantage of the chaos, and the shakiness of more ancient faiths.

At the center of it all, acting as the Skiano's chief aide and major-domo, is *Rety*, the young human female who once seemed such an untamed savage, even on remote Jijo. Transformed by surgery and new garments, she beckons and commands the converts – even sophisticated starfarers – like some haughty lord of an ancient patron clan.

And they take it! Bowing respectfully, even when the parrot on her shoulder squawks irreverently caustic remarks.

I've never seen a human act more confident, or more arrogantly assured of her status.

Meanwhile, the Skiano himself paces slowly, an eerie light flickering in one set of eyes, while the other pair appears to stare at distant horizons.

Naturally, Dwer has failed persuading Rety to leave this fanatical group. She would not even budge when Harry Harms offered a transit pass to his homeworld, a colony located far from the current troubles, where she might possibly find safety and comfort with her own kind.

Harry and Dwer both express frustration. But frankly, I find Rety's adamant resolution understandable. She has learned how pleasant it can be to find a sense of importance and belonging among people who value you.

So have I.

It's nearly time to put down my journal. Dor-hinuf expects me at her parents' dwelling, where members of the local hoon community will gather again for an evening of dinner and poetry. A normal enough occurrence, back home on Jijo, but apparently quite daring and new among my star-god relations.

I must paw through the box of books I brought from Jijo and select tonight's reading. Last time, we had some Melville and Cousteau, but it seems that human authors are a difficult reach for many of these civilized hoons. I expect it will take a while for me to teach them the merits of Jules Verne and Mark Twain.

Mostly, they want me to umble from the odes of Chuphwuph'iwo and Phwhoon-dau, singing melodramatically about taut sails straining against sturdy masts, defying wind and salt spray as a knifelike prow cleaves bravely through some gale-swollen reach. My father would be proud to know that the hoonish literary renaissance of Jijo, so long eclipsed by Earthling authors, is at last finding an eager audience among our distant, starfaring cousins.

It is most gratifying. And yet, I wonder.

How can this be?

Consider the irony! Huck and I always dreamed of how romantic and wonderful it would be to go flitting about in spaceships. But these civilized hoons only see starcraft as conveyances – dull implements for travel between assignments – as they plod through the routine destiny assigned to our kind long ago by our Guthatsa patrons.

So what makes them receptive *now*, to umbles of hope and joy? Is it the growing chaos outside? Or was something lying in wait all along, sleeping underneath a dark shell of oppressive, bureaucratic unhappiness?

Can it really be the simple image of a sailboat that triggers an awakening, a stirring deep inside?

If so, the elation might have lain buried forever. No *civilized* hoon would willingly risk life and limb at sea. The mere thought would be dismissed as absurd. The accounts would not balance. Averse to risk, they would never give it a try.

Besides, what hoon can swim? Nothing in our ancestral tree would logically suggest the way hoonish spines frickle at the sight of wintry icebergs on a storm-serrated horizon, or the musical notes that rope and canvas sing, like a mother umbling to her child.

Only on Jijo was this discovered, once our settler ancestors abandoned their star-god tools, along with all the duties and expectations heaped on us by the Guthatsa.

In fairness, perhaps our patrons meant well. After all, we owe them for our sapient minds. Galactic society sets a stern standard that most elder races follow, when uplifting their clients toward sober, dependable adulthood. The Guthatsa took our strongest racial traits – loyalty, duty, devotion to family – and used them to set us down a single narrow course. Toward prudent, obsessive responsibility.

And yet, only now are Dor-hinuf and her people learning how our patrons cheated us. Robbing our greatest treasure. One that we only recovered by playing hooky ... by ditching class and heading for the river.

To Jijo, where hoons at last reclaimed what had been stolen.

Our childhood.

LARK

The transcendence gateways appeared to have finished their migration, climbing outward from their former position near the surface of a white dwarf star. Now all the huge, needle-shaped devices glistened in much higher orbits, beyond the outer fringes of the candidates' swarm.

The distance traveled was a short one, as space journeys went. But in crossing it, they created murderous bedlam.

Below lay a roiling cauldron of fire and confusion, as millions of vast spacecraft fought desperately for survival. Already disordered by chaos waves, all the prim spiral traffic lanes were now completely unraveled, curling and splitting into myriad turbulent eddies. Engine resonances intersected and interfered, creating mutual-attraction fields, yanking vessels suddenly toward each other. When one giant ark veered to avoid a neighbor, that brought yet another hurtling toward explosive impact.

Eruptions seemed to coruscate up and down the densely packed funnel, converting what had formerly been sentient matter into white plasma flame.

As if intending to make matters worse, each of the titanic needles also *lashed out* during its brief voyage, using beams of fierce brightness to seize several dozen spacecraft, chosen apparently at random, dragging them like calves at the end of a lariat.

Among the unchosen, those who brushed accidentally against the tendrils were instantly vaporized.

Why? Lark asked, appalled by the sight. *Why did they do it?*

He was counting on Ling for an explanation, since she had once been a starfarer and had spent more time exploring the Transcendents' Data Mesh. But on this occasion she was equally astonished and aghast.

I ... cannot begin to guess ... Unless they already had their quota of candidates, and decided that any more would be superfluous ... Or else maybe the chaos waves are getting too strong, and they had to give up trying to send more nominees through to the next level.

He shook his head, dislodging one of the symbionts that had taken residence there recently, devouring his last hair follicles.

But that doesn't explain the callous disregard for life! Those are sapient beings down there! Quadrillions of them! Every one was a member of some ancient race that had studied and improved itself diligently for ages just to get here ...

Ling took his arm and stroked it, pressing herself against him for the warm comfort it provided them both.

Even so, Lark, they were still like animals, compared to the Transcendents. Expendable. Especially if their destruction might serve a higher purpose.

He blinked several times.

Higher purpose? What purpose could possibly justify—

He cut off as a new presence began making itself known, groping toward them across the mental byways of the mesh. Soon, Lark recognized a familiar presence – one that had formerly been his teacher ... then an enemy ... and was now simply a friend.

'X,' the modified traeki, had been doing some independent exploration, and now wanted to report its findings.

The Jophur have despaired of ever returning to their clan, or accomplishing their mission. Moreover, they realize they have very little time. Soon, the macroentity that we now are part of – what you call 'Mother' – will complete its conquest of the Polkjhy *by breaking into the engineering section, where the former crew have made their last redoubt. When that happens, they will cease to be Jophur – at least by their own narrow definition.*

Before that happens, they have decided to embark on a dramatic and conclusive course of action. A final act of vengeance.

Lark cast his mind outward, visualizing the once mighty battleship and its surroundings. Whether by luck or by dauntless piloting skill, *Polkjhy* had apparently succeeded in escaping the candidates' swarm. Only tattered outskirts of the whirling disk lay between them and deep space – a starry night sky that *rippled*, every now and then, with shivering waves of chaos. The prospect of flight beckoned, now that a getaway path seemed clear. But *Polkjhy*'s remaining crew members knew it could never be. Mother would absorb them into the new hybrid existence, long before they reached the first transfer point. Assuming the t-point was still usable.

Engine noises rumbled through the liquid environment, carrying notes of deep resolve. Lark sensed *Polkjhy*'s trajectory – and realized it was aimed almost straight toward one of the gleaming needle-gateways!

Throughout all this struggle and confusion, the Jophur have kept tenaciously – even single-mindedly – to their original purpose. They never lost track of the Earthling ship.

It lies dead ahead, ensnared by the Transcendents in a webbery of light.

Casting his viewpoint outward, Lark verified that each great needle was now surrounded by clusters of captive starcraft, wrapping them in layer after layer of lambent windings. No reason or purpose for this strange activity could be learned by sifting the mesh, but soon Lark noticed that a faint resonance seemed to echo from one of the confined vessels.

Something familiar.

Ling joined his efforts and together they focused closer, until something *clicked* and the circuits abruptly filled with jagged sonic patterns.

A *human voice*, somber but grimly determined.

'... we repeat. This is not a destiny of our choosing. We are not legitimate members of the candidate swarm. Nor are we part of the retired life order. We have no business in the Embrace of Tides, nor do we wish to experience any form of transcendence at this time.

'Duty calls us back to Galaxy Two. Please let us go! We humbly request that you let us flee this doomed place, while there is still time.

'Again, we repeat. This is not a destiny of our choosing ...'

Lark felt the traeki's mental touch, sharing thoughts that seemed to slither, like smooth rivulets of dripping wax.

How interesting. Apparently the Terrans have been selected to perform some honored task. Some chore or service deemed worthwhile by the highest overminds. Yet, they petition to escape this distinction, resuming their forlorn plight in a world of danger and sorrows!

Meanwhile, the remaining Jophur send Polkjhy *charging ahead with but one thought in mind – to deny the Earthlings any taste of a transcendence they have not earned!*

A confrontation looms. One that should prove interesting to observe.

Lark appreciated the traeki's sense of detachment, even though the most likely outcome was for *Polkjhy* to be swatted aside – vaporized – like some irritating gnat, by powers unimaginably more powerful.

He considered ways to avoid this undesired end.

I wonder if it might be possible for us to communicate with Streaker, *via the mesh.*

Ling nodded.

I don't see why not. If only for a few moments.

Their traeki friend also agreed.

I/we have our/my own reasons to wish this. Let us work together, and strive to achieve that connection.

HARRY

When one of the big south pole galleries suddenly collapsed – blowing several thousand gasping tenants into deadly vacuum – the high officials in dominion over Kazzkark finally gave in to the inevitable. They issued the long-awaited directive.

Evacuate!

'My research – sifting through the oldest, most ambiguity-protected archives in the Great Library – indicates that conditions were probably similar during the Gronin Collapse,' Wer'Q'quinn explained when Harry reported for his last assignment.

From a high balcony at Navigation Institute HQ, they watched as crowds thronged down the main arcades toward various egress ports, streaming to reclaim the starships that had brought them here. Meanwhile, Wer'Q'quinn waved a languid pseudopod and continued contemplating the past.

'Then, as now, the Institutes went into denial at first. Later, under instructions from higher life orders, they concealed the truth from most of our civilization until it was too late for any concerted preparation. Indeed, an identical scenario would have repeated this time, if not for the recent warning that was broadcast from Earth. Without it, most of the races in the Five Galaxies would have had scarcely any chance to get ready.'

'A lot of clans chose to ignore the warning,' Harry groused. 'Some are too busy *attacking* Earth to listen.'

After a gloomy silence, he went on.

'I don't suppose there's any chance that all these spatial distur-bances will affect the Siege of Terra, is there?'

Wer'Q'quinn swiveled a squidlike gaze toward the chimpanzee scout, as if scrutinizing him for any sign of wavering loyalty.

'That seems unlikely. We estimate that up to thirty percent of the t-points in Galaxy Two will remain at least partly functional. Of course, during the worst part of the crisis, metric backlash will con-vulse every level of hyperspace. Woe unto any vessel that tries to undergo pseudoacceleration while *that* is going on! But this should scarcely inconvenience the great battleships presently surrounding your ancestral solar system. They will be safe, so long as they remain in normal space, and refrain from using probability weapons until the rupture is over.

'Naturally, we expect the effects will be far more severe in Galaxy Four.'

Harry nodded. 'Which is exactly where you're sending me.'

'Would you withdraw? I can send another.'

'Oh, yeah? *Who* else are you gonna find who's willing to enter E Space at a time like this?'

Wer'Q'quinn's answer was eloquent silence. Of his remaining staff, only Harry had the experience – and talents – to hold any hope of success in that bizarre realm of living ideas.

'Well,' Harry grunted. 'Why the hell not, eh? You say I should have time enough to lay down new instrument packages along the Path, from here to Galaxy Four, and still make it back before the crisis hits?'

'It will be close,' Wer'Q'quinn averred. 'But we have supple-mented our traditional calculations with new estimates, utilizing wolfling techniques of mathematical incantation that were con-tained in the message from Earth. Both methods appear to agree. The main rupture should not take place till after you safely return.'

Another long silence stretched.

'Of course I would've gone anyway,' Harry said at last, in a gruff voice.

A low sigh. A nervous curling of tentacles.

'I know you would.'

'For the Five Galaxies,' Harry added.

'Yes.' Wer'Q'quinn's voice faltered. 'For the Civilization of . . . Five Galaxies.'

Down on the boulevards of Kazzkark, the worst of the exodus appeared to be over. While gleaners sifted through dross and wreck-age from so many hurried departures, Harry strode along with a floating donkey-drone, bearing capsules to deposit in E Space for

Wer'Q'quinn. Telemetry from these packages might reveal more about the strains now pulling apart the connective tissue of space. Perhaps next time – in a hundred million years or so – people might understand things a little better.

And there *would* be a next time. As the universe expanded, ever more of the ancient 'flaws' that linked galaxy to galaxy would stretch, then break. After each sundering transition, the number of surviving t-points would be smaller, their connections less rich, and the speedy lanes of hyperspace become that much more inaccessible.

As it ages, the cosmos is becoming a less interesting, more dangerous place. Everything must have seemed so close and easy in the Progenitors' day, he thought. *A time of magic, when it was almost trivial to conjure a path between any two points in seventeen linked galaxies.*

He squared his shoulders back.

Oh, well. At least I get to take part in something important. Even if Wer'Q'quinn is exaggerating my chances of getting home again.

Kazzkark had seemed so immaculate when he first arrived here from training school. Now a dusty haze seemed to pervade the corridors, shaken from the walls by quakes and chaos waves, which rattled this entire sector at ever narrower intervals. They had grown so frequent, in fact, that he hardly noticed most of them anymore.

It just goes to show, even the abnormal can get to seem normal, after a while.

Approaching the dockyards, he witnessed a large party of hoonish clerks and their families, carrying luggage and tugging hover-carts, preparing to board a transport for one of their homeworlds. The queue was orderly, as you would expect from a hoonish procession. Yet, something appeared different about this group. They seemed less dour, more animated, than others of their kind.

It's their clothes! Harry realized, all at once. *Alvin's got them wearing Hawaiian shirts!*

Indeed, roughly a third of the hulking bipeds had set aside the more typical robes of boring white or silver, and draped themselves instead with tunics bearing garish prints of flowers and tropical ferns – split down the back to leave room for their craggy spines. Umbling as they waited patiently in line, the group made every nearby corridor reverberate with tones that seemed far livelier than the dirgelike chants usually heard from hoons.

One GalSix trill-phrase, in particular, caused Harry to stumble.

If I didn't know better, I'd swear that translates into Anglic as 'heigh ho!'

Some of the older hoons looked on all this with perplexed – even miffed – expressions. But toward the front there stood a crowd of youths – *teenagers*, he noted – who boomed out the refrain with enthusiastic bellows of their bulging throat sacs.

A cheerful ballad about transition, and eagerness for new vistas.

Over in a corner, shuffling behind the hoons, stood a strange figure, looking like a short, shabby Jophur. It was *Tyug*, the traeki alchemist from Jijo, accompanying Alvin on the next phase of his adventure.

Harry tried to catch Alvin's eye as he walked past, but the lad was fully immersed, enjoying his role as the out-of-town boy who had come to stir things up. With Dor-hinuf close to his side, and a pair of tytlal lounging on his broad shoulders, Alvin leaned against a loosely wrapped shipping crate, feigning nonchalance while keeping a close vigil over its contents.

One edge of the tarpaulin shifted as Harry watched. From the darkness within, a single *eye* drifted upward at the end of a waving stalk. Another tried to follow, squeezing through to twist and stare at the surroundings.

Without pausing in the umble song, Alvin silently used one burly hand to grab both wayward eyes and cram them back inside. Then he tied the tarp down firmly. The crate shuddered, as if someone inside were rolling back and forth in protest. But Alvin only leaned harder until things settled down.

'Ahoy!' shouted a hoon at the front of the queue, when the portal opened at last, leading to their ship. 'Avast back there. Here we go!'

Harry tried holding it in. He struggled hard, and managed to make it fifty meters farther along before his splitting sides could take it no longer. Then he ducked around a stony corner, sagged against the nearest wall, and guffawed.

The Official Docks were nearly deserted. Dignitaries of the Library, Migration, Commerce, and War Institutes had already scurried off, leaving empty moorings. Only Wer'Q'quinn's busy teams remained on duty, rushing forth on rescue missions, or using beacons to guide traffic around danger zones. Noble work. Harry's own days might be better spent that way, helping save lives and patching the raveled skeins of Galactic society. After the main rupture event, NavInst must promote recovery by getting trade going again.

But Wer'Q'quinn saved me for this mission. I guess the old octopus knows what he's doing.

Ahead lay Harry's venerable observation platform, designed for cruising the memic jungles of E Space. Although this mission was bound to be the most dangerous yet, Harry found his footsteps speeding up, drawn by strange eagerness.

Humming under his breath, he recognized the same melody Alvin's new in-laws had been umbling as they prepared to depart.

It seemed a catchy tune.

Good for traveling.

A song of anticipation.

More chaos waves struck the planetoid while he was busy loading Wer'Q'quinn's instruments into the hold. Ancient stone walls groaned with resonant vibrations, causing the ship's decks and bulkhead to vibrate violently. Harry had to scoot out of the way when an unsecured crate toppled from an upper shelf. Thanks to Kazzkark's slight pseudogravity, he managed to avoid getting crushed, but the box smashed hard, spilling delicate parts across the floor.

While sweeping up, he listened for the wailing siren to announce a vacuum breach. Only after several duras passed did his fur settle down. Apparently, the dock seals were holding – for now.

Harry stepped outside to visit the stocky little Thennanin-built star cruiser that lay parked behind his station. Stepping through its airlock, he shouted for the pilot.

'Kaa! You ready to ship out? I'll be outta here in less than a midura, if you're still thinking of tagging along.'

The sleek gray dolphin emerged from his control cubicle, riding atop a six-legged machine. Kaa was starting to look weary. It had been weeks since he'd had a swim. Aside from rest periods in a narrow water tank, he'd spent most of that time lying on the float bed of a walker-drone.

'It'sss not soon enough for me,' the pilot hissed. 'Alasssss, I'm stuck waiting here till Dwer returns.'

Harry glanced around.

'Aw hell,' he grunted. '*Now* where's Dwer gone off to?'

Another voice spoke up from a rear doorway, uttering Anglic words with unctuous, almost seductive tones.

'Well, well. I would surmise that the young human is trying – yes, one more time! – to persuade his female counterpart – Rety – to come along. Would you not guess it so?'

Kiwei Ha'aoulin emerged from one of the tiny cabins, working past a pile of supplies tied down by cargo netting. The Synthian had pressed to accompany Kaa, despite warnings that it would surely be a one-way trip. In fact, each admonition just heightened her resolve. Kiwei even offered to finance all the food and other items needed for Kaa's voyage.

She did not believe that a so-called 'great rupture' was imminent. '*These disturbances will pass,*' she had blithely assured. '*I am not saying everything will go back to normal. While the Institutes and great clans spend centuries sorting things out, they will be lax about enforcing minor rules against little sooner colonies – or against smuggling! Can't you scent business opportunities in this? I shall serve as Jijo's commercial agent, yes! In utter secrecy and confidence, as off-planet liaison for the Six-or-Seven Races, I will market primitive autochthonous implements on the collectors' market, and make us all quite rich!'*

Harry had watched greed battle typical Synthian caution. Eventually, Kiwei resolved the conflict by entering a state of pure denial, blithely rejecting any notion that upheavals might change the cosmos in fundamental ways. Harry felt guilty about giving in to her request. But a Synthian trader could be obstinately tenacious, wearing down all opposition. Besides, Kaa needed the supplies.

Kiwei stepped over the crude caricature that Pincer-Tip had carved in the metal deck – a chilling image of the qheuen's murderer, who had probably departed Kazzkark by now, plotting more mischief.

'Indeed, Dwer went after Rety. I was monitoring comm channels, moments ago, when an urgent message came through from the boy.'

Kaa thrashed his tail. 'You didn't t-tell me!'

'Pilot, you seemed well occupied with pre-takeoff checklists and such. Besides, I had it in mind to go now and help the young human, myself! Generous, yes? Would you care to come along, Scout-Major Harms?'

Harry squirmed. His launch window would be optimum in a midura. Still, if the boy was in trouble . . .

'Did Dwer say what's the matter?'

The Synthian rubbed her belly – a nervous gesture.

'The message was unclear. Apparently, he feels urgent action is needed, or the girl will not survive.'

They tracked the young Jijoan to a nearby warehouse chamber, crouching behind a pile of abandoned crates. Wearing a dark cloak and a frustrated expression, he gazed at a gathering of sapients, about forty meters away.

Empty cargo containers had been festooned with blue and gold draperies, a convivial backdrop for the big Skiano missionary, who stood surrounded by about two dozen acolytes from as many races. The Skiano's head jutted above most followers, resembling a massive ship's prow. One pair of eyes gleamed ceaselessly, as if lighting the way into a warm night.

Most of the proselytes had already dispersed to far reaches of civilized space, spreading their exceptional message of personal salvation, but this remnant group remained by their leader, chanting hymns that chilled Harry's spine.

'What's up?' he asked Dwer, stepping past him. Harry quickly spotted Rety, a small human figure, sitting apart from the others, her face lit by the glow of a portable computer.

'Watch out!' Dwer snapped, seizing Harry's collar and yanking him back hard.

'Hey!' Harry complained – till several small projectiles pelted a nearby crate, sending splinters flying.

He blinked. 'Someone's shooting at us!'

Dwer hazarded a glimpse back around the corner, then motioned it was okay for Harry and Kiwei to rejoin him. He pointed toward a pair of blue-clad acolytes – a *gello* and a *paha* – standing protectively near the dais, glaring with expressions of clear warning. Both races had been uplifted to be warriors, with innate talents for violent conflict. Though now dedicated to a religion of peace, these individuals had been assigned a task worthy of their gifts. While the gello brandished a metal-tipped staff, the paha sported a simple device on one arm – a wrist catapult, like the one Dwer was seen wearing earlier.

'Interesting,' Kiwei said. 'Disallowed more sophisticated weaponry, they swiftly caught on to the advantages of wolfling arts. No doubt Rety taught them. Perhaps their new faith disposes them to be more open-minded than most.

Harry shrugged aside Kiwei's foolish commentary.

'They don't want us comin' any closer. Why?' he asked Dwer.

'I was warned not to bother Rety anymore. They said I was *distracting* her. They can't bring themselves to kill a sacred Earthling. But since "it is the Terran destiny to suffer for us all," they won't mind shattering a bone or two. I'd be careful, if I were you.'

Harry's frustration flared.

'Look, Dwer, we don't have much time. Rety's decided to stay with folks who'll love an' take care of her. That's a lot more than most folks have in this universe, and better odds than she'd have coming with us! It's time to let her make her own choices.'

Dwer nodded. 'Normally, I'd agree. Rety's been a pain. I'd like nothing better than to see her make it on her own. There's just one problem. Things may not be quite the way you just described 'em.'

Harry's eyebrows arched.

'Oh? How's that?'

In reply, Dwer pointed.

'Look to the right, beyond the platform. See something there? Beyond that curtain?'

Blowing another sigh, Harry peered toward a flowing veil of colorful fabric between two massive pillars, just past the Skiano's meditating followers. 'What're you talkin' about? I don't get ...'

He paused. Something *moved* back there. At first, the outlines reminded him of an angular machine, with sharp edges for cutting, slicing. Then an errant gust blew the drapes harder against the object, revealing a stark, mantislike outline.

'Ifni's boss ...' Harry murmured. 'What's a Tandu lurking back there for?'

Of one thing he felt sure – no Tandu would ever join the Skiano's heresy! Immortality of some abstract 'soul' could not appeal like a chance to crush enemies, or impose their racial will on a recalcitrant cosmos. Till now, constraints of ritual and law kept such impulses in check – Tandu seldom killed openly without a veneer of Galactic legality. But what if civilization collapsed? There were rumors of secret bases, filled with countless warrior eggs, ready to hatch at a moment's notice.

'Why are the paha and gello just standing there?' he wondered aloud. 'They must not realize—'

Kiwei interrupted.

'They do realize. Note how they keep their backs toward the curtain, as if to ignore what's beyond. Clearly, they have orders. The Tandu is here for some approved purpose!'

Purpose? Harry tugged nervously on his thumbs ... till he had an idea.

'Kiwei, hand me your data plaque. I want to try something.'

The Synthian complied, and Harry started mumbling commands into the handheld unit. Using his authority, he ordered ferret programs to search for transmissions emanating from Rety's computer. With luck, he would soon—

'Got it!' he announced, while his companions crowded close. On a split screen, the left side abruptly revealed the young Jijoan woman, her visage smoothed by recent surgery. On the right, they saw copies of the charts that had her attention transfixed.

'What now?' Dwer asked. 'Use this link to speak to her? I guarantee she'll just get angry and cut us off.'

Harry shrugged. 'I was hopin' to spy a little first.' He studied the image on the right. 'It looks like a list of planets where their cult recently sent missionaries. Most are trading worlds, with good spatial contacts and cosmopolitan cultures that don't oppress odd points of view. These folks are clever. But I don't see what this has to do with—'

He cut off as an expression of smug pleasure crossed Rety's face. She spoke with clear satisfaction.

'This one's perfect!'

The picture jiggled as she stood, slinging the computer under one arm. Harry caught blurry glimpses of blue draperies, and the faces of squatting acolytes, staring at some far horizon. The scene steadied when Rety came to a halt and spoke loudly, to be heard above the murmuring chant.

'Master, I've chosen my own place. See? I have it listed right here!'

The camera view swung around to face upward, briefly catching the image of a colorful Earthling parrot, pacing on a massive shoulder. Then Rety corrected her aim, facing the screen straight at the Skiano's imposing head. Beyond the ramlike chin, its upper brace of eyes shone like headlamps, aimed at posterity, while the lower pair roved in search of final truth.

Rety continued. *'It's Z'ornup! I'm sure you've heard of the place. It has just the right atmosphere and all that stuff, so's I can stay healthy. There's also a human trading post, in case I ever need others of my kind – which ain't likely, but I guess it's better not to close off all my options, right?*

'Anyway, you already sent a small mission there, but I see the planet sits in a good spot, with lots of space trails leading in all directions, where we can send any new converts we recruit. With all that going for it, I figure Z'ornup needs a higher-level apostle, right? That's someone like me! I'll use the last commercial shuttle headin' for Galaxy Three. It leaves in half a midura, so with your permission—'

The Skiano's unwavering stare dimmed at last. The bottom set of eyes turned down to regard Rety.

'Such a posting is beneath you, my dear wolfling child. I will not have you sullied by mundane chores, proselytizing and breathing the same air as unbelievers.'

'But I—'

'There is a reward that awaits the worthy,' the missionary continued, intoning with a remote, pontifical voice. *'It was alluded to by your own saints and prophets, long ago. By Jesus and Isaiah and Mohammed and Buddha ... in fact, by all the great sages of your blessed-cursed race, whose suffering in darkness allowed them to see what remained hidden to all those living in the light.'*

'I know that, Master. So let me go forth and spread the word to —'

'Of course those prophets made errors in recording what they saw. How could they accurately chronicle such glory with crude ink and paper, using languages that were little more than animallike grunts? Nevertheless, destiny has spoken. The beacon they lit will ignite other pyres, spreading the heat of truth everywhere, even as ruins topple around us.'

'I agree! So now let me—'

'But alas, I will not see that promised land, that apotheosis. Like Moses, I must halt before entering a mere temporal Valhalla. My labors have exhausted this poor flesh. It is time to seek the recompense that I was offered in a dream. To bypass the routine of Purgatory, and proceed directly to Paradise!'

Rety's response was quick and restless.

'That's great. Happy travelin'. Now about Z'ornup —'

'My reward beckons,' the Skiano went on, ponderously. 'A personal salvation much finer than the Embrace of Tides. And yet . . . I cannot shake an uneasy premonition. Have I done everything required? What if I arrive only to learn the heavenly gatekeepers do not recognize my strange face and body? After all this time devoted only to Earthlings, are they quite ready to receive nonhuman souls in Heaven?'

The prow-shaped head rocked from left to right.

'It occurs to me that the gatekeepers will be more accommodating if I arrive escorted, with an entourage of those who will testify on my behalf . . .'

The image on the screen wavered, as if the hands holding it suddenly trembled from realization, even as the rhythmic chanting reached its final climax and faded into echoes. Rety's voice came hoarse and nervous.

'This "trip" you've been talkin' about . . . it's not to another preaching mission, is it? You're plannin' to die!'

The answer made Harry shiver.

'To abandon this shell, yes. Accompanied by converts, to demonstrate my worthiness . . . plus a human, a true wolfling from the martyr world, to vouch for me in front of all the angels and saints.'

Harry's shoulder was jogged, so hard that he nearly fell over. Dwer clutched his arm, squeezing with great force. He pointed.

'The curtain . . .'

Kiwei uttered a low moan as the shrouding drapes fell, revealing a regal Tandu warrior, painted and accoutred for ritual slaughter, advancing toward the acolytes with six arms upraised, brandishing glinting blades.

Instead of leaping to defense, both of the soldier-disciples – the gello and paha – joined their fellow converts in a crescent-shaped formation, waiting quietly with their leader centered before them.

Rety, now struggling in the Skiano's adamant embrace, abruptly stiffened and let out a soft cry, staring upward in aghast awe while the parrot squawked, flapping overhead.

'Summon police drones!' Kiwei urged. 'This ceremony is not entirely voluntary. I will attest to it!'

As if that'd do any good, Harry mused as he ran forward,

following Dwer's more rapid footsteps. *The law is crumbling. Anyway, help would never get here in time.*

In which case, a mighty good question would be exactly what he and Dwer hoped to accomplish by rushing toward the debacle, except to join the Tandu's ceremonial mincing session!

The Jijoan youth slid to a halt just twenty meters from the assembled devotees. Flinging his cloak aside, Dwer lifted the compound bow he had brought from his faraway home, with an arrow nocked and ready.

'Those are mine!' the Synthian shrieked from far behind, more offended by theft than ritual murder-suicide. 'You stole them from my compartment. I demand they be returned at once, or I shall file a complaint!'

In the time it took Kiwei to babble that absurd threat, the Tandu finished approaching its scheduled victims, lifting several blades high – and Dwer loosed three arrows in rapid succession.

Harry reached out for the young hunter.

'You can't harm a Tandu that way! It has no single weak spot to disable—'

He stopped as the little missiles seemed to veer off course. Instead of hitting the executioner, they missed by a wide margin and struck the Skiano instead! Two dark eyes were extinguished by plunging bolts of wood and stone. A third arrow vanished down the missionary's throat, when he opened it to scream.

The Skiano's white arms convulsed. For an instant, only one of the four clutched Rety – and she chomped down on the remaining hand with her teeth. Slipping free of his spasmodic grasp, she ducked down to avoid being seized by the paha, then swerved in an unexpected direction, *under and between the Tandu's spiky legs!*

Harry waved his arms.

'Over here! Run!'

A terrifying noise escaped the Tandu. Hired under certain conditions, it had come armed only with weapons appropriate for a formally pious sacrifice. Resistance was not part of the bargain. This amounted to breach of contract!

Its bellow resonated down the hallways of Kazzkark, calling for comrades to come avenge this insult. Meanwhile, one blade flicked to remove the paha's head.

The husky gello warrior reacted impulsively by swinging its metal-edged staff, crushing one of the Tandu's forelegs, then another, before its own turn came for skewering upon a scalpellike edge. Meanwhile, two more acolytes – a flying *glououvis* and claw-footed *zyu8* – also lost sight of the purpose of the gathering. Responding to ancient loathings, they launched themselves at the

Tandu, to peck at it from above and below while dodging its flailing knives.

Amid this pandemonium, Dwer kept firing arrows, taking out the giant mantislike creature's sensory stalks, one at a time.

Harry thought of telling Dwer to save his ammo. That tactic seldom worked against Tandu. But then Rety finally broke free of the melee and bolted toward the edge of the raised platform. Sensing freedom just ahead, she took two long steps, making ready to leap.

Harry's throat caught as he saw the Tandu reach after her. The razor-sharp sword already dripped with multicolored gore.

A new swarm of chaos waves struck. The floor convulsed, bucking like a wounded animal. Dust clouds poured from shuddering walls and gay banners billowed before a rising wind. In the distance, a siren wailed.

Harry staggered, watching helplessly as Rety teetered at the rim of the heaving platform, then sprawled over the edge amid a flailing of frantic arms and legs.

He tried rushing forward to catch her – knowing he would be too late.

Till the moment her head struck pavement, Rety was defiant. She neither cried out nor moaned, refusing to give the universe any satisfaction – least of all by whimpering about bad luck.

GILLIAN

Lucifer means 'light bearer.'

The thought came unbeckoned, while shimmering luminance poured in through a nearby window, playing across her face.

Angels are bright ... though not always good.

The sight before her reminded Gillian how many beautiful and terrifying sights she had witnessed during recent months and years. And how many deep assumptions she'd been forced to revise.

For instance, she recalled that time, deep within a twisty transfer point, when the Earthling crew had confronted the *Great Harrower* as it sifted among countless starcraft, choosing a fraction to aim toward transcendence. That huge glowing specter had reminded Gillian of some mighty seraph, culling the virtuous from the wicked on Judgment Day. No one was more surprised than she when the blinding ball of energy seemed to identify *Streaker* amid a crowd of passing vessels, plucking the Earthship and setting it aside for some purpose the Harrower never bothered to explain.

Perhaps now we'll find out, she thought. Indeed, there appeared to be a definite family resemblance between that earlier 'angel' and the giant needle-gateway now holding *Streaker* in thrall, spinning out radiant tendrils that snaked amorously around several dozen selected spacecraft. The behavior reminded Gillian unpleasantly of a spider, busy wrapping living morsels, preserving them for later.

All the other ensnared ships parked nearby were vast arks filled with merged hydro- and oxy-life-forms – true transcendence candidates – yanked from the maelstrom surrounding the white dwarf. *Streaker* was minuscule by comparison – a tiny caterpillar next to beach balls. Yet, she now wore her own blanket of shiny, billowing strands.

'The material is unknown,' commented Hannes Suessi. 'I cannot even get a decent reading with my instruments.'

The Niss Machine hazarded a guess.

'Someone may have had this in mind for us all along. Even back at the Fractal World. The coating we received there could be meant to serve as a buffer – or perhaps glue – between our fragile metal hull and this new substance ... whatever it is.'

Gillian shook her head.

'Perhaps it's another kind of protective armor.'

Silence stretched for several seconds as they all turned to look at the rearward-facing view screen. Everyone clearly shared the same dour thought.

Something was about to happen soon. Something that called for 'protection' on a scale formerly unimaginable.

At least the earlier orgy of destruction appeared to be over, down below where millions of space vessels once cruised in prim columns and well-ordered rows, like polite pilgrims seeking redemption at a shrine. That procession had been smashed, crushed, puréed. Now, only an occasional flash told of some surviving 'candidate' finally succumbing to forces that had already pulverized millions of others, leaving a turbid stew of gas, dust, and ions.

A roiling funnel now surrounded the ancient stellar remnant, shrouding its small, white disk beneath black streamers and turbulent haze.

According to Zub'daki, that whirling cloud had special dynamical properties. It would not orbit for long, or even spiral inward gradually, over the course of weeks or years.

'The debris storm has almost no net angular momentum,' the dolphin astronomer announced. *'As collisional mixing continues, all the varied tangential velocities will cancel out. When that happens, the whole mass will collapse inward, nearly all at once!'*

Asked when this infall might occur, the dolphin scientist had predicted.

'Sssoon. And when it does, we'll be at ground zero for the greatest show in all the cosmossss.'

Staring at that murky tornado – comprising the pulverized hopes of countless races and individual beings – Gillian's crew mates knew the show would begin shortly. Akeakemai whistled a dubious sigh, getting back to Gillian's original question.

'Protective armor ... againsssst what's coming?'

The dolphin switched languages to express his doubts in Trinary.

* When the great gods,
  * In their puissance,
* Start believing,
  * Their own slogans—

* Or their wisdom,
  * Omniscient,
* Or their power,
  * Invincible—

* That's when nature,
  * Wise and patient,
* Teaches deities,
  * A lesson—

* That's when nature,
  * Keen and knowing,
* Shows each god its
  * Limitations—

* Great Dreamers must
  * Ride Tsunami!

* For Transcendents?
  * Supernova! *

Gillian nodded appreciatively. It was very good dolphin imagery.

'Creideiki would be proud,' she said.

Akeakemai slashed with his tail flukes, reticent to accept praise.

* Irony makes for easy poetry. *

Sara Koolhan commented.

'Forgive my ignorance of stellar physics, but I've been studying, so let me see if I get this right.

'When that big, whirling cloud of dross and corpses finally collapses, it's going to dump a tenth of a solar mass onto the hot, dense surface of that white dwarf. A dwarf that's already near its Chandrasekhar limit. Much of the new material will compress to incredible density and undergo superfast nuclear fusion, triggering—'

'*What Earthlings used to call a "type one" supernova,*' the Niss Machine cut in, unable to resist an inbuilt yen to interrupt.

'*Normally, this happens when a large amount of matter is tugged off a giant star, falling rapidly onto a neighboring white dwarf. In this case, however, the sudden catalyzing agent will be the flesh of once living beings! Their body substance will help light a pyre that should briefly outshine this entire galaxy, and be visible to the boundaries of the universe.*'

Gillian thought she detected hints of hysteria in the voice of the Tymbrimi-built machine. Though originally programmed to seek surprise and novelty, the Niss might well have passed the limit of what it could stand.

'I agree, there doesn't seem much chance of surviving such an event, no matter how fancy a coating we are given. And yet, the coincidence seems too perfect to ignore.'

'Coincidence?' Suessi asked.

'The cancellation of angular momentum is too perfect. The Transcendents must have meant this to happen. They slaughtered the remaining candidates for a purpose – *in order* to trigger the coming explosion.'

'So, yes? Then the big question is – why aren't *we* down there now, mixing our atoms with all those other poor bugs, beasties, and blighters?'

Gillian shrugged.

'I just don't know, Hannes. Obviously, we have a role to play. But what role? Who can say?'

Zub'daki didn't expect mass collapse to occur for twenty hours, at least. Possibly several days.

'The infall may be disssrupted by outward radiation pressure, as the star heats up,' the dolphin explained. 'It could make the whole process of ignition messsssy. Unless they have a solution to that problem, as well.'

He didn't have to explain who 'they' were. The shimmering needle-gateway throbbed nearby, as long as Earth's moon, spinning webs of mysterious, translucent material near several dozen captive ships.

Assured that the crisis would not come for a while yet, Gillian headed to her quarters for some rest. Upon entering, she glanced across the dimly lit chamber at an ancient cadaver, grinning away in a glass cabinet.

'It seems our torment won't go on much longer, Herb. The end is coming at last, in a way that should erase all our troubles.'

The gaunt corpse said nothing, of course. She sighed.

'Ah well. Tom had a favorite expression. If you've really got to go, you might as well—'

Baritone words joined hers.

'*You might as well go out with a bang.*'

Gillian swiveled around, crouching slightly, her chest pounding from surprise. Something – or someone – stood in the shadows. The figure was tall, bipedal, with the shoulders and stance of a well-built human male.

'Who ... who's there?' she demanded.

The answering voice came eerily familiar.

'*No one you should fear, Dr. Baskin. Let me move into the light.*'

As he did so, Gillian's heart sped instead of slowing down. She stepped back with her right hand pressed midway between throat and sternum. Her voice cracked on the chisellike wedge separating hope from dread.

'T-Tom ... ?'

His ready smile was there. An eager grin, always a bit like a little boy's. The stance, relaxed and yet ready for anything. Those well-known hands, so capable at a thousand tasks.

The head – black haired with a gray fringe – tilted quizzically, as if just a little disappointed by her response.

'*Gill, are you so credulous, to believe what you see?*'

Gillian struggled to clamp down her emotions, especially the wave of desperate loneliness that flooded as brief hope crashed. If it really were Tom, she would already know in several ways, even without visual sight. And yet, the careworn face seemed so real – fatigued by struggles that made her own trials pale by comparison. Part of her yearned to reach out and hold him. To soothe those worries for a little while.

Even knowing this was just a lie.

'I'm ... not that naive. I guess it's pretty clear who you really are. Tell me ... did you take Tom's image from my mind? Or else—'

She swiveled to glance at her desk, where a holo of her husband glowed softly, next to a picture of Creideiki, along with others she had known and loved on Earth.

'*A bit of each,*' came the answer while Gillian was briefly turned away. *'Along with many other inputs. It seemed a useful approach, combining familiarity with tension and regret. A bit cruel, perhaps. But conducive of concentration.*

'Are you alert now?'

'You have my attention,' she replied, turning back to face her visitor ... only to be rocked by a new surprise.

Tom had vanished! In his place stood *Jacob Demwa*, elderly master spy of the Terragens Intelligence Service, who had lobbied hard for the commissioning of a dolphin-crewed ship. *Streaker* was just as much his doing as Creideiki's. Dark, leathery skin showed the toll of years cruising deep space, among Earth's many outposts, fighting to stave off the fate suffered by most wolfling races.

'That's good,' her visitor said, in a voice much like old Jake's ... though it lacked some overtones of crusty humor. *'Because I can spare only a small part of my awareness for this conversation. There are many other tasks requiring imminent completion.'*

Gillian nodded.

'I can well imagine. You Transcendents must be frightfully busy, slaughtering trillions of sapient beings in order to set off a brief cosmic torch. Tell me, what purpose did all those poor creatures die for? Was it a religious sacrifice? Or something more practical?'

'Must one choose? You might say a little of both. And neither. The concepts are hard to express, using terms available in your discursive-symbolic language.'

For some reason, she had expected such an answer.

'I guess that's true. But thanks anyway, for not using terms like "crude" or "primitive." Others, before you, made a point of reminding us how low we stand on life's pyramid.'

The image of Jake Demwa smiled, with wrinkles creasing all the right places.

'You are bitter. After suffering through earlier contacts with so-called Old Ones, I can hardly blame you. Those creatures were scarcely older than you, and hardly more knowledgeable. Such immature souls are often arrogant far beyond their actual accomplishments. They try to emphasize how high they have risen by denigrating those just below. In your own journal, Dr. Baskin, you make comparisons to "ants scurrying under the feet of trampling gods."

'In fact, though, any truly advanced mind should be capable of empathy, even toward "ants." By deputizing a small portion of myself, I can speak to you in this manner. It costs little to be kind, when the effort seems appropriate.'

Gillian blinked, unable to decide whether to be grateful or offended.

'Your notion of selective kindness ... terrifies me.'

The Demwa replica shrugged.

'*Some things cannot be helped. Those composite beings who died recently – whose stirred mass and other attributes now form a dense cloud, hovering at the brink of oblivion – they will serve vital goals much better with their deaths than they would as junior Transcendents. Here, and at many other sites across the known cosmos, they will ignite beacons at just the right moment, when destiny opens a fleeting window, allowing heavens to converse.*'

Her brow grew tense from concentration.

'Beacons? Aimed where? You Transcendents are already masters of everything within the Five—'

Abruptly, Gillian hazarded a guess.

'*Outside?* You want to contact others, *beyond* the Five Galaxies?'

Demwa seemed to croon approvingly.

'*Ah, you see? Simple reasoning is not so difficult, even for an ant!*

'*Indeed, an aim of this vast enterprise is to shine brief messages from one heavenly locus to another. A greeting can be superimposed on the blaring eruption of light that will soon burst from this place, briefly achieving brightness greater than a whole galaxy.*'

'But—'

'*But! You are about to object that we can do this* anytime! *It is trivial for beings like us simply to set off supernovas, flashing them like blinking signal lights.*

'*True! Furthermore, that method is too slow, and too noise-ridden, for complex conversation. It amounts to little more than shouting "Here I am!" at the universe.*

'*Anyway, the vast majority of other galactic nexi appear to be mysteriously silent, or else they emanate vibrations that are too cryptic or bizarre for us to parse, even with our best simulations. Either way, the puzzle cannot be solved by remote musing on mere sluggish beams of light.*'

Avoiding the false Demwa's scrutinizing gaze, Gillian stared at a far wall, deep in thought. At last she murmured.

'I bet all this has to do with the *Great Rupture* that Sara predicted. Many of the old connective links – the subspace channels and t-point threads – are snapping at last. Galaxy Four may detach completely.'

Her hands clenched.

'There must be some *opportunity*. One that only takes place during a rupture, when all the hyperspace levels are convulsing. A window of time when . . .'

Looking back at her visitor, Gillian winced to find it transformed yet again. Now Jake Demwa was replaced by the image of *Tom's mother*.

May Orley grinned back at her, bundled in thermal gear against a Minnesota winter, with a ski pole in each hand.

'*Go on, my dear. What else do you surmise?*'

Such rapid transfigurations might once have unnerved Gillian, before she had departed on this long, eventful space voyage. But after years spent dealing with the Niss Machine, she had learned to ignore rude interruptions, like rain off a duck's back.

'A window of time when spatial links are greater than normal!' She stabbed a finger toward the Transcendent. 'When physical objects can be hurled across the unbridgeable gulf between galactic clusters, at some speed much greater than light. Like tossing a message in a bottle, taking advantage of a rare high tide.'

'*A perfectly lovely metaphor,*' approved her ersatz mother-in-law. '*Indeed, the rupture is like a mighty, devouring wave that can speedily traverse megaparsecs at a single bound. The supernova we set off shall be the arm that throws bottles into that wave.*'

Gillian inhaled deeply as the next implication struck home.

'You want *Streaker* to be one of those bottles.'

'*Spot on!*' The Transcendent clapped admiration. '*You validate our simulations and models, which lately suggested a change in procedure. By adding wolflings to the mixture, we may supply a much-needed ingredient, this time. Perhaps it will prevent the failures that plagued our past efforts – those other occasions when we tried to send messages across the vast desert of flatness between our nexus of galaxies and the myriad spiral heavens we see floating past, tantalizingly out of reach.*'

Gillian could no longer stand the unctuous pleasantness of May Orley. She covered her eyes, in part to let the Transcendent shift again ... but also because she felt rather woozy. A weakness spread to her knees as realization sank in.

Instead of imminent death by fiery immolation, she was being promised an adventure – a voyage of exploration more exceptional than any other – and Gillian felt as if she had been punched in the stomach.

'You've ... been trying this a long time, have you?'

'*Ever since recovering from the earliest recorded crisis, just after the Progenitors departed, when our happy community of seventeen linked galaxies was torn asunder. Across the ages since then, we have yearned to recontact the brethren who were lost then.*'

The voice was changing, mutating as it spoke, becoming more gruff. More gravelly.

'*It is a pang that hurts more deeply than you may know. For this reason, above all others, we made sure that starfarers would abandon Galaxy Four, in order for the loss to be less traumatic, this time.*'

Uncovering her eyes, Gillian saw that the Transcendent now resembled *Charles Dart*, the chimp scientist who had vanished on Kithrup, along with Tom and Hikahi and about a dozen others.

'You can truly remember that far back?'

'By dwelling deep within the Embrace of Tides – skim-orbiting what you call "black holes" – we accomplish several ends. In that gravity-stressed realm we can perform quantum computing on a measureless scale, combining the insights of every life order. With loving care, we simulate past events, alternate realities, even whole cosmic destinies.'

Gillian quashed a manic surge of hysterical laughter. It was awfully posh language to come from the mouth of a chimp.

She fought for self-control, but the Transcendent did not seem to notice, continuing with its explanation.

'There is yet another effect of living near an event horizon, where spacetime curls so tightly that light can barely struggle free. Time slows down for us, while the rest of the universe spins on madly.

'Others plunge past us into the singularities, diving headlong toward unseen realms, pursuing their own visions of destiny – but we remain, standing watch, impervious to entropy, waiting, observing, experimenting.'

'Others plunge past ...' Gillian repeated, blinking rapidly. '*Into* the black holes? But who ...?'

A grim smile spread slowly, with her growing realization.

'You're talking about other Transcendents! By God, you aren't the only high ones, are you? All the life orders merge next to black holes – hydros and oxies and machines and the rest – gathering near the greatest tides of all. But that's not the end of the story for most of them, is it? They keep going, *into* the singularities! Whether it takes them to a better universe, or else eliminates them as dross, they choose to keep going while you guys stay behind.

'Why?' she asked, pursuing the point. 'Because you're afraid? Because you lack enough guts to face the unknown?'

This time the transformation took place before her eyes. A whirl of painful color that seemed somehow *vexed*. An instant later it resolved in the shape of her own father, long dead, but now restored to his appearance at the end, lying in a hospital bed, emaciated and bitter, regarding her with grim disapproval.

'I would ponder, Dr. Baskin, whether it is wise or justified to taunt powerful beings whose motives you can scarcely comprehend.'

She nodded.

'Fair enough. And I humbly apologize. Now will you please choose another form? This one—'

In another flashy pirouette, the visitor reformed as a *Rothen*, one of those scoundrels who claimed to be Earth's patron race, gathering around themselves a cult of human thieves and cutpurses. Gillian winced. It served as a reminder of the messy situation faced by all her kind back home, where threats and dangers piled up faster with each passing year, month, and day.

'*Now that I have explained your role, there are further matters to discuss,*' continued the ersatz Rothen. '*A few details have been entered into your computer – some precautions you should take, for comfort during the coming transition. But the new coating we are spinning around your ship is quite intelligent and capable. It will protect you when the star explodes, escaping most of the heat and shock as the gravitational backlash throws you into a hyperlevel far beyond—*'

Gillian cut in.

'But what if we don't *want* to go?'

The Rothen-shaped being smiled, a friendly gesture that brought her only chill.

'*Are glory and adventure insufficient motivations? Then let's try another.*

'*Even now, the defenses surrounding Earth are collapsing. Soon, enemies will own your homeworld, then all its colonies, and even the secret refuges where Terrans stashed small outposts for desperate safety. Only you, aboard* Streaker, *have an opportunity to carry seeds of your species, your culture, beyond reach of the schoolyard bullies who would kill or enslave every human and dolphin. Do you not owe this to your ancestors, and descendants? A chance to ensure survival of your line, somewhere far from any known jeopardy?*'

'But what chance is that?' she demanded. 'You admit this never worked before.'

'*Simulations show a much better chance now that wolflings have been added to the recipe. I told you this already.*'

Gillian shook her head.

'Sorry. It's tempting, but I have orders. A duty ...'

'*To the Terragens Council?*'

The Transcendent seemed dubious.

'Yes ... but also to my civilization. The Civilization of Five Galaxies. It may be an anthill to you. And yes, it's in a nasty phase right now, dominated by those "schoolyard bullies" you mentioned. But the Tymbrimi and some others think that may change, if the right stimulation is applied.'

She nodded toward Herbie, the ancient relic of *Streaker*'s mission to the Shallow Cluster.

'Truth can have a tonic effect, even on those who are lashing out out of fear.'

The Rothen-figure nodded, even as its features began melting in another transformation.

'*A laudable position for a young and noble race. Though, of course, our needs take higher priority than a civilization of fractious starfaring primitives.*

'*In any event, the time is nearly upon us ... as you are about to find out.*'

The visitor's features remained murky, while Gillian puzzled over the meaning of its last remark.

Abruptly, the comm line on her desk chimed. A small holo image erupted. It was Zub'daki. The dolphin's gray head looked agitated and worried. He did not seem to realize Gillian had company.

'Dr. Bassskin!'

'Yes? What is it, Zub'daki.'

'Events are accelerating in ways I hadn't anticipated. You might want to come up and have a look-k!'

Gillian's guts churned. Normally, she would respond quickly to such a summons. But right now, it was hard to imagine anything in the universe more important than this conversation she was having with a transcendent deity who controlled all their lives.

'Can it wait a bit? I'm kind of busy right now.'

The dolphin astronomer's dark eye widened, as if he could not believe what he was hearing.

'Doctor ... let me explain. Earlier I said the infall of the debris cloud might be delayed by light pressure. As the white dwarf heats up, its increasing brightness pushes back against the collapsing disk, slowing the arrival of more matter. It could make for a sloppy, uneven supernova.

'But-t something's changing! The gas and sooty dust are starting to *clump*! All the mass is consolidating into little dense ballsssss! Trillions and gazillions of dense *marbles*, all at once!'

'So?' Gillian shrugged. She was distracted by the sight of her visitor, who now stood in front of the glass display case, gazing at Herbie. The Transcendent's outline kept rippling as it tried adjusting its form. She realized that it must be attempting to simulate Herbie's original appearance, before the mummy spent a billion years in desiccated preservation, back at the Shallow Cluster.

'So? You ask *ssssso*?' Zub'daki sputtered, aghast. 'This means the debris cloud will be effectively transparent to light pressure! As it precipitates onto the star, nothing impedes the acceleration. The whole great mass plummets all at once, with tremendous speed!'

Gillian nodded.

'So the supernova will take place quickly and smoothly.'

'And with unprecedented power!'

While she conversed with Zub'daki, her visitor seemed to be having trouble finding the right shape, as if there was something *slippery* about Herbie's figure. Or else the Transcendents were too busy with other matters right now to apply much computing power for such an unimportant task.

She shook her head.

'I expect we're just witnessing some more supercompetent technology at work, Zub'daki. Clearly, this was all arranged. Perhaps long before we were born. Tell me, do you have a new estimate for when infall-collapse begins?'

Frustration filled the dolphin's voice.

'You missssunderstand me, Doctor! Infall has *already*—' The astronomer's voice cut short, interrupted by a shrill clamor of alarm bells. The dolphin's image swung around as shadowy figures rushed back and forth behind him, hurrying to emergency stations. Then Zub'daki's image vanished completely.

It was replaced by the whirling tornado of the Niss Machine.

'What is it?' Gillian demanded. 'What's happening now?'

The Niss bent slightly, as if starting to note the presence of her visitor. Then the hologram shivered and seemed to forget all about the Transcendent.

'*I . . . must report that we are once again under attack.*'

Gillian blinked.

'Attack? By whom?'

'*Who do you think? By our old nemesis, the Jophur battleship, Polkjhy. Though clearly mutated and transformed, it is approaching rapidly, and has begun emanating vibrations on D Space resonance frequencies, once more turning our hull into a receiving antenna for massive flows of heat—*'

'Stop!' Gillian shouted, waving both hands in front of her. 'This is crazy! Do the Jophur know what's going on here? Or whose protection we're under?'

The Niss gave its old, familiar shrug.

'*I have no idea what the Jophur know, or do not know. Such persistence, in the face of overwhelming power, would seem to verge on madness. And yet, the fact remains. Our hull temperature has started to rise.*'

Gillian turned to her visitor, whose face was coalescing into a visage of humanoid-amphibian beauty, almost luminous in its color and texture. At any other time, it would have been one of the most transfixing sights of Gillian's life – and she barely gave it a second glance.

'Well?' she demanded.

'*Well what, Dr. Baskin?*' the Transcendent asked, turning toward her. There was still a tentative, uncertain quality to the reconstruction, a near resurrection of her longtime companion, the antediluvian cadaver.

'Well ... are you *going* to protect us?'

'*Do you ask for our protection?*'

In amazement, she could hardly speak.

'I thought ... you put so much effort into choosing and preparing us ...'

The Niss Machine whirled in perplexity.

'*Are you talking to me? Is someone in there with you? My sensors seem unable to —*'

With an irritated hand gesture, Gillian caused her artificial assistant to vanish from sight. She gazed in wonder as the Transcendent seemed to shimmer, growing brighter by the instant.

'*Such investment merits confidence, Dr. Baskin. Can wolflings survive the vast gulf between heavens? Have you the fortitude to endure all the cryptic challenges that await you? And the denizens you'll meet, when you arrive at some distant galactic realm?*'

Her guest became radiant, completing the transformation from cadaverous mummy into something truly like a god.

'*It occurs to us that one final test might be called for. In the interest of verifying your mettle.*'

Gillian covered her eyes, and yet the glare soon grew too bright to endure, outlining the bones of her hand. The visitor's words pierced her skin, vibrating her soul.

'*One more trial to pass ... in the slim moments that remain ... before our universe changes.*'

LARK

Despite occasional gaps, a distant voice came through clearly, resonating in his mind.

'*... there are further matters to discuss ... precautions you should take, for comfort during transition ... the new coating will protect you as backlash ... throws you to a hyperlevel well beyond those commonly used by starfaring races.*'

*

Working together with Ling and other members of the Mother Consortium, he had labored hard to achieve this – sifting through the incredible complexity of the Transcendent Mesh for something simple enough for mere organic life-forms to understand. After all their efforts, this was the best result so far. An explanation, in plain Anglic, of what the great ones hoped to accomplish from all the recent violence and turmoil.

Apparently, they would take advantage of rare cosmic conditions to launch specially modified ships, sending messenger-envoys hurtling on one-way voyages across the immense gulf separating clusters of galaxies.

By adding wolflings to the mixture, we may ... prevent the failures that plagued past efforts ... when we tried to ... cross the vast flat deserts between our galactic nexus and the myriad spiral heavens we see floating past, tantalizingly out of reach ...'

Lark felt growing agitation in the surrounding watery medium, where he and Ling floated amid a jostling throng of symbiotic organisms. 'Mother' was clearly both excited and worried by this news. He knew this, in part, because his own fretful thoughts helped shape the overall mood.

Ling's presence made itself known. Turning around, he saw her swim toward him through the living murk, reaching out to clasp his hand. At the instant of contact, he felt her mind stroking his own, bringing dire news.

Can you feel it? The master rings have decided to assail and destroy Streaker, *no matter what the repercussions!*

Lark blinked in surprise. Putting out his own mental feelers to probe the data network of starship *Polkjhy*, he tapped the Jophur command frequencies and soon confirmed the worst.

The priest-stack and the new captain-leader were in complete accord. With stark decisiveness, they had sent *Polkjhy* careening on a new, deadly course. Attacking, heedless of the consequences.

What can they hope to accomplish? Interfering with the Transcendents will only invite those mighty ones to swat this ship – and all of us aboard – out of the sky like annoying insects!

Ling nodded, and Lark saw that he had just answered his own question. From the Jophur leaders' point of view, this offered a last chance to wipe out the hybrid oxy-hydro superorganism that had taken over most of their ship. Apparently, the Jophur would rather go out in a blaze of glory than surrender.

The suicidal decision saddened Lark. If only they would simply wait for the supernova! He had a hankering to watch the run-up to that gaudy event. To feel the first hyperdense flux of neutrinos sleet through his body, heralding a crackling dawn. One that would illumine night on myriad worlds.

Of course, Mother wasn't about to take this lying down. With approval of every sapient member, the community launched an immediate, all-out assault against the remaining vital strongholds held by unconverted Jophur. Soon Lark began sensing the fractious fury of combat, as both sides flung deadly bolts along stained corridors, further melting *Polkjhy's* already tortured walls. Lark's nerve endings responded, turning each injury or death into a pang, physically painful. Personally intense.

Mother is about to break into the engine compartment, Ling noted. *But we may not be able to cut power in time to save the Earthlings ... or to prevent angering the Transcendents.*

Indeed, resistance was bitter as ring stacks and robots stubbornly held their ground against the costly assault. But Zang globules and other members of the Mother Consortium kept up the pressure, storming Jophur defenses with spendthrift courage.

We'd better go help, Lark thought, and Ling nodded. They both had a sense of how drained Mother's reserves were. This was no time to hang back.

And yet, even as they made ready to join the fray, something restrained both of them. A resistance that stopped Lark in his tracks.

Not a *command*, as such. More like a consensus decision – a general feeling among other components of the symbiosis. An agreement that the two humans should not be risked right now.

They would better serve the whole with their intelligence and knowledge, by probing through the Mesh, trying once more to communicate.

With some reluctance, Lark accepted the wisdom of this. Together with Ling, he went back to work, reopening the channels they had discovered before.

'*It occurs to us that one final test might be called for ... verifying your mettle.*

'*One more trial ... before our universe changes.*'

Lark exhaled a sigh that formed bubble trails in the frothy medium.

So. The Transcendents were still tinkering, trying to optimize their experiment till the very last moment. Or else the 'gods' were amusing themselves at the expense of those poor Earthlings. Either way, they weren't about to defend *Streaker* with omnipotent power. Instead, they would let *Polkjhy* attack, evaluating the results.

There wasn't much time left for exploration. With one part of his mind, Lark tracked the great mass-infall of collapsing debris.

Already the white dwarf surged and boiled as the cloud's inner fringes struck its surface at high velocity. Concentric waves of actinic blue fire crisscrossed the ancient, tormented surface, spouting gaudy flares of plasma back toward space, hinting at far greater fireworks to come.

Meanwhile, uncoded insults hurled from *Polkjhy*'s bridge, taunting *Streaker*'s crew as their hull was turned into a betraying antenna, forced to siphon heat from other folded layers of space.

At that point a familiar voice joined in.

It was Lark's old friend, the traeki from Jijo who had once been *Asx*, then *Ewasx*, and now was a wise, multicomponent being, simply called 'X.'

I have finally made full contact with the Earthship's computer, the hybrid creature announced.

Congratulations, Lark replied. *Have you transmitted the information you wanted to send?*

With a sense of waxy satisfaction, X confirmed it was done. Everything that had been learned about Jophur master rings was now copied into *Streaker*'s onboard storage system, including the knack for growing red toruses – the kind that had proved so potent against egocentric dominance.

And yet, what good would the information do? Even if *Streaker* survived the present attack, *and* the coming stellar explosion, the Transcendents would only hurl it away from the Five Galaxies, riding a cosmic tidal wave, careening toward starscapes where no Jophur ever lived.

X showed no sign of recognizing any inconsistency.

You might be interested in something else I have learned. There is a passenger aboard the Earthship. Someone now counted among its honored leaders. A human person, familiar to us both.

Lark sensed anguished irony behind the words. Bending his will toward the indicated path, he finally gained access to *Streaker*'s housekeeping files and discovered the datum X referred to.

Sara!

A spasm rocked him, from sheer surprise. Eddies tugged Lark's body, while Ling grasped his right arm, to help him get over the shock.

What is my sister doing out here ... so far from Jijo?

How did she wind up in such a mess!

The blow was made worse when Mother came up with an estimate of heating rates aboard *Streaker*. At this pace, the influx would reach critical levels in less than half a midura.

Soon after that, all the water aboard the dolphin-crewed ship would start to boil.

The alarm seemed to take everyone in *Streaker*'s control center by surprise.

The others had been so intent and worried about the engorged, enraged star – and about mysterious actions of the nearby needle-gateway – that they seemed to forget about danger from mundane enemies.

But he had not.

Emerson knew better. He had dealt with Jophur before and understood their tenacity – a single-mindedness that had been grafted into their race by careless Uplift consorts, who had failed to grasp the basic value of moderation. When the assault came, he was ready.

Lacking speech or literacy, Emerson could not read the flashing monitor screens or figure out the exact nature of their weapon. Details did not matter. He understood that it somehow had to do with making *Streaker* hot. Already the walls and floor plates were emanating uncomfortable warmth. Large amounts of energy poured in, even though the small sun was still not ready to explode.

Sara reached for his hand, and he felt guilty putting her off with a mere loving squeeze, before dashing away. But Emerson figured that a chance of saving her life was worth more than staying by her side and roasting together.

Running down a torrid hallway, he kept shouting, in hopes that the automatic intercoms would pass on his simple message.

'Suessi! ... Karkaett! ... Now, now, now!'

Would they come? So much labor had gone into making his idea a reality, applying a two-hundred-year-old technology to new problems in survival. And yet, he worried. They might have simply been humoring him, working together as a way to stay busy till the end ...

Clambering through a maintenance tube, Emerson hurried till he reached the small chamber where his last, triumphant encounter with the Old Ones had taken place – and breathed relief when he saw that Hannes and a couple of dolphin engineers were already there, gathered around the big laser. They babbled to each other in the sweet dialect of engineering. Emerson could no longer parse the quick, efficient meanings, but their speech sounded like music, nevertheless.

The graceful lyrics of competence.

Hannes turned his mirrorlike dome to ask Emerson a question. One that was simple enough for his frail remaining language centers to grasp.

'Yes!' He nodded vigorously. 'Do ... it!'

Hannes pushed a switch and the laser abruptly bucked in its mounting brackets – hissing and straining like some great beast, snorting as it sprang into action.

Emerson shifted position in order to sight along the massive barrel, curious to see where massive amounts of energy were now pouring.

He saw nothing but stars.

Sure enough, a nearby view screen showed a red dot, representing the Jophur vessel *Polkjhy*, approaching *Streaker*'s other side.

Of course he had been lucky with the Old Ones. It would have taken extreme luck for this enemy to be within reach. Anyway, a battleship's defenses might deflect even such a potent beam.

He shrugged. It didn't matter. He and the others did not have to smite the Jophur in order to defeat them.

Emerson felt a chill draft. He shivered, and soon noticed a distinct fog begin to form above each dolphin's blowhole, like individual fountains of frost. His own breath began condensing, too. In moments, the small chamber became noticeably colder, and Hannes shouted for everyone to evacuate. It was time to leave, allowing the machine to perform as planned.

Still, Emerson hung back, relishing a flow of icy air that gushed through ducts to far corners of the ship. He visualized the laser beam acting as a great pump, sucking heat as fast as other forces drew it in, then shooting it forth toward the cosmos. Grinning, he took satisfaction in the way an ancient Earthling technology thwarted Galactic foes – as it had once before, a long time ago, in the maw of a torrid sun.

I ... still ... have it ... He pondered, glancing down at his hands.

When his grin became noisy – a chattering of clenched teeth – Emerson finally let Hannes and the others tug him back toward habitable areas.

Anyway, Sara was waiting for him.

Now at least they would have a few moments together.

Until the star exploded.

GILLIAN

'You never asked for volunteers,' she told her visitor accusingly.

The transcendent being returned to her office, assembling itself out of dust motes and particles of air – perhaps in order to resume their conversation, or else to congratulate Gillian for the clever trick worked out by *Streaker*'s engineering crew – creating a *refrigeration laser*, a device for dumping heat overboard, spraying it garishly sky-ward as fast as energy flowed into the ship from D Space.

Few Galactics had ever needed such a crude, gaudy, *wolfling* device. It would seem preposterously primitive, like rockets, or propeller-driven aircraft. But when humans began exploring the depths of their own sun two centuries ago – going there out of pure curiosity – the trick of laser-cooling had proved both useful and fateful, in several ways.

Shortly after reappearing, the visitor seemed to float before Gillian, an entity with lustrous gray skin and a short, powerful tail whose flukes actually stirred a breeze, kicking up midget whirl-winds, rustling the papers on her desk. Coalescing further, it started taking a resemblance to Gillian's dearest dolphin friend, Lieutenant Hikahi, one of those who had been left behind on Kithrup, along with Tom and Charles Dart.

Before the Transcendent could speak, Gillian completed her accusation.

'You say you need wolflings, to add as *ingredients* for your message-probes to other galaxies. Did it ever occur to you to ask? I know my fellow Earthlings. You'd have gotten thousands, *millions* of volunteers for such a trip! Even knowing in advance that it would involve merging with hydros and machines and other creepy things. There have always been enough weirdos and adventurers. People who'd pay any price, just to be the first to see some far horizon.'

The ersatz dolphin rolled on its side, almost languidly, as if rel-ishing a new experience.

'*We shall make note of that-t,*' crooned a close approximation of Hikahi's voice, causing Gillian a lonely pang. '*Perhaps we'll take your advice . . . next time the question comes up.*'

She stared for a moment, then gave a low, dry laugh.

'Right. When another rupture comes, in a hundred million years!'

'*That's not so very long, for those of us who make our true homes next to ssssingularities. We who you called "cowards" for biding our time in a black hole's stretched borderline, rather than plunging into the unknown.*'

'Look.' She raised a hand. 'I already apologized for that. Right now, though, I think we'd better cut to—'

'*The chasssse?*' Her visitor rolled the simulated body in a loop.

Gillian raised an eyebrow. 'Do you already know—'

'*What you are going to say? Your surface thoughts are trivial to read. But even without using psi, we can make good estimates, based on appraisal of your past behavior under varied circumstances. These models were recently revised. Would you like to know what our latest simulations foretell?*'

She answered, guardedly.

'I'm listening.'

The imitation Hikahi brought one dark eye toward Gillian.

'You were about to decline the honor of being our emissariessss. You would claim that urgent obligations beckon you elsewhere. Obligations that cannot be ignored.'

Gillian shrugged.

'Anyone could've guessed that, after our last conversation. Assuming I did decline, how would you have replied?'

'I would have said that you have no option. A conveyance and shield have already been woven around your ship, ready to clasp the opportunity when a spacetime rift opens nearby. With luck, it might carry you safely beyond the limits of known civilization. That kind of investment is not given up lightly. Your request would be refused.'

With her next breath, Gillian exhaled a bitter sigh.

'I guess that answer's inevitable. So. How do your simulations predict I'd respond next?'

The dolphin-shaped being sputtered laughter.

'With threatsssss!

'You would claim readiness to blow up your ship . . . or to interfere with the mission in some other way.'

Gillian felt her face grow warm. That really had been her next move. A desperate ploy. But no other tactic came to mind in the short time available.

'I guess it is a bit of a cliché.'

'Naturally, all such possibilities have been taken into account. In this case, our analyses show you would be bluffing. Given a stark choice between adventure, on the one hand, and assured extinction on the other, you could be relied upon to choose adventure!'

Gillian's shoulders slumped. The Transcendents were quick learners, and with awesome computational power they could simulate whole alternate realities. Small wonder they outmaneuvered any plan she came up with, using her limited human brain.

'Then that's it?' she asked. 'We have no choice. We head for some far galaxy, like it or not.'

'Your linear guess is only partly correct. Indeed, you have no choice. That part of it you have right, Dr. Bassssskin. We can compel you and your crew to depart, and that-t would be that.'

The visitor shook its sleek gray head as it began yet another transfiguration. Hikahi's outlines grew blurry. Her simulated body started stretching.

'But our simulations did not stop with your behavior today. They scrutinized what you might do later . . . during the weeks, months, and years that stretch ahead, until your people arrive at some distant realm.'

Gillian blinked. 'You worked it out that far ahead?'

'*To a high degree of probability. And that is where a problem keeps cropping up in our models. Given enough time, something else will occur to you. You will realize that it is possible to have your adventure, plus revenge as well! A way to visit far-off realms, and also retaliate against those who thrust you on so great a voyage, against your will.*'

She could only stare, blinking in confusion as the Transcendent finished converting to a different body shape ... another dolphin image, a bit longer and stronger looking than Hikahi, with scar tissue covering a savage wound near the left eye.

Creideiki, she realized, with a faint shiver.

'I ... don't ... I don't know what you mean. Unless ...' Gillian swallowed, and tried concentrating. It was difficult, under that strangely powerful cetacean gaze.

'Unless you're concerned about what we'd *say* about you, to whatever high minds we meet on the other side.' This time, the visitor did not respond in Anglic. Rather, the facsimile of *Streaker*'s old commander lifted that tormented head and cast a spray of squealing clicks, filling her office with couplets of ornate Trinary verse.

* What revenge is
    more long-lasting
* Than the cruelty
    of slander,
* Spoken by outraged
    descendants,
* Defaming their
    distant parents?

* Would you escape
    time's death sentence?
* Or entropy's
    cruel erosion?
* We know just one
    surefire method
* To succeed and
    be immortal—

* If you want to
    live forever,
* First earn love and
    fierce devotion
* From those who will
    carry onward,

They will speak your
        name resounding
                Even when the stars grow cold *

Gillian squinted at the replica of her old comrade and leader. The dolphin captain looked so genuine, so tangible, as if she could reach out and stroke his warm gray flank – battered, yet unbowed.

'That's ... the first truly wise thing I've yet heard from you gods,' she said. 'It's almost ... as if you really *are*—'

The Transcendent interrupted. Its sleek form began dissolving, folding inward toward a ball of light.

'*Are you ... entirely sure ... that I am not?*'

She blinked, unsure what to make of the non sequitur.

'Wait!' she cried out. 'What's going to happen? What are you going to—'

The visitor vanished silently. But in her mind a soft presence lingered for another moment, whispering.

We have much to do ... and very little time ...

A shrill whistle filled the air. A holo image of Akeakemai burst in, calling from *Streaker*'s bridge.

'Gillian! Zub'daki says that mass infall is speeding up! The explosion's just minutes away!'

She nodded, feeling tired and altogether unready to witness the end of the universe. Or any part of it.

'I'll be right up,' she said, turning toward the door. But the pilot's voice cut her short.

'That's not all!' he added, with frantic tones. 'The big needle-gateway ... it's—'

There followed a noisy clatter. Gillian saw a blur of motion on the bridge, as officers dashed in all directions, propelled by agitated tails.

'Niss!' she called out. 'Show me what's going on out there!'

Abruptly, a new holo display opened, presenting a view of nearby space.

The planet-sized Transcendent needle took up most of the scene. One of its flanks was now almost too bright to look at, reflecting angry light from the dwarf star – a fuming conflagration, rapidly heating toward Armageddon.

Gillian quickly saw what had Akeakemai upset. The needle was *splitting open*. Moreover, as it broke apart, beams of light reached out to seize three nearby objects.

Flashing labels identified the targets.

Streaker was the first. Gillian felt its hull shudder as the beam struck.

The Jophur battleship was next.

Finally – one of the globelike 'candidate vessels,' now wrapped in a fuzzy mass of special fabric.

All three were being drawn inward.

Then, as if with a surgeon's delicate lancet, the light beams started carving all three vessels apart.

'X'

Can you feel it now, my rings? And my other little selves?

How about you, Lark?

And you, Ling?

Can you sense how *Mother* – the macro-entity we all joined – writhes with uncertain fear as blades of force cut through *Polkjhy's* hull? Can you sense distant walls and bulkheads separate, spilling air, liquid, and creatures into vacuum? For a few moments, it seems our time of destruction has arrived.

Our/my/your end has come, at last.

BUT NOTE! Can you sense a sudden change in mood?

Mother rejoices, as we/i/all realize the truth.

These are *scalpel rays*, slicing rapidly, selectively. Only a few small segments are being removed from *Polkjhy*!

Likewise, instruments tell us that just one or two prim holes are being drilled in the Earthship *Streaker*.

But the third victim seems less lucky!

The nearest mighty globule-vessel – a giant candidate-craft, already prepared for its epic journey – has been torn open and gutted! Horrified and awed at the same time, all our rings and segments watch as the contents are sacrificed ... thousands of sapient-hybrid beings, cast aside like the entrails of some fresh-caught fish ... leaving behind only a lambent shell of glimmering tendrils.

A living shell that now moves rapidly toward *Polkjhy*!

AND NOW, ATTENTION TURNS TO THE LIVID SUN.

How long did it spin in peace? A remnant of this galaxy's earliest days, the dwarf star had long ago finished its brief youth and settled down to placid retirement. Left alone, it might have spent another twenty billion years slowly shrinking as it eked out a flickering white surface flame. Lacking a nearby stellar companion, it would never obtain the sudden infusion of mass required for a more ecstatic death.

Only now that mass infusion comes!

Like pilgrims to a shrine, millions of starships recently answered the Great Harrower's summons. They came to this place, arranging themselves in polite, crisscrossing spiral queues, seeking redemption and advancement ... only to find death on the very threshold of transcendence. Their corpses, compressed into compact balls, now rain upon the star, inciting new ferment, taking its matter/energy balance close to a special value.

An acute point of no return.

MY RINGS ... MANY OF YOU ONCE WERE MEMBERS OF ASX, THAT WISE OLD TRAEKI SAGE.

Back on Jijo, you had no need to contemplate such things. Instead of Chandrasekhar limits and radiative opacities, we/you/i used to adjudge disputes among local villages and tribes. We offered marriage counseling to fractious urrish, human, and qheuen families. We would squat for days on some aromatic mulch pile, happily arguing among ourselves.

Now, Mother obligingly makes available vast stores of information, offering free access to *Polkjhy*'s onboard Library, lately captured from the remnant Jophur.

So it is that i/we/you know all about *critical thresholds* and the *catastrophic collapse* that will soon occur, followed by a tremendous 'bounce,' expelling much of the poor star at high fractions of light speed.

First will come a burst of neutrinos. Not so many as in a 'type two' supernova. But enough so that those phantom particles will impart heat and momentum into any body within ten Jijoan orbits. (We are much closer than that!) X rays and gamma rays will follow ... and then other forms of light. So much that the wave-fronts will carry their own palpable gravitational fields as they plunge through this point in space with the brightness of one trillion suns.

Finally, if anything remains of poor *Polkjhy*, it will be struck by the shock wave of protons, neutrons, electrons, and ions, imparting accelerations of one hundred thousand gravities.

No wonder the Transcendents feel this event will rip holes in the cosmic *ylem*. Apparently, that is their desire. To kindle a pyre. One bright enough to propel seeds across the greatest desert of all.

*

DO YOU HEAR THE LATEST, MY RINGS?

Lark and Ling report what they have learned by tapping into the Transcendent Mesh.

An explanation of the recent violent surgery by flashing scalpel rays!

Apparently, the high ones have decided on a last-minute change in plans.

Quick improvisation is not their normal habit, but now they labor furiously, redesigning. Reconfiguring.

AND WE ARE OBJECTS OF THEIR SUDDEN INTENT!

Transfixed, we all watch as two slim plugs of matter slide smoothly out of the Earthship and head this way, leaving holes that seal quickly behind them. These slender tubes race toward *Polkjhy* ... even as the gutted shell of the third vessel approaches us from the other side, shimmering and alive.

Dolphins, Ling says, identifying the contents of the cylinders taken from *Streaker*. *About a dozen of them. Volunteers, coming to join us, along with some gene stores, and cultural archives* ...

With breakneck speed, the tubes slide into slots prepared for them. *Just in time*, as the rippling shell wraps around *Polkjhy* and seals shut with a blaze of energetic union.

All of Mother's components – even the newly captured Jophur officers – stagger briefly from psychic shock as that mass of luminous tendrils takes hold of our transformed vessel – bonding and penetrating – turning it into a throbbing, vibrating whole.

Something eager. Coiled and ready for what comes next.

CAN YOU SENSE THE NEARBY AGONY OF DYING GODS?

The needle-gateway writhes and flickers as it draws *Streaker* toward it. Glowing and collapsing inward, the transcendent nexus *flexes*, creating powerful fields, causing space to warp straight through its innards, generating a tunnel. A lean passageway.

An improvised escape route for the Terrans to strive for.

Will they make it in time?

AND NOW COMES IGNITION OF THE BRIGHTEST COMPACT DETONATION IN THE UNIVERSE.

Perhaps it will not be our knell of extinction, after all.

A poll has been taken, among Mother's many members. Nearly all agree.

This is what we would have chosen if the Transcendents had asked. (Indeed, with their mighty simulations, perhaps they did.)

Our merged union is a distillation. A combination of life orders.

A mélange, filled with hybrid vigor. Laced with special flavors from Jijo and Earth, our community may have the right mix that it takes to succeed at last, where so many others failed.

To bridge what was unbridgeable. To help unite what was separate.

To bring the cosmos more diversity ... and make it one.

We can feel *Polkjhy*'s new tendrils reaching out, clasping the fabric of space, awaiting the moment when a chaos wave next strikes.

The biggest chaos wave of all.

The Great Rupture.

Have the Transcendents timed things right? Do they really have the skill to trigger their explosion at precisely the moment, so *Polkjhy* can catch that wave?

Yes, my rings and other selves.

i/we/I/you can hardly wait to find out.

THE WHITE DWARF TREMBLES.

It is just ten thousand kilometers across. Ignition will flow at the speed of sound – a few thousand kilometers per second. That means it should take less than a dura ...

STREAKER LABORS MIGHTILY, STRIVING TO REACH THE ESCAPE TUNNEL.

Go, Sara!

You can make it.

Go!

Each passing second seems an eternity, as the Earthship struggles toward that flickering sanctuary.

ABRUPTLY, OUR SUNWARD SENSORS CATCH A BRILLIANT LIGHT!

A blinding flare that flows and ripples with mad speed across the tormented stellar surface, like the sudden striking of a match.

Then—

CAN YOU FEEL THEM, MY RINGS?

Neutrinos in the wax.

What a strange sensation! Like remembering tomorrow.

And now, here we go—

V

THE TIME OF CHANGES

Some life orders are more communicative than others.

MEMBERS of the Quantum Order have no sense of either place or time. At least, none corresponding with the way we view those properties. Though willing to exchange information, they generally make no sense of our queries, nor do we comprehend most of their answers. There must be some commonality of context in order for the word 'meaning' to have any significance. Compared to the Quantum Order, it is almost trivial to converse with hydrogen breathers, machines, or even the most coherent sapient memes.

Once, however, a member of the *touvint* client race presumptuously interrupted its elders at a D-Space rendezvous, and confronted one of the quantals with a naively simple question.

'WHAT can we expect?'

THE answer has puzzled scholars for a million years. Without hesitation, the strange being replied—

'EVERYTHING.'

The supernova's photon front caught *Streaker* just short of a swirling black tunnel – the escape path promised by cryptic Transcendents.

Alarms wailed and dolphins squalled as waves of searing energy struck from behind, crushing the normal protective fields, slamming each square meter with more heat than a normal sun would over the course of its lifespan. The blast would have evaporated the *Streaker* of old almost instantly.

But the Earthship was like a whale whose skin was coated with hard-shell barnacles; *Streaker* toiled under layers of strange stuff – coatings that shimmered in the heat, as if *eager* for the ruinous light.

Sara held Prity and Emerson. A rumbling vibration rattled her bones and the marrow inside. Blinding turmoil swamped every outside camera, but sensors told of staggering photon and neutrino fluxes as the star passed its limits of endurance ... or perhaps ecstasy. In real time, the eruption took milliseconds, but *Streaker*'s duration-stretched field let the crew witness successive stages, in slow motion.

'Our magic coating's impressive,' commented Suessi. 'But these're just photons. No way it can handle what's next. More than a solar mass of real matter ... protons and heavy nuclei ... leapin' this way at a good share of lightspeed.'

Sara had learned enough practical physics to know what fist was about to smite them. *Each atom of oxygen and carbon in my body passed through a convulsion like this one ... cooked in a sun, then spewed into great clouds, before condensing to form planets, critters, people.*

Now her own stardust might return to the cosmic mixing bowl, perhaps joining the life cycle of a new world, yet unborn. It seemed a dry consolation. But she knew another.

Lark.

I got his message – just as that shell closed around the Polkjhy, *spreading its lambent tendrils, preparing to catch waves of hyper-reality, the very moment when galaxies part company forever.*

By now, his ship must already be punching through, catching a great tide of recoiling metric. Outward bound on a great adventure.

Ironies made her smile. Among Nelo's three children, Lark alone never dreamed of leaving his beloved Jijo. Yet now he would see more of the cosmos than even the great Transcendents! An avowed celibate, he and his mate could sire a whole nation of humanity in some far galaxy.

Good-bye, brother. May Ifni's Boss keep an eye on you.

Have fun.

Their escape tunnel loomed, a cave filled with eerie, unnerving spirals. She looked up at Emerson. Moments ago, as a final hail of crushed Old Ones fell on the white dwarf's tormented surface, he had barked a single word—

'*Dross!*'

—and smiled, as if watching a deadly foe collapse in failure.

Someone counted subjective seconds till the matter wave would hit. '... fourteen ... thirteen ... twelve ...'

Meanwhile, Akeakemai crooned. 'Almost there ...' The pilot's flukes thrashed, urging *Streaker* along to the refuge. 'Almosssssst ...'

The suspense was so awful, Sara's mind reflexively fled to a domain where she had some control. Mathematics. To a problem she had discovered recently – while Gillian dickered with the Transcendents to take *Polkjhy*, and let *Streaker* go.

Amid a maze of transfinite tensors, Sara had found a renormalization quandary that simply would not go away. In fact, it seemed *essential* to describe the chaos waves they had seen. Yet, according to the Transcendents' own models, it made no sense!

I thought I knew the whole truth when I foresaw the galactic breakup, arising from the expansion of the universe. But now I can tell – some added force is driving things faster than expected.

It only made sense if she made a peculiar conjecture.

Something is coming in. *Something titanic.*

Details were vague, but she knew one thing about the intruding presence.

It won't be found in any gravity well. We must look elsewhere, in flat space. Far from the Embrace of—

Streaker shook suddenly. Vibrations leaped in force and volume, shuddering her spine. Someone screamed.

'Matter wave!'

For an instant, time seemed to flicker—

Then, across the span of an eyeblink, Sara was surrounded by leaping, yelling figures. Emerson squeezed her as if it were the end of the world. And briefly, she thought it was.

Then she knew Prity's gleeful screech, the dolphins' whistled raspberries of joy, and her lover's gasping laughter. Amid the tumult and confusion, Sara noticed – all the ominous rumblings were gone. Vanished! Replaced by a happy roar of unleashed engines.

The view screens were back on, showing vistas of strangely distorted *ylem* – the walls of a weirdly beneficent tunnel, sweeping them along.

'We made it!' Suessi's amplified voice exulted.

We . . . did?

Sara realized with some chagrin that her math-trance had kept her from witnessing the moment of triumph and salvation.

Well, damn me for a distracted nerd, she thought, and threw herself into kissing Emerson with all her might.

E SPACE

Harry's profession always seemed a lonely one.

Now I know why Wer'Q'quinn sent solitary scouts on missions to E Space. Too many minds can be dangerous here. And embarrassing.

During earlier trips to the kingdom of living ideas, he sometimes had entered a new territory only to find the local matrix crystallizing around symbols that leaked from his own mind. Since there was seldom anyone else around but herds of local memoids, it hardly mattered what the shapes revealed about his subconscious.

This time, the station carried *five* strong-willed personalities, from four different races. Harry worried from the moment his vessel emerged through a drifting purple haze, striding on long, spidery legs.

The initial fog shredded, as if blown aside by his passengers' curious scrutiny. Dwer and Kaa and Kiwei Ha'aoulin pressed the windows rimming the control chamber. Dwer had been in E Space before. The others were transfixed by their first visit to this famous, mythical province.

You wouldn't peer about so eagerly if you'd seen what I have.

Still Harry refrained from closing the louvered blinds. This would be the last chance of their lives to see E Space.

And maybe my last trip, as well.

Soon, the mist cleared to reveal a vast landscape of cubes, pyramids, tilted planes, and other more complex geometric forms. At least, that was how the objects began.

The first time he looked closely at one, it started *melting*, congealing, taking on new, rounded contours. Soon he saw protrusions on both sides that resembled . . . ears! Then a flared nose. Moments later, a mouth full of yellowed teeth grimaced back at him, both unappealing and familiar.

He checked instruments. The memic-monolith stood over thirty pseudokilometers away! Apparently, he had just triggered the manifestation of a gigantic sculpture representing his own head, towering higher than the largest structures on Earth. Glancing left and right, he saw that Synthian, dolphin, and human-shaped statuary were coagulating in all directions. Replications of Kaa, Dwer, and Kiwei soon stretched as far as the eye could see.

'Well, well,' commented the delighted Synthian trader, with both hands folded across her belly. 'Should someone wake Rety, so she might also partake in this opportunity for megascale immortalization?'

Harry shook his head while a mammoth sculpture mimicked his expression of piqued irritation.

'The poor kid is sleeping off a concussion, for Ifni's sake. Anyway, this sort of thing generally doesn't last. Most of these gross memes just fade back into the ylem, soon as the stimulating host mind leaves.'

'But occasionally they *don't* fade? There is a chance this will be permanent?'

Harry shrugged, wondering why Kiwei cared.

'I've seen things – crypto-shapes and frozen images from the distant past. Wer'Q'quinn says reified meme-stuff can sometimes get more rigid than anything made of true matter, like the ideas that become permanently fixed in some living brains. I guess there are concept-objects in E Space that may outlast all the protons an' quarks, an' the whole sidereal universe.'

Kiwei gazed at a range of hillocks and mountains, most of them wearing her own smug, rounded countenance.

'Really?' Her sigh was wistfully hopeful.

Dwer and Kaa both chuckled. But Harry shook his head.

'Let's get moving,' he said. 'Before something else goes wrong.'

So far, little had gone according to plan.

First came that riotous muddle at the Kazzkark warehouse. While Dwer covered their retreat with a hail of arrows, Harry and Kiwei had managed to grab the unconscious Rety and carry her off without being ripped to shreds by the angry Tandu warrior. Nearby hallways clamored with sounds of reinforcements – more of the vicious creatures – charging to help their comrade wreak havoc while chaos waves shook the little planetoid from end to end.

With a backward glance, Harry caught the final moments of the Skiano missionary – hurled into an exploding globe-icon of Earth, the blue 'martyr planet.'

Troubles followed them to the Institute Docks, where slabs of rock wall were already coming loose, toppling to crush vehicles parked at nearby wharves. Screeching alarms warned that a vacuum breach was imminent. Harry hurried everyone aboard and got his station under way – with Kaa's little corvette towed just behind – just before the ceiling started collapsing. By the time he reached the main airlock, there wasn't much point going through emigration protocols. The obstructing wall *dissolved*, revealing fields of weirdly twinkling stars.

It took a while to dodge swarms of hazardous debris before they could make even a simple, short-range hyperjump. Meanwhile, chaos waves rocked the planetoid. *Even if I make it back from this mission, there'd be no sense reporting here.*

There are other Institute bases.

Anyway, they say it's safer to be on a planet these days.

Finally, the chaos waves ebbed, though he knew worse was to come. As Kazzkark vanished from sight, Harry hoped Wer'Q'quinn, the old squid, would make it somehow.

Things got kind of blurry then. He gave coordinates to Kaa and let the expert space pilot take them through a dozen B-Level jumps, then into a small t-point that was already declared dangerously unstable.

Kaa's innovative thread-jumping maneuvers somehow kept them from being torn, sliced, roasted, or vaporized. Still, it was a wild, nerve-racking ride. Harry spent half the time cursing cetaceans and their ancestors, all the way back to the Miocene.

At last, they reached his assigned entry point – a special place, darker than black, where the walls between reality levels were thin enough to pierce – and it was Harry's turn to take over. Soon, materiality shimmered and they underwent transition to a realm whose physics let ideas have a life of their own.

It gladdened Harry to depart the province of giant statuary, entering a terrain covered by endless swaths of undulating orange 'grass' – each blade consisting of some basic concept that thrived free of any language or host mind.

On close inspection, the prairie looked eroded, discolored. Large patches seemed broken or seared, as if raked by quake and fire. Apparently, E Space wasn't immune to the tumult shaking five linked galaxies. Even the memoid herds were affected. He witnessed several great flocks darting to and fro, stampeding as both ground and sky rippled threateningly.

While his passengers stared in wonder, Harry set course for the Cosmic Path. He must find a portion that peered into Galaxy Four and set his instruments, as soon as possible. Fortunately, these new devices were disposable. He could leave them in place till they were destroyed. Their death cries would give Wer'Q'quinn's people vital data about the Great Rupture. This time, his boss promised, the information would be broadcast widely, not kept in secret files for use by elder races and star gods.

That was the main reason Harry agreed to this mission. It might seem odd to worry about events a hundred million years from now. But for some reason he identified with people in that distant era. Maybe his efforts would spare those folks some of the ignorant terror now sweeping Five Galaxies. Even if, by then, the 'gods' were distant heirs of chimpanzees, and the Navigation Institute of that future age was staffed by descendants of today's lice. The kind infesting his fur right now, making him constantly yearn to scratch his—

'*Captain Harms*,' said a whirling circular shape that appeared uncomfortably near his nose. '*I have news! Your goal should now lie in view. Congratulations! And may I add that it has been a real—*'

Harry cut off observer mode holo with a curt headshake. Hustling to a bank of windows, he peered past the ever-present E Space haze ... and caught sight of a thin, sinuous glow, twisting across the countryside just ahead.

'Well, something's going right, for a change,' he murmured.

While laying his instruments, he would find an appropriate site along the Path, put Kaa and the others in the corvette, and shove the little vessel into normal space – hopefully within reach of their destination. Harry might then have barely enough time to get back home to civilization before the whole place rocked and rolled.

Rety was adamant.

From the moment she got up – stumbling into the control chamber with a hand pressed to her head and the other stroking her little urrish 'husband' – Rety made one fact abundantly clear.

She was not returning to Jijo with Dwer and the others.

'*You* may be homesick for filth an' a bunch of low-tech barbarians, but if I never hear o' that place again, it'll be too soon! I'm going back with Harry.'

That was it. No gratitude for saving her life. No mention of her erstwhile religion, or inquiries about her late guru. Just a fierce determination that defied all opposition.

Even so young, she is formidable. I've met some humans with personalities this strong. All were worldshifters – for well or ill.

But most had one trait Rety lacked. They knew the pragmatic value of tact. Of course, she'd been raised by savages. In civilization, she might learn social skills, forge alliances, achieve aspirations, and possibly even be liked.

There was just one problem with her plan.

'I'll be honest, miss. There's a good chance I can get you all to the right quadrant of Galaxy Four. Maybe even the sector. But my own odds of survival after—'

Rety laughed. 'Don't tell me odds! I ain't worried 'bout odds since I was gored by a gallaiter, and given up by my own tribe for dead. Yee an' I are gonna stick right by your furry side, if you don't mind. And even if you do.'

The others were no help. Kaa used a spectral analyzer to peer into the Path – filled with dark nebulae and glittering stellar clusters – searching for the telltale blush of a particular stormy star. Kiwei occupied herself staring at the plain of memes, apparently trying to impose her will again, causing more shapes to appear.

Dwer's sole response was a rolling of eyes. He had no aim to intervene in Rety's life again.

'Oh, all right.' Harry sighed. 'Just promise you'll stay out of the way. And no whining about where you finally wind up!'

Rety nodded. 'So long as it ain't Jijo.'

A buzzer announced the dropping of another instrument package along the curving Path. With luck, Wer'Q'quinn's devices would be positioned well before the biggest chaos wave of all. Then it would be a matter of dropping Kaa and the others off near a mapped t-point and wishing them luck.

He offered Kiwei a chance to withdraw.

'You don't have to enter Galaxy Four. After the links snap, there'll be no more travel between—'

She raised a meaty hand, chuckling. 'Not more fairy tales about a permanent "rupture" please! Scout-Major, you've been misled. The Five Galaxies have always been—'

The station abruptly jolted to a halt. A shrill squeal made everyone turn as Kaa used his tail flukes to thump the pad of his walker.

'C-come!' the dolphin urged. 'Come and see thisssss!'

Harry and Kiwei hurried to join him at a bank of windows. Kaa used his neural tap to create a pointer ray, aimed toward the glittering Path.

'*There it isss!*' The pilot hissed clear, moist satisfaction. 'I found it!'

Dwer asked – 'Izmunuti?'

'Yesss! Just past that oblong cloud of ionized hydrogen. The spectral match is perfect. So are surrounding star formationssss.'

'Wow,' Dwer said. 'I think I can even make out a familiar constellation or two. All twisted, of course.'

Kaa raised a sleek gray head, chattering happily. And though Harry's Trinary was rusty, he caught the gist.

* *It would be enough to do my duty,*
    * *having helped the cause of Earthclan.*

  **It would be enough to rescue Peepoe,*
    * *and to spend a lifetime with her.*

  * *It would be enough to help save Jijo,*
    * *and to taste those silky waters.*

  * *All those things and many others,*
    * *would have let me face death happy.*

  * *But among those counted pleasures,*
    * *this means I reclaim my nickname!* *

Kiwei peered toward the vast sprawl of pinpoints.

'Then Jijo's sun . . . ?'

'Is right th-there!' Kaa turned a dark eye toward Harry. 'Major Harms, if you insert us here, how many paktaars would that leave us from—'

A sudden jab on the shoulder diverted Harry's attention. He swiveled to see Rety, holding her urrish companion in the crook of one arm. The little creature – her 'husband' – craned its long neck, peering at the Path.

'Uh, Major Harms, could we ask you a question?'

'Not right now, Rety. We're making an important decision.'

She nodded. 'I know. But yee just saw something you oughta look at.' She pointed along the sinuous tube, back the way they'd just come. 'There's stuff goin' on in there.'

Harry straightened. 'What do you mean?'

'I mean in the last few duras there's been three or four really bright . . . There goes another one!' She winced as a sudden glare hit her eye. 'Is that normal? Can stars get so shiny, all of a sudden? I figure you'd want to—'

'Observer mode!' Harry shouted. 'Scan the Path for sudden stellar bursts. Are they E-Space illusions, or is something real happening in Galaxy Four?'

The hovering symbol whirled for only a moment.

The outbursts have spectra and brightness profiles of unusually energetic, type SN1a supernova. Such explosions are known to affect the interfacial membrane that you call the Path.

'I can see that!' Harry snapped. The mammoth tube's stable sinuosity had started to move. It shivered and heaved near each sudden point of aching brightness.

'Safety parameters deem it prudent to retreat now from the boundary.'

Kiwei protested. 'But supernovas do not happen this way! Each is an isolated astrophysical event!'

'I don't like this,' Dwer added.

'Maybe we oughta do what the voice says,' Rety suggested. 'Back off. Head for civilized space. Take shelter on some planet till all this blows ov—'

'Forget it-t!' Kaa squalled. 'Harms, keep your promissss!'

Harry nodded. 'Okay. Everone who's going to Jijo, move through the airlock to the corvette. We'll need a few duras—'

His sentence cut off as another little blue star abruptly flared – this time just to their left, almost adjacent to the boundary – expanding its effulgence a billionfold, filling the cabin with blinding glare.

Lightspeed was no impediment to the causality disruption that followed. Some kind of metric wave hammered the fleshy inner surface of the Path, making it buck and heave like a tortured snake. The perimeter warped into E Space, discoloring horribly as new bulges formed, flailing like agonized pseudopods. Several of these curled around the station, lashing spasmodically.

It seemed a rather personal way to be assailed by a supernova. But Harry had no time to dwell on ironies of scale. 'Prepare for transition!' he croaked in a terrified voice.

All at once, the entire Path seemed to *shimmer*, and Harry knew that the estimates had been wrong.

The rupture is coming.

His passengers had just moments to grab some nearby object before the sidereal universe grabbed Harry's vessel with a horrid moan, yanking them all back into a realm of atoms.

SOL SYSTEM

Gillian knew just two living pilots who might stand a chance of maneuvering swiftly through spacial conditions like these.

Keepiru, and Kaa. Both had started out three years ago with Creideiki's carefully picked crew.

Now, both were gone. Each to where he was needed most.

Each to where he belonged.

Fly true, Keepiru. She cast the wish outward, past myriad random glimmering stars. *Wherever Tom and Creideiki decide to go, please guide them through to safe harbors.*

As for Kaa, she had felt guilty since pulling him away from Jijo, where Peepoe needed him. According to Sara's calculations, the route back to Galaxy Four would be perilous, demanding all his skill, as well as a generous helping of his famous luck.

I know you'll make it, Kaa. May you swim with Peepoe soon, and remain Ifni's favorite all your life.

Conditions elsewhere weren't quite as bad as in Galaxy Four. Yet, the remainder of civilized space was raucous and high-strung. The Navigation Institute kept posting detours till it ran out of buoys, then stationed gallant volunteers along every known route, shouting themselves hoarse over subspace frequencies, diverting traffic to a few safe paths. Flotillas set out from countless planets on daring mercy missions, braving maelstroms to rescue lost ships and stranded crews.

It was Galactic Civilization at its best – the reason it would almost certainly survive this chaos, and possibly emerge stronger than ever. After things settled down, that is. In a few thousand years.

Meanwhile, the four remaining galaxies were a mess. While many clans and races dropped their petty squabbles to lend a hand, others took advantage of the disorder to loot, extort, or settle old grudges. Religious schisms spread like poisonous ripples, amplifying ancient animosities.

And where is Streaker *heading, right now? Straight for the worst site of fanatical warfare, praying we get there before the fighting's over. Talk about jumping from the frying pan into the fire.*

At least Gillian had no complaints about *Streaker's* rate of speed. Right now, she probably had the fastest ship in all of oxygen-breathing civilization.

Not to put down Akeakemai, but without Keepiru or Kaa, this trip would have taken months, following the marked detours. We'd arrive at our destination only to find ashes.

So it's a good thing we had outside help.

That 'help' embraced the Earthship's bristly cylinder like a second skin – a blanket of shimmering tendrils that reached out to stroke the varied metric textures of the cosmic continuum, sensing and choosing course, speed, and level of subspace in order to make the best possible headway. Undaunted by warning buoys and danger signs, the semisapient coating steered *Streaker* along routes that flamed and whirled with tempests of unresolved hypergeometry, making snap transitions that would tax Keepiru at his best.

The great Transcendents might hate leaving their comfortable Embrace of Tides, seldom venturing from their black-hole event horizons to meddle in the destiny of lesser races. But their *servants* certainly knew how to fly. Perhaps this special treatment balanced some of *Streaker*'s awful luck during the last three years. But after narrowly escaping a supernova explosion, Gillian gave up tallying miracles – good, bad ... and simply weird.

Just get us home in time, she thought, whether or not a Transcendent might still be listening.

By the time *Streaker* passed the triple beacons of Tanith, Gillian knew the impossible was about to happen.

We're going to see Earth again ... though perhaps only from afar.

When golden Sol filled the view screen, they began encountering new warning buoys, laid down by a different bureaucracy.

BEWARE TRAVELERS!
YOU ARE ENTERING A CONFLICT ZONE
DULY REGISTERED UNDER THE RULES OF WAR!
YOU ARE ADVISED: RETURN TO TANITH AT ONCE!
IF YOU HAVE BUSINESS HERE,
INQUIRE WITH REPRESENTATIVES OF THE
INSTITUTE FOR CIVILIZED WARFARE
ABOUT A SAFE-CONDUCT PASS,
OR ELSE REGISTER AS YET ANOTHER
CO-BELLIGERENT FORCE
EITHER ALIGNED AGAINST THE TERRAN
DEFENDERS
OR FOR THEM.

THE FOLLOWING RACES/NATIONS/CLANS/ ALLIANCES
HAVE DECLARED VENDETTA-ENFORCEMENT
CAMPAIGNS
AGAINST THE OXY-LINEAGE KNOWN AS EARTHCLAN ...

It went on like that for a while, listing some of the factions who had laid siege to Gillian's homeworld – a long, intimidating roll call. Apparently, after years of bickering over who should get the privilege of conquering Earth, the Soro, Tandu, Jophur, and others had agreed to join forces and divide the spoils.

On the defending side, a tally of humanity's allies remained depressingly sparse. The Tymbrimi had remained true, at great cost. And the doughty Thennanin. Material aid – arms, but not fighters – had been smuggled in by p'ort'ls, zuhgs, and Synthians, as well as a faction of the Awaiter Alliance. And a new group, calling itself the *Acolytes*, had lately sent shiploads of volunteers.

The War Institute message went on to describe a long chain of protests, filed by the Soro and others, complaining about 'wolfling tricks' that had stymied several successive attempts to bring their warships within firing range of Earth, resulting in massive casualities and the loss of several dozen major capital vessels, all caused by weapons and tactics not found in the Galactic Library, and therefore suspiciously improper ways for folks to slay their own would-be murderers!

That part made Gillian chuckle proudly ... though apparently the Terragens Council was running out of 'tricks.' In fact, their forces were now reduced to a fiery ring, marked by Luna's orbit.

The Institute buoy finished by officially attesting that the rules of war had largely been adhered to as this conflict wound down to its inevitable conclusion.

'Some rules!' sniffed Suessi. In other eras, the War Institute had formalized combat to a relatively harmless sport, pitting professional champions against each other for privilege or honor. But under today's loose strictures – made almost unenforceable by recent chaos – the battle fleets infesting Earth could do almost anything. Gas its cities. Capture and 'adopt' its citizens. Anything except harm the planet's fragile biosphere. And even that might be overlooked as society unraveled.

There was some good news. Apparently, the so-called Coalition of Moderate Races had finally declared open opposition to the siege, gathering forces to compel a cease-fire. The first units might arrive in a few weeks, if they weren't held up by traffic snarls.

We've heard such promises before, Gillian thought bitterly.

The Niss reported that oddsmakers and bookies (who hardly paused doing business, despite the Great Rupture) gave Terrans little hope of lasting that long.

'Well, a lot has changed lately,' she told *Streaker*'s crew as they plunged toward the shell-of-battle surrounding their home star. 'Let's see if we can make a difference.'

Her plans remained flexible, depending on what conditions were like near Earth.

Perhaps it might be possible to break the siege by causing a distraction. After all, her ship was the great prize everyone had been chasing for so long. Word of *Streaker*'s discoveries in the Shallow Cluster had set off all this frenzy in the first place. Nor would that passion have abated, with the Great Rupture fresh in memory and apocalyptic prophecies crisscrossing civilization, more disruptive than chaos waves. While tumult still rattled every sector and quadrant, each dogmatic alliance would feel more anxious than ever to solve the Progenitors' Riddle before its rivals.

What if *Streaker* suddenly appeared before the besieging forces, confronting the attackers, taunting them, and then turning to flee across a turbulent galaxy? Might that draw the battle fleets away, buying Earth much-needed time? With luck, it could reignite strife between the Tandu and other radical factions, winnowing their ranks so the timid 'moderates' might at last intervene.

Such a move might seem to conflict with Gillian's orders from the Terragens Council. Those instructions had been to hide. Above all, not to let Creideiki's data fall into the wrong hands. *Streaker* should surrender the information only to qualified impartial agencies, or else when the people of the Five ... rather, *Four* Galaxies, could agree how to share it.

Well, I've taken care of that! What agency could be more 'qualified and neutral' than the merged community that took over the former Jophur battleship, Polkjhy? A consortium of emissaries from several life orders, picked by the Transcendents to represent our entire macro-culture to some far-distant realm?

All the Ghost Fleet samples, including Herbie the enigmatic cadaver, were now aboard that transformed starship, racing far beyond reach of even the most dogged zealot. Perhaps some far-distant alien civilization would be suitably impressed, or even be able to answer questions about the enigma.

All that remains from the Shallow Cluster is a set of coordinates. And those are in a safe place.

Heady sensations filled Gillian's chest. She recognized the source.

Freedom.

Along with *Streaker*'s remaining crew, she now felt liberated of an awful burden. A weight of importance that used to hang on them all like a shroud, requiring that they slink and hide, like prey. Too valuable to be brave.

But that had changed.

We are soldiers now. That is all.

Soldiers of Earthclan.

HYPERSPACE

Everything unraveled after the great rupture. All the wonderful structure – the many-layered textures of spacetime – began coming apart.

*

Wer'Q'quinn's experts had warned Harry. Recoil effects would be far worse in Galaxy Four, when all its ancient links to other spirals snapped and most transfer points collapsed. Additionally, all the known levels of hyperspace – A through E – would come more or less unfastened, like skins sloughing off a snake, and largely go their own way.

Not only have I lost any hope of going home, he thought during the wild ride that followed. *We may all be stuck forever in some pathetic corner of a single spiral arm. Perhaps even a solar system!*

That assumed they even made it safely back to normal space.

Harry's station shuddered and moaned. All the louvered blinds rattled in their frames, while unnerving cracks began working their way through the thick crystal panes. Just outside, a maze of transfer threads churned like tormented worms, whipping in terminal agony, Spaciogeometric links, robbed of their moorings, now snapped violently, slicing and shredding each other to bits.

This seemed a frightfully bad time to try evading the speed of light with shortcuts that had been routine for eons. Cheating Einstein had become a perilous felony.

It might have been safer simply to drop to normal space and ride out the aftershocks near some star with a habitable fallow planet. Worst case – if FTL travel became impossible – at least they might have a place to land. But Kaa would have none of that. Almost from the moment they dropped out of E Space, the dolphin took over control, ditching the now useless corvette, and sent Harry's station careening through a nearby transfer point – a dying maelstrom – desperately scouring for a route to the one place he called home.

Harry had never seen piloting so brilliant – or half so mad. His stubby station was hardly a sport-skimmer, yet Kaa threw the vessel into swooping turns, hopping among the radiant threads like some doped-up gibbon, brachiating through a burning forest, throwing its weight from one flaming vine to the next. Kaa's tail repeatedly slapped the flotation pad. The dolphin's eyes were sunken and glazed while floods of information poured through his neural tap. A ratchet of sonar clicks sprayed from the high-domed skull, sometimes merging to form individual words.

Peepoe was one Harry heard often. Having done his duty for *Streaker* and Earth, Kaa had just one priority – to reach his beloved.

Harry sympathized. *I just wish he asked me before taking us on this insane ride!*

No one dared break Kaa's concentration. Even Rety kept silent, nervously stroking her little urrish husband. Kiwei Ha'aoulin crouched, muttering to herself in a Synthian dialect, perhaps wishing she had listened to the inner voice of caution rather than greed.

Only Dwer seemed indifferent to fear. The young hunter braced his back against the control console, and one foot on a nearby window, leaving both hands free to polish his bow while a Gordian knot of cosmic strings unraveled spectacularly outside.

Well, I guess anything can seem anticlimactic, Harry thought. *After watching a whole chain of supernovas go off at once – and having the Path seize you like some agonized monster – one might get jaded with something as mundane as a conflagration in hyperspace.*

Kaa pealed a yammering cry, sending the station plunging toward a huge thread whose loose end lashed, shuddering and spraying torrents of horrid sparks! Rety shouted. Vertigo roiled Harry's guts, threatening to void his bowels. He covered his eyes, bracing for impact . .

. . . and swayed when nothing happened.

Not even a vibration. Around him stirred only a low chucker of engines, gently turning over.

Both fearful and curious, Harry lowered his hands.

Stars shone, beyond the pitted glass. Patterns of soft lights. Stable. Permanent.

Well, almost. One patch twinkled oddly, as a wave of warped metric rippled past. Tapering chaos disturbances, still causing the vacuum to shiver. Still, how much better this seemed than that awful pit of sparking serpents!

Behind the station, receding rapidly, lay the transfer point they had just exited, marked by flashing red symbols.

DO NOT ENTER, blazoned one computer-generated icon.

NEXUS TERMINALLY DISRUPTED.

CONDITIONS LETHAL WITHIN.

I can believe that, Harry thought, vowing to embrace Kaa, the first chance he got . . . and to *shoot* the pilot if he tried to enter another t-point like that one.

In the opposite direction, growing ever larger, stood the red disk of a giant star.

'Izmunuti?' Harry guessed.

Kaa was still chattering to himself. But Dwer gave an emphatic nod.

'I'd know it anywhere. Though the storms seem to've settled since the last time we passed this way.'

Rety reacted badly to this news.

'No!' Her fists clenched toward Harry. 'You promised I wouldn't have to go back! Turn this ship around. Take me back to civilization!'

'I don't think you grasp the problem,' he replied. 'At this rate, we'd be lucky to reach *any* habitable world. Clearly, the nearest one is—'

The young woman covered her ears. 'I won't listen. I won't!'

He looked to Dwer, who shrugged. Rety's aggrieved rejection of reality reminded Harry of a race called *episiarchs*, clients of the mighty Tandu, who could somehow use psi – plus sheer force of ego – to change small portions of the universe around them, transforming nearby conditions more to their liking. Some savants theorized that all it took was a strong enough will, plus a high opinion of yourself. If so, Rety might hurl them megaparsecs from this place, so desperate was she *not* to see the world of her birth.

Kaa lifted his bottle-nosed head. The pilot's black eye cleared as he made an announcement. 'We c-can't stay here. Jijo is still over a light-year away. That'll take at least a dozen jumps through A Space. Or fifffty ... if we use Level B.'

Harry recalled predictions made by the Kazzkark Navigation staff – that the rupture would make all hyperlevels much harder to use. In Galaxy Four, they might detach completely and flutter away, leaving behind the glittering blackness of normal space, an Einsteinian cosmos, where cause and effect were ruled strictly by the crawling speed of light.

But that peeling transition would not come instantly. Perhaps the rapid layers could still be used, for a while at least.

'Try B Space,' he suggested. 'I have a hunch we may need to drop out quickly and often along the way.'

Kaa tossed his great head.

'Okay. It's your ship-p. B Space it issss ... '

With that hiss of finality, the pilot turned his attention back through the neural tap, to a realm where his uncanny cetacean knack might be their only hope.

Harry felt the station power up for the first jump.

I'd pray, he thought. *If creation itself weren't already moaning in pain.*

Almost from the start, they saw disturbing signs of ruin – debris of numerous space vessels, wrecked as they had tried following exactly the same course, flicker-jumping from Izmunuti toward Jijo.

'Some folks passed this way before us,' Dwer commented.

'And quite recently, by all appearances.' Kiwei's voice was awed. 'It seems that an entire fleet of large vessels came through. They must have been caught in hyperspace when the Rupture struck.'

The results were devastating. As Izmunuti fell away behind them, and Jijo's sun grew steadily brighter, Harry's instruments showed appalling remnants of a shattered armada, some of the hulks still glowing from fiery dismemberment.

'I make out at least two basic ship types,' he diagnosed, peering into the analytical scope. 'One of 'em might be Jophur. The other ... I can't tell.'

In fact, it was hard to get a fix on anything, because their own vessel kept heaving and shuddering. Kaa yanked the station back into normal space whenever his fey instincts told him that a new chaos wave was coming, or when a flapping crease in B Level threatened to fold over itself and smash anything caught between.

Crossing this unstable zone of hyperreality – a rather short span by earlier standards – became a treacherous series of mad sprints that got worse, dura by dura. Each flicker seemed to take greater concentration than the last, demanding more from the gasping engines. And yet, there could be no pause for rest. It was essential to reenter hyperspace as soon as possible, for at any moment B Level might detach completely, leaving them stranded, many light months from any refuge. Food and air would give out long before Harry's small group might traverse such a vast distance of flat metric.

Too bad we Earthlings never pursued our early knack at impulse rocketry, after making contact with the Civilization of Five Galaxies. It seemed the most ridiculous of all wolfling technologies, to make ships capable of brute-force acceleration toward lightspeed. With so many cheap shortcuts available from the Great Library, who needed such a tool kit of outlandishly extravagant tricks?

The answer was apparent.

We do. Anyone who wants to travel around Galaxy Four may need them, from now till the end of time.

At least there were clear signs of progress. Each jump brought them visibly closer to that warm, sturdy sun. Yet, the tense moments passed with aching slowness, as they followed a rubble-strewn trail of devastated starcraft.

'I guess that Jophur battleship must have got word to their head-quarters, while it was off chasing *Streaker*,' Dwer concluded. 'Their reinforcements arrived at the worst moment, just in time to be smashed by the Rupture.'

'We should rejoice,' mused Kiwei. 'I have no wish to live in a Jophur satrapy.'

'Hmph,' Harry commented. 'That assumes all of their fleet was caught in hyperspace during the worst of it. For all we know, a whole squadron may have made it safely. They could be waiting for us at Jijo.'

It was a dismal prospect – to have endured so much, only to face capture at the end by humorless stacks of uncompromising sap-rings.

'Well,' Dwer said, after a few more edgy jumps, when the yellow star was already looking quite sunlike. 'We won't have long to wait now.'

He pressed close to the forwardmost window, as eager to spy Jijo as Rety was to evade the verdict of destiny.

The solar system was littered with wreckage from more than two years of seesaw fighting – shattered reminders of stiff wolfling resistance that surely came as a rude shock to invaders expecting easy conquest. Fourthhand tales of that savage struggle had reached *Streaker*'s crew, even at the remote Fractal World. Apparently, the defense was already the stuff of legends.

Ion clouds and rubble traced the inward path of that fighting retreat ... vaporized swathes in the cometary ice belt ... still-smoldering craters on Triton and Nereid ... and several asteroid-sized clumps of twisted metal, tumbling in orbit beyond Uranus.

It must have been quite a show. Sorry I missed it.

More debris was added recently, when the Great Rupture struck. Ships that tried any kind of FTL maneuvering during the causality storm had been lucky to reach normal space again with more consistency than an ice slurpie. Saturn's orbit was now a glittering junkyard, soon to become a vast ring around the sun.

Unfortunately, long-range scans showed more than enough big vessels left to finish the job. Scores of great dreadnoughts – several of them titans compared to the enormous *Polkjhy* – gathered in martial formations along the new battlefront, all too near Earth's shimmering blue spark.

The first picket boats hailed *Streaker* well beyond the orbit of Ceres. A bizarre, mixed squadron consisting of corvettes and frigates from the Tandu, Soro, and gorouph navies, joined in uneasy federation. They were alert, despite the havoc that residual chaos waves still played on instruments. When *Streaker* ignored their challenge and kept plunging rapidly sunward, the nearest ships raced closer to open fire with deadly accuracy.

Blades of razorlike force scythed at the Earthship – only to glance off its transmuted hull. Heat beams were absorbed quietly, with no observable effect, dissipating harmlessly into another level of spacetime.

If these failures fazed the enemy, they did not show it openly. Rushing closer, several lead vessels launched volleys of powerful, intelligent missiles, hurtling toward *Streaker* at great speed. According to Suessi, this was the worst threat. Direct energy weapons had little effect on the Transcendent's coating. But *physical shock* could disrupt anything made of matter, if it came hard and fast enough, in a well-timed sequence of shaped concussions.

As if aware of that danger, *Streaker*'s sapient outer layer suddenly became active. Tendrils fluttered, like cilia surrounding a bacterium. Swarms of tiny objects flew off their waving tips, darting to meet the incoming barrage. Under extreme magnification, the strange interceptors looked like tiny pockets of writhing protoplasm, jet-black, but disconcertingly alive.

'*Reified concepts,*' explained the disembodied Niss Machine, sounding awed and unnerved. '*Destructive programs, capable of making a machine terminally self-hostile. They don't even have to enter computers as data, but can do so by physical contact.*'

'You're talking about freestanding memes!' Gillian replied. 'I thought they can't exist here in real space, without a host to carry—'

'*Apparently, we're wrong abou that.*' The Niss shrugged with its funnel of spinning lines. '*Remember, Transcendents are a melding of life orders. They are part meme, themselves.*'

She nodded, willing to accept the incredible.

The expanding memic swarm collided with the incoming barrage, but effects and outcomes weren't evident at first. Tension filled *Streaker*'s bridge, as the missiles continued on course for several more seconds ...'

... only to veer abruptly aside, missing the Earthship and spiraling off manically before igniting in flashy torrents of brilliance, lighting up the asteroid belt.

The dolphins exulted, but Gillian quashed any celebratory thoughts as premature. She recalled a warning, from the Transcendent being who had visited her office.

'*Do not be deceived by illusions of invulnerability. You have been given advantages. But they are limited.*

'*It would be wise to recall that you are* not *gods.*

'*Not yet, that is ...*'

Indeed, Gillian wasn't counting on a thing. Soon, the enemy would learn not to send mere robots against a ship defended by hordes of predatory ideas. Or else they would attack with overwhelming numbers.

Still, I guess the ends justify the memes, she thought, raising a brief, ironic smile. Tom would have liked the pun – a real groaner.

Right now, in the heat of battle, she missed him with a pang that felt fresh, as if years and kiloparsecs meant nothing, and their parting had been yesterday.

The next line of ships – destroyers – had little more effect. A few of their missiles managed to detonate nearby, but not in a coordinated spread. *Streaker*'s protective layers dealt with the flux.

When Akeakemai asked for permission to fire back, Gillian refused.

'We might damage a few,' she said. 'But they'd notice our offensive capacity is tiny, compared to defense. I'd rather leave them guessing we're equally formidable, both ways. *So* formidable, we can afford to ignore them.'

Of course it was all part of a bluff she had worked out. Her greatest one yet.

A new force rose to meet *Streaker* – this time consisting of sleek, powerful cruisers. Meanwhile, the giant dreadnoughts near Earth began changing formation, arranging themselves into a hollow shell, its cusp aimed toward Gillian's ship. Loudspeakers groaned, twittered and beeped in several formal languages, as commanders of the united fleet beamed a final warning.

IDENTIFY YOURSELF, OR BE DESTROYED.

She wondered.

After all this time, hounding us to every far corner of the Five Galaxies, have we really changed so much that you don't recognize your intended prey – coming now to beard you in your den?

Gillian decided.

It's time to end the silence. Answer their beamed challenge with one of our own.

Pressing a lever, she unleashed her prerecorded message – one that had drawn her entire concentration ever since *Streaker* dived into that cool black tunnel milliseconds ahead of a supernova's fist. It was inspired partly by her own interview with the transcendent being.

More than one can play games of illusion, she had thought. Of all the tricks pulled by her godlike visitor, the one that impressed her *least* had been that showy series of visual poses, mimicking everyone from Tom and Jake Demwa to Hikahi and Creideiki.

Mirages are a dime a dozen.

If Earthlings possessed any craft that was equal to the best Galactic technology, it lay in the art of manipulating optic images.

The play began with one of her oldest disguises – one she routinely used to fool *Streaker*'s stolen Library unit.

Appearing suddenly in the holo tank, a stern Thennanin admiral strode forth, preening his elbow and shoulder spikes, puffing up his extravagant head-crest, and clearing his vents with a deep *harrrumph*, before commencing to speak in stately, formal Galactic Six, addressing his remarks to those besieging Earth.

'Brethren! Fellow high patrons of starfaring civilization and descendants of the Great Progenitors! I come before you now at a crucial juncture of choice. You, along with all your clients and clan mates, may profit or suffer because of decisions made during this nexus of opportunity.

'The time has come to look past blinders of false belief. Your presence here (which my clan had the great wisdom to resist) is

anathema to destiny. It brings you nothing but cascading sorrow, replenished from an inexhaustible supply of hardship that the universe willingly provides the obstinate!'

It really was a very good Thennanin, quite pompous and credible. But credibility – even plausibility – wasn't the point here.

No, it was the sheer *effrontery* of this ruse that should gall them. Her ersatz admiral continued.

'Consider the facts, misguided brethren.
'Number one.
'To whom did the Progenitors reveal relics of great-and-profound value?
'To you? Or even to the Old Ones you revere?'

While speaking those words, the Thennanin started to *melt*, shifting and reconfiguring in a much more gaudy and disturbing manner than the Transcendent had. (Her visitor's intent had been to focus Gillian's thoughts, while her aim right now was to frighten . . . then enrage.)

The big admiral finished transforming into a quite different entity that now floated in midair, glossy and gray, resembling Captain Creideiki at his most handsome and charismatic, before an accident permanently scarred his handsome sleek head.

'No they did not! The Progenitors did not disclose hidden truths to you, or to any noble clan or alliance!
'In fact, the Ghost Fleet was revealed to one such as this!'

Creideiki's image thrashed its tail flukes for emphasis.

'A member of the youngest of all client races. A race whose talents would have made any senior patron eager to adopt them, yet who proudly call themselves members of wolfling Earthclan!
'Next, consider yet another fact. The way the Earthship, Streaker, *evaded all your searches and clever schemes to capture it! Even when you bribed and suborned the Great Institutes, did such acts of treasonous cheating avail you at all?'*

The figure began shifting again, continuing, sotto voce, with teasing GalSix undertones.

('Tell me, brethren. Have you begun to guess the identity of the vessel now plummeting toward you, laughingly defiant of your vaunted power?

'Do you need more clues? You shall have them!')

A male human shape replaced Creideiki. She had tried using Tom as a model, but that proved too hard. So she settled on old Jake Demwa ... which was probably a good idea anyway. The Soro would instantly recognize him from two centuries of frustration, when he had proved their bane on numerous occasions.

'Fact three: Despite great wealth and innumerable lives spent sub-duing the Terrans' homeworld, what have you accomplished here, except to make their legend grow? Even on the verge of apparent suc-cess, can you be certain this is not yet another ruse? A trick, meant to draw in your reserves? To make their unexpected triumph seem all the greater in others' eyes?

'Even if you win, and the last human lies dead – with every dol-phin and chimp readopted by some humorless clan – will you withstand the vengeance others may then take upon you, in the name of martyred Earth?

'Ask yourselves this. Might these wolflings rise even stronger, out of death? Either in fact, or else in a flood of new ideas? Ideas that will span the New Era to come, diverting Galactic culture down paths you can't imagine?'

Streaker shuddered. The lights flickered. On other screens, Gillian glimpsed a brief, violent, one-sided battle, as the cruiser flotilla fired volleys while sweeping past.

Either they were getting a knack for using dumbed-down brains in their missiles or there were simply too many, this time. For whatever reason, about a dozen got through, detonating uncom-fortably close.

Suessi gave a thumbs-up sign, indicating the pattern wasn't focused enough to be dangerous. But it showed the limits of their defense.

Just so long as the enemy can't tell. Let them think we're just shrugging it all off, for a bit longer.

In the holo tank, Jake Demwa faded into another shape – one of the elder races *Streaker* encountered at the vast, chilly habitat called the Fractal World. Without pause, that stark visage contin-ued the soliloquy.

'Or take fact number four: Did any of you foretell the Great Rupture? So conservative were you all, so trusting of your own elders, that you had no idea the Old Ones were manipulating the Great Library, and the other Institutes! For their own reasons, they kept the Civilization

of Five Galaxies ignorant. We had no inkling to prepare, or that this sort of massive spatiotemporal breakup has happened before!

'Yet, a warning did come. Even while beset by attackers, the Terrans did their citizenly duty, broadcasting an alert based upon their alternative mathematics.

'Is it a coincidence that great harm befell those who ignored the warning? Those blinded by their contempt for wolfling science, who chose obstinate ideology over pragmatism?'

('Have you guessed yet, brethren? Have ye figured out who streaks toward you now? Insolent. Heedless of the reverence you feel yourselves due? Can you sniff/sense/ feel/grok the very thing you covet . . . and secretly fear?')

Cruisers fell in behind *Streaker*, cutting off retreat. Looming just ahead, the unified armada of capital ships left their siege positions to meet this challenge, spreading to envelop and enclose the impudent newcomer in an inescapable mesh of fire.

'They're talking to each other,' informed the Niss Machine. *'From battleship to battleship. A lot more discussion than you'd expect for warships going into a fight. It's coded, but I can tell it is pretty heated.*

'Is it possible they don't understand your hints and clues, Dr. Baskin? Perhaps you've been too coy. Shall we go ahead and tell them who we are?'

She shook her head.

'Relax. They're probably just arguing over how best to kill us.'

Streaker had one hope. This kind of envelopment pattern meant the enemy must concentrate their volleys into a very narrow zone, or else risk damaging each other. If the Earthship could create *uncertainty* over its exact position, that might result in a focused blast that was offset just enough, so their Transcendent-shell would not be overwhelmed. Then, amid the blinding aftermath, *Streaker* would swerve away and run for it! With any luck, this amazing survival would make the enemy pause long enough for a good head start . . . before the entire fleet came baying after her.

The aim was simple: to buy time, giving Earth a brief respite – a chance to quickly rearm the Luna fortresses – and possibly get a few mothers and children away before the end.

'They are p-preparing to fire!' announced the detection officer, who then squealed a warning in Primal Delphin.

'Here come sharkssss!'

Gillian felt palpable twinges go off in her mind as several hundred speedy missiles leaped from launching tubes, arming themselves as they raced toward *Streaker*. At this range, many would carry psi and probability warheads, as well as annihilation charges.

Streaker's protective shell cast forth swarms of countermemes, but this time the effort would clearly be inadequate.

'You know what to do,' she told Akeakemai, trusting her life to his skill. This was not a job for a pilot but for a gifted geometro-dynamics engineer.

Lacking anything else to do while waiting for obliteration, Gillian turned back to the scene playing out within the holo tank – the same message being watched on the command deck of every battleship.

The last of her simulated Old Ones started to dissolve.

And yet – (copying tricks she had learned from the Transcendent) – the voice went on, using tones that were intentionally infuriating, patronizing, and serenely confident.

'Can you see the symbol on this vessel's prow? Is it the familiar emblem of five spiral rays? Or has something else taken its place? Can you recognize the nature of our new shell?

'And yet, by now your scans also show the ancient, mundane hull within. The Earthling figures of our crew.

'Well? Can your minds resolve this anomaly? This dissonance? Is there an explanation?'

The image in the tank reformed at last, taking a shape she had recorded during her interview with the Transcendent. A form that was sure to spoil the enemy's composure.

If just one glimpse of Herbie – a billion-year-old mummy – had thrown half the fanatics in five galaxies into a tizzy, what would the mummy's reconstructed likeness do? Emulated in apparently living flesh, the faintly amphibian humanoid now offered an enigmatic smile that broadened to uncanny width, conveying a touch of cruel empathy.

'Come now, foolish youngsters. Surely you can draw conclusions from what lies before your very—'

Akeakemai interrupted with a squeal.

'Impact in ninety secondsss! Let's do it-t!'

Gillian blinked as *Streaker*'s engines let out a wail of exertion, yanking the ship out of normal space.

Too bad, she thought, regretting that it had happened quite so soon. *I wanted to watch the show once through, all the way to the end.*

*

In theory, you could dodge enemies by jumping into hyperspace.

Unfortunately, that idea was older than a lot of stars. The arts of war had long ago adapted to such tactics. When *Streaker* jumped, so did the pack of onrushing missiles, which had no trouble sensing which way she headed.

Akeakemai played the engines swiftly, sending their old Snark-class survey ship leaping *laterally* among the known strata that still overlay Galaxy Two.

Unlike Galaxy Four, the varied levels of hyperspace were still accessible here, though with greater difficulty than before. Gillian was counting on that difference now to disrupt the timing of the incoming barrage. With any luck, there might also be chaos waves – aftershocks from the Great Rupture – to warp space and confuse the death machines.

Alas, it did not take long to realize – she had committed the worst sin of any commander. Assuming her enemies were stupid.

In B Space, where all stars turned into midget rainbows, the detection officer yelled dismay.

'Mines! They've filled the place with —'

Akeakemai was swift, triggering a second jump, but not before several nearby objects detonated, slamming *Streaker* with shock waves, even as the ship flickered over to A Space.

The strange-familiar sensations of that speedy realm crowded around Gillian, as if each direction she turned became a *tunnel*, offering a shortcut beyond some far horizon. Down each of those tubes, there glowed the disk of a single majestic, spinning sun.

'Fifty seconds,' murmured Hannes Suessi, mostly to himself.

'More mines!' came the rapid cry ... unneeded, as a drumbeat of savage thuds rocked the ship, straining the energy-absorbing power of *Streaker*'s new shell. Excess heat brought sweat popping from Gillian's skin.

In our old form, we'd be vapor by now, she thought during the agonized moment it took to flick into D Space.

It was a lousy place to look for shortcuts. Everything looked *far away*, as if you were peering through the wrong end of a telescope.

Unfortunately, D Space was also inhabited, by members of the Quantum life order – glimmering half-shapes whose outlines grew more vague the closer you looked at them. A multitude of these amorphous beings suddenly converged on *Streaker* the moment she appeared.

'Our enemies must have hired local allies to guard this back door.' The Niss Machine sounded bemused by such clever thoroughness.

Gillian saw chunks of the transcendent coating evaporate under this new attack.

'They're mostly small craft – lifeboats, scouts, shuttles. Survivors, I guess, from those fleets who got torn up in B Space, during the Rupture.' He paused, pulling nervously on both thumbs. 'They're headin' for the only refuge in sight. The same place we are.'

Dwer blew a long sigh. 'So, even if the Commons managed to get rid of the Jophur garrison while we were away, the danger isn't over.'

Harry nodded. By standards of his former civilization, the oncoming forces were pathetic and weak. Some of the lifeboats would not make it. Others would burn in Jijo's atmosphere. Still, the remnant would be far more than his little station could stave off. Soon, the Jijoans would face real troubles.

And, he realized, the coming confrontation could have long-lasting repercussions.

Unless there were other sooner outposts, hidden on fallow planets elsewhere in Galaxy Four, this may be the one place where oxygen breathers exist with knowledge and experience of starfaring.

Even if hyperspace is completely cut off, a culture will someday expand outward from Jijo. That culture may fill this entire galaxy, starting a new tradition of Uplift when it comes across promising species along the way.

The implications chilled Harry.

Whoever wins control of Jijo, this year, may establish the morality – the whole social ethos – of that star-spanning civilization to come.

Harry had already been willing to give his life for one community. Now, it seemed there would be no rest. Before even partaking of Jijo's food and air, he must decide to become part of this new world and take on its troubles as his own.

From what I've heard, this Commons of Six Races was a pretty impressive bunch. If Dwer and Rety – and Alvin and Ur-ronn – are any indication, the Jijoans will put up a stiff fight.

He patted the console of his trusty old station.

Maybe we can help just a bit, eh?

Their approach spiral took them over Jijo's dark side, below a big moon that Dwer identified as 'Loocen.' Harry exclaimed when he spied a line of bright sparkles along the day-night boundary. Glistening *cities* shone in a long crescent across the airless surface. Then he realized.

Reflections. Sunlight, that's all it is, caught at an angle as dawn creeps across the lunar surface. The domes are silent, lifeless. They have been ever since the fabled Buyur departed – how long ago? Half a million years?

Still, he admitted. *It is a pretty sight. And maybe someday—*

A piping cry made Harry turn around.

Rety was standing by a far window, obstinately refusing to look at the soft beauty of her homeworld. Sullen, with arms crossed, she ignored repeated calls from her 'husband,' the miniature, male urs called yee. The little centauroid stood on the windowsill, prancing with all four delicate feet, reaching out with his long neck to nip Rety's shoulder, then gesture at the view outside.

'look, wife! look at this sight!'

'I seen it before,' she muttered sourly. 'Scenery. Mountains an' bushes an' dirt. Lots of dirt. No 'lectricity or computers, but all the *dirt* you could ever want to—'

'not scenery!' yee interrupted. *'turn and see fireworks!'*

Rety stayed obdurate. But others hurried to find out what the little fellow meant. 'Douse interior lights,' Harry ordered so glare from the observation deck would not drown the view outside.

Jijo's night stretched below, a dark coverlet that might come ablaze with city lights within a few generations, no matter who won the coming battle. Now, though, the expanse showed no visible sign of sapience that Harry could detect, even with instruments. *Well, the Six Races have been hiding for a long time*, he thought. *They must be good at it by now.*

It was interesting to imagine what kind of starfaring civilization might arise out of the Jijoan Commons, with its fervent traditions of environmental protection and tolerance, and yet an easygoing individualism when it came to endeavor and new ideas. Something pretty interesting, assuming it survived the coming crisis.

At first, Harry saw nothing to justify yee's excitement. Then Dwer nudged him, pointing to the right.

'Look. A spark.'

'How pretty,' Kiwei commented.

It *did* look like a flickering ember, blown upward from a camp-fire, wafting – gently and very slowly – out from that thin film of atmosphere into the black sky above.

'Observer mode,' Harry commanded. 'Zero in on the anomaly I'm looking at, and magnify.'

The computer scanned his eyes, judged the focus of his attention, and complied. A holo image erupted, showing the strangest object Harry had ever seen, despite years spent exploring the weird memic corners of E Space.

A long, slender tube hurtled upward pointy-end first ... and from its tail poured gouts of white-hot fire.

'It ... looks like a burning *tree!*' Kiwei murmured in amazement.

'Not a tree,' Dwer corrected. 'It's boo!'

Curiosity finally overcame Rety, who turned around at last –

barely in time to see the flame go out. While the slim missile coasted for several seconds, Harry's instruments measured its size, which was many times bigger than his station!

Abruptly, the pencil-shaped object split in half. The rear portion tumbled away, still smoldering, while the front part erupted anew from its aft end.

Kiwei uttered hushed perplexity.

'But, what natural phenomenon could—'

'*not natural, silly raccoon!*' yee cried. '*boo rocket made by urs-hooman-traekis! shoot rocket high to welcome Rety-yee home!*'

Harry blinked, twice. Then he grinned.

'Well, I'll be. That's what it is, all right. A multistage rocket made of hollowed-out tree trunks . . . or whatever you call 'em, Dwer.'

He called again to the computer. 'Zoom in at the front terminus. The part that's farthest from the flames.'

Like the tip of a spear, that end flared a bit before tapering to a point. It rotated slowly, along with the rest of the crude rocket.

A brief glint told them everything. A pane of some kind of glass. A pale light shining from within. And a pair of brief silhouettes. A snakelike neck. A crablike claw.

Then Harry's station swerved, making everyone stumble. Kaa reported they were entering the planet's atmosphere.

'T-time to buckle up-p!' the pilot commanded. Soon, a different kind of flame would surround them. If they survived the coming plummet, it would not be long before their feet stood on solid ground.

Yet, Harry and the others remained transfixed for a moment longer, watching the rocket as long as possible. The computer calculated its estimated trajectory, and reported that it seemed aimed at Jijo's biggest moon.

At last, Rety commented. She stomped her feet on the deck, but this time it was no tantrum – only an expression of pure joy.

'Uttergloss!' she cried. 'Do you know what this means?'

Harry and Dwer both shook their heads.

'It means I'm not trapped on Jijo! It means there's a way *off* that miserable dirtball. And you can bet your grampa's dross barrel that I'm gonna use it.'

Her eyes seemed to shine with the same light as that of the flickering ember, till their orbital descent took it out of sight. Even when Harry ushered her to a seat and belted her in for landing, Rety's wiry frame throbbed with longing, and the grim inexorability of her ambition.

'I'll do whatever it takes.

'I'm headin' *out* again, just as fast an' as far as this grubby ol' universe lets me.'

Harry nodded agreeably. One of the last things he ever wanted to be was someone standing in Rety's way.

'I'm sure you will,' he said without the slightest doubt or patronizing tone of voice.

Soon the windows licked with fire as Jijo reached out to welcome them.

HOME

Terrible wounds marred the haggard vessel as it prepared to drop back into normal space. Most of *Streaker's* stasis flanges hung loose, or had vaporized. The rotating gravity wheel was half melted into the hull.

As for the protective sheathing which had safeguarded the crew – that gift of the Transcendents now sparked and unraveled, writhing away its last, like some dying creature with a brave soul.

Gillian mourned for its lost friendship. As she had mourned other misfortunes. And now, for the loss of hope.

Our plan was to avoid destruction, leading the enemy on a wild chase away from Earth.

Our foes planned to thwart and destroy us.

It looks like we each got half of what we wanted. Suessi was down in the engine room, working alongside Emerson and the rest of their weary team, trying to restore power. As things stood, the ship had barely enough reserve energy to reach the one level of space where there weren't swarms of mines – or other deadly things – converging from all sides.

No, we're headed back to face living *enemies. Oxy-beings, just like us.*

At least it should be possible to surrender to the battleships, and see her crew treated as prisoners of war. Assuming the victors did not instantly start fighting over the spoils.

Of course, Gillian couldn't let herself be captured. The information in her head must not fall into enemy hands.

She let out a deep sigh. The ninety-second battle had been awfully close. Her tactics had almost worked. Each time a mine went off, or a quantum horde attacked, or a chaos aftershock passed through, it disrupted the neat volley of converging missiles, shoving their careful formations, reducing their numbers, until the detonation – when it occurred – was off center. Inefficient.

Even so, it was bad enough.

As *Streaker* finished its last, groaning transition into the normal vacuum of home space, surrounded by clouds of blinding debris, she knew the grand old vessel could not defeat a corvette, or an armed lifeboat, let alone the armada awaiting them.

'Please transmit the truce signal,' she ordered. 'Tell them we'll discuss terms for surrender.'

The Niss Machine's dark funnel bowed, a gesture of solemn respect.

'*As you wish, Dr. Baskin. It will be done.*'

While the hardworking bridge crew worked to replace burned-out modules, all the monitors were blinded by a haze of ionized detritus and radiation. The first objects to emerge from the fog were a pair of large gravity wells – modest dimples in spacetime.

Earth and Luna ... she realized. *We came so close.*

Soon other things would show up on the gravity display, objects rivaling moons, majestic in power.

The tense moment harkened Gillian back across the years to the discovery of the Ghost Fleet, so long ago, when she and Tom had been so young and thrilled to be exploring on behalf of Earthclan, in company with their friend Creideiki. It had looked a bit like this. A haze surrounded them as *Streaker* worked its way slowly through a dense molecular cloud, in that far-off place called the Shallow Cluster.

An interstellar backwater.

A place where there should not have been anything to interest starfaring beings.

Yet, the captain had a hunch.

And soon, emerging through the mist, they glimpsed ...

Nothing.

Gillian blinked as stark, astonishing reality yanked her back to the present. A nervous murmur crossed the bridge as crew members stared in disbelief at emptiness.

Laboring mightily, *Streaker*'s wounded engines managed to pull the ship free of its own dross cloud, clearing the haze far enough to reveal more of nearby space.

There was no sign of any vast, enclosing formation.

No fleet of mighty battleships.

'But ... I ...'

Gillian stopped, unable to finish the sentence. Someone else had to complete the thought.

'Where did everybody go?' asked Sara Koolhan, whose hand clutched Prity's with a grip that looked white and sweaty.

No one answered. How could they? What was there to say?

Silence reigned for several minutes while sensors probed gradually farther.

'There's a lot of debris, but I don't see any big vessels within a cubic astron of here,' ventured the detection officer at last. 'Though I guess they could be hiding behind Luna, getting ready to pounce!'

Gillian shook her head. That armada of giant dreadnoughts would scarcely *fit* behind the moon's disk. Besides, why set a trap for prey that lies helpless, already in your grasp? *Streaker* could not run, and a puppy would beat her in a fair fight.

'I'm detecting a lot of fresh hyper-ripples in the ambient background field,' added Akeakemai. 'Engine wakes. Some really big ships churned things up hereabouts just a little while ago. I'm guessing they tore outta here awful damn fasssst!'

While *Streaker*'s crew continued laboring to repair sensors, the Niss Machine remanifested its whirlpool shape near Gillian.

'*Would you care for a conjecture, Dr. Baskin?*'

'Conject away!'

'*It occurs to me that your little holographic message might have had unexpected consequences. It was meant to enrage our enemies, but please allow me to submit another possibility.*

'*That it scared the living hell out of them.*'

Gillian snorted.

'That crock of bull-dross I cooked up? It was sheer bluff and bluster. A child could see through it! Are you saying that a bunch of advanced Galactics, with all their onboard libraries and sophisticated intelligence systems, couldn't penetrate to the truth?'

The Niss spiral turned, regaining a bit of its former insouciance.

'*No, Dr. Baskin. That is not what I am saying. Rather, I am insinuating that a primitive wolfling like yourself, caught up in the emotions of a transitory crisis, cannot see the essential truth underlying all your "bluff and bluster."*

'*The Galactics* did *perceive it, however. Perhaps only instants after they fired upon* Streaker. *Or else later, when they sensed we were returning, having survived the unsurvivable ... and began broadcasting a simple offer to discuss surrender.*'

'But that was—' she stammered. 'I didn't mean *their*—'

'*Either way, the alliance shattered – it flash-evaporated – as each squadron fled for home.*'

She stared. 'You're guessing. I don't believe it.'

The Niss shrugged, a twisting of its dark funnel.

'*Fortunately, the universe doesn't much care whether we believe. The chief question now is whether our foes were sufficiently terrified to completely abandon their goals, or if they have merely withdrawn to reassess – to consult their own auguries and prepare fresh onslaughts.*'

'Frankly, I suspect the latter. Nevertheless, it seems that something noteworthy happened here, Dr. Baskin.

'By any standard, you must accept history's verdict.

'The word has a strange flavor, spoken aboard this ragged vessel. So I can understand if you have trouble speaking it aloud.

'Let me coax you, then.

'It is called Victory.'

The forces of Terra emerged, climbing slowly, tentatively from their last redoubts, as if suspecting some deadly trick. Out of seared mountain peaks and blasted lunar craters, stubby ships nosed skyward, bearing scars from countless prior battles. Together they cast beams of inquiry toward every dark corner of the solar system. Distrustfully, they threw intense scrutiny toward the one remaining intruder, whose tattered outlines were not at first familiar.

'Keep well back,' Gillian ordered her pilot. 'Make no sudden moves. Let's be patient. Let them get used to us.'

Akeakemai agreed. 'We're emitting *Streaker*'s transponder code. But it'll take a while to get other messages out. Till then, I'd rather not make those guys nervoussss!'

It was an understatement. Those tattered-looking units had managed to keep the terrifying Tandu, and many other allied warrior clans, at bay for two years. All told, Gillian would rather not be fried by her own people, just because they had jittery trigger fingers.

After all this time, she could wait just a little while longer.

Jake Demwa isn't going to be happy with the condition I'm bringing Streaker *home in*, she mused. *Without two-thirds of its crew, or the Shallow Cluster samples. He'll grill me for weeks, trying to figure out where Creideiki and Tom went off to, and what strange matters may have kept them busy all this time.*

On the other hand, she did come back to Earth bearing gifts.

The secret of overcoming Jophur master rings, for instance.

And information about the Kiqui of Kithrup, whom we may claim as new clients for our growing clan.

And the rewq symbionts of Jijo, which help species understand each other. Plus everything the Niss and I learned by interrogating our captured Galactic Library branch.

And there was more.

The Terragens Council will want to know about the lost colony on Jijo and the Polkjhy *expedition. Both groups face great dangers, and yet they seem to offer something the council long sought to achieve – offshoots of Earthclan that might survive beyond reach of Galactic Civilization, even if Terra someday falls.*

There were plenty of other things to talk about, enough to keep Gillian in debriefing for years.

Everything we discovered about other life orders, for instance. Especially the high Transcendents.

As powerful and knowing as those godlike beings appeared, Gillian had come away from her encounters with a strange sensation not unlike pity. They were, after all, not the eldest or greatest of life's children, only the ones who stayed behind when everyone else dived into one-way singularities, seeking better realms beyond.

Cowards, she had called them in a moment of pique. Not a fair characterization, she admitted now, though it held a grain of truth.

They seem trapped by the Embrace of Tides. And yet they are unwilling to follow its pull all the way – whether to a higher place or to some universal recycling system. So they sit instead, thinking and planning while time wafts gently by. Except when it seems convenient to sacrifice myriad lesser life-forms in order to accomplish some goal.

All told, they weren't company she'd look forward to inviting over for dinner.

As the haze of battle cleared, Gillian ordered *Streaker*'s cracked and fused blast armor sloughed away from the viewing ports for the first time since Kithrup, allowing her to stand before the glittering Milky Way – a spray of constellations so familiar, they would have reassured even some cavewoman ancestor whose life was spent in hardship, grubbing for roots, a mere ten thousand years ago.

Lightspeed is slow, but inexorable, she thought, gazing at the galaxy's bright lanes. *During the next few millennia, this starscape will flare with extravagance. Supernovas, blaring across heaven, carrying the first part of the Transcendents' message.*

A simple message, but an important one that even she could understand.

Greetings. Here we are. Is anybody out there?

Gillian noticed Emerson – whose duties down in Engineering were finished at last – hurry in to embrace Sara. The couple stood nearby with their silent chimp companion, regarding the same great vista, sharing private thoughts.

Of course the young woman from Jijo was another gift to Earth, a treasure who, using only mathematical insight, had independently predicted the Great Rupture. That alone was an impressive accomplishment – but now Sara was making further, startling claims, suggesting that the Rupture was only a *symptom*. Not of the expanding universe, as Earth's savants claimed, but of something more complex and strange. Something 'coming *in* from outside our contextual framework' ... whatever that meant.

Sara thought the mystery might revolve somehow around a race called the 'Buyur.'

Gillian shook her head. At last, there would be others to pass such problems on to. Skilled professionals from all across Earth – and dozens of friendly races – who could deal with arcane matters while she went back to being a simple doctor, a healer, the role she had trained for.

I'll never order anyone else to their death. Not ever again. No matter what they say we accomplished during this wretched mission, I won't accept another command.

From now on, I'll work to save individual lives. The cosmos can be somebody else's quandary.

In fact, she had already chosen her first patient.

As soon as the spymasters let me go, I'll focus on helping Emerson. Try to help restore some of his power of speech. We can hope researchers on Earth have already made useful breakthroughs, but if not, I'll bend heaven in half to find it.

Was guilt driving this ambition? To repair some of the damage her commands had caused? Or was it to have the pleasure of watching the two of them – Sara and Emerson – speak to each other's minds, as well as their hearts.

Watching them hold hands, Gillian relaxed a bit.

The heart can be enough. It can sustain.

Akeakemai called.

'We're back in two-way holo mode, Dr. Baskin. And there's a transmission coming in.'

The big visual display erupted with light, showing the control room of an approaching warship. It had the blunt outlines of Thennanin manufacture. The crew was mostly human, but the face in front of the camera had the sharp cheekbones and angular beauty of a male Tymbrimi, with empathy-sensitive tendrils wafting near the ears.

'*. . . that we must find your claims improbable. Please provide evidence that you are, indeed, TAASF Streaker. I repeat . . .*

It seemed a simple enough request to satisfy. She had spent hard, bitter years striving for this very moment of restored contact. And yet, Gillian felt reluctant to comply.

After a moment's reflection, she knew why.

To any human, there are two realms – 'Earth' and 'out there.'

As long as I'm in space, I can imagine that I'm somehow near Tom. We were both lost. Both hounded across the Five Galaxies. Despite the megaparsecs dividing us, it only seemed a matter of time till we bumped into each other.

But once I set foot on Old Terra, I'll be home. Earth will surround me, and outer space will become a separate place. A vast wilderness where he's gone missing – along with Creideiki and Hikahi and the others – wandering amid awful dangers, while I can only try to stay busy and not feel alone.

Gillian tried to answer the Tymbrimi. She wished someone else would, just to take this final burden off her shoulders. The ordeal of ending bittersweet exile.

She was rescued by an unlikely voice. Emerson D'Anite, who faced the hologram with a smile, and expressed himself in operatic song.

'Let us savor our folly!
Man is born to be jolly!

'His idle pretenses,
   and vain defenses,
      trouble his senses, and baffle his mind.

'Leaner or fatter,
   we cavort and flatter,
      so let us be cheerful and let us pretend.

'*Fun* is the triumph
   of mind over matter,
      we'll all get home if we laugh in the end!'

DESTINY

The Zang components were better prepared to take all this in their philosophical stride. So were the machine entities who helped make up the macrocommunity called *Mother*.

In both hydro- and silicon-based civilizations, there existed a widespread conviction that so-called 'reality' was a fiction. Everything from the biggest galaxy down to the smallest microbe was simply part of a grand simulation. A 'model' being run in order to solve some great problem or puzzle.

Of course, it was only natural for both of these life orders to reach the same conclusion. The Zang had evolved to perform analog emulations organically, within their own bodies. Machines did it with prim software models, carried out by digital cognizance.

But ultimately, it amounted to the same thing. Joined at last, they found a shared outlook on life.

We – and everything we see around ourselves, including the mighty Transcendents – exist merely as part of a grand scenario, a simulacrum being played out in some higher-level computer, perhaps at another plane of existence – or else at the Omega Point, when the end of time brings all things to ultimate fruition.

Either way, it makes little sense to get caught up in feelings of self-importance. This cosmic pattern we participate in is but one of countless many being run, in parallel, with only minute differences from each to the next. Like a chess program, working out every move, and all possible consequences, in extreme detail.

That was how some of the other Mother-components explained it to Lark and Ling. Even the Jophur-traeki converts seemed to have no trouble with this notion, since their mental lives involved multiple thought experiments, flowing through the dribbling wax that lined their inner cores.

Only the human and dolphin members of the consortium had trouble reconciling this image – for different reasons.

Why? Lark asked.

Why would anyone expend vast resources doing such a thing? To calculate the best of all possible worlds?

Once they find it . . . what would they do with the result?

And what will they do with all the myriad models they have created along the way?

What will they do with us?

That question seemed to startle the Zang components, but not the machines, who answered Lark with strangely earnest complacency.

You oxies are so obsessed with self-importance!

Of course, all the models have already *been run, evaluated, and discarded. Our feelings of existence are only an illusion. A manifestation of simulated time.*

To Lark, this attitude seemed appalling. But Ling only chuckled, agreeing with the dolphins who had recently joined the onboard community, and who clearly considered this whole metaphysical argument ridiculous.

Olelo, a leader among that group of former *Streaker* crew members, summed up their viewpoint with a burst of Trinary haiku.

> * Listen to the crash
>> * Of breakers on yonder reef,
>>> * And tell me this ain't real! *

*

Lark felt glad to have the newcomers aboard, in several ways. They seemed like interesting folks, with a refreshing outlook. And they helped keep up the oxy side of the ongoing debate. There would be plenty of time for give-and-take discussions over the course of many subjective years, until the transformed *Polkjhy* finally reached journey's end.

With a flicker of awareness, he cast his remote senses through one of the external viewers, taking another look at the cosmos. Or what passed for one.

It was a perspective few others had ever witnessed. A *blankness* that was quite distinct from the vivid color, black. None of the great spiral or elliptical galaxies were visible in their normal forms – as gaudy displays of dusty white pinpoints. From this high standpoint, no stars could be seen, except as mere ripples, brief indentations that he could barely make out, if he tried.

Everything seemed flattened, ephemeral, tentative – almost like a crudely drawn rough draft of the real thing.

In fact, *Polkjhy* was no longer quite part of that universe. Gliding along just *outside* the ylem, the modified vessel rode atop a surging swell that was composed not of matter, or energy, or even raw metric. The best he could figure – having discussed it with others, and consulted the onboard Library – *Polkjhy* was riding upon a swaying fold of *context*. A background of basic law, from which the universe had formed long ago, when a perturbation in Heisenberg's Uncertainty Principle allowed the sudden eruption called the Big Bang.

An emergence of Something from Nothing.

What he saw now was not things or objects but a vast swirl of causal connections, linking one set of potentialities to another.

Behind the hurtling ship, diminishing rapidly with each passing dura, several of these junctions could be glimpsed twisting away from a recent, shattering separation. A splitting apart of ancient ties.

He felt Ling's mind slip alongside his own, sharing the view. But after a while, she nudged him.

All of that lies behind us. Come. Look ahead, toward our destiny.

Though nothing tangible existed on this plane – not matter, or memes, or even directionality – Lark nevertheless got a sense of 'forward' . . . the way they were headed. According to the Transcendents, it was a large cluster of galaxies, lying almost half a billion parsecs away from Galaxy Two. A place where enigmatic signals had been emanating for a long time, hinting at sapient activity. Perhaps another great civilization to contact. To share with. To say hello.

Its sole manifestation – to Lark's subjective gaze – was a swirl of faintly glowing curves and spirals. Vague hints that another domain existed where hyperdrive and transfer points and all the conveniences of spacefaring might be found in abundance.

We'll live to see that, Ling pondered. *And much else. Are you glad we came?*

Unlike the dolphins, no Transcendent had ever asked Lark about his wishes. Yet, he felt pretty good.

Yeah, I'm glad.

I'll miss some people. And Jijo. But who could turn down an opportunity like this?

In fact, some already had. Gillian Baskin, striving to remain where her duty lay. And Sara, whose love he would carry always. In sending a dozen dolphin volunteers, Baskin had included other gifts to accompany *Polkjhy*'s voyage – *Streaker*'s archives, the genetic samples accumulated during a long exploration mission.

Plus another item.

Lark glanced at the most unique member of the Mother Consortium, encapsulated in a golden cocoon of *toporgic* frozen time. An archaic cadaver, possibly a billion years old, that had traveled with *Streaker*'s luckless crew ever since their fateful visit to a place called the Shallow Cluster.

Herbie was its name.

The mummy's enigmatic smile seemed all-knowing. All-confident.

'Isn't this your most precious relic?' Lark had asked during those frenetic moments leading up to the supernova explosion, as the *Streaker* samples were stowed and *Polkjhy*'s protective shell closed around it.

'*Herb and I have been through a lot together*,' Gillian answered. '*But I figure it's more important that he ride with you folks. He may tell some distant civilization more about us than a whole Library full of records.*'

The Earthling woman had looked tired, yet unbowed, as if she felt certain that her trials would soon end.

'*Besides, even if* Streaker *somehow survives what's about to come, I figure old Herbie's not irreplaceable.*

'*I know where we can get lots more, just like him.*'

That cryptic remark clung to Lark as he and his mate let their senses roam, watching a soft luminance sweep by – the loose threads and stitching that always lay hidden, behind the backdrop of life's great tragicomedy. For some reason, it seemed to imply a story still unfolding. One in which he kept playing a part, despite an end to all links of cause or communication.

Someone could be felt sliding alongside the two floating humans. A dolphin – long, sleek, and scarred from many travails – jostled their bodies slightly with backwash from its fins, slipping a strong mental presence near theirs, sharing their view of the austere scenery beyond *Polkjhy's* glimmering hull.

Soon, their new companion sang a lilting commentary.

> * *Even when you have left*
> > * *Old Ones, Transcendents,*
> > > * *and gods far behind,*

> * *Who can truly say they are*
> > * *beyond Heaven's Reach?* *

Ling sighed appreciatively and Lark nodded. He turned to congratulate the cetacean for summing up matters so beautifully.

Only then he blinked, for his eyes were staring at an empty patch in Mother's rich, organic stew.

He could have sworn that a big gray shape had drifted right next to him, just moments before – glossy, warm, and close enough to touch! A dolphin he had not met, among the newcomers.

But no one was there.

It would be many years before he heard that voice again.

AFTERWORD

I feel it's a bad practice for a writer to get stuck in a particular 'universe,' writing about the same characters or situations over and over again. To keep from getting stale, I try never to write two 'universe' books in a row. But clearly, the Uplift Storm Trilogy (*Brightness Reef*, *Infinity's Shore*, and *Heaven's Reach*) is an exception. I never deliberately set out to 'go the trilogy route,' but this work took off, gaining complexity and texture as I went. Life can be that way. If you drop one stone into a pond, the pattern of ripples may seem clear. But start tossing in more than a few at a time, and the patterns take off in ways you never imagined. A realistic story is much the same. Implications and ramifications spread in all directions.

Many people have asked questions about my Uplift series. This is certainly not the first time an author speculated about the possibility of genetically altering non-sapient animals. Examples include *The Island of Dr. Moreau*, *Planet of the Apes*, and the *Instrumentality* series of Cordwainer Smith. I grew up admiring these works, and many spin-offs. But I also noticed that nearly all these tales assume that human 'masters' will always do the maximally stupid/evil thing. In other words, if we meddle with animals to raise their intelligence, it will be in order to enslave and abuse them.

Don't get me wrong! Those morality tales helped tweak our collective conscience toward empathy and tolerance. Yet, ironically, I feel it is now unlikely our civilization would behave in a deliberately vile way toward newly sapient creatures, because the morality tales did their job!

The Uplift series tries to take things to the next level. Suppose we genetically enhance chimps, dolphins, and others, with the best of motives, offering them voices and citizenship in our diverse culture. Won't there still be problems? Interesting ones worth a story or two? In fact, I expect we'll travel that road someday. *Loneliness* ensures that someone will attempt Uplift, sooner or later. And once an ape talks, who will dare say 'put him back the way he was'?

It's about time to start thinking about the dilemmas we'll face, even if we're wise.

As *Glory Season* let me explore a range of relationships that might emerge from self-cloning, the Uplift Universe gives me a chance to experiment with all sorts of notions about starfaring civilization. And since it is unapologetic space opera, those notions can be stacked together and piled high! For instance, since we're positing Faster Than Light Travel (FTLT) I went ahead and threw in *dozens* of ways to cheat Einstein. The more the merrier!

One problem in many science fictional universes is the assumption that things just *happen* to be ripe for adventure when *we* hit the space lanes. (For instance, the villains, while dangerous, are always just barely beatable, with some help from the plucky hero.) In fact, the normal state of any part of the universe, at any given moment, is equilibrium. Things are as they have been for a very long time. An equilibrium of law perhaps, or one of death. We may be the First Race, as I discuss in my story 'Crystal Spheres.' Or we could be very late arrivals, as depicted in the Uplift books. But we're very unlikely to meet aliens as equals.

Another theme of this series is environmentalism. What we're doing to Earth makes me worry there may have already been 'brushfire' ecological holocausts across the galaxy, set off by previous starfaring races who heedlessly used up life-bearing planets as their 'Galactic Empire' burned out during its brief reign of a few ten thousand years. (Note how often science fiction tales ring with the shout, 'Let's go fill the galaxy!' If this already happened a few times, it might help explain the apparent emptiness out there, for the galaxy seems, at this moment, to have few, if any, other voices.)

A galaxy might 'burn out' all too easily, unless something regulates how colonists treat their planets, forcing them to think about the long run, beyond short-term self-interest. The Uplift Universe shows one way this might occur. For all the nasty traits displayed by some of my Galactics – their past-fixation and prim fanaticism, for instance – they do give high priority to preserving planets, habitats, and potential sapient life. The result is a noisy, vibrant, bickering universe. One filled with more life than there might have been otherwise.

For the record, I don't think we live in a place like the wild, extravagant Uplift Universe. But it's a fun realm to play in, between more serious stuff.

Pile on those marvels!

Hang on. There's more to come.

ACKNOWLEDGMENTS

I want to thank my insightful and outspoken prereaders, who scanned portions of this work in manuscript form – especially Stefan Jones, Steinn Sigurdsson, Ruben Krasnopolsky, Damien Sullivan, and Erich R. Schneider. Also helpful were Kevin Lenagh, Xavier Fan, Ray Reynolds, Ed Allen, Larry Fredrickson, Martyn Fogg, Doug McElwain, Joseph Trela, David and Joy Crisp, Carlo Gioja, Brad De Long, Lesley Mathieson, Sarah Milkovich, Gerrit Kirkwood, Anne Kelly, Anita Gould, Duncan Odom, Jim Panetta, Nancy Hayes, Robert Bolender, Kathleen Holland, Marcus Sarofim, Michael Tice, Pat Mannion, Greg Smith, Matthew Johnson, Kevin Conod, Paul Rothemund, Richard Mason, Will Smit, Grant Swenson, Roian Egnor, Jason M. Robertson, Micah Altman, Robert Hurt, Manoj Kasichainula, Andy Ashcroft, Scott Martin, and Jeffrey Slostad. Professors Joseph Miller and Gregory Benford made useful observations. Robert Qualkinbush collated the glossaries. The novel profited from insights and assistance from my agent, Ralph Vicinanza, along with Pat LoBrutto and Tom Dupree of Bantam Books.

Emerson's last song comes from the finale of Giuseppe Verdi's opera *Falstaff*.

Some of the spectacles contained herein did not start in my own twisted imagination. The *Fractal World*, that tremendous structure made of huge fluffy spikes, presenting far more surface area (for windows) than any Dyson sphere, was described by Dr. David Criswell in a farseeing paper that can be found in *Interstellar Migration and the Human Experience*, edited by Ben Finney and Erik Jones (University of California Press).

As usual, this tale would have been a far poorer thing without the wise and very human input of my wife, Dr. Cheryl Brigham.

And now ... a lagniappe!

I did it once before, following the afterword to *Earth*. A little denouement – a story-after-the-story – for those of you who hung around all the way through my final remarks. It visits one of our characters a year or so after the Great Rupture, and attempts to tie off just a few (of many) loose ends.

Enjoy.

CIVILIZATION

(DENOUEMENT)

The seas of Hurmuphta are saltier than Jijos.

The winds don't blow steady, but in strangely rhythmic bursts, making it awkward and dangerous to sail a close tack.

That is, till you figure out the proper cadence. After that, you get a feel for the rolling tempo, sensing each gusty surge and tapering wane. With a light hand on the tiller, you can really crowd the breeze, filling the mains till you've heeled over with spars brushing the wavetops!

The first time I did that with Dor-hinuf aboard, she hollered as if Death itself had come up from the deep, to personally roar a Chant of Claiming. By the time we got back to the new dock, soaked from head to toe, she was trembling so hard I figured I must have really gone too far.

Boy was I wrong! The moment we stepped through the door of our little seaside khuta, she grabbed me and we made love for three miduras straight! My spines hurt for several days after.

(Soon I realized, civilized hoons seldom experience the stimulated drives that come from exhilaration! Back on Jijo, that was part of daily life, and served to balance a hoon's instinctive caution. But our starfaring relatives have such sedate lives, except for once-a-year estrus, they hardly ever think of sex! Fortunately, Dor-hinuf has taken to this new approach, the way an urs takes to lava.)

Alas, we seem to have less time for romantic trips together. Business is picking up, as word keeps spreading across the high plateau – where hoonish settlements huddled for a thousand years, confined to prim, orderly city streets, far from any sight of surf or tide. After all that time, I guess there's a lot of pent-up frustration. Or maybe it has something to do with the way the Five Galaxies have been shaken up lately. Anyway, lots of people – especially the younger generation – seem willing to consider something new for a change. Something our Guthatsa patrons never taught us.

Groups arrive daily, flying down to our lodge on the deserted coast, emerging from hovercars to stare at the glistening lagoon, nervous to approach so much water, clearly mindful of rote lessons they learned when young – that oceans are *dangerous*.

Of course, any hoonish accountant also knows that risk can be justified, if benefits outweigh the potential cost.

It takes just one trip across the breezy bay to convince most of them.

Some things are worth a little jeopardy.

My father-in-law handles the business details. Twaphu-anuph resigned his position with the Migration Institute to run our little resort, meeting investors, arranging environmental permits, and leasing as much prime coastal land as possible, before other hoons catch on to its real value. He still considers the whole thing kind of crazy, and won't step onto a sailboat himself. But each time the old fellow goes over the accounts I can hear him umbling happily.

His favorite song nowadays? *'What shall we do with a drunken sailor'!*

I guess it bothers me a little that neither the haunting images of Melville, nor the Jijoan sea poetry of Phwhoon-dau, have as much effect on Twaphu-anuph as a few bawdy Earthling ditties. The rafters resound when he gets to the crude part about shaving the drunkard's belly with a rusty razor.

Who can figure?

I'm so busy these days – giving sailing lessons and reinventing nearly everything from scratch – that I have no time for literary pursuits. This journal of mine lies unopened for many jaduras at a stretch. I guess my childhood ambitions to be a famous writer will have to wait. Perhaps for another life.

In fact, I found a better way to change my fellow hoons. To bring them a little happiness. To change their reputation as pinched, dour bookkeepers. And perhaps help make them better neighbors.

Back on Jijo, all the other races *liked* hoons! I hope to see that come true here, as well. Among the star-lanes of civilization.

Anyway, the literary renaissance is already in good hands. Or rather, good *eyestalks*.

Huck gave in to half of the role assigned to her.

'I'll have babies,' she announced. 'If you guys arrange for hoonish nannies to help raise 'em. After all, *I* was raised by hoons, and look how I came out!'

I would have answered this with a jibe in the old days. But without Pincer and Ur-ronn around, it just isn't the same. Anyway, I'm a married man now. Soon to be a father. It's time I learned some tact.

Huck may be resigned to staying pregnant, since she's the only one who can bring a g'Kek race back to life in the Four Galaxies.

But she absolutely refused the other half of the original plan – to live in secrecy and seclusion, hiding from the ancient enemies of her kind.

'Let 'em come!' she shouts, spinning her wheel rims and waving her eyes, as if ready to take on the whole Jophur Empire, and the others who helped extinguish her folk, all at the same time. I don't know. Maybe it's her growing sense of prominence, or the freedom of movement she feels racing along the smooth sidewalks of Hurmuphta City, or the students who attend her salons to study Terran and Jijoan literature. But she hardly ever comes down to the Cove anymore, and when she does, I just wind up listening to her go on for miduras at a stretch, saying little in response.

Maybe she's right. Perhaps I am turning into just another dull old hoon.

Or else the problem is that g'Keks seldom compromise – least of all Huck. She doesn't understand you've got to meet life halfway. For every change you manage to impose on the universe, you can expect to *be* transformed in return.

I brought gifts from Jijo to my spacefaring cousins – adventure and childhood. They, in turn, taught me what serenity can be found in home, hearth, and low, melodic rituals inherited from a misty past, before our race ever trod the road of Uplift or cared about distant stars.

Those stars are farther than they used to be. Ever since the Five Galaxies abruptly became four, half the transfer points and interspatial paths went unstable, and may remain so for the rest of our lifespans. Untold numbers of ships were lost, trade patterns disrupted, and worlds forced to rely on their own resources.

I guess this means it'll be a while before we get a letter from Urronn. I'm sure she's having the time of her life, somewhere out there, consorting with engineers of all races, up to her long neck in pragmatic problems to solve.

Though urs aren't a sentimental people, I do hope she remembers us from time to time.

All I can say about poor Pincer is that I miss him terribly.

Sometimes you just have to let go.

Death has always been the one great, hopelessly impassable gulf. Now there is another. When Galaxy Four finally ripped loose, it seems every sapient being felt it happen, at some deep, organic level. Even on a planet's surface, it staggered many folks. For days, people walked around kind of numb.

Scientists think the recoil effects must've been far worse in Galaxy Four itself, but we'll never know for sure, because now that entire giant wheel of stars lies beyond reach, forevermore. And with it, Jijo. My parents. Home.

There are consolations. It feels nice to imagine dolphins, swimming with abandon through the silky waters off Wuphon, playing tag with my father's dross ship, then coming near shore each evening to discuss poetry by Loocen's opal light.

Of course the Commons of Six Races can now tear up the Sacred Scrolls and stop hiding their faces from the sky. For the laws of the Civilization of Five Galaxies don't apply to them any longer. Perhaps Jijo's people have already dealt with the Jophur invaders. Or maybe they face even worse crises. Either way, the burden of guilt we inherited from our criminal ancestors can be shrugged off at last. The folk of the Slope aren't trespassers – or *sooners* – anymore.

Jijo is theirs, to care for and defend as best they can.

I have faith they'll come out all right. With a little help from Ifni's dice.

Speaking of strange colonists, I'm now being nagged by a little otter-like creature who wants yet another favor.

Ever since admitting he could talk, Mudfoot has been a real chatterbox, constantly demanding to know if Tymbrimi ships have come to Hurmuphta Port, or if any vessels are bound for the war front in Galaxy Two. Mudfoot's impatience is characteristic. Though he calls himself a *tytlal*, he'll always be a *noor* to me. I prove it by puffing my throat sac and humming a favorite umble. He joins my pet Huphu on my shoulder, and soon they're wrapped up together, dumb to the outside world.

'He will never leave,' Dor-hinuf predicts. Indeed, Mudfoot seems to enjoy his daytime job on the yacht, scrambling among the sails and spars, chewing sourballs and muttering caustic remarks about the landlubber passengers.

Yet, I'm not so sure. A flame burns inside the small creature, like a human with a cause, or an urs with a gadget she wants to try. Mudfoot will never rest till he's taken care of unfinished business.

Knowing what I do about tytlal, it probably has to do with a joke. Something long range and desperately . . . unless you happen to be on the receiving end, that is.

Someday, I figure we'll wake up and find him gone – with all our lanyards tied in knots as his way of saying a fond good-bye.

Mudfoot is reading over my shoulder as I write this, panting and grinning enigmatically, enjoying my speculations without offering a clue.

Enough. Come on, you little rascal. There are customers waiting. The breeze is fine, and companies of clouds march in neat rows past a silver horizon.

Let's go give some stuffy old hoons the thrill of their lives.

CAST OF CHARACTERS

Akeakemai – a dolphin member of *Streaker*'s bridge crew.

Alvin – the humicker (human-mimicking) nickname of Hph-wayuo, an adolescent hoon from Jijo.

Asx – a member of the Jijo Council of High Sages, representing the traeki race. See Ewasx.

Baskin, Gillian – a Terragens Agent assigned as physician to the dolphin survey vessel *Streaker*. In command since the debacle at Kithrup.

Blade – a blue qheuen, son of Log Biter; a wood-carver and friend of Sara Koolhan.

Brookida – dolphin metallurgist on *Streaker*.

Cambel, Lester – High Sage of Earthlings on Jijo.

Chuchki – dolphin engineering mate on *Streaker*.

Creideiki – a male dolphin, former captain of the dolphin-crewed Earth vessel *Streaker*. Left behind on Kithrup, along with several other members of the crew, with just a space 'skiff' to make their way across the Five Galaxies.

D'Anite, Emerson – a human engineer, once assigned to the Terragens spacecraft *Streaker*.

Dedinger – human zealot who wishes all races of Jijo to devolve so one day they may be uplifted from innocence.

Dor-hinuf – a young female hoon. Twaphu-anuph's daughter.

Dwer – the son of the papermaker Nelo Koolhan, brother of Sara and Lark, chief tracker of the Commons of Six Races of Jijo.

Ewasx – a Jophur ring-stack entity made mostly from components of the Jijoan sage Asx, plus a master ring.

Fallon – a retired tracker, Dwer's former mentor.

Foo, Ariana – the emeritus High Sage of Human Sept (retired).

Harry Harms – a neo-chimpanzee scout for the Institute of Navigation.

Harullen – gray qheuen intellectual. Leader of a heretical sect that believes illegal settlers should voluntarily stop breeding and let Jijo return to its time of fallow rest.

Hikahi – former third-in-command of *Streaker*, lost at Kithrup.

Hph-wayuo – Alvin's formal hoonish name.

Huck – the humicker (human-mimicking) nickname of a g'Kek orphan raised by a hoonish family on Jijo. Alvin's closest friend.

Huphu – Alvin's pet noor beast.

Jass – young hunter of the Gray Hills band. Rety's past tormentor.

Jimi – the 'blessed' born higher along the Path of Redemption.

Jomah – the young son of Henrik the Exploser.

Jop – Dolo Village tree farmer, believer in the old Sacred Scrolls.

Joshu – Sara Koolhan's late suitor, an itinerant bookbinder who died in Biblos of the pepper pox.

Kaa – dolphin, pilot of *Streaker*. Formerly known as Lucky Kaa.

Karkaett – engineering mate on *Streaker*.

Keepiru – former chief pilot of *Streaker*. Left behind on Kithrup.

Kiwei Ha'aoulin – a Synthian trader.

Knife-Bright Insight – a blue qheuen, High Sage for the qheuen race.

Kunn – human pilot of the Rothen-Danik ship.

Kurt – a leader of the Explosers Guild. Jomah's uncle.

Lark – brother of Sara and Dwer, naturalist, junior sage of the Commons, and heretic.

Ling – Danik crewwoman of the Rothen ship. A skilled biologist.

Makanee – a female dolphin, the ship's surgeon on *Streaker*.

Melina – Nelo Koolhan's late wife; mother of Lark, Sara, and Dwer.

Mopol – a male dolphin, spacer second class on *Streaker*.

Mudfoot – a wild noor beast, named by Dwer Koolhan.

Nelo – papermaker of Dolo Village, patriarch of the Koolhan family.

Niss – pseudosapient computer lent to *Streaker* by a Tymbrimi spy.

Old Ones – a term given to the 'retired' races of the Fractal World.

One-of-a-Kind – an ancient mulc-spider assigned to decompose a ruin high in the Rimmer mountains.

Orley, Thomas – a genetically engineered Terragens Agent assigned to *Streaker*. Married to Gillian, left on Kithrup with Creideiki's group.

Ozawa, Danel – deputy sage, knowing hidden secrets of Human Sept.

Peepoe – a geneticist and nurse on *Streaker*. Kidnapped on Jijo.

Phwhoon-dau – the hoonish High Sage.

Pincer-Tip – a red qheuen friend of Alvin's who carved the hull for the bathyscaphe *Wuphon's Dream* out of the trunk of a garu tree.

Prity – a female neo-chimpanzee; Sara's servant, skilled at certain aspects of mathematical imagery.

Purofsky – a sage of Biblos, specializing in arcane physics.

Rann – leader of the Danik humans.

Rety – a human sooner, she fled her savage band's hidden offshoot colony in the Gray Hills of Jijo.

Ro-kenn – a Rothen overlord.

Ro-pol – possibly Ro-kenn's mate, killed before the Battle of the Glade.

Sara – daughter of the papermaker Nelo Koolhan, sister of Dwer and Lark, mathematician and language scholar.

Shen, Jeni – a human militia sergeant.

Strong, Lena – part of Danel Ozawa's expedition to the Gray Hills.

Suessi, Hannes – a human engineer on *Streaker*, converted into a cyborg by the Old Ones.

Taine – a Biblos scholar who once courted Sara Koolhan.

Tsh't – a female dolphin, once *Streaker*'s fifth-in-command, now sharing command with Gillian Baskin.

Twaphu-anuph – a hoonish customs official at Kazzkark Base.

Tyug – the traeki alchemist of Mount Guenn Forge, a vital assistant to Uriel the Smith.

Ulgor – an urrish tinker and supporter of the Urunthai.

Urdonnol – urrish apprentice serving Uriel.

Uriel – urrish master smith of the Mount Guenn Forge.

Ur-Jah – the urrish High Sage.

Ur-ronn – Alvin's urrish friend. Part of the *Wuphon's Dream* expedition. Uriel's niece.

Uthen – gray qheuen naturalist. Helped Lark write field guide to Jijoan species.

Vubben – the g'Kek High Sage.

Worley, Jenin – part of Danel Ozawa's expedition to the Gray Hills.

yee – an urrish male ejected from his pouch home by his former mate. Later 'married' to the sooner girl Rety.

Zhaki – a male dolphin, spacer third class on *Streaker*.

CAST OF SAPIENT SPECIES

g'Keks – the first sooner race to arrive on Jijo, some two thousand years ago. Originally uplifted by the Drooli, the g'Kek have bio-magnetically driven wheels and four eyestalks rising from a combined torso-braincase. Due to vendettas by enemies, the g'Kek are extinct throughout the Five Galaxies, except on Jijo.

Glavers – the third sooner race to reach Jijo. Uplifted by the Tunuctyur, who were themselves uplifted by the Buyur. Glavers are partly bipedal with opalescent skin and large, bulging eyes. Roughly a meter tall, they have a prehensile forked tail to assist their inefficient hands. Since illegally settling Jijo they devolved to a state of presapience, dropping out of the Commons of Six Races. To some, glavers seem to be shining examples, having shown the way down the Path of Redemption.

Hoons – the fifth wave of settlers to arrive on Jijo, bipedal omni-vores, with pale scaly skin and woolly white leg fur. Their spines are massive, hollow structures that form part of their circulatory system. Hoons' inflatable throat sacs, originally for mating displays, are now used for 'umbling.' Since their Uplift by the Guthatsa, this race have found widespread service as dour, officious bureaucrats in Galactic culture.

Humans – the youngest sooner race arrived on Jijo less than three hundred years ago. Human 'wolflings' evolved on Earth, apparently achieving technological civilization and crude interstellar travel on their own, or else assisted by some unknown patron. Passionate debates rage over this issue.

Jophur – semicommunal organisms resembling cones of stacked donuts. Like their traeki cousins, Jophur consist of inter-changeable spongy 'sap-rings,' each with limited intelligence, but combining to form a sapient community being. Specialized rings give the stack its senses, manipulative organs, and sometimes exotic chemosynthetic abilities. As traeki, this unique species was originally gentle and unaspiring when first uplifted by the Poa. The zealous Oalie later reinvented them by providing 'master rings,' transforming the traeki into Jophur, willful and pro-foundly ambitious beings.

Qheuens – the fourth sooner race on Jijo. Originally uplifted by the Zhosh, qheuens are radially symmetric exoskeletal beings with five legs and claws. Their brain is partly contained in a retractable central dome or 'cupola.' A rebel band of qheuens settled Jijo attempting to hold on to their ancient caste system, with the gray variety providing royal matriarchs while red and blue types were servants and artisans. Conditions on Jijo – including later human intervention – provoked the breakdown of this system.

Rothen – a mysterious Galactic race. One human group (the dakkins or Daniks) believe the Rothen to be Earth's lost patrons. Rothen are bipeds, somewhat larger than humans but with similar proportions and charismatic features. Believed to be carnivores.

Traeki – second illicit settler race to arrive on Jijo. Traeki are a throwback variant of Jophur, who fled the imposition of master rings.

Tymbrimi – a humanoid species allied with the Earthclan. Known for their cleverness and devilish sense of humor.

Tytlal – a species considered impossible to uplift. Uplifted by the Tymbrimi.

Urs – the sixth sooner race on Jijo. Carnivorous, centauroid plains dwellers; they have long, flexible necks, narrow heads, and shoulderless arms ending in dexterous hands. Urs start life as tiny, six-limbed grubs, turned out of their mothers' pouches to fend for themselves. Any that survive to 'childhood' may be accepted into an urrish band. Urrish females reach the size of a large deer, and possess twin brood pouches where they keep diminutive mates, who are smaller than a house cat. A female with pre-larval young ejects one or both husbands to make room for the brood. Urs have an aversion to water in its pure form.

GLOSSARY OF TERMS

Allaphor – the metaphorical interpretation made by sentient minds of certain features in E-Level hyperspace.

Anglic – a human language created in the Twenty-First century, using many English words, but influenced by other pre-Contact tongues and modified according to new understandings of linguistic theory.

Biblos – a fortress containing the archive, or hall of books; a combined university/central lending library with profound influence on Jijoan culture.

Bibur – a river running past Biblos, joining the Roney at Tarek Town.

Buyur – former legal tenants of Jijo, froglike appearance, known for wit, foresight, and gene-crafting of specialized animal-tools. Departed when Jijo was declared fallow half a million years ago.

Chimpanzee or 'chim' – a partly uplifted variety that accompanied humans to Jijo, mute but able to communicate readily with sign language.

Client – a race still working out a period of servitude to the patrons that uplifted it from presapient animal status.

Criswell structures – fractal shells designed to surround small red suns, utilizing all light energy. The fractal shape allows maximum possible 'window area,' unlike a simple Dyson sphere.

Daniks – a vulgarized term for 'Danikenite,' a cultural movement dating from humanity's first contact with Galactic Civilization. Daniks believe Earthlings were uplifted by a Galactic patron race that chose to remain hidden for unknown reasons. An offshoot cult believes Rothen are this race of wise, enigmatic guides.

Day of Judgment – in prophesy, when the Six Races of Jijo will be judged for their crimes. By that time, many hope that their descendants will be like glavers – innocents, far along the Path of Redemption.

Deconstructor – a mechanical device licensed by the Institute of Migration to demolish remnants of technological civilization on a planet declared fallow.

Dolo – a village on the Roney River, famed for papermaking.

Dooden Mesa – oldest and largest g'Kek enclave.

Dross – any nonbiodegradable waste material, fated to be cast into the Midden, for recycling by Jijo's tectonic fires.

Dura – approximately one third of a minute.

E-Level hyperspace – a dangerous hyperspatial region in which the distinctions between consciousness and reality become blurred. Self-consistent concepts may exist without a host brain or computer to contain or contemplate them. See **allaphor**.

Earthclan – a small, eccentric Galactic 'family' of sapient races consisting of neo-chimpanzee and neo-dolphin clients, along with their human patrons.

Egg – see **Holy Egg**.

Embrace of Tides – a quasi addiction that causes elder races to seek the sensation of gravitational tides, close to very dense stars.

Er – genderless pronoun, sometimes used when referring to a traeki.

Exploser – demolitions expert who mines settlements of the Six Races for quick destruction, should The Day arrive. Guild headquarters in Tarek Town.

Fen – plural of 'fin,' Anglic shorthand for a neo-dolphin.

Fist of Stone – a huge shelf of stone above Biblos that has been mined by the explosers, and would serve to destroy the fortress on Judgment Day.

Fractal World or Fractal System – a place of retirement for races that have nearly transcended the Civilization of the Five Galaxies. A huge, diffuse edifice made of hydrogen snow, constructed to surround and use all the energy of a small star.

Galactic – a person, race, concept, or technology deriving from the eons-old Civilization of the Five Galaxies.

Galactic Institutes – vast, powerful academies, purportedly neutral and above interclan politics. The Institutes regulate various aspects of Galactic Civilization. Some are over a billion years old.

Galactic Library – a fantastically capacious collection of knowledge gathered over the course of hundreds of millions of years. Quasi-sapient 'Branch Libraries' are found in most Galactic starships and settlements.

Gathering Festival – annual fair that celebrates and reinforces the Great Peace among Jijo's sooner races. Incorporates a pilgrimage to the Holy Egg.

Gentt – a river just north of Blaze Mountain.

Great Peace – a time of growing understanding among the Six Races, variously credited to the influence of Biblos, or else to the arrival of the Holy Egg and rewq symbionts.

Great Printing – the sudden introduction of paper books by the humans soon after their arrival on Jijo.

Grok – Anglic term, of obscure origin, that denotes understanding a thing or concept in its entirety. Similar to the Scottish 'ken.'

Gronin Collapse – historical name given to the last time in Galactic history when the expansion of the universe caused transfer points between galaxies to 'pull apart,' thus fragmenting Galactic society.

Guenn Volcano – location of the hidden forges of Uriel the Smith.

'Heresies' – variant views of Jijoan destiny, held by groups who disagree with the High Sages. One holds that Galactic law is just – and Jijo would be better off without 'infestation' by sooner races. Others subscribe to more orthodox interpretations of the Sacred Scrolls, that each exile race should seek separate salvation down the Path of Redemption. One rare heresy is called 'progress.'

Holy Egg, the – a mysterious mass of psi-active stone that emerged from a Jijoan volcano a century ago, accompanied by widespread visions and dreaming.

Humicker – slang term for someone who mimics humans, because Earthlings texts still dominate literate life of Jijo, long after the Great Printing.

Ifni – a vulgarization of 'Infinity.' In spacer tradition, a name given to the goddess of luck. Personification of chance or Murphy's Law.

Illias – a matriarchal tribe of horsewomen living secretly in the Spectral Flow.

Izmunuti – a red giant star, uncomfortably close to Jijo's sun; spews a carbon wind masking Jijo from supervision by the Institute for Migration.

Jadura – approximately forty-three hours.

Jijo – a planet in Galaxy Four. Home of seven sooner races: humans, hoons, qheuen, urs, g'Kek, the devolved glavers, and 'demodified' Jophur known as traeki.

Jophekka – the homeworld of the Jophur.

Kazzkark – a space station operated by the several major Galactic Institutes, including the Institute of Navigation.

Kidura – approximately one half second.

Kiqui – an amphibious presapient race native to Kithrup.

Kithrup – a water world rich in heavy metals, where the *Streaker* crew lost Captain Creideiki and many others in escaping a dire trap.

Loocen – largest of Jijo's three moons.

Lorniks – a domesticated animal, bred as servants by qheuen. Lorniks are radially symmetrical, have four legs and four three-fingered hands.

Midden – a vast undersea crevasse, or subduction zone, formed by plate tectonics, running alongside the Slope on Jijo. All dross generated by the inhabitant races – from skeletal remains to the hulls of sooner spacecraft – is dumped into the Midden, where natural forces will carry it below Jijo's crust for melting.

Midura – a unit of time, approximately seventy-one minutes.

Morgran – a transfer point where *Streaker* was first attacked by war-ships of the most fanatic religious clans.

Mulc-spiders – a life-form engineered to destroy buildings and tech-nological artifacts on worlds declared fallow.

Mulching ceremony – reduction of dead bodies, returning flesh to the Jijoan ecosystem. Often involves consumption of flesh by spe-cialized traeki rings. Nondegradable leftovers are treated as dross and sent to the Midden.

Neo-chimp, neo-chimpanzee – uplifted chimpanzees; humanity's first clients. Fully uplifted neo-chimps can speak; the 'unfinished' variety that accompanied humans to Jijo are mute.

Neo-dolphin – uplifted dolphins; clients of humanity.

Nihanic – another pre-Contact human language, derived from a hybrid of Japanese and Han Chinese.

Noor – bright, dexterous, but mischievous otterlike creatures. Noor cannot be tamed, but the patient and good-natured hoon are able to employ some noor beasts on their ships. Noor are considered pests by the other sooner races.

NuDawn Colony – a world colonized by the Terragens before con-tact was made with Galactic Civilization, in unknowing violation of migration laws. The inhabitants were forcibly and violently evicted by hoonish bureaucrats, supported by Jophur and other vigilantes.

Oailie – third-stage uplift consorts and 'step-patrons' of the Jophur, and fanatical members of the Obeyer Alliance. As expert gene crafters, the Oailie reworked traeki biology and psychology by the addition of master rings, transforming them into Jophur.

Oakka – a planet containing the regional headquarters of the Institute of Navigation, where *Streaker* barely escaped entrap-ment and betrayal.

Orders of Life – seven types of sentient life are known among the Five Galaxies:

oxygen breathers – members of Galactic culture, including humans.

hydrogen breathers – utilize 'reducing' atmospheres, having slower metabolisms. Most inhabit giant gas planets, drifting among the clouds, performing internal simulations of the world.

Retired Order – former patron races that have reached senescence and 'retired' from Galactic affairs.

machine – self-replicating sentient machines. Generally confine themselves to high-radiation areas or zones of deep space unwanted by either hydrogen or oxygen civilizations, though a few types are tolerated for their usefulness.

Transcendent – races that have 'passed on' to a higher plane. Galactics are riven by many beliefs about this stage of life. The first to transcend (it is assumed) were the Progenitors.

memetic – bizarre 'thought' organisms residing primarily in E-Level hyperspace.

Quantum – organisms discovered only during the last 100 million years, existing between the interstices of the universe, making scant contact with Galactic society. Their way of life seems to depend on macroquantum uncertainty.

There is widespread disagreement over whether the number of life orders should equal eight. Even more are suspected. Contact between life orders is dangerous, and widely discouraged.

Parrot ticks – a peculiar Buyur-engineered insect that can memorize and recite short phrases. The first humans on Jijo doubted their sanity when they kept 'hearing voices'.

Passen – Jijo's smallest moon.

Path of Redemption – goal of orthodox religious factions of Jijo, who believe the sooner races should devolve to presapience. Only thus can they escape punishment for colonizing a fallow world, offering a second chance at uplift. Glavers have already trod the Path.

Patron – a Galactic race that has uplifted at least one animal species to full sapience.

Phuvnthus – six-legged wood-eating vermin on Jijo.

Pidura – six-to-the-seventh-power duras, or approximately four days.

Xi – a meadowland in the midst of the Spectral Flow, home of the Illias.

Year of Exile – the epoch that began when the first sooner race arrived on Jijo.

Ylem – the underlying fabric of reality itself.

Zang – a hydrogen-breathing race resembling huge squid. They live in the atmosphere of gas giants. Jijo's entire galactic region has been ceded to hydrogen breathers by the Institute of Migration; oxygen breathing sapients are supposed to stay out for a long fallow period. Zang patrol globes are a rare but feared visitor to Jijo.

Zhosh – the qheuens' patron race.

Zookir – servant animals bred by the g'Kek, able to memorize and recite messages, but not as bright as neo-chimpanzees.

Polkjhy – Jophur battleship that landed on Jijo in search of the *Streaker*.

Poria Outpost – the Danik headquarters, where a small human population serves Rothen lords.

Primal Delphin – semilanguage used by natural, nonuplifted dolphins on Earth.

Progenitors – legendary first spacefaring race, who began the cycle of uplift two billion years ago.

Rewq – quasi-fungal symbionts that help the Six Races 'read' each other's emotions and body language.

Rift – a branch of the Midden located at the southern end of the Slope.

Rimmers – a mountain range marking the eastern boundary of the Slope.

Sacred Scrolls – texts of enigmatic origin, the only written matter on Jijo between the departure of the Buyur and human introduction of paper books. The scrolls taught the g'Kek and later colonists about the need for concealment, planetary care, and 'redemption.'

Sept – a race or sapient clan of Jijo, e.g., the g'Kek, glavers, hoons, urs, traeki, qheuen, and humans.

Sooners – outlaws who attempt to colonize worlds designated fallow by the Galactic Institute of Migration. On Jijo, the term means those who try to make new illegal settlements, beyond the confines of the Slope.

Spectral Flow – a forbidding desert region in the southcentral area of the Slope, thought to be uninhabitable. Covered with sheets of luridly colored, psi-active volcanic stone and outcrops of photoactive crystal.

Streaker – a neo-dolphin-crewed Terran starship. The *Streaker's* discoveries led to unprecedented pursuit by dozens of Galactic factions, each seeking advantage by possessing the dolphins' secrets.

Stress atavism – a condition found among newly uplifted species, when individuals lose their higher cognitive functions under stress.

Tabernacle – the sneakship that brought human sooners to Jijo more than 200 years ago.

Tarek Town – the largest town on the Slope, where the Roney and Bibur merge. Headquarters of the Explosers Guild.

Terragens Council – ruling body of humanity's interstellar government, in charge of matters affecting relations between Earthclan and Galactic society.

Toporgic – a pseudo-material substrate made of organically folded time.

Torgen – one of Jijo's moons.

Transfer point – an area of weak space time that allows faster than light travel for vessels entering in precise ways.

Tymbrimi – a humanoid species allied with Earthclan, known for cleverness and devilish humor.

Tytlal – see **Noor**.

Uplift – the process of turning a presapient animal species into a fully sapient race capable of joining Galactic society. Performed by patron race.

Urchachka – the urrish homeworld.

Urchachkin – urrish clan that gave refuge to human females and horses in the Spectral Flow.

Vlenning – a rare form of traeki reproduction, in which a small, complete stack is budded from an adult.

Wolfling – a derogatory Galactic term for a race that appears to have uplifted itself to spacefaring status without help, or else to have been abandoned by its patron.

Wuphon's Dream – the bathyscaphe built by Pincer-Tip, with the help of Alvin, Huck, and Ur-ronn. Outfitted by Uriel the Smith.